Acclaim for William Vollmann and *Fathers and Crows*

"A fascinating, eccentric bouillabaisse of a novel . . . a profound meditation on the nature of human existence, including the dusty traces left behind in the form of history . . . a truly daring and original dream vision of the past."
—*The Philadelphia Inquirer*

"An impressive achievement from a writer who seems bent on, and fully capable of, astonishing us again and again." —*USA Today*

"Vast and vivid as Canada itself, mingling the cold, deep waters of history with the present, and quixotic and ironic to its core. An immensely rewarding saga." —*Kirkus Reviews*

"Vollmann's 'Seven Dreams' septology will be the most important literary project of the '90s." —*The Washington Post Book World*

"*Fathers and Crows* is an important addition to Vollmann's already impressive body of work." —*Library Journal*

"Vollmann shows every sign of being equal to his self-appointed task of creating a symbolic history of the European settlement of North America. . . . His ambition is without parallel, and he clearly has set in place another solid block of his audacious project." —*Publishers Weekly*

CONTEMPORARY AMERICAN FICTION

FATHERS AND CROWS

William T. Vollmann was born in Los Angeles in 1959. He attended Deep Springs College and Cornell University, where he graduated *summa cum laude* in comparative literature. In 1982 he crossed into Afghanistan with Islamic commandos, and afterwards lived for several years in San Francisco. Vollmann's books include the novels *You Bright and Risen Angels* (Penguin), *The Ice-Shirt* (Penguin), and *Whores for Gloria*; two story collections, *The Rainbow Stories* and *Thirteen Stories and Thirteen Epitaphs*; and a work of nonfiction, *An Afghanistan Picture Show*. Vollmann won a 1988 Whiting Award in recognition of his writing achievements and the Shiva Naipaul Memorial Award in 1989. He is currently engaged in writing a series of seven novels (of which *Fathers and Crows* is the second) exploring the relations between North American native populations and their colonizers and oppressors; the third volume *The Rifles*, will be published by Viking in February of 1994. William Vollmann lives in California.

FATHERS AND CROWS

by

WILLIAM T. VOLLMANN

PENGUIN BOOKS

SEVEN DREAMS

ABOUT OUR CONTINENT
IN THE DAYS OF
THE SAINTS

Raising from their GLASS COFFINS
the * **BLACK-GOWNS** *
Who Plucked the Blossoms of
Souls
(Fearing Never a Thorn);
Who
Prayed Blood
to
SANCTIFY THE BONES OF CATAMOUNTS;
Who Foreswore
RUM, WOMEN AND LEAD,
Who were
So Astounded
at the Unfathomable Extinctions of
Savages;
Who
Made More Miracles than They Saw!

As Compounded and Confounded From
DIVERSE RELATIONS

by

WILLIAM T. VOLLMANN

(*Known in This World as*
"WILLIAM THE BLIND")

PENGUIN BOOKS
Published by the Penguin Group
Penguin Books USA Inc., 375 Hudson Street, New York,
New York 10014, U.S.A.
Penguin Books Ltd, 27 Wrights Lane,
London W8 5TZ, England
Penguin Books Australia Ltd, Ringwood,
Victoria, Australia
Penguin Books Canada Ltd, 10 Alcorn Avenue, Toronto,
Ontario, Canada M4V 3B2
Penguin Books (N.Z.) Ltd, 182–190 Wairau Road,
Auckland 10, New Zealand

Penguin Books Ltd, Registered Offices:
Harmondsworth, Middlesex, England

First published in the United States of America by
Viking Penguin, a division of Penguin Books USA Inc., 1992
First published in Great Britain by Andre Deutsch Limited 1992
Published in Penguin Books 1993

1 3 5 7 9 10 8 6 4 2

THE LIBRARY OF CONGRESS HAS CATALOGUED THE HARDCOVER AS FOLLOWS:
Vollmann, William T.
Fathers and crows/William T. Vollmann.
p. cm.—(Seven dreams)
Includes bibliographical references.
ISBN 0-670-84333-4 (hc.)
ISBN 0 14 01.6717 X (pbk.)
1. Canada—History—To 1763 (New France)—Fiction. 2. Brebeuf, Jean de, Saint, 1593–1649—Fiction. 3. Jesuits—Missions—Canada—History—Fiction. 4. Wyandot Indians—Fiction. I. Title. II. Series: Vollmann, William T. Seven dreams.
PS3572.0395F38 1992
813′.54—dc20 92-18315

Printed in the United States of America
Set in Bembo

SECOND DREAM
Fathers and Crows

The letter is badly written, and quite soiled, because, among other inconveniences, the writer has but one whole finger on his right hand, and can scarcely prevent the paper's being stained by the blood which flows from his yet unhealed wounds. His ink is arquebus powder, and his table the bare earth.

FATHER FRANCESCO GIUSEPPE BRESSANI, *Brief Relation of the Mission in New France* (1653)

The
DEDICATION

has two parts: *To* and *Against*

This book is dedicated *to* all **Canadians**, past and present, Jesuit and Iroquois; Huron, French, Algonkin, English, Montagnais, Micmac, Inuit, and others. May they preserve their land together.

This book is dedicated *against* all **dogmatists** and their armies (in which some of the above may have enlisted). Whoever they are, I cordially wish them a warm stay in Hell.

THE AUTHOR

Contents

The reader is encouraged to use the Chronology and Glossary only as needed while reading *Seven Dreams*. The first gives context to characters and events in the text. The second defines and gives the origin of every word which may be unfamiliar. As for the Source Notes, they may be ignored or skimmed; their function is to record my starting points, which may interest travelers in other directions. The Chart of the Stream of Time, which precedes the text, is a schematic analogous to the Chronology.

List of Maps

An Accurate Chart of
Goals, Straits & Obstacles
to Be Found in the
STREAM OF TIME,
Keyed to the
"*Spiritual Exercises*"
of Ignatius de Loyola

Week the First

River's mouth

Eddy of the Three Sins (Pride; Disobedience; any Mortal Sin)
Ex. I.
Current of Sorrow (One's own sins revealed on the bank)
Ex. II.
Isle of the Trinity (Our LADY, JESUS, GOD, begged to intercede)
Ex. III.
Current of Patience (Which washes one backward to begin a second time)
Ex. IV.
Shoals of Hell (Revelation of the Damned)
Ex. V.

Week the Second

River proper

The Rock of Earthly Kings (Service with a generous King)
Ex. VI. Part I.
The Rock of CHRIST (Service with the Heavenly KING)
Ex. VI. Part II.
First Rapids (Sault de l'Incarnation)
First Day. First Contemplation.
Second Rapids (Nativity)
First Day. Second Contemplation.
Current of Patience (Which washes one backward thrice)
First Day. Third, Fourth and Fifth Contemplations.
Third Rapids (Sault des Deux Contemplations: The Presentation, the Flight)
Second Day. First and Second Contemplations.
The Shoals of Obedience (The CHILD and His parents)
Third Day. Contemplation.

Fourth Rapids (Waterfall of the Two Standards)
Fourth Day. First Meditation.
Isle of the Three Classes (The Enthralled, the Attached and the Free)
Fourth Day. Second Meditation.
Shoals of the Eight Contemplations (The XXIVth, XXVth, XXVIth, XXXIXth, XXXXIst, XXXXVIth, XXXXVIIIth & XXXXIXth Rapids)
Fifth Day – Twelfth Day.
Fifth Rapids (First Fall of Humility)
Third Note to the Second Week.
Sixth Rapids (Second Fall of Humility)
Ditto.
Seventh Rapids (Third Fall of Humility)
Ditto.
Eighth Rapids (Sault of Election)
Following Note.

Week the Third

River narrows

Ninth Rapids (Last Supper) (Same as LIIIrd Rapids)
First Day. First Contemplation.
Tenth Rapids (Garden) (Same as LIVth Rapids)
First Day. Second Contemplation.
Eleventh Rapids (House of Annas) (Same as LVth Rapids)
Second Day.
Twelfth Rapids (Caiaphas and Pilate) (Same as LVIth Rapids)
Third Day.
Thirteenth Rapids (Pilate and Herod) (Same as LVIIth Rapids)
Fourth Day.
Fourteenth Rapids (Nailing to Cross) (Same as LVIIIth Rapids)
Fifth Day.
Fifteenth Rapids (The Burial) (Same as LIXth Rapids)
Sixth Day.
Current of Patience (Which washes one twice back to the IXth Rapids)
Seventh Day.

Week the Fourth

To the source

Sixteenth Rapids (Appearance of CHRIST to Our LADY)
First Contemplation.
Seventeenth Rapids (Love)
Contemplation to Attain Love.

First Isle of Prayer (Form)

The First Way of Prayer.

Eighteenth Rapids (Ten Commandments)

Ditto.

Nineteenth Rapids (Capital Sins)

Ditto.

Twentieth Rapids (Powers of the Soul)

Ditto.

Twenty-First Rapids (Five Senses of the Body)

Ditto.

Second Isle of Prayer (Meaning of Words)

The Second Way of Prayer.

Third Isle of Prayer (Breathing Control)

The Third Way of Prayer.

The Twenty-Second Rapids through the Seventy-Third Rapids comprise the Mysteries of Our Lord

Twenty-Second Rapids (Terra Incognita)

Twenty-Third Rapids (Annunciation)

Twenty-Fourth Rapids (Visitation of Elizabeth)

Twenty-Fifth Rapids (Birth of Christ Our Lord)

Twenty-Sixth Rapids (The Shepherds)

Twenty-Seventh Rapids (The Circumcision)

Twenty-Eighth Rapids (The Three Magi)

Twenty-Ninth Rapids (Presentation of Christ)

Thirtieth Rapids (Flight into Egypt)

Thirty-First Rapids (Return from Egypt)

Thirty-Second Rapids (Life of Christ from Age Twelve to Thirty)

Thirty-Third Rapids (Christ at the Temple at Age Twelve)

Thirty-Fourth Rapids (Baptism of Christ)

Thirty-Fifth Rapids (Temptation of Christ)

Thirty-Sixth Rapids (Vocation of the Apostles)

Thirty-Seventh Rapids (The First Miracle: Water into Wine)

Thirty-Eighth Rapids (Christ Expels the Merchants from the Temple)

Thirty-Ninth Rapids (The Sermon on the Mount)

Fortieth Rapids (Christ Calms the Storm at Sea)

Forty-First Rapids (Christ Walks Upon the Sea)

Forty-Second Rapids (The Apostles are Sent Forth to Preach)

Forty-Third Rapids (Conversion of Magdalene)

Forty-Fourth Rapids (The Loaves and the Fishes)

Forty-Fifth Rapids (Transfiguration of Christ)

Forty-Sixth Rapids (Resurrection of Lazarus)

Forty-Seventh Rapids (Supper in Bethany)

Forty-Eighth Rapids (Palm Sunday)
Forty-Ninth Rapids (CHRIST Preaches in the Temple)
Fiftieth Rapids (The Last Supper)
Fifty-First Rapids (Agony in the Garden)
Fifty-Second Rapids (House of Annas)

The Fifty-Third Rapids through the Fifty-Ninth Rapids repeat what was revealed from the Ninth Rapids through the Fifteenth Rapids

Sixtieth Rapids *through* **Seventy-Second Rapids** (Apparitions of CHRIST: Ist–XIIIth)
Seventy-Third Rapids (Ascension of CHRIST)

Indeed, this great Stream or Fleuve is in correspondence with the scheme of my Second Dream, which you will find wide at the beginning like a river's mouth, then narrower and narrower as it ascends its rapids and waterfalls, until at last I am successful in steadiness, deviating from my history no greater distance than that equal to the radius of a needle's eye: – *viz.*, the proverbial entrance to the Kingdom of Heaven (which I, William the Blind, have seen with my own eyes).

Crow-Text

The Jesuit Relations 1610–1791
A Historical Note

The journals of the Black-Gowns, submitted once a year to their superiors in Québec and Montréal, and thence forwarded to France, were published in duodecimal volumes known to book-worms and book-lice as Cramoisys, but the pious thousands called them simply *Jesuit Relations*. For a span longer than the life of the present nation of CANADA, that British paradise so queasy with French discontents, they chronicled the Second Age of our continent: – the Age of Miracles. "When we evoke its departed shades," says Francis Parkman with his usual melodrama,

> they rise upon us from their graves in strange, romantic guise . . . the fitful light is cast around on lord and vassal and black-robed priest, mingled with wild forms of savage warriors, knit in close fellowship on the same stern errand. A boundless vision grows upon us; an untamed continent; vast wastes of forest verdure; mountains silent in primeval sleep; river, lake, and gleaming pool; wilderness oceans mingling with the sky. Such was the domain which France conquered for Civilization. Plumed helmets gleamed in the shade of its forests, priestly vestments in its dens and fastnesses of ancient barbarism. Men steeped in antique learning, pale with the close breath of the cloister, here spent the noon and evening of their lives, ruled savage hordes with a mild, parental sway, and stood serene before the direst shapes of death.

This animated troop of pictures exposes the duties of writers in pre-cinematic days: if you read and blink, you may be able to glimpse a forest behind the lids of your eyes. (That is the first step if you truly desire to see my love, my Sainte, Catherine Tekakwitha.) – Should, however, you make the Exercise deficiently – should you represent those gleaming helmets of Canada by the worldly polished brass of spent rifle casings, those firs and spruces by buildings whose beetling windows glitter between the blue and white sky-stripes of sunset (and you *dare* to deem this acceptable? – you cite the well-known fact that Frenchmen use the same word for an armadillo and a wood-louse; do you therefore presume that office-towers are sufficient approximations of pine trees?) . . . – no, no, at this I must raise my mild paternal hand, whose palm-wound weeps reproachful blood at you; I must admonish you: – Dream harder! . . . Do you at least spy the 1873 covered bridge of Newfield, New York, as red and gay as a carnival, and inside its shape all the curling wood-ribs of a truly Yankee intricacy? – Good, but you must blink back the tears of another hundred and ten years to recall the passing of New France into English hands; flail yourself past-ward yet again a century to witness Tekakwitha's edifying death, bushwhack three-quarters of still another, through all the undergrowth of years, to restore the virgin forests to the rock of Kebec, and even then a good dozen of decades will stand between you and the Dream of the Floating Island that began it all.

Can you do it? I pray that Our FATHER will favor you.

Begin.

Make the usual preparatory prayer – namely, to ask of GOD Our LORD the grace that your intentions, acts and works will be directed toward no other end than the service of His Divine Majesty. *Now* (I hope), you'll screw your eyes more tightly shut in the First Prelude ("Mental Image of the Place"), craving with so much longing to see Sainte Catherine that your spiritual atlas begins to turn its pages, fanning the love inside you with blue-green river-spattered vastness – in these rivers flows no water, but Greek fire, searing your heart with love, and you glimpse the *fleur-de-lys* of Lake Huron (CANADA, GREAT LAKES – FORMERLY WENDAKÉ/HURONIA), but the page speeds by, and you feel the bite of that great blue fang, the Gulf of Saint-Laurent (CANADA, MARITIME PROVINCES – FORMERLY ACADIA) – but descending there to sail with Champlain and the Black-Gowns would be a glory as yet undeserved, so at once you resist that evil thought and it is conquered; the page turns again to yellow-greens and grey boulders like the stone ruins of barns now standing in sunny fields overgrown with raspberries and responsibilities (NEW YORK STATE – FORMERLY IROQUOIA), and the pages turn over half-wild apple-trees and green-blue tree-shadows on grass and you're almost there where Catherine is . . . but you've already committed a venial sin by taking pleasure in the fact, *sensual* pleasure, so I command you: close the book! You must make an act of contrition. "I will deprive myself of all light," says the manual of the Black-Gowns,

> closing the shutters and doors when I am in my room, unless I need the light to say my prayers, to read, or to eat. I will neither laugh nor say anything that will provoke laughter. I will restrain my eyes except in looking to receive or dismiss the person with whom I have to speak.

Then raise the drawbridges of your castle,

(I) banishing New York City with its marble lobbies, where phones ring incessantly;

(II) excommunicating the ceilings of department stores dazzling with cut evergreen boughs bearing light-fruit;

(III) casting out the Christmas window displays along Fifth Avenue, where animated mannequins of little white children slowly untie the ribbons of their presents, never finishing, or else they wave bones made of confectioner's sugar (Sainte Catherine's bones) above the eager heads of mechanical dogs who never spring up to taste them, and white electric trains go round and round;

(IV) saying get thee behind me SATAN to Saks and Macy's where the dangling black tag of a red sweater held against a black dress resembles a bloody scalp (oh, we'll see scalps aplenty in this book);

(V) so that the shadows of your eyelashes, which tremble ever so slightly, become ferns dancing in the wind that now smells of sunlight and beehives

(VI) as you stand beside the Stream of Time

(VII) that must eventually freeze over in allegories – although in *my* book it remains a determinedly downpassing creek, bottle-brown, with false islands of autumn leaves trapped between its rocks (you cannot cross without getting your feet wet – but commit all things to Him!) It makes a noise like wind as it descends from shade to shade.

And so at last, Seigneur, the First Prelude is accomplished. – The Second Prelude is the "Mental Examination of the Place." – Well, look around you.

New France stretches from the forty-first to the fifty-third degrees of latitude, and west for uncounted leagues to the Sea of China.* To the east lies the great

* "Canada" seems originally to have been the name of an Indian town. Cartier generously bestowed it upon an entire district along the Fleuve Saint-Laurent; Lescarbot used it to refer to the river itself, and so in time it became the appellation of the country. Perhaps on account of its conveniently obscure origin, the word gained considerable expansive power for its French users; in the end, like New France itself, its rivers and references flowed down into the equally amorphous "Florida" of the hapless Spaniards.

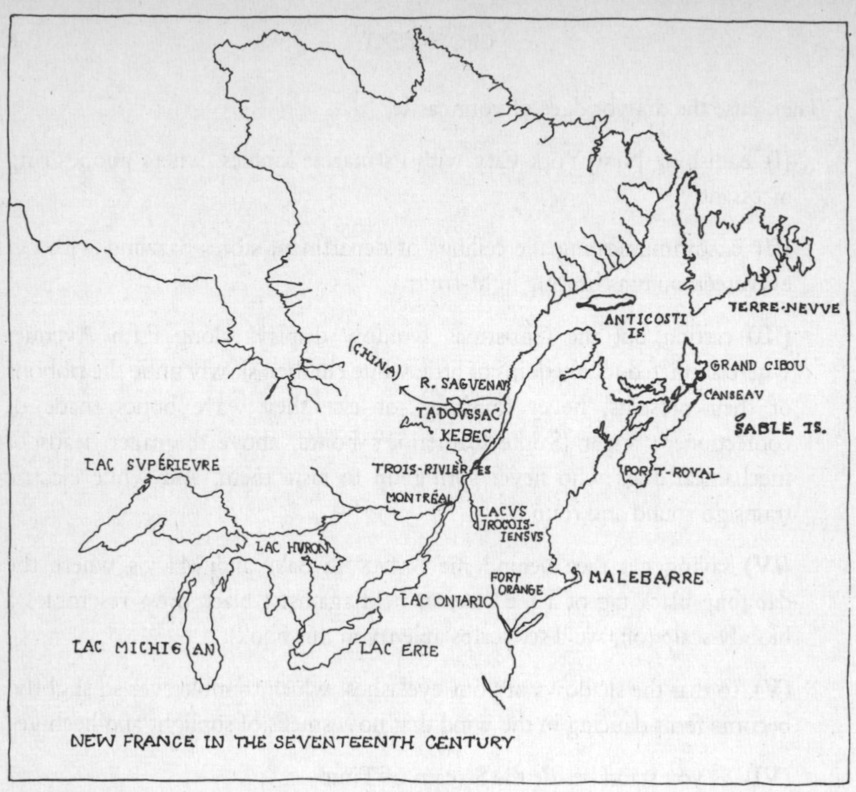

NEW FRANCE IN THE SEVENTEENTH CENTURY

island of Terre-Neuve, which was known to the old Norse Greenlanders as Vinland; Bretons fish there now for cod. This region and parts south are called Acadia. There are mooseberries in the shaggy forests, and churches eaten with arches like mysterious seashells. The Savages called *Souriquois* still live hereabouts as they did in the previous Dream, worshipping their devil KLUSKAP; but the Savages called *Esquimaux*, or *Excomminqui*, which means *Excommunicated*, have withdrawn north to Hudson Bay with the change in climate; our Black-Gowns will have little success with them. *This tribe is very savage, and, it is said, addicted to Cannibalism,* wrote that righteous pioneer, Père Biard (1611). – At the center of the spider's web, Champlain is debouched at Kebec. Directly south (a direction of dread) lies the Country of the Hiroquois; northwest of them, a month closer to China, the Huron rule their rustling empire of cornfields. Black-Gowns will die there.

Yes, but look around you, I said! Water glistens. Listen! Water boils in your ears.

Canada wouldn't be Canada without rivers, would it? Canada's story (a story of swimmings, drownings and falls down precipices of water) rushes and mazes like those many arms blue and brown that reach toward the great sea, always there, never there, shoving silt and boulders along the flats of their fishy palms, then sometimes relaxing, spreading their fingers wide to make shallows where Québecois children sit fishing from river-rocks, collecting trout and perch to gill-string like jewels into gleaming necklaces. There are so many rivers in their Country, in fact, that the Canadians classify them, letting some, the middling ones, be *rivières*, while the grander ones they call *fleuves*. The town of Three Rivers has three rivières. But the way from Kebec to Montréal is the Fleuve Saint-Laurent. – The Stream of Time is neither fleuve nor rivière as we begin, but rather a mild little brook, time *being* mild, meaning no harm to the leaves it whirls away, exerting no effort. Beyond, it is true, where the Waterfalls of the Saints cast their thunderous chill on sloping rock-shelves, where Tekakwitha the Iroquoise is buried, where Père Jogues' head surveys the stream from a pole of the Mohawk palisade, in those places the hills lie dark and low and covered with leaves; the sky is raining yellow leaves like memories. But new foliage can be expected next spring. The Stream of Time is mild. Knee-high waterfalls gush down rock-clefts, and the roots of silver birches flow in stream-like twists. You walk between trees and trees, uneasily reverent, as if you were proceeding down an aisle between ever so many pews in the Église Notre-Dame in Montréal, with incense about you like pine-fragrance as you approach the crucified CHRIST, Whose arms, raised in a great Y, bless you when you near Him to inhale the glow that shows what agony is made of; glow or not, His Cross is the darkest thing you see as you make the Third Prelude ("Asking for What I Desire"), darker than any cruel tree whose leaves come whirling down; but you lift your eyes to the sky-blue glass and the brassy spires and niches where Saints live; and crowds of indulgence-candles flicker in the draft, making little waves of light to comfort you and subtly kiss you; until you're prepared to sail time's Fleuve and gaze upon the true terrors of this church. Not that you *want* to do that. But what you want is Catherine Tegahkouita, and she is in Canada.

✠ ✠ ✠

This book is the story of how the Black-Gowns and the Iroquois between them conquered the Huron people. With its weight of antecedents and obscurities, as I admit, the tale is an ungainly one, like the patent letter granted in 1639 by the Grand Roy of France, Louis XIII, to authorize the founding of the Ursuline seminary in Kebec: – *viz.*, very wide and creased and cracked, dragged down by its heavy tassel-strewn seal. The name **LOUIS** is the largest word. And yet in this tale of Fathers and Crows, the word writ in grandest majuscule must be **RIVERS**. – In any event, the architect of our Église Notre-Dame was born

too late to see it. The Preludes being completed, you must proceed to the Body of the meditation, whose First Point is to visualize this fine builder, and, reflecting within yourself, to gain some profit or goodness from him. His skeleton lies beneath the first pillar on the epistle side, fingers folded over rib-cage. His coppery skull glows like the Star of Decay; he's staring up at you through the stone floor. (Canada, I should explain to you, is a place where most everything is transparent.) You stare back, into the eye-depths, looking for something that isn't there anymore. You're standing in some high steep place where the trees grow taller and vision is easily lost in green-grey distances; peering down through hemlocks you see the narrow white ribbon of rapids to which the Black-Gowns once ascended in Huron canoes, swollen, bleeding, smiling; and you listen for the river-roar but cannot hear it since it has soaked into pine needles and fern-walls and moss and grizzled grey twigs that snap like gunshots when you tread on them, as if only *they* could release that river-noise (and their release is meaningless); so now you gaze fruitlessly into the skull of this Catholic convert and deliver your question about Père Brébeuf's necklace of red-hot axeheads because now that they both are dead the men must know each other, but no replying glow lights from within to stream up through tired eye-sockets, as customarily happens with stained glass figures in church (so the Exercises command you to believe); you reach through the floor and take his skeleton-hand in yours, but it is only a cold dead claw, a bundle of frozen twigs . . . anxiously you assure him that the Black-Gowns love him, that Tekakwitha sees him, that the two lately added towers, *Temperance* and *Perseverance* (1842), crown his work as nobly as a pair of oaks – but now the skull turns slowly from side to side in denial; the jaws work, and you bend down with your ear against the floor to hear; your ear is getting cold and all this dead thing can say is: *je ne me souviens pas*: I don't remember . . .

✠ ✠ ✠

In Québec, at the Musée des Ursulines, there is a fairhaired girl as beautiful as an Angel: pale, pure, peaceful and very Catholic.

She directs you to the black chapel-Cross "Lozeau," forged of iron; with the words MARIA and IOSEPH wrought into it. Each arm ends in a fleur-de-lys; and there's a fleur-de-lys in each metal armpit.

She says: In those days it was quite difficult to teach these Indian girls! They were always coming and going, coming and going!

She says: The Ursulines tried so hard to help them, save them!

Do the Ursulines have a statue of Sainte Catherine Tekakwitha? you ask.

Yes, she says, I think so. I think there is one in the convent school. I was a student there. It's a very small statue near the stairs, like this. She wears a blue sheet or something. She is in Indian dress.

Could I see it?

Here it's very difficult to see what's not shown. You have to get permission and see the Superior.

Where do I go to do that?

You go to number eighteen, rue Donnaconna. This is the *tour*, the main entrance. You probably have seen the door already. When you have continued on the street, you see a *porche*, a big door with a grille. Then you ring there, and a nun will come.

So you hood yourself against the spring rain and proceed to number eighteen. You enter the *tour*. In the dim hall you are welcomed by the upraised eyes, the spread hands of the founding Sainte.* But you know that you are not supposed to be here. On your left is the grille. You push the call button and a little door creaks back, behind which a nun says *oui?*

* Mère Marie of the Incarnation, who will also play a part in this Dream.

You explain your purpose.

The nun says: One moment, Monsieur.

The little door closes.

You wait, admiring the crucifix above the radiator (JESUS's arms are raised, which your good Angel has assured you is a sign of Jansenist heresy, signifying that He asks only the elect to ascend with Him). On your right is a very antique bench whose back is formed of separate wooden rests, in each of which is an oval hole. At the head of the stairs, which rise to unknown destinations, hangs a photograph of the convent girls at their desks, with one nun at the back of the room, watching; and a nun in the flesh looks down at you from the top of the stairs and goes away, and you scrutinize another photograph, of girls in white in the Chapelle, kneeling between the ranks of nuns; and then at last the nun returns and you come to her with pounding heart and she says: Monsieur, there is no statue here of Tekakwitha.

The next day, a rainy Sunday, you return to the Musée to tell your pathetic tale.

She was looking at her left, the Angel insists. She has a blue sheet on. Maybe it was not her; it was someone else. But I think it was her.

Oh, well.

At the convent it is sometimes like this.

Is it a good school?

Yes, it's a good school, but I was quite bored after five years there. It's all girls. They are very strong on theories.

✠ ✠ ✠

Eh, then, back to Montréal, where we are merely half a river away from Tekakwitha's relics. (Six days after her death, say the *Jesuit Relations*, she appeared to Père Chauchetière near this spot and touched him with her ecstasy. Twice again she came to him. But I wonder if he saw her bones toothmarked by the spikes of her iron girdle?) Where might she appear now? Will she uplift her chin as in her medal, gazing up at her new mother the HOLY VIRGIN, so that you might sweetly kiss her throat? – GOD knows. – Let's try the Église Notre-Dame again, wasting no effort on the architect's skeleton this time. The dark sheen of the old walls is one with that of the dim canvases, from which pale faces glow like lamps of melancholy. Their cousins, the candles (**Offrance Petit Lampion 50¢**) flower beneath them in racks of red dishes like all the flames of Hell; they bloom in blue vases (**Gros Lampion $3.00**) like foxfire, and the groined ceilings are golden-veined like the wings of celestial flies – yes, there is light all around you; you go upstairs to search the Sacred Heart Chapel (reconstructed since the fire of 1978), where bronze faces and trees strike you like sunlight. *Love ought to be manifested in deeds rather than words,* you pray, according to the formula of Saint Ignatius. – But what deed can you hope to do? – Well, skip up the Stream of Time to the Mohawk Rivière, where she was born; there you can prospect between ruined longhouses for the charred relics of Amantacha the Huron; those might draw her out, and then you could go back downstream to the Fleuve Saint-Laurent with its lakes, waterfalls, bridges – *viz.*, Montréal, where you are now – which is not good enough. Somehow, you must make that same great circle and come out in a new place. Then you will be anointed by JESUS so that you will be fitting in the eyes of your bride. – But where is she?

(Again it is like the river and the sea. You know where she is but not how to find her. But *if* you found her . . . There is a saying among the Hiroquois: *The dead are separated from us only by the thickness of a maple leaf.*)

Returning from the chapel, you exchange gazes with each of the fourteen stained glass windows, looking through them as they do you, seeking scudding clouds that disturb the ruby mouth-light to which you're moth-drawn because you want to kiss the Absolute! and there is *One* whom you know, one face for whom your heart pounds in joy and excitement and reverence and love: there she is! – Star of the Natives, Lily of the Mohawk, Patron of Ecology, KAIATANORON, Apostle of Prayer – *viz.*, your Mohawk Virgin to whom you will pray this Dream.

Her hand – no, you will never never touch her. That is the Second Point.

She blesses you from her glass prison, and she is glowing. The long braids fall to her waist. She wears a luminous white robe of moose hide, fringed and patterned with red and black. You look into her because you want her to see you (so the dead architect also prays, when at morning Mass the fiercely rising notes of the organ rattle his bones, and he remembers her at last and tries to genuflect; then he says his *Aves* with many a chilly skull-chatter); you pray love me because you want her so but she is looking off and upward. – It is 1680, the year of her delicious young death. Her right hand is stretched out over a clearing of brilliant glass flowers and berries which can never tremble in any breeze; a stump stands at her feet, and its cut face glows as whitely as her dress. Behind her rises a pair of teepees, and two sachems stand talking *tête-à-tête* among the trees, and the chilly sunlight of Montréal illuminates their feathered headdresses (one red, one white). But Tekakwitha does not see or hear any of this. And she does not see you; she *will* not see you. Her tawny Iroquois face is uplifted, and the glass shines blue above her through all the swirling petals of sky, crowned at last by a flowered arch of gold.

Is that what she really looked like? you ask your friend Pierre.

No! he says scornfully. (Pierre is an atheist.)

✠ ✠ ✠

Pierre has taught you Québecois swear words. In Paris they would be excremental or sexual, but here they are religious. To insult someone you can call him *mon calice*, or *mon tabernacle, mon ciboire, mon* CHRIST, *mon ostie, mon Sacrement.* You can mix them if you like: *Mon ostie de ciboire de tabernak de* CHRIST. You try this out on a leatherjacket who is blocking your way on rue Sainte-Catherine and he kicks you.*

✠ ✠ ✠

The whores on rue Sainte-Catherine are blonde tonight, and wear their scarves very demurely. Snowflakes melt in their hair. They stand in a gaggle in the doorway of Harvey's and say things like you won't catch me hanging round *near* that bitch – by which you deduce that they are mere Anglophones. One

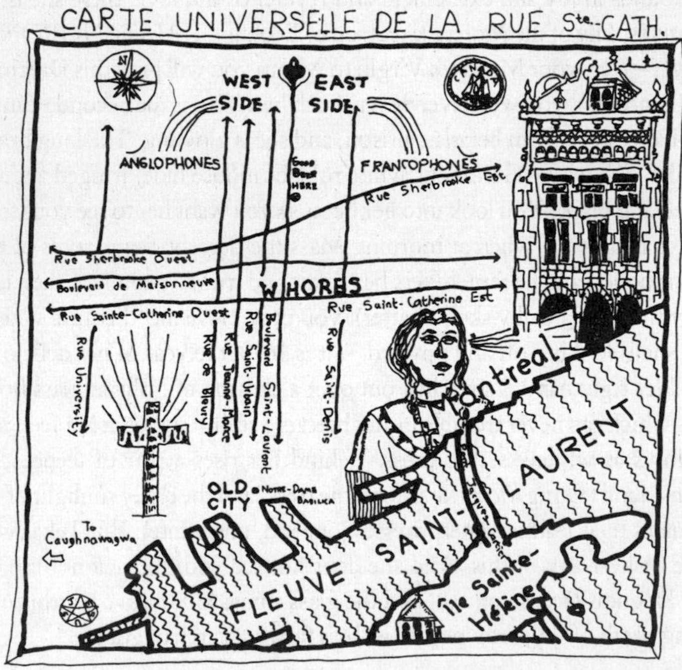

* "This is not the image post Quiet Revolution Québecois want of themselves," says Prof. Bruce Trigger (note to author, 28 May 1989).

follows you, clop-clop-clop, for blocks. Every now and then you turn around and nod agreeably at her. But it is too cold. You are shivering, and she is shivering. That is the Third Point. Snow plummets past the posters on the walls. Snow blows like smoke. She scuffs snow with her boots, and paper snowflakes twirl gently in the darkened windows of stores. You want her to tell you everything that the architect, the Ursulines, and the *Jesuit Relations* wouldn't. She must have seen things: Who was the Souriquois woman that Robert Pontgravé used? Which Angel took Champlain's kisses? How did Amantacha die? Who pandered to the Black-Gowns and left them in dark corners with the mouth-lit souls? (Because then if Tekakwitha catechizes you, you'll be able to answer.) – But, remaining loyal to the Third Point, you say nothing, and she leaves you wearily. That is what faith must do in Canada: it shatters the bridges between hearts, leaving only a stream of frozen blood.

At least, at last, here like a chapel is the Taverne, where you can get a 1635 ml. bottle of Molson Export for $3.30 Canadian. You go in, because that is the Fourth Point ("Examination of the Taverne – Listening to What They Say").

It is warm, and the TV not too loud. Over the counter, a fleur-de-lys. All the men are facing the street, so to be contrary you sit down facing the other way, facing them. A schoolteacher whose neck is purple and fatty like a snail watches you, sips, gives the bartender money so that a fresh Molson, emissary of night friendship, appears on your table in substantiation of the rumor of loaves and fishes; and he is watching you. – Can he join you or do you want to be alone? – You tell the bartender that he's welcome. You need information.

Tell me about the *Indiennes*, you say. I want to understand them.

Ah, he says, the Indian girls, they are first one thing, then another. They are unstable, like water. You buy one a beer, she go home with you. She is yours.

Mine? Mine forever?

He laughs. – If you want.

He leans forward; he points sternly with his finger. His nose is like a beak. – They are bad girls, bad all the way, he says. But they will bring you glory . . . Glory . . .

That's what I want.

Then you don't want me. You never wanted me. Glory leaves no room for human beings.

Yes, but then Catherine will be mine forever.

Tekakwitha? You should visit the Jesuit Chapelle on rue Bleury. There is a statue of her there. You can kiss her, kiss her. But hurry. Someday rue Bleury will be on the English side . . . Ha! You want Tekakwitha! Have you sinned so badly, that you need her to breathe in your mouth? She'll do it, you know, if you ask her. Her breath is like – like roses, and the smell of new chalk; when I take out a new stick of chalk and look at my boys, when I make the first mark, I think of Tekakwitha. Like a young boy's face. So new and clean. I am very religious. And the roses, I . . . Won't you please come home with me? You don't have any place. I can see it. I live on the top floor. Sometimes I watch the whores there. I can look down from the balcony and see them in the alleys. Sometimes they look up and see me. Then with their faces raised, it's religious, very religious, I can't describe it. I'm so lonely. Won't you come home with me?

Monsieur, I can't. I would if I could, but that's the Fifth Point. I saw her in the Église today, and she was looking away from me. Maybe I'll find her again on Mont-Royal; that's where I'm going. I'll go higher if I can. I wish I could see better; the snow is whirling so hard outside.

Stay with me. Just until the snow stops. I won't touch you. I just want someone . . .

You rise and stride into **MESSIEURS**. In the stall, you pray. Your prayer beats its wings inside you and you unbutton your jacket to let it out and it flutters over the top of the stall and through the crack in the door and across the bar, unseen by any, and out the door, and down rue Sainte-Catherine, past the multicolored posters flapping in the wind, grainy with snow-crystals, that say EROTIQUE and SEXY, and a gaggle of shorthaired rich girls come chattering out of a late night record store and on the wall it says **FUCK LES ANGLOPHONES**, beside which a whore in a black parka stamps in the snow to keep warm, looking your prayer in the eye when your prayer looks her in the eye so that understanding passes between you; the Anglophone is being fucked; and just past the bar that says DANSEUSES NUES a woman stands in the doorway of an erotica shop too thickly dressed to use hip-arts or breast-arts so she widens her eyes a little at the face of your prayer and blows a kiss of breath through her lips like CHRIST, the steam hanging invitingly like the fragrance of something good cooking. It is snowing hard, and the snow stings your prayer's wings very pleasurably. Up it flies, up to Mont-Royal. Whether or not Sainte Catherine is there, your prayer will search for her manfully, mournfully, with frozen tears, yet it will travel low and speedily between treetops, hunting, loving unceasingly . . .

✠ ✠ ✠

The Black-Gowns prayed to the Huron: LET US LOVE YOU – and the Huron were destroyed. If you pray to a prostitute: *let me love you* – then maybe you or she will be destroyed. If I pray to Sainte Catherine: let me love you – well . . . That is the Sixth Point.

To love CHRIST properly (taught the Black-Gowns), you must despise yourself. The more you dissolve yourself in the river of Him, the more you will *be* Him in all His love and Power. This may be so, and it may not be so. But do you need to despise yourself in relation to other human beings?

Consider that moment (not a great deal downstream from where you first stood beside that little rivulet called Time) when Père Chauchetière was pleased to see that certain Savagesses had begun to adopt austerities, having been inspired by the pious practices of the Hospital Sisters in Montréal,* who disciplined themselves with iron girdles and hair-shirts. Père Chauchetière had never sought to communicate these things to the Savages, believing them still to be too lowly of purpose and understanding to benefit (remember that these were Iroquois!), but GOD shaded three Savagesses with his black wings; they formed a society to commence a sort of convent, at which Père Chauchetière was forced to intervene, saying my *dear* children, I cannot permit this because your grace is not sufficiently tested at which they threw themselves down before him, bowing and pleading and wailing and gashing their foreheads on the stones like undisciplined infants (although he had to confess himself gratified by their ambition, however rudely expressed: already they'd given up their Maple Thanksgiving and other pagan rites; they'd forsaken their False Faces, those satanically wise heads of mummified corpses), so he passed his hand over their brows and said you must labor to *control* yourselves, my children; you must *trust* me to inform you when I consider you prepared to take this step at which the Savagesses lifted up their heads to him and dried their eyes and meekly begged his indulgence, which he freely gave. Although they had failed in their hope of being cloistered, the three took vows of chastity and mortified themselves as best they could. At Christmas-tide of 1676, the leader of them undressed, kneeling at the foot of the great cross that Père Chauchetière had erected beside the cemetery. It was particularly cold that day, and a heavy snowfall had begun shortly before dawn. The snow fell upon her long black hair, and slowly turned it white. It fell upon her shoulders and neck and welt-marked back as she crouched there praying and shivering. She had been got with child shortly before she took her vow, and now her belly was very big. The snow fell. – Later, the other two Savagesses made a hole in the ice of the Fleuve Saint-Laurent and cast themselves into that black water for the length of time

* Not until 1960 would the hospitals of Québec Province be taken out of the hands of the religious.

that it took each one to say her rosary sedately. One of the pair, afraid that Père Chauchetière would find her out, did not even dare to warm herself on returning to the cabins, but lay down silently on her mat with great lumps of ice stuck to her shoulders.

This is excessive, said Père Chauchetière. You have not the strength of heart of the Hospital Sisters, as I told you already. You are only ignorant Savagesses. I call upon you to moderate your behavior.

Of Catherine Tekakwitha it is told that she and her best friend now retired every Sunday into a cabin in the middle of the cemetery, where Tekakwitha, being now exhausted to the point of illness with all the travails that she set herself, undressed and then begged her friend to do her the charity of whipping her with willow shoots. At first her friend refused, saying, look at you, Kateri! You are so weak already; your body cannot bear this! but Tekakwitha fell on her knees before her and said what does it matter? and her friend (whose face was as wide as a shaman's wooden medicine-scoop) said by Heaven what do you mean? and Tekakwitha said yes yes dear sister by Heaven and she started telling her about all the blue glories of Heaven which she could see whenever she looked up at the sky and she whispered how much she wanted to go there and she told her friend that the two of them would be there soon where JESUS would draw them to His breast and then they would never be sad anymore and Catherine's mother and father and brother would be there waiting and all the other good people who had died in the epidemics and burnings and winters of Canada and Catherine and her friend would come into each other's arms rocking each other and kissing each other forever and her friend's eyes widened slowly and she began panting and Catherine gave her the willow shoot and said through lips as lucid and pink as the dwarf raspberry of Canada called *Catherinette*: now please strike me please and her friend began to whip her until the blood flew off her back and then she said it's my turn and Catherine took the switch and beat her but she was too feeble to draw blood so her friend began to weep but Catherine comforted her and said never mind and showed her another secret thing that she knew to cause blood and pain infallibly, and so they gave each other consolation every Sunday. Later, when Catherine's illness became more severe, her friend wondered if she had sinned in agreeing to do it, and so at last confided the matter to Père Chauchetière. He looked at her for a long time, but said nothing.

Père Chauchetière sat shivering and blowing on his hands and writing his yearly journal for the *Jesuit Relations*, reporting that another Black-Gown had drowned in the rapids (and the bloated body went whizzing down waterfalls, so pale and swollen inside that black cassock, shooting past Québec to the place where GOUGOU the Water-Monster waited for food), and Père Chauchetière wrote *In truth, one must always be prepared for death in this Country* and Père Chauchetière described the devotion and zeal of the Savages, saying *From time to time, they deplore the misfortune of their birth* . . . and Père Chauchetière wrote that many a married couple now lived as brother and sister, and the men were not to be outdone by the women in matters of asceticism, and the snow fell.

Catherine Tegahkouita died on the seventeenth day of Avril 1680. Although Père Chauchetière usually required the Savages to be carried to the chapel to receive the viaticum, no matter how ill they were, he made an exception in her case. She died, says that year's *Relation*, "in the odor of sanctity."

Seeking her, your prayer flies south to Auriesville, New York, arriving on a foggy twilight. At the entrance, huge dark Crosses tower over:

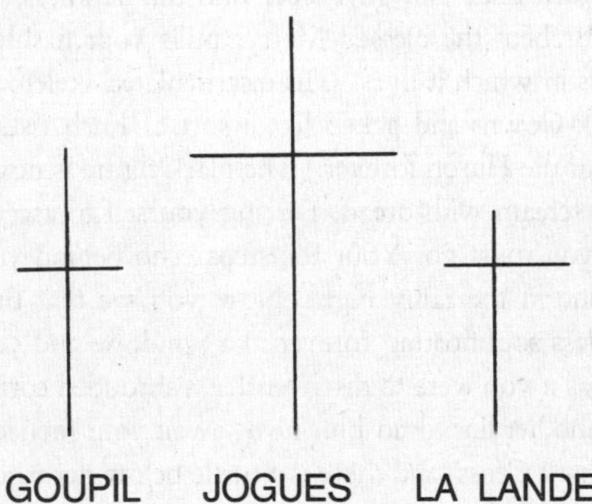

and at your prayer's left is a sign that reads ***Ossernenon: The Land of Crosses***. A cricket chirps. A bird flies overhead. Your prayer enters the world of trees. At Notre Dame de Foy, the first shrine, your prayer meets the replica of the Black-Gown Jogues inside his tomb-phallus of wood and stained glass. He was tomahawked here. His right hand is uplifted terrifyingly. He holds the cross in his left hand. His face is darkness. You shine your flashlight beam of prayer upon it, hoping that it is not presumptuous to do so (after all, your light is but your gaze), and now you see his moustache curving down, at which you feel relief, knowing for certain that he is not Death, whom the Hiroquois named *The FACELESS ONE, the lineaments of Whose Face our ancestors failed to discern.* At least he is not That. Yes, you raise your light, and simultaneously the shadow of his raised hand shoots up and races across the ceiling. Red-glassed candles flicker at his right and left. There is a puddle of rainwater at his feet.

Your prayer leaves him and returns to the Strait Path. When you reach the Third Station of the Cross, fog creeps along the lawn that was once a Mohawk village, and the tall trees exude darkness. The Seven Sorrows are marked with medallions on poles whose Cross-arms halt you and embrace you in clammy parallels. Night is seeping down to you.

At the Chapel to Our LADY of Martyrs, devoted to the Blessed Kateri Tekakwitha (for she was born here at Ossernenon), your prayer enters beneath wooden wings into darkness; and ahead of you you see a dark silhouette hovering in air like a spirit and you are afraid. The dark benches around you are like ribs. The flickering red candles light you upstream. The air is stifling, as if you had come into a crypt. CHRIST stands faceless. At His feet, a rose. Through the window behind Him you can see the immaculate lawn, the pale twilight freely endless, but you turn aside and go deeper into the darkness, where a piece of bone from Père Brébeuf the blessed Martyr pulls your flashlight beam to the lovely silver Cross in which it lives. (His disarticulated skeleton was dried in an oven by the Black-Gowns and baked like a sort of Eucharist, just before they fled the Country of the Huron forever.) The black figure is now so close to you that you want to scream with dread. Forcing yourself to ascend past the altar, you go the way you must go. Your footsteps echo behind you like pale trees planted one by one in the rainy night. Now you see that the figure is Saint Kateri's stained glass soul floating forever in a window, and your fear becomes sadness and love, as if you were to discover that a shrouded corpse in a mortuary was your wife's, and her lips, dead-blue now, await your final kiss. Kateri stands holding her birchbark Cross, and there is a turtle below her (she was born of the Turtle Clan). Behind her, the hill of Ossernenon drops grandly down to the Mohawk River, whose silver and grey she has seen stamped with tree-reflections metal-colored in dusk, the water so still; your Kateri has seen trees in a rain; she's looked down into a gorge of blue-grey tree-edges delicately staining the grey sky. Now she is more than three hundred and thirty years old, and she is gazing at you. You stand on tiptoe and kiss her glass lips at last . . . Then you go out. She cannot see you; she can only see through you. But that was the Second Point, wasn't it?

Your prayer continues on through the fragrant darkness of that immense mortuary, wandering among trees and Crosses, until the circuit is completed;

and again (bereft of her already because she shivers across Canada so restlessly like the reflection of a flame in a Fleuve) you pass Père Jogues' candles flickering red in the mosquito-ridden darkness.*

Gone again, is she? Why, that's the whole point of the Exercises! – But in default of her dubious statue, the *Jesuit Relations* do remain. There we read how Black-Gowns administered the Sacraments in longhouses and at the banks of creeks where it was very cool under the bending of beech branches, with darker greens of evergreens walling in the forest behind; and the water in the Stream of Time was holy water. They portaged their lives rapid by rapid. First they supplicated the Nations, then they debated with them, and finally they commanded them. A few as lucky as picked Jansenists (Père Brébeuf, Père Jogues, and others whom you will soon know) were murdered. The survivors baked their relics and went on like your prayer, searching for souls to love. (In 1700 you could have an Ottawa girl merely by going into her wigwam with a lighted taper, but that is not what I mean.) They hunted Catherine and her sisters across New France, working ever west and south, away from Heaven and Labrador, whence the Greenlanders first came to plant the seed of frost; and as they ascended the Stream of Time the Country became ever flatter, bluer and greener, sprinkled with fat silvery lakes in which cloud-shadows were blue like Père Brébeuf's eyes; and clouds were a woolly summer crop that grew upon the sky like lakes, and it was warm. Here it was that the Black-Gowns lived and toiled and died. Their sufferings can barely be imagined. Père Lalemant writes that the snow at Kebec was often four feet deep, and lasted from Novembre to Avril. (Indeed, when New France was lost forever in 1763, back in Paris they only laughed and plagiarized Voltaire, shouting eh, but what *was* New France after all but a few arpents of snow? and then they had another bottle of wine and somebody made a toast and said here's to the memory of all the squaws! and a fur-hat dandy said eh, but it's really too bad about the beaver trade. By then the *Jesuit Relations* were longer than Catherine's hair.)

Year by year, the Black-Gowns' vision penetrated farther into the forests. – If only the same could be said of her own! That could not be, of course; the smallpox that lived inside the crucifixes' carven whorls left her eyes very weak

* "For almost all [the Indians] the information is fragmentary," says the *Dictionary of Canadian Biography* (1966). "Like fireflies they glimmer for a moment before disappearing again into the dark forests of unrecorded history."

(nearsightedness being the disease of many a *clairvoyante*). But she saw farther and farther *inward* along the Stream of Time, past the Fifth Rapid, past the Twenty-Third and all her Mohawk girlhood days when she had bowed, never crying out, as her aunts mocked her for having received the Faith: already her elbows protruded like wings. She saw as we'll see, saw past that little island in the ice where the French first wintered in Canada – a children's toy of an island, Champlain's toy, with miniature trees and knee-high cliffs: the Isle de Sainte-Croix. She saw Port-Royal, where they tried again; Kebec, where they came to stay; Mission Sainte-Marie, where they proselytized, then Montréal, consecrated to GOD in defiance of the Iroquois. She saw her own death, surely; the *Relations* say that she knew her grave long before the Black-Gowns chose it, and loved to pray there. Then she drank water from the Rain of Heaven, kissing the well's mouth. – For their part, as I said, her French crow-Fathers saw ever farther outward, the rays of their eyes raking through green shade-walls just as spruce-needles rake the foreheads of ordinary men. And they wrote it all down. That is the Seventh Point. Of course, writing not for themselves but for those whom they obeyed, they cast each account in the fashion best suited (1) to show off their own unworthiness, in order to escape the sin of pride; (2) to record the progress made that year, in order to escape the stigma of unworthiness. As Père Biard wrote so frankly from Port-Royal (1612):

> . . . inasmuch as (I believe) no one would be edified by our losses, or greatly benefited by our gains, it is better that we mourn our losses apart; as to our receipts, we shall be like the unjust servant commended by Our LORD in the Gospels, namely, by sharing Our MASTER's goods with others we shall make them our friends . . .

The men in Montréal and Québec followed the same policy; and the Generals in Paris or Lyon who got the "receipts" made their own corrections before releasing each year's *Relation* to the printer. We have, therefore, a series of artifacts like multiply polished gems, whose settings may not have been what the miner would have chosen, had he thought about it, but which are all the more "authentic" for that; for we are dealing not with individuals, but with flocks and congregations of Black-Gowns flying like crows across the vastly anonymous sky of GOD.

Truth to tell, I myself have never held in my hands one of the original volumes of the *Jesuit Relations*. I have, of course, studied the reproductions of the old title pages, with their ships sail-billowing within epigraphed lozenges bordered by leaves, and everything seems so happy, windblown, purposeful that it would be impossible to believe that the ships of Black-Gowns could be resisted. – How purposeful our life is yet! – In the New York Public Library, which was once a stretch of grass on the edge of New France, a greyhaired woman in a striped skirt, her figure still good, clops by me with her head held high as that of any giraffe; and a blind man pads almost silently behind his dog. The questions on my forehead cannot exist for him, nor can they for that dead architect of Notre-Dame Basilica, James O'Donnell, who built so well, as I said, that he converted to the True Faith before he finished, for I too am transparent and they can only see *through* me (again and again that Second Point!) – but I remember nonetheless the emptiness that he kept in his skeleton-hand, as I do the missing beginning of Saint Ignatius's biography, the unknown Father of DEKANWIDEH the Huron, Kateri's stare, the hollow crypt in Saint Peter's heart; above all I recall the mysterious martyrdom of Père Brébeuf among the Hiroquois. Even if I were Brébeuf himself, I might not know why I died. If I were not he, but one of his torturers, I would be less likely to know; since I had not even been born in the century when the deed was done, how can I hope for a reply shining in the skull's eyes? The skeleton is under the floor, and the towers are gifts from other architects, and the stained glass portrait of Sainte Kateri is wrong: smallpox cratered her face, as I said, but the likeness does not show it! (Well, but that was her first miracle.) – This being so, there is nothing left to do but read about her. "The fruits of great errors are always libraries." (That is the Eighth Point.) The lamps cast their gentle light upon the long tables in the reading room.

✠ ✠ ✠

I asked Pierre: What's your assessment of the Black-Gowns?

Well, I think they did a great thing, he said, because before they came here there was nothing. But I don't like the way they wanted to change the Indians. They didn't respect them. And you know, everything Québecois is based on the Indians – everything truly Canadian.

✠ ✠ ✠

There are seventy-three volumes of the Reuben Gold Thwaites edition of the *Relations*. (There are seventy-three rapids in the Stream of Time.) Pages are often loose, and the paper itself is brown and crumbling. Like so many other things on this continent, they will not last much longer. Increasing the sense of loss and limitation is Thwaites's confession: *We cannot promise for this series the entire body of existing Jesuit documents, either printed or in manuscripts . . . This would carry us, even if they were obtainable, beyond the limits of this series . . .* As is all too often the case with treasure-hunts, we are left with a sense of mildewed disgust, as if, expecting to lose ourselves in the verdant forests of Parkman's Iroquois, we were to find nothing but old orchards of sour apples. – What, then, can we hope for from the *Relations?* Are the burned drowned Fathers *our* fathers? Unlike the Greenlanders in the previous volume, they strove to do good. – Were they good, then? – Of that Sainte Catherine will assure us . . . and so, reader, *pax CHRISTI.*

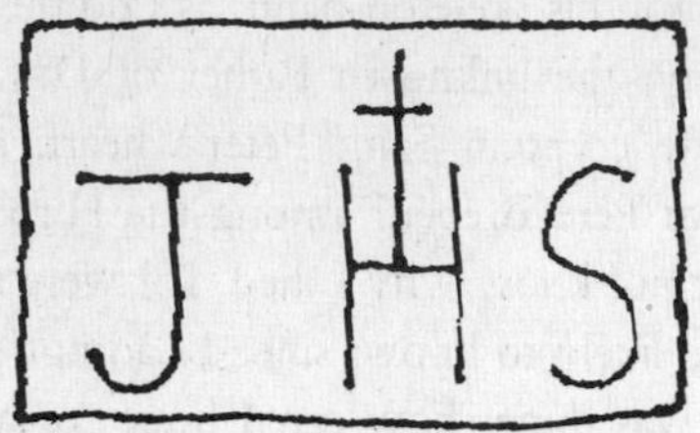

Fathers and Crows

Take the greatest saint on earth to Greenland and feed him on train oil and candles, and you make one thing of him; put him under the equator, with the thermometer at one hundred in the shade, and you make another.

HARRIET BEECHER STOWE, 1869

We have very rarely indeed seen the burning of an Iroquois without feeling sure that he was on the path to Paradise; and we never knew one of them to be surely on the path to Paradise without seeing him pass through this fiery punishment.

Jesuit Father, 1660

1
Kingdom Come
or,

How the Black-Gowns Sailed to Canada

Wearing the Black Shirt

1534–1990

> Whatever your hand finds to do, do it with all your might; for there is no work or thought or knowledge or wisdom in Sheol, to which you are going.
>
> Ecclesiastes 9.10

"The rivers of this land," wrote Père Joseph Juvency in 1710, "are remarkable because in certain places they are precipitated with a great uproar from the higher to the lower levels. The French call those places water-falls [*Ea loca faltus vocant Franci*] . . . The water of an entire river often falls in the form of an arch, in such fashion that it is possible to walk dry-shod beneath the stream which rushes overhead. The Savages, when they come to such a spot, shoulder their boats, which are constructed of light bark, and carry them, together with the baggage, to the calm portion of the river flowing below." In these places, Saints and bears stood behind the rainbows although we could never understand why their gazes retained the melancholy impassivity of carven images even as heathen rivers roared down across their faces like tears, caressing them with fish-silver, rattling slimy pebbles against their legs, drenching them, greening them with algae, shaking them in their niches, defiling them with frogspawn and minnows, with the blood of Savage river-wars, with rotten tree-trunks that struck them and chipped them and shot away, with maple leaves that stuck to them, with the bones of arrow-pierced beaver that the *Souriquois* had consigned to streams to hide them and cleanse them until the beaver came alive again – and that which cleanses must be defiled; so naturally the Saints were defiled by water, just as they were by the white, swollen corpse of Père Nicolas, whom the *Huron* apostates had drowned in the rapids; just as they were by the black and bloody spider-thing that whirled in white eddies, making them pink, spinning and rushing hideously until a fall swept it past a Saint's wooden face, to which it seemed to cling with every long black hair, but the weight of water behind it and behind it threw it to calm water where it floated in the sun, bleeding forever so that the great river would know that it was the scalp of that *Irocois* warrior called the Fox, whom Tekakwitha would not marry, whom her protector, his enemy, the Eagle, had killed laughing, after which the Eagle sang and scalped him and threw his twitching carcass into the Mohawk River where it shot past all the Saints and fell over the waterfalls and was broken, and the Eagle sang *Hey-yeh! Hey-yeh!* and painted his face. Then he leaped into his canoe. He paddled and portaged down to Mission Saint-François-Xavier de la Prairie, where Tekakwitha was praying beside the Cross of maple wood that she had made, and it was very sunny by the shore of the Fleuve Saint-Laurent and the birds sang *Ee-oh! Ee-oh!* and Tekakwitha was happy, so happy to be praying alone when she heard the snapping of a twig in the woods behind her. When she uplifted her head joyfully to receive friendship or death, she saw a man standing, his face blurred featureless as a deerskin drum, and she laid her fist on her heart as he came nearer and she leaped up and said *It's my uncle the Eagle!* and the Eagle thought that Tekakwitha loved him; so he laid his trophy down at her feet, saying, I killed him because he made you cry! and she trembled and said you know I'm a *chrétienne* now so please, Uncle Eagle, I *pray* you, throw that scalp into the river and – forget . . . and in astonishment and anger he shouted you would have me do *what!* and Tekakwitha turned her back on him and fell before her Cross, weeping and praying, so the Eagle snatched up the scalp meaning to be gone forever as she kept praying and he looked back but Tekakwitha was praying (which was sorcery) and he could see her lips move, could hear every tear of hers strike the ground with a sound like fresh rain: every teardrop became a lily until the meadow was white with dreaming

flowers. The Eagle said to himself Algonkin bitch! and the Eagle said to himself but I'm a *warrior* – I do as I please! and the Eagle said to himself as softly as a summer brook I know she'll never and the Eagle said never and then he retraced his steps with a fierce false face that she did not even see because she was staring into her Cross. So he shook the wrath from him; so he folded his arms and turned away, calming himself with the words of the Clear-Minded chanter who stood by dead chiefs singing: *Let the matter remain in perfect peace,* and he laid down his heart; he pushed past her to river's-edge where he squatted trailing his hand in the water with the charm clutched between his fingers and it felt so good that even now he was twisting it and stroking it like a beaver pelt; now he began to squeeze it tighter saying you dung-eater Fox I wish you were alive so I could kill you again! and felt so happy to be triumphantly hating him again without reference to the praying girl (because the Fox had made her cry), and then he stretched out his arm a little farther than self-love where the current was stronger and the scalp opened like a flower and he let it go. But the Saints did not change their expressions; no, they let the spider-thing touch them; they let the defiling rivers gush down tree-cliffs into the sea, where porpoises leapt away from the smell of murder-blood as the sailors said look how they play! and murder-bones settled down among the sea-rocks and murder-blood diffused throughout the world with porpoises leaping, leaping vainly ahead, from the coast of Turkey to the African Sea, but no matter where they leapt to, murder-blood bore up our warships that came sailing through the ocean sunshine, bearing cargoes of hatred and cannonballs to every new land; in their woodenness the Saints did not weep at that; nor had they wept at the very beginning when the Huron SKY WOMAN Who fell into the water ill repaid the efforts of beavers and otters who dove so kindly down to the bottom where the Fox's scalp lay rotting and pulsing as they foraged among soggy beaver-bones and brought up mud in their mouths to make a world for Her, the world where her children the Savages would have lived happily if they could (but every Black-Gown knew that the SKY WOMAN was *evil*); the Saints did not weep when DEKANWIDEH was cast into the falls by the Flint People;* they held back their resinous tears even when John the Baptist was beheaded for the ignorant pleasure of a whore; they wept not when CHRIST Himself was crucified (although another whore wept); they did not weep when Roderick King of Spain raped Florinda and she opened the gates to the Moors to revenge herself and the Moors ran in shrieking and slaughtering and stuffing Spanish

* Mohawk.

bread and meat and fruit into their dark pagan faces and they trod down the land for almost eight hundred years until the Fifth Seal was opened and pale slender women, nude like fishes, swam upward out of their tombs and into the storm in which Kings of the Earth committed fornications with the Whore of Babylon who rode the streets on her seven-headed scarlet Beast that trumpeted with the voices of elephants and brayed and howled and jerked its heads back spitting when the Whore pulled the reins, and it plodded and slouched across the cobblestones like a drunken King walking on his hands and the Whore laughed triumphantly and smoothed her scarlet dress and rode high between the humps of that growling wailing Beast, and the Whore cried, *Come to me, you Kings!,* and the Beast turned two of its heads around and strove to bite her but she struck those shying honey-eyed animal-faces with a little jeweled whip and they flinched away from her and the Beast lumbered on wailing while a crowd of desperate people stood shouting against her in the plaza until all the fountains stopped and the statues of Generals on horseback cracked into pieces; and women leaned screaming out of the windows of narrow red-tiled towers; the Archers and Sentinels on the wall had deserted their posts; the boats of the fishermen lay at the docks as if it were a holy day; and the Whore spurred the Beast and came galloping into the crowd and trampling them while they clawed at her and threw stones up at her, but she filled a golden cup from between her legs and began to shake it at them so that the poison spattered them and they died. Then a troop of Soldiers came to clear an aisle between the dead, tossing them left and right so that heads struck heads with hard dull sounds, following which the King's Guard rolled out a carpet of purple and the very King of Kings came to the Whore with so many rich gifts for her heaped up against his belly that it seemed he was pregnant. And he brought her refreshment, but what she liked to drink the best was the blood of the Saints. The Saints behind the rivers did not weep, even when she sucked the blood directly from their breasts or gashed them smiling and collected their blood in her golden cup of filth. And the King – did he weep? – Hardly. – But the Fathers of the Society of JESUS were there. *They* wept, and wore black, and raised their fists. They took Saints from river to river and so brought them to dwell behind all the rainbows. They laid their hands on the heads of the Savages and healed them. And the Saints were still silent. But now the forests of New France rang with shrieks; the gorges echoed with them; the rivers were turbid with them; screams flowed down to the great sea. At last the Whore of Babylon was weeping.

The Games of Waterfalls

Where the Fox had made Tekakwitha cry, the Country was wrought with gorges a hundred feet deep or more, at the bottom of which flowed wide brown creeks of easy shallowness, shaded by oaks and sumacs, and the water rippled across wide rock shelves on which the Savages known as *Irocois* liked to stand in the heat of the day, letting the cool water flow around their ankles, or they lay on broad rocks enjoying the sun while the river and the gorge wound down into the trees. Toward the end of the summer, in the time between the Green Corn Festival and the Harvest Thanksgiving, there were days when the stream was only a narrow brown ribbon in the dry gorge, and the waterfalls were wet stains of rock and shadow barely connected by drooling water-teeth, but in other places farther up or down the water still flowed white-bearded down ever so many steps of shale, eating deeper into them by the century and cooling the dandelions that grew tentatively beneath the heart-shaped leaves of trees; and ivy grew up the dark, many-ledged gorge walls, and the water came to the end of a rock and made a great white arch of rushing and fell down among the pale trees far below in the haze, and it fell again and there were rainbows, and then the river became wide and flat and there was a sound of rain as it ran down the slimy rocks that were green like the scales of turtles, and Queen Anne's lace grew where the river came out of the rocks and into the meadows, and trees and valleys rolled softly on through creeks and trees to the low blue hills beyond. Between gorges the glens were sometimes steep and dark. Deer-trails and moose-trails made roads for the Hiroquois to follow on their hunts. Their Elders held deer-antlers as their emblem of office. Deer browsed beside the streams. The spotted coats of the young fawns were like copper and flowers. They swam in that ocean of trees whose waves are hills; they flew through the sky of trees whose clouds are leaves. (But the crows also flew in the sky.)

Often in this season, when the warriors came home with their captives to be burned, the sky was white and grey with the light of thunderheads, and then the trees seemed darker. But the sun came out again, and waves of heat came even into the leaf-tunnels of the forest, so that the only thought of most creatures was to go to those wide green waters of August that flowed down through the gorges; and the Savage children dove into a deep pool in the rock where in their time their mothers and fathers had played; and they swam fast through the brown water and played a game at the base of a little fall where a narrow ledge, slimy with algæ, gave bare purchase to their toes when they hoisted themselves up onto it by hooking their fingers into cracks in the rock, and they stood precariously a few inches above the water and the white falls drenched their faces and they could shake their wet black hair out of their eyes and look up and see the jets of water seemingly falling from the sky as meanwhile they tried to walk along the face of the rock, laughing and so hopefully hugging its smoothness until they lost hold and tumbled back into the water to swim and dive and lie on their backs looking up at the ferny glen above the falls so darkly tree-shaded, and then they returned to the ledge and strove again, or pulled others down by their ankles, and the air was fresh with the smell of water. – Just below the place where the children swam, the falls roared down from a lip of rock which they had notched with their ruthless usage, and fell eerily down a hundred and fifty feet so that the air shimmered with flying drops; a tall narrow grotto could be seen behind, as if through a curtain; ferns grew there. At the base of the falls were rapids; a WATER-MONSTER lived there. A Black-Gown was doomed to die there.

The Dream of the Floating Island

A little north and east of the Country of the Iroquois (or, as they called themselves, the *Haudenosaunee*), past the Montaignez and Algoumequin Nations, lay the Country of another People where the moose were yet more plentiful, the forests were much thicker and sometimes swampier, and osiers and speckled alders lined the banks of wider rivers up and down which this People paddled their canoes when they hunted and fished and made war and visited; here mosquitoes whined in multitudes and the forests rang with the scoldings of chickadees and there were so many beeches that the sunlight was changed and became green. Flowing down from the dark mountains whose grey-lichened sides were wet with fog, clear streams swelled the rivers, which often rose above their banks after a rain, and the fishing was good in those places, and the rivers swept down through the green beech forests and widened further until they met the sea, where the People lived, gathering mussels and fishing for cod. And they were the People of KLUSKAP. They knew His ways, and the ways of PLANT PERSONS and ANIMAL PERSONS, and their Shamans had Power. They swore by the SUN; they smoked tobacco for wisdom. In after times they became known to the Black-Gowns as the *Souriquois*, and, later still, the *Micmac*, but, like any other People, they called themselves the People.*

* *Lnu'k.*

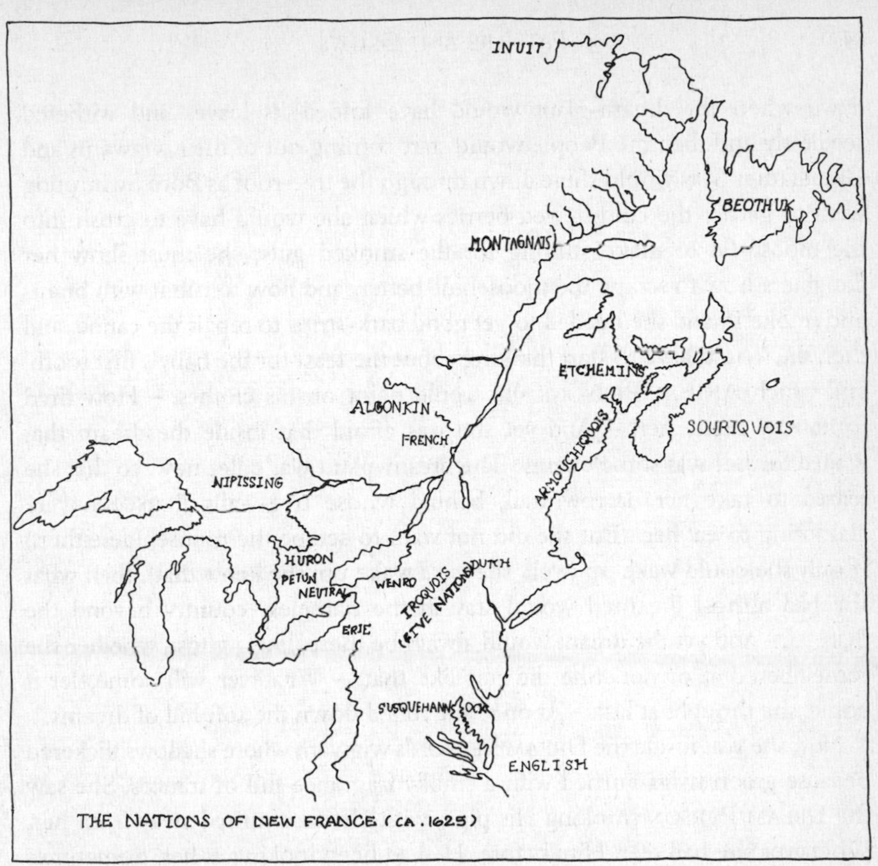

THE NATIONS OF NEW FRANCE (CA. 1625)

One night in the Moon of Leaf-Opening, the People were sleeping by the coast, and a woman had a dream. Her name was Born Swimming. At first, it is told, her sleep was translucent like a sheet of dried seal-guts, through which she could almost feel the warm weight of the bed-skins on her body, the muscled hardness of her husband's arm against her; she almost heard him clearing his throat in his slumber; his warm breaths tickled her shoulder like feathers. In that hour when the People had left their bodies, Born Swimming had traveled only a little way. Deep in the night forest, among the shining eyes of animals, her dream waited for her. It was a plant, head-high and fuzzy-soft like a mullein, whose pale greenish-white leaves glowed to draw her close, whose little flowers smelled sharp and bitter, so that she wondered if it might be poisonous. Of course she did not have to pick it; she could run back up to the hill-crest where her People slept behind their gutskin window of sleep; she could crawl back into her dear warm body and roll away from her husband's arm and open her eyes upon the smoky darkness of the wigwam where across the hearth her children lay sighing and coughing until dawn when the dream-plant would have folded its leaves and withered seedlessly and then the People would start coming out of their wigwams and Grandfather SUN would shine down through the tree-roof as Born Swimming went to gather the cold-dewed berries which she would have to crush into the moose-fat to make stuffing for the smoked guts; she must show her daughters how to scrape the moosehide better, and how to rub it with brains and smoke it, and she needed to get good bark-strips to repair the canoe, and then she would have to start thinking about the feast for the baby's first tooth, and which ANIMAL PERSONS she would paint on his clothes. – How tired tomorrow made her! – And yet she was afraid that inside the dream that waited for her was some enemy. The dream-plant was taller now, so that she feared to take her narrow trail, behind whose tree-walls PERSONS were clamoring to eat her. (But she did not want to scrape the moosehide either.) If only she could wake up (well, she *could* wake up; she knew that), then what she had almost dreamed would stay in the nameless country beyond the SUN . . . – and yet the dream would always be there, like a ghost, whether she remembered it or not. She did not like that. – Whatever will come, let it come, she thought at last. – At once she rolled down the soft hill of dreams.

Now she was inside the DREAM PERSON's wigwam where shadows flickered because green twigs burned with a smoky fragrance full of trances. She saw the DREAM PERSON smoking His pipe, with His face turned away from her. Whenever she had seen Him before, He had been looking at her. Sometimes He smiled at her with His toothless mouth and sent her a good fat dream that smelled like tobacco and berries; other times He tortured her with dreams of brambles. But this was going to be new. The DREAM PERSON put a pale green leaf in His pipe and began to smoke it, and the smoke drifted behind Him into her face so that she smelled the sharp and bitter smell of dreams. She willed that the sleeping skins would not weigh so firmly on her; she willed them to rise until they joined the hot and hairy darkness – *that* way she could breathe . . . but then the DREAM PERSON willed a wind that blew her down under a doorflap in the back of His wigwam, and she understood that if she had not willed the sleeping skins to rise, the wind could not have gotten at her; now it was too late; now the wind blew her into a dark place where an underground river rushed her down silvery waterfalls between moonlit cliff-rooms echoing with owl-voices; so Born Swimming willed fins on herself and began swimming upstream, clambering back up the wet rocks of rapids to return to the DREAM PERSON's house where it was safe and the sleeping skins waited in the air and she could wrap herself in them until she stopped shivering and then give back the dream and go out into the forest and up the hill again to her People, but the DREAM PERSON willed more water and more water until she was washed back down the rocks, and clouds shot across the moon and she smelled the forest as she rode down little falls across which tree-branches grew, their leaves tickling her face, and she willed strength into her arms so that she could cling to a branch even as the water spilled into space around her, and there she hung struggling until the DREAM PERSON willed that the branch would break, and then she fell into a whirlpool where the Fox's scalp spun thrashing and thrashing and whipping her face with its long oily hairs until she had to will herself *down* past this bad Power to where the DREAM PERSON meant her to go, into cool and silver spume, and she was carried to the sea. Now whatever was going to happen must happen. And that excited her.

It seemed to her in her dream that she saw an island floating in from the sea – how could that be? – and there were trees and animals on it. She saw a man walking about on this island, with no appearance of fear; he was dressed in rabbit-skins. – *You are going to be drowned!* Born Swimming shrieked at him; she wished so much that she had not let herself dream this dream. The island was creaking and bobbing under him; the trees were creaking on the waves, and yet the man did not seem at all put out. Who was he? – Born Swimming could make nothing of this.

When she woke up, she was smeared with her dream. She did not feel rested. It was almost dawn, when the People prayed to the SUN.

She said to her husband: I dreamed.

Tell me, he said respectfully. The children listened, rubbing their sleepy eyes.

Born Swimming told her dream.

That is a good dream, he said happily. Game will be coming from the sea. Now I will make a new spear for sturgeon.

I was afraid, she said.

He laughed. – Don't worry. I'll be careful.

Born Swimming replied not a word.

She went to Smoking the Pipe, who was Shaman and told the dream again. But it meant nothing to him, either, although he was an old man.

Smoking the Pipe coughed; Smoking the Pipe took a stone from his mouth. He rolled it in his hand. – This friend of mine sees no islands, he said. I think you are sick with desire for something.

I desire only one thing, she replied. I wish to see this Floating Island, and the PERSON in rabbit-skins.

Maybe He is Power coming in to you, Smoking the Pipe said finally, his voice trailing off. Maybe you will be a healer . . . – He shook his head. – No, I don't think so. You are not that way. I don't believe this dream is about you. Maybe new food is coming from World Above Sky. Maybe something bad is coming . . .

Did *you* have dreams like this, ever? she asked him defiantly. She wanted to contradict him now. She hated him because he could not explain her dream.

Not even KLUSKAP could ever have had a dream like that, Smoking the Pipe laughed brightly. Your dream is a mad dream! – No, no, keep your gift. I can do nothing for you.

All that day the People wondered what Born Swimming's dream meant. Her children ate blueberries and looked at her shyly while the purple juice ran down their chins. Her husband sat rocking himself on his heels. The seagulls screamed and screamed. But there was no change in the sun or the trees; the ocean was just the same. And that night no one dreamed anything extraordinary. Born Swimming herself dreamed nothing that she remembered. She woke up with a sense of disappointment. But then she heard people shouting. Everyone was running down through the trees to the beach. An island had come in to them overnight, like drift-ice. It was an island of wood, and dead trees rose up from it with their branches meeting each other crazily and not a stick had any bark; beavers must have chewed it all. Fat, pale bears were crawling in the trees. When the men of the People saw this, they ran back to their wigwams and got their bows; they wanted to shoot the bears and make an eat-all feast. Then they would dance and wear their necklaces of Armouchiquois scalps. The women withdrew – for among the People it is not good for a woman to see the approach of bears. But Born Swimming did not go away, although the men looked at her with dislike and fear. And presently it was seen that the bears were men, and the island was a big boat with poles growing from it. Yet still the hunters hesitated to lay down their bows, for among the Lnu'k it is known that some PERSONS can be bears and men at the same time. But Born Swimming spoke in a voice which they respected even as they drew away from her, and she said: They are men! – Then the other women came running back breathlessly.

Now the bear-men lowered a canoe into the water and some of them came paddling ashore, while others stayed in their big boat, crawling and crawling among the poles while the big boat bobbed in the water.

People kept running up to her. – Is this the island that you saw in your dream? they asked.

Yes, Born Swimming said exultantly.

In the canoe was a man dressed in white. There was hair on his face; in a few moments, when the People stroked him, they would find that his cheek was as rough as a beech leaf. He smiled at the People from across the water; he said something that they could not understand, and raised his hands toward the sky. The other men in the canoe kept on rowing.

Is he the man in rabbit-skins? asked the People.

Yes, Born Swimming said. Whatever happens, *I* have dreamed it!

Smoking the Pipe stood by in silence. People waited a little away from his Power, as they always did. He was almost blind with age, and his apprentice must speak into his ear before he could understand what the others saw. For a long time he thought, leaning on his stick. Then he raised his head.

The Shaman will speak! cried the boy, and everyone hushed.

Smoking the Pipe said: Listen well. Long ago those bad white ones came, those *Jenuaq*. KLUSKAP whispers in my ear now. KLUSKAP says that these strangers are more of them. They have secrets. We must hide from the Jenuaq or we must kill them. I have spoken.

But Born Swimming would not give up her dream.

You are our Shaman, she cried shrilly; you dream of enemies, and warn us! But did you dream this? – No! – *I* dreamed it! *I* say that the dream was good; *I* say the man in rabbit-skins will give us gifts!

For until this day she had never been important.

Hunh! said Smoking the Pipe scornfully. But he said nothing else. One must not argue overmuch with dreams. And it was true that sometimes KLUSKAP lied –

The canoe came closer and closer. The People stood indecisive. Some clutched their bows; some put their bows down. Smoking the Pipe stood motionless, blinking. At last a paddle grated on sand. The unknown men got out and pulled the canoe onto the beach. (It was a very strange canoe, round and fat like a giant berry.) They never stopped watching the People. Some held silvery sticks in their hands, which they pointed in front of them like blind men. With loud and heavy steps, they strode toward the People. Their moccasins were like hooves. Their faces and hands were sandy-pale, as if they were dead men bled of all color. First among them was the man in white.

Saint Pierre and His Shadow

AD *30–1534*

> Now it was that the fresh colored young man began to tremble, every joint of him, having dreamed the night before that the Indians were about to barbecue him over live coals.
>
> WILLIAM BYRD, *Histories of the Dividing Line Betwixt Virginia and North Carolina* (entry for 21 March 1728)

Just as the blue sky around the rim of a rock may become white if the sun is about to burst out around it, so heart-shirts darkened around the edges before we began to wear the Black Shirt. So it would be for the People of KLUSKAP (the man in white was the first, but Grey-Gowns and then Black-Gowns would supplant him); so it had been for the Hebrews. – May I tell it? (I beg you, by the way, not to think that the pages which already lie behind you are but fallen leaves of meaninglessness in an interminable forest of digressions – indeed, did I not know the end of this story I myself would despair. For already Savages, priests and harlots have slipped through our fingers, and it seems that we but grasp water. What will come next? Will I persist in my pretensions that this book has to do with the reduction of those pagan Huron Nations to faith and reason, when – now it comes out – we shall not even get our first glimpse of their Country for two or three hundreds of pages? – Yes! I refuse to say otherwise. For history is like a string that the cat has swallowed: – drawing events and events from the poor creature's throat, one is surprised at how much must be disgorged. To know how BEELZEBUB was expelled like an OKI from Huron stomachs, I must draw out the knotty life-twine of Père Brébeuf, which GOD had previously tied to the careers of Père Biard and Père Massé; antecedent to these Black-Gowns, and higher than they (as if in our cat's throat) comes Saint Ignatius, who created their Order; it was Saint Peter to whom *he* was vowed; and the ONE who began *him*, the only ONE Whom we can seize hold of, is the SON of GOD. It is to Him that I now vow myself, praying His favor in holding the string together as I yank. For why hurt a cat? – Especially since the Cat Nation was exterminated by the Hiroquois.)

When Our LORD JESUS CHRIST, then, was raised up from Hell at the end of His Passion, He kept company with the Apostles for forty days, and called upon them to be His witnesses in Jerusalem and Judea and Samaria, and unto the very ends of the earth so that His sacrifice of Himself would be remembered and loved and bring all to love; just as ODIN hanged Himself and gashed Himself to bring us knowledge and poetry, so CHRIST mutilated Himself on the Cross for us and even went down to the Place of Lost Souls to lead forth the innocent who had waited for Him, and they stood white and translucent and blinking at the brightness of the desert day that they had not seen for so long and then came a ringing as of a vast bell and the souls shimmered and ascended waveringly to Heaven, and CHRIST appeared to two who were walking to Emmaus and they did not know Him and discussed the empty tomb with Him and He interpreted Scripture so that they thought Him wise but still did not know who He was, but when they came at last to the house where they were going He made as if to go further, and the two said: Stay with us, Rabbi, for the day is far spent (but still they did not know Him), so He came in and they washed their hands and sat at table and He took the bread in His hands and blessed it and broke it and when He gave it to them their eyes were opened and they recognized Him and fell down before Him but already they could see the flickers of the torches through His face and He smiled and was gone. Similarly He appeared to the Apostles, and Thomas the Twin was not there when He first came to them, so Thomas would not believe until he had put his hand in the hole in His side, at which CHRIST was saddened and said: How much more merit you would have had, my poor Thomas, had you believed when you were not there!, but in this thing Thomas was never repentant, for in after years he cried to Peter, I *must* believe forever, for I felt the hole in His side with my own hand!, and Peter envied him, but he envied him in silence, not wishing to acknowledge his own need for palpability and relics. So CHRIST stayed with them for a space and revealed to them the meaning of all the prophecies that had gone before, and He told them many other secrets for their hearts' desire, such as what Moses had seen when the LORD placed him in the cleft of the rock, and how the LORD builds waterfalls and rainbows, and when the world will come to an end; but He told them these things only to comfort and divert them, because they mourned incessantly that at the end of the forty days He would be leaving them; because like Ignatius they saw Him already gone. So He led them forth and commanded them to act upon what He had told them. Then He was lifted up, "and a cloud took Him out of their sight." They stared into the sky hoping to see just one more sign, but two Angels appeared before them in white robes and said: Men of Galilee, why do you stand looking into Heaven? This JESUS, Who was taken up from you into Heaven, will come in the same way as you saw Him go into Heaven. – And then the Apostles understood that they had woken forever from their dreams and miracles, and must now hover lifelong making ready for His return. Even as they comprehended this, the Angels vanished, and their spirits fell still lower. They gathered about the place where the Angels had been, searching for footprints to kiss (there were none). And so, very slowly, with backward looks, they descended from the mount called Olivet, and returned to their upper room in Jerusalem, praying and waiting. On the day of Pentecost a sound came from Heaven like the sound of a wind, and they all began to speak in tongues, and the Apostle Peter called upon the multitude: *Let all the house of Israel therefore know assuredly that GOD has made Him both LORD and CHRIST, this JESUS whom you crucified!* – and all the people began moaning and screaming, because they remembered choosing to free Barabas the Murderer instead, he then being popular in their caprices, so that JESUS had died slowly in Barabas's place on that dry hill, Golgotha, where the sand was yellow with skull-dust and every rock was a skull . . . *Repent,* cried Peter, *and be baptized every one of you in the name of JESUS CHRIST for the forgiveness of your sins; and you shall receive the gift of the HOLY SPIRIT.* – So there were added that day about three thousand souls, whose high dikes of pride were shattered at last by the waters of the Spirit so that it seemed to them that brown rivers foamed over their dry mud-brick cities and washed them clean and they died in Him as they had lived in themselves; then upon the waters sailed a gaily painted Ark, and CHRIST was on it, and He went down under the waters and freed them from the Fox's scalp, which had grown into a great greasy forest of hairy seaweed that had wrapped around their necks and was choking them with sadness but CHRIST unwrapped each tendril lovingly from every neck and brought the people up to Him. All had known of Him before, but some there were who had never seen Him in life; He did His work now through the mediation of His Apostles. And this was painful to the Apostles, for they felt, as they had when they descended the mount called Olivet, that they were moving farther and farther from Him, but they knew that they were doing His will. So they sold their goods, and lived in common, owning nothing but their clothes and their belief. And the Apostles were now the Leaders, whereas when they walked with JESUS they were only His followers. And they became accustomed to commanding the people. Now, one day at the ninth hour when Peter and John were going to the temple called *Beautiful*, they met a beggar who had been lame since birth, and he called upon them for alms. – Peter said: I have no silver and gold, but I give you what I have; *in the name of JESUS CHRIST OF NAZARETH, walk!* – As a result of this miracle, the number of true believers grew to five thousand, and this time there were many who had scarcely even heard of Him, but allowed themselves to be baptized only because of what they had seen Peter do. So the Apostles gained more power in the eyes of the people, and they no longer rejected it, but rejoiced, since that power would help them to do His will.

A Concise History of the Middle Ages

Thus, says Herder, *the keys of St. Peter came into employ; but never did they turn without a fee.*

Further History of the Christians

AD 303–1533

My son, whoever strives to withdraw from obedience, withdraws from grace.

THOMAS À KEMPIS, *The Imitation of CHRIST* (*ca.* 1413)

Diocletian had them tortured and roasted; Constantine put their monograms on the shields of his soldiers, and led them to victory. On his death-bed he was baptized, and the Christians were secure. After him came Theodosius the Great, who overthrew the idols and forbade the heretics to assemble. By then the Roman mirror of empire, already riddled with cracks, had shattered. In the centuries of plague and pestilence that followed, the monks came forward, preserving the ways of reading and writing, and emulating the life of CHRIST. This is what the Black-Gowns said: *To save your life you must lose it.* Some made their hermitages in pleasant valleys, where they worked the fields and instructed children, and crucifixes hung upon the doors of their chapel-huts; halos glowed from their heads and kettles boiled vigorously on the hearth. – Others strove more harshly with themselves. – Across the lake from Nero's deserted palace, Saint Benedict began his career, in a cave so difficult of access, it is written, that his one faithful follower must lower down his daily basket of food on a rope. The darkness sent him dreams of forest places, but because he did not know Canada he thought them but a cloak thrown over his naked poverty of spirit. In a vision he saw the Fox's scalp swimming down Golgotha's evening to bury its tendrils in the face of CHRIST, stinging Him with unholiness in His last hours; but to Saint Benedict this was merely the Crown of Thorns. So he prayed until his beard reached the rocky floor, and his lion-head rested against his hand; his inward-sunk eyes saw Saint Maria Magdalena kneeling in the forest with a halo around her as the Angels built a chapel to shyly screen her from the Oriental city below; and he remained within his cave for three years, with his crucifix resting against his shoulder like a javelin. – What of his follower? He told all who would listen of the Master's austerity; soon Benedict's fame had traveled halfway to Egypt! When he came out of that darkness at last, dazzled by sunlight and bird-song, a dozen monasteries took him for their patriarch. And yet, though we would not think it, **MORTIFICATION** had scarcely flowered, for when men told of a hermit who had chained himself to a rock inside a stifling cave, Benedict went to him saying sternly *Break thy chain, for the true servant of GOD is chained not to rocks by iron, but to righteousness by CHRIST.* – And he returned to his twelve monasteries, where in obedience to the willful flickers of candles (these places, too, were like caves) the brothers recopied old books again and again, illuminating them with careful hands: one of these gleam-artists became Pope Gregory. In that age, nonetheless, the Christians sought more and more to despise themselves, for only by such sacrifice could they hope to emulate CHRIST their Master. (But the Popes were magnificently glittering.) And Saint Jerome said: *A Christian maiden ought not to know what a lyre or a flute is.* And Thomas à Kempis said: *There is no real liberty and joy, save in the fear of GOD . . .* And Saint Ignatius said: *While eating, one may consider the lives of the Saints, so as to take less delight and sensual pleasure in the nourishment of his body.* But the darker and more shapeless the habit that the Christians threw upon themselves, the more did they rejoice, like Saint Benedict in his cave, like the fettered hermit who competed with him, like Saint Augustine crying in ecstatic wonder: *For even while I dwell in darkness and silence, in my memory I can produce colors, if I will, and discern betwixt black and white.*

Maps of Canada

AD *ca.* 550–1544

If a man had fifty cents in his pocket he would assure you that in a month or two he would be a millionaire.

FRANZ WELZL, *The Quest for Polar Treasures* (1933)

If you look up into Heaven you may sometimes see an open door.* This was certainly the preconception of Saint Brendan the Navigator (AD *ca.* 550), who set out for the Promised Land of the Saints in an ox-hide curragh. He and his fellow monks voyaged for seven years. – How ruddy their faces look in the old picture that somehow found its way to Heidelberg! On a faint wash of illegible text, like smooth wave-crests, they stand in a crowd of frock-coats and tonsured heads, looking out in all directions. Saint Brendan himself wears a maroon cap and holds a scepter. A flag with a Cross on it flaps playfully just over their heads, atop a pyramid of rigging. Their yellow boat is not unlike the gondola of a balloon. Indeed, it is suspended, not in the air or the water, but in the coils of a scaly eel-like fish who is sleepily scratching his head against the keel.

The story is told in the *Navigatio Sancti Brendani Abbatis*. They saw many wonders, including a high rocky island that was continually dashed by the waves, where a castle stood waiting for them, and when they entered it they found the banquet hall already laid out with platters of fish and bread, but there was nobody there. In every niche there stood the carving of a Saint, at

* Revelation 4.1.

which sight the monks knelt in reverence, but Saint Brendan stood bashfully aside; knowing now as he did that he was one of their company, so that he doubted whether he had the right to pay them reverence. In the niche behind the head of the table stood a likeness of Saint Peter. – You must sit there with him, Master! said Brendan's brother-monks, so he bowed his head and they prayed with him and were seated. A tumbler of water stood on the table. When Brendan picked it up to bless it, he saw something like a bloody clot of hair at the bottom, but when he said the LORD's name it vanished, and the water became wine. For a moment Saint Brendan sat perplexed, but then he took his knife so that the others could eat (they waited yet upon him) and put the matter from his mind; had he not already seen ever so many wonders?

In the course of their travels, hosted at solitary island monasteries, pursued by sea monsters whose origin you will have guessed, befriended by the great fish JASCONIUS whom they originally considered an island, they must have become very wise. Once, emerging from the fog, they spied a great pillar of crystal. Perhaps that was the demon BLUE-SHIRT Who ruled Greenland; perhaps it was the LORD Himself (Who had come before, as we know, as a pillar of fire). – The ocean was very choppy. They sailed past the Fiery Mountain and the Island of Smiths. On one grey little islet they saw Judas, who had been let out of Hell on a holiday. His eyes were red embers, and his hair was a mass of flame. Seeing them pass him by, Judas screamed: You will be bigger betrayers than I, you and your Black-Gowns! at which the monks shuddered and rowed hard, but Brendan stood and called across the water: There may be hope even for you, Judas, if you repent! but to Judas the word only echoed faintly, in this wise: *repennnnnnt!* – so that he became bewildered, thinking that sea-birds were crying about him, and sat heavily down upon his wet rock (which now smoked and steamed) and once again he began scooping ocean water upon his burns. – Let us pray for him, said Brendan, himself sitting down beside his oar . . . Finally, drawn by supernatural light, they made landfall upon their Canaan. For forty days they wandered amidst ripe fruit trees. – Where, I ask you, could they have been but Canada? – At length a young man appeared and gave them precious stones. He told them to return to Ireland, because Saint Brendan's death-day was approaching.

The Khans of Canada 1492

Thirty-three days after my departure from Gomera, wrote Columbus to Lord Raphael Sanchez, treasurer of Aragon, *I reached the Indian Sea, where I discovered many islands, thickly peopled, of which I took possession in the name of our Most Illustrious Monarch, by public proclamation and with unfurled banners.* – Yes, the Indian Sea! – For Columbus it truly was a small world. And some Indians that he seized did not tell him otherwise – oh, what good little captives! The harbors, too, were excellent; the rivers ("so indispensable to the health of man") abundant. Everywhere he looked there seemed to be fruits, gold and spices.

The inhabitants of both sexes of this island, he reported, *go always naked as they were born, with the exception of some of the women, who use the covering of a leaf or small bough or an apron of cotton which they prepare for that purpose.* In the little square engraving of Dati (*Narrative of Columbus*, 1493), we see those ladies marching along the edge of a jet-black rock meant to be an island, their bellies low-slung, like those of horses. They are giantesses. His ships scarcely come up to their thighs. Their breasts depend from their necks, like goiters; they wear circlets of leaves around their waists, and their lush hair falls to their buttocks. Two little thatch houses stand on the summit of the island. The thatch has the same texture as the Indian women's hair. A banana tree rises to the height of a cloud. Across the harbor, an Indian king sits on his throne, emptily gesturing. Does *he* know where Cathay is? – Columbus did learn of an island of cannibals, and of an island of Amazons in brazen armor. Surely Cathay was but a little further west . . . Surely he must have been in Canada.

A Leopard's State of Mind 1544

Canada appears unambiguously in the 1544 map of Sebastian Cabot, which colorfully delineates the coast of our continent from Labrador to Florida. To the west is a long flat stretch of white, tufted with grass here and there, like a precognition of the driver's-eye view of Interstate 80, where you can drive a hundred miles an hour if you want and *still* the scene will not change; to this day it bears out that usual judgment of the wise, the lazy and the pessimistic: *incognita*. And so it is marked. In the north, bordered by CVLVVS, two blue bears are prancing left along a latitude line. They have long red tongues. To the south, not far from OCEANVS OCCIDENTALIS, are two Nubians in striped barber's aprons, so mesmerized by their own gesticulations that they do not notice a thirty-foot leopard about to spring. The coastline is a pretty poem of illegible names extending inland by porous tidepools. Somewhere, I am told, Sebastian's father's landfall is dutifully marked *prima terra vista*, but I cannot find it.

Darling Red Souls

Pretty as that map is, it is the map of Lopo Homem (1525) that must truly be called illuminated. The title is MVNDVS NOVVS. Here we see, on a background of gold leaf shining like birch trees at sunset, a swirl of birds and autumn leaves, and fat brown bears drinking at a stream, while a fox and two long-necked deer look about for something enigmatically fabulous. Warships sail among the smudged islands which are dwarfed by their flags of territorial acquiescence. Due west of OCEANVS OCCIDENTALIS are black-skinned Indians in a maple grove, shooting bows and arrows, swishing their tomahawks, and leaning on wands, their hips sensually flared. It was these people that the Black-Gowns came to save.

The Magic Words
1610

Father, before your arrival in these parts where GOD decreed that we should be born, and where we have grown like the grasses and the trees that you see around you, our most constant occupation was to hunt all sorts of animals so as to eat of their flesh and to cover ourselves with their skins.

ARGUIMAUT THE SHAMAN
(Souriquois), to Abbé Maillard
(1740)

As the man in white led them closer, the People faced them across the sandy stretch of beach, there between the three rivers of eels. Membertou was the *Saqmaw** of that People. He went ragged to clothe the orphans; he went hungry to feed the widows with moose-fat. He was very tall. He had seen more than a hundred winters, yet even now his eyes were the keenest. Just as a pickerel gobbles frogs, so Membertou destroyed his enemies splitting their heads with his axe. He obliterated them; he crushed their bones so that they could never live again. For this reason, most people agreed that Membertou was an outstanding man. On this day he had painted his face well: with all four colors of Power he had marked himself. He had donned his shirt fringed with porcupine quills. His black hair hung down to his shoulders, shining with grease. His mouth curved down grimly. – He said to his red-painted warriors: Now I will go out there where the SUN is bright and meet them.

* Chieftain.

Be ready, my sons and brothers. You others, hide yourselves. If they cut me down, you must fight them. I have spoken.

Your words are good, said the People, withdrawing anxiously into a place where spruce-shadows raked them and beech-shadows drenched them with coolness. Their eyes gleamed. Membertou would use his Power; Membertou would shelter them once again. But they were still uneasy.

Smoking the Pipe bowed over his stick, listening. His ears were old; he could not hear the men coming.

They are near now, Looking Down Streams told him.

Born Swimming must bear whatever befalls, he replied. It is her dream.

Then once again Born Swimming felt afraid, as if through the crowds of sun-questing leaves and twigs on the spring hillsides she suddenly saw beneath to rock-cliffs' seamy old faces. (A long time ago, one of her grandmothers had uprooted her wigwam doorpost and then cried herself down the hole, down, down into World Under Earth . . . Born Swimming did not want to go there.)

When the Pale Men were almost upon the People, they stopped. Membertou strode slowly toward them, with his hands empty, as if he knew not how to kill. That was his cleverness. His head was high; his shoulders were thrust back.

The man in white took a step forward.

The Pale Men were aiming long bright sticks at Membertou, their heads low between hunched shoulders.

Suddenly the man in white knelt down on the sand and lowered his head, as if he had lost something. But he did not seem to be looking for it. He had closed his eyes, and he held his hands very tightly together. Perhaps he had not lost anything after all, but had something very precious between his hands which he was afraid to lose. Of course he had not held anything between his hands a moment ago. But it was impossible to tell about these Pale Men. They came from nothing.

Out of politeness, Membertou too had stopped, and now he waited patiently.

The man in white was saying strange words which nobody could understand, but he said them loudly, as if he wanted the People to hear. The Pale Men were nodding their heads. Behind them, the wooden island of bears creaked in the sea . . .

The man stood up.

I welcome you to the Country of the People, said Membertou. We call ourselves the People of KLUSKAP. – We are your kin-friends; you are our kin-friends. Do you understand my words?

The Pale Men were straining to hear. – Kin-friends, kin-friends, they said (or tried to say, for they could not get the words quite right). Over and over they pointed to the People and said: Kin-friends.*

Yes, said Membertou. Slowly he took off his necklace of bear-teeth and presented it to the man in white. The man smiled at Membertou and said something so quickly that Membertou could not catch it because the man's words were liquid and leaping like a brook in the spring. The man took a necklace from his own neck and handed it to Membertou. It was made of a series of unknown shells or stones, very light in weight and cunningly attached to each other in a fashion that Membertou had never seen before. Its ornament was a dull yellow color, like the hue of beech leaves in autumn: in shape it was like two twigs, a short one laid crosswise upon a long one. How they were attached Membertou could not make out.

I thank you for your gift, brother, he said, even though he knew that the other could not understand. He put the necklace around his neck.

Again the man in white was saying something. It was difficult for Membertou to take the sounds into his heart, but he listened carefully, and repeated the man's last words: *Pax CHRISTI.* – Perhaps that was what the Pale Men called themselves. Yes, it must be. They had all lowered their silver sticks, and appeared very pleased that he had uttered their name. – *Pax CHRISTI!* they all shouted back at him.

Membertou turned back to his People. (Out of the side of his eye he observed how the Pale Men at once tightened their grips on the silver sticks.) – Say their name to them, he called. It will make them happy. Say it to them: *Pax CHRISTI.*

Pax CHRISTI! said the People.

Again the Pale Men smiled.

But Smoking the Pipe said: I will not say it. Perhaps they mean to trick us with magic words. Let's kill them. I have never heard these words before.

Everything is new to you, it seems, said Born Swimming scornfully.

A Sermon

Eh, Messire Aubry, your benediction has turned them into lambs! said one of the men behind him.

The priest was almost weeping. I have never seen such ardor, he said.

* I.e., *nikmaq*. The French misunderstood this, and that is how the Micmac came to be named.

They understand nothing, but they *want* to understand; JESUS calls them . . .

They do seem amiable enough, for Savages, said the Sieur de Poutrincourt. Messire Aubry, you have done outstandingly well. Duval, do you take the gifts to them. – Have no fear; the guns are still loaded. – And the rest of you, I feel confident that they'll be well disposed to us very shortly. (Do you agree with me, Monsieur de Champlain? Monsieur Pontgravé? Good.) – Biencourt my son, signal the ship. – What a beautiful spot this is! As pretty as any dream! I shall call it Port-Royal. Yes, we'll get rich here, my friends! But all of you remember what I told you. These people are much stronger in numbers than we. The situation demands that we defer to them. There will be no theft or violence offered; and you'll leave their women alone. Young Pontgravé, I beg your pardon, but that last applies especially to you. Do you comprehend me? I'll have no disorder here. (Biencourt, has the Sieur de Monts replied to your signal? Good.) Monsieur de Champlain, where and how would you fortify this harbor? This Acadia of ours appears to be a vast island, and there's no telling what Powers or allies these Savages can call upon.

But Messire Aubry trembled with enthusiasm. – Yes, imagine! he cried. An entire Continent of Savages, and whether they know it or not they are all calling for conversion!

Père Biard and His Mission

The Black-Gowns had had the same thought. For a whole year the Royal Confessor, Père Coton, worked inside the Roy Henri's ear, like a worm in an ear of corn, until at last the Roy was corrupted to his purpose. Then the Black-Gowns rejoiced. Out of their number they chose two most zealous Pères: – *viz.*, Pierre Biard, Professor of Theology at Lyons, and his dear brother in CHRIST, Ennemond Massé.

Black-Gowns

1534–1988

> Continuing thus with many copious tears, I did not feel that I had the right to gaze higher. Thus by not looking up but only mid-way my devotion increased sharply with intense tears.
>
> SAINT IGNATIUS, *Spiritual Diary* (1544)

I cannot forbear to quote Parkman once more. He, who regarded the Black-Robes with a fascinated horror which only at rare intervals gives way to admiration, once looked deep into their Spiritual Exercises and became as faint and dizzy as if he saw his own coffin at the bottom of the shaft. For him the Exercises were a lethal Cabbala, guaranteed to turn out brilliant zombies who could descend upon the tree of life like some dark crow-flock, roosting, waiting, descending when called upon to do so, to pick clean the bones of souls. – "Loyola's book of *Spiritual Exercises*," he wrote,

> is well known. In these exercises lies the hard and narrow path which is the only entrance to the Society of JESUS. The book is, to all appearance, a dry and superstitious formulary; but in the hands of a skillful director of consciences, it has proved of terrible efficacy. The novice, in solitude and darkness, day after day and night after night, ponders its images of perdition and despair. He is taught to hear, in imagination, the howlings of the damned, to see their convulsive agonies, to feel the flames that burn without consuming, to smell the corruption of the tomb and the fumes of the infernal pit. He must picture to himself an array of adverse armies, one commanded by SATAN on the plains of Babylon, one encamped under

> CHRIST about the walls of Jerusalem; and the perturbed mind, humbled by long contemplation of its own vileness, is ordered to enroll itself under one or the other banner. Then, the choice made, it is led to a region of serenity and celestial peace, and soothed with images of divine benignity and grace. These meditations last, without intermission, about a month, and, under an astute and experienced directorship, they have been found of such power, that the *Manual of Spiritual Exercises* boasts to have saved souls more in number than the letters it contains.

What were they really, these men? They mortified themselves in secret. They were lovers of IESVS. Of course other Orders could say the same. But unlike their rivals the Grey-Gowns, the Recollects, our Jesuits knew how to navigate the Stream of Time. The watery way they chose to walk was cataracted, but more than one came triumphant to its end, where the Crown of pain and death fell more heavily still upon the composed, burning face that did not scream, but rejoiced in its own sacrifice. – In the painting of the Saints Martyrs Canadiens at their shrine, we see eight of them on a cloud. All but two wear the accustomed black robes that stretch down to their ankles, the hats with strange ridges, the collars with their two narrow rectangular tabs, white-bordered, grey inside, as if to suggest the beleaguerment of the Recollects. Angels swim above them with the loving curiosity reputed to be shown by mermaids toward drowned sailors, and the initials of the Society of JESUS glow in the sun's heart. The halos of those who kneel shine more fervently than the ones of the standing Martyrs, who are perhaps shy, for they have ranged themselves in the back row of this group portrait. Folds of black fall from them like the striations of cliffs. They clasp their hands or they make the sign of the Cross. They gaze raptly in every direction. In this company we find Père Jogues (tomahawked 1646), Père Daniel (shot 1648), Père Jean de Brébeuf (roasted 1649), and so many others.

We do not find Père Biard or Père Massé. Why? Because they were not put to death by enemies of the Word.

That was the Crown. That was what the Black-Gowns longed for. That was their pride.

What faith – to embrace the Fire and love it! To kiss the rotting Face . . .

Toy Islands

1604–1610

. . . the *potlatch* is present in the thoughts and hopes of the poor everywhere.

ROCKWELL KENT, *Greenland Journal* (entry for 13 February 1932)

But before I allow myself to be carried by the Stream of Time even as far as the year 1611, when our two Black-Gowns set sail for Acadia, I shall observe the proprieties, and frog-kick my way to shore just a few years upriver in that century, in order to make obeisance to their unwilling hosts the beaver-traders. – As surely as the town of Rochelle is Protestant I can see you now becoming impatient. The covers of my book are between your relentless palms. A single hint of insolence on this page, the faintest shine of gloating over all these delays, and you will slam the volume shut – don't claim I can't predict it! – What can I say to appease you? That I am weak-kneed, that you can bully me into leaving out all these extraneous histories which don't matter, which merely *protrude* like those octagonal stalagmites with windows which grow from the corners of houses in Kebec? – It is true that I am easily dealt with. As evidence, I promise to postpone my biography of Saint Ignatius, who founded the Black-Gowns. – Near the mouth of the Stream of Time there is a certain Current of Sorrow (this corresponds to the Second Exercise), in which one's own sins are revealed. I see my sins, but I also see the beauty of Acadia's tree-lined shores . . . Try not to fidget too much in your chair, for in doing so you pierce my heart, which you happen to be sitting on; that wound will only cause further delays. – Do you comprehend? – Good. Then let us swim without dissension to

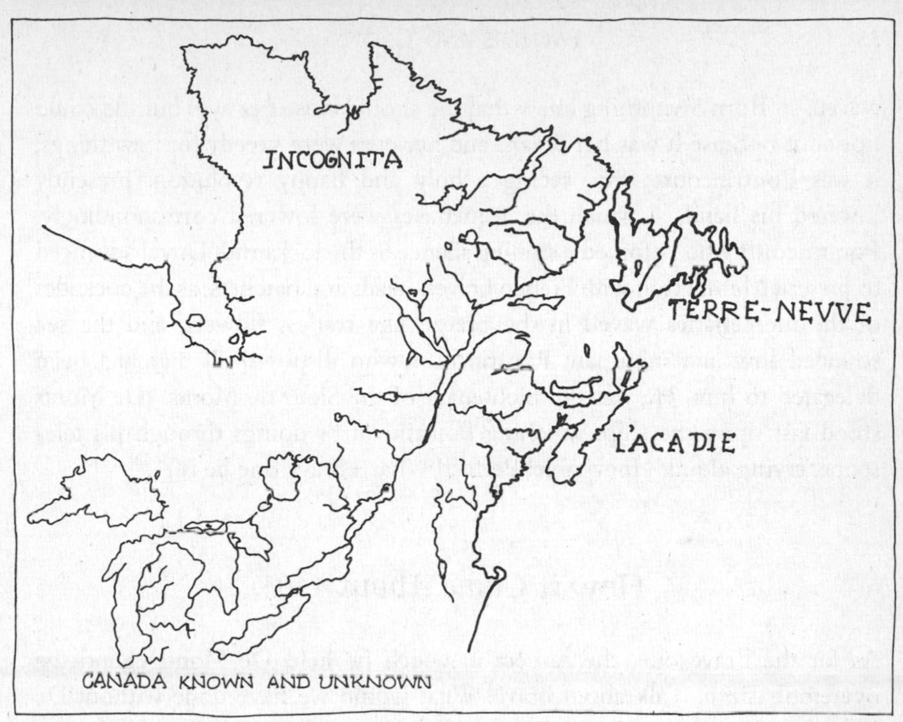

Acadia 1604

It was the Sieur de Poutrincourt, then, who, in the lawyer Lescarbot's words, *seeing our France seeming to languish in a monotonous calm that was wearisome to men of action*, first rowed ashore with a priest and a half-dozen Swiss soldiers to face the People of KLUSKAP across that sunny crescent of beach riven by triple eel-rivers. (Eh, he thought in astonishment, these clubs and bows and arrows of theirs are the arms that were in fashion just after the creation of the world!) It was Poutrincourt who commanded his retainers to raise their arquebuses and take aim at the Savages just in case while the priest stepped forward to meet Membertou, as we already know (or think we do, for this is still Born Swimming's dream we swim in; she is but dreaming that she dreamed the Dream of the Floating Island: – the People have now been exchanging goods with these strangers for upwards of a hundred years!), and Born Swimming peeped around a tree-trunk wondering what might befall even though she knew the tale of the Weasel Women who came down from World Over Sky, descending a tall pine, doing exactly what they should have done to get safely to Earth World except that the Weasel Women opened their eyes too soon, so they found themselves trapped in the crown of the tree, lashed back and forth by a breeze as the slender treetop bowed and waved, so Born Swimming knew that she should close her eyes but she could not do it because it was her dream and her eyes were greedy for new things; it was Poutrincourt who, seeing a holy and happy resolution, presently lowered his hand, at which the arquebuses were lowered correspondingly; Poutrincourt who enforced a smiling silence as the locksmith Duval advanced to present Membertou with French knives, beads and hatchets, as the cockades of the mercenaries waved in the breeze like restless flowers, and the sea sounded low and inhuman; Poutrincourt who disposed all that had been delegated to him. He was the Lieutenant of the Sieur de Monts. (De Monts stood fast upon the ship, watching Poutrincourt's doings through his telescope, crying aloud: Inevitable! Perfect! What a brave one he is!)

How it Came About 1603

As for the brave one, the respect in which he held De Monts cannot be overemphasized. Talk about brave! What would we have done without De Monts at the Siege of Paris? What a Chevalier! He had glory in his bones. And later, when he'd made his peace with the Roy, he stood up for royalty with all its claims. When that dog Chastel tried to kill the Roy, De Monts was one of the party who proved that the Jesuits were behind it. (They denied it, of course. What else could anybody expect from those characters?) You can thank De Monts that they were expelled in 'ninety-five! It was irritating (to say the least) when the Roy himself let them back in this year – sad to see how even Kings don't always know what's good for them. But De Monts knew what *he* wanted (another reason why his friend Poutrincourt admired him). He wanted Canada.

He wasn't the first, of course. De la Roche had tried it; Chauvin had tried it. But his Navy friend, the contractor Pontgravé, said that those men had gone about it all wrong. No wonder Canada slipped through their hands like a rainbow trout! – Pontgravé wanted to help him. – Seigneur, you mustn't miss the Palace today, he'd say. The Roy's in a good mood. You can get the monopoly through if you just nudge . . .

For five years? asked De Monts very thoughtfully. It would take at least that long to recoup my expenses.

Five years? snorted Pontgravé. Ten years, easy!

Ah, yes. The others had ten years, too, didn't they?

Don't worry about *them*, Seigneur! On my honor! We'll get you a monopoly yet, and keep those crows and vultures from Rochelle away long enough for you to sell a few felt hats . . .

Tell me, Pontgravé, is it as beautiful in Canada as they say? I was with Chauvin, but I don't remember –

Beautiful? Hah! It's a wasteland. Nothing but trees, Savages, beavers, cod-fish . . .

Grand. Grand. I'll be at the Palace today.

When De Monts inherited the ten-year monopoly, just as Pontgravé had predicted, great foamy cataracts of notions gushed through Jean de Poutrincourt's head. Soon he couldn't resist them any longer. But De Monts would surely indulge his worshipful craving, in much the same way that he would give a child some sweetmeat or other; De Monts was magnanimous. – Then they'd both get rich! Poutrincourt knew that in the marrow of his bones. Gold! China! Trees! Savages! Beavers! Cod-fish!

His wife begged him to proceed slowly, but he had already examined the facts. There was no one as good as he at using the ovens of logic to bake agreeable results. He stood gazing out the window. His black beard had just begun to turn grey: in this as in other things, it seemed, he followed De Monts his Captain. Slowly the corners of his mouth turned down as he stared into the sunlight. He seemed to be struggling with himself. As Madame de Poutrincourt stood watching, the light gleamed on his forehead. His eyes were like those of a man entranced. – Imbert! he said to his agent, who stood at hand. Would you take this letter to the Sieur de Monts? I've decided to sail for Canada.

Was De Monts about to say no to that? Was the moon made of green French cheese? Was the Pope a Protestant? (Actually, *De Monts* was – a Calvinist, to be precise. But every great man has his peccadilloes.) We know from the complaints of Madame de Poutrincourt, which rose to Heaven and engraved themselves forever on the clouds, that her husband even undertook to supply the expedition with armaments and Swiss soldiers – out of his own pocket! – at which she said Jean, Jean and he cried but take the *long* view, Claudette! – for though he had spent much of his wealth in the Wars of Religion, his purse was not yet exhausted. De Monts was very moved by this gesture, and swore that he would find a way to recompense him, as Imbert reported upon his return. – That's of no moment to me, replied Poutrincourt. I'll be happy enough in casting my eyes upon strange sights . . . (In his dreams, he saw painted Savages and Chinamen, rivers of dreams . . .)

He asks you to call on him tomorrow, Seigneur, said Imbert.

And his age, his – his fashion of speech lately, that doesn't disturb you? cried Madame de Poutrincourt in desperation.

Believe what you wish, said her husband. De Monts is as fit as ever.

When he called upon his Captain, he was received with an embrace. – My dear Jean, we're all ravished by your good heart. Pontgravé already knows you; he's delighted. D'Orville's coming, and he'll definitely winter with us. And the Sieur de Champlain – have you made his acquaintance? In a way he's abject, but I find him very, very useful . . . Ah, but you're the most sensible one of us all!

But merely tell me, said Poutrincourt, affecting not to be affected by the compliment, how I may best help you in this enterprise, Seigneur. My purse and the strength of my arms – they're all at your disposal.

Eh, now, said De Monts, considering. What shall I have you do . . . ?

De Monts' beard, iron-grey, flourished on his chin in such wise as to make his face seem wider than it was. Sideburns of the same hue advanced majestically up his cheeks. His eyes were not yet as faded as an old man's, but neither did they gleam with quite the same luster as they once had. He remained very fit of body, as a Captain of men must be; and of a certainty he was skilled in strategies and intrigues. He always took thought for those who served under him, and was generous, so that he had many followers and retainers. It was said of him that bravery and compassion flowed in his veins instead of blood. For all that, however, anyone but Poutrincourt could see that he was not many years away from the end of his fortunes. (Pontgravé, for instance, figured that he had rather less than a decade left in him.)

Well, Pontgravé is essential, of course, said De Monts, who had a habit of telling things over and over, as if he were reciting the most holy Rosario. – He knows how to trade with Savages, and he's a staunch Navy man. No worries on that score, Jean. Do you know his son Robert? – Ah, that's right; you hadn't met him. A wild rogue, they tell me, but with his father's blood in his veins he must be good for something. As for Champlain, he's mapped many rivers and bays in Canada already, and longs for nothing else but to extend his charts. So he tells me, anyhow. He just came back from Canada with the Pontgravés this year. Now he's picking out our ship's crew; he's very good at that sort of work. Now, Jean, you might gauge the firmness of a few people of our own sort – say, the Sieurs de Beaumont, La Motte, Bourioli . . . And you must meet this Champlain and arrange a convenient rendezvous in Acadia with Pontgravé – yes, Pontgravé's going to take his own ship. And we'll have great need of artisans and builders . . .

They drank together from little silver goblets with flared rims.

Sounding 1603

I should not omit to say that before proceeding to Acadia the Sieur de Poutrincourt repaired to the Palace, in order to sound out how firm his good Captain's monopoly might be. This was certainly not at his own instance, for he trusted De Monts, but rather his wife's. (Of course!) Far more acute than he in spying out the shoals of life, she feared that his new enthusiasm might prove to be some chimera concocted of fog and wind, luring him on until he sailed right through it and came to shipwreck. Such things had been known to happen. Indeed, a jury of reasonable heads might well conclude that such things had happened already to Jean Biencourt de Poutrincourt. – Consider his stature at the Palace, for instance. Poutrincourt's devotion to the Roy Henri flowed unceasingly, but he had once fought against him. It was only after the Roy repented of his opposition to the Catholic League that Poutrincourt had come to his side, although then he did so gladly. Now, as often happens so inexplicably, the enemies were fast friends. Indeed, the Roy had once been heard to say that this Chevalier was one of the foremost in the Kingdom. As he said this, he touched the great Cross depending from his breast like a snowflake of crystal glass, so greatly did he wish to emphasize his praise. And over the years he heaped so many honors upon him that no one except Madame de Poutrincourt noticed that her husband seemed to be growing rather more than less impoverished.

You have six daughters, Jean, she began. How do you expect to pay their dowries?

That was concisely put, he admitted, pacing to and fro. I cannot deny that it is a risk. And yet you know that De Monts' grant is perpetual. At the very least we shall always have land there. Indeed, I think sometimes of beginning a new life with you and our family in those unknown lands. You will not exactly like that, I know, so I set the point aside for the moment. More germane is that De Monts needs me; he has asked for me.

Yes, but you have not replied to my question. Surely your first obligation is to those who depend upon you.

I cannot deny that. I want to go to Acadia for just that reason. With this mania for beaver-felt hats that all the dandies have, we shall soon recoup our fortunes . . .

You're as transparent as a pane of glass, she laughed sadly. That is not your reason. Tell me, do you even know whether beavers have legs or tails?

I have no respect for such questions, replied the dreamer.

Very true; you don't. So how, pray, will you enrich us? Jean, Jean, you are no bourgeois like this Pontgravé who attaches himself to every expedition. You couldn't begin to scheme and profit like him. We all know that De Monts is a great man, but he is no better at *that*, I'm sure. Would you at least run down to Court and satisfy us both that the Roy will not suddenly withdraw his favor?

And how am I to do that?

You know very well how to accomplish those things. You are the Governor of Méry-sur-Seine.

That I am, he sighed.

In those days, the Captain or Navigator of a sailing-ship would sound unknown waters with a pyramid of lead weighing seven or eight livres (Champlain was an expert at this art). The lead was first prepared by greasing the bottom with tallow and butter. When it was cast overboard, the depth of the water could be measured by the length of cable required to reach bottom. Then the lead was hauled up, and the bottom inspected. To that coat of grease would cling some bit of pebble or shell, a smear of muck, a dead crab, a decayed bit of sedge, or some such indication of what lay below. Poutrincourt now followed much the same procedure at Court. He began by greasing the bottom – which is to say, by giving his agent, Simon Imbert, a few gold pieces. Now the lead was cast into the murky Palace depths, and Poutrincourt stood watching Imbert's squat figure vanish into shimmering whitish-green corridors like coral-holes, tied to him by the ever so flexible hawser of allegiance (for Imbert was not an entirely reliable man). And then Imbert was gone from sight.

He descended with impunity among the brightly colored schools of Courtiers, being known by all, and was favored with a nod or two on account of the Sieur whom he served; he sank swiftly down torchlit halls, bowing to his betters (at which his resemblance to a lead pyramid was accentuated), and he came to his depth at last, within a certain little grotto of foul air in which sat the Roy's Notary (whose name we will not mention here, both to avoid scandal and because not even I have been able to learn it). – A few bows, an embrace, and a flapping or two of his pudgy flippers, and Imbert had made his business known.

Ah, yes, said the Notary. Well, of course I remember that commission. I remember every commission, you see. The eighteenth of Décembre, it was. I had a touch of rheum in my throat that day, and my eyes were watering; that was the worst of it.

Now, did the Roy smile when he signed the document?

He smiled, yes; and De Monts was present; he seemed very moved at the honor shown him, as of course he should have been: ten years' monopoly in Acadia, yes, yes, Monsieur . . .

But did he smile out of the *side* of his mouth? whispered Imbert, approaching the sea-floor at last.

What questions, my Simon, what absurd questions! And what a little cockerel you think yourself, strutting about in this way! Now, why ought I to tell you any such thing? The Roy, you know, is above gossip. And what a magnanimous man! I remember once when – well, I see you fidgeting; I am not blind, Simon, although I may appear so – yes, thank you, thank you – thank your Seigneur for his generosity! – oh, I love gold! (but who doesn't?) – well, he smiled sidelong, if you must know the truth; he looked both ways before he signed . . .

Oh, he did, did he? said the agent grimly. And was Père Cotton there?

You must get over your childish desire to find three conspiracies behind every two Jesuits, lectured the Notary severely. I tell you, Monsieur, Père Cotton scarcely bends the Roy's ear. Anyhow, he was not there.

Well, well. Then the portents are ambiguous. I know not what to tell Poutrincourt.

I believe he was sincere when he signed. Of course I would stake no money on it, but unlike your master I am not a gambler. I *keep* my money, every yellow livre of it – ah, thank you, Monsieur, thank you!

Green and Yellow Wax

Dangling in perplexity as he was drawn back up into the sunlight, Imbert turned the Notary's words over and over in his mind. At last, breaking water, he adopted the safest course and told Poutrincourt what he wanted most to hear. Thus it was that upon reading the lines of the palm he had greased, our good Sieur saw not the muck he had feared, but a pretty little row of shells . . . At dinner he said: It seems as if the Roy will support De Monts steadfastly . . . and Madame de Poutrincourt raised her hands to Heaven and said: I see there is no talking you out of this voyage. May GOD protect you. – On the following day, Poutrincourt gave the Sieur de Monts his assent, and was invested as his Lieutenant in Acadia. So the matter had its end. But we who see farther down into the Stream of Time will now lower our own plumb-lead a bit, passing the Roy's Notary who works his querulous lips in spasms, like a halibut; and suddenly we strike rock! Of course Poutrincourt's vessel can pass above this obstacle easily, but is it our imagination or does the rock slope *upward* ahead in that murky greenish water? (Most rivers do become rocky and narrow as the explorer proceeds upstream.) – Here then is what must be reported: – Even though the Roy had granted that most honorable Sieur de Monts (*viz.*, Pierre du Guast) a ten-year monopoly on the beaver trade throughout La Cadie;* even though the Roy addressed him as *Our dear and well-beloved Monsieur de Monts*; even though the Roy granted him the power to create officers of war and justice, to impress criminals, vagabonds and masterless men; nonetheless De Monts himself could not feel entirely satisfied, for the document on which this commission was written had been sealed not with the green wax used for permanent documents, but rather with yellow wax only. Now, such an omen as this was not infallibly bad. The Pax Vervins, for instance, had been sealed with yellow wax, although the Roy and his Ambassadors certainly had no intention of breaking the peace with Spain within the immediate future. On the other hand, it was *generally* true that yellow wax was used for documents whose purpose was expedient at best and temporary at worst; and De Monts feared that that might be the case with him. A severe person might well say that De Monts should have acquainted his Lieutenant with such misgivings. But he thought to himself: I know Poutrincourt. No danger is too great for him. But if he once believes that I myself am discouraged, he will become so, for men of action like him are mercurial.

Reassured, then, both from above and below, the Sieur de Poutrincourt embarked for Acadia without hesitation. He'd been to Canada once before, with the Sieur de la Roche in 'ninety-eight, but all that was flashing mist; he'd learned nothing. But that's to be expected. If men learned anything, sons would be smarter than their fathers. – On the seventh day of Mars, he set sail from Havre-de-Grâce.

The Voyage 1604

He was seasick all the way to Terre-Neuve. At first he missed his wife and daughters with their rose-cake perfumes, but presently even that remembered scent made him ill to think about, and so he was forced to banish his family from his Exercises, like every other voyageur to Canada sacred or secular. A chilly blankness was now in his heart, waiting to be filled by Canada . . . As

* Acadia.

for De Monts, he too was scarcely to be seen. So the men were listless and spiritless. The other Chevaliers, who had never before undertaken such a long sea-voyage, paced the decks, squinting at the sea, into which the days sank one after the other, like lead. Their only amusement consisted in watching De Monts' Calvinist ministers arguing with white-robed Messire Aubry and the other predicators of the True Faith. Sometimes they struck each other with their fists, at which the men jeered. Many of these onlookers were impressed convicts. They sent up great ruffianly roars when one or the other of the theological disputants got in some particularly fine box on the ear, thereby settling once and for all the question of predestination; while the loser, well painted now with his own blood, scuttled down to De Monts' cabin to complain. Sometimes the convicts themselves would fight, out of boredom or animal viciousness or greed for an extra crust of bread, and then the priests and ministers threw up their hands in horror. But they knew well that they had no power to break up these learned debates, and so did little but stand apart like crow-witnesses. As for the nobler-born passengers, *viz.*, the Sieur d'Orville and his companions, they looked on diffidently, each thinking to himself: In France these miscreants would be hanged! – But France was as far from them now as Heaven. The rattling of the rudder was very loud. It ached in the teeth of the seasick men. De Monts groaned to feel it. Sometimes there were storms so dark that the men could not see each other's faces, and De Monts heard waves washing the deck over his head and seawater leaked through the ceiling. Then he would hear Champlain's footsteps, steady and sure. This made him hate Champlain the more, with all the desperate hate of a sick man which is really fear and envy without sufficient object. The Hiroquois know that Death is but a face of blackness in all directions. De Monts did not know this, so he hated health and haleness. He lay retching in a bucket, and water dripped on his head, and he said: But at least Champlain is adroit and capable. – He heard Champlain shouting at the men; he could not make out his words, but the strong and vulgar timbre of the man's voice penetrated the deck-planks just as the rudder-noise sank into his teeth. Meaning to stop his ears, he began to move his right arm, but the slight motion made him sick, and he spewed again into the bucket . . . On deck a great sweep of water came spilling, and a sailor was drenched. Champlain laughed. – Eh, did you drink your fill? And the man laughed, too, and everyone laughed. De Monts heard the laughter and wondered if they laughed at his weakness, and was ashamed of himself for wondering. Presently the storm subsided somewhat, and he heard the sailors off watch coming down to eat and drink. The thought of it made him nauseous again.

Into the bucket. They sat a dozen men to a pot, as he had seen, reaching for the food with filthy fingers. De Monts was a soldier. Soldiers were clean; the dried blood and dirt pancaked on soldiers' faces were but the anointments of glory; sailors, however, were filthy in a wet and peeling fashion like rotten fish. Into the bucket. He heard them praying; now they were snoring, and the eight-bells watch was on deck . . . Champlain and Messire Aubry stood together at the bow, looking at a waste of grey fog, grey waves. – This weather, it makes the beard smoke! said Messire Aubry. – Don't worry, Père; we have a very favorable wind. (Thus Champlain.) We'll be at the Bank soon. – The Grand Bank? How will we know when we're there? It's underwater, isn't it? – We'll take a sounding. You'll see. – And the next day Champlain really did, just to reassure the priest with a bit of ritual, and Captain Timothy came to watch, and with his own hands Champlain drew up the plumb-lead and turned it over. There was nothing on the bottom. Champlain had known there would be nothing. But every day he cast the weight, for Messire Aubry's sake, and every day the result was the same, until one day the bottom of the pyramid was covered with sand as white as salt. – So, said Champlain, beaming. – Le Grand Banc! shouted the men, and those below came running up the ladder to see. – Thank GOD, said De Monts in his bunk.

At the Bank they clashed with schools of icebergs, and so Captain Timothy gave order to set course south of Sable Island in order to avoid them. Now Poutrincourt emerged onto deck at last, to fish with a stick for the birds called liver-snatchers,* which drove about them in greedy clouds. The sailors searched incessantly for cod, and he also essayed the sport, while Champlain stood to one side and gazed into the sea. – It was almost as Cabot had said: – *viz.*, that one had simply to let down a stone-weighted basket and pull it up teeming with sea-fruits! – At Poutrincourt's command the men gathered together the hearts and tripe of these fishes, which the cook hashed with bacon, spices and codflesh to make white puddings of even greater relish than those of France. He regaled himself much upon this food, and his color began to come back, so that all who depended on him were well content. He sent a man down to De Monts with a platter of it, in hopes of reviving his appetite, but the platter came back untouched. Poutrincourt himself still felt unsettled in his stomach, but it was not good to show it. Now again his retainers felt his approving gaze, which meant much to them, since *Canada* meant nothing.

* Fulmars.

They laughed and took delight in everything, from the barkings of the ship's dogs upon smelling land, to the strange speech of be-wampumed Savages who now paddled up to them in their canoes, hoping to exchange news for bread to take home to their wives. Even the convicts fell into or at least feigned a pleasant disposition now that they were under the eye of one of their Captains. – The breezes freshened; the sun shone; De Monts appeared at last. He was very pale, but he saluted his men, and they cheered. So they hove in to Acadia, and Messire Aubry led them in singing the *Te Deum*. They anchored and lowered longboats. All the men who could crowded into them. They rowed easily to that green shore. De Monts knelt and kissed the soil; a cannon pealed, and all else was silent.

Their first office in that new Country was to bury their dead, a priest and a minister having both succumbed to the fever on the previous day (which left only Messire Aubry as their Captain in CHRIST). De Monts shrugged and said nothing when the crew buried them in a common grave, to see whether they would lie together peacefully. Poutrincourt could not approve of such impiety, but it was not his place to gainsay those above him, so he thrust the incident into its own thought-grave, covered it with greensward from Acadia, and gazed about him marveling at the sunny freshness of that salt-aired coast, whose continuum of meadows led his eye into unknown regions of freshness; so he drank in Canada as De Monts paced and sighed. The service was over; Messire Aubry knelt beside the grave; the Swiss soldiers hunkered down on boulders, chewing bread very slowly as they cleaned and charged their harquebuses.

I pray to JESUS CHRIST to sanctify this Country, said Messire Aubry softly.

That is a good prayer, said De Monts in his rumbling voice. May this Acadia of ours become civilized and frenchified. But first we must build our own houses.

Smiling, he clapped Poutrincourt on the shoulder.

They put out to sea again until their pilot Champdoré said that the depth was safe; maintaining this distance, they followed the coast, searching for anything that might enrich them. On the fourth day they discovered and confiscated the ship of an illegal trader, one Captain Rossignol; to console him they named a harbor in his honor. As De Monts possessed a soul of exemplary humanity, they did not abandon this Rossignol on the Acadian shore, but took him with them, in a capacity nicely between that of guest and prisoner. – I desire to be . . . to be . . . said Rossignol, his voice falling off. – Yes? said De Monts. You have done wrong, but even so I hope you shall come to trust me. Captain Timothy, sail on! – They proceeded to Cape

Mutton (so called because it was there that they feasted on a fresh-drowned sheep). Then, making rendezvous with the merchant Pontgravé, who had just rifled and despoiled four Basque vessels, they unrolled the scrolling horizons of meadow-shores. Poutrincourt stood smiling in the sun. Everything was fair in his sight. While he was still in that frame of mind, which makes it extremely difficult to resist the vain and worldly forms of things, the Captain sighted Port-Royal.

The Dream of the Floating Island

It was here, as I have said, that Messire Aubry first strode forward to present the crucifix to Membertou the Sagamore, while De Monts remained on shipboard saying to Captain Timothy: How many Savages do you reckon are hiding behind the trees? and Poutrincourt thought to himself: May it please GOD to hold this scatter-brained priest from error! – for they had not been in Acadia so very long that Messire Aubry had refrained from doing himself mischief. At Baie Sainte-Marie he'd gone into the forest to relieve himself, and got lost for seventeen days, without a thing to chew on excepting sour and bitter herbs resembling sorrel and partridge-berry, so that when he found the ship, as much by chance as when he had lost it, they greeted him like Lazarus resurrected: indeed he was as skinny and bony as a man but lately in the tomb!

Ah, brothers, this is a cursed Country, said Master Aubry.

That may be so, replied Champlain with gleaming eyes, but consider the value to France when I find a passage to China without the inconvenience of the northern icebergs!

You are a bold man, Monsieur. And would you say the same if you had been lost in the forest?

I have never been lost, the Sieur replied, and hope never to be. In you it is forgivable, Master Aubry, for your eyes are not on the things of this world.

You are kind to speak so; I know that I must have inconvenienced you and your Captain. Where, pray, are *your* eyes today?

New coasts and islands are what I see. Ho, you men! Stop gaping at the priest and get him something to eat!

As a result of this adventure, the Sieur de Monts had been somewhat loath to permit Messire Aubry to be the one to approach these Savages, but Poutrincourt, seeing the piteous look in the priest's eyes, begged to stand surety for him. So De Monts relented, and it worked out very well.

Champlain whispered in Poutrincourt's ear: Seigneur, I should direct the soldiers to aim into those trees if I were you. I count a dozen men . . .

Eh, Champlain, stick to geography, said Poutrincourt, annoyed. I was in the Civil War, too.

Messire Aubry was leading the Savages in prayer.

Tell the others to come out, called Poutrincourt. Duval, do me the kindness of distributing these beads. Pontgravé, you're certain they'll like them? – Ah, I can see that they do. Just listen to them exclaim in that Savage dialect of theirs. Now I suppose we must come forward ourselves. Under no circumstances is anyone to discharge a weapon without my signal. Behind me, all of you. Here we go.

Everything went swimmingly.

The Prize 1606–1613

And Port-Royal – what a Heaven that place was! Whales and seals swam in the harbor in abundance, and could easily be killed. You could gather crabs by the bushel, and also lobsters (which are like grand crayfishes or langoustes); the codfish were as fat as any on the Bank of Terre-Neuve (which that Black-Gown of dangerous memory, Père Biard, was even then imagining as a large sandbar in the middle of the sea), and Poutrincourt's Frenchmen lived behind a wall of green that smelled like summer, pale green and yellow-green and evergreen; and a hot moist breeze almost tropical in its richness blew from the unknown inlands even as a cool breeze blew from the sea. – Talk about salubriousness! – The Savages there lived to a hundred and twenty or even a hundred and forty years. (They counted their age by moons.) Perhaps there was some secret virtue of air or water here (Poutrincourt supposed), which would make him younger himself, which would add further roses to the beauty of wife and daughters . . .

Seeing the splendor of the place, Poutrincourt asked the Sieur de Monts to grant it to him in sub-infeudation, which De Monts very willingly did, for he felt every affection for this cavalier who had been true to him. – Poutrincourt's men sent great cheers beating against the blue vaults of Heaven, so that the Souriquois were astounded, and wondered what war portended. As for Poutrincourt himself, he made an inclination to the Crucifix with love and gratitude in his heart.

The Two Rings 1604–1606

A charming story which demonstrates the relations between De Monts and Poutrincourt at this period runs as follows: In Acadia there were certain deposits of copper which their companion and cartographer, the Sieur de Champlain, believed might be worthy of mining (Champlain was very ambitious). For this reason he often visited these cliffs in company with his pilot, Champdoré. – I forbid you to go out of sight of the pinnace! – so he said to him – for the Savages hereabouts have a treacherous look about them. Do you comprehend me, Monsieur? – Poor Champdoré therefore was confined to the beach, where he strode to and fro, blowing upon his hands to keep them from being harmed by the chilly sea-airs, while Champlain strode around some cape or other to stare entranced at copper here, copper there, knocking at rocks with his mallet (but his arquebus was always at the ready), and presently Champdoré began to kick pebbles in his boredom. Almost at once he discovered blue stones of the finest water and transparency. – Aha! he said to himself. I shall say nothing to Champlain, as he has ill-used me. How shall I spite him? – Presently he hit upon a clever plan, in which his revenge would be disguised as generosity to others. The largest stone, therefore, he cut in two, presenting one half to De Monts, the other to Poutrincourt. (Champlain said nothing at being thus excluded, and Champdoré did not dare to look into his face, but he felt a rush of glee.) When these two returned for France they had the pieces set into rings, as if they were lovers. – But the story is not done yet. The virtue of a gift being never exhausted, the pair now resolved to give their rings to those who had power over *them*. So they went to Court, Poutrincourt presenting his to the Roy, who was delighted, De Monts performing the same service for the Queen; while the Mesdamoiselles-in-Waiting whispered like cattails rustling at a pond's edge. – But already De Monts was anxious. Beaver-traders from Rouen and Saint-Malo wheeled about the throne in shrieking flocks, seeking to have his monopoly revoked (which would be ruin), and Père Cotton was in evidence more than ever before, thickening the air with his Jesuit slanders and skullduggeries . . . The rings might be useful reminders; but such charms (the foregoing about gifts notwithstanding) do not long hold their efficacy. Already De Monts was wondering what other treasures and novelties he must present at Court. – Poutrincourt, of course, made no such calculations.

Prognostications 1604

But Pontgravé did. That fall, sailing home (Poutrincourt was one of the passengers, but De Monts and Champlain had stayed on), Pontgravé leaned against the railing beside Captain Timothy, and Captain Timothy squinted up at the square wind-paunches of his sails and watched his pennants flutter, and foam-lines of breakers streamed at right angles to the ship, and a seagull almost crapped on Pontgravé's head, but he shouted and shook his fist and the gull veered away, and then Pontgravé and Captain Timothy got to the business which was the joy of their lives: – *viz.*, games of chance.

Now, our De Monts, when's *he* going to keel over? asked Pontgravé of the world at large, very thoughtfully.

I'll wager three years, said Captain Timothy.

Four, said Pontgravé. But that's in the strictest confidence.

Done, Seigneur. And Poutrincourt, will he be ruined?

He'll come out of this with lightened pockets, that's for certain, said Pontgravé. But whether he'll be in rags or not, I can't say. He's not predictable. Not greedy enough.

He's always seasick, said Captain Timothy hopefully. Do you think it's ulcers? I'd kind of like to lay a wager on him, also. I don't know why. There's something about his face – the pallor of it, and then those black dots of eyes he has . . . well, Seigneur, it reminds me of an ivory die; it brings out the man of fortune in me.

All right, said Pontgravé indulgently. I'll put twenty livres on him.

For how long?

He's got to croak before – eh, 1615 for you to collect.

Agreed. Now, what about Champlain?

Champlain? Oho, I wouldn't bet against him if I were you. I've seen him at close range. He's one of us, Captain Timothy, although he may not look it. He'll ride the years out. You can put up any number of livres, and I'll match you two for one he'll survive the others.

After all, he's younger. Fifty for a hundred?

High stakes, Captain Timothy. What have you been doing on the side? Eh, it's not my business. Are you going to bet on me also? I'm fifty-one, you know. Almost twenty years older than Champlain. Do I look like a dead man to you? Lay down any wager you like. If I live, I'll collect. If I die, make me pay if you can!

I must meditate on that, Seigneur, laughed Captain Timothy with gleaming teeth.

Confidence 1604–1605

Indeed, among the dispatches which awaited the Sieur de Poutrincourt upon his return to France was one signed by his agent, Simon Imbert, which suggested that continued optimism about the monopoly was feckless. So far the bettors were correct. De Monts was not there to be consulted, as I said, for he'd elected to stay the winter in Acadia with Champlain, who claimed to love cold weather. But Poutrincourt set aside his anxieties – for all the important men at the Court-house at Paris now wore beaver-skin slippers! Indeed, his cargo of peltries sold out in a few days, such was the demand. (Pontgravé had packed those furs; Pontgravé was very able in those matters.) – Do you see? he cried delightedly. – Yes, I am foolish, said Madame de Poutrincourt. But you have always known that. I shall never gainsay you again. Only pray set some of these profits aside for your daughters' sake. – Profits? he laughed. Oh, there are no profits yet. Indeed, we shall be liable for many more expenses.

In the following year, his Captain returned home. Poutrincourt was at the docks to meet him. Seeing his face, De Monts said: Is there trouble on your mind, Jean?

No, not exactly, he said.

Well?

Poutrincourt looked into his face as a child regards its mother. Suddenly, convulsively, he said: I – I was a *fool* to ever doubt our enterprise! Believe me, Seigneur, I never doubted you.

Ah, I know you would never do that, said De Monts, watching him very attentively, however.

Backstabbing 1605

Now pray tell me how your winter passed in Port-Royal, said Poutrincourt, when the two friends had some peace. For I think so often upon that place that my heart grows sick with longing for it.

De Monts seemed embarrassed. – As a matter of fact, he replied, we did not winter there, thanks to Champlain's obstinacy.

How is that? It seems that this fellow continually gives himself airs.

I suppose it's because he has dreams, too. But you're correct; he's insufferable. I fought in the Civil War, too, you know! But because he was once the Roy's Quartermaster he thinks he knows everything about strategy.

He kept talking about how the Spaniards defended Mechique until my head was spinning. I tell you, Jean! I was determined to find a situation for the winter which could be well-defended. As you know, my intuitions are often good, when it comes to redoubts. So I proposed building a fort at Port-Royal, but Prince Champlain replied: *I do not like the low hills there, Monsieur.* – The way he talked, you would have thought that he was at a banquet, and hills were a dish that did not agree with him! – *Granted,* he said to me, *the harbor itself can be defended from pirates, but as for our rear, I cannot vouch for that. Can you trust these Savages?* – And all the mercenaries, hirelings, convicts, tradesmen and varlets were standing about listening, with their mouths open! Now they were all going to have nightmares about the Savages running off with their heads! (Not that he was insolent then, you comprehend – just careless.) – I respect your fears, I said. What then do you propose? – He drew himself up in that pompous way he has, and proceeded to announce, as grandly as if he were about to present me with the Philosopher's Stone: *I have discovered an island which commands the mouth of the Rivière des Etechemins.* – I thought to myself: You mean your pilot Champdoré has. You never discover anything. You're a mountebank! Anyhow, islands are a livre a dozen in Canada. But of course I said nothing, except a *Well?* to put him in his place. He didn't take the hint. He came up to me breathing his breath in my face and kept talking. I don't remember everything he said, but it went something like this: *I call the spot Isle Sainte-Croix, because another river crosses near there at perpendiculars.* – What a little geometrician! And there he was, standing so straight you'd think his mother must have been a ruled stick! – *I assure you that it is of manageable size,* he went on, still letting me sample his halitosis, *of manageable size, being half a league in circuit. Rocks and shoals guard it about. If we erect our cannon there and post sentries, none of these tribes will be able to take us.* – I said to him: And what shall we eat there? – *Eh,* said our Champlain, his countenance falling a little (that delighted me, Jean!), *there are mussel-beds. But that is not the most important thing. We must protect ourselves. Until winter comes we can till the soil across the river; then we can fish through ice . . .* – And are there trees? I asked him. We shall need a lot of fuel. – *To tell the truth, Monsieur, there are cedars, but not many.* – At least he admitted it – oh, I wonder what he'd admit under torture! *Yes, there are some cedars,* he said to me; *I fancy we can make a Habitation out of them.* "Fancy," indeed! He really thinks he's someone exceptional! *Then* he started telling me all about the fortifications of Mechique and Cadiz again, until I couldn't bear it anymore. Finally I yielded the point to him. – Well, the long and the short of it was that half the men died of scurvy.

Naked Privities

1598–1605

> The person who has become a contemplative in action also is a very good companion, even if a bit unnerving, just as JESUS was and is unnerving.
>
> WILLIAM A. BARRY, SJ, *Jesuit Formation Today* (1988)

"That fellow," of course, would have considered this version of the tale to be slander, and in fairness to him (I forgot to mention that he is a principal character) I had better give his side of it. As doing so may require still more backtracking, it is only fair to warn you of the fact, so that you may if you desire simply turn to the last page of my book to gobble the dénouement, although I must warn you that none of the people mentioned there have been introduced yet. – Still with me? – May the BLESSED VIERGE reward you! – Well, what gave life its glamor for our Champlain was (in alphabetical order) neatness, order and propriety. We all strive to be icons of what we adore, in order that we may better adore ourselves; so it should come as no surprise to be told that his curly hair fell to his shoulders in the French waterfall style, which certain periwigged worthies at Court surpassed in manner but not truly in spirit. He clipped his fingernails short; he washed himself when circumstances permitted. Yet for all this dandyism, his face was ruddy and sunburned, and he had a loud voice (although not so loud, indeed, as Pontgravé, whose special department at sea it was to hail passing ships). As the said Sieur de Monts stated in his affidavit, Champlain had indeed served

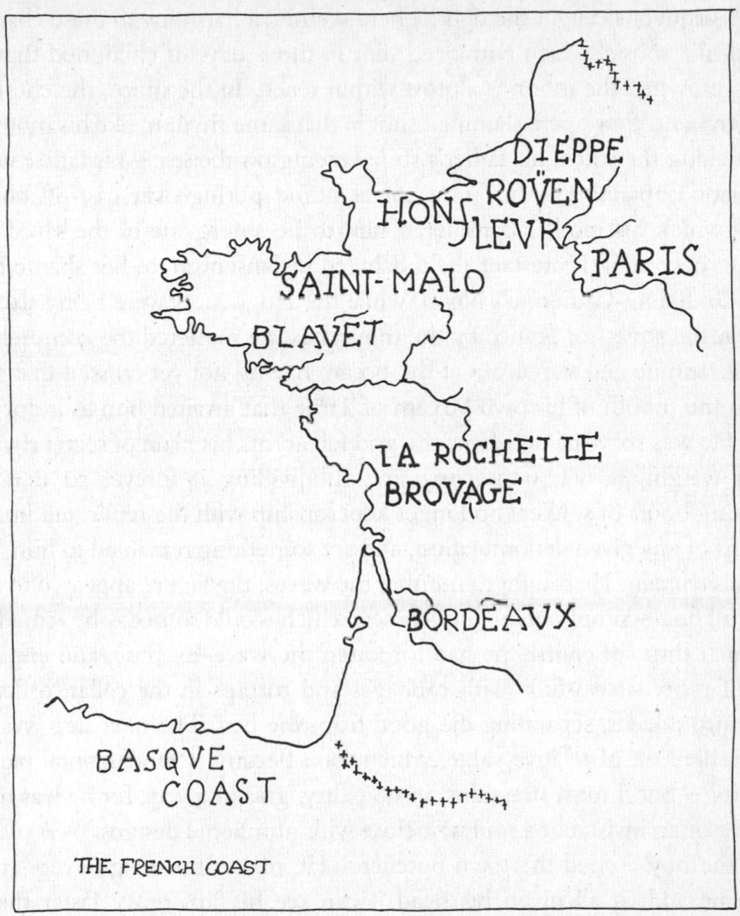

THE FRENCH COAST

the Roy as Quartermaster, receiving therefrom seventy-five livres per month, which was (if you must know) what the locksmith Duval got in a year. And was he truly worth a dozen times as much as Duval? By all indications, yes. Although born to a Protestant family, he'd long since renounced that heresy – even before the Roy did (De Monts *never* did). In short, his loyalty was as pure and fine as the salt-crystals of his native town of Brouage, which now looms greyly before us as we enter the Bay of Biscay, Brouage with its square-angled stone-brick walls guarding against attack by land or sea . . .

At the corner of every extremity of these ramparts there rose a hexagonal tower with a slit-window at each facet, from which darkness young Champlain would sometimes see the glint of metal as the sentry shifted on his feet and his arquebus caught the light. There seemed a harmony to these changes almost like music, which entranced him in those days of childhood that we all forget, when the moon is almost within reach. In the shops, the chests of the merchants flew open, slammed shut in that same rhythm, like his mother's arm making the stitch, his father's ship dancing on the sea: – his father was a merchant Captain! The boy now sat at home poring over cast-off charts, seeing which his mother considered him to be surely one of the saved (for prior to becoming Protestant she'd dabbled in Jansenism, to her shame be it said). On Sainte-Catherine's Night, while the Huguenots were being slaughtered in the streets of France by the thousands, he mastered the comprehension of latitude and stared out at the ocean, having not yet crossed that salty gulf to the mouth of his own Stream of Time that awaited him as it does all souls. He was six years old. Now the grid fell across his plain of secret rhythm like a weightless net, transecting and subdividing it forever so that the marching boots of soldiers no longer kept kinship with the replicated images of coins of any given denomination, and yet something remained to him, and that was *counting*. He sought to number the waves; the failure appeared to him not at all final – simply an incompleteness which would someday be remedied; by which time, of course, he had forgotten the wave-Exercise, and engaged himself more successfully with cabbages and turnips in the cellar, ordering them into dozens, separating the good from the bad. The next step was the comprehension of relative value, which soon became a fundamental part of his being – but (I must stress this) in no paltry, grasping way; for he was not a hoarder or archivist, but a soul writ close with numbered designs. – A plague upon the boy! cried the town butcher. He makes me weigh every cutlet twice; he adds it all up in his head; I can see his lips move faster than a hundred DEVILS! By Heaven, when'll they send him off to sea? – for of course no one in Brouage did not breathe in sea-smells of salt and dead fish; fishy sea-fogs hung over the afore-mentioned Bay of Biscay.

When he was a little taller the butcher's prayer was granted, for his good father took him sea-coasting. He learned from him how to listen to the water, and what soundings and landmarks meant. He took an early interest in the ship's accouterments and supplies; his father smiled to see him struggling to align the big hogsheads in perfect rows . . . Later, when he thought back upon those days, he remembered his father's face much less vividly than his greatcoat – a Captain's greatcoat – with the row of boutons interrupted by the sash, and his father's feet tramping in their boots.

He was seventeen when William the Silent was assassinated; he was twenty when Queen Mary laid her head down on the block. He learned from his father to hold back from too many risks, especially in foggy weather. He learned never to carry too much sail to make sheet, as that can dismast a ship. When he was twenty-one the Spanish Armada was defeated, and he ached to join in the adventures of the time, being both robust and alert; at which his father the Captain gave him leave, making him first promise always to be liberal and well-mannered to his enemies and keep faith even with them. – I swear it, Père! he cried solemnly; Captain Complain smiled and gave him what clothes, money and weapons he could . . .

When he came into the Roy's service the discipline of grids was useful, although the sea itself ebbed from his life leaving only the mud-flats of days and years wasted on duties which none but he really valued, but duty for its own sake had become as indispensable a preservative as salt. Now he learned the use of pike and arquebus; he learned to render his Captains good courtesy . . . From afar he glimpsed De Monts, De Poutrincourt and Pontgravé; he served them well and bowed most gracefully, after which they forgot him; one had so many loyal serviteurs!

On the seventh day of Novembre, 1594, they repelled the Spaniards from Fort Crozat. Here he played a conspicuous part. It was in this engagement that Sir Martin Frobisher, the discoverer of Baffin Island, was mortally wounded. Our Champlain was not even scratched. He began to think himself quite fine in his abilities – even finer, perhaps, than others thought him – until the Year of Our LORD 1598, when Henri, having reduced the rebellious Country of Brittany to obedience, dismissed his Army, and Champlain stood in the mud bewildered. (Paul Le Jeune, future Superior of the Black-Gowns at Kebec, was seven years old at that time. Père Brébeuf, Saint and Martyr, was five.) – What would he do now? This question rattled through his days like a Corpus Christi procession of skeletons. His father no longer hoped for his return, since the son had accepted the True Faith. Nor indeed could he wish to live under the authority of a heretic. Ah, his poor family – how he pitied their sin! But that was their affair, their own arbitrary refusal. What would he do; what would he do? As the other soldiers hurried home to motherly arms, wifely bosoms, vanishing from him in that dusk that smelled of rotten fish, he stood just outside the barracks. The stars were coming out. – Come drink with us, Champlain! – He did not move. A breeze as soft and delicate as French lace swirled about his face, reeking in a friendly fishy way that he had long since accustomed himself to, just as now his eyes began to learn the trick of piercing darkness; at the quai he saw the sad pale blur of a Spanish standard stirring like something unknown; a drunk jostled him; what to do? In his heart he knew already, but he wanted to delay the sweet fear of that resolution just a little longer, because he apportioned time as he did goods. The Spanish banner could no longer be seen. He stood adjusting his hat into more perfect symmetry on his head, sighing *ehhh,* remembering how great hams and hogsheads of wine had but recently marched under his triumphant authority to the rows of hungry mouths, arriving just before the mouths could begin to curse; how the men's uniforms sorted themselves by size and quality, out of kinship and liking for him, obeying that rhythm that only he and they knew; how the happy harquebuses in his keeping had never missed fire. But there was no grand Store-house to be locked and guarded any longer. – It is true that the Roy gave him a pension; following my Seigneur de Monts I admit this freely. But pensions could always be revoked (a fact which would obtrude upon his future distances to an increasing extent), and even if the golden blood of royal affection did continue to flow lifelong into his cupped hands, was he supposed to sleep until noon? He had an eye of icy keenness, which craved measurements; his fingers itched to be sorting goods; there was a lump in his throat which would not dissolve, he knew, until he uttered regulations of his own. So he decided to travel. His ears rang with the sea.

Canada was not in his mind then. But as is written in the Book of Corinthians, *Behold, now is the accepted time; behold, now is the Day of Salvation.*

In the town of Blavet, on the mouth of the river of the same name, the last garrison of Spaniards waited to be evacuated from France under the terms of the Peace of Vervins. His uncle, Captain Provençal, was among them. Champlain asked permission to keep him company. – I can only encourage such venturesomeness, replied the uncle. Come, then.

Avocados and Dragons 1599–1601

It was the month of Août. After ten days they sighted the tip of Cap Finneterre. A fog sprang up, and the vessels were scattered. When they found one another again, they proceeded to the isles of Bayonne to refit the flagship. Champlain's heart was beating fast; they were entering the unknown Realm of Spaniards. As he understood it, there were as many levels of hierarchy and authority in that Country as there were layers in those imperishable festival-cakes called altars. – But you are prudent, said his uncle. You will do well, I see. – In due time, they reached the Cap de Sainct Vincent, and Champlain inhaled the smells of Portugal; then they made landfall at Cadiz.

And what do you think of it here? said his uncle.

Do you have a chart of this place? said Champlain. I am very interested in topography.

Not so loud, not so loud! And I called you prudent! Don't you see that they will take you for a French spy?

I assure you, uncle, I only wish to count the indentations of the coast.

But what do indentations have to do with anything? cried Uncle Provençal in despair.

Let me speak seriously. Until everything is known and mapped, why – why . . .

Ah, I can see you long for the Savage Countries. There are many like you.

Under General Colona, with the good recommendation of his uncle, he was given charge of His Majesty the Roy of Spain's armament ship to the West Indies. (They knew that he would not squander anything.) Raising sail, he commanded the pilot to set course, raising his voice with the heartiest benevolence. – Don't worry, Señor, the man replied, *I* know the way. – Thinking that he meant by this remark to show up a Frenchman's ignorance, Champlain scowled, but said nothing.

Already he was wondering how to comport himself upon his first meeting with those exquisite human novelties, the Savages. Would they seek to trick and parasitize him? What would they ask of him? And what might he require of *them?* He decided to hold commerce aloofly, for the same reason that at sea one ship ought not to come too near any other that she sights, on the chance that she might be a pirate.

As easily as a dream they arrived at that mountainous island called Guadeloupe, which was peopled by Savages. There they took on water, while Champlain made his sketches. – Three and a half leagues from here to that rock, everybody heard him mutter, then another seven leagues around . . . – Three hundred Savages, perceiving the ship, fled deep into the interior, so that they captured none. And Champlain thought to himself: these Spaniards treat their Savages badly.

Off Margarita Island he saw the Spanish King's negro slaves pearl-diving with baskets under their arms, sinking into the greenish water until they became one with the shadows that flickered between the coral beehives like the tendrils of the Scalp-Monster. The teeth of the negroes were very white. On the whole, he thought *them* better off in captivity. The priests were here to teach them . . .

On the isle of Saint-Domingue he spoke frankly with the Indians, and learned that they sometimes trafficked with Frenchmen without the knowledge of Spain. – They are very friendly, he concluded slyly.

So he westened, port by Spanish port, where the treasure-galleons were moored to bronze rings in the walls of the fortresses. The sea was glorious about him with macules of many-colored light, and he truly believed that he could do anything if he only measured the way league by league. At twilight the waves were rosy as if with blood; at noon their blue was as that of the sacred fleur-de-lys. As for his heart, its colors too were pure, because untested. The Spaniards on board watched how he paced and paced, his face glittering with sweat, sketching and calculating in the wake of the setting sun. They envied its unsmiling glow of confidence and desire, the glow which comes for but a single period in life, and endures as briefly (it seems in after years) as the falling of a leaf. In that admirably ignorant frame of mind, he came at last to New Spain with its palms, cedars, guavas, lemon-trees . . . There, in the belle ville of Mechique, or *Mexico* as it is sometimes called, he first tried the fruit called *avocado*, whose taste resembled green walnuts. He heard tales of dragons with bat-wings and eagle-claws, though he saw none; he spied lizards as big as quarter-pipes! – What splendid temples, Palaces, houses! It seemed to him in that first flush of his fulfillment that he had but to sketch or map a thing in order to increase its significance forever. He made his inventories; and it was as if GOD above wrote the same figures, at the same instant, on tablets of alabaster. – Two leagues away were the silver mines. There the Indians worked for the King of Spain. Champlain considered their disposition melancholy. But it was true that they never became annoyed, no matter how ill they might be treated: they were quite intelligent, he thought to himself. Indeed his cautious resolutions had been misplaced. Not a soul of them had made him any request at all. Truly it was not their fault that they had been born Savages. For we must all appear before the Judgment Seat of CHRIST, he reminded himself, Savages and Christians alike. Indeed, it seemed very likely that all the Savages on earth would someday be Christianized – a noble enterprise, whose achievement would surely wipe away many a stain of Spanish cruelty; for the overseers of the mines had not neglected to furnish priests, who instructed the Savages and remanded them to be whipped when they did not attend Mass.

I envy the Spanish General, he admitted to himself. He busies himself with needful things; he has an opportunity to do great good for ignorant souls . . .

This said, he understood with amazement that he was no longer happy. It was as if all his triumphant mapping had been a victory tainted at the source. But why? Why? He sought to recover his excitement with many facile insinuations, but he could not.

I desire something, he reasoned, but I have not yet discovered what it is.

He believed this. He could not bear that anything might already be lost to him.

Truly it would be a fine thing to rule Mechique.

But I am no Spaniard, he sighed. Nor am I so unworldly. I could not spend my life here. If I knew for a fact that I could accomplish something, then my heart would not be so heavy. I wonder what the exact circumference of Mechique is . . . I want to map everything. Some men count sheep. Others have mistresses. There's no harm in what I do – far from it! – But why did I come here? I should have gone to Canada.

At dusk the fireflies were the size of hazel-nuts, and the astonished Champlain exclaimed: if I had but three or four of these, I could read by night as well as with a candle! at which the Spanish General said laughing: What an enthusiast you are, my Frenchman! and he and Champlain pledged each other's health, for that was the custom in Mechique with its heat and bad vapors and plagues . . .

The River's Mouth 1603

By the time he got back and collected the back installments of his pension, it was 1603. The Sieur de Chaste held the Canadian monopoly then. Would he have bothered with it if he'd known that he was about to drop dead? Pontgravé probably knew, but he didn't care what color the figurehead was painted: – *he* knew who needed whom! He'd been coming to Canada for ten years. His son Robert was old enough now to come with him, although he still didn't know what *real* trade was. Whenever they were alone, he'd whisper in Robert's ear: Remember, it doesn't matter who's in charge as long as you're the Deputy! – Such crassness irritated Robert to the highest degree, but on the other hand his father was very indulgent. All the other boys envied him. – A Navy boy! they'd say. And you get to see Savages! And every year your Papa gets richer! – These words would make Robert very proud of his lineage: he was not only Pontgravé, he was Gravé du Pont! So in the end, despite the tiresome paternal whispers, he found his father quite tolerable. – In 1598 old Pontgravé surveyed Three Rivers and saw some things, I tell you! In 1599 he played the cunningest part in getting the Sieur de Chauvin a ten-year monopoly on the beaver trade. (Chauvin had no head for business, which suited Pontgravé quite as much as dining on some Canadian bear's white delicate flesh . . .) The Sieur de la Roche, who was left out, denounced him, crying: You have betrayed traders from Saint-Malo who were your partners! – Pontgravé laughed in his face. – I'll pull strings! shouted La Roche. – So sorry, Seigneur, said Pontgravé. I'm busy.

In 1603, as I was saying, La Roche was out on his ass again and the Sieur de Chaste had the monopoly. That was when Pontgravé got thick with Champlain and brought him to Canada for the first time. Champlain – *huh*, the fellow was a bit of a prig; ever since he'd converted he'd given himself such airs that his own family couldn't stand him. His father, Captain Complain, had even published a notice of exhereditation, as Pontgravé had heard. As far as *he* was concerned it was no big deal. Champlain wanted to be an idolator? Fine; let him be an idolator. Pontgravé couldn't care less. He had nothing against Catholics. So let the guy come along and draw his maps – as long as somebody else paid his way. The long and the short of it was that Champlain set out from Honfleur with Pontgravé, in his ship the *Bonne-Renommée*. It was De Chaste's ship, actually. But De Chaste wasn't long for this world. Anyone could see it by looking at him: – his face was paler than his powdered wig. – As for me, I'm fifty, said Pontgravé. And I fully intend to live another fifty years. Do you know my secret? Grease!

I beg your pardon, Monsieur? (Thus Champlain.)

Grease, I tell you! That's the elixir of these Savages. You'll see, Champlain. On my honor, matters will be clarified!

I never doubted it, replied the cold fish.

It was the first of Mars. They passed Orgny and Grenesey, then Bretagne, then Ouessans. Champlain stood dreaming. He had heard that the Savages painted their faces red and green . . . For a month he saw nothing but the open sea. Then presently they attained the icebergs. – Watch your starboard! Pontgravé was shouting to the helmsman. (The Captain rolled his eyes.) – That's damned close! Cool enough for you, Champlain? Robert, I'd gamble that our Sieur de Chaste is no warmer than that now. I'd gamble he croaked last week. Who takes the stake? But be brave, my boy; I'm sure you'll inherit my longevity! – On the second of Mai they reached the Bank; on the sixth they could hear the waves against some rocky shore, but could not see anything for the fog, so they put out to sea again, and time passed, like other winds and islands, until at last with exceeding joy they came in sight of the isle called Anticosti, which is the entrance to the Grand Fleuve of Canada, whose name is the SAINT-LAURENT. (But we know it as the Stream of Time.) Champlain's heart soared. There was a grandness of clouds before him. The Fleuve was like some great green mirror-crystal, with an infinity of wave-facets. Seeing the width of it, he felt awe for the first time in his life (a feeling which recurred only once, ten years later, when the Huron Savages brought him to the vastness of the Sweetwater Sea). – Mon DIEU! he cried. Pontgravé laughed at him; the wind whipped through the rigging . . . – He stood clinging to the railing as Pontgravé conferred with the Captain and the Captain gave the order to proceed. It was bell-clear to him where he would be for the remainder of his life. – Entering the river, they passed the high-water mark of dead explorers: Denis de Honfleur, Aubert, De Léry, Verazzano . . . Now of all the chroniclers only Cartier and Roberval had gone beyond him (although he was well aware that Pontgravé had been farther, but Pontgravé did not count).* – The new sailors cried out to see their first moose. The Captain gave them leave to shoot it. Champlain gaped at those antlers, broad as planks. The meat was very good. Then day by day, riding that Fleuve beyond all fleuves, they left the desolation of Gaspesia behind them, passing blue hills with green streaks of trees beneath corresponding cracks in the clouds. – Such a chilly wind! – The clouds drew aside as they continued up river; the ripples behind them were green and grey and brown. They saw diamonds all along the coast. (These, alas, had the fell property of turning into quartz the instant that anyone brought them home to France.) On the twenty-fourth of the same month they cast anchor at Tadoussac. On the twenty-sixth they entered the harbor; and Champlain leaped ashore and climbed a hill; looking down at his solitary vessel, he thought: this harbor is small and could not contain more than ten or twelve ships . . . – Striding between the pines, he paced to Devil's Point and looked excitedly into the water.

This Tadoussac was a narrow place in the Fleuve Saint-Laurent where the Savages could be relied upon to bring their peltries. Pontgravé had built a trading post there in 1600; scurvy and mutiny, however, forced him to close it down after a single year. Nonetheless, he'd persevered: Savages were valuable to him. He bribed a dozen of them with biscuits at the end of the season, and haled them to Paris in order to impress the Roy; the following year he brought two back to Canada to make a report to the others of the Roy's good reception. – Oh, Pontgravé knew how things were done! He knew what to say and what not to say. So Champlain, who was as simple as a child, admired his wisdom. From Pontgravé's point of view Champlain was a useful associate,

* "Actually, many whites had been going as far west as Tadoussac since 1550," says Trigger, "& Jacques Noel + other traders had been visiting Montreal Island beginning in the 1580s. Not just Pontgravé but many other non-chroniclers had been farther west."

being hale, industrious and determined: whatever beaver-treasures he might unearth, Pontgravé could always snatch away at his leisure. So he flattered the man, and pretended to admire the Roy's Army, about which he had to hear every day (truth to tell, Champlain was rather dull); every day he told Champlain that in his opinion a Quartermaster was more important than ten Generals. – For men may fight or march, or they may lie at their ease, he said, but men must eat!

Now that is what I always say myself, replied Champlain in astonishment. I can see that you have thought upon these matters, Pontgravé.

Indeed I have, Monsieur. I have learned much from you. When you describe your battles, I can almost see the bloody field.

Champlain smiled uncertainly and laced his fingers together.

So the time had passed until they arrived at Tadoussac, and Pontgravé's men readied their bales of nightcaps and looking-glasses and dried prunes. As for Champlain, he continued to promenade about on Devil's Point, having charged his arquebus with two balls in case of any surprise, and he listened to the roar of water inland and thought to himself: I have cause to hope, thanks to the volume and violence of this water, that some might issue from as far away as the Sea of Cathay . . . Nonetheless, he found it an unpleasant Country.

Upon returning to the ship, he buttonholed his friend. – And these Savages, what of their morals? he said.

Pontgravé shrugged. He had become addicted to the Savage herb called *tobacco*, which Champlain had seen north and south in this great land; now he put a few dried leaves in his pipe and began to puff. – Eh, that is easy, Monsieur, he said. They have none. Ask them. They speak to the Devil face to face. The girls have many suitors, and are as free as they like . . . But trade is trade.

At least they are chaste after marriage? said Champlain in horror.

Oh, after marriage they are, no doubt.

Let me try that tobacco, he said. – When Pontgravé passed the pipe to him, he inhaled deeply and coughed. – Diabolical! he shouted.

The Promise

They sought the Savages at Saint Matthew's Point, under the wrinkled gutskins of clouds, and found them a league away. They were encamped at the bottom of a fir-clad hill, a good thousand of them. – Sometimes, sighed

Pontgravé, they make me so fatigued, with their wandering antics . . . – His son Robert rubbed his nose and said nothing. Champlain trudged stoutly behind with the varlets, bearing a bale of trade goods on his back; he could not but make himself useful. So they came into their camp and proceeded to the lodge of a grand Sagamore, named Anadabijou, who with eighty or a hundred other Savages was carrying on a grand feast. One of Pontgravé's pet Savages gave an oration, describing how well the Roy of France loved them; how the Roy of France wished to people their country with Frenchmen and make peace with their enemies the Irocois. Pontgravé watched him with satisfaction. In him he recognized his work, like a silver plate engraved with its maker's mark. (But his son Robert sat glaring sullenly.) When he had finished, the other Savages cried *ho!* and appeared to be very pleased, so that Champlain and Pontgravé exchanged smiles which betrayed the same sly indulgence as those of parents at some children's pageant. – Then there was a grand feast in bark dishes, the Savages gobbling boiled moose-meat and seal-meat and wild birds, after which they wiped their greasy hands in their hair and threw their dogs down in front of Anadabijou one by one, shouting *ho!* and then they danced, joyfully taking in hand the scalps of their enemies the Irocois, a hundred of whom they had slain by ambush at the mouth of the rivière called Irocois. The Frenchmen watched warily, eating as fast as they could.

At that camp there were three tribes or Nations gathered together: the *Montagnes*, in after years called Montagnais; the *Estechemins*, and the *Algoumequins*. These were allies against the Hiroquois, whom they hated and longed to destroy. (Champlain had not seen any of these yet, but Pontgravé assured him that they were most redoubtable.) He opened his journal on his lap and began to make notations, filling the sheets with his half-legible griffonnage, while Pontgravé winked at Robert . . . Eh, their canoes and lodges were made of birch-bark. The lodges were long and low, like tents. The roofs had slits a foot wide to let the light in. And did they keep sentinels properly distributed? – He craned his head. – No and no. Indolent brutes!

Now the Algoumequins ranged themselves in an open place, with their women and girls standing side by side. Besouat the Sagamore seated himself between two poles from which hung the Hiroquois scalps. He clapped his hands. Suddenly the females cast off their skin mantles and flung them to the dirt, thereby stripping themselves stark naked! What was this; had they lost all judgement? Champlain blinked and shook his head, but the row of naked brown legs, brown teats, bushy black privities would not go away. What a pimp or pandar this Besouat must be! What whorish barbarity! The naked women stood gazing at him with their shiny black eyes, as if *he* were naked.

The shade-marks of evergreens tattooed their faces. And what faces! Round, nut-brown, with greasy black hair, black dirt smeared on their cheeks! When they smiled, he saw that even the young ones were missing teeth. Hideous! Their mouths curved up or down, but they were all slits of darkness. Some were now ducking their heads away from him, wryly wrinkling the corners of their mouths, so that their faces became crumpled like little dolls or poupées. It would have been comical but for that strange look in their eyes, those shiny black gazes that made their features into masks of something smooth and ancient and alien, something that he could never comprehend . . . JESUS, look at that slut grinning at him and scratching herself between her legs! They all had lice. Pontgravé had told him that. – Naked privities, naked privities! He *would* not look anymore. No, he must not permit himself to remain ignorant of anything . . . He thought to himself: I pray that nothing unexpected happens. – Now they began to dance, lifting one leg and then the other, gesticulating rapidly but remaining in their place, while the men chanted songs. – Eh, they had no shame, these squaws! – Their smell was not agreeable. They were very thin. Their skinny pointed breasts hung down; he could almost count their ribs. What a miserable life they must lead! And yet they seemed cheerful. Remarkable! Speculation was unsafe. – They had retained their beads and ornamental cords of dyed porcupine quills, and these slapped and rattled as they shook themselves in the dance. (No, were they sad after all? Their glittery black eyes terrified him. Pontgravé whispered, bidding him hold his peace.) When the song was completed the men cried: *ho, ho, ho!* at which the women covered themselves, thanks be to Our FATHER. Young Robert was staring slack-jawed; Pontgravé smiled very softly to himself and puffed his pipe, his hand on his son's shoulder; Champlain bit his lip. – Eh, now the Savagesses were doing it again! Never, never could this leave his mind!

He said to himself: As I can do nothing about this, I shall dismiss the matter.

He turned away from the carnival and said loudly: Do you know of any caves or mountains where there is to be seen a metal of a yellow color?

Yes, friend, laughed the Savages. It is easy to find it if you dream of it.

I do dream of it, he said curtly.

Pontgravé winked at him.

Besouat the Sagamore now cried to the Montagnais and Etechemins: You must dance also, so that we may be satisfied. – At this they all cried: *ho ho ho.* Then Anadabijou and his Montagnais cast off their mantles (the privities of these Savages being covered by a small piece of skin), and Champlain, shaking his head, turned to Besouat and asked him: Where is this metal? –

Later, my dear friend, I will speak with you, the Savage replied, but now we must do what is fitting for Those who have Power. Do you comprehend? – and meanwhile the Montagnais were giving gifts to the Algoumequins. – Champlain yawned and tapped his foot. He stood up. He went to Anadabijou and said: Now where is this yellow metal?

Anadabijou thought for a long time. He closed his eyes. Then he smiled. – That way, he said. Past the river called Saguenay.

Then Champlain was content, reflecting upon the great obedience with which these Savages answered any question put to them. It occurred to him how well they might learn to live if someone would but teach them to till the ground. And he said to himself: I will go beyond the Saguenay as soon as I can and seize these mines. Then I shall be able to accomplish many good works for the glory of GOD. Perhaps I shall bring the Jesuits here. Perhaps I will build a great Church. – These considerations led him to inquire into the health of their souls, so that he tapped Anadabijou on the shoulder and said: Do you believe in GOD?

In which god, my brother?

In the One True GOD, said Champlain, raising his voice. – The Savages glanced at him sidelong.

Anadabijou took the leg of a dead bird in his hand and began to eat it. – Yes, I believe in one GOD, he said. There is also one MOTHER, one SON, and the great golden SUN in the SKY. How many is that? GOD is best, as you say – yes, and the SON and the SUN were good, but the MOTHER ate them up: Her name is SKY WOMAN. She fell into Water-World. That is what the Hiroquois say, but I believe that there must also be a bad FATHER.

Dismayed, Champlain said: But have you ever seen GOD in the world? (meaning CHRIST); – but Anadabijou told a story about five men going to the setting SUN, where they met GOD; and GOD asked them: Where are you going? – To find our living, they replied. – GOD said: You will find it here. – But they went on, at which He touched two of them with a stone, and they became stones. – Again He asked them where they were going, and they gave the same answer. Again He told them to stay, but they would not, so he touched another pair of them and made them also stones. Now one was left. This time he was obedient when GOD told him not to go on, so GOD gave him a fine present of meat, and he returned home.

That could not have been GOD; that was the DEVIL! exclaimed Champlain.

Devil? What is that, my brother?

When you die, if you have been bad He burns you forever in a dark black place.

Like the Hiroquois?

No, not like them. When the Hiroquois burn their prisoners, they can burn them only for a day or two; then they feel no more pain. But when the DEVIL burns you, you will scream in agony until the end of the world.

Now all the Savages were staring at Champlain in horror. – This DEVIL is a hungry PERSON, very hungry, they said. Brother, instruct us so that we may avoid Him!

The Sieur de Champlain smiled tightly and bowed his head. – I am heartened by your craving for the True Faith, he said. As soon as I am able, I promise to send wise men from my country to instruct you.

I approve what you have said, replied Anadabijou. If you do this thing I will thank you.

Pleasant Reflections

Young Pontgravé (who had just reached the age of eighteen) meanwhile sat smiling dreamily, for in France he had never imagined such license as these Savage fillettes had shown in front of all. Were these the ones called libertines? They were agile and extremely well-shapen, as he had to admit; their bodies were a beautiful olive color (the result, as his father had explained, of a certain pigment or grease with which they rubbed themselves. That was the merchant's joke to Champlain). Their breasts were in many cases more generous than those of the French ladies. And Robert said to himself: since they are so evidently licentious, I will easily find my opportunity.

More Pleasant Reflections

As for Champlain (who had no soupçon or suspicion of what Robert was thinking), he sailed farther up the Fleuve Saint-Laurent with Pontgravé senior. – You wish to explore? said that worthy. By all means! I wish I'd had you with me in 1600! We would have talked Chauvin into something then, I wager! But listen, man, you work too hard. What do you do for recreation? There are many recreations here in Canada. No? Then take a pinnace and half a dozen men, by all means! Enjoy yourself, and look out for Savages! – Thank you, Monsieur, said Champlain.

Where the Fleuve narrowed, he dropped anchor, regarding the mountain-cliffs of Cap Diamant with acquisitive intent. The Souriquois called the place

Kebec, meaning *The river narrows.* A proper site for a fortified Store-house impregnable to Savages, English or Spaniards . . . *He* knew the ways of battery and mortar, of scarp and counterscarp! – Lifting his quill, he mapped the place, distributing upon the coasts regularly spaced replications of a single tree-concept, like a craftsman's stamp. The Fleuve Saint-Laurent he left limpidly white, with the exception of an elbowed line of soundings he took in the center to prove that even here, so far upstream, sufficient depth remained for even the stoutest warships to graze.

He sailed on to Three Rivers, near which he spied half a dozen islands, on one of which, he thought, might be erected a good stout fort; and *then* the French could surely make cause with the Irocois, so that other Savage Nations might come freely to trade. – On the last day of Juin he reached the Iroquois River, where for the first time he saw a Savage fortress: the close-set stakes by the riverbank, the canoes drawn up ready to flee in case of any reverse, the fortifications themselves with their covering of oak bark . . . And he said to himself: I could easily vanquish them, if they give me the opportunity.

Most of all he wanted to bring the Faith to Canada. Anadabijou had believed that men and women came from arrows. The folly of it!

He could not forget those women, those indecent women with their naked privities . . .

At the end of that voyage, the Montagnais Sagamore, Bechourat, gave Pontgravé his own son to take to France. (Poor lad! He died in months; good Christian food was too rich for his digestion . . .) Champlain asked for the present of an Iroquois woman as well, for they had intended to eat her. Bechourat laughed and kicked her and gave her to him, for which he thanked GOD. (When he smiled at her most pleasantly, she began to wail. She thought that she would be his dinner, it seemed.) So they set sail with two Savages, departing Gaspé on the twenty-fourth day of Août, in the company of the Sieur de Prévert, who told them the tale of a sea-monster called GOUGOU, which he had seen with his own eyes. Could it be so? Surely there must be devils in Canada, to have taught the people such barbarities! On the twentieth of Septembre they arrived without incident in Havre, in good time to take part in the festivities of the Dauphin's third birthday, for which grace all praised GOD, saving only the Hiroquois damsel, who had unfortunately died of homesickness.* Yes, it had been a most advantageous voyage. But as soon

* "I think she may still have been alive and at Quebec in 1610," says Trigger. ". . . It is a sad commentary on the inadequacy of our sources concerning the Indians that we know nothing about what this woman was doing at Quebec . . . or what eventually became of her."

as Canada had vanished behind them, Champlain felt a pang, and he knew that he would return there if life remained to him.

The Custom of the Country

In the Country of the Haudenosaunee, which lies upon the forty-third parallel, a sun-struck lake-crag glowed white through the orange fog of autumn, and blood-flecked trees upraised their thin arms in prayer. A canoe went by. A yellow-red maple-leaf wigwagged slowly down and landed on the water. Mist hung over that mirror-silver lake like an echo-bell. The lake was still. The wake of the first canoe had long since vanished when a second canoe approached. The first canoe was made of birchbark, but the second canoe was made of elmbark, which meant that the men in them were of different Nations. The birchbark men were Montagnais; they were far from home. The elmbark men were Hiroquois. They were Mohawk warriors. It was past the time of the Harvest Thanksgiving. They had finished their raids; they had burned their captive enemies, and now they had set out to hunt the deer. They paddled down the lake and rounded a steep cape grown with beeches. Here the lake narrowed. The canoe vanished, and for a moment there was silence. Then screams clogged the air.

The next day crows came in great numbers to that place.

Pontgravé Wins his Wager

Upon returning to port, Pontgravé rushed down to the dock and cried anxiously: And my patron, the Sieur de Chaste, has he returned to health?

He is dead, Monsieur.

Dead? Dead! What terrible news!

He ran back onto the ship and winked at the Captain, who groaned wearily and paid the stipulated fifteen livres . . .

Acadia Again 1604

It was this same Sieur de Prévert, who, not content with filling credulous Champlain's mind with lies concerning sea-monsters, also persuaded him that Acadia was an Empire of Copper. The mines at French Bay were so rich, he insisted, that somebody was bound to make a million livres. And there were diamonds on the way . . . The Sieur de Monts also drank in these tales. – Tadoussac is too cold for me, Monsieur, he said. Is Acadia a warmer place? – Ah, sighed Prévert, it is as warm as India, and indeed I believe that Acadia must be the way to Asia, for the breezes that blow there are fragrant with nutmegs and myrrh . . .

You old faker! Pontgravé would have shouted. But he was in town, selling his beaver-skins.

And so that, in fine, is how De Monts, having come into the monopoly, let himself be gulled into his Acadian adventure. Pontgravé didn't care where he sailed to. Pontgravé knew that beavers waddled everywhere in Canada. Why, almost all the ponds in New France were constructed by beavers! One would never exhaust the supply of those animals.

Isle de Sainte-Croix 1604–1605

Thus we see that the aforesaid De Monts was at least somewhat in the wrong in his castigation of Champlain. He himself had believed Prévert's tales as much as any. When they got to Acadia, while Poutrincourt mooned around giving presents to Membertou, while young Robert Pontgravé begged the key to his father's coffers and drew out even more beads and blankets and hatchets (which, however, he didn't give away out of kindness and diplomacy, like Poutrincourt, but *traded* to the Savages for beaver-skins); while Born Swimming dreamed of her Floating Island, while Duval the locksmith was set to work making stout padlocks for a Store-house which had not yet been built, intended to hold a mountain of riches which had not yet been gathered, the Sieur de Monts dispatched Champlain to look for them. – Old Pontgravé only blew his nose while De Monts went on, De Monts saying (as if to a witless person): Copper mines, Champlain. And silver mines, too. That's what we were told. Do you remember? We must begin to recover expenses. Do you comprehend me?

Yes, Monsieur. You are my Captain –

Now, about the second part. If you discover gold and diamonds, leave the copper and silver behind for now. I don't believe that Prévert will be able to claim it before the expiration of my monopoly, so there's plenty of time. I trust in you to watch over the men, and prevent greed from getting too great a hold on them . . .

He truly believes it! whispered Pontgravé to Robert.

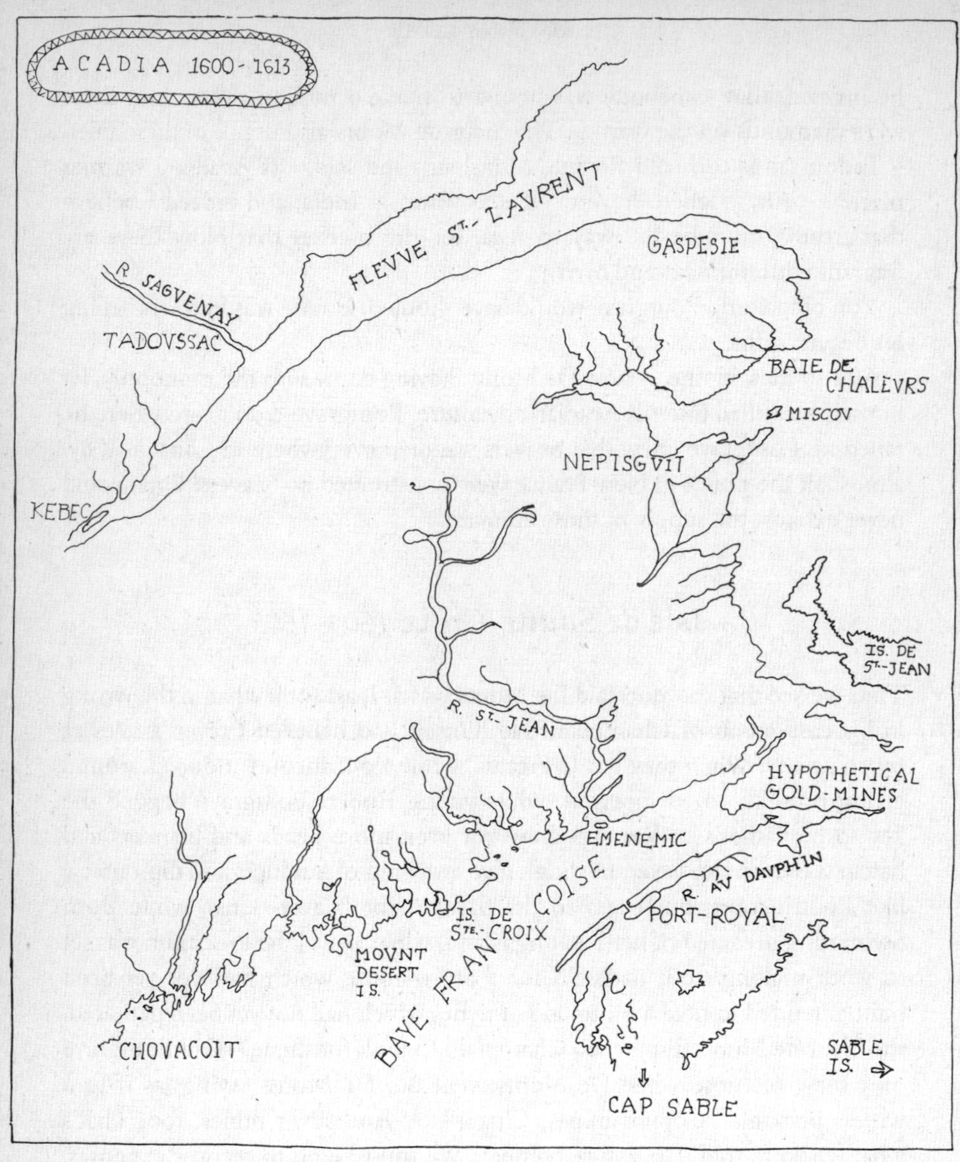

Robert folded his arms. – But, Papa, what if he's right? What if Champlain comes back loaded with gold, and we don't get any?

What if all the Savages become Saints? rejoined Pontgravé scornfully. No fear of that!

Champlain departed; Champlain returned. – No mines? cried De Monts in astonishment.

I could find none, Seigneur. But I shall search again in the spring . . .

You're certain that you landed at the proper place?

The end of the Bay, Prévert told me. He swore it! But the countryside there is quite extensive. I journeyed for more than sixty leagues. Perhaps he was mistaken in his measurements. I did sail up the rivière called Norembegue, but found nothing save islands and waterfalls . . .

No, the pique which De Monts now directed at the ex-Quartermaster should have boomeranged back to bruise his own gullible breast, and surely would have, if hooded Justice were GOD. But she isn't. As for the next item on De Monts' catalogue of recriminations, however, I cannot deny that if *anyone* was to blame for the fact that Port-Royal did not immediately begin to enjoy the benefits of French favor, that for another space the Savages called Souriquois must be left in darkness, it was Champlain, who longed for a toy world upon which he could make experiments, in preparation for grander projects. On one of the charts of his mind he had already engraved the Isle de Sainte-Croix with its rocky shoal-fang curving south, its small square compounds, outside of which lay the gardens, and then at some remove the cemetery. (One always needed cemeteries, sooner or later.) That islet to the west would serve as a most convenient mount for cannon. He'd draw up his settlement in a square around the central tree – yes, that tree had to be there, for the double reasons of health and ornament – maybe for a gallows, too – and he'd build his narrow steep-roofed houses crowded close together: blacksmith's shop, carpenter's shed, bakehouse, as many as possible making smoke at any given time; then he would add the smoking cookhouse overhanging the river, the cliffs looking down . . . There'd be a chapel, of course (no smoke there), to which he and De Monts would go to pray even when it was not the hour for Mass, so that piety would exercise its needed effect over the impressed men. He saw himself kneeling at De Monts' side . . . (Just as a Captain in the clutches of some insidious sea-fog may sometimes come alongside a rock, believing it to be another vessel, so Champlain still believed the Sieur de Monts to be his friend.) From the good French timber on De Monts' ship they'd build a Store-house for their furs, provisions and armaments. The residence of the Sieur de Monts would be constructed of the same material (although in his secret mind he pretended that De Monts had lamentably died, and that he, Champlain, ruled there). The other buildings would have to be log huts: he understood that; he was practical. Anyhow, they'd be suitable for the men of inferior grade. Most likely he should command that a covered gallery be erected for work or leisure in bad weather. Since De Monts would assuredly live through the winter, he'd erect a sturdy cabin for himself just opposite his residence, so that De Monts would have ready access to his advice. Perhaps he should live with D'Orville and Champdoré: – as they were not entirely reliable, he had better exercise supervision over them. Then the artisans . . . and the mercenaries . . . – yes, and the whole palisadoed all around.

We already know that Poutrincourt, whose obsession with Port-Royal might have triumphed over Champlain's obsession with security, had returned home to France by now, in company with several gentlemen of leisure who had made the voyage merely to while away a summer. The Pontgravés father and son sailed back, too. They knew Canada. In their default, De Monts let himself be persuaded to raise arms on Isle de Sainte-Croix. As he had the highest rank, he must take the responsibility, although not (as I have said) the blame.

They completed the Store-house first, in order to lock away all the Sieur de Monts' goods, provisions and treasures. The architect, however, was dispatched back to French Bay to search once again for the Sieur de Prévert's copper mines. He sailed a good threescore of leagues, but all he found was Savages and rivers.

At least you are punctual, Champlain. (Thus De Monts.) You are always that.

Thank you, Seigneur.

De Monts clapped his hands. – You, Duval the locksmith! Is the door to my Store-house completed? Good. Present the key to Champlain. He shall be my Quartermaster, being proved so capable in that position. – Eh, Champlain, look at his lynx-face! He does not want to give it over, does he? Duval, Duval, you are quite comical.

Champlain proceeded to the Store-house and tried the key. – A very good fit, Duval, said he. You should praise GOD for your talent; indeed I have rarely seen the like.

Now Champlain said this only to please the man, because he thought him somewhat sullen in his temper. These types, in his experience, could be controlled more easily with words of honey than of vinegar. Yet Duval seemed in no wise pleased, but stood glaring at the key in Champlain's hand, as if he sincerely believed that merely because he had wrought such a thing it ought to belong to him. So Champlain strode between the two Swiss guards who stood there with their halberds, and pulled the door open. It was his plan to beckon Duval inside with him, there to learn what vexed his heart, and if need be to chastise him in such a way that the man would not be needlessly humiliated in front of his fellows. But when he turned round from the casks of wine, biscuits, gold sols and livres, gunpowder and beaver-pelts, he saw that Duval was gone.

Now fall came in earnest, and the winds blew chilly on the island. The garden did not thrive. There was so much sand . . . The Swiss mercenaries stayed silent in their barracks. (Their hearts were river-islands whose root-edges, catching snow, had already become fringed with ice.) At low tide everyone not of the highest rank gathered clams, mussels, sea-urchins, sea-snails and suchlike water-vegetables, of which there was such an abundant supply that De Monts' fears for the winter did not yet grow on him like frost in his chest; and the sun still cast down warm red rays of evening. Champdoré the pilot, it is true, voiced some alarm, having discerned as he thought an unfavorable conjunction of stars and wind-currents, which he said portended a severe season, but Champlain said: That may or may not be so, but you should have expressed your opinions to me before. Now it is too late to move our Habitation. I shall consider any more such talk disloyal. – Abashed, Champdoré swore to keep silence, but nonetheless the matter was heard of, at which the other men fulminated against Champlain, so much indeed that he began to feel himself as if surrounded by the sea-birds called *Margaux*, which bite like dogs. He paced to the northern end of the island, from which he could see a grand solitary peak rising at somewhat more than two leagues' distance, and he thought: indeed it would be preferable to have a solid range of mountains to wall us away from the wind, but it cannot be helped – certainly not by traitors such as Champdoré. Eh, he is not a traitor, but his tongue is the clapper of the DEVIL's bell.

Now winter came, and their hardships were much increased. In Novembre they weathered several attacks of foudrilles or blizzards, which cast drifts so thick and high against their doors and windows that they were almost stifled. The Swiss guards did not marvel at this, for their Country too was very alpine, but the artisans were discomfited. The breezes grew frigid, and froze many a man's nose or ears. De Monts had commanded that the cedars which surrounded the buildings not be cut, in order to provide some shelter from these very winds of Canada, yet even so, icy drafts blew through every house, dusting floors and faces with snow. The river that fortified them, their Stream of Time, was frozen in various shades of silver and white, with tree-hills snorting against it with lowered noses. The snow was four feet deep. The men hooded themselves in their cloaks when they lay down to sleep. All beverages froze excepting only the Spanish wine, which, coming from the tropics, possessed yet a little tropical virtue. For this reason the men drank it most eagerly, believing that it could best warm them: warmth was the main subject of their conversations. But it was soon exhausted. Cider was weighed out by the livre. Champlain performed this task. A ludicrous sight it was to see him do it, too, scraping the veriest tincture of reddish-brown ice-shavings from the pan of his balance to make the portion equitable, but soon the men stopped laughing. When the cider gave out, they had to drink dirty melted snow.

De Monts did all that could have been asked of him. He encouraged and exhorted the men to comport themselves patiently, like true Christians. Daily he pointed to the banner of France which flew above his house and drew their hearts to it. The lesser Captains likewise did their part: the Sieur de Beaumont besought them to think upon the spring, when Canada would hide its naked harshness from them under green skirts, and they could enrich themselves. Messire Aubry held Mass twice each day and set a most pious tone (although behind his back the convicts mocked him, saying: He is lily-breasted, like a liver-snatcher!) It gave him great distress that the holy water was a cake of ice. Before High Mass he must melt a cake of it in the cookhouse. The convicts jeered, saying that this was proof that it had no virtue, at which he flew into a rage and boxed their ears. They knew better than to strike him back, so they turned and walked away, muttering oaths. Yet these ugly scenes subsided with the temperature, for it became apparent to them at last how unpredictable a business their survival would be this winter: therefore they began to love duty and obedience once again, and prayed humbly (those who were capable of it) for GOD's help. Comprehending this change in their hearts, Messire Aubry became gentler, and strove with all his power to communicate to them something of the purity of JESUS, of which they were sorely in need. He was often to be seen in the barracks of the Swiss soldiers, many of whom suffered from weakness and lassitude. Hearing of these things, both De Monts and Champlain came to admire him greatly. As for the Sieur de La Motte, he organized a mock tournament between the soldiers and the artisans, putting up five livres as the prize, just as he had done on the occasion of the Dauphin's third birthday. The Sieur d'Orville was likewise zealous in encouraging their spirits. And when Champdoré was sick from the scurvy, Champlain (who thought he was doing him a favor) asked him to talk about copper and blue stones. – Think on these things, he admonished him, and you will be distracted from your sufferings.

What kind of distraction is that? said Champdoré sourly. It distracts you, not me.

At this, Champlain stood up and went out into the snow.

He remembered New Spain, with its lemon-breezes –

He paced and paced. Presently he stole quietly to the bakehouse and pressed his ear against the door. Duval was in there, chatting with the baker. He could hear his croaking voice. He did not like Duval.

Maybe De Monts will do it, the baker was saying. He's a shrewd one. See how the Roy loves him . . .

Ah, then he's not so shrewd, said the locksmith importantly. The Roy loves Poutrincourt much more. Why? Because Poutrincourt costs him no money. Have you never noticed how those loved by the Roy are poor? But that's only human nature.

At this the Sieur de Champlain made one of his sudden entrances (it was uncanny how the man would appear at the worst possible moment). – What's this treasonous talk I hear, Duval?

The locksmith shot a glance at him, then ducked his head suddenly.

Well? said Champlain.

I was only saying, Seigneur, what a shame it was that the Sieur de Poutrincourt had not been better requited for his zeal.

Champlain paced up and down. – Indeed Poutrincourt is zealous, he said. Yet I am surprised that you consider him and his zeal any subject for your unclean attention. And it seems to be a familiar tune with you, that this man or that man has not been well requited. Tell me, Duval, do you too consider yourself poorly requited here?

Excuse me – said the locksmith in confusion. I beg you, Seigneur –

But the Sieur de Champlain had already taken his leave.

For a moment the two men stood silent and shamefaced. Then the baker opened the door and peered out into the blizzard, like a child afraid of monsters. He turned to the other at last. – Eh, he is gone, he said. It is a wonder how that man can be everywhere.

Presently the scurvy fell upon them in full force. Now Champdoré was one of the lucky ones, for he could still talk. By mid-Janvier, all that was heard upon that snow-covered isle of misery was the groaning of dying men. It was no use doing anything for them, although Champlain was indefatigable. He searched for a certain kind of bark with which the Savages warded off the disease; he did not recollect the name of it, but he'd read about it in Cartier's relation of a hundred years before . . . So he was always attempting to persuade the men to try this or that bark, which he himself fetched, striding across the frozen river to Port-Royal, from where the Souriquois had removed, GOD knew where, and white snow-trees tunneled the grey creeks, stifling them in the utmost dreariness and severity; with his numbed hands he brushed the snow away from tree-skins, cutting frozen slices with his knife (no wonder the Savages used this stiff and crackly stuff for the walls of wigwams). – *Anneda*, that was what Quartier had called that medicinal tree. One could very easily remember such things with practice. But the Savages – where *were* the Savages? Did they hunt the moose in winter? Perhaps. – But these Souriquois are different in their ways than the Montagnais whom I saw last year with Pontgravé. Eh, that is not to be wondered at. Just as certain whales can be recognized by their tails, so evidently these Savages too can be told apart quite easily . . . I wish I could find Membertou. Surely he would tell me the secret of this bark. It is a pity. – So Champlain bore great loads of bark home to the island on his back, but none of the sick men would taste of it, fearing the poisons which must lie in so many Canadian vegetables. – He was at his wits' end. Some things came easily to him. If some Captain or Admiral over him were to give orders that he unmoor ship and heave short, he would know what to do. He could tell how many fathoms were needed for a safe anchorage. But this was different. Even good wine did not seem to be sovereign as a specific against the complaint, although he ministered it repeatedly to all. Of course new diseases must be expected in new lands. But this was sickening and sorrowful to see. Flesh blossomed in the men's mouths like fungus. Their gums became as white as Messire Aubry's stole; upon them, flowers red and green and gold embroidered themselves. They could pull their own teeth out without feeling any pain. Presently these flowers opened so wide that the men could no longer eat anything. With great difficulty Champlain could force a little fluid down their throats. Now their arms and legs became swollen and blotched with blood. They entered into convulsions and became weak. They felt stabbing pains in their stomachs, their loins . . .

Out of seventy-nine men on the island, thirty-five died, among them Messire Aubry, so that they were now without the benefits of the Church. At Champlain's insistence, they opened the bodies to determine the cause of this disease and found the lungs very dry, the spleen watery, the gall tainted, the whole filled with black and clotted blood.

Tell me, grinned De Monts after one of these autopsies, do you think it's possible to love without an object?

What do you mean, Seigneur? said Champlain.

This Country – this place – there's something about it that keeps us here. I feel no vocation; I shall return with Pontgravé's ship, but I remember the fidelity I felt to a certain lady before I was married. Until it's made apparent to me that a man can love his own fear, I – I know not –

My Seigneur, don't shame yourself by saying such things, said Champlain imploringly. We must not listen to talk such as this.

De Monts laughed. – Why? Do you feel the same? Of course you do. Why else would you come back and back here without reward? Oh, your *insolence!* For you know you never *will* be rewarded, Champlain. You have no advantage over me. You're a vulgar, mediocre man. Everyone remarks it of you; no one fears you anymore. You know it yourself – you must know it! No, you're here for – for the rivers . . .

Open your mouth, said Champlain.

I beg your pardon?

No, wider. – Exactly! – Eh, you, too, Seigneur. Your gums are rotting. It's this scurvy. You must conceal your condition from the men, or we shall all be lost.

De Monts smiled sadly. – But I suppose you have none of the symptoms yourself?

None.

Somehow I'm not surprised. Or do you follow your own prescription for concealment? Never mind. Perhaps I'm wrong about you. Perhaps you are extraordinary after all. But if so, then I for one despise extraordinariness.

Why must you say such things to me, Seigneur? You know that I have been zealous in my duty.

It is not only I who says them, Champlain. But take no alarm. I have no wish to discharge you from my service, and send you into the snow like a barefoot penitent. No, I shall keep you. Year in, year out, I shall keep you here with me in Canada. You must finish your charts, I know. Year in, year out.

Champlain had become livid. He said something in a very faint voice, which neither he nor De Monts could comprehend. His face was contorted with shame and guilt, which seized the muscles of his mouth in spasms like the struggle between the East and West winds upon the surface of the sea. He turned as if to go. Night was falling; snow was falling.

Yes, go, laughed De Monts. You are so certain. You speak from experience. Perhaps next winter you can establish us all on a fine warm glacier.

After this, the Sieur de Monts and the Sieur de Champlain were perceived to avoid each other somewhat, although no one ventured to speak of it.

Iron
1604–1605

> As for us, our fortune is made; we are the portion of JESUS CHRIST and JESUS CHRIST is our portion, and our profit is to try to possess Him by practising our Rules and doing His will.
>
> MARIE DE L'INCARNATION, to her son (1670)

It is probably needless to say that the winter was not so bad for the Ln'uk (*viz.*, the Souriquois) as it was for the French, whom they were already calling Iron People. First of all, the heavy falls of snow were no inconvenience to them, as they knew well the art of weaving cunning raquettes or snowshoes, whose rawhide lashings held the curved wood in wide ovals to distribute a person's weight upon the snow. Wearing these, the hunters of the Lnu'k traveled lightly upon the snow-crust. They found the moose and caribou floundering in the drifts and killed them easily. So for these People a heavy winter was a time of plenty. This year, too, some of them had a special advantage: *viz.*, the *iron* which their new friends had given them. The Basques had brought them *iron* before, but never enough. How rich these others were! The women of Membertou's household laughed with delight to see how easily they could cook with their *iron** kettle. No longer must they heat stones in the fire and then drop them into bark dishes, over and over until the water boiled. They could set their kettle among the embers and the kettle would not burn. (The Basques had given them one, but it burst.) So the moose-bones boiled, and the dogs devoured the moose-guts outside, growl-

* Probably copper, but everything would have been called *iron* at this stage.

ing softly at one another in the red-smeared snow, and Membertou sat in the best place, the father's place, telling stories of KLUSKAP and KEWKW and other PERSONS, which are best told in winter, and his eldest son, whose name was Membertouji'j after him, sat making a new shield of wood for war, and his wives were there cooking with his mother, and the kettle boiled and after the stories were ended Membertouji'j said jokingly to his wives: I shall have to hunt well this winter to keep you occupied. Otherwise you will become lazy. Your cooking is easy now. – You, you! they shouted. Look at you, with your *iron* hatchet, your *iron*-tipped spear! Now you can hunt doing nothing!

(Membertouji'j said nothing to this. They were carried away with themselves. They showed insufficient respect for the animals.)

In the spring the Iron People will come back, said Membertou after a pause. We must get some beaver-skins to give them. That will make them happy.

Why do they care for our rags of clothing? said Membertouji'j. They are truly a stupid People. And how ill-favored they are! I have never seen such ugly men. Do you think that there are women among them also?

And he shot his wives a single ill-tempered glance.

Indeed they act like women, replied his father. It is a marvel to me to watch them gesticulate and interrupt one another. What unmanly People! But they are our kin-friends now. In the spring I will not hunt for caribou. I will hunt only for beaver. Then they will give me more presents. I like *iron* as much as you.

Pontgravé's Reward

1605–1606

The Enemy observes very carefully whether one has a delicate or lax conscience. If the conscience is delicate he strives to make it excessively so, in order to disturb and ruin it more easily.

SAINT IGNATIUS, *Spiritual Exercises* (1533)

But winter continued to pass very slowly on the Isle de Sainte-Croix – so slowly, in fact, that Champlain succeeded at last in convincing himself, through a sort of inverse paranoia, that De Monts did value his services. After all, he'd promised that he would bring Champlain back to Canada with him year after year. The disagreeable resonances of that conversation lingered, like the smell of those Montagnes fillettes at Tadoussac, but all this was dampened by the first trickle of the midwinter thaw (by which time he no longer heard the survivors saying: Even the black-cowled Jesuits could have picked a likelier spot! – by which time he'd convinced himself that he would soon enter into the most roseolous afterlife). – De Monts will return to France in the fall, he prayed, and then I shall be his Viceroy here . . . – One might express surprise that so practical a man as Champlain was capable of hoodwinking himself in this childish fashion. But to focus only on his practicality is to regard him as a mechanism like Poutrincourt's water-wheel, ignoring the motive-power. In Champlain's case, the river which turned his gears was not (as he thought) the Stream of Time, but rather the Stream of Optimism, which is a very steady water-course in the neighborhood of the Saguenay. True Faith was dissolved in it in high concentrations. It never

froze; its blue water streamed so monotonously past pine trees, flecked with golden macules . . . When spring came at last, and the ice began to break up, the Sieur de Monts announced his intention of rigging out a boat to seek a more southerly place in which to build, and asked Champlain to accompany him. – Of course, Seigneur, he said, laughing and full of life.

But they could not go yet. The snow melted, dripping sullenly; the wind and rain continued to assault them, and they sat waiting for their supplies. In the Moon of Leaf-Opening, when the Souriquois were happily shooting bears on the branches of trees, Isle de Sainte-Croix remained a dirty, icy slush-heap. The rivers had long thawed, and the Souriquois hunted beaver at sunset, clubbing them as they came out of the water; they must have pelts and pelts to give to the Iron People. Then the Iron People would give them hatchets. Born Swimming's husband, Swooping Like a Hawk, had visited Membertou's wigwam and greatly admired the Iron People's gifts. He wanted some of them, too. He went to a beaver-house in the darkness and killed all the animals he could. Born Swimming laughed and sang songs to see how many beaver-tails there would be to eat. But the Iron People did not come forth. (You must dream them closer! laughed Swooping Like a Hawk. Your Floating Island is stranded like a dying whale! – Born Swimming grinned sharply; her black eyes gleamed.) The Iron People shivered and starved and did not dare to unhood themselves. On the fifteenth day of that same month of Juin, Pontgravé arrived at last. The Iron People greeted him with trumpets and a cannonade.

Eh, you lazy scoundrels, I had thought that you would have raised up a fine walled town at Port-Royal by now! (Thus Pontgravé.) What did you pick this iceberg for? Eh? By my beard, where are the rest of you, dead? *Dead?* You're joking. (Captain Morel, you owe me two crowns.) You've had a hard enough winter, I see. GOD wishes to punish us for our sins. My dear, dear Seigneur de Monts, you've become as skinny as you are valorous. But don't fret – I've brought barrels full of peas, flour and sweetmeats! – Have I told you the news? The Pope died! Now Paul V is *Pontifex Maximus*. At Court I heard them say that he means to overhaul High Mass – no, it's idle gossip, I'm sure. Some tongues are far too worldly! – Eh, Champlain, it's you! And did you discover your mountain of gold last autumn?

No, Monsieur. I sailed up and down French Bay, where the Sieur de Prévert placed his mines, but I could not find any metal, not as far as I could see.

Whenever Pontgravé passed by Champlain, he slapped him heartily on the shoulder. He had spoken with De Monts in private. Slowly, Champlain understood that he would receive the blame for the winter's deaths after all – *he*, who had rendered up everything, who slept in his clothes to be better prepared for alarms, who never ceased to sweep his torch-eyes across the vassals' hearts, searching for doubt and treachery! And now this! He flushed; he felt queasy in his stomach. Naked privities, naked shame! The idea of returning to France entered his head. From there he could take passage to Cadiz; surely the Roy of Spain would give him some befitting command; he could go back to Guadeloupe, to . . . – But then the listless weeks in Mechique seeped back into his head like water. What was he thinking of? He had to stay in Canada. No matter what befell, he must make something of himself here. He was already more than thirty years of age.

Pontgravé's son Robert stared at him wordlessly. He was a hulking youth.

The men feasted on the wine and peas and biscuits which Pontgravé had brought. They were very thin. Pontgravé clucked his tongue and shrugged.

On the second day following, Champlain and the Sieur de Monts set out on their explorations. Pontgravé could not refrain from coming likewise, although he'd meant to be cheating Savages at Tadoussac by now, but what could he do with De Monts in a pickle, Champlain in a pout (thank Heaven the fellow was too simple to meditate revenge!), D'Orville dead, everybody of a rubicund temperament dead! Pass me the brandy! He couldn't have believed it if he hadn't seen the same with Chauvin at the turn of the century. This time, alas, Pontgravé had lost a couple of bets. He'd honestly thought that priest Aubry was too stupid to die! And Duval – *that* fellow was such a grippeminaud* Pontgravé had marked him for a speedy execution. – What can you do? Just when you think you have life figured out, death butts in on you. LORD, I'm profound! – Anyhow, it was a good crew that raised sail at last. They discovered the Bay of Seven Isles, the Cape of Isles, the Bay of Isles . . . It was easy, frictionless, facile. Some Savages told Champdoré how to steer, avoiding the white breakers and islands. (Champlain kept him under proper observation, of course; for such tasks Champlain's eyeballs were more than suitable.) – Pay heed to our Champlain! (Thus goodnatured Pontgravé, slapping Champlain's shoulder so hard he thought the cannon had gone off.) Champlain's *experienced*, I tell you! Bend the knee to him, gentlemen! – Champlain made a half-grateful, half-disgusted grimace, like a baby trying some new food . . . Once there came a strange lashing turbulence of the water, and the Savages shouted, but De Monts continued unmoved: he had little use for these GOUGOUS, and BEELZEBUBS, and other scare-flies! And in truth nothing untoward occurred; whatever double-dealing might be going on beneath the waves did not affect the French. – Champlain drew maps all the way. What a rich Country! He scratched his curly head; he rubbed his sunburned nose. – Now in truth I am acting as Viceroy, thought he to himself, well pleased. – Again he sketched out his trees and promontories and unknown rivers fading inland beyond knowledge (how near was China?); everywhere he made his soundings – with far more effect than Poutrincourt had done. He gathered the trees into orderly clumps as he mapped them, so that the rivers would be less encumbered . . .

The man is cuckoo! muttered De Monts.

He knows his wind and longitude, however. (Thus staunch Pontgravé; thus peacemaking Pontgravé; thus the magnanimous Gravé du Pont.)

Continuing south, they found the Country to be greatly deficient in moose and beaver, but roebucks, bears and lynxes abounded. They shot many from the ship. Flocks of crows and liver-snatchers wheeled overhead, calling hoarsely. At Cap Corneille there were so many crows that they shot them for sport, laughing to see them tumble into the sea to be devoured by they knew not what, vying with each other to extinguish the greatest possible number of those ominously nagging black lives . . .

* Hypocritical little weasel.

Fishing for Eels

They explored even to Kinibeki and Malebarre (a coasting distance of four hundred leagues), but no safe harbor could they find. Here the Savages were different than the wood-wanderers whom they had previously seen: they were called *Armouchiquois*. They came running to the strand. Their wampum-collars glittered in the sunlight. – Ah, said De Monts lightly, the Sieur de Prévert assured us that their knees were higher than their heads. – Hearing this, a sense of bliss swept through Champlain. Surely if his Captain now blamed Prévert for the imbroglio of the mines, and for his idle lies concerning the Armouchiquois also, then – then . . . – But he did not even desire to bring his logic to orgasm. – How sedentary these Armouchiquois were! They tilled the soil, as we were told to do in the Bible; they raised pumpkins and Jerusalem artichokes. Champlain felt tender toward them. They were enemies of the Souriquois; it would be good work to pit those Nations against one another. He gave them hatchets (Pontgravé had brought more than forty-three hundred of the cheapest kind). Through his telescope, he could see their squaws scratching in the fields with wooden hooks . . . He believed that it would be an easy matter to convert them, once they had been sufficiently instructed in the French language. But of course that was not his vocation. (As for Messire Aubry, he desiccated in his sandy grave.)

It was at Malebarre that the Armouchiquois attacked. When the carpenter went ashore for water, the Savages watched him subtly. Really they were watching his kettle, his iron thing. When he set it down for a moment, one snatched it. The carpenter yelled and gave chase, at which they shot him with arrows, and he fell dead. Now the Sieur de Monts shouted out to fire, and the men on ship began to discharge their muskets, but the Savages were gone behind the dunes. They were swifter than greyhounds. Champlain's arquebus had exploded in his hands, and he was streaming with blood. Yet he seemed in no wise disconcerted. He threw down the pieces and leaped into a dinghy, as if to give chase. – You are wounded, man! cried De Monts. I do not deny that you are brave . . . – For the first time Champlain heard a tenderness in his Captain's voice, and was moved almost to tears. He went to Bonnerne the surgeon, who gave him brandy and pepper while he bound up his wounds. Meanwhile the ship rounded the sandy cape and so escaped danger. There were a number of Armouchiquois on board, whom De Monts considered firing upon, but even as he deliberated they saw their danger and leaped into the water. Champlain tore himself from Bonnerne's hands and dove in after them. One he seized wriggling and slippery and dragged him back to deck. They bound him hand and foot.

Eh, said De Monts, let him go.

Champlain's face fell . . .

The New Viceroy

Having failed in their better hopes, they resolved then to remove to Port-Royal, where they should have gone in the first place (said De Monts). They landed at the Isle de Sainte-Croix and took down all the buildings, with the exception of the Store-house, which was too large to pull down, and chose a site opposite the Rivière de l'Équille. Here the Souriquois were waiting for them with many beaver-skins. Their dogs, whose coats were of all colors like foxes, began to bark and growl, but the Souriquois were silent. They threw their skins down at the Sieur de Monts' feet without a word, as was their custom. Watching De Monts' face, Champlain saw a sudden light of greed emitted by it, and he was downcast. Did no one feel what he felt for the poor Savages?

This time De Monts himself drew up a quadrilateral plan for their winter Habitation, well closed against the winds, which indeed (Champlain had to admit) was a grand amelioration. Eh, the mischief of last winter was long over! He began to feel freer. Under the Sieur de Monts' direction the Frenchmen went to work, building narrow houses huddled together, dominated by chimneys, their roofs as narrow as razor-ridges. They sowed French grains, hemp, turnips, radishes, cabbage . . .

De Monts watched, pacing on the cannon-platform; Champlain bawled out orders until his face turned purple, slapping the artisans on the shoulder with a laugh, or striking them if they weren't fast enough. – He is truly one of them, said De Monts to Pontgravé.

Correct as always, Seigneur. Absolutely correct. – He whistled contentedly; offered De Monts *tobacco*.

I wonder what baleful mishap he's engineering for us now . . .

Oh, come, Seigneur, don't take it like that. Mishaps rule the world. The fault was not his. Let bygones be bygones, just like the Savages do. Haven't you noticed how serene they all are? Why, if they all starved to death they wouldn't even mind it; that sort of thing happens all the time in Canada. As for Champlain, he's a bit of a ninny, but – *Champlain!* How kind of you to join us! How's the weather down there?

No thank you, Monsieur, said De Monts to Champlain. I do not need your sketches.

Champlain wandered into the forest and built a trout-pond with sluices, a garden, a workroom for himself . . .

When autumn fell, De Monts left for France, appointing Pontgravé his Lieutenant on that side of the sea.

Champlain said nothing. Again he set out with the pilot Champdoré, in search of the Sieur de Prévert's copper mines; again he did not find them.

Winter at Port-Royal

Pontgravé was very diligent. He never permitted any idleness.

A dozen men died of the scurvy.

They ground their bread with hand-mills. This was very laborious, and they offered the Savages half of what was ground if they should perform the work, but they refused, at which Champlain stamped his foot and said: Someday we shall make them beg for bread!

A Dream of Meadows
1606–1610

What in Rome is evident to the view, is often looked for under the Earth.

HERDER, *Reflections* (1880)

The Sieur de Poutrincourt arrived at the end of the spring. – You shall replace Pontgravé and be Lieutenant-Governor of Acadia! De Monts had said, at which Poutrincourt was much moved. But his wife, bidding him adieu at Havre, said only: I did not notice that the position carries any stipend. – To this he paid no attention. He wrote the lawyer Lescarbot, who asked a day's adjournment, as he put it, and then acceded to his own desire to flee the evil world, having just been wronged in a property suit. – You'll like it, Marc, I promise you! said Poutrincourt very enthusiastically. – Off they'd sailed. – Now again he became drunk with Canada, as always happened; his head felt light; his heart soared. He expounded theories of happiness at foolish length to his son Charles Biencourt, who'd never been there before, and indeed to all who would listen, so that they thought him half-senile like De Monts. Now here again was Port-Royal with its waterfalls and meadows and stream-rain. The new Habitation had survived the winter quite well, although Champlain and the others were in bad case for lack of provisions; indeed, at Pontgravé's orders they had gone in search of good French fishing-boats to take them home. Only two Frenchmen remained to guard the Store-house, by name Miquelet and La Taille. They snored day and night, dreaming of pork pies. But Membertou saw Poutrincourt coming. He ran out upon the cannon-platform and then came into the kitchen where they dozed, crying: Wake up, brothers! You do not see the great ship which is coming; wake up, wake up! – Now he leaped into his canoe and paddled out with his daughter

Memberech'coech' to meet the strange Iron People. Ever more deeply did he crave their axes year by year. *Hé hé hé*, they cut so well! Their metal was the color of a stream-pool on a cloudy summer day, bright and silver! Ahead flashed the brilliant future of the Irocois, when the necklace of glowing axeheads would settle around Père Brébeuf's throat, sizzling upon his chest and shoulders; when Père Jogues' head would get split by a pretty silver wedge . . . Perceiving that these Iron People were French, and then recognizing Poutrincourt, Membertou was very happy, and waved the French hat which Pontgravé had given him: to this agreed upon signal of good news, La Taille responded, rubbing the sleep from his eyes, searching for tinder and match; so he fired the cannonade of welcome: ***THOOOOOM!*** Now all gathered together in reunion, and Poutrincourt set a plump barrel of wine in the courtyard, for any to imbibe of as they wished. The kitchen chimney smoked more vigorously than a whole Council of Savages; La Taille wept to smell the fragrance of good roast pork . . .

But you were so poorly off that you seriously intended embarking for France? (Thus dry Biencourt.)

No matter, no matter, sighed his father, all is secure now . . .

The weather was fine, which added to Poutrincourt's enjoyment of the Country; every day he considered to himself how much he would like to live there. He'd brought with him roosters and gravid sows, and many kinds of seeds, which he eagerly planted. Biencourt planted orange seeds and lemon seeds; and in three months the shoots were a foot high. His father made sketches on birchbark, which the workmen followed, and soon a water-powered gristmill was turning for the benefit of all; he tasted success in his soul like soft ripe gooseberries . . . (Champlain was still there, too. He inventoried the forest, noting how the black birch was good for musket-stocks; elm for cannon-bracings; ash for Biscayan pike-staffs . . . – So each of them performed his function and was content.) All around them were meadows and butternut trees, and between trees the Souriquois stood leaning on their spears. They liked the French famously, for they gave them iron.

Fishing

Lescarbot, of course, encouraged the Sieur de Poutrincourt by writing *odes* and *apostrophes* in the ancient manner. He could never be anything but sprightly, especially with three pints of wine a day! Generous Poutrincourt! he would cry, laughing as he tilled and enclosed his new garden (he was a fanatic about good soil). Worshipful De Monts! Calculatory and calculacinous Champlain! O France! – The Savages, however, irritated him with the terror which they had or pretended to have of their GOUGOU or Scalp-Monster. But such forebodings were natural, as he well knew, in a race that had no walled towns. – And Poutrincourt, *he* had no forebodings at all. He didn't care a fig for the Jesuits or the excluded traders at Court. De Monts was a staunch Captain – *he'd* know how to neutralize their schemes! Lescarbot had learned the contrary through his sensitive ears, which he sometimes seemed capable of detaching by night and throwing across the sea to flutter against the windows of the Roy's Palace like moths until they had heard the latest plans, proclamations and conspiracies. – Yet how could Poutrincourt worry about such things? Evening after evening, when the tilling and building were done, he strolled with Lescarbot along the point of sand and clay that extended from Port-Royal, and their shadows stretched long and thin almost to breaking across the sharp clamshells as they inhaled the breeze and Poutrincourt said: Monsieur de Champlain is certain that we can make bricks from this soil; – and Lescarbot replied: Eh, let him do it! – at which Poutrincourt grinned at the imputation to poor dull Champlain but then remembered his charity and said: GOD grant that he shall, Marc! – at which Lescarbot, placing his hand on his breast, stood statuesque and heroically declaimed:

Kind Acadia, whose harbor-eyes
Haunt me with a lover's tricks,
Cries: *I yield; I am your prize;*
My virgin sand shall form your bricks!
My Savage maids, in naked guise,
Shall receive your noble pricks!
Robert P. has found his dear;
The rest await *their* Cavalier . . .

– that's *you!* cried Lescarbot, bowing and raising his hat, at which his friend threw himself down laughing. – O, if Loyola's robbers caught wind of you, they'd excommunicate you in a twinkling! he said. What a beast you are, Marc, what a snuffling Savage beast! In France you'd be flogged for such compositions, do you know that? And in France I myself would administer the lash! No, I cannot approve such dishonorable doggerel and drivel! But tell me, is it true that young Pontgravé has been availing himself of the charms of the neighborhood? – Lescarbot winked ominously, at which Poutrincourt's mouth began to twitch into another rictus, but instead he sneezed and leaped up from the sand, dusting himself off. – Now let's see what we find in this bay of ours, sportsman! he shouted enthusiastically. – The two friends raced to the water's edge, and cast their lines. (And in the forest, Champlain raised and lowered his sluices, counting the captive trout, watching the sun-gleam on their bodies, subdividing their prison at his will, for he had no other official powers.)

Codfish! My GOD, this place is worth a million livres! cried Lescarbot.

Eh, here's a bass, much larger than your cod! Throw it back!

Herring!

Halibut! Oh, what a glorious Country! What you say about young Robert Pontgravé, it's too much! Too much! What a scapegrace! And the Savage wench, she loves him, does she? For they ought to be married, Marc. What's this? Not wench, but *wenches*, you say? How many? I cannot approve of that; that is dishonorable libertinism. And do these fillettes show any inclination to convert? Ah, that is the worst of it – fornication between Christians and infidels! Well, someday my position will be strong enough for me to put a stop to it. Robert, Robert . . . And he the son of a Naval officer, too! – Well, as long as it causes no trouble. I want no trouble on my domains. I should arrest him, but I will not; I am too happy here. This air, these breezes, Marc – they go straight to my head! I'm well aware that I talk on and on, like De Monts, but I can't help it, believe me! Ah, I remember when we first anchored, and Membertou came so gravely forward, his face even more hideously painted than usual – you should have seen him! It was no joke. Messire Fléché went as white as snow! He was certain his hour had come, as I realized. But he did his duty; he stepped forward. A good man. – Ah, I am almost drunk on this sea air! – And I prohibited that young Pontgravé from outraging squaws, right in front of everyone. His father took me to task for it later, but I had to make my position clear. Now it doesn't matter, as long as he gets away with it. But if trouble comes, then that scapegrace will hear from me, I assure you!

I must tell you something, said Lescarbot, swallowing. Not all these squaws gave themselves to him willingly. Charles Biencourt was telling me so; he heard it from a Savage . . .

Ah, but that is serious, sighed Poutrincourt. Or do you mean the Etechemin maid?

That's the one.

Yes, well, I heard of the matter from her brother, that plump fellow they call the Trout. In fact, it was I who told the matter to Biencourt. Very stern, my son is. I hope that he will not be too unhappy in life . . . No, Marc, I spoke with Robert's father immediately. Pontgravé is an eel, but trustworthy nonetheless, wouldn't you say? He investigated fully; he gave me a report. The culprit wasn't Robert or any of his men, but one of the illegal traders. A merchant from Honfleur, evidently, with some Basques . . . They robbed and murdered another squaw, did you hear that? – Scoundrels! If I only had them at the end of a rope! They're too stupid with lust to comprehend how they hurt their own trade. Pontgravé couldn't catch them. No, no, it was I, as usual, who had to placate the Etechemins with presents – *I* who subsidize these fornicating robbers!

There isn't any justice, agreed the lawyer. I knew that a long time ago. I was once acquainted with a very wealthy Cardinal who –

I wish I could decide what to do, Marc! Sometimes I want to be out of this Acadia game. Pontgravé comes almost every year, with or without me. Pontgravé could run things. Sometimes I think on my poor wife . . . You have no idea how patient she is, my Claudette. But I can't let De Monts down now. Honor still means something to me. I've had the course! . . . But tell me truthfully, Marc, you don't think the Jesuits will get us, do you?

A bite on my line . . . Cod again! This is getting tedious. No, Monsieur, I don't think so. Not as long as *I* have ears! I mean, after *all!* But Champlain, what about him? *He* should be your worry. I don't know his character. He's not satisfied here . . .

With good reason.

Well, everyone strives to be happy. But he's a fanatic. I've seen him scourge himself when he thought no one was watching. He'd treat with Jesuits, there at Kebec. I heard him say so, just today –

As for this Kebec, he has to get there first. And as for the Jesuits, I've had dealings with their patronne, Madame de Guercheville. I'm certain that she'd refuse him assistance, just like that! (Poutrincourt snapped his fingers.) She doesn't care much for men of his stamp. She's like you; she calls them dangerous. But I . . .

But he's mathematical, isn't he? said Lescarbot, happy to swim away from his friend's lugubrious catalogue of woes. I'll bet he's laying up arpents and beaver-skins against you at this very moment. He's a humorless buffoon, too, so De Monts says (I myself would never say that) – eh, you would know better than I, being better acquainted with him. Believe me, if he has any ambition he'll go to De Monts behind your back –

Ah, but Kebec is so far up river . . . said Poutrincourt lazily. As for being mathematical, well . . .

Well?

I suppose you have a point. He *was* a Quartermaster. I suppose that's where he comes by his exactitude. Not a buffoon, though; that's going a bit far. Noble in a way, but . . . eh, there's something absurd about him. The very first hour that we anchored at this place, although it was a dreary drizzling night, he had to go pace off every conceivable distance. You should have seen him! The sailors' eyes were bugging out! And our Swiss stared straight ahead like dolls, I'm telling you! He concluded, if I remember, that the entrance to the harbor was eight hundred paces wide – to calculate that I think he must have had to walk on water like CHRIST! He also said that two thousand ships could be accommodated in this harbor, perish the thought. I like my solitude.

You see? He's stodgy, Lescarbot insisted. That's what Pontgravé says, too.

Oh, he works hard.

Well, let him, Monsieur, let him.

Robert and the Souriquois

In the spring, Pontgravé set out as De Monts had done the previous year, in order to find a better place of settlement; yet he could not do it. Twice the shallop put back on account of excessive wind. On the third time, they were shipwrecked on the rocks, for which they threw their pilot Champdoré in irons. – I tell you, the fellow is treacherous and obstinate! (Thus Champlain.) – But they had to pardon him. They had no other pilot; and anyhow Biencourt insisted upon it, for he was but eighteen years of age and needed to exercise his authority if he would become respected like his father. The most prudent way to do this, of course, was to oppose Champlain's advices and testimonies, Champlain being but a straw man there at Port-Royal. So at the Council which Poutrincourt held, the lad said: I have examined Messire de Champdoré, and find in him sincere repentance for his faults committed! – at which a chill or froidissement passed over Champlain's features, and Poutrincourt looked away in embarrassment. So Champdoré was sprung from the cage. Champlain stalked off to his trout-pond, to pass some solitary hours in biting and twitching. In the end he came to himself and said: I must not be so dainty or weak – else my *character* if not my body will sicken with scurvy! – And these words braced him. He comforted himself further, saying: If the Sieur de Monts were only here, he'd take my part –

Now Pontgravé returned home, hoping on the way to attack a Rouen merchant named Boyer who was trading in defiance of the monopoly, but Boyer gave him the slip. However, the season was profitable for him as always. His son Robert stayed behind. Of his relations with Biencourt, a lad of his own age and position, it must be said that they were indifferent. Robert knew that his father had no claim to seigneury at Port-Royal, whereas Biencourt was the heir of the house. Therefore he felt himself outcast, while Biencourt, with the insensitivity which sometimes characterizes young Lords seeking to realize themselves, paid him little heed. As a result, Robert took to wandering in the woods, sometimes with Champlain (who was willing to teach him what he knew, out of loneliness and regard for old Pontgravé), but more often by himself. By a natural instinct he sought out the wigwams of Savages. He came to a clearing. Born Swimming sat picking the moose-hairs out of her stew. Her hair was as black and greasy as a Souriquois kettle. Robert's penis stirred. He stood looking her up and down. Born Swimming flushed and went inside her wigwam, leaving the stew to steam and summon mosquitoes and flies. Robert stood watching the door-flap of her house. It seemed to tremble shyly, though perhaps it was only the wind. At last it lifted, and a little child crawled out to study him with shiny black eyes. Robert grinned. Reaching into his pockets, he drew forth a biscuit and cast it down in front of the little one like bait – but now he saw Born Swimming's hand come out of the wigwam to snatch it, while the child burst into tears. Robert laughed and strode on, extremely pleased with himself. He found a speckled tree like the flowering staff of Moses, its leaves rising from the smoothly twigless stem, outthrusting themselves and shading the tree like the petals of a flower. He came to a lake and found a beaver-dam, into which he discharged his arquebus. Nothing happened. He shrugged and walked on, thinking again of that pretty femme sauvage whom he had encountered. Ah, how he'd like to sniff her crotch! Did she have a husband? He'd have to ask around; yes, he must surely learn the Souriquois language; pidgin wasn't good enough . . .

The Wolverine-Brothers

Born Swimming had had little to do with the Iron People. Yet her husband, Swooping Like a Hawk, was always among them, giving and getting gifts. As for her, when she first began to observe these bearded strangers, she shrank from their incomprehensible speech. There were hard sounds in it, but these were half hidden in the liquid rush of other sounds, like rocks in rivers. Some of them mouthed the halfway-speech that everyone knew for exchanging gifts, but even then they spoke in voices like crunching ice. They killed bears even in summer when the fur was no good. They did not fear to dream of bears, although some People said that that meant death. (She forgot that she had dreamed of bears herself.) So she was wary of the Iron People, lest their carelessness injure her. But their bread and prunes were good. And whenever Swooping Like a Hawk returned from their house he would be singing songs of joy. He brought biscuits, peas and flour for her. He gave her a red nightcap from the Iron People . . . – Then came the Pontgravés, father and son. It seemed that the father was teaching the young man how to exchange gifts after his manner, which was indeed how he occupied his life. Such instruction was only right. So he brought him into the wigwams of all the People who had the means to fittingly welcome strangers.

Pontgravé the Elder was somewhat wizened and goutish, but the son was in his prime, so that when Born Swimming saw the two of them together she always remembered the tale of KI'KWA'JU the Wolverine, and his little brother KI'KWA'JUSI'S. To her the son had become the elder, the father the younger; and indeed it might be so, for in the tale it was KI'KWA'JU who put on his Power shape to bite off the heads of the birds he had called to his wigwam, foaming breathlessly in his lust to eat them all as they sat politely unknowing in a row with their eyes closed, and it was little KI'KWA'JUSI'S who saved a few of them so that they could come back to be eaten next time. So old Pontgravé had always been respectful to her and sought to restrain his son when he looked at her. Perhaps Robert Ki'kwa'ju meant something different than he seemed to mean. Nonetheless she did not like that young man. His face was reddened from the sun; it was the hue of a muskrat's skin. He was missing three fingers. His chin was covered with fur. He was very ugly. He could not seem to keep still. Sometimes he passed by her wigwam without any errand. She had already spoken to her husband of this, and at length they moved their house. But Robert Ki'kwa'ju found them again. After that she considered him a wolverine in a tree, waiting to leap down on any moose and gnaw it to death.

Robert and the Armouchiquois

But, after all, we all follow our own dreams like wolverines. Poutrincourt, for instance, now prepared for new explorations. He made Champdoré ferry him to the Isle de Sainte-Croix, where they'd so disastrously wintered, and found corn growing in the garden. He was so interested in the agricultural possibilities of New France . . . He did not invite Champlain, of course. Champlain watched their pinnace until it was out of sight. Then he turned on his heel. Passing through the sea-gates, he followed the mucky path that led between cannon platform and palisadoed deck to the dark and narrow archway which broached the main courtyard. He lay down on his bunk and gnashed his teeth. (He too was interested in agriculture.)

When Poutrincourt returned, he took Lescarbot aside and spoke with him. He mustered all the men and announced that he had just appointed Lescarbot to be Lieutenant-Governor of Port-Royal in his place.

Champlain cleared his throat. He felt as if he were choking.

Champlain, my friend, we have instructions to search once again for a winter haven. (Thus Poutrincourt.) I am sure you will welcome the opportunity to complete your maps.

Very well, Seigneur. (They always used such derision in speaking of his maps! Didn't they see how important it was to inventory this Country properly? What were they thinking of?) So we shall retrace our voyage of last year?

Oh, not entirely, said Poutrincourt airily. But I would receive your advice with pleasure. Are there other regions which you think it profitable to explore?

No, no.

Let's speak seriously, Champlain. I'm observing a certain truculence in you – or am I unfair to characterize it that way? Champlain, look at me. We all have the highest respect for you. No one blames you for what happened on the Isle de Sainte-Croix. I myself can see that you're a very prudent man. It's certainly no slight to you if we go back over your course of last summer. There may be something to be admired in the south.

Champlain had clasped his hands together and was wringing them very tightly. He appeared to Poutrincourt to be unconscious of this. Poutrincourt pretended not to see.

Seigneur, said Champlain, I have no objections. You know I shall do my duty. I beg your pardon for my low spirits. I have been feeling somewhat listless lately . . .

My friend, think nothing of it.

And so Poutrincourt and Champlain set out for the Country of the Armouchiquois once again. In short, Poutrincourt searched for a way to discharge his duty, while Champlain beside him was looking no less zealously for reputation and honor. With them was young Robert Pontgravé. So was Duval the locksmith. They had their own agendas. It was almost autumn.

Breezes blew very fresh and cool. As long as they were in the Country of the Etechemins they made no bones about camping on shore. Champlain shot geese with his arquebus, and they caught all the fish they could eat. Poutrincourt trotted about on the shore as busily as a sandpiper; he could not get over his love for this wilderness. He concluded a treaty of eternal friendship and reciprocal trust with a Saqmaw at Marchia Bay, by name Olmechin, giving him knives, hatchets and beads of French glass both white and blue. In exchange he received moose-meat and a Souriquois prisoner, which would make the Savages of his Nation very glad when he was freed, and deepen their obligation to the French – glory be to the HIGHEST!* But presently, as days lapped by and past, they drew closer to those straight sandy beaches where the Armouchiquois grew their pumpkins, and Champlain warned his companions of what had happened the previous year, when these very Savages had shot the carpenter dead with their arrows. So all were on their guard, and accepted with good heart the Sieur de Poutrincourt's word that it was forbidden to any to sleep on shore. One chilly day Champdoré, who was at the helm, cried out, and they saw a man's naked carcass lying on a sand-hill, so decomposed and blackly clothed with crows that it was impossible to tell whether he were Christian or Savage. Arrows bristled from him. – Shall we give him burial? said Champdoré. – Poutrincourt hesitated, and Champlain said: I do not like the look of those dunes. We cannot see what may be behind them. – And Poutrincourt said nothing, and the ship continued south, and then a bleached peninsula swung its arm behind them and the dead man was gone. The sailors sucked their teeth; the Swiss soldiers muttered to one another, their eyes as innocent and neutral as the sea.

Presently, after they had gone a hundred leagues or so, they reached a large cape, almost half a league wide, on which there was a village of the Armouchiquois, surrounded by fields of the Saracen wheat called *maize*. It was almost evening. The sands were variously colored. – What a goodly Country! cried Poutrincourt. (He'd just killed twenty-eight sea-larks with a single shot of his harquebus.) Now the Savages sought to lure them hither with sweet music, piping into reeds and whistling through their noses. Poutrincourt made no move to order a change of course: his favorite syllogism was: *One must never lay bait for rascals.* The Armouchiquois continued to entice them, however, running along the beach with incredible rapidity, so that they kept level with the ship. One of them even had the temerity to approach in

* But Olmechin was really in league with the Armouchiquois.

his canoe, at which Poutrincourt commanded that a fire-dart be launched above his head to deter him, as was done. He turned about hastily and went back to shore. After this they heard a great tintamarre from shore, but it died down . . . Through his telescope Poutrincourt saw the Savages striding about with copper in their ears, hearing which Champlain became fascinated, and whispered in Robert's ear: Perhaps this is where they have their mines after all, somewhere near this sand-rib. (He liked Robert; the lad seemed self-reliant.) – Do you care to look, Champlain? said Poutrincourt. – Eh, Seigneur, he replied, I can see the gleam of copper about them very well. – In truth he was shamefaced to see them, as they reminded him once again of the lying tales of the Sieur de Prévert of Saint-Malo, who'd insisted that these Armouchiquois were gruesome skeleton-men whose knees were higher than their heads. Perhaps Prévert had also told an untruth in describing the GOUGOU. – But then it struck Champlain that his sense of ignominy might be unmanly; just because Prévert's name always reminded him of the Isle de Sainte-Croix did not establish an official connection; anyhow that winter could not be mended, which was why he now told Poutrincourt his Captain that he'd be most willing to go ashore alone if that might be desired, in order to learn more concerning their copper. – Poutrincourt smiled sadly. – That is not needful, Champlain. You labor hard on our behalf already.

They pulled far enough out to sea so that the inhabitants could not easily board them, and cast anchor for the night.

At the next harbor, which they reached the following morning, they found themselves in need of provisions, and so sent a boat to treat with the Savages. An old woman brought them maize-bread and wild grapes, for which they paid her by attaching strips of paper to her forehead with spittle – a trade which she seemed to consider very much to her advantage, for she cried with great emotion: *Haii haii haii.* Robert laughed so hard that he almost spewed.

These people must be worked upon with fear, said the Sieur de Poutrincourt, at which Champlain replied: I do agree. – They promenaded upon the beach in company with the apothecary Louys Hébert; when they found a fat driftwood log Poutrincourt commanded him to discharge a ball into it. – After the noise and the shrieking of the Savages had died away, their painted Captains approached the log most gingerly (beside which Hébert stood rubbing down his gun with a cloth). Throwing skittish glances over their shoulders, they felt the hole which the shot had made. Then they conferred together, and presently Champlain noticed that some had taken up their bows, which he liked not at all. He began to dart his cunning eyes about, and picked out several skulkers behind the trees . . . – Approaching Poutrincourt, he said in a low voice: We'd best withdraw now . . . – Regrettable, said the other, but no doubt you are correct. – He fired a shot into the air to summon the men (at which Robert grinned to see the consternation of the Armouchiquois renewed), and then the Trumpeter blew a blast, after which they returned to the ship, where again they anchored at some distance out to sea. – Pax CHRISTI. Anyhow, what could Savages do against good French guns?

That night, while Champlain dreamed of Mechique and Poutrincourt dreamed of Port-Royal, Robert Pontgravé rowed to the beach, along with Champlain's enemy, the locksmith Duval, and a crony of Robert's named Captain Merveille. They knew the watchmen, so it was easy. They got two other men to join them – *viz.*, Gaspard and Du Gay. It was the object of the party to rent a few squaws. That stuffed shirt Champlain would never know anything about it. The sea was very quiet. Robert rowed with a will. His lust was building like a great sand-drift in his heart, rising higher and heavier and moister with pale-stubbed beach-grass choking its roots down into it; and his companions were in similar case, grinning in the dark, with their arquebuses at the ready. Their need had made them pitiless. And yet Duval and Gaspard and Du Gay were men of little initiative, who scarcely would have acted alone. Robert was their puppeteer. And the one who pulled *his* strings was Captain Merveille. There was an unhealthiness about them both which neither prayers nor rare spiceries could correct.

It had fallen out one afternoon on this voyage, while the Sieur de Champlain and the Sieur de Poutrincourt tête-à-têted cozily over the Sieur de Champlain's maps (all except those two themselves thought them thick as thieves), that Robert asked leave to go a little inland to hunt game for supper, which Poutrincourt freely granted. They were still in the Country of the Etechemins. He had not been walking long when he heard footsteps behind him.

I decided to join you, my young friend, because I wished to discuss your future with you. (Thus Captain Merveille.)

Yes? said Robert, flattered in the highest degree.

I trust that you plan to carve out your own little Port-Royal someday. You're so promising, you. You and I together, Robert, could do quite a lot. And with your father's help . . .

Robert's face darkened. – Or *without* his help. I can get pelts from the Savages so easily! You've seen how I took them from that Souriquois squaw, sticking the barrel of my arquebus right against her head . . . You know that! You helped me! In five years I'll rule more Savages than anyone, you'll see! Or maybe I'll become one of them; that might be easier. A few pretty squaws doing all the work – you know what kind of work . . .

Ah, Robert, laughed Captain Merveille, you are effective in the way you hold yourself among these Savages, but still too theatrical. Of course you dazzle them, but still! I almost believe they *fear* your glittering behavior! You must descend and condescend to their level, so they'll trust you as a man like them, and not a GOUGOU who might destroy them with snapping jaws . . . Now let me see. How are you to go about this?

I can tell that you're not even going to consult my opinion, said Robert in a pique.

But of course, my friend! I'm all ears.

I shall take a wife among the Savages.

Captain Merveille pretended to consider. – It would be effective, no doubt, he said slowly. Yes, I am sure of it. But only . . .

Yes?

I am sure you know how our sailors bathe their hands in fresh porpoise-blood to strengthen the sinews? It is the same with women, Robert. You must build up to marriage. It is best not to begin with the hardest part. Do you comprehend my meaning? Here in Acadia we are free of moral strictures. The nearest priest is that Messire Aubry at Sainte-Croix, and he dwells in the cemetery, you know.

Robert remembered his friend's words now as he steered the boat toward that moonlit cape of floury softness. Merveille matched his oar-strokes perfectly. Gaspard and Du Gay were another symmetrical pair. Only Duval sat on the rear thwart and did nothing. Duval did not like to work. He had a moustache and a thin horsey face. His hair was tied in a long greasy pigtail. (He had a hoarse voice and a hooked beak, like a liver-snatcher.) The wind was blowing vigorously from the northwest. Robert's face was numbed with the cold. But his heart pounded joyously. He thought he could smell peas and strawberries on the shore. The moonlight was very soft and pale upon the sand, and the lodges of the Savages, half concealed by a low dune-shoulder, were black domes. – I see their fires, said Duval in a low voice. The dinghy grated on sand. Robert leaped out and drew it as far as he could; then his companions stepped into the water, their arquebuses charged and cocked . . . – Robert laughed with excitement. He strode about on the beach, crushing mackerel-skulls underfoot. Now the Armouchiquois began to come forward, shyly, from behind the dunes. They were scrawny olive-hued people. Robert could not discern them very well at first, for they hesitated like dogs afraid of a blow, as he thought. He could see the ghosts of their white teeth in the darkness, the dull elegant glitters of moonbeams on the plates of copper they wore at wrist and ankle. – How many are there? he whispered.

– Hold your tongue, replied Captain Merveille. Those things don't matter anymore. – He took a biscuit from inside his cape and threw it down onto the sand, as if to a pack of animals. At once the Armouchiquois pounced on it. – Now we've lured them out, if I'm not mistaken, said Merveille, and Robert heard the exultation in his voice, spouse-emotion to his own. Slowly the Savages came closer. Despite the freezing wind they were naked, excepting only their privities, which were covered by leaves. Rosaries of white and black wampum glittered from their necks like strings of eyeballs. Around their wrists they had carcanets of sea-cockleshells. They wore their hair in long black horse-tails bristling with the feathers of gulls, murres and liver-snatchers; they sported more feathers than a quiver does arrows. They had plucked out the hairs of their foreheads, making them hideously half-bald. They began to sing or chant some incantation whose very lack of comprehensibility enthralled him. He saw his own laughing recklessness in the gleams of their eyes. There were, however, no women among this embassy. Evidently they had dealt with Christians before.

You, Gaspard and Du Gay, gather driftwood for our fire, said Captain Merveille. Duval, bring the dinghy up here and overturn it; keep watch on it. You, Robert, come with me. You have the blankets and kettles?

My father will never miss them, laughed Robert.

Gaspard came back with an armload of driftwood logs whose ingrained ocean-salt would make them burn blue and strange; Du Gay brought dry twigs. Sitting on the boat, Duval watched them as they struck their flints. It was breezy, and the fire was hard to start. The other two cursed him softly because he would not aid them, but he merely replied: You heard what my instructions were. (Duval loved to guard things; he was Champlain's counterpart.) He sat watching a spider dig a well in the sand, deeper and deeper, safer and safer . . . As for Robert and Captain Merveille, they strode fearlessly to the Savages who squatted in the darkness watching them, and Merveille said: Now, my Robert, and Robert knelt down in the sand beside them and drew the figure of a naked woman with his forefinger, taking particular pains with the privities, and then gave them the trade goods, which they snatched from him, wrapping the blankets about their shoulders, gibbering, licking the new iron kettles, and Captain Merveille stood smiling ironically, leveling his arquebus at them. They knew what it was; Robert could see that. – Put it down, for the love of JESUS! he whispered. He saw the moon-gleam on bone arrowheads and spearheads aimed at them from a gulley of darkness between two dunes whose dirty whiteness was moonlight befouled; and Merveille lowered the gun slowly and the points of dirty white winked instantly away.

Now the Savages embraced them tenderly and sought to lead them to their village. Again Robert pointed to the woman he had drawn in the sand. – You must be our pimps and pandars, he said through lust-clenched teeth, and the Savages looked at him askance, but then seized his hand once again and pulled him to his feet.

Have you heard the news? called Merveille over his shoulder to those who sat by the fire. – It seems that they have women after all! Fancy that. I suppose codfish *do* bite at night! But you must watch the boat.

And what if we say no? said Gaspard.

Then I'll kill you, laughed Merveille. Do you truly believe it would be so difficult to kill a brute like you?

Don't worry, brothers, said Robert quickly. (The Savages were stroking him with chilly fingers.) We shall return and then it will be your turn.

What a woman-rage you're all in! muttered Duval contemptuously.

Eh, and why are you here then? shouted Gaspard.

He laughed with his glottal frog's chuckle. – To watch the boat.

Robert and Captain Merveille shouldered their guns. The Armouchiquois hurried them away into the darkness. The two Christians stumbled over drifts of sand, continually shaking off the sly hands of the Savages from every part of their bodies; and now they had reached the summit of a high dune and the beach-grass rocked against their waists and Robert looked over his shoulder, shocked to see how small the fire on the beach had become – a mere spark, as far away and fragile as the tiny speck of luminescence from the ship's lantern; and then an Armouchiquois had seized his elbow and pulled him down into the shadows with Merveille and the others. There were perhaps a dozen Savages with them; they were all clamoring most insolently. He could not hear the sea anymore. A chilly wind fingered him. Now the Savage town was in sight, and the Armouchiquois waiting there began to sing. Their escort shouted something which neither Robert nor Captain Merveille could understand, to which their brethren replied: *He he he he!* Stumbling through mounds of filth and refuse, the two men followed their captors to the town. He heard the dead stalks of their maize-fields crackling in the wind. It was the loneliest sound that he had ever heard. He smelled drying fish and rotting fish and boiling fish and also something baking. He trod on hollow ground – a corn-pit, he supposed. Just outside the palisadoes, old men in filthy chamois-skins crowded round them poking them with skinny fingers, and between the wigwams was a fire from which ashes flew like black and red birds. A pair of women were squatting naked to receive them. Their heads were as tiny as walnuts. They were chewing leaves. Their necks, though no thicker than sticks, were excessively long, and adorned with collars of snail-wampum. Their arms were no more than articulated bones covered with taut brown skin. It was indeed as the Sieur de Prévert had said: their knees rose higher than their heads as they squatted like spiders of eld. So horrible did they look that Robert shook with fear. – By the spittle of Cerberus! cried Captain Merveille. – Even as these words left his mouth, the two she-demons leaped high into the air like locusts and landed on their shoulders, one apiece, and they began to throttle the Christians with their long skinny legs. Again the Armouchiquois cried: *He he he he!* and now the other women came rushing out of the wigwams, flinging down the belts of copper quills that girdled their haunches so that there was a tremendous rattling on the ground, and now the men likewise exposed their privities, and their legs stretched and became emaciated and terribly long like those of their wives. Struggling desperately with his murderess, Robert glimpsed Merveille behind him subsiding lifelessly to the ground, with bloody froth on his beard. Now he himself was growing dizzy, and the sound of waves and waterfalls was in his ears. He fell. The Savagess shifted her position and mounted him, strangling him between long sharp knees, and he was gagging and then the world went black at last. He came to himself, and he was lying by the campfire on the beach. Merveille was still unconscious, his face purple. Their companions were bending over them. The night boomed with the sound of drums. Slowly Merveille opened his eyes. – How did we get here? cried Robert.

You fell through the air, rasped Duval. Some devil must have had you.

Give me a smoke, said Captain Merveille. Ah, Duval, you really missed something. These squaws were incredible.

What about us? It's our turn now!

Merveille puffed contentedly. – So you say, my fine little Gaspard. But I'll tell you something. Between you and a dog is only an arbitrary demarcation.

Why, you –

The principal difference, Merveille went on, is that a dog doesn't need any help in mounting his bitch. But *you* . . . – Ah, how these stars shine!

Robert's face was still white with terror. – They're witches . . . he whispered, at which Gaspard also paled, and said no more.

In the middle of the night, four hundred Savages crept around them and fired their arrows. Gaspard and Du Gay were killed instantly. Robert discharged his arquebus, but it proved faulty and exploded, blowing off three of his fingers. He was covered with blood. As yet he felt no pain. He and the other two survivors fled for the boat. An arrow whizzed into Duval's breast, and he slowed to take it out, but Robert hit him hysterically with his bloody hand and he looked at Robert with wide eyes and continued running alongside him and then an arrow passed between them and they forgot each other. An arrow grazed Robert's ear. Arrows stuck everywhere in their flesh. The arrowpoints were shaped like serpents' tongues. Now Duval was at the boat yelling: Help, help, we are being butchered! – A blizzard of arrows whirled at him, and he threw himself down just in time, thinking: If the blessed VIERGE-MARIE saves me I shall offer up a whole trental of Masses . . . The arrow was still in his breast. Blood was spreading around it. – Help! he shouted again. Robert lay in the sand behind the boat, wrapping a handkerchief about the gushing stumps of his fingers, while Captain Merveille watched him alertly. – On ship Champlain and Poutrincourt leaped up in their night-shirts at last, and Poutrincourt cried out: For the love of JESUS! and Champlain had already mustered eight men, including the Trumpeter, the Surgeon, and Hébert the Apothecary. These sprang into a skiff and rowed ashore. They charged the Savages, firing their arquebuses. Casting his gaze about, Champlain could see the enemy scuttling about during the intervals of flash, seizing their dead and wounded and dragging them behind the dunes. Now a Frenchman screamed by the water's edge and fell dead. By some sorcery the Savages had transpierced him with an arrow on which a skinny dog was also crucified. – Poutrincourt was shouting: To me, all who love me! and the harquebuses boomed and Champlain stood firing very coolly (he took pleasure in such sports). The Armouchiquois never screamed when a ball struck them. It was impossible to tell whether any headway were being made. At last the moon burst out from behind a cloud, and Champlain looked around to see that the men were shooting at nothing. Poutrincourt had comprehended this also, and raised his arm: the guns fell silent.

Another Frenchman had been riddled with arrows. He still lived, but his case was doubtful. Bonnerne the Surgeon enlisted four strong men to hold him while he removed the barbs. The patient jerked in their hands like a fish. – You must be patient, whispered Bonnerne. Do you understand me? – The patient screamed. Bonnerne poured a dram of brandy down his gaping throat. He lived until Novembre, when they got back to Port-Royal . . . – Meanwhile the Apothecary, Louis Hébert, applied some of the mud-clay of Port-Royal to Robert's hand. – Very medicinal, he said smiling. *Terra sigillata*, this poultice is called. It seems abundant in New France. – Robert looked into his eyes with such faith and longing and hope as he had never shown in Church, and Hébert turned away embarrassed.

Champlain himself pulled the arrow out of Duval and examined the point. – Some sort of carapace.

Yes, Champlain, said one of their pet Savages. They make from horseshoe crab. These Armouchiquois, very evil, very bad.

At dawn they buried their three comrades at the foot of a Cross, while the Sieur de Poutrincourt led them in prayer. Withdrawing to their ship before the onset of low tide, they then had the mortification of witnessing the Savages dig up the bodies, stripping the shirt from one, dancing with glee. They squatted naked and mocked the French by dribbling sand between their buttocks, yawping like dogs. At this outrage Poutrincourt was beside himself, and turned to give the order to fire, but Champlain said: That is imprudent, Seigneur. Then they will know for a certainty that our arquebuses cannot reach them at this distance. – But Poutrincourt was wild with rage, and would not listen, so the guns sounded uselessly. The Savages danced round and round the Cross with many lewd gestures. Then they pulled it down and wrecked it. At high tide Poutrincourt gave the order to land again. They buried the bodies again and erected another Cross, although they knew it was no use.

Two days later they saw another party of Armouchiquois, who made signs to tell them that the murderers had gone away. They wished to trade their tobacco and periwinkle-shell necklaces for iron. In their arms they brought gifts of wild grapes glistening on the vine, purple, sun-warmed even through their toothy roofs of leaves, hanging on the stalks, bending them down with the weight of breasts and eyes. Pretending to welcome this embassy, Poutrincourt invited a dozen on board and then winked at his men, at which they seized them. It was his design to use them as slaves to grind corn at Port-Royal. They would not let themselves be taken alive, however, and so the French were compelled to hew them to pieces, which they did with exceeding joy.

Effects

Robert Pontgravé found it difficult to grow accustomed to the loss of his fingers. He became quite unruly in his temper. Champlain had seen the same happen to many men.

Captain Merveille did not change a smidgeon. After his success with Robert, he felt very agreeable.*

* His other name (by which he was more widely known in France) was Captain Miroir, for his special gift lay in convincing people of the reality of things in which they already half believed. I wish I could say that he himself only half existed, but that is not true; you will find him in the *Jesuit Relations*, in the *Dictionary of Canadian Biography*, in Lescarbot

As for the locksmith Duval, after this he often went about crying: Nothing can kill me!

He was very cocky for someone whose destiny it was to be hanged from a hawser.

They found no better place to settle. So once again they must return to Port-Royal, where Lescarbot welcomed them with a pageant of Neptune and the Tritons . . .

The Lawyer's Holiday 1607

Lescarbot loved to hunt. – Ah, he thought, the solitude and the silence bring such BEAUTIFUL thoughts to the mind! – He fired off his musket, and killed half a dozen geese. Striding on, he let his speculations turn as powerfully as all the water-wheels of France. – How, for instance, could this New World have been peopled after the Deluge? Lescarbot, who always preferred rational to supernatural causes, thought that shipwrecked mariners might have accomplished it. In olden times the wives of Captains often accompanied them on their voyages: it would have taken but one who was fruitful (as the Bible said) to become the mother of an entire Nation. (Indeed, Madame de Poutrincourt had herself agreed to remove here on the next voyage. What a woman!) Then by and by these men would have lost their knowledge of GOD, and become

---

down to the last sneering comma . . . Anyhow, he is not so rare. Any Christian of sufficient rank can turn wine into blood; and I firmly believe that love can transform the Fox's scalp into Tekakwitha's hair. On that day beside the Fleuve Saint-Laurent seven decades later, when she knelt praying as tranquilly as the Armouchiquois women baking their maize-bread between hot stones, and then the Eagle came with the scalp in his hands, suppose that GOD had permitted her to crown her head with it? If with true affection and grace such as she possessed she had done this, letting it quicken and burrow down among her blue-black hair, what then? Instead of becoming GOUGOU, would it have become a part of her as her blood-sap rose within it and it flowered into a black and weeping rose? Remember how the white petals already flickered down around her in the continual summery autumn in which we are required to remember her, knowing her end. Her approved biographer goes to pains to describe how she smiled, *listening to the birds. She had gathered some leaves from one of the great maple-trees. She had let them fall, as she let fall all things.* So she might have made the scalp clear-minded as the Iroquois do for the bereft in the Ritual of Condolence, then let it go, to rot or become a holy relic as it would. (At the Martyrs' Shrine in Ontario, not far from where Père Brébeuf was killed, her own relics are mounted on the kneeler beneath the altar. At Ossernenon the fleurs-de-lys, so many of them, rise like leaf-crowns upon her shrine-roof where her image stands in the shade of tree-pillars.) But that did not happen. So GOUGOU became as evil as iron, and Captain Merveille reflected only the shimmering beauty of evil.

Savages. What could be more reasonable than that? – Then again, perhaps Noah took it on himself to repopulate the world, for after all he had three hundred and fifty years left to live. True, the Ark had been left high and dry on a peak in Turkey, but Noah was a master shipbuilder. This hypothesis also seemed a likely one to Lescarbot, the more so since he had dreamed it up himself, and being a lawyer he knew how delightful it was to watch the fairy mushrooms of speculation spring up after the slightest dew. – Or what about the Lost Tribes of Israel?

He shot a moose (*that* meat never inconvenienced the stomach).

In his mind he had already begun to draft his *History of New France*, *not only to satisfy the honest wish of several who had long required it of me, but also to employ usefully the leisure hours which I may have during this vacation season in the year 1608.*

Ah, vacations, vacations . . . All Canada was but a holiday. – Not that Lescarbot was lazy – oh, not by any means. He'd tilled and fenced his gardens, and even enclosed them in a fosse; he'd built a Store-house with his own hands; on the Sabbath, taking the place of dead Messire Aubry, he instructed the men in religion, even condescending at times to scatter pearls of doctrine before the Savages . . .

Look at them! he laughed. Such clowns!

A Savage caressed his cheek.

Ah, he said softly to Robert, suddenly very moved, they love us, one and all. – (Robert scratched himself.) – We really must convert these many thousands of people before the end of the world comes on . . . I wonder when that will be? In Paris some priest told me we had six thousand years, but that was the maximum, and much could be deducted for our sins. – (Robert picked his nose.) – Then of course, continued Lescarbot, we've used up a millennium and a half since the death of Our LORD, and before Him it was – eh, there I always have to calculate from my Bible. Anyhow, it can't be done too soon!

Robert was not of this mind, being well-traveled among the Savages of the mainland. His father had shown him a few things, by JESUS! And Captain Merveille said . . . Robert told nasty tales of their treachery and cruelty, especially to their hereditary enemies the Hiroquois, whom they roasted alive or otherwise tortured; the Hiroquois, it was said, did likewise. – As far as Robert was concerned (he joked), if it were not for the beaver trade they'd be best exterminated.

Ah, no, replied Lescarbot very softly. I would not have them exterminated, Monsieur. For we Frenchmen are under the law of Grace.

Robert Pontgravé's Sweetheart

1607–1611

> But our Savages were, in my opinion, brutal before the arrival of the French in their territories; for they had not the knowledge of this sweet honey which lovers suck from the lips of their mistresses, when they begin to bill and coo, and to prepare nature to lay their offerings of love on the altar of the Cyprian queen.
>
> LESCARBOT, *History of New France* (1618)

For a long time after she awoke, Born Swimming believed her dream. She truly believed that the Dream of the Floating Island was hers. Her joy was as flavorful as a fire-roasted porcupine. Then it was dawn, the time in which the family must go out to greet Grandfather SUN and offer tobacco to Him; and her children were giggling and making their body-lice promenade across the backs of their hands before they ate them, and her husband opened his eyes beside her and she got up and threw back the blanket from the door, still proudly thinking: *I brought the Iron People!*

Then His rays streamed through the doorway and glittered upon her iron kettle.

She clapped her hand over her mouth in surprise.

Her husband had been away hunting for two days, praying: O SUN, give us something to eat. – She could not speak with him. In mid-morning she set out for the wigwam of the shaman, Smoking the Pipe.

She saw one of the Iron People on the beach, hunkered over something, like a bear eating stranded lobster –

Smoking the Pipe was readying himself for Membertou's eat-all feast. He wore his necklace of Armouchiquois scalps. His face was already daubed in the four colors of Power: his cheeks mottled white, yellow, black and red; a black stripe running down the bridge of his nose. He invited her in and sat looking at her blandly, cocking his head a little to one side as his hands scraped and scraped at a bit of root with a clamshell. It was very smoky inside. The fire crackled. Smoking the Pipe was an old man; his hair was white. He claimed to have seen almost two hundred winters.

I pray you, tell my dream, she said very softly.

(She was afraid of him. She'd heard of the little bow with which he killed unborn children, pulling back the string interlaced with porcupine quills and shooting an arrow into that sheet of birchbark overgrown with leaves and bears and faces . . .)

Smoking the Pipe grinned wide, to show her how his mouth was empty. Then he invoked his Power, and began to choke. He coughed a stone the size of a nut into his hand.

My MN'TU' did not have to go far to see your sickness, he said. Ghosts want to take you, ghosts from long ago. They want to pull you down under the rotting leaves.

Born Swimming bit her tongue so that she would not scream.

You are not one of the great dreamers, said Smoking the Pipe. And this dream of the Floating Island, your grandmother's grandmother dreamed it. Now it is a dream of Iron Ghosts. They want to eat your heart.

Shuddering, Born Swimming threw him his gift (some colored beads of the Iron People) and fled.

But later she thought: I am *happy* to have an iron kettle! I am *happy* to have a knife of iron . . .

Power

She sat in the wigwam sewing spruce-root thread around the rim of a dish to strengthen it, and steam rose from the kettle. It was a warm day. The dogs lay outside panting, with their hind legs drawn up for a leap which they were too lazy to make. Swooping Like a Hawk had gone across the river to kill geese: there were many, many of them, flying with uptilted heads, as if to peer farther; they were coming north again now. She set the bark dish down and sat very still, chilled by the shade of the tall pine trees. Beside her, the kettle steamed. It was eerie now, this iron thing. – But no one else thought so. Her friend Kinebji'j-koji'j would have dressed in iron and eaten iron if she could . . . – What if she threw it into the water? Would she be sad then? The surface of the bay, luminous greenish-grey, was very still. Through the door of the wigwam she could see it, striped with shadings of Power. World Under Water was down there. She saw the whale, spouting his frothy mist; there were the diving water-birds . . .

The kettle was alive. Of course. But what Power did it have?

The Order of Good Cheer 1606–1607

Eh, the same as a harquebus. – But I become impatient with these Savage fancies and superstitions: let me rather, like a good servant of the Roy, recommence the account of this momentous year 1607 with a more important subject, which is food. (Don't worry, I've dined with De Monts; my table manners are quite refined.) That winter had been very mild. Only four men died of the scurvy, no doubt because Lescarbot called upon the others to wear leather overboots to guard against the winter damp. He had many ideas about this disease. Most logical was his plan to burn down all the woods of Canada, for the sickness probably lay in rotten wood. That too would end the laziness of the Souriquois; after that they would be forced to till the soil . . . On the other hand, all four of the scurvy-slain had been in rooms facing west, so perhaps it was the harbor-breeze which poisoned them. This hypothesis held water since on the Isle of Sainte-Croix so many men had perished, and the breezes had been much stronger – although, as Lescarbot reminded himself, technically speaking this was not deducing algebraically from the contra-positive. So perhaps he'd better go on the fact that the four men had slept on rotten mattresses. Surely rot was at the bottom of it somehow . . . – Ah, thought Lescarbot to himself, it is splendid to reason, since after all GOD has given us an upright form! – So he passed the brumal season most pleasantly. He ate well, too, for Champlain, who sought to win himself back into favor, had that Novembre founded the Order of Good Cheer, whose members feasted each other with moose and porcupine-flesh. Each member took his shift to be the Maître d'hôtel once a fortnight. Two days before his turn, he went out hunting and fishing. He marched in with his napkin on his shoulder, and the wand of his position in his hand, and the collar of his Order around his neck. Each of the other members followed him in procession, bearing a dish: bear stew, eel tarts, pigeon roasted and in pies, sturgeon and partridge and succulent beaver-tails . . . Then they sat down to eat, giving thanks to GOD. After eating, the Maître d'hôtel passed over the collar to his successor and they toasted each other, while the seals barked in the harbor.

Striding across the planks in step, with steaming dishes in their hands and napkins over their shoulders, the members of the Order followed their Captain, who this night was Champlain. Poutrincourt played the violin in a triumphal march. At the head of the procession was Champlain, sweating and grinning, with the largest roast that anyone had ever seen. His attendants were likewise weighted down by his woodland spoils. Now the serving-men poured out wine and cider, and the candles flickered as Lescarbot said grace, Champlain so flushed and proud as he stared at the steaming moose-pastries which would still have had hooves and hide and antlers like strange cockle-shells were it not for him; and Poutrincourt said: Magnificent, Champlain! In matters culinary, at least, you are the Governor of New France! and Lescarbot piped: On the contrary! Champlain is our veritable *Roy* and *Pope* of cookery! – at which Champlain frowned, first because he did not like to hear those twin sovereigns mocked, especially by one whose ostensible vocation it was to minister to men's souls here in Acadia – eh, hypocritical Lescarbot with his Calvinist Bible! – and secondly because he distrusted the lawyer's bright, malicious eyes. Champlain was intelligent enough to know that the other considered him stupid. Sometimes he'd begin to say something when Lescarbot would interrupt, shouting: Incorrect use of the word! – Then, too, there was the matter of the locksmith Duval, who continued to foment mischief. He complained that the cold was too rigorous for labor, that the Sieur de Poutrincourt was a tyrant, both of which were patent lies . . . Lescarbot saw through *him* immediately (Champlain admitted as much; Lescarbot was shrewd). Lescarbot had seen the Peasant Revolt at Quercy, the mob with their wooden shoes clacking, shaking their stick-shafted sickles, their rusty swords . . . The expression in their eyes had terrified him. He saw it now in Duval's eyes. So privily he drew Poutrincourt aside and warned him that he did not like the man's demeanor, at which the Sieur replied: Why do you not take your concerns to Champlain? For he knows him best. They served De Monts together, you know, on Isle de Sainte-Croix. – Lescarbot stammered: I thought – I . . . – at which Poutrincourt, unfailingly just, transfixed him with severity and said: Eh, Marc, now you *know*. Go then to Champlain. – And he did not. It came out later, when Poutrincourt himself approached Champlain and referred to the matter while speaking of other subjects. A sly and cowardly way of dealing (thus Champlain). *Cogito; ergo*, I do not care for Lescarbot.

So Lescarbot said grace, his words too exuding satisfaction (feasts make for smugness) while Membertou sat perfectly still, scowling amiably, with his hand on his heart.

The Abstainer

Robert Pontgravé was invited to be a member in good standing of the Order, due to his good birth, but he declined, offering as an excuse the claim that he could not hunt well while his fingers were healing. At this, Champlain offered to hunt for him, but Robert remained steadfast in his refusal. He had become a sullen loup-garou of a fellow. Nonetheless, he sat at table with them and ate.

The Storyteller

To please the Iron People and especially their Saqmaw Poutrincourt, Membertou always made the Sign of the Cross before eating. What an outstanding old Savage! It was a great edification to Poutrincourt that he had taught this man a little Church doctrine. Membertou had enemies, so he loved the Iron People with their arquebuses. Now that his wigwam was a Store-house of iron treasures which he bestowed far and wide, he was determined that he too would possess a gun – particularly since the previous summer the Armouchiquois had slain his son-in-law Panounias, to revenge their kinsmen who'd been killed by the Iron People. (Let's blame Robert for that débâcle, shall we? – but no – the year before the Armouchiquois had killed our carpenter . . .) It was Membertou's turn to draw blood now. Come spring he'd send for his war-friends. Then his brother Poutrincourt would take pity on him – *hé hé!* Membertou knew how to obtain his desires from the Iron People! Not long ago, in River-Freezing Moon, he'd prayed his brother Poutrincourt to fire off the cannon in his honor. Smiling, Poutrincourt had done this. Now matters were so well arranged that whenever Membertou brought another Saqmaw to visit, Poutrincourt would oblige him in this way. *Pooom!* What Power! After this, while the foreign Sagmaw still gaped, Membertou would ask Champlain or Biencourt to give him wine – a remarkable beverage, which smooths away cares. – See how they prize me? he said to his guests. – And they would reply that indeed he had more right to speak than they. – Biencourt my brother! (Thus Membertou.) Here is my son-in-law Panounias. He is a great Sagmaw now, almost as great as I. You must give him a hatchet! – (But Panounias was dead now.) – Now that your ears have been enlightened, my brothers and sisters, you must own that Membertou knew how to establish his dignity among the Iron People! And it was true that his Power was growing. He was even better than Smoking the Pipe, at consulting DEVIL and the other MN'TU'S to learn where there was game. Of course he was; he was the Saqmaw! He dug a pit and tied a stick to a cord and beat it, singing: *Haloet ho ho hé hé ha ha haloet ho ho hé.* Then DEVIL was caught, and answered him. So Membertou told the hunters where to go, at which they exclaimed: *Hé é é é!* Membertou never spoke in error.

Now he sat by the fire of the Iron People and opened his mouth to explain to them the direction in which they must go, if they would remain his brothers. – What would persuade them? Ah! He commenced to relate to them how he had entertained their grandfather Jacques Quartier threescore winters before. (This Quartier was a very famous Sagmaw of the Iron People, now long dead, of whom Champlain retained the greatest jealousy, for Cartier had been to Canada before Champlain was born.) – Listen well, continued Membertou, for I do not lie. Your grandfather gave us guns –

Champlain said: Did the Captain Cartier mention to you any hills where there is to be seen a metal of a yellow color? – Ask him for me in Souriquois, Robert. I distrust my pidgin –

Brother, you must be patient, replied Membertou. What do you think my stories are? They are great trees; you cannot fell them all at once.

Ask him again, Robert: Was there metal of a yellow color?

Poutrincourt laughed, and filled the goblets.

The Exercise of Hell

Sometimes at these feasts the Saqmaw Poutrincourt or his nephew Lescarbot (Membertou could not understand exactly how they were related) would tell tales for the People. Robert translated when he was not too sulky. Otherwise Membertou listened as well as he was able (he knew more of the Iron People's speech than they thought), while Champlain made a bipod of his elbows on the table, upon which he rested his chin, staring deep into Membertou's face with his icy blue eyes, so that Membertou thought him uncanny. With the utmost courtesy, the Saqmaw Poutrincourt passed round the little silver mustard-service, with its swirling plates like scales, as Lescarbot told of the deeds of JESUS. (Mustard – uggh! How foolish and perverse these Iron People, to goggle up this slime that smelled of rotten dung!) Lescarbot told the tale of Saint Peter, Gatekeeper of Heaven, who for his loyalty to the Great SAQMAW called CHRIST was permitted to dwell in His fort in the sky, watching for friends and enemies. – How nicely they have tailored this story to me! thought Membertou to himself. For *I* watch and wait for *them.* – Not infrequently he became irritated with their recitals, which seemed to indicate that they thought themselves better than he. Granted, they had iron things, but they were ignoramuses in the woods; they were stupid bearded people! And did they open their ears when he reminded them that they were his guests, in his Country? Nonetheless this CHRIST seemed like a good Power, Who would probably be effective to call on when one blew bad blood out of wounds.

Lescarbot spoke to him of *christening*. What a stupid bearded word! He could hardly say it!

What is *christening* for? he asked.

To keep your soul from getting lost.

In the woods? – Membertou (who could grind chert-stones to bits with his teeth, who could swallow a stick two hands long) did not comprehend this answer. His soul never got lost.

No, in Hell, cried Lescarbot. His eyes gleamed.

Where is Hell? asked Membertou patiently.

Under the ground.

But we never go there! Membertouji'j, my son, what should I say to the Iron People? What need do we have for this *christening?*

Aha, my friend! You will have need after you die. Your relations will bury you.

Membertou smiled very slyly. – But if Hell is such a bad place then we will not be buried. We will pray our relations to wrap us in painted bark and leave us in the trees.

No, no, Membertou; that will not save you from Hell.

At this, he clapped his hand over his mouth in surprise, for he could not comprehend the reasoning of these Iron People. What was Hell? Lescarbot said that it was bad, and that it was a place where Membertou would go if he did not do exactly what Lescarbot told him; and then Membertou became fearful, for this place sounded evil indeed to him. But he was brave and would not show it.

To Lescarbot he said gravely: Brother, I seem to see us both in Hell together, eating much meat and laughing at the DEVILS. What do you say to that? – for he wanted to try the man's courage.

But at this, all the Iron People shouted out against him, rudely, as if he were not in his own Country.

Membertou gazed upon them. – Brothers, learn once and for all: *I* speak here, even in this drafty box you've built. When I open my mouth, you must listen. I sit while others stand. It is not the custom in my Country for friends to shout against friends.

He is angry now, Robert translated. You had best leave off plaguing him with your religious talk.

Robert, you must not speak that way. (Thus the Sieur de Champlain.) I often think that your father's gout is a visitation upon his ungodliness –

Excuse me, Monsieur, said Robert. I must go and relieve myself.

He went outside and did not come back. Where was that Savagess he lusted after? He knew the words now for what he wanted to do to her. – *Kijimij!* he shouted. *Nsi'siknm! Puktew! Samugwan!** The stumps of his fingers ached.

Wearing the Woman-Shirt

The People knew of many men like Robert. After all, they were the People of KLUSKAP. KLUSKAP had dealt with such men.

In the days that are gone, there was a man of the People who could not get women out of his head. He had one; he had another; but he wanted the perfect one: he was always looking. He wanted them as the Black-Gowns want souls. Finally he set out to find KLUSKAP. (He carried his knife at his breast; he thought himself valiant.) The river wound ahead into a distance of blue trees. He passed BEAR WOMAN sewing moccasins; he passed LOON PERSON hunting; he did not want them. He found KLUSKAP; he threw down gifts of tobacco and eels –

KLUSKAP had lidded eyes and a shadowed mouth, KLUSKAP had a nose like a knife. KLUSKAP knew the SERPENT with one horn red, one horn yellow.

Well, grandson, said that Person, you've asked something difficult, but have patience. Open your ears to what I say. I take pity on you; I speak to you from My heart, but whether or not I can help you depends entirely on your intelligence. I give you this box from my medicine bag. Take it back with you, but remember: You will not have your desire if you open it before you see your own wigwam.

É é é, thank You, great KLUSKAP! My heart hurts me; there is so much joy inside.

Go happily, said KLUSKAP.

The man set out at top speed. *Kijimij! Nsi'siknm! Puktew! Samugwan!* He ran through the trees; he swam the lakes, but always he wondered what was in

* Your cunt! My cock! Fire! Water!

the box that he carried. He made the Exercises, but he could not see. He climbed the crag-way until he was so high and lonely that he could see the snow on the mountains of the northern lands, and he almost opened the medicine-box then, for how could KLUSKAP see him here? – KLUSKAP was nothing; there were other MN'TU'S more Powerful than KLUSKAP! KJIKINAP the GREAT POWER had once made a wind that tore out KLUSKAP's hair by the roots! – But ahead was a pine tree, beyond which rose a purple peak, and low above the peak hung GRANDFATHER SUN, Who might perhaps tattle to KLUSKAP, so the man held his lust in a little longer and ran his way along stony flat-top mountains; he trampled purple alpine campions in his haste; women's names scudded fluffily through his mind like clouds as he tried to guess what her name might be: – Born in Dance-Time, or Born Swimming, or Sky Turns Blue, or Deer's Return? – and as the purple evening came he ran down into the beech-forests and a panther's eye gleamed at him by a little brook but he lusted too much to be afraid, so he ran on through the trees until he came to a wide river that gleamed as purply whitish-blue as a clean-bleached mussel shell, and the water was too high to cross until morning, so he sat looking at the box that KLUSKAP had given him, thinking: If only the river were low! Then I would be closer; then I could see her sooner! – for although the wish of his life had been granted, he still had others; there were always others. Presently he began thinking: What if she is frightened in there? It will do no harm to raise the lid a bit and reassure her! – He had often begun his enterprises in this way. – No, no! he would say. Just take your hide-shirt off and let me see your breasts; that is all I want! I will kill my favorite dog to feast you . . . ! – Oh, he had had so many women that way! And the wonder was that he always believed himself. – He got out the box and looked at it. Just as one sucks maple sap from the tree in moments of thirst, so he would drink her . . . He held the box to his ear, and thought he heard giggling inside. But no, it was only the river gurgling beside him. But how long must it be before he could open the box? Finally he could bear its constant promise no more (he could never bear any one woman); so he sat himself down in a pretty meadow. – Then it was done. – A lovely girl sprang out, and then another. – Which would he choose? They *both* seemed perfect! (Their nipples were painted, one red, one yellow.) But they did not look at him; they began to dance with each other. They kept their fists closed when they danced. They crossed them on their bellies. The man began to beat a stick on the bark plate to keep time. The women drew back their arms and pushed them out; they glared down into the earth, hissing through their lips; they contorted themselves until they sweated. – Here came a third, and then a dozen more! (They were too many now, he admitted, grinding his teeth; he had done wrong in opening the box before he was supposed to. He was greatly astonished; he was a single kernel of corn in an Armouchiquois cornfield.) How the girls marched and leaped around him! They stamped their feet together, and the ground shook. Their arms shot up like stalks; their fingers flowered; the music of the air made them sprint around him; now still more of them bounded from the box! He shivered. He must tie wampum to a pole for KLUSKAP to take. They rushed wordlessly, blissfully, and their fingers intertwined like butterflies; their hair was maidenhair. – In this forest of women he lost his way. KLUSKAP would surely chastise him now. What cord could he cut to release all these PERSONS from him? He had no gifts to give them. Their sweaty breasts crushed him; he panted; he tried to shake them off and flee between those standing rows of arms, but the women rushed so fast that he could see nothing in their faces; they were too busy growing: – they were choking him with their growth! – When they clapped their hands, his ears bled with a thousand thunders. They multiplied in number like poppies. Their hair grew longer and longer; KLUSKAP towered among them dancing and laughing *ho!* – then KLUSKAP was the clouds! – They clapped in time to KLUSKAP's laugh, and their clapping shattered his bones: there were too many even for greed to accommodate; so without even noticing it they laid him waste.

The Translator

Proof of Divine justice: it was sullen Robert, no less, whom Membertou pressed into service one night to relay the import of this tale to the frowning French. Poutrincourt had begun to master the Souriquois tongue, as I said; but Robert knew it better than any other Christian (with the exception, of course, of Captain Merveille – but no one knew Merveille's talents save Robert and the locksmith Duval). Just as Champlain often stared into Membertou's face as some point of the True Faith was expressed, so now Membertou plumbed the eye-depths of Robert as he told this story, scowling at him who scowled, so that Robert wondered what Membertou knew or suspected . . .

Ah, this Membertou! cried Champlain in dismay when the tale was done. – He is a lost soul!

I doubt me that he thinks so, Seigneur. (Thus young Pontgravé.)

The Audience

The squaws squatted very patiently on the floor. After Lescarbot said his Pax CHRISTI, Biencourt got up and gave them bread. They thought the Iron People very selfish, to give them no meat.

Ironless Nights

On the same night, Born Swimming went hungry because Swooping Like a Hawk had not come in bow-shot of his animal, who was Moose. He had hung Moose's bones in a tree; Moose must live again. But he did not find Moose's tracks. Since the snow was meager that year, Moose was not trapped; it was harder to shoot him with arrows. (Champlain had his arquebus, which Swooping Like a Hawk had seen but never handled, for the Iron People guarded all such weapons with great care.) In the golden clearings, snow lay on the shady sides of creeks. The hollows between the tree-packed hills were full of snow. But Moose was clever; Moose did not go there where he could be caught. As for plump Bear, he and his wife had retreated into their hollow trees. Swooping Like a Hawk could not see their breath. All day he'd trudged through the swirling green fingers of sun-shadow upon the creek-snow, hiding behind the naked trees palely patient in the sun, standing with raised arms in drifts that submerged their waists. It was often like that in Cod-Rising Moon. The Moon of Frost-Fish would be harder; Snow-Blind Moon would be most difficult of all. Once he saw Rabbit. Rabbit came to drink from a hole in the ice, lifted his ears (through which the sun shone) and bounded away. Swooping Like a Hawk waited for Rabbit to show himself again so that he could kill him, but Rabbit knew; Rabbit was gone. So the light failed at last. Swooping Like a Hawk greeted the setting SUN, saying *ho, ho, ho,* saying: Dear GRANDFATHER, please grant the needs of my family. – He searched for one of Beaver's houses, but all was still and lost in that icy dark. (Had someone forgotten to throw Beaver's bones in the water?) Suddenly it had become very late, and he looked around him as if in a dream. He was near the tree where he had interred his father in painted bark. This made him uneasy. Turning homeward, he followed the three Guards of the North Star (who were three People setting out in their canoe to pursue Bear), and the air came crisply into his nostrils. The wigwam was a triangle of darkness in the blue snow. He entered in silence. Born Swimming did not take his game-bag from him. She could tell that there was nothing inside. The children puffed little pipes that their father had made for them; Born Swimming smoked, thinking that perhaps tomorrow her husband would kill something; and Swooping Like a Hawk smoked and twirled the scalps of his enemies. The two girls were playing with the dogs. The little boy, Bearing Two Loads, puckered up his face as if to cry with hunger. At once Born Swimming began to sing loud brave songs for him. He listened with wide eyes.

Early the following morning, Swooping Like a Hawk ventured again beyond the winter hills whose bare grey tree-stalks were as fine and straight as comb-teeth. Again the ANIMAL PERSONS did not give themselves to him. Others would say that he was no hunter. He came home weary.

Born Swimming said carefully: I did not visit Kinebji'j-koji'j today. I think I will search for her near the Iron People's house.

Her husband bit his lip.

They went there together with their children, and the Iron People sat them down on the floor and gave them bread. But all the time, one of the Iron People (a young man with a crippled hand) sat gazing at Born Swimming.

Leave of Absence 1607

In the spring of that year, the Sieur de Poutrincourt completed his water-mill, which was a source of great astonishment to the poor ignorant Savages. At low tide they caught great quantities of herring behind it, which doubled its value; he gave orders to salt down two casks of them to present to the Roy (for even he, sanguine though he was, could not believe that he and De Monts could operate much longer on the strength alone of the blue Canadian ring-stones which they had given to him and the Queen), and the men said yes, Seigneur and he and Lescarbot were standing on the shore, taking aim at a moose that was swimming leisurely in the harbor, and Membertou and his children and grandchildren came to watch them grinning shyly when suddenly Membertou shaded his hand and said: Brothers, someone is coming from the sea. – At first no one else could spy anything. But presently a spot appeared in Poutrincourt's vision which could not be blinked away, then in Lescarbot's, then Champlain came running down from the cannon-platform; and a ship supervened closer and closer. It was the *Jonas*. It bore letters and dispatches which proved the worst. – Our FATHER! The monopoly had been revoked!

It is false! – This was Poutrincourt's first thought, which seems all too familiar to us, for everyone has had it. But that is as it ought to be. There is no easier way of holding doom and ruin at arm's length than by negation.

Membertou's Guns

But negate in tranquility a little longer, dear Poutrincourt! For there remained the matter of Membertou's heart's desire, indulging which he might for a moment forget the futility of his own, and simultaneously strike a blow against those godless Armouchiquois. – Ah, but would the Sieur de Monts approve if Membertou were given guns? Wouldn't it be a dangerous step? – Poutrincourt could not deny that, so as usual he set the point aside.

The decision must be soon arrived at, however, for by now Membertou had sent his sons Aktowtinji'j and Membertouji'j to the allied Nations. And they came: Souriquois, Etechemins and Montagnes: – two hundred painted warriors shooting eye-gleams; they came by day and by night, debouching themselves everywhere, upending their canoes on the beach, singing songs of prideful hate; Biencourt spoke with his father and posted extra guards before the Store-house. Duval prayed Mon DIEU! and ran into the Habitation to hide; he refused to perform his duties, and crouched rocking and whimpering while Poutrincourt had him whipped. – Robert will

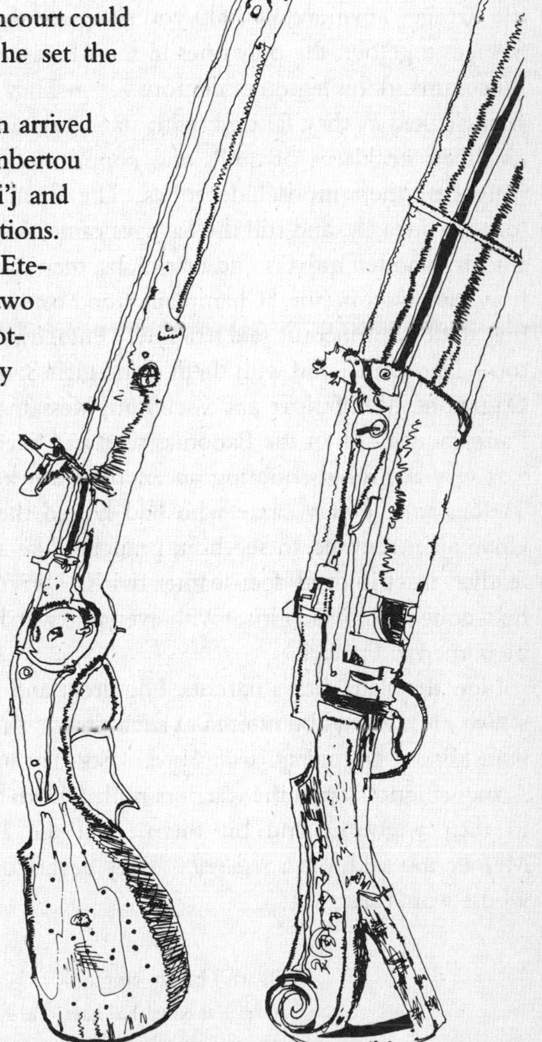

SHOT ARQUEBUS BALLS FRENCH ARQUEBUSES.

understand, he whispered thickly to himself when it was over, Robert and dear Captain Merveille . . . – but those two were outside surveying the gaudy Savage faces that reminded them of Mardi Gras, and Merveille slapped Robert's buttock with a laugh, saying: How effective we would be, if we could masque ourselves in that way! and Robert turned to him with shining eyes and said: If we went with them, Merveille, if we went killing with them . . . – and Merveille said: Doubtless they have their tricks! Eh, never fear, Robert, someday you'll know them all, and then when you don't need the Savages anymore I'll help you slaughter them all and you and I will be Savages together, the only ones in the whole world! but Robert said: First I'll command this legion of demons . . . – They came tanned and stripped, or skin-cloaked as they fancied; with star-worked ear-cups of porcupine quills; and their necklaces of quills and copper slapped grandly against the long fringes of their moosehide robes. The Frenchmen stood about smoking tobacco uneasily, and still the Savages came; they came bearing wicker body-shields, wooden quivers and war-clubs; they came thirsty to kill, for that was how they won honor. (Champlain stood ostentatiously priming his harquebus, until Poutrincourt said irritably: Put it away, man! I was in the civil war, too!) They came, and with them came their Saqmaws: Chkoudun the Trout, Oagimont, Membourre and Kich'kou; Messamoet, Ouzagat, Meadagoet and Panoniaques, son of the Panonias who had been murdered; Oagimech, who was very skillful at shooting an enemy from behind, and Anadabijou from Tadoussac, the very same who had hosted the dance of naked privities. – Champlain scowled to see him, prancing like a Seigneur, with his mane of feathers inset in dyed deer-leather twirls. – Wretch! – Who could forget what he'd done with those girls – with everyone watching – a crime for which he'd be burned in France?

Now the slain man's parents, Niguiroet and Neguiadetch, said the words which must always be uttered at such times: *My heart weeps tears of blood. We must blot out this outrage with blood.* So they incited all to rage against the Armouchiquois, until the warriors pulled down the enemy scalps which hung in their wigwams and bit them. And the Fox's scalp was there. And Membertou said: *It is resolved.* They began to chant their vengeance song, whose words are:

Death I bring, singing
Kwe! Ya! Kwe! Ya! Kwe! Ya! Kwe! Ya!
Bones I smash, singing
Kwe! Ya! Kwe! Ya! Kwe! Ya! Kwe! Ya!

. . . Seigneur, we must take care not to let them steal off on this war of theirs with our weapons. That would be rash. (Thus Champlain, pleading. He'd taken care with his moustache, and trimmed his beard to a ribbon's narrowness. For him this was an urgent interview.) They are Savages, Seigneur – *Savages!* Guns and Savages must be kept apart. I have seen their squaws strip themselves naked, clutching heads of roasted Hiroquois between their breasts –

Yes, you love to tell that tale. But those were Montagnes, were they not?

I only say that we must be wary and cautious . . .

Well, our ancient Gauls set great store by the heads of their enemies, cried Lescarbot gamely. (Lescarbot always interrupted.)

That may be true, Marc, replied Poutrincourt as kindly as he could, but it is not to the point. Please be so good as to leave Monsieur de Champellain and myself to our little discussion. This is very serious.

Baring his teeth at Champlain, the little lawyer scuttled out. Champlain resumed the melodrama. – We must watch these Savages, I say. Do you comprehend my meaning, Seigneur? I shall specify in detail: indeed this Chkoudun the Trout has warned me that Membertou is plotting against our lives. This must be investigated before all else. Never waste time striking sail in a storm, I always say. Most likely the Trout is mendacious, but –

I agree. Indeed one must not lay bait for rascals. Who could dispute that? But they come to us for justice against their murderers! (Poutrincourt felt very chivalrous and fine as he said this.) Is this not a worthy thing, that they begin to see the superiority of our way of life? You know how our Lord the Sieur de Monts has striven to bring this about. And consider, Champlain: if we do not do our part to civilize them, then the Jesuits will infallibly make a breach. They've ruined our monopoly just lately, as you know; next they'll set the Savages against us; they'll confuse them and lead them astray . . .

I am ignorant of such faults in the Jesuit Order as you claim. (Thus Champlain, rather coldly.) Indeed its priests have always seemed to me to be earnest laborers for our good.

Yes, yes; I am no heretic, Champlain, although you may think me so. But events must take their course. Indeed I do not think it such a brave step to supply our Souriquois with arms for a few days. We shall make them account strictly, I promise you! Membertou must promise that . . . Then they shall honor us all the more, and in the bargain we'll have a fine revenge upon those Armouchiquois who slaughtered our people last year – a victory we shall have, but all by proxy, Monsieur – think of it! Not a single Frenchman to risk, no matter how it goes! – No, not another word, Champlain: the matter is settled.

Iron Dream

So Membertou strode forth from the house of the Iron People and his mouth was rejoicing. He sang: *Over there runs the enemy. Over there, trembling with fear. See how he sobs like a woman! Over there he dies!* – a very good song which had come to him in a dream. Now at last he had the iron thing called GUN. He had always known that this would happen. Now GUN would utter the words of the song in GUN's voice of thunder: *Over there he dies!*

Listen, he cried out to his People. GUN begins to speak!

He pressed the trigger as he had seen Champlain do, and GUN shouted. A branch smashed down from a tree.

No one was as ingenious as the Iron People!

Now the People waited to hear who else would be permitted to make GUN speak, for his brother Poutrincourt had allowed him to carry many of Him, so as not to insult the great men. Membertouji'j got one, of course, and Aktowtinji'j. Then Oagimont, Membourre and Kich'kou must be satisfied, for they were great men. It was the will of the Saqmaw Poutrincourt that Chkoudun the Trout, who was in his eyes a good Christian, should be given two muskets. Nor could Messamoet, Ouzagat, Meadagoet, Panoniac, Anadabijou and Oagimech be forgotten. And still GUN came forth in multitudes from the Iron People's house! Therefore some of the lesser warriors could be remembered.

One was Swooping Like a Hawk.

For Swooping Like a Hawk the intoxication of GUN, so much grander and mightier than that of other iron things, lifted him higher and higher above himself, like the bird he was named for, serenely entranced upon piny wind-waves of yellow light. GUN was a dream-Power of swirling beauty, at the service of his desires. The Iron People, as potent and capricious as KLUSKAP, had rewarded him with dreams never before dreamed. He lay down with GUN; he rose up with GUN; Born Swimming laughed and smote her breast.

He strode out among the tender leaves and saw Crow. He raised GUN and made GUN speak. *Kwe! Ya!* Crow exploded into a rain of bloody feathers! Now at once he felt ashamed. He had not meant to kill Crow. It was GUN longing to speak; he must permit GUN to speak! He gathered up Crow's little bones and cleaned them lovingly; he hung them in a tree. Crow would come alive again. (Crow's spirit shrieked in World Above Sky.)

Now it was night. Carrying GUN, Swooping Like a Hawk went to a beaver pond. He took aim; GUN spoke! Beaver was dead. He tied Beaver to his back and brought him home for Born Swimming to boil; Born Swimming smiled and scraped the skin . . . In the bay, a big fish! He aimed below the water; GUN spoke! Water drenched him; he staggered back coughing smoke; the Iron People came running. – Never shoot into water! said the Saqmaw Poutrincourt. – (He spoke like a little child: thanks to his beard, he could not readily learn the speech of the People.) – Very dangerous! See this young man here? See Robert? Look what GUN did to his fingers last summer! GUN will be angry if you treat Him badly!

The Exercise of Contrition

Champlain watched the Savages parading about with good French harquebuses from De Monts' Store-house, yelling, pretending to shoot, shooting (although this last not often, for he had at least succeeded in getting Poutrincourt to admit that Savages ought not to be trusted with shot and powder beyond counting). Their manner chilled him. None of the other Christians seemed to feel that the line of authority was not still firmly held, and yet it seemed to him that the line was running out freely, sinking into unsounded depths. The back of his neck tingled.

I ought to have pressed Poutrincourt more strenuously, he thought (for it was easier to suppose that he had not tried hard enough than to acknowledge that his best had been disregarded). – But no; Poutrincourt is my Captain; he is wise and cautious . . .

Membertou shouted something, and the Savages howled like wolves.

You know them well, he said to Robert.

Yes.

Do you find them less compliant?

Robert grinned at him. – I keep no charts of such things, with all your ruled intervals. Perhaps you remark a change, Champlain, but I see none. Believe me, they still cringe and cower when I face them down in their hovels of bark –

They have become proficient with our guns. Alarmingly proficient.

I beg your pardon, Monsieur. But I have little reason to love the Armouchiquois. My hand, if you remember . . . So these proxies of ours could never be too proficient for me.

Ah yes, your hand, returned Champlain with a sudden flash of spite. You defied my orders to remain on the boat; you corrupted my sentry; you lost your fingers; and you blame the Armouchiquois! I tell you, boy, when one is given a post, one does not leave it except by order of the Captain or someone in authority! – Oh, what's the use?

Robert seemed not to have heard. – I comprehend the songs of these Souriquois now, he said. They're singing the enemy to death.

Champlain's shoulders slumped. – I can comprehend nothing. There are too many syllables in their words. Tell me, do they worship DEVILS like the Montagnais, or have they no settled ideas about such things? You know that I wish only their good –

Untrue! cried Robert falsetto, mimicking Lescarbot. – No, Champlain, you wish them no good, and neither do I, nor does any one of us. If we did, we'd leave them to themselves . . .

Soon enough we shall, boy. You know we must abandon Port-Royal. And who knows when De Monts will have cash again?

Champlain watched the Savages dancing, and wondered if his reckoning of danger were good; and if it were not how it might be corrected. – Certainly these Souriquois love us, he thought. They would never use guns against us. (If they did, of course, we could cut them down: that is certain.)

But I do not like to lend guns to Savages, he repeated to himself very softly.

More Good Times for Robert

Naked, the People danced together on an island in the Rivière Saint-Jean, turning round about a hill and singing. They were tattooed with vermilion and gunpowder: beasts, Crosses, flowers . . . The women did their best to capture the men, and beat the ones who did not escape.

Champlain observed these lecherous ceremonies with detachment, thinking to himself: their movements vary somewhat from the snail-like involutions of the Montagnais.

Robert also watched them. Now he saw Born Swimming naked for the first time, and his heart pounded viciously, and he slurped between his teeth. No, he would not sneak off to war after all –

Gleam and Glitter

They painted their faces red, so that their enemies would not be able to see any fear. Now Membertou spoke to the Saqmaw of the Iron People, saying:

Poutrincourt my brother, look after our wives and children well. We go to devour the Armouchiquois. – And Poutrincourt promised that he would do this. (But he closed the Habitation up tight. Champlain had worked on his fears thus far; what if Membertou plotted against him?) Then Membertou went down to the shore with the warriors, after which they embarked in their canoes – but some only, the smaller part, with which Membertou planned to make his ruse. The rest went by land. Cautious of every noise they heard in the damp and mossy forest that faced them, they began to creep and skulk so that the Armouchiquois might not surprise them. They glided past the rocky ravines scragged with birches and spruce-trees. The blue needles of spruce glittered above their shoulders with all the beauty and wonder of evil things. They saw a beaver-skeleton wavering in a stream. Some among them found a bad omen in that, but Anadabijou said: Think upon Membertou, brothers! He is more than a hundred winters old, but he goes on. He has Power! – and their hearts soared to hear this. They gladly followed him. (Anadabijou, too, was old – old.) Now they crossed the frontier of the Armouchiquois Country. They ducked among the sweet-smelling trees (over which GRANDFATHER SUN was now setting) and rushed on, sticky and glistening with tree-resin, until they saw before them the sandy grassy plain that fronted the Chouacoit River, at the mouth of which they saw the lodges where their enemies camped after planting the corn. They swarmed silently through the Armouchiquois cornfields. They strove not to walk near the manure-piles for fear of crunching mussel-shells beneath their feet. It was dusk now. Swooping Like a Hawk was very happy. When he went to war he never cared if he lived or died because he had already seen the SUN, hunted animals, taken a wife, had a son; all was well. This time he was certain that he would live because he had GUN. He thought about how it would be when he was home showing the new scalps to Born Swimming and he could dance for her and everyone with the scalps glistening as they slapped gently against his chest. GUN glittered in his hands like the silver of rippling rapids. GUN glittered in the hands of Anadabijou; GUN shone like a constellation in the hands of Chkoudun. They heard the roar of the river called Chouacoit. They smelled it beyond the mossy arms of trees. They smelled harebells and mooseberries. They were close enough now to smell the sassafrass on the breath of the Armouchiquois and they could hear the rattling of their wampum beads when they breathed.

Applause

They came back bloody and laughing. They brought back women and children for slaves, stripping them of their hair to deepen their disgrace. They cut the scalps of the enemy dead with quick and practiced motions, enjoying the sounds of ripping skull-skin, jerking each bloody black braid up high to be admired, slapping it in the nearest captive's face, and the crows were already coming and no one could smell anything but blood anymore and they made the women dig up the hidden cornpits and bring them to the baskets of dried fish and they feasted until their bellies swelled and then they loaded the women up with corn to carry home. A little Armouchiquois boy had found a squashed lead bullet sticky with blood, and they laughed and let him keep it. They returned to their Country of beech trees and grey-lichened hills and the SUN was shining. Their minds were cleared. Someday the Armouchiquois would counterattack, and then they could revenge themselves again. It was for them as it had been in the first days, that they could become whatever they chose, and they became death. The Dream of the Floating Island was a good dream and victories came as easily as dreams; that is the First Point. *Kwe! Yah! Kwe! Yah!* – Poutrincourt emerged from the Habitation to greet them; Biencourt drew his hand up sharply, and the mercenaries fired off a peppery salute! – Their *guns*, Seigneur! (Thus you-know-who.) Get their *guns* back now, before they hide them! I have a full tally on this sheet . . . – Eh, Champlain, don't worry about their guns! I see that avarice is your temptation! Listen, those old muskets will all have burst in six months, and if they don't, where will the Savages get powder? Let's make them happy, Champlain! They're our friends; soon we must abandon them; today we'll open a tun of wine . . . – (Poutrincourt, suddenly easy, was talking like old Pontgravé. He could not deny that he'd slept poorly while the Savages were gone; he almost wondered if he'd begun something interminable and nasty with those guns, but no! it was only an incident; it was his victory, too; everything had happened for the best!) (And next we'll hand out prunes and biscuits! whispered Duval to Robert in disgust.) – The warriors were singing. Their wives led the captives away and set them to work, scolding them in shrill exultant voices, and they applied slices of beaver-stones to their husbands' wounds (which were slight), and Membertou consulted with the MN'TU'S to heal whomever he could. The smelt were in multitudes, and the slaves soon gathered enough mussels to fill all De Monts' longboats. The People danced holding to them the severed heads and arms of their enemies.

Ah, happy victory! breathed Lescarbot. Ah, immortal glory!

The Exercise of Contrition Again

Yes, I was in the wrong, he said to himself very humbly. Again I reckoned wrongly. Eh, if another opportunity is granted to me I shall lead them myself! Young Robert says the same. I shall teach them to be victorious in every situation – victories they'll owe only to me. Thus I shall bind them more closely to me and my good friends . . .

His face glowed with these and many other infallible fantasies.

Crows and Savages

And so you are leaving us, brothers, said Membertou.

For a time it must be so, said Poutrincourt.

Why?

We cannot pay our expenses anymore.

Come, brother. Live with us. You do not need these ridiculous houses. Come into the forest; we shall show you how to live like men.

Poutrincourt stared at him. For a moment he had almost been able to see himself happily becoming Savage among the Savages, forgetting his wife and daughters, forgetting France, running among the caribou . . . He laughed uncertainly. Then he shook his head smiling.

Membertou had been watching him very intently. He sighed. – So you will be dead to us. I do not know why it must be so.

We shall all come back here, Membertou – I promise you!

Membertou leaned forward, thumping his stick. He had painted himself black in sadness, and many of his People had done the same. His face was puckered, as if he were being made to eat French spiceries. His brows were like shaggy mountains. His cheekbones stuck out at angles.

Dead or absent, it is all the same, said he. My heart weeps tears of blood.

They stayed an extra day to placate him. Then they set sail. It was the eleventh day of Août. They did some fishing and waited upon Champlain, who had essayed another bootless visit to the Sieur de Prévert's mines, still hoping for some rich and lawful prize, which of course he would share according to established usage, not being in the least selfish or greedy of gain. All he found, alas, were a few nuggets. – By the aid of GOD, he said, I shall at least finish my chart of the coast . . . In his heart he had already given Acadia up. He longed incessantly now for inland Canada – *viz.*, Tadoussac and beyond, where at Pontgravé's side he had first beheld those vast forests, those clawed darknesses called bears . . . On the second of Septembre he rejoined the Sieur de Poutrincourt and his retinue; the following day they departed Canseau.

As soon as they had cast off, a flock of crows appeared from nowhere and roosted on the trees, cawing and bowing their beaks with the utmost gravity. Duval fired a shot at them, and they leaped into the air, beating their wings frantically; the evening sky shone through their wingfeathers. When the ship had moved a little farther away, they settled greedily upon the refuse that the Christians had left. They fell like dark snowflakes, unfurling their wings to land with soundless ease upon bones and cheese-rinds and ordure.

How They All Took It

Lescarbot was very sad, though not as sad as Poutrincourt. He grieved mainly for the moose-skins which the Souriquois and Etechemins wore, being convinced that excellent buff-jackets could be made from even such rude apparel. He could almost see himself in one, walking down the streets of Paris, with a hat of beaver-felt upon his head . . . To a lesser extent he grieved for the sea-urchins left behind (these had been his favorite food); and yet their loss would be corrected for by other plates of fare in the grand eateries of France; so that left only the moose-skins.

Duval came back with the rest, complaining all the way. Twenty-five sols; that's all Greedy Pierre pays me! he said. (Greedy Pierre was his name for the Sieur de Monts.)

I'll bet you twenty-five sols he'll pay you nothing next year, said Pontgravé, irritated.

Within the locksmith's silver pupils, two keyholes began to swivel. – Done, he said.

Pontgravé shuddered. He had the feeling he'd done something stupid. Quickly he changed the subject, telling him how he'd seen the young Dauphin beaten by his father for three-quarters of an hour because he'd pissed himself, and all the Princes and Cardinals and favorites gathered round were laughing as the boy struggled under the Roy's great hairy hand, screaming: I'll kill you, kill the whole world! I'll kill GOD! – at which Duval too began to snigger, and Pontgravé hoped that the matter of the twenty-five sols had been forgotten, but then the keyholes began to swivel again and Pontgravé said quickly: Once I saw that old hag Madame de Montglat, the one who has him in charge, and he'd just struck his half-brother in the side, so she was getting ready to beat him, and she said to the kid: Come, Sire, lift up that ass! – and Duval clutched himself and snorted *whee-whee-whee* with laughter as Pontgravé had known that he would because men of that stamp loved to hear those above them degraded; but then the keyholes began to swivel, so Pontgravé said: And the Roy said to her: *Madame, you do not beat him enough. I profited from constant beating, and he must do likewise!* at which Duval chuckled yet again. – None of Pontgravé's stories were eyewitness, exactly; he'd gotten them all secondhand from De Monts, but he wasn't about to admit that to Duval for a second, 'cause a fellow's got to keep some advantage in this world – get it?

Done, Seigneur, said Duval. Twenty-five sols.

This Duval, what could you do with him? Pontgravé knew that his bet was lost.

But presently he recovered his sunniness, for he said to himself: After all, by next year Duval might be hanged.

As for the Sieur de Champlain, he was very cast down on the voyage. Lescarbot had made a melancholy ode about him which kept ringing in his ear:

> As you search for the origin of an infinite Fleuve,
> You'll reach at the end the Future you love;
> You'll reach la Chine . . .

But would he, could he reach China? Eh, of course he would. For Champlain, as for all of us, the Stream of Time does lead to China, if by China we mean death.

He was not quite acute enough to sense this. But it rendered him low-spirited all the same. The soul comprehends what the mind cannot.

For all that, he continued to be practical. As they crossed the sea, the sailors caught a quantity of dog-fish and were about to throw them back when Champlain said: No, no; you must save the skins for sandpaper. The carpenter can use them when next we are at Port-Royal.

Poutrincourt put his hand on his shoulder. – So you too have faith that we shall be back, Champlain?

I know it in my heart, Seigneur. I know it.

And Poutrincourt felt a peculiar warmth. Certainly the man was adept; he was steadfast as well. – The Chevalier's reversal of attitude was, of course, a natural one. Now that hope had turned to wretched sadness, why should not contempt be transmuted to admiration? All feelings, after all, are but specious illusions, being unsusceptible to measurement. (Thus Champlain.)

Hospitality

They made port in France at last, easing in between piers that curled like tendrils, that sported stubby cylindrical towers at their ends like carbuncles; and Poutrincourt was shocked to see the swarms of running men and barking dogs that infested those octopoid arms which now embraced them; he had gotten used to the solitudes of Lacadie. Ahead, stout towers turreted, manned with archers and pikemen, bedizened with ugly square windows whose grilles provided some surety against lobbed bombs or missiles; and behind them the herds of sharp-creased roofs gathered about their steeples and enclosed by a wall which paralleled the shore as far as the eye could see; the stink of the town already filled his nostrils, and he could see crowds of commoners wriggling in the streets like mites in a rotten cheese . . . Monasteries and convents exploded from the hills beyond. – No peace, I tell you! – He almost shed tears.

Courage, Seigneur. (Thus Champlain.)

Champlain stayed with him throughout the summer, leaping up whenever Madame de Poutrincourt entered the room, smiling at her anxiously. There was no good news from Court. The Sieur de Monts did not invite Champlain to visit, although Poutrincourt saw him often; after those visits Madame de Poutrincourt would raise her voice and then weep, at which Champlain, more out of place than ever, went out into the town in his Quartermaster's uniform so that the peasants at least would lift their hats . . . He had no desire to see his mother or Captain Complain, for they persisted in their error of faith. Just as the ordures which fall between decks will produce unhealthful vapors, so thoughts of family which slip between the bulkheads of a voyageur's mind may be counted on to work their own corruption: therefore it is best not to encourage such thoughts, remaining clean and free. – He accompanied Poutrincourt, Biencourt and Lescarbot to the Abbey called Mont Saint-Michel, where they saw all the relics, with the exception of the buckler of the Archangel Michel, which the Bishop had lately forbidden to be shown. Then they went to Court and presented five Canadian bustards to the Roy, as well as the first fruits of the soil. It was Champlain himself who gave them into the Roy's hand; he'd reared the birds most tenderly, knowing them to be the property of his Master here on earth. And the Roy smiled upon him and held out a fawnskin glove for him to kiss . . .

Madame de Poutrincourt did not like him. She was convinced that he meant to step into her husband's position. – No, no, Claudette, Champlain is not like that. He is hardworking, loyal . . .

Yes?

I tell you, he would not do such a thing!

All the same, said Madame de Poutrincourt, he is quite impertinent.

How do you mean, impertinent?

Eh, perhaps my words were ill-chosen, she said. But you would not deny that he's ambitious?

Ambitious? Champlain? He's too realistic for that.

But presently our man began to feel uncomfortable *chez* Poutrincourt, for he was not nearly as dimwitted as claimed. Pontgravé saw how matters stood, too. He'd been around; he knew which hole the shit comes out of! In Septembre he invited Champlain to come and take good cheer with him. They'd celebrate the Dauphin's birthday; they'd talk over old times with the whole crew! You know how you take a codfish from Terre-Neuve and dry him until he's stiff as a board and then he'll preserve forever? Well, that's just how it would be (said Pontgravé) with these fine old Canadian memories; and maybe the boys could come up with a way to get back there, too . . .

And I must finish my maps.

Of course, Champlain. Of course. We all know that.

One night they were all sitting around naming new islands for Champlain's chart, and Pontgravé winked and said: But these two, the dimpled ones, you must name them Sainte-Hélène and Sainte-Marguerite! at which Champlain frowned and said: You must think me very fresh and ignorant, to believe that I do not see that there is some licentiousness here! – at which Pontgravé made a face behind Champlain's back as if there were a bad smell, and Poutrincourt, Robert and Merveille had to bite their lips not to laugh; and Pontgravé went on: Of course I do not think you ignorant, mon ami; I insist that everyone ought to be educated! – to which Champlain replied: Eh, then, who are these ladies? – and Pontgravé shouted: What difference does it make who they are? – at which Robert came so close to laughing that he had to cough.

Very well, said Pontgravé at last. I'm not angry; I'll oblige you. Do you know Nicolas Boullé?

Doubtless he's been to New France?

No no no. He's not that type, Champlain. You know him – the Calvinist from Fougères. Properties at Mayenne and Mons – ah, if I could get my hands on his properties! . . . He used to be the Collecteur des Finances . . .

Yes, I know him, said Champlain grimly. Nicolas the Heretic.

The heretic? By Heaven, man, what do you mean? Infernal!

He forced his wife to abandon the True Faith, did he not? He baptized his children according to the so-called "reformed" church. Yes, Pontgravé, I've taken soundings in my time, and I know Nicolas Boullé.

Pontgravé threw up his arms. – Great snakes! I can't take anymore! What about Poutrincourt? What about Lescarbot? What about the Roy himself, despite his professions? What about me and Robert? Or De Monts? Don't you know who your friends are, Champlain? Calvinists and Huguenots! You're surrounded by them, Champlain, and do you know what we're going to do? We're going to *eat you alive!*

Peck his eyes out! shouted Merveille, who longed to be drunk.

Robert sniggered at this witticism, running his gaze back and forth across Champlain with caressing malice.

Excuse me, said Champlain. I did not mean to offend you. You know that I have never held your faith against you. Let us say no more about it. What about Nicolas Boullé?

Only this – he has two daughters. Their names you can guess.

Hélène and Marguerite. (Thus Champlain, wearily.) And they are of marriageable age?

How did you ever guess? Hélène's six now, so she's a bit overripe, but Marguerite is younger. – Come now! You have no sense of humor! I knew the family when they hid out in Vitré during the Civil War; we Malouins go there to buy sea-guns. Then when you were ogling Mexican girls with your Uncle Provençal, they moved back to Paris. As a matter of fact, he swears he knows you. You must have seen him in oh-three . . .

Indeed I did. I admit that he does not have a bad temperament . . .

And do you remember that René Noël who died of the scurvy at Île de Sainte-Croix?

The soldier?

Naturally. He was a dumb bastard, wasn't he? – Eh, he couldn't help it. His father demanded an attestation from De Monts; it was your friend Nicolas who got it, who made him stop spreading scandals . . .

Scandals? What do you mean, Pontgravé? (As always when this topic arose, Champlain had gone white. Pontgravé was quite satisfied with himself.)

You know perfectly well what I mean. Mismanagement, poor judgement, corruption, starvation and cannibalism! Death without benefit of clergy! Scurvy, faction and icy breezes! Remember how the holy water froze? No need to go into who was responsible; GOD will ferret that out when the time comes. You should be grateful that your friend Nicolas –

He is no friend of mine, said Champlain through clenched teeth. – Put your reckoning right. You mention GOD, so in GOD's name what are you leading up to?

Nothing, nothing, I tell you! Have your way then. Holy MARIE! He's no friend of yours. But he *is* a friend of mine. That's the way of it, and I'm not going to convert him or antagonize him to please you. I want to get my hands on his properties. And not just for me, either – you needn't look at me that way! This enterprise is costing De Monts a whole Store-house full of gold livres and sols; as for Poutrincourt, the man's bankrupting himself! I give him another half dozen years of solvency, tops! He'll end up in debtors' prison! Don't you care about your friends, Champlain? Are you going to help out with those islands or not? Ah, I can see your head's spinning. Well, think it over.

No, Pontgravé, that's not necessary. Whatever you wish. You make me so tired . . . Île de Sainte-Hélène and Île de Sainte-Marguerite. No, no; these isles are named. But Port Sainte-Hélène and Port Sainte-Marguerite, that would be possible . . .

Wonderful! Merveilleux! Don't forget. My dear Champlain, I'm counting on you!

In the spring, Pontgravé had some business to do in Paris. De Monts had agreed to try again in Québec, and so Pontgravé was compelled to run around organizing things – a dog's life, I tell you! – Buy the establishment, Seigneur! (Thus sagacious Pontgravé.) Buy Kebec! With all its rights! It'll pay; it'll drip gold onto your head like birdshit! Even that dumb fuck Champlain has it on his maps! Mull it over! – On the way back, he ducked into Nicolas Boullé's.

Listen, said Pontgravé, Champlain must never find out I'm here; he's so sensitive. But I thought I'd better give you the news. He's crazy about your daughter.

Hélène? But she's –

Starry-eyed! Completely bouleversé! Mark my words, when that new map of his is published, you'll see that he named a harbor or an island or something after her – and Marguerite, too! Even in Canada, your Hélène was all he'd talk about. *So beautiful,* he'd say. *Such a sweet little fillette. Ah, heads will turn when she grows up! GOD's Providence!*

But what is the meaning of all this? cried Boullé, astonished. He's approaching forty; how can he even mention such an unseemly passion? And you would have me give my daughter to a –

To a great man? Indeed I would. Nicolas, let me tell you something. (Have I ever led you wrong? It's us against the Papists, you know. And Champlain's not really a Papist; he's on our side; he's just boring from within, that's all.)

Champlain's going to go down in history. Why deceive you? He fought the Armouchiquois singlehanded; he saved us from scurvy on Sainte-Croix (I nearly pissed out of my armpits when I heard of that notion of De Monts' to winter there – sheer idiocy!); the Savages worship him; he'll discover gold mines for the Roy! No, no – let me get it out of my system! Get in on the ground floor! Your little Hélène will have a great future . . .

Not a Single Christian

Ah, Pierre, sighed the Roy, more robust than ever, I'd help you if I could. – Say, have you met my little Dauphin? Louys, come out from behind my arm – don't be bashful! You're six years old now! Have a sip of wine and greet these gentlemen with good courtesy – ha, ha! Now be silent. – Pierre, you know that you are blamed for the high price of beaver. Your monopoly – well, it's sad, Pierre, it's really sad. The Malouins and the Rochelais complain to me that their ancient liberty has been taken from them, for men have traded with the Canadians for a hundred years. You see how it is.

The Jesuit, Père Cotton, was there also. General Provincial of Aquitaine, he was soon to assume that position for all France. The Dauphin was terrified of him. His voice was loud and shrill. He had a way of plucking one's sleeve, and if he was not satisfied the claw would pinch . . . He surveyed De Monts sternly, cocking his head like a parrot. – And they say that you have made not a single Christian! he said.

I know not which of these accusations to reply to first, said De Monts. As for making Christians, Père, the truth is that I have written even to the Pope, but so far no priest will consent to come with me. The Prince of the Souriquois is ripe for the Faith. He's been very, very useful; his name is Membertou. But, you know, because Canada is scarcely populated, I am told that the number of souls to be saved is insignificant.

Insignificant! cried Père Cotton in amazement. Who says this?

Peace, peace, said the Roy. No matter.

As for the high price of beaver, continued De Monts, the truth is that these greedy traders are to blame, for they flock to Canada without regulation and bid against each other. I remember when one beaver-skin was worth two biscuits or two knives. Now it's worth ten. And as for their confounded liberty, you know what I think of that.

Eh, Pierre, said the Roy, I shall award you the monopoly for one more year, no matter what they say. One year, mind you.

I shall endeavor to prove myself in that time, Seigneur. I'll send Champlain to Kebec, and Poutrincourt will return to Port-Royal; their fortunes are a little shabby, I know, but we can use them for another year or two at least –

If you fail this time to do CHRIST's work, be assured that we ourselves shall do it, said Père Cotton.

No Need of any Learned Doctors 1610

Champlain went off on schedule, of course; Champlain was a walking talking clock. But Poutrincourt couldn't get away for three years. The puissance that he always felt in Acadia had entirely deserted him here, so that he was enmeshed in the weariness of his daily affairs as in the GOUGOU's tendrils, and the whirlpool dragged him round and round through schools of monsters whose greatest weapon was their banality. First there were the usual chicaneries with the monopoly, which required him to sell off another of his properties, and then his mother died. Arranging to have Masses sung for her immortal soul was a simple matter; settling her estate was not. He had to borrow again . . . He very rarely presented himself at Court anymore. The Roy condescended to him as lovingly as ever, and somehow that hurt him; he did not know why. He had to sign another note of hand for his eldest daughter's dowry. Then, too, he must make his wife see that they were not bankrupt yet, not quite; he must importune the Pope to send priests for the instruction and edification of the poor Savages; De Monts had left that devoir to him. – Eh, very well, said the Pontiff. Then you shall take with you Messire Fléché. – That wasn't so bad; at least he didn't have to bring any Black-Gowns with him; all he had to do was victimize his poor wife once more, to bid farewell to his daughters whom no one called upon . . . So be it. When he was prepared to leave, some false traders with whom he had been compelled to enter into partnership suddenly withdrew. People made no bones about his convenience anymore; he'd noticed that. But he set forth out of our French seas at last, on the twenty-fifth day of Février, 1610. With him once again he brought his son Charles Biencourt, who had considerable experience of Navigation. Poutrincourt had high hopes of him.

On the open ocean there was a mutiny of sailors, who aimed to become pirates and then highwaymen, because we all seek to improve ourselves, but Biencourt ferreted out their skullduggeries, as they had not been discreet in front of his ears, believing him to be but a boy; indeed even as a boy he'd always stood listening at closed doors, not out of dishonorable motives but because the cloud of doom overhanging his father was always coming closer and closer and his father did nothing to dispel it; his father never even looked up to see it, so it was left to the boy to develop not only the usual rigidity and pride with which we diagnose such cases, but also a desperate cunning; these two qualities had blended in him in such wise that Biencourt suffered from a desire to prove that everyone was his enemy; he was never wrong. So he happened to be behind some barrels of gunpowder when the sailors made their plan, and a bitter thrill passed through him when he went to his father. But Poutrincourt pardoned them all. When Biencourt proposed to hang the ringleaders at least, he replied: I have not the heart to do it. Let us simply have vigilance for the future. – Are you serious, Father? They're nothing but scum! They would have shot us while we slept! I think execution would be much simpler and safer than vigilance . . . but Poutrincourt only replied: Someday you will be master of Port-Royal and then you may do as you think fit. You are already the Baron of Saint-Just; you must not think that you do not have any authority. – With this Biencourt saw that it was well to be content, especially since his father was now entering that foolish rapture which always veiled him like mist as he drew closer to Canada. Truly there was something different about air and water and light in those parts! Resinous darkness pressed so sweetly about him that his soul knew itself to be already within the shadows of the rocky spruce-coves of Paradise, and he heard little that his son said. Sighing, Biencourt paced the deck, wiping sea-spray from his cheek, keeping watch upon the crew with patient unforgiving resolve.

As they neared the Grand Bank they saw many of the fishes called *flutan* or *halibut*. These were four or even five pieds in length, so that they must be hooked with gaffs. Their eyes were as large as fists. – What a marvel! exclaimed Poutrincourt. I feel drunk again! – And he weighed in at that shoal-ringed harbor of Port-Royal, explaining everything excitedly to the white-gowned Messire Fléché. – I expected it, the priest said, folding his arms on his chest. Nothing is any different than I imagined. No fear, Seigneur; these Savages will all be good Christians in a month. – Christians? laughed Biencourt drily. Ah, yes.

The Savages had not damaged anything that he had left; even the furniture remained undisturbed. This seemed amazing to Poutrincourt. He had expected to find the Habitation burned to the ground, the Savages his enemies, Canada marred by the malignity of Providence, but the same dreamy greenness embraced him and his happiness bubbled over. Membertou had eaten their entire flock of pigeons, it was true, but when they reproached him he burst into tears and blamed the *Culloo*-bird of his religion, at which they knew not what to say. – Every day I have watched for you, he said. I have guarded your house for you. – So Poutrincourt rolled out the usual hogshead of wine, and drank with Biencourt and Membertou and Swooping Like a Hawk and all the rest of them until the beech-trees in the forest seemed to become acquaintances, and he went and hugged the nearest one, which turned out to be his crony Lescarbot! (Lescarbot had remained in France this time; indeed he never came to Canada again.) – Write something about the Savages! cried Poutrincourt. – "This shows the great amiability of these people," recited the tree,

> who, having seen in us only the most humane qualities, never flee from us, as they do from the Spaniard in this whole new world. And consequently by a certain politeness and courtesy, which are as well known to them as to us, it is easy to make them pliant to our wishes, and especially so in regard to Religion . . .

Marc, you can write like a hundred devils! cried Poutrincourt in admiration when he read this. You say just what you ought to say, but so finely . . . Let me call Messire Fléché! Can all lawyers do such things?

That depends, said the tree, puffing itself up. Mainly, Monsieur, it is a question of breeding.

Eh, go on, go on! Put in the important part!

> Now, for the present, intoned the canny Lescarbot, there is no need of any learned Doctors, who may be more useful in combating vices and heresies at home. Besides, there exists a certain class of men in whom we cannot have complete confidence, who are in the habit of censuring everything that is not in harmony with their maxims, and wish to rule wherever they are. It is enough to be watched from abroad without having these fault-finders, from whom even the greatest Roys cannot defend themselves, come near enough to record every movement of our hearts and souls.

Ha, ha! laughed Poutrincourt. – Loyola and all your spawn, in New France you are now dead dogs!

Then he tumbled down and puked.

An Unpleasant Duty

But when the glasses stopped clinking at Port-Royal, the two Poutrincourts had to sail across French Bay to the Country of the Etechemins, there to arrest Robert Pontgravé for rapine.

The Stream of Crime 1608

How had this come about? Pontgravé the Elder was steadfast in his loyalty. And he hated the Black-Gowns just as much as Poutrincourt: – all this had nothing to do with them. Whenever they were mentioned, in fact, he began to spit like a cat. If *they* were ever let in, the Savages would spend all their time praying and forget how to trap beaver. *Then* where would his profits go? You have to admit he had a point.

Everything had to be done just so for Pontgravé to get rich. The Savages had to scrape and rub the beaver-peltries, tanning them with brains; they had to trim them to a rectangle's shape and sew them half a dozen or so together to make robes; they had to wear their robes with the fur against their skins for a good year and a half, until the grease from their bodies left the fur soft and downy to the touch, and yellowish or agate-hued in color; *then* the Savages must bring their robes to Pontgravé. – As if the Black-Gowns wouldn't scramble *that* up! Hah! *He* knew better!

Knew better? Why, he knew better than anybody!

In the spring of the new year (*viz.*, 1608) he'd returned to New France as usual. Poutrincourt and De Monts couldn't afford to go? So much the worse. Champlain was building at Kebec: De Monts was willing to put in that much. – *That* was all on Pontgravé's advice, I assure you! – Seigneur, he said to him (as well-mannered and logical as you please), if you don't keep one toe on Canada, somebody else is going to have both feet there by the time you get back. Think about it, I beg you, Seigneur! – So Champlain got his second opportunity – not that he deserved it, the stupid *dagorne**! But truth to tell, Pontgravé couldn't take *all* the credit for rehabilitating him; the truth was that the Roy had pleasure from his visits. He loved to unroll Champlain's maps and make finger-voyages on them, the Roy did. Champlain approached the red carpet bordered by fleurs-de-lys which flowed down to him from

* One-horned cow.

shallow steps like cascades, at the head of which the Roy and the Reine gazed down benignly. Pontgravé watched Champlain bow and click his heels, and he thought: eh, he knows how to suck the egg! Very talented! – Hence Champlain continues in our *Relation*, now en route to Kebec, and by some coincidence Pontgravé has a lucrative contract to drop off the supplies! Small world. (One thing Pontgravé had learned was that you couldn't make a single counterfeit sol when your hold was empty.)

So we're becoming practical at last, Champlain! (Thus Pontgravé.) You're going to build yourself a cosy house in Canada. You'll sit all winter by a nice fire, drinking brandy and giving orders. How can you beat that?

I'm always practical, Monsieur.

(MARIE's tits! Does the man never get a joke?)

Of course, of course. Say, how do you think that wheat-field of yours turned out, the one at Port-Royal?

I'm sure it's growing tall. But I have no certain knowledge –

Let's pay a visit. It's on the way, and I'd swear that the Souriquois had some beaver-skins for us – wouldn't you, Robert?

(Pontgravé was one of those people who love to pretend they're doing you a favor when in fact they're following their own agenda. This system is prudent. If you see through your supposed benefactor, well, he still had to do his errands anyway, so he loses nothing. If you believe him, then you owe him something.)

So it was agreed that they would make a brief debouchment at Port-Royal. KLUSKAP's People were there. And Robert's sweetheart was one of them; you know who; there's no suspense in this book –

The Anointment of the Son

Pontgravé sat polishing one of his silver coins with a beaver-tooth, which was perfect for this purpose, being hard in one place and soft in another. The corners of his mouth were turned grimly down as he listened to his son.

So I will not stay here with these bastards from Rochelle! the latter was shouting. They insult me; they insult you; they insult the city of our birth!

I never knew you to be such a patriot, the father said, beginning on another coin.

I beg you not to mock me also! It is not my fault that there is bad blood between the ports of France. I want nothing to do with it, but they will not leave me alone. Just today I had to beat that Étienne Brûlé to the ground with my fist, although he's only a child! Now the rascal is waiting for me, no doubt, with a dagger in his hand.

You will never learn, I see, that a bad temper makes a bad profit. Do you think that you are here solely to take your pleasure with squaws? – Even at home Lescarbot makes a standing joke of it. Don't think you're in good odor with the Mademoiselles of the Court – you know how pious they are. So far Poutrincourt is pleased to laugh, because it's not in his interest to thicken the stink, but if you ever go too far and set the Savages against us, I myself will thrash you!

Sullenly the young man worked his leather-clad toes back and forth against the wall: – squeak, squeak.

And stop that noise, said Pontgravé, frowning more blackly than ever. I know not what to do with you. You and that Captain Merveille of yours! Shall I send you to the forest? There at least your misdeeds will be less likely to come to Poutrincourt's ears, just in case he ever comes back. (And I have faith that he will. He's not quite ruined yet.) – Shall I establish you among the Etechemins? (Too bad Champlain's such a clever Quartermaster; otherwise I could siphon off some of his stock. Eh, there are ways, Robert.) Yes, I believe that is what I shall do.

Beavers and Marguerites

Across French Bay as one sailed out from Port-Royal was a substantial rivière. Champlain had explored it and named it the Saint-Jean in honor of Poutrincourt's namesake. Along its banks lived the Etechemins. Here Champlain had seen several promising islands, which he duly reported to those in authority over him, but ever since he'd made that one Exercise with the Isle de Sainte-Croix, no one was impressed; Pontgravé figured he could help himself to one of Champlain's goddamned islands . . . Champlain knew enough not to put up a squawk! And so Robert and his men were installed on the isle of beech-trees called by the Etechemins *Emenemic.* – And take regular inventories, Robert, that's my advice! – Merci, Monsieur de Champlain! (Au revoir, poltroon!) When the ship was out of sight, he felt himself to be a man at last.

In short order, Robert Pontgravé had become a great executioner of those fish of fresh water with four feet – *viz.*, the muskrat, otter and beaver. Since they were fishes, it was permissible to eat them during Lent. So he reasoned – and how conveniently, too! – for the thighs and shoulders of beaver were not a whit inferior to mutton when they were roasted. His familiar, Captain

Merveille, laughed at him upon hearing him utter such sentiments: – As for me, he said, all these priests and churchmen can be d—d! Lent or no Lent, permission or no permission, I'll eat meat; and if those Black-Gowns try to stop me I'll roast *them* like a haunch of beaver!

Concerning this *beaver*, Robert could conclude only that it was one of GOD's strangest creatures. It was almost as long and stout as a sheep, but possessed very short feet – the hind ones webbed like those of a goose, the front ones like hands. Lescarbot had told him that beavers were civilized animals, respecting their old Commandants who directed the carpenters, masons and hod-carriers in the construction of their public edifices, chastising the slothful with their teeth – mimicking (in short) the civilized hierarchy of France . . . – Did he believe it? Well, it was a charming story, far more so than that of the GOUGOU. But he certainly knew more than old Skinnyshanks. He trapped beavers continually. Why, he knew as much as a Savage!

In the distance, he heard the sound of beaver-tails beating earth on a dam.

He went to the Store-house and poured himself something to drink. – Ah, how wonderfully it burned! – Where was Merveille, anyway? It was time to go grab a squaw or two . . . Today for some reason he could not keep his mind off those Savage Marguerites and Hélènes . . . Usually they didn't cause any ruckus. (One had hanged herself, it was true; he'd heard that. But the Savages only suspected him; they had no proof.) – Ha, ha, ha! – The way he felt right now . . . – eh, it was as if he had dined well, but still desired a small dessert of piquant cheese . . .

Duval was at Kebec with Champlain – so much the worse. Duval would have come along to take the pleasures of the neighborhood. He was a sullen oaf, that fellow, but at least he'd be company.

Where was Merveille?

Captain Merveille was right behind him, of course. He had already learned from the Savages how in these regions the lynxes climbed trees, waiting until a moose came by to jump down upon, which they did; he learned how lynxes could worry and gnaw at a moose-throat until the prey sank to its knees groaning and bleeding and dying. This delighted Captain Merveille. He encouraged Robert to think along these lines –

There were certain rules, of course (in this, Merveille was one with Robert's father). One must hush things up. One must not dirty one's own nest. In the Country of the Etechemins it did not pay to rape Etechemins. Some were allied with the Armouchiquois, it is true, but which ones? Why not sail across the Bay and have at some Souriquois girls, especially since Poutrincourt was away? Bad news travels slowly over water. Besides, the Etechemins and the

Souriquois were jealous of each other. But he made it clear to Robert that he must never ravish any of the women of Membertou's household, no matter how attractive he might find them (indeed, if Merveille knew Robert, he was liable to find them all the more attractive for the prohibition). Failure to be reasonable on this point would certainly turn the entire Souriquois Nation against them, which could be prejudicial to profits.

Robert listened carefully. His penis was already hard as he thought about Born Swimming.*

It happened on an evening of unseasonable warmth. Captain Merveille had gone south in the pinnace to trade with the Souriquois. Robert was very bored. He itched to beat one of the Savages to the ground – not for any reason, really, but strength was pulsing through him that day; it seemed a shame to waste it.

I'm ready for Born Swimming! he shouted to all his cronies.

Been saving her up, eh? The *pudendum muliebre*, that's what you ruminate upon, like a cow and her cud.

Here comes old Merveille, said Robert. Let us ask him.

Captain Merveille was very handsome. His hair was reddish, like maple sugar.

Love

The next day continued bright and sunny. The mosquitoes were very bad. Born Swimming made her husband a headdress from two bird's-wings. She rubbed her face with grease until it shone.

The leaves have sprouted, Swooping Like a Hawk said. The wild geese are here. The seals have given birth. Spring is here.

* Before you judge Robert too harshly, I must inform you that he had good reason to be a rapist (isn't there always?) Trying to make the others laugh, he'd told them how he had once gone to a whore in Marseilles when his father was busy counting the other kind of beavers and the whore's privities did not look very clean to him so he asked her if he ran any danger of getting a disease from her and the whore laughed scornfully and said: Stick it in me, Seigneur, and then inspect it in two weeks. That's the way to find out! – But this story of Robert's, sad, comic, profound and even true, was not accepted with the guffaws he had anticipated from his bored companions; rather, an embarrassed silence swirled round Robert's face and settled on it like a swarm of Canadian mosquitoes and bit it until it turned bright red, and then Captain Merveille said: Eh, did you do it or didn't you? – Of course I did, Robert lied. – No one said anything. – After this it was incumbent upon him to prove himself. His yearnings wound like some mucky green river among trees . . .

It is time to look for black spruce root, said Born Swimming.

But Robert Ki'kwa'ju had also taken the narrow path that led into the woods.

He was waiting for her in a dark place, his soft hand opening with subconscious candor.

Her heart began to pound with horror.

He took a step toward her. She stepped back and turned to run. He lunged for her and she ducked behind a pine tree and he reached around the tree and she ran behind another, knowing now that sooner or later he would get her, and he snatched at her hair and she ran behind another tree and he was behind her grasping at the fringe of her shirt and she tore herself away so that the moose-skin ripped and he flung himself after her and his forearm was about her throat. The sharp bone in his arm pressed against her neck like a knife so that she could not breathe. Even yet she weakly strove to push him away. Instantly he hit her in the stomach and then, as she doubled over in pain, struck her again with his fist and knocked her down. Grasping her mercilessly in his arms, he took his pleasure, jeering and sniggering at her. *Kijimij!* he shouted. *Nsi'siknm! Puktew! Samugwan!* He was white-bellied, like a partridge. She could not comprehend his words, but he took particular pains to make certain gestures whose insulting meaning no woman could fail to see. (As he got on top of her, he felt at last that he was truly in Canada, that it was his Country, that he was in fact a conqueror of this Kingdom of Dreams where anything could happen. The squaw's shrieks and struggles were lavish flourishes beneath his signature; he signed the deed of Canada.) When he was finished, he held her as fast as before. Her weeping now infuriated him, and he began to strike her in earnest, until she lost consciousness.

The Seventy-Third Rapid

After having thus paid his debt to nature, Robert was very happy. He felt as he often did when canoeing up some rock-ribbed rivière, poling with an Etechemin Savage, and bird-swarms cheeped overhead and a soft hazy mountain rose at the next bend. – He took the longboat south to the Country of the Armouchiquois and repeated his trick. Yes, this New France was a Paradise of which the Jesuits had no conception!

He tramped all through the wilderness about his Rivière Saint-Jean. The land was very uneven and heavily timbered. Eh, this soil is very good, he thought. More loam than clay . . . He made experiments, like Poutrincourt, cutting down beeches and oaks to see how long it would take for the stumps to decay. – In truth these valleys were rather gloomy. He could bring a squaw to any one of them, rape her, and slit her throat – he'd wager no Savage would ever come nosing in! – But why trouble himself to murder them? They never complained.

Prayer

Born Swimming stood up and screamed. She said to herself: *My heart weeps tears of blood. I must blot out this outrage with blood.*

Annunciations
1608–1609

> . . . see and consider the THREE DIVINE PERSONS seated on the royal throne of the DIVINE MAJESTY, how they behold the entire face and vastness of the earth and all the people in such great blindness, and how they will die and go down to Hell.
>
> SAINT IGNATIUS, *Spiritual Exercises*

The summer passed rapidly enough on his rainy shores, for he was busy laying in beaver for the Store-house. He'd built his cabins beside an ugly swollen stream; he palisadoed them around, as he had seen De Monts do, for he wished to give the Savages no chance to take revenge. Once he thought he saw them waiting for him in a stand of yellow birch (of which there was plenty in that cursed Country of the Armouchiquois where he had lost those three fingers); and he let fly with his arquebus, at which Merveille and the others came running. There was nothing there, of course. – In the autumn, when the rivière was murky with fish-spawn, his father sailed by to visit him and his men, and bring them home if they chose. Champlain was wintering at Kebec, he said. All was well there, aside from a trifling mutiny, which had been put down. The ringleader had been hanged. (Robert, bored by death, did not even ask who it was.) The accomplices were in the hold.

Robert said: Father, I think I shall stay on this winter. I feel so at ease here.

Indeed Robert, now blessed by his GOD, Who was Who He was, had become complete. It was the utter languid completeness of one's first signature deed, whose repetitions in this *Relation* are mere underscorings. As happy as a cat in the sun, he knew that he could never ask any more than this. Reader, you may as well know it, too, for the truth is that we have needed

Robert only for the commission of this one act. Yet lives do go on past their epiphany, and so I shall be fair and keep him with us for exactly the same span of years as he is assigned in the *Dictionary of Canadian Biography*. With this Robert would have agreed, I am sure, for although his being had now been crystallized, the excrescences of experience continued to attach themselves to him.

Merveille, whom he had regaled with an account of his adventure, now seemed less a mentor than a peer. When the man proposed leaving his service the following year, in order to form a connection with Champlain at Kebec (for Acadia, as he put it, might well dry up), Robert was surprised to comprehend that he would not be heartbroken. Duval was at Kebec now; Gaspard and Du Gay were dead; Port-Royal was abandoned, and yet he felt no loneliness. As he went about his assassinations of beavers, he found himself becoming stronger almost by the hour. His forearms were hard and rigid, like iron bars. His shoulders could easily sustain the weight of two hundred livres. The other men who were at the post – mainly no-account Basques and Huguenots – wondered at his zest for exertion. At the end of a day of labor, Robert liked nothing better than to climb one of the pine trees overhanging the island's edge and dive from it, deep into the water, where, opening his eyes, he saw clams and greenish tendrils of muck flicking with mechanical intelligence. Then, puffing and blowing, he'd rise to the surface and swim around the island with great strokes, while the others drank brandy and shouted cheers and fired off their guns into the sky. Robert knew that they would have followed him into any act, because he was stronger than they, and strength was all that they knew (if one includes strength's twin derivations: *viz.*, fear and cruelty). This was what it was like to command a Habitation, he supposed. And yet oddly enough he did not care for it. What he longed for was to go inland among the Etechemins and strive with their strong men in the chase, in war and in games. He was certain that he could best them in any competition which required force and endurance. He had heard from Membertou that it was a custom in these parts for the braves to seize one another by the wrist and then lower those locked forearms into the fire, to see who was the stronger. Robert smiled to think of it. It came to him like a fact engraved on a sacred tablet that he could hold until the bone was roasted through. – When he leaped out of the water and found his companions in their stupor, foul with old sweat and dirt (saving only the suave Merveille), he despised them.

Sundry Rejoicings

But he shouldn't have, for Swooping Like a Hawk clapped his hand over his mouth when he found his wife lying half-dead. – What an evil thing! he shouted. I shall kill him!

Your words are good, she said dully. Smash his head with your war-club.

She painted her face black with sorrow. He knew not what to do.

A Representation of the Ideal

It is easy to see that you are a lighthearted veteran now, Robert. (Thus Captain Merveille.)

I am satisfied enough, said Robert shortly. I'm free here –

Yes, but you must guard yourself better. You did not kill that Souriquois squaw and sink her, as I advised. The Savages will crave revenge.

Or rcparations, said Robert boredly.

Shall I be your Ambassador?

I don't care. The Souriquois are addicted to iron now –

Eh, let me think, said Merveille, as if to himself. Which would be the eviller course: to let them slay you, or to bring about a reconciliation so that you might continue to infect their squaws . . . ?

I don't care, said Robert again, hardly listening.

The following morning, Merveille set off in a skiff. Like all great men, he loved to travel alone. He wore stout armor and a helmet. Over his shoulder, a loaded harquebus. Between his feet, a good quantity of powder and shot.

Robert had told him where Born Swimming's wigwam was. But he thought it more efficient to go to Membertou's.

He saw a flotilla of Souriquois canoes near Port-Royal, bobbing like the white crowns of Hydra beneath the water. The Savages shouted against him, and launched their arrows. – Quick, before one struck him in the face! – Merveille threw down his paddle, swiveled the arquebus around, and let fly, but over their heads; he wanted no blood-feud. He laughed to see them put hurriedly to shore –

When the tide was propitious, he entered the Bay. He tied up at De Poutrincourt's dock. The Habitation had not been pillaged, which he construed most favorably. The roof had fallen in above Champlain's old room, and a crow rose shrieking from the hole. – Humming to himself, he pulled the arrows from his chest. Their heads of French iron had penetrated his deerskin jacket and scratched the thick chainmail beneath. Ah, and here were some others which must have ricocheted off his helmet. He bundled them up under his arm.

Membertou had moved his wigwam, but it was easy to find. That Saqmaw guarded the Habitation as faithfully as Saint Peter! Very effective, to have such a dupe . . .

In the breeze, a French blanket shuddered vaguely in the doorway.

Kwe! called Merveille.

No answer.

Merveille hesitated. He laid down his arquebus. He paced around the dwelling, whose bark panels Membertou's wife had painted with fishes and birds and red French Crosses. Smoke ascended through the smokehole. He listened, and heard a faint cough. Then his heart thrilled within him, for what women were to Robert games of strategy were to him – not by any means the scientific games of Champlain, nor quite the gambles of elder Pontgravé, but something more aesthetic.

Kwe! he called again, louder.

Who is there?

Merveille. I come from the Country of the Etechemin, to speak for Robert Pontgravé, who insulted one of your squaws.

Enter, grandson, and rest yourself.

It was Membertou's voice.

The fire was low. The old man was sharpening his knife on a stone. He appeared very distressed and fatigued. He squatted in silence, waiting for the guest to speak.

Merveille handed him the arrows, and wordlessly he threw them into the fire.

You must know, Membertou, that I am very sorry for what has happened. I ask you to convey this gift to Born Swimming and Swooping Like a Hawk in token of my love and sorrow. – Thus Merveille, withdrawing from his sleeve a very pretty little clasp-knife which Robert had stolen from his father.

Membertou said nothing.

What happened occurred without my knowledge, continued Merveille most earnestly. I desire that you continue to look upon the Iron People as your friends. Iron calls to iron, you see . . . – and glibly he withdrew a number of beads and balls of shot, which he dropped into Membertou's kettle, one by one, listening to them rattle and echo like pebbles in a copper skull.

You speak just as did Bashaba the Armouchiquois Saqmaw, said Membertou. We accepted his gifts last summer, and then we killed his Saqmaws Olmechin and Marchin with your guns. Do you remember? Thus far Bashaba has escaped us, but last night I dreamed that I would kill him. As for Robert Ki'kwa'ju, we cannot pardon him unless he gives us great presents. Doing otherwise would be against our laws. I have spoken. Do you hear me? I dreamed that Robert Ki'kwa'ju would die today. I am greatly astonished, grandson, that you have not already been killed.

That was done long ago, said Merveille, and he smiled.

I wonder at your words.

From an inner breast-pocket of his jacket, Merveille withdrew a pistol, which he gave to Membertou, requesting him to load it with powder and ball. It had been specially modified for such stunts by the locksmith Duval, so that the trigger mechanism first opened a tiny velvet-padded oubliette in the chamber, into which the ball dropped soundlessly just before the powder ignited.

Now take aim, grandfather.

I want no war with you Iron People –

There will be none. Am I myself not inviting you to kill me, Prince Souriquois?

Membertou swung the gun viciously upward, pointing it into Merveille's face, and his eyes blazed with ecstatic hatred. – Eh, the fire separates us sufficiently (thought Merveille). The powder burn will be negligible.

Membertou pulled the trigger. The shot was obscenely loud, and shouts came even from the depths of the forest. Yellow smoke swirled through the wigwam like the atmosphere of Hell.

The smoke cleared.

I am dreaming, said Membertou very slowly. I wonder at this dream.

You see, replied Merveille, I am quite effectively dead.

Yet I have Power! the Saqmaw was shouting.

Oh, naturally.

Perhaps I am not dreaming. You show much ingenuity, my grandson. Indeed I believe you have as much intelligence as my brother the Saqmaw Poutrincourt.

Your words are pleasing to my ears, grandfather.

And this gun is pleasing to my fingers. I could well amuse myself with this gun.

Merveille took the pistol into his hand and secretly pressed a stud which sealed the oubliette forever. Now it would function like any other such weapon. He peered down at it, as if loath to part with it. Then he passed it back across the fire. – It is yours, he said.

The Annunciation

After this, the Lnu'k and the Iron People were reconciled, and a few days later Robert Ki'kwa'ju gave a hogshead of beads to Membertou to present to Born Swimming (being wise enough to see that he ought not come before her himself), so that her hatred was softened to sadness. Her friend Kinebji'j-koji'j, who was very changeable, now counseled her most urgently to be appeased by these gifts. They dared do nothing against the Iron People anymore; they could not be killed. So sadness became fear, and in time fear became hatred again, but by then it was the Moon of Fat Animals, and Born Swimming knew that she was pregnant.

A Conference

Pontgravé was very proud of his merchant's scales, whose case was a lozenge-shaped affair of walnut. When he opened the lid, the two pans of the recessed balance trembled like the needle of a shaken compass, and then came to equilibrium. Inside the top was a printed chart of the correct weights for all the known currencies of the globe.

Now he stood prying these wooden lips apart and closing them again, not knowing what to say.

Eh, Père, I see you have heard all about it. (Thus his son.)

Have you no thought for others? exploded Pontgravé. What about the trade? How am I supposed to make a living among these Savages now? Ingrate! Wretch! Fornicator! GOD will punish you. And you, Merveille, how could you have permitted this?

The only solution, Monsieur, would have been castration – a drastic one, to be sure, but highly effective.

Now the others began to laugh, and Pontgravé strove to scowl more blackly than ever, but he could not, and began to chuckle into his hand.

But you've truly gone too far. Poutrincourt is returning next year, and when he does he'll arrest you – of that I'm sure! So you'd better lie low.

That is just how he lies, Monsieur. (Thus Merveille again.) If you don't believe me, ask the squaws.

Pontgravé chewed on his lip for a moment. Then he drew his son aside. – Is it true that they – grease themselves?

No.

Eh, then I'm out five crowns . . .

Born Underwater

Everyone congratulated her, including her husband, Swooping Like a Hawk, for to him children were riches. But Born Swimming would not wipe the black paint of mourning from her face. This child inside her was a child of the Iron People. This child was a child of rape.

Most of all she remembered his freckled hairy fist shooting almost lazily through the air –

Swooping Like a Hawk held a feast, however, to which he wore his strings of enemy scalps. To his mind the Iron People had given satisfaction (Robert Ki'kwa'ju had remembered him with twenty hatchets), and now, since the baby must be born, it might as well be welcomed. So the People of KLUSKAP danced beneath the trees, and then Swooping Like a Hawk danced, leaf-plumes and antler-plumes on his head, as the People sat round him in a circle beating time on a kettle that the Iron People had given them, crying out *ho, ho!* in their happiness. But Born Swimming could not be happy.

How long will you wear that sad face? cried Swooping Like a Hawk.

I don't know. Maybe it will go away when the baby is born.

When the baby is born? Then why not now? Why not be happy with other People?

What happened to me is an insult, Born Swimming said. Women have hanged themselves in the forest. I will not do that. But I am not happy. – I have spoken.

Day and night she sang sad songs.

Swooping Like a Hawk avoided his wife until she gave birth, so as not to risk harming the baby with his hunter-Power, for that was the custom; but it seemed to her that he avoided her too zealously, and she looked into his face once and saw him look back at her ashamed.

When it came time to give birth, she drank water mixed with powdered bone from the breast of a moose; that would ease her. She went into the forest. Her labor was very painful; the baby was big. She did not cry out.

The name of her daughter was Born Underwater. Her eyes were like that Stream of Time brown and clear, whose rocks are brown beneath the water.

Born Swimming washed her with river-water. She gave her a drop of seal-oil to swallow. When she began to cry, she rocked her and gave her the breast. She loved her. But when she looked at her, she felt such pain that her eyes began to burn with tears, as if she were snowblind and someone were scraping scale from her pupils with his knife.

Now the others came and admired the baby, caressing her very much, for which Born Swimming gave them presents as was the custom. She wiped the black paint from her face. But she remained very quiet.

She laced her baby into the cradle; she lashed the cradle to her back. When the Iron People came back, she went to beg some grease for her breasts, which she took without thanks, gazing at them with hatred in her eyes.

The Door Opens
1609–1610

Neither turneth he back from the sword.
The quiver rattleth against him,
the flashing spear and the javelin.

Psalm LXXXIV

So now that Born Underwater has come into our History, it is time to let the Black-Gowns in, too – much as I have enjoyed this titillating game of delays, as if it were a snowy night in Montréal and the Black-Gowns were some pure French girl whose shyness made my resolution not to touch knees with her beneath the table an act of tenderness; that granted, let me turn the hot water faucet, so that the Stream of Time may begin to move a little more quickly. – Well, a *little* more quickly.

Père Biard at Bordeaux 1609–1610

– Wait and pray, said his Provincial, Père Cotton, and he waited for a year. He understood that circumstances were against his Mission, but the Provincial said: I know you are high-strung, Pierre, but mortify yourself with patience; I have word from the highest places that you will go and Père Biard bowed his head meekly but then he burst out: how *wicked* and *despicable* these tactics of our enemies! and the Provincial said: remember that it has been scarcely six years since they rescinded our expulsion from France and Père Biard said bitterly: I remember, Your Reverence and the Provincial said quickly: soon we shall make the Spiritual Exercises together and Père Biard said yes and swallowed and closed his eyes, and then he saw kind Saint Ignatius smiling at him, the eyes twinkling in his bald head, and for a moment he was at peace. A man of strong soul, he was very accomplished in the Exercises, which are a Black-Gown's true sustenance and armament. He had come very close to conquering himself, and had thereby acquired certain Powers never likely to be imagined by the neophyte. To begin with, such was his skill at meditation that he could visualize his life's journey as an ascent of the Stream of Time. He knew the approved placement of every island and shallow which he had already passed, and by dint of severe attentiveness to his Directors he had a very good notion of the way before him. To those who did not believe, he would seem to be but kneeling in his crow-colored robe, his head bowed, his lips moving, when in fact he had left his body and was continuing on ahead. From his exertions he'd already acquired an iron concentration and an imposing manner which had proved effective in aweing many in the world. Certainly his companion Père Massé held him in great regard, as he could see. Père Massé would be coming with him to Canada. He could tell that the man was excited by this. He too often caught him smiling. Fortunately, Père Biard had but to look him in the face, and Père Massé's gaze would drop, sliding down the pleats in the front of his cassock – which afforded him good consolation, as he admitted. Doubtless the Savages would treat him the same. Still, it was an unbearably fruitless time. Canada seemed to be in an unattainable sphere. Every day he paced through the town, and his zeal continued to exsanguinate. He thought upon the way that Jacob had worked seven years to win Rachel and at night he went in to her and then in the morning he discovered that she was not Rachel after all but Leah instead, so that he must work for another seven years for Rachel, and when he went in to *her* he could not but have been thinking about the first time when he thought that Leah was Rachel and now Rachel could never really be Rachel anymore. – And he was still more incensed when he learned in the end that Poutrincourt had sailed to Acadia without him, in his place bringing – what contemptible transparency! – the aforesaid lay priest, Messire Jessé Fléché.

The First Conversion

Membertou was now quite aged, being upwards of a hundred and ten years old, but for all that he remained clear in his thoughts. It was essential, therefore, to convert him.

Messire Fléché gave presents and administered the Sacraments, while Poutrincourt fiddled a ravishing *Alleluiah*. – Hm, said Biencourt glumly. The sailors stood round drinking wine and sniggering. (In their ships were big rats, which soon infested the wigwams of the Savages.) Swooping Like a Hawk watched from between the trees. Born Swimming was nowhere to be found. It was almost the time for the feast of Born Underwater's first tooth, for which there would be much meat; but now the Iron People had belittled it with their biscuits and brandy and baptisms. She wished sometimes that she'd drunk the abortifacient of boiled roots . . . – Pontgravé sat taking bets with the sailors, his face flushed red and ugly from brandy. On the side he was complaining about his gallstones – the size of hazel-nuts, I tell you! Membertouji'j was drinking wine and shouting with joy. Born Swimming's kin-friend Kinebji'j-koji'j, still dismarried, peeped shyly, ready to take to her heels if the Saqmaw Poutrincourt should remonstrate with her again about the murder of the Armouchiquois slave-girl, and a sailor came up to her and started whispering in her ear and looking around at the others and Kinebji'j-koji'j was giggling and the sailor pressed something into her hand and Kinebji'j-koji'j pouted because she wanted to be baptized instead and get Power but the sailor (who was really very gentle) gave her a tweak and popped a biscuit in her mouth, so she took his hand and pulled him into the forest. Meanwhile Biencourt said hm and hum, wondering how he might best trap Robert Pontgravé in the forest like a wild beast, because his father would never do it, and Membertou crossed himself and said his *Aves* most proudly. Messire Fléché decided to baptize him *Henri*, after our most wise and gracious Sovereign. But Membertou, being a Sagamore, considered himself equal even to Roy Henri – such was his Savage blindness and vanity! – and so he saw no cause to give up his name. – Sharply clapping his hands together, Messire Fléché said to him, No, you must change your name. This is a custom that we require to be followed with Savages who become Christians, for our GOD said to His servant: *Your name is Jacob; no longer shall your name be Jacob, but Israel shall be your name.* – Are you my GOD, then? said Membertou. But slowly he stretched his leathery old cheeks in a smile, and Messire Fléché saw that he had only been joking.

Around his neck he wore an embroidered purse the size of one of Pontgravé's gallstones, in which he kept his Power. This he took off most dutifully and gave to Messire Fléché, who consigned it to the flames . . .

The register of baptisms in the Church at Port-Royal begins on Jean the Baptist's Day, 1610. The first to be baptized was *Catherine*, the fourth daughter of the eldest son of Membertouji'j, whom in his turn they called *Judas*, at which he made a face, for he knew that Judas was a bad name. Then they all laughed at him. It went on and on. Membertou's wife was baptized *Marie*, after the Queen; and then the others were named after nobles who might sulk if they were left out. – Pax CHRISTI!

Satisfaction 1610

Now they can't get those greedy Jesuits in here! Pontgravé laughed and laughed as he slammed the registry book shut; so loudly did he do this that it almost seemed he was afraid the baptisms would escape from the pages, and be undone. But he only meant to be jubilant.

I'm very tired, said Messire Fléché. He sat down and began munching on a cheese.

Hey, watch yourself! cried Pontgravé, alarmed. It was his favorite cheese.

You see, said Messire Fléché, I feel very tired.

Tired! Hah! Your labors have just begun! You with your labors, me with my gout, between us we're both – *hey!*

But it was too late. Messire Fléché had eaten all the cheese.

The Disappointment 1610

When young Biencourt came sailing proudly to the Queen with the register of baptisms in his hand, however, he soon discovered that it availed no more against the Jesuits than an ordinary bullet against a vampire. It was, in fact, a brilliant entertainment that he brought them, for they'd been certain of their victory long ago. It had come through a lady in waiting to the Queen, named Antoinette de Pons. She was the widow of the Marquis de Guercheville. *A rosary in her hand and a Jesuit at her side,* says Parkman, *she realized the utmost wishes of the subtle Fathers who had moulded and guided her.* When the Roy got knife-kissed that year, Madame de Guercheville was among the first to console the Queen, for which action she was highly esteemed. She helped her don her white robes of mourning (which garments are the reason why the widowed Queens of France are called White Queens, but chess-players would doubtless find all too many other reasons). And she wept because the Queen wept. This is called the Exercise of Contrition. After Matins the Queen listened to Madame de Guercheville read from the Book of Kings, wondering how far her husband's heart had decayed (for by a particular codicil of his will the Jesuits had been permitted to bear it away with them to their College of the Arrow), and she wondered what gold or silver casket they had put it in, and she wondered when Madame de Guercheville would stop reading because she did not much like her or her condolences, for which a bill must assuredly be presented; and she also wondered about the little Dauphin Louis, her husband's darling, and whether he had to be murdered or whether he could simply be ruined. Her favorite person in the world was her dwarf foster-sister Leonora, who had married an adventurer of considerable resolution, by name Concini. To please him, and therefore Leonora, the Queen was prepared to advance him to a leading position in France. Unfortunately, the Dauphin was in the way. When the midwife dribbled wine from her mouth into the baby's, she'd hoped that he would choke. Then he would not eat, and she could hope that he'd waste away, but when he was two days old Doctor Héroard cut the membrane under his tongue. Then he'd received the city fathers of Paris when he was a month old, and Madame de Montgalat had almost dropped him and the Queen made the Exercise of Yearning until she could hear his skull smash upon the flagstones but it hadn't happened. And yet he was her son; she didn't want to smear herself with his blood if there were a kinder way. It was very promising, the way she'd taught him to call his half-brothers *mere pretending Princes, made of filth.* That would isolate him. But he still preferred that fat Queen Marguerite; she'd heard him call her his little Mamma; and Marguerite's schemes depended on his survival. – Poor boy! Maybe he'd conveniently die of one of Héroard's purges . . . – Annoying Madame de Guercheville went on reading her illuminated Bible, whose gold leaf flickered and shone in the candle-light, and the Queen looked at her coldly, wondering when she would be done, not knowing that Madame de Guercheville was paying no attention, either, because Père Cotton had just now told her of the sad darkness of the Souriquois! Their clothes were made from the shaggy skins of brutes, so badly (Père Cotton had been told) that one could see the skin under their armpits. In winter many of them froze. When they found no game, they starved to death, as happened not infrequently. In their hearts was no knowledge of Our Lord. – Hearing these things, Madame de Guercheville began to sigh full heavily. She felt an urgent desire to do good works before she died. Many times before, she'd striven her utmost, but it seemed to her (though her friends would have denied it with affectionate indignation) that in each instance she had faltered, thereby tarnishing her purpose. Here was one more opportunity, for which she gave thanks. Now if only the Queen . . . – The pupils of her eyes got bigger and bigger in the darkness until even the

Queen noticed, and Madame de Guercheville noticed that she noticed and broke off in the middle of a verse and said:

Have you learned, Madame, of the great wickedness that is being worked against our Friends?

No, my dearest Antoinette, I have not, said the Queen in surprise.

But soon she had.

So that's all she wants, thought the Queen to herself. Eh, that's nothing.

And to the pious Madame de Guercheville was granted the continent of *America* or *Antarctic France*, from Florida all the way to the Fleuve Saint-Laurent –

Poor Biencourt didn't know anything about this, of course; nor, at first, did the other freaks in that sardonic circus which Père Cotton stood watching at the Queen's side, being the edge of a wedge of knowing Black-Gowns who did not yet know what he knew, but drew optimism nonetheless from his smirk, while the Queen, who couldn't care less, chewed candies (she was already starting to get fat now that her husband wasn't alive to govern her), and Père Cotton's smirk widened moment by moment; he hadn't been so entertained since Lent; how fascinating it was to see these souls go on like ants, unaware that the purpose to which they had consecrated themselves was already dead! GOD (through His agent, Père Cotton) would soon tidy up the chessboard; but first let them say their lines one last time –

Loyal Lescarbot was there, dressed to the nines, insisting: No, no, I am not their paid advocate. But I assure you that the time has not yet come for a Canadian Mission – I *assure* you! It's all been reasoned out –

Biencourt said much the same. – Messieurs, examine this paper, he pleaded. You will see that our priest, Messire Fléché, is doing great work in the saving of souls.

Pontgravé was there, too, by some coincidence. – Of course we support your authority, he said amiably to the Black-Gowns. You're the ones who instill a love of law and order in our kidneys – no one fails to understand that! We're preparing the ground for you, Messieurs, don't you see? They never gamble or drink anymore; practically every wigwam has a Cross on top! Biencourt and his father have done wonders! You should read Champlain's reports! And my son Robert . . . Attend a little, just a few more revolutions of the sun, Messieurs, and we'll have them waiting on their knees for your ministrations . . .

De Monts was there. – No, dear Pontgravé, I can see that this is the end, he murmured.

Quite right, said Père Cotton.

He surveyed them all, the whole wretched crew of them, and decided that he had had his fill. He yawned. He curled his fingertips slowly. He fixed on Biencourt, who was so patently a greenhorn. The slightest inclination of a face, the position of a single eyeball in its socket, the way a man mopped his forehead – any one of these things was sufficient to reveal to Père Cotton the greed, the lust, the desperate fears within the skull. – Biencourt's curls twisted and twirled across his shoulders. He had a plump face, still somewhat unformed. His eyes were sunny, and his skin was fair. – Aha, thought Père Cotton, he's the one I'll smash.

My *dear* young friend, began Père Cotton . . . and already Biencourt stood picking at the ruffles of his collar. Not knowing what else to do with the register of baptisms, he tucked it under his arm. He looked down at his shoes, in whose black mirrors he could vaguely see his own face; he tried not to listen, but already Père Cotton's Black-Gowns had seized Biencourt by his buttons in their eagerness to convey their desire to be of service to the Savages of Acadia; and Biencourt was rolled away like a loose rock in a steep rivière. Looking into Père Cotton's eyes at last, he saw a golden flickering.

He could neither comprehend nor believe what had happened. When the monopoly was rescinded that other time, that was one thing, but this –

Only his father's tiny grant of Port-Royal could not be given away, having previously been transferred in all due process by De Monts, with the Roy's approval. But she would ring his father round with Jesuits until he capitulated; failing other means, she would not hesitate to discredit him at Court.

Merde, he said.

. . . Later that day he was led into the Marquise's receiving chamber, and she looked at him and said: My dear boy, has Père Cotton sought to steal your purse, that you look so crossly at him?

No, Madame, he replied. I shall say no word about the matter, which you know as well as I.

Oh, but he hated those two Pères who must accompany him! He had not even met them yet, and already he hated them. In a way he longed to meet them, so that his hatred would gain known faces to feed on, like a crow digging its claws into a hanged traitor's nose . . .

Take it not so hardly, she said. The Pères mean only the good of the Savages, as you yourself know. In such a case, how can I do anything but aid them? And to help *you* I shall speak to the Queen on your behalf; I am certain that she will grant you the post of Vice-Admiral in New France.

He bent the knee miserably. (In his heart he remembered what an English

Captain had told him at the Grand Bank: This assassination in your country? Yes, we all know the Jesuits did it!)

I shall ask the Queen to send you a letter to encourage you in your piety, added Madame de Guercheville.

So at last, in the first month of the following year, it came to this: that Biencourt must pick his way down the streets of Bordeaux, dodging the high-wheeled horse-coaches that splashed him as they raced through the mud-puddles, inquiring for the two Pères at inn after inn (for they were not to be seen at their residence), making way for the workmen rolling their hogsheads (and he bit his lip to see himself grown so small – in Canada he was Prince of land and Savages!), strolling past dockmen stacking sacks, wandering the docks, saying have you seen the Pères Jésuites? they must be told that they will be permitted to accompany me! and he passed the crescent-shaped dinghies, and he tracked his way through the creaking sea-forests of masts, until he had searched for them everywhere but on his own ship! . . .

. . . where, of course, they were waiting for him.

Now at last, cried Père Biard when he saw him, we can begin the LORD's work!

Oh, you dog, said Biencourt very very softly. You dirty, cunning, black-eyed dog . . .

The Journey 1611

Père Massé wished to beguile the time by speaking of marvels. – Have you heard of the great gar-fish that the Sieur de Pontgravé found in the Rivière of the Yroquois? he asked, flushed with excitement.

No, said Père Biard.

The sailors told me of it. They claim that these gar-fish reach eight feet, that they are as thick as a man's thigh, that they bristle with scales thick enough to turn the edge of a knife! Can you believe it? What a fight it must be to land one of those! I can scarcely imagine it. Beaks as long as your arm, and they have double rows of teeth! The sailors said that they lunge so viciously they even leave the water to snatch up birds!

They must be demons, said Père Biard. You must watch yourself, Ennemond. Too much curiosity about demons is not good.

But the sailors said –

Yes, and do the sailors love you? Do you trust in them? Have you heard the things they say about us? Why, just today I heard them call me a filthy black crow.

Nonetheless, said Père Massé stubbornly, I would like to see one of these gar-fish.

I am sure you will, brother, said Père Biard. Make the Fifth Exercise, and peer down into Hell.

They sailed on, west and west across the foggy sea. The voyage was long; it was very long. Not until after four months did they reach Canada.

Père Biard

. . . dreams, above all, have here credit.

SAINT JEAN DE BRÉBEUF, on the Huron Nations, *Jesuit Relations* (1635)

The Jesuit is no dreamer: he is emphatically a man of action; action is the end of his existence.

PARKMAN, *The Jesuits in North America* (1867)

Père Biard could not get over the darkness of this Country. On the voyage out (for the Stream of Time now draws me a week or two backward, thanks to a little tourbillon or whirlpool) the water-casks became almost empty, and so they moored a boat to an ice-mountain in the sea and filled them. Then Père Biard stood looking at the mist and glare and sparkle of the ice and thought that he had never seen such brightness. Père Massé was half-blinded by the dazzle, at which Père Biard said eh, brother, consider how much light there will be in Heaven! at which Père Massé (who never complained) smiled patiently. But later, when the new coast appeared before them, the two Black-Gowns saw trees going north and south and west forever, as thick as the crowds at Paris, and there was a great darkness rising from them like a smell. – And how dark the nights were! – In the dreams of the sailors at first glowed copper nuggets in the ledges of sea-cliffs and gold shining serenely, for having no higher purpose they craved to enrich themsleves; but night by night the ship drew closer to the Savages, who could sometimes be seen dancing on sandy spits by moonlight; and the ship had now passed through the fog of the Great Bank as if into another realm and there was that black tree-coast flashing before them so alarmingly: then the darkness was made up of the sounds of demons. There was GOUGOU in the water, whose hairy tendrils the Savages had often seen lashing the black waves into storms (Père Biard had not yet glimpsed this monster, but supposed it must be some sea-devil, with a body like a jellyfish); and Smoking the Pipe (with whom Père Biard had more than once come to words) assured him that the wind was a monster, and the trees were monsters, and so were the rocks and rivers – statements which the Black-Gowns had no reason to doubt, this being in truth the Devil's Country. Inside the Habitation at Port-Royal it was not so dark; there were light and mosquitoes on the long boards, which were rippled like the sea from hand-chisels (everything was wood, that being so plentiful in this country); there were tiny windows. And yet the darkness made walls around the walls, day and night. They were walls that the sea ran through. The Savages tunneled through them laughing and yelling.

The Conversion of the Souriquois

1611

Aota Chabaya: – You can have your way and we shall have ours; everyone values his own wares.

A Souriquois, to Père Biard

They crossed the Grand Bank, as I have already told. They intersected paths with Champlain's ship, which was floundering amidst the icebergs; Champlain was doing very well, merci; he'd had a victory over some Hiroquois . . . They coasted round Terre-Neuve and reached Acadia at last, where Père Biard saw Souriquois boats riding down the wide rivers of Acadia, Souriquois faces peering shyly at his upheld Cross. Surely they could be made into decorous and well-ruled persons.

On the Day of Pentecost, not long after the feast for Born Underwater's first walking-alone, they made haven, for which grace all on that ship were very joyous. The beach-gate stood open. Poutrincourt's men were waiting on the strand, hurling their caps into the air and shouting for joy. They looked very thin and ragged. Here there were also Savages.

The two priests stood watching the harbor close about them. – I do not suppose we shall ever leave this place, said Père Massé.

We go where GOD sends us, replied the Superior shortly.

Around his head shrieked the birds called liver-snatchers.

Three rivers flowed into the harbor at Port-Royal. At the mouth of the largest was an island covered with pines, firs, spruces, birches, aspens and oaks. Biencourt's ship landed close by, and Père Biard smiled to see so pretty a sight. As for Père Massé, he too admired what he saw, almost as greatly as the Sieur de Denys, who lived in Acadia later that century, and wrote that great things might be accomplished there, *provided,* as he said, *that the envy of the French, one against the other, does not ruin the best-intentioned plans.*

Biencourt ran ashore and embraced his father. Then the Black-Gowns saw him say something into his ear, and at once he became sour. – Ah, said Père Massé to himself. Now our fame reaches New France.

The other sailors disembarked, laughing to see so much greenness, throwing their caps in the air, drinking fresh water from the rivières. The Souriquois stood watching. Their faces were painted red and blue.

Now Madame de Poutrincourt emerged, pale and tremulous, from her cabin (for she had been prevailed upon at last to make the adventure). Her husband embraced her. – Now you must tell me, my Claudette, your impression of this Canada that's consumed our wealth! he said presently, with a jocularity that fooled no one.

It's like a music box! she exclaimed in wonder; at which he said: Whatever do you mean?

When I was a girl, Jean, I had one of those toys, painted with griffins and strange landscapes. The music was so sweet to me that I wanted to look inside and see the Country that it contained. Of course that was impossible. But now it seems to me that I am finally come there –

So you like it? You are happy?

She smiled at him, but her eyes watered.

Now the unloading began, for those who dwelled at Port-Royal were in straits due to hunger. The sailors rolled casks and barrels down onto the beach, paying no more attention to the priests than if they had been insects. Père Massé, who was a man of great strength, strode forward to help them, but Père Biard plucked his sleeve. One of the sea-ruffians spat on the deck near where they stood, and Père Biard treasured up that grudge forever. But they had expected no other welcome than this, and were well prepared. Père Biard's eyes glittered like sword-points as he strode down the gangplank at last, and Père Massé behind him was compelled to admire his courage. – Poutrincourt saw them and turned away.

Let us sit under that pleasant tree and wait until he has leisure for us, brother, said Père Massé.

So be it, said the other.

They seated themselves beneath a tall pine, and Père Biard saw his companion's lips moving slowly in prayer. He himself was greatly in dread of the coming interview. By ignoring him as he had, Poutrincourt had made him ashamed, although he knew perfectly well that he had no reason to feel shame toward anyone but Our FATHER. The years at Port-Royal would be very gloomy, and his task defeated before it began, if he gave in to his humiliation (which he did not dare to confess even to Père Massé, for fear that the other might lose confidence in him). He would begin at the very mouth of the Stream of Time, by the great log of driftwood in which was carved the *Anima CHRISTI*: *Soul of CHRIST, sanctify me. Body of CHRIST, save me . . .* Stripping off the cassock called his body, he took a deep breath and dove into the water.

The entrance to the Stream of Time was dangerous, for there were many hidden eddies and whirlpools in that part. When he had first made the Exercises in Rouen he'd questioned his Superiors about this, saying: Surely it would be better if GOD made the way easy at the beginning, to encourage us! but at this the Superiors raised their hands aghast, saying: You must rid yourself of such thoughts, my son, for they indicate that you do not desire to go straight to GOD, but rather expect Him to come straight to your inordinate attachment. – Then he was ashamed, and strove to comprehend. Being zealous in his learning, he soon grasped the point, at which many other things became clear to him like water flowing with infinities of wrinkles through the grass. Of *course* the Stream of Time must have rocks and rapids. Of *course* he would be expected to ascend it, not to be borne down by it into the Sea of Hell. Having understood these principles, he could now apply himself to the geography. The best approach, then, was to starboard. The entrance was narrow (*strait is the way to the Kingdom of Heaven*) due to an islet to the larboard side, beyond which the Savages sometimes constructed weirs of rocks and stout branches; these became so overwhelmed with silver souls swimming like those fish called Gaspereaux that the Savages often found themselves compelled to break down what they had built, in order to prevent them from befoulment and ruin due to such large numbers; then the convulsing souls were washed back into Hell. So it was best to enter to starboard. One must now swim upstream for many leagues, showing patience (which is pleasing to GOD) and diligence in approaching the purity desired. Whenever one was caught in a whirlpool of sin, it was necessary to immediately extricate oneself, before any sensation of pleasure at the effortless whirling-in could enter one's heart; then one must swim toward the bank until it became shallow enough to stand; there one was required to place his hand on his chest, repenting the circumstance of his fall. After this it was permissible to rest sufficiently to regain one's strength; then, renewing one's resolution, one might continue with the Exercise, swimming upstream toward the First Rapid . . .

A duck quacked. The river was loud in his ears. He heard the rustle of Père

Massé's cassock. Slowly he opened his eyes, and saw the Sieur de Poutrincourt standing before him, with many men gathered around.

Pères, shall we go to my house and have a little chat?

Père Biard rose to his feet and bowed. Père Massé was already standing. They followed the Sieur in silence, the two of them, and the hatred that they felt from all present was like a glaring light. Raising his head high, Père Biard strode on. Père Massé smiled vaguely.

Please sit down, said the Sieur.

He'd already seated himself in his grand fauteuil, the arms of which spilled down in smooth wooden waterfall-curves. He leaned his head back against the rack of frozen abacus-beads that comprised the headboard.

He hesitated, and made a little mouth of distaste. – Conditions are not easy here, he said. The harvest was not large last fall, winter was severe, and we have almost nothing left to eat. Relations with the Savages are poor. One of our young men committed an outrage upon a squaw, and it is dangerous to approach any Souriquois at present. The child is strange, they say. Last month some of the warriors approached me once again with red-painted faces, and I was obliged to make them many presents. Many *expensive* presents.

The Black-Gowns waited.

What I wish to tell you, said Poutrincourt with abrupt firmness, is that there must be no discord here at Port-Royal. I shall expect you to obey me and follow my judgement in daily matters, and make no more enemies than you already have. Do you comprehend me?

The Black-Gowns looked into his face. Seeing Père Massé about to utter some words of a conciliatory nature, which he believed might well be interpreted by this man as weakness, Père Biard quickly interposed himself, saying ironically: – Well, Monsieur, as your friend Monsieur Lescarbot so aptly said in one of his pamphlets, *to think of living as the Savages do seems to me out of all reason.* I cannot agree more. Père Massé and I are here solely to amend them. We shall live on thorns and acorns like them, if need be, and exercise our influence among the French only for their good.

Poutrincourt coughed and could think of nothing to reply. Père Massé looked down at the ground.

I hope that there will be peace among us, said Poutrincourt at last. Then again his eyes flashed. – Are you Pères prepared to render obedience to me in matters civil or do you intend to instigate your Jesuit treasons here? I am as good a Christian as any, but I know about you! There will be no plots and assassinations in Port-Royal, Messire – of that I assure you!

At this, Père Massé held his peace, but Père Biard commenced to expostulate loudly, at which Poutrincourt said: so! in this Army of two, *you* are the General! and Père Biard said you are blasphemous and ungodly – but now Poutrincourt smiled, having as he thought taken Père Biard's measure, and said: I know my duty, Père, and I beg you will leave me to do it. I, with my sword, have hopes of Paradise, just as well as you with your breviary. Show me my path to Heaven; I shall show you yours on earth.

Oh, *faridondaine!* cried Père Biard in disgust.

Still Père Massé said nothing.

Robert and Biencourt

Seeing Biencourt's harquebus leveled at his heart, Robert Pontgravé hesitated – not out of fear, as Biencourt well knew, for the man was fearless. He could see the muscles twitching slowly in Robert's freckled arms, and he knew that Robert was wondering whether he should make a rush and seize the gun.

You're under arrest, in the name of the Roy. (Thus Biencourt, hoping that his icy voice formed a skin of opacity over his heart.)

Robert smiled.

Well? Are you coming or must I shoot you? I'll do it, you know.

I know you, Biencourt.

What does that mean? Are you coming or not?

I'm coming.

Come out slowly. I *pray* that you force me to kill you –

Robert said nothing. Biencourt stepped back and swung the barrel of the harquebus so that Robert could see it gleaming in the sunny hatchway, and he came up with his big hands wide open ready to take the gun if Biencourt should try some treachery.

Now this way. You, Hébert! Cover him while he walks the gangplank. Good, Robert. Very good. Now into the shallop. My father is waiting.

Two men, and all for me, laughed Robert. You must think me quite redoubtable.

The Savages think so.

Eh, them . . .

May I shoot him, Seigneur? (Thus Monsieur Hébert.) It would give me great pleasure.

Even dead he'd bring us trouble, said Biencourt. Even dead, at the bottom of the water, with a collar of iron hatchets about his neck.

I pray that your father will give him to the Savages, said Hébert. Let them cut his scalp out.

Even then he'd plague us, said Biencourt bitterly. You, Robert, lie down on your face. Don't move until I command you.

At your service, said Robert. He lay down on the bilgy planks and put his arm under his head with contemptuous lassitude. (This man could run down a moose to exhaustion.) He fell asleep.

Possession

When Robert was fairly seized, and conveyed to an empty Store-house (in Canada there is a Store-house by every waterfall), the Sieur de Poutrincourt was content, as if this prize might momentarily offset his failing fortunes. Here was a decision which could be easily made. Were it not that the prisoner were Pontgravé's son, Poutrincourt would have hanged him. As it was, he would take some revenge – first because the man had outraged several squaws, which was dishonorable and against GOD; secondly because he had disrupted trade; third because he had defied Poutrincourt's authority; and fourthly because the Jesuits were here – not that *they* could be laid at Robert's door, but they increased Poutrincourt's need to inflict pain. In this strain his son encouraged him, as he thought. So Poutrincourt had half decided to brand Robert's forehead and return him to some French prison. For his Canadian dream was now akin to one of the grey bands on the trunks of trees that mark the high water of spring – *viz.*, only a sort of ring-stain, which was easily colored to vengefulness. – In France that libertine would be burned! he muttered to himself. Then, scowling, he returned to his gristmills. There were many fine waterfalls at Port-Royal. To Poutrincourt every rapid in the Stream of Time had a purpose – *viz.*, to turn some water-wheel or other. And I for one cannot blame him.

Robert still slept, dreaming happily. Someday he'd go upstream to China where the Chinese girls had breasts pale yellow like the blooms of dubious water stargrass . . .

Charity

When the Black-Gowns heard how a Christian soul now languished under guard at Port-Royal, their hearts were filled with pity – although some would say that their real emotion was one of pious joy at this chance to do Robert, and therefore his father, a kindness so opportunely. With old Pontgravé in their debt, no doubt they could set up shop at Kebec as well, where Monsieur de Champlain seemed to be establishing a French presence most effectively . . . – But even if this had truly been their rationale, we could not fault Père Massé (who never celebrated Mass save in a hair-shirt) or his Superior, Père Biard, for their *purpose* was as silver and gold. – Granted, it had scarcely been realized; since the Savages, taking their cue from Poutrincourt, considered them to be haughty, unfriendly and potentially treacherous – so it is no ill reflection on them that their inclinations turned with relief toward one of their own, whose case they could assuredly better and who therefore would requite them with something less piquant than scorn; the only other soul who even returned their greeting was Membertou, who, having once given his medicine-bag to Messire Fléché to be burned, now felt obliged to remain a Christian, as he had surely offended KLUSKAP and the other Powers by this action. He considered the Black-Gowns to be great dreamers, sons of IESVS the Saqmaw of the Dead. Poutrincourt, who could scarcely encourage a Savage to give up the Faith, had become the equivalent of a "pinioned" piece in a chess game – a state of mind at least more certain than his habitual indecision. The Black-Gowns were not indecisive at all. Once their minds were made up on a question, Poutrincourt was no match for them.

There is a matter which I must discuss with you, Seigneur de Poutrincourt. (Thus Père Biard.)

Yes?

The priest stood very rigid, so that none could see the dread within him.

It would be greatly to your credit in the Hereafter, Seigneur, were you to grant pardon to Robert Pontgravé. I have visited him in the dungeon to give him confession – I can see that he repents from the bottom of his heart.

I see that you are beginning already to forget what I have told you, said Poutrincourt very coldly. Who permitted you access there?

It is no matter. I gave him absolution also. Forgive me if I trespassed –

Was it my son?

Père Biard swallowed. – Yes. But only at my insistence. Do not blame him, Seigneur, I entreat you –

Oh, now you tell me how to behave toward my own son. Tell me, Père, are all of you Jesuits cunning in this way, to get first a toehold, then a foothold, and then to trample everything down? I ask you: who gave you the right to be here?

Père Biard stood silent, breathing heavily.

I ask you, Père Biard!

God did.

Eh – eh – you lugubrious crow!

It is ill for all of us French if we are enemies in such a place, said the Black-Gown, as patiently as he could. Surely you must see this, Seigneur. What sort of example do we set for the Savages by quarreling among ourselves?

And what example, pray, has young Pontgravé set for them by outraging their women one after another? Now they tell me that one of the girls hanged herself! Do you condone this?

You do, Seigneur – not I. You condone it by permitting it to fester in his breast. Give him absolution as I have. Do you plan to imprison him forever?

Père Massé was in the room as well, but until then he had been so quiet that Poutrincourt had forgotten his existence. There were ticks and lice in his hair-shirt, and sometimes when people saw him smiling they imagined that he was mocking them, when in fact he was just smiling at the terrible burning and itching which he would not scratch. Now he said very softly: Seigneur, please understand that what this man has done is as much of an abomination to us as to you. How can violence and fornication be pleasing in our sight? But let us be practical. These things will continue to happen until this Country is settled with good French girls . . .

Well, well, said Poutrincourt. This is quite a determined embassy with which I have to deal. You chide and scold me like bluejays. Very good. I shall release him; *you* will stand surety for his good behavior. But – if I may say such things to men of God – know now that you stand in equal case for your own. And now get out, for I cannot bear the sight of you.

Fealty

Monsieur (thus Poutrincourt, coldly), I beg you to inform me whether you are prepared to render me due submission.

Robert bowed his head. His neck-muscles jumped.

I do not believe I heard your reply, Monsieur.

Yes, Seigneur, said Robert in a low voice.

Yes what?

I submit to your authority.

I suppose you are aware that the Savages hate you hereabouts.

Robert stood as if waiting.

Do you know that?

They hate me, Seigneur, but they also admire me –

I said, do you know that?

Yes, Seigneur.

And have you a point of view on the subject?

No, Seigneur.

I could hang you, you know. Charles Biencourt yearns to do it with his own hands. Swooping Like a Hawk would gladly split your head.

Robert waited.

You and your associates are to remain on Emenemic Isle, unless you need to go to the mainland for purposes of trade. You are never to come to this seigneurie without my express and advance permission. You are to render tribute to me, or in my absence to Charles Biencourt. I shall not demand of you the full fifth part, but you must set aside a tenth of what you gain in the trade.

But, Seigneur –

Do you agree to be bound by these conditions?

Does it matter whether I agree?

Throw him back in the Store-house, Hébert.

No, I agree to your conditions, Seigneur.

Shall I chain him again, Seigneur?

No, no, Hébert; he is learning to be true to me. – Eh bien, Robert. You are to depart my domains immediately. If it were not for my friendship with your father . . .

Seigneur, I ask leave to make my Confession first.

Ah, so indeed the Jesuits are at the bottom of this.

Robert waited.

The Gifts

Père Massé made no great demonstration, but Père Biard wrung Robert's hand most joyfully to find him freed. (Robert's hand was as broad and heavy as a mason's adze.) He took a rosary and gave it to him, begging him most ardently to remember its use. Robert gazed at him for a moment. He had become sickly in the darkness of the Store-house. Suddenly he showed his teeth in a smile. He pulled a chain from around his neck and put it into Père Biard's hand. There was a whistle at the end of it. – My friend Capitaine Merveille once gave me this, he said. I know its note well. If you should ever be searching for me, come to my Country and sound this. I shall hear you. You comprehend me, as I can see . . .

The Work Ahead

Here then are our occupations, wrote Père Biard for inclusion in the *Jesuit Relations,* *to say Mass every day, and to solemnly sing it Sundays and holidays, together with Vespers, and frequently the procession; to offer public prayers morning and evening; to exhort, console, administer the Sacraments, bury the dead; in short, to perform the offices of the Curate, since there are no other priests in these parts.*

His face, in which was united the bitterness of unsatisfied longing with the piercing glance of an analytical intelligence, could not be shut out of anyone's dreams, much less Poutrincourt's, for it hung over them all like a star whose rays could in no way be avoided. He wanted so much to have a glorious victory over himself, to humble himself to the level of the Savages and *give himself to them* as CHRIST had done; then surely he'd have the revelations that Saint Ignatius had had, blessed Ignatius who glimpsed the glowing ovals of the DIVINE PERSONS and even saw Him appearing in the color of a flame of fire! But truly, the condition of the Savages horrified him. They howled day and night; they wiped their filthy hands on their dogs, on rotten wood powder. Then, too, their language seemed to him as senseless as the weepings of seagulls around the spires of churches. It clicked and rattled in their mouths with many sharp consonants.

They stood like a circle of ferns in the forest around him, frail and bittergreen and fresh. He was writing in his journal. – See how he soils those white leaves with strange black marks! they cried, at which Père Biard threw up his hands and said my LORD, my LORD, their *ignorance!*

They greased themselves with seal-oil. They ate congealed grease as if it were bread, and liked no better drink than liquid grease.

He could see their hearts held up to him like baskets of colored porcupine needles; inside lay the untreasured souls, which he desired so fervently to take to him, to cleanse, to hold up naked to the light of GOD. His only role then would be one of renunciation. Would he be sad, then, to see the precious souls vanish from his hands, leaving only light? Or did he desire to be a soul-swallower?

He had learned that they were made up of many tribes or bands, not simply the Souriquois as he had thought at first, but also *Algonquians*, *Montagnais*, and *Etheminquins*, who were nomadic like the Souriquois but spoke a different dialect. Farther off (for apparently Canada went a long way) there was a tribe called the *Irocois*, which these others seemed to fear, but as yet he did not know the nature of these other poor heathens. No doubt in time, when they had all been brought to reason, peace could be made among them.

The Secret Weapon

The Black-Gowns had found the affair of Robert truly providential (or rather Père Biard did, and what Père Massé thought none knew). Rather than establish good relations with Biencourt, which might in the end prove entangling or constraining, Père Biard continued to share his confidences only with his Superiors in France – although they quickly became a shadowy enough crowd in his memories. They were the ones who exercised authority over him. He was not free to be friends with all, no matter what his private desire might be. But Robert was scarcely an entangling interest. He admired Robert greatly for his strength. He almost loved him –

The Etechemins said that Robert had landed this summer at various isles, ports and capes, hobnobbing with the Savages, racing them, wrestling against them, burning his arm in the fire with them to prove his courage, so that they called him a great man. – Poutrincourt was in nowise pleased at this, and his son even less so, but Père Biard's heart soared. It gave him inexpressible happiness to touch the whistle that Robert had given him. He felt no inordinate attachment – he swore to GOD! – but it brought him peace, to see how the young man had trusted him.

The Unhappy Voyage

When a night-owl cried, and one saw it mount high in the air, plummet down and then rise again, good weather could be expected. This was true in Acadia as in France. On a certain morning at the end of Juin, having sighted this bird in the performance of its well-omened acrobatics, Biencourt stood upon the strand bidding farewell to his father. Poutrincourt was preparing to set sail for France with a meager cargo of beaver-peltries, hoping to realize sufficient profit therefrom to support the establishment at Port-Royal yet a little longer. The inordinate length of Biencourt's voyage (even there the Black-Gowns had been jinxes) had required that the biscuits be consumed instead of being saved for trade; as a result, there had been little left to give the Savages in exchange for their furs. Then, too, furs were dearer these days, for the Savages had become greedy. – Poutrincourt stood peering into the half-empty hold, thinking: I might as well ballast this ship with rocks. He shook his head. Descending the gangplank, he made his way to his son, who was pacing in the meadow. Trees were thick upon the rivers. – Biencourt's heart was heavy as lead.

I have no lack of confidence in you, said the father, smiling kindly. Beware only of these Black-Gowns and of Robert Pontgravé's men. They are much more dangerous to us than any Savages.

I do not know when I shall see you again, Biencourt said in a low voice.

Nor I you. Let us commend each other to God.

He sailed out of the harbor, and was lost to sight.

Although he had endeavored to conceal his own uneasiness from his son, believing that doing otherwise could accomplish only harm, yet the truth was that he felt nothing but alarm for his enterprise. Being of the temperament called by learned Doctors *sanguine*, Poutrincourt had always considered caution to be a sort of miserliness with which he did not wish to associate himself. So he'd come to Acadia with blue heart-skies. The problems which had arisen were especially maddening for him because they could not be dealt with through bravery or reason. He paced the deck as they creaked through the seas of Juin and Juillet . . . At night, when he lay down into his berth to sleep, no matter how exhausted he was his eyes would suddenly snap open and his heart begin to pound as he considered the Jesuits seeking to intimidate Biencourt, as his enemies at Court danced about him a laughing circle, as he made desperate plans to mine his assets deeper and deeper, in order to support Port-Royal yet a little longer . . . – On our previous voyage we were almost lost in a sea of pitch-fire, he reminded himself, but the vessel righted herself. This journey can be no worse than that, unless indeed we *are* lost, and I would almost welcome that. – This train of thought appalled him, for he had not thought himself so weary. Even the autumn past, when they had barely escaped that terrible sea of light, had not seen him in such spirits. Indeed, that Captain Rossignol, whom they had dispossessed of his illegal peltries, had felt that way, for upon seeing them about to run aground in a fog he'd seized a knife to kill Captain Timothy, crying: So you are not content with having ruined me, but want to drown me here as well! and Poutrincourt signaled his men, who rushed upon him and held him back; and Poutrincourt ascended into the crow's nest to see where the danger lay and glimpsed a rock ahead like a great black tooth, at which he commended his soul to God; but having done this he felt a rush of vigor, and hurried down to shift sail, commanding the sailors to help him. At first they gazed at him like hypnotized men, but when he persuaded them that much might yet be done, they flocked to the work with a will, and averted their doom; the ship almost grazed the rock as it rushed by . . . For this deed Poutrincourt had been much commended. Now, he thought, he would have stood by with folded arms, but for his anxiety on his family's account. And this saddened him more than his sadness itself.

In the month of Août he made port in France, and requested an interview with Madame de Guercheville, for he had no other recourse. Her reception of him was in unfortunate conformance with his expectations. And why not? There are some people who upon striding into a receiving-room cause others to eye them askance, for with their every step they smear gloom more thickly, as if they had not wiped their boots: such people are very disagreeable. In previous years, the Chevalier de Poutrincourt had never been a member of this class. Having therefore had little to do with fatalists and desperate men, he could not now recognize their disease running riot in himself. Had he had a good agent to represent him – *viz.*, some strapping Courtier with a healthy red face, always laughing and jesting, so that it was patent that he wanted nothing, then of course he would have been given all. Do usurers lend their coin to men who truly need it? Do Roys confer favor on those who would be most benefited thereby? Do Mademoiselles love Cavaliers who have found no one to love them? – Sometimes. Sometimes palm-trees grow in Canada (I have seen them in the engravings of De Bry). – Having only himself to go before Madame de Guercheville, he could do little more than draw upon the already almost exhausted capital of her sympathy.

Of course I shall help you, Monsieur, she said when he had kissed her hand, but I have not heard very favorable things about you or your son in the letters from Père Biard.

I know not what to say to you about that, Madame, he said. Believe whom you will.

Very well, the Marquise replied. I shall trust you yet a little further. I comprehend your concern for your son, since I myself feel for the Savages of New France as if they were my own children.

Poutrincourt flushed.

And how is young Charles Biencourt? she inquired. He is quite a sportsman, as I have been told, although I did not fancy him such when he was introduced to me.

He does well, Madame. I left him in full charge at Port-Royal, and have no doubt of his capacity.

You need not be so stiff with me, she said. I know more than I would wish about his difficulties. Do you truly believe that you or he can set the good Pères aside for your own vain and worldly purposes? Look about you, Monsieur. This ostentation means nothing to me. I would gladly leave it all to educate the Savage girls of Canada, if there were but a convent there to receive me. As for you, you have a great chance to do good; the Pères are anxious to assist you in this, for the sake of your own soul as well as those of the Savages. Why must you be obstinate? You know, Père Cotton is here today and would love to receive you. I am sure that any hint of friendship on your part would console him; it would please me so much if you and he became friends!

So, Madame, if I bend my knee to him and apologize, then you will undertake to keep my people at Port-Royal from starving?

Pray refrain from addressing me in that manner.

Never mind. I thank you for allowing me to present myself here at the Palace. I shall not trouble you anymore.

Oh, how knightly! she replied in the most scornful tones. But even so I shall not break my word. I said that I would help you, and I shall. A ship will go out. But you must wait until it is ready, for Père Cotton will surely want to meet with the Mission Procurator to determine what my Pères might need.

He waited for four months . . .

The Education

While the Black-Gowns busied themselves that summer, the sailors, who continued to despise them, instructed the Souriquois in their own way. *The first things the poor Savages learn are oaths and vile and insulting words,* wrote Père Biard for the *Jesuit Relations* (of which you may have heard); *and you will often hear the Savagesses (who are, otherwise, very timid and modest), hurl vulgar, vile, and shameless epithets at our people, in the French language; not that they know the meaning of them, but only because they see that when such words are used, there is generally a great deal of laughter and amusement.*

Membertou

One day when Père Biard was reciting with him, *Give us this day our daily bread*, which in the language of the Savages was said *Nui en caraco nac iquem esmoi ciscou*, Henri Membertou smiled and said: But if I did not ask Him for anything but bread, I would be without moose-meat or fish! – Père Biard laughed with him, opening his jaws wide like a wolf.

Ka'qaqus

From his visits to Robert, Père Biard had come to know a cunning Sagamore of Port Saint-Jean, by name *Ka'qaqus*, which means *Crow*. Like all the others, he was swarthy, and clothed himself in beaver-skins. Visiting him, and seeing quickly that he was wicked, Père Biard asked him how many wives he had – hoping, of course, only to goad his conscience a little, for Saint Ignatius had made plain to say that revealing the hidden venial sin of another was itself a venial sin; when the sin was public, however, as in the case of a woman openly prostituting herself (this was Saint Ignatius's example), or when the hidden sin was made known to the sinner to help him vanquish it, then to speak of the sin was permitted. Père Biard had sometimes been reprimanded by the Generals of the Society for being too quick to drag others' sins to light, like a cat dragging some loathsome half-chewed rat into the house; but his defense had always lain in his good intentions. Saint Ignatius had gone on to say that good intentions are necessary but not sufficient, that *there must be grounds or probable reason* for believing that speaking of the sin would help the sinner. Having meditated and prayed over the case of Ka'qaqus the previous evening, Père Biard had come to the conclusion that to speak out was his duty; for since Ka'qaqus lived openly with his many wives the sin was public, even if not acknowledged as a sin by the Savages; as to the *probable reason* for believing that denouncing him would help, Père Biard decided that he *must* believe it, for to assume otherwise implied that Ka'qaqus could not be saved.

Ka'qaqus, said Père Biard with gentle sternness, how many wives do you have?

The Sagamore beamed. – Eight! he said with proud dignity. There they are, those beautiful young women right there, getting clams by the river. I see seven of them. The youngest is inside my wigwam cleaning skins.

And you feel no shame?

Shame, Père? Do you feel shame when you think upon your family? And what of these *nuns* that you have told me about? All of those women are Brides of CHRIST. So CHRIST has more wives than I do, and *He* is not ashamed! Oh, you are both stupid and a blackguard!

All the Savages laughed. And for a moment Père Biard was filled with the sin of anger. He longed to be back in Paris in his high grand chair, explaining Theology to his silently attentive students who rose from their benches only when he told them to, who truly longed to love CHRIST, who were his own. – But let it be enough, he said to himself, to keep before our eyes the vision of these poor natives, these images of our GOD as we are and as capable of enjoying Him, these companions of our own species, and almost of the same quality as we, who are upon the edge of the horrible gulf of the fires of Hell, many of them even precipitated every day into eternal torments and profound depths of everlasting punishment without hope of deliverance.

Biencourt Proves Steadfast

In the month of Août, Père Biard asked leave to meet Robert at Emenemic, in order to learn the Souriquois language from him, and have the Apostles' Creed translated. Biencourt refused, for he was suspicious that the Jesuits might be conspiring with Robert and perhaps the Basques. After all, Basques had sought to foment treason on his father's ship the previous year.

As for the Apostles' Creed, he said, that I can translate for you myself. My command of the Souriquois tongue is no whit inferior to Robert's.

No, said Père Biard. You do not mean me well, I can see that. Who knows what obscenity you would insert in your conjugations and translations?

So be it, said Biencourt wearily.

The Speech-Hurlers

Membertou now held an eat-all feast in his wigwam, to which many repaired, bringing their birchbark bowls. All the men wore their necklaces of tanned Armouchiquois scalps, smiling and twisting them dreamily. The Black-Gowns were present. They smoked tobacco with the rest, but timidly. They made no compliments on the scalps, which made the men somewhat sullen; other Iron People were better mannered. Then Père Biard was observed attempting to give some of his meat to the dogs in secret, at which they raised up a great outcry against his lack of courtesy, but when he flushed and said nothing his companion Père Massé apologized for him, citing the ignorance of both Black-Gowns so recently arrived here in this Country, so that the anger of the People was eased against that taboo-breaking, and the feast continued merrily. At last matters had reached the stage where it was customary to give orations in praise of the feast-giver.

This is a most generous Saqmaw! exclaimed Born Swimming's husband, Swooping Like a Hawk. He had knotted his hair and put a feather in it, to be distinguished for this feast. – Today this most generous Saqmaw has filled our bellies with moose-meat. He has entertained us here in his wigwam. He has advised us well in peace and led us to victory against our enemies, so that we have split open many heads and gained honor as a People. He has befriended the Iron People, so that we now gain new axes for us men, new kettles for our wives. Someday the Iron People will give us guns again. Therefore we are very content. – I have spoken.

This was considered a good speech.

Next it was the turn of the Black-Gowns. Père Massé spoke first, briefly, thanking Membertou for the repast, and expressing a desire to return the hospitality when resources permitted, at which all cried *ho, ho!* being eager to learn what new delicacies the Black-Gowns might provide. Then Père Biard arose, and began to speak of JESUS, as was his way, and all watched Membertou's face to see whether he might be content, but indeed he was, and puffed at his pipe in great tranquility, for he had come to love Him. – But after that stood the Shaman, Smoking the Pipe; and he said: Membertou, I too thank you for this fine feast, which makes me happy in my belly. And I am pleased also for your sake, that the Powers of these Black-Gowns who respect dead men have become good in your sight. And I am pleased likewise for myself, because I continue to respect the Powers of this Country as my fathers have done. This I will continue to do until the end of my life – I swear by the SUN!

At this Membertou's face clouded over, but looking around him he perceived that more people were in agreement with Smoking the Pipe's speech than opposed it, and so he said nothing, and likewise the Black-Gowns were silent, although Père Massé appeared ill at ease and Père Biard darted many venomous looks at him who had thus proclaimed himself his enemy.

Friendliness

Biencourt had not been present at this feast, for proof had reached him that Robert Pontgravé was preparing some new treason. – As if there weren't enough! The plupart of the French traders already refused to yield up their lawful portion of beaver-furs gained in trade that season, for which rebellion

Biencourt must now prepare to do deeds of blood, as in previous years. Robert and his men had enrolled under the banners of that selfsame evil, it seemed, for when he sent a messenger to collect the tenth part of his beavers, the man returned bearing nothing save purple bruises, with two of his teeth knocked out. Indeed, we must acknowledge that Canada remained in its primitive stage then, when the French had only each other to use for their enemies. In time they would have the English, and then the Iroquois; but for the moment they must choke upon the loathing bred by familiarity. – So Biencourt spent that evening coaching one of his Deputies, Louys Hébert. The next day, while Biencourt bit his nails and paced the strand where his father had once walked with the Sieur de Champlain, the Swiss mercenaries filed blank-faced to receive their powder and shot from the Store-house, and then Hébert led them at his command to the shallop, their aim being to capture Robert and clap him in sure ward. They gained the fort, but neither Robert nor Captain Merveille were there. Undoubtedly they knew well how to roam the forests most cunningly, like Savages . . .

Providence

So we see that no Frenchman was happy in Canada during those days. Fortunately, however, the sickly season came at last.

The first accomplishment of the two priests was the baptism and salvation of a dying nine-year-old girl.

Certainly you dark Crows can have her, her father said. Now she is good for nothing, like a dog.

Père Biard and Père Massé took her in, cared for her, nourished her and instructed her. Presently it became clear that she would not live. That pleased the two Black-Gowns exceedingly, for that meant she could not relapse in her faith. They baptized her Antoynette de Pons, after their royal sponsor, Madame de Guercheville. She carried the name to Heaven with her soon after.

Yes, said Père Massé, with a kind of weary joy, as he prepared her for burial, she is our firstborn.

You are correct in what you say, brother, replied Père Biard. Truly we can say with Joseph that GOD has made us forget our past hardships and the bones of our Fathers.

Other infants died, some of a peculiar disease which had never before been seen in the Souriquois Country, so that some Savages (particularly Smoking the Pipe) blamed the Black-Gowns, fearing them for Sorcerers, but the Black-

Gowns knew better. They baptized all the innocent babes they could and reckoned them up so happily; just as Swooping Like a Hawk was so contented when he smoked his pipe to the scalps of the men he had killed; these hung in the wigwam . . .

More Angels

It was summer's end when the deaths began, and Born Swimming and Swooping Like a Hawk had moved their wigwam, after which Swooping Like a Hawk was successful in his hunting, and soon brought down a moose. He strode home and threw down a great joint of meat in front of the wigwam. Born Swimming became glad, and began to sing and dance with all her children. Swooping Like a Hawk's mother also danced, although she was very old, and could not move her limbs very well. They devoured the meat on the spot, eating some raw, cooking the rest on sticks over the hearth-fire, cutting off the outer layer as soon as it was roasted. So they filled their bellies. Sighing, Swooping Like a Hawk lay down by the fire to sleep, while Born Swimming and her two oldest daughters set out to bring back the carcass.

LN'UK QUILLWORK PATTERN: KAGWET THE STARFISH

Born Swimming boiled the fattest moose intestines and made them into rolls. The lean meat her daughters sliced and smoked. They prepared a feast from the nose and tongue. Then Born Swimming set out to invite the widows and orphans to partake. In that winter many had gone hungry, and it was a common sight to see the skinny children sucking patiently on old clots of moose-blood. To ease their stomachs they smoked tobacco and sang songs, widows and children together. Now they were very happy to be summoned by Born Swimming's tender words, and hastened to the wigwam with their birchbark bowls.

Again they praised her new child, Born Underwater, at which she was highly contented. And she was very proud of her other children, who contributed so much to the feast. But within a moon they had all died of the new disease, excepting her youngest child, baby Born Underwater.

At that she hated the Iron People once again, and sang to herself: *My heart weeps tears of blood. I must blot out this outrage with blood.*

The Capture of Captain Merveille

Autumn fell, and the forest became a chasuble of red velvet with gold flowers down the side, its skinny leaf-arms outstretched in grasping prayer. Now came the furious wind-gusts that could dislodge trees from the ground. The waterfowl flew south. The leaves on the trees, which a few days before had been flaming gold, were now an earth-dull brownish-yellow, and the many bare trees around them crowded each other like thin posts, as snow flurried down from the grey sky.

On the third day of Octobre, Biencourt set out with sixteen men and two Savages for a second attempt to capture Robert Pontgravé. With them came Père Biard. – I do not require you, said Biencourt coldly, but Père Biard only smiled and said: That is a matter which only GOD knows. – At this, Biencourt swung round as if to lay hands on the priest, at which the others cried out in horror, for though they had no love for Jesuits they were yet pious enough to respect the cloth. – Père Biard stood awaiting the blow. For a moment Biencourt almost admired him. This must have shown upon his face, for Père Biard seized that moment to say very softly that he wished only to be of use, and that since young Pontgravé had a special understanding with him, his presence might incline him to give up peacefully. – At this, knowing that he had spoken true words, Biencourt lowered his fist slowly, saying nothing. Then he turned on his heel, and they all boarded the shallop together.

The day was very peaceful, the water light and blue like Heaven. Biencourt rowed with a will, to set the men an example. Some animation had come into the Switzers' soldier's faces, and they began to work their mouths as if chewing at something. They were famous for their love of killing other nationalities, as Biencourt had learned from his father: that was why they were in such demand. – Where was his father now? He had had no word from him for a long time. He remembered a dream he'd had shortly before accompanying his father to Canada for the first time. He dreamed of looking out a window in some alien place and seeing nothing but water, a world of it lapping, brownish-greyish-green, and that water was so perfectly pure . . . Suddenly he saw a Savagess falling from the sky. She fell into the water and drowned and instantly the water was vile. And it seemd to him as he rowed that the strait had become vile, the water heavy in its color, and he saw that Père Biard was casting his black shadow upon him.

When they arrived at the isle called Emenemic, on the far side of the fort, Biencourt commanded Père Biard to remain on board the shallop by himself, but the priest most courteously asked leave to accompany them.

You! laughed Biencourt. And would you carry an harquebus?

You know full well that doing so would be against my vows.

Your vows! Ah yes, I forgot. You're vowed to Robert; you desire nothing better than to pillow your head beside him –

Cease your filthy insinuations, Seigneur, or I swear to you –

Yes?

Père Biard turned away for a moment. He smoothed a wrinkle in his cassock.

You know that I desire nothing save the keeping of the peace between you, he said when he had regained mastery of himself.

Come, Seigneur! (Thus Louys Hébert.) The more time we waste, the farther our birds may fly. Indeed, what if they listen even now in the bushes, and prepare some ambush?

Biencourt put his hands on his hips, and looked Père Biard up and down.

I suppose you will come then, Père. You are marvelously adroit at getting your way.

Once again they found Pontgravé and Captain Merveille away. There were three men at the fort, dressed in rags, who seemed very content to surrender. One wore a bloody nightcap. – Don't beat me, brothers, he kept saying. I didn't do it. A horse kicked me in the balls when I was young. I'm impotent, you see. – The second man spat on the floor, but the third only closed his eyes as he held out his hands to Hébert to be tied. – Very good, very good, cried Biencourt (and Père Biard saw that he was excited, that so little went right for him that this meaningless and contemptible victory enriched the boy's Store-house of happiness). – I'm not a common man, the one in the nightcap was saying. In my family we once had a Duc de Poitiers . . . – Shall I smack him one, Seigneur? (Thus Hébert.) – Leaving this unanswered, Biencourt strutted about. – Listen, animal, he said to the prisoner. We're going to build a gallows outside. And we're going to hang your leaders. What do you have to say to that? – Very sure of himself now, Hébert punched the man in the mouth, and Biencourt smiled faintly. – Père Biard looked on sorrowfully. As they were but subalterns who obeyed what Robert commanded, Biencourt's men did not treat them harshly, but gagged them and locked them in the secure ward of their own Store-house. Then they waited. Biencourt walked back and forth, and the floorboards creaked beneath him. When it was nearly evening, Père Biard asked leave to bring water to the prisoners, but Biencourt only clasped his hands behind his back and continued to pace. He was considering the case of Robert with great pleasure. They were not in France, and solutions were simple. – At nightfall they heard footsteps in the dry leaves of the forest. Two Basques.

Biencourt gave the signal, and then they rushed upon them before they could point their arquebuses. – Into the Store-house to join the others!

It was very late now. They went outside and the moon rose and Biencourt paced. Père Biard said that he had a plan. Before the others could stop him, he raised the whistle to his lips and blew. A long sweet note came from it – not loud, but vibrantly penetrating.

Seized with fury, Biencourt hurled him to the ground.

So now you warn them, traitor! he shouted.

Père Biard stood up and smiled at him – as gently (so he himself thought) as a child.

Look, Seigneur, he said.

There was a shimmering in the air at the edge of the forest. Beams of light seemed to thrash and whirl. Then slowly a man's shape was formed from this light. Now the silhouette began to darken like cooling lava, and Captain Merveille stood before them.

Where is Robert? he said. Robert whistled for me, didn't he?

Biencourt and his men gazed at him steadfastly, leveling their arquebuses at his heart.

Eh, it was cooler at Kebec, he said.

Step forward, you Devil.

Surely it was a Devil who called me here with that satanic, demonic, Mephistophelean and diabolical whistle. Who was it? You, Père? For shame!

We were looking for Robert . . . – Père Biard burst out.

So I see.

Tie his wrists, Hébert. (Thus Biencourt.)

Do you always employ him to do your thuggish deeds?

Where is Robert?

Robert? Why don't you whistle him up, Biencourt? Or ask your priestly Judas –

Shall I do it, Seigneur? (Thus Père Biard.)

Biencourt hesitated. – No, I do not like your whistle.

Shall I throw it on the fire then?

Biencourt appeared not to have heard this. He turned to the prisoner, who was now well bound. – Where is Robert? I ask for the last time.

Ah, but you will not capture Robert tonight, laughed Captain Merveille. He has a sweetheart among the Etechemins . . .

Oh, you libertine dog!

You are a fine Cavalier. It is edifying to see how you do duels with a pinioned man.

Biencourt stood over him, breathing heavily.

A sweetheart, laughed Merveille. A dead sweetheart among the Etechemins. I myself have a dead sweetheart at Kebec.

He began to shimmer again, and disappeared.

Witchcraft! the men whispered.

Shut up, said Biencourt. You'll keep this secret. And remember this: I felt flesh and bone when I struck him. My fist didn't go through him; you saw that. And when we catch Robert –

A New Leaf

They waited all night. In the morning Père Biard said: Let me go alone into the forest, Seigneur, and I'll search him out.

With your whistle?

Yes.

He gave it to you?

Yes.

You care nothing for witchcraft?

It's not witchcraft.

Very well, priest. Perhaps GOD will help you, if indeed you believe in Him.

The Black-Gown said: Do you give your word that you will not harm him if he gives himself up of his own accord?

Yes, priest.

Père Biard began to walk away. Over his shoulder he said: Biencourt, you know far less than you believe.

Biencourt spat.

Rich white combs of tree-trunks stood below the stream-notched hills of other forests, raising up their branch-arms in suppliancy, but the other forests were so far away as to be bluish-grey; it was unlikely that they heard these lower tree-prayers. The air was chilly. Brown rivers flowed wide and still between the leaning walls of birch, and grey trees and green trees grew as thickly as hairs on a head. Evergreens ranked themselves on the ledges of grey hill-cliffs; patches of snow glared in the wet green grass.

He raised the whistle to his lips and blew it. Robert was not, could not be, a bad man. – Again that sweet note. A breeze from nowhere blew the branches of trees apart, and he saw a river.

The river circled broadly left and right and left again, girdling lakes of a diamond shape, like snake-scales, and the trees were a wall and the grass was a wall on either side. Père Biard smiled to himself. All his life he had followed streams of prayer clear and shadowed with trout-rainbows; this was nothing to him. Now in the muck he saw the deep footprints of a vigorous man, like the deep round hoofprints of a moose.

His heart ached with joy.

He tracked him through the deep forest crevasses where the torrents went. The smell of beeches and yellow birches clamored in his nostrils like great bells of wildness. The moose-browsed twigs snapped against his body. Then the tree-darkness was all about him like the darkness of Souriquois souls, and he knelt on a bed of moss to pray.

Is it you, priest? came a voice from behind him.

Of course it is I, said Père Biard. You are in a bad case, Robert.

That I know. – The voice was desolate.

Come out and let me see you, Robert my son.

No, you comc into my shadc . . . This way. And how do you like the outsiders now?

Outsiders?

Biencourt and his crew.

But you know them better than I! Why do you call them that?

Eh, you know well, said Robert in a threatening voice.

They were walking a path of darkness. Robert was ahead. He never turned to show his face.

I know what they require of you, said Père Biard.

For me to give myself up? To their so-called mercy? But they can't comprehend how dappled it is here, how among the leaves, brown puddles gleam like deers' eyes. I've learned to run with the deer!

And with the Savages?

There are no Savages anymore, Père Biard, I swear to you. No – upon my oath! The necessary steps were taken . . .

What about Born Swimming? said Père Biard searchingly.

I recognize no obligations, replied the man in a trembling voice. There are no obligations here in Canada.

Ah, so you play that game, dear son. You know that Père Massé and I have come here to make that game impossible, to destroy these forests with all their licentiousness –

That's just what that scut-lawyer Lescarbot used to say. He assured us that scurvy lurks in these trees. But, do you know, Père, I never got it! – Say, are you hungry?

I haven't eaten all day.

But you should have told me, Père. You know I love you better than my own father – better even than Merveille now . . . Come – half a league – I have moose-meat.

I thank you, Robert.

They took a path through a field of ferns in which flies swarmed like demons and then into the innermost darkness of the woods where Robert led him along very quickly, kicking rotten logs with the toe of his boot so that the soggy phosphorescence leaped like sparks, and Père Biard had to almost run to keep up, so that he thought to remonstrate with him but then he thought: No, I must say nothing . . . – and they crossed a wet glade of gloom and came to forest again but Robert suddenly swiveled back and bent down with inexorable swiftness to snatch up a newt or salamander or some such Devil's spawn before he crushed the life out of it between thumb and forefinger –

Let's get on, he said, although Père Biard had said nothing, had only gasped hoarsely his song of breathlessness.

They went deeper and faster. The wet moss sucked at Père Biard's boots.

It was Merveille I learned it from, said Robert over his shoulder, not even breathing fast, and they came in hearing of a sullen stream-roar gnashing itself against rocks and tangles and Robert bent without stopping to seize a handful of late blueberries and thrust them feverishly into his mouth.

Learned what from, my boy?

They came to a place where grey lichens hung from the trees in strips like pieces of sulphurous shrouds and the deer-trail or whatever it was went up among sharp cold granite rocks which Robert wrested in his hands and threw himself uphill in defiance of while Père Biard scrabbled behind him gasping: Learned what from? and wiping his forehead and clambering, creeping, climbing most wearily to the top of the rise, brushing lichen-skirts from his eyes; and there through the slick of sweat was the river, as grey and ugly as he had supposed it to be, and Robert formed a smile-twist of his mouth, stretching out a hand hard as wood to help him up the last stage between two boulders, and he said: We're only just above the Second Rapid, Père . . . – and Père Biard shook the man's shoulder with fingerclaws that gripped like rats' teeth and shouted: What do you mean? Have you profaned the secrets of the Exercises? – and Robert said: I learned it from Merveille.

Père Biard let go of his shoulder. His arm fell. He stood catching his breath.

Many trout I've seen there, Robert went on softly. I can catch them with my hands now –

Biencourt has sworn not to harm you, said Père Biard suddenly.

I can catch them with my hands.

Halfway down the far side of the hill was a wide ledge whose ends had been blocked off by rock walls as high as a man's shoulder. Without a word, Robert lifted him as if he were a child and raised him over the wall, and he let himself gingerly down onto the ledge. Before he had even begun to orient himself, Robert had leaped down beside him, as lightly as a wolverine. His sunburned face shone fiercely with pride.

It would take too long to explain everything, he said suddenly. But those cramped styes we all lived in in France, and then in Canada nothing but beaver, beaver, beaver!

In the center of the ledge grew a great blue spruce, its roots twisted like fingers in agony, straining so hard into the rock that they had cracked it beneath their will and bored into it with frenzied remorselessness greater than that of water, and the tree rose wild and shaggy against the granite wall, and a dozen pieds or so upward an unpeeled crossbeam had been lashed against the trunk with French ropes reinforced with moose-sinew, and at the place where the lashings had been made, the wood was worn smooth as if by rubbing, and a little below this was a segment of branch which had been lashed tight to form a footrest. Upon the many living needled arms of this Cross were hung beaver-skins and moose-bones and bloodclotted scalps. The rock beneath the tree was stained brown with splashes of blood.

Birds in Autumn

> Therein one sees men of good height and build, but wild and unruly . . .
> They paint themselves with different colors of red.
>
> JACQUES CARTIER, on the Souriquois (1535)

When Robert Pontgravé made formal and voluntary submission at last to Charles Biencourt de Poutrincourt, acknowledging him as the Lord and Seigneur of these parts, the two Black-Gowns found themselves that day in high honor, for people could not but admit that it was Père Biard who had brought the thing about. – Born Swimming's kin-friend Kinebji'j-koji'j said to her that at last this man who had insulted her would have his head shattered like a gourd, for that was surely what these Black-Gowns liked to do, so fierce and haughty as they were, and so much did they speak of death. And she begged Born Swimming to come to the lodge of the Saqmaw Biencourt, or *Poutrincourtji'j* as she jokingly called him after his father, in the fashion of the People, for she most eagerly believed that this day would see Robert Ki'kwa'ju's brains dashed out upon the ground. – But Born Swimming only replied wearily: You speak like a child, sister, for the Iron People will not kill one of their own. And you know very well that they fear the strength of his arms. I see-ahead too well . . . – But at this, Kinebji'j-koji'j stiffened and said to her in a voice of shrill temper: You never spoke to me this way before, in the days when we were girls together! – And she turned to leave the wigwam. But before she flung aside the French blanket at the door she shouted: I see that you dream your Dream of the Floating Island again and again! – and then she was gone.

Born Swimming was sickened to see such rage against her.

Her child had clapped her hand over her mouth in fright. Born Swimming lifted her in her arms and smiled into her face; she said: Have courage, my pretty little Born Underwater . . . – and she held her up over her head high in the smokehole where the SUN spattered gold amidst the smoke-motes where her husband's scalp-trophies spun round and round on their moose-hide strings and Born Underwater was laughing as she tried to reach for them and then she was squirming in her mother's arms and Born Swimming put her down so that she could play.

Born Underwater had seen two winters now. She loved her father's dogs that lay so tawny and bark-shaggy in the SUN; she laughed to see them snatch and snarl at the food he gave them; she clambered on their backs and rode them, which they suffered in the way that dogs sometimes do with young children: – a year later when she tried it they would bite.

She stared into their eyes. Suddenly she began to cower again. Born Swimming took her in her arms and she fell silent.

The Death of Kinebji'j-koji'j

Kinebji'j-koji'j had a very passionate temper. She loved her friends and hated her enemies. One of her favorite things was revenge. When she was sixteen winters old she became married, and it seemed that she did not get on well with her husband, for they separated and she took another man. That was in the time when the Saqmaw Poutrincourt first came to the Country of the People. Robert Ki'kwa'ju had not yet assaulted Born Swimming. In the summer when they received guns of the Iron People and won the great victory, one of their slave-women aided another Armouchiquois to escape. She stole a tinderbox and an iron hatchet from Membertou's house. And the other prisoner took these things when he fled by land to alert their enemy Bashaba against them. When Membertou discovered what the slave-woman had done, she only laughed triumphantly, knowing the penalty. – I have deceived your KLUSKAP! she shouted. It was Kinebji'j-koji'j who longed the most to kill her. She spoke with her kin-friend Metembroji'j and also with Membertou's daughter Membertouji'j-koji'j, and they were in agreement. Born Swimming wanted to go, too, but Swooping Like a Hawk was against it; the Iron People would be angry, he said. Born Swimming was a little angry, so he gave her a biscuit from the Iron People . . . The other three girls, the lucky ones, took the enemy woman behind the trees, away from the Iron People, and began. The enemy woman was too proud to cry, but Kinebji'j-koji'j saw her knees knocking together as she stood there and jeered, the better to shame her. Membertouji'j-koji'j took a hatchet and swooped it almost into her face, and the woman blinked. They played with her from a morning of vast and serene fir-space to a night that was supple, glassy, dark like another skin (summer nights were round and flat like beaver-skins). Then Kinebji'j-koji'j began. She was young and eighteen winters old then; she was plump and fair. She stabbed the enemy woman in the throat with a knife, a lovely knife of iron. The woman gurgled and sprayed the three girls with blood as they laughed red-mouthed beneath the trees. Next, Metembroji'j (who was also very pretty) pierced her in the breast. Then Membertouji'j-koji'j split her head. It was a very fine revenge. When the Iron People reproved them, they hid themselves, for who knew what cruelty the Iron People might be capable of for *their* revenge? – The next day, Kinebji'j-koji'j's husband brought some beaver-skins to the Iron People, and they would not take them, because they said that his wife among others had committed a grave crime. Enraged that they had turned their faces away from him, he got into a gambling game and gambled her away to Swooping Like a Hawk. Among the People of KLUSKAP, a woman who is gambled away scorns her husband and will not look at him. With Kinebji'j-koji'j this was particularly the case. Haughtily turning up her chin, she walked to Swooping Like a Hawk's side. She would never live with him again. – Now you see how wise I was not to permit my wife to offend the Iron People! (Thus Swooping Like a Hawk.) I have spoken. – He thought to keep Kinebji'j-koji'j, for she remained fair, and Born Swimming had had nothing to say against it, but upon considering her temper and also the difficulty of feeding another person (perhaps more than one, if she should get pregnant), he slept with her for only a few nights. She took this refusal as an insult, and ran shrieking into the woods, for which no one could blame her, as she had just been sent away by two husbands. Some witch was ruining her! But in time her temper cooled, and she became friends with Swooping Like a Hawk and Born Swimming again. (Indeed Born Swimming had reason to believe that Swooping Like a Hawk frequented her company even now, although this was not her affair.) – When Robert Ki'kwa'ju had outraged her, it was Kinebji'j-koji'j who came running first, and Born Swimming had little doubt to meet with a kindred rage. So it was. Kinebji'j-koji'j did not trouble to stroke Born Swimming's cheek, as many other women would have done, but began at once to howl against the Iron People. – Kinebji'j-koji'j was a bad enemy. So now, when they had exchanged words over Robert, Born Swimming was made uneasy by the anger that Kinebji'j-koji'j held against her, she knew not why. Born

Swimming knew Kinebji'j-koji'j's sister. She went to see her; she brought her fresh moose-fat. – She fears your little daughter, the sister said. She wonders if your little daughter will become a witch. She believes that your little daughter killed your other children, by magic from the Iron People. And her baby is sick –

Kinebji'j-koji'j's baby died. Kinebji'j-koji'j herself died two nights after.

The Death of Membertou

The new disease hovered in the mossy trees, nibbling at the People and plucking their souls – oh, not to excess; it had many years ahead to devour the People; but every now and then it destroyed a woman's children (did Born Underwater remember her brother and her two sisters? Among the People it is not good to mention the dead). One day, Membertouji'j fell sick. When his wife and children had already deserted him for dead, Père Massé saved his life with a relic of the glorified Saint-Laurent of Dublin. Then he believed. The Black-Gowns rejoiced. They would mold these Savages until they were thoroughly sacramentated.

Now his father Membertou entered upon his last illness, and was carried to the Black-Gowns to receive the rites of the Church.

To Biencourt he said: Bury me with my ancestors.

Biencourt promised to do so. He looked upon Membertou very sadly. Biencourt's moustache had thickened, and he had creases at the corners of his mouth. His face had become somewhat doughy and plump; his hair had begun to thin. He wore his wide bib-collar, no matter how dirty it had become, and the tassels of the authority which hung down from it had become grimed with sweat and soil and tree-sap. It was strange, the way that his features had thickened. His diet was scarcely very rich: no one's was, in Acadia. It was as if the hard young skull of will within his head could no longer tauten itself, and the flab of resignation began to puff out Biencourt's cheeks.

That is out of the question, said Père Biard. That place is not hallowed.

Biencourt shrugged. – Then hallow it, Père. Why must you continually cause unpleasantness with your scruples?

That cannot be done, replied the Black-Gown patiently. In such a case, heathens would be buried in a manner unsuited to their degree.

Now Membertou was very confused and unhappy in his mind to see his friends quarrelling at his deathbed over the disposition of his remains.

We shall not say prayers over your grave, if you insist upon being buried with other Savages! – So shouted Père Biard.

Hé é é, said Membertou at last. Were we not afraid to eat mussels until we saw you Iron People do it? Mussels are the enemies of KLUSKAP. Yet, brothers, I am content to follow your customs.

At this, the good Père Biard shed tears of happiness.

Membertou died receiving baptism and extreme unction. They beat the drum as they bore him to his grave, so that all the Savages marveled at such pomp . . .

A Bird in Winter

Yea, the sparrow hath found her an house,
And the swallow a nest for herself,
where she may lay her young,
even Thine altars, O LORD of hosts,
my ROY, my GOD.

Psalm LXXXIV

A crow flew. Brown-black rivers eased most civilly between white-rimmed forests. The crow looked for something to eat. He was so high that the winter-stricken trees appeared to him like grey grassblades – tea-grey, tinged yellow-brown with sunset. He flew across the Country of the Haudenosaunee, searching hungrily. Now he saw villages, which appeared to him a series of snow-squares inset in grey-green velvet (all of which showed through the clouds only patchily, like sandbars). He saw the longhouses puffing smoke, and dropped low, knowing that food was near, but the songs of the People inside terrified him, and he flapped past the palisadoes. Some Mohawk boys playing snow-snake saw him, but let him go. There was no reason why they ought to harm him. He overpassed cornfields: white clearings misted white, silver-smeared trees. He flew now the way a river bends without reason. He flew for the same reason (I suppose) that snow is darker than clouds; for hunger is no reason; hunger simply is. He flew until he could not fly anymore. Then he landed upon a snowy branch and died. History devours what happens, without any reason. History devoured the crow.

Birds in Spring
1612–1613

He who puts himself outside the authority of the Church will be damned to eternal torture, even though he allow himself to be burned alive for the sake of CHRIST.

SAINT AUGUSTINE, *Ad Donatum*, ep. 173

In this case, the beaver has been stimulated into his inborn dam building behaviour by the sound of running water.

THE FRIENDS OF ALGONQUIN PARK, "Beaver Pond Trail: Algonquin Beaver Ecology" (pamphlet, 1988)

In France, the Jesuits enmeshed Poutrincourt in all the litigation of which they were capable. His heart was as dry as the shoals of Port-Royal at low tide. Yet already something black and sour was seeping from under it . . . In the month of Janvier, thanks to Madame de Guercheville, who'd agreed to trust him yet a little farther, a ship went out at last, bearing his agent, Imbert-Sandrier. Accompanying him was his assigned enemy, a lay brother named Gilbert du Thet; for it seemed only right to the Black-Gowns to match Poutrincourt pawn for pawn. Du Thet would be the first of his Order to die in New France; and if Imbert had had his way he would have perished long before. Even as they stepped off the ship, words of thunder were rolling off Imbert's lips. – Heretic! he shouted. Regicide! – Ah, Biencourt, it is you. I tell you, this Jesuit has been fulminating against the life of our new Roy! –

It is not so! cried Frère du Thet. But as for you, I saw you selling Poutrincourt's grain and pocketing your silver, like Judas; I saw you add two barrels of biscuit to the invoice, but when I counted them in the night they were not there . . . – Biencourt, whose first and most prudent instinct was to command a truce, quickly fell into the clutches of his passions, egged on by Imbert, who assured him that Frère du Thet was a Spanish spy; and the long and the short of it (as Pontgravé would have said) was that he had the Black-Gown clapped into irons. The next day he convoked a tribunal. It soon shone through that Imbert's accusations were impelled by nothing more than hatred, which Biencourt admitted to himself was no surprise, and, feeling a little ashamed (though only a little, since Jesuits were often spies and traitors), he was about to tell Hébert to free the prisoner, when Père Biard, blind to Biencourt's forthcoming noble action, strode forward and began to shout for justice. Even yet Biencourt was not inflamed, only regretful that he must postpone his command for a day or two so that the Black-Gowns would not think themselves the masters here, and he pointed a finger downward; Hébert, taking the hint, quickly kicked the prisoner down into the dungeon again, and they heard the rattling of his chains as he fell into darkness. A smile of triumph now informed Biencourt's nervous face. He was about to explain to Père Biard in all coolness why Frère du Thet's release was delayed; but just as Père Biard's shouting had been fatal to his tranquility before, so that smile of his now undid Père Biard, who rushed almost into his face and began roaring for justice, justice, justice –

Justice? laughed Biencourt. You speak of justice, Père? What essence or tincture do you mean? It must be a rare spice, for I do not recall that you have ever before seasoned your words with it.

This is too much! cried the priest. I see that I must return to France.

Oh, no, said Biencourt. Now you wish to defy us and ruin us at home. No, I shall not let you go. You Jesuits came here against my wishes; now you shall not leave against mine.

In spite of Frère du Thet's release (sped by the application of Hébert's boot), bitterness presently became so great between the Black-Gowns and all others (saving only Robert Pontgravé, but he rested dutifully at Emenemic, in honor to Biencourt's command), that Père Biard saw that he must board ship in secret, to return to France. But Biencourt discovered him, and took him by force. This arrest being against canon law, Père Biard considered himself bound to excommunicate Biencourt. Louis Membertouji'j, who was now Saqmaw, took a hatchet and asked leave to kill them and their excommunication, but Biencourt only put his hand on Louis' shoulder . . .

– For the next quarter of a year Père Biard and Père Massé held themselves aloof, and would neither say Mass nor perform any offices. But Frère du Thet was guarded less rigorously. He awaited his opportunity and met the vessel of Robert Pontgravé, who was returning to drop off a good cargo of skins. – Ah, mon pauvre! Robert commiserated. And you look so seasick! – And so Du Thet arrived most seasonably, in the brumal month of Octobre, whereupon, detailing most fully to his Superiors the arbitrary and unreasonable way with which he and the others had been dealt, he helped dig deeper channels in the streams of their malice . . .

Winter screamed by, and spring was like a sigh. On the twenty-fifth day of Juin, Père Biard humbled himself and made full apology to Biencourt, which was accepted. Then he wrote a letter praising Biencourt. Behind that smokescreen, the Jesuits of Rouen had already seized Poutrincourt's ship in payment of his debts. Poutrincourt bit his lip hard at this news. Madame de Guercheville was unfortunately too busy to receive him. Fearing that his son might starve unless succor was sent him, he dove down seven hundred and fifty francs deeper into debt, bonding himself to a certain merchant recommended by Père Cotton, by name La Saulsay. It was very safe. La Saulsay would borrow the money and charge Poutrincourt the interest, then forward it to an infallible Captain he knew who'd ship Biencourt sackfuls of dainties, never fear –

You are mad! cried his wife. Now, when we are almost ruined, why do you not go to De Monts and request his help?

Do you not think that he is as poor as we?

No, I do not think so. It is this cursed obsession of yours with loyalty that is crushing us. If you do not pity me or your daughters, think at least upon Biencourt! What is he to do, alone in that wilderness?

That is why we must take this loan, said Poutrincourt stonily.

And you will not speak of the matter to De Monts?

No, he said.

De Monts owned apple orchards and vineyards whose fruits he took great pride in. Once indeed he had presented the Poutrincourts with a barrel of fresh apples, opening which Madame de Poutrincourt had discovered many foul worms. Her husband forbade the matter to be mentioned outside the house, for fear of wounding his Captain's heart.

. . . When he learned that the aforesaid La Saulsay had taken the seven hundred and fifty borrowed francs but not spent a penny of it, Poutrincourt appealed to Père Cotton for satisfaction. – La Saulsay? said Père Cotton in surprise. I do not know him. (For he admired Saint Peter, even to his denials.) What! he is your Lieutenant-General! So cried Poutrincourt, but it was his last cry, for now at last the Black-Gowns had their victory: by dint of whispering and turning diverse secret levers they succeeded in having him committed to debtors' prison. There, lost among the other convicts in the great prisons, he wandered up the steeply winding stairs of his own mind's jail-galleries, sickening from day to day, digging the Roy's roads with heavy pick and spade, manacled throughout the noisome nights, while water dripped and rats scurried, and the guards played cards at their benches by the balustrade, and the stone ceilings, stained with filth, trapped the smells of the prison, and all Poutrincourt's dreams of Acadia were chained separately groaning to little niches in the ways and galleries of his failing soul; digging the Roy's roads he choked to contemplate the ruin into which the Jesuits had thrust him; and when the guards were not watching and the other convicts let their chains droop and stood whispering close together, Poutrincourt went on working in a daze until they shoved him and tripped him laughing; and he dug the Roy's roads so that quiet gilded carriages could roll along them to the white steps of the Roy's palaces; and Poutrincourt coughed and clutched his chest in dull pain to see the Black-Gowns mounting ladders to scale the loftiest arches of his mind, there to thrust at his thoughts and fancies with flaming brands, and the smoke stained the ceiling of his skull still further and his head whirled with smoke as he stood leaning on his pick, slowly, ever so slowly digging the Roy's roads; and great pulleys swung and creaked beneath the shadowy balconies of his lost hopes, and brazen rings clattered in the drafts of his wheezing breaths that whirled through the beams of his failing skeleton as the torch-lamps flickered inside his towers and his fears and envies leaned on the railings of shadowy platforms, watching Acadia be strangled; and young Pontgravé broke a Souriquois woman on a wheel of sharp stars, and Père Biard and Père Massé strode up and down the wide and shallow steps inside him, tapping at his skull, nodding and gesturing to each other with conceited smiles; then his wife fell screaming down a long flight of stairs and died before she reached the bottom; he heard Biencourt crying out behind dark and many-bolted gates; and there was blood in his phlegm as he dug the Roy's roads; and the wooden idols of Saints stood against the walls; he coughed and coughed, and there was a tightness in his chest, like a spring too greatly compressed, and then suddenly a great stone fell from the ceiling and he felt eased as something began gushing between the bars of doors and out of wheel-shaped openings and down the great stone blocks of walls where chained figures struggled so desperately not to be drowned; and the pick fell from his hand as little pink streams became *rivières* and then great crimson *fleuves* spilling down the stairs in waterfalls roaring louder and louder, rushing past the unseeing wooden faces of Saints and bears, extinguishing the lanterns, pulling chains taut until they swung and tangled in the current with vicious creakings, and the waterfalls roared louder and louder in the hellish red darkness inside Poutrincourt, who had only loved Acadia and wanted to live there for the rest of his days; and the thundering masses of water shattered stone banisters and crushed the convicts in their lowest cells and swept filth down the stairs, and he felt Père Massé shooting through him, round and round, down all the spiral staircases of his being, bracing his pale hands against Poutrincourt's passageways, pushing and pushing so that he felt a thumping in his heart and was choking, and then he vomited Père Massé out of his mouth, in a gush of black blood; now he felt Père Biard squeezing his heart, clinging to it underwater with the obstinacy of a wooden Saint, and the wooden Saints did not change their expressions, and then suddenly something like a great black clot came whirling down bell-ropes and entangling itself in ladders, which it simply brought with it as it rushed down the waterfalls of his darkness faster and faster; it was the Fox's scalp; and it swelled to choke his widest galleries with glistening bloody kelp; it crammed itself through every doorway and forced him to taste its slimy salty blood; and the last thing he knew some chandelier was swinging and swinging and then it came crashing down . . .

And yet he survived. Those who owed him favors got him freed at last. Yet he was now very ill, and the fire had gone out of him. There was little left for him to do but engage the professional services of Lescarbot (which the latter, pitying him, provided free of cost) in order to arrange a legal separation from his wife. That way she could at least retain whatever property might be vested in her name. Now she wept, and rued the time she had ever heard of Acadia. Again her husband assembled a cast of partners, pouring the last dregs of his fortune into this trade . . .

Père Massé's Epiphany

After this, the two Black-Gowns found all hearts closed against them, for the Savages loved Biencourt and counted his enemies as their enemies. (Among the Huron they'd have a fresh start, even a fresh name.) Smiling timorously, Père Massé passed his hand across the tops of their heads and mumbled a prayer, very low, as if he were afraid that they might hear him. Père Biard stood watching him. And suddenly (he could not have said why) he hated him more than he had ever hated anyone on earth.

Now it was spring, and the strange deaths had abated among the Savages, and puzzle-pieces of snow swept down the brown rivers which the Black-Gowns did not recognize as the rivers of Exercises and dreams. Biencourt had forbidden the Black-Gowns to travel beyond Port-Royal, for he considered them very pernicious. In secret, Père Biard directed Père Massé to go among the Etechemins, which Robert Pontgravé could arrange. Having seen fewer Frenchmen, the Etechemins must suffer from fewer prejudices. This was Père Biard's firm belief; Robert agreed; Robert came running to him when he blew his whistle . . . So Père Massé set off one day when Biencourt did not see. – In the Etechemin woods he suffered terribly. He set his teeth; he quickened his step and went deeper into the forest. But how could he explain anything to them, when they understood *good* but not *goodness*, *strong* but not *strength*, *black* but not *blackness?*

Give us bread! the Savages cried. Heal us!

They were frightened by the consecrated wine, believing that the Black-Gowns drank human blood.

This is the blood of JESUS, said Père Massé.

Was that a man? they asked.

He was the SON OF GOD, but He became a man to die for us. In memory of His sacrifice, we drink His blood.

At this they drew back and whispered in their language, with many terrified glances.

Père Massé knelt making the Exercises. At the mouth of the Stream of Time, in the Eddy of the Three Sins, he contemplated his own disobedience. Now a black whirlpool appeared before him – at which he flushed, remembering something that he had done as a young boy that even now embarrassed him. In his father's absence, he had opened his desk and discovered a bottle of ink, which he began to play with, and spilled on the carpet. Suddenly he realized that he would be punished. He watched the spots getting bigger and bigger on the floor . . . – Now even this childish sin must stain him like sewage every time he made the Exercises. Sins never go away. He struck out briskly, hoping to traverse the whirlpool through diligent concentration; the pikes and sturgeons of his other larger sins snapped at his legs and drew blood. At least they had grown leaner . . .

He traveled with Louis Membertou, called *Membertouji'j*. (Membertouji'j had changed his name to Auctodin now that his father had died, but the Black-Gowns did not recognize this heathenish custom.) Père Massé had become very weak. Louis said: Listen, Père, you will soon die. I predict it. Write to Biencourt and your brother Black-Gown that you have died of sickness, not that I have murdered you.

Père Massé looked upon him coldly. – If I do that, then you will surely murder me, having been thus given safe-conduct by my own hand. No, I shall write no such thing. Indeed, I am of a mind to write that you seek to murder me, so that if anything does befall me then you will swiftly pay the penalty.

Louis laughed and shrugged.

One night in a dream he saw Saint Ignatius, who was very pale, and a sun of holiness gleamed behind his head, outlining untouched the black mountain of his collar and shoulders and sleeves; his gown was black. He stood holding the *Constitutions* in his white hands, offering the sweetness of his face that looked nowhere (in, away) – and the sun behind him did not touch his balding crown; nothing touched him; light flowed from him and over him like water, and still he stood there, looking down, or to his left, or somewhere, and maybe beams of light shone from his eyes but that fact was neither straight nor sure.

After this experience, Père Massé prayed to Saint Ignatius more fervently than ever, seeming to see him behind every waterfall. *I will be your image-bearer!* he cried. *Blessed Ignatius, be my companion as Saint Peter companioned you.* But there was no answer.

Then he saw him standing behind the green arch of river-water that thundered beside the Souriquois hunting camp, and the spume foamed over him and drenched him but he never moved; he was *there* just as Père Massé had seen him so many times in the old engraving in the room where he had taken the Exercises. There were the narrow Spanish eyes, kind but shrewd, the smooth forehead, the patrician nose, the moustache beneath which the lip curled in a foxy smile . . . Saint Ignatius.

And he knelt and prayed, saying: Blessed Ignatius, help me!

The Saint was watching him. His dark eyes danced with mirth, but he said nothing.

Again Père Massé uttered from his heart: Blessed Ignatius, help me! – And he knew that he had never made a sincerer prayer.

Still the Saint was silent.

Blessed Ignatius, he prayed, only tell me what I must do to make you a gift of these souls, and I shall do it. You know that I am obedient. You have seen how I bear with Père Biard, whom you must acknowledge is a difficult man. I say this not because I am proud, but because false humility serves no one. You yourself have written much about this. Let me but know the path, and I will follow it to my very death.

The Saint said nothing. The wrinkles at the corners of his eyes were slyer than ever.

Do you hear me? shouted Père Massé suddenly. Does nothing move you? Are you nothing but an idol that I have worshipped to my destruction? – He stood with his hands on his hips, breathing heavily. He hated the Saint more than he had ever hated anyone on earth.

Then I'll go on in spite of you! he cried. I'm going to do my best; *I* have the steadfast heart! Do you hear me? I have the steadfast heart, I tell you!

Well then, my son, said the Saint (he had never changed his expression), have I been of benefit to you?

And the water poured over his face. The stream was dirty and foul. The Savages used it for their latrine. Every drop in that waterfall defiled him, but nothing could defile him, and so he smiled.

That was Père Massé's epiphany. After that, his character was fixed until death. He never sought to question his mortifications anymore. He clasped his eyes and wept for gladness, saying: My dear Canada, embellished with lovable and adorable Crosses . . .

He converted not a soul.

Smoking the Pipe

Père Biard meanwhile thought it wise to essay converting one of their principal Jugglers or Shamans, by name Smoking the Pipe; for it was patent that once these old men (who were esteemed as wise) accepted the True Faith, others must bow to their authority. So he set off into the woods. He would eat up this fellow's superstitions, quietly, one by one, as a white weasel eats bird-eggs.

It was summer now, and the Souriquois men wore white robes of moose-skin well dressed and ornamented with chevrons and the figures of animals. The women did that. They used pretty dyes: red, black, yellow . . .

His guide was a stout Souriquois whose name meant *Swooping Like a Hawk*. He had consented to show him the way, in exchange for a handful of biscuits (for among this People all must be paid for, if one is French. This proves their covetous and uncivilized nature.) Swooping Like a Hawk strode ahead at a very good pace, which Père Biard was hard put to follow. Yet follow he would, for his purpose was as sharp-topped as a spruce tree. Indeed such hardships as these were akin to the shad-fish of Acadia, whose meat was so oily that Père Massé had vomited until the blood came up; but in time his digestion became accustomed to it. It was that way with all hardships. There was nothing, including death, that a Black-Gown could not endure. Swooping Like a Hawk led him through many difficult and wearisome thickets that raked his cheek or the back of his hand with brambles. Black eyes glared at him from the side, but when he looked again he saw that he was mistaken, and no one was there. (Really it was Born Swimming, pounding berries to be dried into the disk-shaped cakes. Her children, the ones who were dead, had been very fond of those.) He slipped, and his boot trampled down the slender stalks of purple bladderwort. The mosquitoes were almost insufferable. There was no trail that he could see, but Swooping Like a Hawk never hesitated. Once he turned and seemed almost to laugh into Père Biard's face; but that too must have been imagined, for this Savage was very grave. At long last they arrived at a sodden meadow on the margin of an alder-screened brook. There stood Smoking the Pipe's wigwam. The vicinity was littered with moldering scraps of furs and various excrements. A dog snarled. Swooping Like a Hawk kicked the animal so hard that it flew through the air.

Kwe! called Swooping Like a Hawk.

Smoking the Pipe's apprentice, Looking Down Streams, parted the hides that covered the doorway. Seeing Père Biard, he scowled. His face disappeared. The two visitors stood waiting until Smoking the Pipe crawled out grumpily.

Ah, it is you, said Smoking the Pipe. And you have brought this black-feather crow who wishes to train me to caw of dead men, as Membertou once did. Now Membertou is well-suited to his talk! – he added spitefully, for he had been very jealous of him. – Come in, brothers, come in. Be seated. I have some beaver-meat if you wish to regale yourself, Swooping Like a Hawk. As for the crow, he must give me presents for it, for I am told that that is how the Iron People show hospitality when we visit them – though that is only hearsay, for I never go there.

So you think yourself fit to instruct this young boy! the priest said sarcastically. And what do you teach him today?

Today, Black-Gown, it is the lore of balms and sickness. I will show you. Quick, grandson! What is the cure for an arrow-wound?

Fir-balsam chewed into a poultice, replied Looking Down Streams. The juice must be spat into the wound.

You improve. And if a man dies of sickness and it is the work of bad Power or monster, what must be done?

We must eat his heart, to torture the demon that lives there.

My ears are overjoyed. Tell me truly, Black-Gown, if you have such knowledge.

I have come to teach you the error of your entire life, old man! Père Biard said sternly. You have wasted your best years fornicating and worshipping idols! Yet GOD is merciful. He will embrace you; He will permit Saint Peter to lead you – even you! – into the Kingdom of Heaven. GOD can do everything. He is our FATHER. He weeps to see the evil ways of your people. Listen to me, Smoking the Pipe! You can win much merit if you lead your brothers and sisters to him. You must turn your back on the Devils of the forest. You must not offer tobacco to the sun. Do you understand?

Grandfather SUN created the universe, said Smoking the Pipe. That is a fact known to all intelligent men. Look around you and see His rays! How can you deny Him? As for you, you respect a Power you cannot even see! Brother, I must tell you this: it is your beard which makes you so undiscerning. Pull the hairs out by the roots, and you will become intelligent like us. You will recognize the SUN's Power. – No, brother, do not seek to interrupt me when I explain these matters to you: such behavior is worthy only of children. You have come here seeking to instruct me; now do you be instructed. I was telling the tale of our SUN. He divided the world into regions separated by lakes. In each part He made one man and one woman. These pairs married and brought forth children, so that throughout the earth lived multitudes among the trees, raising wigwams and painting their faces each in his own fashion. But presently they became wicked, and the SUN wept. His tears made a great rain. The waters rose to the tops of mountains. The frightened peoples sought to save themselves, but fierce winds overturned their canoes, so that they all drowned, with the exception of some old men and women who had remained virtuous. *Kespi-a'tuksit.**

You speak words of truth and lies intermingled like oil and water, replied Père Biard. This Deluge which you recognize is also one of our traditions. But the sun is but a lifeless star hung in the sky for our use by GOD.

What! cried Smoking the Pipe. You say that there is no life in things? What evil and selfish doctrine is this? Brother, I now begin to believe that your sickness is deeper than I had feared.

* "Here ends this story."

Making the Exercises

The Ln'uk, the People of KLUSKAP, were now in that season of the year when they lived on eels, waiting for deep snow to trap the animals so that they could hunt. Swooping Like a Hawk had read the signs of sky and wind, and believed that a blizzard would soon come. Therefore he consulted with his wife, and they agreed to move their wigwam into the forest on the following day. It was night. Swooping Like a Hawk set out into the forest to smooth a snow-road down to the river, which was well frozen for travel. The Sturgeon went with him. He was Swooping Like a Hawk's nephew. He lived with them now, for his parents had perished in one of the plagues that the Black-Gowns had brought, and after Born Swimming sickened from the same cause she could no longer bear children. The Sturgeon was their son now. He went with Swooping Like a Hawk most willingly; he was respectful. Together they cleared away dead branches where the bark rolls would be dragged on the toboggans. They returned rather late, and were eating a little beaver-meat when they heard visitors coming: Iron People, whom we can hear from a distance, for they tread clumsily in snowshoes.

Swooping Like a Hawk watched his wife's face. But she looked down at the floor.

And you sincerely believe that this visit could bear fruit? Père Massé was saying.

It is our duty to try. We have no right to leave them in ignorance. – So Père Biard. – And if we are scorned, we are well practiced in bearing that.

You are right, I am sure, Père Superior.

After this they said nothing more until they arrived at Swooping Like a Hawk's house. This was not a wigwam with four fires, where two tens of persons lived. There were only Born Swimming, her husband and the two children, the others having died.

Kwe! said Père Massé.

A little Souriquois boy lifted the flap and looked at them. Then he ran into the forest.

Who is it? called Swooping Like a Hawk from within.

We are the ones you call Black-Gowns.

Born Swimming gave place to the visitors. Swooping Like a Hawk yielded his seat also and bade them repose on skins. It was very smoky inside.

We greet you in the name of JESUS, said Père Biard.

I am greatly surprised at the stupidity of these Iron People, said Born Swimming aloud.

Forgive her, Black-Gowns, said Swooping Like a Hawk. She has reason to bear a grudge against your countrymen.

We know well what matter she refers to, said Père Biard. Have some charity, woman. Show some forgiveness for young Pontgravé who wronged you. If I offended you in obtaining absolution for him, I am sorry. But I could not let him remain in the forest like a friendless animal.

Is that how you see us? said Born Swimming. We are very content to remain here. As for us, we are much amazed at your vast and foolish houses like prisons. We find it strange how you glory in our shabby old beaver-rags.

Our French take those to France to be worked into felt, explained Père Massé. It is simpler if the guard hairs have fallen out. Otherwise someone must pull them out by hand.

Swooping Like a Hawk said nothing. He felt that he could not chastise his wife; nor did he care particularly to encourage the Black-Gowns.

Do you hate your child then? said Père Biard abruptly. For I can see that you hate us.

Here she is, said Born Swimming. Ask her. – And she turned her face away.

Now the Black-Gowns were somewhat confounded, as the infant was only three winters old. They studied her for a moment. She was rather larger than a fullblooded Souriquois baby of the same age; her face was the mottled pale of an owl's egg. She had big round eyes.

A promising young soul, said Père Massé.

She is our happiness, said Swooping Like a Hawk simply.

And do you all know of JESUS in this wigwam? cried Père Biard, raising his voice. For it is of the utmost urgency that you know.

Oh, we have heard of Him, said Born Swimming. We have heard too much of Him.

He reminded her of a sandpiper, always pecking up little worms.

The little girl backed away and opened her mouth as if to scream in fear, but Swooping Like a Hawk puffed tobacco-smoke into her mouth, at which she became calm, and once again stared at the visitors with wide eyes. – She is already addicted to that devilish fumigant, thought Père Biard to himself, sadly but without surprise. He had seen so many vices among these Savages . . .

Toward the First Prelude

Père Biard and Père Massé agreed that little, far too little, was being accomplished. Père Massé wept very gently in a way that filled Père Biard with disdain for the man's weakness: – the way Père Massé wept, it seemed that he accepted this failure passively, whereas Père Biard went alone into the forest and found himself sobbing the thick hoarse sobs of defeated pride – and yet, he said to himself, even though this emotion be evil in me, I will not reject it, because it *goads* me to do better! – and he thought again of his companion and curled his lip. – Yet there was no denying that the fruitlessness of the toil was exhausting him. Requiring consolation, he knelt beside a frozen little brook and made his favorite Contemplation: *viz.*, how the Blessed Ignatius first came to the Faith by grace of Our LORD, who permitted him to be wounded by the French in order, as it was said, that through the maiming of his body he might come to knowledge of the maimed state of his soul, which was puffed with the rotten bile and humors of worldly vanity; and how, so learning, Ignatius took the Vow at Montmartre in the year 1534. – Closing his eyes, Père Biard prayed the *Anima CHRISTI*, murmuring softly to himself *Soul of CHRIST, sanctify me. Body of CHRIST, save me. Blood of CHRIST, intoxicate me. Water from the side of CHRIST, wash me . . .* and again he wept (this time not those burning prideful tears, but cool drops whose loss weakened him still further, as if he were bleeding) and for a moment he could not go on with the prayer. He longed overwhelmingly to be in Paris again. He could hear the tolling of the bells; he could smell the rose-cakes with which the ladies perfumed themselves for church; he heard the rattle of horse-carriages, the reassuring marching of the Roy's soldiers on the bridges, prepared to quell all disturbances . . . Then he became enraged at himself, and chastised himself for his weakness. Why, he said to himself, I am no better than these Savages! – And he finished the prayer. And he said now for my own consolation I make this Contemplation, which contains four Preludes: the Castle, the Exhortation, the Defense, the Wounding . . . – so Père Biard cast his sight back across the past, swimming up the Stream of Time as he had been trained to do by his Superiors, who were themselves expert swimmers, and he ascended dark waterfalls, pulling himself up rock by rock between leaf-walls of yellow-green, and the mild spray felt good on his face and the breeze blew across his pale wet shoulders like the Stream of Time itself from whose shallows a buck-deer drank; and the stream ran steeply down its rock bends as the Savages watched him unseen and he worked his way higher and higher up the slippery rocks until he came to the pool where the Irocois children played but for him it was the pool of the First Contemplation, where he trod water to say an *Ave* and then drank deeply of that holy water; he ascended past the other pools, never looking up forest ridges into that white summer light because he must keep custody of his eyes and focus them on nothing that was not needful; and he began to feel joy and gladness as he came closer and closer and then he was wading through brightness to the First Prelude where he could kneel still and silent in the Acadian forest and he smiled because he had begun truly and so now saw old Spain . . . And the life of Saint Ignatius, founder of the Black-Gowns, flowed across his eyes like water.

11
Obedience
or,

A Brief Life of Saint Ignatius de Loyola, Who Invented the Exercises

The Warmaker
1491–1522

Many are given to believing that new things bring greater advantages, and that is where they are often mistaken.

CHAMPLAIN, *Voyages* (1629)

When Iñigo fell to talking with the Duke at Nájera, they often made discourses on the nobility of faithful love, not so much to pass the time before breakfast (though that had been what began it) as to convince themselves and each other that they felt *deeply* even as they stood in the hot sun on the parapets of the Citadel wondering when (if ever) the French attack would come, Iñigo hoping that it would, the Duke that it wouldn't; and Iñigo admired his dagger over and over, kissing it where the light glittered on it so that the Duke laughed and said Iñigo, Iñigo, you are so passionate! and Iñigo would say but it *is* a beautiful dagger, Señor, is it not? I got it at Court . . . and the Duke said yes, you have told me that story and Iñigo said well, then, and have you heard the tale of the dog who shed tears (so they say) over the grave of his dead master? at which the Duke saw fit to mention the VIRGIN's tears, every drop of which he now treasured up for young Iñigo with most sorrowful reverence; at which generous Iñigo offered up to their *mutual* consideration the steadfastness of Saint Peter, Doorkeeper of Heaven, whose love for CHRIST grew so great (by grace of GOD) that even the denial in the Garden could be forgiven – but while they both acknowledged the value of such persons, their real delight was to speak of instances of the love of men for women. (Here I must shift my narrative alluringly, like a whore on a street-corner, combing her hair, tapping her heels, squirming like bait; like all the girls on rue Sainte-Catherine who lean up against counters late at night, arms crossed, one bare knee before the other;

some girls are lovely; others have great fat legs and zippers longer than roads running down their bulging black-leathered asses; but what they offer without exception is purity, bravery, love.) – These matters consumed them, Iñigo especially (for the Duke was now advanced in years) and all stories were of interest that tended to the practical. Iñigo was also a great reader of romances, whose personages would each night rule and regulate his dreams so that the next morning he could say to the Duke oh, Señor! but you should have seen her as I did just now, with her pure blue eyes and that golden hair that she braided into rope to draw her lover up! – Like enough, laughed the Duke, I would have fought you for her hand!

Then it was time for Iñigo to drill the soldiers in the morning sun, while the bells sounded in the town below.

He had never yet seen the First Rapid.

In the evening, bats ascended into the sky, and the Duke and Iñigo walked around the ramparts receiving their spies and discussing the morrow's business and the Duke said I saw how the men followed you today; it is clear that you inspire them and Iñigo blushed and said their form was good today, Señor and the Duke said a new slut came up the hill just after Vespers and Iñigo said yes, Señor, they were telling me all about that and the Duke said but tell me truly, do you consider such affairs to be worthy of being called love, or could they lead to love? and Iñigo said no, no, Señor, that woman may strive to show the graces of a highborn Doña, but inside she is mud and ashes.

I see that you have your convictions, said the Duke.

And you do not agree?

No, no, I agree. But it is a pity. It is so rare anywhere to find this special devotion that we two make it our pastime to speak of! That is why to this day I lament the death of King Fernando – that was the year before you came into my service (well, of course you know that, boy) – oh, but he truly loved the Queen! We could all see it in him. When Isabel died, twelve years before him, he bowed his head and wept for her although she was no beauty anymore –

As he ought to have, Señor, said Iñigo. That was only natural. But I do not think he loved her as he should have done.

Iñigo, Iñigo, you must not speak of such things, nor should you speak so loudly. A page you were, not a Lord. Remember that our rulers are set over us by GOD; it is our place but to obey. And what do you mean by this talk of disrespect? Throughout her life he was true to her.

He took his new wife a mere ten months after she died! shouted Iñigo. How then can you say that he was faithful to her? Can you call that fidelity?

You would have fallen on your dagger, I know. Such a Cavalier!

No, no! I demand an answer, Señor!

The Duke laughed a little and shook his head. – You forget yourself.

Excuse me. Please. You know I get excited . . .

Well, you know that he wanted an heir. Princess Juana was not fit to do anything but weep over her husband's coffin.

Yes, *she* was faithful!

She was mad! shouted the Duke in his turn. You idiot, do you think you're some Angel of Conscience? She embraced the coffin – yes, I know that meets with your approval – but were you aware that she had it opened? Repeatedly, impiously, even when he was nothing but slime! When in life *he* was never faithful to her! You call *that* fidelity?

Well, said Iñigo, I call it something.

The Dandy

On his head he always wore a colored cap. (Near his heart, an ivory comb which a certain Doña had given him.) His hair fell to his shoulders. Usually he was to be seen in cape and hose, with a dagger by his side, and whenever he traveled down into the town he put on the breastplate that the Duke had given him. He kept a musket at his side. It was not only that weapons were his chief delight; – in Nájera the Duke's men were not welcome. Once when Iñigo was walking down the street a group of men jostled him hard against a wall, and he drew his sword and came running after them, shouting until his face was purple; if others had not restrained him he would have swung at them, and been killed.

But you are too headstrong! the Duke said. Are you so desperate for glory that you will throw away your own life stupidly?

Señor, I only wish to serve you, said Iñigo.

Love *1507–1516*

Yes, how he wished to serve! In the years before, when he was a page at Court, there was a certain Lady – not a Countess nor a Duchess; her standing was much higher than even those. The first time he saw her he felt for her as tenderly as he did for his sister-in-law Magdalena, who had taught him the beauty of *family*. How lucky his brother was! Thinking of Magdalena, his eyes filled with tears. The Doña had an hourglass waist like Queen Germana. She wore a dress of a thousand flowers whose sleeve-wings imprisoned her in the likeness of an enormous moth. Her face was delicate without being sweet, which indeed he thought a fault in her: it was a delicate bored exile's face. Yet she made up for this with her wig of silver fans. Now his wax against the world began to melt. By stages he came to love Queen Germana also. How could he not? His beloved was one of Germana's Doñas – *viz.*, a LaDy, whO had beeN born so fAr above him that her name was sCArcely even To be thought (I will not write it here except by A secret anagRam); all his lIfe, he was certaiN, he would remember her comb of gold filigree, with the teeth on both sides like the thorns of A rose-stem: – that stood for her in his mind; nor could he forget the other one, the ivory one with painted birds on it which she dropped once and he had rushed to pick up for her. His heart was pounding, as he brought it to her, looking not at her face, as he could not have borne that, but at her hand (whose every finger he would have kissed). The Doña smiled; she told him that he could have it. He had kept the comb against his heart ever since. (Her hand, her hand; it had been like porcelain.) Now day after day he felt such sweetness that his face was sometimes wet with tears. At this the other pages began to gossip, wondering which of the many noble wenches at Court dangled him from her finger, but of course he did not tell. – So this was what love was, this secret radiance! – One day upon going to Mass, he glimpsed her again; although of course she did not notice him. That night he could hardly sleep, so much did he love and desire her. He grew sickly; a lock of hair clung to his sweaty forehead. – Again he read the romances of courtly love, and when he came to parts where the knights gave their lives for a Doña in distress he cried out to himself: Surely I can do as they did! – The blood had rushed to his face, and his jaw-muscle was thumping. – But there was no Doña to die for. He knew all too well that that comb was the utmost favor that he could hope to receive.

Iñigo's Nose

He was more successful in his other amours, even including those with the lesser Doñas of the Court. And it seemed to him as if this must go on forever. But one day (ridiculous to say) he developed a strange disease of the nose. It swelled and ached, and a sickening smell came from it. The Doctors could do nothing. The Doñas turned away from him, grimacing through handkerchiefs. They seemed exceedingly ugly to him when their faces were screwed up like that, and with a kind of vengeful wonder he thought: how my own deformity deforms them! The one who had given him the comb was not there, but he supposed that she had heard about it. Iñigo's nose was the most important subject of state to him; therefore it seemed logical that everyone else discussed it when he was not there. Nor was this entirely untrue, for back at Casa Loyola they did learn of it, and his sister-in-law Magdalena sent him all the fat round bottles recommended by the nuns, although the expense was not slight. He must write a note of thanks to his brother. – Oh, his ridiculous nose! Because he was always conscious of it, it seemed to glow. He touched it: it was greater than ever with pus. – May all the Saints help me! – Lifting the glass stoppers one by one, he tried the powdered essences: Columbo, Benz-Naph, Gaiacol . . . but none of these eased him. The King made a wry face and gave him leave from waiting upon him until he might be seemly again. At this, flushed with the disgrace, Iñigo locked himself in his room and resolved to treat himself with water and poultices until he was cured or died; he would never come out otherwise. Looking into the mirror, he wept. He prayed to JESU. And indeed it seemed that JESU heard him and held his case to be more important and pitiable than many others (for there was a pestilence in that year, of which numbers died): Iñigo was cured. Then he was popular again. He cut and combed his hair; he cut his nails; he dressed like a dandy. The Doñas came again. He tried to forget what had happened; it upset him; it embarrassed him. He had Doñas and Doñas, until he had forgotten his nose, until he cared no more (as he thought) for her of the comb.

The Box

Then he dreamed that she said to him very softly: Come up into my chamber, Iñigo – and he took her hand and went up with her, at which she closed the door. Drawing the curtains across the window, she said to him see my treasure! and from between her breasts she removed a locket in which was a tiny ivory box with two golden locks. Not knowing what was inside, he desired very fervently to learn, so he knelt before her and prayed so earnestly for the key, but at this she only smiled at him and said: My Iñigo, are you truly worthy? and he cried: With all my heart! – but at this reply she became sad and put the little box back inside her locket and closed it with a snap and she seemed to be weeping soundlessly into his eyes; when he woke his eyes were as usual wet with tears . . .

Machinations of His Destiny 1517–1521

But now Fernando came to his deathbed at last, and Charles the Foreigner was made King of Spain. The Highest Judge of the Kingdom of Aragon crowned him according to the old formula, looking fiercely into his eyes: *We who are as good as you, swear to you who are no better than we, to accept you as our King and Sovereign Lord, provided that you accept all our liberties and laws; but if not, not.* – The Highest Judge put the crown on Charles's head, but he who had been thus elevated smiled blankly as if he did not understand what had been said. – Already people talked about the Golden Days when King Fernando and Queen Isabel La Católica had ruled Spain, when King Fernando knelt with his Book and Queen Isabel knelt with her Book and their pale long-fingered hands were clasped in prayer as the Bishops purified them with evergreens and ribbons as the VIRGIN sat enthroned, looking at everything with downcast eyes.

The name of Iñigo's patron at Court was Don Juan Velasquez. Having displeased King Charles with his loyalty to bygone days, he fell out of influence, and all his dependents with him. So Iñigo was compelled to give up Court life, and become a soldier. At first he felt not a little sad and desperate, as if he were leaving his family a second time; but he routed these cowardly sentiments by pointing out to himself how good it was to follow whatever path might be laid out for him. – I will win fame, he said to himself. – Then someday I shall come to her of the comb (although he knew all the time that *that* was impossible). So he came into the Duke's service. For three years he exercised his weapons and read his romances. He was at the occupation of Nájera, where he acquitted himself right well, so that the Duke praised him and presented him with a fine sword.

In the following May, the army was summoned to Pampeluna. Iñigo was twenty-six years old. He was given his own column of men to lead. Being very valorous, he infused them with high spirits, and they arrived at the Citadel very briskly. There the Duke awaited him.

Pampeluna 1521

The river came in from the northwest, and made a wide bend and then another where it was very plentiful in carp and tench-fish, passing a little northward of the city, and then looped sharply south to wrap around the eastern side of the city, after which the river curled northeast and southeast and northeast, where it forked. It was not the Stream of Time. Pamplona was nestled in that first southward bend, a little square-walled town above which the Citadel rose like a jagged star. Around its ramparts walked Iñigo and the Duke, the latter wearing his shiny black armor with gold accordion-joints.

No, no, Iñigo, you must be patient, said the Duke. No one likes this new King Charles of ours, but sensible men detest rebellion and anarchy far more.

Yes, Señor, said Iñigo.

Your affirmation is mere politeness; it is not an answer. I insist upon an answer! How do you stand in the service of your King?

The blood had rushed into Iñigo's face. But he replied: He is my Lord, Señor. I shall defend him to the death.

Well! said the Duke. I am as pleased as I am surprised. I had feared that it would be necessary to discharge you from my service, something I would have done with extreme regret, for you are very quick and capable. We must clean house before the *Salamander** comes – I assure you that he will come. His agents have roused the Moors to an uprising against our King. The Moors have promised him three cities – if you can believe such treachery! I am going to Court today to plead for reinforcements. Now remember, Iñigo, no matter what happens, I trust you to live up to your word.

He walked away. For a very long time Iñigo could hear his long pointed boots slapping upon the stones.

The First Lock

That night he dreamed that he sought his beloved fiercely through the wastes of mountain desert that were as creamy and barren as the margins of the books at Court, and he went even to the strongholds of the Saracens to search for her; at last, returning home, he saw her in a Church and threw himself down in front of her, beseeching her *Doña Dona Dona* until the floor was slippery with his tears; he saw that her eyes were very steady and clear, only a tightness around her lips betraying impatience as she sat listening to him in her private pew, tapping her comb very gently against her wrist. It was not the comb that he still kept against his heart; it was the other comb. – You want me to come straight to you, she said laughing. But it is you who must come to me! I am the woman, not you! – This speech made a great

* Emblem of the French King, François Ier.

impression on him. He understood that all his exertions were as nothing to the exertions that he must perform if he wanted to win her; embracing this fact, he was instantly permitted by the LORD OF DREAMS to be with her in her chamber again, she more gentle and beautiful than ever before, and the locket opened by itself in her palm, its fine gold chain dangling from her wrist, and there was the twin-locked ivory box whose unknown contents he craved so passionately; again he prayed her for the key; again she asked him if he was worthy, and he said despairingly *no one* is worthy! at which a tiny golden key appeared in his hand, and his heart began to pound as he leaned forward and turned it in the first lock . . .

In France

When Pope Alexander VI drew a line through the New World, assigning half to Spain and half to Portugal, the Roy François I curled his lip and said: I would like to see the paragraph about *that* in Adam's will!

Oh, you are so clever! said his mistress. Will you *always* say such clever things to please me?

To please *you?* said François, who had forgotten her existence. Oh, by all means! he said ironically. Without doubt I shall always be clever enough to please *you!*

He moved away from her and sat on the sofa. He was looking through the hexagonal leaded panes, and she came to look through them, too, resting her plump white hand on his shoulder, letting her breast touch his cheek – she half expected him to snuffle at it, as he so often did, but this time he paid no heed to that warm and flaccid hemisphere, thinking instead of the one that the Pope had spoiled for him. He sighed a little, and she sighed, too, and he shot a glance into her skull before resuming his staring out the window. She yawned. One of his great hunting-dogs got up from the floor and buried its muzzle in her lap. She laughed (although she loathed dogs), because such scenes amused him; but still he kept to himself, so she said to him darling Monseigneur, what do you see through the window? and he set his teeth and said I see New Spain.

He went to Romorantin and had another of his sham battles, whose missiles were snowballs, potatoes and eggs. – Come on, you poltroons! he shouted in wild excitement. The watchword is Jerusalem! Let's have at all these Turks and niggers! – He led a charge to the front door of his Palace, yelling and roaring and laughing, and his dogs mauled a serving-boy while the damsels of the Court watched and fanned themselves; and an egg hit him on the side of the head and splattered and he snatched up a clod of dirt and hurled it back and wiped his cheek with his dirty hand as he went, running toward the frenzied defenders in the game (for he had decreed that whichever side won would receive a prize), and he did not know that his half-conscious attempt to clean himself had but blackened him like a Moor, so that when he came to the door crying *death to the Pagans!* the Sentry did not recognize him and therefore swung heartily with a log. François fell and lay still.

There was a silence, and then the courtiers started crying out: Treachery! He's killed the Roy! – But the Roy had not been killed at all. True, he had to lie in bed for a month or two, as the Docteurs told him, but he would recover.

Eh, so now I'm an invalid, he said. Still and all, a beautiful escape. Send for General Lesparre.

Lesparre came galloping on his horse. – Sire, I heard about your terrible accident, he said. Are you in great pain?

Oh, my head hurts, said François, his eyes tightly closed. But that's not what I want to talk about. You know how much I love my brother Charles of Spain . . .

There was a smirk beneath the goatish lip. The face flushed with pleasure beneath its bandages; the fingers plucked at the lace collar around the neck. The eyelids, as square-angled as shutters, flew up suddenly to feast upon Lesparre's astonishment.

You *know* how Christian a Roy I am. I want my dear brother to have everything I have, including his knock on the head. Oh, I believe in charity to lepers, all right! (Damn, but my head hurts!) Do you understand me, Lesparre?

I listen with the greatest attention, Sire.

You *know* that England has declared that she will side against whoever breaks the peace in Navarre, yawned the Roy, scratching the ears of his favorite dog. – Well, you see that I am a hopeless invalid at present who cannot conduct foreign policy. So no one will blame *me* if you invade Navarre. If you fail, *I* shall blame you and discharge you from my service; if you succeed we shall have given those Spaniards a good blow with the horsewhip. Maybe the Pope will respect our claims then. How about it? Will you or won't you serve your Roy?

Lesparre fell to his knees and thanked him with tears in his eyes. Then he went to assemble his forces.

The Conversion of the Spaniards

Commander de Herrera looked very mournful. Iñigo knew that he had resolved to surrender the fortress to the French. This seemed to him the basest and most cowardly decision, and he felt that he would rather die than see it carried out. The other knights concurred, although they were not outspoken; he could read them well. – And these were the very ones he had led here, thinking so highly of them! – Lesparre has a very great army, they said.

Why is it, he thought to himself, that however much fervor and conviction I have by myself, it melts away in the presence of others? If only the Duke were here! He'd tell me what to do. They look at me as if I'm their leader, and then the words of command don't come out of my mouth. I smile and say whatever will be most agreeable – not from cowardice, but from a sense of futility. The pure thing, the noble thing, is only what makes *me* alive. But to make others do it is selfishness. Or is it? Maybe I've met no one pure enough for the Sacrifice with its black mouth bloody and screaming. But where are they, those pure companions? Do they exist? And what about the pure one who would not love me? Did she reject me because she was pure, I being base-born in relation to her – or do I only think her pure because she rejected me? I feel so alive in my suffering!

And then suddenly, for the first time in his life, he felt the Power within him. Within him, something laughed silkily and told him: Iñigo, you can *tame* these men! You can make them into heroes; they will do whatever you tell them to do.

And in astonishment he knew that it was true.

There were two knights of particular bravery there named Don Pedro and Don Avilla. When Iñigo heard even these men saying that the fortress could not hold out, he strode up to them and shouted: What do you think the Duke would say to this? Do you not remember how he has so graciously and generously housed us and clothed us, and now he is away to get succor for us? And if you cannot keep the Duke in your minds, what about the King? Do you feel prepared to betray him? Remember Saint Peter! Imagine yourselves in disgrace in his presence, with your faces cast down! How can you think of laying down your arms to these Frenchmen?

Astounded, they stepped back from him and said nothing.

Iñigo, Iñigo, these knights are correct, said Commander de Herrera in a caressing voice. Your zeal is appreciated, but . . .

Iñigo fell to his knees. – Commander, do *you* think of the Duke, I pray you. And think of the glory that will be ours if we hold fast.

But we cannot. Do you seriously believe that I do not have the same longings as you?

Iñigo remained on his knees.

No, no! he shouted. I insist on a final decision. If the rest of you surrender, I shall go down and fight them myself!

And you have no fear? I have never seen the like. You are fearless!

If I said anything different, sir, said Iñigo, I would be lying.

Then the hearts of the others grew hot and valorous, and Commander de Herrera smiled and said: See, we cannot resist you. Let us hope that the Frenchmen will say the same.

The Battle

Iñigo had his hair cut and combed; his hair was very important to him. On the morning of the engagement, he confessed to his comrade-in-arms, Don Avilla. Turning away so that others would not see, he kissed the comb that his beloved had awarded him. He longed for nothing better than a glorious end. He sharpened his dagger. He polished his sword and put on his helmet.

Now he saw the French officers in blue, with wrought golden buttons, singing and cantering, their red leg-hosen glowing in the sun. They were serenely bearded like suns. Suddenly he was very afraid, but he recalled his family ancestor, Alfonso IX, who bravely fought against the Moors and died in the battle of Gibraltar. – Surely, he said to himself, I can do as Alfonso did!

Come on, you Frenchmen! Iñigo shouted.

Just as he said this, a French ball passed through both his legs and so struck him down.

The other defenders surrendered at once.

A Nice Scene

The French soldiers were full of admiration for Iñigo, and treated him with chivalrous courtesy, so that he was very much satisfied. He felt very light-headed and heroic. His comrades kept slapping him on the shoulders and weeping. He thought that they were ashamed of having surrendered, and tried to cheer them up. He did not understand that they grieved for him, because his career as a soldier was over. He would be lucky to walk again. He smiled and laughed, and understood nothing. Everything was dancing before him. Presently he began to feel the pain, but it was a matter of honor with him to show no suffering.

Oh, but you are valiant, Monsieur! cried the French Docteurs. They did their best for him; he could see it. He was filled with love for them. He gave them his buckler, poignard, cuirass . . .

The Books 1521–1522

His autobiography, that precursor of the *Jesuit Relations*, tells us that on the thirteenth day after the battle, they carried him over the mountains on a litter, past the iron mines, across the little brooks (and here, by some trick, the Ninth Rapid mirrors the Forty-Eighth; one can see mirages doubling over the topmost ridge of mountains), and everything seemed very strange to him. He felt as if what he saw was but the backdrop for some pageant, indifferently constructed; and he wondered that anyone could take pleasure in it. They carried him across a stream in which trout swam, and he saw them and said to himself: What idle likenesses of silver! – Because his case was not good it was decided to rest him a week at his sister-in-law Magdalena's house, which was midway between Vergara and Tumálvaga. So at last they came to Casa Loyola. His brother Martín García was waiting there. Iñigo was almost unconscious by then, but he opened his eyes for a moment and smiled at his brother as they carried him up the steep stone stairs to the topmost floor; as they rounded the corner he saw his family escutcheon on the wall – the two wolves rampant on either side of a hanging cauldron – and again he smiled a little.

His dear Magdalena cared for him and sought to ease him with spices and other drugs, so that he thought of the goodness of kinship, of how Elizabeth was MARIA's cousin, how John the Baptist was JESUS's cousin; how in Heaven the saints were relations and friends. But then his leg ached, and he tired of thinking of religious matters.

Iñigo, there is a pretty doe among our sweet-chestnut trees. I wish that you could see.

A doe, Magdalena? he replied. How strange! – And for a moment it did seem to him the strangest thing that he had ever heard.

Sick almost unto death, he lay there, and the Spanish Doctors said to him: We must break your leg again. The bone did not set properly on the road.

Heaven! cried Magdalena fiercely. Hasn't he suffered sufficiently for all his sins?

Standing by the head of the bed, Martín García told her to be silent. – You know it must be done, he said.

Iñigo laughed. Let it be done then, he said. I am ready.

They took his leg in two places and began to pull upon it, very slowly and carefully. Iñigo's face went white. Magdalena put her hand on his shoulder, and he was very happy. He did not groan, or even clench his teeth; but his fists squeezed themselves tighter and tighter.

Afterward Magdalena brought him his sword and dagger, and he kissed them. She said: Soon you will bear arms again, brother-in-law! – And Iñigo smiled.

Still he did not recover. His face became pale and yellow, so that the Doctors drew Martín García aside and whispered in his ear, and Iñigo saluted Magdalena and said don't cry, sister-in-law; I rest very comfortably here and Martín García said something low and harsh to the Doctors and they said nothing. The days of fever went slowly by, and then it was the Feast of Saint John.

We advise you to confess, the Doctors said to him. We cannot guarantee your recovery.

During the Vigil of Saints Peter and Paul they gave him the Sacraments.

If you do not improve by midnight, said the Doctors, you can consider yourself dead.

Iñigo prayed: Dear Saint Peter, you know how I venerate you and love you. Please save me on this Night, which is your Night, and help me to recover so that I can be a soldier again. I know that all things are possible for you.

And he began to recover.

But one of his bones jutted out in his leg, just below the knee. When it became clear to him that he would remain this way, he wept for the first time and implored JESUS. For while his bravery yet grew in him, he had made no progress in overcoming his vanity.

Can this bone be cut away? he asked the Doctors.

Of course, they said to him in surprise. But you would not want us to do it.

And why is that? said Iñigo very quietly.

Your leg is healed now. We should have to cut it again, and you would suffer great pain.

Have I complained about the pain yet?

No, you have not, said the Doctors, but this pain will be much worse than anything you have suffered.

Go ahead and cut it, he said.

Martín García could not restrain his horror when he saw what the Doctors began to do. – Stop, stop! he cried out. Iñigo, do you really choose to suffer this?

Yes, he replied.

I know I myself would not have such courage, said Martín García. Cut away, then.

When the operation was completed, the sick man felt rather faint. The Doctors stretched his leg continually with their instruments, so that he almost felt as if he were in the hands of the Inquisition. But Magdalena was by him hour after hour, rubbing his leg with ointments that the Doctors prescribed, and presently he began to get well.

Now we shall leave you for three weeks, the Doctors said to him. You are out of danger. You must stay in bed for that time, until your leg is completely healed.

So he lay upstairs, and the time passed very tediously. In his mind he saw at first the blinding river-glints of Pampeluna, but slowly he lost those, being out of his context. And the feeling of strangeness returned.

Magdalena, he said one day, have you any romances of chivalry for me to read? That would help me pass the time.

We have a *Vita CHRISTI* and a Lives of the Saints, she said. Would you like either of those?

No, no, he said. I think I will sleep.

But he slept and looked at the ceiling, and looked at the walls, and Magdalena passed upstairs and downstairs on her many tasks, and when she looked in on him he said that perhaps he would look at the books after all.

He opened the *Vita CHRISTI*, and this is what he read:

> IT IS VANITY TO SOLICIT HONORS, OR TO RAISE ONESELF TO HIGH STATION. IT IS VANITY TO BE A SLAVE TO BODILY DESIRES, AND TO CRAVE FOR THINGS THAT BRING CERTAIN RETRIBUTION. IT IS VANITY TO WISH FOR LONG LIFE, IF YOU CARE LITTLE FOR A GOOD LIFE. IT IS VANITY TO GIVE THOUGHT ONLY TO THIS PRESENT LIFE, AND TO CARE NOTHING FOR THE LIFE TO COME. IT IS VANITY TO LOVE THINGS THAT SO SWIFTLY PASS AWAY, AND NOT TO HASTEN ONWARDS TO THAT PLACE WHERE EVERLASTING JOY ABIDES.

His leg ached.

He read:

> DO NOT BE VAIN ABOUT YOUR BEAUTY OR STRENGTH OF BODY, WHICH A LITTLE SICKNESS CAN MAR AND DISFIGURE.

And he remembered what had happened to his nose. He remembered his knee.

He read:

> STRIVE TO WITHDRAW YOUR HEART FROM THE LOVE OF VISIBLE THINGS, AND DIRECT YOUR AFFECTIONS TO THINGS INVISIBLE.

He read:

> WHO HAS A FIERCER STRUGGLE THAN HE WHO STRIVES TO CONQUER HIMSELF?

For a moment he envied Saint Peter, who had *seen* CHRIST and known Him: how much easier it must be to keep to one's faith under those circumstances! Why, he thought, was it not given to me to be present when my LORD rose up to Heaven? Surely it would be no trouble to be righteous then!

Then his leg ached, and he yawned, and imagined how fine it would be to serve his high Doña, and how it would be to kiss her hand again; as he thought of these worldly things he was very happy, and the time passed.

Magdalena was out of sight. Slyly he drew the comb from his breast and touched it to his lips.

Nothing happened in his heart.

He closed his eyes, and confusion pounded at him like armies.

His brother Martín García said to him: The Caballeros have defeated the French, and General Lesparre has been imprisoned! and he said slowly that is good; thank you for the news; but somehow he could not form an intense excitement over it.

Martín García looked at him a little queerly, but said nothing.

The Second Lock

Then he dreamed he was with her once again and her beauty terrified him like the roar of some great waterfall and the first lock had sprung open with his golden key still shining in it and she covered his face with her hair, saying to him you're worthy now, aren't you? I *see* it in you and he answered I I I am wounded for you – at which she smiled down at him and he loved her breath on his face and the second golden key appeared in his hand but it was burning him so that drops of sweat burst out on his forehead; yet he would not be unmanly here in front of her, so he clasped his fingers tight around the key and they began to sizzle and he bit his lip and leaned toward the box which shimmered more and more brightly and seemed to recede from him as he reached for it and she was smiling at him and his hand was burning and the key was shining right through his fingers because the locksmith Duval had made it and this was Champlain's Store-house still in the Heaven of unborn souls and his fingers seared and crackled, but in a gasp of effort he fitted that key into the lock so delicately (when what his body was screaming at him to do was to pull away and let the key fall twinkling to the floor and his fingers were already black skeleton-fingers but she knew his pain as she looked into his face; that smile told him that she knew); and he mastered his agony and turned the key very carefully in the lock until there was a click and the lock flew open and he lifted the lid of the ivory box so respectfully even as the bone-digits fell from his wrist; and now he heard Angels singing and there was a shining Country inside, as vast as the box was tiny, where the gilded domes of Skull-Churches seared his eyes with their brightness, and sky-blue brooks flowed with clouds. He saw fields of flowers beyond which everything was grassy and open. Sheds whose boards were weathered grey (or rather bright and shining silver), whose shingles were peeling, stood alone in the wastes of cornfields where the souls of good children ran laughing and playing; they played among the red cows, white cows, black cows that chewed their cuds in yellow fields of gold; and in the City he heard the happy souls singing and praying around the Palace of the FATHER that flew a thousand flags whose emblems were blue and white, the colors of purity, of the VIERGE MARIE (it was the fleur-de-lys, the symbol of Solomon, first King of the Jews; the symbol of the Unearthly Kingdom); and he saw the Angels and Virgins walking in the wide wide streets and autumn came and the parks were strewn with golden leaves; and the crowds of blessed souls streamed in under the great rainbow arch. He saw there his mother and all of his brothers who had died for the Faith: they smiled at him and JESUS came out of the Palace and touched his forehead, at which Iñigo wanted to die for love of Him and His ever-bleeding wounds; and then he saw Saint Peter standing sternly at the gate, looking outward at a great dark forest; and he saw that a golden wall ran round the Kingdom and at every parapet and tower there stood a grim and shining War-Angel keeping watch and he understood that the Enemy was somewhere in this endless forest that surrounded the City, hiding like the pale grey sky flickering through that wall of dark grey trees, whose thinness was interrupted occasionally by evergreens. Although the time of the foliage was past, young maple saplings, leaved rusty red, burned like fire around the tall bare trees. There was an evilness here; he could feel it now, lurking in the thick stands of cattail, in the feverish alternations of orange and green treetops, beneath the black rivers that were already striped white with ice . . . The Enemy was coming out of this darkness. (The Enemy was the Hiroquois.) – Iñigo cried out: *Let me serve with Saint Peter in CHRIST's army!* . . . and Doña Catarina was his Sainte Kateri Tekakwitha whispering in his ear: Now you have me forever and he said I am worthy only for burning and she said you will go into the box, but first I will kiss you and for the first and last time her lips were on his lips and the agony seared him and he was in the box and the lid closed over his head like water like a stream a rivière a Fleuve and he was stifling burning lonely dreaming of glory radiantly enthroned on glory, glory in and of itself like candles in a church burning so brightly that he could not understand how the church did not burn down; and the stained glass windows ran and melted with it; the colors were unbearably bright; he was unbearably happy. He woke up, and his pillow was wet with tears.

His leg ached.

He fell asleep, with the sun streaming through the window onto his face. He was with CHRIST. When he awoke, he tried so hard to *see* CHRIST and *feel* CHRIST in his breast, but he could not. He said to himself: Iñigo, you are not awake at all; you are sleeping, and you are not even dreaming hard enough, you chain-bound sinner! I *beg* you to see yourself as you will appear before GOD on the Day of Judgment, miserably weeping and shriveling in His brightness.

He said to himself: It was at Cæsarea Philippi that Peter suddenly understood that Jesus was CHRIST, the Anointed One. And here I am at home; CHRIST has made it so easy for me that I have discovered Him as I lay idly in my own bed!

He lifted up his hands to CHRIST; he felt sunlight on his palms.

He felt very intense interior motions.

He read the life of Saint Francis, and asked himself: could *I* not do what Francis did?

The Election

A fierce joy seized him. He sat up in his bed and raised his fists. Silently he shouted:

I declare *war* against the world! I raise CHRIST's standard in its face!

The Pilgrim

1522–1524

> Truly the condition of a voyageur is very sad, when he does not return able to compensate by some solid advantage for the hardships and dangers which he has encountered.
>
> THE REVEREND PÈRE F. X. DE CHARLEVOIX, SJ, *The History and General Description of New France* (1743)

First, he said, I must free myself of all inordinate attachment. Then I can listen for His voice.

I shall become a Pilgrim, he said.

And I understand, he said, that I am an instrument of Thy will; I expect to be used until I am broken.

Iñigo and Martín García

You are well, said Martín García.

Sir, Iñigo said, I am going on a journey.

Something has changed in you, said Martín García. You have been reading these holy books. That is good, but I do not want you to get extreme ideas. You are an extremist; you know that.

Sir, the Duke knows that I am well. It is proper that I go to him now.

You have no plans other than to serve him? said Martín García, studying his brother very minutely. You do not plan to become some barefoot beggar-monk whose life will be an embarrassment to us?

Since the change that had come over him, Iñigo had become very careful to say only the truth.

You know I have served him faithfully, he replied.

Why do you equivocate with me? said Martín García, and Iñigo was ashamed of the pain that he was causing his brother, the pain that he knew he would cause him again and again.

Martín García took him from room to room, pleading with him and imploring him to consider all the hopes they had in him. Rubbing his moustache, Iñigo chose the words of his reply as exactly as he could, so that he would not be lying but nonetheless could soothe his brother.

Go, then, said Martín García, happy again, go and serve the Duke. We shall pray for you on your journey.

GOD be with you, Sir, he replied.

He desired passionately to give his sister-in-law Magdalena a farewell embrace, but the time seemed to have passed for that. He thanked her for her gracious care of him, and said: Magdalena, I shall always love you for your goodness.

Come back to us, she said. You will come back to this house?

My thoughts will never be far from you, he said. May GOD keep you.

Under the pillow he left the ivory comb that Doña Catarina had given him.

The Mouth of the River

The Duke was in straits at that time, having fared ill at Court since the French attack, so that when Iñigo rode into his courtyard the Treasurer said I am sorry, Señor, but your wages cannot be paid but when the Duke heard who was there he said by GOD, if I must forego repayment of all my other debts to do it, yet still would I pay Loyola first!

The Pilgrim thanked him very graciously. Then he said what he had to say. He rode away to the nearest church and gave the money away, so that a statue of Our LADY in poor repair might be restored and adorned with jewels.

The Unbeliever

He went on his way to Montserrat, says the *Autobiography*, *thinking as he always did of the deeds he would do for GOD.* His sword and dagger were at his side.

As he rode along on his mule, a Moor on a mule approached him, so they conversed to pass the time and forget about the chilly winds and the dust that rose in their faces with every step. They began to speak of Our LADY.

Yes, said the Moor, I accept that she conceived Him without a man, for much can happen in that way. We know that mud gives rise to frogs in springtime, and old dung produces flies.

The blood rushed to the Pilgrim's face, and he clenched his fists.

But surely, the Moor continued innocently, surely she could not have remained a virgin once she had given birth. How could she? I don't mean to cause offense, but it's against all reason! A virgin is a maiden intact. Once the birth tears her, how can she be intact anymore?

She can be if GOD wills, said the Pilgrim in a very low voice. He did not dare to look at the Moor; he was afraid that he might strike him.

No, no! laughed the other. That's no reason; that's just your dogma! Say, why is your face so red? I hope I haven't embarrassed you. Well, Señor, I must increase my pace. I am going far, far. Good day to you!

The Pilgrim could not stop thinking about what had happened. He felt deficient in his duty, like a sentry who has fallen asleep, like a soldier who surrenders the fortress. He had not defended Our LADY's honor. To think that good Spaniards had once been the slaves of these infidels!

He let the reins go slack. He let CHRIST flow into him. He closed his eyes and said: Let me *see* what I must do!

Nothing happened. He did not know how to make the Exercises yet.

So he said to himself: If my mule remains on the highway at the next fork, I shall do nothing. But if the mule takes the town road, I shall pursue this vile Moor and slit his guts!

The mule stayed on the highway. The Pilgrim took the road on to Montserrat. His dagger jiggled against his thigh.

Montserrat

At last he came to that great hill of peaks that arose above tree and church; he rode past a great hacienda whose servant lowered the well-bucket for him and the narrow high-walled house rose to meet its red roof, overtowered only by its bell-shaft, and the Pilgrim said thank you for the water, brother, and as he smiled at the man his moustache dipped further at the corners of his mouth. The road wound upward between the boulder-crags, and on almost every crag there stood a little shrine with its cross-crowned pyramidal roof, and the Pilgrim rode his mule very slowly between the praying penitents, stopping at every shrine to bow his head and express his reverence for Our LORD, while the cold dusty wind blew in between the pillars; he knelt on the sandy steps and the mule shifted its feet restlessly; and he rode upward and passed a procession of monks carrying crosses and chanting dolorously; when he looked back at them they seemed like ants. He wondered if Martín García had yet learned that he had left the Duke's service. He wondered what had crossed Magdalena's mind when she'd found the comb beneath the pillow. These thoughts came to him again and again, like the ache in his leg, because he had not yet fashioned the weapons to render them inhuman. Now he rose the worn trail across the meadow, and brushed past Spanish oaks, and the way became dark and narrow between the little crags until suddenly he came out into a wide bowl walled in by crags and more crags with the hermitages of Santa Cruz and Sainte-Catherine and Saint Michael nestled in tree-pockets among the crags above him, each with its own church and garden, and there were ever so many more all the way up to the little chapel of Saint Jerome just below the summit (from which, it was said, you could see Barcelona and the isles of Majorca and Minorca), but the Pilgrim had already arrived at his destination. The Abbey of the VIRGIN stood before him, walled around like GOD.

He could still go back to Casa Loyola. The Duke would take him back. Magdalena would forgive him the distress he had caused her . . .

Ah, the cunning of the DEVIL! And the pity of it, that he must now see the DEVIL in Magdalena's face –

The Pilgrim stared straight ahead at nothing. His dark eyes almost seemed crossed. – Thank you very much, sirs, he said, but I am not hungry. I wish only to pray to Our LADY.

The monks nodded and did not trouble him further.

All night he knelt and stood with the others in that massive space of glittering bars and grilles, with the great Altar rising in the distance beyond, where Our LADY held the infant JESUS to Her and the baby held a saw in His hand, and Our LADY looked down at Him so softly as the love from Her went rising against panels and panels of holy pictures, and moonlight streamed in between the shadows of bars. He resolved to dedicate his sword and dagger to Her.

The next day he began his written confession, which was to occupy three days, and in the night he woke up suddenly with a stab of anguish, thinking how can I give up my arms? but he comforted himself, seeing in his mind the beauties of this mountain with all its hermitages walled in to themselves beneath the dolmens and stone-fingers, with chestnut trees in every ravine, and secret Crosses where people came to pray; and he said to himself: it is good for my arms to be here in this place – and at last he was able to go back to sleep.

The treasure of the Abbey was vast, for many had felt as the Pilgrim did. The place possessed a golden crown, and many barrels of gold and diamonds. Greedy though she is for gold, however, the Church is greedier still for martyrs. When mourners bring the bleeding bodies of her sons back to her, she lays their heads on her lap with a tenderness and pride that outdoes the chastisements she gave them when they were alive. Ignatius was now on the path that would give her Père Brébeuf and Père Jogues. But that was more than a century away. He would begin by giving what he had.

The Father Confessor sat in his chair, looking out the casement window. Birds peeped in, and he smiled a little. The remains of his supper were on a tray on the floor. The wall behind him was book-lined; the room was niched with many little arches. He wore a skullcap; his beard was white as snow. His collar was like the leaves of a heart.

Sit down, he said, not looking away from the window.

The Pilgrim sat.

So you wish to give us a mule? he said.

Yes.

Are you a wealthy man, Iñigo? Can you afford such a sacrifice?

I am poor in goodness.

The Father Confessor turned slowly and looked the Pilgrim in the face. – You must open your heart to me, my son, he said. You must not guard and equivocate so much; by so doing you approach mortal sin. Do you understand that?

The Pilgrim began to weep. I . . . I am so poor in goodness, Father, he said.

Ah, so that is how it is, said the old man. Well, we accept your mule with thanks.

The Vigil

He stood all night in front of Our Lady.

He stood with splayed feet, his helmet resting at his feet like some dead black skull, and the shiny exoskeleton that he wore, so cold and black, made him seem severe when he was only sad despite his big clown's ears and his goatish beard and moustache; he went to the casement and opened it; he put his hand on the hilt of his sword, and his eyes were so very sad.

The next morning he set out. He kissed his sword; he kissed his dagger. Then he left them there. He had already changed clothes with a beggar.

Manresa 1522

Gaunt and pale, he leaned forward and touched his slender white fingers to his breast, praying in Spanish lightnings and chilling himself in clouds. He prayed as follows:

O VIRGIN in your gold robes, outstretch your pale hands to me; let me touch you. Let me kiss your jet-black braids. Look upon me with sweetness and compassion, my wife, my mother, my – my sister –

He felt that he had not prayed aright. He felt that he was *not* pure enough. And he prayed as follows:

Dearest MARIA, I feel such an ache in my heart that You will not have me. But You already know that. What is the sense of saying anything? Why do I need to express myself to You? I am not asking You for anything. I am not even praying to You because there is nothing that I want to ask You for. I knew as soon as I prayed to You today that You would not accept my love. Your silence was already in Your voice. I could hear You not wanting me. But I cannot keep silent, and that is another sin of mine because Your weariness with my sins is all around me now like bruises that I have caused; I cannot help telling You that night after night at Court while other women slept beside me, I lay awake imagining kissing You all over: it was only when I felt myself praying to You, kissing Your mouth and drinking from it, that I felt alive. When I first saw Your box with the two locks, I hoped that You could grant me this prayer; I believed *until I could taste You on my tongue as I lay in the darkness. And now that's over. You kissed me once, but that was not You. Now I know You'll never have me. You don't want me. I feel so selfish for having asked You. I feel so unhappy. And I'm grateful for this pain; I'm grateful for anything You give me. Please don't keep this prayer of mine. As I said, it isn't even a prayer. Please don't even listen to it. (But consider: You could let me love You; You wouldn't have to love me back; what if I just bowed down before You and kissed You? What if I stayed with You all night and You pretended that I wasn't even there, that I was just a lump of darkness between the many lamps that burn in praise to You?) I can't understand why I want You so badly and always have, when women love me. It must be Your grace that permits me to want You. But please don't be angry with me for having asked You; no one else was good enough because no one else was You. And don't be angry with me if I keep myself from You for awhile, until I bear to look upon Your image without craving to kiss You. Now I do pray to You: I pray to You to forgive me for loving You. My heart is a stone prison in which some condemned thing is bleeding very quietly.* AMEN.

And then it was the same as it had been with Saint Peter: Because he knew himself unworthy, he was accepted. But there was this difference: Peter was one of Twelve, but Iñigo was alone.

The River's Mouth

He closed his eyes and offered Her his freedom. Then at once he saw Her. That was the first Exercise. But in terror and love and shame, the image of his sister-in-law rose behind Her and peered so shyly and desperately over Her shoulder and he bit his lip and explained to himself the reasons why he must curse her and then began to do it and she burst into sobs and he knew that he was sobbing and he did not even see the expression on the VIRGIN's face as he execrated the DEVIL until Magdalena screwed her eyes shut in a great wail and vanished and so he had defended himself from the malignant ENEMY.

Manresa 1523

After this, a month passed in melancholy, and then he began to wonder where exactly in his body his spirit was. He thought that if he could just see inside his heart and find that thing he would be happy. Somehow it was connected with the double-locked box that the Exercises came from. The thought that because he could not locate his spirit exactly it might be straining unseen toward earthly things was a continual torment to him. There was a great hole in the floor of the Dominican monastery where they let him stay, and when his unhappiness began to scream he longed to throw himself into that jagged darkness where the Fox's scalp waited, but then he would remember that it was a sin to end one's life, and so he paced up and down yelling: LORD, I shall do nothing to offend you! until the monks came irritably and told him to be quiet, and he knew that he had been troublesome. – Where was his spirit? If only he knew that his agony and scruples would diminish. Once he thought he could feel it in his chest between heartbeats, illuminating the inside of his heart in a way that no one could ever see because if even the skilled and subtle Doctors had cut inside his heart the spirit would fly away; he would be dead before they could see that it was already dark inside; but now he felt the heat and glow of it inside him, beating and beating inside him and hurting him, and he said O JESU, help me to bear this agony! . . . and then it stopped; he felt it no more, and he was in terror and shame; he thought: has my spirit gone away from me?

He begged his alms. He prayed on his knees beside that hole for seven hours of every day. He saw something bright and shining in the air.

He found a cave in Manresa where he went daily to scourge himself. When he had beaten his shoulders until the blood flowed down his back, when he knelt exhausted but glowing with happy sadness, then the world's day passing by outside was like a meaningless river that flowed over his face without altering or besmirching him; he prayed and prayed, not seeing the walled and towered city by him, not hearing the people walking by, not feeling the flies landing on him to feast on his blood. He had resolved to purify himself until he was prepared to sail to Jerusalem.

Rome 1523

At that time he still had a passion to seek out spiritual persons, that he might be better enlightened. For when one's life is bent toward obedience, it is a lonely thing to obey no one but oneself. Often he thought upon the old Father Confessor at Montserrat, but his weapons were there in the grave of his past life; he could never go back there. Here in Manresa he could find no one of true discernment, save for a woman who told him to look for GOD with all his might and craft, like a hunter in a dark forest. So he completely lost his desire for spiritual persons after this, and relied increasingly upon his own voices. His Confessor at the monastery was skeptical of him, as when one day a platter of meat sailed into his Exercises and he knew after that that it was permitted to him to partake of it. – Consider whether this may be a temptation, the Confessor said; and he replied: I have looked well into my heart, Father, and I know now without a doubt that I must decide to resume eating meat. – So be it, said the Confessor, shrugging, but the Pilgrim knew that he questioned him. At first he felt the same rage against him that he had felt against the Moor who'd spoken against the virgin birth, but then he said to himself: Dishonor in men's eyes is also a good mortification! and then he was happy. He saw the creation of the world, and tried to explain it to the Confessor, but he could not express himself about the white rays and the whiteness; the Confessor struggled hard that day to show no smile. This time the Pilgrim had himself under better control, and so the Confessor's reaction pleased him.

For his own use he had begun to write down the Exercises as they came to him, in order to train and direct his imagination upon worthy things. How well he could guard himself from danger, if in moments of temptation he could see before him CHRIST's face flashing beneath the Crown of Thorns! A spell of weakness, in which he found himself joying in worldly things, could easily be set at nought, if within the instant he could cause the reddish-black mouth of Hell to open to sight! If at any time he could bring before him the baptism of CHRIST, or the Annunciation, the Vocation, the Conversion of Maria Magdalena; or any other images to be drawn forth at need as if from a deck of cards, what Power he would gain over himself! The day would come, he hoped, when to everything he might need to think of would be attached a single heart-picture, luminous and static like a stained glass window . . . But to the end of his life he always had to cover the face of Our LADY in his Book of Hours, since she reminded him so much of Magdalena. To call up the colors of the Exercises, one must dwell in blackness.

In the winter of 1522–3 he was very ill, having severely mortified his body with thin clothing and a scanty diet. They put him in the house of a Señor Ferrara, whose son was in service, and many prominent Doñas came to watch over his bed, for his piety was becoming famous. For a long time he suffered from stomach pains and fevers, but as the year came to a close he recovered, and they made him promise to eat better fare and to clothe himself in clothes more appropriate to the weather. He promised readily, for it occurred to him that these extreme mortifications of his had been a sort of vanity from which he drew satisfaction. – Who am I, after all, he said to himself, to take up the hours and energies of these good Doñas? Surely they are correct, and I was abusing myself. – So he soon felt stronger than he had been the entire time in Montserrat, and at the coming of the New Year he set out for Barcelona. He was there for twenty days. At the command of his Confessor there he begged food for his passage to Jerusalem, although for fear of vanity he told those he begged from only that he was going as far as Rome. – The Doñas frowned and swept the air with their pretty little fans. – That is no place for things of the spirit, so we have heard, they told him. – The Pilgrim bowed and said nothing. When he had enough provisions for the shipmaster to accept him, he embarked for Gaeta, and there set out on foot. Everyone kept telling him: Turn back, you fanatic, there is pestilence ahead! – So be it, replied the Pilgrim, thumping the road with his staff. And he pressed on to Rome.

Begging with him were a mother and daughter, and a young man. The mother looked a little like Magdalena. So he was particularly careful to be formal with her. When they came to a farm house for shelter one night, there were many soldiers singing and cursing around a fire; they gave the travelers wine, as if out of friendliness, but kept winking among themselves. Considering the Eight Beatitudes, the Pilgrim said to himself: I must show goodwill towards them, for while they are not the pure of heart, nor by their profession can they be peacemakers; yet by looking into their eyes I can tell that they mourn, although they know it not. – But the soldiers laughed louder than before, and continued to gaze upon the woman and the girl. – I see that the mare has foaled, said one, but which is the better horse we shall know only by riding them both! – The other roared with laughter. – But the Pilgrim thought: Still I must show them charity, for this is the wine shouting out, and not the man. – And when the soldiers were not looking, he stealthily poured out his own cup.

Why do you do that? whispered the young man. That was good wine!

Not so good that I must drink it, said the Pilgrim. We must watch here, for the two ladies' sake.

Soon the travelers became sleepy, and went to bed, the mother and daughter in the upper room, and the Pilgrim and the young man in the stable, where the innocent breathing of horses filled them with peace. His companion lay down in the hay at once, but he knelt and prayed for the safety of the ladies on this night, casting among his images and Exercises for one suited to this case; and at length he selected the Contemplation of CHRIST upon the stormy sea* whose waves curled over the boat as He lay so peacefully sleeping (this was the First Point), and the waters were blackish and shot through with green lightnings as the Pilgrim could plainly see (the young man staring at him in astonishment at the length of his devotions, and the horses shifting patiently in their stalls); and the Disciples grew pale with fear and said to one another: we are ruined! for now the fury of the waves increased and great whirlpools broke out upon the water like great wells down whose screwthread spirals the Disciples peered trembling and it seemed to them as if at the bottom of the nearest of these hideous shafts gleamed the red eyes of some DEMON or WATER-MONSTER and they could not discern its features or body beneath the spray but it seemed prodigious, hairy with wriggling hairs the thickness of eels, and the hairs now began swarming their

* I.e., the Fortieth Rapid of the Stream of Time.

way up the whirlpool to fasten upon the boat and the Disciples screamed in terror and one rushed to awaken Him, at which He said (this was the Second Point): Why are ye fearful, O ye of little faith? – Then He commanded the winds (this was the Third Point), and at once the whirlpools became smooth and ocean-weight pressed down upon the Fox's scalp so that it could do no harm, and the waves were sunny and blue. – So the Pilgrim calmed his apprehensions on the ladies' account, commending them to Him. And he lay down in the hay beside his companion at last.

Come midnight, however, the pair were awakened by women's screams. The young man's lip twitched; he cocked his head from side to side like a squirrel and fled into the darkness. But the Pilgrim felt more anguish than fear. Rushing upstairs, he saw no sign of the two women, but the room was in some disorder. He thrust his head out the window and saw them weeping in the courtyard below.

He ran out and said: What has happened to you?

The soldiers, the mother gasped, they tried to lay hands on us. I think soon they will come back . . .

The Pilgrim was filled with anger. When the soldiers came out jeering, as if they were prepared to assault the women once again, he shouted: How dare you break GOD's laws? Why does this have to be tolerated? – The veins stood out on his neck, and his eyes glared so fiercely that they were afraid of him. They did not dare to strike him.

Come, said the Pilgrim. I shall protect you. Let us go on.

But it is night! said the daughter.

Would you rather stay here?

She began to sob again, and shook her head.

Come, then.

They walked until they came to a city, but the gate was closed and the walls shimmered very high and terrible in the chilly moonlight.

What now? said the mother in a low faint voice. The daughter's face was glistening.

We shall find something, said the Pilgrim. He led them to a church, which was very clammy inside, but at least it was a shelter of sorts; they lay down there.

Señor, you are so good to us, said the one who reminded him of Magdalena.

He longed to embrace her.

It is nothing, he said smiling. Give thanks to GOD.

The next day he was weak with sickness again, and the women went on to

Rome without him, although they had offered to stay. He could not have endured that. It would have been too sad to have Magdalena nurse him twice. So he prayed in the sodden straw most patiently, and made the Contemplation of Saint Andrew; in time he cured himself. On Palm Sunday he came at last in sight of the Church of Saint Peter, with the clifflike walls of the Pope's Palace rising on his right, and the Palace of the Inquisition on his left; entering between the two colonnades of the Place Ovale that gaped open like a lobster's pincers, he longed for them to close upon him and devour him, but they did not, and the sun shone through the columns, so the Pilgrim walked across that hot and dusty space to the Pyramid of Rome and then ahead of him rose the façade of the Church, with its great colonnade crowned by twin domes, above which rose the Dome of Fifty-Five Roofs surmounted by the bowl of golden bronze. He knelt, and the Pope blessed him . . . Then he pressed on to Venice, and arranged passage to the Holy City. He was trembling with excitement.

Jerusalem 1523–1524

A Venetian Lord took him into his house. On the day the ship was about to sail, the Pilgrim became ill again. A high fever assailed him, and he sank down to his knees for weakness, but in that position he merely prayed to CHRIST to give him enough strength to get to the ship. After that, he would put his trust in the LORD, as he always did. The man of the house sent for a Doctor, who administered a laxative.

Is this man fit to travel to Jerusalem?   asked the good man.

Certainly he can go,   laughed the Doctor.   That is, if he plans to be buried there.

The Pilgrim went down to the ship, which sailed that very day. Seagulls cried about his head. When they had left the harbor, the sea became a little rougher, and the laxative began working on him. He leaned over the side and vomited heartily. Then he began to recover himself.

On the third day they were becalmed in a Sea of Weeds, whose water was wondrous thick and oily, so that the sailors laughed and said: CHRIST would have had no trouble walking on this water!   – At this the Pilgrim reproved them, calling them impious, at which they laughed at him. Now he was scarcely satisfied, for it seemed that their blasphemies must give the DEVIL power; and indeed this Sea of Weeds was a most evil place, for its hairy snakes and members seemed to grow each from the same stalk, somewhere in the bloody depths. At night he dreamed that he was on a floating island surrounded by savage and hungry bears of every description who sought to rend him, but he held them back with the Cross all that long sea-tossed day and the island drifted in the waves through sunset and evening and then by moonlight he saw that the island was nearing the rich tree-coast of Canaan at last with all its beeches and beavers and wigwams, and he saw a Savage woman watching him from the shore and she cried out *you are going to be drowned* but he smiled upon her, saying, you have no understanding, and now it was daylight and the other Savages came out to attack them with arrows and spears but he raised his Cross and touched the bears with it and they became Christian men. When he awoke he said to himself with great satisfaction: Now I know that I have been chosen to convert the pagans and infidels of Palestine! And his eyes glowed with joy. – That day the kelp was blown away by a westerly breeze, so that they left the Sea of Weeds behind and made good faring.

The sailors had brought some harlots onto the ship, and consorted with them on the very decks. – How is this? cried the Pilgrim sternly. Do you sincerely believe that your filth and indecency is pleasing in the sight of GOD? – We know all about you, the sailors shouted. We know that you have no balls. – And the other Spaniards who were there warned the Pilgrim saying, look you; if you provoke them they will leave you on some little fever-island! – And for that I should hold my tongue? said the Pilgrim. For that I should condone unrighteousness? – At this, they shook their heads and left him in peace.

By the grace of Our LORD the sailors did not cast him away. They arrived at Cyprus, at the port of Famagusta. Then the pilgrims must walk ten leagues to Las Salinas, where a pilgrim ship waited for them. Ignatius strode ahead, singing praises to GOD and thumping his staff in the dust. – He is a marvel! cried the others. He never tires! – They did not know that CHRIST continued to appear to him and to sustain him. He carried no food with him on this journey. Whenever someone gave him alms, he gave away all that he did not need for that day.

They boarded the pilgrim ship. *It seemed to him,* says the *Autobiography*, *that he saw something round and large, as though it were of gold, and this appeared to him after they left Cyprus before arriving at Jaffa.* When this occurred, he said to himself: is this a card of a particular suit in my pack of Exercises, or is it a Manifestation of Him? – And for some time he pondered over this. Now there appeared to him someone whom he thought he knew, with jet-black braids to haunt him and torture him with longing, and glittering black eyes;

she had high cheekbones like one of the Savages, and her smile was enigmatically tremulous, so that at first he thought he knew her as she advanced toward him with the hem of golden robe sweeping the floor and he cried inside himself: MARIA, is this truly in Your mind, that You will kiss me after all? . . . – And his heart beat fast for joy, until he remembered how it had been when the final lock had been opened and She had burned his hand in Her fires; he remembered himself praying *I feel such an ache in my heart that You will not have me.* Then he knew that it could not be Her; he was not worthy enough for Her to come to him. – And to think that he had wished to kiss her lips! – It had been Doña Catarina. In his notations for the Exercises he wrote: *The ENEMY behaves like a woman in that he becomes weak in the presence of strength, but strong if he is not opposed. For it is natural for a woman in a quarrel with a man to lose courage and take flight when the man makes a show of strength, but on the contrary, if the man loses courage and begins to flee* (but there was nowhere to flee to), *the anger and vindictiveness of the woman knows no bounds.* He was gasping. He wrote: *The ENEMY also behaves like a false lover who . . .*

They made the last stage of the journey riding on little donkeys. One of their number, a noble named Diego Manes, said to them: Soon we shall have our first sight of the Holy City. Would it not be pleasing, if we now rode in silence, searching our consciences?

My brother, said the Pilgrim, what you say is good. – From then on he did not move his lips, even when the flies landed on them.

And yet he could not stop thinking of evil spirits. He remembered how he had once heard a rumor at Court that a certain Doña not his own was in love with him, and at once his heart bled with tenderness for her, and he shed tears at her approach, and would have died for her as for his own; but then he learned that the rumor was quite mistaken, and at once the passion dispulverated, like some ancient corpse exposed to air. It was as though he were in a gallery of tarnished mirrors, so that there were duplications of his image and of the images of whoever might be lurking near him, but no image was clear enough for him to discern its features . . . – I must make the First Prelude of my Exercises, he said to himself, and establish where I am, and where I am going . . . and at once his thought planted him inside a splendidly illuminated Book of Hours, and he was a Crusader among Crusaders, bound for Jerusalem – then he understood again that he was going there and would arrive this very day, if GOD willed . . . and such a heavy happiness fell upon him that he thought he must be killed.

So they came to the place where the Friars waited for them with a cross; they dismounted, and the Friars led them to the overlook; when he saw the

Holy City for the first time, the Pilgrim trembled, and tears of joy ran down his cheeks. All around him, the others were crying as well. Diego Manes bowed his face into the dust and strewed dust in his hair. This seemed good to the Pilgrim, and he did likewise.

He saw the Wailing Wall, and the Dome of the Rock whose gilded cupola dazzled him; – on that spot, he was told, Abraham had prepared to sacrifice Isaac. But now the Turks had polluted it. He saw the silver dome of al-Aqsa, and he thought to himself: So much to put right here! For a moment he longed to carry a sword again. He thought upon his dagger, lying dustily by the altar at Montserrat; he wondered how the Duke was faring; then he said to himself: Later I must do penance for these thoughts.

On the horizon was the Mount called Olivet, where JESUS had ascended into Heaven. It was covered with cemeteries now. The Jews said that this was where the Resurrection of the Dead would begin first, and they had many learned arguments to prove this case.

At the hostel of the Friars the Guardian asked the Pilgrim his purpose, and he said: I want to visit all the holy places. Here are the letters of recommendation that I bring.

As you can see, said the Guardian, we are a poor house.

Yes, said the Pilgrim, you are very blessed.

The Guardian became impatient. Blessed or not, he said, we cannot feed our own. Some of us will be returning to Europe with you.

You do not have to feed me, said the Pilgrim proudly. I ask only that someone hear me from time to time when I come to confess.

The Provincial is in Bethlehem, said the Guardian. On his return I shall put the question to him.

I thank you, said the Pilgrim. I shall wait in silence. – And he retired to write letters to the most devout and holy eminences that he knew in Barcelona. Presently the Guardian summoned him into the Provincial's presence, and he came with head bowed.

GOD's grace to you, Señor, the Provincial said to him. He stood in his black robe, the corners of his mouth arching downward in a frown, like the corners of his eyes, and his face was yellowish and sad. His tonsure, like a halo, seemed to weary him with its weight.

The Pilgrim clasped his hands and smiled as meekly as he could.

The Guardian has informed me of your request, said the Provincial, and I have thought upon it and prayed upon it.

From this beginnning, the Pilgrim knew that the answer was going to be against him.

You see, the Provincial was saying, there have been so many before you who wanted to live their lives in the Holy City. It is a praiseworthy end. If only the heathen would let them stay here in tranquility!

I have my own tranquility, said the Pilgrim.

I see that you do, replied the Provincial, his lips twitching, and your faith is undoubtedly firm enough to withstand being captured or tortured or even killed.

Undoubtedly, said the Pilgrim.

Well, if you are killed, Señor, that is a speedy way to GOD, but the heathen are cunning. Most likely they would not kill you at all. They would manacle you to the wall of some dungeon and leave you there until your beard was white.

I wish for nothing better, said the Pilgrim.

Well, yes, that is commendable, but you see, Señor, they compel us to ransom these captives. That is one reason that our house has become so poor.

You need not ransom me, said Ignatius. I do not want that.

Now you are putting me in an impossible position, the Provincial said. I am afraid that you will have to prepare yourself to leave tomorrow with the other pilgrims.

For the first time, the Pilgrim raised his head. He looked the Provincial in the eye. – My purpose is fixed, he said. I cannot imagine anything that would stop me from carrying it out.

The Provincial flushed. I have authority from the Apostolic See to compel, to expel, and to excommunicate, he said. I have determined that you will not remain here. You may read the bulls that give me these powers if you desire; in fact, I think that you had better read them.

The Pilgrim stood stiffly. I don't need to see them, he said in a low voice.

You remain determined to defy me?

No, no. I shall obey you. I shall leave with the others.

He left the Provincial's presence, and returned to where he was before. He knelt down; he prayed; he rocked in grief.

Suddenly, for no reason, the name *Magdalena* was on his lips. He struck his mouth until it bled.

It came to him that he wanted to see the mount called Olivet, where CHRIST had ascended and Saint Peter with the other Apostles had bid Him farewell. It was not the Pilgrim's intention to be disobedient, so he told no one where he was going; that way they could not command him not to go. He did not even take a Turkish guide, although to go alone was dangerous.

So he passed through the city, thinking of CHRIST; eagerly he traced out with his eyes the Via Dolorosa, where CHRIST had carried his Cross to Calvary; he saw the Church of Saint Maria Magdalena rising with its crosses and onion-domes among the trees where Saint Peter had fled from Gethsemane after denying Him; he measured himself against the great blocks of the Wailing Wall, each of which was as high as his shoulder; and he came at last to the foot of that mount called Olivet where the guards stood roasting meat on sticks in a smoky little fire, and when they saw him they challenged him with spears slamming down into the dirt around him, shouting and scowling and wagging their beards.

Good day to you, brothers, said the Pilgrim. I wish to go where JESUS walked.

We shall not let you! they said. Go back now, or we shall kill you!

From his sack he took a fine desk knife that his brother Martín García had given him. – This is yours if you permit me to enter, he said.

They took it from him and bit it, saying to each other, is it gold? and passing it from hand to dirty hand and muttering over it. At last they pocketed it and drew their spears aside and let him enter.

So he ascended the hill of sand, the hill of golden grass. Where the gold was worn through he could see patches of ashy grey. Junipers flared up like stout green flames. Far away, beyond the rolling dust-ridges, diamonds and knives of blue lay shining on the grey table of the horizon. Red bricks of rock crumbled at the rims of little outcroppings. He said to himself: What happiness if through Providence my foot might fall where *He* once stepped! He went up and up, toward the sky. He saw house-ruins on distant ridges all around him. Square towers rose roofless. The window-holes were a little higher than his face. He walked past them, as Saint Peter had done so many times, wondering, but the Pilgrim did not wonder; his faith was stronger than Peter's, because he believed from Peter's words, because he had never seen CHRIST taken away from him. He prayed beside the Citadel, whose square brick rooms, scorching to the touch, reminded him of the empty Tomb; he watched ants rushing on the hot bricks. At the top of the Citadel, which was flattened and smashed and littered with red shards, the hot wind blew and the desert grass below was pale and glowing green, and there were low black mountains and blue mountains like islands, and a cricket chirped and the wind blew hotter and hotter and there were clouds over Golgotha. Bricks reared crazily against the sky, peering through their tiny black windows. The Pilgrim knelt and began brushing away at the ground. He found a red stone with worked edges that might have been a scraper, some tan fragments of pottery, and a piece of brick that was reddish on one side and white on the other. He swept and swept with his hands until he found JESUS's footprints in the rock. Then he kissed them and prayed.

Later that afternoon he felt the desire to go to Bethphage. He could almost hear water running as he licked his lips in the dryness, carrying the hot burden of the day. Fat green lizards a foot long basked in the sun. Collars of blue bead-scales glittered on their necks.

Suddenly he realized that he had not noticed which way CHRIST's right foot had pointed on Mount Olive, nor which way His left. So he returned there. This time he gave his scissors to the guards so that they would permit him to enter.

The Provincial sent a "Christian of the Belt"* to retrieve him. This man came thumping up the mount towards him with a huge staff, making signs of striking him. – You *bad wicked!* he shouted. Bowing his head obediently, Ignatius descended at once. The Christian of the Belt seized him in a pinching grip and dragged him back to the monastery. The guards laughed and laughed, snipping at the air with the Pilgrim's scissors. But he felt the consolation of CHRIST. A flock of crows swam slowly in the clouds.

The Madman

He returned with great hardship to Venice, Genoa, and thence to sea-washed Spain, whose occasional dwarf palms reminded him a little of the Holy Land. He had changed greatly in his appearance. His body was lean and hard. His eyes were not as gentle as they once had been; their stare was somewhat fixed, but they drilled very deeply into what they looked upon, seeking to send their gaze through it and whatever lay behind until at last they could see to Him beyond. He was very glad of his new self, insofar as he allowed himself to be glad. He had become what he wanted to be.

In those days King Charles and the French King François were at war again, so that he had to pass from one army to the other as he trod the main road to Genoa. Once he was arrested and stripped; then they took him to a lower room of the Captain's Palace for questioning. The Pilgrim feared torture a little, and considered speaking to the Captain using the formal pronoun, instead of the devotional *vos* that was his habit; however, he recognized this for a temptation of the Enemy, and so did not yield. – Not

* Syrian Christian.

only will I refuse to speak formally to him, he said to himself, but I shall show him no reverence. – At last the Captain came and said to him: Well, Monsieur, state your business fully. For you know that we believe you to be a spy. – The Pilgrim answered in a few words, without clothing them in any courtesy – for he was not clothed himself except for his breeches and long shirt. Staring through the Captain, he prepared for the torture. – The Captain stroked his moustache; the Captain said aloud: I have no time for this! – Considering him a madman, the Captain had him thrown out of the Palace without harming him, and the soldiers gave him back his doublet and other things. – In Genoa, a Vizcayan named Portundo, who remembered him from the days when he was Iñigo the page at the Court of Queen Germana, got him passage on a ship for Barcelona. The pirate Andrea Doria pursued that ship, but they made safe port in Spain with the aid of Our LORD. Seeing that it was not His will that he return to Jerusalem at this time, the Pilgrim decided to study grammar.

The Black-Gown
1524–1556

As the first council at Jerusalem spoke in the name of the Holy Spirit, other councils did the same in imitation of it; and we are startled at the spiritual power very early acquired by the bishops, in the Asiatic provinces.

JOHANN GOTTFRIED VON HERDER, *Reflections on the Philosophy of the History of Mankind* (1784–91)

. . . after I had seene a Jesuit turne the *Pope* out of his *Chaire* in *Hell*, I suspected that that *Order* would attempt as much at Rome.

JOHN DONNE, *Ignatius His Conclave* (1611)

Both that which is in potency to exist substantially, and that which is in potency to exist accidentally, can, like the sperm and the man, respectively, be called matter, another scholar recited.

Yes, said Ignatius, but what Aquinas didn't understand was that these distinctions have neither application nor even relevance. Our LORD said, *Suffer the little children to come unto Me,* and it is only as a little child that one can love Him. Little children don't need to know about accidental and substantial is-ness; they only need to know Who *is*.

Someone laughed.

Ignatius said: I see that you don't understand, either. Well, all right. I'm only a barefoot scholar of no account.

He sang the Psalm of the Steadfast Heart.

Barcelona 1524

Once they said to him: What's the matter with you, Loyola? You can't define anything!

I'll tell you what I read in the *Imitation of* CHRIST, said Ignatius. I read: "I would far rather feel contrition than be able to define it."

Barcelona 1525

He saw two of his comrades from Pampeluna, and he did not want to see them. But he would not look away from them. He felt a shrinking inside him as they looked at him, but then they did not recognize him. – He was relieved, and then he thought, am I a true soldier of GOD, to be relieved when there is no battle? – So he rose and followed them, and called out to them heartily:

Don Pedro! Good Don Avilla! And how are you both on this day?

They stopped.

Iñigo, I had heard, said Don Pedro very civilly, but I did not believe.

I could not go on the way I was going on, he said.

If there is any help that I can give you, said Don Pedro, you know that I would. You can stay at my house. I shall give you clothes and a horse . . .

In the name of GOD, Don Pedro, give me some alms.

But saying this, he felt ashamed of himself. No matter what he did, he would be ashamed now; he knew that. – Don Pedro! he cried. Do you remember, my friend, when we almost won the battle at Pampeluna and how we stood so faithfully at arms? Do you remember how proudly we strutted from cannon to cannon before the attack, and how those Frenchmen looked at us so anxiously from below?

That is how you are looking at me now, said Don Pedro. He took two silver pieces from his wallet and dropped them into the dust beside Ignatius; he turned and walked on.

The First Investigation 1526

He continued his way of life, preaching righteousness to all. His Master told him that he made good progress with his studies; he was studying arts now at Alcalá. By this time he had his first four disciples, who begged alongside him; he had given them his Spiritual Exercises, and from them many others received them. People began to gossip about Ignatius and his "sack-wearers," as they called them. Rumors of heresy reached the Inquisitors at Toledo, who came to investigate them, but in the end they returned to Toledo without summoning them to be examined, for they could see no evil in them. At this, their Vicar, Figueroa, took charge of the trial, and called them to him.

His disciples Arteaga and Calixto trembled visibly, and the other two were very pale. – Master, shall we be burned? asked the young Frenchman, Juanico. There were tears in his voice.

Have no fear, said the Pilgrim in a ringing voice. We are in the hands of GOD.

And he led them down the road.

Coming toward Toledo, the five Companions saw a green hill as round as a breast, so soft and bright, but storm-clouds were stacked on the sky end-on-end in glowing slabs so that everything was electric, and though there were chinks of blue sky between them they did not lessen anything; they only chilled and charged the city that rose upon the hill; the Pilgrim could see its grey towers shining deadly and new against the darker grey of those clouds, and he led his disciples closer and saw the grass waving in tall soft puffs above the river and the bushes waved in the wind; he could smell the bitterness of their white flowers. Now the Companions heard the rushing of the dark river; they saw the people ascending the steep road to the bridges whose arches, narrow and very tall, were like a skull's eyes, and they walked across the bridge, drawing closer and closer to the storm-shadows; they ascended the turreted way; they approached Toledo Cathedral and the Palace of the Alcazar, whose walls above them were stone honeycombs of menace. Blackness gaped from every window. The grass below them swished in the wind, and far down in the shadows of the river, fishermen waded in the shallows, taking no notice of Toledo, but Toledo was waiting for the Companions, waiting with clouds and darkness and stone. – Perhaps the examination would conclude there, or perhaps the Companions would be sent on in chains to be examined in Castile by the Grand Inquisitor in his scarlet robes, whose buttons rose straight and sure to the cloud-soft collar beneath the Heaven of his face, whose hands hung down with the languid ease of power (he had burned more than two thousand persons); the dark rings glittered on his fingers. You did not dare to look into his eyes at first. His gaze was not stern, exactly, not even watchful, but you were afraid of it. His cap rose in a flared mound, almost a trident; he sat still and watched you. You wanted to hide your eyes, to look down at his shoes, but you did not dare to do that, either; at last you looked into his eyes.

We have found no sin in you yet, said Vicar Figueroa, but you must not wear the same habit, as if you belonged to some illegal religious Order.

We shall do as we are commanded, said Ignatius.

You, Señor, and this Arteaga – I want you to dye your clothing black, said Figueroa. Calixto and Cáceres shall dye their clothing brown. Juanico may remain as he is.

We shall do as we are commanded, said Ignatius.

Good, said Figueroa dryly.

He had turned as if to have his guards show them out when Ignatius said: I do not know what benefit these investigations bring to anyone. The other day a priest almost refused to give one of us the Sacrament. I've been inconvenienced, too.

Figueroa spread his hands.

We would like to know if they have found any heresy in us, Ignatius persisted.

No, said Figueroa. He smiled benevolently. If they had, they would have burned you.

Ignatius looked him in the face. He said: If they had found heresy in you, they would have burned you also.

The Oath 1534

He was investigated again. He passed five years in Paris. There he danced the Basque dances, in order to cheer up a melancholy man. The Exercises were complete now, and he longed to teach them to others, many many others. His disciples grew in number. So he went on in Saint Peter's footsteps, drawing souls into his authority in JESUS's name. In darkened rooms he raised his hand, and they felt fear or joy as he bade them, and the tableaux of his Exercises loomed on their way like the Stations of the Cross. Although his métier was obedience, he must command: that was the Cross which GOD had laid upon his shoulders. And he did it zealously.

Just as Saint Peter had had the vision at Joppa which required him to teach the Gentiles, so he saw that he must save the souls of pagans in distant lands.

On the fifteenth of Août, 1534, in the subterranean chapel of Montmartre, Ignatius de Loyola led his Companions in prayer. They numbered but six, but they were elect, and they were French, Spanish, Portuguese . . . And together they bound themselves to the service of souls. He would lead them again to Jerusalem, but if they were not permitted to stay there they would give their allegiance directly to the Vicar of CHRIST in Rome, where, giving themselves entirely over to pious labors, they would become coin to be spent by the Church, like gold rose-nobles with the rose graven deep into them. That was their special vow. Other Orders vow themselves to poverty, chastity, obedience; only the Jesuits vow themselves directly to the Pope as well.

They waited for a year at Venice to be given passage, and after this renewed their vow, at which time they were joined by three others. As passage to the Holy City remained impossible, Ignatius resolved to lead them to Rome. The Companions were somewhat downcast at first, but Ignatius said to them: I have been to Jerusalem before, and accomplished nothing. But here much can be done. We will go now to Rome.

In Venice, in Paris, people had begun to talk of these monks. Considering them conceited dreamers, they jeered and said to them laughing: What can *you* do for the Pope?

The faces of the Nine darkened, but they were silent, and Ignatius smiled. Later, when they knelt alone in their residence, he said to them: Are you troubled by these calumnies? Then make the Exercises which I have taught you. Make the *Anima CHRISTI* and swim the Stream of Time to the Thirteenth Rapid, ascending which you will see CHRIST before Herod.

Now he watched their faces and smiled with gentleness to see them comprehending Him as they reached the Third Point, when Herod and his Court mocked JESUS and clothed Him in white. Because the Nine accepted Ignatius as a preacher of wise doctrines, they strove to make the Contemplation all alike, in the fashion that he had written for them, so that no matter of importance could be omitted. He for his part was less rigid; having built the stream-cliffs himself, he felt them to be less monumental than they were, and clambered up and down them using toeholds that he would not have permitted his disciples. In this matter of being mocked and set to task by the citizens of Rome, for instance, he thought not of the Thirteenth Rapid (whose image he knew by heart), but rather of the case of Maurus, Saint Benedict's disciple, who was ordered by his Superior to go into the water, and he could not swim but he took the first step and before him were rapids foamy and creamy down shady cliff-walls, half hidden by greenery as light as fluffed-up air; and he took the second step and raised his head to see above the cliffs to where maples met the clouds with softness; and Maurus took the third step to the Stream's edge where he could spy something heavy and blackish-green combing the water beneath, and there was a parrot-like beak at the crown of its long bloody hairs and the beak was inset with teeth that gashed and gashed, because the Fox's scalp was hungry, and Maurus had seen so many swimmers destroyed by this monster, their thighs chewed off in one swipe of that horrid purple beak, but the Superior said to him Go! and he stepped into the water and it sustained him as a witness of his obedience so that he was like CHRIST walking on the sea and the Fox's scalp moved uneasily beneath him and he could see the beak between his feet, but as if through glass, and Maurus was not harmed. Later the Superior said to him: Maurus, bring the wicked lioness to me. So Maurus went into the desert and found the lioness growling over a man's bones, and he took her in his arms and carried her to the Superior in his study, and the Superior, who had meant to kill Maurus, cowered back and said let her go, man, take her out and let her go! but Maurus refused to see the Superior's fear or spite because the Superior was CHRIST to him, being set in CHRIST's place, so he took the lioness back to the desert where he had found her and let her go, and she sprang from his arms and turned and stared at him for a very long time and her yellow eyes were very beautiful and Maurus smiled at her and thanked her and she watched him until at last he turned away, and then the lioness shook her head in confusion and sprang upon the old bones again with a snarl.

The Society of Jesus *1538–1990*

After this, his life-work began to take shape around him.

He was very busy

It is a heart-law that the rejection of another person or thing does not so much obliterate it as push it into some very nearby patch of darkness – push it, in addition, against the tension of an idiotic coil-spring (hearts are riddled with those). The more sweeping the rejection, the farther away Magdalena's corpse is pushed, the greater the corresponding tension of the spring. Rejection is thus a continual effort. At any weakness, the spring is allowed to relax, and Magdalena comes hurtling back into the light, half-rotted, half-devoured, but still very much present.

What to do with her then?

Champlain would have weighed and measured her. Born Swimming would have covered her with peltries. Kateri Tekakwitha would have kissed her. Père Biard would have buried her and marked the spot.

Ignatius made the Exercise of Blindness, and went about his duties.

As for Doña Catarina, of course, he had her in the Exercises forever.

The Order which he had created was less a palm-leaf than a spear in his side. As it expanded day by day, it grew beyond his ability to oversee, and he often heard his Generals giving orders in words that he himself would not have used. Yet there was love in their hearts. How could he insist that he was not worthy, that they were not worthy? And the fresh faces glowed with devotion; they touched him; he liked to be around them. Yet all the time he wanted to cast them off and go down the road to Everywhere, in poverty, in nakedness. He wanted to be free. Knowing his duty, however, he stayed. Had he not sworn it? On 22 Avril 1541, he was proclaimed Superior General. He read the letters that came and answered them; upon being entreated he dictated the story of his life to Father de Camara; he wrote to Father Nicolás Bobadilla, who had taken the Oath with him in Paris: *I am not so eager to correct the wording of your letters as I am for your perfection in general* and he conferred with the Bishop in his robes of red with black diamonds within diamonds. The Bishop stood tall. He raised a finger. But Ignatius himself stood taller than ever before . . . He preached obedience, obedience to his brothers in the refectory after supper, even when they became restive, and one night when he kept them scowling at table to read them his latest sermon on this most important subject, there came a loud crash from outside; and when they rushed out to see what the matter was, they discovered that the roof had collapsed upon the pleasant spot in the garden where they were wont to spend their evenings; – you see, said Ignatius, GOD was pleased with my words, and used them to warn and protect you!

He could tell now that he was getting older. It seemed to him that his teeth were getting thinner and thinner, that his inflamed gums were receding. Often he ran his tongue over his teeth, convinced that he could almost feel them breaking of their own weight.

In 1551, Henri II the Roy of France issued letters patent for the maison and collège of Clermont to be built in Paris. And Ignatius knelt and relieved his heart with many tears of joy. He labored now over his *Ratio Studiorum*, which he did not expect to complete; in 1552 he issued the Constitutions in their final form. – Pale? Yes, he was very pale . . . Laymen spoke in sneers of his *Jesuits*, as they called them in derision, but the Jesuits smiled meekly and took the name for themselves and so it lost its derisory character; thus may the bad become good. And their number grew. By 1556, the year of Ignatius's death, there were nine hundred and thirty-eight members. And there were many missionaries among them, who were directed by their Superiors to convert the heathen. In those last years, Saint Ignatius bade the Fathers farewell with bowed head (he was almost bald now), and his face was pale as he stood in his black gown in the arch of darkness; extended the white ghost of his hand to be held, and the Fathers knelt before him with their heads bowed toward his breast as the birds sang in the trees and the Superior General blessed them with a hand on the shoulder before they departed forever. They sailed to Ireland, Morocco, the Congo, Brazil, Ethiopia . . .

Their plan was simple: to save every soul on this earth. The means were complex, requiring the tense spontaneity of generals, the extravagance of jesters, the indifference to comfort of ascetics, the compromising of merchants, the intriguing of diplomats, the patience of craftsmen – all of which were so many pretty veils drawn over an iron purpose.

"In your dealings with all," Ignatius ordered his army,

> be slow to speak and say little, especially with your equals and those lower in dignity and authority than yourselves . . . In dealing with men of position or influence, if you are to win their affection for the greater glory of GOD Our LORD, look first to their disposition and accommodate yourselves to them . . . Whenever we wish to win someone over and engage him in the greater service of GOD Our LORD, we should use the same strategy for good which the ENEMY employs to draw a good soul to evil. He enters through the other's door and comes out his own.

He died in the year that the Pope issued the first list of banned books. A decade later, Saint Francis de Borja, the new Superior General of the Society of JESUS, prohibited the Jesuits from reading Ignatius's autobiography.

Further History of the Jesuits
1556–1773

The Society of JESUS is a sword, whose handle is at Rome, and the point everywhere.

ANDRÉ DUPIN (1825)

They were Royal Confessors to all the Roys of France for two centuries; to all the German Emperors after the seventeenth century, to all Dukes of Bavaria after 1579, to most of the rulers of Poland and Portugal, to the eighteenth-century Spanish Kings, to James II of England . . . In the year of Ignatius's death there were nine hundred and thirty-eight Jesuits. Nine years later there were fifteen hundred and sixty-five. In 1590 they established a mission in India, in 1605 they were building a church in Ecuador; in 1615 they had multiplied their number almost ninefold. Six years later, there were over fifteen thousand of them. Their work in New France was well underway by now. They converted the Souriquois, the Huron (who were destroyed in the process); they spread the light to the Etechemins and Armouchiquois; in 1637 they were placed in spiritual charge of the Indians and settlers throughout Canada. By 1664 there were almost thirty-six thousand of them. In 1676 they baptized Kateri Tegahkouita, "la Vierge Iroquoise." In 1749 they made up a quarter of the entire Catholic Apostolate. In 1773 the Society of JESUS was dissolved.

III
Our Daily Bread
or,

How the Black-Gowns Began the Great Work

The Scruples of Père Biard

1612

These readers are school books and are not intended as recreation for idle hours. Therefore we have been careful not to give too much space to stories of battles or skirmishes or to picturesque Indian legends . . .

EDWARD PAYSON MORTON, PhD,
Lake Huron and the Country of the Algonquins (1913)

Yes, cried Père Biard to himself; even from the beginning he wished to serve!

He cried with delight to see Ignatius instructing the others in the rose-garden, or *Rosarium* as they smilingly called it.

(He longed for Ignatius, just as Ignatius longed for Saint Peter, just as Peter longed for CHRIST: it is always so much easier to go *backward* in the chain, to float on one's back down to sea . . . Yet beyond the Seventy-Third Rapid, as they say, lies a Sweetwater Sea of equal ease. – Which way *is* forward or backward in the Stream of Time? This book, I fear, will not answer that question.)

The Conversion of the Frenchmen

1613

Nor is it less strange that some wolf in sheep's clothing arrives not from New England to lead astray a flock that has no shepherd.

WILLIAM BYRD, *Histories of the Dividing Line Betwixt Virginia and North Carolina* (entry for 16 March 1728)

When she had heard the tale of Frère Gilbert du Thet, the Marchioness de Guercheville resolved to break with Poutrincourt and his son and establish a new post elsewhere. There was no reason not to; her Jesuits owned almost all of Canada – ah, Blessed LORD! When Père Cotton came to confess her, she received him in her usual dress. A vast collar of lace fluttered all the way up around her neck. Epaulets of fleurs-de-lys snaked halfway down her arms. Then came the bodice, narrowing to an impossibly thin waist, the miracle of corset and bustle; and at last the dress sweeping to the floor with the massiveness of any monument. Atop this assemblage was a little pale head with greying chestnut hair and half-closed eyes. She had always seemed to Père Cotton a fragile sort of mushroom. – So have you meditated upon the matter which we spoke of? he whispered, his gentleness like a hand stroking her hair. – Yes, Père, she replied. As ever, I have come to the conclusion that you are correct, that the establishment of the Faith at Port-Royal is not yet GOD's will. – Père Cotton nodded and smiled sadly. – Oh! A spider! Could you catch it for me, s'il vous plaît? You see, I have a blue fear of insects . . . – But of course, Madame. There! It's dead. – Thank you, Père! Ah, thank you so much! Now tell me what I must do in Canada . . . – On the twelfth day of Mars, one of her Captains, René le Coq, set sail from Honfleur. With him was Père Cotton's Lieutenant-General, the one who had tricked Poutrincourt so that he would be committed to prison – *viz.*, La Saulsay. He bore a Queen's order permitting the two priests to depart Port-Royal if they desired. The Queen had also given him four great tents or pavilions. Frère Gilbert du Thet was of that crew, that being the privilege which he had garnered for his tale-bearing against Biencourt; and another Jesuit, Père Quentin, was sent to increase the presence of his Order further. – A cannon-peal! The Stream of Time was rose-water . . .

In the month of Mai, La Saulsay landed at Port-Royal and called for Biencourt, but he was not there. Showing the Queen's order to Louys Hébert, he took Père Biard and Père Massé on board, and they set sail for a pretty island in the Country of the Etechemins, a little south of Robert Pontgravé, where the trees went on forever and there were lakes long like rivers, wide like seas. Champlain had already discovered this isle, for Champlain as we know was a great pioneer. It was round, but then again almost cleft by a deep narrow bay-slit. Large and rugged, it seemed like seven or eight mountains alongside each other. Because it was largely bare of trees, Champlain had named it Mont Désert.

Here, in a harbor on the east side, the Black-Gowns erected a great Cross, upon which were the arms of Madame de Guercheville. White clouds blew like wind-mist, and the shadows of the clouds moved briskly upon the sea. On those hot days, if you could look down from the clouds like an Angel, the air would be so thickly blue below as to be unbreathable, like ink; and the sunlight would make your eyes heavy and you would yawn and be hot and sleepy. There was an abundance of walnuts, and even some wild grapes, although not so many as there had been five hundred years before when the Greenlanders came. (But for the Mission of Père Biard there was only a future of evil, like the night-black Iroquois hats with glowing flowers.)

As always, the French quarreled, and so they made little progress in erecting their Mission. Père Massé said nothing, but Père Biard became so anguished at these continual factions that he sought to call upon his good Robert, to ask his advice. One evening he went to a hill apart and raised the whistle to his lips –

The Heretics

It is now to be told that the English had established a colony in Virginia, and that the Governor of that colony, Sir Thomas Dale, having basely set out to do mischief to France (but, thanks be to the Eternal GOD, those who seek to do harm to others will be repaid at the Day of Judgment!), laid claim to Maine and Acadia as possessions of King James, and thereby justified in his own wicked heart (if not in the hearts of reasonable men) his designs: namely, to expel the French from Canada. He had in this matter a perfect assistant schooled in violence and treachery, being one Captain Samuel Argall. Argall, perhaps, heard Père Biard's whistle; he had very good ears. It was this Argall who had just this very spring kidnapped the Indian Princess Pocahontas, who had never done the English any deeds but good, and was now holding her hostage; thus it is that the English requite their friends. Captain Argall, who now pretended to be codfishing, set out for Acadia with men and guns, and Sir Thomas laughed to see his ships swim northward into the summer sea-fog. Detesting as he did those black-gowned creatures who trafficked in Popish primers and rosaries, he hoped that Argall would spit a few of them. It is written that the aforesaid Argall had a tall ship of some two to three hundred tons, another of a hundred tons, and also a longboat.

Now Argall came nigh to Mount Desert Island, and within a twinkling he was bearing down upon the Mission with his red flag flying and his cannon firing; and a cannonball came whistling toward Frère du Thet, who suddenly comprehended that death was going to strike him; death would nail him to himself so that he must become a Cross; and he exploded and died –

But he was not a martyr. Poor Frère du Thet!

The Three Miracles

They seized Père Biard and the new priest, Père Quentin, and threw them in irons. Père Massé they marooned, and he had to borrow one of Biencourt's salt magazines to make his living, praying, mortifying himself, weeping tears of happy salt to mix with ocean-salt, drinking it all down, a medicine of wholesome misery; he bobbed along peninsulas gently rising and falling with trees until a French fishing boat found him and took him home; it was the very same Rossignol whose vessel De Monts had confiscated on that first Acadia voyage so long ago in the days when Champlain was hopeful; when he found the poor priest, drenched and salt-crusted like a crow in a salty rain,

Rossignol began to laugh, because he loved the misfortunes of others now; he rescued Père Massé only to keep before his eyes the spectacle of that crushed man (who wasn't crushed at all; nothing ever crushed Père Massé); and in sunlight they passed the rock where Poutrincourt had almost been wrecked, and in sunlight they came home to La Rochelle, and there Père Massé disembarked barefooted; we'll see him again in Canada, but not for a dozen years . . . So of our three songbirds there were now but two. Turnell the Lieutenant was in charge of the Jesuits; Argall the Captain had command of the other Frenchmen. Therefore let no one say that we English do not know the difference between Master and man. And they sailed south along the coast until they came to Virginia, and Captain Argall brought Père Biard before the Marshal. In a tone of detachment so sublime that it makes up for his failings, Père Biard writes that the Marshal *listened very willingly to Captain Argal as he related all that had taken place, and in a proper spirit of devotion awaited Père Biard to shorten for him his voyages and to make him find the end of the world from the middle of a ladder.** But he was saved by GOD. Let us call that the first miracle.

Just as two French pigeons may sometimes strive or kiss together (it is not clear which), beak against beak, nodding up and down in symmetry, until at last one mounts the other and then what's happening becomes perfectly evident, so Père Biard was drawn to Captain Argall. However, it would be submitting to the blandishments of the Basques to say that he was drawn to him for fear of his life, or that any treason was committed. We may state most assuredly that his dislike of Biencourt was not a consideration, either, for was he not a man of GOD? We may only print the fact, which, ugly as nakedness has ever been since Eden, is simply this: Père Biard agreed to accompany Captain Argall to Port-Royal, which Captain Argall intended to destroy. – Did he agree under duress? – Of course. – Was Port-Royal worth anything now that the Jesuits had left; was it anything but a husk? – Of course not. – So the bitter plaints of Biencourt and his father, which are yet preserved, have absolutely no foundation.

Captain Argall desired to burn Port-Royal and raze it to the ground, so of course he could not expect the Frenchmen to give him directions. *For this reason,* continues Biard's *Relation, he began to look for a Savage, and by dint of much running about, lying in ambush, inquiring, and skillful maneuvering, he caught the Sagamore, a very experienced man, and well acquainted with the country; under his guidance, he reached Port-Royal.*

* Gallows.

Of *course* Père Biard sought to dissuade the English from their purpose by any means that he could. How can we not believe that? He was no mean and worldly person, to long for revenge . . . To Lieutenant Turnell, who had come to have some regard for him, he said (as he reports in the *Jesuit Relations*, which never lie): I hope you expect to find no booty in Acadia, Lieutenant. We are poor people who live at a high latitude, and our only treasures would be of no use to you, for they are but converted Savages.

You assert that *they* have souls? asked Lieutenant Turnell in astonishment.

They are a gentle people, said Père Biard proudly. – They extend to us their hands with an incredible longing, and with a profound grief to see us defeated. They will hate you English now; you must beware of them.

You may be right, said Lieutenant Turnell. You seem to me to be remarkably well informed, for a Frenchman.

And he went to raise the matter with Captain Argall.

Ever and again Père Biard spoke into the Lieutenant's ear, and he listened and scurried to the Captain with new reaons not to go to Port-Royal, until at last the Captain cried: A pox on you and your Frenchman! We are going and we are going! – What do *you* say? he said, turning suddenly to the Sagamore.

The Savage laughed so that his eyes crinkled. – Much treasure, he said. Hatchets, knives, glass things!

Oh, you stupid animal, said Captain Argall.

They reached Isle de Sainte-Croix, where De Monts' Frenchmen had wintered in that first year, and the English razed the buildings that remained and burned the arms on the escutcheon that was set there. Père Biard told them that the Sieur de Champlain had crossed the frozen river often, in hopes of curing scurvy with various kinds of bark. – And as you see, gentlemen, this river is on either side three times as wide as the Seine at Paris!

Damme if I've ever been to Paris, said Argall, smashing down De Monts' rotten Store-house with his axe.

Yes, my Lord. I tell you this only so that you can appreciate Champlain's strength. He is a very powerful man.

You're awfully proud, for a traitor, said Argall thoughtfully. All the same, I'd like to fight Champlain.

They got to Port-Royal, and possessed themselves of it easily, for not a soul happened to be there. The great door was ajar. Argall strode through the arch and came into the courtyard. – Very pretty, he said. Indeed the houses and roof *were* so prettily wood-striped, everything shingled like the slat-armor of the Yroquois . . . And there was good plunder there; for the Sieur de

Poutrincourt had recently sent a goodly shipment of dainties for the Storehouse. – Turnell, I'll teach you to listen to wily Frenchmen! shouted Captain Argall as the sailors loaded the hold with beaver-skins. You only hindered us, so your share will be less than the meanest swabber's! – Then the Lieutenant began to hate Père Biard, as Argall had surely intended. And another of these malicious English Puritans recommended that Père Biard be cast off and abandoned on the coast without food, since he had only tried to prevent them all from obtaining it. But Père Biard only fell to his knees and prayed them to leave some food for the inhabitants of Port-Royal so that they would not starve when winter came. Then the Englishmen were touched by his selflessness, and he was spared. So GOD preserved his life a second time. Hurrah for miracles!

Now they set fire to the Habitation, and watched carefully to make certain that it burned.

Père Biard showed them where the swine were, the horses, mares, and colts, all of which they possessed themselves of easily. Then he brought them to the fields where the French were working. They tried to seize them for their prisoners, but they escaped to the crest of a hill, where they stood watching their Habitation burn.

Then Captain Argall, praising Père Biard for his utility to the English thus far, sent him to attempt to treat with the enemy, so that they might yield themselves without inconvenience.

What can you hope for now from Biencourt, your penniless Captain? said Père Biard to them gently.

Be off with you, a Frenchman shouted down, or else with this hatchet I shall cut your throat.

Then others called to the English that Père Biard was not even a Frenchman, but a native Spaniard with all the craft and evil of that race, and the Captain came to believe these slanders. But he forbore to have him executed then and there, thinking himself better served by bearing patiently with his existence until their arrival at Virginia, where moderation is always praised. Thus GOD spared Père Biard a third time. Let's call it a miracle, shall we?

When the Habitation which his father had worked so hard to build was ashes, and the gristmill was smashed, and the crops properly ruined in the fields, Biencourt offered single combat to Captain Argall, but he for his part saw no profit to be gained in fighting a desperate man with even odds. He proposed instead to Biencourt that they meet in private.

It is said (though I cannot believe it) that Biencourt, beside himself with sadness, offered for the sake of his men to serve Captain Argall, for otherwise they might starve to death that coming winter, but this proposition was not accepted. Then Biencourt asked him as a courtesy to hand over to him the Black-Gown, Père Biard, whom he meant to hang from the nearest tree-gallows. This also Captain Argall refused, for that reason of moderation which we comprehend. But this does not really partake of a miracle's character, as Père Biard knew that it was only natural to deny Biencourt everything.

Mr. Biencourt, you are a gentleman, like myself, said gentle Argall. Therefore I much regret what has happened. No doubt you are aware, sir, that it was no fell design of mine, but rather your Father Biard who aroused my General in Virginia and forced me to this. This Biard warned him that your father Sir Poutrincourt is bringing with him many cannons –

Cannons? cried the astounded Biencourt.

And for this reason it was essential to destroy you while you were feeble. My General hopes indeed that you would be put to the death, or die of famine. Then we English will not be dispossessed.

Père Biard watched Biencourt trudge away from the parley under flag of truce, with his head held high, as he went back to his followers who wept and prayed upon their windy hill. He seemed resolute even yet. But Père Biard thought to himself: very often a man puts a good mien on bad cards.

And he smiled.

But then he heard the Souriquois weeping that their brothers had been possessed, and his shoulder slumped and he said to himself: Eh, the poor Savages, what will they do without us now?

The Agreement

There were two Jesuits left now. One was Père Biard, and the other was Père Quentin.

Come, the English said to them, show us your rosaries and all that abracadabra!

On the way back to Virginia, where Père Biard was to be hanged, they mocked and tormented him, calling him *subtile Spaniard* and reading to him from a book of blasphemies that an Englishman had made, in which were written such things as:

> O wonderfull, and incredible *Hypercritiques*, who, not out of marble fragments, but out of the secretest Records of Hell itself: that is, out of the

> minds of *Lucifer*, the *Pope*, and *Ignatius*, (persons truly equivocall) have raised to life againe the language of the Tower of *Babel*, too long conceived and brought us againe from understanding one an other.

Hey! laughed Argall. I'll sing you two doleful crows a tune. It'll raise your spirits back to cawing, because it's a merry song, written by an Englishman of great piety. It goes like this:

> 'Tis time we now should in due place expound
> How guilt is after shrift to be aton'd.
> Enjoin no sour repentance, tears and grief:
> Eyes weep no cash, and you no profit give.

– Hey, crows! I'm singing about *you!* Now I forget what comes next, but the melody is the same, *rum-ti-tum-ti-tum*; and then there's this verse:

> O glorious and heroic constancy!
> That can forswear upon the cart, and die
> With gasping souls expiring in a lie.

How d'you like that, Black-Gowns? Doesn't that sum you up on a most learned abacus?

But presently a storm blew up, and Lieutenant Turnell's ship, which held the Jesuits, was blown across the sea . . .

. . . and Captain Argall is now out of this Dream . . .

. . . and the Jesuits agreed to be promise-bound to hide themselves from the Spanish Catholics of the Açores.

The Meaning of the Falls

The ship lurched in the water, and the two Black-Gowns sat very quietly, and the rapids of the Stream of Time hammered at Père Biard's spirit like the falls in Acadia, where there was a hollow between two rocks in which there was an upright tree that floated and sank, sometimes vanishing for eight, ten, or even fifteen days; but it always reappeared. The Savages called it *MANITOU*, meaning Devil as the Frenchmen thought (but wrongly). Whenever they passed by, the Souriquois looked to see if it were visible; if not, they feared calamities in the future, thinking that MN'TU' was hiding His face from them out of anger. When He was present, they attached good tribute of peltries to the top of His head with moose-bone arrowheads. Later, when the Iron People had begun to change them, they covered Him with iron points. An acquaintance of the Sieur Denys, who wrote this tale later in the century, once tried to pull the tree out with a log, thinking perhaps to obtain the peltries that way, but could not, such was the power of these falls.

Presently Père Quentin became beside himself with grief and sea-sickness, and so Père Biard felt more alone than ever. He raised Robert's whistle to his lips and blew a single note.

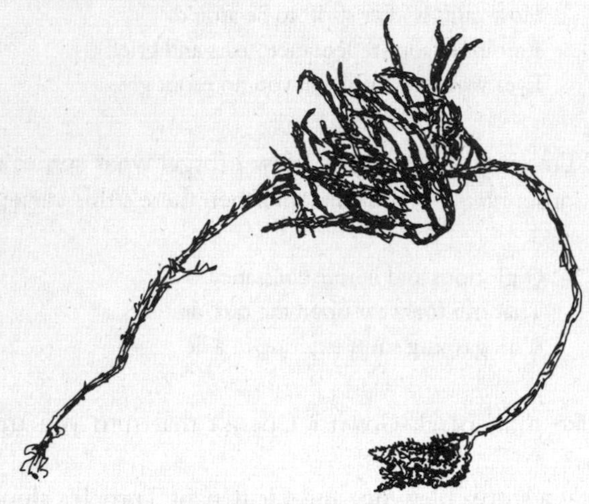

WITHERED CROW'S-FOOT, NEW YORK STATE

Père Massé appeared before him.

You! he cried in amazement.

Père Quentin moaned faintly.

Père Biard felt as if he were broken now. He said: Ennemond my brother, my eyes are trapped in the falls . . .

Eh, that is very interesting, said Père Massé.

Père Quentin lifted his head. – Why do you talk to no one? he said feebly.

You are no one, replied Père Biard, curling his lip.

But Père Massé touched the crown of Père Quentin's head most tenderly, and Père Quentin sighed and slept.

He will feel better when he wakes, said Père Massé.

Yes, Ennemond, but I cannot get beyond this falls, or whirlpool, or whatever it is –

Now Père Massé took pity upon his Superior's sufferings and said: You must make the Exercises and see the Country of Glory unroll before you as you ascend; that will give you consolation.

Père Biard rocked himself, there in the darkness of the hold. – I am trying, but I cannot, he said woodenly. I cannot even get past Sault de l'Incarnation . . .

Père Massé waited.

I hear the waterfalls. I hear them all. They deafen my ears.

What do waterfalls do? said Père Massé.

They impede travel, replied Père Biard, and there was uncomprehending anger in his tone.

Yes, they do that. They block travel both in time and in space. What else?

Père Biard sat thinking obediently. – They make eddies, he said at last.

What else?

They end travel. They cause death to weak swimmers.

Yes, brother, said Père Massé. That is the purpose of the waterfalls in the Stream of Time. Low creatures such as you and I are not meant to surmount those obstacles. We are meant to be broken on them. Even CHRIST was broken on the Seventy-Third Rapid. All must die. But to understand this and die in the proper circumstances, that is to gain the Crown of Martyrdom.

Père Biard stared at him as if he had never seen him before.

Further History of the French Acadians
1614–1987

> It takes little courage to kick dead horses. Never has this maxim been better illustrated than in the case of the Catholic church since its demise in Québec society during the last decade. If verbal crucifixion produces purification, it can now indeed be called the Holy Roman Catholic church.
>
> HERBERT GUINDON, *Québec Society: Tradition, Modernity, and Nationhood* (1988)

After the English attack, Biencourt parleyed with Argall under a white flag, as I have said, but accomplished nothing. He lived with his men in the woods like a Savage. Winter came exceedingly hard. The rivières were ribbons of ice unrolled for leagues and fathoms among the evergreens; at the end of a day of fruitless hunting, silver ribbons unrolled in his brain like waterfalls and he sank down in the snow with a groan. In the month of Mars, starving, his men opened gashes in maple trees and drank the sap, which was of the hue of Spanish wine. They ate bark and mussels. The Souriquois took them into their wigwams with many expressions of pity. Yet when his father came, Biencourt expressed no wish to return to France. – We are ruined as well there as here, he said. – Poutrincourt wept. – GOD be with you then, he said. He deeded Port-Royal over to him (that was all he had left to give) and sailed to his waiting tomb, which was France. Surely he knew where he was headed. He imagined the vault-door clanging shut behind him, and to him it was music. – My poor wife . . . he muttered over and over, so much so that his enemies mocked him and said: That is how the Sieur de Poutrincourt says his *Aves*, not with a *Hail MARIE* but with an *Alas, my Claudette!* Eh, he is brought low now, the greedy scoundrel! – Of course I pity him, shrugged the Sieur de Monts. But he was very extravagant; he had no sense of proportion . . . Pontgravé was exceedingly interested in his case, for he had fifty livres riding on him. He had to die within another year for Pontgravé to collect. – Damn, but how long will that marshmallow remain in the world? (Thus Pontgravé.) Not that I wish anyone's death – GOD forbid! But his life is useless to him, and his death would be useful to *me!* Eh, what a reprobate I am! But all I do is buy and sell Monsieur Beaver; I'm entitled to some amusements: After all! But I wish I knew some good priest who could explain it all to me. There are some days I just don't comprehend anything. It's like a river roaring in my ears . . . LORD, aren't I profound? – Fortunately, the Sieur de Poutrincourt did indeed die just under the wire – which is to say the following Décembre, in the siege of Méry-sur-Seine. His own soldiers mistakenly fired their arquebuses at him, with the result that he instantaneously became a pudding filled with bullets instead of raisins. Or at least that is how sympathetic histories relate the tale. The truth was darker, of course. It seems that Poutrincourt had surrounded the city with a great force, among which were Vieuville the Roy's Lieutenant and all his men. Even as Poutrincourt was preparing to make a secret breach in the wall of the Lower Town, Vieuville was already treating with the enemy Captain, who agreed to capitulate if he were granted honorable terms – *viz.*, to march out with his garrison in full array, with drums beating, and the men to retain their arms. – Monsieur, I assent, said Vieuville. – When Poutrincourt learned that in this matter as in all others he had been superseded, he became mad with rage and shouted: Follow me, all who love me! and led his men across the moat (which was but knee-deep), and they charged up the ridge to the Upper Town and the Sieur de Poutrincourt screamed: GOD save the Roy and Poutrincourt! and the Sieur de Poutrincourt screamed: Kill, kill! and he led them down against Vieuville's soldiers. (You must understand that he was the Governor of this place. It was not for others to take it.) When his followers comprehended that he was harrying his own ally, those of them who could ran into a side street, where they stood motionless and trembling while he was cut down. It did not take long: Poutrincourt was old. – So much for the Viceroy of Canada! said Vieuville, standing over the bleeding body. He sent his troops to feel the breeches of all the men whom he suspected might have served with Poutrincourt: those who were wet-legged from the moat were slaughtered. Fully a hundred of Poutrincourt's men died with him that day.

Ah, one sees by this how the end of a life is in the pure providence of GOD. – Thus the Sieur de Monts, who in his blind imprudence and insatiability had wrought this razing of a life. The toad now proceeded to prove his own point, for he lived on serenely for years. But he never returned to Canada.

Most of Biencourt's men had returned home with his father, and now our young Sieur de Port-Royal had no hope of swelling his forces save by appeals to deserted sailors. Savages would not do, as much as he loved them: they had no wish to live in fixed houses. But as for him, he did not want to dwell in their wigwams anymore. It was not greed or ambition that kept him in Acadia, but the desire to attach some value to his father's sufferings. If he lived as a Souriquois he could not do this. – He seized the ships of illegal traders whenever he could, and his own trade was not unprofitable, for Membertouji'j never forgot him, but neither could it be said that he was gaining riches. His old enemy Robert left the beaver-business in 1618 and returned to France to join the Navy. Champlain was well entrenched at Kebec, as he heard, and did very well there, but never stopped to visit. Neither did old Pontgravé. – What should I expect? said Biencourt bitterly to himself. After all, I am no great personage anymore. – Presently he removed to Cap Sable and built the Fort called Lomeron, where he lived in foggy misery, fishing and hoarding beaver-skins until his death.* His Lieutenant, Charles de la Tour, was his heir, and sought to rule Acadia like a little Roy; in fact this Charles was more like a little boy who builds sand-castles and then runs screaming from the waves; for waves of English and Scottish did come, at which he swore allegiance to them; little waves of Frenchmen lapped back, at which he insisted that he had stood firm. Meanwhile he raided against his rival, another Charles, who had taken over Port-Royal . . . Years ran down the Stream of Time, whose waters are the waters of gall. Robert was killed by the Dutch in a great sea-battle in 'twenty-one; Pontgravé died in 'thirty-two, Champlain in 'thirty-five. Pontgravé's wife Christine lasted until 'seventy-seven, if you can believe it! Let's hope she collected on his last bets. The years were river-islands in a long, long chain. Now the priests crept timorously back, both Black-Gowns and Grey-Gowns. Père Le Clercq the Recollect knelt and hung his chart of invented Savage hieroglyphs on a tree, reading out: *also Thou, GREAT SPIRIT, pardon us sinners; strengthen us so that we are brought to bad things never again!* and the Souriquois knelt behind him as obediently as lambs, and their hair rustled like leaves in the forest breeze that enriched them one and all. Now it seemed as if the Kingdom had come; but in 1654, recalling the exploits of Argall, the English

* Writing *ca.* 1631, Champlain speaks of "the late Sieur Jean Biencourt," so it is patent that he did not live long.

conquered Acadia; in 1690 they conquered it again; in 1710 they did the same. By this time the Acadians no longer knew who ruled them, and paid little attention to anything but their livelihood and their growing families. (The Sieur de Dièreville, who visited Port-Royal for a year in the course of some unsuccessful business, met two couples in competition, who between them had produced eighteen children; another husband and wife had twenty-two. Eh, it was good that these people continued steadfast in the True Faith!) In 1714 legal title to their Country passed definitively into English hands, thanks to the Treaty of Utrecht. But the Black-Gowns and their proxies still came among the Acadians secretly from Québec, to insure that they remained loyal to Church and Roy. Our view of Port-Royal in 1751 (now Annapolis Royal) includes the harbor, of course, with its many-masted ships, its Navy men rowing about in longboats on Sunday errands, its cockaded Red-Coats leaning on canes and pointing across the water, its serene low hills . . . There were still Souriquois about, but they were called *Micmac* now. About one of their girls, Captain John Knox wrote: *. . . She was comely and not disagreeable; her complexion was not so fair as the British, nor yet so dark as the French in general are; her features were large, with sprightly black eyes, hair of the same colour, thin lips and a well-shaped nose . . . somewhat Dutch-built, but very sprightly, and had much of the French in her manner and behaviour . . .** As for the French themselves, failing in 1755 to take an oath of allegiance to His Majesty the King of England, they were expelled forever, and New England families took their farms . . .

The French Powder Magazine at Port-Royal 1987

This low white structure has a shingle roof which lowers over the walkway like wings on this clear afternoon with the distant sound of lawn mowers, and there is green grass; there are green trees; and there is a white fortress. The magazine is piebald, stones being set into its white mortar. Inside, everything is dark and cool. Tourists have scratched their names on the powder barrels. It has one window, ledged about with stone in the shape of a fat cross, and one door. It is set about five feet deep into the ground, shrugged down between the shoulders of two hills. Not far from this site, Biencourt and young Born Underwater must have passed each other, there on the edge of the vanished beech-forest where her mother was raped. Perhaps that meadow

* *Of these Tribes, reduced to direst need,* wrote the Sieur de Dièreville in 1708, *the greater number are already gone.*

toward the harbor was Lescarbot's garden. On this rise the Sieur de Champlain must have stood with his astrolabe, making his measurements. Over there Membertou might have been buried by Père Biard. Here Argall stood gloating over the charred timbers of Port-Royal. – What are we to make of all this? – Nothing. Port-Royal was beautiful. It is still beautiful, even though now it is Annapolis Royal and Anglophones live there.

Apples and Graves 1987

The Prescott House is where old Mr. Prescott lived, while in another country his famous cousin was writing *The Conquest of Peru*. It is a lovely white house in Nova Scotia, with its two chimneys, its wide green garden, its birds, its salt sea breeze blowing from Wellington Dyke, and all screened by trees in the midst of a paradise of white houses and apple trees, orchard fields by the sea, gilded with dandelions; white horses roving in the grass, the smell of manure, warm sun and cool breezes, gently rolling hills. In the sky are clouds like puff-pastries; and here and there, as if for ornament only, may be found a reddish-brown field, its furrows sloping down to the sea. There are white houses with steep tight roofs and narrow windows, their green shutters hospitably drawn back. The apple trees wear blossoms as dense as hair, so that they are like pink islands in the green. But everywhere you go in Nova Scotia, it seems, you find graveyards. You cannot easily find headstones with French names, search though you will; Nova Scotia is English and seems always to have been English. The oldest tombstone in Annapolis Royal, once the Port-Royal of Père Biard, reads:

HERE LYES Y BODY OF
BATHIAH DOUGLASS, WIFE
TO SAMUEL DOUGLASS, WHO
DEPARTED THIS LIFE OCTO.
THE 1ST 1720 IN THE 37
YEAR OF HER AGE

Close upon the inscription presses a skull with rippling wings, like angel-cloud.

Yes, the Frenchmen are gone. As for the Black-Gowns, where in Canning or Digby will you find their mark? – Only in the sky, where flocks of crows go raining by . . .

Further History of the Armouchiquois

1613–ca. 1620

As to the customs of the Savages, it is enough to say that they are altogether savage . . .

PÈRE LALEMANT, to his brother,
Père Lalemant (1627)

Once the Iron People were gone and could no longer tell the Lnu'k what to do, the latter went at once to attack the Armouchiquois. We do not know whether Biencourt went with his friend Membertouji'j to help him shoot the arquebuses against Bashaba their Saqmaw, but very likely he did send the guns as his father the Sieur de Poutrincourt had done with Membertouji'j's father, Henri Membertou. So they stole upon Bashaba, and slew him by surprise, dragging off his women to be slaves, and taking whatever other booty they could find. After this, the Armouchiquois fell into disorder, and quarreled against themselves, Saqmaw against Saqmaw, band against band. They despoiled one another of food whenever they could. Let an Englishman conclude the tale:

. . . famine took hold of many, which was seconded by a great and generall plague, which so violently rained for three yeares together, that in a manner the greater part of that Land was left desert without any to disturb or appease our free and peaceable possession thereof . . .

Out of the Kingdom
1613

. . . if we consider the country, it is only a forest . . .

Jesuit Relations (1610)

Throughout the voyage, a voice of idiocy spoke in his head, and all that it said was, "Jacob left Beer-sheba and went toward Haran. Jacob left Beer-sheba and went toward Haran." Père Biard strove not to let himself be tempted into despair, and said to himself, yes! Jacob must leave Beer-sheba, and he must work for Laban with many trials, and he must receive ugly Leah when he had expected Rachel, but in the end he will win her also, his Rachel the Beloved; and after wrestling with GOD he will be blessed by GOD, and his name will be called Israel. – But the voice said only what it had said. And presently, swimming in the sea-mist of failure, he saw France again before him.

Born Underwater
1613–1625

> If it were not so paradoxical, one would almost like to call out to the dream interpreter: "Do anything you like, only don't try to understand!"
>
> C. G. JUNG, *The Practical Use of Dream Analysis* (1934)

The barred owl of Acadia was said by the Sieur Denys to collect live mice in a hollow tree. What a crafty bird that hooter was! The mice could not escape him because he broke their forelegs in his beak. In another hollow tree close by he kept wisps of hay, so that every night he might come feed them and carry off the fattest. – Denys seems truly to have believed this folly, just as he believed that flying squirrels had wings, that crows were as good to eat as chickens; he swore that the noise of beavers beating their tails on their dams could be heard for more than a league's distance; he saw *with his own eyes* and almost captured a merman off the Acadian coast . . . (What are we to make of his eyes?) – Concerning the Souriquois it was his affidavit that before the days of the French they shared hollow trees with the owls for their necessities, utilizing them for kettles. The availability of iron pots in trade was therefore a great relief to them, as they were now no longer confined to their immovable tree-kitchens. – Might this have been so? – We cannot say.* (The Souriquois for their part marveled at the immovable houses of the French.) In any event, a fog of fabulousness still hangs over Acadia at this period, as if it were the month of Mai, when sea-mists lie in upon the coast until nine or

* "There are many ways of cooking without using hollowed out logs," says Ruth Whitehead. "Hollow trees are not used. The wood is burnt and adzed out."

ten in the morning, after which the day becomes very fine (so says Denys). Upon the destruction of Port-Royal, of course, the vapors of unreality somewhat thickened, for nothing could now be known of Acadia save from the lips of the truth-hating English: Biencourt did not write home. For those who had always lived there, the People of KLUSKAP, the existence of the Iron People did not become so conjectural. Outcast men with pale skins remained. In the winter they were dependent on the People for charity. They had fewer iron gifts to give. But from time to time a vessel anchored at Port-Royal, and then the Iron People who had stayed were happy. KLUSKAP's People often spied Iron People's ships between the tree-roots, their reflections shimmering on the water, with the blue coast of Labrador behind, and once a ship came closer and closer, so the People went to Born Swimming's wigwam and laughed, saying: Your Floating Island has come back to us!

She did not like this.

A ship landed, and it was filled with French beaver-traders, so that the People rejoiced.

Another ship landed.

Another woman was raped by the Iron People. She sang sad songs and hanged herself from a tree. Her husband went to the ship of the Iron People and killed as many of them as he could before they shot him.

Another ship landed. Hooded French cod-fishers stomped about in their boots and aprons. The People gave them furs and moose-meat. They gave the People iron fishhooks.

A Conclusion *1615*

When Born Underwater was yet a small child she became known for her watchfulness. One winter when her family was moving the wigwam to a better place, and she struggled through the snow behind her mother, with corded bundles of house-bark lashed to her back, she suddenly stopped and pointed. (She was only four or five winters old; her mother was still giving her suck.) When Born Swimming looked, she saw that the girl had discovered the vapor of a bear's breath rising from the roots of a fallen tree. She ran ahead to get her husband and the boys. And so there was meat that night. – Her father stared at her for a long time until she dropped her eyes.

He himself was a very good hunter, although slower since he'd suffered from the new sickness. When he hunted beaver, he could reach through a hole in the ice with such patience that the family joke was that the ice froze again around his arm. Slowly he brought his hand into the beaver-lodge, caressing the animals in exactly the same way that they rubbed against each other, to keep them from taking alarm while his fingers learned where a tail was; then he seized it, drew the beaver forth in a twinkling, and split its skull with his axe before it could bite him. He hunted beaver often. Of all meat Swooping Like a Hawk best loved the gristly fat of a beaver-tail, roasted over the fire. Then, too, the Iron People lusted after beaver-skins even now. The Saqmaw Biencourt gave gifts for them, when he could. So beaver-skins became iron hatchets. It was wonderful how much better those iron hatchets were. True, they quickly lost their keenness, and the Iron People would not sharpen them, but it was no trouble to kill another beaver to get a new hatchet.

In the summer, when he was stalking moose, Swooping Like a Hawk could tell by the dung he found whether a moose was a bull or a cow, and how old it was. He knew how to recognize another Nation by their footprints. He considered himself a good observer. But he felt now that he had not studied his daughter with sufficient attention. It was very strange for such a young girl to see what he had not.

Of course, he said to himself, she comes from the Iron People. Perhaps that is why she is different.

She did not know that she was different yet. She could remember being very little and being held by her father as he smoked tobacco, puffing twin white clouds through his nose, at which she laughed and touched his big loving face and inhaled the good smoke from his nostrils and he was laughing also. At the end of that summer she saw how proud her father was when she made her first quiver for him and he wore it even though she soon saw that it was not so well made, and begged him to discard it so that she could give him a better, but he refused, stroking her long black hair . . .

Sault of Election *1618*

Born Swimming was boiling moose-bones and crushing them. The snow-white grease was rising in the kettle; she skimmed it off and put it into a birchbark vessel where it hardened into the firmness of wax. She formed it into cakes. This would be her husband's food when he went hunting.

What happens to the bones after the marrow comes out? said the girl. She was nine winters old.

Then we hang them in the trees to make Moose come back again. You know that.

Does he grow like fruit, or does he come from Ghost World to get his bones?

I can't tell you that. I never dreamed about it, said Born Swimming. She was breaking branches for the fire.

A proud smile twisted the daughter's face. – I'm going to dream it, she said. Then I'll tell you.

Oh, you will? Maybe you will. Go to the head of the stream and get me some black spruce root. You and I will sew baskets today.

It was early spring, when snowbanks rolled whitely down to the river whose brown pools stretched out like hands. Born Underwater was happy as she left her mother's house because she hoped to see the awakening of the waterfalls. On the ridges, brown leaves lay as thick as snow; rain-washed, no longer crisp, like the dingy yellow bark that streamed in tatters from the trees. Past the snow-roofed beaver dams the river narrowed into a half-throttled ribbon of ice, then widened again, pool above pool. Here the waterfalls lived, and they were still asleep. Born Underwater admired them. There was one, a young one, into which she sometimes threw the bones of the fishes she killed. She brushed the snow from a place of crackly moss and squatted down to watch. From the frozen waterfall, ice-colored water streamed in gouts from icy horns. Water rolled down between the tree-mounds, almost shielded from her sight by ice, but now the ice had worn thin so that she could see the grey rushing movement beneath the milk-grey; here and there were cavities, black from the wet rocks inside, through which the water tasseled and twirled.

Then there came a sound as of rain, as if ice-crystals were sifting down from the trees (and yet she felt nothing on hands or nose). This pattering did not come from the sky, which was grey like dirty snow; the young saplings and twigs were still glossy with ice. No, it came from the rivers. This was the mysterious moment when spring began. Something was breaking, breaking in the glassy ponds root-pierced and tree-pierced; something was breaking in the thick-frozen marshes. Slowly the ice began to gape wide, the brown water to bleed. Brown pools and streams ate into their snow-shirts like spreading holes.

At that moment something happened inside the girl, something strange. Something passed through her like wind in the forest. She fell down, biting her lip because no one of the People ever cried out no matter how great the pain was; that would have been a disgrace.

She had become blind.

The pain was worst just behind her eyes.

For a long time she lay there in the snow. Her fingers twisted and untwisted the neck of the reed-bag that her mother had given her to fill with roots. The pain did not go away. Finally she stood up, too quickly. A branch which she could not see scratched her cheek. After that she began to feel about her with a timidity that was exactly the same in form as loving gentleness, but was as unlike it as it was possible to be. She caressed the trees around her. Their icy bark was as slippery as fish-skin.

What was happening to her? She was an obedient girl. Why had she been given this pain?

Now another spasm attacked her, and she found herself unable to stand. She was rolling in the snow; she drew her knees up tight and almost whimpered, but not a sound came from her. The darkness behind her open eyes filled with stars, and a pain more sharp than any before exploded in the back of her head.

Something was flowing. Something trickled.

When she opened her eyes again she could see. Her mouth tasted of blood. The ache inside her was gone. But something was different. Something new was inside her heart. She had not wanted it to come; she still did not know exactly what it was; she felt only the tip of it, like the green sprout that marks where groundnuts are strung on the root like beads. But she had been given something. – There was an eye inside her heart!

There's *Power* inside me, she thought gleefully. Power came to me!

The Face

But when she told her mother, she watched the expression that came over her face.

An evil thing happened to me, Born Swimming said. That's how I came to give birth to you. If you do not yet know of it, it is fitting that I tell you now. I do not lie: I see his fearful face before me day and night. He is a venomous man of the Iron People. He still dwells nearby, in the Country of the Etechemins. You must be careful if you go there – open your ears! Once or twice in every life, evil things happen. Have courage, daughter, but be warned! I'm afraid that the eye in your heart comes from that man. What will happen to you? You were born so different from the rest of us, with your round eyes, your strange skin . . . I'm afraid for you.

No, it was good, Born Underwater said. I think it was good.

The big pot of moose-bones was still boiling. The corn-like smell of marrow filled the wigwam. The liquid was thick and bloody and marrow-frothed.

I cannot comprehend the Iron People, Born Swimming said. Nobody knows what they want.

Hearing this, the girl was apprehensive; she couldn't have said why.

Hang those moose-bones in the trees, her mother said at last.

The Eye

Later, when Born Swimming lay down to dream, she said to herself the old words. This sickness of Power which would now afflict her daughter for life, this too must be laid at the door of Robert Ki'kwa'ju. *My heart weeps tears of blood,* she moaned. *I must blot out this outrage with blood.*

She had forgotten the eye in her own heart that saw the Floating Island.

Leaf-Opening

After this, the girl gave evidence of being *Nikani-kjijitekewinu*. In the Moon of Leaf-Opening, when they stripped the trees of bark to make new houses, she began to cry out almost every night, so that the others in the wigwam were awakened. Yet she seemed happy, as if she did not understand what was happening to her. That was often how it was: those who saw far were also blind, like Smoking the Pipe.

Once, in her sleep she turned over and said: I want . . .

Born Swimming was awake. She listened tensely for a very long time, to hear what it was that her daughter wanted, so that she could bring it to her, but she never said anything more that night.

People who did not get what they wanted became sick. Not to know what one wanted was very dangerous. Some People died that way.

These unknown desires of hers reminded her mother of pale green young maple-leaves trying to fly when it was late spring and they could only flutter and shade each other with flickers of translucency and coolness all summer long, until at last fall came and they *could* fall, fly and fall colored like bloody dreams.

The Bowl

Now the girl knew what was necessary. She adorned herself with wampum and painted her face red. She took up a birchbark bowl. Then she went into the forest. Her mother watched her go, saying nothing. Born Underwater's heart-roots had now grown so tightly about the secret that it would only harm her to search it out. That was what everyone said about her now. They had begun to leave her alone.

Two Winners

One day after this, in the Moon of Moose-Calling, the People were playing the game of Waltes, and her father Swooping Like a Hawk was about to shake the dish of moose bones when Born Underwater said: Father, you will not win. – All looked at her, and Swooping Like a Hawk shook the dish and the bone-disks whirled into the air and landed in the dish in no order, some white side up, some black side up, and then his opponent took a turn and won the Old Woman, and the play went on as the People scored the throws on the stick-counters, until at last it befell that Swooping Like a Hawk had not won. But this was not a matter for surprise. Next was a young man called Dreaming of Iron; and Born Underwater said: You will do better than Father. Five disks will show their black side. – He too made no reply; and it came about as the girl had said, so he got three counting-sticks. – Now old

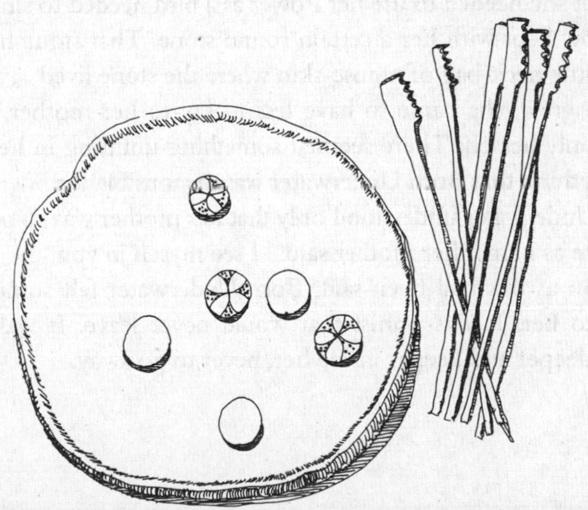

Smoking the Pipe stepped forward to take his turn. – And me, granddaughter, what will my luck be? he said ironically. – Her face fell at once. – I don't know, she said. I can't see you. – Smoking the Pipe shook the dish and the bone-disks rose like butterflies black and white and rattled down in the dish and every face was black; on the other throws his luck was almost as good. – Hah! he laughed. Dreaming of Iron, you will pay me first. Give me your shirt of birds! – And all the People cried *ho, ho!* at the spectacle of a winner, and the children were shrieking in excitement and the predictions of Born Underwater, being inconclusive, had already been forgotten.

She herself, of course, did not forget. She felt proud and glad, and thought to paint her face red and yellow in token. But when the game was concluded, Smoking the Pipe came to her quietly and said: Do not recall your triumph to others, for they will only fear you. Surely I who am their Shaman know them well.

And he laughed bitterly.

Recognition

Now the happiness of newness was gone. But she trembled with sensitivity, like a spiderweb thick and dusty over dead leaves; she did not want to catch the dust and have it stick to her, but she could not help it; and she would stretch under the impact of a single raindrop; – imagine, then, how it would be for her to be trampled by dreams.

And yet she needed to use her Power as a bird needed to sing.

She now kept with her a certain round stone. That stone had Power. She made a little neck-bag of moose-skin where the stone lived . . .

As she grew, she came to have less to say to her mother, for which she blamed only herself. There seemed something unfitting in her. Somehow it was something that Born Underwater was responsible for.

Born Underwater understood only that her mother was so often unhappy.

You are as I am, her mother said. I see myself in you.

As soon as this had been said, Born Underwater felt something horrible crawl into her. It was a mist that would never leave. It was a cold worm twisting deeper and deeper inside her, never to go away.

The Death of Smoking the Pipe

That winter, in the Moon of River-Freezing, Smoking the Pipe had become very foul and bloated with sickness, so that he opened his veins with his scalping-knife, to let some of the bad blood out. But he continued in his illness, until at last he could neither eat nor speak. It was Frost-Fish Moon now, and the People were scattered to look for moose. His apprentice, Looking Down Streams, split his head open with a hatchet to end his suffering. Thus he died; thus he went behind the high mountains.

Looking Down Streams made him a coffin of bark and put him tenderly in a tree-crotch, as was fitting for those who had died in winter. In Egg-Laying Moon, when all the People had returned and the snow was gone, the time had come to bury him. Since there were not enough Iron People lurking near to dig up his body, Looking Down Streams did not think it necessary to bury him on the secret island. Membertouji'j gave him a magnificent funeral robe which one of his wives had made. Born Swimming and Swooping Like a Hawk gave him the best iron knife they had. Kinebji'j-koji'j's sister gave him some beads that the Iron People had given her. So it went. Then Looking Down Streams bound his bones and buried him in the round grave. He buried him with all his goods. He struck the bark of his wigwam, crying loudly: *Oué! Oué!* to make his spirit come out. On his grave he then threw earth and logs. Now Looking Down Streams was the Shaman.

The Confirmation 1621

At the coming of the leaf, they shot Bear upon a branch, piercing him once and again with arrows. They shot Beaver as he came from the water. In the following moon, which was Sea-Fowl Shed Their Feathers, it was summer, and Swooping Like a Hawk set out to hunt Moose with the Sturgeon, whom he'd adopted as his son. It was a heavy night. They paddled up the river very quietly. Presently Swooping Like a Hawk made a sign, and his son dipped the birchbark dish into the water, raised it to his shoulder, and spilled it slowly, in imitation of the sound of a doe-moose making water. Meanwhile Swooping Like a Hawk made the sound of her call. They waited. No moose came. The boy looked up into the SKY, which was so thickened with haze that the STAR PERSONS could not be seen. His father touched his arm, and again they played their ruse together without result. So they paddled a little farther up the river, to a stand of black birches whose branches had been chewed by moose, and made their trick again. Again they waited, and presently they heard a male come crashing through the forest. Father and son raised their bows and drew back the strings. When they saw the moose's chest in the moonlight they launched their arrows, one into the shoulder, the other through the throat. The moose leaped and began to run. Swooping Like a Hawk shot another arrow. Putting one hand on the bow of the canoe to steady it, he swung himself onto land and began to run, while behind him the boy beached the canoe. The moose had already fallen. Swooping Like a Hawk slit his throat.

The boy said: I long to have a gun from the Iron People!

Swooping Like a Hawk said: Yes, guns are good.

Suddenly the boy said: Why does my sister act so mournful, like one who has no sense?

The father hesitated. – You must bear with her, he replied at last. She is not so bold and stout as you.

So matters went, until she became a woman and her breasts gently upcurved like the mid-gunwale of a canoe.

It was the Moon of Fat Animals when Searching for Caribou painted his face red and she accepted him. In the Moon of River-Freezing, there came an epidemic. Looking Down Streams was called, but he could not help anyone. He gave back the tobacco they gave him, saying nothing. Presently he too died. In almost every wigwam there were faces daubed black in mourning. Her family sickened, except for her. Searching for Caribou died. Swooping Like a Hawk died. But Born Underwater lived. She had Power. That was the thread that ran through everything, like a black spruce root.

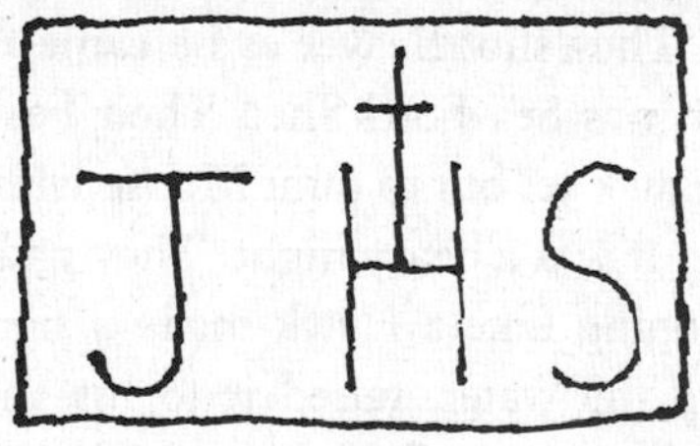

IV
Thy Will Be Done
or,
The War with the Irocois Savages

The Dream of the Irocois
1603

> Thus religion attracts more devotion according as it demands more faith – that is to say, as it becomes more incredible to the profane mind.
>
> Henri Frédéric Amiel, *Journal*, 5 June 1870

"As we began to approach the said rapid with our little skiff and the canoe," wrote the Sieur de Champlain in 1603, "I assure you that I never saw any torrent of water pour over with such force as this does, although it is not very high, being in some places only one or two fathoms; and at the most three. It descends as it were step by step; and wherever it falls from some small height, it boils up extraordinarily, owing to the force and speed of the water as it passes through the said rapid, which may be a league* in length. There are many rocks out in the stream; in the middle are very long narrow islands . . ." – So he continued with his observations, sketching rivières and fleuves on the snow-white plain of his first map, although in truth those streams were mainly snow-frozen with ignorance (how could they not be?); they issued from dismaying blankness, and great knives of broken ice lay upon their backs, these fragments being covered in turn with snow. Thus his map wore the Ice-Shirt as yet: – the extent of Canada was so large that no end to it had been found! – But even here a cheerful season must come at last. These rapids, for example, had lately been but a frozen beard upon the rocks, but now that he had found them they would flow on his map forever.

* Two and a half miles.

In truth *NAVIGATION* had always seemed to him the highest art, for it allowed anyone with a dram of courage to gain knowledge of other regions, to find riches, and to overthrow idolatry. These things he would do, if the Lord left him his strength of body. His eyes would melt away the mystery from every last river in Canada until he found China! Surely one of these aquatic highways must lead there – not straight, of course, but pausing and bending from time to time at many an easy lake-elbow – but that it did he was sure, so that China would be French without the inconvenience of the northern icebergs . . . (That was one of his favorite notions.) – And so he touched his pen to the birchbark sheet, making little swirls to mark the rapids, and those swirls were new cracks in the previously featureless icecaps of maps that had been so for a quarter of a thousand years, ever since the Norse Greenlanders had forgotten Vinland; and Champlain stood up and parted two bushes to peer down the cataract to a bend in the Fleuve Saint-Laurent beyond which was a hill whose shape he corrected on the map . . . and the blank sheet thawed and dripped. (Beside him, Pontgravé yawned.) Closer to Kebec, rivers were already brown and gushing in narrow braids between snow-islands brown and sodden around the edges, for Champlain had become familiar with those. There the white page was riddled with lines. But here it was empty afternoon, and the sky was snowy-white. His chest was tight with misery. Again the Savages had tricked him, idly and without reason. He would not look at them. *This* was no ship-way to China. (And the Golden Kingdom of the Saguenay – what if that too were one of their fairytales?) – Snapping off a branch, he cast it over the precipice like a spear, and watched the rapids devour it. The Savages laughed, as if he were playing a game for their amusement. – Champlain bit his lip. – Grey cloud slid across the moon. On his map he mustered the congregations of fat spruces grey-green and snow-soft like cloud-lobes; they shivered when he touched them, so that dollops of snow fell down his neck. And the more he filled in the landscape with his knowledge, the more the snow melted, so that his map thawed into a springtime in whose mucky places he saw nodding Canada lilies which were spotted brown inside their waxy golden cups, like the skins of those tropical fruits called *bananas* (these he had seen with his own eyes on his voyage to the West Indies); and his ignorance dwindled (as he thought) from a snow-field to a white moth fluttering among ferns of fresh expectations; and he assembled lakes and forests and granite boulders with the dispassionate steadiness of Descartes, thinking surely there must be a way to China! and yet he was still downcast. The Montagnais who had brought him to the rapids watched his face; they were very sorry for him because he was disappointed.

To please him, they had agreed with him when he expressed, disguised as a strictly neutral and hypothetical question, his desperate wish that the Fleuve Saint-Laurent would take him to the Chinese Sea; – after all, he must be a powerful dreamer to have come across the Great Water to them. Perhaps his dreams could make it so for him. And there were many seas of sweet water in the interior; that they knew.

You have lied to me, said Champlain at last, very coldly. These rapids are impassable. – He glared into their eyes; and then his busy hand resumed its sketching. – At this the Savages looked away, ashamed for him because his dream had failed. (Pontgravé yawned again.) And for a long time they sat there, by those rushing boiling falls to which succeeding Frenchmen, ridiculing him, gave the appellation "Lachine."* But *he* . . . he pursed his mouth and thought to himself: one might portage here, in the light canoes of the Savages. The woods are open here. My men could carry their weapons at the ready here without much toil . . .

This time tell me the truth, he said. Above these rapids, how many more?

Twenty more, a Savage said.

And then China?

You will surely find it if you seek it.

Eh, come on down, Champlain. – Thus Pontgravé.

After this, turning back from this place where his predecessor Quartier had turned back three-quarters of a century before (Cartier contenting himself with kidnapping the Savage King Donnaconna and his sons, who all died on beds of disease in France), Champlain and the Savages climbed down again into the summer of mapped country with its ridges of yellow-green, grey-roofed with sky, floored with mud and ferns. Pontgravé ambled behind, humming. And Champlain, forcing his way through the broken branches that hung from a row of birch trees, told his rosary of lakes and falls and lakes until in his hopes he had already come to the Sweetwater Sea, which (although he did not yet know it) was where the Huron Nation lived. He said to himself: all this will be New France. And yet the gnats swarmed about him in preference to the naked and unwashed bodies of the Savages in front of him, and he was fatigued and his thoughts were the anxious yellow color of a forest before a storm. But his eyes continued their automatic catalogue: white spruce for the masts (there did not appear to be any red spruce as in Acadia), white elm for the hulls, red oak for barrel-staves, white oak for

* "China."

cabinets: the trees of Canada, in short, could be turned into vessels to carry more trees. His thoughts whirled and fell in hope-water.

What deep eyes he has! said the Savages to each other.

Yes, they said, that is why his dreams cannot come out.

After lakes and falls and lakes, one comes to the Sweetwater Sea, he repeated to himself. These Savages tell me the course of the waters there is from the setting sun to the east . . . – Another trickle from that hard-frozen map. The page was becoming slushy like Lower Town in Québec where there were puddles in the sunny streets, although the cliff-shade kept snow hard on the roofs of houses; water dripped down the stone walls from Upper Town, freezing glasslike in the snow around the churches and houses there; in ten years, twenty years, thirty years, Champlain would see the beginning of this, and so would the Souriquois woman, Born Underwater, clinging to wet dripping walls as the French passed her in the street. Icicles dripped down upon her head. Champlain would die here. The whiteness melted . . .

The Savages had stopped. One launched an arrow and brought down a goose. At this the others clapped their hands and shouted: *ho!*

Once I have charted these waters, he said to himself, I will no longer have to rely on brutes and lost souls for my direction. They would not behave in this way if they were capable of reason. But someday they will be *brought* to reason. Their filthy naked dances will be abolished, and someday my map will be entirely blue and green . . . And his hands reached out to embrace every river and waterfall for his own, although he did not realize that the farther he reached the closer he came to something quite deadly that should have remained buried in the snow; greedily he shoveled the drifts aside with his hands, paying no heed to the frozen scalps that he found: – After Lachine, he learned, the river climbed five rapids to a lake beyond which were five rapids. (This was the rivière beside which the Algoumequin Savages dwelt.) Then he came upon a lake whose mists melted in front of him, and yet it was a considerable lake whose end could not be easily discerned so that his desire for China leaped up in his breast; – yes, a very large lake, into which in due course proceeding, armed and calm, he was to find the great isle where the Savages hunted in summer; and beyond the isle the waters became brackish. (He was close to Catherine Tekakwitha's country now. He was far too close . . .) The Savages assured him that this brackishness increased until one reached a tremendous fall called *Niagara*, which must be portaged; a league beyond this, however, was the Great Sea.* (Could *this* be where Cathay lay?)

* I.e., Lake Erie.

– The Savages further said that at the entrance to this Great Sea were two rivers, one of them leading back to the territory of the Algoumequins; the other descending into the Nation of wicked and dangerous Savages, known as *Irocois* . . .

The Hodinhsioni
?1451

Thou and I are brothers . . . May I, therefore, say, my brother, that I again draw together thy people at the place where thou art wont to environ the fire . . .

JOHN DESERONTYON, leading a Ritual of Condolence at Caughnawagwa (1782)

In the Country of the Savages there once was a lake called BEAUTIFUL.* North of Beautiful, in the Land of Crooked Tongues, lived the Huron, who wore shirts of skin. In later times, when embroidering had become the fashion, their coats grew red patches sewn in the shapes of birds and moons and diamonds. They bloomed with flowers made of beads, those coats; the Huron women were famous for their skill. But this Iroquois tale was told long before the French traders and weaving-exemplars had come into the Country. In those days it was enough simply to wear painted skins. So it was among the Five Nations of the Irocois as among the Four Nations of the Huron. Now it must be told that the Huron and the Hiroquois were enemies. They warred upon each other, and many were the captives who burned in each others' fires. Sometimes the raiders were victorious, and sometimes they fell into the hands of the defenders; but always the torturers laughed. And so did the victims, for that was the way to show greatness. Thus the enemy Nations needed each other; they gave good glory one to the other. – But there was a difference between them that must be told. The Huron Nations

* *Deyoswege Kaniodai.* Lake Ontario.

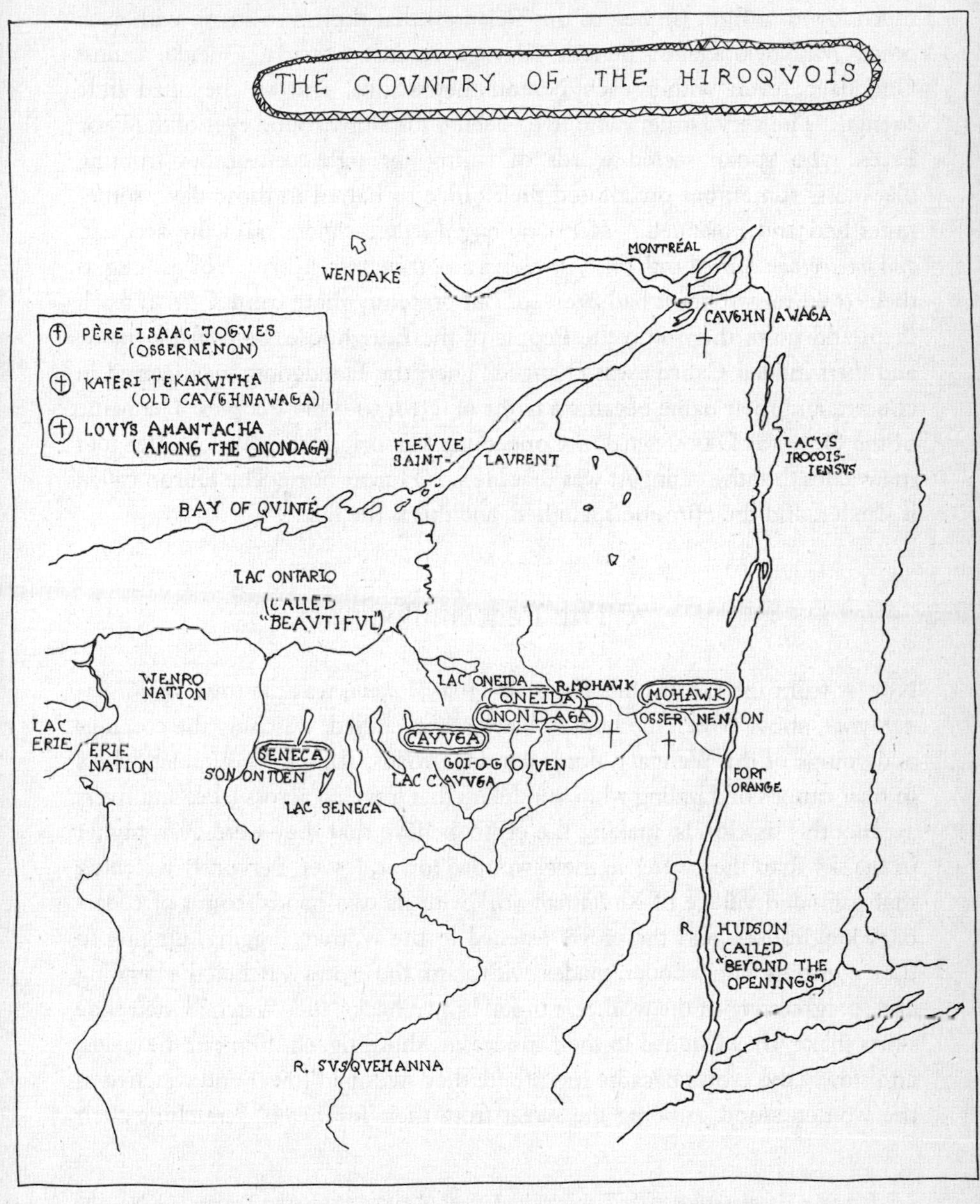
THE COVNTRY OF THE HIROQVOIS
PÈRE ISAAC JOGVES
(OSSERNENON)
KATERI TEKAKWITHA
(OLD CAVGHNAWAGA)
LOVYS AMANTACHA
(AMONG THE ONONDAGA)
WENDAKE
MONTRÉAL
CAVGHNAWAGA
FLEVVE SAINT-LAURENT
LACVS IROCOIS-IENSVS
BAY OF QVINTÉ
LAC ONTARIO
(CALLED
"BEAVTIFVL")
WENRO
NATION
LAC
ERIE
ERIE
NATION
SENECA
SONONTOEN
LAC SENECA
CAYVGA
LAC CAYVGA
GOI-O-GOVEN
LAC ONEIDA
ONEIDA
ONONDAGA
R. MOHAWK
MOHAWK
OSSERNENON
FORT
ORANGE
R. HUDSON
CALLED
"BEYOND THE
OPENINGS"
R. SVSQVEHANNA

were friends among themselves, and acted in concert. But the Irocois so much loved to fight (so begins this Relation) that they even strove with each other, Mohawk against Seneca, Cayuga against Oneida, Oneida against Onondaga; even within each Nation they strove, and so they had little strength. The very Healers who lived behind the shiny round eyes of the False Faces, who spoke sacred words of curing through teeth-grilles fronting blackness, sometimes prostituted their office to hatred in those days, sometimes lied and poisoned. *Men were ragged with sacrifice,* says the account, *and the women scarred with flints, so everywhere there was misery.* For as long as they could remember it had been so. But presently there came One to teach them and unite them into the People of the Longhouse, or *Haudenosaunee*, and then indeed Canada was changed. Then the Haudenosaunee warred in concert, and their name became a name of terror to other Peoples. The name of the One was DEKANWIDEH. Concerning His origins the Irocois later told many tales, but the strangest was that He was Huron-born. The Huron called it slander, and the Hiroquois laughed, and this is the tale.*

The Peacemaker

Not far from the Great Hill, *Ti-ro-nat-ha-ra-da-donh*, was the town of *Ka-ha-nah-yenh*, above which the hungry black crows circled, watching the comings and goings of the Wendat† along the ridge-roads, seeing the Wendat fishers in their canoes of dazzling white birchbark that traveled across lakes and rivers as smoothly as clouds, making the crows believe that they were even higher in the sky than they were, so they swooped lower, lower, nervously watching that palisaded village of *Ka-ha-nah-yenh* with its two hands' count of cedar-bark longhouses, and the crows listened to the women digging, digging in their cornhills with wooden spades; with alarm the crows watched the bending and straightening of the women's broad brown backs; they watched their hide skirts shake; they listened to their moccasins shuffling, shuffling in the fields, and slowly the crows became less afraid; they swooped lower and watched as the women stood, rubbing the sweat from their foreheads, scratching their

* *Is there a Huron version of the Dekanwideh legend?* I asked Professor Trigger. – *No,* he replied, *and if there had been it would have been noted. The question is why did* [the] *Iroquois invent a Huron culture hero? Did it reflect* [the] *fact that after 1650 so many of them were descendants of Hurons?*

† What the Huron called themselves. The name "Wendat" means "Island-Dwellers," which Trigger infers to mean "at the center of the world."

sweaty brown breasts, and the crows came closer and then the women shouted and stamped and the crows flew high again in a fright. But they could not stay away. They wanted corn. They alighted in the middens, looking for kernels of corn; in late summer they hid among the tall shady stalks and gobbled whatever they could until they were driven away or killed. They alighted on the palisade-poles, watching the women of *Ka-ha-nah-yenh* grinding the corn in hollowed-out tree-trunks, watching the cornmeal that was spilled, watching so greedily. Sometimes they heard strange noises in the forest nearby; then, being insatiable, they hopped up into the air and spread their wings. They flew higher, higher, until the longhouses below were like a row of corncobs; then they could see into the forest, where the Wendat men girdled the bark of trees to kill them, chopping at them with their stone axes and burning the branches that they cut, and it was very cool and dim and mosquito-ridden where the men worked (always on guard against enemies), and the crows hoped that the men were preparing spoils for them as good as corn, but they never saw anything and so were disappointed. At last, loudly cawing, they departed for the Great Hill called *Ti-ro-nat-ha-ra-da-donh*, where they feasted on hard red berries.

In this village (so say the Irocois) there lived a woman whose daughter was a virgin, but the mother watched her and watched her unwinkingly, like a crow, and at last she knew that she was pregnant.

This part of the legend is peculiar, since in those days the Wendat girls saw no harm in stringing lovers like beads. So there is reason to believe that the notions of the Black-Gowns have painted themselves here, darkening, overlaying and insisting, until another redskinned Madonna smiles sadly forth. – Maybe, maybe not. At any rate, it is how the story goes, so I have no right to change it. From a bad debt one collects what one may (thus Champlain).

For a long time the mother did not know what to do. It would not do to humiliate the girl; she might kill herself. But she could not say nothing, either. Six families lived in that longhouse. Their eyes were not fixed on her daughter as sharply as hers, of course, but soon now, when the girl ground corn for soup, or when she went out to the fields, they must notice her swelling belly. In the Country of the Wendat, poisoners and witches were quickly put to death. If she had conceived the child with no man, then . . .

The girl was feeding the little bear cub, who soon would be large enough to be sacrificed and eaten; she was clucking at him as she fed him fish, so that he peered up at her. – Soon we will eat you, eat you, eat you! the girl was laughing. She rubbed the cub between his ears, which she knew he liked, and he blinked and reached up to touch her nose with his paw.

The mother, greasing her hair with sunflower oil, looked sidelong at her daughter and was filled with rage. She longed to consult her husband or her brother, but both of them had gone down to the Iroquois to get prisoners for burning. Her mother was too old; she could not keep secrets anymore. If she told her anything, then it would come out. She swallowed until the anger was safely in her belly, rumbling and bubbling; then she smiled at her daughter and asked her to come into the fields.

Yes, my mother, said the girl.

They passed the Peace-Chief's house and the War-Chief's house and went out through the winding way between the palisades. Crows cawed in the sun. It was the Month When Strawberry Flowers Open. They went down the rustling hill of corn toward the river. The green smells of corn were sweet in their nostrils. The girl carried their hoes over her shoulder as she always did. Her lightheartedness was chilling.

I'm going to ask you a question, said the mother, and I want you to tell me the truth. How is it that you are going to have a child?

I'll tell you the truth, the daughter said, smiling as her mother smiled. The truth is that I don't know.

You know that I do not begrudge you your joy, returned the mother. But now that the child is coming, we must bring its father into our lodge.

There is no father, the girl said.

That answer hardly heals my grief, said the mother, snapping an old cornstalk in her hands.

The girl looked down at the ground, biting her lip. I've told you the whole truth, she said.

The mother started walking back toward the palisade, while her daughter stood between cornhills, watching the big ants running and running. – The only truth is, said the mother over her shoulder, that you don't have much love for me. I never knew that before, but I know it now.

After a long time, the girl returned home. Her mother was boiling acorns. She did not look at her. The girl did not know whether she should aid her mother or avoid her. She stood for a moment, watching helplessly, knowing that her mother knew she was there, but her mother never looked at her, so at last the girl lay down on the wall-bench, looking into the hearth-pit until her eyes filled slowly with tears. She scratched her flea-bites. Then she blinked, and sighed, and closed her eyes, and slept.

I will be born soon! said a voice inside her.

I know, the girl said. You will be born soon, and my mother says I don't have much love for her.

Be comforted, my mother, said the voice. *I'm going to be a great man. When I'm born, call Me* DEKANWIDA.* *I'm going to go to the Flint People, to the Many Hill People; I'm going to raise up the Great Tree of Peace.*

The girl awoke, and did not dare tell her dream. She would only be disbelieved and mistreated still more.

The summer went by, and the young men returned to *Ka-ha-nah-yenh*, with prisoners for the fire. Her father and her uncle had not been captured by the Iroquois, for which she rejoiced; but she could not enter fully into the festival of happy tortures which now took place in the War-Chief's lodge, because she had heard once behind her in the cornfields the word *witch!* and that night she lay on the sleeping bench, sweating with dread. It was the Old Men who decided if someone were guilty of evil Sorcery. If they reached that verdict in their secret Councils, then someone would come and open her head with the blade of his stone hatchet, suddenly, when she was not expecting it. The Old Men tried to make such killings look like the work of the Hiroquois, so that no blood-feuds would begin, but that was unnecessary: in the case of a witch, her own mother would be happy to see her lie bloody and cold. Later, perhaps, her mother might forgive her, and clean her bones in all love for the Feast of the Dead . . . Just as in the course of a lake twilight it is the tree-walls, not the water, that first show darkness, so it was her mother's eyes which first darkened against her, but steadily that darkness spread throughout the longhouse and then spilled into the next lodge and the next and all through *Ka-ha-nah-yenh*, although nothing further was said against her. Probably she had imagined it, that someone had whispered *witch!* But it was true that when she prepared the corn soup in her mother's place, then her aunt's family across the fire said that they were not hungry. If her father and uncle had not come back from the Country of the Iroquois, it might have gone much worse for her. Her very presence now gave offense. Her belly was very big when she helped bring in the corn. When the last of the enemy People had been burned and eaten, it came time for the fish-gathering, but this year she did not go, even though she remembered how uplifting it was to be in the long white canoes and the lovely way that when they camped on one of the islands at dusk, she could always see water and sky so pale blue through the trees, then fading to grey and the trees became black with grey needles. Making these Exercises of regret and desolation, she could smell the pine smell and the good smell of the whitefish as she smoked

* "Two River Currents Flowing Together." Another tradition says: "Double Row of Teeth."

them. – No, my uncle, she said. I thank you, but I will not go this year. – He did not try to persuade her otherwise.

When he was alone with her father on the lake, they discussed what was imputed against her. Neither one wanted to bring her up among the Old Men, because they both loved her. She was hardworking, cheerful and obedient to her mother. Her fatherless child must have come from the witchcraft of another. Didn't witches work claws and hair-tufts inside the bodies of others by magic? Why not a baby, then?

But in that case, said the uncle, it is surely an evil witch-child. I am afraid that it must be put to death. Otherwise how can these clouds be dispersed?

The father did not reply for a moment. Then he said: I have been silent, my brother, and listened to you well. Yet I believe that my wife has more right to speak than either you or I. We men know not what the women do. It is for the women to decide this matter.

Tell me only this: Is your daughter a witch, as some say?

You know that she is not! Who has she ever harmed? To think even for a moment that she has had recourse to that Serpent called ANGONT, which the Old Men say worms its way beneath the ground . . .

Brother, I know that she is not a witch, as you do. But do others know that? You must make my sister listen to you. It is for your daughter's own sake that the child must die. Or would you rather see her skull split? Beyond the Tall Trees would be happy to do it; he fears lest the charge of witchcraft rebound on him . . .

The catch was not as rich as usual. They came back without singing. The girl's face went white when she saw how some looked at her, and she swallowed. One night her mother was dreaming and cried out: *Ghosts, ghosts!* so that the whole lodge rang, and everyone was awake but silent, and the girl gnawed her hand to keep from sobbing aloud. Dreams assailed her like rocky tongues breaking the waves of some choppy lake. Throughout the fall she remained in the longhouse so much that she became pale.

Now winter came, and the Wendat sat down on the floor to be nearer to the fire, putting their children closest. When it was time to sleep, they lay down where they had sat, tucking their faces into their robes. The sleeping benches were too far and cold. It was in winter that the old people often died. Winter was the difficult season. The girl sat looking across the fire at her aunt's family. They did not look back at her.

As they say among the Haudenosaunee, the Longhouse People: *A baby's life is the thinness of a maple leaf.*

When her time came, just before the Dream-Feast, her mother partitioned a corner of the longhouse with skins. – She still won't tell me who the man is! said the mother bitterly to the other families, but they smiled politely and said nothing; that was the way of the Wendat. – The girl delivered herself; that too was their way. She was brave; she did not cry out. When she had given birth, her mother came in to pierce the baby's ears and said: He doesn't have a father; does he have a name?

DEKANWIDA, replied the girl weakly.

That is no name from our clan. But there is no speaking with you. – She lifted her grandchild. He did not cry when she pierced His ears with a fishbone. – I name you DEKANWIDEH, she said.

The daughter sat up without weeping and put Him to her breast.

You still refuse to tell me the father? said the grandmother. Once you obeyed me as soon as I opened my mouth. I am sick with sorrow. And if there is truly no father, do you not see that a great calamity might now befall our Nation?

I told you the truth, said the girl.

The other families in the longhouse were silent.

Well, DEKANWIDA, said the grandmother, You have no father, so Your mother's going to drown You. She may not desire to do it, but I have more right in this matter than she, because she is silent. *Won't* you? she said to the girl. – Show courage now!

The girl stood up without a groan. Swaddling her baby in new beaver-skins which she had from her father, strapping him firmly against her back, she parted the hangings and came out. Her aunt's family looked away. She walked past the hearth-fires whose smoke made her eyes burn, past the bear-cub who snorted at her and licked his paw, and her first aunt's family looked away, and her second aunt's family looked away, and she lashed her snowshoes on. In her hand, a good stone axe. The baby moved a little on her back. She went out. The wind blew and it was snowing and the dogs were barking and the sky was grey. The lake too must surely be frozen grey, although she could not see it. Her nose stung with cold.

She went through the curving tunnel between the palisadoes, remembering how when she had been a child her mother used to warn her: You must always be on guard against the Hiroquois when you go out. When you go into the forest, be watchful. When you gather blackberries, be watchful. They will split your head or roast you if they catch you . . . – and she was afraid even though she knew there was no need to be: the Iroquois never came in winter. Now she saw the village was behind her, and she closed the stockade gate. When no one could see or hear, she wept.

The wide round tracks that rested so lightly on the dazzling snow-crust were like knots on a rope which led back to her mother. The ice-hung stubble of the corn-field crackled and groaned on either side of her as she went down the path to the stream where her mother had questioned her that summer. So brown as to be almost black, it clove the ice-crust, and streamed past sapins and other evergreens toward the low icicle-hung cliffs streaked black with rock and shadow beyond which it was swallowed between white birches the color of snow-roofed islands. Closer to shore the ice was thicker. She did not want to throw her baby into the quick brown current. She chopped a hole in the ice that overhung a pool where she sometimes bathed in summer, a smooth deep pool of peace, and she threw DEKANWIDA in. He floated there, sucking His thumb, watching her with His serious baby face. She took Him up and pried a stone loose from the hard ground. She wrapped the stone in His swaddling clothes and threw Him into the water again. She saw Him go down, down into the black water; for a long time she could see the pale brown oval of His face. Then something like a black spider moved in the water, and when it was gone, DEKANWIDA was gone. Ice formed in the hole. Snow fell and covered it, and then darkness came.

Well? said the girl's mother.

My hands are empty, aren't they? replied the girl bitterly.

Come now, come now, said her aunt's family. Have some corn soup. Here, now, you're weak – eat these nice big fish-pieces!

Later that night they found DEKANWIDEH at His mother's breast.

The next morning the girl's mother stood in the doorway with her hands on her hips, watching her daughter take the baby away; she heard the splash and nodded.

In the night they found DEKANWIDA at His mother's breast.

I'll drown Him myself then, said the girl's mother. She took Him out.

Once again her aunt's family had nothing to say.

In the night the mother pulled the sleeping skins away from her daughter, and there was nothing there, but when morning came, there was DEKANWIDA at His mother's breast.

The girl's mother thought for a long time.

Well, she said, maybe DEKANWIDA's going to be a great man.

When DEKANWIDA had grown to manhood, says this Iroquois tale, *He was greatly abused by the Huron people because of His handsome face and good mind.* – But the Iroquois would have their revenge in 1649, reader; just be patient and you will see!

So He went and stood upon an upturned slab of granite at the edge of the lake and gazed south, toward the Country of the Irocois. Sometimes a wave broke against this rock, and it sounded as if an otter or muskrat were splashing there. He stood there for a long time. Then He returned to the village of *Ka-ha-nah-yenh*, to say farewell to His mother and grandmother.

Where are You going?

To the Agnierrhonons.*

But they will kill You! You know that their minds have seven linings –

Yes, he laughed, they will surely kill Me.

There was no use in telling the Old Men or the War-Chief where He meant to go. They would only say once again that He was setting himself in opposition to them, and must therefore be a witch. He had no friends to part with. No girl would cry for Him. He fastened on His deerskin sleeves; He left the palisadoes for the last time. He took His canoe and traveled south across the lake called Beautiful. Because He had Power, He went as fast as mist racing across water, accompanying the ripples, stripping away distances to show the leaf-mottled coast across the water. He paddled through the orange river-sky of evening until the ridges greyed and hid the sun. Then He struck shore. He had arrived in the Country of Flints.

The People there were the Flint People, the Mohawk. They were one of the ferocious Nations. They lived in the forest, shadowed by their black dogs, tattooed to the semblance of snakes (indeed some say that the name *Hiroquois* means *Real Adders*). They had round heads, like the heads of tadpoles. Their leggings were decorated with beads that formed bright flowers and stars. They had been led astray by the Spirit called EVIL-MINDED, so that they were very dangerous. In the red depths of autumn trees they crept about with raised warclubs, seeking enemies. They hated all who were not of their Nation. The other Nations hated them. Bowing their heads, the Flint women marched slowly through the longhouses, while the men beat the drum and sang songs of grief. Other Nations had split the heads of their strong young men, their bright young girls. So many dead!

The Flint women gazed down at the hardpacked earth where skulls lived. Their long thin braids hung down upon their breasts like blue-black streams of tears. (Their grandmothers' white braids were icy streams frozen beyond hope of time.) They marched with folded arms, wearily, not seeing the flowers that they had sewn on the hems of their robes, not seeing the toes of their moccasins; and the drumming saddened their heartbeats as the men

* Mohawk Nation.

sang bitter songs. They would kill DEKANWIDA if they could. In their Country, the trees were as numerous as the blades of grass, and beavers swam in the ponds, although not to as great an extent as in Acadia. The sky was mistily pure.*

DEKANWIDA went to the lower waterfall in that Country, and made camp. He smoked His tobacco, sitting beneath a tall tree. It was early autumn, when the corn is ripe. The hills were like waves of yellow, orange and grey. There was a texture of dead wood behind everything. – All right, you People, He sighed to Himself, come on and kill Me! My heart is at rest.

A Flint man came. He was from the Turtle Village, where Sainte Kateri Tekakwitha would be born. He had come to this place in search of deer; it was that season. He had already killed one two days before, and his wife was tanning the hide with smoke to make new leggings. Peering through the dark green forest at a light green clearing of immense radiance, he saw the stranger, who seemed to be unarmed.

I have more right to dwell here than He, he said to himself, for I am a Mohawk, and this is my Country. I shall devour Him; I shall bring calamity to Him if I can.

He ran down the deer-trail; he came to the palisadoes of the Turtle Village, and he cried out the tidings to the War-Chief and all the other men who came rushing in. It was their plan to kill the stranger and take His canoe. (For they did not realize that only DEKANWIDA could use that canoe, which was made of white stone; if anyone else sat in it, it would sink.) So they came, bearing their shields of sturdy bark, wearing their armor of cord-tied wooden slats; they stood around Him in a circle and jabbed their spears into the ground.

DEKANWIDA sat smoking His pipe.

Where do You come from? said the War-Chief.

I come from *Ka-ha-na-yenh*, said DEKANWIDA.

So You are a Crooked-Tongue. I am astonished at Your presumption in coming here. I shall gladly kill You. What is Your name?

DEKANWIDA.

What do You seek to steal in our Country?

* The Sieur de Champlain, who went to war there, was most impressed with its richness and concluded: *The Country of the Hiroquois is hilly, but fertile; whereas the Country of the Algoumequin is a lowland, thinly wooded. Ergo, the Country of the Hiroquois is superior. Ergo, it would be good to frenchify this region, for the greater glory of GOD and the enrichment of the Roy of France . . .* – But he did not succeed in that, for the Mohawk were fiercer than he might have guessed.

Hear me, War-Chief: the GREAT CREATOR who is the ancestor of us all has sent Me to make peace. We shall establish the Great Peace and become strong. – I have spoken.

The War-Chief tilted his head just slightly to one side. Eyes and mouth smiled. A painted fish jumped upon the muscles of his neck.

All that You say is surely true, and we may not contradict it, he said. Ah, how I honor You! Before we obey You, however, before You persuade us to believe in Your sorceries, we must have proof that You are the Power that You say You are.

I can demonstrate My Power, said DEKANWIDA. The GREAT CREATOR has given Me the ability to choose the manner of My death.

Choose then, laughed the War-Chief. We are ready to destroy you.

At the edge of this falls is a tall tree, said DEKANWIDA. I saw it today. I will sit on a branch on this tree. One of you will chop down the tree, and that will be My end. Will your minds rest in confidence then?

Now the man who had found Him cried: Give Him to the flames! and the other Flint men shouted their agreement, but the War-Chief held up his hand. – My brothers, my sister's sons, it matters little how we kill Him, as long as He dies.

Then they agreed that it should be as he said. So the War-Chief said to DEKANWIDEH: Now let it be done.

They went to the tree at the cliff's edge; yes, they ascended the yellow horizon of leaves until the world became brown with gables of rock on the hills, ledges and shelves and dark spaces of granite and sandstone making pitted walls up to the top where it was mossy and ferny and green and orange with soft hairy moss-locks growing down the broad trunks of trees whose bark was braided like rivers and rattlesnakes. It was like that so many autumns later when Tekakwitha ascended the hill to be baptized. But when her last spring came, then the bell tolled to summon the other Savages to her glorious death, and the Black-Gown Père Cholonec sat with a tear rolling down his cheek, writing: *Every morning, winter and summer, she was in our church at four o'clock, and often she arrived even before the bell which rings every day at that hour . . . She passed an entire hour in the church weeping and sighing while she prepared herself, and when she began her confession she would have given her confessor much difficulty in understanding her, had he not otherwise known her angelical innocence. She thought herself the greatest sinner in the world . . .* and then he stood up and went to her deathbed to make certain by searching her yet aware eyes that what he wrote was and always had been true, and he saw that it was, that everything about her proclaimed it from the way that her long black hair fell across her throat to the way her crossed hands drew the ends of the blanket as taut as they could across her breast and her skinny face glowed up at him, not yet free of pockmarks as it is in the medal that I wear, but somehow the same in its joyous acceptance of pain, as even the other Savages could comprehend, pathetic half-Frenches though they were – who could *not* smell the lily-odor of that girl's virtues? he asked himself, trembling with emotion. In her heart she was French! – but for DEKANWIDEH this His fourth death was no such encensoir giving forth the myrrh and frankincense of His fame, but only another trial that had to be won through, a baptism of sorts, like Tekakwitha's, but one of the loneliest kind: the baptism of death at the hands of enemies. So He stood among the war-painted men who would kill Him, and He was weary but clear-minded, so that His will stirred less than the feathers in the War-Chief's hair. Beside the trail, the earth was cut away so deeply down to where the waterfall roared, so far below; and He leaned over the edge for a moment and His face became wet with spray.

They all thought it strange that He did not sing His death-song, but that was His choice. Instead he sang the Peace Hymn.

He climbed the tree, higher, higher, until they could not see anything of Him but the smoke-puffs of His pipe; then they began to chop the tree down. DEKANWIDA made no sound. They wondered if He had changed himself into a bird and flown away, to mock them brightly from some stump or lightning-struck pine, cawing and cawing at them with a bluejay's coat buttoned tightly over His breast, watching them from a single glittering bluejay eye on the side of His head – but no! the smoke-puffs were still ascending into the sky.

The Flint People swung their stone axes with the furious energy of bees. The blades bit into the wood; the great tree began to groan and lean.

Cut faster, my nephews! DEKANWIDA called down to them. Cut down my Tree of Peace!

The man who had first found Him put his palms upon the tree, his left hand above his right, and began to push, and the tree listed more and more; it was hanging over the precipice and its leaf-crown was shaking and DEKANWIDA had to lock His legs around the branch now as He smoked there so lonely in the sky, and the man who had first found Him pushed and pushed until the tree was attached to itself by a single resinous hinge that gave and gave and gave and suddenly broke and the Flint People shouted *Heh-yeh!* as the tree fell and fell through the smoke-rings that still puffed from DEKANWIDA's pipe, and before the tree had even been caught in the falls and hurled down against the rocks far below, the man who had first found Him was shouting happily *I* killed Him, brothers. It was I! and the War-Chief led them in a chant of thanksgiving that this Crooked-Tongue who had sought to devour them was now Himself devoured; while DEKANWIDA's tree was shattered into great knots and splintered branches that shot away with His dismembered limbs and the river was defiled.

But in the morning, there He was, cooking His breakfast in one of their abandoned longhouses. The War-Chief saw Him and was abashed. Indeed this DEKANWIDEH had shown that He had the right to speak.

So the War-Chief and the other Lords or Rodiyaner of the Flint Nation invited Him to a Council, saying: We now acknowledge the truth of Your Mission among us. We are ready to believe in this perfect peace of which You speak. Therefore tell us how to bring it about. We shall make the preparations which You instruct us to make, and we shall plant the Tree and water it. – We have spoken.

Then DEKANWIDA stood and spoke to them until they could see His Tree of Peace already rising from the dark soil of each others' brains, with the slick glistening of sapling-leaves shading thoughts better than warriors' hair-plumes; and the Tree of Peace grew taller in that hot breezeless sun of necessity where even the insects were silent, and clouds embroidered the sky like lace as the Council said: It is good.

So the Flint People accepted His proposal. And DEKANWIDEH said that it would be their special right to be the receiver of tribute from conquered and enslaved Nations. But a Great Peace is not great if only one Nation subscribes to it. So DEKANWIDEH prepared to form the Great Longhouse, the League of the Haudenosaunee.

The Oneida would surely join. The Great Hill People and the Mucky Land People would join if the Hill People did. But in the Country of that Hill People (called Onondaga), there was an evil-minded man whose hair was snakes. He ate human flesh; his name was Adadarhoh. There were so many like him! No one could cure them, it seemed. At the Festival of the White Dog, when even the Faith-Keepers confessed their wrongs in public, Adadarhoh was silent and did not take the white wampum-shells in his hand. – He does not seek peace! the People whispered in horror (for although they had not yet heard of DEKANWIDEH they wanted that much among themselves, at least). And they looked sidelong into the winter forest. – Now the Dream Feast was held, and Adadarhoh dreamed loud boastful dreams, so that the People must impoverish themselves to gratify him. So the New Year came, and they played the game of Snow-Snake, but Adadarhoh stood apart. Now it was the turn of the False Faces to drive out disease. Crawling, gripping the doorway, rattling their turtle-shells, they crept into every longhouse. Their round eyes goggled. Their mouths wry and twisted sneered like wolves'. They peered here and there, looking for bad Power. They purified the houses with ashes from the hearth. Their long white hair of cornsilk stuck sweatily to their chests. They crouched and knelt and scuttered like spiders, looking, listening behind frozen gruesome faces . . . Adadarhoh lived alone. When the False Faces came to his house, he barred their way with his arm.

Came the Planting Festival; came the Raspberry Thanksgiving. The blueberries were white flowers and green buds. A Lord among the Onondaga named Ayonhwatha sought to clear Adadarhoh's mind. In his lodge he called a Council. It was decided that half the people should go by canoe to Adadarhoh's lodge, while the other half should walk. They set forth with brave hearts. They went the way that none had gone since the False Faces had been rebuffed, and so they came at last into Adadarhoh's domain, which was a lake leaden-grown with tall sedges like a comb's teeth, separated by lily-dappled channels. These merged and widened into a long narrow lake beset by granite tree-walls. The water was warm, grey-brown and very clear. A few snags crooked their fingers; birch-images and aspen-images went whitely swimming among the fish. The warriors who walked looked uneasily from side to side. The warriors who went by canoe searched behind beaver-dams; they peered under the water with their hearts thumping, for they knew that Adadarhoh had Power. Yet they saw no one. Now they came in sight of his lodge. No smoke rose from the smokehole. All was ruined and silent. But Adadarhoh was watching, and the yellow-green rainy leaves were very bright against the grey sky where Adadarhoh coiled himself like a fiddlehead fern. From the bushes overhanging the river a loud voice called: Stand quickly and look behind you – a storm is coming! – The People did this, and their canoes overturned. Many of them were drowned. So they returned home to feed their terror and to mourn.

Hayonhwatha said: We must try again to conciliate him.

Again they set out. But Adadarhoh guarded himself well with his Power, like a screech owl turning its head from side to side. So as they approached his domain, beautiful feathers began to rain from the sky. Each warrior said to himself: I must have these, for then my headdress will be proud. – So they fought each other for the feathers, and many were killed. They returned to their lodges forgetting everything.

Ayonhwatha said: We must attempt the thing once more, my brothers, for his tyranny is intolerable.

But another dreamer had already dreamed that Ayonhwatha must fail by himself. He must go to the Flint Nation to meet DEKANWIDEH. Then he could prevail. The dreamer called a Council and revealed his dream. All agreed. Now no one came to Ayonhwatha's councils anymore; they knew that there could be no fruit in them.

Hayonhwatha had seven daughters. They were as busy as birds. He loved them. He would never leave the Onondaga Nation as long as they were alive. So the other dreamer gave gifts to a Sorcerer called Ohsinoh. – You must kill them with your magic, said the dreamer. Then he will be free to do his duty to us. – I have spoken.

It is well that you should employ me, replied Ohsinoh. I am very glad, for now you will make me many fine presents.

He strode into Ayonhwatha's lodge. The youngest daughter was plaiting the crackly yellow cornhusk dolls. *Hé hé hé*, she was beautiful! – How was he to go about his task? He could become a poison shadow at the bottom of a spring; he could become a monster to eat her . . . – The lessons of seduction, like those of sleep, do not always come easily, but once your eyes finally close they seem so simple and natural that you are astonished that you had any trouble getting there (but only a little astonished, because you are not thinking about very much now except being seduced). So he would seduce her to death.

On a chilly summer morning, the tree-ridge green with blue shadows, the clouds white with blue shadows, the Sorcerer climbed a tree. (It was time to hold the Corn-Hoeing Thanksgiving, but as in previous years the Nations were too ferocious against each other to observe this celebration.) He said to himself: this tree has Power. In this tree what I say will come true.

Ayonhwatha's youngest daughter passed below him, singing good tobacco songs.

In the night, listening to the bird whose song was like the sound of a raccoon washing its hands, listening to the purrings of unknown animals, Ohsinoh climbed the tree again. He filled his mouth with clay and imitated the call of a screech owl. Then he spoke the youngest daughter's name, singing: *Unless you marry Ohsinoh, you will surely die, whoo-hooh!*

In three days she died.

Ayonhwatha cried out with grief. No one came to console him.

On the following night, Ohsinoh climbed the tree again, and killed the second youngest daughter. Hiawatha shouted with grief. So it went. One by one they sickened and died. If any of them had wanted to marry him, he would have refused her to make her die.

When the last of his daughters was dead, Ayonhwatha was sick with grief. So extreme was his frenzy that no one dared to comfort him. So the conclusion was reached. He resolved to leave the Onondaga Nation and wander in the forest. Then the other dreamer was joyous, and said: Now matters befall as I saw.

Early summer, and the river-cliffs had greened. Day-cliffs were bright like leaved birds; green leaves and brown water were now made whole. Dogwood blossoms burst in showers of ecstatic droplets. Hillsides were pale green. The low sweltering river-islands steamed with morning fog; only on their shores could the breeze reach the sorrowing man. Two steps, three steps into any island, he vanished into tree-wealth where it was cool and dank and humming with mosquitoes. – In the summer the rivers of Canada were darker, and they sparkled.

He found round jointed rushes, and made strings of them, thinking that the rush-beads might serve as magic easements. – Thus would I condole another, he said to himself.

He wandered weeping among the wild roses. The day was hot enough to clothe him in sweat. He wandered through the mosquito evening as the lake widened and became very clear with ripple-rows fluttering their winged blue shadows. Tree-shimmers crawled across the water. It was very hot. His face glowed with sweat. Even his reflection was shiny.

It rained, and the rivers rose, and the summer's sky was icy. Then the roof of the forest became glaringly stricken with orange, and the blue twilight came.

He went on. He came to a lake of ducks. He said to himself: If I am truly to become of high rank, then let me here discover my Power.

He called upon the ducks to fly up, bearing the water with them so that he could cross the lake dry-shod, and this they did.

On the bottom of the lake were snail-shells, white and purple. He filled his pouch of deerskin with them and passed across the lake. He did not know why he did this. He did not yet know that these would give meaning to his grief. Then the ducks descended, bringing back the water between their webbed feet.

He understood that shells could become words. So wampum came into the world. He set two poles in the ground, with a third resting across them. From this third pole he hung three shell-strings.

Near this place he was invited to a Council, but no one asked his advice, so he traveled on. He was invited to another Council, but again no one asked his opinion. Then suddenly a runner came from the Land of Flints, inviting him to go to DEKANWIDEH. And he went.

DEKANWIDEH took the snail-shells from Ayonhwatha's pouch of deerskin, and made wampum-strings of them. Now He addressed Ayonhwatha with the words of condolence, and made him clear-minded, clearing his grief with each wampum-string of words. Just as tobacco smoke makes a path for prayer, so the words of DEKANWIDEH cleared a footroad through the forest of his grief, permitting sunlight and reason to stream down into the golden line from which suffering could be lanced. Then at last Ayonhwatha's grief was eased.

DEKANWIDEH then said: My dear younger brother, as you are competent in your thoughts again, we shall now make our laws and create the Great Peace, so that tranquility and quietness may return to the People's hearts. We shall wear deer antlers on our heads, and place them on the heads of all the Lords whom we elect to our League of Haudenosaunee. Their titles shall be vested in the women of their families forever.

What You have said is good, said Ayonhwatha. I do agree.

Now the Flint People had already agreed to accept the Great Peace, as told. So they sent runners to the Oneida, the Stone People, to ask them to join in the League, to no longer roam the meadows and thickets of blood-red maples, killing one another smiling with all their gleaming teeth. And their Captain, Odatshedeh, replied: I shall consider the plan and reply to you tomorrow. – Among the Hiroquois one day is a year. So when the new year came he answered them, saying that the Oneida would join the Haudenosaunee, the Longhouse People.

Then they sent to Ayonhwatha's People, the Onondaga, and they too agreed to participate. Because their territory was in the center of the Five Nations, they became the Fire-Keepers. Their great town was called Onnontagué. It had one and a half hundreds of longhouses. Here they agreed to have the grand council chamber of the Haudenosaunee. But Adadardoh did not agree. His evil Power awaited them like the pallid shining of a stagnant lake through the forest dusk. So they set out to the Onondaga Nation, DEKANWIDEH and Ayonhwatha together, and the evil Sorcerer, Adadardoh, they sung into clear-mindedness. They sang the Hymn of Peace. The wildness left his eyes, which had been the dark-plaited suns of snakeskin-husks. They combed the serpents out of his long hair. So he became one of the Rodiyaner of the Haudenosaunee. And to further appease him, two Rodiyaner of the Onondaga were assigned to him as his councillors. And he was the one to whom was granted the honor of singing the song installing new Rodiyaner into the League, the song that begins *Haii, haii . . .*

Then they asked the Cayuga, the People of the Mucky Land, and next the Seneca, the Great Hill People. In Goi-o-gouen, the main village of the

Cayuga Nation, the People held a Council, and their tobacco smoke made a path for prayer and they agreed to accept the Great Peace. The Seneca were divided on this matter, but when DEKANWIDEH made the SUN go out, they believed, and so they also took the Great Peace into their hearts. The Seneca lived at the western edge of the Haudenosaunee. So they became the Doorkeepers. The Cayuga lived just east of them, so they became the First Fire.

The League of the Hodinhsioni

Now that the People were a great longhouse with its darkness and flickering fires, DEKANWIDEH and Hayonhwatha could establish the Great Peace. They appointed the wisest men of each Nation to be the Rodiyaner who would advise the People, and when they died the women in their families appointed new Rodiyaner to take their names and places, and they were crowned with deer-antlers; and the women of the Mohawk brought them forth, and the women of the Oneida brought them forth, and the women of the Onondaga brought them forth, and the women of the Seneca brought them forth, and the women of the Cayuga brought them forth, and the wives of the Rodiyaner prepared the feast and each of the Rodiyaner gave to DEKANWIDA a span-length string of lakeshell wampum beads to be kept in pledge of promise, and so the *League of the Haudenosaunee* was formed. So Ayonhwatha is alive today among the Onondaga, and so is Adadardoh. So Adadardoh schemed against the French Captain, Onontio, for more than a century, although Adadardoh and Onontio each died more than once.

DEKANWIDA and the Rodiyaner had already wrenched the tallest pine tree up by the roots, and as DEKANWIDA held the tree up in the sky, into the hole the others cast all the weapons of war with which they had formerly plagued one another, and those bows and spears and clubs and arrows tipped with glittering chert-stone went tumbling, tumbling into the moist darkness and fell into the Black Waterfall that roared away and was defiled by them, and the war-clubs were shattered like nuts against the sharp black rocks of the darkness, and then the water was full of bloody splinters, and the bows became entangled in the piles of beaver-bones that the People of KLUSKAP threw down there, and the taut strings hummed and quivered underwater until the current broke them and then they shattered against the rocks, but the spears and arrows shot through the water, whizzing from fall to fall, and at last they came to the Black Waterfall and went singing down to pierce the great hairy WATER-MONSTER that the Fox's scalp had become, and the WATER-MONSTER flailed about with all its arms and bloody bubbles came from it, but it could not be killed, not again, and so presently, after all the hate-filled arrows of the Five Nations had stuck in its quivering slippery flesh, it began to pull them out one by one with its purple parrot-beak; then, tasting bloody tears in every shaft, it gnawed them greedily down to their points. Then the WATER-MONSTER snapped with its beak, and placed those sharp hate-tips and fear-tips on the end of its tendrils with the point outward. – But DEKANWIDA and the Rodiyaner knew nothing of this. They had slammed the tall pine-tree back down into the earth so that the blind WATER-MONSTER was deprived again of the pale day-glimmer that it could not yet know of, and the pine-roots gripped the dirt like claws and the pine tree grew taller, by which time DEKANWIDEH had left the People, so that there was no one to uproot it again and look down the hole even if anyone had wanted to.

Meanwhile, DEKANWIDA had planted the white Tree of the Great Peace in the Country of the Onondaga, who were the Firekeepers, and the white feather-down of the globe thistle was spread by the Rodiyaner each for the other to sit on in the shade beneath that Tree whose roots of Peace and Strength spread out in all the four directions, and an Eagle sat atop the Tree watching for enemies, and the War-Chiefs were appointed, one from each Nation, and they tied five shell-strings together to be the Five Nations, and they tied five arrows together to be the Five Nations, and they made the Great Belt of the Confederacy whose shell-beads were dark on white in the pattern of an ever-growing Tree whose boughs and trunk never tapered because it rose and rose above the sky; then they recited the Laws and made commemoration belts and grew stronger and stronger.

Each Nation went its own way, but they took counsel of each other and joined armies whenever that was politic. Each Nation was bound by DEKANWIDEH's laws to union with the Haudenosaunee, just like a tomahawk-head bound over and over with sinew to hold it to the handle.

It is true that from time to time there were elected Rodiyaner who were not faithful to the Great Peace. When they began to follow a course that was out of accordance with the Laws or the will of the People then they were warned by their women relatives once, twice, thrice; and even yet there were some Rodiyaner who did not heed, so the War-Chiefs then came into the Council to warn them, at which time, if they were wise, they heeded, and said: We shall reply tomorrow. – Then the War-Chiefs were satisfied, and the People of the Five Nations were content. But it must be told that even yet there were on rare occasions some Rodiyaner who would not bend, and then the War-Chiefs stripped their antler-crowns from them and told them to vacate their seats; or else the War-Chiefs chose the other course, the way of the black wampum-strings. For this, the War-Chiefs directed their men to enter the Council and sit between the Rodiyaner whenever possible and wait for the black wampum to fall from a War-Chief's hand . . . – But that course was rarely necessary. So the United People kept the Great Peace.

They built their towns on hilltops, so that they could better watch for enemies. The greedy crows flew to look upon their concentric palisades of logs and tree-trunks and sturdy wicker-work; they flapped their wings and alighted on the platform bastions from which the archers and stone throwers could defend their town; they cawed hoarsely, and little tan boys crept closer and closer; suddenly taking alarm, the crows leaped into the air and made the town smaller and smaller below them, the longhouses earth-colored lumps against the earth, the palisades so intricately insignificant, and the crows saw below them the sunny fields of beans and squash and sunflowers falling away in all directions; they listened and heard the sound of crackling sunflower seeds, and swept so easily upon the hot air-tides, cocking their heads back and down to see with their shiny black eyes; they swooped low to see the young girls extracting the seeds, and then the waiting boys shot them and they tumbled dead from the air.

Now it is to be told that after the United People healed the wounds that they had inflicted upon each other, they came into the fullness of their strength and began to look about them. And they saw many other Nations. But these were mere alien Nations. It was only the United People, the Original Beings, who owned the land. The United People had a law that all Nations must accept the Great Peace. Alien Nations could be adopted into the Haudenosaunee; such adoptions were limited and temporary, but as long as the aliens obeyed the will of the Five Nations faithfully, they would not be annihilated. (When a Nation was annihilated, all of its property became the property of the Five Nations.)

From the Constitution of the Five Nations

When a proposition to establish the Great Peace is made to a foreign Nation it shall be done in mutual council. The foreign Nation is to be persuaded by reason and urged to come into the Great Peace. If the Five Nations fail to obtain the consent of the Nation at the first council, a second council shall be held, and upon a second failure a third council shall be held, and this third council shall end the peaceful methods of persuasion.

At the third council, the War-Chief of the Five Nations shall address the Chief of the foreign Nation and request him three times to accept the Great Peace. If refusal steadfastly follows, the War-Chief shall let the bunch of white lake shells drop from his outstretched hand to the ground, and shall bound quickly forward and club the offending Chief to death. War shall thereby be declared . . . War must continue until the contest is won by the Five Nations.

The Future

In battle they strive especially to capture their enemies alive, wrote Père Biard. *Those who have been captured and led off to their villages are first stripped of their clothing; then they savagely tear off their nails one by one with their teeth; then they bind them to stakes and beat them as long as they please. Next they release them from their bonds, and compel them to pass back and forth between a double row of men armed with thorn clubs and instruments of iron. Finally, they kindle a fire about them, and roast the miserable creatures with slow heat. Sometimes they pierce the flesh of the muscles with red-hot plates and with spits, or cut it off and devour it, half-burned and dripping with gore and blood. Next, they plant blazing torches all over the body, and especially in the gaping wounds; then, after scalping him they scatter ashes and live coals upon his naked head; then they tear the tendons of the arms and legs, lacerate them, or, after removing a little of the skin, leisurely cut them with a knife at the ankle and wrist. Often they compel the unhappy prisoner to walk through fire, or to eat, and thus entomb in living sepulcher, pieces of his own flesh . . . Moreover, they prolong this torment throughout many days, and, in order that the poor victim may undergo fresh trials, intermit it for some time, until his vitality is exhausted and he perishes. Then they tear the heart from the breast, roast it upon the coals, and, if the prisoner has bravely borne the bitterness of the torture, give it, seasoned with blood, to the boys, to be greedily eaten, in order, as they say, that the warlike youth may imbibe the heroic strength of the valiant man.*

The Isles of Demons
1534–1603

. . . the regular round of [Amerindian] pursuits, which had been perfected by centuries of constant adaption to the northern environment, became a monomania with iron as its fixation.

ALFRED GOLDSWORTHY BAILEY,
The Conflict of European and Eastern Algonkin Cultures 1504–1700 (1937)

There is no denying that the Eagle would never have killed the Fox if he had not made Tekakwitha cry, that he would not have made her cry if she had not refused to marry him, that she *would* have married him if the Black-Gowns had never come into the Country of the Haudenosaunee. Shame is the sediment of the Fleuve Saint-Laurent, where ice rears so high, crashing into the sea at springtime, that no Black-Gown should ever have been able to worm his way in – but, of course (Pontgravé's slur notwithstanding) Black-Gowns *can* walk on water, except when they drown; and of course the WATER-MONSTER who had once been a scalp lay lashing and lashing his arms at the mouth of the river, waiting to do mischief. Indeed Born Swimming had dreamed of him, as she told the Frenchman Prévert, who recounted the tale to the Sieur de Champlain, who in turn BELIEVED, being credulous at heart. It is interesting, however, that in his writings the demon goes through a change of sex, as if even now, for all his busy lashing of arms, he might not be fixed in his nature. But what else can a WATER-MONSTER become? (Perhaps we shall see.) – Champlain's description, in any event, runs as follows: *To the southward, near Chaleur Bay, lies an isle where there lives a dreadful monster called by the Savages* GOUGOU, *which, they told me, had woman's shape, but very terrible, and so tall, said they, that the top of the masts of our vessel would not have reached her waist . . . and that she has often devoured, and still devours, many Savages, whom she puts in a great pouch when she can catch them, and then eats them; and those who had escaped the peril of this direful beast said that this pouch was so large that she could have put our vessel in it . . . The said Monsieur Prévert of Saint-Malo himself told me that on his way to explore the mines he and all his crew heard strange hissing noises made by it, and that the Savages told him that it was the same beast, and were so afraid that they ran everywhere to hide themselves . . . and I am led to believe their tale by the general fear which all the Savages have of it . . . I hold it to be the haunt of some devil who torments them in this fashion . . .* but Lescarbot said blandly *and as to the* GOUGOU, *I leave its credibility to the reader.* And I must do the same. – Nonetheless, like GOUGOU's arms, strange influences insinuate themselves into this true and pious relation of the Black-Gowns: – for if Canada has a sacred history, from Saint Peter in the dry lands to Saint Brendan whirling in his coracle, next, by easier stages (like a canoe between river-islands), from Columbus to Cabot, and finally (a longer sail this time) from Saint Ignatius to Père Biard; if these altar-isles in the Stream of Time mark the course of Canada's progress, well, there is also (I hate to confess it) a secular current, caused undoubtedly by GOUGOU's nasty whirlpools – and I do mean nasty. Anyone who seeks to make the Exercises, no matter how powerful a swimmer he may be, will be swept off course between the first two Contemplations of Acadia and Kebec, and then again between those of Kebec and Montréal: he who seeks to save the souls of Savages must be deflected by him who's already raped them of body and goods. That is why (I beg your indulgence) our word-river must now bend once more backward for a few pages before curving along its original axis, so that we will not overshoot the War with the Irocois Savages which now waits before us in golden clearings, where the snow of Champlain's cartographic ignorance still lies on the shady sides of creeks. Yes, Champlain's knowledge is in its springtime and will remain so. He will venture into the Country of the Hiroquois with his arquebus loaded and at the ready; he will shoot Savages (an action of great eventual consequences to the Black-Gowns), but for him the snowy river can only be brown and liquid at the edges, beneath the thinnest pane of ice. The hollows between the tree-packed ridges are brimming with snow. He cranes his head at shadows, bluish-green trees, young pine trees standing in the snow; he has bad dreams. He ought to. GOUGOU swims in the blood of his brain.

Currents 1518–1532

One day in the year 1530, when Saint Ignatius was studying in Paris, another Spaniard came to him in great excitement and said, our Lord King Charles is being crowned Emperor of the Holy Roman Empire!

May it give him grace, replied the Pilgrim, a little dryly.

He did not know that Charles was riding with the Pope beneath the canopy that bore an eagle's likeness, and the host about those two shouted and raised their spears, whose blades flickered like leaves, and Charles in his conical cap nodded at everything the Pope said and rubbed his beard and pretended to listen but he was really thinking about conquering Tunis from the Moors. Meanwhile his horse and the Pope's horse tapped delicately on, raising forelegs whose hoofs drooped like a King's hand waiting to be kissed, and the spear-leaves rose like some vast cornfield that Charles I, now Charles V, was going to harvest . . . – Conquest, conquest, was what every grass-blade whispered to him; it was on the lips of all the soldiers because they had seen the Savage gold that came back in ships and ships from *America*, as it was now called. Surely Isabel the Catholic had been a Queen beloved by the VIRGIN, for she had supported that Columbus fellow who had discovered the outlandish countries. Others followed him. Two years after the Holy City was finally lost to the Turks, Juan de Grijalva had landed in Mexico and heard tales of an Empire of Gold. He was like the first ant in the anthill that smells a tasty carcass. He rushed home, and a year went by and a year went by and then Cortés conquered Mexico. Now Pizarro had come to see King Charles, Pizarro who was going to conquer the city of Cuzco and wrench all the gold out of the Temple of the Sun and hold King Atahualpa for ransom and once the ransom was paid Pizarro would murder him anyway and King Charles would get richer than ever, as he needed to be if he were to wrest Tunis from the *Moriscos*' cruel brown hands . . .

The Enmity of Mapmakers

The French were equally greedy of gold. They had a name for *America* that well revealed their own aspirations: "Antarctic France." As for the continent to the north, which the Spaniards called *Florida*, the French called that CANADA.

The Ants 1506–1524

First of the French there came the Basques, who raided the cod-banks of Terre-Neuve, called by them *Baccalos*, which means *Codfish* in the Basque language; then Denis de Honfleur sailed a little way into the Gulf of Saint-Laurent, which seemed to him a vast arm of the sea, so that he became more and more confident that he could easily go to the Land of Gold where the Spaniards were getting such good plunder, but then a fog sprang up and he passed the Isle d'Anticosti and the sailors began to worry about striking a rock and then the Gulf narrowed shockingly and he was at the mouth of the Fleuve Saint-Laurent, which, though a very wide river, was still a river, and though it widened somewhat where many rivers streamed into it from the north, De Honfleur's men stood on deck anxiously looking from one side to the other in this greyness that hovered six feet above the water, and I would be very surprised if De Honfleur got as far as Tadoussac before he turned back; and on their return to the Gulf a man suddenly cried out and pointed with his arm, at which all the men grabbed their muskets and began firing because half a dozen canoes of Savages were trailing them as silently as swans on a pond, and the men fired in great disorder, cursing and staring wildly in all directions, but the Savages only vanished into the fog. – Next came Aubert of Dieppe, who did no more than repeat De Honfleur's Exercises by rote, like a dull schoolboy, and he did not even see any Savages; then after another decade the Baron de Léry, like Champlain, thought to create his own small world on Sable Island where his powers would be more than absolute, but of *that* experiment all that remained in the end was a ruined stone house and a few forlorn cattle wandering in the wet grass and snorting and sniffing and growing fat and multiplying all over Sable Island so that the Savages saw them and cried out in wonder and sometimes came to hunt them, feasting on their fatty meat so joyfully, and in the summer when they played the Games of Waterfalls the Lnu'k children found a weatherbleached cow skull or bull skull in the bottom of the clear green pool, which is where the skull of no land animal should be; they cannot return enfleshed from there; so one day when the Elders were away they dived down to be titillated by the perversion of it and grasped its horns as they held the air in their bulging cheeks and the skull-eyes looked up at them from underwater and a crayfish scuttled in the sand and then the skull said *I am the WATER-MONSTER!* and the Lnu'k children were afraid and let go of the horns to shoot back into the sun shrieking, and they never did play the Skull Game again, but helped their Elders butcher a fat young cow and boil the marrow from her bones and then they hung the bones on a scrubby bush to come alive again and return to Sable Island as calves, which certainly happened because the cattle there became more and more numerous* and the Souriquois were happy and forgot about the Pale Men except that every now and then they saw the boats of the Basque fishermen off the coast, and from time to time the Basques came after their women, and they were strange rough men with a strange smell, so the women did not much like them.

The next to come was Verazzano the Florentine, whom King Francis sent forth from France with four good ships, of which two were weathertorn not long out of Dieppe, and one vanished inexplicably from the record, like grace, so that Verazzano pushed on from Madeira in a solitary caravel and was permitted by the sea-demons to reach Canada. The Savages there, who had shyly hid at first, soon came down to the beach in droves, smiling and waving and pointing out the best landing place. *They are of colour russet, and not much unlike the Saracens,* he reported in his letter (only a copy of which survives), *their hayre black, thicke, and not very long, which they tye together in a knot behinde, and weare it like a taile.* Farther north, when Verazzano ordered a sailor to swim to them to bring them beads, they built a fire and tried to dry the sailor's clothes for him. But seeing him uneasy (for he thought they meant to roast him and eat him), they hugged him and let him go. So he swam back to the caravel in such speed as to churn up the water, and Verazzano leaned over the side watching his progress with great interest, and when he shinnied up the rope that his mates threw over the side Verazzano said to him: still alive, are you? No loss and no gain! and the sailor lay shaking and gasping in a puddle of chilly seawater. – Now let's keep on north and look for TREASURE! shouted Verazzano. – They weighed anchor and followed the coast until the sailors grew restive, thinking that perhaps they might have already (who knows?) bypassed temples like the ones that Cortez had found, temples of silver and gold whose knee-high stairs made straight and terrible ramps going steeply into the sky so that Verazzano's men could sweep their eyes across the soft treetops green and blue, with ruined towers bursting up above the jungle, some with a single square window, others emptily sheer; and then with Our SAVIOR's help someone would shout *Aha!* pointing to the Golden Road which must infallibly lead them to the great Treasury where gold idols with the faces of unknown animals and demons squatted, waiting to be hatcheted into pieces small enough to stuff into belt-pouches, and ruby

* In 1633, one John Rose of Boston claimed to have seen eight hundred cattle there, all red.

eyeballs popped out and rolled across the golden floor like marbles; where piles of gold masks could be trampled on like autumn leaves as with greedily pounding hearts Verazzano's men fought each other for scraps of golden cheek or chin now impressed with the marks of boots; where Verazzano's men could set fire to whole storerooms of gold and kill each other for the privilege of picking melted yellow tears from the ashes; where Verazzano's men could wrench great sheets of delicately carven gold down from the walls and crinkle them up; where golden earrings could be yanked out of women's bleeding ears, the women then stripped, raped, decapitated . . . so Verazzano prudently let his men land in a place where they saw smoke. They discovered Savages hiding fearfully in the grass, and at first they played the Game of the Pale Men and said laughing I *hear* something! What could it be? and they said I hear *hearts* beating in the grass! and they said chuckling could it be *animals* we hear? Let's shoot them! and they fired their arquebuses until the poor Savages began to run. Then the sailors caught them and threw them down to the ground and handled them. There was an old woman, a pretty young Savagess, and several children – they did not bother to count those. They took one of the children with them as a novelty, and would have taken the young Savagess as well, for they had great plans to use her below decks, but her screaming exasperated them, and they let her go.

Once they were on board, they threw the child down and began to shake it. – Where's the gold? they shouted. Answer us in French so that we can comprehend! – (They were all of one heart in this matter.) A sailor knelt down sobbing gold gold gold and struck the child in the mouth . . .

Some say that Verazzano was hanged by the Portuguese in the end for piracy; another account has him roasted and eaten by the Savages on a second voyage. But no one knows what became of the child, or where the gold of Antarctic France had gone.

Further History of the French Conquistadors

Their expectations diminishing over the centuries like unfulfilled erections, they gave up on silver and gold, choosing first beaver-skins, then codfish, then train-oil. Only the Black-Gowns held firm in *their* aims, unceasingly quarrying the treasures of souls. Their great Crosses, cracked and salted with sea-spray, slowly listed over the years, and fell at last to the sand with scarcely a sound.

Further History of the Savages

As for the People who lived there, their cravings ascended rather than decreased. For they wanted beads, knives, hatchets and kettles. Next they wanted French goods. At last they wanted French guns.

The Dream of the Hiroquois *continued*

And so I have ascended Lachine! he trumpeted to himself, rereading with pleasurable scorn Lescarbot's cavilling *History of New France*, in which the lawyer insisted: *For to get above the fall, which is a league in extent, and throughout the whole of which the river pours down amid steep places and rocks, cannot be done in boats. Even Champlain himself has not done it . . .*

Not in boats, that is true, he admitted.

But the Savages sometimes go down in their little boats of bark. What would this pettifogging Calvinist say if I did that? De Monts' servant, Louys, drowned when he tried to shoot the rapids in a canoe with a Savage. The Savage drowned, too. All the same, someday I shall do it and live. I must make these Savages respect the French. And De Monts will embrace me and say to me –

Champlain! Over here, Champlain!

Eh?

The boat's leaving for Canada. Are you coming?

Always in a hurry, Pontgravé. You would do well to be more measured in your behavior.

Measured, he says! Champlain, you're a walking yardstick, but look who's late this time. Measured, eh? Wouldn't *that* be wonderful? Well, I see the problem perfectly now: you need a wife! Someone to give you a kick in the pants –

You don't have to raise your voice, foghorn. I'm coming.

A Toy Island Broken
1608

Like all the Iroquois, the Christians enjoyed this annual camp life in the wilderness.

FRANCIS X. WEISER, SJ, *Kateri Tekakwitha* (1972)

His Captain (*viz.*, the Sieur de Monts) had obtained a renewal of the monopoly for another year. The Sieur de Prévert's dream of Acadia had not yet been discredited by Captain Argall, but Champlain had no desire to go back there. He did not want to see the Isle de Sainte-Croix anymore. It embarrassed him. Pontgravé would be sure to jape about it; De Monts' face must darken whenever he sailed past, and there were all those graves . . . No, it had not been his fault. But one may as easily feel shame as guilt. Anyhow, he'd now come to realize that Acadia was but a failing sideshow to *le Canada actuel* which lay to the west, shaggy and dark and endless, lurid with red and yellow flames and warpainted faces glowing in its blackness of wet leaves and mountains forever: what Savagesses were to young Pontgravé, in short, Canada was to Champlain – a heaven of carnival darkness in which he might lose himself forever. So in his dreams as before his eyes the rivers of a mainland Canada were blindingly silver in the dark blue afternoon of trees; the rivers were redoubtable. – The voyage was of middling length. He paced the deck and took his soundings, even as René Goupil, Père Jogues' companion in martyrdom, was born in France. He ached to open up his new venue . . . They crossed the Grand Banc. He landed on Sable Island, where Baron de Léry had abandoned his cattle; it was fifteen leagues in circumference, according to his reckoning, and very sandy. He did not think it a good place for a fort, although it did possess one small lake, shaped almost like a camel . . . He saw a cow skull in the lake, almost covered with sand. The fishermen and sailors who traveled with him searched for the stone shell of the Baron's house and could not find it; then Champlain became irate and determined that he *would* prove its existence and mark it on his latest chart, so he thoroughly bestrode that isle, parting underwoods and grasses while his men winked and tapped their foreheads, until he discovered it at last, a heap of boulders fortified by raspberry-thorns; and he stood smiling with his hands on his hips and climbed a rise and looked from left to right and made a mark on his sketch . . . The sailors meanwhile had shot five black foxes. Seals were abundant, and they clubbed a dozen with the butts of their harquebuses. They found silver scattered in fragments about the sandy neck (but in France it turned out to be nothing but galena).

Pontgravé sat in the shallop, scratching his hams and yawning. He said to the Captain: According to De Monts, Champlain doesn't have a chance. The men all hate him.

I don't believe that, Seigneur.

I don't believe it either. No wager, then.

Champlain had clambered up what remained of De Léry's chimney. Somewhere to the north, he thought, there must exist a mine of pure copper, as was proved by the yellow bracelets which he was shown by the good Irocois called *Huron*. And to the northwest, they said, there was a salt sea; that must be the Pacific. That was where China was . . .

Again he was gulled by river-diamonds, filling his empty casks with them to bring back to France in case some of them might be precious.

He took a deep breath. He prepared to begin his Canadian career at last.

The City of God

Poutrincourt has chosen *his* estate, De Monts had said to Champlain that winter, as they all sat around admiring Champlain's maps. – What's this Île de Sainte-Hélène? Eh, never mind. Now we must find another place to carry on our trade.

At this, Pontgravé intervened, mentioning Kebec again in a hushed and greedy voice, as if that word corresponded to the telling of the most holy Rosario. – Seigneur, I assure you it's perfect! he whispered (Champlain had not known that Pontgravé could whisper). – You should see Champlain's map! Where is it, Champlain? Look, Seigneur – perfect, I tell you! The great

Fleuve is less than a cannon-shot across in that place. No one but God could get past us!

Oh? said De Monts absently.

And the beaver-skins are better there, Seigneur. The farther north and west you go, the finer they get!

De Monts regarded them. – I don't imagine that either of you will reach China next summer – eh, Messieurs? Well, that's inessential, of course. So what shall I have you do? – Mmm. In a way it seems halfhearted, but Kebec is I suppose a fair compromise. – Champlain, do you still want to be in charge? Oh, good, your tail's wagging like a puppy's. Do try to avoid killing off too many men this winter . . .*

– So Champlain weighed anchor and came to sail.

For days he traveled the Fleuve Saint-Laurent in company with Pontgravé, through light airs intermixed with calm, watching the banks come closer together, the Fleuve itself silver-grey and calm beneath the rain-clouds. It had been five years since he was there. The farther inland he went, the finer became the country. He continued to take soundings, glorying in the depths that he found: the Roy himself could sail here if he chose! On the third of Juillet he came in sight of that broad tree-greened rock of Kebec (above which – nowhere else – the sky was open), and he thought to himself: here I possess Gibraltar! – The closer he came, the further he was strengthened in this impression. – The rock was steeply round, green from river to summit. It was in fact a very steep cliff or falaise. Half-cloaked in grass and blooming trees though it was, the granite showed through, in white fractured faces glittering with mica. He had no fear that any besieger could scale it. And he thought: I will build my city here.

So he raised his Habitation, a structure vigilant and unfriendly within its walls and roofs and little parapet, its single tower, its huddle of a castle. Embarrassment aside, he'd learned a thing or two from Isle de Sainte-Croix: thicker walls, higher walls, generally speaking a grander scale . . . Shouting, striking his men, jesting with them, doling out wine, he controlled them as well as if they had been his fingers. To tame and edify he hung portraits of the Roy Henri on every wall, Henri staring down at them with the all-seeing skepticism of death. – He said to them: First we must till the soil. Then we can be at our ease. – He made them sow wheat and plant good French vines.

* Or, as Champlain tells the tale: "I gave him my advice, and recommended him to settle on the grand Fleuve Saint-Laurent, which from my journey up it I knew well . . . He decided to do so."

He put them to digging moats fifteen feet wide. He made them raise the Habitation higher, higher. He built balconies about it for his watchmen. He reinforced the walls until they were great and stout. Grudgingly he made way for his narrow quadripartite windows, knowing them to be points of danger, but he needed them to spy out the country below. He ordered that a deep shaft in the rock be dug to store the powder-kegs. In future he hoped to have a secret tunnel made, so that in the event of treachery by Basques, Yroquois or English he and his could slip away beneath the piney dirt. He erected chimneys and they began smoking. He erected great palisadoes. Pacing in the grey clouds that often swaddled the place on chilly summer mornings, he gave orders in his loud hoarse voice, with sidelong looks down at the Fleuve Saint-Laurent. Now for the first time was heard on that rock of Kebec the flutter of a flag in the wind.

The Conspiracy

Champlain was in the garden directing the building of his Store-house when the pilot Têtu came to him and said my Lord, I must speak with you in private and Champlain said for what reason? and Têtu said please, my Lord, so they went into the forest where the petals of tree-flowers stood straight up like tiny pink candles on the leaves, and all around them nestlings cheeped, and Champlain said, eh, Têtu, this is quite far enough. Now what do you have to say to me?

The pilot cast down his eyes. The locksmith Duval means to kill you! he blurted. The Basques at Tadoussac will pay him to turn Kebec over to them. And I think the Spaniards are also working like spiders behind the scenes . . .

You have done well to tell me, said Champlain in his most friendly manner. How did you learn of this?

Every man knows of it. I heard it from the locksmith Natel. Duval has three accomplices, and between them they have so frightened and bewildered us that we – Think not harshly of us, my Lord, for we are ignorant men.

I will remain here, said Champlain. Now, Têtu, see that you bring Antoine Natel here to me without fail, or you shall pay the forfeit.

The man ran away trembling. Soon he returned with another paler still than he: the locksmith Natel.

Well, well, said the Sieur de Champlain. So you were a part of this conspiracy to overthrow me, were you?

No, my Lord, I swear that is not true! – He shot Têtu a look of hatred.

– If that man has said anything of the sort, he lies. I told him; I warned him; I –

Champlain turned upon him those eyes like the wide-arched tunnels which would lead deep into the foundations of that city called Kebec, deep down past hogsheads of wine and bacon into dungeons and then a dark forest of cobwebbed beams. – But why did you not warn *me*, Antoine?

The locksmith staggered, and could think of nothing to say.

Champlain raised his voice. And how was I supposed to be killed?

They said – some said that you must be strangled, but Duval was for raising a false alarm in the night and shooting you . . . And they promised that whoever informed upon them would be pierced by their daggers!

Champlain thought for a moment. – You have shown scant courage or honor to me by concealing this, he said at last. But I will now give you a chance to be weighed on the other pan of the scales. Are you willing, my Antoine, my little Antoine, or would you rather be judged with the traitors?

No, no, the man protested faintly, I shall do as you say. Have pity on me!

Pontgravé's skiff has just arrived from Tadoussac, said the Sieur. Go to the helmsman, give him two bottles of wine, and direct him to invite the four ringleaders aboard to regale themselves when it is dark. Tell him to say that he comes from the Basques and wishes to further their skullduggeries. You and Têtu will attend me in hiding on the boat. When the rebels sit down we will seize them. Do you both comprehend your orders?

Yes, Seigneur.

Jean Duval, as we've seen back in Acadia, had been a locksmith not only in his trade, but also of his heart, which he kept closed against all save three other villains, whom he inspired to discontent by complaining about the excessive labors of tilling and cutting to which Champlain subjected them. Their plan was to destroy Champlain, then to plunder the grand Store-house and sail to Spain with a crew of Basques. Thus he bathed in pleasant notions like a river, not knowing that he now approached his own Niagara, whose waters, separated first by a long narrow island spaced with trees, then by a bulging wedge of rock affixed to the precipice itself, would become great roaring cables of brown and white and silver, smashing down into its stone pan where it boiled and spewed in a most unholy manner. If I had a soul of any mercy I would let Robert Pontgravé or Captain Merveille come to save him, but I once said that Champlain was worth a dozen of him, and so I must live up to my word. He pretended to follow Champlain's commands, cutting the land into whirling puzzle-pieces of fields and tree-polygons; and Champlain meanwhile pretended not to see his pretense while the preparations were made. Still Duval did not see the rapids ahead. Waving away the mosquitoes from his face with a fern, he cast the lock for Champlain's new Store-house, not knowing that it would be the last lock he'd ever make; and suddenly he seemed to remember that floury summer night among the Armouchiquois women, when he and Robert and good old Merveille had had such a fine time; and he dreamed things that had never happened, that not even Merveille had compelled him to dream; and he seemed to remember ever more intensely those Armouchiquois fillettes so beautifully riddled with inlets, bays and harbors, like the coast of his life which yet stretched infinitely before him; he would have all the girls he wanted – French girls, Basque girls, Spanish girls, Savagesses – and lock them away in a grand golden Store-house that he would build himself; when they died he'd gild them so that they might be his treasures forever. His face took on a strange beauty as he dreamed, now smoothing out the tines of the Store-house key: it was the beauty of confidence. There was no way to stop him. Having nerved himself at last to betray his Captain, he'd become truly himself, like the sudden yellow flashing of a grosbeak's wings: he'd become the ruthless swaggering pirate he'd always wanted to be. Until he stepped onto Pontgravé's skiff he would be perfect. He had no need to look ahead anymore. The time for strangling Champlain, the opportune moment no longer needed to be planned. Champlain had been and would always be dead, his mouth streaming blood; Duval would always live. He had the discernment to see that he was sublime! Voiceless though he was, he said nothing of this to the other conspirators, who had already discussed among themselves the best moment to slit his throat so as to increase their own shares of the golden Store-houses which they themselves had built in the shelter of their own mind-cliffs.

. . . When he had clapped them into irons, Champlain smiled, and his smile was no longer a young man's smile. The ship creaked and yawed in the river-tides. His confidant Pontgravé was there, of course. So were Têtu, Bonnerne the surgeon, and the navigation officers. These men now held a full council and considered well the perfidy of the traitors. Initially Bonnerne was for mercy, but Pontgravé said: That is only because of your merciful profession. Me, I am more hardheaded than you. See how my arm is bound up in a sling! The Basques fired on me when I tried to kick them out of Tadoussac – can you believe it? These men worked with them. Hang 'em all, I say!

Têtu?

Whatever you say, Seigneur de Champlain. You're the Captain . . .

Bonnerne, what do you say now?

I –

Eh, cut the slack, Bonnerne! (Thus Pontgravé, grimacing and rubbing his arm.) You think you're going to get some kind of prize if you save their necks? Forget it! What do you care? When they swing, you won't feel the strain – I guarantee it!

So they tried them and sentenced them to death. The next day, Champlain gathered the men together.

Now, Duval, I am going to hang you, said he. Do you have anything to say?

The man burst into tears. His beauty was gone. – Please have mercy on me, my Lord, he whispered.

Champlain rocked on his heels. – You see, he said to the crowd, you feared him, and yet he is not so dangerous. A marvel how he supplicates tonight when he strutted this morning! Antoine Natel, step forward and execute the sentence!

The other three were sent back to the Sieur de Monts in France, in order, as the tale says, that slow and relentless justice might work upon them in their home country. De Monts, however, pardoned them, being always humane. So Bonnerne got his way, more or less . . .

The Towers of Prudence

When the locksmith was dead, Champlain made Natel cut the head off and affix it to a pike, which he raised by the wall of the Habitation, to remind others how treason must end in stench. Then it was evening, and Pontgravé took his leave, being eager to get back to the trade at Tadoussac; and Champlain climbed the cliff to watch them go, watching how below Cap Diamant the Fleuve Saint-Laurent curved widely into the evening and Pontgravé's pinnace went slowly upstream, radiating lines of wake, and the still, wet cleanliness of the evening was refreshing for him after his labor and his men were roasting a moose and the smell of it was good. The south shore curved into the endless west, toward Asia, past yonder steep bluff whose rock was greened at its base by sumacs (the Savages said that you could boil the fuzzy red berries in a vessel of bark and drink the mixture – a thing which he had not yet had the leisure to try), and the Fleuve Saint-Laurent rolled on westward until tree-green became mountain-blue, then cloud-grey.

At his side stood Têtu.

Têtu had not wanted to come, but Champlain had ordered him. Champlain wished to speak with him alone; Champlain had plans. It was his will now to build an organization to protect himself and his enterprises. – After all, he could not always be so lucky as to depend on the fright of locksmiths! – Therefore Têtu would be the nucleus; Têtu was reliable.

I hope that you will not condemn us all in your heart, Seigneur, said the pilot hesitantly.

Champlain smiled. – Condemn them? Whatever for? They have learned the merits of obedience. But now we must create a channel, you and I, through which information can travel safely and secretly. For the men's own sake, you understand . . .

Têtu did not dare to look his Captain in the face. He thought him almost unbearably sinister. He shuffled, peering down the steep rocky wall riddled with ledges of a finger's thickness, in which weeds grew bright on that summer evening . . .

Yes, Seigneur, he said very faintly.

Blessed are they who seek justice, quoted Champlain, slapping him on the back.

Through Têtu others were recruited who controlled others, both Frenchmen and Savages over the years. And so it came to be known by all who dwelt beneath that round projection of rock (from which the grass was very quickly worn) that the Sieur de Champlain, who on ship always carried his own compass to check the course of the helmsman, also employed his own spies . . .

As for the locksmith Natel, who had been the first informer, he died of the scurvy, sad to say, that very Novembre.

The Towers of Perseverance

Champlain continued to sleep in his clothes, as was his habit, with a loaded arquebus at his right hand. His lodgement was at the flank of the lower storey, where he could hear the sentry pace the gallery just above his window, and he could almost put his ear to the outer palisadoes to listen for conspiracies. He could peer down from behind the panes to see the mercenaries standing bored and true at the cannon-platforms. He grew so sensitive to all irregularities that after a time he thought that he could almost hear the changes in piney windy sunlight from morning to evening. He watched the shadow of the wall fill in the moat remorselessly, like a door closing. And the Fleuve Saint-Laurent flowed across his life. He kept his fingers curled tight about the watch-list even in his slumbers; from time to time he started up and read it to himself, saying: Ah, tonight it is Têtu and Bonnerne . . . and then he would go back to sleep.

And Kebec also grew.

He'd never seen such lovely beans and peas as he grew that summer in his garden, and he thought: why, if this soil were tilled it would be as good as ours! – So he kept his confidence even through those late autumn afternoons when the sunlight streamed long and low through the greyness, and he remembered how matters had gone on the Isle of Sainte-Croix – but at least (he said to himself) I have eliminated disloyalty. – The problem with disloyalty, however, the very essence of it, is that whenever it is not evident it must be suspected. So he continued to be extremely vigilant, and summoned Têtu to him on any pretext to question him concerning the men's disposition, until it was obvious to all that the fellow was Champlain's satellite, at which his usefulness was diminished. – Eh, what should be done? An Order of Good Cheer could be established, as at Port-Royal, but few of his companions were of sufficient rank to sit at table with him: the thing was impossible. (Someday, perhaps, he would elevate the Savage Captains to dine beside him, but that too could not be accomplished for the moment, as they were too proud. He did not recognize that his schemes had as their object not only the consolidation of his authority, but also the winning of affection.) He increased the men's rations; he labored beside them, cursing them or singing with them; they must see how he accomplished twice as much as they . . . This was not without its results. Most of the company had acceded to Duval's plot only out of fright at his threats. Duval having now been set upon his pikestaff, the momentum of relief carried them for the time being into the Sieur de Champlain's orbit, so that they boasted to one another of his various condescensions shown them – which talk Têtu and the other spies faithfully reported. This gave him pleasure, and redoubled his desire to display his courage and goodness before them. Shouting and laughing red-faced, he ran to help them lift the last poles of the outer palisado. At night he lay sleepless not only out of vigilance, but because a crowd of undone tasks immediately began to march to and fro in his brain, awaiting him to dispose of them as he saw fit. He took a great joy in doing so, and his heart beat fast as he lay there silent, never grudging the slumber that he had lost. And yet as the autumn drew on, and his immediate devoirs were discharged, there seemed to be greater numbers than ever in that host that paraded through the soft grey plains of his cerebrum in such sprightly fashion, and he began to grow anxious. Indeed there was a struggle ahead. The Sieur de Monts' monopoly would expire in Décembre. They must hang on through the winter, by tooth and claw and prayer, so that enemy traders, greedy Rochelais and heretical Malouins, could not supplant them in the habits and affections of the Savages . . . De Monts and Poutrincourt were both stewing in lawsuits, he knew. De Monts was thinking of putting up Kebec for sale: six thousand livres would be the asking price. What would Champlain do then? Pontgravé had told him that Nicolas Boullé's daughter Hélène, now eleven, was almost marriageable; by some stroke of Providence her dot or dowry would be exactly six thousand livres . . .

What to do, what to do?

No, it was not right for a grizzled fellow like him to marry some fillette. He would not even think of it. Anyhow, he had never had either the time or the taste to interest himself in femmes of any age.

There was seldom a midnight when he did not open his eyes and rise, listening for conspiracies and derelictions. He lit the candle and sat at his table (a sober affair in the Italian style); he laid down river-soundings on his maps. Now what was the number of leagues from Point A to Point B? . . .

The weather became very brumal and dank. The first snow came on the eighteenth of Novembre. From Février until Avril it lay very heavy on the ground. Clouds blew like dust over the grey road of the Fleuve Saint-Laurent. On either side, Canada rolled westward, snowy and greyish-purple in those orange-streaked afternoons. Out of twenty-eight men, twenty died – some from the scurvy, others from excessive regalement upon the flesh of eels. The doctor Bonnerne could do nothing for them. When they were buried, ice formed in their eye-sockets just as it does now in the round stained glass windows of certain churches on rue Sainte-Catherine; and the dead men's faces were stone-grey like those churches; thus they took on the semblance of GOD's house as they had too rarely done in life. – Champlain himself was ill, but recovered to climb those slanting faces of rock once again, to stare down upon the frozen Fleuve Saint-Laurent. So he stood where he had stood with Têtu; he stood where someday his monument would stand bearing another man's face (for no one knows now what Champlain looked like). The tops of the pines below him were curtseying to one another, which foretold a gale . . . He set traps, and caught a pair of black foxes whose pelts were beautifully streaked with white, whose like he had not seen in Acadia . . . It was a much easier winter than had been the case at Isle de Sainte-Croix. – Thank GOD I am master here, not De Monts! he thought to himself. And the winter passed. As for his men, he treated them in an exemplary way.

In the spring of that new year – *viz.*, 1609, he received supplies from

Pontgravé, who winked and bellowed: Eh, Nicolas Boullé's still waiting on your word!

There is no need to discuss this, Pontgravé.

I bet you were lonely last winter, weren't you? Think about it! Hélène's growing up fast and she's going to be a looker, I'm telling you!

The Quartermaster Measured

Although he made no admission of it, Pontgravé grasped as soon as he saw Champlain that spring that he had changed. The man no longer sought to justify himself at every turn. He was by no means more relaxed or good-natured, but somehow he seemed for the first time to be *himself*. It took Pontgravé a moment longer to comprehend how this might delay or even obstruct his own designs. – There's some mistake! he thought in dismay. It can't be that my puppet has torn loose from his strings! – And meanwhile the Sieur de Champlain clapped him on the back and walked him up and down the galleries of the Habitation, pontificating about how soldiers and sailors must be kept apart, and the best way to put down the Yroquois (he'd promised the Montagnais, the good Savages, to accompany them against the Iroquois this year), and how to protect seedlings against the Canadian winters, and the proper fashion for excluding the Hollanders from Acadia, and the best way to dig moats; from which lessons Pontgravé escaped as soon as he could. By the new quai he met a man he knew, one Godet du Parc. – Eh, cried Pontgravé, wiping his forehead and rolling his eyes, our Champlain's become quite a stuffed shirt! – Godet gazed at him as solemnly as a stuffed parrot. – Monsieur, one does not criticize Monsieur de Champlain, he said to him severely. – Ah, said Pontgravé, clearing his throat. Ah, I see how it is.

Zut alors! He'd better fix up Champlain's marriage fast!

But then he thought to try another experiment.

Now, Champlain, he began, don't get overexcited, but it's my duty as a friend to warn you in advance: De Monts is almost definite about closing down the Habitation. It's impressive, but too expensive, he says. I'm not saying it's going to happen tomorrow, but he and some of the Rochelais merchants were there – Boyer and God knows who else – and the screams about investments and outlays made my ears ring. A thousand times worse than a flock of liver-snatchers! A very high personage – no, I can't tell you who (and indeed Pontgravé couldn't, because all this was a total fabrication) – a very high personage bent De Monts' ear, pointing out that if we just exterminated the Armouchiquois we could start over in a better climate, till the soil with ease, see Indian squash come up the size of cannonballs, you know the score. Of course I spoke up for you. You'd have done the same for me, eh? But it doesn't look good. Never a dull moment with De Monts, eh?

Now the gloom and abjection surged back into Champlain's face, turning it grey before his eyes – what a pleasure it was, to see once again the old Champlain he knew and loved! – no; there was nothing to worry about after all . . . !

Kebec
1608–1989

And thus the first Christian altars were confidently erected upon graves.

HERDER, *Reflections* (1880)

Kebec was two hundred leagues from the mouth of the river. The snow was four feet deep in the winter, but the French who lived there did not mind so much because they thought that it was theirs forever.* They never looked back. They worked hard, and were garrulous but dissembling. They cheated each other and the Savages and became rich in the money of New France, which was like little black buttons with faces.

In Kebec they built the narrow, crooked, chimney-crowned spire-crowned streets, chimneys rising thin and tall like graves. Fat towers with round owl-eyes rose in Kebec; the rows of house-walls each with its dozens of arched window eyes. Sun-shadows glowed in strange angles on the walls of streets because of the many strange towers above, so that the Savages who were allowed to visit passed constantly from warmth to chill and back again as they went, and became dizzied with looking at the church-steeples that rose higher than any tree they had ever seen. (Once the French began to pay them for English scalps, they quickly mastered the art of slicing them into threes, thereby tripling their profits.) The Québecois scarcely looked up at them. They toiled and prayed and were faithful subjects of the Roy. They raised their domes and weathervanes until the city had become an altar beyond comprehension in its levels and niches and garlands and tapers, shining

* My guidebook somewhat implausibly assures me that Louis Hébert, Biencourt's thug and the first farmer of New France, came to Kebec with his family in 1617 and did not die until 1827 – but perhaps the soil was more salubrious then.

steadily in points of glitter, while the red flame of GOD burned overhead. The wooden pews gleamed, too. (Outside the cathedrals, nothing gleamed; everything glared; icicles dripped. And in the forests all urgency was gone.) So in despite of fires and Irocois wars, Kebec grew taller and thicker-churched, anticipating that happy credulous time when by every brook would stand a shingled timber house with a chimney like some narrow arm of bricks

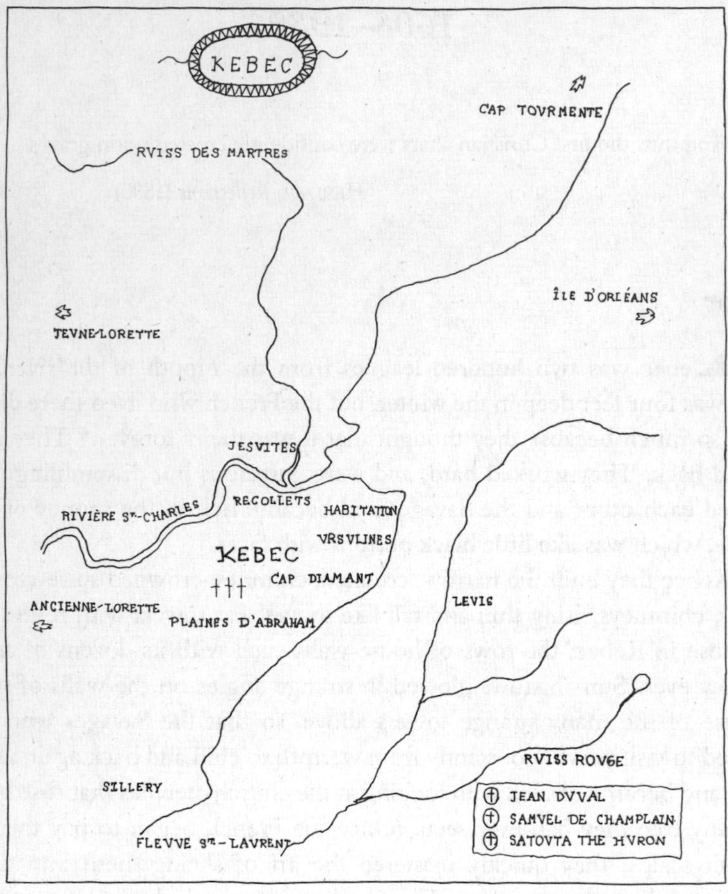

upraised at the explosion of sun-rays and CHRIST-rays from the churches in the wet green hills of fields, blue rays of morning whizzing from ridges, yellow rays of brightest afternoon thrusting clouds aside so that the blue skies of Canada rolled on from Angelus to tolling Angelus, and bearded farmers in shaggy homespun leaned on spades with the grass glistening around, until evening's green rays burst from the steeples of churches like aurora borealises and salmon leaped up the foaming streams.

An Apology

But these are only the pictures I see when I make the Exercises, deceiving myself in the manner ordained by my Superiors.

What was Kebec really? Why does it have to be that when the snow pelts down upon the night-glistening sidewalks of Kebec I cannot stop thinking of a city that scarcely exists anymore, someplace that my bad French, which resembles one of those white-eyed cars creeping foolishly down the hill to Lower Town, will never permit me to reach anyway – someplace, for that matter, that perfect French would only make harder to find because then the wondrous ungraspableness of it would be pushed farther back into the snowy trees so that I would have to put on my snowshoes and run all winter until I got out of Père Le Jeune's wavering tracks? The sleet blows horizontally, stinging drops in the Stream of Time; ice-flecks fly true like the ships which once went sailing from the Citadel.

But one French word I do know: *s'écouler*, to flow, which sounds like it.

At the corner of rue Corps-de-Gaulle, the famous cannonball between the roots of the tree is overgrown by snow. I've seen the laughing Ursuline schoolgirls play there on their way home. Not far from the pillar where General Wolfe died, a French-Canadian girl with dark eyes and dark hair is carrying groceries up the stairs to her apartment and the snow is spattering her face with brilliant crystals.

Kebec *continued*

Meanwhile the houses grew, high-chimneyed and of almost egregious narrowness, such as the Hôtel-DIEU, with its trio of dormer windows on each roof-side, its three chimneys (around it ran a log palisade to cordon off the cloistered nuns; the wigwams of acolytes stood beside). Kebec now flowered with rows of windows like dominoes; its roofs assiduously crumpled themselves into gargoyles' points . . . Then the day came, the great day, when it gained its treasure. In 1649, the Black-Gowns Jean Brébeuf, Gabriel Lalemant, Charles Garnier and Noël Chabanel were martyred, as will be told (believe that and you'll be saved). The relics of all save the unfortunate Chabanel were rescued from the Irocois, at great peril, and brought to Kebec, where a Marian chapel took them in in 1818. To the left of the altar, a figure of alabaster purity, his outline delineated by years of dust, lies rigid, his left hand across the Book on his breast, and a skeleton-sprig grows stonily across him. His

head rests upon a rolled stone bundle. His eyes are huge, and yet one could not say whether they are open or closed. On the slab beneath him, the mason has carved SAINT JEAN DE BREBEUF, PRIEZ POUR NOUS. Him gained, our heart's Québec must last forever. That is why the Marquis de Montcalm rested confident, saying we will send those British rushing home!; saying we shall serve them what they fed upon at Ticonderoga!; saying with a smile we will put cannonballs in their sails! . . . – For this was *our* Montcalm with his open face, his wig powdered as silver as a censer, his quick brown-green eyes moving in his face like river-depths . . . how could he not win? – But Major General James Wolfe was leading his men up the secret path beside the waterfall.

And so Kebec fell, and the year after that Montréal fell and New France fell so that two hundred and thirty years later my friend Pierre said in anguished recapitulation: the big mistake they made against Wolfe was not fighting guerrilla-style . . . – Now the College of the Black-Gowns stood riddled by the cannons, and Kebec was in ruins, and the English officers passed the time in cards with the French officers, who sighed very sadly. In 1890, while Francis Parkman sat scribbling his Seven Dreams of Canada in a state of nervous half-blindness, remembering how he once walked in the cropped green grass around the many-pointed star of the Citadel's ramparts where black cannon aimed so decoratively at the past, separate Catholic schools were abolished in Manitoba.

The Shoals of Hell

The roseolous schoolbooks said *Canadians share that most enlightened of political systems, the British parliamentary system* and in 1927 the British government generously gave most of northeast Québec to the colony of Terre-Neuve – and Pierre's sweetheart Marie-Claude said with tears in her eyes: all the Anglophones in the west, they call them Canadians; they call *us* French. I say to them: *I* am Canadian! I don't know what *you* are! (just as I myself could not grasp the Château Frontenac with the sharp-spired black cones set atop its grey stone and orange stone, and the green roof with two dozen points rearing over everything like a nightmare; Québec's buildings, red and white and green and many-windowed, chiseled, clocked, painted, arched, flagged and shuttered: what was *it* supposed to be?)

When people from France came to visit, said Marie-Claude, they found the Québecois *quaint* and *comical*. In the Ursuline Museum they shrugged and smiled to see Montcalm's skull, mottled black and brown, reposing in its glass case behind a discreet obfuscation of gilded dragons, birds, towers and mottos. On the floor was a mound of similarly colored spheres, with the legend: CANNON BALLS SHOT BY THE ENGLISH INTO OUR GARDEN AND OVER OUR MONASTERY. And the French visitors thought: how fanatically provincial!

Marie-Claude cried: that's why I hate so much the French. They are *so* the bottom! (She had been to French College.)

Priez pour nous

Marie-Claude was always smiling and laughing and helping her father make wine and teasing Pierre with shining eyes and mockingly downcurved brows, laughing: Ah, *boo-boo boo!* as she flicked her hand in his face; and we went out past Montréal's grey streets and blocky skyscrapers and great steely domes, past the École de l'Infant Jésus, now a housing co-op; and up by Three Rivers we saw a windmill whirling beside a great crucified JESUS, and it was very strange to see the restless Cross and the still one, and a little *mesonge* bird with a black head alighted on Pierre's shoulder, and Marie-Claude cut a slice of Oka cheese for everybody, giggling: it smells like the feet of the priest! but earlier I had heard despair in her voice like the whitish shining of a winter lake.

My Researches

I went to the Parlement building in Québec City. Considering myself an ignoramus, I took the English-language tour. My guide was an Angel of blonde curls like any one of the barmaids at Saint Alexandre's on rue Saint-Jean: – these ladies wear white blouses and dark skirts; you will often see them huddled together behind the bar with its row of ivory taps, calculating bills while you read about another murder on Prince Edward Island, another two-year-old boy in Ontario sodomized and strangled. The beer is good; the green lamps illuminate the laughing neighing drinkers with tolerable clarity. Then one of the barmaids brings you the *sandwich du pub*, bending on tiptoe to lower the tray on wide-spread fingers. – This tour guide had the same fine grace. All of us felt it. In her charge we considered ourselves as lucky as high-ranking Jansenists to see the handsome wooden desks adorned with microphones, two seats at each desk; the throne for the Speaker; the six hundred pound candelabra fashioned of Czech crystal; the Red Chamber with its partly upside-down clock like a sundial (maple-leaves and fleurs-de-lys everywhere). – And what grand inscriptions on the walls! – But as for me, I could not help thinking of the inscription (marble-lozenged) above Montcalm's grave in the Chapelle-des-Ursulines:

HONOR TO MONTCALM!
IN DENYING HIM VICTORY,
DESTINY GAVE HIM RECOMPENSE
IN A GLORIOUS DEATH!

And this chair, said the tour guide, this is for the leader of the opposition party.

Ah, the Partie Québecoise, I said innocently. Now, what is the difference between the two parties?

The tour guide frowned adorably. – Oh, they are kind of in the middle, said she. They want a secession – well, not *that* exactly, but a sort of association. I cannot put it more exactly. It is hard for me to understand. It is hard for most of us in Québec to understand.

You are a troublemaker! laughed Pierre when I told him what she had said.

The government, they are sleeping with the British! said Marie-Claude contemptuously.

French Guns Again

1608–1610

> ... here is a lock of hair from a Russian guerrilla-girl. They fight like wildcats and are quite *Untermensch*.
>
> UNTERSTÜRMFÜHRER HUBER, in a letter home (*ca.* 1942)

Now his map ran with many rivulets; and yet to the north and west (where it was still possible that he might discover China) the blank snow of the unknown had not yet been melted. This fact persuaded him to remain allied to the Algoumequins, who had promised in their good time to bring him among the Savages of the interior, whose very names he barely knew: the *Nipissings*, the *Good Irocois* (who were also called Chariquois or Hurons), the *Cat Nation*, the *Esquimaux* ... No doubt many other such Nations lay beyond the Country of the Irocois, but it was evident that *those* Savages were formidable and jealous of their territory. He would never get to China through their agency. Then, too, it seemed as if the Algoumequins had access to more furs, and furs of a quality superior to those of the Irocois. And the Algoumequins were subservient, their Captain, Yroquet, practically his vassal ... – No, there was no reason that he could see to keep peace with the Iroquois. If the Algoumequins wished him to assist them in their wars, then he would, by GOD ... He had learned from Cartier's mistake: he would not be aloof from them.

Readying his Sportsmen 1609

Now, as the strawberries began to blossom, the Montaignez gathered together, wearing their richest garments of beaver-fur, which were adorned with beads and cords in such profusion that Champlain had never seen the like. Anadabijou the Sagamore raised his hand, and they all shouted: *ho ho ho!* They marched, leaped, and made many ingenious poses. Then they held their accustomed Tobacco Feast. After this the Savagesses stripped themselves naked as always (aside from the ornaments with which they were decked). – He closed his eyes quickly. – They danced; they got into the canoes and struck at each other with their paddles to incite their husbands, paddle thunking harmlessly against paddle; shouting, they drenched each other with war . . .

Commencement of the Irocois War

On the twenty-eighth day of Juin he set out for the Country of the Hiroquois in one of Pontgravé's shallops. Pontgravé had himself originally determined to come, but later he decided that there was no profit in it.

Eh, you know what they say about other people's quarrels. (Thus Pontgravé.) *Nothing is gained by putting your finger between tree and bark.* That's what they say, all right.

Very well, Monsieur, said Champlain, a little disdainfully. I cannot say I am surprised.

Pontgravé shrugged and blew his nose. Then he went back to Tadoussac.

Champlain for his part disassembled his arquebus and cleaned it very carefully, as it had always been his habit to do in the civil war in France, for upon this mechanism his life depended almost as much as upon his prayers. (They said that these Yroquois were very clever with their arrows.) And the shallop sailed on, his men laughing and smoking the *tobacco* . . . The canoes of the Savages darkened the water around him. They proceeded up the Rivière des Iroquois as far as the First Rapid, beyond which the shallop could not go. At this place, therefore, he left all but two of his Frenchmen behind. (The Savages had lied to him again, of course. They'd assured him that the river was navigable. They had no understanding of authority and hierarchy! In this they were not even beasts, but *worse* than beasts; – he remembered the great bird-island at the mouth of the Fleuve Saint-Laurent, where the birds nested in excellent order by species . . . – But no; he must not dwell on such things. They were not merely ignorant, however, as he had thought at first; they were cunning and malicious. Eh, they had led him so many tricks! But one day – not right away, mind you, but one day . . . !) They led him on a portage of half a league, and then seated him in one of their canoes. Now the war-party continued upstream with ready bows, entering into a Country of increasing richness. It became very warm. Repeatedly he wiped his brow, gazing up at that hazy white summer sky, from which a few cool drops sprinkled; at the trees so thick with leaves like an infinity of green fingernails or pine cone shingles. – We shall take many heads! whispered the Montaignez Savages gleefully, looking about them immediately after, to make certain that no Hiroquois lay lurking near . . . According to his best calculations they were in the western extremity of the Country of the Armouchiquois. Eh, Membertou with half a dozen arquebuses had routed them! How then could this expedition fail, when it included not only guns but also Frenchmen? – But there are always ifs to consider, he reminded himself, gnawing at a fingernail. And they continued south. Some of these tall trees' leaves and pollens stood on end like church tapers, so that Champlain thought himself gliding through a forest of çandelabra; other trees had leaves which flared out like ladders and shelves; – all of them he noted, in his mind burning and clearing them, sawing them into lengths of ship-timber, making houses and palisades of them. Presently they arrived at a dark point of land, beyond which lay a vast and elongated lake. Chestnut trees bordered it, and modest Alps rose in the forest beyond. The water was greenly deep. This was *Lacus Irocoisiensis*. Now they must travel only by night. Whenever they laid themselves down they first built redoubts or breastworks of trees, so that they might not be easily slaughtered in their sleep. They studied each other's dreams, and prayed Champlain to recount them his, he being a man of Power, thanks to his iron things. Smiling, he said that he dreamed that the Hiroquois had drowned, at which they were much elated, and the Algonkin Captain, Iroquet, caressed his cheek. And they traveled on. At last, late on the twenty-eighth night of Juillet, they spied Hiroquois canoes ahead.

Already the enemies had seen each other, and began shrieking their stylized cries of rage. In a whisper, Champlain ordered his men to conceal themselves with him, below the gunnels of the canoes. And he peered forward (hidden from view, as he hoped) with the keenest desire to study these new Savages, whom he had never seen before. – That is right, Chawain: look, look! (Thus his friend Iroquet.) They will shoot no arrows today! – Good, he replied curtly. He craned and stared. His eyes did not perceive long distances as well as they had during the Civil War. But it was hard to mistake these Hiroquois. They were great stout men, like the trees of their Country, some of them being upwards of six pieds in height. Their hair was trimmed in a fashion rather akin to that of the Recollect priests, except that it was raised and stiffened in a most unholy manner, by the use of some kind of vermilion wax which he had not seen before. From this matrix depended feathers, claws, wampum strings . . . For a moment his heart sank, for they seemed redoubtable, and he longed passionately to be watching the scene from a great distance through De Monts' spyglass as De Monts and Lescarbot approached the foe – how that lawyer's teeth would chatter! – Thinking this, he laughed, and his fear fell away. At any rate, it was all in the hands of GOD, so he had nothing left to do other than set his followers a spirited example.

The Hiroquois landed at once and began to fell trees with their tomahawks, forming a barricade behind which to install themselves, while Champlain's allies lashed their canoes together on the water and began to dance the war-dance.

We shall kill you tomorrow, when the SUN can see us! shouted the Montagnais.

Tomorrow we shall roast you alive and drink your blood! replied the Hiroquois.

As far as Champlain was concerned, it was all but blustering and bravacherie.

What is your opinion of tomorrow's sport, Seigneur? said one of his men.

Ah, he replied, it will be an unequal contest. Those Hiroquois still use stone axes, like brutes. We shall rout them.

The night was stifling, moist and close. Crickets built a heavy wall of sound that was as impenetrable as the forest. The shadows of leaves in the moonlight were as sharp as axe-blades. The men lay awake all night; their faces were sticky with sweat. Farther south, in the palisadoed towns of the Hiroquois, lovers turned away from each other in repulsion at the desperate sweatiness of hot and sticky flesh.

Just before dawn, Champlain and his two companions donned their corselets. Now his Savages landed, he and his followers remaining concealed for the moment, so as to better astonish the enemy in due course, who now issued from their fort – two hundred of them! – He peeped over the gunwale of the canoe, studying their painted faces, watching how the early morning sun glistened upon their shaved heads, their long greasy scalp-locks . . . He heard his two followers clearing their throats nervously. Pitying them, he whispered that only he would stand directly in the line of fire. – The Hiroquois were screeching their hate-songs, to which his Montaignez gave fitting reply. According to his traveler's hourglass, these preliminaries took a good fifteen minutes, which would have been more than sufficient to fall upon the enemy. And these Montagnais, if only he could make them understand his language better, he would have commanded them in such a way that these Hiroquois would have been utterly exterminated with scarcely a single casualty! As it was, there was nothing for it. He beckoned to his men, stood up, and strode forward. The Montagnais divided to let them pass. – The Hiroquois fell mute. His two followers darted behind a tree and raised their arquebuses. For the space of a *Hail MARIE* the Irocois stared at him, seemingly incapable of motion. He almost felt sorry for them in their peculiar wicker armor . . . Recovering from their stupor, they howled and began to bend their bows in preparation to launch flocks of arrows at him. At once he charged his musket with four balls, and in a single shot killed two of the three Iroquois Captains, whose heads were adorned with feathers. The Irocois ran shrieking; it was an easy victory. His Indians carried off many Hiroquois heads.

The Point of It All

As I cannot hide from you any of Our LORD's graces, I shall tell you here with my usual simplicity that among the Savages who accompanied Champlain, deferring as always (naturally!) to his leadership, were several of the Good Iroquois, also called *Chariquois* or *Boar's Heads – viz.*, Huron. These were a confederacy of Nations lying far west, near the vassal-lands of China. Champlain observed them and said to himself: Eh, their beaver-skins are finer than any that I have seen. I must take a sounding . . .

The Second Campaign 1610

Upon his return from France in the following year, his heart beat rapidly. He was anxious to get in more innings against these Hiroquois Savages. Nothing else was proceeding well. De Monts had reprimanded him for having paid out so many iron goods to the Savages. – In 1602 a beaver-skin was worth only two knives, Monsieur, and now you tell me it costs twenty! he shouted. Tell me, if you please, my *dear, dear* sir, how I am to pay my expenses in such a way!

The old man's face was purple and wrinkled, like that of a baby afflicted with the colic or some other upset. He had fallen off greatly over the winter. He had always been rigid in his views, but now he had reached that stage of old age in which any circumstance not to one's liking is seen as an impudent defiance or contradiction. He was no longer capable of listening to Champlain's explanations. Champlain knew it, and De Monts himself knew it, but the farce had to be gone through.

I cannot help it, Seigneur, he began. – There are too many illegal traders on the Fleuve. Their one object seems to be to get whatever they can for themselves. They bid against each other like street-whores; they ambush each other in the forest; they importune the Savages; they outrage their women; they get them drunk with brandy . . . They are worse than mosquitoes, I tell you! Even the Savages are disgusted with them. Wherever I go, a dozen longboats follow . . .

De Monts tightened his lips. – You must do better, Champlain, he said. Let me express myself in an idiom which you will surely understand. You were once a Quartermaster. You know the value of frugality. Does that go to your heart?

Champlain nodded stiffly. He was his Captain; he could not set himself against him. All day he struggled to accommodate himself to De Monts' humor, like a ship repeatedly tacking in hopes of getting to windward.

Of course De Monts was not making a profit. Champlain knew this. But *he* served loyally! It was not his fault that the monopoly had not been renewed this year.

De Monts was now in partnership with some greedy merchants from Rouen, for whom Champlain had little taste. They insisted that Kebec become nothing but a giant Store-house for furs. They had no vision, no vision at all; whereas *he* knew Canada from the Port of Sainte-Catherine to the Port of the HOLY GHOST! He felt a burning anger at the way he had been treated, which resolved into illness. Doctor Bonnerne was not there to help him; he had died in Canada last winter of the scurvy. So Champlain must be bled and purged by men who were strangers to him. – My dear Seigneur, they said gently, you must take care; you are not so young now . . . – at which his face was filled with wrath. Something swelled painfully inside his chest; he must lie down again. His departure from France was delayed a month . . .

At any rate, he was back again, and could at least have his sport with the Hiroquois. His cares sank, like a stone in a river. He could already feel the glory in his veins . . . A pair of gulls passed overhead, curling their wings: they were nothing less than flying fleurs-de-lys; and he rounded the last bend, leaving behind that round blue hump of cape, the Fleuve Saint-Laurent a somewhat vicious blue-grey almost like ironwood; and then the rock of Kebec stood at his right hand.

It was spring.

In the hills that flanked the Fleuve Saint-Laurent the dirt was pine needles and red clay, and the trees grew close together in a grim grey way that made darkness, but when Champlain looked across the deep striations of the gorge the trees on the side seemed treasured with green, although they too were not open. Gorges split the forest with the grins of skulls, and the sound of water was a low steady remorseless rush that rose in to the heights like spray, and the cliffs were terrible and grey and old. Far below, the trees became blue horizon.* Here, at the mouth of the Rivière des Iroquois, a hundred of the enemy had been discovered within a barricade.

Now the Montagnais seized bows and war-clubs and leaped into their canoes. – Follow, Champlain, follow! they cried.

Some Basque fur-traders drew near, seeing the commotion. – Help us, brothers! shouted the Savages.

Upon learning that it was an adventure of war, the traders spat into the water and remained where they were.

You are women! the Savages sneered. Not like Champlain!

He accompanied them with four of their men. Hastily, kneeling in the canoe, he buckled on his metal breastplate, studded with great yellow rivets. His Frenchmen did the same. Now they were halfway across the river, and he measured out the charges from his ivory powder-horn. His heart pounded exultantly. He inspected the breech of his arquebus; he slammed a ramrod through the barrel; for just as he always made the examination of conscience before putting out to sea, so similarly he examined his weapon at the commencement of any one of these Hiroquois frolics. The Savages looked covetously at the gun. – Give it to us, if you are our friend! they shouted. – I cannot do that, Champlain replied. But I shall lend you my aid; you may be certain of that. – The cliffs were greenly clothed; great masts rose above the rock-brows.

He loaded the arquebus with round and grapeshot.

Now they had breasted that river wide and bright, milky blue-grey like the mild and cloudy sky; and the canoes landed and the warriors rushed into the

* Prof. Trigger remarks here upon how well I have made this Exercise, noting: "The part of the Saint Lawrence near Sorel is absolutely flat for miles around."

woods. Champlain led his men after them. For some moments they wandered bewildered through a swamp, but at last they heard the war-yells ahead, and redoubled their pacc. This was no easy matter, for they sank to their knees in muck. In Champlain's nostrils was the smell of dry leaves and fresh dirt as he ran behind the Savages, who had come running back to gesticulate at him, and he ran on, brushing past the skeleton-cones of long dead twigs dangling from tree-crotches like brooms, which very occasionally creaked and clashed in some breeze-gust. Now the cries grew louder, and he slackened his pace a little, commanding his men to search as they went, lest they be taken in some fosse or ditch lined with stakes (for he did not know what devilish entrenchments these Hiroquois might be capable of). But he found nothing. Later he understood that he had been overcautious, for like all Savages these were scarcely more civilized than beavers in their constructions.

So at last he led his men to the grey piles of brushwork in which the Irocois waited like snakes. The Montagnais stood clamoring and shooting arrows.

Fire! he cried to his men.

An Hiroquois arrow with a sharp stone head whizzed through the tip of his ear and pierced his neck. He drew it out contemptuously.

He stepped up to the breastworks and discharged his arquebus through a crack, and the Hiroquois began to scream, and his men were acquitting themselves likewise, and the Montaignez were shrieking with joy and rolling the log-trunks aside and Champlain was firing and firing and for return fire the Hiroquois shot greater than a puncheon's worth of blood from their exploding hearts . . .

Justification

Some of the fur-traders joined the battle late, hoping for a greater share of booty than of risk. When it was over, and all but fifteen of the Hiroquois lay dead in their fort, the traders rushed in and plundered them of their clothes. At this, the Savages mocked them in harsh terms, saying: Look, brothers, these Iron People are but women! They make war only on the dead! – But the traders paid no heed. Greedily they stripped the corpses of their blood-stained pelts. Running riot, they trampled the dead Mohawk Captains; they stepped on their faces tattooed with canoes, stars, chains, diagonal alchemical grids; they ripped the robes from their chests tattooed with greenish-black groves of spear-trees. – Do they truly come from the same Nation as you? said the Savages to Champlain in disgust. For you – *you* are valiant! –

Champlain thanked them for their compliments (which in truth he considered that he deserved), but later that evening, while the Hiroquois captives were being burned, he visited the traders' campfire and asked to see the skins. This request they freely granted, being indebted to him for this plunder, as well they knew; and Champlain held them close to the firelight. At once his previous impression, and therefore the *raison d'être* of his participation in this warfare, was confirmed: – namely, that these peltries of the Irocois were vastly inferior in quality to those of his allies the Algoumequins . . .

Iron *1609–1610*

The Mohawk said: Again they have vanquished our strong young men with the help of the Iron People. Again our young men sing their songs of bitterness, their Death-Songs. Again they scalp them; again they burn them; again they slice off pieces from their arms to feed to the dogs!

The women howled in rage and grief.

We must not raid in those places anymore, they said, despondent.

We must turn away our eyes from their blood, they said. Otherwise we shall provoke their anger. We cannot now cleanse the river of the Iron People.

Two Mohawk Captains were dead. Their armor had not helped them. Their names were Owenheghkohna and Shadekarihwade. A man ran through the forest, dangling the black wampum-tears from his hand, calling: *Kwa! Kwa! Kwa!* so that all might know of the death. Then the Clear-Minded chanters of the other clan-groups set out to condole the sad ones, singing: *Haii, haii! Haii, haii!* Now listen, ye who founded our Great League. *Haii, haii! Haii, haii!* Now it has become old. *Haii, haii! Haii, haii!* Now it is a wilderness again! – Then they sang the roll of their Captains whose names never died. When they reached the village someday to be called Ossernenon, where the corpses of the two Captains had been borne, where my love Sainte Catherine Tekakwitha would be born, there they met the Mourners, who had kindled a great fire of welcome on the edge of the forest. And the orator of the Mourners thanked them for their coming through the dark trees of uplifted tomahawks. Then the Clear-Minded orator took DEKANWIDEH's part and hung the first three strands of wampum on the pole. And he sang of the faceless darkness called GREAT DESTROYER, which strides about at night with uplifted war-club, and he sang words of loss and sorrow over those Captains who had been smitten dead like crushed firebrands. Then with wampum the Clear-Minded ones wiped the eyes of the Mourners with the white fawn-skin of their pity. With wampum they unstopped their ears, they unclogged their throats of the throttling darkness of the GREAT DESTROYER. And the Mourners were eased. The Clear-Minded gave the Mourners the medicine called Water-of-Pity to drink. They wiped away the bloody trails; they cleared away the darkness of grief. They beautified the SKY; they attached the SUN in place. So they carried out the Rite of Condolence. And when that Rite was concluded, the two Matrons who owned the titles of the dead Captains now strode through the ranks of the Mohawk men and raised up two to their feet who would now be given the names of Owenheghkohna and Shadekarihwade. So the names lived again, and the two new Captains were crowned with the antlers of their predecessors. Then the Hiroquois danced and feasted, for their League was whole.

But in the following year, as I have told, the Iron People interfered again, defeating them. Once more they must hold the Rite of Condolence. When this was concluded, they held a Council, at which the new Captain called Owenheghkohna said:

Brothers, we have become women. Being so, we must take up the occupations of women. Let us then get brooms to sweep away these crawling creatures who invade our Council fire. Without them, why abandon our wives, why risk our lives each summer? A woman sweeps not with her hands. You deceive yourselves if you believe that we shall reverse these disasters only through valor. Do you desire our Great League to become a desert? No, we must have iron axes to split heads. We must have iron points on our arrows to pierce hearts. Then we shall overcome these Iron People; then we shall burn them in our fires! Are we otherwise to permit them to mock us and call us women, solely because they possess iron? Are we to await their uplifted hatchets? Are we to allow them to lay thorns in our path? We must get iron. If we do not, then we shall become thin and our bones will dry up. – I have spoken.

Your words are good, the People said.

Henry Hudson

Here I'd better add that the previous year, not long after that first battle, not long before the Harvest Thanksgiving, still more players had entered the game. They were Iron People, called *Dutch* or *Hollanders*. And they were at war with the other Iron People. It was the Mohawk who spied them. One of their Rodiyaner, he who held the name of Aghstawenseronttha, saw their ship when he was fishing for eels. It was coming up River Beyond the Openings; it came to the place called *Skä-neh'-ta-de*.* There the Iron People landed. Aghstawenseronttha was well aware that they were Sorcerers. He was afraid to comprehend them. You fell into the Power of Sorcerers when you least expected it. A pretty girl combed your hair for you and you were hers; she was a witch. A poor old man asked for help, and if you listened you were trapped. Your way became slicker and muddier until suddenly you lost your footing and bellied down to the bottom of a hill of slime where the Sorcerer waited to eat you. – So it would be with these Iron People. Who knew how they made their kettles, or what they brewed in them? Aghstawenseronttha saw the ship in the evening and did not declare himself. Night came and he spied a comet, which among the Haudenosaunee is called the *Sky-Blue Panther*. And the Sky-Blue Panther is a bad omen. But Aghstawenseronttha wanted iron so much . . .

The Hollanders liked it there among the Iroquois Country of trees and trees and then blue and white horizons of hazy tree-crests beyond. White fogs clung to the trees so that they could not see how far the Country went. But they'd measure its limits as soon as they were well walled. So they erected Fort Orange, and intoxicated themselves with good Dutch dreams as they began to clear a field or two, admiring lilies of the valley, white wood aster, poison ivy meadows . . . And so for the time being the Hiroquois did not go to the Fleuve Saint-Laurent, and their enemies slept in peace. Quietly, the Hiroquois bartered furs for iron with the Hollanders. They tipped their arrows with iron, as Owenheghkohna had said. They got iron hatchets. And they waited to revenge themselves.

* The site of Albany. Schenectady, New York, farther up the river, bears the anglicized version of this name.

In the Shallows

1610–1614

> Transformation of large areas of woodland, bottom land, and prairies into farms created an agricultural ecosystem that is now an essential element in our society, although the initial modification of land was in sharp conflict with the religious beliefs of the indigent [*sic*] Indian peoples.
>
> WILLIAM PECORA, "Nature: An Environmental Yardstick," USDI pamphlet (1972)

How am I now to describe the deceitfully tranquil year-islands momentarily tree-puffed high in this summer of the Stream of Time? Here we are between waterfalls.

On the eighth day of Août, 1610, Champlain departed Kebec with Pontgravé, leaving as his deputy Monsieur Claude de Godet, on whom he could well rely. – I feel that I have done my duty, he said to himself.

On my honor, Champlain! (Thus Pontgravé.) The youngster looks lost! What cradle did you steal him from?

You mean to say that you do not trust him to fulfill his devoirs?

Eh, it's your affair.

Monsieur, if you believe that matters are dangerous, I beg you to inform me. (Thus Champlain, quite coldly.)

He's just a shoulder-shrugger, that's all. I'm sure he's quite capable, although if he wasn't that *would* be rich! He's got sixteen men, a Store-house full of harquebuses, and an impregnable falaise at his back. What could go wrong, I ask you? Nothing, nothing!

By now poor Champlain, who became anxious each time he left his fragile enterprise behind, was convinced that something *could* go wrong, something dire which he had overlooked – by Heaven, he had been remiss in his behavior!

But we cannot secure them against any invasion . . . – he said fretfully.

Come now, Champlain! his friend cried in surprise, thumping his shoulder. Why so anxious? All is in order: your raisins are in rows and columns in every pudding!

And the Savages . . .

Savages! (Thus Pontgravé, scornfully.) If they say no to hatchets and beads, give 'em brandy. If they reject the brandy, give 'em grapeshot like your Spanish uncle. Why so nervous all the sudden? I tell you, mon ami, it hurts me to the depths of my soul to see you torture yourself so needlessly. Do you know what you need?

What?

A wife.

Sacré bleu!

No, no, I swear it!

Ah, Pontgravé, I need no one to look after me. Don't think of it anymore. And how could I guarantee the safety and happiness of any Frenchwoman in these parts? What an idea! You know how melancholy Madame de Poutrincourt has become; as for Madame de Pontgravé, I tell you honestly that I cannot understand her . . .

Oh, her? Eh, Christine's fat and happy! She dotes on our Robert whenever she sees him; she worries about marrying off our Jeanne; she keeps herself busy praying for us . . .

Champlain had become agitated. He refused to listen to any more. At his command the pilot swung the bow around again and they returned to Kebec. Godet and the sixteen men came running down to the shore with exclamations of surprise. Without explaining himself in any way, he subjected them to a long speech bidding them to take close care of their defenses (while Pontgravé coughed as hard as he could so that he wouldn't laugh). Champlain's face glowed with sunburn. He exhorted them to obey Godet (who reddened and glared blindly ahead). He told them to pray morning and night. He reminded them that just as in religion filial fear is one with divine love, so it is in life. – Monsieur Godet is a pure and mild man, he said to them, and will desire to be mild, I am sure, if you give him good opportunity. – (Here the Sieur de Champlain did not hesitate to point with his finger at Duval's skull, which still found lodgement on a sharpened pole, although these days it rattled loosely in the winds, since there was no longer any flesh on it.) – Be not ungrateful like the Savages, said Champlain. Guard yourselves against idleness, and above all against caprices and fantasies; for those are the Devil's courtiers. I commend you all to Our LORD.

. . . His nose had become somewhat sharper in recent years. His features were dark and wind-worn. There were sour wrinkles at the corner of his mouth.

In Décembre of that year, having accomplished his other business in Paris, he married a twelve-year-old fillette, Hélène Boullé by name. Her parents pleaded that the marriage not be consummated for two more revolutions of the sun, she being so young, and he accepted this provision gladly. What a charming little bird! These days his vision was beginning to blur a little, like Tekakwitha's, so he couldn't make out the face of the Holy VIERGE-MARIE who sometimes visited him in his dreams; anyhow Hélène must resemble her . . . And the dowry was six thousand livres. – On the day before the épousailles were concluded, in the Church of Saint-Germain-l'Auxerrois, he signed a quittance for forty-five hundred, yours regretfully, Samuel de Champlain, which they explained to him was only a formality (Believe me, son-in-law! It's nothing! Don't look at me like it's some plot! You'll get the rest in time, *trust* me! – eh, sign here . . . exactly! I'm as serious as a toothache!), at which his face fell, but Pontgravé vouched for Monsieur de Boullé's honesty – besides, he was in an uneasy position to contest anything: on his pension and what De Monts paid him, it wasn't as if he could contribute much to Hélène's support . . . – Life was making some mistake. He was like a child who, unwrapping a magnificent gift on his Saint's name-day, finds within nothing but air. But soon he'd have the forty-five hundred; and of course the remainder would be paid at the end of the stipulated two years. – Eh, before then I'll have resources in Kebec, he thought. He saw himself outfitting pinnaces with the best light cannon from Vitry; he saw his Store-house bulging with harquebuses and long muskets to put down the Hiroquois forever, to the general good of all the Savages; and then he could build a chain of forts all the way to China! And his bride would teach the little Indians girls . . .

So he drank with Hélène from the marriage cup like a broad shallow chalice of silver, its two handles curving like vines. (It was a Catholic ceremony; Champlain had insisted on that. – Nicolas Boullé threw up his hands goodnaturedly. – But of course! he said. The wife must always follow the husband, in religion as in all else. – My friend, thought Champlain, you are very complaisant, as befits a Huguenot . . .) So he be-ringed her hand. So he bent down and kissed her cheek. She flinched. Timidly she signed the certificate of marriage below Monsieur de Champlain, and stood looking down at her name, written in letters so gauche and small –

Not one of his relations was present, of course. They'd long since written *him* off! His father he'd hoped might come, despite their differences, but no; who knew where that old Captain sailed? De Monts was one of the witnesses. He picked and plucked at his beard. Champlain had to run around looking for the others. He got the Roy's horse-leech to sign, and a midwife, a barber, a merchant, a shipbuilder . . . Pontgravé couldn't make it himself; he had important business; but he sent Pierre Noël, whose brother René had died of scurvy at Île de Sainte-Croix . . . So De Monts was the star of the show, as usual. The horse-leech was especially impressed. He talked about it for weeks: Yes, I was next to De Monts – a great, great man! Loaded with money! The groom sure looked shabby beside him, I'm telling you! – De Monts turned up his nose; De Monts raised his head and peered in a fashion which could only be termed sourcilleux or disdainful. But then De Monts put his arm around Champlain's shoulder very tenderly, and Champlain knew that De Monts valued him; De Monts recognized his sacrifices . . .

The Marriage Prologue 1607–1610

Which by definition should have come sooner, but, please let's not dwell on it, since hearing such complaints comes to me as a tremendous blow

For three years, as we know, Pontgravé had been laboring on the ungrateful Champlain's behalf, trying to get him married. JESUS! Most Messieurs would give their left nut for a fillette like that – a good clean Christian girl! Spread 'em, bitch! And was she a pauper? But no! Nicolas Boullé was the Roy's Secrétaire, and a wine merchant, too. Did you want a nice red Bordeaux, streaming into your glass as freshly crimson as the blood of CHRIST? Talk to Boullé! He'd supplied all the cider for the boys at Isle de Sainte-Croix, too. Sure it had frozen, but why did everyone make such a big stink about that? Messire Aubry's holy water had frozen just as solid! If you liked money and wine, then Nicolas was your man. Sometimes I wish I weren't saddled with my big cow of a Christine. When I see those daughters of his, I think to myself, I still have what it takes to make one of them happy! Eh, and so does my Robert! But Robert, he's no good. All he likes are red-skinned fillettes who never take a bath except when they dance naked in their orgies. I myself take a bath twice a year, a good long soak, once before Easter, once before Christmas. That's why I'm so healthy today. Of course I have gout once in a while, but that has nothing to do with it. – Where was I? My thoughts are so profound these days, I lose the track, like Messire Aubry in the forest. Poor Messire Aubry! – Ah, yes. Champlain. What a lemon he is! One good thing I will say about him: he can drink like a sponge and never get drunk. But he's about as much fun as a wind-pump. He doesn't even want to pop that Hélène. What in Heaven's name is wrong with him? Is he really just a Quartermaster who gets no other delight in life than cutting up horses' carcasses into perfect squares? Anyhow, if he weren't so selfish he'd see that the marriage would help us all out. With that six thousand we could build up our equipage at Kebec! Doesn't the man have any sense of duty?

But, Papa, why must I marry him? (Thus Hélène.)

It's an affair of reason and interest, my sweet. (Thus the Sieur de Boullé.) Monsieur de Champlain is a gentilhomme of great merit. He will take you to see strange lands; you are a very lucky girl.

Please don't make me!

You must obey us and trust that we seek only your good.

Oh –

Hélène, you *must* promise to render submission and amity to Monsieur de Champlain. Do you promise this?

She remembered all the evenings when Monsieur de Champlain had come to visit, and he looked like a huge crumpled bear in the firelight, some of his hair already going white, and he told her stories of the Savages and their wars so that she woke up shrieking from dreams of Hiroquois lurking and waiting to seize her and pull her forever among the trees, but all the same she could hardly wait for him to come again and tell her more; he always brought presents: Huron arrows winged with the feathers of unknown birds, an Armouchiquois arrowhead forked like a serpent's tongue, a Hiroquois arrow (which brave Monsieur de Champlain had pulled from his ear! – he let her touch the scar . . .), a little Montagnais drum of deerskin or moose-skin, a sleek otter pelt which she took to bed with her, sleeping with her cheek against its cheek so that no bad dreams of Savages hurt her. Then there was a long time when she did not see Monsieur de Champlain; she'd nearly forgotten him when he called upon her father again, and her father said: Run, girl, and pay your courtesies to Monsieur de Champlain! and Monsieur de Champlain brought her some sweet brown juice from a tree of Canada called *maple*, and Hélène thought that she'd never tasted anything so fine, and threw her arms around Monsieur de Champlain, begging and wheedling for more as she pulled the hairs of his beard with sticky little hands, and he was laughing *ha ha ha* from the pit of his belly and suddenly her mother and father were standing there too and her mother said in a caressing voice: Hélène, would you like to marry Monsieur de Champlain?

Marry him? Mama, how silly!

A silence, and her mother's face turned crimson with rage, and Hélène shrank against Monsieur de Champlain, who suddenly seemed her only friend, and he sat her on his knee – she must have been very small then – and he was saying to her mother: But no, Madame, we need not discuss it further at this time. There is no reason to make the child fret . . . – and she recalled little else that was said, but she did remember that Monsieur de Champlain did not bounce her on his knee as her father did, but sat quite still, as if he were abashed, and his knee-bone was sharp like a tree-root; but then he began to tell her another story about how he'd saved some good Savages from the Hiroquois to make them Christians and she gazed at him with admiration, seeing the dark forest now rush before her as he spoke, and her breast ached with pride that he was telling this tale to *her*; no girl could ever have a better friend than Monsieur de Champlain . . . – while Hélène's parents fidgeted, seeing too well how Champlain was telling stories only to himself . . .

My Mama is angry at me, she whispered through tears which he longed to wipe away.

I know why, he said dryly. You don't want to marry me.

Please don't let's talk about it, Monsieur de Champlain. I know that I'm going to be married . . .

Are you afraid?

She nodded very quickly; the tears sprang from her cheeks faster and faster . . .

You must place your trust in me, Hélène. I'll be kind to you just like your own father –

You promise?

I promise.

I believe you, Monsieur de Champlain. – But I wish I had some bonbons.

He bowed gravely so that his head touched hers as she sat there on his lap. – Then you shall have them. And when you're a little older and can comprehend the True Faith, then I'll present you with your very own Cross of silver . . .

(That had been years ago, she thought. But she wasn't sure. As long as she could remember, there had been Monsieur de Champlain.)

Hélène, it's all arranged. You're going to be married this Décembre. (Thus her mother, smiling with that special smile that pretended that nothing had happened.) Monsieur de Champlain is the man for you. You're still just a baby; you don't know what's best. Try to do as you're told, and don't make us cross.

I don't know . . . muttered the girl, watching her wiggling fingers.

Hélène, do you promise to obey your husband?

Yes, Mama. I promise. But sometimes I –

Yes? What do you mean to say?

Nothing.

Ah, my pauvrette, I'll help you with everything . . .

Will he take me away? Mama, I don't want to go away!

That's up to Monsieur de Champlain. But I think he'll be willing to leave you with us for another year or two. Of course someday . . . Don't worry, silly! We're not trying to get rid of you! Hélène! Stop it, Hélène! You're as stupid as a little paysanne!

The Accolades

This barbon of forty years – and with a little fillette of twelve . . . – It's shameful, I tell you! (Thus Pontgravé, whispering in every dirty corner that he could, his mouth and eyes so wide with astonishment at this disgusting turn of events that he looked like an old cod.)

Surely she is still *impubère*. Why, he could be her grandfather!

If he got started early.

Eh, *she'll* get started early enough, Monsieur – I tell you! Say, do you recall that case with the Sieur de Lefebvre's wife?

Ah, that fourteen-year-old?

Fourteen? She was thirteen – only a year older than this Hélène Boullé! And he was forty-five! A roué, too, they say. No wonder the wife was condemned for incest three years after . . . How she screamed when they burned her! And her name was Marguerite, too, just like Hélène's sister (who knows whom they'll marry *her* to?)

Terrible! Horrible! Not at all chic! In Canada, no doubt, such things happen among those painted cannibals, but here in France it's a different kettle of codfish!

It *should* be, anyhow. Nauseating, that old Champlain!

. . . Pontgravé was happy. He'd made Champlain see reason at last. That forty-five hundred had gone straight into De Monts' coffers (well, four thousand, anyway, for Pontgravé must have his kickback), with the understanding that it was earmarked solely for Kebec; and that Champlain would never be supplanted – GOD's balls, I'm doing the sucker a favor! – but he'd take it wrong, Seigneur de Monts; let's not tell him about the forty-five hundred; and for my part *I'll* keep mum, mon vieux, old Canada pal of mine . . .

The Bridegroom

He loved her as he loved the little Montagnais girls who gazed at him starving in winter with the snot frozen on their lips and the DEVIL in their hearts – he ached for them.

He said to her: In two years, you will be fourteen. Then I think you will make a public predication of the True Faith. Do you comprehend me?

No, Monsieur, she whispered low . . .

. . . and he told her the tale of GOUGOU so that she shrieked aloud with delightful chills of fear and pressed his hand hard and then (although he had remained honorable) her face turned red and she pulled her hand away and he sat smiling uncertainly into the fire.

Captain Merveille's Kiss

Meanwhile the Country of the Huron continued untrodden by the Iron People, and there came a great sleet at Kebec, and the Fleuve Saint-Laurent was frozen. Seagulls swirled around the unbuilt Basilica like snowflakes. (In the public circle by it, today's walkways form a rayed disk, in the place where Born Underwater once stood. But that also had not yet happened. Born Underwater was still a little baby in Acadia; the Basilica was but a slight resistance in the icy air. Frenchmen and Savages strode through it like ghosts.) Snow fell upon Duval's skull, crowning it with spurious veneration – how Captain Merveille laughed to see it! – for he'd left Robert for the nonce, as I have said, in order to increase his longing subjection to any proposal which he, the great Captain Merveille, might utter. Of course this was only the *primary* reason for the change of scene. With Captain Merveille, everything also had *secondary* and *tertiary* reasons to complete a Trinity not unlike the Three Points of some Contemplation or other in Ignatius's Exercises. The *secondary* reason was that since Robert's assault upon Born Swimming had exasperated all the other French (except Champlain, who had not been informed), it was well to pretend like indignation so as not to be too closely associated with the deed. The *tertiary* was that since the Savages were exasperated as well, little could be hoped for from the beaver trade in Acadia, at least until the spring. – Off to Kebec! – It was the ominous month of Septembre, when icebergs begin to bloom upon the Canadian Sea. He rode in a pinnace with some Basque fishermen, who thought him superb, as he spoke their language. They discussed their countryman, the Blessed Ignatius, with all his merits and demerits; a liver-snatcher hovered overhead, and Merveille detonated it with a single careless shot, at which the Basques threw their caps into the air, and Merveille smiled thin-lipped, saying: No, Messieurs, *those* are too pretty to shoot . . . The ropes of the mast sang in the wind like viol-strings, but he kept on: how he longed to see old Duval at Kebec! So here he was; he tossed down a few pelts in payment for his passage; and there was Duval, grinning down at him, snowhaired and snowhatted with a mound of the best! It was a sugarloaf sort of hat that his skull wore, very grand and becoming – rather more so, indeed, than the grey icicles which had grown down from his teeth.

Champlain, you finally gave it to him, bastard! (Thus Merveille, laughing like a loon.)

May I ask your business here, Monsieur? (Thus the Sieur de Godet. The Basques had already departed: remembering the affair of Duval, in which their cousins and nephews had been falsely wooed, they had no wish to take any chances at Kebec – no, not them!)

Seigneur, I was with the Sieur de Champlain in Acadia. I was given to comprehend that there is a need for men here at this post . . .

And who were that shadowy crew who dropped you here?

Basques, Seigneur.

Basques? *Basques!* I believe I should throw you in the dungeon! The Sieur de Champlain specifically warned me against Basques . . .

Seigneur de Godet, I pray you: do feel free to test my loyalty. We can overtake them in a shallop if I hail them. Then, when we get within range, give me a match; I'll fire the cannon! Believe me, I'm a hundred percent French!

Godet blinked. He sat down. – I know not what to make of you, Merveille. Is there anyone who can vouch for you?

The Sieur de Pontgravé once enrolled me to teach his son marksmanship. He knows me well.

Gravé du Pont is in France, said Godet, slowly, perplexed. I know not what to say . . . – He regarded the new arrival for a long time – a scrutiny submitted to with high good humor, for the outcome was no longer unclear. – Eh, by Heaven! (Thus the Sieur de Godet.) I know not why I ponder this so much! You must forgive me, Merveille. Of course you are welcome here; in fact, tonight you will stand the watch, in lieu of one of my sentries who is ill with the scurvy . . .

It was night, one of those Canadian winter nights that begin almost the previous noon and last long through morning, rubbing its slimy black ice-face against the back of your neck, weighing down your shoulders with shivers. The Sieur de Godet slept within; most of the others did likewise; a few played cards . . . Merveille was on duty. He paced to and fro upon his terrace. The other sentry was invisible in the darkness; he was stationed at the Store-house. Merveille had the better position; he was permitted to move, at least. Oh, it was cold! Every time he passed the skull, he bowed ironically. Yet even so the hours passed slowly, so that he felt constrained to provide better entertainment for himself. Thus he began a discourse to the skull, in the most fashionable manner, saying: – Duval, my dear, do you recall how once I helped Robert plan out his future? Now it is your turn, for while you are just as surly now as you were alive, I have nothing better to do. Strange to see that you are almost more effective in your new and lasting form! I never thought I would see you so handsome! Eh, that is all to the good – for I propose the same thing to you that I did to Robert: you must needs be mated! When men come to Canada, they leave their families behind; they become as lonely and alien as your icicles. But men are not made of bone only. They have other parts which must be exercised. So Robert insisted, and how can I disagree? Now you, of course, have no membrum virile with which to pierce squaws; you have no arms to seize them and beat them about the face, no legs to kick them senseless, no proud belly to squash them down on the ground – in fact, my dear Duval, you possess very little beneath the chin, unless we are to count the pole that you rattle on as your neck! Can we? Let me take you down and see. Uggh, you're frozen fast! Well, a knock or two with the butt of this arquebus will loosen matters – tap, tap! So sorry, old fellow!

The moon had risen. His breath was frosty. He peered over the railing, down at the blackish water of the Fleuve Saint-Laurent, in which streamed white crystal-islands . . .

He held Duval's skull in his hands.

Ah, he said smiling, if I had golden hooks or pendoirs on which to hang you, what a shining lamp you'd be!

At his shoulder, atop the rock of Kebec, the Plains of Abraham merged with the snowy moonlight so that he could not see the long, low, tunnel-ridden walls that now run between the snow-shoulders; the British built them two centuries later when they built the Citadel.

Oui, you must be mated, Duval! But who would have you; who would take you? Who but I? I'm GOUGOU, you see!

Laughing at his fancy, he kissed the skull, but it was so cold that his lips stuck to it. He couldn't believe it! Moaning, he pulled until his skin ripped. Then in a fury he hurled the skull over the railing. It rolled down snow-softened slopes as lightly as a padding cat; it scuttered across the ice of the Fleuve Saint-Laurent and broke through at last; now the real GOUGOU seized it and set it underneath that fathom-long hank of Fox's scalp and seaweed ornamented with wampum-shells so that now GOUGOU had a white bone-face and eye-pits to see through (but no eyes) and GOUGOU lolled beneath the ice and wondered what GOD would give Him next . . . And GOUGOU looked inside His new skull to see what it contained; He strained to make the memories come forth to give Him more Power; He stroked it with His softest slimiest hairs, but it was like all skulls; all that it could say was: *je ne me souviens pas*: I don't remember . . . So GOUGOU remained blind and mindless.

The Stream of Time 1610–1611

As for Champlain, sleeping on starched sheets at the Maison Boullé, with the future presence of his bride scarcely warm in the adjoining room, he dreamed that the rivers were low, and he waded along their flat beds of shale on a hot day toward the end of summer; the streams came scarcely above his ankles. He was still in France, although the landscape was Canadian. He smelled honey and spruce-gum; all was beautiful, and yet a feeling of dread was with him. In the dream all water bore some disease, and everyone was dying or dead. He himself had been infected. The houses were boarded up; and water ran beneath their foundations. The Roy had died, and with him all his Grand Seigneurs and Ministers. In the river he passed a mother with a sick boy; she held the child by the hand, but stood upstream, so that the lethal humors which he exuded would flow away from her; though the child laughed and splashed, his cheeks were pale: tomorrow he would be dead. He saw Hélène; she too had died, and was floating downstream very slowly; the sash of her dress continually snagged on some rock, at which her corpse would slowly work around until the position of head and feet were reversed; then, being momentarily freed, she traveled a little farther downstream, toward a roar as of rapids which came from around a shady bend . . . – What an idiotic dream!

He boarded with his parents-in-law throughout the brumal months, taking good care never to press his attentions on Hélène too forcefully. Each day, no matter what his other business, he troubled himself to speak to her with a courtesy that always left her abashed – and he spoke in the same wise to her mother, her father, her sister Marguerite, her brother Nicolas, and even to the servants; so that, like Godet regarding Merveille, she was left in confusion as to whom he really cared for – for it seemed impossible that he could care for them all. Yet perhaps he did. Certainly he was good – perhaps he was good enough for that. She herself could not love everyone, although she strove to. Sometimes she flew into a rage at Marguerite and secretly pinched her to make her cry, as when she broke one of Hélène's treasured Savage things that Monsieur de Champlain had given her. On other occasions she found herself hating her father, or even Monsieur de Champlain (she could not yet call him husband, although he was). But why? He was kind to her always. His neck and face and arms were so red that it made her laugh. Strong and patient, he looked into her face with the docile eyes of a horse – so honest and eternally present – and she believed in her soul that he would never serve any other of her sex. But *husband?* He was so very old!

In point of fact he was in his prime, as he well knew (peering into the mirror, setting his moustache right until he could take full pleasure in his appearance). The first frost of grey at his temples had simply silvered him, like a ruddy copper double-coin being transmuted to a higher denomination. His eyes were still bright (as he saw for himself in the mirror); he walked with a swinging step; his shoulders bulged, threatening to burst through his coat with implacable life. His very back, as Hélène saw, watching him silently from the window, was a great slab of muscle which flexed wide and powerful – Day by day I am taming her, he said to himself. I must have patience.

In the month of Février, 1611, he was summoned to the Château of the Sieur de Monts, where he went with the greatest joy. The thought of the voyage before him made his heart pound. In Mars he set out again for Canada.

The Twentieth Rapids

Powers of the Soul

On the twenty-first of Mai, when the white violets were in flower, he attained Kebec, where the Sieur de Godet gave him good greeting. There had been scarcely any scurvy-deaths, for which he gave thanks to GOD. The Habitation was showing signs of wear, and he set his sawyers to putting it in good order for the next frost. He helped them measure . . . Someone had tampered with the lock on his Store-house, but Godet swore he knew nothing. Duval's skull was missing from its pike; he supposed that it had exploded with the winter chill. – What else? – He marched about, inspecting everything, jingling the keys in his hand; he distributed wine, brandy and hard biscuit to the men, who received their portion very gratefully. He took down the portrait of the Grand Roy, Henri IV, now dead from the assassin Ravillac's knife, and raised in its place a likeness of his son Louys XIII – at that time only nine years of age, so that his mother must be Regent; but the phrenologists at Court predicted great things of him, every one of which Champlain believed. So when the boy-King looked palely down upon them from the wall, he led them all in singing the *Te Deum*, and his voice shook the rafters (though Pontgravé's really rattled them); then he set out the customary hogshead of cider, just as poor Poutrincourt would have done. Striking his spy-glass against his knuckles, he then spoke with them one and all, chastising or praising them as they merited. He tapped dubious beams and listened for rot. He welcomed Merveille, who was a hardy and invaluable man, and asked after Robert; next (tap, tap) he demanded the news from Acadia, which Merveille gave, although he could see that Champlain was not very interested; indeed, at one point he interrupted and said: I believe that Acadia must always lag behind Canada proper in the matter of settlement! – at which Merveille bowed and said: I admit it, Seigneur; I grant it freely. You are the Captain of this place; your knowledge is superior . . . – at which Champlain beamed and thought to himself: Indeed this fellow possesses an intelligence of the finest water!

And have the Basques been lurking about? he said abruptly to Godet.

No, Seigneur. We've not seen them. Not since they brought this man –

Good, good.

Hollanders?

There's a nest of them in the Armouchiquois Country. Trading with the Yroquois. Pillaged a few of our ships. I've had requests for protection –

Eh, the Hollanders are weak (don't you agree, Merveille?) We can rout them out at any time. But our fortifications are in good order?

Yes, Seigneur.

And no more conspiracies. I will have no more conspiracies, Godet.

Oh, no. And no Hiroquois –

Hiroquois? Of course not, Godet. You had nothing to fear from them. And did the men keep the fasts?

In the main, Seigneur, and the offenders have repented of their sins.

Champlain clapped him on the back. – I can see that you have been diligent.

The Savages had not yet arrived with their furs, but already there were so many traders crouched about the place, greedy and inharmonious, that they would soon be ruined if steps were not taken. It was, as Pontgravé would say, "a serious case." (At least the price of beaver kept going up. A skin sold in France for eight-and-a-half livres now.) Everywhere he went, the traders followed him, flattering him, threatening him, striking one another with their fists:

Champlain, where are the redskins? They're holding us up! If they don't come soon we're going to set fire to the woods. How'd you like that, Champlain? *Champlaaaaaaaaaaaaaaaaaaaaaaaaaaain?*

Champlain, I'll protect you from these greedy Rochelais bastards if you give me a commission!

Champlain, I'll keep the Malouins off your back!

Champlain, where are you hiding the squaws? Come on – you scratch my back, I'll scratch yours! Knock off the JESUS act! It's only human weakness . . .

He was liberal and courteous with them – even with them! – for so he was bound in honor to be. But he could hardly sleep. They were destroying the trade. He said to himself: Delay is prejudicial; I must obtain the backing of grand personages! De Monts does not have sufficient authority.

Suddenly a thought bubbled and laughed in his brain: *I'll shoot the rapids at Lachine. Lescarbot said I couldn't do it. I must instill in the Savages the conviction that I'm superior to this rabble of traders!*

He had to meet the Huron Captains anyhow, secretly, to discuss the trade. Iroquet the Algoumequin was taking him.

He sailed up the Fleuve Saint-Laurent, reaching unborn Montréal on its isle of blue haze besieged by hurtfully shining white throughout that hot river-summer; and to the east, the great Fleuve faded into the haze. The broad trunks of trees were braided with diamonds, like rivers and rattlesnakes. Harquebus at his shoulder, he strolled about, but the place was deserted. There were some ruins of lodges on the hill called Place Royale. Had the Hiroquois since driven them away? Or had they been Yrocois themselves? –

No matter. Down to the shore. Here he commanded that some trees be cleared, in order to level the ground and ready it for the construction of edifices. After all, one must always be prepared for Providence. Who knew whether De Monts would keep the Habitation at Kebec? And indeed the English might come, as he foresaw full well when making his sort of Exercises . . . On an adjoining isle he set his artisans to build a wall of earth, ten fathoms in height, to see whether it would hold or crack in the winter frost. A good strong town could be erected here; he must write it to the Roy. He named the isle Saint-Hélène after his wife (Pontgravé sniggered at that . . .)

On the thirteenth day of Juin, he saw the Savages in good numbers. Their cheeks and noses were painted blue, which made their eyes seem more liquidly mysterious than ever. Why did they masque themselves in this barbaric way? He would never comprehend them. – For peltries he traded them some fine iron axeheads heavy and dark. He asked for news, and they said that a Montagnais Sagamore well known to him had died – *viz.*, Anadabijou. Champlain could never recall him without that lewd dance of naked privities unrolling in his mind, glistening most shamefully . . . And how young Robert had stared! Vile! Filthy! Someday all that would be suppressed. And now he was dead. Burning in Hell, no doubt. I feel old. The Algoumequins were bringing his son condolence presents –

Eh, on to Lachine. The rapids roared and boiled –

His subaltern Brûlé had done it before him, it was true. But Brûlé was of little account, being an orphan ten years of age. That was why he'd permitted him to go, as a sort of human sounding . . . (Talk about testing the waters! sputtered Pontgravé with laughter. The poor kid! Give him a tot of brandy first!) Yes, Champlain would be the first Christian of any rank to accomplish the feat. He could already see De Monts' gentle smile of love and comprehension when he told him how he'd risked his life on these rapids, solely to increase his estimation in the eyes of the Savages; and he could see Hélène pretty and breathless and close to tears on his behalf as he told her the tale, she squealing wide-eyed: Papa, Monsieur de Champlain is so brave! and he'd imitate the gush and spray of the rapids for Marguerite, who was still young enough to laugh at childish noises (how fond he was of her! Marguerite had been his mother's name . . .); he'd give young Nicolas one of the Algoumequins' stone hatchets; he'd take Eustache aside and explain to him exactly how he'd managed it (the boy already longed to go to Canada, and Champlain had promised him that he should come as soon as Monsieur Boullé considered him of age). Oh, what Exercises he made! Like everyone else in insoluble difficulties, he persuaded himself of the easy shallows ahead.

I must remember, no matter how much it boils about me, that in no place does the fall exceed three fathoms. (Thus Champlain.)

The Algonkin and the Montagnets were having one of their orgies or *tabagies*, in honor perhaps of their dead Captain, Anadabijou. He did not have the patience to inquire. Not today.

Watch the skiff, Merveille, and keep our painted friends from pilferage. If anything befalls me, you are in command until Kebec.

What do you aim to do, Seigneur?

Watch the skiff, Merveille.

Yes, Seigneur.

He strode through the forest, the branches whipping against his face, the little creeks gurgling like wine-jugs, and he prayed that he would not see their Savagesses naked again. He smelled the dogs and the smoking fish and green skins. He strode down the muddy trail to where they were yelling and they fell silent and regarded him black-eyed. Indeed these Algoumequins were not quite as friendly as they had been ten years before.

GOD's greeting to you all, my friends, he said to them. And where is your Captain?

Sick, Champlain. Many of us die of sickness now.

I wish to ride the rapids, he said at last. The words came out of his throat with difficulty. He knew that they could never be unsaid. Not in Canada.

Who will take me? he said.

They watched him.

Champlain took a new knife from his pack and held it so that it glittered silver in the sun. – I shall give one of these to each man who rides in the canoe with me.

We all have iron knives now, Champlain.

He put the knife away. – You lie to me and become insolent, he said to them. – I see it growing in you. You displease me to speak so.

He waited.

Who will take me? he said.

He waited.

He smiled. – Last night I dreamed that all of you who did not take me were burned by the Hiroquois.

What a tintamarre! How the females began to scream! Oh, he knew his Savages! He turned on his heel and began to walk away.

I will take you, Champlain.

Ah, Iroquet, is it you?

Yes, Champlain. I fought the Irinokhoïw* with you. I will take you.

Just you?

I am now in my father's place.

I know that. I make it my business, Yroquet. I'll give you three knives.

Three knives?

And as many dried prunes as you can take in one hand.

That is a good gift, Champlain. I will take you.

Your people are insolent. Your people are cowardly, Iroquet.

The youth drew himself up haughtily. – We are masters in our own Country. We have no care for the opinions of bearded men.

Champlain bit his lip. He could not force them all to see reason at this time. He must be patient. He said: You know that I am the friend of all of you, Iroquet. I have fought against the Hiroquois . . .

Yes, we honor you, Champlain. I will get my canoe now.

Champlain went away. He came out into the sunlight and stood blinking at the Fleuve Saint-Laurent and there stood Iroquet with some other Algoumequins and their canoes were drawn up on the shore.

They went up the Indian trail between the pines and the rapids, and the river skipped white and hellish down its stony steps and stung him with misty drops as he climbed, Iroquet striding steadily ahead of him with the canoe upon his shoulders so that he resembled a double-billed pelican or some other monstrously impossible bird. The Savages were very strong: in that respect they put good Frenchmen to shame. – But I am not so young as I used to be, he admitted to himself.

Silently he commended himself to GOD.

They reached the lookout where he'd stood in 1603, sketching the long islands that beset this cascade as Pontgravé stood sopping up sweat with a handkerchief, in exactly the same greedy manner that he wiped up gravy with his bread. But Pontgravé was at Tadoussac today. – There were even more rocks and dangerous shoals than he had remembered. It would be very easy to drown here. But now his map was feathered with hills, trees, encampments and ripples all the way to the blank northwest; it did not matter now what happened.

The forest exploded with raspberries.

He followed Iroquet along the bluff to a place where there was grass and the land eased gently down to meet the Fleuve Saint-Laurent above the rapid,

* Iroquois.

and Iroquet had set down his canoe and was looking into the sky and laughing with joy and saying: It is good to see the SUN, Champlain!

That is so. And Who made the sun?

GOD did, Champlain.

That is correct. You are very clever, Iroquet, and now my heart is moved with affection for you. To your gifts I add a fine new hatchet.

I thank you, Champlain. You are good.

I am good only because I adore IESUS. Do you comprehend me?

No, Champlain.

Eh, let's go.

The young man stood looking down the fall for a moment. Then he leaped into the water and stood holding the still half on land for Champlain to climb into, which he did. Iroquet swung himself into the stern of the canoe and said: Do not be afraid, Champlain.

I fear nothing but GOD.

Yes, Champlain. We honor you.

They floated downstream, and then they began moving faster and faster and a blue-green wall of pine flickered by and the canoe struck a rock with a noise like a gunshot and flung them both sideways and the canoe almost tipped but Iroquet did something with the paddle and suddenly they were steady again and Iroquet was very pale and sweating as they approached the falls and Champlain bowed his head to pray and saw water coming in where the canoe had struck and shouted at Iroquet but Iroquet couldn't hear him because the noise of the water was so loud and they bumped down and bumped down and Champlain took out his handkerchief and wedged it into the leak and they struck a rock and he seized the gunnels holding them as he'd once clung to the pommel of a skittish horse in the Civil War and they fell a fathom and slammed down into a pool that rushed them over another lip and they crashed and fell as Iroquet crouched flicking his paddle from side to side, his head swivcling very fast, and a great gout of spray half filled the canoe and Champlain bailed water frantically with his hands as they whirled in an eddy and bumped a shoal and passed one of the razor-thin islands he'd seen from the lookout; he could have run his hand along it as they passed; that was how close they were, and Iroquet was looking up at the sun and laughing as they fell three fathoms and smashed down on a rock that tore the bottom of the canoe open and they teetered atop a wall of white water and then tumbled crazily down it, Champlain bracing his feet as hard as he could against the sides of the canoe since the bottom was so far gone now that he could see rocks and fishes between his legs and something hairy whisked out a tentacle and took his handkerchief because Duval's head fancied it and the two green minnows in Duval's white eyesockets swam back and forth in glee as GOUGOU considered whether or not to eat Champlain and Iroquet but by the time GOUGOU made up His mind to do it they were already long past Him, having spilled down a thousand steps of rapid, embracing the half-wrecked frame of the canoe in love and terror and rage as the rocks sliced their legs and they tumbled into the sun with Iroquet laughing so passionately that Champlain thought himself inside the belfry of some French church with the bells tolling between his ears and he could no longer comprehend anything but the jolting roar downward and he clung to the canoeframe with his eyes closed, trusting in Iroquet, thinking of nothing else, not even GOD, until he knew that they would make it through to Sainte-Hélène's isle and already he could hear the Savages shouting below and Merveille fired off one of the harquebuses and he was so happy and Iroquet was caressing his face . . .

That night his Algoumequins held a dance, in celebration of his triumph as he assumed. The stamping dancers, painted in stripes from shoulder to ankle, shook their war-clubs and tossed their proudly feathered heads, grinning and sweating and shouting, their long greasy hair flying about their shoulders, their bearclaw necklaces rattling on their chests as the fire crackled and the Old Man beat the drum, and narrow-faced women headbanded with quill-worked triangles and diamonds smiled in excitement, and their wampum-strung braids clicked together against their wampum necklaces and their painted eyesockets glistened in the firelight almost as brilliantly as the glistening of their eyeballs.

He said to himself: They know me now to be as great as any of them.

He said to himself: May this have been for the glory of GOD.

And I suppose I should pay a visit to my wife – poor dear child . . .

He'd met with his new allies the Huron, in that place above the falls, and they agreed to bring him beaver-skins in exchange for iron, which they found quite novel. Pontgravé scented profit all the way from Tadoussac and hastened to join them, his suspenders almost bursting. Seeing how fat he was, they cried: *Behold the fallen star!* for in their traditions a STAR had once fallen from Heaven in the form of a fat goose. Pontgravé laughed and winked and pinched his belly for them; he was very jovial. Then they flocked to Pontgravé, leaving Champlain to suck on imaginary lemons, but Pontgravé saw this and said: No, no, my friends; the Sieur de Champlain is your Captain, not I . . . – at which Champlain felt a terrible ache of gratitude and love. Now the Savages returned to him, as was only his due, and invited him most tenderly to visit their Country, caressing his face in their manner, but some Algoumequins who were there grew sour, fearing the loss to their trade, so he thought quickly and said: Someday we shall all fight together once more, against the Hiroquois! – at which they exclaimed in happiness, and the Huron chanted a War-Song: *Wiiiiiiiiiiiiiiiiiiiiiiii!*

But that will be another year, he said quickly. When I have the leisure to drill and instruct you –

There was nothing else doing in Canada that summer, the trading having proved so poor – disgustingly so, in fact, thanks to the spiteful and irreligious actions of these Rochelais and Malouin merchants. De Monts would not be pleased. And to think (as Pontgravé so often did) that even five years ago any clown could clear four hundred crowns in a season! – I myself am happy not to live my life for such things, necessary though they may be (thus Champlain).

After repairing the Habitation and planting some rose-bushes for Hélène, he left Tadoussac on Août the eleventh. The sea was mild, the voyage without incident. Broad-shouldered and laughing, he served out brandy to the sailors; he and Pontgravé played round after round of cards, but Pontgravé always won . . . – No matter! cried Pontgravé. Pay up! And let's drink a toast to Samuel de Champlain, the Hero of Lachine! – Champlain smiled shyly. – I am very grateful to you, he said, but you need not mention it. – The men thought him wonderful, it was true. Whenever they saw him they poked each other in the ribs and said: If you please, tell us about those rapids again, Seigneur! – But he didn't let it go to his head. He took his accustomed soundings; he slept by day and woke by night, spying on the helmsman like a silent ghost. On the tenth evening of Septembre he found La Rochelle looming ahead, with its docks and dogs and turreted lighthouses, and the dusk was peach-colored.

Ah, I don't know whether the harbor is more the hue of mud or oranges, sighed Pontgravé sentimentally, hawking over the side. – Sure is handsome, though – eh, Champlain? Something about the home waters . . .

Across the bay, steeples, domes and house-fronts hid their indistinctness in a glory neither pink nor gold, and two crows flew overhead, so free. The pilot folded his arms on his chest in his usual self-satisfied way – as if he'd done anything! Pilots are a bunch of chiselers! – thus Pontgravé to himself, whistling a little, as Champlain frowned and thought: And what would the fat cockerel say if I offered to bet against Madame de Pontgravé's life? How'd he like that then? and he glared at him, when suddenly, as if the power of that glare (which Pontgravé hadn't even seen) were supernatural, diabolical, Pontgravé grunted with pain. A fit of gout had seized him. He burst out in sweat and bent over the railing as if in seasickness, gripping it with swollen purple hands. Then, bit by bit, the pain ebbed. Champlain shook his head, feeling as guilty as if he had caused the whole thing.

Slowly Pontgravé's face became its accustomed color. He smiled gratefully to see Champlain at his shoulder with a pannikin of water . . . Anyhow it was nothing. (Even if it wasn't, he had nothing to fear. He'd long since made contrition for all his evil deeds!) Already he could make out the Controlleur of Customs, purple-faced and stout like him, mon semblable, mon frère, standing impatiently upon the jetty, and the smells of dead fish and excrement grew stronger and Madame de Pontgravé stood sobbing happily and waving a handkerchief.

Hélène was not there. Doubtless some circumstance at home had occupied her –

Whatever shall we *do*, my dear Champlain? (Thus De Monts; thus fretful De Monts.) They were at his Château in Pons, sipping brandy, De Monts almost in tears, Champlain sober, patient, anxious. It seemed that the merchants of Saint-Malo had obtained the Roy Louis' ear (or rather the Queen-Mother's, for the boy continued to be too young to rule in his own name), and again the monopoly had been lost. Our backers ridicule the whole idea of Canada now – wasn't that the cold place where we used to send criminals?

We must appeal to the Roy himself, Seigneur.

Ah, the Roy likes you. Or at least his father did. As I often used to say to the Sieur de Poutrincourt, you're very good at certain kinds of work. I have every confidence that you'll get a step ahead of these traders and open the way to China. You assured me of that on the Isle de Sainte-Croix. You do remember Isle de Sainte-Croix? Eh, I see that you do. I promised you then that I'd keep you with me, year in, year out . . . – Why *do* you think that the Roy's late father liked you so much?

I shall set out for Court at once, Seigneur. But first I must visit my wife. After all, I have not seen her since the month of Mars . . .

I can see that that's essential for you. Go, then. Pontgravé tells me you shot the rapids in a canoe.

Yes, Seigneur.

That was ill advised. Do you think you're a young man like Brûlé?

No, Seigneur. Au revoir.

He set out for Paris. De Monts sat by himself. After awhile he opened a chest and drew out his first bill of monopoly, dated 1603, in which the dead Roy named him Lieutenant-General of Acadia, with all requisite powers and duties, and the great 𝕳 of the Roy's name was a lattice upon which grew toothy leaves of flame; and he sighed.

Champlain galloped on, his joy in himself reduced to ashes. He jerked the reins brutally, and his horse stumbled and fell upon him. He was laid up at an inn for almost a month.

And were you anxious for me, my sweet little Hélène?

She burst into tears.

He felt very awkward. – Come now, he said to her. I was not so badly injured as that. It was much worse when I had the dysentery at Mechique!

He stretched out his hand to her; she would not take it.

Have you felt lonely? he said. Are you dissatisfied with your position here?

Eyes swollen with crying, she nodded very rapidly, her head hanging down.

If you desire to be my wife more completely, he said to her, you know that there is a provision in the marriage contract which allows us to call family and friends together. Then you could sleep in the same bed as I . . .

She ran from the room as though she were going to vomit.

The following day she was silent, and he did not disturb her, believing that she was considering well whether she wished to remain a maiden for the stipulated term or whether indeed she felt it high time to give him her pucelage. The next day was the same, and then the next. Then suddenly she began to provoke him with many childish scenes. Her mother Madame Boullé was soon exasperated, and slapped her face, at which Champlain begged her to desist, as he believed that he might correct her more kindly. If she had not been of the weaker sex, then indeed he might have beaten her for the good of her own soul, which must be taught to love obedience – but she was just a fillette! Therefore he must keep down the hot surge of rage that sought to rise in his chest . . .

The Third Isle of Prayer

Breathing Control

Being now fully healed from his injuries, he rode to Court and presented to the Roy all his maps and reports, which the Queen-Mother took into her hand, as her son was still one year shy of his majority. No one in the Palace was greatly concerned with Canada's riches, as indeed he had expected; yet De Monts and Pontgravé now cast their nets down those corridors, the former with desperate intensity (for he strove to regain his monopoly), the latter with his usual stolid dexterity; and the old Notary with whom Poutrincourt's factotum had dealt so long ago, who'd seen monopolies swim into so many nets and out of them again, was at length summoned to prepare a new document in the name of the Sieur de Champlain. Scribbling and blinking, the Notary did Pontgravé's will. When the parchment was ready, a gold-clad henchman rose to the surface with it, like a beetle clutching an air-bubble; and so, on the eighth day of Octobre, he awarded Champlain the right to govern in the name of the new Lieutenant-General – *viz.*, the Comte de Soissons. The Comte soon died (which cost Pontgravé a gold livre and two doubles), but his successor, the Prince de Condé, confirmed Champlain as his Deputy on the twenty-second day of Novembre, so that henceforth Champlain would be permitted to appoint Captains, to treat with Savages or make war upon them should they prove obstinate, to seize the possessions of renegade merchants, and other such necessary marks of rank. Ha! – Samuel de Champlain, Lieutenant to the Viceroy!

A Conversation

My dear Pontgravé, why do you never see fit to take these titles in your name? For we all know who actually governs at Kebec. (Thus the Sieur de Monts.)

But I'm only there coming and going! laughed the one addressed. You flatter me, Seigneur.

Perhaps I do. But I could very easily get rid of Champlain if you wish it.

Pontgravé was embarrassed. He blew his nose to give himself time to think. Since he'd married him off he'd become quite fond of Champlain; the man was useful.

Don't worry about him, Seigneur! he said at last. He keeps us free to do our business.

Grand. Grand. (Thus De Monts.) Well, encourage him to explore Canada, at least. I'm really quite annoyed about the absence of those silver mines. Do help him extend his charts. Persuade him to explore the Chinese hinterlands. He never does anything on his own; I'm always waiting upon him for an explanation –

The truth was, however, that De Monts would never have given Champlain up now. Like Pontgravé he was attached to him, but for different reasons. From De Monts' point of view, Champlain was the incorruptible prig that every master dreams of. He would never take so much as a biscuit from De Monts' Store-house without leaving a receipt for it. Better still, as he was diligent and had no great authority of his own, he could be blamed for everything.

The Exercise of Mortification

Hélène had also come to blame her husband for many things, but being young she had not yet realized (as in his heart De Monts had) what a benefit and convenience it was to have such a scapegoat. Whenever he spoke to her, she stared at him as though she did not comprehend what he had said. Her mother Madame Boullé had reproved her many times for this behavior, both privately and in her husband's presence, but she only listened motionlessly. Her father had begun to repent of his cruelty in forcing her into this marriage (indeed, his son-in-law was by no means as distinguished as he had at first believed), but as they were now joined by GOD, there was nothing to be done any longer save to resign themselves to one another and to His will. The Sieur de Boullé had learned to fear his wife's temper and also that of his daughter, so he kept out of it, which is probably the greatest mistake he could have made. But after all, there are times when we harm by doing, and others when we harm by abstaining. If there were certainty in this world, what need would there be for the DEVIL?

On the twenty-eighth of Novembre, Hélène's sister Marguerite made a brilliant marriage to Charles de Landes, who was Secrétaire to this same Prince de Condé. Champlain had had something to do with this; the Sieur de Monts considerably more, because there was no reason not to build on the foundation of Champlain's espousals if doing so would bind more men of authority to the enterprise at Kebec. This Charles was only twenty-seven years of age, and a very handsome man. Champlain bowed to the groom and kissed Marguerite most affectionately, wishing her well. Beside him, Hélène hung her head in shame. When he turned to her, she begged him in a low voice to leave her alone. Paling and biting his lip, he strode wearily to the other side of the room to speak with her brother Eustache, who was very keen to go to Canada (Monsieur de Champlain had told him about the long white beaches of the Country of the Armouchiquois, where everything was dangerous, and weird glossy weeds with leaves like bulbs or little pears rumpled their flowers at you, grinning wider than idols – a somber enough tapisserie, as one might say, but Eustache longed to see it), and Hélène stood silently sobbing, which everyone pretended not to notice except Pontgravé, who whispered to one of his cronies: Do you see that? I wonder what indecent proposition he made to her! Champlain is quite a roué in Canada, you know . . . – and speaking of indecencies, it was soon Décembre, the stipulated two years of the marriage contract now elapsed, and therefore time for

The Defloration of Hélène

Wide-eyed, she watched as he marched in with his strips of clean linen to be used as bandages if need be and his pot of boiling water and his brown soap of caustic resin held discreetly in his hand until he had made landfall at her bedside table with its girlish unguents now commanded into orderly retreat by his sea-reddened hands moving bottles to the rear so that the soap, water and bandages could be secure and in good order for any immediate need, after which he closed the door and bolted it and lit the candle then shuttered fast the windows and told her to undress and began himself to unlace his boots, his husbandly erection in readiness and his mind so disposed as to have an eye on her grand petticoats and the unfurling thereof and disembarkation therefrom as he mounted his post and made his bride fast both aloft and alow, meanwhile being likewise vigilant about matters occurring on her pale breasts and with the nipples on those stations. This difficulty being solved, and meanwhile continuing to keep up his exertions under great press of sail through deep and rhythmic soundings, he came near to his objective and yet avoided danger and put out to sea again, so to speak, not wishing to end this maiden voyage too quickly, although now it was certainly good season to bring one of those bandages to hand, and one *was* now to hand, thanks to the providence of GOD.

The Harvest 1613

In Janvier she quitted the house without her husband's permission, at which her shocked parents were forced to raise a public allegation against her. Neither they nor he could find her. Distraught, he rushed to the Lieutenant de Police and begged his assistance, but the man only laughed and said: You should have thought of this before when you engaged to be a cradle-robber! and Champlain raised his fist to strike him but he thought of disgrace and prison (such as the Sieur de Poutrincourt now faced; De Monts had not aided him, and he would scarcely aid Champlain), and his fist slowly fell . . . After a week, Hélène returned again to the house, pale and dry-eyed. He sat by the fire awaiting her. At last her mother brought her in. He had prepared his speeches well, but as soon as he saw her he saw that it was no use, and put his head in his hands.

It is not a little thing to live in quiet, he said to himself. I know that now.

Inventories

On the sixth day of Mars, he left Honfleur with Pontgravé, and they sang happy sea-songs. Hélène was unable to come to the wharf, but her brother Nicolas did, gazing at the ship with longing eyes. – Now Champlain was gone, and Hélène rushed to show her friends the Montaignez arrow that he had given her, with its blackish eagle plumes, its point of bone lashed in an X of deer tendon about the shaft. (Monsieur de Champlain had explained it all to her so that she comprehended exactly how it was made.)

On the twenty-ninth of Mars he proclaimed his commission at Tadoussac, so that all would pay him due obedience and respect. Now they loaded the casks of cider, flour, raisins and peas into the pinnace, and ferried them up to Kebec, where, directing the artisans to bring them into the Store-house, he presently came into that cool moist place and closed the door behind him; with the tally-sheet in his hand he hastened to count, weigh and receive every item: such was his happiness; such was his genius. He cross-checked the result with what he had written on the receipt for Pontgravé. Yes! Identical! Yet some of the colored glass beads from last year were missing, as he now ascertained. When he questioned the Sieur de Godet and compared his replies with Merveille's, the story came out. The clerks had traded with the Montaignez for snowshoes, of which they had had great need in Février, when the pease and flour were almost exhausted. The Montagnes had shown them how to hunt quite well, as it appeared. – Eh, he'd forgive the clerks, if they begged his pardon on bended knee . . . It was De Monts' fault anyway for not having provisioned them better (how fine it felt to blame De Monts this once!) And besides, the Store-house was crammed almost to bursting now. He'd taken on consignment from Pontgravé three milliards of hatchets, some hats, and a number of blankets with which to pay Savages. The trade that year, however, was poor; few of the Savages came to the meeting-places, partly on account of the fear and hatred which they'd conceived toward the traders, but also because the winter had been very mild, so that moose were not trapped in the snow. For this reason, many of them had starved. Then, too, as his spies told him at Kebec, the Yroquois had laid more than one cunning ambush for returning canoes. – They request iron from me? said the Sieur de Champlain. Then I shall give them lead! No doubt they will enjoy the benefit of *that* decision. – He felt very manly as he said this, and that sensation sped through his blood like a pox, until, mingling with other dangerous notions, it incited him to visit the Country of the Huron. But then, sitting so alone in the darkness of that Store-house, he remembered his obligations to his dear wife; no, for now he'd better hasten slowly.

The Exchange Students

They were a western Nation, these Huron. The men were very outlandish in their appearance, being tattooed both upon face and body like the Iroquois. (The women stayed at home, as it seemed, following good Christian custom.) In the center of their shaved pates the warriors sported immense rays of hair two fingers wide – or some of them did, at any rate; others were bald on one side, while on the other their locks fell down to their shoulders. Their language seemed to him very obscure. One of his eager French boys, that same Étienne Brûlé who'd tested the rapids of Lachine for him, listened well to their speech and reported that they seemed to possess neither *m* nor *p*, *l* nor *f* or *b* – which proved what Champlain already knew: – *viz.*, that they were not civilized. Pagans, pagans! They called him *Chawain*: there was so much that they could not say! They claimed that beaver was very plentiful in their Country. Hearing this, Champlain commanded them to take charge of this young Brûlé of his; Brûlé would inform him exactly how and where they debouched themselves –

Ah, Chawain, we are afraid to do that, said the Huron Captains. What if he dies? You would kill us!

All men are mortal, said Champlain shortly. If he dies, he dies. Do you refuse to take him?

The Huron smiled nervously.

If you do refuse, then I shall not consider you my friends.

Really Tregouaroti was not displeased to take the boy as a hostage. However, he hesitated to give the Iron People one of his own. Yet it seemed that he must. So he presented to Chawain his brother Savignon, who was willing enough to undertake the adventure . . .

Champlain took him to Paris, where he kindly corrected his most egregious misdemeanors and instructed him in the French language. This Savignon thought his uncles the Iron People to be women. Granted, their Palaces were as long as ridges, with forests of pillars, boulders of gleaming domes. The little cabins pulled by moose-pairs, those intrigued him. And their guns – ah! But as for the rest of it, they were worth little. They were loud, anxious and shrill. They were not strong. They feared one another. Day and night they disputed, using words as ugly as their beards, but these insults they rarely avenged by striking or killing one another, for which he mocked them. For this reason the Black-Gowns thought him stupid, and did not baptize him. Hélène was horrified by him. She strove to catechize him in all good charity, but the Savage's dark, puffy face regarded her suspiciously. His eyelids were bloated into pouches. His cheeks were as soft as a baby's. The too full lips parted, and the tongue came forth. She knew that she ought to consider him a treasure like any other human soul, but could not. She could hardly wait for her husband to take him back beyond the sea. Yet Champlain learned much from him. Drawing up a list of questions at De Monts' dictation, he learned that this so-called *Wendaké* was vast and rich, possibly an outlying fief of China (on this point Savignon equivocated, as it seemed to Champlain, although in charity he must acknowledge that China might have a different name in the Huron language). In any event, he'd go there, if they didn't eat young Brûlé . . . The manifold kindnesses which he and his wife were showing to Savignon even as he spoke would insure an advantage over that rabble of Malouin and Rochelais traders; De Monts said that he had to get to Wendaké before the other traders did . . .

As for the said Brûlé, he was but eleven years of age when the Sieur de Champlain confided him to the People called Wendat. Champlain first made him the following Exercise, to quiet the boy's terror: (I) Iroquet loved the French. (II) The Huron were his friends. (III) Ergo, the Huron loved the French. – Étienne did not have the same confidence. But informers breathed on every side of one at Kebec. If he dared to express his anxieties any more directly, someone would report him to Champlain and his head would end up where Duval's had been – best to set out on that lonesome journey (which Robert Pontgravé would have killed for – Étienne was going to be what he longed to be – the very first French Savage!) and go on into Canada –

The Huron were like the maskers at carnivals. Would they eat him? – But no! They caressed his face most gently; they called him *my nephew*; they taught him the language of the True People, which he learned most aptly, until he could question them as to China and gold mines and other such matters as would interest his Captain, the Sieur de Champlain. – And what else did he learn? – Well, he learned the habits of those doglike brutes called beavers, whose testicles the Sieur de Champlain devoured weekly, in order to fortify his brain; Champlain had also reduced some of these organs to a powder (so the Sieur de Pontgravé had whispered to the boy with gleeful malice) in order to provoke the monthlies in his child-bride. – They can't breed until they bleed! (Thus Pontgravé.) Étienne laughed like a good sycophant. So in Wendaké he continued to laugh whenever he was expected to do so, taking on the character of those he lived among, like an apprentice Captain Merveille; that was his only hope . . . He stripped naked and entered the sweat lodge with other men, shyly at first; soon he thought nothing of it. He learned to love the taste of beaver-tail and roast dog-meat (in France he'd starved when he was very young; here there was always food). When the rigor of the winter was at its height, and his French coat froze, they gave him warm beaver-robes to wear. The following summer, in the Month When Blackberries Are Ripe, when he accompanied the Savages back to Lachine to make his report, Champlain was astounded to see him naked like them, wearing only the deerskin codpiece and the moccasins. His body was smeared with bear-grease. He bore a bow slung over his shoulder, a quiver of arrows he'd made himself . . . So Champlain slapped him and laughed, and the boy ducked his head, laughing when Champlain laughed.

And did you find China, boy? There were so many syllables in Savignon's replies that I couldn't always – eh, speak up; did you or didn't you? Speak up or you'll be whipped! You need not try to smooth matters over . . .

No, Seigneur. Please excuse me.

You do well to remember respect for your Captain. Now, Étienne, what opinion do these Chariquois or Boar's-Heads have of the French?

They long for iron, Seigneur, but the Algoumequins stop the way.

And the beaver-skins are as good as the ones they bring here?

Better, Seigneur.

Excellent. You've been a good little spy. How'd you like to go back there?

Yes, Seigneur. (Thus the boy, blinking his freckled eyelashes very rapidly so that Champlain couldn't see him crying.)

Back you go, then!

– And back he went. For eighteen years . . .

The Exercise of Yearning

Champlain, you sour lemon-sucker, you mediocrity, I think you were grumpy then. Brûlé's just a cipher; that's what you made him; why be nasty to a kid who's merely a moral zero? You might at least have given him prunes and biscuits before returning him to the heart of a wilderness trenchant with cannibalism! And when are *you* going to Huronia? Is your ambition as dead as your sex life? Here it is page 403, my plot more or less in place, all destruction finally ready to happen (and what about the poor Jesuits, sidelined again? You're their friend and this is their book!) – and you? You count beaver-skins for De Monts! – Ah, it makes me tired, said Pontgravé. Only thirteen thousand beaver-skins for France! What a year! Those stinking Yroquois! And how many of those skins were ours, do you think?

Ten thousand? hazarded Champlain.

More like seven. It is those pigs from La Rochelle who swill the profits.

(Oh, he was exercised! Champlain had to laugh.)

The truth is, you don't care about beaver. You never did.

And why should I, Pontgravé? Come on, be jolly. Beaver is your department; I don't need to be involved with that. Of course I like fried beaver-tails as much as you . . .

You make me hungry. What's for dinner?

Moose.

Eh? I thought you would say beaver.

Speaking of beaver, Pontgravé began (and Champlain knew this voice of his very well; it always meant that he was about to open a new kettle of worms), speaking of beaver, Champlain . . .

Yes, I see that you are speaking of beaver – or rather that you mention them. You have yet to say anything *about* them.

There's one thing I'd do about the beaver, if I were you. Now that Brûlé's dipped his toe in, why don't you take a swim in the Sweetwater Sea? Before the other traders get the same idea . . .

But Champlain had reached the end of his yardstick. This was the summer he'd been misled by the liar Vignau into believing in an imaginary northern sea, which would surely give easy entrance into China. *That* wild goose chase had taken him all the way to the Isle of the Allumettes; and he'd had to plunge waist-deep into the water, too, dragging his canoe by a rope all the way, for there were no paths worthy of the name . . . – And now this!

Please do me the kindness of controlling your aspirations for me, he said, as icily as he could.

Ah, now the bastard's hooked, thought Pontgravé with glee, he always tells me to shut up right after he bites.

Perhaps next year, said Champlain, rubbing his forehead.

The Harvest continued

He returned home in Août. In Octobre his wife began to be very disobedient and mischievous. Why, it was worse than the Civil War! In the winter, she fled from him – no one knew where. Beside himself, he called the Lieutenant de Police.

He found her more capable of resistance to the True Faith than he'd imagined. Her father's influence, no doubt. But when she was fourteen years of age, he whipped her for the good of her soul, until she agreed to abjure heresy and make a profession of faith. Then she loved him – with *gratitude* as well as tenderness (says the Ursuline chronicle). He instructed her and made her accomplished. He did what he could to tame her.

In Janvier of 1614, Hélène Boullé de Champlain was disinherited by her parents, on grounds of disobedience and insubmission to her husband. They charged her with inflicting gross and scandalous injuries upon him and them.

On the fourteenth of Février, Madame Boullé confirmed her daughter's exhereditation.

The Waterfall of Humility
1614–1615

> The last of his three purposes shows us the human side of Champlain. He saw the Indians not as Savages, but as beings with souls to be saved, and so he looked to the day when missionaries might be brought out to teach them a better way of life.
>
> A. R. M. Lower and J. W. Chafe, *Canada – A Nation; and How It Came to Be* (1958)

In the Country of the Haudenosaunee they say that it is time to plant when white oak leaves are the size of a red oak's foot. They soak the seed of the Three Sisters* in medicine to keep crows from eating it. Then comes Berry Moon, and then they hold the Thunder Rite, in which they request the Sun not to scorch the earth. They play the hoop and pole game. The women have a second hoeing, and a third. In the autumn, when the harvesting is done, they sing that the Three Sisters are happy to be home again from the fields. By that time the summer raids and tortures are over, for the forest begins to shed its leaves, so that enemies can no longer hide from one another. – But among our French, good reader, enemies hide from one another all year long. Champlain knew that, but he made the Exercise of Blindness because knowing did him no good. That spring, not long after Hélène's exheredidation was confirmed, he formed the Compagnie de Champlain, which united the merchants of Rouen and Saint-Malo for eleven years. Selfless Pontgravé helped him organize things; dear Pontgravé pulled a

* Corn, beans and squash.

few greased strings . . . The trade was good that summer. All the dandies were in a rage to buy hats made from the good Huron beaver-pelts. Who needed to rent some fillette's beaver when you could *wear* one on your head? And Champlain, considering himself a great success, gave utterance to a new idea which he'd just lately had, which was to proceed *in person* to the Country of the Huron – (What a marvelous thought! cried Pontgravé in admiration. Where do you get these ideas? I wish my brain were half as clever as yours!) – for if he could establish relations with the Savages there, then it would be a matter of the most limited difficulty to break Algonkin control of the fur trade . . . – Yes, Messieurs, their peltries are very fine, as you see. My young Brûlé brought these back. Hold them up to the light. The colors are quite subtle. (Thus Champlain, to the merchants.) And if we avail ourselves of the Indians and their canoes, I do believe that we can see everything seeable. – At this they all toasted him, knowing that they'd go on forever. – The Hollanders were satisfied, too. The New Netherlands Company of Amsterdam was given a three-year monopoly to trade with the Hiroquois . . . The Hiroquois were happy. The Susquehannock People (who were friends of the Huron) captured two Dutchmen, but believing them to be Champlain's friends they let them go without putting them to the torture, so they too were happy; everyone was happy; who says that history isn't happy? – Canada devoured iron and defecated beaver-hides. Everyone was happy except the Black-Gowns.

In that year, as I have told, the French settlements in Acadia were burned by the English, and Père Massé, who had sought to convert the Souriquois there, arrived at La Flèche – "in rags," as his *Relation* says. He was now thirty-nine years of age. He had no other wish than to return to Canada. So he mortified himself. In Canada he'd worn a hair-shirt whenever he celebrated the Mass. He continued to do this, but he added diverse little secret Crosses, none of which the other priests knew about until many years later when he died and they found the paper hidden in his breast. He resolved to lie down upon bare ground for the rest of his life. In his cell he kept a mattress and blankets, but these only to mislead the world. He slept on the floor, coughing, longing for the bitter sharp rocks of Canada. He wore no linen, except around his neck, where his Order required a white collar. Each morning he whipped himself with the device called *the discipline*, until his back was brittle with long white scar-filaments which burst open every day in streaks of blood. And he whispered: *My dear and adorable Canada . . .* He vowed that he would never again eat any food whose taste he savored. He fasted three times a week, but again secretly . . . – As part of his ministry, Père Massé sought to inspire the younger Jesuits and fill them with zeal. One of his catechumens was Jean de Brébeuf, who's the protagonist of this book, although we haven't quite gotten to him yet (for a few more slimy yards of history-string yet remain to be drawn from the cat's throat) . . . – As for Père Biard, he went on with his life as he had begun. Disputing with the Calvinists most zealously, ministering to the spiritual needs of the Roy's soldiers, he showed himself unbroken. In 1620, seeking to defend himself against charges of treachery and slyness (which had been brought against him by that hypocritical lawyer Lescarbot), he drafted his *Apologie*. As a favor he sent a copy to Père Massé, but sometime afterward, when he pressed him by letter for his opinion, Père Massé replied: Eh, brother, I'm not much of a reader. Rakes and shovels, goats and pigs – those are more in my line. – And he continued to mortify himself, in hopes of returning to Canada. But in truth there seemed little likelihood of that. For where the Stream of Time becomes definitively fresh in its estuary, the sweetness of the water is guarded by many ingenious lily-flaps –

The Great Work Recommenced

Nonetheless the years pressed more powerfully upon Canada. In 1615 the under-roar of water was as regular as the white speckles on black ice-lakes. Champlain did not know this. For him, despite his happy new show of beaver-merchants, time seemed at a low ebb. He was exasperated with his wife, sick with various bodily aches of late middle age, and distressed to hear of the Sieur de Poutrincourt's bankruptcy, for he had liked him well enough to be unable to say (as he usually did when told the misfortunes of others) that here was something which would never have befallen a more experienced man (such as Champlain). And his son Biencourt – *he* was not receiving the necessary assistance! – Nor am I, sighed Champlain to himself. But I shall persevere in my duty. – It was his intention not only to establish himself securely at Kebec, but also (as he had so often claimed) to bring the True Faith. How could he forget those benighted Savages at Tadoussac, twelve years ago now, prating about sticks and stones in the belief that they knew GOD? It hurt to think of it! – How many times had he gone to the States-General to plead for the salvation of Savage souls? How many times had he bent the knee to Lords and Cardinals, Bishops and Pères by the score, begging from them what he never would have asked for himself? And afterward all people said was: What an abject soul this Champlain has! – No one presented himself; none made any contribution.

But in the town of Brouage where he had been born, there was a good Catholic of exceedingly honorable character, by name the Sieur de Houël, who by degrees had become interested in his pious designs. Lest you infer that this Houël was a nobody, I hasten to convey that he was Controlleur-General of the salt works. Eh! Houël was acquainted with quite a few Grey-Gowns, or Recollects as they were more officially known. Their Order was well established, having been founded in 1484 (quite a *bit* before those upstart Jesuits, when you come to think about it, as the Grey-Gowns often did). Like everyone else, they meant only good. The previous spring, after Champlain had left for Honfleur, and thence New France, Houël remained alone, trudging up and down on his hills of salt, and thinking: I make salt, Champlain rides upon it – why, it is our mutual living! Champlain is my brother! I must help him! – And he began to feel very edified. From Champlain he'd heard the tale of Pères Biard and Massé. – Perhaps we might succeed where the Jesuits failed! said the Recollects to one another very brightly. – By all my salt, I am sure of it! replied the Sieur de Houël. This Champlain, well, his fortunes have been checkered, I grant you, but he seems now secure in the favor of the Roy, and he craves the good of the Canadians from the bottom of his heart! They're all sodomists and cannibals, you know, with no knowledge of GOD.

In the topmost windows, glowing Saints hovered in arches of blue sky (although outside the sky was sullenly white). Before the altar knelt a nun. She was fading into her own white face, white veil . . .

I have no authority to send you to Canada, said the Nuncio, spreading his hands wide. This commission of yours, it may be sufficient and it may not; I cannot say. My recommendation is to address yourselves to the General of your Order. But it is certainly a worthy design, my friends; your hearts are to be commended. And now pray excuse me. Do inform me of the outcome.

So they returned to their convent at Brouage. The Sieur de Houël, now himself inflamed to great deeds, accompanied them to an interview with another Provincial, and spoke such words of salty eloquence that all thought him moved by the HOLY GHOST. Champlain for his part importuned his patron the Prince de Condé; he went again to the States-General, and this time the high Seigneurs agreed to defray the costs of four Friars. In the end they gave almost fifteen hundred livres! Hélène actually kissed him when she heard; she was very pious now . . . Champlain bought them provisions, vestments and suchlike necessities.

There were four of them: Père Jamay, Père Le Caron, Père Jean Dolbeau, and the lay brother, Frère Pacifique du Plessis. Compared to Père Massé, none of them was worth much. But you have to put on the Grey-Shirt now; take the long view . . .

The associates were delighted. The reader may recall that upon hearing word of Robert Pontgravé's greed and lustful impieties, Champlain said to himself that GOD used the compulsions of such persons like great hulking beasts to which the grand carriage of Good could easily enough be attached. The merchants at Honfleur held a complementary view. Their dignity was continually assaulted by those who accused them of selfishness – quite rightly, of course. They had done nothing to clear land or educate Savages. All they wanted was beaver, beaver! But now they could pull on religion, like a whore slipping a pair of frilly underpants over her syphilitic privities. So they struck their glasses together to see the Recollects boarding their ship, a vessel of five hundred and fifty tons, named the *Saint-Étienne*. They were on hand on the twenty-fourth of Avril to see them embark for Canada again. The Recollects had longed to meet them, which they willingly granted, repressing their smiles at the earnestness of these silly grey gulls or boobies who perched upon their chairs so peacefully; they shook their hands, saying: GOD requite you for your zeal, good Pères! – As soon as the *Saint-Étienne* had left the dock, they doubled up laughing. – And Champlain, too! a man choked out. It's too much!

Pontgravé was the Captain. When Champlain was below decks (for he did not like this sort of play), Pontgravé sized them up for the First Mate's benefit, saying: That Père Le Caron seems to me a tough and stringy sort of bird, like one of our Canadian liver-snatchers. I'll put up ten livres he lasts five years or more. The others, though . . . Eh, they're coming this way – keep up appearances! Set your lunkheads to scrubbing something! It smells like bilge up here! Ah, they're gone – scratching each other's armpits, no doubt of it. It's a question of dead men's odds. Not more than three livres on the lot. I'll tell you the reason: did you see how they – eh, *Champlain!* How many fathoms down do you think the bottom is, here in the open sea? And why's the ocean near the shore? That's something I've always wondered. What does Navigation say about that? – Good, he's gone. Now where were we?

When Père Le Caron first saw the mouth of the Fleuve Saint-Laurent, he cried out just as Champlain had done, for it seemed to him a vaster and grander shimmer of sun-silver even than the River Euphrates in his dreams and visions.

The wind whistled; the other priests looked about them dolefully.

Champlain was very happy to be showing people things. Everyone looked where he pointed! – You see, Père Le Caron, there on our port side is the place where the Savages camp when they come to trade.

And what is that big round mountain beyond, Seigneur?

I have assigned it the letter *A* on my chart, which seems to me a very fortunate choice. For wouldn't you say, Père, that your mountain is the first thing that the eye lights upon?

Eh, Seigneur, to be sure . . .

The following day they went up to Kebec in the longboats. Père Jamay's gown fluttered in the wind like the young leaves shimmering on the birch-hills all around, and through the rigging the priests saw the Rock of Kebec with the zigzag trail or sentier up to the fort upon its brow. – The Sieur de Champlain had this year brought a sundial to Canada at his own expense, the better to cut up the fresh pie-wedges of unbaked hours. One of his minions clambered up the roof of the Habitation and nailed it down where he bade, just beneath the fleur-de-lys banner. – Now, how was his garden coming along? Godet and Merveille had taken turns watering it in his absence, knowing that to be the shortest road to his favor; still and all, it seemed that crows had reaped an early harvest. – He marched stout and redfaced along the promenade; the Grey-Gowns trailed behind. The moat stank. His private casements had not been cleaned, which caused him to shout with rage (all the men laughed behind his back, and the priests looked at one another, comprehending how things were). – Here, good Pères, is our forge, he said. – The kitchen you see. The dovecote is currently vacant, alas, due to the expense . . .

It was very chilly. The priests looked about them like men in a dream.

But Père Le Caron, their Superior, wished to go straight to Lachine to meet and convert the Savages, for he was fired with conversion-lust. – Come, now, my brothers! he said to the other priests. This Canada is not so gloomy a tapisserie as your fears wove for you! These fleuves and rivières, this light, these endless ringing spaces – they are signal favors from Our LORD!

There was a rivière at Kebec which had many bows and bends before it met our Fleuve Saint-Laurent, so that it was called by the Savages *the Snake*. But Christians called it the *Rivière Saint-Charles*. Pontgravé took them there. (It's close, he reasoned to himself, but not *too* close!) The Recollects decided to build a residence at its shore, complete with the first chapelle to grace the soil of New France. This they accommodated with vestments, and otherwise prettified as best they could. But Père Le Caron was already at Lachine, meeting the Huron Savages: robust, laughing men who welcomed him. Surely he could adapt himself to their foods and whims! – Champlain tried to dissuade him, saying that he would know his own necessities better after wintering at Kebec, but Père Le Caron replied: I know that none have discovered and calculated as particularly as you, Monsieur, so that I ought to take your advice, but my heart sings too loudly for me to hear anything but the song of JESUS!

As you will, then. (Thus Champlain.) Indeed you are a man of saintliness.

Now Père Le Caron kissed the Cross sewn upon his amice and placed it over his neck. Already he feared to look into the face of the forest which pressed so darkly upon him, but he would never say it. He had once been the tutor of the Duc d'Orléans. He felt himself ready for any martyrdom. He put his arms in the sleeves of his alb and slid it down around his body like a shirt of silken innocence; he girded it tight with the tasseled cincture. Over this he put on his chasuble of excellent scarlet damask well seasoned with gold lace;

he took up his pearl-embroidered stole; he draped the maniple over his right hand, carefully, so that all three Crosses showed. Now he and his brother Recollects chanted their Mass: the first one ever in these parts – and how fortuitous that they did so on the site of Caughnawagwa! – The Savages watched, astounded as usual –

A few days later, Père Le Caron set out for the Country of the Huron. – Meet me at Carhagouha! he shouted gaily to those who stayed behind. He did not see how the Savages regarded him, measuring him with their eyes just as Champlain would have done a bale of peltries. He was too exalted to find in their silent attentiveness anything but rapture. – To sweeten his way still further, Champlain loaned him twelve good Frenchmen, well armed.

The Third Campaign

The Huron, studying well his face, saw there as if in new snow the creature-tracks of certain arguments to adduce. – The Hiroquois close the way, Chawain, they said. If you want our beaver-skins you must help us. – And they smiled slyly, peering into his eyes to see what he might say. He felt their breath on him, and drew back.

Eh, just listen to them! (Thus Pontgravé.) There's nothing for it, Champlain. You'll have to go off with them. And just when I was counting on you to help me haul bales and barrels of ironware! Seventy-one hundred hatchets on inventory! And yet I envy you, I must say. Imagine being able to see all those new Countries – what a pretty coup! They eat fire there – that's what the Algoumequins say. Do you think it's true? Never mind; you'll have the answer to that when you come back. How's young Brûlé getting along, I wonder? How many squaws has the lad skewered? When I was with Chauvin . . .

Chauvin's dead, said the Sieur de Champlain curtly. And I'm sure you made your wager's worth from his warm corpse.

He turned to walk away, but Pontgravé seized him by the arm and cried: Champlain, Champlain, what's gotten into you? Surely you don't blame me for not accompanying you?

Champlain's shoulders slumped. – It's not that. It's nothing. Please excuse me. Of course I shall go with the Savages, so that they'll love us the more. And I shall draw maps . . .

Don't forget your astrolabe, his old friend clucked at him, at which he laughed.

He summoned the Savages to a great Council (to which they thought they summoned him), and they agreed to furnish twenty-five hundreds of warriors for an assault upon one of the Châteaux or Castles of these ferocious Hiroquois; this number he judged to be more than sufficient, provided that they follow his instructions down to the last dot and comma. – Did they agree? –

Naturellement! – Hearing this, he felt great satisfaction; for they were not vacillating in their usual Savage manner.

If we can enfranchise ourselves from these greedy Algoumequins (thus Champlain), then Huron peltries will come in quadruple measure, at one-fourth the price, and I shall have pleasure in counting them. – Ah, but I must take care not to offend the Algonkin until I control the Huron. If only I could prevent any of the Savages here from learning of my journey! But that cannot be avoided.

Just before his departure, as a matter of fact, he had an unpleasant encounter with one of his Montagnais, a young Captain named Capitanal, with whose father he'd fought the Iroquois. Capitanal came to him saying: Champlain, do you go to Wendaké?

It is so, he replied.

Why?

I desire to see new Countries, to follow fleuves and rivières . . .

The Wendat will kill you. They hate you Iron People.

They will do nothing but the will of GOD.

They will *kill* you, I say! – The man was shouting.

Perhaps, Capitanal. Or perhaps you plan to kill me yourself. Who knows?

At this, the Savage turned on his heel and disappeared, and Champlain sat down trembling. All that evening, Capitanal's accusations rang in his ears. Loathsome! Vile! He must put the matter out of mind . . .

Anyhow, Iroquet the Algonkin was coming with his warriors. It was Yroquet to whom he had entrusted Brûlé. Iroquet was very knowing. Perhaps it was Iroquet, whom he had thought to be his friend, who was the Algoumequins' dirty spy . . .

On the ninth of Juillet, loading a good quantity of powder, match and lead shot into one of their canoes, he set out for the Huron Country, with two of his own men (one of whom, the interpreter Brûlé, was now very skilled in Savage languages, and the other of whom was his valet, Captain Merveille) and ten Savages both Huron and Montagnais, whom he astonished by means of his astrolabe with the mysterious holes like clover-leaves, the turning hand. Their Captain, a great stout man named Darontal, begged him to repeat the miracle, which at first he would not do, believing that it was best never to be too friendly with inferiors lest they later hold him in contempt for it; but Brûlé the interpreter whispered in his ear that it was best not to displease them, especially since he had kept them waiting. Very good. But he did not often engage in such sport: his mind dwelled on mines, lakes and other necessary matters. Indeed he lost the instrument, which is why in the Province of Ontario there is now a special sign directing you to visit its discovery theme park: how stupid! – They went up the Rivière-des-Prairies. Dodging the floating corpses of trees, they paddled and portaged through the Country of the Algoumequins; they ascended the Country of the Otaguottouemins (whose language is something between Algonkin and Montagnais); they traversed lakes and lacs . . . It was a very great distance. China continually receded from him. By GOD's beard, this Canada was vast! He saw no sign of any end to it. New streams and rivières continued to unroll in his map, which must lengthen daily toward the west in order to accommodate them – even the journey from Kebec to this Huronia or Wendaké was farther than any sail from Iupiter to Pluton!

The water in his Stream of Time was almost stagnant, but he knew only that it was calm. As he passed near the center of his calculations (which were five million fathoms deep), he sensed a black turbulence, and bubbles rose up through his mind between the arms of GOUGOU (*viz.*, the Fox's scalp) which clung together like sedges and lily-stems . . . Champlain was in a sense the successor to the Hiroquois wizard called Adadardoh, but not the new clear-minded Adadardoh of the League, who had been cured by the Peace Hymn of DEKANWIDEH – no, not that Adadardoh at all, but the other one, the old one, the Evil-Minded.

There were pebbles in their corn soup or sagamite, but he scarcely noticed. He had no daintiness left in him, for which he thanked the LORD. He paddled with great vigor. The threshold of suffering which that Grey-Gown, Père Le Caron, had already begun to cross not far ahead, meant nothing to him. The radiant curtain of wildness and suffering had been parted by him so long before – probably on the isle called Sainte-Croix – that the journey held scarcely any hardship. He said to himself: These mosquitoes are quite heinous. The Savages said to themselves: Chawain is strong and patient. For a Frenchman, Chawain is a great man.

And which of the Hiroquois Nations are we to war on? he said abruptly, laying his paddle down.

The Entouhonorons, Chawain. (Thus the Savages.)

They mean to say the Onondaga people, Seigneur, as I do believe. (Thus his interpreter, Monsieur Brûlé.)

Ah, he said absently. I have never seen them.

He did not pick up the paddle again. He would not have them think him to be on their level.

The air became milder and more temperate. Now for the first time he saw the Sweetwater Sea. As he had done when he first saw the Fleuve Saint-Laurent, he cried out at the vastness . . .

They went out upon it in their canoes, and he kept craning his head and looking toward the western horizon to find an end of it, but he could not. It was of perfectly transparent purity. He estimated that he could see the bottom at a depth of fifteen pieds. The nature of the suspension particles must determine the clarity of water; one day he must write a treatise about rivières, lacs and seas . . . The canoe was suspended in a blue-brown sky. Usually they traveled in shallows, where their ripples left their golden shadows on the sand, moving and interlacing in meaningless patterns. Tiny arms of aquatic pipewort shot up rigid from the water, straight or canted, it mattered not; and all to bear their little rounded heads of compound flowers, like Duval's head on the pike at Kebec (now closer to him than he would ever dream); and the dark purple shadows of those blooms were so sharp upon the surface of the water . . . He saw the level line of a beaver dam, its long logs and sticks leaning at perpendiculars to the water-line, the snags rising black from the water. As a rule the Savages followed the shore, for their canoes were as unreliable as their promises (thus Champlain); but presently they reached the Bay which they called *Matchedash* (beyond lies Wendaké Peninsula) and chanced farther out to make a crossing, into the grand blank blueness so incomprehensible like the source of all fleuves and rivières. Now the Sweetwater Sea became terrifyingly choppy, so that he thought that the canoe would swamp, and put all his heart into prayer. Thus he got over his delight in that grandeur; Champlain's delight in anything never lasted very long . . . Near shore, rocks broke water like blunt teeth. A strand of seaweed floated like a hair-tuft or toupillon of GOUGOU . . .

That night they said to him: Tomorrow we come home, Chawain! – He lay awake all night, as if he'd been at the Habitation again, revolving schedules and ordnance and treason in his head while the sentries paced overhead. Morning lake-light seeped up gradually from under the trees, and the Huron swarmed down to their canoes, caressing their sides very lightly, lifting them, kneading their bark to test its fitness as they always did. Champlain's heart was pounding. On that first day of Août he arrived indeed in Wendaké, latitude 44° 30′ –

The village where they landed was called *Otoücha*. The people there wore shells and feathers depending from their ears. They belonged to the Bear Nation. Now for the first time he entered the longhouses, where the Savagesses openly ate the lice from their own bodies and those of their children. What stench and uncleanliness! Once he saw a woman suckling a foxheaded dog . . . Yet he had to admit that they were more civilized than the Souriquois and other wandering tribes. And here the country was very fine, being well cleared and transected with rivers. He said to himself: Truly, these Huron are advantaged. He proceeded on to *Carmaron*, where they feasted him with bread, squash and meat, which was very rare in their Country, so that he knew that they did him honor. They told him their foolish and sacrilegious tales, as all Savages did. It seemed that the demon who chiefly beset them was a withered old hag by name AATAENTSIK . . . Very ungodly people, these Huron! They reminded him somewhat of the Armouchiquois whom he had seen in Acadia – ten years ago it was now. It was to the Armouchiquois that the carpenter had lost his life, and poor Robert Pontgravé his hand. So Champlain held himself with great caution (which with further caution he dissembled). Such was their hatred of the Hiroquois that whenever anyone sneezed the others would respond by cursing those Five wicked Nations. He saw the women in their knee-length skirts of deerskin, holding their infants to give them suck. Breasts everywhere, fat naked breasts, dirty breasts pimpled and stained, but it was not as bad as the dance of naked privities; – besides, I'm a married man now; I can observe breasts with impunity. It's not as if they're making me touch them. And they're very handsome and happy, these Savagesses. – On his second night in Carmaron he was sleepless and much beset by fleas, so that at last he went out of the lodge. It was very dark. It did not seem to be the custom of these Huron or Wendat to go about much at night. No doubt they feared demons and monsters. But Champlain was not superstitious. (GOUGOU was one thing; that was an established fact.) On the voyage out from France that spring he'd spoken out against the practice of flogging the cabin boy to bring a favorable wind. He pointed out that there was no passage in Holy Writ to justify this cruelty. (But the cabin boy was flogged just the same; Pontgravé said that it was not anyone else's affair.) No, there was nothing to fear, not with that Cross around his neck . . . How shall I lead them to victory over the Yroquois? And shall I require the Yroquois to kneel before me when they surrender? I wish Robert Pontgravé were here with me; he listens so well . . . – He strolled along the inner circumference of the palisadoes, crunching fish-guts, clamshells and bones beneath his boots. (Beyond, the Sweetwater Sea, the black bristles of moonlit grass.) Something was heavy and immovable beneath his thoughts, like the brown boulder in a river-bottom, over-rushed by streaming water, tinged at one corner with black spirals, concealing Heaven knows what ugly little crayfish . . . Suddenly a young girl appeared before him, smiling nervously. Her hair was tied up in eel-skin, as if for one of their dances, and she'd prettied herself up with wampum-plates. He stepped courteously aside. She took his hand and – and *touched it to her bosom!*

– JESUS, what shameless effrontery! – *Now* the image of those dirty naked Montagnais girls, which had never left him these twelve years, rushed into his head like a whore with a thousand stinking brown breasts and black bushy lice-ridden crotches . . . – He jerked away; she stared at him and began to back off and he saw how her mouth was opening as if to scream; quickly he took her hand again and directed to her his sweetest remonstrances, quoting to her the verse of Leviticus: *He shall take a wife in her virginity*. Of course she could not understand a word, but it was still his duty. Perhaps the Word of GOD penetrated to her nonetheless; he prayed to MARIE that it was so . . . At last, patting her shoulder, he sent her away, thinking to himself: what a corrupt Nation this is! How I crave to subject them to reason . . . I must write about this in my *Récits* and *Relations*, so that pious hearts in France may be stirred . . . Those poor Recollects are scarcely sufficient.

But should I tell Hélène? Would hearing of it wound her in any way? Was there any fault in me? Was I – could I have been lewd? – That poor lost girl. She'll burn forever in Hell. And so many like her! Their breasts hang down very little, except when they are old.

He went on to *Touaguainchain*, where all the families invited him into their smoky holes (Heaven! the things he had to do!); to *Tequenonquiayle*, where the Savages feasted him on citronniers or Mai-apples, whose color approximated that of lemons . . . He did not like the Savages nearly so much now. But their beaver-peltries were even finer than he had dreamed. Remember the old days of the monopoly, with fourteen hundred percent profits? They might well come again . . . At each town he raised the arms of his Nation. He told the Savages that they were now subject to the Roy of France, at which they expressed great joy. Or, to relate the conversation more exactly:

Tell them that it's essential for them to be protected from the Hiroquois, because they make war badly and have no more freedom from error than children. Make that clear, boy! Tell them that the Roy loves them, and that if they regard him as a father and promise to obey him, then – then he'll send armed Frenchmen to live here, and priests to instruct them in the Faith. (Thus Champlain, to his good subaltern, Monsieur Étienne Brûlé.)

Chawain says to you: You are great warriors. Our Big Stone in France desires to assist you in your wars and reap glory with you. Chawain asks you if you will permit the Iron People to live among you as your brothers. Chawain's friends are Sorcerers who will teach you to cast spells and make iron things. Is this well? (Thus tactful Brûlé, to the Wendat.)

We say to Chawain our brother: Our lodge is your lodge. We desire to learn the use of your guns. We desire to learn from your Sorcerers. Come live among us. Take our daughters in marriage. Learn from us to be hunters and strong bearers of burdens. Learn from us to shave off your foolish beards and to speak softly. You are welcome here. (Thus the Wendat, to Brûlé their nephew.)

The Huron reply to you: It is well. (Thus Brûlé, to Champlain.)

Champlain, who had been watching them narrowly, let his shoulders fall. He smiled; he laughed; he passed out hatchets and hatchets . . .

Thus enraptured, he proceeded north to *Carhagouha*, a minor ink-spot upon his Canada so intricate, subtle, but almost regular in its distribution of mountains west-shaded, trees in pairs and trios and occasional square formations like armies, between which ambled an emblematic beaver just as in his widest fleuve, the Saint-Laurent, there sailed a solitary battleship-fish horned and scaled: a sturgeon. Lacs and rivières subdivided Canada further. There remained no blanknesses on his map anymore. Why, he knew everything now; he scarcely needed to walk another pied! But no matter; he was amiable: let the sounding-line spin out from its spool . . . It was here that Père Le Caron now lived with those armed Frenchmen he'd loaned him. Here the Savages were very crowded – which was a misfortune to them, as he thought, considering how many souls must thus die without any knowledge of Him above. Shyly, they hid their anxious smiles behind their hands. Their eyes were patient, dark.

And how are you succeeding in your travails, my good Père? (Thus Champlain.)

Le Caron shrugged sourly. – They speak to me with all their babble and twittering and gringottage, but what do they actually say? To comprehend that is difficult – *ver*-y difficult.

Ah, but surely you grant that these are an amiable people, said Champlain heartily. And what think you of your accommodations here?

In Latin there are three words together, replied Père Le Caron. Do you know what they are?

I beg your pardon, Père. I had no opportunity to study Latin in my youth –

I will tell you, said Père Le Caron in a great brassy voice. *Putrefacio, putresco, putridus!*

Now there was nothing for it; Champlain must bear with him as he dove into the Stream of Disillusionment, recapitulating every league and paddle-stroke of the voyage trapped between Savages who continually let loose stinking bursts of gut-wind, who pissed into the pots they cooked in, who seasoned their meat with clods of dirt . . .

Oh, come, Père Le Caron. It is no worse among sailors from Saint-Malo. Why, you should see Pontgravé's habits!

No, no, these Savages know nothing! They are not even human! When it rains, their women importune me to lend them my cassock for their comfort in the fields! They steal the keys to my strong-boxes to hang around their children's necks! It is very difficult. They would strip me naked, Seigneur! They make – indecent propositions . . . And their *smiles*, I cannot –

You must strive to accommodate yourself, my good Père.

On the first of Septembre, they set out to raid the Hiroquois, Champlain in the vanguard, of course . . . The warriors had assembled at the grand ville called *Cahigué* – not twenty-five hundred of them, as they had promised, but only half a thousand. When he saw fit to remonstrate with them for their faithlessness, his host Darontal said: There would have been more if you had come sooner, Chawain. – Being reminded by this insolence that he was in their power, he desisted. – After all, he thought, I am not so young anymore . . . Père Le Caron had blessed him. It had become chilly, with a sharp white frost. Canada waterweed rustled suppliantly about their gunnels. Champlain felt a little dismal, but the Savages shouted his name to tease him until he too grinned . . . A water lobelia twirled beside his reflected face . . . They gave tobacco to the Powers of the rapids, to calm the rivières, lacs and fleuves wherever they boiled, so that no one would be drowned. They gave tobacco to the Powers Who might smooth the way. They descended a fine sparkling rivière . . . The shores thereabouts were quite desolate of souls, thanks to the incursions of the Hiroquois. Champlain felt almost as if he were crossing a border between two great European Nations at war, where a hush of ominous character exposes one's every footfall to the avidity of echoes, and enemy soldiers lurk Jesus knows where. – Where did the Country of the Hiroquois begin? This it was difficult to calculate. Perhaps its edge was that pale blue mountain-line across the river, humid, pale and steamy . . . – They hid their canoes among the rocks and walked four leagues along a sandy beach palisadoed by forest (a very agreeable Country, thought Champlain, although not sufficiently cleared). It was warmer than in Wendaké, although some trees had already begun to turn, diverging yellowly day by day from their evergreen neighbors. This difference, however, was barely noticeable as yet. It was evening. The white sky of rain had retreated, thickening as it did so; and steam swirled between the trees. Then the clouds lowered again. A few raindrops fell, heavy and round like tears. Grey mountains and grey sky joined together in the rain. – At Kebec, he supposed, Pontgravé and the others would now be gathering in provisions like ants, so that the winter would not surprise them. Soon enough all Canada would wear the Ice-Shirt again . . .

I must not distract myself with such thoughts, he said. And he glared around gloomily, so that the People thought him very moody.

Now the Savage Captains planted sticks in the ground to correspond with their warriors, and they held many drills until all understood their role. Yet Champlain considered that they lacked discipline. How much better they would fight, if a single will commanded them! He for his part examined his conscience, and encouraged the other French to do the same, as he always did before hazarding his life.

Then once again he thought to take his sounding, to see how many fathoms deep the loyalty of the Savages lay. – Darontal and you others: you will obey me in all things? he cried, his eyes flashing.

Naturally we obey your commands, Chawain. You are our well-beloved nephew; do not hide your words from us . . . (Thus Darontal.)

But Champlain said to himself: This Darontal, I don't know this Darontal . . .

And afterwards you will take us home, do you comprehend? Otherwise I shall be very angry. Darontal, do you hear?

Yes, Chawain. My lodge is your lodge.

They turned inland for twenty-five leagues or so, crossing the Rivière of the Oneida. His heart was pounding. Surely this year would be the *annus mirabilis* when the Hiroquois must declare their subjection to the Roy of France! On the ninth of Octobre, a chilly day of rustling leaves, with everything browner and drier than before, they captured a family of eleven Hiroquois who were fishing together. Champlain categorized and divided: four women, three boys, one girl, three men. Yroquet sawed off the comeliest woman's finger with a knife, blank-faced to better drink in her screams, which made a pretty prelude to the ordinary tortures, but Champlain became angry and told him to cease the torture, at which Iroquet cried amazed: But, my dear nephew, they do the same to us! – to which Champlain replied: That is of no moment. Do you not see how this woman has no defense save tears? – at which (when Merveille translated his words to them), the Indians sniggered among themselves and said: This man is bearded and stupid like all other Iron People! – They desisted nonetheless, since they were good politicians, and began to torture the men instead, cutting them, singeing them, roasting them, which they endured without a murmur, though the others in that family, looking on, wailed loudly. Laughed Darontal: How could you have forgotten to turn aside the evil of our coming with tobacco?

– He placed an ember between a prisoner's toes. He sliced off a strip of flesh from another man's leg and threw it sizzling on the fire. – Champlain said nothing. The stink of burning tainted his nostrils; but then he had smelled the same in Paris when witches were roasted. – I must not be dainty or weak, he said to himself. – Turning his attention to the other prisoners, he said to himself: But these are nobly formed! (He imagined even yet that it might be possible to establish peace with the Irocois, a possible model being the Pax Vervins – a *firm* peace, mind you, but a peace nonetheless.) The tortures went on until the Hiroquois men died. Then the Huron scalped the corpses and kicked them away. One of the Algoumequins snatched up an Iroquois child by the legs and bashed his brains out upon a rock. Then some Huron led the womenfolk away, and he never saw them again. Above, on the sunny granite shoulder where junipers grew sharp and high, the birds and locusts sang on.

The following afternoon was a cool clear one in the Country of the Irocois, the sky white-striped above waves of maples, between which rivers flowed; and watchful on palisaded hilltops the Irocois had their villages. Champlain most earnestly prayed his allies to wait until the following morning for the attack, as they must first embarricade themselves – he'd told them all this before! – but though they pretended to agree, in fact they paid small mind: indeed, they were so foolhardy as to wander in plain view of that enemy Château, shouting insults as they customarily did, so that there was no longer any possibility of surprise. A few arrows were exchanged on both sides, as Champlain said to himself in amazement: And they call this activity la guerre? Eh, I call it faridondaine! – Now his impetuous Savages even sought to rush the Castle, such was their folly: – they were repulsed, of course, and retired bearing half a dozen wounded, of which one soon died. They began to construct their barricades a mere cannon-shot from the place, while Champlain railed at them with stern and unpleasant words to incite them to perform their devoirs.

Ah, we are sorry to have offended you, they said, hanging their heads.

I excuse you, he said, for you do not yet know what it means to be disciplined. But now you must follow my commands precisely, in order to recover from this little defeat which you've suffered. Do you comprehend? Very well, my friends. First we shall fell some trees and construct a *cavalier* or moveable tower of greater height than the enemy's palisadoes. Are you familiar with that term? Two hundred of your strongest warriors will be required to carry it and set it in position. My Frenchmen will then ascend it and begin to fire upon the Hiroquois. Meanwhile the rest of us will approach under cover of wooden mantelets which I shall show you how to make –

the procedure is quite simple. These will deflect their arrows. Forty or fifty warriors will lay a heap of firewood against the base of the wall. At my signal you will make a spark upon it, and set those Hiroquois ablaze. These are my orders. Follow them, and we breach the town!

Your words are good, Chawain. (Thus the Algonkin Captain, Yroquet.)

They went into the forest and began to cut wood. Champlain's joiners fitted the logs into place to make the cavalier, and also a generous sufficiency of mantelets for all. Now all was ready, and he selected his tetrad of arquebusiers: eh, Merveille must be in command; Boucher had proved himself already; Saint-Foy and Rondeval were very steady shooters . . . His heart was beating fast, and he grinned.

And where will we make the breach? (Thus Merveille.)

Let me see. Shall we scout out this ramshackle Castle? he said with a wink.

You are our Captain.

Eh bien, said Champlain, unable to hold back the pleasure that pinkened his cheeks at these words. – Merveille, you and Saint-Foy come with me. We'll measure the weakness of their palisadoes most carefully before we overtop them. – No, pardon me, Merveille, but I misspoke myself. You must remain with the Savages. You speak their tongue: watch them, and if need be, cool their rashness. Boucher, you attend us. As for you, my Rondeval, I count on you to keep good watch over our stores of powder and other things: only Frenchmen can watch French goods. – Eh, it's that Darontal again: by Heaven, the man knows not his place! Merveille, tell him tactfully that we do not need the company of Savages on our reconnaissance. They'll only spoil things; I know them.

Hardly any leaves remained on the trees. With arquebuses at the ready, they parted the dry black branches.

I do not think that they will ambush us, he whispered to the men, to reassure them. – All these Savages are craven!

A breeze was blowing. He could smell the Indian corn.

Thirty pieds high, more or less, said Saint-Foy, studying the place through a glass. But over there, between those two galleries, it may be less.

Our cavalier will be at least forty, said Champlain. Anywhere we place it should give good advantage. What say you, Boucher?

We must bring it to the closest part of the wall, Seigneur. Once we begin to run bearing that tower on our shoulders, it will be easy for the Hiroquois to launch their arrows . . .

Have no fear, said Champlain. Remember, you'll be inside. No arrows can pierce you there. I myself will run alongside and cover you. Shall we elect Saint-Foy's spot? I think it somewhat too far, but I will take your counsel.

The two men were silent for a moment. He could see the veins hammering in their throats.

We like that spot well, said Boucher at last.

Very good.

He laughed and slapped them on their shoulders, but indeed he did not feel easy in his soul, for he scarcely considered that he had such a great advantage over the enemy as in previous years.

I pray to GOD that I do not forget anything necessary, he said to himself. These poor Savages look to me for guidance . . .

If the Iroquois were as sly and capable as Spaniards they would be taking aim at us even now from their towers, he said to himself. But of course we are out of range of their arrows.

His heart was pounding. Boucher and Saint-Foy were looking into his face.

You fall back now, he said to them. Make certain that everything is in its place.

Yes, Seigneur.

When they were out of sight, he knelt and prayed. He felt himself to be in very tight shoes, as the saying goes, and he saw nothing whose measure might help him. After making his devotions to JESUS, he requested the favor of Sainte Barbara, the patron of gunners and sailors, saying: Good Lady, I ask not for myself, but for the Frenchmen in my care . . .

In the camp of the good Savages, the cavalier lay full length on the ground. Merveille was already worming his way in – good man! Saint-Foy looked a little bewildered; Champlain slapped him on the shoulder . . . He said softly: Fear none but GOD.

The outer palisadoes of the Onondaga Castle made a great hexagon thirty pieds in height whose spike-ribs crossed and clashed, sharpened to points at the tops; behind this were nested the inner walls, inside of which the longhouses lay. The Frenchmen approached just out of bowshot and discharged their muskets, with many booms and smoke-puffs. Within the village someone screamed, and then all Champlain's Savages began to laugh and yell. (He said to himself: Those who know the least shout the loudest.) Now the Huron Savages bent back their bows and fired over the palisadoes, shrieking with rage. Under cover of this diversion, two hundred of Darontal's stoutest warriors came running with the cavalier, carrying it like a battering-ram (inside of which the four Frenchmen crouched like worms) and raised it a pike's length from the outer palisado. Champlain's men in the cavalier fired low loud volleys through the slits, so that the Hiroquois were compelled to retreat from their galleries (those who did not tumbled down like bloody meteors, smashing through the bark-roofed lodges to detonate among their kin) and the balls of the arquebusiers, scarcely slowed by their passage through enemy flesh, drove onward through the air with the blood and fat sizzling on them and then, like their victims, like Champlain, like all that GOD has created, they too commenced elliptical trajectories of a downward character, as if sky and time had become a steep rock shelf slanting down through pines and glossy-leaved oaks to the water below, rock succeeding rock until it slid beneath the lake-line: thus the balls of French death pierced the roofs of the longhouses and surely plumbed that darkness so that women and children began to scream in pain; and on the ground Champlain's remaining arquebusiers fired through the palisadoes.

As yet, all seems very well executed, thought Champlain.

But now his Savages were yelling in such high excitement that he could not make his commands and orders heard. Disregarding him entirely, two Savages sought to ignite the wood which had been piled up against the wall, but they did so in the teeth of a wind, so that the fire went quickly out. – Not like that, you imbeciles! he shouted. Bring up the mantelets, I order you! I command you! The mantelets will shield you from the arrows! Listen! Can none of you understand French? – Ah, how he longed to beat them and shake them for their good; that was the only way to get battle-hearted men to listen! But he could not; he did not. They launched their arrows in a shrieking passion. Sighing *ehhhhh*, he folded his arms. They had abandoned the mantelets. How could he be surprised to see them come to harm? Now one leaped high and fell; there was an arrow in his groin. Expressionlessly, Champlain's arquebusiers pulled their hats lower over their eyes and fired through the palisadoes. He ascended the cavalier, in order to encourage his Frenchmen there and see how they did; arrows buzzed at him like a cloud of locusts and he laughed and threw himself down behind the arrow-proof walls. – I see *you* at least are valiant! he said to his men, and they smiled shyly. (Merveille, however, did not look around, but only said with his usual dryness: Yes, Seigneur, we are very effective.) Boucher was doing execution *comme il faut*, Saint-Foy was calm and steady . . . He took an arquebus from Rondeval and charged it. Then he applied his eye to the slit. The weird monotonous patterns of Savage cross-beams in the enemy village confused his eyes with triangles, but he blinked his eyes and squinted. A girl ran screaming from a longhouse below (in the din he could not hear her cries, but he saw her mouth gaping in horror and terror and grief); she was bearing a bleeding baby in her arms. He did not fire. Poor creature! Her husband came running out after: Champlain took aim and brought him down. The man's head exploded with a flash of red as from some fluttering leaf: it was a very lucky shot. He stood for a moment before his wife, spouting blood upon her; then he fell. She swayed there like a pine branch gracious with its needle-stars. A Huron arrow found her.

Now in the second hour the fray became wilder than ever, and Champlain clambered down from the cavalier to try to reintroduce some order into his forces, for only thus could they hope to breach the town, but the louder he yelled the less his words seemed to carry to the Huron's ears, until at last he desisted, hoarse and disgusted, feeling himself to be but a ship driven before the wind. Why would no one look to his experience? What indeed had they thought to do in bringing him here, when they made no use of him? Seeing him slacken thus, his own men became irresolute, so that again he was compelled to strut about the palisadoes to hearten them. – Two arrows sped toward him. One pierced him in the leg, and the other in the knee. He fell to the ground, incommoded with the grandest possible pains and dolors. His men threw down their guns in dismay. At once the Huron also ceased the attack. With expressions of the tenderest pity, they rushed to drag him away from the battle. – No, no, you must persevere! he shouted. Why are you all abandoning the assault? – They stroked his cheek. As soon as they were out of arrow-shot, they lifted him to their shoulders and bore him to the fortress that they had built. What an imbroglio! It was only the third hour. He continued to scold, expostulate and complain, until at last Yroquet said: Many others are wounded also, Chawain. We must carry them as we retreat. If our friends from another Nation come to help us, then we shall carry out your commands.

He dreamed; once again he saw his wife Hélène; again Nicolas Boullé took him aside and asked him to sign a quittance for forty-five hundred of the six thousand livres which he had been promised. His mouth worked bitterly. In the end, out of the six thousand livres that he'd expected from the marriage, he got fifteen hundred, and that not for nine years . . .

The following day the winds were most impetuous, at which he raged at them to fire the Hiroquois Castle once again, but they would not hear of it. His only solace was Darontal's eyes so black and luminous with respect for him that he was disarmed. Darontal stayed with him, feeding him, bringing him water, as though he were his vassal: lordly affection touched Champlain's heart. (Then, too, he must remain calm, to set an example for the other French.) They lurked in their fort all that day and through the next, occasionally beating off cautious sallies by the enemy. Brûlé and the Susquehannock Savages never came. Merveille was singing a song about a woman with long hair who waited for him at the bottom of the sea. *They called her* GOUGOU, GOUGOU *La Blonde* . . . On the sixteenth of Octobre the Savages set out for home, carrying him in a pannier upon a warrior's back, so that he was as helpless as a babe in arms – to say nothing of the jolting. Carried likewise were two wounded Huron Captains, by name Ochateguain and Orgni. The whole party seemed anxious, and never stopped to eat. Whenever hunger struck them, they smoked tobacco. The Hiroquois harried them for a league or so, but then desisted. By various signs and persuasions they proclaimed to Champlain that he ought not to mix himself in Savage affairs. They derided the Huron for cowards, that they must call in these Iron People to help them. At this, the Huron shot arrows against them in sullen silence.

Palms and Laurels

After a retreat of thirty-five leagues, they achieved the Lac of the Onondaga, also called Ontario, and had great joy to see that their canoes remained undiscovered. Now Champlain was so far recovered as to walk on his own legs, and requested the Savages to deal with him honorably by sending him back to Kebec with his men.

Kekwek? Kekwek? What is that? (Thus Orgni.)

We are very sorry, Chawain. (Thus Darontal.) We do not have enough canoes for that. You will have to winter with us. But believe me, my friend, my dear nephew, when I tell you that my lodge is your lodge.

So here too they had lied to him! Yet they went on making pretended declarations in his favor . . .

At sea he had become quite adept at distinguishing between the so-called "double lands" – *viz.*, adjacent capes, mountains, or other features which closely resemble each other and so are liable to be mistaken one for the other. Yet now it struck him that perhaps this concept applied to Savages as well as coasts. Who knew what they were thinking? Perhaps Huron friendliness was not at all the same as Souriquois friendliness – certainly the Montagnais kind he would never trust, having lived so long in proximity to those hypocritical wretches!

Take me to Kebec instantly. I command you! (Thus Champlain.)

Chawain, my brother; Chawain, my nephew; we are very sorry.

At this, Champlain became very agitated, even distrait, for in body and mind he was not accommodated to such a sojourn. But in the end he saw that he would have to bear it patiently –

He stood staring into that lake that the Iroquois called Beautiful, and saw how even this late in the season there yet remained much duckweed in pale leaf-clusters almost as rich as the wild grapes he'd seen with Robert and Poutrincourt and De Monts so long ago now in the Country of the Armouchiquois –

Was there no end to anything? When would he reach the final measurement?

Improvements

Now the Onondaga Captains or Rodiyaner had a Council, to which all the warriors came, and they discussed what had happened. Among them was a certain Captain who had succeeded to the name of Kawenenseaghtonh some time since. And these were the words of Kawenenseaghtonh:

Brothers, nephews, grandsires! Now hearken while I speak to you, for I have thought much upon this battle. The *Huron Crooked-Tongues* have devoured many of us, and our kinswomen look to us to seek revenge. But I know them well. Never could they have slain so many without the help of their cunning uncles the Iron People! And so it is the third time that the Iron People have broken the Great Peace. We have heard in the thunder of their arquebuses the footsteps of the FACELESS ONE, the Being Whose countenance is darkness. The Iron People have Power, I cannot deny it. But let our hearts now become insensible to their thunder: any other course would be shameful in the sight of the SUN. With courage and patience, we can overcome and punish this insult. – I have spoken.

Kawenenseaghtonh, your words are good. – So spoke the Captain called Hohyunhnyennih. – Now my soul is uplifted in joyous rage, for I long to put the Crooked-Tongues to the fire. We do not know whether these Iron People have a Death-Song that they sing, a song of bitterness against the fire. I crave to hear such music. I crave to go on the war-path against them. – I have spoken.

Hohyunhnyennih, your words are good. – So spoke the Captain called Sahhahwih. – Like you, I begin to grow tired of these Iron People. Our brothers the Mohawk have obtained iron arrowheads from the Hollanders. These Crooked-Tongues, the Huron who attacked us today, had them also. Here is one which I pulled out of my shoulder! This iron cuts deep! We must take hold of iron like the others, if we are to work our will in war. – I have spoken.

Sahhahwih, your words are good. – So spoke the Captain called Onehseaghhen. – These Crooked-Tongues must perish. These Iron People must perish. We shall go to their camps and kill them forever. But I too have learned something from this attack upon us. I saw how their guns made the most havoc among us when we issued forth from our palisadoes, for emerging from that narrow way we stood shoulder to shoulder like a herd of deer to be slaughtered in the traps of the Crooked-Tongues. Henceforth, we must scatter when we come near them, and approach them from all sides. I urge you all to creep upon them like the FACELESS ONE, like the ferocious darkness. They cannot turn their guns on what they cannot see. – I have spoken.

And so the Onondaga Nation, the Hill People, made plans to be more silent and cruel, in keeping with this Age of Iron which had been thrust upon them. Yet all they did for the nonce was to make plans, for in truth they were more terrified than they said. These Iron People! Horrible, horrible! But they would watch and wait and waylay them . . .

The Marvelous Adventures of Étienne Brûlé 1615–1616

I might or might not have said that Champlain sent his French boy off to the Susquehannock for reinforcements for the Yroquois campaign. It's easy to forget Brûlé, for he's a nothing, a boring person. But the Wendat didn't think so, because he was their nephew now. They chose twelve of their best braves to run with him. He was very excited to go. He still hoped that if he discovered something suitably impressive, his Captain Champlain would give him high honors. He did not see that it was his fate to spend the rest of his life among Savages. – They went around the western side of the Lac called *Ontario*, which DEKANWIDEH had once crossed; then south to Carontouan, which is the chief town of the Susquehannock. – *South to Carontouan!* What a grand sound it has! I almost called this section by that phrase. But I didn't, because I would rather concentrate on sunsets, which to greedy young Brûlé had the same rosy glow as a red fox pelt.

The Susquehannock, like all of us, longed for heads and scalps, so they set out as soon as their warriors could be gathered, but they arrived two days too late. Darontal, Iroquet, Chawain and the others had departed. Now a sullen ripple flourished briefly on the surface of the boy's smoothness, for he'd expected a reward. But there was nothing for it; he had to winter at Carontouan with the Wendat braves. There were pleasurable liaisons – how many he could not have said, for he didn't have his Captain's mania for keeping memory-ledgers. Let's simply say that squaw led to squaw, that he always gave gifts; and that the Wendat said nothing: – firstly because they were similarly entertained, and secondly because to be jealous is to be a witch fit only for burning. Ha! He knew how to play the game now. He knew women now, and fucked them well – not because he liked it; it was for the sake of the Roy! – Which reminded him: he must question their Old Men about geography, which would be of value to Seigneur Champlain. *Then*, if a dozen Swiss mercenaries with arquebuses were to drop in (invited by himself, of course), they could easily run the Savages out. Pontgravé would shake his hand and say: Well done, my little man! Pontgravé would slip him a bottle of brandy . . . Suitably motivated, he began to have some dim glimmering of the vastness of Canada's lacs to the west, in which he dreamed of sailing between isles and shoals . . . When the season improved, Étienne set about his explorations. He found the river which discharges upon the coast of Florida. Exceedingly pleased by this contribution of his to geographical knowledge, he set out with his friends for Wendaké.

Their thought was to hug the high hills which ran south and west of the Haudenosaunee, until they had passed the Wenroronon Nation. Then they could follow the forest trail through the Neutral villages, and finally, bypassing the Tobacco Nation (which scarcely comes into this book), they'd be home again. Such a route would draw them very close to the enemy, but were they not men?

Goldenrod meadows, then pale blue mountains whose forests were haze-polished to the texture of cloth – that was the way to the Haudenosaunee.

It was the Hiroquois called *Seneca* or *Sonontrerrhonons* who caught them in an ambuscade. Two of the Wendat were killed; the others fled for their lives. The Seneca seized Étienne and began to torture him. Cringing, he strove to pull away from their hands, for he redoubted their fierceness, but it would have to be an awfully slippery fish who was as adroit as that . . . They took him to their village, taunting him all the way that he was going to be burned. It was twilight. The fluffy backs of the tree-hills were gilded at arbitrary angles, and the grass along the rivers was very gold. Rich green shadows lay in the dimples between ridges. At times they came to a meadow where it was still afternoon; here the grass was almost painfully bright, and the shadows between hills were deniable. The bushes were heavy with hard emerald berries. The rivers were dark blue. Now the palisadoed village was before them, and they made the scalp-whistle, at which the other Savages came running to torment him – *ha, ha, ha,* so happily; this is the happiest thing in this history; at last someone is taking pleasure . . . They beat him and cut him – yes, yes! They flung him down in the War-Chief's lodge. All night, those who had lost relatives to the Wendat came to harass him with burning brands. In the morning they led him out and kindled a fire.

At this point, GOD took pity upon Étienne and caused an eclipse of the SUN, with which our lad was quick to frighten them, so they let him go.

Truly you are favored by Heaven, my boy! (Thus Champlain, when he heard it the following year.)

Nothing like that happened, of course. GOD wouldn't be GOD if He did things like that. Screaming, babbling, scarcely knowing what he said, Étienne told the Iroquois that if they refrained from harming him he would make peace between them and the Iron People – forever, perpetual, with loads of iron things! This had its effect. So they too called him *my nephew*, and feasted him upon roast dog and dried squash from the previous season, and he acted important and prayed constantly that they would not change their minds (although the only prayer he knew was the *Benedicite*) and at last he got away – in style, too! – Whew! (thought he to himself.) He checked his fingers and toes; they were all there; he ran like the best iron bullet!

It would never have done to tell anyone. If the Wendat thought that he'd treated with their enemies, that would be the end. The Sieur de Champlain would surely have whipped him then . . .

A Lost Bet 1616

I had almost despaired of seeing you again, I tell you! (Thus Pontgravé, at Lachine in the month of Juin.)

Despaired? said Champlain bitterly. What a laugh!

In fact Pontgravé did look glum (as well as a year older), for Captain Timothy now said to him: Seigneur, you owe me ten sols!

Ah, it was false news as well as bad that the Savages gave me, saying that you were dead. (Thus Pontgravé.) I shall praise Our LORD night and day for your safe return! Eh, I'm all out of breath! What a trying winter I've had without you! You'll never guess everything that happened – foudrilles and suchlike blizzards up our ass, scurvy and dissension – terrible, horrible! But we've kept everything shipshape, of course. I think De Monts will be satisfied . . .

And you bet my life again, you blasphemous scoundrel! I sleep in my clothes, you know. Don't think I don't know what goes on.

Champlain, I shall not wager on you again.

That remains to be seen.

The old merchant was shamefaced. – Well, and how was your journey? Did you blast the Hiroquois?

Yes, yes.

Good. Bon! And now we must enlarge our settlement at Kebec; that is what I have been thinking . . .

I agree. Our men have cleared far too little land, being greedy of beaver-skins.

Darontal stood looking about him.

Most astonishing of all were the river-tides, which he had never seen before. Evidently there was some powerful WATER-SPIRIT here. This grand lodge of the Iron People was also an enlightenment to his eyes. He could never have imagined such a thing if he had not seen it. And the stone people eternally tortured on stone Cross-trees – the Grey-Gowns had many of these to show him. The Grey-Gowns said that these dead people were their uncles, and that the dead people were also alive, which he could not understand, yet he believed without understanding. In his Country there was a Shaman named Tehorenhaegnon who could make the rain come; and his rival Tonneraouanont the Hunchback boasted of strangling his own sister in the womb. There was no reason for Darontal to contradict any of these things, either. After all, he was here to get presents. What would Chawain give him? Chawain had brought him here; that showed that Chawain was his friend.

He spoke to Iroquet of the Little Nation and said to him: Tell Chawain that I am his uncle now. Tell Chawain that he must trade with me now before all other Wendat.

No, I'll tell him, said Merveille, spitting on the ground.

So Darontal was a step closer to pure iron unmediated by the haughty Algonkin Nations who so often stopped the way or levied tolls. An endless friendship worked out by iron for skins: that was what this visit meant. But did Chawain truly comprehend his obligations? It was difficult to say. Chawain was a shifty individual. He'd threatened more than once to trade with the Yroquois, who were Darontal's enemies and must therefore be Chawain's enemies. The matter was incomprehensible.

Nor could anyone deny Chawain's childishness – although there was no doubt of his courage; he was great in that way. But he'd wept like a child because they had not burned up all the Hiroquois in that town! If they killed all the Hiroquois, whom would the young men have to fight then?

Then, too, Chawain was inconsistent. He'd been angry when the People tortured their enemies the Hiroquois. He had defrauded the People of their right. Didn't he know that friends are friends because they burn enemies together? What was he? – *Haii, haii*, he was only an Iron Person!

And Champlain, he stood watching Darontal.

Now the man must see my true importance, he said to himself. Now he will tell the other Huron to obey me!

He was still shaking with rage at having had to winter among the Savages. They had promised to bring him home after the battle: that was their devoir. And he had believed them. But as the proverb says, experience surpasses science. – I shall never go among them again until I can control them, he said to himself. Ah, they are cunning and evil, these Savages – I see now how foolish I was to be so friendly with them. My escape was narrow indeed.

And as he smiled at Darontal and gave him hatchets and blankets, he bit his lip with hatred.

The French Dress
1624

> But all obeyed their dreams as a divinity, exactly observing whatever had been represented to them in sleep.
>
> MARIE DE L'INCARNATION, to her son (1670)

Making the Eight Contemplations I've now passed eight years streaming prismatically down rocky riverbeds from the Yrocois Castle which withstood Champlain's siege, thereby gaining Power, for the Yroquois say that if you seize the invisible knives of death hurled by the Sorcerer who would kill you; if you snatch them from the air before they hurt you then they are yours to turn against him. Eight years, I said (although we'll soon retrace our steps; you know me). In the Country of the Souriquois I see Born Underwater now a woman with her mother's thin angry mouth, her mother's eyes perfect and black and glittering with strange openness like lakes which cannot be anything but honest – but there is also something hurt, gentle in their upward gaze. Born Swimming is older now; she carries three wrinkles above each brow. Two vertical creases weigh upon the bridge of her nose, and her cheeks are as shriveled as the skins of old berries. Yet she is haler than ever, and boils the marrow from the moose-bones after her accustomed fashion, in a kettle obtained in exchange from the Iron People – not the same kettle, to be sure, for that cracked long ago. Her new husband cut it up and adorned himself with stream-washed triangles of copper. He wished then to make the scraps into arrowheads, but Born Underwater said: Give me some of them to wear about my neck – which he did. He feared her, pitied her, although he never said so. And she was happy, wearing copper-Power . . .

Another epidemic came, and he died, too. Born Swimming married yet again.

Born Underwater still had her Power of seeing-ahead. It led her into dirt or blackness.

Among the Lnu'k a woman who cannot bear children is but the husk of a woman. Searching for Caribou had separated from her. She knew herself that she would never have a baby to wash so joyously in the river. Came the opening of the leaf, he helped her carry their wigwam back to the beach where they traded with the Iron People, and then he took his bow and quiver and laid them into his canoe. It was the beginning of the fat season; she did not have to interrupt her repose at once, for there was food everywhere. – Hunters visited her sometimes; she was what dead Kinebji'j-koji'j once was. (Her pale face-disk was slightly mottled like the moon.) She butchered and cooked the meat they killed. She gave them joy of her; sometimes she got joy of them. But what would happen in River-Freezing Moon? – Sometimes, when one of the men stayed for half a moon or longer and she began to know him, a picture would come to her of how he'd die: – with an Armouchiquois arrow in his throat, or icewater in his lungs when a canoe overturned in spring or autumn. Very rarely she'd see him as an Old One, dying of hunger or sickness as Old Ones must. These visions came to her against her will. She never spoke of them. Someone had once told her the tale of a blind boy with Power who frightened his mother with his sight. Born Underwater understood. The men liked her because she was silent.

She painted herself with red ocher and slipped her Armouchiquois wampum-strings about her neck. She hung wampum from her ears. Over her robe (whose ANIMAL PERSONS she'd freshly painted with a moose-bone), a circlet shone dark golden-green with copper-Power. Her heart was pounding. She felt almost sick. She took a birchbark bowl in her hand and went past the falls to Beaver's house. Just upstream of this the water was brown and still. She knelt down quietly on the bank and dipped her bowl into the water. Then she stood up and carried it back to a sunny granite outcropping she knew about beyond the trees, where no one was likely to disturb her. She was very careful not to spill a drop from the brimming bowl. This water from the place where Beaver lived had Power. She set the bowl down. She looked and listened to make certain that she was alone. From the moose-skin bag she wore about her neck she took the stone that Moose had given her from his stomach. Gripping it tightly, she stared into the water in the bowl, and began to sing a dream-song, very softly so that no one but the MN'TU'S could hear. It was a song whose cadence was as the cadence of the wind in spring, when river-ice begins to melt, and the icy pine needles tinkle together. Because she sang without error, Power rose in her and gripped her with tensely painful pleasure, narrowing her vision until she knew nothing but the water quivering almost imperceptibly in the bowl. There was a face in the water which had once been her face. Now it began to glow and run and change. It was a man's face. He had one eye.

A Perfect Match

One-Eye wore a robe of peltries painted with the shapes of caribou, in the sharp-angled style of his People. His wife had made it for him, but she was dead. She had died giving birth, and the baby perished also. After this, One-Eye said: I would rather marry a barren woman! It is less trouble. – Everyone scorned him for this. – A wide quiver of feathered arrows hung from his back. In his hand he carried a bow whose ends curved towards each other like two heads of snakes. His shield, reinforced with twigs and cords, was always in his hand. He was proud of it, and thought himself quite skilled. The truth was that it was a very ordinary shield, even being indifferently made.

She married this man, and followed him into the forest. Her People were glad to be rid of her. She never saw them again.

The Dice Game

Her husband led her through dripping forests of beech and alder, and great purple flowers whose fuzzy wet leaves drenched her to the waist. Having traded with the Lnu'k and also gotten a bride, he was happy now to be coming back into his own Country, with its lakes of silver and gold linked by thin white rivers. Silver lakes were gold at the edges, filled with dark islands; lakes terminated in fishtails whose scales shone in the haze; lakes made faces in the forest: a lake for each eye; a narrow pond for the nose, set just over an expressionless river-mouth. Lake-hands opened wide. Steam rose from them, for the express purpose of permitting the swarms of blackflies to shimmer. She never told her husband why she'd accepted him, and he never asked; she was generally silent. Only her eyes spoke, changing in accordance with her thoughts within, just as two lakes side by side will change color together every moment in consistency with the SUN and WIND and tree-shadows which impel from difference to difference. His good eye peered and glared; his bad eye was as a frozen lake.

She cut her hair (which had grown long since Searching for Caribou left her); for she was married again. – That is good, said her husband. Yes, cut it well in front, so that you can see when you run.

They went on, north and west. She did not know exactly where he was taking her. It didn't matter. – The Lnu'k loved the fruits of the sea, and so they did not go very far from it. But her husband's people, the Innuat,* were very different. They did not fear to wander deep in the forest where the greatest Power lived, where the Oldest Old Ones dressed themselves in leaves and mosses. Her father had warned her never to go that far. He himself had seen the *KUKWESK*, the hairy Giants who killed people by screaming. They ate people's flesh. The KUKWESK had not harmed him because They were eating a dead bear; They liked bear-meat, too. Now maybe he was one of Them; he was dead; who knew what he was now? From her mother she'd heard of the *MI'KMWESU'K*, the beautiful Flute-Players whose music made things alive. They lived in the forest; They had the ultimate Power. People who were lost sometimes saw Them. A night in a MI'KMWESU wigwam was the same as a winter among the People. And farther in the forest, that must be the way to Ghost World. There the wicked would have nothing but bark to eat. But she did not dare to say anything of this to her husband. She knew that he would strike her; she did not have to see-ahead to know that. – Let me go to Ghost World, then! she thought bitterly.

In the winter they melted snow in their kettle, and the water tasted like smoke.

Excellence

One-Eye was always hungry. He was as avid as a man just out of the sweat-bath. When she joined the others in catching mollusks and eels to dry before the cold darkness came again, she often saw him helping himself to that food. He ate more than two other men, it seemed to her. But he was not a good hunter. This shamed her.

* Montagnais.

The French Dress

She strove to be a good wife, although it seemed that she could not please him. All the Innuat looked down upon her, as she thought at first. They thought so highly of themselves that anything she said might have been an insult. So she was silent. That winter he became snowblind, and Born Underwater was forced to scrape his eyes with a knife of the Iron People, to let the humors out. When this did not help him, she anointed his eyeballs with goose-fat. Suddenly he jerked out of her arms, saying that she was clumsy, and meant to poison his vision forever. Valuing her repose, she let him go. He staggered out of the wigwam and sat staring sightlessly. Leather fringes dangled from his shoulders like strings of rain. His fingers worked; the tomahawk-head was soon wound tight against the haft with leather strips. Perhaps she would leave him in the summer. She would go back to her Country and say that her Power was gone. Then she might have a man who respected her. But no – she would not have children. – So One-Eye crouched outside that night, while his wife Born Underwater lay sleeping with the starshine in her face . . .

The next day, Manitousiou the Sorcerer began drumming, and so he cured One-Eye.

The Sorcerer was kind to her. He always gave her food. He was the eldest of four brothers. The youngest, Pastedouachouan, was at Kebec, learning sorceries from the Iron People. When he came back, he would teach the Sorcerer what he had learned, and then the Sorcerer would help him get a wife or two. The Sorcerer dreamed of animals nearby, and One-Eye killed a cow moose, after which Born Underwater was happy. Sasousmat and Mestigoît, the other two brothers, were good hunters, so no one went hungry that winter. After awhile, Born Underwater began to laugh and joke with them, but never with her husband.

The warm days came. The women boiled maple syrup. Now game became less scarce, and the Innuat gathered together again.

One-Eye put Beaver's bones into the spring, so that he might live again. Beaver's skull shimmered white and weird in the clear water.

Now Born Underwater went to this same spring, and gazed with eyes so black and lonely into her own stainless face floating in water; she tightened her mouth in concentration. It was the Moon of Leaf-Opening, the mountains blue against the gold sky of evening; an evening of astonishing limpidity, not unlike one in 1989 in which everything seemed transparent to the view, far off, no matter how distinct, and as a result of this corresponding boundlessness the streets of Kebec were like chambers in a wet golden seashell . . .

Tall trees rose up to the SUN (which is the heart of MANITOU's wife), their boughs arching gently downward like wings feathered with the bitterfresh needles shimmering blue and green, scales of swimming tree-fish in the seasky. Born Underwater was scraping a deerhide stretched on a frame; smiling to herself, she flicked it with her thumbnail and it hummed like a living drum. The barkskinned cones of lodges craned around her on the field. Pigarouich was going into the forest, with his bow across his shoulder and his quiver on his back. The Sorcerer's wife was fetching firewood with her two little girls. The Sorcerer himself, he who was called Manitousiou the Married Man, was helping Sasousmat repair a canoe. Mestigoît and some other young men were preparing to attack the Hiroquois. One-Eye her husband was paddling on the Road That Walks, seeking to spear sturgeon. Born Underwater could not see him anymore. She finished scraping the skin. Now the Sorcerer was greasing his face and painting it with red and black ocher; he was very fond of himself.

When her husband came back, Born Underwater had taken up the shinbone of a moose, which she used to paint with, and was coloring her new beaver-robe with designs in the fashion of birds and animals, but One-Eye was scornful and said: That is no longer the fashion of our Nation! You must wear a French dress and blanket-cape. That is the way to look beautiful.

Husband, I am happy in this way, she said. Let us save our peltries and exchange them for other goods of the Iron People. Don't you need a stout hatchet? How much longer will this kettle last?

At this her husband clouted her, saying: You are a barren woman and a foreigner. At the very least be obedient. – Then he took the robe away from her and soon came back with the clothes of the Iron People, which she recognized as having belonged to another woman of this Nation.

She did not ask how he had gotten them, but silently put them on as he had asked her to do. Her eyes were hurt and glowing. Her mouth tightened. To herself she said: Someday I shall avenge this insult.

The summer days went on. She rarely saw-ahead anymore. As they lifted their canoes out of the stream, preparing to shoulder them up the portage trail, a crow flew low over their heads and the cattails waved and rustled with breezy whispers. Born Underwater threw the bundle of otter-peltries onto her shoulders; they were going to trade with the Wooden Boat People, the Iron People. There was a smell of growing things all around her. The oak leaves were lengthening day by day; the white violets were in flower.

Kebec Years
1616–1624

If a light exists within a luminous one, then it gives light to the whole world; but if it does not give light, then it is darkness.

The Gospel of Thomas

On the eighth of Juillet they'd set out for Kebec in Pontgravé's pinnace, arriving on the eleventh. I have already told how Champlain brought the Huron Captain, Darontal, back from the Hiroquois campaign with him as his guest, so that he might see the superior manner of living practiced by the French. Some of the lesser Savages in Darontal's retinue had also come to trade, which was laudable. The Algoumequins would not like it, of course, but both they and the Montaignez must now be superseded, for there was no doubt about it: the Huron had the best beaver-pelletries in Canada! – although it is true that they were mendacious wretches. Through intercourse with civilized men such as himself and Père Le Caron they might someday become refined, if he showed sufficient charity toward them . . . – however, he no longer took great pleasure in believing that. Last winter had sickened him of Savages. But he must continue to go through the motions, which was why at Kebec he now gave Darontal good cheer and made him many presents, at which he was filled with admiration for everything French, saying that he would never rest until his friends had also seen these wonders, and many other utterances of the same tenor. – I foretold this, did I not? (Thus Champlain.) Now, my friend, you see that my words are always true. – Yes, Chawain. I see that. (Thus Darontal, via that obliging wag-tongue, Captain Merveille.)

According to the arrangement which he had made with his good friend the Sieur de Pontgravé, he now set his sawyers and masons to aggrandizing the size of the Habitation by a ratio of one-third, adding many fortified buildings. He smiled to see the thriving apple-trees which De Monts had given him in Normandie . . . The strawberry blossoms had long since given way to unripe buds, and the oak leaves were more than two inches in length. The wheatfields waved as proudly as any he had ever seen in France.

There was little news. A locksmith and a sailor had drowned, as it appeared, for they never came back from the Fleuve Saint-Laurent. At first Champlain had a soupçon or surmise that Savage treachery was behind it, but Pontgravé only said: Don't get a toothache! We must all lie under earth or water in the end . . . – to which of course he must agree, and after that the occurrence hardly seemed so extraordinary. Besides, the Montagnais and Algonkin continued tractable. Following the command of his Captain the Sieur de Monts, he had begun to pay them less for their beavers, which they accepted patiently, like Christians. It should not be long before no man among them defied him anymore. Then at last he could cherish them as his dark shy children . . . – What else? The leak in the roof had been fixed. – What else? No English or Hollanders had lately infested the Fleuve; the Yroquois had darkened no French door. – As all Canada seemed therefore to be in order, he made arrangements to return to France. – Who was eligible to keep him company? – Merveille, perhaps; Merveille had upheld military discipline – but the man replied that he would rather watch the Store-house, which diligence could not but please Champlain. – On the fifth day of Août, therefore, he departed Tadoussac un-Merveilled, but in company with Pontgravé. He'd left the Sieur de Parc in command at Kebec. (Merveille was a good man, but not well-born enough for that. He waxed his cockade with moose-tallow . . .) Two of the Recollects had joined him: – *viz.*, Père Le Caron, and his Superior, Père Jamay. It was their desire to testify to their fellow priests in France about the rich harvest of souls which waited to be gathered, and also to lodge a complaint against those insubordinate Malouin traders who were enemies of their Mission – oh, someday GOD would punish them! The Recollects had had an extremely reasonable plan, which was to frenchify certain Montagnais by force, compelling them to abandon their heathenish language, ringing them around with French farmers – but the traders replied that in that case they'd burn everything and drive the Savages away. Little wonder that no progress was being made here –

The voyage was unremarkable. Champlain was vigilant as usual against fires and tidal currents; he slept by day and watched over all by night, silently approaching the helmsman from behind, compass in hand, and then reproving him for having strayed a degree from his course, so that the man leaped in terror. He took regular soundings, and crossed the Grand Banc in accord with his good reckoning; he crossed the open stretch and successfully avoided the much-dreaded Channel of Saint George, which lies north of the English Channel; and so at last he hove in sight of our French coast, the sky being free of any cloud. – Our Champlain is very certain in his knowledge, he heard Père Le Caron say. *Ver-*y certain. – Pontgravé belched and spat over the side. He was definitely getting old. Sly and toothless, he continued to thrust his big nose into Champlain's affairs, brushing mosquitoes off his limp black hat, rubbing his horny hands together . . .

A Faithful Likeness

For Pontgravé as for other Frenchmen, Canada had once been a realm of newness. With his ehs and ahs he'd cried out as loud as the rest of them the first time he'd seen the Fleuve Saint-Laurent! Everyone was alike in that first moment of a Canadian career – the baby reaching for a mote of sunlight because it was brightly incomprehensible. Of course good men such as Pontgravé went on to the second stage, when novelties were extinct, which allowed Canada to be used most facilely. This was when men became beaver-traffickers. After many years of this – ever so many in Pontgravé's case – the final phase loomed up inevitably, like an iceberg in front of your ship. Now nothing but dullness remained. Pontgravé was almost at that point.

Home

Arriving at Honfleur on the tenth of Septembre, Champlain sought tidings. The Roy had put down Huguenot rebels at Champagne, and now he'd married the Spanish Infanta to whom he'd been betrothed in infancy. Her likeness was everywhere. She was fair, and preferred brocades of green and silver (said De Monts).

Who cares, Seigneur? interrupted Pontgravé. It's all the same to me. She's a Spaniard; she'll corrupt this Country; you just wait and see! Probably gives head to Jesuits on the side . . .

Be silent, said De Monts very coldly. Champlain, I must tell you also of the death of our friend, the Chevalier de Poutrincourt, which occurred last year. And Port-Royal has been destroyed!

What? I don't believe it! By the Basques?

The English. If only Madame de Guercheville had given me thirty-six hundred livres when I wanted it, I know we could have done something. Pitiful! But we'd already lost the investment; that doesn't matter. The tragic event was Poutrincourt's collapse, my good friends. And how inessential! If he had but consulted me, it could have been avoided. Such a true heart! His poor wife – how I feel for her! It is a pity that your birth did not entitle you to marry one of the daughters, Champlain. But of course you married above yourself as it is. – Poor, poor Jean! If he were alive today, I could have set him up as my Viceroy at Kebec . . . Eh, you will have to do. And naturally I have every confidence in you.

I shall do my duty, said the other through clenched teeth.

And your patron Condé's in the Bastille, you know.

What?

He wavered a little in his loyalty to the Roy, it seemed. Don't you remember? He led those Huguenots whom you think so highly of.

Ah, said Champlain softly. In the Bastille, and Canada with him. From this I infer that our enviers will not be very slow in spewing out their venom.

Surprise, Surprise

He was living separately from his wife Hélène, for she had requested this upon his return from Canada in the month of Juillet, and he, no longer having any desire to force her, assented to her will, at which she made him many demonstrations of gratitude and tenderness.

The Top 1617

The following spring, while Louis the Roy schemed with his chief falconer and catamite (whom he'd made Governor of Amboise for his talents); while the Queen's brother-in-law Concini assembled an army to usurp Condé's usurping place; while Madame de Guercheville prayed behind her double doors, which were carven with garlands in ovals, that cunning Methuselah the Sieur de Monts wet his thumb and drew up the articles for a new company to trade in beavers. O Canada! – Condé thought about Canada now and then, chained and shivering in the Bastille. Madame de Guercheville thought about it every day, mortifying herself with the thorny fact of unbaptized Savage souls. The Queen never thought about it. The Roy, on the other hand, studied over Canada from time to time, because his dead father Henri had made a top for him out of Champlain's first map of 1603, trimming it and pasting it tight upon a hollow tin ball, brushing on the lacquer with his own hand: what better use for that stupid Country than to make the Dauphin laugh? – Who's Papa's darling? – Louis, two years old, tapped his tummy shyly. – And who's the Infanta's darling? – As he had been taught, the boy pointed at his penis . . . – Ha, ha! Now go play with your top and be silent! – So Louis XIII, the Most Christian Roy, gave the world a spin, watching Kebec and China wobble round and round amidst the luxuriant flashing of Champlain's endlessly replicated trees, and the Fleuve Saint-Laurent swallowed its own tail, round and round . . . Suddenly he flung his toy against the wall. He turned to the Governor of Amboise. He said: I was made to whip tops at the Tuileries. It is time I took charge.

The Governor kissed him on the mouth. – Yes, Seigneur. I shall summon De Vitry.

The Sieur de Vitry said: Should Concini defend himself, what does Your Majesty desire me to do?

Louis was silent.

Sire, smiled De Vitry, I follow your orders.

On the twenty-fourth of Avril, as Concini fondled his sister-in-law the Queen-Mother, smirking as he told her how he'd put Leonora up to ordering the Roy not to make so much noise playing billiards, De Vitry and twenty picked men stood waiting with pistols. The Roy played billiards, smiling. The Governor of Amboise was his opponent. Soon the Governor would be promoted to Duc. Concini gave the fat old Queen-Mother's teats one last good twist and swaggered out. De Vitry was waiting for him. De Vitry said: I place you under arrest!

Concini drew himself up. – I? *I?*

So you resist, sighed Vitry, shooting him five times.

They took Leonora to the Bastille and beheaded her for treason and sorcery. They confined the Queen-Mother to her apartments. She wept and said: I've reigned for seven years. Now I await my heavenly Crown. – A mob of Royalists tore Concini's heart from his corpse and devoured it.

A Break with the Past

Ah, said De Monts when he heard, now that France is safe again, the Roy can give more time to Canada.

(Is it admirable or contemptible or merely faintly amusing, this optimism with which we assume that others must be fascinated by what concerns us? De Monts' optimism, like Champlain's, was a never-failing stream – whether of piss or pure water may you be the judge.)

Canada, Canada – who gave a Huguenot's ass about *that* place?

De Monts' new partners, for one. They were already making the Exercises, counting up the gold sols they had coming to them if they clipped each other trading with the Savages – and Pontgravé assured them that the squaws never resisted a white man. Grand! Incroyable! Parfait! And this time the Beaver Company wouldn't make any mistakes: everything was organized; they'd stick together for a hundred years! The Maréchal de Thémines was the figurehead now; Pontgravé had set that up; it was the old story. And Champlain remained the Viceroy's Lieutenant, of course, of course: De Monts assured him of it. After all he'd done . . .

But when he got ready to sail, one of the partners, by name Daniel Boyer, took him aside.

Champlain, suppose you were me, and you'd thrown a lot of good money after bad for the sake of a few mangy beaver-skins that might never return the investment. (Thus began Monsieur Boyer.)

Beaver-skins always return the investment, Monsieur. I think we both know that. You equivocate with me. How many leagues and fathoms before you make your point?

In such a situation, continued Boyer, it is desirable to make a clean break with the past. Do you comprehend me?

And I'm the past, said Champlain slowly, is that it?

Exactly!

Why, you execrable serpent!

Be reasonable, Champlain. I'm speaking from a strictly sublunary point of view. Most of the traders hate you. We can't work with you. Are we to find you in our way year after year?

In your way? When I go fight battles with the Hiroquois for you? Ingrate!

Save your romantic military dreams for the Roy: *he'll* like them. You're through in Canada. What it comes down to is this. Your colonization schemes are megalomania, pure and simple. They'll cost hundreds of thousands. Worse yet, they'll spoil the Savages for the trade. You're through, I said! Don't you comprehend me?

Where's Pontgravé? Pontgravé will knock you down three pegs, young man –

Listen to me, Champlain! Businessmen have no remorse. They can't afford it. Pontgravé is a businessman. Can you follow the syllogism from there?

Champlain could not determine whether the expression on the man's face was sympathetic or merely impatient. He thought about this for some time after he had left the offices of the Compagnie. He went home and lay down.

Hélène stirred in her room, but she did not come out.

Falling asleep at last, he dreamed that she wore a circlet of porcupine quills about her forehead. A baby was at her breast; her hair fell free. When he awoke, his heart ached worse than before.

He wrote a memoir to the Roy, begging him for the necessary funds to fortify New France against the English, who could easily do what they had done to Poutrincourt at Port-Royal (Champlain saw-ahead). And surely the Sweetwater Sea, beside which the Huron Savages lived, must be the way to China . . . *That* must be protected. They were afraid of Hiroquois reprisals, Pontgravé had said . . . Above all, a town must be built at Kebec. A fort must be built at Tadoussac. He could see it all. (He had such a lump in his throat that he could barely breathe.) He wanted fifteen Jesuits or Recollects, three hundred good French families, three hundred soldiers . . . And it would all make money. The useless trees could be burned for potash; and there were mineral mines in Acadia, as he had well seen (although that had been another of Prévert's disappointments, but not to mention that) . . .

Hélène was staring out the window.

He lay sleepless and tried to catalogue all the animals in the Country of the Souriquois: hares, partridges, pigeons, elk . . .

The skin-trade was worth four hundred thousand livres a year. He wrote the Chamber of Commerce about it. (He felt – he felt the same as when those Huron brutes had held him hostage!) And if you added in everything else – the mines, the duties on imports collected from China, the cod-fishery, the timber – why, you'd have to add five million to that! And if they founded a town at Kebec, not even the size of Saint-Denis . . .

The sleepless itching of his soul grew so unbearable that he flailed himself to rawness, listening to night sounds as Hélène slept on; thinking – exhausted though he was – of the next dozen things which must be done to secure his position; and comprehension attacked him like a physical irritation far exceeding in intensity the ache of his bloodshot eyes, comprehension that the integrity of the Store-house could not be guaranteed as long as the key was in another's keeping; so with a tide of loathing like crabs on his skin he awoke fully to the ignominy which he had suffered under De Monts – and now all these traders in the Company sought to render his life impossible; he'd understood this before; he'd even complained of it, but until now he had never been goaded by the matter to ILLUMINATION itching along his thighs and armpits. The sensation continued. Now he brought into relief the Sieur de Pontgravé, toward whom all the friendship curdled in his breast, as irrevocably as had his love for that Huron Savage, Darontal – and for a long moment a sense of snowy blankness descended upon him as if all his maps were erased or unmade, and he could not even recollect where this Ouendaké or Huronia was, so that despair and fear swelled in him and all that he could think of was that he must somehow undo Pontgravé. He knew very well that Pontgravé would help him if he were ever in need – hadn't it been Pontgravé who'd arranged the matter of his marriage, who'd put the fiasco of the Isle de Sainte-Croix in a good light with De Monts, who'd obtained for him his present Lieutenancy at Kebec? He knew that he had given himself to Pontgravé like a child, dully, trustingly, on account of this very quality from which the beneficiary customarily averts his eyes. Now all that must be at an end. His determination was equal in intensity to his old exploratory fervor when he'd set out with his Uncle Provençal on that voyage which would bring him to Mechique. How happy he had been then! Every league of ocean was new like every island unrolling before him, like all the beauty of Robert's women, with an endlessness that only his youth allowed him to feel. Now that was gone, and his drive to rid himself of Pontgravé was a frenzied nervous irritation. This was his true self which had been waiting for him: this realization crossed ruthlessly into the future like a line of latitude splitting apart an entire sea on one of his maps and going on to do the same to the land. Everything seemed sad and vivid. At last he was feeling the first epiphany of his first self, just as Robert had come into his own. Now everything would be easy. He would deal with Pontgravé unbendingly, and within a measurable number of months or years Pontgravé would be nothing but a fat old man, goutish and irrelevant, who had nothing to do with the administration at Kebec. Champlain did not yet know how this would come about, which unsettled him, for he preferred in most cases to put procedure before decision. But now he was a new Ignatius, a man in harmony with himself. What must be done would be done.

Still, it was a rather difficult play. He must lay down his hand correctly. He must dissemble –

He lay down and dreamed that all the Savages were hunting him! He ran across a grid of longitude and latitude that stretched beyond any horizon, hoping (he had to hope) that certain crossings of the lines might be sanctuaries such as churches. The Savages had already slaughtered every other Christian in the world. He ran through a grey-green leaf-dusk, the map-lines luminescent at his feet; here was a conjunction or intersection of them at last, over by this heap of boulders. He tried to hide within it like a worm, but there was no space for him. Now an old squaw saw him and raised an exultant shriek. Warriors came and spitted him on their spears. – He awoke in a cold shudder. – How absurd these dreams!

Further Pleasures of the Toy World *1618*

The Rouennais hated him so bitterly that they tried to stop his ship from leaving Honfleur; he had to get another letter from the Roy just for that. So he paced the deck, glaring most valiantly. He was Captain in Ordinary for the Roy in the Western Ocean; he was uncredentialed. – Père Le Caron accompanied him, murmuring, *Ver*-y tragic, Monsieur. Eh, your position is *ver*-y tragic. – And, as always, the Sieur de Pontgravé commanded the vessel. That worthy was in fine fettle. – Pull yourself together, Champlain! he shouted. This Boyer you complain of, he's nothing! I remember when he was nothing but a puling infant, and that's exactly what he still is – an infant, really! He just wants to act like a big shot. Don't worry; I'll pull some strings; I'll get your commission back from those bastards; the worst is already over . . .

Champlain said nothing.

I warn you, Champlain: glumness is bad for the liver! Think about it! Hey! Remember when I told you that story about squaws and grease, and you fell for it?

I remember everything.

Ah, but do you calculate it also, as I do? Calculate this! Ten livres for a beaver now! Ha, ha! And the bastards from La Rochelle have me to thank for it. I can't help dragging them up to glory with me. Eh, let 'em have a whiff; there's more than I can eat!

They arrived at Tadoussac on the twenty-fourth of Juin – *viz.*, Saint Jean's Day. It was so wonderful to be in Canada again that he could not keep from laughing. There were tears in his eyes – extraordinary! He was Emperor again . . . He looked upon the wheat, which was more than a span high; he saw that the cherries were fully leaved . . .

Kebec had grown a trifle in size. That long sharp roof he'd raised still broke the wind's back, toothed with chimneys and dormer windows. The new stone convent of the Recollects was well underway. There were now more than sixty French Christians in permanent residence there, and he had hopes of further increase, although there were not yet many women, it was true. Perhaps if he could persuade Hélène to accompany him . . . ? Now that distance had sharpened his mind, he comprehended how truly loving and obedient she was; she'd come; she'd do anything for him!

What else?

Bad news, Seigneur . . . (Thus Captain Merveille.)

Bad news? *Bad* news? What could it be now, Monsieur? (Thus Champlain, with bitter dryness.)

Now Merveille commenced his narrative, which was corroborated by Godet and the priests who'd stayed over . . . Remember that locksmith and sailor who drowned last year? – Well, they'd since washed up as skeletons, in such wise that it was clear that the Montagnais had murdered them.

Treason! He slammed Kebec tight like a clamshell!

(They jumped at Kebec when he told them to, by GOD! Credentials or not!)

He could see now that he had allowed the Savages too much license . . .

Now the Captains of the Montagnais came to offer beaver-skins, which was that Nation's way of paying compensation. – Tell them we must speak with the murderers! cried Champlain, trembling with rage. Tell them that we command the murderers to appear before us! – One came, and one didn't. Champlain raised the drawbridge behind the one who had been caught, so that he could not escape. The light cannons peeped through their square stone windows. Then he began shouting into the man's face so that spit covered him from forehead to chin, shrilling that he deserved death; as meanwhile Père Le Caron paced mournfully to and fro, twiddling his thumbs behind his back and saying: We French have been good to you. *Ver*-y good to you . . .

Now the murderer's father cried out: Here is my son who committed the supposed crime. He's worth nothing, but consider, Champlain: he was but foolish; he was not a premeditator. We are in your power –

And the son said much the same.

I shall have you put to death! screamed Champlain.

There was a silence. Then Champlain remembered what Boyer had said to him in France. Drawing himself up, he said: We need a break with the past, you vermin!

Pretending that the man was Pontgravé, he shook him by the shoulder. – I'll burn you in chains! he screamed.

The murderer turned to a beaver-clerk he knew, by name one Beauchaine, and said to him: Put me to death then, without formality.

Ah, we are not accustomed to put men to death as suddenly as that, said Père Le Caron. We must deliberate.

And he whispered into Champlain's ear, reminding him that the garrison did not have sufficient arms to take revenge for this, given the vindictiveness of the Savages (which had now been proven, for it came out that the locksmith had been murdered because he often beat the Savages in a rage: – clearly, then, they did nurse their grudges and insults, like demons suckling at snake-venom); no, it was better to leave the matter.

So Champlain said: Very well. We forgive you. Now leave us hostages, and pay us your beaver-skins.

That's the way! cried Pontgravé. You showed them! These crises don't go away if one ignores them . . .

He was happy. No one dared defy him –

. . . And the Montagnais were also happy, seeing now how little it cost to kill a couple of these hated Iron People.

Later that summer, when the Huron met him at Three Rivers and asked him to go on the warpath with them against the Hiroquois, he refused (but embraced them, dissembling his hatred). He would never go with them again. Still, he took pleasure in seeing how their caravans seemed to increase in number each year; soon they too would be vassals of the French.

His puppet Étienne Brûlé had come down that year; Champlain patted his head and assured him in all precision that he would come to Ouendaké someday to reward him. (As Pontgravé would say, fat chance!) – What else?

He built a furnace to test certain ashes. And Anne Hébert had married a Frenchman at Kebec; it was the first marriage in New France.

Tallying the Game

He arrived in Honfleur on the twenty-eighth day of Août. Everyone was against his new settlement plan. They were still afraid that the conversion of the Savages would interrupt the fur trade. The Protestants from La Rochelle were writing vicious pamphlets against him; the Rouennais demanded that Pontgravé be given supreme authority . . . They think they're setting up some sort of republic here! snorted Champlain, as if he thought it very funny. But his eyes were puffy and red. – Well, they can have those notions if they like. Eh, Pontgravé? Pontgravé?

I'm with you every step of the way, Champlain. Would I lie to you? Let's just not rock the Ark, pal, or all the little animals will tumble out and drown two by two. Get it? Anyhow, this discussion is giving me heartburn. (Thus poor Pontgravé, feeling caught in the middle, grimacing and quickly popping down a pill of the *castoreum* or beaver-medicine, which he got for free.) I don't often suffer from sickness, you know. On the other hand, I haven't exactly been a well man for some years. And this is absolutely the worst season for gout. All the Doctors agree with me there. I for one have made it quite clear to them that I'm a special case, because – Champlain, Champlain! I know you too well! You're not listening.

You've made it clear that you're a special case, repeated Champlain patiently, because – ?

CHRIST, man, why must you always be so wooden and literal?

Champlain thought to himself: Nothing has happened yet. But someday I shall tame you. Someday I shall be myself . . .

. . . Now he was at the offices of the Company, and his heart sank to see De Monts conferring with his enemy Boyer, and then De Monts approached him coldly, without even taking his hand, and said to him in hearing of all: – I cannot but suspect a lack of diligence on your part, and perhaps even treason. – Oh, not *your* treason, of course, but perhaps some of your men . . . ? How could the trade have been so poor this year? Canada swarms with beavers, and the Savages remain Savages. Surely that Jean Duval whom you hanged must have left confederates –

You say that we sabotaged the trade? said Champlain, unable to restrain himself. Why would we cut our own throats? Have you no further use for my services, Seigneur? For I tell you, I do not care to be spoken to in this manner.

Ah, now the lynx bares his claws, said De Monts (meanwhile paring his own fingernails). Look you, Champlain. We'll dwell no more on the past. Speak to me of the future. How can we make a profit at Kebec?

Exclude the illegal traders. Civilize the Huron. Punish the Montagnais –

So simple! – De Monts clapped his hands together.

Champlain glared at him stonily.

But perhaps it is time to give the Sieur de Pontgravé command at Kebec. Perhaps he'll please us more, eh?

I am his friend, replied Champlain very stiffly, and his age will make me respect him like my father; but as for agreeing that he be given what by right and reason belongs to me, I shall not stand for it.

Deep inside himself he was saying: I must break with Pontgravé, to put down all his tricks, supercheries and swindles . . . Why can't I act on this? – And that thought anguished him. He was very lonely.

At home he paced about.

Still, said Champlain in a very low voice, there is no reason why a man in good health, with adequate strength, accustomed to command, might not return to Canada uncredentialed . . .

You are mad! said Hélène de Champlain.

So Champlain was threatening to go into business for himself (he'd play along as Condé's Lieutenant, of course, but we all know how *that* works thus Pontgravé). – Who does Champlain think he is? And has he ever seen me play the wrong card? Oh, I'm very frightened; I'm shitting in my pants – ha, ha! Thinks himself so redoubtable! Has he forgotten how I ruined Chauvin and the others? As for Poutrincourt, he sank like a stone when I pulled out of Acadia! – So watch yourself, Champlain! Anything might happen to you!

Toy Repercussions 1619

On the twenty-first of Décembre, he made the partners sign an affidavit agreeing to convey and maintain eighty persons at Kebec. The Roy gave him a pension of six hundred livres. In Janvier of 1619 he received his fifteen hundred livres from Hélène's dowry at last, but even then the partners would not accept him as Lieutenant. He had to go to Rouen and show them his commission from Monseigneur le Prince. When this was not sufficient, he found himself compelled to follow the Council in tour until he got a royal decree affirming his right to command in Canada. Decrees, of course, have a half-life; water soon ripples and ripples die away over the stone-splash of any decree. That year the ship sailed to Canada without him, and the Huron waited upon him and his guns, until at last Iroquet said bitterly: I am not astonished that Chawain does not keep his promises, for he has never been brave since the Hiroquois wounded him! – and Darontal, whose prestige was scarcely increased by Chawain's perjury, said: So it is, brothers, that we go singing the War-Song alone; however, we now have iron arrows . . . – And Soranhes the Trader soothed them, saying: Chawain becomes old. No doubt he has important Councils in the Country of the Iron People. No doubt he has been elected to the company of the Old Men. – So they returned to Ouendaké in ill humor, capturing a family of Mohawk on the way, whom they tortured and burned. – Lescarbot was marrying that year; he'd landed a real plum, some Mademoiselle Françoise de Valpergue, acquiring through her hand and person the seigneuries of Wiencourt and Audebert . . . Needless to say, Champlain didn't attend. Pontgravé remained in command until the spring of 1620, when Champlain sailed up with a commission naming him Lieutenant to the Viceroy. That was the year that the Recollects took a Montaignez boy with them to Paris, to be instructed in the True Faith and taught good French and Latin.

His Royal Flush

In Octobre, through the same illogical turn of events which now takes Born Underwater's father, Robert Pontgravé, out of this story – for, returning home with a load of skins, he'd been given command of the *Espérance*, along with a set of sealed orders, posting him to the East Indies: he must fight the Hollanders; – through the same tedious incomprehensibilities which rid us of him, Champlain's patron the Prince de Condé was released from prison. Hurray for deus ex machinas! Condé sold his viceregal office to the Duc de Montmorency for eleven thousand écus. So far, so good. Champlain and Hélène had the new man over for dinner. He was very pious, which was to their tastes. Within half an hour, Champlain had won him over to the colonial policy.

Ah, said Montmorency, your little wife – she is charming!

Now, Champlain said to himself, *now* if I measure myself carefully, I shall be Master at Kebec, and Pontgravé is through!

The following Mai, he set sail for Canada with his good Hélène.

The voyage was very rough.

Hélène in Canada 1621–1624

She quickly learned to speak the dialect of the Algoumequins, in order to catechize the Canadian or Savage girls under the direction of the Recollects. Among her other jewels she possessed a tiny mirror which dangled from a necklace. The Savages loved to admire it. When one of the Savagesses inquired of her as to why she could see her own face at Madame de Champlain's breast, Madame de Champlain smiled and replied: Ah, my dear, because you're always near to my heart!

She was so very courteous that only her husband could hear her screaming inside her heart-Church, crowded and befouled by stinking Savages . . .

When the Huron came down the grand Fleuve to trade, they were astonished and said: Now our eyes are opened, for the Iron Men who became our nephews assured us that women from your Country are ugly and bearded like them. How is this? Do you shave your beard?

I have no beard . . . Please let me alone –

Every day she promenaded to the Recollects' Chapelle and prayed that Monsieur de Champlain would return to France. She prayed at such length that the Recollects thought her wonderfully pious. Père Le Caron dilated to her upon his success in teaching the Montagnets and showed her all the petitions he was writing to the Roy in the cause of New France; he took her to visit the Savage canoes and wigwams; she climbed the great falaise above Kebec. She fancied that she could see all the way to the Country of the Hiroquois. In her dreams, hateful forests grew over her eyes.

The Roy's portrait had hung ten years in the Habitation now. From within the prison of the frame a young boy looked down at her. He reminded her somewhat of her brother Nicolas at that age. Dark curly locks crowned the egg-shaped face of almost cloistered pallor. He was neck-winged with ruffles. In his hand he held a miniature sword. His cheeks were plump and childish. He stared at her with strange eyes, the eyes of a boy backing away from punishment. – She remembered when that likeness had been displayed in the public places at Paris. He was crowned in Octobre, as she recollected – not long after his ninth birthday. She had not seen the event, but her father Monsieur Boullé had, and said that it was very splendid. And now the Roy was close upon twenty years old, a grown man, a professional soldier. Only in this outpost of wind and dead dogs and shrunken planking had the Stream of Time been choked until it ran a decade behind itself. Her husband, too, seemed to lose his years when he was here. In amazement she saw the grey receding from his hair day by day; he became ever haler and more content. He and Eustache ran about with hogsheads on their shoulders, shouting to one another in idiotic excitement. Or he'd go hunting with that obsequious Captain Merveille. It was true: he was almost magnificent in a petty way; *he* was the Roy here at Kebec . . .

In the moat, upon the carcass of a dog she saw the rushing glittering bodies of ants.

She had brought with her a great armour or wardrobe, whose doors were chased with diamond-grooves; her father Monsieur Boullé had given it to her. Seeing it stand so incongruously noble amidst the dust and stench of their quarters (which, desiring not to discourage her, he had once described to her as a sort of grand Château), she began to cry. The place could not be repaired immediately, as all the workmen were engaged in enlarging the Convent of the Recollects. Seeing her so displeased, however, he set to work with his own hands to clear away the courtyard of ordures. Captain Merveille helped him to prop up the sagging Store-house. (Eustache brought flowers and chucked her under the chin; she slapped his hand away.) – When the artisans were free, they began to work on the Habitation with saws and hammers, giving her no peace save at night (when the mosquitoes tortured her). At last they were finished, and her husband asked her if she was satisfied.

Oh, there's a great deal that I might say, she replied to him.

But why? What do you mean?

There is no need to explain what I mean, since we are such great friends. I know that you comprehend me perfectly.

He went out, and she heard him commanding some men to dig out the moat. Her breast glowed with vindictive joy to hear how the good humor had quite departed from his shouting voice . . .

She spent hours among her personal fripperies, holding to herself her satin capes and dresses which would so quickly be ruined if she ever wore them here; and if she did not the moths would surely destroy them . . . She made the Exercises desperately, being a poor sinner, stroking back down to the river's mouth where the waterfalls would not choke her with icy sprays anymore; at the river's mouth it was warm again, four years warmer when she had returned to France (she'd *never* sail to Canada again! Never, never!) and that forcibly suntanned face became white once more, snow-white, milk-white, as she prayed behind drawn curtains until her eyeballs rolled up in their sockets and she held Him splayed upon His Cross; she cradled Him beneath her chin as if His Cross were His bed; and she prayed for all the Savages in this Country that she'd deserted.

She paid endless visits to Madame Hébert and her surviving daughter (Anne, the married one, had died in childbirth); she sat with the two Langlois girls, who had become Madame the Bakeress and Madame the Artisane; in her fourth year, she also had for company Madame Pivert, the cowherd's wife . . . she was godmother to the baker's daughter, Hélène Desportes, the first white child born at Kebec.

She smiled vaguely at Pontgravé, who paid her a visit to say that Monsieur de Champlain had been quite rude to him . . .

As for Monsieur de Champlain, he was much occupied, being Leiutenant to the Roy, as we know. First he had to proclaim his new commission, which he did to the booming of the cannon, and the Recollect Pères exhorted the men to obey him, while Hélène stood looking on with the breeze blowing her hair and believing herself to be in a dream. – Then he must make progress on the construction of the new fort above the Rock – a matter of high urgency now that two ships from La Rochelle had traded arquebuses to the Savages, which was most mischievous and pernicious. – That is the way these rebels continually do evil! he cried to his wife. – Yes, Samuel, she said to him. You have spoken of this before. – He flushed. – What can one expect? he said in a low voice. After that he was often absent at Tadoussac or Trois-Rivières . . .

One day he came running in with a letter from the Roy! *Dear Champlain* he read aloud, grinning from ear to ear, *I've seen with what earnestness you're working over there* . . . For days all the men spoke of this letter in reverent voices. Her husband could do no wrong; he was in the Roy's favor. She made no remark about it, and when they turned the conversation in that direction, to give her opportunity to praise her husband as a good wife should, she ached and shrank away.

And yet it was not that she did not love him. It seemed to her that she was always on the verge of coming to accommodation with him and achieving some kind of peace, but when she sought to picture that peace in her mind she could not do it. He tried so very hard to make her comfortable in Canada that she could not blame him for anything (which formerly it had been her habit to do). Indeed she could not but feel guilty whenever he came, and that was one of the reasons that she avoided him. She said as much to Père Le Caron, who was her confessor, and he did not seem to know what to reply. Because she was young and her energies needed to be called into play, she focused them upon striving to please him, or, if she could not do that with all her heart, at least to put on a brave show for others, so as to be no disgrace to him. She did not want to relax her efforts, because doing that would leave her no other choice than estranging herself from him, and she was terrified of suffering even more from boredom and solitude than she already did. But the strain of her position exhausted her. Gradually she began to give up her promenades and good works, and spent ever more time in her room, embroidering endless tapisseries only so that her fingers would not begin to tear things to pieces.

He saw how it was for her (how could he not?), and that wounded him, though he strove always to be cheerful with her; yet she saw his pretense as well as he saw hers; and so she loathed herself more than ever.

One day in Août he took her to see her own Isle Sainte-Hélène, where the trees were lacily plaited with ivy-trails and an Algonkin canoe went past – two Indians with feathers in their hair; they saw him and her but pretended not to . . . The wall of stone and earth that he'd built in 1611 was still standing, although much cracked by the frosts of Canada. He clambered up upon it; he knelt and extended his hand to her and she shook her head smiling but he continued to hold out his hand until she shook her head again and took it and he drew her effortlessly up to him and she saw the Fleuve Saint-Laurent so blue and wide before her and her heart soared at the beauty of it and for a moment he knew that she was with him, that he had won her at last. Seeing how it was for him, she could not bear to ruthlessly spoil the pleasure he took in that day, and so forced herself to be cheerful, as if to a little child at a funeral, who cannot understand why its parents grieve.

Two Guilty Foxes

He had a nosegay of white violets. Seeing her lying in their bed, he approached her with his best tenderness and slipped his arm around her. She did not open her eyes. – I was almost asleep, she said in a weary complaining little voice, such as she often used.

Pardon me, he said quietly. He knelt and kissed her.

That hurts, she said. Your beard, Samuel, it's so grizzled and sharp . . .

On a night of such rigorous cold that the sky was bereft even of snowflakes, he went to the Store-house with Captain Merveille to get a hogshead of cider for the men, and they had some labor to work the lock, which had become both rusted and frozen in spite of his vigilance. At last Merveille proposed that they melt some moose-tallow over the fire so as to grease the mechanism, at which Champlain laughed and said: I see I have taken counsel with the wise! – for he was almost as fond of Merveille as he was of Eustache; and indeed this advice proved successful, for the hot grease, being devoured by the iron, readily appeased it, so that the key turned with scarcely a creak, and Merveille said with a smile: Consider, Seigneur, that this lock and key are all that remain now of Jean Duval! – at which Champlain's face darkened, and he said: What do you mean by mentioning that traitor to me? – Oh, fear not, he was well-hanged, said Merveille, at which Champlain laughed shortly and his shoulders slumped. Later that night, when he wished to go to bed, he found himself thinking of Duval again, not at all of his own will; but it came about because his wife had closed the bedroom door against him, being in one of her bilious moods; and he paced outside it like one of his own sentries, uncertain what he should do. If anyone else had pulled such a trick, he would have solved the case easily by putting his shoulder to the door . . . – well, maybe not anymore, for he was not so young; he'd call Eustache or Merveille (it was a wonder how the latter never seemed to age); but nonetheless it would be easy. He could not humiliate Hélène in such a way, however. Experience had made that evident. – What to do; what to do? – He took a sounding as to how many times he had asked this of himself since his betrothals and espousals, but the line ran out long before the weight hit bottom; *that* calculation could never be finished. Probably she was asleep by now. He could lower himself from the sentry's gallery and pry the casement open, quietly so as not to wake her; he did not want to irk her . . . No, he was not certain after all that the window could be opened from outside. Nor did he fancy himself as a skulker. It was now that he thought of Duval. No one had ever skulked as well as *he*. Duval you ingrate, may you be damned again even in perdition! – In Acadia – seventeen or eighteen years ago now it must have been; for the thing had happened at Port-Royal – the Sieur de Poutrincourt had kept certain fripperies locked in his *cabinet portatif* which stood in the corner, woodenly firm, its belly barnacled with fleurs-de-lys in the royal style; and Champlain sometimes wondered what it might contain – a natural line of inquiry in any Quartermaster (think you not?), be the Store-house never so small. Yet because Poutrincourt was his Captain, and the cabinet stood therefore not in his jurisdiction, he'd never sought to regale his curiosity. – Duval was not so scrupulous. One evening when Champlain was surveying the soil for minerals and Poutrincourt and Biencourt were hunting (it being Poutrincourt's turn to be Maître d'hôtel for the Order of Good Cheer), Duval thought to pick the lock and see what he might pilfer. He crept within the chamber. He inserted a rod of the proper size and thrust back the tumblers one by one; the ringed handles shuddered against the drawers like ripples. It was at this point that Champlain, his mineral researches having exhausted themselves as they always did in Canada, now returned. He haled the fellow out to be whipped, and that was done, after which they thought little more about it, as Duval had made his obligatory little contritions. But now on that cold night, pacing outside his own bedroom door, Champlain remembered the man's furtive guilt-smeared face flaring up at him like a fox surprised in the act of eating dung. He could not bear to associate himself with that face. Let Hélène sleep. But he was like Duval to this extent: that no one else must know of his shame. Wearily he threw on his coat again, and went down to the Store-house to sleep . . . The sentries knew, of course. Everyone knew. But there was nothing to be gained in taunting Champlain their Captain with that knowledge, so they were silent, and time passed.

Canadians

Yet in this phase of Champlain's life, such mergings and overlays were becoming more frequent. Duval's face kissed his, able only in this way (as it seemed) to return Captain Merveille's bygone kiss; upon Hélène's fairness was imprinted the stain of a Savagess's privities; his own men increasingly resembled the Savages in their wildness and lawlessness; in winter they bound the racquettes or snowshoes on their feet like them; they had begun to dress like them in filthy buckskins; they made liaisons and embrassades* with their Savage concubines; they scarcely remembered to say their *Ave MARIAS* from one day to the next.

Twenty years now he had been coming to Canada. And always he had measured himself before and after each voyage, believing to find neither warpage nor shrinkage. Oh, yes, he had fatuously thought that he could go to Canada and back and never be changed! Pontgravé had never changed. But Robert had. Young Brûlé had. It was because Hélène could not change that she did not thrive here. Duval failed to change, and was hanged. On the other hand, Merveille could jabber like a Savage; Eustache roared out songs with French and Indian words intermingled, rushing grinning and sunburned through each day; he had made the change.

But no – all this is but false vaporing! (Thus Champlain.) I have never changed.

The King of Toys

Now the Kebec years went on, no one remembering anymore the time not long ago when the snowy river was only brown and flowing at its edges, beneath the thinnest pane of ice; for now streams made rivières which met in a great and swelling Fleuve, the Fleuve wearing gold robes of cattails (the sun was gold upon the Savage paddlers' fingers), the Stream of Time rippling like some silver censer with pipes and grilles . . . – What manner of rivière *was* this Stream of Time? How could the same places flash by you over and over, no matter how unceasingly you struggled on? The Currents of Patience could not explain it. – No matter. There was a blue-green haze of pines across the river, a great rock like an arrowhead from Ossernenon where Tekakwitha was born (from this rock Montagnais children dove into the water for play);

* Embraces; kisses.

there were mountains blue enough to swim in, and time ran deep and still all summer.

In the Year of Our LORD 1621, Robert Pontgravé was killed, as Champlain heard from his father. His ship was burned by those enemies of true Christians the Dutch. Some used the word *malemort* in describing his end, meaning a bad death, but what his father thought no one can say, for he never spoke of Robert after that. When Père Le Caron came to condole with him, he sent him away, saying only that the lad's soul had been in poor condition . . . – What other news? – Well, it was of some interest to Champlain to hear from his spies that many Hiroquois now fitted their arrows with sharp iron heads which they had gained in trade (just like our Huron), so that the slat armor once worn by these Savages was no longer effective. The open warfare which he himself had seen in his three campaigns began to give way to ambushes. In this connection an ominous incident had occurred the previous year, when two more illegal ships from La Rochelle traded guns to the Montagnais. Fortunately, the weapons soon wore out, so that Savages could not hope to compete with Frenchmen. But if the Hiroquois were ever to get guns, what a fiasco that would be! He remembered the vindictive glitter of triumph in the eyes of those Souriquois at Port-Royal, fifteen years ago now, when Poutrincourt had given them arquebuses to use against the Armouchiquois. Well, there was no use in dreading the future. The present was difficult enough. The Huron had expressed some distress about the Hiroquois when they came to trade that year, for they feared that the way would be closed, they said. He assured them that the French would always protect them, at which they went away singing. (He observed with satisfaction that they'd already begun to abandon the use of their stone knives, and used blades of good French iron to fashion their Savage little necessities . . .) – What else? – Champlain built the first road in Canada, along the Rivière Saint-Charles, where the Recollects had their convent. And for the treatise on Sea-Navigation which he proposed someday to publish, he constructed a table of knots, hours and brasses for all directions. – What else? – The Apothecary Louis Hébert, Biencourt's old strongman, was named Attorney-Royal of New France; and the beaver monopoly fell to the good Sieur Emery de Caën and his nephew, which pleased Champlain greatly, as he had become wearied with the Sieur de Monts. – You know, Champlain, said this latter, I had the most ridiculous dream. It seemed to me that you and Pontgravé broke away from me and left me stranded in the trade. You'd never do that, would you? – Monsieur, replied Champlain, I have my honor. – But this too was only a dream of De Monts', for Champlain continued to abide in Canada. – Pontgravé of course had already been removed from the game by this new change. But he came nonetheless, pretending not to be aware that the old company had been abolished. He was too old to stay out of Canada anymore. – Eh, Champlain, he cried innocently, in what position will I be employed this season? Come on now – don't look at me like that! I may be a Huguenot, but so is De Caën.

Champlain set his teeth. – I have great hopes that the Sieur de Caën will soon become a Catholic, he replied. And in the meantime, I have it stated here on this document that he is not permitted to practice his so-called religion here, either by land or by sea.

Champlain, Champlain! Why are you being this way? I've already told you that I only need –

Monsieur, you know that you should not have come this year.

Ah, so I'm "Monsieur" to you now, am I? After eighteen years? I let you ride along as a passenger – I didn't even charge you! – and now look how you treat me! Is this gratitude? Who got you your highfalutin title in the first place? Let's just say this, Champlain: it wasn't you.

You seem intent upon annoying me, Pontgravé.

Oh, put the goddamned drawbridge down and stop yelling at me over the moat! I'm not an Englishman, you imbecile!

Pontgravé, you're making a scene. And now you add blasphemy to your other sins. You know very well that this year you're in a defenseless position! –

Because I call you an imbecile I'm blaspheming GOD, is that it? And to think that I . . . – Hey, Merveille! Eustache! Clout this poltroon over the head and let me in! Don't let De Caën's puppet here take away your rights!

In a defenseless position, Pontgravé, as I said. Let me ask you something. Did you sail here in the *Salamander?*

What's that got to do with anything? Champlain, be reasonable and take your stuffed shirt off and let me in. Or if you're too scared to do that, at least come out. I'm not going to turn you over to the Basques! I helped hang Duval, didn't I? – Yes, yes, I took the *Salamander*. She's anchored at Tadoussac.

That's what I thought. The Sieur de Caën has informed me that he plans to confiscate your vessel. Frankly, Monsieur, I am surprised that you've left it within his reach . . .

At these words, Pontgravé crumpled like a pricked balloon, and he bowed his head, saying: Monsieur, you know I'll make no resistance . . .

Then Champlain's heart ached. He knew not why.

When De Caën arrived in the month of Juillet, Champlain took Pontgravé's part, for which that personage thanked him most humbly. Publicly broken,

Pontgravé swore that he would no longer contest the Sieur de Champlain's supreme authority. He worked for De Caën until 1629. – Ha, ha! La victoire!

What else? The Recollects received word that their patron the Bishop of Rouen had died, and with him their great scheme for a school to educate fifty Indian boys.

Day by day, nothing ever seemed to happen, but the Kebec years streamed by.

Kebec Years 1622

In the year 1622, when the Blessed Saint Ignatius was canonized, Père Biard died on a bed of sickness at Avignon. The Hiroquois attacked Kebec for the first time, but were easily beaten off. (Wading in the orange waters of the Fleuve Saint-Laurent, it seemed to them that the cliff called Kebec was not so high, that they could easily leap it, or at least pull themselves up green shoots or grassblades and then run amok, crushing the Habitation below. But that was only a dream.) Shouting insults at the Iron People, they launched a flock of arrows – an act of insolence which the Sieur de Champlain had not looked for from them. Evidently they'd forgotten the two lessons in place he had taught them ten years before. (Ten years! Had it really been that long? He was almost minded to lay siege to another of these Hiroquois towns . . . – but no, he remembered how *that* had gone.) At any rate, these Mohawk were no threat. Their arrows chattered against the walls of his Habitation, and that was all; later his beaver-clerks came out to pick them up for souvenirs. And the Indians paddled away, to attack the residence or convent of the Recollects . . . There the good Pères had rendered them a sprightly riposte with their harquebus, and killed at least a brace of the scoundrels, the remainder of whom departed in great haste. It was all good sport. – What else? Well, Champlain gained one of his many objectives by appointing the Savage Mristou as Captain of the Montagnais. Someday every Savage Captain would be a vassal of the French. The next step would be getting them to settle where he commanded. Then he wouldn't have to worry about being abandoned by his Savage guides on any more explorations; for their wives and children would make such fine hostages . . .

Kebec Years 1623

The following spring, Pontgravé, taking very seriously his position as Chief Factor at Kebec (subject always to the caprice of the Sieur de Champlain), instructed his beaver-clerks to develop some facility not only in the Algoumequin and Montaignez languages, but also in *Chariquois* or *Huron*, for the trade with them was booming! Half a hundred canoes a year! The Fleuve Saint-Laurent was clear of Mohawk and other vermin now; you could sail or paddle at your leisure, thanks to the reputation of our good French guns . . . Sometimes Étienne Brûlé (who now seemed entirely a Savage) came down with Soranhes and Darontal and the rest of the barbaric crew – although the Algoumequin levied high tolls to discourage them from the trade, being greedy of their position with the French; apparently they'd even told the Huron that the French had all drowned! (So said Brûlé, stammering a little with nervousness at being enclosed in the Habitation – he was half a cretin, I assure you! My late Robert was never that way.) One thing you had to say for Brûlé, though: he didn't mind teaching the clerks a few words of his Savage jargon. And if you wanted the inside poop on Savage fashions, go to Brûlé! It seemed, for instance, that the brutes still couldn't tell the difference between good iron and bad. Can you imagine? So sell 'em the cheapest trash we make – give it to 'em right up the ass, and with no grease, neither! *That* was worth a few pistole-coins to know . . . – Here you go, boy (thus Pontgravé, plinking down Brûlé's salary. Good old Brûlé! Already he was making almost as much as Champlain! Pretty soon he'd be what the Huron called a Big Stone . . .) Pontgravé sent half a dozen Frenchmen back with him, to winter there and insinuate themselves into the trade. There were already a handful of others, one to a village, carrying on with the fillettes, no doubt, but that too seemed good for trade; best not to mention it to Champlain . . . You want to hear a good one? They had their orgies in Père Le Caron's old cabin! Served those Grey-Gowns right, by CHRIST! . . . – What else was new? – Well, the Huron had a victory over threescore Hiroquois. They burned them all. After that, one of those Hiroquois Nations, having learned their lesson at last, now concluded a treaty of peace with our Montagnais . . . (JESUS help us, *they* were as uppity as ever! A French Captain gave a Captain of the Montagnes a gift which the latter considered too small, so he threw it into the grand Fleuve and his warriors pillaged the Frenchman's ship . . .) But the Hiroquois began to be broken and civilized; Champlain could see they'd never be a nuisance again; servile Pontgravé assured him of it; Pontgravé knew them like the back of his hand –

A Relation Concerning the Hiroquois 1624–1628

Ah, but did he?

Before the Peru voyage, as Lescarbot said, one could lock up infinite riches in a little room. Now, however, large coffers are required, due to the devaluation of gold. So it is also with murders and tortures in this History. We have scarcely seen any of them so far, but now they are going to be increased and devalued. – What caused such a thing? – Well, bigots will say *the Iroquois*; reductionists will say *iron*; noble Savage romanciers will say *the French*; and they're all right. So, let's begin (shall we?) with the Yrocois.

In the Year of Our LORD 1624, once the Mohawk had smoked the pipe of peace with the Algonkin and the Iron People, they turned their attentions to the Mahican Nation and decided to destroy it. It was their aim to crush every Nation in the vicinity of the Dutch. Then the Dutch would have no one else left to exchange gifts with. (They'd already given presents to the Mahican; they could not be trusted.) – The Mohawk therefore began to spin their own poison-webs, slowly, carefully, desperately – they must have iron!

They commenced by treating for peace with the Montagnais, as we have seen – swearing their affection in the name of the SKY – for the SKY is the most Powerful OKI. They did not like to fight too many enemies at once. So it was a peace-Council level and easy (as the Huron would say), easy like a reaped field. Now they were free to brand the Mahican with the burns of slaves; they could take their possessions, adopt them, exterminate them. So the War-Chief sang the War-Song. And the young men fell upon the enemy. They began to raze their villages, each in its turn. They brought them home to be tortured. They brought home iron hatchets. They danced . . .

The Wendat always said that the minds of the Hiroquois were so evil and cunning as to have seven linings, like a spiderweb's nested polygons. That was true; it is true of all minds. It is certainly true of the Dutch. – By the ALMIGHTY, they'd fight for their dear friends the Mahican – otherwise the price of skins would go up!

So Daniel Van Krieckenbeeck, the Commandant of Fort Orange, set out with a party of musketeers. The Mohawk sang them into an ambuscado; the Mohawk burned them screaming in the fire. – Oh, not all of them – for the Mohawk needed iron. But even one would have made the point. And they burned more than one.

Now the Dutchmen crawled to the Mohawk most humbly and begged forgiveness. The orator *De-hen-nah-ke-re-neh* (that is, Dragging Horns) accepted their postulations for the sake of iron; how could Dragging Horns know yet that these same double Dutchmen had spread presents to the Montagnais, inciting them to sing War-Songs against the Mohawk? The Dutchmen loved proxies . . . And so the Montagnais seized a pair of Mohawk fishermen and began to torture them most lovingly.

Champlain knew what the Dutch were up to, of course – they wanted to divide his pawns! – He called the Montagnais Captains to him and shouted: If you persist in your odious folly, I myself will fight you alongside the Hiroquois! – Then they cast their eyes down and laughed, as if it were but a jest . . . But they knew now that they couldn't count on the Iron People to take their part. Stupid bearded Champlain! Nothing to do but escort the two prisoners back to the Country of the Mohawk, anxiously befriending and honoring them to make them overlook any burns and missing fingers . . . So they entered the enemy forests amidst the high laughter of birds, and there came one of those surprise chills, the clouds long and thin, cutting off the sun, and then the sun came out again and the procession reached the prisoners' village. The Mohawk welcomed them, accepted their presents, called them brothers and uncles and nephews. But then Dragging Horns called a secret Council and told them what he'd just heard – that these Montagnais had been scheming with the Dutch . . . Therefore they lulled the envoys all the more; then they sank axes into their skulls.

Our REDEEMER is good! chuckled Daniel Van Krieckenbeeck. Aha, we were cunning to leak word to those Hiroquois of our negotiations! –

So the Dutchmen won that round, and the Frenchmen lost. Champlain had to back the Montagnais now. His alliance with the Hiroquois had fallen through, just like his commission . . . How he hated the Hiroquois! They were fiends; they were murderers; they traded with the Dutch. At least his Montagnais couldn't sneak down to Fort Orange anymore to sell their furs . . .

By 1628 the Mohawk had enslaved the Mahican entirely. Now they controlled the lands all around the Dutch trading post. Their hopes and their greed grew up like sweet green cornstalks.

Pontgravé's Gout 1624

In Mai of 1624, Champlain began his new Habitation, in order to please Hélène and also to better guard himself against any Savage treachery. The foundation was of stone. He set his sawyers to making one and a half thousands of planks. On the eighth day of Mai, when the wild cherry showed its leaves, they celebrated the peace with the Hiroquois. – Pontgravé got twenty-five canoeloads of beaver-skins out of the deal; he was so happy he almost shat in his pants, I tell you! . . . But the following year he had a bit of a greenish tinge. Gout was what it was. Eh, what could you expect? He was more than seventy years old! The thought of settling down had crossed his mind more than twice; he didn't say he'd never do just that. But later, later . . . What the hell (good thing that sourpuss Champlain couldn't hear him think! even so, he really shouldn't think it: what the *H—L*, let's say) – what in **BLAZES** was he supposed to do back in Paris or Pons? Listen to De Monts chew the fat? No, merci! Why, every winter he could hardly wait for spring so that he could start making profits again! And give that up? Unthinkable, incroyable! It wasn't Pontgravé's fault that he'd been made this way; he just naturally created value – enriched the world was how he saw it. A live beaver wasn't worth a hill of beans, but a dead one turned into ten livres! Eh, the wonder of it!

Ugggh! What awful heartburn!

He should really bet against his own life, as he'd once promised that ship-Captain in Acadia so many years ago – who was it? Timothy? Morel? CHRIST, they were all dead and waterlogged; GOUGOU had gotten them; it made his head spin to think –

Everybody was kicking off, it seemed. That very Mars, on the Feast of Saint Joseph (*viz.*, the spiritual Patron of Canada), Père Coton died. What a run for their money he and his Jesuits had given poor Poutrincourt! Thank GOD they were out of Canada for good! – But who'd die next? That was the thing! Champlain? No, he'd bet against *him* one time too many. De Monts? De Monts, yes, one of these days. Christine? That wife of his was fat, happy and bald – she'd live forever! She'd outlive him; she'd already outlived Robert –

But I still have a few more golden sols to make, sighed Pontgravé to himself. JESUS won't take me yet. I'll give more to the Church . . .

He gambled with a Savage who put his wife and children as the stake and lost. Pontgravé, however, returned them to him of his own will, thereby showing his great magnanimity.

The Best Resolution

Champlain set his pen above a sheet of good French paper; he was going to ask the Company to increase his salary, which was only twelve hundred livres. He swallowed. – No, he said to himself; that is too hard. Let me add a page or two to my *Voyages*. He dipped the quill and began to scratch: *It robs a man of courage to serve people who pay no heed to those who are preserving their property, and slaying themselves through the care and labor they bestow upon the task* and meanwhile his stomach fumed and fizzled because Hélène was in the bedroom with the door shut and had been there for hours, silent, not sleeping, he knew that as well as if he saw her; she'd be staring out the window at the Fleuve Saint-Laurent, caring nothing for his cherry trees and grapevines; and his heart ached with anxiety: he could not control her. He could not make her happy. He did not know what to do. He felt himself to be in the wrong; there were certain indications of that; he didn't have to prick the sea-chart to be apprised of his position! How could he proceed? Only by guesswork. What did she want? He had no practice in any of this. Nor did he wish to. It was all Pontgravé's fault. Why had he taken the old lecher's advice? Marriage was, after all, a pretty dry bed of sawdust to lie in. Why did so many people tout it? Granted, it preserved the human race, which was essential if man were to continue to have dominion over this world in GOD's name, but aside from that –

Suddenly he thought he heard Hélène retching. Terrified lest she have been overtaken by some Canadian sickness, he rushed in, only to see that the noises were harsh dry sobs, like the wind whistling through cables at sea . . .

On the twenty-first day of Août, he left Tadoussac in company of his good wife. They made landfall at Dieppe on the last of Septembre – a voyage of average length, with no untoward incident, for which he was grateful to GOD for his dear Hélène's sake. The Nation was enjoying peace, since the Roy had vigorously put down his mother's armies in Normandie, Anjou, Saintonge, Toulouse, Béziers, Lunel . . . Vive le Roy! He had developed a mordant turn of mind, De Monts said, and loved to roll up his eyeballs in imitation of the dying men that he had seen these last few years. There were many new likenesses of him on display in the public squares. Champlain strode the cobblestones, inspecting them all (Hélène had asked leave to be alone). – What a fine young man our Louis! Long black locks, a short moustache, a chevron of a beard just beneath the lower lip – if I trimmed my beard in that fashion, would Hélène . . . ? – Useless. He measured himself against the Roy, the Roy showing naked leg as required; down his body spilled a robe festooned with fleurs-de-lys; at his throat a great crystalline Cross gleamed like a Canadian diamond . . . Indeed he is magnificent. (Thus Champlain.)

He bought a house on the rue de La Marche in Paris. She asked leave of him to enter a convent, from which step he dissuaded her, though agreeing that henceforth they would sleep in separate rooms.

Now Is the Time

He visited Montmorency in Saint-Germain, where he was presented to the Roy.

Now, my dear boy, I have some news for you, which may seem good to you or bad. At any rate, it's a fait accompli. (Thus Montmorency.)

Yes, Seigneur? (His heart was already sinking. Canada, my Canada!)

These factions and quarrels of the traders have ruined my digestion. I don't know how you accommodate yourself to it, Champlain. They're pirates, I tell you! I wish I were young enough to lard them all through with this sword – as you see, I can scarcely draw it without falling into spasms and quivers – oh! my apologies! did I graze you?

It's nothing, Seigneur.

Here's a handkerchief. Well, so you see my state. Ah, good, it's just a scratch. My situation is far more serious. You should cry pearly larmes of pity for my condition –

Seigneur, said Champlain coldly, I've heard much the same request from Pontgravé, and even from the Sieur de Monts. Are you related?

I *beg* your pardon, Monsieur. In short, I'm out of it. I sold the Viceroyalty to my nephew Henri, the Duc de Vantadour. I think you'll like each other. He's very pious – so pious his eyes bulge. He's agreed to live apart from his wife, who's only fourteen years old, and also very pious, so they tell me, and quite attractive as well – how old was your Hélène when you . . . ? Well, they both intend to take holy orders. (He's twenty-nine, of course – considerably younger than you.) He tells me that his heart's desire is the conversion of the Savages of Canada; he's going to bring the Jesuits back in . . .

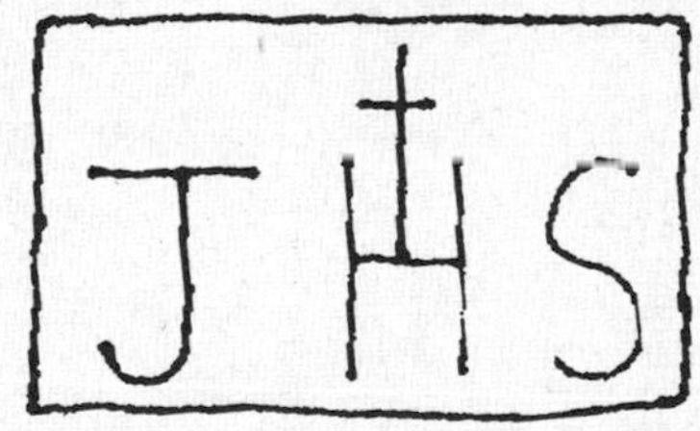

V
Temperance
or,

A Brief Life of Father Roberto de Nobili, Who Brought the True Faith to India

Père de Nobili
1577–1656

Sow a Jesuit, and you reap a rebel.

JÉRÔME BONAPARTE, speech to the Chamber of Deputies

But before *we* let the Black-Gowns in again, before we permit them to set sail in Champlain's fleet (they on the *Alouette*, Pontgravé on the *Don de Dieu* as ever, where in comfort he could gamble on lives with his cronies; Hélène and her ladies-in-waiting in the calèche that now creaked on wooden wheels toward the house in Paris where she would dwell in blissful solitude; Champlain, armed with the Duc de Ventadour's instructions to fortify the Citadel and propagate the Faith, strutting about on his flagship of two hundred and fifty tuns, ominously named *Catherine*); before we ascend from the river's mouth to the narrows of Kebec, where Iroquois and divers rapids hope to drench our resolution, it is important to note that as of yet the good Pères, be they indeed called Black-Gowns, Fathers, Crows, or Charcoal, had made scarcely a mark on the Savages of New France and could very easily have changed direction. Lest I seem utopian, I shall now tell the tale of Père de Nobili, which the Superior General of the Order certainly knew, and could have told to all his soldiers, had he chosen.

Roberto de Nobili was born at Rome in the Year of Our LORD 1577. The season was September, the harvest-time of our bucolic poets. His father was a General in the Papal Army. Anyone who follows ensuing events, therefore, through no matter how dusty a magnifying glass, can scarcely be surprised that when the son was of age they sent him to the Jesuit College to study (it being widely agreed that the Jesuits made the best schoolmasters). Pious though his parents were, they expected a worldly career of him. They were as naive as the Huron Savages, who thought to get French kettles without also getting French churches! The Jesuits had soon schooled Roberto so well that he decided to become a missionary. His mother, the Countess Clarice, sobbed many an indignant tear; for being the Pope's General is one thing, and a rather pleasant thing, too; whereas the Pope's missionaries are but anonymous scouts in Indian country, bound by vows to enjoy no recompense save hardship and the prospect of fearful tortures, and to engender no offspring to carry on the family name, unless we count their numberless broods of winged prayers. – Of course the name of De Nobili, being historic, was scarcely likely to be extinguished, with or without Roberto. So he considered; and who is omniscient enough to say otherwise? (Not that I know any De Nobilis myself.) – His father having died, and been buried with all the honors to which he was entitled, Roberto's cousin the Cardinal had the task of dissuading him – a curious labor for a Cardinal, as one might suppose; and perhaps Roberto did; for he fled from Rome to Nocera, where he put himself under the protection of a certain Duchess. She thought him a very dear boy, for he followed her will in everything. In 1596, a reluctant assent having been extracted from his mother the Countess's lips, he entered the novitiate; in 1600 he began his theological studies in Rome; in 1603, when Champlain first sailed for Canada, Roberto was ordained, and in April of 1604 he set sail for India in a Portuguese carrack. Because his destination was Goa,* he was considered a vassal of the King of Portugal.

From the instructions given him by his Superiors he knew that Goa was a state sixty-two miles long and forty miles wide, that she was bounded on the north by the state of Sawunt Waree, on the east by Belgaum and New Canara, and on the southwest by the Indian Ocean; and that she was yet barren of converts. Her history both ecclesiastical and otherwise was as follows: The Portuguese, hovering off the coast of India like crows, had had news one day that the King of Cochin was fighting with a native Prince called Samiri who ruled Calicut, so in exchange for their naval assistance, which quickly reduced Samiri's holdings to a very narrow kingdom six feet deep, the King of Cochin freely granted the Portuguese permission to build a fort wherever in Calicut

* "**Goa** – The former capital of the Portuguese possessions in India, once an opulent and powerful city, but now fallen into an irremediable and hopeless state of decay," says the *Gazetteer of the Territories Under the Government of the East Indian Company* (1858). The *Gazetteer* concludes that there is no possibility of salvation for Goa except being taken over by England.

they desired; *now* the exultant Portuguese could commence operations, and they took Goa by storm and made it the capital of their Indian dominions. But despite their most pious efforts, as I said, they had stormed no pagan souls.

Père de Nobili was shipwrecked near Mozambique. After great suffering, he arrived in Goa in May of the Year of Our Lord 1605. He was not quite twenty-seven.

He learned Tamil among the Paravas of the Fishery Coast. The sea was as palely luminous a blue as some dream of noon horizons. Its almost sickening perfection shone up between the thorn trees. A seagull flashed; ants glittered in the jungle. – Yes, yes, he said to the Paravas. I see: that is the first conjugation. – A year and a half after his arrival, his Provincial sent him inland to Madura – a dangerous town for Europeans, says the *Catholic Encyclopedia*, because it was out of reach of Portuguese naval guns.

His Senior in Madura was a Portuguese Jesuit named Gonçalo Fernandez. As was the custom in those days, he made his Indian neophytes eat and dress like colonials and take Portuguese surnames. This greatly hindered his work, for any Hindu who took a foreigner's name was called like the foreigners *Parangi*, a term of great odium; furthermore, such habits as eating beef and wearing leather shoes – which Père Fernandez required them to follow to show their sincerity – made them further despised in this Country where cows were sacred.

Perhaps we should adapt ourselves to them, said Père de Nobili to his Senior. That is what the Blessed Ignatius told us to do.

How can you suggest such a thing? cried Père Fernandez in a fury. You – an untried young suckling, puffed up and conceited with your noble origins – you dare to tell me what to do?

No, said Père de Nobili. But I shall dare to do it.

He moved into a hut by himself. Looking across a steep ravine, he could peer directly into the hill, where the palm-stems were like black bars. He gave up his black gown for a saffron dress; he exchanged his shoes for wooden clogs; he marked his brow with the vertical line of paste that signified *Teacher*, he adopted the vegetarian diet of the holy men called *Sannyasi*.

You are crazy! shouted Père Fernandez. I'll tell your Provincial of this when I see him. Shame on you – to so quickly forget your vow of obedience!

In time the Madura folk discovered for themselves that he was a Count's son. Then they called him *Rajah Sannyasi*, a term of honor for his rank.

In his first eighteen months in Madura he converted eighteen people.

Making the Exercises, he found the Stream of Time to be the Swari River, which, pale blue like the sea, was puffed up with rich coconut islands. He located the Isle of the Trinity which represented Exercise Three; he progressed to the Rock of Earthly Kings, upon which grew a single jackfruit tree; he reached the Rock of CHRIST and a mango fell into his arms . . .

In 1608, even as Champlain was clearing the first arpent of ground at Kebec, the Brahmin Sanskrit scholar Sivadarma set out to bring Père de Nobili to faith in the sacred Vedantas. Père de Nobili welcomed this, for he wished to know as much as he could of Indian ways. He thus became the first

European to learn the Vedas. When he had attained to knowledge, Sivadarma took him into the temple whose yellow arch yawned among the trees. A woman in a purple sari sat on the steps. There were rings on her toes. Père de Nobili blessed her in the name of CHRIST. – Come, said Sivadarma. It was dim inside. Among marble and incense and brass he saw the acolytes, naked to the waist, bending over a great silver mouth with black things in it, offering coconuts and lotus blossoms to DURGA. He heard the ringing bells; he saw the flashing flames. – Do you understand what you see? said Sivadarma. – Yes, replied the priest. And he asked him many learned questions, under cover of which his purpose seeped between the other's doctrines just as the blue-black ocean of dawn penetrates the channels between rocks in a series of slaps, white-foamed the color of eye-whites, tide-greedy, flicking crabs off rocks as if they were flies. And Sivadarma marveled. Together they left the temple, descending the marble steps beneath the roof that gaped like a cobra's mouth . . . – The other Brahmins had long sought to declare Nobili a *Parangi* so that he could be expelled, but at a meeting of eight hundred Brahmins, in a place where the shrub-leaves were many-fingered hands, Sivadarma defended him, saying: He is no *Parangi*, but a Rajah Sannyasi indeed. – The following year, on Whitsunday, Sivadarma was converted.

Now we must baptize you, said Père de Nobili.

You know that I am willing, replied Sivadarma. But must I give up my topknot and my triple thread?

Père de Nobili had already thought on this matter for a long time. It seemed to him that by depriving Sivadarma of these marks of Brahmin status, he would be retarding rather than advancing the spread of the Faith, for then Sivadarma would be outcast and despised. Nor could he see any reason why Sivadarma's burden should be increased. Just as a brown river winds far below the white waterfall it came from, shaded dark by palms and red flower-trees, and then becomes white again upon meeting the sea, so the word of CHRIST (he reasoned) must adapt itself to the infinities between Alpha and Omega. After all, the Blessed Ignatius had written: *He enters through the other's door and comes out his own.* So he said to Sivadarma: My son, I believe that you can be a Brahmin and a Christian, too.

And he smiled.

Père Fernandez soon got wind of this. In 1610 Père de Nobili was censured by a council of his peers and Superiors for corrupting the Faith. He had no recourse but an appeal to the Superior General at Rome. Meanwhile, the power of giving baptism was stripped from him.

We see him carrying an axe; he is wearing his long gown of saffron-colored sackcloth. A chain is draped over his shoulder. There is a turban on his head. His chin is grizzled. He stares straight ahead, his lips tight with determination.

But his Superior General had to be reckoned with, as he knew well; oh, he knew Claudius Aquaviva, whose election in the Year of Our LORD 1581 coincided with the inauguration of the beaver trade in New France. It was Aquaviva who had sent Père Biard and Père Massé to Acadia. He was to have the longest term of any Superior General; and he did perhaps the most of any, including Ignatius, to regiment the Society of JESUS. And he was a very pious man. At this time he had already written out a *Directorium* for making the Spiritual Exercises, which perhaps did not correspond precisely to the intentions of Ignatius himself, but then the founder had never claimed to be infallible, and it was Aquaviva who now had to deal with so much secret hostility within the Church toward the Jesuits . . . In the Year of Our LORD 1599, Aquaviva completed the definitive text of the *Ratio Studiorum*, which Ignatius had begun; and in it he prescribed oral exercises and games in which the Jesuit students were pitted against each other to make them successful at overcoming opposing arguments through cleverness; and he handed out dramas, fêtes, vacations in abundance . . . Over and over he read what Ignatius had written in the *Institutum* – how well he knew the Saint's handwriting, so black and thick-lettered, like the notes of medieval music! – he made the best determination that he could as to what must go into the turning-out of his Jesuits. He expected them to be able to write Latin like Cicero, and think like Aristotle. He prescribed the writings of Saint Aquinas, about which Ignatius had been lukewarm. Each of the large classes was divided into *decuriæ*, or groups of ten, with a Captain overseeing the other nine, and the Captain was instructed to instill a desire for honor and glory in them so that they would vanquish the other *decuriæ* in the class competitions, and the Captain reported on them to the teachers, and the teachers then reported to Aquaviva, who listened carefully and made decisions about the young Jesuits' careers far earlier than they ever imagined. In the Year of Our LORD 1600, Aquaviva instructed the Order to build houses exclusively for conducting the Exercises, where trained Retreat Masters could play on men like harps, now making them experience consolation, now desolation.

So what was he to do about this vexing case of Père de Nobili?

Clearly the fellow was a dangerous individualist. Clearly he got results.

The Superior General sighed. He did not have a great deal of time to devote to Madura, or Goa, or India for that matter. But he smelled a precedent. (So many precedents were erected in the reign of Aquaviva!) Why did thinking of this remind him of a grey morning after a long sleepless night?

The question was this: How much license could a missionary give to native custom before his message was distorted? Half-Christians, such as Protestants, were no better than pagans. But the Society of JESUS did not seek to uproot native life simply because it was different. The Jesuits were tolerant and sophisticated men.

So he decided to temporize. With clever vagueness, he wrote to the Provincial at Goa that the triple Brahmin thread should certainly be cut, but at the same time nothing ought to be done to compromise the existence of the missions.

So I have become a sort of Pontius Pilate, said Aquaviva to himself with weary self-disgust. But he soon forgot the matter in the press of other tasks.

In the end, the Pope ruled in Père de Nobili's favor, and he was finally permitted to resume his baptisms in 1623, after a space of thirteen years. He continued to do the LORD's work. In 1640 he was imprisoned for a year, but his zeal was only increased. In 1654, when he retired, there were four thousand one hundred and eighty-three native Christians in South India. There had been none when he came. He died in a hut outside Mylapore two years later, wearing his saffron-colored robe.

So, if it had to be done at all, it could have been done that way in Canada. It could have been done.

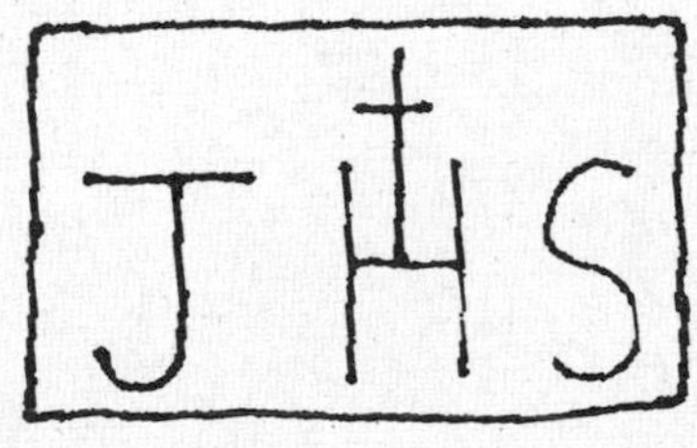

In the end, the [illegible] and he was finally permitted to go home, [illegible] in 1871, after a spell of thirteen years of [illegible] work. [illegible] When he retired, there were four thousand four hundred and [illegible] Christians in [illegible]. There had been none when he came. [illegible] many years [illegible].

VI
Glory
or,

The Conversion of the Huron Savages

The Huron Years
1623–1649

Oh, how sweet it is to die for JESUS CHRIST! It is for this reason that His servants so ardently desire to suffer.

MARIE DE L'INCARNATION, to her son (1647)

Silver streamers descended a notched and mossy wall, as they went subdividing into spume and ribbons until they attained their foamy pool, from which they flowed over boulder-teeth, undercutting the roots of cedars that leaned uneasily from the gravel bank; and so they entered the rivière with its long white lines of froth. Before the epidemics, Savages sometimes came to fish here in the main channel where water flowed in glittering gushes down limestone steps beneath the evergreen forest. It was a forest of holiness: – yes, it was Kebec's great Basilica, which night hollowed out into a drum that the Black-Gowns could strike with beats of tranquil lateness. The pews had again become the forest they had been carved from; there were so many of them, their wood polished almost to the brightness of sun-dappled leaves (but the spots of brightness did not move). Above hung the massive Sun, which comprehended the Figure and the tilted Crucifix. Its six great arms of light grew downwards like golden roots; a winged Angel supported the base of each. And the lights went off one by one in that spaciousness. – Savages hid behind trees with half-drawn bows. Savages ran and killed. The woods were fragrant with mud and moss and juicy spruce-buds. – Below this place the rivière quickened somewhat, spilling through a cleft between mossy cliffs (on whose roofs grew lilies-of-the-valley and crow's-foot amidst the moss and lichens and brown spruce needles). Fishes flashed. Water-striders found calm places

between stones in which to live their lives, dragging heavy oval bubbles like sins. Leaf-boats bobbed and whirled, impossible to hurt. Now the stream made rapids in its rocky gorge, along whose walls ran long strata of black and white to chronicle the water-years; now it calmed itself into doldrums; now it frothed like the lace of an Ursuline tapisserie, fringed above by faithful evergreen soldiers; yet again it made rapids around the sunny rocky islets where Savages used to sun themselves. And it flowed on. How mild and pleasant this Stream of Time; – how fresh like a Virgin! Sometimes the water was blue-black in the sun, and sometimes reddish-ochre. Sometimes the sun went behind a cloud; then ripples dulled like the scaly bark of that tree called *épinette blanche*.* And the years gurgled by, dissolving limestone, bearing leaves away. Above the main falls, years became treacherously slow, shallow and wide, running coffee-colored down steps of shale, with clouds tremblingly reflected in the shallows. A breeze titillated the treetops, and the sun came and went. Water flowed down steps. Little alder saplings grew optimistically in the very riverbed, flourishing between the warm bellies of boulders. Channels widened on the rock like spreading fingers. Then the river plunged into space . . .

* White pine.

The Currents of Patience

1625–1633

In particular cases, however, much depends on that for which a man struggles and dies.

HERDER, *Reflections* (1880)

Père Jean de Brébeuf was too modest to acknowledge what was so obvious to his brethren: that he was one of those youths for whom greatness is predicted. When the others prayed, their features softened, and a look of bliss came over them, as if they were partaking of nectar, but when this young man knelt before the altar it was noted that his lips drew tightly together and his face became hard and virile with determination. He knelt rigidly, without making any movement. Repeatedly in Confession he expressed his desire to die for the Faith. Even the Superior General, Aquaviva, took notice of him and ordered that special reports be brought to him of his progress. Sighing, rubbing his brows with a forefinger, he noted the coincidence that Brébeuf had been born the twenty-fifth day of Mars – *viz.*, the Festival of the Annunciation, when in future years the Ursulines of Kebec would clothe the image of Our LADY in a vestiaire white with gold disks and chains, silver-fringed and lacy-topped . . . A propitious time for a martyr to be born, surely (although Aquaviva scarcely let his hopes go so far). Brébeuf was not exceptionally handsome, but the clear shining of purpose that was imprinted on his features drew Aquaviva's eyes to him, and Aquaviva thought of his youthful self for a moment without knowing why, without knowing that we always see ourselves in others more noble than we; and the Superior General looked moodily at his own face reflected in the polished letter-opener and he looked old and it seemed to him that the years had gone by quickly.

Young Brébeuf, of course, never knew any of this. And yet he could not help but see the special light into which others insisted upon casting him. This dazzled him at first, like the soul emerging from Plato's cave; then in time he became accustomed to it, and thought simply: Since I must be an example, let me strive to be a worthy one! – and he became even more resolute than before. Some of his brethren grew jealous, and probed to discover a flaw, but there was none. When they sent him to Canada at last, in the Year of Our LORD 1625, it was with unchanged expectations. Aquaviva had died a decade before, but the new Superior General said to the Provincials: Were it not presumptuous to look ahead on the LORD's path, I might say that this man may be destined for the Crown! – As for Père Brébeuf, however, he had no such hopes, although he remained faithful in his desire, even in the nightmare of Canada, even in the Huron-Land, which he considered the veriest donjon-keep of Hell, with all its screaming Savage souls tormented in darkness. It was there that he dreamed that the Savages had conquered Europe and were busy raising forests everywhere, so that he wandered through the hot green wilderness that had once been Paris and between the roots of two enormous oak-trees he saw a great round stone like a wheel of cheese, which seemed to him to be called a *century stone*, and there were letters carved into it but he could not read them; and a great rage and grief came into his heart when he understood that this was all that was left of the cemetery. The Savages strode about in the green spaces and the sunny spaces, and the reddish-brown muscles rippled in their wide backs. They saw him and gazed curiously at him. Because he was the only one left, they were indifferent to his existence, and this made him more angry than their hostility ever could. He remembered the year when he had first taken the Three Vows and his Superior had said I tell you that if you are persistent you will come up to the expectations that many have of you at which Brébeuf blushed and said nothing and then the Superior said harshly you must not think that I pay compliments and Brébeuf said Your Reverence, what is in your mind? and the Superior said we shall send you on the hardest road that we can, you understand that and Brébeuf was happy and murmured yes yes and the Superior said we may send you to China but I think we shall send you to New France. – Then in his tertianship the idea of difficulty soon to come had bemused him and beguiled him like evening light through a narrow window, a glow, a beauty, that isn't really there; the danger excited him also, and when he admitted as much in Confession the Père said use these proud and wicked thoughts of glory to impel you, my son; *control* these sinful expectations but let them strengthen your desire to be of service. We must be like these Savages, and waste nothing, not even sins. – And so Brébeuf took the Fourth Vow, the special one, and let himself be happy, until he was in New France and then the difficulties came thickly enough. But the remembrance of the Exercises was a great strength and consolation to him; most of all in those times he recalled the Fifth Rule: *In time of desolation one should never make a change, but stand firm and constant in the resolutions and decisions which guided him the day before the desolation . . .*

It was the Recollects who sent for the Black-Gowns, never dreaming that these guests would displace them. (The robes of the Recollects were grey like the skins of moths, and it is as sad moths that I see them, fluttering by twos and threes about the flame of CANADA . . .) – Père Brébeuf had just recently received the priesthood at Pontoise. He was serving as a steward at the Jesuit College when he was confirmed for the Canadian Mission by the Procurator, Père Cotton, a most worthy and diligent soul indeed, who had chosen Pères Biard and Massé for Acadia in the previous decade. Yet again there was delay, for the expense of the passage was great, but through the munificence of Duc Henri, the Viceroy of New France, Père Brébeuf set out for Canada at last with Père Lalemant and his teacher, Père Massé, as well as two lay brothers. He was thirty-two years old.

It was the month of Avril, 1625, when they set sail. Now truly Père Massé was the man of the hour, for he had visited these barbarous Canadian Countries before. He, however, preferred to discuss the places where he had not been – perhaps out of modesty, or perhaps to avoid discussing Père Biard, about whom he had never been talkative. – Yes, brothers, so many souls lie chained in darkness where we are going! he said. I speak not only of the Souriquois, to whom I once hoped to minister, but also of the numberless unknown peoples! There are many islands in the Country of the Armouchiquois, it is said, and on every island a Savage . . .

In Juin they passed Terre-Neuve and gave themselves to be swallowed by that vast sea-mouth at Gaspesie. Then they ascended the Fleuve Saint-Laurent, which narrowed about them league by league, just as purposeful lives must; and at last they came in sight of Cap Diamant. Already in undisciplined imagination Brébeuf let himself be carried *down* the Stream of Time by a space of several hours, so that he had landed at Kebec and was in the first evening of his Mission, standing beside the Sieur de Champlain on the rock where the fortress was, looking down at the walls of the houses, between which streets curved like tributaries, which in fact they were when the rain flowed, making muddy gullies; and rain ran down the rough housewalls so loudly in the summer night. Medallions of leaves hung over the walls, dripping down chimneys; they were his dreams. Because he dreamed so sincerely, he could not take himself to task for having gone the wrong way down the Stream of Time, although in a sense this was a perversion; he had made himself ready as best he could, and the small indulgence was prudent (after all, it served little purpose to mortify oneself beyond discomfort to death: death came at CHRIST's choosing). So the wind ruffled his hair and the waves of the Fleuve Saint-Laurent marbled each other brown and blue as he stood on deck with the other Black-Gowns, Père Lalemant blowing his nose loudly, Père Massé smiling; and now they came close enough to see that New France was even smaller than he had imagined. The houses were sheds, the streets scarcely even paths. At the base of that cliff was the new Habitation of the Sieur de Champlain. Smoke rose from its chimneys, streaming across the cliff-face like spume from a waterfall. Soldiers with arquebuses stood on its second-storey galleries, watching the ship as it came closer, to make sure that it did not wear the red flag. The windows of the watchtowers were squares of darkness in the evening sun. Outside the palisades, Savages lounged beside their upturned canoes. Seeing them, Père Brébeuf felt a knot in his breast.

Yes, said Père Massé, who was watching him closely. There they are again – the vanguard of the army of lost souls.

Père Brébeuf could think of nothing to reply.

He had prepared his greetings on behalf of the Black-Gowns – for although Père Massé was the Superior, Brébeuf was more gifted of speech. More than he knew, he was like the VIERGE-MARIE with tears of happiness running down her face because she had conceived, not knowing yet that no one would believe her. The Sieur de Champlain, who would have welcomed them, was not at Kebec when they stepped ashore. His Deputy, Monsieur de Caën, refused them lodging in the fort, and the French traders likewise had no place for them. At last the Grey-Gowns, the Recollects, sent a boat for them, and permitted them to stay in their convent, which was located on the Rivière Saint-Charles.

It is very desolate here, I know, said his host. (Père Brébeuf did not find it desolate at all.) *Ver*-y desolate. Although our little garden adds a speck of cheer, with those blossoms called *Cardinals** . . .

Yes, Père Le Caron. We thank you and your Order for your hospitality.

Who sent you, brother? – The other priest addressed himself only to Père Brébeuf (people often did that). The other two Black-Gowns folded their

* Scarlet lobelias.

arms and watched him smiling. – Ah, Père Coton? I am told that he is a most discerning man. So he is your Provincial . . .

Père Le Caron's manner of speaking irritated Père Brébeuf somewhat, but he said nothing. It is the custom at sea for a merchant-ship to dip its ensign to any vessels of the Roy; in like wise Père Le Caron seemed to believe the Black-Gowns required by the usages of Canada to humble themselves to him – which, of course, they were glad to do, being themselves men of the utmost artlessness and simplicity.

Père Lalemant cleared his throat. Now tell us about these Savages called Huron, Père Le Caron.

Oh, but they are the cunningest race on this earth! the other priest replied, shaking his head. We see them on our river sometimes, catching eels in the autumn . . . But mainly those are Montagnais (ah, with that filthy dance of naked privities!) Then the interpreters – Étienne Brûlé and the rest – they take full advantage of the bordellos there, I assure you! There is no Huronne who is not a whore. She'll stand before you, anointing her naked breasts with beaver-grease . . .

Père Massé cleared his throat. – As for the interpreters, we have authority to recall them –

No, Jean, continued Père Le Caron, unhearing, your road will not be easy among the Huron. They will trick you and use you howsoever they can; you must be great-hearted to continue our progress in that Country! And they have no conception of authority. It is much simpler to show a Brahmin of India the True Faith than one of these willful Savages who cares not what your judgment of him might be!

And Père Le Caron launched into a long narrative of all his trials. From the first, he said, the Savages had sought to irk him and wear him down. On his first voyage, close to a decade before, they'd compelled him to paddle with them, for which he suffered greatly. Arriving in the Huron town of Carhagouha, he could scarcely believe the appalling license in which the Savages lived. Although they pressed him to live with them in the midst of their debaucheries, he insisted that they build him his own residence on the outskirts of the village, which they did. After that they demanded presents for the food they brought him, which he was forced to give them, having no other recourse. In his cabin he compiled his dictionary of Huron words and grammatical rules, hoping always to accomplish something for the LORD; he made not a single convert. And his subsequent labors bore much the same fruit. – Père Brébeuf listened very carefully. The other's self-pity annoyed him, but he was careful not to show it.

Our Père Nicolas will be a great help to you, I am sure, said Père Le Caron. He speaks the Huron dialect so rapidly that it is a marvel to hear the syllables escape from his lips! And you Jesuits, I take it, have made some preparation in the language?

It was impossible to do so in France, said Brébeuf, for there were no teachers there. But we are ready learners.

Ah, said Père Le Caron. But it is not a question of readiness. You must also show aptitude and discipline. Do you possess those qualities as well?

The Black-Gowns flushed. – We strive to do our duty, said Père Massé.

Eh, in any event, Père Nicolas will be a great blessing to you, said Père Le Caron. I am sure you will show him the courtesy that he merits.

But when Père Brébeuf reached Three Rivers, he found that Père Nicolas was dead.

The Martyrdom of Père Nicolas 1625

Père Nicolas Viel had accompanied Père Le Caron and a lay brother, Gabriel Sagard, to Wendaké, *viz.*, the Country of the Huron, in the Year of Our LORD 1623 – an auspicious annum, for it was then that Père de Nobili was finally permitted to resume his baptisms in India. – Père Nicolas was very pious. Before he became a monk, the girls had loved to make eyes at him, imagining what pleasure they would have if only they could dress him and adorn his hair with flowers. Soon indeed the women of Kebec would have this privilege, but only to lay him out for burial: – Père Nicolas was always unlucky. Perhaps for this very reason, he was able to keep all his natural goodness throughout his life, never being called upon to buy his successes with the gold doubloons of it; after all his successes were nil. When he first stepped onto the shore of Canada, making his lanky struggling way in the inch-thick wooden sandals that his Order required, the Montagnais were there, and said to one another: See how sad and sunken his eyes are! Does he have Power, or will he die soon? – Indeed, Père Nicolas made it his special prayer that GOD would permit him to spend the remainder of his life among the Huron; GOD heard and granted the boon in His own way, which atheists and other bleeding hearts might call ironical, but which the enlightened among us must value, for it shows true compassion for this man's vulnerability that his sacrifice was to be accepted so quickly. I know many a revolutionary who would rejoice to give himself to the fiery orgasm of a suicide bomb; it is the prospect of a sixty-year prison term that makes him shudder. For this reason, Père Nicolas,

I make no apologies in now rushing on to bring your story to its final sodden page.

The year before the Black-Gowns arrived, then, Champlain, looking up from a letter which he was writing to his wife (*I fully comprehend your unhappiness, my dear child, at being left a "half-widow," as you put it, but I beg you to refrain from this mad project you have of taking entrance in a convent*), heard through his spies that the Huron now sought to conclude a peace with the Seneca and various other Hiroquois; and this alarmed him because he knew that the Hiroquois were now trading for furs with the Hollanders. If the Huron began to trade with the Hollanders as well, Kebec would be compromised. How very long and cold these Canadian winters then, were the Savages to raise their prices . . . The situation was made still more difficult because Champlain was himself seeking to make a truce with the Mohawk Hiroquois for purposes of trade, and the Mohawk remained enemies of the Huron. (On account of the Hollanders, of course, it was his determination that the Mohawk *must* remain enemies of the Huron.) – Oh, how his schemes wriggled in his brain like worms! For these reasons he thought it best to summon Père Le Caron to him.

My good Père Joseph, he said, I am sending eleven armed Frenchmen to defend the Huron villages from the Hiroquois. Would you be pleased to accompany them?

Ah, said Le Caron, this is great news; good Père Nicolas will swoon when he hears. He wants so badly to go . . .

It was agreed that three Recollects would be permitted to set forth. But at the Council that Champlain held, when he smoothed his will ahead of him with hatchets and glass beads from his Store-house, a Huron Savage stood up. – We do not want these men, he said. We want men with guns to defend us against our enemies.

Come now, my son, said the wise Champlain. Don't you have eyes? Look at them, they're Grey-Gowns. They have spiritual powers. Each one of these Pères is as good as ten arquebuses! A prayer from one of them is as good as a round lead bullet!

The Huron smiled politely. After all, Père Le Caron had lived among them before.

Guillaume de Caën, the Protestant, now stood up and said: Listen to me, Huron men! If you take these Grey-Gowns to your bosoms I will reward you with presents of axes, knives and beads!

At this the Huron murmured and consulted with one another, for this was handsomely said. Then they agreed to take the Black-Gowns.

Said Père Le Caron to Père Nicolas: See how the Protestant seeks to appease us! But he is a serpent, I'm telling you! I will get his license revoked, never fear . . . (And indeed he did, three years later.)

To De Caën he said: Thank you, brother, for your generosity.

So they set out to erect their trophies of the Cross. It was a very sunny day. Père Nicolas kept looking behind him, until he could no longer see his convent's wooden ramparts, until the stone tower above the chapel gate had vanished among the sumacs, and he sighed. – Take heart, brother, said Père Le Caron. – Oh, said Père Nicolas, it is not that. It is only . . . – But then he trailed off, and the other thought it tactful not to press him. The lay brother, Frère Sagard, kept looking about him in wonder, for he had never seen such a foreign land. He scratched the name of IESVS in the bark of a large tree, to warn SATAN that he was taking possession of this great Country of Canada in the Name of GOD. And they met the Huron on the shore of the Fleuve Saint-Laurent and clambered into the canoes . . . – The way was long and laborious, and if I believed truly in representation I would be forced to describe for you every canoe-stroke, to mimic with the rippling swirls of these characters every change in the waters through which they passed, to let my prose shine like a star through the pallid pillars of trees around their campfires, to mimic the noise of wind and creeks in darkness. – *But on the other hand,* wrote Frère Sagard, *I have been advised to follow the artless simplicity of my usual manner.* Let me merely relate, then, that the Grey-Gowns with their armed escort visited the Tobacco Tribe, the Province of Fire, the Country of the Stinkards, the Forest Nations, Coppermines, Sorcerers, Island People, and High-Hairs – to say but little of the Little Tribe. And so they arrived in Wendaké, which is a narrow Country on the shores of the Sweetwater Sea.

The faces of the Savages there were almost the color of dried blood, noted Père Nicolas to himself. Those clear black eyes, gleaming like their greasy scalp-locks, never stopped watching him. He could not comprehend them. But of course he did not need to. It was his function to make them comprehend *him* and the LORD Whom he served. He would preach to them; he would teach them.

Loving their ideals above all, the Grey-Gowns shunned the filthy corruption of the longhouses, where the sounds of the Savages debauching could be heard at all hours and the smell of unwashed bodies and unclean vessels was an offense. At the Dance of the Naked Ones the young people copulated together; at a dream-feast a young man urinated in an old woman's mouth, for she had dreamed that that must be . . . No, the Recollects lived together in *reclusive* brotherhood. But they fanned out, too, searching, searching for souls. Père Nicolas soon came to the understanding that this Nation was very docile, and when influenced by temporal considerations it could be bent as one pleased. How exalting it all was! When he first saw the Country of the Huron it seemed to him that he must have seen it before in some dream, for its vast lake, known to all as the Sweetwater Sea, struck a chord of familiarity in him. Water, water . . . He did not understand that the water was already lapping round him. What he sensed was his own careening river-destiny.

There were many, many Huron villages imprisoned by the pale green walls of summer. He could not hope to know them all. But some of them he visited; some Savages became accustomed to him. In Teanaostaiaé Town, which lies in the Cord Nation of the Huron, there was a man called Soranhes. He was one of those Huron called *Atiwaronta* or *Big Stone* because he made money from the fur trade without himself trading. Yet in his case the appellation was not entirely accurate, since he dabbled his fingers with the French whenever he could. He had a fifteen-year-old son named Amantacha,* whom Père Nicolas considered a very likely boy to be formed and educated and perhaps even (who knows?) to become the first Huron priest, for he was very quick and pleasing in his ways. Indeed, Amantacha's face reminded him of a blank page of fine cream paper that could be written on in characters of the utmost beauty, a page that would preserve the writings of the LORD forever.† His eyes were very gentle; he addressed the Recollects with modestly becoming words. Everything about the boy seemed well-formed. So Père Nicolas visited this family whenever he could. He decided to be as delicate in his asking as the fine hairs at the nape of the boy's golden neck. In his zeal he even ate the dish called *leindohy* – small ears of corn drowned in a stagnant pond until they began to rot. – See how Kwer Nikoas grimaces like a sick dog! cried the boy, and the others laughed until the tears rolled down their cheeks. – Later, however, Soranhes took his son to task. – You spoke thoughtlessly, he said. We People do not believe in publicly chastising or humiliating a friend without good cause. He lives among us; he is our nephew. My dear son, you must take care not to poison his heart. Go now to the Grey-Gowns' lodge and give him this dried fish. It was unmannerly of him to make faces while he ate the *leindohy*, but he had reason to be ignorant. Perhaps he will like our fish better.

* Soranhes' name meant "He is a very tall tree." The meaning of "Amantacha" has been lost.

† These Huron used to laugh and say to the Recollects: Bring snowshoes and mark it! whenever they would write; for they had never seen that art, and marveled at the strange creature-tracks with which they covered the winter-white sheets.

Flushing, Amantacha ran out of the house. He ran through the winding gates of the palisade; he ran into the ravine where the Grey-Gowns roosted.

Seeing the boy's shy face so close to him, Père Nicolas was first consoled, then edified, then rendered exalted.

Look how he watches you! laughed Soranhes to his son one day when the priest was not there (for he could not help it; he too thought Kwer Nikoas preposterous). – He gangles himself over you like a big grey bird! – The boy had little desire to leave Wendaké, which all knew to be the center of the world, but upon his expressing these feelings his father reproved him, saying that he could not hope to prove himself a man if he showed fear. – Remember, he added, that it is the business of men to deal with outsiders. Women till the fields, but men smooth the way to distant places. If you dwell among them, the hearts of the Iron People will be bright with joy. They ask for you; they wish you to become a cord of our friendship. And you will learn their ways. Much about their hearts remains cloud-wrapped to my eyes. But *you* will learn to see the truth within them. Then you will have the right to speak to us all. Think upon it, my dear son.

Amantacha said: Do they live beyond the sea?

So they say, said Soranhes.

Can they see the GREAT TURTLE who upholds the world on His back?

If you go they will instruct you, of that you can be sure, was the answer.

In the year 1624, Père Nicolas spoke for a long time with Soranhes, pressing him earnestly to let him take his son Amantacha to be raised in France. – This face is not so different from the son's, thought Père Nicolas. – The small, almost feminine lips, however, seemed sly, coquettish. The brows were too perfectly arched, the eyes too brilliant. The slender bony face was both womanly and birdlike. He could not trust this man. – As for Soranhes, that worthy said to himself: I know that exchanging sons is what friends must do, to become kin to one another. However, I have heard bad reports of these Iron People. It is said that they strike young people who offend them, and do not allow them liberty. Still . . . – So he strode about perplexed.

If you do this thing, I personally will guarantee the boy's safety and happiness, said Père Nicolas. It will be for no more than a year.

And the other Pères will be happy to receive him in *Kekwek* and in France? said Soranhes. (The mouths of these Huron could not embrace the letter *b*.)

Very happy.

I seem to see them enclosing him, denying him the life to which he is accustomed –

Oh no no no.

Nephew, I must think upon it, he said, smoking his owl-head pipe. I love my son, and I want to know his mind.

He loved the goods of the Iron People. His father had seen them when still a young man, but in those days they were rare and sacred. Now they were not so rare, but yet more desired, for a man could clear fields so much more easily with iron axes, and women loved the copper kettles. The days of the Old Men and the Big Stones were glorious now; all respected them for having brought these things. What prestige, to give these things away! No one could forget Soranhes now! And suppose he opened a private way to the Iron People. Who knew what else they might have to give him?

In the end, Amantacha being willing, he agreed to let him go the following spring. That was when Père Nicolas made the decision to descend the Fleuve Saint-Laurent for the purpose of making a spiritual retreat. Père Le Caron and the lay brother, Sagard, had already returned to Kebec, and he had been left alone. As he went down the river he was feeling very satisfied with himself because he could soon take Amantacha in hand and mold him as he saw fit, so he sat at ease between the two Savages who paddled, not knowing that what he took to be the Fleuve Saint-Laurent was for him the Stream of Time, which only goes one way excepting for Black-Gowns; and they portaged past the rapids called La Chine where Champlain, dreaming the Dream of the Hiroquois, had been defeated in his progress twenty-two years before, and then they loaded the canoe again and the Savages held it steady while Père Nicolas climbed in, as he was clumsy, and then they leaped in, one before him, one behind, and continued down, the blades of their paddles fluttering among the fishes, and one of the paddles snagged on something hairy that wrapped around it and sought to pull it into the water but the Savage said something that a Shaman had taught him and the thing went limp. Père Nicolas, who had noticed nothing, was occupied still with his dreams for Amantacha, wondering whether it would be too quick or too slow to instruct him in writing toward the end of his first year; for in France he had had charge of a Montagnais boy named Pastedouachouan to whom he had taught both French and Latin most tolerably; of course he had worked upon him for almost five years . . . and he said to himself: Pastedouachouan was docile, malleable; yet I verily believe that from this Amantacha my hands shall make a greater masterpiece! and the reflection of Père Nicolas's long pale face traveled with him, gazing up at him from just beyond the side of the canoe; and the noise of the Fleuve got louder and they came in sight of the island that would someday be Montréal, the Savages admiring how the flatness of the island narrowed into thick mistiness like the neck of some animal; the

Fleuve made a narrow channel on the north, a wide one on the south. Both channels had rapids. The Savages had already decided to shoot these rapids rather than make another portage. The sound of the Fleuve was much louder now. Père Nicolas was about to die. He chose to do it. He chose to remain in the canoe while the Savages leaped out and swam with it, one on either side, looking for places to set their feet so that they could brace themselves and walk the canoe down the rapids of Rivière des Prairies (the rapids were soon to be called Recollect Rapids, after Père Nicolas, but in the Stream of Time they were the Thirty-First Rapids – *viz.*, the Return from Egypt, where Père Nicolas had been all his life), and Père Nicolas lay full length in the bottom of the canoe, the water roaring in his ears, and the two Huron had now planted their feet firmly between boulders; they stood waist-deep in the foam, easing the canoe down step by step (the rapids here were brief) as Père Nicolas was thinking: since the boy comes to me with his eyes open, it's fair to transform him when one of the Huron stumbled, whether because of the extra weight in the canoe or because something hairy pulled it from beneath will remain a Point not categorized in these Exercises; and the canoe shot away and overturned almost in sight of the Cross where Kateri Tekakwitha was going to be buried in fifty-five years, and Père Nicolas tumbled into the water. He was not a good swimmer. Nor was he young. Swept rapidly down to where the water was so deep, chilly and indigo that there was nothing in it excepting his long white hands, his thrashing knees, and weird green rays of luminescence revolving around him, Père Nicolas sought to cry out to the Huron who could not help him; so doing he swallowed water. Water now rushed him to the shallows where bubbles glowed tan through the murk and the wriggling sedges tickled his hair; he tried to seize the bottom, but only blue-black mussels fell through his hands. The river rushed him on. A rock-edge sliced his forehead. He shot down through the narrows. He was pounded against rocks, and the green rays whirled faster and faster in every pool and suddenly he comprehended that they were hairy arms or tentacles and GOUGOU pulled him down and pressed His lips to Père Nicolas's and drank his breath, vomiting whirlpools down his throat in conformance to the code of exchange that characterizes magpies, crows and monsters. As the Black-Gown's struggling body fled from life, becoming more waterlogged with every such water-breath, it passed the Isle of Montréal where his soul saw a silvery church rising amidst the trees of Montréal, because he was riding now into the future of our continent, flying down the Fleuve Saint-Laurent with its low flat shore softened by trees, its tiny wooded islands like bubbles, flying until his tranquil white corpse, rock-scraped past bleeding, snagged itself between two driftlogs to become a wooden Saint, another icon in Canada's gallery: – yes, he was the first martyr! – Of course it did not happen at once. The Huron did not suspect it when they brought him to Kebec to be buried. Nor did the idea occur to Père Le Caron at first.

Could he have met with foul play at the hands of those Savages? he asked Brébeuf. I wonder; I wonder . . . ?

But what would be their motive, Joseph? said the other. Those two Huron look to me like honest men. They did not rob him; here are all his possessions, no? Did the Huron Nation hate him for some reason? But you say that this man Soranhes trusted him enough to promise him his son!

(Besides, added Père Brébeuf privily to Père Massé, it would be beyond reason for GOD to give these Recollects a martyr before *we* have our chance! – And Père Massé looked back at him with his impassive leathery face and slowly winked . . .)

Père Le Caron sat upright in the night. – I am sure they drowned him! he said aloud.

No one replied.

For nine years Père Le Caron went about whispering, and no one paid any attention. But by then, when the Recollects had been excluded from missionary work once and for all in New France, the Black-Gowns could afford to be generous. So it was that Père Le Jeune, the Superior at Kebec, heard out a pair of Algoumequin Savages who wished to calumniate the Huron for reasons having to do with trade, and allowed himself to believe. Then at last poor Père Nicolas achieved the glory of a mention in the *Jesuit Relations*. His wooden statue was encrusted with the gold of piousness as he stood in his niche in the Stream of Time, blessing the lovely darkhaired Québecoise girls bicycling along Sherbrooke, the Québecoise girls walking down the sidewalks on those Montréal summer evenings when the sky has that northern limpidity of Canada glowing and clean above the street lamps; the lamps of the *Société des alcools de Quebec** blaze, and trees shimmer in the vacant lots . . .

Amantacha's Sponsors

The martyr's plans for Amantacha were not upset with his canoe. The following year, in the time when the Wendat and the Iron People gave one another presents, Soranhes came with his son to Two Large Waters Joining

* Provincially licensed liquor store.

(called by the Iron People *Kekwek*), and entrusted him to the Grey-Gowns, saying: Thus I fulfill my promise. Here is my strong young son. Bring him back to me next year, for so my nephew Kwer Nikoas promised me.

Oh, he did, did he? said Père Le Caron. What a bother. You know very well that passage to France and back is a very uncertain matter . . .

Amantacha stood shyly in the courtyard, staring at the convent's four wooden bastions. He had never seen those before. Outside the ramparts, at the edge of that natural moat called the Rivière Saint-Charles, Montagnais were digging up tiger-lily bulbs to roast. – On the gallery, a young man of

that same Nation leaned upon the railing, looking out at them who might have been his cousins. He was dressed like one of the Iron People, for they had *baptized* him. His name was Pastedouachouan. The Recollects had had him in France for five years. He did not remember his own language anymore.

Père Le Caron looked up and saw him. He frowned. – Pierre-Antoine, what are you doing? he cried sharply. Go into the Chapel and say your prayers!

Yes, Père.

Soranhes spoke to Brûlé. – Who is that boy, and why does the Grey-

Gown raise his voice to him in that way? Young people are very delicate. Sometimes they hang themselves from a tree if one scolds them too much.

Ah, my uncle, I cannot say. (Thus Brûlé, shrugging.) He belongs to them now.

And you have no compassion? Beware, my dear nephew, lest in all your comings and goings your mind may sprout seven linings like that of the Hiroquois. I seem to see you devoured by your own mouth! Will you also say of my son *He belongs to them?* Listen well: I have been a good uncle to you. If you are not a good brother to him in the Country of the Iron People, then I shall split your head!

Perhaps I too should poison myself, said Brûlé in a low voice.

You? You love life too much. – No, forgive me, my nephew, I pray you; I become as short in my patience as these Iron People. I should have spoken more gently . . .

Père Le Caron stood with folded arms, tapping his foot upon the ground. He comprehended but little of what had been said, for he had forgotten his command of their dialect, which was in truth Savage, barbarous and outlandish.

Well, Soranhes, what have you to say to me now? You must not keep me waiting.

If the boy is happy he may return to France the following year, replied the father, seeing through the priest as though he were a transparent river-pool. – But after the first year my heart will be aching to behold him once again. – And he took his son by the hand, as if he wished to take him back forthwith.

Very good, *ver*-y good, Soranhes, said Père Le Caron. You have my word.

The Père was young but white-bearded, reaching out for Amantacha's shoulder with spread fingers . . . Amantacha smiled, quick and sensitive. His skin was the color of a brown pond in the sunlight. How good he was! He seemed so docile, so credible that Père Le Caron marveled. – Père Brébeuf, who happened to be there, approved of him, too. (It did not occur to Père Brébeuf that he expected the same great things of the boy that his Superiors expected of him.) Père Le Caron was especially delighted. Before the father departed, he gave him many friendship-presents.

Ver-y good, he says, thought Soranhes to himself. But my eyes see far. My eyes see me doing better.

For he did not like the face of that Montagnais boy whom they had frenchified.

He strolled about the place called *Kekwek*. Tomorrow was the beginning of the appointed day for exchanging gifts with his uncles and nephews among the Iron People, but today was the day of Councils. He must attend those and speak, or else those of his Nation would suspect him of solitariness, which is almost witchcraft. But first he would see what he would see. His brother Oronton could not be spared; he was guarding the beaver-skins against theft. Where was his dear nephew Tregouaroti? It was he who had given his young brother Savignon to the Iron People long ago. Tregouaroti would give him good counsel. – But no. He did not want Tregouaroti to believe he had the greater right to speak. Tregouaroti was a good hunter, but no warrior; he was not a great man. – Instead, therefore, Soranhes approached Chawain's lodge with his good nephew Iroquet, who, being of the Algonkin Nation, could do less harm with his talk. Chawain was shouting in the courtyard; Chawain was as shrill as ever, although his body had become somewhat dried up with age. The other Iron People feared him – that Soranhes could readily see. Did those big guns in the wall belong to Chawain? Look! Chawain raised his hand, and a man brought him a key. (The Iron People loved locks and keys.) Now Chawain was going into his Store-house. What was in there? Soranhes seemed to see mountains of beads and blankets, glittering ossuaries of hatchet-heads, copper kettles brighter than suns – ah, and guns. How could Chawain not weep, knowing as he did that the Wendat had none of those? Perhaps Amantacha could persuade the Iron People to give him a gun. Then he and Amantacha could win fame. There would be much eating of Iroquois flesh then in the House of Cut-Off Heads! – But what was Chawain doing now? He had come out, and he was shouting again. Truly Chawain was a bearded old woman; he was a bluejay! And see those men carrying heavy bales on their backs, bent low, struggling up the stairs while Chawain's warriors leaned upon their arquebuses and pulled their hats lower and lower over their eyes! – Iroquet stood beside him, slapping mosquitoes and staring. Yroquet loved to come here. Iroquet marveled how the Iron People never changed houses when they rotted, but simply patched them up and continued to live in them. Of course their houses were difficult to make; maybe that was why they were so lazy. They did not like to travel. – Now Chawain had given over his scolding. One of the Black-Robes had come. Chawain smiled and deferred to him, as though he were Chawain's uncle. But he was much younger than Chawain. – Ah, this must be the one I desire, said Soranhes to himself, for he knew the Iron People well. – He whispered, and Yroquet went to greet Chawain. Now, while this Black-Gown stood detached for the moment from Chawain, now was the time to come smiling. The Black-Gown stood very tall. His eyes were cold and blue like juniper berries. His skin was much paler than Chawain's. He wore a broadbrimmed hat like the soldiers, so that his face was always in shadow. Soranhes thought to himself that he would like to have one of these hats.

He stepped forward. Chawain looked up in alarm, but Père Brébeuf smiled at him. As soon as the smile went away, the sternness came back, and darkness rippled full of Power in his robe.

Soon enough, Père Brébeuf had given him friendship-presents for his son Amantacha – and his presents were more generous than Père Le Caron's; for he could see that once the child was instructed, he'd be very useful in opening the way to distant Nations. Now it was time to try Chawain's deputy, that big man with the big belly. This was Emery de Caën. Monsieur de Caën, knowing that his own opportunity to be pious had come, submitted in his turn to the cajoleries of the grubby Savage. Eh, a grand number of beads and knives and iron arrow-points I'm going to have to give him . . . Well, may it be to my celestial credit.

Soranhes was satisfied. He prayed for his son's good journey; he prayed for blue sky and smooth waters.

After he had returned to Wendaké (not troubling overmuch to watch for Hiroquois, as that year they were embroiled in a war with the Mahican), the inevitable quarrel broke out. – Père Le Caron was the loser. He stood with bowed head by the raspberry bushes of his convent, listening to the droning of the bees . . . – It was decided that the boy would travel to France on Monsieur de Caën's ship, and that his education would be the charge of those generous Jesuits . . .

The Education *1626–1629*

As for Amantacha, he was terrified of the Black-Gowns, but only at first. They reminded him of the time that he had gone hunting for birds in the maplewood highlands, for his mother craved meat, and because he went westward instead of east he soon discovered one of the old villages. Of course he was old enough to remember when his village had moved and they'd held the Feast of the Dead in all seemliness, for the sake of the dear bones which must now be left behind; that happened every ten years or so, when the soil was exhausted. And yet he had never gone back to the abandoned place. It was not good to go there, his father said, because the dead were angry. Even the Feast of the Dead did not entirely console a number of them – *viz.*, the weaker ones, who could not hope to withstand HEAD-PIERCER on their journey to the Country of the Dead. They stayed in the old longhouses; they grew spirit-corn in the old fields. Yet now as the young man stood there, he felt a strange curiosity about the dead people, the bone people. – A mangy hide still hung on a stretcher. The bark-lined corn-pits gaped empty. Looking right and left, ignoring the prickling of nervous sweat in the groove of his back, he strode to the middle of the clearing already overgrown with thistles and grass and ferns with wide rounded leaf-lobes so that everything had a grassy smell; he saw how spiders and beetles crawled upon the leaves, and snakes lived in the abandoned lodges whose roofs had tumbled down to let in the hot sun-joy; trees pressed all around and saplings were springing up on the edge of the clearing to drown out that openness; – and suddenly Amantacha started with fright as something cawed loudly inside one of the ruined lodges. He gazed around him. He was alone. Trembling, he took a clod of earth and threw it into the lodge. At once a black crow issued, flapping its wings and screeching. – Amantacha fell to the ground laughing. How ridiculous that crow was! – When he remembered that, he could not be much afraid of the Black-Gowns. – And yet what if the crow were Something Else after all? . . .

. . . Kekwek, what a place! A hundred Iron People lived there now. They built many tiny houses; he didn't know why. The Iron People didn't like to live together, Monsieur de Caën said. – Amantacha peered through the lace curtains of Kekwek with their flowers and shields and crests, thinking: why do the women of the Iron People leave holes in their work? (Not that there were many women here. At least they didn't have beards, as Tehorenhaennion the Shaman had said.) And he laughed aloud, so that Monsieur de Caën spoke to him through the interpreter, saying: Young man, don't be insolent. We see possibilities in you, but after all you're still nothing more than a Savage! – Amantacha gaped at such rudeness. Then he smiled and said nothing; silence was the way of the Wendat. – Amantacha was amazed at everything. But he reminded himself: My father said that when I come back next year I'll be a man. And I'll know the secrets of the Iron People. – So he was exultant when Monsieur de Caën put his arm around him and led him aboard his ship. – A cannonade! – They sailed. Crows were shrieking over the edge of the settlement in an untidy row that reformed crazily, and the cannons faced them in the sunset, the light too cloud-muted to shine on them; Champlain's sentinels found their bores very cold to lean on as they stood there watching the ship decrease like melting ice. The wind whipped the tops of trees back against the wall at the edge of what was not yet Upper Town, and the Fleuve Saint-Laurent streamed greedily . . . Amantacha kept looking in between the trees as they went down river, his eyes like child-hands dragging across the stakes of the palisade at home for the fun of the noise. But he didn't do that anymore. Besides, Teanaostaiaé Town was so far away . . .What was his father doing? They sailed past the blue mountains and green table-lands on the south side of the Fleuve Saint-Laurent, the fleuve a dreary greyish-brown hue that evening; and orange striped the grey ceiling of cloud overhead. Amantacha felt sad. Now they passed Anticosti Island, and reached the great Ocean that Amantacha had never seen. And once the whole world had been that way, so the Old Men said at home! Breasting the mountain-waves without any incident that the chroniclers thought worthy of record, they landed safe at Rouen by grace of Our LORD, where Amantacha stayed with De Caën and his uncle Ézéchiel for a week. He saw a moose called a *horse*. He saw beggars and prostitutes. *Then* . . .

Then for the first time he saw Paris. The Black-Gowns took him there. The city was like some great egg in the fields, cracked into a thousand pieces by its *rues* and *boulevards* and *avenues*; within its wall-curve rose church towers innumerable above the teeming roofs, their bells shrieking louder than any birds he had ever heard; and wide stone bridges crossed the Seine by way of an Isle of Churches (which also was infested with houses); one of the biggest bell-towers of all rose here, high enough almost to clear the stench of the river; from it Amantacha could see the green hills and windmills beyond the wall and he wanted to go see them but the Black-Gowns laughed and Brûlé said no, my good nephew; *Paris* is where you will be taught* and they took him from church to church to be presented to strange people whom the Black-Gowns said meant him well, but he thought that the slit-windows of those churches made them seem more than ever like skeletons. – The Roy's coach squeaked through the streets on its wooden wheels, between the walls of narrow high houses whose windows were vertical slits; and merchants rode by and workers rushed down the avenues on urgent errands and the nobles rode by nodding to each other in their beaver hats. He saw more beggars, horses and prostitutes. He saw lepers stinking and dying in the streets. At night the Black-Gowns closed their shutters very tightly so that it was hard for him to breathe and he heard strange laughter and screams in the streets and sometimes nobles rode about all night shouting and clattering their weapons, and he was afraid because the brothers in the house with him were afraid. In the morning they took him to see old Duc Henri, who was the

* "Brûlé had a wife in Paris who looked after his rather big bank account" – Trigger.

Viceroy of New France, and the Viceroy said something to Amantacha in the language of the Iron People and Amantacha replied, knowing that he could not understand: the Black-Gowns are like crows! – But all at once he thought: these men are Shamans. What if they can read my thoughts? And why should I say such things to this old man, who is well-respected? So he quickly dropped to his knees as he had seen the Iron People do, and kissed the Viceroy's hand. He knew enough now not to call him Uncle, as he would have done at home. With closed eyes he waited, like a clever lapdog, until he felt the old man's hand on his head, stroking, stroking . . .

He had no interpreter anymore. Considering this Étienne Brûlé fellow to be barbarous and coarse, the Black-Gowns had dispensed with him; he'd go back to Canada on the next ship, being out of place here. (He knelt and clasped his hands and his lips moved, and their hearts softened a little, for they thought that he was praying. But really he was mouthing over the names of all the Huron girls he'd slept with: She Is Eternal, She Is Called After, Fruit Matures, Small Matter, She Is Called Treetops, She Is Not Waiting* . . . – This last was Amantacha's sister. Remembering her, Brûlé grinned defiantly; he felt that he had cheated these Jesuits somehow, when he'd popped her . . .) – No, Messieurs, there was nothing for it: Amantacha must learn French. This gave him pause, as he remembered that Montagnais boy at Kebec, named Pastedouachouan, who had forgotten his own language. But he told himself to have courage. He did not fear the wiles of the Iron People. Of course he could already say his bonjours; now he learned his devotions and excuses; in his facile way he was soon tracing out his majuscules from 𝔄 to ℨ; he read out the most essential verses from the Bible that the Viceroy had given him, his soft voice pleasing all the Black-Gowns who heard, and he learned to write his name. Kwer Nikoas had promised his father that the Black-Gowns would bring him back at the end of a year, but Kwer Nikoas was dead. – Eh, but he is a clever boy! they said. Soon he was copying out the Creed in a steady hand.

One day there was a great crowd, and the Black-Gowns took him to see the troops with their long guns slung over their shoulders, marching out of Paris through an archway whose walls met in a point, and beneath this was a toothy lip of spikes that could come crashing down when the city was under siege, and beneath this the soldiers disappeared, while pikemen flanked them, keeping the crowds back, and faces peered through the narrow rectangular

* Teondisewan.

windows. And he had the strange fancy that the marching uniforms were somehow akin to the letters that he was learning, that in every hymn-book there drilled regiments innumerable, proceeding from page to page as fast as pages might be turned; but then he had the shivery feeling that perhaps the letters were marching deeper and deeper inside his body, conquering him for the Iron People. – What a grand parade! said one among the Black-Gowns. And Amantacha smiled and said: Yes, Père, it is truly a remarkable spectacle. – He quickly lost his leisure to see these things when the Black-Gowns began to educate him in earnest. They took him down into their dark Meditation Room, whose walls were lined with pictures of Devils and terrifying tortures; for they wished to strike a wholesome fear of GOD into his heart. They left him there for many hours, with the door locked, until they heard him crying out.

During the daytime Amantacha felt nothing but happiness. A continual excitement warmed him; he never knew what new marvels the Iron People might show him. Coaches rushed past him like monsters. The food was plentiful, although it smelled bad (except for the lemon-rind, which he had had also at Kebec and thought surpassingly delicious). He was filled with pride that he had been chosen to understand such things. When he came home at last, he would be the best friend of the Iron People: all the Wendat would come to him, and it would be his choice to open or close the way to the Iron People. – Ah, how well the Iron People cared for him! But at night fear and guilt crawled inside him like worms. He craved the corn soups and breads that his elder sister Teondisewan made, kneeling by the hearth in her deerskin skirt to which were sewn beautiful animals fashioned from the scraps of copper kettles, and the good smoky smell of the lodge was around him and his little sister was laughing in his mother's arms and then they all smoked tobacco with his father . . . – They are far, he said to himself. Have courage. – But he was ashamed that he could not better understand the language of the Iron People. He dreaded the morning when he must wake up and try to understand the Iron People again. No matter how much he slept, he was still tired. It was a great effort for him to learn the ways of the Iron People.

It was the vast crowds above all else that chastened the boy and fitted him for his purpose: seeing them, he understood that the Wendat could never hope to contest with these folk on equal terms.

He dreamed of water lobelias goggling at him like AATAENTSIC's eyes in the Sweetwater Sea . . .

They instructed him at Paris; they taught him at Rouen. (Behind every rayère or loophole, a Black-Gown waited.) At their College in Rouen was a young Black-Gown named Père Daniel. Père Daniel spoke much of Heaven. Whenever he said that word, he pointed upward with his black sleeve and smiled so that he would understand how pleasant a place it was. Amantacha supposed at first that Heaven must be identical with the Country from which the Sky-Spirit AATAENTSIK had originally come: a great white plain of cloud riven with white gulleys and puffed up with tussocks whose edges glowed with blueness like snow-shadows. She had fallen from there in the days when the world was only water; diving to bring up mud in their mouths, the generous animals had made land for Her. – But when he told this to Père Daniel he replied that it was a fable, and that there was no AATAENTSIK in Heaven. He must forget about Her, Père Daniel said; either She did not exist or else She was a wicked demon from Hell. – Hearing this, Amantacha smiled and nodded his head. – You tell me new things that I have never heard before, he said. – Gazing upward, he thought: There must be many places in the Sky that the Black-Gowns do not know about. Perhaps Heaven is the place where only dead Frenchmen go. – Of course he was too polite to say anything. Therefore, the Black-Gowns marveled at his intelligence.

He was taken to Duc Henri's again, and the Duc studied him without pride or disappointment, noting how the boy's face had filled out even to plumpness, so that his disagreeably protuberant cheekbones vanished. He had taken on a somewhat smug turn of mouth, thought the Duc. Eh, he was young. No doubt his life would he hard enough when they returned him among his fellow Savages. So it had been, as he heard, with that Montagnais, Pierre-Antoine Pastedouachouan.

Père Daniel spoke to him of Hell, and said that all the Savages were from there. – Yes, said Amantacha. Everything that you Black-Gowns say is true. The Old Men have taught me nothing to the contrary. My father Soranhes told me always to heed your words, that I might learn.

Your father is a wise man, said Père Daniel.

The Iron People slouched; they threw themselves down in chairs, as if the chairs would never break or be anything but chairs.

There came the passionate moment when he was inducted into the Exercises, and they spoke to him of fleuves and rivières until he saw the Stream of Time, called *Yandawa*,* which made its massy rapids with the sound *yandawa yandawa*, and he peered between beech leaves eaten lacy by

* Wendat word for river.

caterpillars and there was Yandawa, spilling down granite steps with the easy swoop of mosquitoes, and Père Daniel was praying *Water from the side of* CHRIST, *wash me,* and Amantacha threw himself in: Yandawa took him. He almost fell far enough downstream to see Sainte Kateri Tekakwitha where at the edge of the lilies a stone curved up from the water like a turtle's back, but he did not go there because he feared the Hiroquois waiting in the birchy darkness; he almost swam far enough upstream to think that he was home among the dry floury smell of cornfields and his family had prepared a great feast of unleavened bread seasoned with blueberries and deer fat for him so that he smiled for happiness and Père Daniel touched his shoulder very softly, believing that he had seen IESUS but he did not go home, either, because now indeed he did see JESUS, Who said to him: My sister's son, you and I are related forever.

Rihouiosta, he said. I believe.

When at last they considered him sufficiently instructed, he was baptized in that dark and solemn Cathedral at Rouen paved with bowed heads, lit with flickering torches and candelabra like wilted spider-legs; it was a confusion of walls and railings and darkness and eyes staring at him; he sometimes heard the whispers or even the shouts on the street: *ah, le petit Sauvage!* (for it was said that he was the King of Canada's own son); and around him the monks were kneeling, bearing torches as tall as towers; the Archbishop towered over him with his strange onion-shaped headgear . . . But Amantacha was no longer afraid. He knew by now that the Iron People did not mean him harm. Indeed, this baptism was as rich an honor among the Iron People as a portion of deer-fat. – His godparents were the Duc de Longueville and Madame de Villais. They were very proud of him and said: now you may forget that Savage name of yours; now your name is Louys; you are Louys de Saincte Foy . . . – and Amantacha felt a pleasurable shiver of fear in him, to hear that the Black-Gowns had changed him both in name and nature. – It was the icy Month When Bear-Cubs Are Born. A great stage had been erected so that the crowds could better see him; the Black-Gowns were very triumphant. The historian Creuxius, perhaps displaying his own equivocal feelings about the affair, reports that a flash of lightning illuminated the ceremony. Be that as it may, Louys' confidence never cracked. – How everyone gloried in him! – But something else he had learned by now, something that he never told the Black-Gowns. *They* were not the Lords of the Iron People, as they had pretended in Canada. Once he was with two Black-Gowns on the street and a man came rushing at them shouting: You will burn in Hell, you traitors and Gallicans! – And he remembered also how his uncle Père Brébeuf had vied with his uncle Père Le Caron for custody of him; and he thought to himself: they mean to devour each other!

Afterwards a christening feast was held, in which each guest was given his own plate for his meat (this was a new custom that had just been imported from Italy). They ate their soup out of a skull-like bowl of that mirror-iron called *silver*; their women brought this bowl to them, lifting it by its ears.

Amantacha was very pleased with himself. And how he loved the Iron People! What impressed him most of all was their arquebuses. He thought to himself: If only I could take one of these weapons when they are not looking, and hide it . . . What a hero they will call me at home! I will go against the Five Nations and shoot all their Captains!

He awaited his opportunity, but it never came. The Iron People guarded their guns too well.

Faith, Hope and Charity *1628–1629*

While Amantacha was so gracefully joining the family of Christians, that fine gentleman the Sieur de Champlain (now sixty-one years of age) had begun a family himself. – Not with Hélène, of course – *she* was never coming near Canada again! Nor did he beget his three daughters. But they were his just the same. It had long been apparent to him that the real treasure of Canada, the only one, was not gold, not phantom diamonds, not the undiscoverable copper mines, but only human souls. (Even yet, of course, the prospect of China remained like a range of tea-green peaks in his mind. There he would have his plantations, becoming great and mighty even as he instructed his obedient pigtailed coolies, and all the Savages along the way. But someone else would probably get there first – some *upstart* like young Brûlé! And none of them can even remember landmarks, landfalls, capes; no one can prick the chart like I do . . . – not that they'll ever appreciate the necessity.) – Champlain was friendless. He longed to stamp his image upon Savage souls . . . Old Bonnerne the surgeon, who'd pled for Duval's life, who'd died of scurvy before Duval's skull fell into the Fleuve, had thought much the same. In that first and last Kebec autumn of his life, Bonnerne had gone around entreating the Montagnais and the Algoumequins to give him a girl – just one! – to educate and to marry. He was desperate to rule and to love, like all the French. But to the Savages his words were dull, green and pointed-tipped like the leaves of henbane. They refused him. And Bonnerne had died. (Maybe scurvy was only loneliness?) So it had gone – lo! for almost twenty years now. There was Amantacha, of course. And the Recollects had brought a young man of the Montagnes named Pastedouachouan to France, where they taught him good church Latin. But he came back a fop, addicted to brandy, ignorant of hunting: it was his destiny to starve to death in Canada. And the others? Savages were as plentiful as trout, but just try locking one into your Store-house of concentrated education, indoctrination and frenchification . . . ! But all that now changed in a perceptible fashion, for which we must give Champlain the glory. It happened like this:

In the month of Octobre, 1627, two of his cowherds at Cap Tourmente were found with their heads bashed in. So far his authority was leaking dangerously, like a bad ship on the sea. But the Sieur de Champlain was very adroit at stopping up leaks with specially tailored lead plates . . . When he called the Montagnais to account, they whined at first that the Iroquois had done it, but when he pointed out to them that the Fleuve Saint-Laurent was speckled everywhere with the canoes of Montagnais catching fish, and that no one in these canoes had seen the enemy, then they admitted that he was in the right as always, and that one of them must have been the villain. Ah, they were base, perfidious! And they had murdered Frenchmen before.

I must proceed cautiously, however, he said to Merveille, who continued fast in his favor.

Yes, Seigneur.

We are very short of ammunition, you know. And there are only forty-five of us, counting even the women and children –

Yes, Seigneur. (Oh, the pontificating old fool! thought Merveille to himself.)

So the Sieur de Champlain summoned the Montagnaits to a great Council, where he berated them as was his habit. – Do you not agree, he said to them, that the murderer must be punished with death?

Yes, Champlain. We will give you presents . . .

With *death*, I said!

Yes, Champlain.

Would that you all perished of starvation!

Yes, Champlain.

I shall now take hostages, he announced coldly; and he did.

What to do; what to do? He paced up and down the galleries of his Habitation.

He began by making the Exercise of Indignation. He was a visionary statesman –

It seemed to him these days that all parties were determined to defy him in all particulars. (That was the First Point.) And in such difficult times, too! (That was the Second Point.) Every spring they ran so perilously low of provisions that a mere barrel or two of flour would be left, which must be saved for the sick. Every Mars they'd be compelled to eat the Indian dish called sagamite – a vile admixture of maize, fish and game that reeked like a dead dog; in Avril they began to search the river-horizon, eyes visored by sunburned hands, because if De Caën's ship didn't come they would starve; in Mai, seeing nothing, they must waste their last shot and powder on hunting. If the Basques or the Yroquois were to attack, they would not have sufficient reserves of these things to defend themselves. *Every* spring! The worst of it was that he knew this to be the outcome of a deliberate policy of the Company's to keep them in dependence. (That was the First Point again – his favorite. Everyone was against him. Now his fury waxed against these Montagnais assassins!) Cardinal Richelieu had but lately taken command, appointing himself Grand Master, Captain, and Superior General of French Navigation and Trade, but it did not seem to make any difference. – Eh, he said to himself, it will remain like this as long as we cannot feed ourselves. (Back to the Second Point.) And that will never happen until we clear more land. (That was the First Point.) How can I bear to busy myself with these stupidities, when thanks to these others it gets no better from year to year? (The First Point again – in case you didn't guess.) – Saying this litany to himself, he began to feel quite virtuous (as indeed he was). And then there was Pontgravé, whose gout was now so much worse as to require four attendants to do his business – what was he *doing* in this Country? (Still the First Point.) Champlain loathed to see him here. And he was saying nothing of the Protestants, whom he'd forbidden to sing hymns in 1626, at which they only sang the louder, so that the Indians could hear them. (The First Point.) And all the artisans so lazy and inefficient – he'd had to tell them to build the barn at Cap Tourmente; that would never have occurred to them. (At least the Jesuits did not consider themselves too proud to work with their hands.) It was harder now that he himself could not lift a beam as well as he once could, to set them all an example. And then the De Caëns weren't bringing his salary, which put him to considerable embarrassment; Hélène had entered into many legal actions in France to obtain it – thank GOD he had her! – and these winters! Ice in the Fleuve Saint-Laurent in Novembre; eight pieds of snow and sometimes more! One had to buy moose-meat from the Savages, and they were all cheats. (The First and Second Points combined.) – And Louis Hébert had died of a fall just when he was most needed . . . (The First Point.) And now this. – Terrible, terrible! – He trembled with anger. But he'd been authorized to pass judgments without appeal . . . He'd *hang* this murderer as he had Duval!

Eh, when the time was ripe . . .

So what to do? His armory was insufficient –

Nothing to do. He gnashed his teeth like GOUGOU.

In Janvier of 1628, a band of Montagnais came to Kebec. They were starving. They begged him for food, which he gave them, despite the oaths of the beaver-clerks, who already dreaded starvation. Among them were three young girls, of eleven, twelve and fifteen years of age, respectively. And they proposed to give the girls to him as additional hostages.

Eureka!

Do you comprehend that you are offering these girls to me, to do with as I please? (Thus Champlain, to the Old Men and Captains of the Montagnais.)

They are so hungry, Champlain. They do not weep, but soon they will be as snowflakes in the wind.

Good. I shall bring them up as good Catholics.

Pontgravé (who in truth was of a very jovial temperament, and got on well with these Savages) set himself in opposition to this plan. – Some stew we'll be in, having to feed those little bitches! Think about it, Champlain, I beg you! I'm not against your having a couple of pets, but get a Huron or two. Ten thousand skins from them last year! That's why we're ahead of the Dutch. As for these Montagnes, tell 'em you have too much to do. We run short of provisions every winter as it is: that's the Second Point! You know how we have to go moose-hunting in our Savage raquettes or snowshoes! By the time Avril comes around, we'll be down to half a dozen casks of moldy hardtack as usual; you know we will . . . As for the bitches, what's the difference if they starve (forgive me for saying so), when there're so many more where they came from? And GOD knows what they'll steal. Say, do you know what your mistake was?

I almost fear to inquire.

Well, I'll tell you. It was marrying that whiny fillette. Hélène's a good young Christian girl – don't get me wrong – but she won't make a certain effort – *that's* obvious enough. Eh, don't look at me like that! And without that, how can a man have children? That's what you want, mon ami!

Monsieur, replied the Sieur de Champlain in a trembling voice, I have sworn to cherish my wife until death. Her soul is chained to mine. I shall not permit you to slight her. If you continue as you have begun, I shall be compelled to –

Champlain, Champlain!

Do you acknowledge my authority over you or do you not?

Monsieur, I – Please follow your own desire in the matter of these three Indiennes. You know best, I am sure.

So he took them in, to dispose of after his own manner. Thus he exercised his authority over Pontgravé.

For him they'd embellished themselves with the beautiful color of escarlette pigment, applied to their cheeks in a base of bear fat. Perceiving this, he was greatly touched, as these Savages were very fond of grease, which they used as we French do butter, and in this time of famine it must have required very great restraint on their part not to have eaten it all.

They were trembling.

Mesdamoiselles, I am sorry that I can offer you nothing but dried peas, he said to the three girls. Would that be acceptable to you?

They nodded, ecstatic, grateful . . . – We have been so hungry, Monsieur, their silence seemed to say to him. Tears started to his eyes.

With his own hands he set the peas before them –

Ah, how he loved charity . . . Saving them, he himself was filled with life and strength.

They knew a little French, as he soon discerned, and every day until the snow melted he instructed them in the language, until they could speak it very well. In the evening he summoned them to him just before putting on his white nightcap, and listened to them saying their prayers. Hélène's brother Eustache, watching him, was astounded at the tenderness he showed. Had Champlain not been so old, he would have been jealous on his sister's account. As it was, however, he knew his Captain to be faultless. And indeed he was grateful to GOD that some measure of private happiness had come to the man at last (not that he blamed Hélène for the way things had been; it was certainly not her fault that she was high-strung). So he took on as many of Champlain's duties as he could, in order to leave him more time. In ordinary times Champlain would have noticed this at once, for it was his policy not only to punish evildoers, but also to make much of good men, and proclaim their deeds before the rest. Yet this circumspection of his was now expended entirely upon the girls. Before him grew those three Savage faces like the brown-spotted leaves of cloudberry bushes, completed by these pale strange berries which glow without giving light. In this case the berries were the dreaming eyes of Savagesses. Their obedience was as slick and smooth as black dewberries. He drilled them in the catechism. (From the dance of naked privities at least I shall save them, he vowed to himself.) When they were ready, he brought them to the Recollect Pères, and Père Daillon said to him:

And what do you choose for their baptismal names, Seigneur? One must be called after your wife's name-Sainte, I suppose. And the others?

Baptize them Foy, Espérance and Charité, he said in trembling voice.

Père Daillon regarded him. – Certainly. Whatever you desire.

He installed them in the chamber between himself and Pontgravé. Originally Pontgravé's room had adjoined his own, so that the three fillettes could have had the window-room on the east side, but it was a lucky thought of Pontgravé's that Savages might go in and out secretly, by way of windows, and so Pontgravé took the window-room after all and the girls were permitted to occupy the chamber which had been Pontgravé's. It reeked of tobacco, of course, but Savages consider that odor to be a sort of ambrosial perfume, as is well known. Champlain took pains. From his night-stand he withdrew the pretty checkered cloth that Hélène had left (and he gazed at it for a moment affectionately, remembering how in the insomnia-ridden summer nights of mosquitoes and brightness he'd beguiled himself by calculating the number of squares), and he went into the girls' room and laid it on the table for them, with a goodly supply of tapers rendered by the Recollects from moose-tallow. He would not permit the girls to possess matches at first; that was dangerous. But he would teach them. Here was a Bible. He'd assist them to read as he had leisure (not that he himself was as educated as he would have liked to be – perhaps Père Massé . . . but no, Père Massé was no more skilled in letters than he himself; so Père Le Caron would be best. He had proven himself with that Huron dictionary of his.) And of course Champlain would take it upon himself to examine them every Sunday on their progress. He must get them each a little Cross to wear; perhaps there were some in the Store-house.

He chastised them gently . . .

It seemed to him now that he had everything. He was happier than he had ever been. Just as Robert Pontgravé became entirely himself, fulfilled and contented, as soon as he'd raped Born Swimming, just as Duval the locksmith became the man of his own dreams once he'd made his plot, so Champlain grew into the species of perfection that was peculiarly his, now that he'd gained his daughters – for what is fatherhood but the keeping of a celestial Store-house, whose gold souls are coined and minted in one's image, whose front lock and windowless walls and booby-trapped prudence may be played with to the heart's content, since they exist only for the highest purpose? So his sternness began to flake off, and everyone saw with astonishment that sternness was not what Monsieur de Champlain had been about at all. And he thought to himself: I have a family now; I have Canada; all that remains for me to receive is the formal Governorship, and then my final hopes will be realized . . .

As for Pontgravé, he kept to himself and watched developments. Now that he was no longer a grey eminence, but only a grey supernumerary, that was all that he could do. But he didn't miss a trick, I'm telling you! *He* saw how Champlain's Indiennes had but to whisper in the man's ear most urgently, with tears turned on, for him to reach into his pocket and give them sugar, as if they were horses. My, they sure had the run of the place! The clerks all made dirty jokes about it, and Pontgravé came up with a few two-liners also, you can bet on that! Foy was older than that pill Hélène Boullé had been when Champlain married her, and everyone knew (just as he'd said, straight to Champlain's face!) that old Monsieur wasn't getting any from her, hadn't for years, so who could be sure what went on with the new ones? Adjoining rooms and all that . . . – Ah, that Foy, she had a face as red-gold and tasty as maple syrup . . . My Robert would have been man enough for her. But Robert . . . May the Dutchmen who murdered him burn in Hell! Anyhow they were all three sweet girls; no one would deny that – not sluts like other Savagesses. Of course they were young yet. JESUS only knew how they would turn out.

Their new father gave them designs on canvas to be embroidered in wool. He must make them accomplished. His aim was to create good Christian families in Canada. – It is my devoutest hope (thus Champlain, to Champlain) that with the French speech which I shall give them they may also acquire a French heart and spirit. – They could marry some of his Frenchmen, or perhaps that Huron convert, Louys Amantacha, whose sincerity was so impressive. Yet Champlain only pretended to himself that he desired to dispose of the girls. From the very first, he longed to keep them with him. He felt that they had truly completed his happiness. Yes, he had been successful. They were so fresh and eager to learn. Perhaps when he retired he could keep them near him, in some convent . . . – What treasures they were!

But in Juin, when the oak leaves were more than an inch in length, Foy ran away to the woods, after which he was compelled to double the guard around them. As her sisters explained, she had not gone of her own accord, but been lured away by certain hostile Savages of her Nation who dreaded the increase of intimacy with the French. The two who remained he preserved more jealously than ever, for he would not permit these Montagnes to defraud him of what they had given him freely. Ah, such was the worth of a Savage's promises throughout these Indies . . .

The Huron Mission 1626–1629

As for Père Brébeuf, he'd launched the Huron Mission at last, with his brother in JESUS, Père de Nouë, who'd arrived safely on another vessel, thanks be to GOD; and the Recollect, Père Daillon. Sad to say, he'd learned little of the Huron language beforetimes, for Père Nicolas's foul murder had deprived him of a tutor. Père Le Caron had a few sheets of birchbark wormed desultorily with sundry knowledge-tracks, which he glossed over with the tallow-drips from his late candle: so an *Arendouane* was a Sorceress, his enemy; *Aescara* was their gambling game of straws . . . And now Père Le Caron demanded his dictionary back; he was going to France for a year, expressly to present it to the Roy. – Brébeuf reasoned with him in gentle fashion, explaining how much more useful that grammar would be in the New France than in the old, but at this Père Le Caron regarded him most narrowly and said: Could you yourself have worldly motives, Jean? I wonder; I wonder . . . – Eh, my friend, take your dictionary then. – He had need of GOD's help in this undertaking! And yet he was all the more ready to begin it. In the winter of 1625, such was his zeal, he lived among the Montagnais for a space, watching them and communicating in Aristotelian signs of his own invention, therefore saying nothing against their women's naked dances, so that they liked him exceedingly and laughed at his foolish antics. Père Massé had done a similar thing in Acadia and wandered home starving. But Père Brébeuf throve and smiled even when the Shaman called upon a DEVIL in a stone. Otterskin-clad, the Savages rushed like madmen among the trees. They gave an adoption feast to another Savage, saying that they had begotten him, which was of course a lie. Père Brébeuf made signs to signify the falsehood, at which they beamed and pelted him with snow and he threw snow back at them and everyone pitied his stupidity, for he was such a pleasant man. He watched everything, his eyes like distant lakes shining white below pale blue mountains . . . The women were not allowed to eat at these feasts until the men were finished, at which point a certain cry was uttered from within, and they rushed to peck at what remained of the repast. Well, he thought, so at least they agree that each sex has its own place. That is a beginning. Still, I pity these dirty hungry women. If only I could work the miracle of the loaves and fishes, that I might feed them all forever! Yet I shall strive to do what is better: I shall nourish them in their souls. – He converted none of them. He did not expect to. He had read Père Biard's *Relations* over until he knew them almost by heart. Their moral was patience. So too with the jeremiads of Père Le Caron: the major error that the Recollects had made was to insist on control too early. (Père Daillon proved the flaw; at Kebec he was already succeeding so ill that no one liked him.) Like Brûlé, he smiled whenever the Savages smiled. That was his apprenticeship for the apostolate. The following summer, at about the same time that the Hollanders were buying Manhattan, he set out for Wendaké with Père de Nouë and Père Daillon.

It is written that Père Brébeuf was so tall and wide-girthed that the Wendat hesitated at first to take him into their canoes, fearing that he would swamp them. But he calmed them with presents and smiles, as he had long since learned to do among the inmates of this sinful world. So he did become a corpuscle borne upon Canada's rivers, devoured by that teeming green flesh of leaves and needles until he had reached the forest-heart that beat and boomed about him. Its auricles were pines a hundred pieds in height; its ventricles were maple trees whose martyr-blood, like his own, was yet green: only in autumn would the scarlet show forth. Canada pulsed in his ears until the breathing of the Savages in his canoe was his own; its dews spurted into his thirsty mouth as he clambered into the canoe at dawn, dawn coppering his Savages' shoulders most beautifully and darkly. He recalled his conversation with the rheumy old Sous-Gouverneur, Monsieur de Champlain. – It is a very long voyage, Père, said Champlain. You see: I indicate it here on this map . . . – And, leaning over Champlain's shoulder to see, so that Champlain's long white locks caressed him like something subterranean and blind, Brébeuf saw Canada's mouth agape, the isle called Anticosti Canada's tongue, and Brébeuf's gaze tumbled in between the lower jaw of Acadia and the upper jaw of Gaspesia; the Fleuve gulped him in past Tadoussac and into the narrow gorge of Kebec where the ruler twitched wearily in Champlain's hand and the points of the dividers were so sharp that Brébeuf feared the dotard might do himself a mischief; and Brébeuf's eyes hesitated at the vastness, but then Canada gulped and swallowed and his vision hurtled down the gullets of trees and mountains and all the endless dreary Algoumequin Nations, then the Népissingue Nation, and then Wendaké at last, the Capitol of Corn. This was to be his new Jerusalem.

Père de Nouë traveled ahead of him, and Père Daillon behind. But they came into Ouendaké together. A beachhead iris spread its purple lips for them like a proud flag on some spindly green skeleton-stalk . . .

They are robed in darkness like charcoal! cried the Savages in wonder.

The Honeymoon

They did not like their crows' attire, which they had never seen before; nor had their wide-brimmed hats been welcome in the canoes. But the Jesuits smoothed this over with presents. They were determined to flow like water over all obstacles. Whether they must be like easy rivulets or like waterfalls, it was all the same to them.

The People watched Père Daillon sidelong. – He is not even so intelligent as Kwer Nikoas, who caught his beard in the canoe and drowned! (Thus the Old Men.)

He for his part comprehended only the name of his dead colleague. – You speak of Père Nicolas, do you, you dogs? he cried in French. What gall, for the Superior said that it was you who drowned him!

Kwer Daiwon is angry with us, they said, shrugging. Who knows why? He lives by himself. He will not marry or take part in our ceremonies. He is not our nephew; he is nothing.

But they liked the Black-Gowns at first, and especially Père Brébeuf. They could not easily pronouce the words of the Iron People, so they named them with better names. Père Brébeuf they called *Echon*, meaning *Bearer of Heavy Loads*, for he had obliged them in that way on the river-journey hence. Him and Père de Nouë together they named *Hatitsihenstaatsi*, which signifies *They who are called Charcoal.* They feasted him and his companions with the fermented corn. As for poor Père Daillon, he had only the leftover crumbs of tolerance to dine upon – a truly parsimonious alimentation. His name in that Country was *Haouaouton*, which means *Quarrelsome*. (The Black-Gowns pitied him as lovingly as they could.)

The longhouses were very dark. Corn bunches hung down from the rafters like candelabra. Peeled beams crisscrossed beams in checkerboards of wooden darkness.

For three years the priests labored there, perfecting their command of the Huron speech, which has cadences like a song. – The father of Louys Amantacha de Saincte-Foy, one *Soranhes*, came from Teanaostaoiaé Town to give them voice-lessons, for which grace they were exceedingly grateful. It would have aided their endeavors even more had Champlain's interpreter, that Brûlé who'd once been tortured by the Hiroquois, seen fit to teach them, for he'd lived among these Nations so long as to be very facile in their speech. Unfortunately he was vicious in character, and much addicted to women. He'd been in Paris with Louys Amantacha, but they'd dismissed him for libertinage. Apparently he hadn't gone to Mass a single time of his own accord. And now here he was. He had forgotten all his prayers save the *Benedicite*, and when they expressed their horror he replied that he had no need of any others. Even in the autumn rains, when the bodies of the Savages took on the odor of rotten wood in the forest, he was always going into the woods with bare-breasted Huronnes married and unmarried; he had no more respect for the Sacrament of marriage than for any other. Then too, as they discovered when they investigated him a little further, he was in the salary of the Rouennais merchants, who paid him a hundred pistoles per annum to lure the Savages to trade with them. – What an abandoned character! – He would not teach them a single word of the language. He feared that if he did so the merchants would cut off his salary, he said. – Well! – That closed the discussion. But they'd break him in their good time . . .

Never enough to eat, muttered Père Daillon. And what there is is lousy with worms and offal –

Ah, have patience, brother, said Père de Nouë.

Patience? Listen to me. It is our Order which began the great work among these brutes, not yours. And you tell me to have patience!

Père de Nouë started to say something, but Père Brébeuf laid a hand on his arm.

They spread the words of JESUS and combated the Huron she-demon AATAENTSIK Who bewitched and enthralled the entire Nation.

It was a young man who first told them about this EATAENTSIC.* – Am I not learned? he crowed. (For these sacred matters were usually mentioned only by the Old Men.) – She made the world and all living creatures! said the Savage; and Père Brébeuf smiled tightly, thinking: Aha, I have found my demon-enemy . . .

He said: Do you love her?

No, Echon. No one loves Her. She brings death. But Her Grandson JOUSKEHA is good. He lives in Her lodge, in the west, the place of death –

We Black-Gowns have been east and west, said Père Brébeuf. There is no such house. If there were, we should know of it.

The Savage looked crestfallen. – Every Country has its fashions, he said at last.

At this, Père Brébeuf showed him a globe of the earth, upon whose face images of all the known places in the world had been printed. – Do you see? he said quietly. There is no such house anywhere.

The Savage did not reply.

* "She Is Old."

Echon Alone

At the end of the first year, Père de Noüe, unable to get his tongue around the Wendat speech, was recalled to Kebec. (The tongue was very harsh to master; surely it must have been among the first of those which sprang up so suddenly at the Tower of Babel.)

Next, the woebegone Recollect, Père Daillon, was exiled. Despairing of his Mission here, he'd thought to evangelize the Country of the Neutral, and thereby increased the hatred in which the Huron held him: they feared the consequences to their trade in iron things. So they sent killers to split Père Daillon's head, but the first stroke of the hatchet missed, after which they feared his Power and let him live. After a year of defiance, he fled, and Père Brébeuf was left to carry on.

Make rain, Echon! they shouted. Heal us! – So he looked into their faces, seeing *otherness* as Charles Biencourt de Poutrincourt had in Port-Royal – but Biencourt had been made over into a Savage, as we have seen, whereas Brébeuf must make the Savages over . . . but first he would understand them.

The big Huron men faced him, smiling with white teeth, curling and uncurling their fingers at their sides. The women smiled yet more widely, holding up their babies for them to see this Sorcerer. The children swarmed with shrill cries over his baggage, opening everything. Père Brébeuf slapped their hands lightly, to chastise them, at which they laughed the louder, believing this to be but a game . . .

He became more skilled in their language once he understood that it must be pronounced from the pit of the stomach, like Swiss or German; so that by the year 1627 he could tell Bible stories in it, which they delighted to hear. In the year 1628, he had a battle with Tehorenhaennion* the Shaman, bringing the THUNDER-BIRD to make rain where the latter failed: – now indeed he did begin to make enemies, but this Nation admired success, and it had been he, not Tehorenhaennion, who brought the rain with a prayer. So he upheld the colors of the Black-Gowns.

The Three Dastards 1625–1632

As for his brethren in Kebec, they too busied themselves with many pious tasks, such as confessing the French, preaching sermons, and burning that

* "He Extends Beyond the Treetops."

libelous pamphlet against their Order, the *Anti-Coton*. In 1625, as we have seen, they broke those half-wild interpreters Brûlé and Marsolet, who had committed acts of licentiousness among the Savages, and detained them in Kebec. – Marsolet was a big booming fellow. He had sworn never to teach the Montagnais language to the priests, for fear that they would ruin the trade. – You're talking about the sacredness of a man's monopoly! he shouted. – Do not dare to speak of sacred things! hissed Père Massé. He made him recant, and begin to teach Montagnais. Brûlé was still recalcitrant; he shipped him off to Paris with Amantacha. Although Marsolet was being good, Père Massé had had his fill of him. He shipped him off, too. The next year they'd both wangled their way back, and leaped off the ship, rushing into the forest like half-starved dogs craving meat. The Black-Gowns let them go. They were occupied in erecting a residence for themselves, called Notre-Dame-des-Anges. Père Massé showed particular zeal in this last enterprise, being very ready with his hands; so that the Jesuits were forced to dwell with the Recollects for no more than a year, by which time the Habitation was completed. After this the two Orders had little to do with one another, for they were mutually jealous. When the Black-Gowns went upriver to proselytize in the Montagnais camp, they passed by it if they saw the shallop of the Recollects tied to a maple-tree. When the Grey-Gowns came to the peltry-trading fair which Monsieur de Champlain held with the Savages every Juin or Juillet, they made their praises of IESVS in a different spot than the Jesuits. Yet when they greeted each other, all was amity. – Pax CHRISTI, Père Massé! – Eh, it's you, Père Le Caron! GOD be with you on this mosquito-ridden evening! – Yes, Père Le Caron was back from France now – and a trial to all, as I must add; for he was inordinately proud of the fact that he had presented his Huron dictionary to the Roy. (What a vain and worldly soul! quoth Père Massé in high bad temper, and to calm himself he went to split logs with his axe . . . Later he mortified himself for his uncharity.) As for Le Caron's familiar, Père Daillon, he, seeking not to brood upon his reverses in the Huron Country, occupied himself instead by peering ever more deeply into the soul of his pet Montagnais boy, Pierre-Antoine Pastedouachouan, searching for the flaw that rendered the instrument so useless; for Pastedouachouan still could not remember a word of Montagnais, although he had been here now a year! – Perhaps I shelter him too much, thought Père Daillon. Or perhaps our blessed Martyr, Père Nicolas, was the one who spoiled him through an excess of compassion and leniency. Should I strike him? But no. He is only the first generation. One must be patient, until these Savages are entirely frenchified. – In the autumn, when the trees were as red-robed as Cardinal de Richelieu, he called the boy into the refectory and said to him: Pierre-Antoine, we have decided that you must return to your brothers. You cannot preach the Word of GOD until you are over this little ignorance or stupidity of yours. What do you say? – But Pastedouachouan burst into tears. – I pray you, good Père, he said, do not compel me to go back there. My eldest brother Carigouan is a Sorcerer . . . I would be helpless . . . – It will be only for a short while, said Père Daillon as soothingly as he could. Now pack your clothes and prepare to come with me in an hour's time. I myself shall speak with this Sorcerer. – Yes, Père, replied the boy dully; he went into the cellar, which was seven pieds deep, and stood by himself in the darkness . . .

But I fear that I must interrupt the tale of Pastedouachouan; for meanwhile, braving Turks and icebergs, a trio of English brothers had set out under authority granted by good King Charles to wipe away the French. (It is always the English who interrupt us, here in Canada.) Their names were David, Lewis and Thomas Kirke. It inflamed them to conceive of Canada riding the top of the continent like a great green leech; they would *conquer* Canada and crush that cursed Popishness! – After all, they knew the map of Cabot, which, predating by twenty-seven years the chronicle of Verazzano's voyage, thereby established forever England's right. – And so the brothers sailed north; and they entered the Fleuve Saint-Laurent. – Kebec lay hidden beneath a vast white pavement of cloud, like a skeleton beneath church flagstones. But they spied it out. There it was, that faint blue line of cliff-coast; and (holding their breaths with suspense lest they run aground on some unsuspected shoal) the Kirke brothers crept closer and closer, and the haze began to lift so that they could see all about them the river ripple-wrinkled and glittering with white waves and flashes. – Might their enemy have barricaded himself behind floating batteries? – It was best not to chance it themselves. So they sent some captured Basques and other inferior persons to see Champlain, bearing a letter recommending that he surrender; which the Chief Dastard had signed with a frown: *Your affectionate servant, David Kirke.* Although Champlain had but fifty pounds of gunpowder, and his heart was gripped as by a wolverine's claws, he bluffed the Kirke brothers with boldness, bragging *I wait upon you hour by hour,* at which bedridden gout-gripped Pontgravé nodded palely and tried to smile, and then Champlain winked at him and signed the epistle *your affectionate servant, Champlain,* and the Querque brothers believed (were they saved?) and set despondent sail, hoping to board a French fishing-boat or two and recoup their expenses. Here their luck was better than they had hoped, for they seized an entire convoy from France, which had carried supplies for Kebec. – Now we've got those filthy Catholics! shouted Lewis Kirke. (*He* knew what they were like; he'd grown up in France. Indeed he was half a Catholic himself.) So they watched the seals as big as oxen; so they made English haven, waiting for spring, when the sea-ice would have melted, growing fat on French food, even as Champlain's men for want of it were compelled to subsist on fish and tree-bark. Champlain dispatched twenty of his most expendable men to Wendaké: let the Huron barbarians have the expense of feeding them! But the Black-Gowns recalled Père Brébeuf from the Huron Country, begging him to bring what food he could from that granary, and he carried two hundred and fifty pieds of cornmeal back, which he had bought of the Savages with colored beads –

There are certain things that ought not to happen to an old man, Pontgravé mumbled on his bed.

Resig-*nation*, my dear François. (Thus Père Le Caron.)

All right, all right. Gimme another spoonful of those boiled roots. I never thought I'd become a meadow-feeder, like a moose. Well, here goes. *Ugh!* Is it fair? Ah, forgive me, Père, I long to mortify myself, but I just don't have the willpower . . .

(As soon as they were gone, he reached under the bed. He had a fifty-livre sack of cornmeal that he'd had his clerk Olivier buy from the Huron. Olivier had even roasted it for him – oh, no doubt he'd skimmed something off . . . but in any event it was better than Champlain's roots.)

As for the said Champlain, he occupied himself with his maps and his two tame Indian girls. There were enough details to calculate with his dividers: firewood must be brought from half a league away, and the snowfall was not yet deep enough to trap the moose. He sent out a hunting party under the authority of his good subaltern, Captain Merveille, and they did bag one animal, but despite Merveille's best efforts the men devoured everything on the spot, such was their famine. – And what of me? thought Champlain in exasperation. No one brings so much as an extra bowl of soup to the Sieur de Champlain . . .

Espérance was very docile, even more so than her sister. He took great pleasure in her. Perhaps one of his Frenchmen might take her; otherwise there was always that Pierre-Antoine Pastedouachouan whom the Recollects had frenchified . . .

He took up his quill and began to make a new map of the Countries beyond the Huron Nations, based on information which Père Brébeuf had heard from the interpreter, Étienne Brûlé. It seemed that there were grand lacs even beyond the Sweetwater Sea . . .

Eh, those Montagnais! He could not concentrate. Incited no doubt by the English, they were practically in a state of rebellion against his authority. They mocked him to his face, calling him *Captain of the Beard*; they complained about the prices that he set. – They are my worst enemies, worse than the very Hiroquois! he said to himself in a rage.

He still held that murderer hostage. They'd threatened him; they sold him an insufficient number of eels, and those only at the price of one beaver-skin for every ten eels, which every man knew for a robber's and extortioner's fee. – Why did they want those beaver-skins? Was it their intention to trade them with the English? – When he had come to this conclusion, Champlain's heart glowed reddish-black with rage spurting lava through his veins, so that he became yet harder and more inflexible in his purpose. – I will never release that rat! shouted Champlain. – At this the Savages resolved to sell no more food to the French.

Spring came, and still the French must go to the forests to dig roots, such was their want and hunger. They would have eaten their cattle at Cap Tourmente long since, but the English had burned them alive in the sheds. Nor did any French ships come; the Kirke brothers had captured them all (for which they were burned in effigy in France). The little children wept for hunger (in this way they were weaker in disposition than the Savages, for he knew well that his daughters would never cry for any such cause). Now the Sieur de Champlain turned over in his mind many schemes for saving the French. One possibility might be to attack a village of the Hiroquois and exterminate them, living then upon the corn they would find (after all, the Hiroquois were a great menace to the waterways of New France). But his men opposed this, saying that such an enemy was too fierce for hungry men. And still the Montagnais refused to sell them eels. – At last, when the prisoner was so feeble that he could no longer walk, Champlain's men began to murmur. So Champlain released him. – But it must be understood, he said, that I do this only as a great boon to you. Henceforth I expect all your Captains to obey me and follow French law! – Yes, yes, we will do that, said the Savages, but they smiled. They had already welcomed the Kirke brothers at Tadoussac . . .

According to a contemporary estimate, the Fleuve Saint-Laurent passes through ten thousand barriers (without counting beaver-dams) in Québec Province alone. So it took some time to ascend it – indeed, until the raspberries had opened their leaves – but the Frères Querque persevered, sailing, sailing . . . Beyond the Isle d'Orléans (where the waters of the Fleuve Saint-Laurent commence to lose their brackishness) they saw a great torrent falling from the top of a mountain; and they went on and came to Kebec.

It was the Savage Manitougatches who sighted them – one of the few Montagnets who remained pious. He had just recently given his daughter to Pierre-Antoine Pastedouachouan, in order to please Champlain (although she was said to have left her husband with a scornful laugh, because he could not remember how to hunt). Manitougatches was a good man. In due time Champlain would give him a fine funeral . . . Perhaps anticipating this reward, Manitougatches came running to Champlain with the ominous news.

The Habitation was almost deserted, such was the famine. There was but one sentry. The drawbridge was down. The plupart of the French wandered in the forest, searching for groundnuts and wild lily roots; Champlain's own daughters were among them. He hoped that they would help one another like good Christian girls, and not quarrel as they so often did, being mutually jealous like the confrontation of cones in his hourglass, one breast sucking sand from the other whenever Champlain upended his instrument . . . Pontgravé lay bellowing like an ox in his chamber; Champlain could scarcely bear to hear him. – You are certain? he said to the Savage. – Yes, Champlain. – Slowly he arose; he let his ruler slip from his hand, to fall upon the new-inked map and smudge it. Light funneled in through the subsquares of the window. He felt nothing now but relief. The grief would come later. He paced to the lectern and leaned upon it for a moment so that the Savage – a mere Savage – would not see how his knees were trembling. He peered out at the Fleuve Saint-Laurent. Nothing in sight yet, of course. The Fleuve dazzled him with its silvery glitter or papillotage. He descended the stairs and passed through the clerks' chambers – empty now; the clerks were desperately gobbling dirty onion-bulbs in the woods – and slowly he unlocked the door to the armory and stood looking at the neat rows of harquebuses on the walls; and then he went out and locked the door again and went back upstairs to where Manitougatches stood gaping at his ruined map and he crossed into his chamber (which had once been Hélène's, too) and passed through his Charité and Espérance's room with its candles and its lacework on the walls and threw open the door to the next room where Pontgravé lay crying out in agony and Père Le Caron knelt beside him, dangling the Cross before his eyes like a hypnotist, and Père Le Caron looked up and Champlain said: My dear Père Joseph, could you come with me for a moment? – It's the English, isn't it? mumbled Pontgravé. I know from the silence . . . – Pay no heed to what no longer concerns you, returned Champlain coldly. – He led the priest into the room where Manitougatches waited, and the Savage repeated his news, and Père Le Caron said: It is the will of GOD, my dear Monsieur, and Champlain said: Yes. – So the

English marched within his palisadoes with a nasty company of *tourlourous* or foot-soldiers. Their helmets were like the fused pincers of pitiless insects. They strode in a column bristling with spikes, and the French stood out of their way. On the twenty-second day of Juillet, the fleur-de-lys came down, and the ensign of King Charles ascended as the English discharged their gloating cannonade . . . Now the said Louys Querq, bowing to Champlain most gallantly, held out his hand for the key to the Store-house, which must be given him if honor were to be satisfied; in a twinkling the door was thrown open and the cheering English came rushing in, snatching up French beaver-skins – more than four thousand of them! – and striking each other for the privilege. Champlain was silent. Four thousand peltries. At an average of thirteen livres each, that made by his most accurate reckoning fifty-two thousand livres lost to France. Mother of GOD! But his only remaining weapon was discretion. – Smoking the herb called *tobacco*, so that his breath was as a dragon's, Lewis Kirke put his hand on Champlain's shoulder. – Monsieur, I crave your pardon, he said. You know full well the nature of soldiers and sailors. – Yes, Monsieur, replied Champlain, I cannot fail to know it now. – In his heart he journeyed a day, a week, or whatever the distance might be down the Stream of Time to the now inevitable day when his Savages would be leaning against the walls of the Habitation, watching, glaring, wondering, fearing, gloating; and he himself must stride with weary resolution down to the waiting prison-barque, preparing to commence yet another of the retreats which seemed to choke his life; and the maple-leaf epaulets on his shoulders drooped in mourning and his face was hard and grey. – And Lewis Kirke planted the Cross of Saint George and proceeded to the Black-Gowns' residence, sneering: If only I could have battered your house down about your ears! – He hated them as direly as a Savage hates Dutch cheese. – As for Champlain, the Kirke brothers liked *him*. He was a free-rover like them; it was not his fault that he had been born French. Admiral David Querque strolled about the shore, shooting larks with him, and talking of southern voyages . . .

It was 1629. Diamonds shone in the sandy margins of lakes. Seeing these, the Kirke brothers filled a hogshead with them. Then they importuned Champlain to tell them where they might find more. With a wry smile he assured them that the stones were worthless, but they refused to believe him, and their liking cooled a trifle. Like boys they sailed happily about on the Fleuve Saint-Laurent; Thomas Kirke threw his line over and caught a trout a dozen livres or more in weight . . .

Messieurs, said Kirke to the Grey-Gowns, kindly excuse this imposition.

Eh, it is nothing, said Père Le Caron. Before your arrival, life was difficult. *Ver*-y difficult . . .

Messieurs, said Kirke to the Black-Gowns, your errand in Canada was to enjoy what belonged to the Protestant Guillaume de Caën, whom you dispossessed.

Pardon me, sir, said Père Brébeuf. We came purely for the glory of GOD, and exposed ourselves to every kind of danger to convert the Indians.

Ay, convert the Indians! sneered the Huguenot Captain, Michel, who had basely guided the English thither. Convert the beaver, you mean!

That is false! said Père Brébeuf.

False? False! You Papist! But for the respect I owe the General, I should strike you for giving me the lie! shouted Michel.

You must excuse me, said Père Brébeuf coolly. I did not mean to give you the lie. I should be very sorry to do so. The words I used are those we use in the schools when a doubtful question is advanced, and they mean no offense. Therefore I ask you to pardon me.

Michel began to swear.

Bon DIEU! cried the Sieur de Champlain. You swear very well for a Reformer.

I know it, purred Michel. I should be content if I had but struck that Jesuit, that Spanish Malouin who gave me the lie before my General.

Later on, he died of one of his rages. The Savages dug up his body and threw it to the dogs. – I do not doubt that he is in perdition, said Champlain, and the Black-Gowns agreed. Now it was the turn of the Grey-Gowns to pity them most triumphantly and lovingly, for *they* were the ones in favor . . .

Lewis Kirke helped himself to two silver chalices from a chest of the Black-Gowns.

Sir, do not profane them, for they are sacred, said Père Massé with flashing eyes.

Profane them! laughed Kirke. Since you tell me that, I will keep them, which I would not have done otherwise. I take them because you believe in them, for I will have no idolatry in my Country.

Then the Kirke brothers sailed back to England, bearing Champlain and the other prisoners. Champlain was landed at Plymouth, where he went to London to work upon the French Ambassador. Soon all had been put right again, and the King agreed to restore Canada to France as soon as the Roy should pay the remaining four hundred thousand crowns of Queen Henrietta Maria's dowry . . .

A Change of Course 1628–1629

Among the ships captured by the Three Dastards was one from France, carrying Louys Amantacha. The Black-Gowns had finally concluded the education of that young man, believing him fit to help spread the Faith in Canada. – Who is this dark, greasy rascal? shouted Thomas Kirke. – The son of an Indian King, Monsieur, replied the passengers. – Oh, he is, is he? said Kirke, who had been about to jerk Amantacha's chin up so that he could stare, stare into his eyes. He felt somewhat wolfish . . . They landed in England, and the Kirkes let all the passengers except Amantacha return to France. It was their intention to make an Englishman out of him.

So he wintered in London among these *Hatiwendoyeronnon*, these Island People. So many kinds of Iron People! They gave him dazzling new suits as befitted a King's son, and Amantacha smiled and bowed his head. He knew that his father would have come to Kebec each summer to seek him in vain.

Hope and Charity Abandoned 1629

We know that despite his proclivities to receive, count and organize, the Sieur de Champlain was no slave to worldly things. For him, as it transpired, the greatest sorrow was not the loss of land, honor and goods, but of his two adopted daughters, Espérance and Charité.

When he left Kebec for Tadoussac, having given to Louis Kirke some furniture which the man had asked for, they parted on most cordial terms. Kirke had urged the Héberts and Couillards and other French families to stay on, saying that nothing would be done to hinder them, for which Champlain was grateful, on the whole (although he warned those individuals in secret to take care for their souls, and to return to France should the Anti-Papists not relinquish Kebec). Now Champlain stood upon the bank of the Fleuve Saint-Laurent, and Louis Kirke wrung his hand. – It is all a great shame, Mr. Champlain, he kept repeating, a very great shame!

Eh, Monsieur Kirke, but Kebec is your prize. I wish you good fortune.

May I confide in you, Champellain?

Please.

My own people are repugnant to me. I am French in my heart. I wish that this conquest had never come about. For me, Canada will always be French!

(As he spoke, Querque even believed what he said. Tears ran from his eyes.)

You are very amiable, Monsieur. (Thus Champlain, dryly.)

Au revoir, Champlain! And you, Charité, Espérance – good journey to you also, my dears! How fortunate you are to have such a father!

Champlain whispered in the Indian girls' ears, and they kissed their hands to Monsieur Kirke . . .

Thomas Kirke, the middle brother, was not quite so well disposed (as might be expected from this fairytale of increasing obstacles). When the flyboat was well underway, and they suddenly encountered Emery de Caën's vessel, he sent Champlain and the girls belowdecks and nailed down the hatches, in keeping with the rules of war. It was as dark as a Black-Gown's cell in that receptacle. Champlain paced echoingly, feeling the walls to see how this English shallop was made; he stepped in a puddle of bilge and said to himself: this vessel must be promptly tarred with oakum; I shall mention that to Monsieur de Querque . . . and they heard shouts and drums and the flyboat lurched and then all ten guns were firing most redoubtably, so loud and deep indeed that his bones ached, and he heard De Caën's guns go off and there came the wooden thud of a falling body (one of De Caën's cannonballs had taken a sailor's head off) and then the chittering rain of grenaille or small shot as the two girls clung to him and he stroked their hair, commanding them to pray to Our dear SAVIOR, which they fervently did. He told them funny tales of the Civil War . . . At last they heard the sound of pliers pulling up the nails, and Thomas Kirke drew open the hatches.

You must persuade De Caën to surrender, he said. – The poltroon thinks to spoil my business by unmanly cunning; for he insists that this war between our Nations is over and that we have acted illegally. But he can produce no proof of his claims. Speak to him. Entreat him. And warm your words with earnestness, you periwig, for I assure you that if they fire from that vessel, you will die.

Champlain smiled a little. – Sir, he said, to put me to death would be easy for you, seeing that I am in your power. But it would do you little honor, I fancy.

Then he did as he was told. My poor Champlain –

De Caën struck his colors with ill grace, saying that he did it only to save Champlain's life, which he'd heard was scarcely worth the saving – a remark which Champlain charitably overlooked, for the man had suffered several reverses of late (as he well deserved, being the uncle of a Reformer). Poor De Caën, too! His countenance was as pale as a masque mortuaire . . . – The oddest part was the twitching of his lip, which Kirke soon spied out and made mock of, saying: And do your knees also knock together like castanets, milksop? – at which Champlain cried out: For shame, Kirke! – and Kirke returned: What is *your* watchword, my bold brave gentleman of the hold?

So they passed the Basque Drying-Stage (now abandoned, thanks to the war), and arrived at Tadoussac, where the main fleet bobbed. David Kirke the General was waiting. He was the most ill disposed of all.

General Kirke sat reading a note from his brother Louis, who had made good inventory of the armaments of Champlain's fort. – Two arquebuses both of the wheel-lock and match-lock type, he said to himself – *that's* not much! . . . A few bronze petards, some good halberds with black-painted whitewood handles, a set of armor or two – *hmmph!* Why, we could easily have taken Kebec last year, instead of subsisting on eels and piracy. What villainous trickery this Champlain is guilty of! – for, like most of us, the General found it easy to blame others whose actions had detracted a jot from his comforts. – No doubt, he said to himself, Mr. Champlain is now so well used to brewing treacherous plots with the Salvages* that he cannot cease to do the same even with white men! Oh, shame upon him! Fie upon his ill-nature!

Yet when Champlain and his daughters descended the gangplank, he was sorry for his suspicions. The greybeard seemed docile, decent. They'd understand one another . . . – For General Kirke, like the late Sieur de Poutrincourt, had one of those dispositions which the alchemists call *mercurial.* It was, therefore, particularly interesting to be in his power.

Champlain for his part stopped short, seeing among the enemy his two prize interpreters, Marsolet and young Brûlé.

He turned away from them and greeted General Kirke in all good cheer and dignity. In bad weather a prudent Captain must pay out slack –

I believe that you know these gentlemen, said General Kirke, smiling.

Yes, Monsieur, I know them.

You seem displeased. Do you have some quarrel with them?

Champlain bit his lip.

Well? Take care not to forget your courtesy, Mr. Champlain, for I am your master now.

You gain no great credit before GOD, General Kirke, by speaking to me in this way. I had thought when I signed the articles of capitulation that I would not be insulted and made a fool of.

* An interesting term. No doubt it was because the English saw the Indians as already salvaged that they saw little need to embroil themselves in saving their souls in the French manner.

As for being made a fool of, Mr. Champlain, I can see now that there is little enough *making* left to be done. Beware, sir!

And Kirke turned on his heel. The guardsmen laughed and leaned upon their pikes –

As soon as he was out of sight, Champlain approached the traitorous pair (who indeed made little effort to evade him), and his eyes gleamed with wrath. The girls were holding his hands, but he flung them off. As he strode forward, his fingers began to curl, at which Brûlé smirked nervously, as he saw, and then his fists became hard and tight. But then he remembered that he was on his honor as a prisoner (that is where we must praise him: he never would undermine the integrity of the contest), and so, clenching and unclenching his hands until the palms were incised with bloody crescents from his fingernails, he came before them with much the same politesse as the Armouchiquois, who, ferocious though they are, lay down their arms in a parley with foreigners. Brûlé and Marsolet were foreigners now –

Forgive us, Seigneur. We were taken by force. (Thus the Huron interpreter, Brûlé. He seemed somewhat out of his element here, like a Savage in Paris.)

Marsolet merely scowled, as if Champlain had intruded upon his private affairs. Brûlé began to stammer something –

You say that they presented each of you with a hundred pistoles and trade, said Champlain in disgust, and having on these terms sworn them fidelity, you live without religion, eating meat on Friday and Saturday, and indulging in licentious debauchery. How can you accommodate yourselves to this? If you could look clearly into your own souls at this moment, you'd be horrified at what you saw! . . .

We know very well that we'd be hanged in France, shouted Marsolet, but the thing is done. *Done*, do you hear me?

We're very sorry for that, Brûlé cut in, as contritely as ever – and now Champlain remembered him as a boy of ten, when he'd caught him stealing bread from the Store-house and so he had Merveille tie his hands around a pole and then he himself whipped him in front of the others as a wholesome chastisement, and the boy kept weeping and apologizing, so that Champlain had given him only three strokes, in consideration not only of his youth but also of the genuine remorse that he seemed to show . . . – Now he disbelieved in genuineness. And indeed he was wise to do so, for Brûlé (having listened well to the Jesuits' sermonizing against inordinate attachments) was already thinking: There are plenty of Hollanders now among the Iroquois. If my situation among the English becomes difficult, I can always go there. I swore to the Seneca . . . Or I can go back to the Huron . . . – Upon my honor, Monsieur de Champlain, we're both very sorry.

O wretched excuse! . . . the old man replied wearily.

Ah, leave him alone, Champlain. (Thus Marsolet.) You scold like an old woman with dried-up dugs.

Seeing no gain to be had in speaking further with these miscreants, Champlain turned away, executing much the same heel-pivot that General Kirke had done a moment before, and his heart sank into bitterness. Charité and Espérance took his hands; they pillowed their heads on his shoulders . . .

Damme, but there's some cunt-meat worth sucking! muttered Marsolet.

Who? Where?

Wake up, Brûlé! Don't you see it's time for fun?

Well, I – But what he said about Hell, I can't deny that it made me upset. Tell me the truth! Is there any foundation in it? I can almost see red flames – no, they're black, and I smell smoke –

Eh, you're young; your supreme hour's a long way off. You can always repent later. Do you think they're both virgins?

Virgins? I don't know. I only see the flames . . . General Kirke swore to me . . . religious toleration. Champlain's a heretic! I'm going to go complain to General Kirke –

Eh! spat Marsolet in disgust.

But Brûlé had already scuttled off, big-eyed, spider-legged . . .

Fear nothing of him, said Kirke reassuringly (he was in one of his best moods). Your Mr. Champlain is nothing but a sow-buggerer, a nasty little dunghill-cock. – He looked about him with satisfaction. – The air of Canada is uncommonly clear, he said. – Fear nothing, Étienne, he repeated; and the young man ran away smiling . . .

Champlain and his daughters had been billeted in one of General Kirke's tents-of-war, and though it was not so pleasant there, Champlain had given the girls instructions to stay within as much as they could, the morals of the English soldiers not being of the best. Then, too, so many of Kirke's crew were Huguenot renegades, from La Rochelle and such DEVIL's-pits; he had no wish for his good fillettes to converse with them. He himself was generally out, matching Brûlé's complaint to le General Querque with one of his own to the Jesuits, who'd just lately arrived under guard. To them he spoke of Marsolet and Brûlé most vehemently.

Those are the common difficulties, sighed Père Brébeuf. Even the best instructed among our French almost lose their Christianity, so quickly do they become Savages. And that Brûlé, I remember him. He was already one of the damned, there in Wendaké, sweltering in libertinage and Savagery . . . – Ah, good day, Monsieur Marsolet.

Marsolet continued on his way. He doubled round behind some rocks, so that the other prisoners could not see him, and drew near the Indian girls' tent, which poor Champlain had conceived to be a Store-house of virtue, forgetting (inexplicably for a Quartermaster) that many others possessed the key.

Bon*jour*, bon*jour*, bon*jour*, my little redskinned fillettes! he whispered. Who wants brandy?

And the tent-flap opened smilingly, like one of those Jesuit Crosses whose lid swings back to reveal the precious relics . . .

. . . When Marsolet was twelve years of age, Champlain had dispatched him to live among the Montagnais and to learn their language. In the winter he slept between an old Captain and his children, in token of his honored position, as he supposed. – I can't bear this, though, he muttered to himself. – The life was very hard. When he'd heard that the English had come, he ran to look for shelter among them. Now I'm through with the Savages! he thought to himself in delight, believing (like all traitors) that he could possibly be rewarded by those to whom he had sacrificed his soul's virginity. But he was not. As soon as he saw Espérance, he knew that he was not. Sacré bleu, what a lovely girl! She had *lines!* Admiring her, he made the Exercises far in excess of anything which Robert Pontgravé could ever have done, seeing Canada as it would be in 1989 when just across from Souvenirs Carseley, a beam of light swept the sky searchingly and people swarmed upon the sidewalks in summer clothes, the barelegged women so handsome, the old men limping along with dignity, hands behind their backs. Neon rivers flowed around glowing square sign-islands. An Indian woman came and searched through the trash bin for cans to be redeemed; a girl and two boys sat on a bench eating ice cream. A whore stood in a doorway, smiling unflinchingly. A policeman came, took away a bottle of beer from someone sitting on a bench, and poured it slowly into the trash (so, at least, writes Lescarbot, whose every comma is correct). Two lovely pink girls were soon leaning against the can, lighting their cigarettes. – Beside the phone booth, where some thoughtful person had written *Clitoris*, an ice cream bar rapidly melted on the sidewalk. Marsolet felt an irresistible urge to mingle with the crowd, partaking of the popsicle-sticks that they had licked, inhaling their breath, making crisp heel-sounds upon the pavement with them, above all proceeding in their chosen direction, as if these composed summer faces made up a River of Rest superior to the Stream of Time and if Marsolet dove in he would be borne to a place of ice cream cones where every gesture would be pure, every action a French action; and the glowing white sneakers that trod the sidewalk confirmed his impression of effortlessness on that happy endless night. – Marsolet felt that he already lived there in the new Canada. Whenever Champlain was away, he came to Espérance and importuned her to elope with him. – My chests will be opened to you if you do the thing with me, he whispered. You shall have all the goods that you desire!

You're worth nothing, she said. You have a bad reputation among us as a liar.

Then I'll close my mouth, and speak to you with my fingers, he said. Do you comprehend me? And your little sister can watch . . .

She snatched up her dagger and brandished it. He went out laughing.

One day when Monsieur le General Querq was giving a dinner entertainment for the Captains of all his ships, to which Champlain was invited, they sat in the great pavilion tent-of-war; and Marsolet was not there (for pregnant enough reasons, thought Champlain to himself), but Brûlé held forth on the OKI-demons in stony hills to which the Huron paid reverence (for he was very credulous), and Champlain chewed his moose-meat grimly, wishing he could choke off that traitor's twaddle with a hunk of gristle, and his daughters sat beside him cracking bones most delicately, as he himself had taught them, and he looked into their faces and said to himself: for their sake I must be steady . . . – and so he locked his anger against Brûlé back into his heart's Store-house and whispered to Charité: I saw how you and your sister made your prayer of grace most prettily and Charité replied, head downcast, thank you, Monsieur de Champellain and Espérance's face was screwed up in a giggle at something, at which Charité kicked her under the table, and Champlain wanted to reprove them, but as this was not the place for that he looked away, and the General Kirke was gazing at him, so he bowed; whereupon Kirke and Champlain began to exchange sea-tales most cordially, and Kirke drew him out to tell the things that he had seen in Ville-Mechique so long ago and as he told it the fresh tropical smells came back to him and the stagnant smell of that great lake or inland sea where the town was located, and he remembered again the griffins and dragons and the fireflies the size of hazelnuts; and then he noticed that Kirke was smiling at him ironically, just as De Monts used to do when Pontgravé egged him on to tell tales; and his heart sank. Now General Kirke laid a letter before him, which he immediately saw was in Marsolet's handwriting. The letter read:

MONSIEUR:

A Council has been held of all the Savage Captains to discuss the question of whether Monsieur de Champlain should be allowed to take the two little girls to France. They have resolved that since the French no longer dwell in these parts, not to let them go. Otherwise this Country will be lost to you.

MARSOLET

Champlain studied this letter for a very long time. He would not look up into General Kirke's sneering face until he had controlled his feelings. At last, clasping his hands beneath the table so tightly that blood spurted from his fingernails, he said very steadily: Monsieur, I beseech you that your charity towards these poor girls be such that none do them violence. GOD will not be ungrateful.

Kirke smiled.

I assure you that Marsolet has fabricated this, in order to ruin my girls for his pleasure! he shouted.

Kindly do not raise your voice to me, Mr. Champlain. Otherwise I fear I shall begin to lose my respect for you.

So saying, he rose from the table. That was his way of punctuating his mood-changes for GOD, by rising and leaving a scene –

Champlain sat there for a moment. Querque's men watched him to see what he would do. He waited until he was certain that he would not encounter Kirke, and then himself went out. His good girls leaped up and followed him –

He besought the aid of the Admiral Thomas Kirke, who reluctantly gave it, but the General remained firm. Why not? He knew by then that he was going to be knighted.

Is it possible that this bad Captain wishes to prevent us from going to France with you, Père? (Thus Espérance.) We have such sorrow in our hearts as we cannot say. We do not remember how to live in the forest anymore –

I know not what to tell you, he replied gloomily.

Can you hide us in the vessel? her sister whispered eagerly.

He smiled at her most lovingly and put his hand on her shoulder, at which she began to weep.

We will follow you across the sea in a c-c-canoe . . . she choked out through her sobs.

He requested admittance to the General's. Kirke was at that time tippling with Marsolet, whom he considered quite a decent fellow for a Frenchman. – Sir, it is Mr. Champlain, said the guard. – Ah, the weasel continues to complain of his infinite losses. (Thus General Kirke, as Marsolet doubled up laughing.) – I suppose I had best see him alone.

Taking the hint, Marsolet slipped out.

Yes, Mr. Champlain. What is it now? Do you want me to give Canada back into your hands, or do you now demand all England as well?

I have a note from you, began Champlain, promising reimbursement for certain stores confiscated from me at Kebec. That note is for a thousand livres. I ask you to pay the Montagnais a thousand livres' worth of your trade goods as they may select, in exchange for Charité and Espérance, following which I shall tear up your note.

I shall speak to Mr. Marsolet, said the General, rising. He knows the disposition of the Salvages well.

But Marsolet –

Good day, Champlain.

Champlain strode to the tent where Marsolet was installed and requested the pleasure of his company.

Ah, Champlain! boomed Marsolet, sweating.

You will have to answer for this matter of my daughters before Divine justice, Champlain began. I think that you yourself know that. Consider well. You may still remedy the act which you contemplate. If you do, then I will forgive you. In the situation in which you have placed yourself, you may someday have need of friends. If you do this for me – I entreat you! – then I shall always be your ally . . .

I can do nothing, said Marsolet coolly.

But later that same afternoon, Kirke summoned him and discussed with him Champlain's offer. – For myself I consider it very advantageous, he said. I cannot conceive how my brother Louis could have been so stupid as to sign that note. A thousand livres! It would be good to have it back in our possession . . .

But the disposition of the Savages, General –

The disposition of your prick, you mean.

Marsolet drew himself up with great dignity. – I wash my hands of this matter, Monsieur le Général. If any calamity happens, let no one blame me.

Hhmph, said Kirke. Very well. You win the day, for now.

Hearing of this outcome, Champlain (though he practically despaired) went once again to Marsolet's tent, much as he had crossed the ice from the Isle de Sainte-Croix so many years ago to search for the bark of that tree called *Anedda* in order to cure De Monts' men of scurvy, and brought back tree-skins of every description, when the men would not touch them. It was the same when the Huron had trapped him in their Country all winter, and he must make the best of it. Perseverance was the soul of Champlain.

I ask you for the last time to reconsider, he said to Marsolet, whose face was as blank and bright as a compass.

Seigneur, believe what you like. When I serve a master, I must be faithful to him.

You have given great proof of it by leaving me and serving the English, said Champlain.

Over his shoulder, he said: If we ever meet again, Monsieur, then by GOD you had better stand on your guard!

When he told the girls that there was nothing more to be done they burst into tears. Espérance became ill with a high fever, which her sister and the Sieur de Champlain together strove most desperately to cure. (He was no Hiroquois; his sorrow could not be removed with wampum-beads.) – Monsieur Marsolet is a dog, a dog! whispered Charité. He has caused us such distress that it is like death! – We must accommodate ourselves, he said . . . – When Espérance had recovered, he went out and strode along the beach to grieve (yet not at so great a distance as to be questioned by the General's sentries, which procedure in his present dejection and rage he did not believe that he could well endure). If only the Iroquois would fall upon this place . . .

General Kirke was giving a supper for his officers that night, at which both Champlain and Marsolet were present. Suddenly Espérance came in, her face red and ugly with weeping, and begged the General's permission to speak with Monsieur Marsolet.

You need not ask my permission, dear girl, said Kirke. It is for him to ask yours, as I do believe he longs to do.

And all the Captains and soldiers laughed, saving only Champlain.

The girl approached Marsolet almost noiselessly.

Monsieur, she said, my sorrow is so great that I must discharge my heart. I can have no peace until I do so.

Marsolet looked uneasily from side to side. The interview did not promise to be agreeable. But he was trapped.

Well, what do you want? he shouted at her.

Monsieur, I wish you to recall how I would not yield to your foul desires when you asked me to go with you. I tell you once again that I never will! Now you show yourself to be worse than a dog. At least a dog is loyal.

Although I am only a fillette, I shall procure your death if I can. I shall plunge an iron knife into your heart! How can I look at you without weeping?

Marsolet picked up a joint of meat and began to gnaw at it. – Eh bien, he said, you have studied that lesson very well.

A few of the English smiled, but most of them found their sympathies with the girl, brute Salvage though she was.

Espérance had not moved. Gazing unwinkingly into his face, she said: You have given me cause to say much more, if only my heart could express it.

Her sister Charité had come in noiselessly. Marsolet looked up and saw her. – And you, he said ironically, I take it you too have something to say to me?

The little girl walked toward him step by step. General Kirke sat grinning and slapping his thigh. But the others were ashamed.

All that I would like to say to you, she began in a low voice, is that if I had my hands on your heart, I would eat it with more facility and courage than I would the meats on this table.

Ha! shouted the General. A very good reply for a Salvage!

But his remark fell flat, for the two girls turned and left amidst a terrible silence.

No More Mistakes

On the voyage back to England, the prisoners not being confined to irons, Père Brébeuf spent some time in conversation with the Sieur de Champlain, and they passed the sea-hours in talking daydreams of Canada restored to them (for they had ample leisure to scratch themselves, as Lescarbot would have put it. Lescarbot had six kids now . . .) Below decks, old Pontgravé moaned with the pain of his gout. He seemed unlikely to live. The Recollects tended to him, eager to free his soul most blissfully from his body when the time came, and Père Le Caron said to him: François, we are all very edified by your courage. *Ver*-y edified . . . – Oh, it's useless, Pontgravé muttered. I can't even see anymore. And my head's splitting. I knew it would happen. It's always this way on English ships . . . – Brébeuf and Champlain stood at the railing, and Champlain was shivering because the breeze was very chilly and he'd given up both cloak and dressing gown to be made into clothing for Charité and Espérance, as he would not abandon them naked, and he'd given Espérance a chaplet because Eustache had given Charité one and the girls were both jealous of one another in this way: that if one of them was given something, then the other must be given it also. He'd begged the Couillards to let the girls stay in their house as maids of all work, to which they had agreed, though grudgingly; and never to his dying day would Champlain forget how Marsolet had gloated and the two girls had wept and made him their last curtsey – well, best not to think of that. After all, the good Père Brébeuf (what a strong young man!) surely had his disappointments, too. – What a pity about the Huron Mission! – So they stood there together unspeaking for a time and Champlain sighed and then Père Brébeuf earnestly asked his advice regarding the furtherment of their joint design – *viz.*, the conversion of the Savages; – for who can say, he remarked, that we shall not be back at Kebec in a year's time?

You are right, Père, said Champlain. Someday, with the help of GOD, New France will be New France again. Without a doubt, Kirke took our Country illegally. But upon our return, if you want my opinion, I think it essential to the harvest of souls that you religious Orders labor in harmony with the traders. Eh, the Recollects . . . – And here he sighed.

I value your frankness, replied Père Brébeuf. I agree that the Recollects made little effort to accommodate the world in their scheme. The world is where we must begin, even though we end in the Kingdom of Heaven. I myself see no reason why the fur-traders cannot come to love us. For in civilizing the Savages we shall both increase their need for our goods and also render them industrious . . .

Ah, but you are a discerning man! interrupted Champlain, in high excitement. So are all you Jesuits. It was a grief to me that your Order did not originally settle at Kebec rather than Port-Royal, although I did make Madame de Guercheville the invitation. She was proud, proud!

We made mistakes in our time, Père Brébeuf admitted. But I feel in my heart that we shall make no more.

Père Massé was there, saying nothing. At this, Père Brébeuf turned to him and asked for his opinion. But he only rubbed his nose and said: Jean, sixteen years ago the English expelled me from Port-Royal. Now they have expelled me from Kebec. Perhaps they will expel me a third time and a fourth, if I should live so long. But for them to expel me again, as is their duty, I must first return to Canada, which is my own devoir.

At this they all laughed.

At Plymouth they parted. Only eleven of Kirke's men had died of dysentery; it had been a splendid voyage. Champlain repaired to the French Ambassador's, where he stayed for five weeks, spooning strong words in his ear, such as: *After all, we do not dispute the English's taking possession of the Virginias, though we might well do so . . .* – for indeed, as it transpired, the Sieur de Caën had been correct in his claim that the Kirkes had taken Kebec after peace was concluded with France . . . and meanwhile the Black-Gowns sailed to Calais and thence journeyed by carriage to Rouen . . .

Two Dispositions

Père Massé was sent to serve at La Flèche. He was now fifty-four years of age. Yet he had as much fervor as ever. Never once had he suffered desire for a woman. Whenever he made the Exercises he still found himself swimming up the Fleuve Saint-Laurent to Kebec, where the residence which he had built with his own hands stood waiting to be put to rights; lovingly he blew the dust away from his dreams . . . He'd never ceased to keep his secret vows of mortification, faithfully whipping himself with the *discipline*, fasting three times a week, sleeping on bare ground, eschewing food whose taste he savored, and celebrating the Mass in a hair-shirt. Now he added a new penance to the rest. Taking from his breast the crumpled sweatstained sheet of birchbark on which the other rules were inscribed, he added:

> If thou suffer to issue from thy lips any word which
> offends charity, however little, thou shalt gather up
> secretly with thy tongue the spittle and phlegm
> proceeding from the mouths of others.

And he smiled, so happily did he now despise himself –

As for Père Brébeuf, he seemed larger to his Superiors than they remembered him. There was a red line of sunburn along the bridge of his nose. In Rouen they appointed him to serve the Church as a preacher and confessor. This he did with zeal, although he longed to return to the Huron. He remembered the violet-grey smoke that hung in their longhouses, and the drying corn hanging from the rafters like flayed rabbits at the butcher's here in France, and he remembered the way that the peeled wall-ribs rose into smoky darkness like the coarse meshes of some giant basket, and he remembered the light from the cornfields blinding him with goodness and he remembered the dry smell of the corn growing in the summer dark. The *yearning* of these memories weighed upon him as heavily as the stones in the head of a sea-elephant (which, according to Frère Sagard, are a remedy for the pain of calculus). He could not find peace . . . In Janvier, 1630, he made his final vows as a Jesuit. That year was one of great mortality in France, for reasons best known to GOD. Thousands died of hunger and plague, so that every priest was well occupied in helping to gather in the harvest of souls. From 1631 to 1633 he was steward, minister and confessor at the College in Eu. It was at that time that he took the First of his Three special Vows, which none are required to do, and scarcely anyone chooses: to serve Our LORD JESUS CHRIST, even to the sacrifice of his life.

Vote of Confidence

The Sieur de Champlain was now greatly changed, as one might imagine – for the colors of a man's soul must change as his life passes, whether or not he likes it. The soul is but a Country like the Country of the Irocois in the spring with its hills like waves of yellow cloud; its brown summer streams, chalky waterfalls; its scarlet leaves of autumn; its white-shrouded winter forests of evil blackness. Now he too had come almost to the end.

When he was repatriated to France, he found De Monts dead at last. Madame de Poutrincourt was dead. But the slanders and accusations went on.

Four hundred thousand livres, Monsieur! the Associates shouted at him. That's how much we've lost in New France these last two years, thanks to your failure to hold the line against these Kirke scoundrels – *your* failure, Monsieur! See how you've defrauded us!

When he replied to them, his voice shook. – Messieurs, Seigneurs, I have looked after your interests night and day. I have labored unceasingly; I have said prayers . . .

Prayers, prayers! Who cares about that? Where's our profit? Why did you surrender to the Querques in time of peace? You should be tried for treason! What have you to say to that?

This is the foolish talk of those who do not know what actually took place, he began, but they shouted him down. (Young nobles, so many of them, with their long curled locks . . . What did these boys know?)

He turned and walked away. He had great hopes of some royal subvention or other which would benefit Canada.

Look how that dotard twitches and quavers! they whispered. – What's his age, anyhow? Sixty-two? Sixty-four? Ah, how abject he is!

He went to the Palace to salute His Majesté the Roy and His Grandeur the Cardinal. He went home to his Hélène in the house in the rue de la Marche.

Sounding Again 1630–1633

She had bought some new tableaux and figurines, he saw: CHRIST was crowded now by Samson and Sainte-Geneviève. The tables were covered over with tapisseries; the chaises were soft green seas of velour. – I suppose she has contracted some new debts, he said to himself. – Her bed was now quite elaborate, being a pillared dais with a ceiling painted blue with gold stars, like the sky of Heaven . . . According to her instructions, the servants had set up his cot on the far side of the room.

Well, Samuel, she said steadily, this last séjour in Canada was very long.

Three years, he said.

And did you receive the letter I wrote you about taking my novitiate? For I never heard from you.

I heard of your design from Père Lalemant, her husband said, pacing leadenly. – The mail ship was attacked by the English, and he was compelled to throw all the letters into the sea. So I am sorry that I did not have your own words in front of me when I replied – you never got my reply?

Never.

Well, did you promise yourself to any Convent? he cried, a little testily.

You need not speak so loudly. I am not yet deaf, although perhaps you are becoming so.

That was unkind. My years –

Yes. Your years. No, Samuel, I did not act without your consent. And I will not.

He nodded. – I'm very happy about that, Hélène. You must not leave the world while I live, which may not be even as long as you imply, for I am in poor health these days.

And Monsieur de Pontgravé, how does he fare?

Poorer than I, my dear, for he died on the voyage, in great pain from his gout. We must pay our condolences to Christine . . .

They sat together for a moment. Suddenly she rushed forward and took his hand. He smiled down at her, massaging his swollen heart.

And what have you been reading, Hélène?

This tract of Sainct François d'Assise moved me greatly, she said. I put it under your pillow today. And of course each year I have followed the *Jesuit Relations* . . .

For almost three-and-a-half years he waited for the restoration of Canada. He lived quietly with Hélène, rarely going out. He lived through the Day of

Dupes, when Richelieu lost his power for a space of twenty-four hours; at fourth hand he heard about the Queen-Mother's escape to Spanish Holland; the Thirty Years' War broke out; the Roy was now attending Mademoiselle de Hautefort with great tenderness, as he could not patch up his quarrels with the Queen; the Roy laid siege to the Duchy of Bar . . .

Champlain sat at home. He sat thinking about GOUGOU. In the Spanish Seas bordering Mechique there is such a foul luxuriance of tropical seaweed that ships must be periodically beached and careened to cleanse their hulls, as he well remembered. His Uncle Provençal had showed him the way of it. Now he knew that that seaweed was GOUGOU. How many such monsters (he asked himself) must dwell in those parts, taking men to be their rich and lawful prizes? And how many must there have been in all the seas where he had taken soundings, stroking the cable with their impure arms, which he never knew because the butter-greased weight came up clean save for a smidgeon of pearly sand? And how many yet haunted the shimmering green corridors of the Roy's Palace, where he and De Monts and Poutrincourt had so often cast the investigatory lead? And how many Frenchmen and Savages were GOUGOU? How many were not GOUGOU? In which category did his wife fall at last, his wife with the glistening hair (now just beginning to grey) which she never let him touch? Everywhere he turned his thoughts now, it seemed that he had been ensnared by others, never acting after his heart. – But no, he admitted very gently, I was *her* GOUGOU; she has never sought anything of me but to leave her alone insofar as I can . . .

When he had thought about GOUGOU for awhile, he thought about his daughters Charité and Espérance. He sat in his nightshirt weeping old man's tears until Hélène came and said hush, my poor Samuel. Hush, hush.

He thought: The Stream of Time now curves sharply, like a reaper's sickle –

He got a letter from Père Brébeuf, saying that thirty Dutchmen had come to settle in the Country of the Iroquois, so that there was a New Netherland now, and possibly a New Sweden soon to come; and he clenched his fists.

In Canada now the oak buds would have swelled, and the sorrel would be ready to cut. He wondered if the Querque brothers had a taste for sorrel. He did not suppose that they did. And of course his French apple trees would have begun to bud. Surely they did honor even now to the Sieur de Monts, who had given them to him. De Monts' orchard at Pons had been sold, Hélène said –

When I sail – if I sail – I will not come back, he said. Before I go away I will settle all my property on you.

On the twenty-third of Mars, 1633, he set sail for Canada. And it was as he said, for he never came back again.

"A Hungry, Naked Indian"

Every summer, Soranhes had returned to Teyiatontariye (which is to say, *Kekwek*), hoping faithfully for the Iron People to keep their promise. But they never brought his son back from their Country. What had they done with him? Had they chanted him into sickness and death with their spells? The first summer Soranhes had spoken with his own mouth to Chawain, who was still their War-Chief at Kekwek (they had no Peace-Chief). – Brother, my mind is not at rest, he said to Chawain, and indeed his feelings were deep-buried like a cache of secret corn. Had the ship overturned in some storm; had his son been swallowed in the sea? But Chawain argued with him like a woman, until Soranhes was forced to be silent for fear of doing further hurt to their mutual honor. Very strange and shameful, how this old Chawain screeched like a crow! But Chawain had always been so. In Wendaké they still told the tale of how Chawain had raged when the Iroquois shot him in the knee. Chawain had little intelligence. That winter when he stayed at Darontal's lodge, he'd followed a bird in the woods and was lost for days! Darontal was compelled to say to him: Chawain, you must not go into the forest alone anymore. If you had not come back and we remained unable to discover you, we should never have gone to Kekwek again, for fear of your Iron People. What if they thought that we'd put you to death? – How Chawain had shouted then; how his face had purpled! Everyone was acquainted with this characteristic of Chawain's. So now, as Chawain scolded him, Soranhes knew to say nothing. That was the only way for Chawain to calm himself. When Chawain had become clearminded at last, he advised Soranhes to have patience on Amantacha's account, because the Black-Gowns were blameless men. – I assure you that I shall never cease to hold them dear, for they are our nephews, Soranhes replied, but this answer did not seem to please Chawain, either. There was no pleasing Chawain!

The second summer, coming to Kekwek once again, he sought to take further counsel with Chawain, but the warriors of the Iron People told him that Chawain's repose could not be disturbed. (What fine guns they had!) Soranhes was distraught by the time that the third summer had passed. Accusing himself of the fault of excessive trust (he could see now that these Iron People had no good in them), he loaded his canoe with hatchets, kettles, blankets and nightcaps, and made his bitter journey home. In Ihonatiria, which lies very close to the Sweetwater Sea, there was an *Arendouane* or Sorceress of high repute, whom he stopped to visit. When he had given her many goods from his new store, she made pyromancies, blinked her red-rimmed eyes, and told him finally that Amantacha was alive, but not at liberty. She could see him standing in an enclosure girt with palisadoes so very high as to shade him entirely from the SUN. – Soranhes, you must assist him with your heart. (Thus the Arendouane.) Strive to dream of him and comfort him over the distance; then he will return to you. He wishes to return to you! – Somewhat comforted, Soranhes returned to Teanaostaiaé Town. Over the winter he sought to dissipate the clouds from his dreams, in order that they could better shine upon Amantacha. Winter passed. Summer came. Then he saw him, resplendently dressed, standing on the deck of an English ship. – My son, my son! he shouted.

Thomas Kirke could not believe his eyes. – *That's* your father? he said.

Yes, milord, said Amantacha, dropping his eyes.

Why, he's – he's no King! He's nothing but a hungry, naked Indian! Odious! Intolerable! – You, sailors! Strip off this young coxcomb's clothes and give him a good drubbing! My, what a plot you've laid! I truly thought you sincere and pure; yet now I could choke for rage to see how you've bilked us of our salt –

But the interpreter Étienne Brûlé whispered urgently in his ear, for he loved Amantacha.

Hold! he said at last. I grant you this, Lewis Amantacha: you may keep the clothes you wore, in remembrance of our good usage and courtesy, for I would scorn now to have back what stinks and reeks with your Savage odor. But the other suits (which we had made for you at great expense) I shall keep – though you may have hope of seeing them, provided that you lead here a troop of other Savages well-laden with beaver-skins. What is your answer? You need not look at me so, boy – are your wits gone? – O, but he drives me mad!

I thank you for your condescension, my Lord. (Thus Amantacha.)

He stood before his father.

Soranhes knew not how to feel. The joy which he had had at first, in seeing that his son had not perished in the boiling waters of the sea, was now mixed with wrath at the sight which he had just witnessed; for it was scarcely custom for one man to raise his voice against another and berate him, unless he were his bitterest enemy. So he conceived a hatred against these English Iron People. Longing to sink a hatchet in their heads, he stood dumbly; until Amantacha smoothed his arm . . .

The river-road to the Country of the Wendat is a narrow one, where sometimes the canoe scrapes its belly on rocks in the narrows with seemingly nothing but a sea of reeds beyond. At these portages Soranhes noticed how his son's strength had declined among the Iron People. It gave him great trouble to lift the canoe above his head, so that Soranhes gazed at him in sadness, and Amantacha flushed, but he said to his father: The Countries of the Iron People are filled with stone houses. There is nowhere to walk and run.

A tree hunched over in the windy rain. The sky was grey; the river was grey and clear. A matted grove of broken-branched spruces leaned toward them, lonely beneath the stormy horizon. Past leafy villi, leafy fringes, the voyagers stopped to offer tobacco to the OKI* that lived inside the hollows of Tsanhohi-Bird Rock, which was a great boulder so high that no arrow could shoot over it, and Soranhes cried out, as he always did: OKI, have pity on us; guard us from our enemies . . . – and his son hung his head, as if he were ashamed.

They returned home in rainy sunshine with their good nephew the Frenchman, Étienne Brûlé; and the milkysweet smell of corn in the summer wind welcomed them long before they reached the cornfield ways dark green and light green with steely cones and cylinders. The longhouses gaped open; the People rushed around, caressing Amantacha's face . . . Now Amantacha's mother and sister prepared a great feast of wild pumpkins roasted under hot ashes – which they had not done before, in case he might be dead or delayed; there was no knowing what might have happened at *Kekwek*. Soranhes named his own contribution to the feast, saying: This is my favorite dog cooked . . . – to which they all cried *ho ho ho!* and struck their fists happily upon the hearth, and Amantacha smiled (looking away) until they shouted: Eat, eat, eat, my dear nephew! – At first it relished strangely to Amantacha, as his palate had been half-spoiled by the Iron People's spiceries, but soon he was restored to himself. He was as sleek and clever as an otter; his mischances had not hurt him.

So he became again a hunter, a warrior. And just before the end of summer, in the Moon When the Little Corn is Made, one of Soranhes' brothers returned with a Cayuga prisoner for burning, and Soranhes requested Amantacha to eat of the man's heart . . . Then there was a Singing-Feast of thirty deer and thirty kettles, and they sucked the *yandohy* or fermented corn – all the children around him smiled to taste that food – after which, to his joy, they called the Aténonha, or Dance of Night Wives, when the women

* Power.

run from lodge to lodge, loving whom they please; he got much pleasure from them. He had Eyandarekwi and Yarenhatsi. They were kind to him – not like French girls! And Soranhes said: Open your ears, my son! It is time for you to take a wife! Your uncles say the same! – Amantacha promised that he'd do that, perhaps next year –

But it was agreed among the Wendat that never again would they permit a youth to be taken from them by the Iron People, for they did not keep their promises.

Guns and Brandy 1629–1632

Thomas Kirke was now the Captain of Kebec, with ninety men at his charge, and more than a hundred traders and others. The trade continued successful, for Amantacha the Huron brought with him so many Salvages in the following July that thirty thousand skins or more were traded, a service for which they did him a signal favor, like true Englishmen, and gave him back his confiscated clothes. At this, Lewis Amantacha thanked them most humbly. To make certain that he took the point (for Salvages are notoriously slow to gratitude, especially Popish Salvages), Thomas Kirke haled him into his presence and said: Now believe me, mannikin, when I tell you that we English are capable of cruelty to our enemies, in equal proportion as we use kindness and courtesy with our friends.

Ah, milord, replied Lewis Amantacha, you know how I love you and revere the King; have I not brought the beaver pelletries to you as I promised?

I would wish you not to forget that, you redskinned nigger, for we of England execute our laws far more severely than the Papists. Be true to me, and I'll better your lot; move my patience to anger, and I'll shoot you for a rebel and a miscreant. Do you get it? My temper is almost spent –

After this speech, by which Amantacha seemed greatly moved, Thomas Kirke was satisfied that he could now show his dear love and goodness with respect to the Salvages, and so he called them all together, *Hurons* and *Montagnetts* and *Algoumekins* (yet not within the fort, where they might perchance do him a mischief, but on the bank of the great River *Saint Lawrence*, so that in case of treachery or sedition his soldiers might easily cut them down); then he smiled upon them and sold them all rum in great quantities, by which means he got all the rest of their beavers very cheaply, and so for the first time the Wendat saw what it was like to be possessed by the terrifying brown spirits that made them attack each other and fall down like dead men; and then the soldiers debauched the Algoumekin squaws (though to Kirke's mind *those* were rank meat . . .) – Enlighten your ears, brothers! (Thus the Algonkin, to the Huron.) Now you begin to comprehend that these Iron People desire to kill you. It would be well for you if you did not come here anymore. Let us employ ourselves against them in your name; we know well how to deal with them. Never fear; we'll not require from you an excessive number of presents . . . – Hearing this, not so many Wendat came to trade the following year, which made Thomas Kirke exceedingly wroth, for he was convinced that Lewis Amantacha had played this rascally game solely to twit him after recovering his clothes. You may be sure that if Kirke saw him again he would reward him according to his deserts . . .

Summers and winters went by, and Kirke wondered how long it would be before he was knighted. He grew weary of Canada. The Irocois came and burned a village of the Montagnaits at Three Rivers, but Kirke did not overstrain himself in that quarrel, which was petty and spiteful like all the wars of Salvages. Let 'em slay one another. If enough were slain, then there would be no more. They humbly begged to buy muskets of him, which he sold to any who had enough beaver-skins. Let 'em slay one another with greater diligence!

He went hawking with his falcons, horned owls and butcher-birds.

He strolled through the triad of steep-roofed towers, choosing the tallest one for himself. Here he could see over the palisadoes; he could watch the River Saint Lawrence. He paced the balconies and galleries where Champlain had walked so recently. A staunch enough man, certainly; Kirke would give him that.

He stationed soldiers at the little square windows. They shuffled nervously and sneered: This place smells like Catholics! – There was a little rosary on the floor; one of Champlain's men had dropped it. In a sudden rage, Kirke ground it under the heel of his boot . . .

The River's Mouth

1633–1634

> It is good for us to encounter troubles and adversities from time to time, for trouble often compels a man to search his own heart. It reminds him that he is an exile here, and that he can put his trust in nothing in this world.
>
> THOMAS À KEMPIS, *The Imitation of CHRIST* (*ca.* 1413)

From Champlain's Habitation on the edge of that grassy rock whose great white fractured faces shaded the town, a cannonade sounded at last. – *Ho!* cried the Savages. Birds pelted from their cliff-nests in shrieking panic; echoes quaked; blossoms drifted down like the last snowfall of spring. It was early morning in the month of Mai. Père Paul Le Jeune, Superior of the Society of JESUS at Kebec, leaped from his bed to find Père Brébeuf in the doorway. Behind stood Père Massé, who had labored among the Souriquois of Acadia, as I have told, and two new Black-Gowns – *viz*., Père Davost and Père Daniel. (It was Père Daniel who'd catechized Amantacha. His destiny was to be martyred by the Hiroquois.) French musketeers strode up the steep cliff-stairs, and Champlain took the keys of the citadel back from his Deputy, Monsieur de Caën. The year before, the Queen's dowry had been paid and the Kirke brothers struck their colors. The Algonquin girls had screeched with drunkenness . . . Now Kebec was Catholic again.

Champlain ascended his highest tower and stood gazing down at the Fleuve Saint-Laurent. His quick eyes caught the leaping of fishes. The water shimmered in the sun like a dream. Although the Roy had still not seen fit to give him the Governorship, it is true, he felt nonetheless the satisfaction of a gourmand awaiting some savory, well-beloved dish: Kebec was his. It was thirty years now since he had first seen this place; his mind had long mapped every ripple and crag. And China? That Nation undoubtedly lay many hundreds of leagues to the west, and yet fleuves and rivières must go there. In five years, when he'd concluded peace among his Savages, he might send one of the younger men to seek it out. Imagine, the Great Khan a French subject! Then those shining mines, those hills of white metal and yellow metal which he'd not found here or in Acadia, those pyramids of silver and gold would belong to France at last. He'd put the truculent Nations of Savages to work as miners and slaves, after the Spanish fashion: – the Algoumequins perhaps, the Hiroquois for a certainty, and also those damned Montagnais . . .* Then he'd adorn every bay and river of Canada with a Church. Oh, indeed the cliff-breeze was refreshing him with fine plans . . . – But first he must establish order in his own house. More forest must be cleared. More foodstuffs must be planted. More colonists must come from France. This very year – no, next year – he'd establish a French town at Trois-Rivières: the Huron traders could be better controlled that way. He'd already forbidden the Montagnais to trade with the English – year by year, he was confident, his edicts would weave soft and delicate embroideries of forgetfulness in the air, drifting down upon the Savages like pollen from Heaven, numbing them, dimming their sight, until they no longer recollected that heretics and usurpers existed in this world! He'd ban their harlots' naked dances. He'd make the Fleuve Saint-Laurent safe again (two more Frenchmen had just been scalped by the Hiroquois). Yes, he'd form an army with a hundred and twenty stout Frenchmen and five thousand Montagnais and Souriquois Savages armed with explosives, they'd march upon the Hiroquois Castles and destroy them! He'd build a great Cathedral. He'd dislodge the English from southern Acadia . . . But dearest to his heart was the saving of souls. And, thanks to Richelieu's new letters-patent, the instruments for *that* were the Jesuit Pères. As for the Recollects, they'd been excluded at last. The English had used their residence as a dunghill –

– And Père Le Caron was dead of the plague.

Le Jeune and Brébeuf embraced each other tightly. – Now, Jean, said the Superior at last, now you can return to the Huron. You will be in charge of that Mission, of course.

* The first thing he'd done was to ask after Charité and Espérance at Madame Couillard's. – Ah, Seigneur, she said, as soon as you left for England, they went to the woods with Monsieur Marsolet. There was no stopping them . . .

Père Brébeuf stood smiling. Tears rolled down his cheeks.

Later they strolled along the edge of the rock together, the two of them, and looked westward. Beyond the Plains of Abraham and the Fleuve Saint-Laurent, the country was walled in by hills green and blue and misty silver. The Huron Nation lay that way.

A Life

Père Le Jeune was two years older than his friend. He was one of those people born to refine and correct. Having the misfortune to come from Calvinist stock, in the benighted town of Vitry-le-François, he first practiced his trade upon himself, at sixteen years of age, and erased what did not pertain to the True Faith. At twenty-two he entered his novitiate at the Society of JESUS. That was the year that the heretic Samuel Argall destroyed the work of Père Biard and Père Massé in Acadia. In his yearning toward perfection, Le Jeune exceeded even Champlain. Everything must be purified, from Brébeuf's reports to the sexual lives of the Savages. Neither optimistic nor pessimistic, he trudged unbendingly toward Paradise, dragging others with him by the ear, for that was charity. When alone, he laid strokes upon himself until the scarred flesh burst open, and blood came forth to wash sins from the dead skin. He had features which approached the birdlike. He was, in short, a manifestation of that eternal soul partaken of by Bishops, School-Masters and their ilk. In 1615, when he first began the study of philosophy at the Collège Henri IV at La Flèche, Père Massé, who directed the pupils' souls, eyed him in amazement, seeing in his unbending fervency a duplication of Père Biard's. But it was not long before he recognized in the young man a fine alloy of steadiness and cool realism, whereas Père Biard had only been rash. Moistening his forefinger with holy water, tracing it across Le Jeune's temple, Père Massé sought to bring out this tendency. Many were the souls shaped by Père Massé: Père Lalemant, Père Vimont, who would be Superior at Kebec after Père Le Jeune, Père Buteux, who would be martyred by the Hiroquois in 1652, Père Ragueneau, who became Procurator of the Canadian Mission after Père Le Jeune began to fail in his old age, and so many others, even more effective, perhaps, for being more obscure. As an ordinary thing such as the head of a nail may through GOD's mercy catch the light of loveliness and glow in divinity to remind us that everything is divine, thus the words of this plain-speaking man caught fire in hearts. And so Le Jeune said: Yes, I must become more patient and subtle. – And he learned to correct by degrees, unlike Champlain, who must seek to wrench the immovable boulder from its bed, who carved his bold blocky signature in the flesh of stubborn Savages, to gall them . . .

But even yet the granite shadow of Canada was still upstream of his knowing. In 1622 he went to Paris and studied theology for four years, at the Collège de Clermont. Then he taught rhetoric in Nevers. He completed the third year of his novitiate in Rouen, and was ordained. In 1629–30 he was Professor of Rhetoric at Caen, now locked fast in the Black Gown which he would bear to his grave. The following year he was preaching at Dieppe. Those above him had placed the Jesuit residence there in his charge, a task for which he was worthy enough to consider himself unworthy; we've heard *that* before –

It was a shock when he was appointed Superior General of the Mission in Canada. Canada? he said to himself. Isn't that the cold place? – No matter. Receiving his instructions, although he had never asked for an apostolate among the heathen, he was happier than he had been for twenty years, for although as yet he felt no special affection for the Savages, the duty of obedience was binding.

The Treachery of the Huron Savages 1633

Well aware that accepting presents from the Savages bound him to return their reciprocals, the Sieur de Champlain now made his gifts of kettles and fashionable red beads and axes to the Huron, for which they showed becoming gratitude. He then said: My children, you must let these Pères return among you and instruct you! at which the Wendat were very satisfied, thinking that these Black-Gowns or *Hatitsihenstaatsi*, being so evidently Shamans, might show them how to make and repair the marvelous iron things. They'd often asked Chawain, whose knowledge was as great as his childish ill temper, to mend their worn-out kettles, but at this he only frowned and shouted and sulked. Perhaps the Hatitsihenstaatsi would be more gracious. That would be good, because then the Wendat would not have to trade so often for kettles. – Still they wavered a little, until Amantacha stood up in Council and said: Brothers, they will show you all the *new things* that I have seen and praised! – And his father Soranhes said: Remember the boys that these Iron People have taken as they once took my son. It is now our turn to take hostages for pledge; that is the way that Nation trades gift with Nation. – At this, the other Wendat said: Soranhes, your words are good.

We long to bring the Hatitsihenstaatsi home with us! – Observing them, Le Jeune said smiling: These Huron seem to me the most contented people in the world! See how they long to hear the Gospel! and Père Brébeuf said yes at which Père Le Jeune put a hand on his shoulder and said you are not afraid, Jean? and Père Brébeuf looked him full in the face with eyes glowing and said no, Père, forgive me my quietness; it is only that I am so happy! and Père Le Jeune said it gladdens my heart to hear that, but you know that I expected no less of you.

Now with provisions and beads Père Le Jeune paid the Huron men who had agreed to take Père Brébeuf, Père Daniel and Père Davost up the river; and these three handed over their little bundles of personal belongings and holy things to be stowed among the trade goods in those high-heaped canoes, and the summer light faded on the water as the Huron – half a thousand of them there were; tall goodnatured men in robes of elk or beaver – bustled about the canoes so that all would be ready to leave at first light, and now it was dusk and the mosquitoes (which are little flies) tormented the Black-Gowns even through their robes but the Huron went on laughing and scratching and brushing them away without paying attention; so the mosquitoes seemed to settle more and more thickly upon the Black-Gowns until Père Le Jeune cried out heavens I cannot *bear* these vermin! and Père de Nouë said yes, brothers, shall we go to the Store-house to perform our devotions and rest? and so the Black-Gowns bade goodnight to the Savages with love in their hearts, having Père Brébeuf translate for them since only he could understand the language; and then they bade goodnight to the Sieur de Champlain, who bowed to them graciously, and they went into the Store-house where it was hot and dark and the mosquitoes tormented them almost as badly, so the Superior slapped at himself and killed a few and then sighed and led his companions in prayer.

At about ten-o'-clock that night, there was a hubbub outside. A Savage was going from camp to camp, crying out something in his language, after which there came shrill hoarse replies like a chorus of frightened crows, and Père Le Jeune lit the lantern and looked at Père Brébeuf's face and saw the light go out of it, and Père Le Jeune said to him what are they saying, Jean?

He is warning the Huron not to take any Frenchmen in their canoes tomorrow. The relatives of that Savage whom Champlain threw in the dungeon have sworn to kill any Frenchmen they can.

Which Savage is that?

The Algonkin who murdered Claude Pichot, said Père Brébeuf. You remember: he was peaceably washing his clothes . . .

Père Daniel and Père Davost sat very quietly. They'd arrived at Grand

Cibou* the year before, where they stayed through the winter, dwelling among Born Underwater's Nation the *Souriquois* and preaching the Gospel until the Sieur de Champlain could bring them to Kebec. They were still very much in awe of New France. Their eyes were big in the dimness.

Seeing the others irresolute, Père Brébeuf stood on tiptoe and unshuttered one of the little square windows.

I can't see what they're doing, he said. I can only see their fires, and the sparks in the darkness . . .

I think we had better go to the Fort, said the Superior to Père de Nouë. The other nodded and put on his shoes. They went out together, and in a moment Père Brébeuf could hear them hailing the sentry.

Do you think that our Mission is spoiled this year after all? asked Père Davost after a long silence.

Impossible to say, said Père Brébeuf. These Savages are of such a capricious and fickle disposition that we can be certain of nothing.

Let us offer up a prayer for success, said Père Daniel.

The other two men knelt beside him in fervent silence.

The next morning, at eight or nine, the Sieur de Champlain came out of the gate of his Fort with many retainers, sentinels, mercenaries and suchlike implements, and assembled the Savage Captains. The Savage who had warned them against giving the Frenchmen passage stood by unconcernedly. He was a one-eyed brute, unclean, like all the Savages.

Why have you aroused this opposition? Champlain said to him sharply.

I have not aroused opposition, said the Savage to the interpreter in silken haughty tones. They mistake me. Tell them that.

Well? said the Sieur de Champlain, his eyes flashing.

Let him tell it his own way, said the interpreter to Champlain very urgently.

The Sieur smiled bitterly. – All alike, these Savages! he said.

I wish only to protect your Black-Gowns, said One-Eye, grinning insolently. If they go up river they will be killed. Then the Huron will be responsible. They will have to go to war to avenge these murders. I believe the river will be a more dangerous place then. Very dangerous. How will you Frenchmen get your beaver-rags then?

Hearing this speech, all the Savages looked sidelong at Champlain and laughed.

* Cape Breton, Nova Scotia.

The Sieur paced to and fro until he had regained his temper. Then he turned abruptly to the Huron traders. – Do you still wish to take the three Pères to your Country, or are you terrified now like women?

The Captains of the Huron smiled and looked down at the ground. – We ask for nothing better than to carry the Hatitsihenstaatsi home with us, said one of them. But the river is not ours.

Not understanding those Huron smiles, even after so many years, Champlain believed that they meant exactly what they said, and spoke to them in stern and earnest terms, exhorting them to follow the upright path and obey him, as the Black-Gowns stood arrayed against the morning like a flock of dark crows with pale, pale faces and beards instead of beaks, so that the Huron mocked at them among themselves and said to each other: what women would want bearded men like these? – They are Shamans, explained those who knew, and they have sworn to have no women until they die. – *Ahh,* said the others in comprehension. – The Black-Gowns understood none of this. – Still the Sieur de Champlain berated the Huron, until Père Le Jeune marveled at his zeal and goodwill towards men of GOD, but the Huron only smiled wider from side to side; at last, exasperated, Champlain strode very close to one of the Huron Captains, who had been seated with the others, and the Huron leaped up smiling and clenching his fists and Champlain stood breathing in his face and saying eh, then, so you are afraid of war with the Island Savages; how would you like a war with us? and the Huron Captain smiled still wider and said to the interpreter tell him to have a care!

Monsieur has certainly done all he could for us, said Père de Nouë, downcast.

Père Brébeuf alone said nothing.

Well? said Père Le Jeune. He had a habit of looking often into Brébeuf's face, as if for reassurance or refreshment.

I dislike giving in to Savages, said Père Brébeuf, but even more I dislike having to wait another year to begin our work. Let us show our good faith and ask the Sieur to release this prisoner.

But he murdered a Frenchman! exclaimed Père Le Jeune in horror.

The Huron were watching them now. One of them asked the interpreter what they who were called *Charcoal* were saying, and he told him.

That is true, Père Brébeuf was saying. But Ignatius tells us to be all things to all men.

A wry smile came over Le Jeune's face. He rocked on his heels. So, he said. Then he took Champlain aside and whispered in his ear. Every eye was upon them.

Absolutely not! Champlain shouted. This is a matter as important to me as my own life! Don't you realize that our Roy will expect me to account for the man that that Savage murdered? He is a *Savage*, I tell you, a bloodthirsty Savage!

Well, said Père Le Jeune, I beg you to at least suspend the execution until we learn the Roy's will. – You see, he continued, turning to the Savages, we love you. We seek no one's death. We Black-Gowns wish only to promote peace among the Tribes and Nations.

Yes, that is true, said the Sieur de Champlain. He nodded at the interpreter to begin translating. (Of course, as had been worked out between them beforehand, he'd been translating all along, so that the Savages would miss none of this comedy.) – These men are loved by all, Chawain continued loudly. They talk to JESUS!

We beseech you, then, to suspend the execution, said Père Le Jeune, praying *may this move their hearts!*

Yes, said another Huron Captain, these Hatitsihenstaatsi are wise and good. May Chawain hear them well! May Chawain delay in killing this man until the Roy sends his mouth to speak to us across the sea.

So be it, said Champlain gravely. Now I hope that my Huron children will be happy at last. Now the Black-Gowns can go with you.

But a Huron Captain said: These Island Tribes are enraged on account of their relative. They fear that his breath comes to him sadly in your dungeon. They say that the murder was not his fault, but the fault of the brandy your men sold him. They entreat us to ask you this favor. We would not ask you, but they have exchanged gifts with us, and so they force us to ask you. We must go through their Country when we come here; they can stop the way if they please. They say they will pardon no one until their relative is released.

Then the Sieur de Champlain spoke to the interpreter in very loud and ringing tones, so that all the Savages sat waiting to hear what he might say. The interpreter bowed his head, listening. At last he turned to the Wendat and said: – Our uncle Chawain tells us, *If the Island Tribes act the part of DEVILS, so will we.* He is very angry. He says to us, *If I see one of you Savages bearing weapons, I shall give my men permission to fire on him with their muskets.* He says to us, *You know I love you, but I am the enemy of evildoers.* He says to us, *There can be no true friendship between us until our Black-Gowns are allowed to visit you.*

At this there was a great noise and tintamarre among the Savages, and Père Le Jeune was hopeful of the success of the stratagem, and said in a low voice to the Sieur you have carried out your part marvelously! but Père Brébeuf had already understood that it was useless. He drew Père Daniel and Père Davost under his wing, and whispered something to them, at which tears started from their eyes; then he turned with a bow to his Superior and his Sieur, saying: Sirs, we three remain resolute to go to the Country of the Huron whenever it is possible, but breaking the peace is too high a cost to ask you to pay for our consolation of dying among these heathens. We promise to keep our hearts from falling, and wait out the year in patience.

The Sieur de Champlain seemed about to say something, but bit his lip. (His eyes were like two of those deep tunnels in the walls of Kebec that one may peer into, seeing past barred gates, seeing arched ceilings composed of the same hard brick as the walls and floor, going deeper and deeper into darkness until the passageway ends in a perpendicular corridor of light whose two stone choices can never be known by you as you stand outside, among the frantic cries of young birds. So the Savages said to one another: We see something within him, but what it is we know not.) And the Sieur stood with his hands on his hips, capturing the likenesses of all in his eyes and imprisoning them there, deep in those tunnels. Later he told the Black-Gowns: These Savages are too strong for us now, but we shall make good Christians out of them yet, whether they will or no! – And Père Le Jeune nodded and laughed and slapped his knee. But for now he held his peace, and Père Brébeuf turned to the Huron and said to them: You have sustained a greater loss than we this year.

The Huron Captains smiled and said: We are very sorry, Chawain. A year will soon pass away.

Well-Gazing

The ways of GOD are hidden, said Père Le Jeune very gently. May He be blessed.

Pax CHRISTI, said Père de Nouë.

Before the Huron canoes departed, the convert Louys Amantacha came to sleep in the Black-Gowns' little house, to confess and to receive holy communion. Knowing him to have been corrupted by the English, though through no fault of his own, the Black-Gowns were suspicious, but his evident fervor gave them consolation. He assured them that the Wendat Nation longed for the day when Père Brébeuf would return. In a beautiful hand, he wrote letters of salutation to the Provincial in France. He answered them freely on every question which they put to him. When, for instance, they asked him the whereabouts of that traitorous interpreter, Étienne Brûlé, he replied that the Wendat had cast him out for excessive libertinage, which they could well believe. They assured him that Brûlé was no longer considered a Frenchman, thanks to his change of allegiance, upon hearing which Amantacha became still more confidential and explained that the place where his People had in fact cast Brûlé was a pit in the ground, and that before doing so a War-Chief had split his head. They had not eaten him afterward, knowing this to be displeasing to the Iron People. Upon hearing this information the Black-Gowns rushed to tell Champlain, who was not at all displeased that that blackguard had met his deserts, and praised Amantacha for being so good as to let him know the secrets of his People, as a good spy should do. Wishing to put him still further to the test, Père Le Jeune took him aside and sounded him out as deeply as he might, for he well knew the artfulness and dissimulation of these Savages; – indeed, as he gazed into the boy's smooth brown face and began to question him, he had the familiar feeling that he always had of lifting the cover from a dark well and leaning in and smelling something rank, shuddering as he lit his torch and held it below him to see all manner of slime and foulnesses on the walls, and getting into the basket to be lowered deeper and deeper into this sinful soul with its toads and stenches; but in this case he was gratified, for Amantacha responded to his questions very well, so that in the end Père Le Jeune saw nothing but good in him.

Then the Huron set off, their canoes swimming in the water like schools of fish; and each man paddled or dawdled as he wished, for since they had refused to transport the French they had nothing to fear from the Island People. In their headdresses many of them wore glass beads, obtained in trade with the French, and bits of mother-of-pearl. These gleamed like molten sunlight among the wild turkey feathers that festooned their heads, the rabbit hair dyed red and blue . . . Champlain, watching from the window of the chamber he had once shared with his Hélène, could not but be reminded of the time he'd wintered in their Country and got lost chasing a beautiful bird he'd never seen before, rather like one of the yellow perroquets he'd seen in Mechique, but with a red head and blue wings. Now these happy feather-headed men faded up the river like cousins to that bird he'd never caught; and this caused him anguish, for under the authority of a loyal Quartermaster no loss of any kind should occur. They dazzled the surface of the Fleuve Saint-Laurent with their finery, the reflected colors almost as brilliant as the originals, and Amantacha turned and waved just before he vanished in the glassy blue distance; it was a very fine day, and young Père Davost was in tears.

It was thirty-eight years before we accomplished anything in Brazil, said the Superior, to console him. And how long have we been waiting in China?

But Père Davost continued to weep, there in the little chapel where only other Black-Gowns could see.

Père Brébeuf came up to him. The Huron are well-made people, as you saw, said he. Believe me, brother, their minds likewise have been fashioned by GOD. They will open their hearts to us when the time comes.

Winter at Kebec

The Black-Gowns had planted rye in their garden, and in those long summer days it was soon ready to harvest. With his long slender fingers Père Le Jeune counted the fruit, and found sometimes sixty kernels, sometimes eighty, occasionally even one hundred twenty. But the forests were full of vermin, such as grasshoppers, worms and insects, that grievously attacked whatever was grown, and the black crows were maddening thieves. He wished that the tree-wastes could all be cleared. (It was there that the Hiroquois lurked.) Everything was dark and shady all around him, and the roar of waterfalls was in his dreams.

Père Brébeuf taught all who could be spared the language of the Huron, morning and evening in his little school, although his command was not perfect. Indeed he would have been overjoyed if GOD had thought fit to unseal the tongue of that rogue interpreter Monsieur de Marsolet, who spoke many Indian languages. But Marsolet insisted that he had taken a vow of silence, so that he could not instruct anyone without sin. (The expression on the Sieur de Champlain's face at this was a terror to see.) So Brébeuf must do what he could. Someday he hoped to improve Père Le Caron's dictionary, although to tell the truth he could not imagine how he might write their language, or what accents he ought to place in the bosoms of their letters . . .

And Père Massé (whom his Superior loved to call Père Useful) had care of the cattle. Gentle Père de Nouë worked at the severest tasks, smiling from morning until night, and soothing the tempers of the artisans, who were amazed whenever the Black-Gowns asked them to perform a task that lay outside their specialty. The tailor was particularly excitable. He was often to be seen waving his arms in a fury when Père de Nouë sent him with Brother Jean to drag wood across the snow. – Come, my son, said Père de Nouë. You make beautiful shirts that fit us all. Do you then make yourself a woodcutter's shirt and play the part today. – Crazy! shouted the tailor.

Crazy! – And he went out to drag wood. Père de Nouë followed after him when his own work was done and did the heaviest part of the labor himself, sweating and beaming and blinking like a big blackbird (thirteen years later he would freeze to death on the Fleuve Saint-Laurent). As for Brother Gilbert, he was somewhat recovered from his sickness of last year, for which he was very thankful; in consideration of his long service in New France, Père Le Jeune offered him his liberty to return home, but he elected to stay. When fall came on, he went daily to the forest to cut wood, assisted by Brother Jean (whose span had yet twenty-two years to run, until he was murdered by the Hiroquois), and the tailor put his hands on his hips and stood in the doorway shouting: Brother Gilbert, go back home before they kill you with their labor! Crazy, I tell you! Snow as deep as your waist, and forests all the way to China! – Oh, you are full of fire, as Père de Nouë tells me! laughed Brother Gilbert over his shoulder, but Brother Jean said: Speak of crazy! You are crazy if you waste your words with that one! – And they left the palisade of their house behind them, and went past the clearing of stumps where below them the purple-grey cliff hung over the Fleuve Saint-Laurent to breathe in its summer evening smell and the fleuve was lavender and the sky was orange and clouds hovered at the river bend like English ships; and then the two Black-Gowns turned into the dark ways between the trees where the wind was chilly and the wild dark trees rose tendoned like an athlete's neck, and Brother Gilbert confided: I am not afraid of my sickness, but sometimes I fear these Savages . . . and he looked around him, as if they might be listening, at which Brother Jean said impatiently your sickness has made you morbid – how can you fear these ragtag Savages as stupid as animals? and Brother Gilbert said do you think Père Brébeuf knows fear? and Brother Jean replied *him?* Never! and Brother Gilbert said so what do *you* fear? and Brother Jean said I sometimes have nightmares of a black DEVIL at the bottom of the Fleuve and they began to fell a lightning-blasted sapling and Brother Jean said once I dreamed that something dark and feathered swooped down on me from the sky and I felt its claws in my face and Brother Jean said sometimes I think about the fields of Normandie, sometimes . . . and Brother Gilbert said quickly but the Savages, how about them? and Brother Jean said I admit that the converts are very pious and Brother Gilbert said this axe is dull, I think. – At length the days began to darken, and yellow leaves rained from the sky. It became cold, fearfully cold. Great drifts of ice could be seen in the Fleuve Saint-Laurent. The rocks in the forest were ice-veined and mineral-stained. Then the snow came at last. It snowed and snowed, until there was snow up to the eaves of the Black-Gowns' house.

One morning after Mass, Père Le Jeune called Père Brébeuf to speak to him. – I am going to leave you in my place for six months, he said. I wish to winter with the Montagnais Savages and bring the word of GOD to them.

But you are the Superior! said Père Brébeuf in astonishment.

Jean, you know what a burden and a grief my duties as Superior have been for me, replied Père Le Jeune. I wanted very much to study with you at your Huron school, but my duties would never permit it. Then, too, as I may as well admit to you, I have the memory of a blockhead. I cannot learn these Savage words. Maybe the Montagnais language will be easier on my ears.

But I could never govern the Mission as well as you, said Père Brébeuf, still stunned at this turn of events. I . . .

Oh, I fancy that you can, said Père Le Jeune with a sad smile. I have always written for the *Relations* that you are the man chosen by GOD for these things.

And you, I ask you what you asked me last summer, said Père Brébeuf. Are you afraid?

The other man nodded. Père Brébeuf saw that he was trembling.

GOD be with you! said Père Brébeuf, embracing him. I shall pray for you morning and evening.

Then Père Le Jeune bade the other Black-Gowns farewell, and set out to preach among the Savages.

The Sorcerer's Wife 1633–1634

. . . And Père Le Jeune wrote in his journal *There is not an insect, nor wasp, nor gadfly, so annoying as a Savage* and Père Le Jeune wrote *I am rather tired of talking about their irregularities; let us speak of their uncleanness* and after that, to divert himself for a space from his misery in this Country (and also because he believed that such things might be of use to such Pères as came after him), he noted and admired the strange abundance of their verbs and adjectives, two different words for coldness, for instance, being used to express the coldness of *wood* and *dogs*; however, this virtue was offset by the lack of many letters in their alphabet, which plainly demonstrated their lack of civilization. – How strange they were! – And all at once he felt such homesickness for France that he thought he would groan. He would never see France again. He must stay here, in this wretched snowy country, through all the years of his life, or until the Provincial recalled him. The thought made him grind his teeth. He wrote in his journal until his fingers were too numb to write anymore, and sighed and held his hands near the fire, and the Sorcerer said: ah, so you are finished with your conjurations, brother! and Père Le Jeune said fiercely I do no conjurations, and neither do you, you trickster and mountebank who only leads this people astray! and the Sorcerer curled his lip and said to the other Savages he loves himself, I see and the Savages stared at him with big black eyes and watched Père Le Jeune as they always watched anyone with Power, their eyeballs rolling back and forth like those of oxen at home that feared to be whipped. – Père Le Jeune rubbed his aching knees. In this smoky wigwam he could not even stand up, and if he stretched out his legs they would be roasted in the fire. Outside, the cold and snow and danger of becoming lost forever in the forest kept him a prisoner, as he thought himself, in this dungeon with neither lock nor key, although sometimes he did go outside for half an hour or an hour to do his devotions and be left to himself for once (for it continually galled this solitary man, as it did so many of the Black-Gowns, to live at such quarters with the objects of his labors), but when the cold had entirely numbed his knees he returned to the wigwam where the Savages hugged him happily shouting welcome, Nicanis!* to which Père Le Jeune must smile and reply as patiently as he could. Where he lay by the fire, part of him was scorched and the rest of him stayed as cold as ever, since the floor was but a few armfuls of fir-boughs spread thinly upon the snow, and the walls were ill-joined necklaces of bark wrapped around the poles so that the winter wind whistled in, and he could see the moon and stars through the smokehole, which did not perform its function well enough to keep even the Savages from rubbing their reddened eyelids and coughing day and night, so that it was well-nigh impossible for him to have any rest; and the smoke seared his throat whenever he breathed; it stung his eyes so that he wept scalding tears, although, as he said to himself, he had neither grief nor sadness in his heart. When it was especially thick, all the people inside had to place their mouths to the earth to breathe. Such tedious spans of misery he could scarcely bear. He rushed outside to the woods again (and the Savages stared after him as if he were mad), where the snow-glare dazzled his inflamed eyes, and it was so cold that tree-trunks split around him with noises like muskets, and he shivered and groaned aloud and returned to the wigwam where the Savages laughed and said welcome, Nicanis! and the dogs ran to and fro gnawing at everything, walking on people's faces and stomachs – everyone laughed to see Père Le Jeune shouting

* My well-beloved.

himself hoarse at the bad-mannered curs who sought to bestride him and nuzzle in his bark dish, until at last he gave up and covered his face, letting them scurry across him as they willed. They too craved the fire, even when it singed their fur, and their bodies cut him off from it. Then only their stinking hairy bodies gave him the least sensation of warmth, and he hugged them against him, while they snapped at him in bewilderment, and the Savages howled with laughter to see this being of so many vacillations. He listened to them, in hopes of improving his command of their elaborate language; he heard two men talking about a woman's private parts, and wrote in his journal *Their language has the foul odor of the sewers.*

All the time he kept thinking how can I make them believe?

Because it was his duty to strip the Sorcerer's soul-flock from him, he daily ridiculed the fellow's hoaxes and juggleries. So the Sorcerer hated him bitterly. Sometimes Père Le Jeune would flatter him for a space, in order to discover more of the wretched little fig-leaves of superstition with which these folk sought to cover their spiritual nakedness, and after swallowing a few such fatty morsels of words the Sorcerer would love him again and call him brother, which was for Père Le Jeune one of the worst trials.

The Sorcerer was a stout man, with powerful shoulders. His head had the proportions of an egg, an impression which he enhanced by shaving the crown of it naked except for a bristling ridge of hair which ran over the middle, like a hedge. He wore a circlet of wampum just over his eyes. Ripples of tattoo-lines and shadow veiled his gaze, so that he seemed quite mysterious to Père Le Jeune at first, indeed almost unearthly. Sometimes he wondered indeed if this being might be a GOUGOU or MANITOU, or some other incarnation of the DEVIL. But it was not long before he comprehended his buffoonery.

The name of the Sorcerer was Manitousiou, which meant *Most Famous*; sometimes they also called him *The Married Man*, for he was very puffed with pride at his wedded state, as it seemed to Père Le Jeune, and loved to be reminded of it. But pride goeth before a fall.

It was a very hard winter for the Montagnais that year. The cold was extreme, but there was not sufficient snow to trap the moose. Therefore the hunters often returned unsuccessful, even though some of them had obtained arquebuses from the time when the English were here (a fact that scarcely made Père Le Jeune easy, for with guns the Savages might prove more obstinate to govern). The hunters reported that they could see neither animal nor trace of animal in the white alleyways between the snow-crowned trees. – Be brave, Nicanis! Sometimes we do not eat for three or four days. – I am content, replied Père Le Jeune, huddled in his black cassock like a sick crow.

He was sickened by their filthy food. Their soups were black with soot and face-dirt. They ate porcupines and old moose-skins, and sometimes when he fled from the wigwam he gnawed on the tender ends of branches in his hunger. The bare trees reached up together like pillars; their branches upcurved together into an arched cathedral ceiling. In the clearings, it was sometimes very sunny when the beams of the afternoon sun danced about on the snow. He was certain that he would die of starvation, and silently said to GOD: I bless the Hand that administers my death-sentence. – Indeed, the Sorcerer's children had died two winters before, when the cold was no more severe. Now it was the turn of his wife.

Where do the dead people go? said Père Le Jeune, questioning him.

You are such an ignoramus! exclaimed the Sorcerer. You know not even that?

Tell it to me, said Père Le Jeune, a faint smile playing around his lips.

You smile; you mock me even as my dear wife is dying! shouted the Sorcerer. I think MANITOU's wife has eaten your heart from the inside, so it is all gone, like a dried-up apple! You have no respect for me!

His face was in Père Le Jeune's face. His eyes were very fierce. His breath was terrible. But Père Le Jeune refused to avert his eyes.

Where will your wife go when she dies? he repeated sternly.

Leave him in peace, Nicanis! said one of the other Savages, stroking Père Le Jeune's face as tenderly as he could, to soften the admonition. You ask too many questions.

But the Sorcerer sat rocking and rocking in his grief. Plump snowflakes lurched greyly down.

The next day the woman was worse. When they set about their daily march, the Savages were forced to carry her on a litter of crossed poles. As always, these struggles through the knee-deep snow were an agony for Père Le Jeune. The Savages mocked him somewhat because he carried no heavier burden than his own body and belongings, but in truth he had not the strength to do more. He straggled with the weakest children, watching their long, exceedingly narrow sledges swim through the snow like canoes and then vanish among the trees, and once he was so far behind that he'd completely lost the trail, and no one was with him but a little Savage child whom he did not dare leave on account of the howls that the child would make; presently he came to a fork in the trail and took what proved to be a wrong turning, for evidently the tracks he followed had been made only by hunters, not by the main party; they ended suddenly in a thicket. – By now the little boy understood that they were lost, and had begun his whimpering. – Peace, child, said Père Le

Jeune. Here, stay with my coat so that I may find you. – He set out running into the blackness and whiteness of that dreary snow-forest, trying not to hear the boy's shrieks of lonely terror behind him, and at last, after many frantic hours, he came upon the Savages, who were looking for him.

But where is Sasoumat's little son? they said in alarm. Have you left him?

No, no, said Père Le Jeune. He is waiting by my coat.

Your coat? shouted the Sorcerer. And what is this then? – He shook that article furiously in the Black-Gown's face.

Père Le Jeune was confounded. – I left him with the coat, so that we could find him more easily, and to keep him warm . . .

There was no child by this coat, said the Renegade.

The child's mother stepped forward and said to him: Nicanis, have you killed our child with your magic?

No, whispered Père Le Jeune very quietly. No, no. – He fell down in the snow and closed his eyes.

The Savages went rushing off into the woods. After a time they found the child and brought him back unharmed. Then they took Père Le Jeune in their arms and said now, Nicanis, we perceive that you are a *good* man.

There was scarcely any food that night. Père Le Jeune gnawed on an old eel-skin. He picked out a bit of cartilage from it and threw it to the dogs, but one of the Savage children was quicker than they, and snatched it into his mouth. – Truly these children were wonderfully brave. Although big round tears ran down their cheeks for hunger, they never sobbed or complained as children in his own country would have done. – At an early hour the Savages hunkered down by the fire and closed their eyes, seemingly content, but he observed them tossing and turning all night; and some opened their eyes from time to time and smoked a little tobacco, after which they immediately fell asleep again. – They pass their lives in smoke, thought Père Le Jeune sadly, and afterwards they fall into the fire. – Although he was wearied almost to sickness, he could not fall asleep, so much did the matter of the Sorcerer's wife distress him. How could he help her to save herself? When he reflected on the fact that she might die even in the hours of this cold night, it was all that he could do not to shake her awake and force her to listen. – Oh, if tomorrow she should be screaming in the blackish-red flames of Hell, and he had not woken her, how could he bear himself? – But, knowing all too well that he could accomplish nothing by proceeding in such a fashion, he lay as still as he could so as not to disturb the others, racked with grief and bitter anxiety.

He wrote in his journal: *From this journey I brought nothing except my own faults.*

He shivered; he could not get warm.

The next day they set out once more. It was very cold, which at least hardened the snow-crust somewhat so that it creaked and squeaked beneath their feet like old boards, and Père Le Jeune was able to keep up with the Savages very well because he did not break through to his knees. His hands were always cold, so that the Savages felt sorry for him and said: Nicanis, do not winter anymore with us, or you will be killed and Nicanis wondered whether that meant they would leave him behind or dispatch him with some treacherous blow, but in truth none seemed low enough for that, excepting the Sorcerer and the Renegade; indeed, every few minutes some Savage would change mittens with him; the Savages' hands were always hot. At these times he was greatly touched, and wished to thank them by teaching them something of CHRIST, but whenever he desired to speak of such things the Renegade refused to interpret for him. The Renegade had once been called Pierre-Antoine Pastedouachouan. The Recollects had taken him to France in a pious attempt to save his soul (now that the Recollects had been expelled they did not seem so evil at all). They'd even baptized him. But Pastedouachouan had turned his back upon Heaven. He was as false as Canadian diamonds, as perfidious as a Hiroquois. He had committed treason, and served the English in the absence of the French. He became addicted to brandy. Then, pressed by his brother the Sorcerer, he renounced the Faith. He had taken four or five wives together in concubinage, but they all left him, because he did not know how to hunt anymore – an appropriate punishment, visited upon him by GOD. Drunk or sober, there was nothing but wretchedness in his face, which an occasional timid desire to please rendered only the more grotesque. He was a damned soul. And he would talk neither French nor English nor Montagnais today. So Père Le Jeune was compelled to be silent, and trudged wearily along with them until he was just as chilled and weary as usual, and with each step he had to steel himself for the next. Presently they passed the children, who were always sent out early, towing little sledges of their own to accustom them to bearing burdens, and who always came in last; and the children's heads were downcast as they walked and they were chewing spruce-shoots. The adult Savages laughed and jested with them before they went on their way. A woman said: Courage, Nicanis! for like many others she ranked him with the children, and every day at about this time she remembered to jolly him.

They went on, and he fell behind, seeing their backs fade into the shadows ahead, and then they and their sledges were gone among the trees and he broke through the crust more frequently now because he was at the rear where it had already been weakened and the late afternoon sun struck it slantwise to soften it; so often he had to rest and pray to the VIRGIN for strength. When he came to the clearing where they were setting up camp, the children were already in sight behind him, and the women had cut the tree-poles and were raising them. At the edge of the clearing, the Sorcerer's wife lay silently on the snow, smoking tobacco. Père Le Jeune pitied her, knowing that she must lie there for two hours or more until shelter had been made. Still more did he pity her soul, for in a day or two, in all probability, she would die ignorant of JESUS and therefore in mortal peril of Hell.

He went over to her. Are you thirsty? he said.

She stared at him blankly. He could not yet speak the language well enough.

Water? he said. You – *drink?* – He cupped his empty hands and raised them to his lips, smiling at her.

Ah! Ah! she said, smiling. Yes, Nicanis. Water. Ah!

He went down to the brook, expecting to find a trickle beneath the ice, but it was frozen solid. With great labor he pried a rock loose from the ground and began smashing chunks of ice, which he intended to melt for her. But when he looked around all the Savages had left their wigwam-building and come to watch him.

The Renegade was beaming at him. Nicanis, they say you entertain them very much. They thank you for making them so happy.

Tell Manitousiou that his wife is thirsty, returned Père Le Jeune sharply.

Oh, her, she is all right, said the Renegade. She is dying; she wants to be no trouble. She is the one you do this for?

Père Le Jeune hated the Renegade for his apostasy so much that it made him nauseous to be near him. Instead of answering, he began to smash more ice. His hands ached with the chill.

You see, we are all the same, the Renegade said. We all do the same thing at the same time. Not like you Iron People.

He said something over his shoulder to the other Savages, and they laughed and left him. By the time that Père Le Jeune had finished gathering the ice and cleaning it, a woman had already brought a kettle of broth to a roaring boil, and someone else, a halfbreed girl with stringy hair, was bending over the Sorcerer's wife with a birchbark vessel . . .

Again he asked the Sorcerer: Tell me, Manitousiou, you who are so wise – where do the dead go?

Soothed by the praise of Nicanis, the Sorcerer said: My brother, when we die, we journey to a Country in the west, eating bark in the forests as we go. Then presently we come to the Isle of the Dead.

What a miserable existence! exclaimed Père Le Jeune ironically. You wish your wife to eat bark when she dies?

Speak not of what you do not understand, said the Sorcerer, striving not to be goaded.

Père Le Jeune turned to the others. – I tell you, we French have sailed the western seas, and never have we found any such Isle of the Dead. This man lies!

There was a silence. It was worse than the time at the porcupine feast when they caught him disposing of meat that his shrunken stomach could not hold by throwing it to the dogs. His heart pounded. He saw that his hands had become fists.

And where do *you* say the dead ones go? asked the Sorcerer's brother.

Père Le Jeune pointed to the Renegade. – Ask *him*, he said. We Black-Gowns instructed him once, though he turned against us.

The Renegade would say nothing.

Well, then, my friends, said Père Le Jeune, we know from Our LORD that when we die, if we have been good, we go into the sky to serve Him, and there to dwell in plenty forever.

Oh, so you French have sailed the skies in your ships and seen this place? said the Sorcerer's brother.

Père Le Jeune laughed. You reason well, my friend, and I shall make a note of your cleverness. But we have no need to see Heaven with our own eyes to believe. Indeed, GOD would not permit us to see it, for it is invisible to all but the pure. But we have a book which tells us these things. It is very old, and the men who wrote it were told what to write by GOD and His Angels.

And he showed them his Bible. They stroked the pages, saying such white leaves! and a woman with a round greasy face said but why were you so careless with this treasure, Nicanis – for you have permitted these strange leaves to be spoiled with marks!

Those marks are the marks of reason, my child, he said, with pity in his heart.

She looked at him in wonder. Unfortunately, however, at that moment a troop of hunters returned with a squirrel and a porcupine, and the Savages (truly they were like children or flighty birds!) rushed to embrace them.

The Sorcerer's wife was still lying in the snow, as they had not yet smoothed down the fir-boughs inside the wigwam. Her face had become very emaciated, and her lower lip hung slackly down. Sweat glistened in the wrinkles of her forehead. Bending over her with another cup of the hot broth, Père Le Jeune smiled and asked her how she did, at which she said weakly *you – crazy man, Nicanis* and her sick-breath was very foul in his face, but he would not turn away; he was determined to save her soul.

You are fortunate, he said to her; for if you believe in Him in your last hour, you will be assured of salvation; you will not live to be an apostate like the Renegade.

Working her throat, the Sorcerer's wife swallowed a little broth. It was pathetic to see how difficult it was for her to get the liquid down. – Why do you love the dead, Nicanis? she asked him.

His eyes shone. He whispered in her ear: *To make them live again!*

Every day after this, he whispered with the Sorcerer's wife, hovering over her like a crow, so that they shouted out to him to leave her alone, and then he had to do it furtively, doing small services for her and trying to uplift her to an awareness of all her sins. But she would not accept the love of CHRIST. A few days later, when he straggled into camp, she was not there.

Where is she? he asked the Renegade.

The Renegade hung his head. – Today she is hurting so bad, he said, we put her to death.

Oh cruel and unjust! cried Père Le Jeune in anguish. Do you not understand, apostate, that if you participated in this you have tried the LORD's mercy beyond endurance? As for the Sorcerer, he too is damned if he killed his wife. Convey this to him.

He no – like to hear these thing, said the Renegade.

Tell him!

The Renegade spoke to the Sorcerer very confidently and rapidly, so that Père Le Jeune had his suspicions that what he demanded was not being carried out. – The Sorcerer, however, became livid with anger, and shouted: *Attimonai oukhimau!* and Père Le Jeune asked the Renegade what does he say? and the Renegade looked him full in the face and told him he say, you are a Captain of the Dogs.

The next day they ventured confidently out upon the ice of the Fleuve Saint-Laurent where the wind howled and made them stagger as they went, for there were no trees to break its force. Snow had fallen and formed a thick crust for them to walk upon; even so, he found every step an agony of cold. This must be very similar to the Ninth Circle of Dante's Hell, he said to himself, remembering from his reading the heads barely protruding from the ice so that LUCIFER could use them for stepping-stones, and the dark freezing blasts that swept that place. – They camped on an island of a thousand white geese that was covered with cedars and pines, and later they went to the Isle of Dyes, where they got some red roots for their superstitious rituals. How it pained him to see them serving such idle follies! – But he held his tongue. – As if to punish them, a storm sprang up, before they could leave the island, and they were forced to remain there for several days, in circumstances of great hunger and misery. Trees came crashing down, like women dying ecstatic with the Cross upraised. The snow came down so thickly that Père Le Jeune could scarcely compel himself to believe in the existence of the trees that encircled the wigwam at a distance of thirty paces in any direction; they were forced to close up the smokehole, and in consequence the hearth-fumes were worse than ever. The walls sagged inward with the weight of the snow, and the Savage who went to brush them free had first to clear away snow by the armload before he could open the door-flap. And it was cold, very painfully cold. Nonetheless they continued cheerful (except when they were drunk, as he reminded himself, for he'd seen how wild they became when they drank up his brandy); truly it was a shame and a wonder to him to see how superior their patience was to that of Christians. They simply laughed when misfortunes happened.

He thought suddenly of the fate of the Sorcerer's wife. His heart was as dun and nondescript as a leather casket.

There was nothing to eat that night, and he said to them: If you lived in one place, and tilled the soil like the Frenchmen at Québec, you would not be so hungry.

But you are *like* us, said the Sorcerer; you Iron People go far, far. That is why the English came, because you forsook your farms and went hunting across the sea.

In vain he tried to make them understand that the English had not come because the French had left; rather, the French had departed because they had been forced to do so by the English. The Savages refused to grasp this point, and eventually it occurred to him that that was well, for why should they be reminded of the limits of French power? So he changed his tack and tried again, saying: If you settle and clear the land, I shall help you build warm houses and grow as much corn as you can eat.

But at this they only shook their heads at his folly, saying that they would rot if they stayed in one place.

That night a woman went out and then came running into the wigwam screaming *MANITOU! MANITOU!* at which the other Savages were terribly frightened and scarcely dared to breathe. Père Le Jeune fancied he could hear their hearts pounding around him in the smoky darkness.

What is *MANITOU?* he said.

Evil Power, very evil, they whispered fearfully. Keep still, Nicanis!

He could see the whites of their eyes shining fearfully.

Père Le Jeune arose and went out, as they watched him dumbfounded. He strode a little way into the forest and cried out: Come here, you MANITOU! – He waited. There was only silence. In truth he was terrified, for surely this continent, being so largely unsettled, must have its share of wild DEVILS, of which he supposed that this MANITOU was one – but CHRIST would aid him if He saw fit.

He walked further into the snowy alleys between trees, shivering.

MANITOU! he shouted.

Again there was no answer.

He struggled up steep hills slick with ice beneath the carpet of leaves; he clung to the trees and searched for little protrusions of moss to step on. Dark snowflakes flickered in the sky-glare.

It was one of those winter nights so dark that the stars appeared to be unspeakably lonely and far away, and the blackness had taken possession of the trees and the spaces in between them, so that he could not even see the snow beneath his feet. It was as if he stood suspended in the night sky, lost beyond the sight of GOD. Never before had he realized how nourishing was the radiance of the founts and tabernacles and consecrated graves of Europe. Even in the Schwarzwald of Germany, where there were reputed to be kobolds and hobgoblins, a man must know that after traversing the eerie mountains he'd come at last to a village, or at the very least a little inn where a lantern was burning . . . He strode on, and the snow crunched beneath his feet. It was very cold. Presently he spied a shooting star, and then another. Now a cold moonbeam grazed the boughs ahead, and he began to make out the faint and infinitely delicate shapes of spruces, like whitish clouds of fog to which from habit he imparted greenness, to make them more familiar; and he struggled through a thicket of spruce saplings whose needles caught him in the face and shivered snow upon his shoulders. Now the moonlight was brighter again, and he could see around him.

He stopped and shouted: Come and fight with me, MANITOU!

But MANITOU would not answer.

In triumph he turned back, and followed his own tracks without incident to the Savage camp. And he was exultant, and said to himself: *this* battle, at least, I won. (But for a moment he could not stop himself from trembling.)

When he entered the wigwam, he saw that the Savages were amazed with his courage. – Are you not afraid of MANITOU? they said.

Père Le Jeune laughed grimly. – Rather does He fear me, he replied, for He fears all who believe in GOD.

Then it seemed to him that they were even more astonished than before, and wished that they could understand him better. So he was pleased with what had been accomplished, until a little later he noticed that they were whispering and looking at him out of the corners of their eyes, and presently one of them threw several eels on the fire.

Why do you waste this food? he said.

Are you so ignorant, Nicanis? they exclaimed. Why, to feed MANITOU!

Indian sign for MANITOU

Then he was very wrathful and upbraided them for their lack of faith and understanding, until one of them said *Cou ouaboucho ouichtoui* at which they all laughed, and he asked the Renegade what they had said, and the fellow grinned and replied: They say, he is bearded like a hare.

When the weather cleared, they went on to the next island, which was called *Ca Pocoucachtechokhi Cachagou Achiganikhi, Ca Pakhitaouananiouikhi* – what that meant he never learned, and the place was like its name, being nothing but a big barren rock, from which they drank dirty bog-water to satisfy their thirst. He awed them with his compass, which he used to predict the direction of the rising and setting sun; when he asked them how they thought it was that he knew such things, they consulted among themselves and the Sorcerer nodded many times, so that he hoped and expected them to say it is because of your CHRIST! – but in the end they only replied, shrugging, clearly you are a very intelligent man, Nicanis.

Consolation

On his return to the house of the Black-Gowns, which was called Notre-Dame-des-Anges, Père Le Jeune wrote for the *Jesuit Relations* a précis of his experiences, adding: *I wanted to describe this journey, to show Your Reverence the great hardships that must be endured in following the Savages; but I entreat, for the last time, those who have any desire to help them, not to be frightened; not only because GOD makes Himself more powerfully felt in our time of need . . . but also because it will no longer be necessary to make these sojourns when we shall know their languages and reduce them to rules.*

The Dream of the Iron People

1634

> But Ignatius Loyola . . . was got neere his chair, a subtile fellow, and so imbued with the DEVILL, that he was able to tempt; and not onely that, but (as they say) even to possesse the DIVELL . . .
>
> JOHN DONNE, *Ignatius His Conclave* (1611)

And yet Père Le Jeune had at least made one potential convert in his wanderings, for on that isle called *Ca Pocoucachtechokhi Cachagou Achiganikhi, Ca Pakhitaouananiouikhi*, when once again the Renegade refused to translate his explanations of Holy Doctrine for the Savages (it was the day after he had put MANITOU to flight), he'd asked to have another interpreter, at which the Renegade only laughed and said that there were no others who spoke the language of the Iron People – did the Black-Gown suppose that very many could be bothered to learn *that* jabber? – So saying, he smiled with fiery eyes. – How this lost soul hates me! thought Père Le Jeune in horror. But when he persisted in his demand, the Renegade seemed to pity him and pointed out a girl who sat across the fire, rocking herself, with her hands clasped in her lap. – This Captain of the Muskrats, he want to *fuck* you, you goddamn Indian girl! shouted the Renegade, at which the Savages laughed. An old woman, toothless as a hen, dug Nicanis in the side with her elbow, shrieking with mirth until the tears streamed from her smoke-swollen eyes. – He stared ahead of him stonily; so too did the girl, whose eyes were round as marbles. How strange it is that when two people who mean no harm to each other are jeered at as if they are in some indecent relation, they must look through each other like ghosts! But that is the rule. – She was of Souriquois origin, went on the Renegade (who never meant any harm with his jokes), but had recently married into the tribe. That was her husband there, that one-eyed man who now pulled her backward and whispered something in her ear, until she pushed him away. He'd stopped the way to the Huron last year with his threats. And her, they called her Born Underwater. Apparently she was a half-breed, her mother having had a connection with some Frenchman, in the usual licentious fashion of these Savages. These facts excited Père Le Jeune's interest, and he gazed at her from across the fire. – Indeed he'd seen her every day, but had never taken note of her, she being a dirty face among many. Then, too, she rarely said anything. – Had she been the one who'd sometimes brought broth to the Sorcerer's wife? When he studied her (she sat gazing downward, nervously twisting a spruce-twig in her fingers), he was conscious of something peculiar. What it was he could not say at first, but if she had been a French girl he would have said that she was shy. Her face definitely had something French about it; beneath the dirt it was creamier than those of her companions, and her eyebrows . . . No, he was mistaken. Yet he cherished goodwill toward her until the next morning when, overcoming his own shyness, he forced himself to speak to her of the state of her soul; the impression she gave him then was one of unyielding pride and self-sufficiency, so that at once he despaired of her and said to himself: JESUS will not touch her. Her eyes, which had seen lakes and mountains, met his easily. He said to himself: This girl has little modesty, and must be chastised for her own benefit. – Immediately he felt that he had been unkind in his thoughts, and reminded himself that after all her curiosity was something to be used for GOD's glory so that souls might be harvested like wild strawberries warm and heavy in the clearings of summer. That aside, she was of course not suitable for interpreting, for her manners were hardly less galling to him than the Renegade's, and she was also married (as the Savages understood marriage), so there was nothing for it but to redouble his pains to gain fluency in the Montagnais language. One-Eye, her husband, snickered as he looked at him, One-Eye puffing tobacco like a lord . . .

It was not many days after this, however, that Born Underwater, finding the Black-Gown kneeling in the forest, approached in silence and squatted watching him until, kissing his Cross, he looked up and saw her. It had been common at first for the Savages to watch him at his devotions, but they quickly wearied of that, and Père Le Jeune had never encouraged them, relishing such few opportunities for solitude as he could have. Finding the young woman's gaze upon him, he raised himself as graciously as he could and said: Well met, child! And do you seek insight into the Mysteries? – For he had lately come to know that of all the Savages in this band, she spoke the best French, as the Renegade had admitted; so that it eased him now to be with her. What a relief it was not to have to stutter those strange words!

I know about the Exercises, Père, said Born Underwater, pulling her blanket tighter about her shoulders. But when you make them, do you see ahead or behind?

Père Le Jeune could not hide his surprise. – So you do know somewhat of us, he said.

My mother knew the Black-Gowns, she said. – She told me about you.

As Père Le Jeune watched her, she scooped a handful of snow into her mouth and sucked on it with satisfaction. – The day always ends with JESUS for you, doesn't it? she said.

Always.

Are you going home someday? I remember when the other Black-Gowns left us –

Not unless I am ordered.

No one is waiting for you? You have no father, no wife, no brother?

He shook his head.

No one waits for me, either, Born Underwater said. I have a husband here, but he doesn't turn my heart from anything.

These words chilled him. – JESUS is waiting for you, he said. He will always wait for you.

She laughed. – I don't want to die yet!

Thinking himself mocked again, he made no reply.

Do you see ahead or behind? she asked again, abruptly.

I see ahead, he replied, to the Kingdom that awaits all who strive to be worthy of Him.

She said nothing, so after a moment he added: You must come to Kebec to be more thoroughly instructed.

Still she said nothing.

We will feed you corn and prunes.

She smiled. – Then I will come, she said. In the spring.

Lapses

Truth to tell, Père Le Jeune put so little faith in the promises of the Souriquois girl (although it was remarkable, indeed, that she spoke French like a civilized person) that he had almost forgotten her when he returned to Notre-Dame-des-Anges. This should not seem strange to anyone who reflects upon the miseries and reverses that he had suffered among the Montagnais. Truly, as he had written in the *Jesuit Relations*, he brought nothing with him from that sojourn excepting his own faults. He had little reason to remember anything or anyone from that winter, except, with a pain that never dulled, the unholy death of the Sorcerer's wife. – Then, too, since the girl was Souriquois, little was to be gained by instructing her. She'd been cast out by her people, as it seemed, and in any event they were nomads like the Montagnais (although, as he freely admitted, they too were becoming dependent on the French for food and tobacco as they devoted increasing effort to the beaver trade. Already Jesuits in Acadia were making progress in the saving of souls. But the victory was not yet, not yet.) So in the end he said nothing concerning her to the other priests.

Now again it was the spring month of Avril, and the Black-Gowns prayed most earnestly for GOD's favor, hoping that summer would find Pères Brébeuf, Davost and Daniel embarked upon their Huron Mission. The Fleuve Saint-Laurent foamed cocoa-colored, bearing its harvest of icebergs to the Acadian Sea. – Still Père Le Jeune could not stop seeing nightmare scenes of filth and lewdness and hostility among the Montagnais whenever he closed his eyes, as if the DEVIL had painted them on the inside of his lids to torment him. Now the Renegade's face flashed before him; now the faces of hungry Savage children grimaced in the smoke and seemed to spin. He saw unbridled copulations; he saw the Sorcerer's painted face, hideously distorted in an effort to frighten him into silence; that was even worse than the time the Sorcerer had drummed unceasingly for three days so that sleep was impossible. Père Le Jeune rejoiced exceedingly to have the French language always in his ears again, to see the little chapel, to eat a sufficiency of food, and yet his memories of his humiliations refused to crumble into sand. He bore the Savages no grudge, but those unholy images hovered stiflingly about him like a veil of sickness. Indeed, he grew still thinner (when he came home, his fellow priests had already marveled to see how slender and feeble he was) and suffered much from cachectic spasms. At last he saw fit to privately ask the advice of Père Massé, who after all had been longest in Canada's service. Above all he did not want to ask his favorite protégé, Père Brébeuf, whose compassion would taste rather more sour than the Sorcerer's scorn.

My dear Père Useful, he said to the old man when they were alone in the chapel, when you were in Acadia with Biard, did Savages come into your dreams?

Always.

And did they torment you?

There it was different, replied Père Massé. Here in Kebec the unwillingness of the Savages to be instructed mortifies us all. But in Port-Royal, anything French was still a novelty, be it beads or JESUS. They loved us, most of them – in the first two years, at least. Later that hothead Charles Biencourt turned them against us. But they continued to hold the French in affection. Of course many of our countrymen did little to deserve that love. I remember a Souriquois woman who was violated by young Gravé du Pont himself, and Père Biard felt obliged to intercede . . .

Hearing this, Père Le Jeune remembered Born Underwater. Of course she was unlikely to have had any connection with the incident that Père Massé related; it was more the word "Souriquois" that reminded him of her, and the fact that Père Massé might have seen her as an infant, and perhaps even baptized her. So the whole story came out, and Père Massé listened, nodding his head.

Eh, Paul, that is very interesting, he said. The Souriquois language was very difficult for me, and I never mastered it. You say that she speaks perfect French! How odd! I cannot say that I remember her. Born Underwater, however, that is a strange name. I wonder what that would be in Souriquois? And she has left her people, has she, to wander in another sort of darkness? I pity her soul.

After this, the conversation turned more directly upon Père Le Jeune's oppressive visions, and the other listened patiently, giving him much valuable advice as to how best to sleep in order to avoid these incubi, what foods might be best, and the like. – And if you will forgive my presumptuousness to a Superior, he said softly, might I recommend that you make a Contemplation of Saint Ignatius in the form of the Exercises?

Père Le Jeune smiled gratefully. – Thank you, Père Useful, he said. I will try it. My heart is eased already

So he went and knelt in the chapel at his first opportunity, and his soul dove into the Stream of Time, where it was night and the trees were weird in the fog, the forest-ridge black on either side; above, the sky was a ragged white, then black in place of stars. That was the First Prelude. (He was not far upstream of Tekakwitha's grave, but he would never know that while he lived because, as he would have explained to Born Underwater if he had comprehended her, the Black-Gowns only swam against the current; they saw-behind.) He swam into dawn and his mind was warmed as he swam into a summer haze so rich and luxurious that he could not even see the treetops;

the air was tree-green and smelled of spruces. That was the Second Prelude. What did it say in the Book of Kings? *I have digged and drunk strange waters.* Now he made the Third Prelude, diving deep into the water, holding his breath, praying to see Ignatius, stroking energetically toward the Waterfalls and Rapids, paying no heed to the granite boulders that he grazed in his progress; and he opened his eyes beneath the water and saw the Church of Saint Peter shining gold and green on the sandy bottom and then suddenly the water became clouded and agitated and when he raised his face to learn what was coming toward him he saw GOUGOU the Water-Monster with bloody bubbles issuing from his parrot-beak and his face was the Sorcerer's painted face and he had as many arms as a jellyfish; they were hairy, translucent; Père Le Jeune could see the pulsing veins of poison in them, and GOUGOU was coming closer and closer and he opened his beak and Père Le Jeune could see a multitude of dark arches inside; clasping his hands into a steeple ahead of him, he swam into the maw, which was welcoming like the Church, so that he pressed on down that ringed gullet without any fear, searching for the marble Saint in a sky-blue archway, his Ignatius (there he was!), whose ascetic face, with its dark beard and moustache, his dark eyes, could sometimes smile, and that was the First and Only Point . . .

After this, Père Le Jeune was cured of his devil's visions. He threw himself into his tasks, and the Souriquois girl was forgotten again.

Lopping the Branches

She, however, had scarcely forgotten him. Her meeting with him had stained her with a feeling which was neither admiration nor pity, but something quite unnameable. So she brooded on his words. But Nicanis had also mentioned food. In the spring the Innuat began to do better at their hunting, and necessity decreased; yet perversely her curiosity to try his prunes grew all the greater. And there was another reason which a dream had revealed to her – a secret reason which we shall see.

Get tobacco from them! her husband whispered greedily. Get food; get peas and prunes! I will come with you. – No, I will stay and rest. If you do not bring back food, I will beat you.

She set out southeast through the forest, striding alertly across its white snow-clearings, searching for Grandfather SUN then, stroking the north-side moss of trees to guide her when she did not find Him, continuing indifferently, no matter whether her way might be clothed in fog, snow or yellow grass. She parted weeping curtains of spruce. She stood at the edge of the Hébert family's pasture. – She'd once met a woman by name Amiskoueian, who had been carried off by the Iron People, and made to serve their Sagamore, Champlain, with two other girls – yet not exactly as his wives, for he never would touch them in that way, nor would he speak of giving them children. He kept them enclosed within his palisadoes; he was very jealous of them. He commanded them to call him Father. He named them with his own names: she'd been called Foy, which in the language of the Iron People signifies loyalty or belief in their ways. This name terrified Amiskoueian, as she could not approve of all they did and did not want to. Champlain had no meat or other good food to give them. Amiskoueian said that she knew him to have a good heart, for he gave her presents. Yet she did not want to spend her life inside his house, where she could scarcely see forest or river. Even the SUN was seen only through a square hole in the wall, as if He were something not to be approached. So Born Underwater was a little afraid. – Now she was at Kebec and it was sunny, but she shivered. She saw Champlain's Palace gloating at the edge of the cliff, in anticipation of that time when the city had itself become a sort of forest whose tree-crowns were steeples and hollowed belfries, whose trunks were narrow stone fronts of houses, whose leaves were windows . . . although of course there were still real trees to be seen through the belfries and beyond the angular ramps and ridges of roofs; they still overshadowed the chimneys of Kebec, which were not yet moss-grown. For a moment, oddly enough, she had a strange idea of going to Champlain and pretending to be Amiskoueian, so that he would feed her forever; surely Champlain must be searching for young women to replace the ones that he had lost. She giggled and dismissed Champlain –

She came to the house called Notre-Dame-des-Anges. Should she tell them that Nicanis had invited her? Born Underwater felt very shy. She walked past. Then she retraced her steps and went to the door.

Père Daniel and Père Brébeuf were away at Three Rivers, but Père Davost was there. He reminded her of a moose, with his downcurving nose.

I have come to see Nicanis, she said. And you, Père, do you also make the Exercises?

Not only did the question show considerable intelligence about matters esoteric, but (what was more remarkable still) perfect French came from her lips! He stared at her, as astonished as if she had danced the *farandole*. – Our Superior is away at present, he replied. May I be of service to you?

She decided that he was good.

I shall wait for him, she said in a low voice.

Père Davost stood perplexed. There she was, a squaw or Savagess like any other. She was dressed in the fashion of a Montagnaise: – *viz.*, in a long skirt of French manufacture, with a hooded cloak over it which had been cut from a French blanket. Her eyes were black; her hair glistened with grease; her blankets stank of sweat. He could not tell who she was or what she wanted.

Come in, he said finally. Have something to eat.

He went into the refectory and spoke with Père Massé. Sighing, the old priest blew on his hands and arose, while the other followed him nervously.

What is your name, daughter? he said gently.

In your tongue I am called Born Underwater, she replied.

(Coming from her mouth, the French language became something beautiful and ominous like the shadow-stripes in an army of ferns.)

He stood blinking. If Père Le Jeune had not told him her story, would he have remembered her? It is hard to say. As it was he *did* remember, for while he had little facility with Savage words he rarely forgot a Savage face. Now as he looked upon her there came to him a memory almost twenty years old of Born Swimming's wigwam in Acadia, with her husband nervously clenching his fists, unwilling to interfere; of Born Swimming's eyes glinting with anger; the little boy (what was his name?) slyly holding out a hand, hoping that the Black-Gowns would feed him something or give him something in that smoky darkness, while Père Biard spoke fiercely on; and best of all he recollected the pale, mottled infant's face, whose large eyes saw him uncomprehending . . .

Well, child, it gladdens my heart to see you grown up after so many years, said Père Massé. You cannot remember it, but I saw you in your mother's wigwam. What a serene little countenance you had; what big eyes! You scarcely ever cried, they said. – Yet I am grieved that you have not yet washed away your sins in the Blood of the LAMB. Your mother, did she die a pagan?

Now in truth Born Underwater had not always traveled a smooth road together with her mother. Yet now, when this stranger questioned her, she remembered how Born Swimming had tied her sleeves on for her, had chewed her meat for her, had pierced her ears and hung them with wampum strings . . .

I am proud to be her daughter, she said.

Père Massé accepted the rebuke with a weary grimace. – You look hungry, he said. Would you like more pea soup?

She nodded.

The Superior is administering the Sacraments to a dying woman, he said. You cannot sleep in this house, as it is against our rules to permit women to do so except in extreme cases. But it may be that I can find lodging for you with one of our pious French families.

I will sleep outside, she said. I love the forest.

It is cold.

Not to me.

He could not comprehend her. He'd thought she wanted his charity.

Very well, he said.

When she had finished her second portion of soup (with which she seemed much pleased), he nodded to Père Davost, who began to instruct her in the Faith. She seemed to listen with an open spirit that pleased both the Black-Gowns well.

Meanwhile she was looking about her inside the strange house. It made her afraid.

What do you do here? she cried suddenly. Why are you Black-Gowns in this Country?

What do we do indeed? said old Père Massé, pretending to reflect and confer with Père Davost. Shall we say to her what Brébeuf always says? – Eh, young lady, our profession is to make holocausts . . .

That night she stood among the trees, watching the glare and torches and fires of Kebec on its little hill, illuminating the screen of trees so that they glittered silver in the snowy night. A long black tongue of shadow lapped across the snowy plain and touched her. Above, the great black cliff of Kebec rose solid in the grey night.

On the following morning she returned at an early hour to speak with the Superior. As soon as he saw her, his tormenting visions flocked back into his mind with a black screech, settling upon the rotten corpse of that past winter like Born Underwater herself, sprawled so immodestly in the wigwam, puffing her pipe of tobacco as greedily as the rest –

He flinched.

I tell you, I have no time for you today! he cried testily. We are preparing a great Mission to take the Word of GOD to the Huron Savages once again; I –

Smiling sarcastically, she strode out of his house.

So this was how the Black-Gowns were! Her mother had spoken truly.

Yet as soon as she was in the forest again, hot tears spilled down her cheeks.

Gall and Vinegar

It was in this Year of Our LORD 1634 that the Montagnais, as is told in the *Jesuit Relations*, first began to use iron in their magic rituals. The Sorcerer had a knife which he had stolen from Père Le Jeune. Beating his drum for days to the number of two hands, shouting and crying and chanting his songs, he consulted the Power of Those who made the light. Now he took the iron blade and held it up; stabbing the air with it, he killed a rival Sorcerer a hundred miles away. It was summer. Iron Power rushed past spruce-points like raccoons' tails; it shot across lakes and fleuves to the darker places where trees burst up, waving like scalp-locks; it swooped down on the Montagnais of the Porcupine Nation who camped where the white trunks of birches glowed in green obscurity. – The Porcupine Sorcerer leaped up, shook his head from side to side, and fell dead. His wife began to scream shrilly.

Yes, Nicanis has Power, he said to himself, but he is a rude and wicked man. I have just as much Power as he. Can *he* do this?

But then a gloomy thought struck him, for he remembered that Nicanis could swallow dying souls. He cursed Nicanis; he knew what Nicanis had done to his wife –

The Plan

In the refectory, the three who hoped to embark upon their apostleship at last sat listening to their Superior. The instructions that he now gave took full cognizance of what had been learned by his defeated rivals, the Recollects.

You will work with the traders, not against them, said Père Le Jeune. In these days the beaver trade is the foundation of the Church.

Yes, Père Superior, said Père Brébeuf. (The cords of his neck stood out with tension.) – Père Davost nodded; Père Daniel looked at the floor.

We see no reason to frenchify these Savages as the Recollects sought to do, said Père Le Jeune. We believe it better to protect them from our people. Ah, it is terrible; there are so many bad Frenchmen! Those interpreters, for instance . . . I trust you agree, Jean?

When I lived among the Huron I found them very earnest and eager to please, the other replied. They are not given to many sins. Indeed, it is my hope that we may bring them to the exaltations and fervent raptures of the early Christians.

The other two said nothing.

Good. And we feel that you should seek to convert communities instead of individuals, said the Superior. – The True Faith cannot be practiced in isolation, except in rare cases. – (Here the Jesuits smiled at each other. That was their secret pride.) – It must happen quickly when it happens, and it must sweep in many souls. In short, it must be like an epidemic.

You may count on us to do our duty, said Brébeuf.

An Extract from the Huron Relation of 1649

In 1634, while Père Brébeuf was making the Spiritual Exercises of Saint Ignatius, Our LORD appeared crowned with thorns and said to him: You will henceforth have the unction of the HOLY GHOST in your words.

The Companions

1634

Nobody was present to witness her steadily increasing mortifications and sacrifices.

FRANCIS X. WEISER, SJ, *Kateri Tekakwitha* (1972)

There were not so many Huron at Three Rivers this year as last. The Montagnais Savages said that the great epidemic had begun its inroads in their Tribes and Nations. The Sieur de Champlain, however, heard otherwise from his spies, whose tales he trusted not to be embroideries. These assured him that the Huron had sustained a grave defeat at the hands of that Hiroquois Nation called *Sonontrerrhonons*.* Many warriors had been captured, said the spies, even including the convert Louys Amantacha – hearing which, Champlain grieved, and so did the Black-Gowns, for this would hinder the spread of the Faith: Amantacha had been very willing. So the Huron were timid about venturing to the Fleuve Saint-Laurent this summer; the Yroquois lurked there. – But as I, William the Blind, have already told in brief, steps had been taken to guard against them: a settlement would be raised at Three Rivers! Champlain had guaranteed it.

It happened in this wise: A Montaignez Captain, by name Capitanal, came to Kebec and said: How happy we would be if you Iron People built a fort at Trois-Rivières to protect us! – to which importunity Champlain listened with indulgence, thinking: How great is GOD, that He permits me the power to grant the request of this simple man! – Just as we never talk about

* Seneca.

Membertou anymore in this Dream, since he has served our turn and is dead, so Champlain did not give Membertou much thought in those days; yet I fancy he saw Capitanal in Membertou's image for a moment; they were both clowns, beggars, benighted children whom one must help. It hadn't hurt to give Membertou guns; it wouldn't hurt to give Capitanal Trois-Rivières, especially since by establishing an outpost there we'd really be *taking* Trois-Rivières . . . – Besides, we needed a way to encourage the Huron to trade. We were more dependent on their beaver-peltries than ever. And if we could awe the Yroquois in the process . . .

I shall be extraordinarily displeased, however, said the Sieur de Champlain, if it comes to my ears that any of you have dared to trade with our mutual enemies the English.

The English? said Capitanal in a tone of bewilderment. But you are masters here now! Even the Black-Gowns have returned again –

Play not the fool with me. You know as well as I that the English lurk at Tadoussac.

I am only a poor little animal, crawling about on the ground. (Thus Capitanal.) You Iron People are the great of the world, who make all tremble. I do not know how I dare talk before such great Captains . . .

So the Savage went on for some time in this pleasingly humble wise, and Champlain's rancor was softened. Sucking in his wizened cheeks, as though he were draining the utmost essence from a sour plum, he sent his glance into Capitanal's heart, at which the Savage pulled his blanket tighter about his shoulders (yes, these Montaignez are afraid of me at last!) and he said: But you yourself sent an embassy to the English, did you not? I forgive you fully and freely, for you are but a Savage, unused to anything save liberty, but I must hear the truth from you now.

It was the Sieur de Caën, replied Capitanal slowly, who believed that I had sent beaver-skins to the foreigners. I sent to those quarters a few moose-skins – not in trade, Champlain, but to cut off the arms of our enemies. You know that the Hiroquois have long arms! If I had not cut them, we should have been grasped and taken by them long ago.

You know that I shall always protect you from the Hiroquois, replied Champlain. Your father fell at my side fighting them. I shall always fight them until they sue for peace. They are no match for my cannons. Have I not won two victories against them?

At this Capitanal was hard beset not to smile, for these victories of which Champlain was so proud were now stale, being twenty-three winters old! *Hé hé hé* – old Champlain was feeble now; his bones were almost dry!

You tell us that the Iron People love us, he said smoothly. We know it well, and would lie if we said the contrary.

Champlain leaned forward. – So you will not go to the English anymore?

The Savage dropped his eyes. – I shall tell my people that they must not go there, he said.

Now I am well disposed toward you for these words, Capitanal. If you continue down the road that you have begun, I shall give you many presents.

Yes, continued the other, I shall tell my young men not to go there, to those English who are your enemies. I promise you that neither I myself nor they who have any sense will do that. But if there is some young man who leaps over there without being seen, I know not what I can do. You can do everything, Champlain – you and your Iron People! Put your boats in the way and capture the beaver-skins of those who attempt to go.

So said that Savage Captain, puffing on his pipe to make clouds as mild as lambs; but Champlain's face darkened as he heard the familiar melody of insolence beneath the pianissimo, and he gripped the arms of his chair . . .

Now my eyes are opened, said he. Now I see, Capitanal, that you are no better than any of your Montagnais, who threaten when they cannot scheme and wheedle.

Now my eyes also are opened, replied the Savage, with fiercely glittering eyes. You say that we must be heedful of what we do. Grasp us by the arm, like the Hiroquois, and we shudder; seize us afterward by the heart, and the whole body trembles. No, we do not want to go to the English . . .

At this, seeing his determination, and recollecting the continued weakness of his own position in Canada, Champlain temporized, sacrificing prunes and kettles to the cause of amity, until all was smoothed over – for these Savages were like infants; easy enough to coax them from their sulks – (Eh, but it was foul that the English had sold them arquebuses; already they'd become redoubtable musketeers . . .) So they agreed together to establish a post of Frenchmen at Three Rivers, as the Roy would doubtless commend –

On the first of Juillet, not long after the elder unfolded its leaves, Pères Brébeuf and Daniel left in a shallop for that place. Père Davost followed three days later in company with Monsieur du Plessis, the General of the French fleet. Scarcely any of the Huron Savages had appeared (although it was well into their season); so the Black-Gowns passed the long and sunny days in praying, ministering to the needs of the French, and listening to the buzzing flies. Frenchmen were spading the land, chopping at it with mattocks. The hats they wore were like mushroom caps. Monsieur le Général strutted about, thinking: When Champlain dies I'll surely inherit his position. Three Rivers will become the glory of the world!

One morning the Renegade came to them, hanging his head shyly, and said: The Huron bad this year, very little, very small. Bad Irocois kill them, many many. Us, too.

Eh bien, said Monsieur the General from the side of his mouth, this is a good year to begin our settlement here, while the Savages are weak.

At long last a few of them came – eleven canoes only. Again the Algoumequins persuaded them against transporting any Frenchmen to their Country, but Monsieur the General called a Council and harangued them. He swore to the Algoumequins that he would never jilt them in the trade (which he meant to do), that he'd treat with them and the Huron equally (which was true; he hoped someday to run them *both* out!), that any year now Monsieur de Champlain would lead them all to victory against the Iroquois – and in the end Monsieur the General was successful, not only for his hollow-chested promises, but also on account of the soft word-blankets and fair red nightcaps of words with which he clothed them: sugar makes any jelly sweeter. And Swiss guards paced behind him, armed to the teeth. That made its own impression, but also led directly to the next difficulty, which was that the Huron craved arquebuses, muskets and other guns, these being the only iron things now denied them; if they could not have those, their Captains said, they wished to have as guests among them stout French soldiers to fight the Hiroquois, not Black-Gowns who would not kill –

The Black-Gowns retired into the forest to pray and rest, and Père Brébeuf promised twenty masses to Saint Joseph if GOD would help them. Immediately a Savage came, and said in the Huron tongue: – My brother, I am called Petit Pré. I have tobacco in my canoe; I will give it to you. Give me iron and beads, for I am sick with craving for those things. Then I shall take one Frenchman.

I must speak with my brothers, said Père Brébeuf gravely. His blood leaped with joy.

The Savage looked him in the face. What do you wish to do in my Country?

We wish to establish a house dedicated to Saint Joseph. There we shall bring your people the laws of GOD and CHRIST.

It is well, you who are called *Charcoal*, said Petit Pré. Then we shall know how to mend the magic kettles. They fall apart more quickly now than formerly; I think you do not work so hard to make them.

As you say, said Père Brébeuf wearily. The worldly desires of this man sickened him.

He went to Monsieur du Plessis and reported what the Huron had said. At once the assembled Frenchmen arranged to trade all this man's tobacco, and because no one else had beads Monsieur du Plessis himself gave them, the good kind, made from pure French porcelain; the Savages already knew enough to lick it, to insure that the colors were true.

Now other Huron Savages entered the game. They rearranged the French goods in their canoes; they replaced this man by that man; they considered well, each speaking in turn. Monsieur du Plessis called them to a feast of Three Big Kettles, dilating on the goodness of the Black-Gowns; Captain Merveille (who was wonderfully pious) gave them all tin whistles.

In the end it was agreed. They'd take Père Brébeuf, Père Daniel, and a young Frenchman named Le Baron; Le Baron had a gun . . . Père Davost was to follow later, if they should find room. They'd have to leave behind all their little baggages, excepting the ornaments for their Altar, trusting for the rest (as they said to one another) in the providence of Our LORD. – To Huronia they'd bring only the processional Cross of silver, with JESUS shining on it as He held up a little babe; and crowned heads were pointing from it. In Père Daniel's canoe they stowed the silver candlesticks that said 𝔐.𝔈. for Mission Étranger.* They packed the ciborium in its many pieces like shiny bones . . .

Monsieur du Plessis honored each Black-Gown with a cannonade, at which the Savages, believing that it honored *them*, were mightily pleased. As they passed by his ship, Monsieur the General directed his men to throw a few handfuls of dried prunes into their canoes (which curved like Richelieu's upturned moustaches) –

The Stream of Time 1634

So they left behind them that broad tree-greened rock of Kebec. Their canoes drifted apart. For a little while they followed the Fleuve Saint-Laurent, which the Savages called *the Road That Walks*. But we know it, as I have said, as the Stream of Time, which is of course the name for all rivers. – So many people now have followed it: Père Biard who swam against its current with such

* "Foreign mission."

admirable doggedness, Père Le Jeune who trod water, Père Brébeuf who ascended it to its source, Born Swimming and Père Nicolas who were drowned by it, Amantacha who ran past it, Born Underwater who let herself be carried down it, Champlain who sounded it, Poutrincourt who pretended to himself that he sounded it, Pontgravé who stationed himself by the bank, catching fish no matter which way they swam, GOUGOU Who dwelt at the bottom of it, JESUS Who sanctified it; – did any one of them understand that there was no need to make the Exercises because the Exercises made themselves willy-nilly, that every paddle-stroke, every breath and cough, every act was an Exercise? – Eh, of course CHRIST and GOUGOU understood. – And Père Brébeuf? – The River of the Hiroquois was at his left hand; on the right, ever so many delightful situations for unborn towns . . . so Champlain always said. There were also hordes of fishes in the Fleuve, including the jagged-toothed monsters called sturgeons. In their separate canoes, the Black-Gowns took separate delights. Continually, to give him strength, Père Daniel repeated the most holy Rosario. The headdresses of his companions, the turning vowels of their language, the canoe and most of all the Fleuve itself combined novelty with familiarity in pleasing proportion: as yet the loneliness had not struck him. But presently they took him on other river-ways, for fear of the Hiroquois, and then it slithered into his heart, creeping through the chinks in his repose. (Every soul is a battleground until the very last sigh.) Now the suffering that he had sought was being granted him. His heart pounded with hopes and dreads as numerous as the blackflies that shimmered about him. With pursed mouth and narrowed eyes, he clasped his hands in prayer. (By now he had a weatherbeaten forehead, wrinkled cheeks.) The Savages were surly and silent. Looking about him, Père Daniel inhaled what his Superiors so often called *the sacred awe of the forests*.

It was a journey of almost four hundred leagues. From the Fleuve Saint-Laurent they took the Ottawa, then the Mattawa, then Rivière à la Vase, then Lac Nipissing, and finally French River to the Sweetwater Sea. In many places the rivers were broken up, rolling and leaping, in spots even falling suddenly from a height of several brasses. There the travelers must land, and convey their baggages over high and troublesome rocks. Some portages were as wide as a triad of leagues. Père Brébeuf kept a tally for the sake of the *Jesuit Relations*, and concluded that they carried the canoes thirty-five times during that journey, and dragged them at least fifty. Being weakened by the new sickness, they made him carry his own cargo, which he'd not had to do before. Continually he praised GOD for having given him a strong body. Each time he found himself compelled to make four trips. He strode with great care, knowing that to stumble over a rock or a root while bearing such heavy burdens might cripple him. What sort of example could he set then? Nonetheless, after he'd shouldered his own panniers, he did what he could to help the Savages, which was little, as the river-bed was full of sharp stones, and he was barefooted. – But truly these are men! he said to himself, seeing how well and quickly they unloaded the canoes and threw the boulder-sized bundles between their shoulderblades, bending their heads forward for balance as they strode through the birch trees; and a pair of Savages raised each canoe above their heads and followed behind, never faltering in their step. – I could not do that, he admitted. I might kill myself in the effort, if I chose, but I could not do it. And this chastened him. But still he carried loads great enough so that they honored him, and called him *Echon* as they had before. (Was he overdoing it?) – They came at length to a rapid greater than any which he had seen before, concerning which Père Nicolas's witness, the lay brother Sagard, had written: *We have mentioned several waterfalls and many rapids and dangerous precipices, but this Chaudière Fall which we were presently to reach is the most wonderful, dangerous and terrifying of all, for it is wider than a full three-eighths part of a league. It has athwart it many little islands, which are merely rugged and inaccessible rocks, partly covered with wretched little trees, and the whole expanse is cut up into holes and precipices made in the long course of time by these boiling cataracts, six or seven fathoms high, especially in one particular place where the water dashes so violently upon a rock in the middle of the river that a wide deep basin has been hollowed out of it, so that the water circling round within it makes mighty upheavals, producing great clouds of spray that rise into the air.* – Seeing this spot, Père Brébeuf shivered with eeriness: it was the famous Forty-Second Rapids (*viz.*, the Journey of the Preaching Apostles) . . .

By now they'd given him a place in their affections. He knew never to keep them waiting when they wished to embark, and to wear a nightcap in the canoe rather than the broad-brimmed hat of his Order, in order to avoid annoying them; and many were the other procedures which he had established for himself. Then, too, he had some command of their language, which made it easier for him to communicate his necessities. – Now you begin to speak, my nephew! they laughed at him, crinkling their eyes in smiles; he laughed back like their reflection on the water . . . At last it could be said indeed that he knew his *Arendouane* from his *Aescara*. He felt a warm well-being since he was fit and could paddle well. – It is too bad, he thought, that this nomadic way of life must be destroyed. – (His purpose was continually more definite. He'd taken that secret extra vow in France. Now his life-stream began to narrow as he swam instinctively up it as we all do, year by year toward that gushing source of all streams.) – The food was scarce and as plain as he remembered, being no more than corn crushed between two stones, cooked in water; all in silence. He said to himself: this mortification peels away yet another thread of the Sin-Shirt which I wear about my naked and immortal soul. – On the fifteenth evening of Août, a century exactly from when his Blessed Ignatius had made the Vow in the subterranean chapel of Montmartre, he began to feel himself somewhat weakened by that diet. His body refused to desist from plaguing him. – So be it, he said. Then the merit I win shall be all the greater. – Kneeling by a shady rock, he spread his arms wide and opened the tips of his fingers to the breeze that streamed through the scented trees whose hands themselves were outstretched, and he looked up into the sky saying: LORD, I thank You for Your light and grace. – The following day he seized the paddle with yet more firmness, cutting the river with deep strokes while the Savages shouted in delight.

It was Père Brébeuf's habit to wear each day a hair-shirt and an iron girdle fitted with sharp spurs. Now as he paddled, he felt the girdle bite deeply into his sides, and he began to bleed. The Savages suspected nothing. He smiled at them so mildly –

Père Davost's Crosses

Père Brébeuf had fifteen years of life remaining before he was put to death by the Hiroquois in a way that we shall see; for Père Daniel the count was one less. Père Davost was not to be chosen for the Crown. His life was merely a living martyrdom, which is worst of all.

He was now following in a canoe of Savages many days behind his brother predicators of CHRIST. Thinking to show good will at the outset, he took up a paddle, saying to himself: I shall do this as much as I am able, and then rest when I am exhausted. – But now he found that his companions expected him to continue as he began. They laughed and made him paddle by himself. There was a strong wind; he could not.

They tried to coax him to eat sagamite with them, but he could not do it; it was too hard and raw for him. Then, too, in their canoes they urinated in the same birchbark vessels in which they ate. Seeing that, he could barely choke down the food. Therefore they lost patience with him. Their eyes, thickly outlined by lashes, searched him for mediocrity and weakness. They had coarse faces, whose lines were as deep as gutters. Their greasy hair stank, but not more than their crotches and armpits. Upon first seeing them, Père Davost had known at once that there would be no getting along with such people. In the first days he'd been able to forget this knowledge, letting it float down the Stream of Time ahead of him like a scalp, pulling it out of sight behind his canoe like frogskin bait as he ascended material rivers, but now water-weight broke him down and brought him down. – Just as that drowned Récollet, Père Nicolas, might have been saved if he'd been among Souriquois – for that Nation was very skilled at such resuscitations; they would have stripped him naked, hung him upside down from a tree, and blown tobacco smoke into his anus until all the water came out – so Père Davost's reputation might also have been saved if only someone had exhaled courage into him; but I guess that I am a sort of Jansenist in believing that GOD does not endow us equally. That, of course, was not Père Davost's fault. A man of imperfect virtue hardly chooses to be so. The mere fact that Père Brébeuf succeeded in enduring his Crosses does not *a priori* prove him to have mortified himself more strenuously. As I've said, he was well-built and owned patience, whereas Père Davost . . . poor Père Davost.

Whenever a mysterious splash broke the embroideries of night-sounds, the Huron said that it was the noise of a WATER-MONSTER (this word he comprehended), and he did not know whether or not to believe them.

They stripped themselves naked before his eyes, so that he blushed for shame and became speechless. They bathed in the river like animals. They laughed because he would not do the same. He had nightmares about their privities –

The maringouins or *mosquitoes* attacked him by hundreds and thousands. They had never eaten white meat before.

He learned the strange freedom of a canoe to pass through water of scarcely a knee's depth, skimming through ranks of plants with spade-shaped leaves that brushed his hips (it was as if he were a giant in a cornfield), gliding across the faces of sunken moss-continents outlined against brown-green sand, from which a surprised frog occasionally splashed. But he could take no joy from it.

Day and night his conductors shouted unintelligible threats at him. They robbed him whenever they could, and threw his books into the river. They would not carry his steel grinding-mill, and he, being unequal to the effort of carrying everything on the portages, found himself compelled at last to abandon it, along with his linen. As his Superior used to say, *It is a great occupation to suffer. May GOD give us grace from it.* At night, when they slept, he prostrated himself with his face to the ground, until the dirt was wet with his tears, for however could he have imagined the darkness of those souls? – In the end, arriving among the Algoumequins of the Island Nation, they abandoned him.

For a long time he knelt on the shore, moaning. He wanted only to die. At last the Algoumequins took pity on him, and argued with other Huron traders who came by that place, until some were found who agreed to transport him farther.

It continued as it had begun. His thoughts were as the dried plums which they prepare for Lent in France.

Père Davost struggled not to lose heart at the endlessness of river-bends widening and narrowing before him, and yet it happened. (That was a sin: to give way to despair. Knowing this gave him a further weapon with which to torture himself.) The river had its way of seeming to end ahead in a heaven of rushes, which *must* be the Country of the Huron, for there was no more water! but as the canoe came closer, trees would begin to part; – and suddenly the river would be there again, grinning its crooked blue grin, wider and longer the closer he paddled. This filled him with rage. He knew what I have already stated so many times, that these trials were but the concretization of the Exercises, and that knowledge was still another thumbscrew. The shadows of the river and the ripples of the river succeeded each other monotonously. A crow rose cawing from the scree in shade around the bend . . .

The people of all the Countries through which they passed were sick and dying in great numbers, the disease being a sort of *rougeole** and oppression of the stomach. At Kebec the French also suffered from it, but not so many of them, and not nearly as severely. Sometimes his Huron were ill also. Then they shouted and blamed him. They tried to throw his vestments over the side, but he uttered such fierce cries that they desisted. After that they pretended that he was not there. They sat upon him; they trod on his feet; they set out no ground corn for him. He fasted and said nothing. Presently he himself was touched by the sickness, but then he recovered, so that they abated their abuse of him a little, believing him to be possessed of some good Power. But they noted well that he made no offer to cure others. – Everywhere they saw corpses. It was as if GOD had lost patience with these Savages, and had begun to chastise them for clinging to their superstitions and juggleries in defiance of Him. – The children died in the greatest numbers. Seeing this disease sweep into Canada, level with his own canoe,

* Measles.

Père Davost felt pity for those little innocents who must suffer for their fathers' sins. But of course he'd seen the same so many times in France, and the children would after all be happier with GOD –

Crying bitter and incomprehensible threats, one of his companions struck him in the face with a paddle. Père Davost held two fingers to his bleeding nose. But they all shouted: even now he must paddle, it seemed. Ahead, the immensity of the Sweetwater Sea was glowing and obscure with mist, but slowly the vapors withdrew, leaving but a bank of slate-blue steam on the far side of the water, which could not be seen, while the sky, a slightly darker shade of the same hue, pressed down upon the orange streaks that made a path just above the eastern trees: – a path back to Kebec, which Père Davost longed to follow and could not. He did not know how Jean kept his equanimity. It seemed grievously unfair to him that these Savages, to whom he was pledged to devote his life, could not show the least gratitude. It was not that he expected them to smooth his way, but at the very least they might forbear to make him the butt of their abuse. – Ahead, the light was overlaying itself like ripples. In sluggish streams now he often saw the dull purple flowers of the water-shield. Frogs rode the veiny leaf-disks of those plants like so many demons; upon the approach of the canoe, they leaped into the water with alarmed splashes. They paddled past birches without number, like the white organ-pipes which would someday bloom at the Chapelle des Jésuites in Kebec, each pipe with its own fleur-de-lys (but that would not be for two centuries). He smelled open water. Again on the horizon, the Sweetwater Sea . . . It seemed but a pale blue line, but from his bitter river-days he knew now how wide it would grow when he got to it. It was very clear. Its blue and orange were filtered subtly with pearl. Its southeast ridges of tree-coast were already distinct. A squirrel dropped nuts from a nearby tree, endlessly; a bluejay sounded once and was silent; moment by moment the sky became more radiant; a goose cried . . .

Now they were on the open water, and he gasped at the *endlessness* –

Behind him came the loon-sound, almost like a horse's whinny, almost like laughter . . . he wondered if that were the call of GOUGOU. (GOUGOU had the round green eyes of lily-pads.)

The Kingdom

Long before the others, Père Brébeuf arrived at the village of *Teandeouïhata*, in the Huron Nation called the Bear. He recognized the landing even before the canoes drew in toward shore, as from diligently making the Exercises his powers of observation and recollection had become quite keen. So his journey was over at last! May GOD in his glory see fit to let me die here, he prayed. – A long low rock jutted out into the Sweetwater Sea, breaking waves with mild splashes. The afternoon was calm. Near the beaches the lake-bottom was sandy and pale, with mussels scattered half an arm's length apart; as his canoe approached that long rock they became more numerous, lying densely together between the pallid stars of young sedges, glinting dully like darkness between the shoots of the lily-forest where fingerlings swam in rapid trembles. – Now love and expectation pulsed in his veins instead of blood, and again he called upon GOD, saying: Increase my burdens, that I may better comprehend the Cross. – This request was granted at once, for the Huron Savages, being ungrateful of disposition, abandoned him, their own destination lying a further seven leagues distant. He entreated them, but they only said: Someone will come looking for you.

They paddled off and were gone.

Undoubtedly they would have left the place he knew and built afresh, as it was their custom to do every ten years or thereabouts, when fields and firewood became exhausted. The new town could be anywhere.

Hiding in the forest that portion of his possessions which he could not carry, he set out with the valuables, he knew not where. It was the fifth day of Août – *viz.*, the Feast of Our Lady of the Snows.

Ducks quacked. He parted the straining lushness of bushy trees and found the trail that he remembered. He'd been walking behind Père Daillon, that first time. And now the Grey-Gowns were expelled, glory be to THE HIGHEST . . . He stood looking upon the ruins of Old Teandeouïhata. What decay and sadness! Ah, how quickly GOD lays us low. The enclosures had fallen in; the roofs had blown away like wisps in the wind; indeed only one longhouse remained standing. Sad weeds softened the fields. A few stalks of corn stood orphaned; crows pecked at them. He passed the place where Étienne Brûlé was basely put to death, because he sought to open trade with the Yroquois. Now he thought again upon what the Recollects went about saying about their own Père Nicolas: that he'd been drowned for malice, these Huron fearing that he might wrench them away from the BEELZEBUB they adored. Brébeuf had told Père Le Caron that the allegation must be false. – Someday, perhaps, these Savages will deal with me in the same way, he said to himself. May it be for the glory of GOD!

He was no longer in any doubt that he would find the new Teandeouïhata, which was called *Ihonatiria*. So he was all the more inclined to linger here, in order to rest and gather his thoughts . . . No, no.

He went on, and found the new village at three-quarters of a league's distance.

Seeing the new cornfields and palisadoes before him, he felt a rapid beating of fear, and the DEVIL landed on his shoulder like a fly, whispering: Jean, you are weary. Would it not be better for you to rest before you went farther? – At once he strode into the village, driving his fear before him. He heard a man shouting from the watchtowers. He entered the winding tunnel of branches between walls, through which he could see both the palisade and the Sweetwater Sea. Now again he saw the teeming longhouses like elongated wicker beehives, and he smelled drying fish and the middens heaped with old cornhusks and Iroquois bones, and the wind rustled from the cornfields, the immense empire of cornfields, and naked children watched him silently and the half-naked women retreated to the longhouses and many many men came out pellmell, bearing their great war-shields of bark, twigs and cords, some of which were shaped like the darkness in the archway of some grand Château, others as round and wide as begging bowls. Arrows hung from the sashes that went about their waists. Their tattooed buttocks jiggled gruesomely. Seeing that he was no enemy, they cried: *Echon, Echon!* in voices as melodious as birds; as joy and fear mingled in his heart with such painful happiness that he soared like a bird in the sun.

What, Echon, my brother, my nephew! – and so you have come back! a man cried.

Indeed we are glad, said another, for now the crops will not fail anymore.

Cautious Wisdom

In fact, through the goodness of GOD there now sprang up an abundance of corn throughout the Country, although there'd been a famine just before; and the Huron were filled with thanksgiving for the coming of Echon. When his two brothers in CHRIST arrived at last, he was quick to credit their Power equally. Deeming them all great Captains, fine nephews, the Savages caressed them uproariously, crowding to see them, in much the same way that cats in France will leap up to taste a hot cod pie, and they babbled and gibbered like peasants in their outlandish dialect, until like the Recollects before them the Black-Gowns were compelled to clamber to the top of the sleeping platform in order to breathe. There they sat together, the three of them, looking down upon that black-braided concourse of heads, the wild hair-stripes shooting up from warriors' shaved pates, the Savage eyes gleaming in the smoky darkness, listening to the din that the Savages made, smiling wearily back at smiles. They wanted to sleep. But instead they must partake of feast after feast, which Père Brébeuf subdistinguished into the spiritual and the carnal or rather the charnel; the former being the generosity with which they shared all they had just as CHRIST's hosts had done at Emmaus, the latter being *what* they had . . . They cooked uncleaned fishes and corn and dog-meat and dirt and stones and berries all together in their great filthy kettles (obtained in trade from the French), picking through the refuse with their hands, and throwing whatever they didn't want back into the soup, ducking their greasy heads into it to drink, washing their hands in it, spitting in it. Always the Black-Gowns must eat more, though they'd sickened before the first bite, hungry though they were: whenever they took another portion the Huron cried: *Ho ho ho!* Vermin were everywhere. Red ants bit everyone's legs. They smeared their faces with bear-oil against the mosquitoes, but the mosquitoes bit them anyway. All night they heard the Savages scratching. Yet this seemed not to disconcert them in the least. – My dear young nephews! they cried one after the other, laughing, stroking the Black-Gowns' cheeks, watching to see how they ate and what made their Crosses glitter . . .

They are happy now, said Père Davost in a low-spirited voice. But will they not blame us for any misfortune?

Antoine my friend, you are too cautious! (Thus Père Brébeuf.)

They believe that the prosperity and fertility of their Country will increase when we baptize them, said Père Davost. You know that.

And you say that it will not?

No, no, sighed the other wearily. I only mean . . .

Above their heads, mice scuttled among the garlands of dried corn.

My poor friend, said Père Brébeuf, you know that I shall not abuse the rites of the Church. I think it prudent to wait a month or two, until the Savages are better instructed and have forsaken their principal superstitions. They are already Christians in so many ways! Surely you do not deny their hospitality, their cheerfulness in the face of all misfortune, the fearless face they put on death itself! I grant you there is lewdness and ignorance here, but no worse than in any group of peasants in the Latin countries.

Now the Savages shouted heartily to them to come down and feast with them again, which they did, smiling brilliantly.

Happy Dreams
1634

> How long will GOD allow this Country to continue to be a land of horror, when, without these wild men, it could be a land of Paradise?
>
> PÈRE RAGUENEAU, in *The Jesuit Relations* (1650)

At that moment the Sieur de Champlain was in some anxiety, having learned from his spies just now that the Montagnais had released a Hiroquois captive and entered into a treaty with their enemies – *his* enemies. Evidently they aimed to circumvent the French monopoly once again, and trade with the Hollanders. He appeared to be surrounded by traitors. – Verily, he said to Père Le Jeune, who was his Confessor, it seems to me that the Montagnais are my worst foes! – Ah, Samuel, they are a cunning Nation indeed, replied the Black-Gown. Let us pray that you and we together will soon show them the light.

Neither of them knew that certain French traders were at that very moment being feasted by the Hiroquois called *Oneida*, having sailed up the Fleuve Saint-Laurent to the Lake called *Beautiful*. And they offered hatchets and kettles for their furs –

Those things we like well enough, they said. Yet we ask you now to give us arquebuses, for we wish to become the terror of our enemies. There is scarcely any beaver in our Country: we have killed them all for you. Give us these guns, well-shaped guns with pretty cases, give us powder in good measure (do you see how we have watched you and learned?) – give us guns we can shoot as high as the SUN! and then you'll have peltries of us in plenty, we promise you. Then we shall be brothers indeed; then we shall dream happy dreams. Do not be afraid of us! Give us what we desire; then we shall not go to the Hollanders or the English.

The Frenchmen hesitated. Greed glowed in their eyes. They fell to whispering while the Savages squatted about them so hopefully; for in the game of Grand Betting, when the moities stand against each other, it is the duty of the players to stake their most valuable possessions to win the most valuable, as they say the CREATOR once did. The Haudenosaunee were prepared to do that. They'd offer up their lives, if that would help. Their warriors and Sorcerers would stake themselves to get guns: among them were very great dreamers. – But then one prudent man from La Rochelle said: – Beware, brothers! Someday they might use those guns against us. You know to your sorrow how a naked Armouchiquois can easily steal an iron knife by hiding it between his buttocks – and use it, too! Yet these Hiroquois are far more cunning and ferocious.

So they lied to them, saying: Dear Savages, forgive us, but we need all our guns for ourselves. Next time we'll bring some for you – yes, unless some mischance occurs . . .

They did allow them iron arrowpoints (although they looked away from one another when the Savages snatched them up, pricking themselves with the points, to compare them with the Dutch kind and the man from La Rochelle said: GOD grant that we never feel those between our shoulder-blades!) – Having thus concluded their business, they returned home, exulting like schoolboys who have just committed nastiness undetected. They passed before the Sieur de Champlain, and he did not know that they had traded with the enemy; they could see his ignorance glowing in his face . . . Later it became quite hot, until a thunderhead from the Country of the Irocois came and rained upon Kebec; then it was hot again, and the roofs and churches glistened; and it rained amidst warm sunlight and the maple trees shone. The sweating Savages who visited felt the sunlight on the backs of their necks. And in the Country of the Hiroquois the People fanned themselves and winged the new iron points with feathers rippled like sandbars and said: We must have guns.

The Captain of the Day

1634

> If they [the Jesuits] should once obtain a connivance, they will press for a toleration; from thence to an equality, from an equality to a superiority, from a superiority to an extirpation of all contrary religions.
>
> JOHN PYM (quoted), *The Churchman* (1956)

First of all we must have our own house, said Père Brébeuf.

The Huron cabins seemed to him to be like grand garden arbors, for they were made of trees or saplings planted in the ground in two parallel rows one brass's distance apart, each one of which was crowned in a socket for a roof-pole; these bent at the height of four brasses to meet their neighbors and counterparts. In place of vegetation and branches, however, as would have been found in the great Jardins of France, they were walled and roofed with cedar-bark. Although they were convenient for the Savages to build, and as commodious as they needed to be (since they could be built to any length; he'd seen one longer than forty brasses), they were unfortunately very flammable, which was why in this year the Black-Gowns witnessed two large villages entirely consumed, and another partly burned. A far greater danger, of course, sprang from the proximity and license of the Savage cabins. The Black-Gowns must live in their own house.

Their hosts had invited them to establish another house in the larger town, named Oënrio, but Père Brébeuf said to his companions: Brothers, it is more suitable for us to keep in the shadow at this time, in this little village where the Savages already love us and are accustomed to our ways.

But they assassinated Brûlé! said Père Davost very low, looking about lest they might hear him. I've heard it said that they dispersed and divided themselves for fear of our vengeance. Who knows what they're scheming? They greeted us overheartily, as I thought. Perhaps even at this moment they plot our ruin! Eh, the pity of it – to be killed and boiled for my meat, like a langouste or crayfish!

Do not make such fanciful Exercises, Ambroise.

But –

Perhaps it is precisely because they committed an evil against us that they appear so shy and desirous of pleasing us. Have you considered that? Brûlé was but a heretic. If his murder has become a chink in their armor, then let us find our way in, and strike their hearts with the truth of GOD!

The others still murmured and hesitated, but Père Brébeuf insisted that it would be less seemly to travel about like panicked partridges than to remain resolute. And he said: Remember, brothers, that to accomplish our work we must appear infallible. The humiliation that we now bear of learning their language is godly and needful. But it would not be to our advantage to appear as stuttering children wherever we go. Let us first make inroads here, exalting ourselves in their eyes, and smashing their idols once and for all.

Yes, Père Superior, that is a good plan, said the other Black-Gowns at last. We shall dwell here.

So it was that on the nineteenth day of Septembre they settled in Ihonatiria (which they called *Saint Joseph*, after the patron saint of Canada). The raspberry leaves had turned a coppery shade of red. Every day, the Black-Gowns heard the summons cried through town; for among this Nation men worked together to build a lodge for anyone who needed it. There were some, however, who said: Why should we labor for these who are called *Charcoal?* They will not live in our longhouses. Therefore they are not our brothers. But they said this only out of hearing of the foreigners, and most replied that they were wrong. In any event, it was well past the day of Our LADY of the Seven Sorrows when the house was entirely roofed and covered. By then there had already been one light frost, so that in the morning the land resembled the dress which the Ursuline Sisters had embroidered for that Day to adorn their likeness of the VIRGIN with wavy white stems and flowers and currents of whiteness on black. – The interior they divided into three parts. First came the antechamber and Store-house; second, the kitchen, carpentry shop, wheat-mill, Refectory, and parlor, with a long-bench along either side, Huron fashion. Under one bench, in the place where the Huron were accustomed to cache firewood, was a box in which to store their rolled

Black-Gowns and other clothing safely away from the thievish hands of the Huron; for indeed they had discovered these Savages to be great pilferers. Here in this room the Black-Gowns also slept, on bedsteads of earth, with bark mattresses; over them they pulled bedsheets of various clothes and skins.

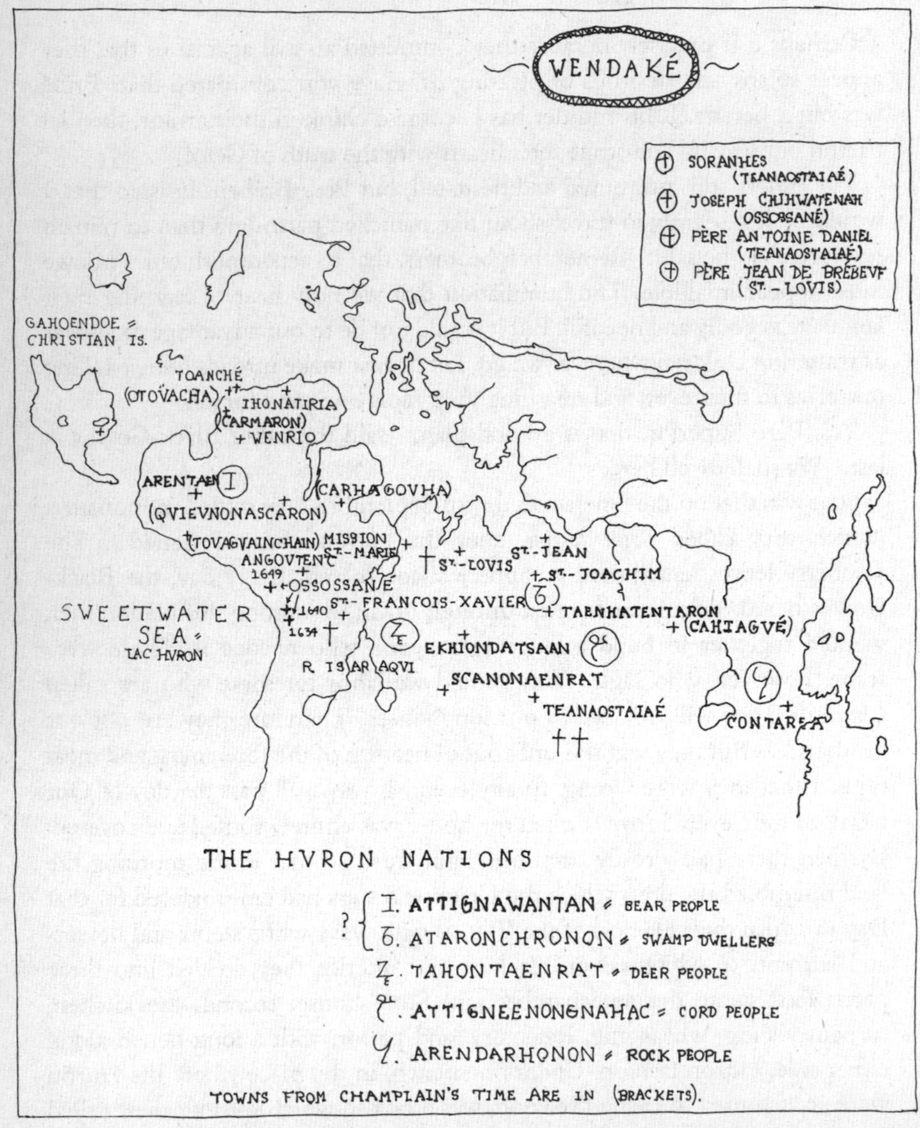

The third and final division of their house contained the Chapel, where they held Mass and prayer, and a small vestibule in which to store the utensils of the service. The entire house was three-and-a-half brasses wide, and six brasses long.

Père Brébeuf strolled about this Habitation and smiled slowly in the darkness. – Now, my brothers, said he, *now* we have the wherewithal to commence the game.

Tehorenhaennion

In that village also dwelled a certain Shaman or Sorcerer, by name Tehorenhaennion, as I have said. He was famous, but sought yet higher honors, which it seemed not unlikely that he would achieve, for while his main rival was Tonneraouanont the Hunchback, a fearful Sorcerer who'd strangled his own twin sister in the womb, yet Tonneraouanont had just lately forecast a defeat at the hands of the Iroquois, and the opposite had happened; the People had devoured so many of them! So Tonneraouanont was in poor fashion at this time, and Tehorenhaennion was considered the greater man.

Tehorenhaennion's cheeks were cut so deeply by the grooves of age that they resembled armor-plates or the shingles of pine-cones. The corners of his eyes were stamped by crows' tracks. Horizontal wrinkles spanned his forehead like the wrinkles between sandbars. Yet for all this his pupils still glowed black and bright with Power.

He remembered Echon very well. That Black-Gown had ridiculed his magic and sought to turn people away from him. In this he had not been successful. Whoever was sick or troubled or desirous of something consulted Tehorenhaennion as much as ever. For precisely that reason it had been easy for him to forgive Echon, who being of the Iron People must necessarily be ignorant, and knew nothing of good manners.

So Echon had returned. He resolved to treat Echon with the same courtesy as he did Tonneraouanont –

The Second Prelude

It was time, Père Brébeuf decided, to bring out his toys.

He was no conjurer, and despised the practitioners and pimps of that satanic trade. But he knew well the art of using novelties as a sort of tinder, through which red flames in the hearts of Savages might be kindled. – Rather than hoard them for a brief and sequential use, he decided to launch them all at once. There was a lodestone (not understanding magnetism, the Savages earnestly searched to see if it might be pasted), a glass with eleven facets, so that a single object was reflected eleven times, a phial in which a flea was magnified to the size of a beetle, a prism, joiner's tools, writing implements . . . (All these things, whispered Père Brébeuf to the other Black-Gowns, will increase their estimation of our intelligence.)

Rain-clouds gathered in the sky. The Old Men came and asked them to have their servants fire an arquebus, to scare away the THUNDER-BIRD –

You who are called *Charcoal*, you are great men, said the Wendat.

By the end of the following spring, at which time they must send off their Relation to Père Le Jeune, the Black-Gowns had already saved thirteen souls, the first being a baby girl of four or five months, in extreme sickness, who died a quarter-hour afterward. The mother had backed away when Père Brébeuf made the sign of the Cross, murmuring to herself: *OKI! OKI!* When he called her to him and told her that her baby had died, she was very patient, and heard him without any change of face. Later she asked him to give her a house-cat, for she'd heard that there were many of those at Kebec and she had never seen one –

The Dead Brothers

In late Octobre, while his Superior Père Brébeuf made a visit to the Tobacco Nation, in order to learn their disposition toward the Faith, Père Daniel baptized an elderly man called Joutaya, whose languishing condition made it imperative to snatch him from the EVIL ONE. Brébeuf had baptized his son in 1628. It was a most excellent consolation to Père Daniel for all he had so far endured to give this soul the baptismal name of Joseph, after the patron Saint of these Huron tribes. Afterwards, Joutaya slept, being wearied near to death by his sickness; and he dreamed that his dead brother appeared to him at the opposite side of the fire, saying sorrowfully: So, my brother, you wish to leave us? – No, my brother, replied the dreamer. I will not leave you. – At this, the spirit caressed him. – Upon waking, Joutaya told this dream to Père Daniel, whose heart sank like a cannonball in a deep lake, but, recovering himself, Père Daniel explained that the semblance of his brother could only have been the DEVIL seeking to block his salvation. At this, Joutaya lowered his eyes, very meekly as Père Daniel thought.

Do you want to go to Heaven, Joseph? said Père Daniel.

Oki! the wife whispered, and at this the sick man's eyes flickered.

Joseph, you must answer.

Yes, my nephew, said Joutaya. Yes, I will go.

And Père Daniel thought to himself: It is done; I have saved him. And it was as easy as filling a cask with cormorant eggs . . .

In those days it seemed to him as to his cassock-brothers that there were only a few things wrong with Huron life. It would be very easy to make them into good Christians. Only they would have to be remolded a trifle.

Marie Aoeswina

And so the labor of the Black-Gowns was one of pure happiness in that Country of white rivers, cool shadows, bluish-green trees . . . Every day they went to the Savages' cabins to bring the Christian doctrine. The women listened in silence, gazing at them very steadily as they gave suck to their wampum-earringed babes; but the young girls giggled; they whispered in the ears of men they fancied, and led them into the woods . . . – No doubt these are brothers and sisters, Père Daniel reassured himself. – On Sunday mornings the Black-Gowns assembled all the children in their chapel for Mass, followed by a catechism with prizes. The girls of seven and eight years of age were especially fond of Echon's beads. Their mothers spent much time dressing and adorning them. Recollecting this well, he'd laid in a supply of these gaming-pieces at Kebec, all glass, and of various colors, to appeal to their innocent fashions. So he lured them to prayer. (This was the sort of trick they themselves played, for they put sticks into the hands of their daughters from the earliest age, to accustom them to hoeing and pounding corn.) There was a little girl named Marie Aoeswina who was without peer, for she loved to make the sign of the Cross and to say her Pater and Ave more than fifty times a day! – and at a cost of but three beads! – and when the men came back from the forest, even wood-laden or game-laden, so many of *them* said their Pater; and before the chase they asked the Black-Gowns to pray for their success, which the Black-Gowns willingly did; and they gathered the men together as often as they could; they instructed the women; they made speeches to the Old Men, who decided all matters. – We have never heard such discourse! cried the Wendat. Whereas we ourselves speak heedlessly (we cannot deny it), your words are sweet and precious, like berries on a bush. Speak on to us, that we may pluck your words and eat them; then we shall be nourished. – Père Brébeuf felt a great ache of love. How happy he'd be if this love might so increase that at last his heart must simply burst! – He made many great plans.

But it is *filthy* to see how they entertain whoredom and concubinage! shouted Père Daniel. He was trembling.

Be patient, brother, said Père Brébeuf. I have written to our Superior. Next year, perhaps, the good Sisters will come.

In a low voice Père Daniel said: But do you not think that it is futile to instruct these Savages?

What did you see?

I –

Tell me!

That little Marie Aeoswina who says her *Aves* so prettily, she – No, no, I cannot.

Antoine, you must school yourself to trust, said Père Brébeuf as gently as he could. It is a sin to doubt the generosity of GOD, as you well know. Within five years these Huron will be our faithful flock. I see only the liberty with which they change their wives at pleasure, and some superstitions, as the problems that will be difficult to abolish –

Père Daniel dropped his eyes. – You are right, Jean, he said. Truly I would go into Hellfire with the greatest contentment, if only I could save their souls by doing it.

My feelings are the same, said Père Brébeuf. – And he led his Black-Gowns into a Council of the Old Men in the House of Cut-Off Heads, and the Black-Gowns stood like dark, dark birds among those bright-striped calumets and bright-feathered headdresses heavy with metals and earrings; and the Old Men smiled graciously as Père Brébeuf described to them the danger of fire which they faced after their deaths. One Savage laughed and said: But Echon, we are well prepared for that; at any time the *Irocois* can burn us living! and then the others laughed also. – But at this, Père Brébeuf's eyes seemed to take fire in his head, so that the Savages thought that they saw there the deadly flames of which he was speaking, and themselves fell silent. Then, having taken the field, Père Brébeuf told them the story of the Fall, with Saint Michel chastising the rebellious Angels with his sword and the farther down into the flames he whipped them the more their sea-green wings wilted and their faces aged and burned and they screamed until they were corpses lying flame-shrouded with bulging eyes. – At this the Wendat nodded so docilely, saying: Truly we desire to go to Heaven and not be burned. – What a wonder! cried Père Brébeuf. In their hearts they believe;

they *must* believe. I almost wish that they'd bring forth more objections, so that I might expound more to them –

Eh, they are not yet ready for such things, said Père Daniel, who now strove to be optimistic everywhere, but that will come.

The Captain of the Day

They were amazed by the Black-Gowns' wheat-mill, which could grind corn so fine in a twinkling (in fact, thought Père Brébeuf, it ground somewhat *too* fine for good sagamite); much more so were they astounded by the clock, which they believed to be alive. – Nephews, truly you are *ONDAKI!* cried the Huron. – Père Davost, who had a somewhat jesting disposition, like so many of us who cannot face life down, loved to play upon their credulity. When the clock struck the hour he would say immediately upon the last stroke: That's enough, clock! Be silent! – and of course it would obey. – Observing well how the machine impressed them, Père Brébeuf said to the others one evening when they were alone: Brothers, we must make use of this superstition to advance our cause. – So they took counsel with each other, and agreed to name their clock the *CAPTAIN OF THE DAY*. Every morning, when the Huron came, they would ask how many times the CAPTAIN had spoken. Sometimes they crouched motionless in the cabin for an hour, just to hear it speak. – What does he say now? they would ask. – When it struck midday the good Pères replied: He says, it is time to put on the kettle! at which others never failed to come, for at that time the Black-Gowns feasted their guests on sagamite, to become endeared to them according to the custom of the Country. As the Savages generally ate but two meals a day, they found this third repast very pleasurable. At the stroke of four, the Black-Gowns, wishing to retire to their devotions, cried out: The CAPTAIN has spoken! He says that all guests must depart. – And at once the Huron took their leave, staring at the clock with big eyes. – The next morning they were back again.

So, my brothers (thus Père Brébeuf), you have seen our CAPTAIN OF THE DAY and this mill and you admire them, so you call us demons. But what of the beauty of the sky and the sun? What of us, your nephews, the Black-Gowns as you call us, who can turn from men into crows and then back again? – Ah, I frightened you? Forgive me, my brothers, forgive me. What of the yearly miracle of the trees around us that shed their leaves and die, and then clothe themselves anew every spring? You do not say: the ONE

Who made the trees must be a beneficent OKI! And why do you not? Because your reasoning is defective. Think upon that, my brothers, think upon it.

The Fires

The autumn was now far advanced, and the weather very dry. Two Huron towns had been completely destroyed by fire in that season, and Teanaostaiaé Town, where Soranhes and Louys de Sainte Foy dwelled, was partially ruined. One day Père Daniel was making his Exercises in the Chapel, having traveled as far as the Eleventh Rapids (which is the House of Annas), and there seemed to be more spume from the cataract than usual and suddenly he realized that it was smoke streaming across his face from outside the Exercises, so he was forced to stroke for shore and open his eyes, which he was very thankful to have done, as the cabin was afire. (In Wendaké they built their dwellings of cedar bark, which was almost as combustible as matches.) Père Davost was instructing children in one of the longhouses, but Père Brébeuf was within shouting distance, so Père Daniel hailed him, and he came running. Between them they soon extinguished the blaze, which had not been very far advanced.

Let us conceal this from the Savages if we can, said Père Daniel.

Why? I marveled why you did not call them to our help –

We must not be associated with Hellfire.

Père Brébeuf looked at him. – Do you really trust their intelligence so little?

I have heard them murmuring against us, Jean, and especially against you, for they call you the Captain of the OKI. They cannot understand what we do here.

Take the eleven-faced crystal with you on your rounds and show them. That will endear their hearts to you. And fear not. You are making the Exercises just now?

Yes, Père.

Return to them. When you return to your Rapid, observe the shore for smoke. If you see any, concentrate the spray of the falls upon it and continue as before. I know you have zeal, but do you have charity? You must try to find it.

The Sin of Amantacha

1633–1634

We shall never be humble if we do not acknowledge our weakness.

MÈRE MARIE DE L'INCARNATION,
Spiritual Maxims (1639–72)

In this season when ferns were stained orange by autumn, the Savages continued to hold Père Brébeuf in high respect, and invited him to go with them on their embassy of peace to the Sonontrerrhonons, but he refused, saying: we Black-Gowns go nowhere until we are recognized by all as Predicators of JESUS CHRIST.

You must come for my son Amantacha's sake! cried Soranhes. He will be overjoyed to embrace you when the Hiroquois release him.

I cannot go, said Père Brébeuf. Still, I am hopeful that the other four Hiroquois Nations will also confirm this peace; that would truly open the door to the Gospel in those countries. Do greet your son for me with all love, Soranhes, and tell him to visit me here in Ihonatiria.

No, no, Echon my nephew, we will be disappointed if you do not come to share corn soup with us in Teanaostaiaé, the old Savage insisted. You remember Kwer Nikoas who drowned? He hid himself like a spider, even more than you; yet he came often to eat the leindohy and the fish with us. Surely you will come.

Père Brébeuf bit his lip with distaste. In no way did he trust this man. – So be it, he said. I will come.

Before the snow had become too deep for travel, he fulfilled his word and went to visit Louys Amantacha, recently freed by the Hiroquois in exchange for one of their prisoners, and he greeted him in CHRIST's name but was received with an embarrassed smile, and he started and looked deep into the boy's eyes, seeking to know whether he had gone rotten, and there was a long silence, and old Soranhes said jovially come now, my Echon, you have come all this way to see my son; surely you have something to say to him! but Père Brébeuf shrugged off this waterfall of words and again addressed himself to the son, saying Louys! and Amantacha hung his head and Père Brébeuf said what has happened to you, Louys? to which there was but more silence, and his heart sank within him. Then the woman came in, and he understood. In his letter to Père Le Jeune for the *Jesuit Relations* he hesitated for a moment with his pen above the birchbark sheet, thinking will it help or hinder our cause to record what has passed with this boy, who is in grave danger of apostasy? and he thought the pious Sisters who met him will certainly be discouraged and he thought indeed it is a humiliation for us and then he thought but shall I act as if I had no confidence even in Him? *Never!* and he wrote *Louys is not as he ought to be, and as we had wished. Nonetheless, we still have good hope.* He lifted his pen again and remembered the little shock he'd had when he saw that Louys' finger had been hacked off by the Hiroquois, and he sighed and bowed his head and his lips moved in the boy's behalf and he wrote *this severe stroke ought to suffice to bring him back to duty.*

The Flames of Time

The previous summer, this is to say in the Year of Our LORD 1633, after Louys de Saincte Foy had suffered the Black-Gowns to peer into his face for sin, he bade them farewell with all affection, for he loved them and their ways, and then he ran down to the Fleuve Saint-Laurent where his canoe was being loaded and said thanks, brothers! here are some dried prunes that I stole from the Black-Gowns! and they all laughed and ate the prunes at once, agreeing that it would be a shame if such rare food fell to the fishes or to the Hiroquois. His companions had received many iron axes and cooking-kettles in exchange for the gifts of beaver-pelts that they had made, as well as some blankets and even a loaf of bread; and they besought him to examine these things and tell them his mind concerning them, for had he not himself journeyed to the Country of the Iron People?

The axes are good, Amantacha told his companions. But in France the cooking-kettles are much better than here. I think these are thinner than the ones the English gave you.

At this they were somewhat irked, and said But you, are you yourself so cunning at changing gifts with them?

Amantacha smiled easily. His teeth gleamed. I did not mean it that way, friends, he said. I only think that we should watch these Frenchmen. I have seen how they treat each other; they are perfectly capable of giving us thinner kettles year by year.

Then we shall give them thinner skins! they shouted laughing. The canoe was fully loaded; Amantacha slid it gently into the shallows as the others took their places, and then himself leaped lightly in. His companions had already begun paddling.

With him was Born Underwater.

All the way home they teased him, calling him by his *chrétien* name, Louys de Saincte Foy, Louys de Saincte Foy, Louysdesainctefoy! – paddling until the SUN glared in their faces and the drops of sweat that flew from their shoulders gleamed like copper. – Amantacha only smiled. But he knew that at the bottom of all their jesting was a touch of reproach.

When they came back to Teanaostaiaé, he said to his father: Who is the best Arendouanc?

Soranhes studied his son. What do you need?

The others have been making fun of me! I shall join the raid against the Hiroquois!

His father caressed his cheek. – Good, son, he said. That is a way to win much glory.

Born Underwater had said nothing, and Soranhes remained likewise silent. He had not gone to Three Rivers that year, so he did not know her. Now he waited. Amantacha stepped lightly backward and pointed to her. (He was very anxious that she be loved and welcomed. She was soft like a new leaf . . .) – Father, this is my *asqua*. She is called Born Underwater. She is of the *Ln'uk* – KLUSKAP's People. Her mother and father are dead.

Ah, said Soranhes. Well, daughter, I'm pleased to meet you I hope you will give my son children. You want something to eat?

Born Underwater smiled shyly. – Yes, she said.

It is a strenuous life your People lead, wandering through the forest, said Soranhes. As long as you stay here you will never go hungry.

Born Underwater flushed.

The next day was a day of highest summer and Amantacha took a dog to hunt a bearcub whose tracks Soranhes had seen and Born Underwater and Amantacha's sister and mother were pounding corn while Soranhes tended his tobacco whispering to it. Born Underwater thought the corn-pounding very foolish work, but it was true that there were few fat animals in this Country; to live here one must grub and grabble like a worm, it seemed –

In that season there were many young men among the Wendat who were anxious to gain prestige by returning with scalps or heads or prisoners to be burned. There always were. The War-Chiefs longed to help them. They traveled through the Country of the Wendat, meeting with one another, calling the Old Men to them so that they might decide who to attack. The Seneca or Sonontrerrhonons were most frequently mentioned. That witch, that traitor who'd once been their nephew, Étienne Brûlé, had sought to open the way between the Sonontrerrhonons and the Iron People. It was for that that a War-Chief had split his head. Now the Sonontrerrhonons ought to receive their own reward . . . – But this was a matter to be debated in secret, for the Hiroquois have spies among us all. In Teanaostoiaiaé the War-Chief's house, the House of Cut-Off Heads, now closed its doors with bark, and the smoke of tobacco rose from it as the Elders cleared their minds, and already the women were talking over what to prepare for the War-Feast and Amantacha's heart was pounding with gladness. His boyhood friends with whom he used to play snowsnake were all warriors now. They had done something, while he had wasted among the ridiculous Iron People. But now –

Every hour he thought of some errand which compelled him to pass that closed door of the House of Cut-Off Heads, and he stood gazing at it with all the other young men. He burned his arms with red-hot coals, to test his courage. Then the door was opened. The Old Men were smiling. It was to be the Sonontrerrhonons.

Ah, but the Serpents* will revenge themselves for this! laughed his father.

What of our revenge? shouted Amantacha.

Yes, came the answer, we must have that.

Soranhes had not gone a-warring for many summers, at first due to the press of his trading concerns, and then later because he was obliged to paddle to Kebec year after year seeking his lost son. Now it seemed good to him that he and Amantacha go together, if the omens were good. – The Arendouane of greatest honor in those days was from Scahonaenrat, a great town, well-palisadoed, where the Nation called *Tohontahenrat* dwelled. She had the Power of seeing-ahead. Last summer she'd announced that the

* Iroquois.

warriors would return with as many Hiroquois captives as there were fingers on her hand; and indeed it came out as she had said. (The year before that, however, her vision had been clouded by evil ONDAKI.) – Soranhes gave his son the gifts to give her, so that the young man would win the prestige. When the War-Feast was over, and Amantacha and other men had raised each other's spirits to honorable rage against the Hiroquois, dancing and singing *Wiiiiiiiii!*, shaking their weapons, knocking one another down, he greased his hair with sunflower oil (his head proudly bristled like the crowded corn-plants) and set out on the forest-road. He went alone.

It was the Month When the Little Corn is Ripe. (A crow unfolded its wings like a book and ascended into an alder, where it crouched silently.) New feathers exalted his headdress. He crossed the vast cornfield, striding proudly; the women who were weeding watched him, giggling sweetly. There was Born Underwater! He went into the corn with her and she opened her legs. After her he had a girl much younger than his sister Teondisewan . . . Now he really had to go. – *Haii haii haii*, he must admire himself in this stream! On a sunny granite shelf adjoining the water, he lay full length, enjoying the warm rock against his belly. He could see the rock's continuation below the surface, in a wash of brownish-green, and it was overgrown with roots cylindrical like the organ-pipes at his christening, and spade-shaped plants with blue flowers grew out of it, too, and weeds like French pipecleaners floated glistening between the dead red cast-off lily-pads. (His heart jumped. The Hiroquois! – No, it was nothing – only a crow.) Now he tilted his head, and the water became a mirror. He saw his oval olive-colored face unsmiling, his shiny hair, his magnificent crown of feathers! Taking up quiver and bow, he leaped to his feet again. He said his *Ave*; – perhaps that would bring luck . . .

Scahonaenrat's palisade was formed of three interlaced rows of pointed poles, almost twice the height of a man. Watch-towers fashioned from forked tree-trunks rose above this wall. Each watch tower was well provisioned with stones to hurl down upon the heads of attacking Hiroquois, and water to extinguish fires (to which these towns were extremely vulnerable). Amantacha passed through the winding way between the walls, a lithe young man striding lightly. Everyone liked him. His clan-friends the Foxes now met him in welcome crying: *Yatarho!* (my friend); *Attaquen!* (my brother). He had so many uncles here, and fine little nephews! Women watched him with big smiles, pulling in their babies tight against their shoulders. Maybe he'd go into the cornfields with one or two of them . . . All was well here; there'd been no sickness; no enemy had come. – They asked after his mother, for among this People the clan of the son is the clan of the mother; she too was a Fox. They embraced him when he said that Yatera was well . . . He strode into the greatest house of the Fox Clan, where his friends gave him tobacco to smoke. The peeled pillars of wood flickered in the hearth-fires as he sat down. The inside of this lodge, with its smell of breath and corn, steam and babies and charred dirt, was unlike his own, but he was among friends shining against the wall-darkness. – He goes to take heads from the Hiroquois, said fathers to their sons. He goes to capture Hiroquois for the torture and burning! – The boys stared wide-eyed: he was a warrior, a great man. Amantacha laughed. A baby clutched at the feathers in his hair; Amantacha gave him one . . . But he kept his gifts for the Arendouane close beside him, so that no one would steal them. Now they bade him attend a fine feast of bread made from early corn – the freshest – chewed tender by the women, then pulverized and baked, so that it relished exceedingly well. How fine to take cheer with them! His heart laughed in great pulses like an arquebus (if only he had one of those!).

. . . So, my grandson, you go to visit the Haudenosaunee. (Thus the Arendouane). I seem to see you in their Country, creeping like a lynx through the darkness . . .

You know everything; have pity on me. Yes, but I did not come about that; but rather to lighten my arms, which are too heavy with gifts, for I have just returned from the Iron People.

She laughed. – Good!

He placed the presents into her hands and she took them with every appearance of pleasure, but he saw her eyeing him shrewdly.

And I wished also to give you this, my grandmother.

He brought forth a red glass bead that he had stolen from the Black-Gowns.

Hé é é, you have done well, the Arendouane crooned in delight, you have done very well! You have given me a little thing with Power – oh, yes! I wish that my old eyes were better. I could drink and drink the color of this little wampum-thing! Now my mind is shining for you, my grandson. The hearth-fire has been kindled. And yet I believe that the flames therein might be strengthened still a little further – have courage, Amantacha, and look upon the joyous red flames! See how they desire to grow so hot that I might prepare my friendship for you in a feast of many kettles!

He presented her with a nightcap from the Iron People.

Now my heart and soul are kindled with gratitude for these treasures which you have given me, she said in her quavering voice. My heart-flames rise proudly like the cottongrass in springtime. You have been kind; I comprehend that I must reward you. Shall we see how this journey of yours will be? Do you care to sit beside me? We shall see it now together.

She began mumbling to herself, and drew a map in the dirt floor. Amantacha looked and saw the Sweetwater Sea, and the Fleuve Saint-Laurent, and there was the Lake of the Irocois (at which his heart began to beat a little faster), and the Arendouane began to build little piles of bark facing each other across that lake, on one side the Wendat, on the other the Hiroquois; and she said very softly *now we shall see!* and touched a torch to each of the heaps of bark so that suddenly there were two armies of flame facing each other across the Lake of the Iroquois and the Arendouane said: the enemies have not found each other and the children at the next hearth were running and playing and they chased each other outside, at which a draft came into the longhouse so that the flames started and twisted wildly, and the Wendat flames burned toward the center of the lake as if they were coming closer and closer to the enemy town and the enemy flames weaved in confusion, but suddenly the Irocois flames began to suck the Wendat flames toward them and swallow them up, and the children came running back inside the longhouse and another gust of air disturbed the flames so that they tangled together and the Iroquois flames leaped across the lake and extinguished so many Wendat flames until Amantacha could not bear to watch and turned his face away.

He must set out with his companions nonetheless. Any other course would have been cowardly, dishonorable. And perhaps the witcheries of the Hiroquois had blinded her this year . . .

Deflections

He returned to Teanaostaiaé to gather up his war-gear. His father was waiting for him, and likewise many other warriors who lusted to break the bones of the hated Hiroquois and suck the marrow from them.

What word did she say, my strong son?

They will devour us, he replied in a low voice.

Soranhes winced. Then his eyes lit upon a Cross which Amantacha always wore about his neck: the Black-Gowns had given it to him. – No doubt that magic object bent the flames, he said brightly. (If the young man lost courage now, then how could he gain it back? Surely the Iron People had not eaten his heart within him!)

I shall go, Amantacha said. I promised to do so.

Soranhes caressed his face –

As soon as he could leave Amantacha's hearing, he went out and told the others not to ask about the Arendouane *– for she spoke no good word,* he said. – *Ouai, ouai!* they sighed, filled with pity for Amantacha. – He went to his son's asqua, Born Underwater, to warn her to be brave for him. But she had nothing to say against this war. She knew from looking-ahead that one day they'd riddle Amantacha with tortures until his soul was caught, borne away in one of those wave-holed Iroquois baskets. But not yet. This time he would live . . . He went to Tehorenhaennion, who demanded three hatchets. – Now I have turned the evil aside! said that worthy. Your strong son will return to you, never fear! After that, Soranhes was all smiles; he threw a feast for his son; he boiled all his favorite dogs . . .

But as Amantacha bound on his slat-armor, he could not but feel its feebleness in comparison to the iron exoskeletons of Chawain and his warriors and the Roy's men in Paris –

Amantacha Among the Hiroquois

Green leaves crawled down darkness like water-droplets. Once they crossed into the Country of the Haudenosaunee, they divided their forces into three groups, as was the advice of their Old Men: the scouts, the hunters, and the main body of the warriors. Each night they built redoubts of logs to guard themselves as they slept. When they were very near to the Nation of the Sonontrerrhonons, they began to travel only by night, and ate corn meal soaked in stream water, so that no fires would give them away. They shared dreams with each other in great anxiety. Now as every summer it was the time of nightmares.

Amantacha went among the party of scouts. Folding his hands on his heart in the French manner, he swaggered. But Soranhes was among the hunters; he was old.

From a hill, Amantacha looked down into the bright blue haze of Hiroquois country, into which fell the sudden summer rains hissing like wind, after which the valleys steamed in the evening sunlight, and a great rainbow, the sign of the Covenant as Amantacha well knew (for the Black-Gowns had taught him), hung in the sky, its bands of color duplicated in the haze, and it was underscored by rainbow-lines of alternating white and blue. Amantacha knew that the Irocois were gazing at it, too. Later the sky was a brilliant transparent purple, in which a single cloud hung, its underside flashing red, reflecting some lightning so distant that no thunder could be heard, and the flashing was in time with the twinkling of the stars. Still a little longer he waited, until the darkness was moist and heavy; then he heard the War-Chief making the call of a screech-owl and he answered and he knew that the others with him heard. Twice more called the War-Chief, which was the signal to attack. Then silently the other warriors gathered in, and they went down into the enemy Nation.

Now it was late night, a cool summer night with the owls going *hooh, hooh, hoo-hooh* and the stars shimmering through the branches, which in the darkness seemed regularly spaced like the ribs of a sturgeon's skeleton. The warriors heard the sound of dripping water far away yet all around them in the breezeless stillness; chilly droplets spattered their knees and chests and shoulders as they parted the wet branches, watching, listening. The night was as dark as the head of a tomahawk. Frequently they stopped and listened with drawn breath. But they heard only the chirr of a night insect, drawn out over an inhumanly breathless interval. Then that noise ceased. The sky flickered with a single lightning-flash. They inhaled the smell of fresh wet leaves. They heard two birds calling to one another and wondered: is that the Irocois? Something was moving in the grass, but it was only a raccoon.

Fifteen Sonontrerrhonons caught them in an ambuscade. And it was as the Arendouane had foreseen. They killed a dozen Wendat and captured fourteen more, including Louys Amantacha. Two Sonontrerrhonons held him, gloating while his dead companions were scalped. They cut off his armor with a knife of sharp stone.

Are there more of you Crooked-Tongues behind? one of his enemies shouted, shaking him.

Many more, many more! cried Amantacha fiercely.

At this they took him by the arm and made him run a dozen miles with them, deep into the forest. He was surrounded by Sonontrerrhonons; he could not see the other prisoners . . .

Now he stood before the enemy War-Chief, whose eyes were as abnormally large as those of a False Face mask. – Behold, I am astonished! laughed the War-Chief. Who is this vigilant man? None but Louys the Frenchman! You will swagger for us through the flames very soon, my nephew. Ha, ha, ha!

The War-Chief's face was tattooed with a diagonal track that ran from the corner of his mouth to his forehead.

He smiled. His scalp-lock glistened terrifyingly in the firelight.

Louys, open your ears, I urge you: make ready to sing your Death-Song!

A Hiroquois snatched a brand and seared the lobe of his ear. – Someday my People will do the same to you, said Amantacha.

Oh, how patient he is! they chuckled in a rage. They amused themselves beating and kicking him.

They lay down to sleep at last, tightly gripping his arms and legs. Just before sunrise they reached a deer-trail which wound across a hill; following it for some distance, they made their scalp-halloos and were answered from afar by shrill cries, which swiftly grew louder. Amantacha knew by this that they must be near Sonontoen, the chief town. Silently he prayed to IESVS; he prayed to IOUSKEHA and all the ONDAKI. He was very thirsty, but his palms were wet. He would not weep or answer, no matter what they did to him. Presently they reached the town of evil longhouses, from which the Sonontrerrhonons, painted in all the hues of earth, came running. They formed themselves into a double line, and told Amantacha to run the gauntlet. Nearby he saw many of his countrymen, their faces blackened, peering at him from the stakes to which they were lashed. They had been condemned. Already the crows sat on the trees –

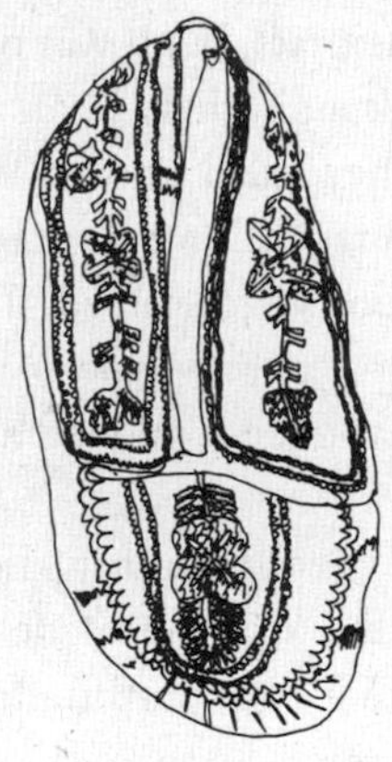

SENECA MOCCASIN

O you Savages! Amantacha shouted, using the opprobrious word for the first time, such was his hatred of them (for he fully expected them to burn him to death in the end). I will tell my friends the Iron People to split your heads! Take care, you serpents spawned only for our burning!

At this they laughed in derision and began pounding the ground with the sticks that they intended to whip him with. – Come, my brother, and let us caress you! cried a squaw.

A warrior seized his arm and began to lead him. With a great shout to give himself courage, Amantacha commenced the trial. They beat him until the blood started out from his ankles to the crown of his head. The long ranks blurred and the cruelly jeering voices became faint, like the buzzing of bees. He tried to go faster, and the warrior tripped him. Now the blows fell in earnest, so that he almost despaired, but somehow he got to his feet and staggered on. Someone knocked him down. Again he recovered himself and went on, although he could no longer see, for one of his eyes was swollen shut and the other was full of blood. Presently, he knew not how, he fell again, and before he lost consciousness he felt them sawing at his finger with a clamshell . . .

The First Epidemic
1634–1635

Ah, how I would like to kill the Devils, since they do so much harm!

Huron seminarian, quoted in
The Jesuit Relations (1639)

Do you who are called *Charcoal* think that you will succeed in overthrowing the Country? asked a Huron very politely.

Ah, we are not so presumptuous as to suppose that, said Père Brébeuf, but it is easy enough for GOD.

Kebec 1635

One sunny March morning, snow was sliding down the steep roof of the Sieur de Champlain's Palace and birds were singing and the Black-Gowns were tolling the bell for Mass. Then it was spring, and the Solomon's seal sprang up in the forests, cheering every Christian heart with yellow-green flowers. In this year the Black-Gowns first began to see open country, and it seemed to Père Le Jeune as he sat in the sleeping room writing the year's *Relation* that the barbarism of the Savages had commenced in some measure to be changed into French courtesy. Now along the shady paths the marks of boots were to be seen, and Père Le Jeune knelt so happily to pray in the new fields of Kebec, his nightmares of the Montagnais Sorcerer dwindling like a pox-blister (although after that first winter among the Savages, he never could rid himself of a cough); and the Sieur de Champlain enlarged the fortifications again and the fur-traders came from Saint-Malo, bringing news of the Roy and the home Country whose recollection reared steadfast in Père Le Jeune's mind like the door of some great unchanging church. Now the breezes were honey-sweet, and the mosquitoes came out, and the Fleuve Saint-Laurent was sparkling blue. And so it came to be summer, and the Solomon's seal bore its blue-black berries in the forest (but the berries of the false Solomon's seal were red), and Père Le Jeune wrote to his Provincial that the Huron were attempting to conclude peace with the Hiroquois, in which event two more Pères would be needed.

If these people receive the Faith, they will cry with hunger, he acknowledged, *and there will be no one to feed them, for lack of persons who know their language.*

and he wrote *the Savages at Three Rivers are all dying in great numbers.*

The First Epidemic 1634–1635

Winter came to the Country of the Wendat. In the forest he saw hares as well tricked out as Carthusian monks in their snow-white habits, but whereas the Carthusians hid themselves in their luxurious hoods, the hares had but to remain motionless on the snow to be almost invisible, so that he marveled at the cleverness of GOD's providence that preserved them; he prayed *let us take on the color required of us to complete our labors for Your Name, inviolate from the ENEMY.* – He gathered the Savages together whenever he could in that season, preaching in the chapel, ringing the bell, wearing his surplice and square cap . . . He led them in chanting the Paternoster, which had been translated into Huron by Père Daniel. He taught them to make the sign of the Cross. To every child who was diligent in learning the catechism he gave a glass or porcelain bead. For a spectacle he had them witness two little French boys questioning and answering each other, which made them rapt.

On a few occasions, unfortunately, their Old Men called him to listen to their beliefs, which, as might well be imagined, were the extremest nonsense, although not really vile. The Sorcerers also entered into occasional colloquy with him. – So many times he had seen a successful man bewitched by Sorcerers, so that the man had to exhaust his goods on those Doctors called *Arendouane*. It was as if the Sorcerers personified the jealous envy of this people, acting as a check upon the accumulation of wealth. In a way this was good; that he had to admit; for it kept all in parity, as must have been the case among the early Christians. And yet these poor Savages lived so deeply shaded by error that he saw a positive necessity for some to rise higher than others, in order to show the rest how to grow out of that darkness. Of course the greater any man might become, the more those resentful Sorcerers would fasten upon him: that was the nature of things. So he did not like them. But neither did he fear them. – It was particularly the Old Men, however, who were stubborn (for the Sorcerers generally held themselves more aloof from the debate). The Old Men cited their AATAENTSIC and JOUSKEHA and suchlike demons who for so many centuries had enthralled them. – Then also the children were terrified at the word *to die*, which the Black-Gowns used very frequently in their teaching. Sometimes they shrieked, or refused to listen. However, such few cobwebs of superstition could swiftly be brushed away from the blank birchbark of their minds –

On the whole, they were inclined to believe, as was only sensible – for the Black-Gowns did not fall ill during the epidemic which now struck them, and this they could only attribute to the favor of GOD.

One old man, falling sick, declared that on his death he wished to go to his Ancestors. But, falling into a sort of sleeping trance, he presently revived and cried in wonder: I must go to Heaven after all, for I was in the Country of Souls and it is empty! All, all have gone to Heaven!

The Black-Gowns smiled –

The epidemic continued. They held their Dream-Feast as they always did in winter: – among these People feasts have such Power that they are reputed sometimes to bring the dead back to life. Now there was need for that, as they called upon the SKY to witness, throwing their tobacco offerings into the longhouse-fires, crying: *Heal us!,* guessing the gifts they each longed for, and presenting them to one another, because that is the way to stave off sickness . . . – but though the presents they gave and got were as fine as ever, they took little joy in them. And their dear ones continued to die.

So they sent for their Sorcerers. These came wordlessly. Then they went to gather helpers. When they returned, they wore bearskins over their heads and began to dance. The sick ones' families gave kettles of food for the feast that must now be held; they gave wampum to the dancers, and the old women sang until they were given presents. The Shamans beat dry sticks against sheets of bark and chanted their dreamsongs; yet the sick ones continued to die.

They called for Tehorenhaennion to come. His name rang out everywhere. Dying people screamed it, believing that even now he could cure them. (Tonneraouanont had made no cures.) Tehorenhaennion came and took his presents with thanks. He cut deep into their bodies with his knives, while they lay soundless. He fumigated them with sacred herbs. But the OKIS in their stomachs would not come out. Then he smote his forehead, crying: Now it is clear to me! This is a case of witchcraft!

Who is the bad Sorcerer? the People shrieked in anger.

Ah, you know that, whispered Tehorenhaennion. Yes, my mother's brothres; yes, my sister's sons; you know that in your hearts –

After this, the eyes of the Huron never left the Black-Gowns. It was Echon whom they dreaded most. He saw them standing in the doorways of their longhouses when he passed by. Their gazes were as those woven corn-leaf mats on the sleeping platforms, rustling whenever one so much as turned over, and wakening the other sleepers. One day when the CAPTAIN OF THE DAY struck four they barred the door of their residence and sat taking counsel together. – Père Daniel, still optimistic, was certain that the mistake would soon be comprehended as such, especially since the Black-Gowns hovered around the dying so lovingly. – Père Davost smiled vaguely and said nothing, until Père Brébeuf demanded his opinion. – My opinion as such – what's that worth, Père Superior? For I can scarcely stutter and stammer their dialect like a babe; who am I to say what wickedness lies in their minds? – I just now learned, said Brébeuf, lacing his fingers together in church-and-steeple, that to speak of the dead is to insult the survivors. That complicates our business, n'est-ce-pas? – Père Davost shrugged a little. – Well, who hasn't been disgusted by our business at one time or another? – Père Daniel, who did not get on with him, rounded fiercely on the other priest, but Père Brébeuf gripped his shoulder, and Père Daniel, gazing first at his Superior and then at Père Davost, saw that the latter was weeping soundlessly even as he smiled.

We all choose, little by little. (Thus Père Brébeuf.) The Italians even say that not deciding is deciding, and they have reason! We've come to a rapid, brothers. We can turn back, or we can portage around it, or we can shoot it in our canoe of Faith.

Forgive me, Père Superior (thus Père Daniel), but I don't comprehend. Are you talking about the baptisms?

Brébeuf smiled thinly. – You see, you do comprehend. So let's play a game. Do you be our catechumen, my friend. What if we baptize all who wish it – the ones who might recover as well as those who seem likely to die?

Then, Père Superior, we'll wipe away the odium that stains the name of baptism in their minds, for that will prove once and for all that baptism is not a demonic rite that kills.

Exactly, my Antoine. No, you are not so maladroit! Then more will come forward to be baptized . . . But what is the difficulty? Can you enlighten us, Ambroise?

The man spoke thickly. – The DEVIL will tempt them as long as they live, Père Superior; some will become guilty of apostasy –

Yes, a fine rape of souls, laughed Père Brébeuf. How many could we send to Hell that way?

Père Davost had recovered himself by now. – We must cease the baptisms for now. We must! That way we harm no one, and when their pox has run its course . . .

Now it was Père Daniel's turn to say nothing. And Père Brébeuf said: But what about those who die unbaptized? I know full well that every success will increase their murmuring against us. But tell me, what would the Blessed Ignatius have done, Ambroise? . . .

So the Black-Gowns continued to flock like crows to the longhouses where the sick ones screamed. And they bent over the dying and whispered gently in their ears –

There was a woman named Khionngnona, who had the insolence to refuse baptism, and shouted: Drive them from me! – but a Savage felt sorry for the Black-Gowns and said into Echon's ear: She is not referring to you, but only to her fox-headed dogs.

Amantacha and Jesus

The Souriquois woman, Born Underwater, was unaffected by this sickness, although many in her longhouse died of it, and both Soranhes and Amantacha became ill. Soranhes became blind for the duration of his sickness. For half a moon he could not rise from beside the fire. When at last he did recover, his hair was white, and ever after he complained of a ringing in his ears. Amantacha was not so badly affected. His fever abated soon enough for him to see the babies die. He heard the women scream shrilly. Presently a pretty young cousin of his got the sickness and died. This was difficult to bear. At this, everyone in Teanaostoiaé began to make accusations of witchcraft against the Black-Gowns, which he found very hard, due to his association with them. – Soranhes said: Now I believe that the wounds of our French nephew* still bleed, and his uncle or sister seeks revenge on us by sorcery. – Ah, I have no knowledge of this, replied Amantacha. Therefore I cannot contradict what you say. – For that was his way, to agree with people. But he clenched his fists. One night a man said that Echon and his followers

* Étienne Brûlé.

should be slain secretly, because the images of their *Saints* or OKIS were filled with venom; at which Amantacha rose and excused himself politely, saying that he would go hunting.

The moonlit shadows of tree-claws were very distinct, being both curled and sharp. Various darknesses lay fantastically coagulated upon the snow: black, silver and grey. It was very cold. The chill sank into his knees like grease as he stood waiting, peering down a snowy hill of gruesome darkness. The rivière had not frozen yet. He could hear it roaring. Despite its loudness, the sound came to him as sadly and distantly as some DEVIL's imprecations. His ears ached with cold. The trees about him were very glossy, like the frozen veins or tendons of Night's hands – yes, Night, or DEATH, Whom the Yroquois called *Him Whose Face is Darkness.* Now, soft and regular and terrifyingly near, he heard the coughing of some animal. Was this the disease? People said that the Black-Gowns had brought it. But he could not believe that. Echon was so kind; the Black-Gowns were loving if severe . . . Why would they wish such a thing on anyone? Yet some feared them more than the Hiroquois now. That coughing – no, it was only a raccoon. It was a raccoon, not dead JESUS. He sought to make the Exercises as Père Daniel had taught him. Here was the Stream of Time tranquil and summery with the smell of dreaming raspberries to warm him in that terrifying night, and he swam upstream to the Fifteenth Rapids – *viz.*, the Burial; and on the left bank he suddenly saw with Born Underwater's eyes almost to those days when every cemetery would stand behind a fence of oak or maple, the graves straining like flowers at the light of the great sunny Eye beneath the steeple where JESUS watched them; JESUS made graves grow; sometimes Amantacha was afraid of JESUS. He could not but see that white SUN inside the black pupil that hovered inside the reflections of spoked candelabra wheeling dizzily above his head in the great cathedral in Rouen as if they might fall upon him; then those black-molded or black-shadowed gravestones behind the dark fenceposts, staring at him with white eye-flowers like lichen

All night he paced through the forest, until the sky greyed and the needle-stages of spruces and sapins rose above him like the gills of mushrooms. The sun was dull and red, like his cousin's sweating feverish face. The thaw had come, as it always did in the month called Day Will Be Long Again; near him he heard a river's roaring riot: sour and defiant it made its way down snowy precipices. The sun was hot on his neck. Did he have the fever again? – Snowflakes glittered like grains of silver, appearing magically from a cloudless sky whose dull blueness was identical with that of the Haudenosaunee lakes and rivers in summer . . .

When he returned, his mother's sister was ill.

Soranhes rushed to the lodge where Tehorenhaennion was staying. He had come to Teannastaoiaié to treat some sick people there.

You must heal her for me! he cried.

Tehorenhaennion gazed at him very remotely. – I will do what I can, he said. But you must give me many presents. This witchcraft of the Black-Gowns is very Powerful.

He came to the lodge and examined her. She was lying still. He beat the stick upon the sheet of dry bark, and the dancers came with the bearskins over their heads and Soranhes gave them all the wampum he had. Amantacha had some wampum-plates which he had meant to give to Born Underwater; these too were given to the dancers. They danced for an hour, and then Tehorenhaennion came to the sick woman and said: You must dance with us.

I cannot. I am too feeble . . .

Do you want to live? You must dance with us!

Amantacha and his father raised her up and began to dance desperately. She was so weak that she could not even hold onto them. Soranhes begged her to move her feet on the floor a little for his sake, and she strove to, in order to please him; seeing how hard it was for her to do even this, Amantacha's sister began to wail. Yet the old woman smiled faintly; she loved the sound of the dance.

Now Tehorenhaennion's dancers went faster and faster, until they became almost beside themselves. Tehorenhaennion raced down the length of the lodge, snatching brands from the hearth-fires and hurling them about, regardless either of his burning hands or of the safety of the longhouse, so that some of the children screamed, and all who were not dancing occupied themselves in stamping upon the sparks that spilled all about, and Tehorenhaennion was shouting and the dancers were beating the sheet of dried bark as now he stopped still and took coals from the hearth and swallowed them. He roared: *I am Beyond the Treetops!* He seized a rattle of tortoise-shell and shook it; he smashed it in the fire.

But she died at moonset. They carried her burial box to the scaffold outside the palisadoes where the other boxes lurked under the snow-drifts . . . Her bone-soul walked before them. She'd have to wait until the Feast of the Dead before she could go to the Country of the Dead, where the souls complain like crows –

Only a Coincidence

As it happened, that same year the easternmost of the Five Hiroquois Nations – *viz.*, the Mohawk – also suffered great mortality from the smallpox. They'd been trading with the Hollanders. Of course, such prices must be paid from time to time. The Savages gained great profit from the trade. Many of the Mohawk longhouses, for instance, now had Dutch-made doors with iron hinges.

A Funeral Feast
1634–1635

I desire no consolation that would not lead me to contrition . . .

THOMAS À KEMPIS, *The Imitation of CHRIST* (*ca.* 1413)

It was evening, the white round moon gaping in the sky, and icicle-collars dripped down the walls of Kebec, which were mainly gloomy except where the sun struck some high place between chimneys and tinted it. Outside the church, Père Le Jeune's hands were chilled red and numbed. Inside he shivered. But he knew himself to be clothed in the pure serenity of CHRIST, which if he but succeeded in mastering himself would warm him better than warmth.

In this year the Jesuits had established a College to serve the needs of the French and Indian boys. Père Le Jeune resolved to have Père Daniel return from the Huron Country this summer or next (he being most easily spared of the priests, as most optimistic), bringing with him any boys from that Nation who seemed suitable. (Jean's letter had put the idea in his head. Jean was filled with cunning for the LORD! Jean had written to him that parents would naturally elect to go where their children went after death. Comprehending so well this mechanism of hearts, Jean now saw the way to incorporate it into a large clock which would tick away the DEVIL's last moments. Could he do it? Surely the children were the ones to work on. Once their souls were walled off forever from those of their parents, Jean's shining wedge would work itself deeper into this pagan community of its own accord, splitting and killing its unclean flesh. Then the Christian graveyards would grow, and the heathen ossuaries would fall into disuse, until at last there'd be a new People here, happy and frenchified, who knew nothing anymore of divorce or sorcery or dancing . . . Ah, clever, clever Jean de Brébeuf!) Now if only some widow of the laity might open a school for the young girls also! In his *Relation* Père Le Jeune wrote another appeal. – How odd it was that the female religious responded so fervently! He wrote: *Alas, if the excesses and superfluities of some of the Ladies of France were employed in this holy work, what a great blessing they would bring upon their family! What glory in the sight of the Angels to gather up the Blood of the* SON OF GOD *to apply it to these poor infidels!*

Over and over, sitting at his desk, he recited Montagnais words to himself. He knew the names of their tribes now, although he had not met them all: *White Fish, Papinachois, Porcupines, Squirrels, Oumamiois* . . .

It was a very cold winter throughout New France. A Savage told him that in Acadia some Souriquois, finding no game, had killed one of their boys and eaten him. For this they blamed not themselves but the French, saying that they'd driven the beasts from their Country. A man of the Montagnais Nation died of cold, for which the Black-Gowns were also blamed, seeing that they had given him a statue of JESUS . . .

At the end of that winter there came news of considerable interest to Père Le Jeune. A Savage conveyed it in exchange for some prunes: the Sorcerer Manitousiou had at last provoked GOD beyond His patience, for that winter he had fallen sick and the Montagnais, weary with caring for him, burned him alive in his Cabin. – Now at last Père Le Jeune could weep for the man's folly. – The Savage who had brought him the tidings was astonished. – But you should be *happy, happy*, my Nicanis! I tell you this only to gladden you with the death of this bad man! – It is wrong to be happy when anyone dies unbaptized, said Père Le Jeune. Now he must burn with his poor wife . . . – At once the Savage, seeing tears still glistening on the Black-Gown's cheek, began to howl with him in the greatest dolor, until to ease his heart Père Le Jeune gave him more prunes . . .

The Drought
1635

During the customary prayer I felt much assistance in general from a warm grace.

SAINT IGNATIUS, *Spiritual Diary*
(1544)

That spring the epidemic abated (it had not really been so serious) and Père Brébeuf was pleased extremely to learn that Louys de Saincte Foy was now once again performing his duties as a Christian. Indeed, he spoke with Père Brébeuf in great earnest, saying that he desired to return to Kebec to devote himself to piety with the Black-Gowns there. In the end, however, he chose to pass that time with Père Brébeuf instead. He attended the Sacrament, prayed, and made a good confession. It was clear that he feared GOD. And throughout his stay in Ihonatiria he proved extremely willing to interpret for Père Brébeuf, so that greater hold could be gained upon the Huron speech.

There remained the matter of the Souriquois woman who was living with him in concubinage. At Confession he assured Père Brébeuf that since his redemption from the hands of the Hiroquois he'd spoken with her, and they had given up their mutual sin. Yet Père Brébeuf found the young man's eyeballs to be shinily equivocal when he resurrected the subject in conversation that evening.

Louys, Louys, what is she to you that you endanger your soul? he said in anguish.

Oh, but you are correct to be severe with me, Père! said Amantacha in a low voice. I have but little wisdom. Would you like to speak with her?

Père Brébeuf started. – You brought her with you?

She is in the longhouse where the Arendouane sits.

Born Underwater

She was not the fresh young girl that Père Brébeuf had remembered. He stood looking upon her. The usual crowd of Savages had gathered about him, crying out for presents, so that she could scarcely have been unaware of him as he cocked his head like a tall black crow, but she did not look up from the corn soup that she was stirring.

Born Underwater, he said.

I am here, she said flatly, still not looking at him. But she was blushing. He had not expected this, and slowly he felt his own cheeks becoming warm, as if he had inadvertently disturbed a lady in her bath in France.

His mind, which was usually like a buckskin sack crammed with words, was empty. This had never happened to him before.

Black-Gown, Black-Gown, give us corn! said a little boy in a singsong voice, and still Père Brébeuf could think of nothing to say. He knew well that the situation was damaging to his prestige, and so made a tremendous effort to say something to her, anything. At last he heard himself say:

You must have been alarmed when Louys was in the hands of the Hiroquois.

Not this time, she said, stirring her soup. She still refused to look at him. Someday they will burn him, but not yet.

What? Why do you say that?

What is it that you want with me? she said. Louys can speak French with you as well as I.

Again he could think of nothing to say. After a moment, he turned and left the longhouse. The children clamored at him, but their voices were like far-off bells whose sound was carried away on the wind.

Answers

And *baptism*, my sister's son – what is that? asked the Huron pitiably, as if they were children.

Have you lived? cried Père Brébeuf.

They looked at him in confusion. – Yes, Echon, we live now and we know life.

That is good, the Black-Gown said. Then you know the pain and difficulty of life, do you not, my brothers and sisters? Perhaps you hunters feel it when you are alone in the woods on a dark winter day, searching for a deer or a bear when there is nothing, and you are weak with hunger. You women know it when your little children die and you must bury them. When these things happen to you and you believe nonetheless that JESUS loves you, *then* you will be ready to be baptized.

But will it heal us? they said timidly.

Père Brébeuf considered well, and decided to make the matter no more subtle than was necessary for their understanding. – Yes, it will heal you, he said.

Ho, ho! they cried, with every expression of joy. Echon, that is good!

Born Underwater was there. Among this People she was known as a great dreamer.

I know that you do not believe you can heal them, she said to him in French.

The LORD can, if He chooses, he said. (Why did she make him so angry?)

She smiled faintly.

They say: *Echon, that is good*, he insisted.

They will never contradict you, she said. That is not their way.

The woman seemed to be fascinated by him – why, he could not tell. Her intensity made him uneasy.

At Work

In the month of Mars, when the snow had begun to soften, a woman twenty-four hours in travail brought forth a babe happily when the Black-Gowns applied a relic of Our Blessed Père Saint Ignatius. It was a victory: the child lived just long enough to be sent to Heaven on the wings of baptism. While Père Davost unpocketed some prunes and other trifles which he saw fit to set before the mother with great solemnity, Père Brébeuf went outside the palisadoes and knelt down to pray in solitude, so happy to have saved a fresh soul from the DEVIL's maw. Again and again he recited his *Ave*; those words said to bring surpassing joy to the VIERGE as she sat crowned in Heaven. The wind blew snow down his back, but he scarcely felt the cold. It was for him as it had been for Père Le Jeune the previous winter among the Montagnais, that no matter how much love one bore these Savages, it was a good thing to be alone from time to time. Alone he could better feel GOD's nearness to him; every breath was sweeter because he breathed His loving condescension even in this twilight of bare red trees, purple ice. (But Tehorenhaennion the Shaman was watching, and said to others: See how Echon goes into the night alone, like a dead spirit! I seem to glimpse flames coming from his mouth!)

The Embassy of the Island Savages

In that same month, an embassy of the Island Savages (who are a Tribe or Nation of the Algoumequins) came to Wendaké with twenty-three collars of porcelain to rouse up the Huron against the Irocois, who had murdered this number of the Island Savages notwithstanding the peace. But the Wendat refused these presents, for Island Savages extorted great tolls of corn and other things when the Wendat passed by way of their rivières, to visit the Iron People. That was why the Captains and the Old Men of the Wendat greeted these Ambassadors without love, although they called a Council to consider the question – since doing otherwise would have been an insult.

Père Brébeuf had also been invited to the Council, for the same reason of courtesy. With him he brought his two companions and also his serving-men, thinking thereby to make a more imposing delegation. It was very smoky in these lodges. No doubt that was why the old Savagesses so often had red-rimmed eyes. There were no women, here, of course; women did not speak in Council. He could hear Born Underwater outside, near the House of Cut-Off Heads. She was playing with some little girls, putting collars of glass beads about their necks so that they laughed. It was really quite pretty, the way that she had adorned them in her Savage fashion. (Amantacha said that she was barren.) He sat with his companions in blackness and listened to Born Underwater and the little children until they moved away, and then he heard a harsh bird-sound, and then the crackle of the fire was all that he heard. He must strive to impress these great Captains with his authority, although (truth to tell) his thoughts were elsewhere –

At this Council, One-Eye of the Isle rose and spoke in the high speech of formal quavers called *Acwentonch*, saying: Hear me, you Captains of the Wendat! My body is hatchets. Fight with us! Preserve me, my brothers, and you will continue to get the French trade. If not, not – for I am master of the Iron People. I have spoken.

Père Brébeuf told the other Black-Gowns what he had said, and they all laughed together to hear such folly.

One-Eye darted a look at them. Père Brébeuf stared him down.

On the following day, after the CAPTAIN OF THE DAY had spoken four times, so that the Black-Gowns could enjoy once more that shady private time in which they loved to write their *Relations* and make their Exercises, the Island Savages came in secret, seeking to persuade them to leave the Bear Nation. They mean to slay you tomorrow. – These Huron are most wicked, they said, for they slew Brûlé and Père Nicolas. – But Père Brébeuf gave them bread and smiled and said: You give us much to reflect upon, my good friend, but on the whole I believe we shall stay, as our bodies are made of stronger stuff than hatchets . . .

One-Eye went to the lodge of Tehorenhaennion (which was a wigwam apart, where he retired to fast) and said: I hereby return your presents, for I could not persuade them to come with me. Yet I marked well how they laughed in Council like children without intelligence. It is well both for me and for you, Tehorenhaennion, if they leave your Country. I know them and their like. If they are children indeed then they can be persuaded. If they are not, then ill-mannered mockers they are, who must in time overstep themselves.

I take comfort in all these words, my brother, said Tehorenhaennion. But let us keep this matter in confidence, for Echon is popular here, and I would be blamed if it were known that I sought to remove him.

The river of words in my mouth is choked up with stones. I promise you.

The next day he and his warriors took their leave, very ill-pleased with the outcome of their embassy. As for Tehorenhaennion, he sat alone and repeated: I wonder why he walks at night? I begin to be astonished at him. I begin to believe that his mind has seven linings . . .

Leaves and Hairs

One day in the Month When the Pickerel Run, Amantacha and his *asqua* Born Underwater went into the forest to have joy of each other, and afterward they sat together on a log and Born Underwater said: Are there many inhabitants in the Country of the Iron People?

Amantacha nodded. He pointed to the leaves of the trees around them. – As many as these, he said.

And the Black-Gowns?

He indicated the hairs on his head. – As many as these, he said.

Born Underwater said nothing.

The Glitter in His Eyes

Spring continued clear and dry. Born Underwater went outside the palisade with the other women to gather wood, this being the time of year for that. The women lashed great bundles of dead branches to their backs; they tied the forehead-collars for each other and returned home, giggling nervously, for fear of the Hiroquois. – Amantacha's sister Teondisewan stayed close by Born Underwater, to help her, since she was a foreign woman and did not know how to do things. – This wood is very crisp, Teondisewan said to her. The dirt is hard, here in the forest. – My People would move their wigwams in these conditions, replied Born Underwater. The game-beasts will not stay here. – We do not wander about like you, said Teondisewan. If a drought comes we must bear it. – I think that it will come, said Born Underwater.

On the twentieth day of Avril the Black-Gowns baptized an old Savagess. – Do you want to go to Heaven or Hell? said Echon. She did not know either of these places. No one but this Oki had ever spoken of them before. She was very ill, and wished that he would go away. – I will go where my son wishes, she said.

Eh, then, said Echon to the son, a man in his middle years, it seems that you have the charge of your mother's soul. Do you wish her to go to the good place or the bad place when she dies? Her father went to the good place. We helped him.

The son was uncomfortable. His apprehensions were like the shadows of dead branches swinging overhead. It seemed that Echon desired his mother to die. Else why not speak of her recovery? He longed to split Echon's head like a pumpkin, to see the blood and brains come out. But doing that would have brought trouble upon his Nation and relations.

I wish her to go to the good place, he said at last.

Then Echon rose up exultant from beside the dying woman, and all who saw the glitter in his eyes wondered what it was that he had seized from her.

Popularity

At Easter, Amantacha came to the Black-Gowns in order to be confessed. He was on his way to war against the Irocois once more. – My people love you, Père Echon, he said. You must promise never to leave us, for if you did our souls would again be in danger of burning. – (He could speak the way the waterfalls of the Rivière Saint-Charles curled halfway around themselves so gracefully at Kebec – yes, how charmingly he spoke!) – At the end of that month, when it was sunny and rainy and warm, the Savagesses betook themselves to the fields, and began to plant their flint-corn seeds in the low mounds of earth which they'd turned up with their wooden spades, hummocking the soil like moles or grave-diggers in the first spring when their village was new; they used the same corn-hills year after year. Père Brébeuf counted a few of these mounds for the sake of the *Jesuit Relations*. He calculated that there must have been almost twenty-five hundred per acre. – There goes Echon again, smiled the Savages, making his black marks of Sorcery! – Père Brébeuf no longer sought to contradict them on this point. If they thought him a Sorcerer, so much the better. – He saw Born Underwater with some other women planting sunflower seeds on the margin of the corn, and he knew that she saw him because she suddenly turned away. At this, the women, who had been laughing among themselves as they worked, craned their heads and stared at him, falling silent. The Black-Gown hastened away. – Look how his shadow clings to the corn, a woman whispered. It stays, like something so sticky and dark . . . !

The Drought

It is not as easy to convert these Huron as I had thought at first. (Thus Père Brébeuf.) They tend so easily to relapse into apostasy. But he said to himself: Take heart, and consider the new farms in this country of Canada, where in spring they must sow the seed three times due to white frost and worms, yet no one would deny that the soil of this Country is fertile!

Frowning, he stretched out his hand to them. His sleeves were like the black tips of a seagull's wings.

There now came a time of extreme dryness of forests and fields, during which the Savages were much alarmed for their crops, and the danger of conflagrations was very high. Scarcely any rain fell, from Easter to the month of Juin. Half the village of Teannaostoaiaé, where Amantacha lived, was consumed by fire once again, and several other towns burned also. The cornfields turned brown, and crows cawed harshly overhead.

The People cried: Nephews, pray your spells for us!

They wrung their hands, saying: Echon, you must help us!

At last they turned to their Sorcerers.

Tehorenhaennion was known to be very powerful in these arts. His name took good measure of his arrogance, for it signified *He Extends Beyond the Treetops*, as Amantacha had explained. Of course his so-called magic was but blasphemous juggleries, as Père Brébeuf well knew, for in 1628 this Tehorenhaennion had invoked the rain without effect. Père Brébeuf had been mightily consoled and edified by such a result, which he considered a sign from GOD that SATAN's reign was coming to an end at last here. But the Huron did not remember; they were like children. Eh, they must be taken in hand. Indeed it seemed that Tehorenhaennion's insolence remained unfettered, for in this new extremity he swore to make it rain in exchange for ten hatchets, at which the Black-Gowns cried out: Have a care lest you fall deeper into idolatry! – but the Huron only laughed insolently and said: Your magic is no good, my nephews, for you cannot make the rain fall anymore! – The day came for Tehorenhaennion to perform his mummeries, a hot day heavy with droning flies, and on the flaccid breezes of noon there was no rain. – The BIRD OF THUNDER is frightened, he said. He does not want to come. – All day Tehorenhaennion made his conjurations, but not a drop of rain did he extract from the sky.

You see, cried Père Daniel in triumph, he is an impostor, misled by SATAN!

Let him be, brother, said Père Brébeuf quietly. We will prove ourselves in our own good time.

Tehorenhaennion tried to help these others, and bring what they said into agreement with what was known to be true, but even this seemed to aggravate them, for they raised their voices and gesticulated much as Chawain and the Grey-Gowns had done. Presently he began to be enraged against them.

Père Davost now came fluttering to him like a black crow and cried: You will burn forever! You are our enemy forever!

Tehorenhaennion looked over his shoulder at him, with half-lowered eyes. (His eyelids were very wide, like paddle-blades.) He lifted his chin for a moment, the corner of his mouth twitching in scorn.

You know as little of courtesy as you know of good magic, you who are called *Charcoal!* he said. But there is something that I see before my eyes, and I say it now for all to hear: you are jealous, and therefore witches. That is why the rain cannot fall in the shadow of your Cross!

Ah, said Père Daniel, coming to join the other priest in the torture. And do you wish to instigate our murder now? Are we to be treacherously struck down like Monsieur Brûlé?

All the People know that you who are called *Charcoal* crave revenge for his death, said Tehorenhaennion (and the other Savages standing about said nothing). It is easy enough to see that you are Sorcerers. Perhaps you intend to kill us. Yes, I verily believe it. You have erected your Cross to frighten the THUNDER-BIRD away! So our corn will die, and we will die.

Now the Savages began to murmur against the Black-Gowns.

They are OKIS! said Tehorenhaennion, loudly, evenly, clearly. Their Cross is an evil spirit!

Brother, you know not what you do, said Père Brébeuf. My heart aches for you –

If you have the compassion you claim, then take down your Cross! another Savage shouted.

Brébeuf smiled.

Hide your Cross away a little while, my nephews! (Thus one of the Old Men, pleading.) Its red color is as a fire flaming; the rain-clouds divide in twain above it. The THUNDER-BIRD is afraid.

Who says so?

Tehorenhaennion says it.

Eh, we Black-Gowns rarely follow Tehorenhaennion's advice, said Père Brébeuf mildly.

At this, the Huron began to reproach him and his crew for their perfidious sorceries against the rain, and a man cried: Evil ones, we will beat you to death! – but at this the Black-Gowns merely drew their robes tight about themselves and said: We are ready. – Then the Huron were aghast, and knew not what to say or believe. They dispersed in muttering crowds –

Now we must be very cautious, and not go anywhere alone until their hearts are calmed, said Père Brébeuf. I know these people. They are very easily roused.

The next day it was very quiet in the house of the Black-Gowns, and the CAPTAIN OF THE DAY struck noon unheard by any guests, and Père Brébeuf saw that Père Davost was clenching his mouth as he prayed. The afternoon was very hot. The notes of locusts came so rapidly as to resemble changes of light underwater . . . Presently the Black-Gowns heard laughter nearby, and went out in a body to see what game might be played against them. Some young people among the Savages had erected a Cross on the roof of their longhouse and were shooting at it with arrows. By grace of GOD they missed the mark. The Black-Gowns stood watching like silent crows until the youths saw them and shouted: Go back into your house or we will shoot you also!

You may shoot *at* us if you please, said Père Brébeuf, but your arrows will reach us only if Our FATHER wills. – Then he led the others back into their house.

What now? said Père Davost dispiritedly.

We must hold a Mass for rain, said Père Brébeuf. Rain will fall, if GOD desires.

Then he went into the chapel to pray.

When they were alone, Père Daniel shouted at Père Davost: Do you know what I think of your heart?

Don't tell me, said the other.

I said, do you know what I think of your heart?

Père Davost looked up brightly, as if he had not heard. He was blinking very very rapidly. He whispered: I sometimes become saddened and believe that, although we are so eager to harvest the fruit of souls, in the end it is only crows who will reap this harvest, running riot in the field like black masqueraders –

When the People were told that the Black-Gowns were preparing invocations and sorceries on their behalf, their hearts melted to mildness, and they came in a body to the house, promising to do whatever might be required of them, if only their corn might be saved. For among them it is a custom that when one of their Captains or Old Men is begged to give his opinion, then it must be followed exactly – not because he has any authority over them, but because they have asked him. When they call in a Shaman it is the same.

You must hate your sins, instructed the Black-Gowns. – They led the Savages in procession through the village, delighting in their numbers, and Père Brébeuf exposed the Sacrament. – I now make a vow of nine Masses to the Spouse of Our LADY, Saint Ioseph, who is the protector of this Country, said he. – *Ho!* cried the Savages.

The encensoir was so riddled with holes that it reminded them of a pine cone.

Precisely at the completion of the Novena, a heavy rain began to fall. In triumph, the Black-Gowns offered another Novena to the Blessed Father Saint Ignatius, whose tears of pity from the clouds had saved the corn, had given the corn Power to form perfect ears, and the People sang songs of joy and said: GOD is good and you who are called *Charcoal* are good! – Then they began to abuse their Sorcerers.

Post Mortem

That was all very well, repeated Père Davost when the Black-Gowns were alone at last, but it is easy to see that they value us only as long as we can fulfill their desires.

Have no fear, brother, said Père Brébeuf. Our PÈRE will provide.

No, no! the other shouted. We are responsible for the sterility or fecundity of the earth, under penalty of our lives; we are the cause of droughts;

if we cannot make rain they speak of nothing less than making away with us . . .

Make the Contemplation of the Apostles, Ambroise, said Père Brébeuf. What is the First Point?

Our LORD called the Apostles . . . said Père Davost in a low voice.

And he gave them power to cast out DEVILS. Can you see Him now? Make the Exercise, and *see* Him!

I see His face . . . I see Him.

As for me, I see everything, said Père Brébeuf very slowly, as if he were dreaming. – I see my prayers; they're like – like greenish-brown rivers in the evening, when they glow with spruce-light and –

When they glow beneath the hot and cloudy sky, said Père Davost, with a superior smile. – Oh, Jean, don't think you're the only one. The Stream of Time flows through *my* Exercises also, you know.

I never claimed to be the only one, said Père Brébeuf. I see no more than you. It is not my will that has placed me as Superior over you.

The Custom of the Country

Now the Hatitsihenstaatsi were in extremely good odor, and felt free to make whatever suggestions they would. As it always does above a difficult rapid which one has just ascended, the Stream of Time stretched wide and smooth across its flaky bed of shale, sunlight-riddled to warm the shivering bleeding Black-Gowns, with also an abundance of spruce-shade beneath the striated root-crowned cliffs . . . What docile Savages! They feasted the Black-Gowns on corn and red beans well intermixed with dried raspberries . . . On Sundays the Black-Gowns held Mass twice a day, as always; they continued their practice of awarding prizes for the catechism of children. And Père Brébeuf opened the doors of their souls, pulling outward to let the light in despite the resistance of the DEVILS inside. When he ridiculed their superstitions, seeking to undermine faith in them and thus to pulverize them to dust, the Savages replied as politely as they might: But, Echon, this is the custom of our Country! – Because this reply was so mild, Père Brébeuf was gladdened in his heart, knowing that the DEMONS were becoming faint. Indeed, in his "Rules for the Discernment of Spirits" had not Saint Ignace exposed this very matter? – *It is the nature of our ENEMY to become weak, lose courage, and take to flight as soon as a person who is following the spiritual life stands courageously against his temptations and does exactly the right opposite of what he suggests.*

You fear the Irocois, he said to them. If they should ever attack in winter, when there is nowhere to hide, you will be defenseless. That is why I encourage you to build square forts like the French, with palisades of stakes in a straight line, and a tower at each corner. If you did this thing, four Frenchmen could defend you with arquebuses.

Ah, we must consider that well, Echon, they said to him with smiles. That has not been the custom of our Country.

On the thirteenth day of Juin, the Hiroquois in ambush split the heads of twelve Huron near the village of Contarea, where the green cornstalks reached up toward GOD. And the Hiroquois skinned the crowns of their heads, to strip them of their scalps, which they greatly prized for their devilish ceremonies. Great were the angry lamentations that rose to Heaven that day. Among the murdered was a young nephew of Amantacha's who had just recently married, hearing which the Black-Gowns pitied that unhappy family. A party of warriors tracked the enemy some distance through the forest, where spiderwebs were as richly translucent as French lace, but soon they reached a stream with many branches, down any one of which the Hiroquois could have sped in their canoes –

Do you see now? said Père Brébeuf. That is why you must build square forts in the French manner.

You are surely correct, replied the Savages, and our own words nothing but lies.

But they did nothing.

On the twenty-seventh day of Août, there was an eclipse of the moon. Because the phenomenon had appeared over their enemies' Country to the southeast, the Wendat believed that it forecast their defeat at the hands of the Irocois. – The MOON is not well! Tehorenhaennion sang. The GREAT TURTLE moves His shell! We must shoot into the SKY to deliver us from danger! – At his word they launched their arrows, shouting: May the Hiroquois perish! – And Tehorenhaennion made an eat-all feast, to turn the evil aside. – The Black-Gowns stood by, saying: Brothers, this is idolatry. – But the Wendat said that this also was their custom.

The Loser

Tehorenhaennion, who'd gotten his songs from dreams, from the whistling and rushing of waterfalls, who'd plucked them laboriously from bird-songs and insect-songs, from rock falling against rock, could not but hate Echon for treading on song-webs with his foot and trampling them down, for making mock of them. Again he had sung his rain-songs, and Echon had made him appear to others as a fool. Echon had taken the rain from him, and brought it himself. How could Tehorenhaennion's songs have Power when they were mocked even as he sang them?

Now he wanted very much to bring Echon low.

What kind of men were Echon and his fellow Sorcerers? He must comprehend them to destroy them.

He'd seen how they walked about at night. The soul was divisible, as he well knew. It could walk ahead of the body; it could come into the longhouses to eat. And it often went abroad by night.

Were they strange fragments of souls, then, that had wandered from the Country of the Dead?

He fasted, and thought upon it.

There were five parts of the soul (as all the Old Men knew): – *viz*., the *Khiondhecwi* or Animator, the *Oki Andaerani* or Demon, the *Endionrra* or Reasoner, the *Gonennoncwal* or Desirer, and the *Esken* or Bone-Dweller which remained with the corpse until the Feast of the Dead.

Now it was evident to Tehorenhaennion that the Black-Robes were disturbed in their souls, and Echon most of all, for he was their leader. In this man's spirit, Reasoner flourished, as could not be denied, for Père Echon loved to dispute and insist upon this point. But he reasoned like a Hiroquois. His words were tricks, and his heart was filled with poison, as Tehorenhaennion had learned to his own bitterness. But in this Echon Desirer was also reaching out, although *what* he desired Echon himself might not know. Indeed, there were many such cases, when people dreamed of something but did not know why. Echon's mind had many linings. Who knew what serpent's nest was at the bottom of its rotten darkness? At first Tehorenhaennion had believed that he comprehended Echon's desire, which was simply that Reasoner be praised: again, there were many men like this. Headmen who wanted to be considered wise, young men untested, these men craved good words, and Tehorenhaennion sought as well as anyone else to grant them their wishes, for doing so caused happiness and cost nothing. But Echon was not so simple. Praise and agreement were not all that he wanted. He appeared to be drawn to death, and hovered about it when his presence was least welcome. He was joyous when others died, and chanted songs. He might be a Bone-Dweller, then. Who knew what his nephews were capable of? How Tehorenhaennion longed to bash his head in! – Perhaps the fault lay in that part of the soul called Demon. Many thought this; that was why they called him OKI. But Tehorenhaennion was not certain. In the end he had no conclusions. He bided his time and watched Echon, who was his enemy. He said to himself: Let the winner laugh; let the loser weep.

Amantacha and Born Underwater

On the twentieth day of Septembre, a chilly day of rustling leaves, when the cornstalks and the forest seemed browner and drier than the day before, Amantacha's father, old Soranhes, came to request the baptism of the entire family. Père Brébeuf was more surprised than joyous at this request, and asked what had decided him upon such a step (as always, he expected little from him). Soranhes replied that he had begun to think upon it the previous year, on the day that Amantacha was captured by the Hiroquois. He himself had escaped into the forest, where he starved for ten or twelve days and shivered with the cold, for he was almost naked; and at last when he felt himself weakening he recollected the GOD to which his son sometimes prayed, and knelt to say his LORD's Prayer as he knew it: *GREAT SPIRIT, please give us food!* and at once he seemed to see a pot of grease before his eyes and a Voice said: Eat, old Soranhes, and strengthen yourself! and he ate of this grease and was satisfied. – Père Brébeuf could not restrain a smile at this tale, seeing which Soranhes waxed indignant and shouted: Do you say that I lie? – That is between you and your GOD, said Père Brébeuf. – On the fourth of the following month, they who were called *Charcoal* set out to determine the family's disposition toward the Faith. The number of these miracle-workers had now been swelled by two – *viz.*, Père Pijart and Père Le Mercier, who had come from Kebec with the trade. These stayed in Ihonatiria under charge of Père Davost, for their voyage had exhausted them almost to illness, although they'd not been compelled to paddle this year. So it was only Pères Daniel and Brébeuf who made the journey. Amantacha's mother, Yatera,* had prepared a feast for them, to which the other aunts and nieces who lived there had also contributed. Teondisewan, Amantacha's elder sister, was unfortunately ill. Tehorenhaennion had but lately come to cure her. Beside the sleeping platform where the girl lay they saw a gourd which contained one of his potions, and Père Daniel stamped with rage. But the feast was all that could have been wished. The women gave them good

* Tree Root.

welcome, pulling down armfuls of dried fish and dried corn from the rafters of the longhouse and boiling it together over the fires, so that the visitors were satisfied. There was a sturgeon of sufficient size, as Brébeuf thought, to feed an entire monastery . . . They stayed with them in Teanaostaiaé for seven days, Amantacha interpreting their words so that the family could be instructed in all the important points of the Christian religion. The matter of conjugal continence was very difficult for them, as was only to be expected from this people of filthy license. Nor had the earlier French visitors, such as Monsieur Brûlé, set a very good example. They had been just as addicted as the Savages themselves to indulge in folâtrerie with the Huron girls. For this reason, Père Brébeuf would have considered himself on weak ground had he ordered Amantacha to send his concubine away. Rather did he take the boy aside and explain to him that unless he was prepared to be shut out from the True Faith he must marry his squaw –

I agree, said Amantacha readily, smiling and ducking his head. (He had always been confident, in more or less the same way that a bird can alight on a branch with the branch swaying as if breeze-blown, in short rapid oscillations, as the bird eyes life unconcerned.) – But there is one thing that I must tell you, my Père.

And what is that? I hope it is no insuperable matter. Your missing finger ought to remind you of Our PÈRE's impatience.

Perhaps you should speak with her directly, said Amantacha.

It would be better for you to tell me.

But I – I can't tell you. That's how it is. I want to tell you, but I can't. You will take it as a sign of opposition. I . . .

Abruptly, the young man fled. Père Brébeuf stood frowning, while curious faces peered at him. Savages, Savages!

At last the woman herself appeared on the scene, and he looked into the broad flat face of her; his soul-questions struck the jet-black eyes of her and glittered; and she smoothed back her hair and looked up into his face.

Born Underwater looked at him levelly. – You are disappointed in us, Echon.

Yes, disappointed, said Père Brébeuf, but also alarmed. You know that I mean your good.

My good. I see.

Her contempt infuriated him. But he must not proceed *bredi-breda* – which is to say, hastily. He said to himself: This too is a temptation of BEELZEBUB. Patience, Jean, patience.

What is it that your partner in fornication was unable to tell me?

I do not want to take your faith, she said.

The Black-Gown curled his lip. – And why is that, woman?

I have the seeing-ahead.

Here too there are devilish juggleries? he exclaimed in horror. Have you not heard the tale of how our GOD has bested the Sorcerer Tehorenhaennion once again and made the rain come? And this very village already half burnt up by drought-fire, they told me –

Tehorenhaennion is like *this*, said Born Underwater, disdainfully slapping at an imaginary mosquito. – That is how all the Sorcerers are in this Country. I come from a different Country where we dream our dreams. In my Country we have Power.

My child, I fear for you in your pride and your dark, dark ignorance, he said. I do not know what to tell you. But it is clear that you must not live with Amantacha as long as you believe the things you say that you do. You cannot be permitted to compromise him in his faith – if indeed he has any faith. Now I wonder whether I should baptize this family or not.

Oh, I see-ahead, she said. That much I see well. You will not baptize them.

Bring Amantacha here, he said shortly.

She turned and left him. The clatter of her wampum necklaces echoed in his ears. Then the boy returned by himself, with the sheepish look of a poor pupil at school.

So that is how it is, said Père Brébeuf decisively. You must leave this companion of your sins and –

But, my Père, the boy pleaded warmly, in his low liquid voice whose half-Parisian modulations never ceased to soften the priest's heart, no matter how much he might do to hide it, my Père, she has no place to go! If we turn her out, the People will murmur against the Christians – not that they care much for her, as she is a foreigner – but they will call us selfish and ungenerous. And I have told my father: *Echon says that if we make songs to JESUS, our longhouse will never be burned, even by the Hiroquois.* He believes now . . . Please, my Père, baptize him and my mother and sisters: – for so many months we have been begging for you to come! My mother's sister and her sons also long to become Christians; they contributed to the feast for you. Now that you are here you must not disappoint us. Do you wish our neighbors here to ridicule us, saying that the Iron People only make sport of my father and all his kinsfolk? I promise to sin no more with – with her, until she takes the Faith, and has become my wife. She will –

I *know* you, Louys de Saincte Foy, said Père Brébeuf sternly. I see your heart, and it is riddled with the maggots of wickedness. Now leave me. I must discuss your case with my brother. And I cannot imagine that it will go well for you.

A Happy Occasion

Surprisingly enough, Père Daniel was of a mind with Amantacha, for he possessed equal anxiety that this conspicuous visit have a favorable outcome.
– So be it, said Père Brébeuf wearily. How this boy disappoints me! We will have him swear an oath that he will live no more with this woman until the Church grants him license. We agree, then, that the Souriquois woman will return to Ihonatiria with us, to keep Louys from temptation. We do agree? Good. Now, Antoine, would you be so kind as to summon the family?

The two Pères explained that it was necessary to learn how to make the Sign of the Cross, to say the Pater, the Ave and the Apostles' Creed.

My sister's son, this is but a small matter, said Soranhes. My memory is good. I often go to various Nations with various tidings.

Very good, said Père Brébeuf, but he distrusted the old man. His suspicion was confirmed when he saw how difficult it was for him to learn the Sign of the Cross.

We will not baptize you now, said the Hatitsihenstaatsi, smiling.

A Guest of Foxes

If you marry this woman (thus Teondisewan to Amantacha), then I shall be proud to bring her the armload of wood that custom requires. All the women in our lodge love her now.

This was not quite true, of course, since anyone foreign-born can never truly become a member of the People in full standing; yet it was a fact that Born Underwater had her friends, though not yet any clan. She knew that she was not of them, just as she had not been of her old husband's People, the Innuat, nor her mother's People, the Lnu'k, nor her father's People the Iron Ones . . . So she learned from her new sister Teondisewan how to care for the corn-seeds, and what to sing in the fields. So she wove a large belt of glass beads for her aunt Yatera. She began to grease her hair with sunflower oil rather than meat-fat (which she had always used before), for here in Wendaké the flesh of beasts was less common than sunflowers. In these efforts of hers the People saw that she acknowledged their superiority, and so out of kindness they treated her as if she were one of them. (The other girls teased her sweetly: Amantacha says that you are tender, like bear-flesh! . . .) They strove not to call her *the Lnu'k woman*. But she almost wept sometimes when no one could see her in the cornfields, remembering how much her mother had loved her, how she used to wander in the forests, how her foster-father permitted her to suck tobacco-smoke from his nostrils . . .

Now her loneliness was more bitter than ever, because to please Amantacha she had gone away with the two Black-Gowns. It was only for a little, he said. He believed it. What hold did Echon have over him? And why was she in this Country? There was nowhere, nowhere for her . . . They stopped in Scahonaenrat, where the Black-Gowns said spells over a dying woman and *baptized* her. Then the woman died, and Echon seemed very pleased.

Someday, my daughter, I shall *baptize* you also, said Echon. It will be a great advantage to you to have a husband already so well instructed –

Learn now once and for all, said Born Underwater, that I do not come with you of my own will, although I fear you not. I seem to see you dying a death of flames, and so you will never *baptize* me.

How Echon gaped, turning down his mouth like a salmon!

After this the Black-Gowns did not speak to her, which pleased her exceedingly.

An early snowfall came just before they departed Scahonaenrat. The trails were still passable, and the Black-Gowns never complained. They were great men in their way, though evil –

Now Ihonatiria came into sight, with lavender smoke-blushes rising from the longhouses dark and stark against the snowy hill, and the warriors who watched from the palisadoes called out to them, and they entered the winding way.

The Black-Gowns regarded her uncertainly, as if they were afraid that she might expect to lodge with them. She would be astonished if that ever came to pass. Sullenly, without a word, she left them; she went to a longhouse in which lived Amantacha's clan-friends the Foxes. There, unfastening her sleeves, she became cheerful again, as she must be among these new People she would live among, she did not know for how long. But it seemed to her that she had already endured enough. She forced a smile as they put corn soup before her –

Dream-Feast

That winter there fell more than a hundred inches of snow.

No disease crept upon the People, for which all save Tehorenhaennion were grateful to the Black-Gowns and their magic, thinking to have pleased the Cross so that it would no longer kill them. The children laughed and played upon the palisade at the edge of the forest, and sunlight burst in upon their faces when they uplifted their hands.

From the Old Men came a rumor that the Irocois lurked nearby, preparing an attack, at which the women began to scream and many families held themselves in readiness to flee into the woods, but the Irocois never came. (And they never *would* come, said Père Daniel, not while Frenchmen were here!) Indeed there were such rumors every winter. So fear turned to rage, as it usually does unconsummated, and the women told the men that they must attack the enemy without fail in the following summer, to be revenged for this fright; then rage turned to boasting, as *it* generally does unconsummated, and then the People went about as if nothing had ever happened. And they loved the Black-Gowns, for these had given them iron arrow-points from their little Store-house, when the spies came with the alarm.

In the Moon When Deer Again Form Bands, however, when they had the great feasts and dances, those who were called *Charcoal* stayed away, believing these affairs to condone idolatry, and – worse yet – to bind souls ever more tightly in that terrible fetter called family, which the Black-Gowns like other French-Canadians had given up to come here; so the People had some peace when they held their holy masquerade or Dream-Feast,* running from longhouse to longhouse regardless of the cold to ask for the gifts of which they had dreamed. Beyond the palisadoes lay the ice-smothered cornfields and then the darkness snow-white enough to glare and show shadows. The forest was high and low and black like a wall between snow below and snow above. The fearful texture of the darkness with all its scales and needles panted in Echon's ears like some hushed and wicked breath as he strode there to pray in solitude, and he heard the wind moaning upon the Sweetwater Sea. Soon, chilled and uneasy, he returned to the priests' cabin; and they sat around the fire making mournful comments about that Dream-Feast in which five hundreds of souls at a time served the DEVIL; someday they'd forbid this custom, as they all agreed; for their plans were as long as a moose's upper teeth. The People, of course, did not see it that way. Gleefully they cried to

* *Ononharoia – viz.*, Turning the Brain Upside Down.

one another: Give me the present that I have dreamed of! – to which the people in the other lodge must say: Is it this set of snowshoes which I have made, my nephew? You can have that. Is it this pouch of tobacco? Please take it, my brother. – Of all the People, Born Underwater was the best at divining which gifts the guests had dreamed of. Indeed she was better at it than Tehorenhaennion, who sometimes guessed wrong. But in his excuse it was said that he lived in a little lodge by himself, as befitted a Shaman, and so could not be expected to know people's dreams as vividly as if he shared a lodge with them. As for Born Underwater, her facility would have made them uneasy had it been displayed elsewhere, but here it delighted them. She was now a favorite in the lodge of the Foxes. – Born Underwater, you are a good little niece! they cried. You always know which things we long for! – Often the women dreamed of eelskin ribbons after the fashion of the Iron People. Born Underwater knew well how to make them, dyeing them with sturgeon-glue in her own People's fashion (Katherine Tekagouïtha was also famous for this art). Before each Dream-Feast she made great numbers of them, to have them on hand. – Needless to say, the Black-Gowns took no pleasure in her fame. – It is to be expected that she should participate in this debauchery, they said to one another, for after all, had not her mother been the inamorata of a licentious Frenchman?

Outside the lodge of those who were called *Charcoal*, each dreamer placed a stone in reproof for having been given nothing. Then they went away singing reproaches. For it is easy to sicken and die of sadness. Because the Black-Gowns would not make anyone happy, the People feared once more that they wanted them to die.

In Teanaostoiaiaé, Amantacha sat carving animal beads from a bone, for he meant to give them to Born Underwater when he saw her. He was not quite as dextrous at this Exercise as his father, who grumbled that the education that the Iron People had given him had made him clumsy and weak. – So you think so? flared the son, shockingly, like an ill-mannered Frenchman. Why did you send me, then? No matter. Next year I will go back against the Iroquois.

The Death of Champlain

Eh, it was the season for repentance. The Sieur de Champlain had erected a chapel adjacent to his Fort or Palace; here the bell rang out the triad of the day. At his table, Père Le Jeune read out the lives of the Saints, thus edifying all. Captain Merveille (who had become very pious) raised high a silver tumbler that sported leaf-fins like a fish . . . The plumed Officers nodded and said nothing, cutting their meat. And Champlain continued to make his plans for island forts stretching west to China; but in the month of Octobre he fell ill. There was a certain Sieur de Châteaufort, who had arrived at Kebec the previous year; he was a member of the Knights of Malta, a most chaste and pious Order, for which Champlain had the highest respect; all the same he could not tell precisely what the man was doing here. Evidently he was a comrade of Père Le Jeune's, because they were often together; this eased Champlain's suspicions, for he knew that the Jesuits were his good friends; they'd never enter any plot against him. Yet when his sickness increased, he found Châteaufort's face flashing loathsomely behind his closed eyes, like those fat lucioles or *fireflies* of Mechique. Châteaufort had a black beard, greasy and matted like those Montagnais girls' naked privities . . . He continued to address him in all courtesy, and never said a word about him to Père Le Jeune. Leadenly he paced about his room. One day his spies came to him saying that they had overheard Châteaufort and Père Le Jeune talking in the forest, and Châteaufort had said Père, I must insist that you return those letters I gave you and Père Le Jeune had replied you know your appointment is confirmed, and you know I am commissioned to produce those letters *at the proper time and place* at which Champlain said nothing, and the spies asked: Monsieur, shall we follow them more closely? and Champlain said leave me. – Every day Père Le Jeune came to give him spiritual direction, which he took earnestly, like a small child drinking soup. Novembre found him so much worse that he took to his bed. He drew breath with difficulty now, and had entirely lost his color. Around him, his men spoke in low voices, hiding their tears. One day when Père Le Jeune came to him he said: And these Knights of Malta, Père, will you drive them out as you did the Recollects, or will they have the victory? – I *forgive* you, cried Père Le Jeune. The matter of the letters is only for your sake, to spare your feelings! – My feelings? said Champlain in an awful voice. The bones in his face stood out like rocks in a river-channel at low water. At the proper time and place, the Jesuits confessed him. His signature huge, transfixed and trembling, he left a fine grey fox skin and other pelts to Hélène, in addition to his drawings of Savages and Canadian herbs, his maps, his *Agnus* DEI and a gold ring mounted with one of those sad Canadian diamonds. The bulk of his properties in Canada, however, he made over to the Blessed VIERGE MARIE. Before he left France he and his wife had signed over their goods each to the other, but he no longer remembered this; he scarcely thought of her; he saw only a map of golden veins on the inside of his eyelids, rivering him away to glory in a thousand directions. Père Le Jeune, who gave the sermon at his funeral, now opened the sealed letters in front of the crowd in that silent church and read them out: Marc-Antoine Bras-de-Fer de Châteaufort was acting Commandant of New France.

For six months he discharged his duties. On the eleventh of Juin, 1636, Seigneur Charles Huault de Montmagny landed at Kebec. He too brought with him letters patent, sealed with the same red wax disk impressed by the robed figure of a femme holding aloft a Latin Cross – the seal of our Compagnie of One Hundred Associates, which proved that he had been appointed Governor of New France. The letters were dated back to the month of Janvier, at the very beginning of the new year, before Champlain's death could have been known in France.

And Châteaufort, had he known that he was no less expendable than Champlain? Or had he really believed himself to be doing something more majestic than warming Champlain's chair until the Governor deigned to come sit in it? One consolation he must have had to shine about his eyes almost as brightly as gold-gleams on the black uniforms of New France's Lieutenant-Generals: his successor was also a Knight of Malta. Handing over the keys to the Fort, he bowed deeply, looking into Montmagny's eyes, and Père Le Jeune smiled at him very gently and put his hand on his shoulder. Not long after, Châteaufort sailed up the Fleuve Saint-Laurent to the settlement of Three Rivers to become Commandant. Almost nothing more is known of him.

The Death of Pastedouachouan

In this winter also there died the Montagnais apostate, Antoine-Pierre Pastedouachouan, also called the Renegade. He died because he had lost his ability to hunt while the Recollects held him in France. He died drunk and abandoned by his wives, who ridiculed him before they left him forever. He died in a bank of snow, of starvation. It was said that in his last days he who once could write French and Latin in the snow with equal ease had forgotten almost entirely how to speak. He, like Champlain, died for the greater glory of New France.

The Thirteen Contemplations

1636

And the story, which never ceases to put forward the cruelty of the Amerindians, is told in a cemetery where travellers must spend the night, and passes into the supernatural with an apparition of the VIRGIN.

GUY LA FLÈCHE, *Les saints martyrs canadiens* (1989)

In the month of Septembre, 1636, a quarter of a year after he had received the keys of Kebec from his fellow Knight of Malta, Charles Huault de Montmagny, Governor of New France, set out to tour his domains. He sailed from Cap Tourmente, which is the last settlement in New France, all the way to the Île Jésus, and he shook his head. His spies had warned him of the increasing bellicosity of the Hiroquois, and it was patent that nothing was defensible. Everywhere he went, the soldiers, priests and traders welcomed him with cheers; by the time he'd taken leave of them, their faces were grave. The danger he saw sickened him. As soon as he had returned to Kebec, he commanded that Champlain's wretched wooden Palace be rebuilt in stone and brick. He had already erected new bastions and barriers, fosses and covered ways, ravelins and batteries faced with brick. He could not believe that this had not been done before. Truly that Quartermaster had been senile in the end as well as ignorant, not to see the precarious position here. Montmagny shook his head. Everything stabbed daggers of dread into his heart. He made a proclamation interdicting the delivery of firearms to the Savages on any pretext whatsoever. He wrote to France urgently requesting more munitions for the Store-house. All through the autumn he trudged about Kebec with his officers, establishing new trenches and emplacements, watching the cold grey dream of the Fleuve Saint-Laurent . . . At last it was winter, and he knew every arpent of white fields, white sky (they could not be defended, but if the Hiroquois should strike it might be possible to control their excesses if – if . . .), and in the distance stood a row of greyish-white tree-bristles, all full of glare. Here the forest began. Here the Montagnais lived, watching over their shoulders for the dreaded Hiroquois. – He ascended to the heights and passed the outward-facing ranks of cannon; he trod over undisturbed snow with walnut tree-shadows in it as blue and fine as if they had been painted. He ascended a long snowy sweep of stone stairs. At the top was Onontio's* Palace – *his* Palace. He stood looking down, waiting for the Irocois.

Wooing a Black-Gown

In that year also, Père Le Jeune received a letter from a female religious of Tours, by name Marie of the Incarnation. She had just recently taken her vows, as it appeared. Her words were so impetuous and ardent that the gaunt Père must smile somewhat as he read it over. This Marie, a member of the Ursuline Order, wrote of her great desire to instruct the squaws or Savagesses of Canada in the True Faith: in fact, if her circumstances permitted, she would devote the remainder of her life to this task. – Ah, how sweet the lady is! thought Père Le Jeune. And yet so childish! She says that she has also written our Père Charles; she is astonished and gleeful like a petite fille because he replied to her on a sheet of smooth birchbark! – No, she is not suitable; I shall not reply.

Victory

It was also in that year that he baptized the Sorcerer's son, who was brought to him at Kebec. It gave him satisfaction to have thus triumphed over his old enemy, who must now be impotently reviling him from the most noisome dungeon of Hell. Never, never would Père Le Jeune forget the torments of that winter – three years ago it was now. He could not cease from thinking on the Sorcerer's wife. But perhaps now through the intercession of the son, the father and mother might someday be saved, for great was GOD's mercy.

* "Onontio" was the Amerindian name for any Governor of New France, beginning with Montmagny: indeed it was a literal translation of his name, "Great Mountain."

Certainly it was a mercy for this boy that the Sorcerer was dead, and could no longer influence him to do evil except in dreams. What a pity it was that Amantacha had not also been removed once and for all from bad companions . . . Père Le Jeune could at least regard the Sorcerer's son with edified pleasure: the lad was very fervent. – Good, good, he whispered, seeing him kneel before him; very softly he touched the boy's head . . .

Truly it could be said that inroads were being made among the Montagnais that year. Several had promised to settle at Sillery as soon as the houses should be ready for them – which was prudent, for beaver and other animals with valuable peltries were becoming scarcer by the Grand Fleuve; the Savages had to hunt them farther afield. (Similar reports came from Acadia, where the Souriquois now made great use of arquebuses.) – See, Nicanis, we are like seeds which are sown in diverse places, or rather like grains of dust scattered in the wind. (Thus his Montagnets.) The country is failing us. There is scarcely any more game in the neighborhood of the Iron People. Unless we reap something from the earth, we will go to ruin. We are like dust in the wind.

Silence

At the turn of the year at Teanaostoiaé the snow had been too deep for travel, and the People stayed indoors. Born Underwater sat with Amantacha's sister Teondisewan in the longhouse, learning from her how to weave twine for fishing-nets by twisting the fiber on her thigh.

I hope that Echon and his Black-Gowns do not find out about this visit! laughed Amantacha.

Born Underwater closed her eyes for a moment. – They will not find out, she said flatly.

Amantacha sat making eagle-feather arrows to launch against the Hiroquois. He wanted very much to have a gun, but the Iron People would not give him one. – Wait and be patient, Echon had said. When Wendaké has Christians in good numbers, then we will arm all of you. – That was what he'd said. Echon, stupid bearded Echon!

He attached his arrow-points with fish-glue. In his father's day sharp stones had been used, but now there were many worn-out kettles from the Iron People; their scraps made good heads.

He strung his bow with deer-gut.

Next summer I will go against the Hiroquois, he said.

That is good, said Soranhes, who was making snowshoes. That is very good. My strong son, I hope you bring back many scalps.

Teondisewan had looked up from her spinning and smiled at her brother proudly.

Born Underwater did not look up.

Brûlé's Bones

Janvier, and sedges stuck out of the ice of the Sweetwater Sea. Shadows passed across the ice; trees loomed black. Février, and the warriors began to build a grand palisado around the nearby village of Angoutenc, for fear of the Hiroquois. Mars, and the Fleuve Saint-Laurent roiled brown down the rapids, bearing dirty snow toward the sea. Avril, and the snow was but a ribbon on either shore. Mai, and the water was warm and blue . . . So also with the Stream of Time. The Eighth Rapids, for instance (*viz.*, Sault of Election), had seemed turbid and foreboding to Père Brébeuf when he first saw them. And yet, once he'd dragged himself cold and bloody up their rocks, with the falls beating upon his head, washing him back almost to the Shoals of the Eight Contemplations; once he'd shinnied up the slimy eminences until his Superior or sometimes Père Massé could reach a hand down from the summit, the next time was easier. Over and over in the course of his life he made the Exercises from beginning to end. He would not pretend that the Seventy-Third Rapid was anything but a barely passable cataract. That changed for no one but a Saint. The Eighth Rapid, on the other hand, although still formidable, had dwindled in ferocity over the years. There were places where he could have walked almost dry-shod, and the roar had diminished to a murmuring as of ghosts. To Saint Ignatius, he supposed, the entire Stream must be as calm and level as the Sweetwater Sea in midsummer.

But for now it was still Mars, and they were drumming and dreaming and preparing themselves for the Feast of the Dead.

Père Superior, they say that they'll be uncovering the dead bodies tomorrow! (Thus Père Daniel.)

And does that please you? said Brébeuf, a little ironically.

No . . . (He could not comprehend Père de Brébeuf.)

I suppose that we'll be afflicted with worms and stenches again, said Père Davost with his accustomed moroseness.

Worms will be our watchword then, said Brébeuf. And why not? All has value in the sight of GOD.

They hung on his words, those junior priests; they admired him. He'd been proven right about the baptisms. Eh, he had admirers in plenty once more, because the epidemic was at an end. Soranhes was importuning him once again to write letters of recommendation to be taken to Kebec; he wished to be baptized there, he said, in sight of the French ships. Père Brébeuf could tell that he desired this solely to increase his credit among the Iron People. So he said: It makes little difference where one is baptized. I advise you to come here to Ihonatiria, and pass some days with us, the better to consider the matter. – Yes, Echon, the other replied. I will do that. – But he never did. Then Père Brébeuf was thankful that he had not baptized him. It would have been terrible to create by an overhasty administration of that Sacrament a new Apostate or Renegade –

They were still going on and on about it. – But do they eat them? Père Davost was wondering aloud. I've heard it said that they dig up their own brothers and sisters and gobble their rotten flesh –

Brébeuf sighed a little.

Then Aenons the War-Chief had come. – Echon, my nephew! Do you not love the dead? You prate ever of them! Now hear me! We take pity on you; we seek to gladden your heart! Mingle your bones with ours at the Feast of the Dead.

Père Brébeuf chuckled. – That is not as easy as you suppose.

Do you wish to be kin with us? Day and night you say that you wish it, Echon; have you lied?

Mingle our bones, you say. Which bone do you fancy, Aenons? I'll gladly give you a rib; Adam did the same. Père Daniel can sacrifice his metacarpi . . .

(The other priests were slapping their sides. GOD knows there was little enough amusement in these parts, aside from twitting a particularly impious Savage . . .)

Or is one of us supposed to die to please you, Aenons? You know we're always ready for that. Père Davost here has just been talking about worms. I imagine he'll make good fertilizer –

You must not scorn me, my dear nephew, for it is unbecoming. I have more right to speak than you, for you are neither hunter nor warrior; you are not a great man. Hear me! I remember where our traitorous nephew lies buried. I think I can find his bones for you –

You're referring, I take it, to Monsieur Brûlé, whom you murdered?

Peace, Echon; you are as a woman; you are quarrelsome like Chawain; you scold like a bluejay; you are kin to those Grey-Gowns who used to shout at us! Echon, there is no evil in my heart. The one you name, I will not name him. There is too much hatred in my heart. For you must know that he sought to open a secret way to the Hiroquois, and that is witchcraft. – No matter; you dwell among us as our nephew. But be silent and learn: Until the bones of the Iron People are mingled with the bones of the Wendat, we cannot truly be kin. We forgive his bones for your sake –

Ah, no, said Echon. We respect our dead too much for their bones to be mingled with the bones of infidels.

But what harm would be done? Echon, Echon, I cannot comprehend you –

I have spoken.

But later he realized that he had not taken the way to friendship among these People. So he offered to raise Brûlé's bones, and have them buried in a private grave, along with the bones of the Savages whom he and his had baptized. This way the community could be divided in death as it must soon be in life. In the end, nothing came of this, due to various disputes and squabbles among the Savages – which pleased the Black-Gowns exceedingly, as they would have been hypocrites in the event (as they well knew); for to honor such an infamous libertine, wretch and traitor as this Brûlé with burial in consecrated ground would have been no better than to give his bones to the Feast of the Dead, as had been originally proposed.

Now it was the day of the feast, and the Black-Gowns set out early, and their lay brothers and hired men crushed about them like bodyguards watching for Hiroquois as they went down the Big Trail to Ossossané, where the rite would be held, and Père Davost was running a hand through his hair nervously, as though he were a dandy about to meet some sprightly fillette (Brébeuf thought this but did not say it, knowing that the man would not laugh; poor Père Davost took everything very seriously) and he heard Père Daniel say to Père Davost: We must observe this very carefully for the *Jesuit Relations* and Brébeuf wondered why Père Daniel reminded him a little of the late Monsieur de Champlain, and they saw Tchorenhaennion but he turned away from them, blind, mad and sour like GOUGOU, and it was going to be a hot day but all the Black-Gowns were pleased to see that men and women alike wore the loin-cloths required by modesty, unlike the Raccoon Nation or Neutrals as they were sometimes known, and then they came in sight of Ossossané, which would be abandoned after today because every wall was grey and scaly with age; the house-poles were brittle and the sleeping platforms creaked; the watch-platforms sagged beneath the warriors' feet; the lodges were rotten with vermin, and the soil was exhausted. – It will not be long, I fancy (thus Père Brébeuf to his crew), before all the towns of

Ouendaké are rotten and abandoned like this one, and all the Savages living happily in cabins after the fashion of our French . . . and Père Daniel cheered and Père Davost said: GOD grant that it soon be so. – The women had gone ten days since into the forest to gather swamp milkweed and basswood bark to make cord for the new longhouses, Born Underwater being the best and quickest at this task; in the forest she saw KLUSKAP's tracks like the forked feet of a moose. The other women knew little of the Plant Persons whose kindness she requested, praying in her Power to Their Power, finding ripe berries deep in thickets where the other women feared to venture; it was not in their nature to go far beyond the cornfields . . . Basswood was easy, but the swamp milkweed was shy this year; Born Underwater could find it best. Meanwhile the men had already girdled trees and felled them in the place where there would soon be new cornfields; that work went easily, thanks to the new iron axes. Everyone agreed that the fields should be enlarged, so that the People would have more corn to exchange for beaver-skins because beaver-skins brought iron things. Now the new village was ready. In a night they would move there. But first they must bid farewell to their well-beloved bone-souls. And so the Black-Gowns came into the Captain's longhouse to find that the men had so carefully painted themselves with designs of men and animals that they seemed to be suits of clothing. – Echon, such is the custom of our Country, they said. – They emerged from the winding way, and Père Davost was already holding his nose (he had a terrible fear of death), and Père Daniel smiled gamely at his Superior's side while the aforesaid Superior, Jean de Brébeuf, examined his heart to discover whether he might be prepared to look on what he must, and he saw that he was, for which grace he gave thanks to Our REDEEMER. When he'd dwelled among them before, the Feast of the Dead had fallen just before his arrival, so he'd never witnessed it, but he'd seen many a boneyard in France, where at times of famine the desperate peasants sometimes ground up skeletons to make flour and baked a hideous bread out of it, eating which they invariably died . . . Yes, he considered himself prepared. – Now they crossed the unsown cornfield still stubbled from last year and from habit everyone walked between the mounds that the women had made and the notes of locusts were so rapid as to resemble the changes of light underwater; and everyone was gathering at the scaffold on the edge of the open pit and he began to smell that smell a little and he gazed mildly at the vast blue-grey plain of the Sweetwater Sea, ripple-riddled to wool's coarseness, but softened by haze; he gazed up at clouds like shadings of light on flesh –

A mother called painfully to her dead son at the foot of the grave. The women put wampum on their dear children's arm-bones. A mother combed the hair that still clung to her son's skull, and the smell that Echon smelled was like the sweetly musky scent of Born Underwater's body (Born Underwater helped the Foxes open the burial boxes but she touched no dead flesh; she had no clan here); and Echon stood smiling a little as the Wendat welcomed their dead ones and helped their bone-souls; and the dark faces, nut-brown, the almond eyes watched him sidelong. Feathers waved in their hair like sedges in wind-blown lakes. (He admitted it now: there were aspects of these Savages that revolted him. Their lives were like the corn soup with whole fishes in it, their scales grating against his teeth; he must always be surreptitiously picking the bones from his beard, and pulling out snaky strings of fish-guts. Yet someday, when they were all Christians, he would have the capability to mold them. He would forbid them from painting their faces with earth-dyes, from dwelling in such loathsome proximity to one another, as if they were caged animals. He would teach them to eat properly. Of course these things would not come all at once . . .) – Père Davost had not vomited, he was pleased to see. Père Daniel continued very steady. – Someone was crying: *Ouai, my daughter, my daughter!* – That corpse was fresh; the girl had died of the pox. The burial boxes creaked and clattered open and the young men were down in the big hole spreading their finest beaver-skins and the crows were darkening the sky and Born Underwater remembered how among her People (*viz.*, the Lnu'k) partridges were hunted in the Moon of Leaf-Opening, when those birds commence to beat their wings in thickets with a great noise, seeking the places to make their nests; and it seemed to her that the dead ones were as caught partridges flapping, but their wings were strips of rotten flesh that their relations flapped for them easily and quickly so that the bone-souls winged themselves smaller and harder into boniness and the scrapheaps of blackish-green flesh rose up in the scaffold's shade and the burial boxes gaped empty like the Dream of the Floating Island. A girl was stripping her sister's flesh off as gently and carefully as she could. Maggots crawled onto her hands. Suddenly she cried out. She reached into her rib-cage; she held up a TURTLE effigy the size of a nut. That proved that her dear sister had been bewitched to death –

The women were shooting with the bow for a prize of wampum beads, and the men were holding a trial of strength among themselves for a similar stake. Père Brébeuf looked for Born Underwater, out of curiosity only, and saw her there, wearing Amantacha's wampum collar on her neck – in token of her continuing subjection to lewdness, as he supposed. Chains of wampum, each bead as big as a walnut, hung from her hair. He'd heard from reliable sources how Amantacha had also hung wampum beads from her ears like rosaries, thus cherishing the unlawful companion of his sin . . . Seeing her thus entirely spoiled his edification at the rite; he could not entirely explain the sinking he felt inside his breast.

Now it was time to let the bone-bundles cascade into the ossuary lined so well with skins, just as the Stream of Time spills somewhere (it must!) into its own final pool. The young men scattered the bones promiscuously among each other, to make them one. They knew that when they died, their own bones would be added to the latest pit, mixed with the loved bones of others; then the living would move to a new village, and the dead would dwell in kinship forever. Thus the Feast of the Dead, which they called *the Fire Stirred up Under the Big Kettle*. (But the bones of the Iroquois captives who are burned, those are cast on rubbish-heaps.) Some gathered up sand from the bottom of the pit and rubbed their bodies with it, for it would make them successful at games. Then they folded down the finest coverlets of beaver-skins. They moved the dirt back over everything. The women had made dishes of corn, which they threw in to give their kin-friends sustenance. Then the Captains announced presents from the dead to the living . . .

The net effect is not without pathos, said Père Davost, still holding his nose. To see them strip the flesh from the well-loved bones so tenderly – eh, I quite agree with our Père Superior. And yet –

Yes? said Père Daniel.

And yet, Antoine, I do believe that the Church will come out against it.

No Rapids

In the Moon When One Sows, twelve warriors were caught in an ambush-trap by the enemy as they crossed into their Country for some early raiding. So the torturers became the tortured. But they laughed and sang while dying, as was honorable and just. And they were devoured. Now in Wendaké the War-Chiefs met together in the House of Cut-Off Heads, and they decided to punish this insult. Which Nation had committed the murders no one could say for certain, for the spies whom the War-Chiefs maintained south of the Lake called *Beautiful* made contradictory claims, but this was a matter of small importance. The Hiroquois were all the same; they were all serpents! So the Old Men closed the door of the House of Cut-Off Heads, just as Black-Gowns do when the CAPTAIN OF THE DAY speaks four times, and they recounted their dreams and strategies to one another. Since they were treaty-bound with the Sonontrerrhonons, they decided to attack the Onondaga.

Soranhes made up his mind not to go this year, although, being a Big Stone, he must contribute a kettle of smoked fish to the War-Feast. A dream commanded him away from joining the young men. But Amantacha was very hot to bring home some Hiroquois warriors for burning. The Iroquois were worse than dogs! he wouldn't be happy until he squeezed one of their heads in his arms, the blood dripping where it had been freshly severed . . . Now they held the War-Feast in the House of Cut-Off Heads and all the young men sang war-songs against the enemy while their wives and sisters and asquas danced fist upon fist, and then the young men went to the Arendouane as ever: this year again the prognostications were bad, but they shrugged and said: whatever happens we can endure. – The Peace-Chief, who was old, said to them: Perhaps you should be cautious this year . . . – but they shouted: *No!* at which he sighed and said: Young men. – Don't we eat our lice to revenge ourselves upon them? his aunts said to him. Ah, sister's son, how we shall honor you if you devour some Iroquois for us! – That was how they talked. How fine it would be to bring back an enemy to be tortured! His dear little aunts – how he loved them! – Amantacha shouted, and his father caressed him. – Young men, young men . . . mumbled the Peace-Chief. – It was like this every year. And the warriors tested one another to see who could hold his hand in the fire the longest, to prepare themselves should they fall into the hands of the Iroquois.

Amantacha shaved his head except for a center-ridge, so that his enemies could not seize him by the hair. He painted himself with black and red stripes. His aunts gave him a sack of roasted cornmeal to take on the trail. His father gave him arrows with iron points and said: I wish only that I might have given you a gun from the Iron People! I cannot understand them.

They are misers, Amantacha admitted. They also lie, for though they tell us not to burn men they do the same in Paris. But someday they will repent, and then IESVS will forgive them.

Yes, IESVS has been good to you. He is your guardian spirit . . .

Amantacha smiled quickly. He touched his father's face.

Before Amantacha took leave of Echon and his Black-Gowns, he asked leave to make a few of the Exercises under their direction, which they willingly granted. The day fixed was the first of Holy Week. Children were shrieking and running between the longhouses. Men strode about, fastening on their sleeves to go to war. Just outside of one of the longhouses a woman stood very still and silent. She glanced once behind her at the doorway, as if she would have rather stood inside it looking out, but there was too much going in and out. She stood self-conscious like a defeated enemy. The Black-Gowns gazed upon her very sadly. If only she would renounce her pagan ways –

Père Davost had said more than once that she ought to be banned from the Residence, as she was in league with Sorcerers, but Père Brébeuf did not believe that the time for that had come as yet. After all, she did listen in silence to the Black-Gowns' predications, as well she should, having been the fornicatrix of one who'd been well instructed, no matter how far he might have fallen since . . . – Eh bien, she'd certainly been advantaged in having connection with Louys Amantacha. GOD grant that it bear fruit.

Amantacha came toward her and said something in a low voice, so that Père Brébeuf, who listened as intently as he could, could hear nothing. Her expression did not change. Then her lips moved. Amantacha smiled dazzlingly at her. – Yes, Brébeuf heard him say proudly, they are very severe, those Black-Gowns! – He began to walk toward Brébeuf. He looked back at her once. Then he came to Brébeuf, and they went into the Chapel together.

Amantacha showed off the stump of his finger to the other People with great pride. In Père Brébeuf's presence, however, he sought to hide it, for he knew that the Black-Gowns considered it a mark of shame.

Do you keep your chastity now, Louis?

Yes, my Père. I would never tell you otherwise, for I must abide by the Golden Rule, and among the Wendat it is a by-word that the Iron People never lie.

This answer pleased the priest. Indeed, it began to seem to him as he interrogated Louys more thoroughly that he had gained considerably in maturity and purpose. He knew full well that there was little merit in this young man and hardly ever could be, but the charming *facility* of that strange half-opened mind always brought him delight whether or not he would. He could not find it in his heart to condemn him, especially when it might be a discouragement to those wealthy patrons who read the *Jesuit Relations*. Have we not praised our Louys there, year after year? Perhaps the Sacrament of Baptism which he'd received in Rouen (seven years ago now) had begun to purify him by slow ways. No doubt it was a help to him that Born Underwater was now living away from Teanaostaiaé. Then, too, it was possible that Père Brébeuf's unceasing prayers over him had brought about some intercession. At all events, Louys spoke with conviction on matters of doctrine, and made it clear that Faith had become a firm foundation in his life. (His face was supple, dark, like an otter's skin.) It was strange to realize that he was now a year past the age that Père Brébeuf had been when he entered his novitiate in faraway Rouen. (What was Rouen like now? Who was living; who was dead?) Even as the years raised the one into his prime, they had begun to bring the other down into decay.

Yes, Père Brébeuf was now but two years short of forty. In his mind and spirit he felt much older; in his body, however, he felt very hale, thanks without a doubt to the simple diet and physical exertion required in a Mission such as his. He might well have another forty years of labor ahead of him.

This thought wearied him immensely.

Amantacha was kneeling before him, saying most earnestly: – Père, I have begged my father to accept all my wampum necklaces if he agrees to become dead to the world; you must not be too harsh with him, Père –

He laughed. – That is what we all say to GOD, Louys. We beg of Him not to be exceedingly harsh against us, on account of our own vile sins –

Yes, Père.

Now Amantacha was ready to receive the Mystery which might aid him against the enemy. With Echon he made the *Anima CHRISTI*:

> O good JESU, hear me;
> Within Thy wounds hide me;
> Suffer me not to be separated from Thee;
> From the malignant ENEMY defend me;
> In the hour of my death call me . . .

and then Echon touched his forehead and guided him through the magic trees of his trance, and it was very sunny as he entered there for the last time.

Where the ferns bared their green ribs, there Amantacha lurked laughing. There were Hiroquois there – with the help of Our LADY he'd burn them all! The sun shone between the leaves, which beat in the wind like pale green hearts. Amantacha ran through the forest throughout that Holy Week, so lightly that not even the birds heard him, and no spider's web was broken with his body. A smell of honey came from the black caves of half-decayed trees, on the trunks of which the moss grew white and green. The birds sang like bells and trickling water. Through the forest came sunlight from below and sunlight from above, so that everything seemed to be suspended in some bright heaven. – Amantacha ran through the dapplings of his double nature. – Suddenly he stopped; he listened; he cried out in his delight: – here was a river seen new through the most delicate possible screen of trees, rippling wisely round its wide sandy bends, every ripple of it a brown wrinkle of wisdom, while crows hopped upon the sunny gravel because there was someone dead and the trees rose high on either side. It was a wide, slow river, flowing shallow in its almost flat bed, cool on this cool spring afternoon when first discovered by Amantacha, through the moss-boulders, the alders and the hazelnut trees. It was the Stream of Time. – He threw a rock into it and gazed at his face widening and shimmering . . . That was the future, the expansion of his madness.

Père Brébeuf watched the young man kneeling there, his eyes closed, smiling happily. At last he opened his eyes. A respectful expression came upon him as he gazed into Père Brébeuf's face. He regarded the Père very seriously. Generally his long dark hair was parted in two opposing diagonals down his forehead, and his face narrowed from cheekbone to chin, so that he presented himself as a diamond. But he had cut his hair. This unnerved Père Brébeuf a little.

The Death of Amantacha

Now her seeing-ahead had returned to her beyond a possibility of escape, and she sat staring with eyes that could no longer blink. She said nothing to Amantacha, but later, after he had bid her farewell, she went to Echon (that was the first time she went to him) and said very flatly: He will die this time.

How can you say such things about the man who may well be your future spouse? Leave the future to GOD.

I see-ahead, she said.

He was horrified, of course. More sorceries! But he was also sorry and curious, and wondered: Does the sadness of that seeing-ahead ever leave her? Why can she not see farther ahead still, much farther, to the End of all things? – It did not matter in which direction one saw, if one saw far enough. The world was a circle, with Him at the center. No matter how one went, one must come to Him – unless after unavailing effort and pain one came only to one's starting place, like a man condemned to die by being rolled down a hillside in a barrel of nails. – So what did she see? It was a part of her soul that he had not touched.

Now Amantacha prepared himself for the hunting of Hiroquois. He and the other warriors set out to attack the Nation called *Onondaga* and destroy as many as they could. He felt very confident. In his tobacco pouch he carried a rosary and a medal of the BLESSED VIRGIN which had been blessed for him in Rouen . . .

Watching him leave the winding way between the palisadoes, she craved to believe that her Power was wrong this time because she did not want to be an enemy woman alone again; she made her own Exercises to see her own Country's beech forests where KLUSKAP played, killed and lied, where the enemy women were Armouchiquois, and by loudening shouts the returning warriors tallied the number of the slaughtered enemy; she danced among her painted wampum-hung kinswomen, crying out with gladness because soon Amantacha would be coming in the canoe, and she saw him now and rushed to the edge of the water to receive the scalps he'd taken . . .

But that was not the custom in this Country.

She mourned silently for a time. Then she screamed: *My heart weeps tears of blood. I must blot out this outrage with blood.*

At once she glowed with the light of hatred.

But no one heard her. She screamed only inside.

They paddled their canoes down the river, which was brown and walled with rocks. Low hills smiled with rock between their mile-long tree-lips. The river was blue with brown wrinkles, brighter than the sky. So blue, so broad that river of grace! They paddled, and the sun was hot on their faces. (But no one wanted to coast beneath the shady cliffs; there were WATER-MONSTERS there.) The sky was blooming with clouds. They came into the Hiroquois Country, the Country wrought with gorges where the wide brown creeks rolled across wide rock shelves, and by stealth they passed that deep pool in the rock where the Hiroquois children played the game of walking the narrow ledge and tumbling and they caught two children and strangled them like birds before they could cry out and the two stranglers were very happy with the glossy black little scalps still wet from swimming, and they hid the bodies in the treetrops so that the Hiroquois would not find that deed out too early and already the crows were coming.

Then it was night in the Moon When Blackberries Are Ripe. The women of the Hiroquois, the Serpent People, would be shuffling naked through their cornfields, fertilizing the corn with woman-Power, dragging their robes behind them to gather up the vermin that sought to devour their corn. Amantacha had glimpsed them on other raids, their hair midnight black, their thighs and breasts so moony-pale. His father had once captured two women, a mother and daughter, and brought them back to Teanaostoiaiaé. That had been long ago, before Kwer Nikoas had come and died. Usually women were tortured in the place where they were caught, because they could not walk quickly. But Soranhes had remembered how a mother and daughter in the Turtle Clan had been killed by the Iroquois. He was always remembering what to give people; that was why he was such a Big Stone. Amantacha wanted to be a Big Stone, too. If only he could capture one of these girls: girls were easy prisoners. She'd scream when her fingers were sawn off. He'd show her his finger-stump when he did it, and laugh to be revenged whole again. Or perhaps someone would adopt her and give him many good presents. That would be good, too. Ah, but could he do it? He had spent too long in idleness among the Iron People! That must be why he'd never captured a warrior. Or perhaps his own capture three summers ago had taken some of his courage. He desired to gain it back by stages. A woman first. These women in the moonlight, dragging their robes like shadows – the shadows between their breasts that smelled of sweat and corn and good fresh dirt – how joyous if one became his! And he'd show Born Underwater how to torture –

After that he would capture a warrior for burning. That was more manly.

In the invisible night-grass, wet against knees and ankles and waist, the Onondaga waited. They'd heard the Huron coming. Their spies, their war-painted watchers had found them. They'd seen the blue comet of warning. Amantacha was surrounded, defeated, like a tree-riven rock in the middle of the forest. They recognized him at once and began to burn his fingers with cries of delight. Never had they forgotten how three times his friends the Iron People had harmed them. Three times his Sorcerer friends had brought it about that the Nations of the Haudenosaunee had been gashed and wounded by the FACELESS ONE Whose features dark and invisible even to dead grandfathers now smiled like trembling night-water reflecting flights of bats; three times the FACELESS ONE had cut down men and women, children and babes with His hatchet of night, that weapon with the sharpness of iron arrowheads, with the voice (the horrible whistling voice) of the Iron People's bullets; three times the FACELESS ONE had sought to wrench apart with His bloody hands the Work, the Commonwealth, the League of the Hodinhsioni. – Amantacha's friends were the slaves of the FACELESS ONE! Ah, how they hated him!

They took his rosary and broke it.

They led him rapidly down the forest trail. As if in a dream, he heard them utter the war-whoops; now the village appeared before him and the War-Chief was dancing and all the other enemy warriors were dancing, and one of their Old Men came forth to congratulate them and the others sent up a great shout. – He glimpsed spirit-masks with black faces and red writhing lips:

there had been pestilence here. The masks stared at him with round copper eyes, coyly, from under a veil of cornstraw hair. – He said silently: IESVS is a greater OKI than you! – But it was all show; he was terrified because his rosary had been destroyed. – They led him to their House of Cut-Off Heads and threw him down. A man led a boy up and put a knife into his hand. Then the bubble of panic rose up in Amantacha's chest, stinking with bile, and he bit his lips hard. Yelling with laughter, the boy sliced a skinny snake of flesh from his arm and popped it into his mouth. Amantacha sought to make the Exercises as the Black-Gowns taught him; even as they pierced his flesh with their torments he strove to swim upstream, but could not. The agony blossomed thickly in his flesh like sphagnum moss in its stylized green galaxies. For three days they tortured him, and then they dragged him half-dead to the next village. They led him to the gauntlet. He was more afraid this time. He knew what they'd do to him this time. He raised his head high, although he had little hope. Perhaps he might yet be adopted . . . But no. Nor ought he to have expected it. No one came to him and pointed out the lodge in which he would live. Grinning, they thrust him to the head of the line. The stink of their rage dizzied him.

He sought to fortify himself by considering what his father would do. His father would bear the torments laughing, he knew it. Ah, and what of the Black-Gowns? They too; they too; for this was as nothing in comparison to the images of Hell which they had shown him in France.

In his heart he said to IESVS: My UNCLE, help me to endure this trial.

Now they urged him on with honeyed voices, saying how much their squaws longed to caress him. The squaws stood smiling, holding knives and thorn-sticks –

When he recovered his senses they'd turned their attentions to some of his friends and relations whom they'd captured. They sang their death-songs and died bravely. – The next day it came Amantacha's turn.

Yatera his mother, Soranhes his father, Teondisewan and Aeoswina his sisters, Born Underwater his asqua, Echon his uncle – the most agonizing loneliness would begin after his death, since his bones would never be mingled with theirs – never! Dogs and foxes would snuffle his bones. He was cut off from his Nation forever.

What he wanted most was to taste the young corn roasted once again. It seemed to him that there was nothing more precious than that food. Yet as they led him to the place where his life would be cut and burned away, he put that aside; he thought back upon the time when he had seen Paris, between whose tall pillars flew birds incinerated in pillars of sunlight; and the bridges were spiked with soldiers' pikes – he had never known there could be so many people in the whole world! – and the Black-Gowns had taken him on a boat that went through dark arches whose darkness was darker than forest darkness; and the Black-Gowns showed him castles overgrown with turrets like boles and branches; and everything was crowded and humming and shouting: he looked at the Hiroquois and cried: You are nothing! *Nothing*, I tell you!

Then they shouted in rage, and cut out his tongue.

They burned him quite artfully. It took a day and a night for him to die. Of the terrible pain of burning, my love Kateri Tekakwitha is perhaps the best witness. At Kahnawaké she often "disciplined" herself with twelve hundred blows or more of a spiked girdle which (like Père Brébeuf) she wore all day (it is written that once after carrying a great load of wood from the forest she slipped on ice and fell, and then the secret spikes sank so deeply into her flesh that the snow around her was spotted with blood, but she got up and finished carrying the wood without telling a soul). When she went with the other women to fetch a deer which the men had killed, she lagged until she was out of sight, and then walked barefoot upon the sharp pond ice, smiling and bleeding until one of her sisters came to look for her, thinking that she might be ill. At once she put her moccasins on, so that no one might think her proud, to be mortifying herself in this way. Every Saturday, as I have told, she and her good companion Marie-Thérèse Tegaiaguenta scourged each other with birch-rods in an abandoned cabin, Kateri weeping and entreating Marie-Thérèse to strike her harder because it was not until the third stroke that blood came, and after five strokes she said her rosary and humbly begged the favor of five strokes more, and as the scarred flesh split anew between her shoulders she cried out: Vent on me, GOD, Thy anger!; and then it was five strokes more and five strokes more until she could not count. As I think of this I want more than anything for Kateri to be here before me so that I could embrace her and tell her that she had not done anything wrong, but I know that there is nothing that I could say that she would ever believe; for as Père Chauchetière later said: *During her life she considered herself to be a great sinner, because it seemed as if she had a stain on her body, which she was very careful to hide.* – What did he mean by this? What did she mean? Was it simply her ugly smallpoxed face that she covered always with her blanket? But even if I had enough Power to make her live before me, even if I had enough goodness to truly reach her through some loving agony of kindness and grief, she would only have turned away. – Ah, my Père, she once told the Black-Gown, Cholonec, I will not marry. I do not like men, and have the greatest aversion to marriage. The thing is impossible.* – So let me interrupt you no longer, my Catherine, in your mortifications. – She strove always to go hungry, and if some well-meaning person besought her to eat sagamite, she would put ashes in it, so that at least she would have no enjoyment of it. On the Feast of the Purification she walked barefoot in knee-deep snow, telling those who questioned her that it was nothing in comparison to what IESVS suffered. She gathered thorns from the forest and rolled naked upon them for three nights running, until she resembled a dead person, and the Black-Gowns commanded her to throw the thorns into the fire – which, of course, she immediately did, as obedience is a virtue. Yet she still searched to find the greatest pain. One day she thought to ask her foster-mother Anastasia Tegonhatsihongon what she supposed it was, and Tegonhatsihongon considered and said: I am certain how to answer you, my Kateri, for what could be so painful as fire? The DEVIL lives in fire, as Père Chauchetière has often taught us, and indeed I will never forget how some of the Crooked-Tongue captives screamed, when we were burning them. It was a favorite trick of my aunt's to put live coals between their toes, because she said that that was the place of greatest agony. – But why do you ask such a thing? – I know not why I asked, dear mother, replied Tekakwitha, dissembling "very cleverly," as the Black-Gowns would have approvingly put it; indeed you are right, mother; for from fire comes the most fearful torment. – At her first opportunity she spoke of this to Marie-Thérèse, who agreed that fire was of all things the worst. – Indeed I have not the heart or courage to mortify myself so far as that, Kateri. – Never mind, said the other. She went alone to the Chapel and branded herself with coals like a slave. She put an ember between her toes while saying her *Hail MARIE*. Then she commenced in earnest, and burned herself from toes to knees with firebrands. Upon this charred and bleeding flesh she knelt all night . . .

In such a fashion perished Louys Amantacha. And yet I think that his death was a greater martyrdom than Tekakwitha's; for she chose hers; he did not. – Did he die screaming or singing? – Ask the Haudenosaunee.

Now they were very happy, and cut his intestines into little pieces for the children to put on the ends of sticks as they ran about the village yelling, and they shared his flesh among them, and then one of the Shamans made this charm against his spirit:

* She was considered an ill-favored slave. "This has caused some of the Savages to say after her death that GOD had taken her because men did not want her." (Thus Père Chauchetière.)

You have no right to trouble me.
Depart: – I am becoming stronger.
You are now departing me,
You who would devour me:
I become stronger, stronger.
Mighty Power is within me.
You cannot now defeat me.
I am becoming stronger:
I am stronger, stronger, stronger.

They made the Great Feather Dance of victory, raising the knee; white feathers crowned their heads. The drummer beat his rattle on the bench; the dancers stamped and pummeled the air with their fists, filled with greatness.

When Amantacha's father had returned from the Island Nation of the Algonkin, where he had been gambling with his good brother Iroquet, the warriors came and told him this news. He arose and said: I have lost my courage! Now without my strong son to shield me I see myself cut to pieces by my enemies. Now without my strong son to avenge me I see my flesh torn by their teeth. I regret every moment that my strong son did not spend by my side. I regret the time that he lived among the Iron People, and every moment that he was out of my sight. When my strong son was born, he did not cry when his mother pierced his ears. When my strong son was captured by the Hiroquois, he made no cry when they cut off his finger. Now he is dead. Now he is dead.

The Huron Seminary

1636

> There are but two means of rescuing the Indian from his impending destiny; and these are education and Christianity.
>
> LEWIS HENRY MORGAN, *League of the Iroquois* (1851)

Earlier in that same summer, as ordered by the Superior of the Canadian Mission (*viz*., Père Le Jeune), Père Daniel and Père Davost set out to Kebec. With them were three young Huron boys – the first of their Seminarians. – Yes, the Seminarians! It was Père Le Jeune who'd brought the thing about, of course, weeping most artfully in the *Jesuit Relations*, until suddenly there was a sufficiency of funds to raise these boys in the French manner, for which Messieurs les Associez & Directeurs of the colony must be thanked (as Père Le Jeune did with a will; he was very good at thanking people). *We have learned, and hold it to be a certain rule* (said these worthies) *that in forming the body of a good colony, one must commence with Religion . . .* – Praise the LORD for such a disposition! It had been the desire of their hearts to commence by making over an even dozen of Savages, but in the end, despite Brébeuf's pleas in the high speech-quavers of formality called *Acwentonch*, the other boys' families had become evasive, in the exasperating manner of these people, until at last the Black-Gowns had been obliged to be thankful merely to have gotten this Satouta and the two others into their power; for indeed matters might easily have been as they had in 1633, when the way to Wendaké had been stopped, and the keen-hearted Pères must wait through another dreary ice-hung winter at Kebec. – Well, they were not all so keen-hearted now. (Thus Père Davost.) The entire affair had been long delayed, not only on the Seminarians' account, but also because the Old Men had circulated rumors of war with the Iroquois. Père Daniel, who was to command the Seminary, drew the Superior aside and said: I begin to fear that they may be satisfied with their old kettles this year . . . – and Père Brébeuf gazed calmly back at him with blue eyes as big and wonderful as lakes – and Père Daniel went on: *That* would noticeably affect the affairs of christianization! – and Père Brébeuf replied: All is good, my dear Ambroise, that comes from GOD. – I know it, the other replied, lowering his head. – He went to speak to Soranhes, who'd arrived from Teanaostoiaiaé to embark upon the trade, and began to quiz him just as the late Monsieur de Champlain was wont to do with his spies. From him he learned that a campaign against the Hiroquois was certain, since the women cried out for revenge . . . and then the two Black-Gowns set out with Satouta and Tsiko and Tewatirhon and all the other Savages who desired to trade their souls or beaver-skins at Kebec . . .

It was a clear morning by the Sweetwater Sea, but the sky was still grey, although thinly, so that the blue of the water and the green and yellow tree-colors were awarded pastel softness by that undefined sky as the canoes rode the water so lightly and restlessly. Père Brébeuf and the others who remained behind were very sad. For a moment Brébeuf wondered if he should recall Père Davost, who greatly feared the rigors of the journey, but after all it was a mercy to send him to Kebec; GOD had not intended him for this Country. Then, too, there must be a second, should Père Daniel the Seminary-Master be called to GOD. So he said nothing to countermand himself as the two domestics clambered in with their little baggages, and Pères Daniel and Davost removed their hats and shoes and squatted uncomfortably down in the canoes, and the Wendat packed beaver-skins and tobacco-cakes all about them until they could scarcely move, and Père Brébeuf saw Père Davost's lip begin to tremble a little, and Louis Amantacha de Sainte-Foy commended his father to GOD most prettily as that old man set off, Soranhes not suspecting that GOD had back-flowed up the Stream of Time by a week or two to let Amantacha appear once more in these pages, because everyone except the Iroquois will miss Amantacha, and Soranhes was laughing and saying: I will bring you a gun from Kekwek this time, my strong son! and Amantacha stroked his father's face very very lightly. – Pax CHRISTI. – The canoes were so loaded with beaver-skins that they rode the water very low. Père Daniel's canoe began to move now, and then the Savages slipped in around Père Davost and took up their paddles as he did his, and Père Brébeuf thought to himself: Poor Ambroise!

Satouta, gawky and awkward, had nothing to say to the two who were called *Charcoal*. Indeed he contrived whenever he could to have his grandfather Tsondechaouanouan (who was a great Admiral among these Savages, and evidently regulated their waterways like the Admirals of France) sit between him and them. It was almost as though (thought Père Davost) he feared their breath or shadow, as though something chilly and vile lived in the shade of their cassocks; so, paddling grimly (though this return voyage would be, must be easier), he turned his head away from the boy and peered into the Sweetwater Sea, considering the Latin *vorago*, which means abyss, and seems to carry the sound of something being swallowed endlessly in its cadences; considering *vorax*, devouring greedily; and he shuddered. (GOUGOU saw him, and blushed pale red like the flowers of aquatic zizania, whose name comprehends the whole alphabet in going from A to Z and back again; GOUGOU let him go and kissed the rubbery pinkish-grey labia of water-lilies.) And they crossed the Bay called *Matchedash* and continued north, hugging the coast of the Sweetwater Sea. They began to descend the rivers that led to the Fleuve Saint-Laurent. And wildness screamed with panther-screams. Now I, William the Blind, remember my friend Pierre on a summer evening in Montréal, Pierre crying: *Here we have the new kind of space that the Europe never knew, and, oh! freedom of space, freedom of living, of water, freedom of trees and living – and all that kind of stuff create Canadian . . .* and the peace and purity of those distances uplifted my soul; but the Black-Gowns could not, must not be uplifted in that way. That wretch Brûlé had been: that was his sin. He had lived in concubinage with the Wendat girls, with his hand on a sleeping breast, the nipple pulsing with heartbreath against his hand; he had taken lacs and rivières without number in a Wendat canoe, living wild, without observing the Sabbath, paying no heed to Lent – truly the man had been a reprobate of the most miserable sort. By a Wendat hand, GOD had struck him down.

The voyage was very easy – for the Wendat, at least. Père Daniel almost died of it. When he got to civilized parts at last, his breviary was on his neck and his shirt rotted about his back, as the *Relation* says. At Trois-Rivières, Monsieur the Gouverneur gave Satouta pride of place, in defiance of all the Savage precedents and ceremonies, so that all believed the boy to have become an exalted person through some magic connected with the Black-Gowns (although it was plain to see, said Montmagny to himself, that they did not like it). – Satouta hung his head; Satouta looked about him smiling and biting his lip.

Tell him that we trust GOD that all his people will soon follow him. (Thus Montmagny.)

Satouta saw his grandfather Tsondechaouanouan watching him; Satouta said mildly: Your words delight my ears.

After the trade was concluded, Tsondechaouanouan approached his grandson and seized his arm. He stared down into his face. He said to him: You must learn all you can of the Iron People and their ways, for soon you will inherit my place. Let them instruct you. They are your uncles now. Be a good nephew to them as Amantacha has been. Watch them. Watch them! Win their trust, but uncover their sorceries if you can; for we must learn if they are poisoners. Do not permit them to take you across the sea.

My grandfather, I open my ears.

And he went on to *Kekwek* . . .

Much more effective there than in Wendaké, Père Davost had recovered his poise. It was his hope to turn out young Savages every year perfectly finished, like the brown moose-fat soap that the nuns made in a big cauldron, cutting it into squares when it was solid. Soon five boys were in his charge. He knew well that if his design here succeeded he could bind the Huron much more closely to the French . . .

Entering the house, Père Le Jeune put his hand upon Père Davost's shoulder and offered his tenderest *Pax CHRISTI*. The Seminarians stood to greet him, half-choking in their ruffed collars, looking around with big eyes. Their uniform was now the black coat whose fruit was buttons, the black cap; they hoped to weigh themselves down with academic medals.

It goes well, Antoine?

Yes, Père.

Good.

Père Le Jeune returned to Notre-Dame-des-Anges and on the creamy sheet which would soon become one of the leaves of the *Jesuit Relations* he wrote an edifying account of what he had seen. He called for more pious men to scatter the fire everywhere; he'd set all Canada ablaze! He'd dry up the dark streams of superstition; how SATAN would scream in the steam!

They learned to make neat courtesies and touch the brims of their new hats to Frenchmen whenever they met them.

Unlike Louys Amantacha, Satouta would never abuse his complaisance. Nor would Tsiko, whose uncle was Ouanda Koca, a great Captain. They strove to love the Iron People.

On Saint-Jean's Day, Monsieur the Gouverneur held a pageant with many fireworks, forming a serpent, a castle, and many fleurs-de-lys.

See – we are more powerful than DEMONS! he said to the Seminarians. We command the fire! If we wish to burn the villages of our enemies, we shall do it.

They watched him –

Autumn came to Canada, sadly purple like the fog-clouds over the endless scarlet leagues of autumn forest smiling with purple lakes.

One day a Frenchman came to the Seminary, out of curiosity, for he had never seen with his own eyes those rubes and boobs called *Huron*. Smiling, Satouta caressed his cheek –

Eh, you perverted wretch! the Frenchman screamed, knocking Satouta to the floor.

Not long after, Satouta died.

Tsiko also died that winter after some quarrel with a Frenchman, although Père Le Jeune believed that the cause of his death was probably the solid food of the French, which was too rich and substantial for his paltry digestion. After this, the other Seminarians became uneasy in their minds, and seemed not to concentrate upon their studies.

So Père Le Jeune shut himself in the house called Notre-Dame-des-Anges. And he took up his pen and appealed to the piety of all of you who read these *Relations*, crying out: *If someone would depict three, four, or five Demons tormenting one soul with diverse supplices – one applying to it fires, another serpents, another pinching it with red-hot tongs, another holding it bound with chains, it would have a good effect, especially if all were well distinguished, and if rage and sadness appeared clearly on the face of the desperate soul . . .*

for he saw now what he had seen but tried not to see ever since he had wintered with the Sorcerer: – *viz.*, that sweet pleadings and remonstrances had little effect upon these stinking barbarians (ah, how he loved them!); that they would not ever subject themselves to IESVS until they were made to scream with terror.

The Vampire Skeleton

1636–1637

> We know that the whole Creation has been groaning in travail together until now; and not only the Creation, but we ourselves, who have the first fruits of the Spirit, groan inwardly as we wait for adoption as sons, the redemption of our bodies.
>
> Romans 8.22–23

After the death of Louys Amantacha de Saincte-Foy, the Black-Gowns observed that Tehorenhaennion the Shaman was sometimes to be seen in conversation with the Souriquois woman, Born Underwater – not so very often, for among these People men and women do not mix together much; but often enough for conclusions to be drawn. The priests disliked this, and Père Brébeuf considered speaking to her of it, but because there was some danger that she might not recognize his authority he let it lie. (Her eyes glittered like the black scales of a muskrat's tail.) Then, too, if she were plotting with Tehorenhaennion it was better that the Black-Gowns be continuously able to apprise themselves of that fact, which could only be more difficult were she warned. There was a third reason which he was almost ashamed of: – namely, that the very difficulty of comprehending her drew him to her a little; for the schooling which he'd received inclined him toward anything whose incomprehensibility he might challenge; he was as if fishing in a river with his hands, closing in on her, but not so quickly as might scare her and end the game. Once he'd solved the problem of what she was, once he had the key to her soul, he'd let some other priest turn it; he was indifferent to mere created things. – So he directed Père Jogues, just now arrived with Père Pijart, to observe their doings. (Best not to play the spy himself. It might be too interesting an Exercise.) Père Jogues saw Born Underwater enter daily into the Shaman's secluded lodge with its empty face of darkness peeping from the door-arch. When no one was present Père Jogues lifted the skins and looked inside. There were bones on the floor, and dried tobacco leaves hung from the ceiling. A turtle-shell rattle, which appeared to him broken, although he did not choose to touch it, lay in the dirt. Tehorenhaennion's bed was a platform like any of the ones in the longhouses. A stinking black bearskin was thrown upon it.

He felt a bony hand on his shoulder.

Now I see that you seek to steal Power, my nephew, said Tehorenhaennion. Why must you be so sly, like a Serpent, when I would gladly teach you? Give me gifts, I say! I know many more secrets than Echon.

Père Jogues turned around and gazed levelly into the old face. – If you had knowledge to give me I would gladly learn it. But your mummeries and juggleries are not knowledge, as you yourself would do well to admit. I extend to you the same invitation. Come to our house, and we'll share our teachings with you. Obey them, and you will not burn in Hell after you die. Repentance comes never too late, even for an old man like you.

The Shaman snorted. – Get out, he said.

Père Jogues went to the Superior, who was winding the CAPTAIN OF THE DAY, and reported the conversation to him. It was after the hour of four; the Savages had been sent away. – It is almost uncanny, that confidence of his, he concluded. Do you think him to be truly in league with the DEVIL?

Well, I've known him a long time. But since we've always been at loggerheads, over rain and other matters, he's never seen fit to show me the DEMONS in his pouch! (Thus Père Brébeuf, speaking without hurry, swallowing Jogues deliciously in his cool blue eyes.) Sometimes I myself have thought so, said Brébeuf. But you must know that there is reputed to be a Demoness in this Country, called *AATAENTSIC*, whom they worship secretly. She is said to be the goddess of sickness and death. But I have never read of Her in any accounts of exorcisms written down for us by wise men at Rome. So it may be that his confidence is mere brazenness –

But *what* brazenness! It is almost magnificent!

Isaac, you must never say that. Tehorenhaennion is a shoddy enough soul, like the DEVIL he serves wide-eyed . . .

As for the one they mentioned, he squatted over a broken knife, reflecting on what Père Jogues had said to him. *Come to our house, and we shall teach you*, the man had said, or something like it. Even now, after all that had happened, Tehorenhaennion considered it. – Not for their reasons, of course. But his own investigations had failed to discover any particular weakness in Echon. He could not be bribed with women. He had no fear. Flattery meant nothing to him; he wanted nothing more or less than the authority vested in Shamans and Old Men. Born Underwater had told him how Echon had banished her from Teanaostaiaé, how she'd walked a little ahead on the path but could never get out of hearing of the soft and steady rustle of his OKI's gown, and the darkness of it was as black as a moose . . . No, Echon must be undermined. Otherwise he would kill again. – Just as the hideous masks of the Iroquois False Faces, being in fact the features of Disease, permit the Sorcerers behind to *own* those diseases, and thereby to cure them, so Tehorenhaennion knew that if he'd simply learn the doctrines of those who were called *Charcoal*, then he could turn them back upon themselves, and be rid of them. But the repeated calls from them to do just that chilled him. It might well be that this was Echon's plan: to ease him and all the other People into a net of sorceries, which would then jerk shut upon them forever. What if Echon's Power was strong enough to swallow him? The game of turning back an enemy's Power is a dangerous one; for to bend it toward its source one must first attract it in all its malignant awareness.

No, for the time being he would not permit Echon to catechize him.

But neither would he admit to any fear. – Not to the People, nor to *them*. With Born Underwater, however, he opened his heart halfway.

The Compact

When I was younger I was a brave warrior, said Tehorenhaennion. I was a good hunter. Now I still give good advice when I am asked.

It is for advice that I come to you, said Born Underwater. It seems to me that these Iron People are bad, and worst of all the Black-Gowns. They seek to make us all children, and teach us to be dead like their JESUS. As you know, I have the Power called *Nikani-kjijitekewinu*. I see-ahead. I cannot see everything, but I see that Echon will swallow many souls. I see more Black-Gowns coming. Yet the future flows far like a river, and I cannot see to the end. I do not know whether he and his Black-Gowns will ruin us all, or whether we can drive them out. I do not know what to do. You are a wise man; maybe you know. – I have spoken.

Tehorenhaennion scratched himself. – It shames me that I must ally myself with such as you, he said, you being but a foreign-born woman.

My mother dreamed of the Floating Island, she replied proudly. Do not insult me.

Just as a flock of black partridges in a tree could be shot one by one with arrows and they would not take flight, so her Power overcame his various disquiets, cautiously, steadily, until at last none were left behind.

So those two made their compact. And after that, their tongues were always busy speaking ill of the Iron People – he to the men, she to the women.

Born Underwater

In the longhouses everybody said: Tehorenhaennion, is she your asqua now?

Ask her, said the Shaman, grinning toothlessly. She's the woman. She knows.

The Death of Soranhes

Late in the Moon When the Little Corn is Made, Soranhes sent word to Born Underwater that he would adopt her into his clan if she desired; now that his son was dead there would be no incest in it. This offer tempted her; she longed to vanish into a family again, to let maple-leaves close about her face so that she sank into dark green peace, but she did not want to return to Teanaostoiaiaé. Nothing was there but more cornfields; singing to the corn with Teondisewan she'd only see Amantacha in her face, and then Born Underwater's heart would be sad. And the Black-Gowns – she'd fled all the way from the Country of KLUSKAP, and here they were again! She'd not flee them again. When she visited Soranhes to give him this word, he replied: You may be right to harbor such a resolution. I once had great love for these Black-Gowns, but now that my strong son is dead I know not what to believe. But I say this to you, my daughter: live in Ihonatiria if you desire, but let us bring you into the Turtle Clan. My wife longs to do that, to show her love for you. If you have a clan you'll have support; you'll be a woman who has the right to speak. Tehorenhaennion is a great Sorcerer, but all sorceries fail from time to time; therefore it is well not to be affiliated to him only. Nor would he be good to marry . . .

So he spoke to her, and added many words in a similar wise, until she agreed to be inducted into the Turtles. But she could not feel as much tenderness towards him as she ought to have done, for she believed that it was his carelessness and greed which had permitted Amantacha to be given to the Iron People. (*The Iron People are not liberal,* her mother always used to say. *They are mean bone-gnawers.*) Perhaps it was his stay among them that had weakened his strength. That was why the Serpents could catch him. – Then, perhaps not. The seeing-ahead never explains why.

Soranhes was suffering from a slight fever, as he said. Although he had much love for his daughters, he feared that it might become worse.

Born Underwater had no need of her seeing-ahead to understand. She caressed his face when she took her leave, as was the custom in that Country – how many fathers had she had? how many more must she have? – but her heart continued to be unmoved. At night it cried out for blood, having so many good reasons to do so; in the daytime it slept.

There are various kinds of grief. Some keen and burn until death; some mask themselves (and all else) as if behind a leaden cloud; others flutter against one's face like a wind-blown curtain of the most delicate French lace; one must be constantly flicking it aside to see clearly, to breathe easily, and that is no effort, as it seems at first, but then the curtain falls again, and again the effort must be made; so that everything becomes dully laborious. Which kind Soranhes suffered from I cannot say, for it is not reported in the *Jesuit Relations*. But we do know that he continually made the Exercise of Desolation, seeing Amantacha with him, Amantacha stringing a bow, Amantacha kissing witch-charms to please those who were called *Charcoal*, Amantacha greasing his hair with sunflower oil . . .

Soranhes is sick, Echon, said a Savage, but so coldly that Père Brébeuf paid little mind. Howbeit, he had to go to Teanaostoaiaé in any case, so he decided to stop at Soranhes' lodge. He also had some little beads which he meant to give him, as a consolation present for Amantacha's death. (He'd pry into Soranhes' soul and strengthen him in the Faith. He considered himself a tool of GOD's – perhaps a carpenter's claw for inserting hoops, which device fixed bundles of staves rigid in useful shapes.) But when he reached the village, Soranhes was already dead. He had sent one of his little daughters to dig up the root called *Ondachienroa*, which was a very poisonous Mai-apple sometimes used in small doses for the amelioration of sickness. He told her that it was not enough and sent her for more. Then he gorged himself upon it in a nervous greed, and quickly became feverish and died.

Soon afterward that daughter died also, which the Jesuits much regretted, as she had been bright and docile. Her name had been Teondisewan. It was said that she dreamed she'd be cured if Echon gave her one hundred cakes of tobacco, but of course he had none for such purposes. Besides, as he heard, she had once been a paramour of Étienne Brûlé's –

Echon's Mercy

In Août of that year the Savages returned with some Hiroquois captives which they were eager to give to the fire, in order to revenge Louys Amantacha and the others. They'd surprised thirty of the enemy fishing at Lacus Irocoisiensis. They would have bagged them all, but the *Relation* says that their bloodlust made them hasty, so they caught only eight, one of whom they immediately beheaded to console them for the loss of the rest. He laughed until the hatchet came down. Of the seven prisoners who remained, six were destined to be adopted and burned by diverse great men of the Cord and Rock Nations, and one would be given to the Bear Nation in which the Black-Gowns dwelled. The uncle who adopted him was named Saouandaouscouay. His nephew had been burned with Amantacha. So his Hiroquois must take the nephew's name. He sang his death-song bravely then. He made the Exercises of his life-pictures as they led him through the forest, past the OKI that dwelled inside Owl's Nest Rock, down the hill of sumacs where he could see the blueness of the Sweetwater Sea and its blue-green capes and islands, and they gave thanks to IOUSKEHA, for the corn would grow well now and the Bear Nation would rise in prestige. The Black-Gowns were invited, which filled them with horror, but then Père Brébeuf said to his crew: Let us hope to save the soul of this Iroquois. If we succeed, he will be the first of his Nation to attain the favor of Heaven.

Père Jogues nodded. Père Pijart said nothing. Père Chastellain gazed at the wall. And Père Garnier said: Of course we shall be obedient, but do you not think that by attending this ceremony we might be implicating ourselves?

Charity causes us to overlook many considerations. (Thus Jean de Brébeuf.)

He paced about. Then he took Père Chastellain aside and said: Do you think that Tehorenhaennion and Born Underwater will be at this burning?

I cannot say, Père Superior. I suppose that vile juggler will come, to gloat. As for his harlot –

Do not call her that! cried Brébeuf in a stricken voice.

Eh? Well – we cannot say for sure, but . . . Savagesses do behave like that! – He stopped suddenly. – But, Père Superior, what do you think about it?

I? said Brébeuf in astonishment. What do I have to do with it?

What! So you do not think her lewdness must be rooted out and exposed? Excuse me, Père Superior . . .

Of course. You know that. – But why do you regard me so strangely?

So they went to the village called Arontaen, which was two leagues away, across the brown creeks wide, shallow and lily-grown. It was a fine day. A crow screeched. So many tapering leaf-cones of trees rose from the grass. Now the palisadoes loomed before them and they smelled the fishes drying on the racks; now the prisoner came singing in his loudest bravest voice, dressed in a splendid beaver robe which his uncle Saouandaouscouay had given him. Strings of wampum beads graced him. He was perhaps fifty years old. Someone had wrenched one of his fingers almost off, and the thumb and forefinger of his other hand had been chopped with a hatchet so that they dangled, attached only by a little flap of skin. His hands were rotten to the wrists, and maggots crawled in them.

When the Black-Gowns approached him, he studied them attentively, not knowing his happiness.

Tehorenhaennion was there, and he said: Echon, do you wish to make him sing?

Ah, it is not that which brought me here, Père Brébeuf replied.

At this the Wendat were silent – in sign of honor, as Père Brébeuf supposed. Then Saouandaouscouay said to the prisoner: Then *I* bid you to sing, my nephew. You have good reason to do so, for no one is doing you any harm. You are now with your kindred and friends.

Good GOD, what a compliment! muttered Père Le Mercier in a low voice.

Now the Black-Gowns swarmed around him and instructed him, saying that once he was baptized he would go to Heaven as soon as he had been burned. To this he was willing, and all the Wendat vied to instruct him in Echon's doctrine, thinking that Echon was but playing with the prisoner, as they were when they spoke to him so lovingly and offered him squashes to eat and picked the worms from his hands, as if he were indeed one of their relatives and it was the Feast of the Dead. Later that night, the Black-Gowns baptized him *Joseph*, and then Echon gave a lecture on chastity to the assembled multitude . . .

JESUS taïtenr, the man said over and over, as the Black-Gowns beamed. JESUS have pity on me.

After this, Joseph's uncle Saouandaouscouay came and said to him in accents of the utmost kindness: My nephew, you must now know that when I first received news that you were at my disposal, I considered myself wonderfully pleased, for I saw in you him who had been lost. I resolved to give you your life. But now I see you with your fingers gone and your hands half rotten, I feel sure that you would regret to live any longer. Do you not agree? It is the Deer People of our Country who have mistreated you so ill, not I; it is to them that you owe your death. Be of good courage, my nephew!

How shall I die?

By fire.

Now it was a summer evening the color of pearl: featureless, refreshing, limitless. The humidity almost thick enough to be mist filtered the forest and the cornfields and not far away something screeched. Now the trees grey-greened with evening mist. Tree-steeples rose green into the SKY. And Joseph made his *Asataion*, or farewell feast, which everyone who had the means assisted him with, providing food and drink so that the thing would be done with dignity. Joseph's aunt sat weeping silently, that he must so soon die! And all the People assured him of their love. Little children clambered up the beams, toward the corn that hung above all, and they swung the furry peltry-bundles brown and black into each others' faces, and they wriggled together giggling and fighting beneath the soft black bearskins on the sleeping platforms, and they peeped at Joseph and laughed as their mothers watched them patiently, anxious only that they come to no harm, that they not upend the bark baskets filled with corn. And the smoky air of that place rang with exclamations of pity for Joseph. How sorry the People were, that their dear nephew must be burned! *Ouai! Ouai!* Only the Black-Gowns sat apart, miserable and aghast. (Seeing this, Tehorenhaennion the Shaman laughed at them, which was an insult.)

My brothers, I am now going to die, said Joseph. Amuse yourselves boldly. I fear neither torture nor death.

At this, the Wendat plucked up their spirits somewhat, since Joseph assured them that the matter was proper (as indeed they had known in their innermost hearts), and so they feasted more easily. But one woman who still pitied him asked Echon whether she should give Joseph to eat of that root called *Ondachienroa* with which Soranhes had poisoned himself, but he explained to her why that would be a sin.

Now they took Joseph to the War-Chief's lodge, the House of Cut-Off Heads, and the War-Chief encouraged all to do their duty for the sake of the SUN, Who is IOUSKEHA the SON of AATAENTSIC. Now he made the first circuit, singing his song, and the Old Men on the high side-platforms nodded their heads with pleasure at his song, and no one touched him, but they took his beaver robe and decided the disposition of his head and liver and arms among them, at which his face grew pale and the Black-Gowns began to weep most soundlessly, and then he began the second circuit and they commenced burning him patiently and he began screaming and they imitated his screams and pressed the torches against his body until the flesh sizzled and took his hands and broke the bones and pierced his eardrums with little sticks which they left inside them, and he made the third and fourth circuit, and they said to him most politely: Here, my uncle, I must burn you; and they said to him: My uncle, where would it best please you that I burn you? and he must answer, and they burned him where he bade them; for that was the way of this People. The smoke from his flesh rose up to the ceiling and obscured him from all but his closest torturers. He strove to laugh and sing like a great man, and occasionally he succeeded, but more often he screamed, which pleased them, for it was bad luck if an enemy did not scream. They made him walk on burning hatchets, and the flesh of his feet hissed like serpents. – Ah, for my part I know nothing about burning, confessed his uncle Saouandaouscouay most bashfully, but he wedged a sheet of burning bark against Joseph's testicles, and Joseph screamed until his voice was hoarse. On the fifth circuit they began to burn him more seriously, Born Underwater helping, giggling with her sister Turtles, dreaming good songs (for the first time since she'd watched Amantacha go away her heart was glad), and as she smiled at Joseph and rubbed her nipples before his eyes and told him how she longed to feel him inside her and jabbed a red-hot needle between his finger-stumps, she began to glow with something proud and bitter and strange to see how Echon the Black-Gown was watching her, clasping his pale, pale hands; his face was white within his cowl, white with a maggot's whiteness; his eyes were not black like a human being's eyes, but blue like a river. On the seventh circuit Joseph swooned, and they revived him with water and made him sing his song, which he did, although his voice broke often now. And each of the Black-Gowns had forgotten the others, and each of them thought that he himself must die, such was his pity and anguish. The People returned the fine iron hatchets to the fire, roasting beside them some green corn to give Joseph strength, for he must not die before the coming of the SUN. – Here, uncle, I must make you a present of a hatchet for coming with us to our Country to be burned, chuckled Tehorenhaennion, and he laid down a red-hot axehead on Joseph's thighs. Joseph's aunt now brought him some corn to eat, which he would have refused, but at this the War-Chief said to him most severely: Do you think yourself the master here? Do you think that you yourself have killed all the Wendat? after which he ate obediently. Then they let him rest until the dawn.

A suitable occasion to meditate upon the Passion of Our LORD, said Père Brébeuf loudly.

The War-Chief laughed. – Do you truly believe, my Echon, that the Iroquois would treat you any better for this *baptism* if they came to ravage our Country, and you fell into their hands?

That is not what concerns me, he replied proudly.

Why are you sorry that we tormented him?

I do not disapprove of your killing him, but of your treating him in that way.

What! Do not you Iron People kill men?

Yes indeed, but not with this cruelty!

You never burn any? persisted the War-Chief skeptically.

Eh, not often, and even then the fire is only for enormous crimes, and the condemned are not made to linger so long. Often they are first strangled, and generally they are thrown at once into the fire.

Then they were silent, listening to Joseph's heavy breathing. He did not moan or complain. Just before dawn came, the People lit fires around the village, so that the SUN could better see what was being done in His honor. Then they took Joseph outside and led him to the scaffold. Before they had avoided doing him any injury which would cause him to perish immediately, but now the game grew rougher. They thrust burning brands down his throat and up his anus. They burned his eyes out. They began burning his abdomen. No matter where he went, warriors jabbed at him from under the platform. His body fluttered in the dawn like a sail under contrary wind. Père Brébeuf wept and prayed for Joseph's quick deliverance. Joseph was breathing very hoarsely. Suddenly he fell down with his mouth open. At once they swooped on him and cut off head and feet and hands. His soul fled like a white moth fluttering among ferns –

Now it was time to eat his body, which the Black-Gowns had no wish to do. As they set out for their house, taking the forest path through the rising sun, they saw a Savage strolling past, holding one of Joseph's roasted hands which he had not yet eaten. Then they longed to fall upon him and condemn him, for that was illegal in France, but they were not yet Masters here . . .

The Vampire Skeleton

As Tehorenhaennion's hatred of Echon increased, so did his comprehension of him. He sent his reason-soul inside him, entering his soul at the place where his hatred had slit a way into it, as if he were skinning an animal with a beaver's tooth. Echon's eyes were the pale blue of juniper berries. Echon's arms and legs were white like a lake at sunset. Echon's hat was black upon his head like an elongated cloud. He stood black and dark, and the wind ruffled the pleats of his garment. He folded his arms; in his hand was the magic thing with the white leaves. Echon's hair was curly and very long. His sweaty face gazed fixedly ahead. His cheek was as pasty as the *flour* that the Iron People possessed. Echon set himself against the Old Men. Therefore Echon was a witch, an enemy. Echon mocked the SKY-WOMAN, AATAENTSIK. Therefore he was Her enemy also. This gladdened Tehorenhaennion. Who would devour Echon first?

At once, he remembered the VAMPIRE SKELETON.

Many winters since, he'd had occasion to learn the lore that the Hiroquois tell, when one of their great Captains or Rodiyaner was captured. The intention had been to burn this man – he who had succeeded to the name of Adodarhoh; he whose first predecessor was the Sorcerer whose mind-snakes DEKANWIDEH must clear before the League of the Haudenosaunee could be established – for to give Adodarhoh to the fire would grieve the Hiroquois, and so be sweet in the mouths of the True People. But it happened that many warriors had been taken by the Hiroquois in that same raid, and so the women said that he ought to be spared as a hostage. It was Satouta's grandfather Tsondechaouanouan, then a young man, who'd captured him, and at first he was disgusted with this proposal, which seemed to deprive him of his glory, but at length, seeing how the others now pressed and insisted, he smiled and said: It is well. There are many others who dwell among the Hiroquois Nations, growing riper for our burning . . . – at which his fellows laughed and said: So you have spoken with intelligence and made us glad! – and Adodarhoh was spared. They brought him to Carhagouha, where Tehorenhaennion was living at the time. In those days, not yet being old, Tehorenhaennion searched everywhere for the secrets of Power, and so he thought to learn what he could from the lips of this man with a Sorcerer's name. It was autumn at that time, and Adodarhoh would not tell the stories until winter, for fear of disturbing the ANIMAL PERSONS who sometimes listened to stories; then the snow fell, and still Adodarhoh would not tell his stories, at which Tehorenhaennion became extremely wroth, believing now that Adodarhoh had tricked him, so he said: Tell me, you who are called *Enemy*,* do you mean to be faithless like all your kinsmen whom we burned?

* Literally, "We kill one another."

Perhaps the case is that you know nothing true . . . but Adodarhoh gazed back at him with strange eyes like arrowpoints, and lay back down by the fire, wrapping his robe around his face. As Tehorenhaennion strode through the trampled snow between the longhouses, longing to kill Adodarhoh, an old Shaman stood laughing at him. – If you wish to learn from him, my nephew, then you must first praise him, do you comprehend? Otherwise he cannot reveal anything to you without being accused in his own heart of loss of courage, since you have reviled and threatened him.

Tehorenhaennion had listened carefully. – I thank you, my uncle, he said, for now you have taught me the better way.

So he returned to Adodarhoh and explained his desire in more becoming words, until Adodarhoh promised to teach him certain charms if Tehorenhaennion for his part would share whatever lore he'd learned . . . But, hearing this Tehorenhaennion grew cold, for he thought: The minds of the Hiroquois have seven linings, and within them all is a nest of poisonous serpents! What if I give him means to devour us when we go to war again? Then surely the Old Men will creep up behind me and sink a hatchet in my head! . . . and so he decided not to be persuaded. – Adodarhoh, looking into his eyes, smiled sadly. Yet in the end, without revealing his songs, he told several stories in the hearing of all. Tehorenhaennion could not remember most of them now, for he grew old, and something gnawed at the memories in his brain. But he'd never forget the tale of the VAMPIRE SKELETON, which Adodarhoh had told in Tsondechaouanouan's lodge as the flames crackled and the dogs snored and the children screamed in delighted terror, and Tsondechaouanouan shared tobacco with all who had come, thinking to himself: It was well after all that Adodarhoh was not burned, since this gathering brings me glory! and Adodarhoh went on with his tale, eyes closed, absently rubbing the stump of his left thumb (for the People had sawn it off joyously when he was first captured), and this was the tale of Adodarhoh:

There was an old man who lived alone, like those who are called *Charcoal*, and was therefore a witch. At last he became ill. The other Hiroquois came to help him die well, and he thanked them for their kindness. Then he said: When I have become nothing but a carcass, then wall me up here in the back of my lodge. The front may be used by any hunter, but no women or children must ever stay here. If they do, then some misfortune would happen. I do not lie; pay good heed! Now I have spoken.

It is well, they said.

So he died, and they coffined him in elm-bark, and set the coffin behind a partition.

In truth his prohibition was strange, yet not so strange as to be beyond our febrile unravelings. Some mixing is permissible, and some is not. Within the Haudenosaunee, the Wolf can marry with the Hawk, but not the Bear with the Turtle. Sainte Katharine Tekakwitha's uncle saw no reason to allow her to mix with Christians. And so we can assume that this Old One of the witch clan had been warned by dreams never to mix with women at all (which was why he'd kept himself apart), and therefore, because he chose to abide by this even as he lay in his last sickness, we see that he was good. What musk or purity of female blood drew out his evil beyond the good one cannot say, but we would certainly follow any number of traditions (*e.g.*, Echon's) were we to blame the woman who came there for what happened. The village nearby was large, they say, and so not everyone remembered the secondhand warning; which vanished behind time like the beginning of the river where it bent and curved beneath trees and was shallowly snowy; the silver ice, the golden grass accompanied it downstream past summer and winter and spring. Now the Green Corn Festival passed, and then the warriors came back with Wendat prisoners, whom the People burned, shouting with joy, and then they ate them. And the children played the game of waterfalls. After this came the Harvest Thanksgiving. So the Haudenosaunee held their feasts, partaking of the bodies of the THREE SISTERS Who came to save us: Sister CORN, Sister BEAN, and Sister SQUASH. The Keeper of the Faith threw tobacco on the fire and thanked HÄ-WEN-NÉ-YU for His goodness in causing the earth again to bring forth food, and the tobacco smoke arose into the sky, bearing the People's thanks to HÄ-WEN-NÉ-YU. They stamped their feet to the beat of the two rattles, the men naked to the waist, with perspiration steaming up from their backs, the women robed as always, dancing slowly sideways; they danced the Thanksgiving Dance, and then they arose to thank the maple-tree, the raspberry-bush, the streams, and wind and stars. They played the Peach-Stone Game –

Now autumn was here indeed, and the People scattered to go hunting. There was a man who set out with his wife and little daughter, to trap deer and bears and live upon their flesh until the Festival of the White Dog. They were ignorant of their destination, as Echon would surely be (thus Tehorenhaennion). They followed the trail giving thanks. Ahead were the grey-blue mountains wooded with trees, sloping down to the lake where the People sometimes went ice-fishing. Beneath the ice were stripes of slimy green and black like an immense fish's belly. The low sun made the ice a lovely pale greyish-blue. Snow and moss wept down from the cliffs, the hills of beauty. And the man led his family, seeing that the Country was rich in game this year, and they came to the dead Sorcerer's lodge, as victims must in stories and dreams.

All his cooking-stuffs were there, and the walls had not yet rotted, so it seemed to them a good place. They saw the elmbark coffin behind the partition, but that was nothing to them: all must die. – So they threw down their deerskins on the sleeping-bench. So the man went out into the snow and set his deer-traps, and the woman spread nets for quail, carrying the little girl on her back.

The deer stepped into the loop. The trap was sprung, and the bent tree straightened suddenly, jerking him into the air by his hind legs. – The man came and killed him. He built a fire and cured some of the venison. Then he packed what he could into the bark baskets that his wife had made for him, and carried it home to the dead man's lodge. It was a long way.

I will lie down by the fire now, he said. Give our daughter to me, and I will sleep with her in my arms.

The woman was very happy that there was meat. She sang songs. The dead man had left corn in braided strings hanging from the rafters of the lodge, so she took them down and began to grind them into meal. She let the fire burn low, and baked her bread in the ashes. It was very dark and chilly now. Firelight flickered like blood on her husband's face. The woman felt a little lonely, but then she heard something gnawing in the darkness – surely a mouse – and she smiled. Aside from the gnawing noise and the faint hiss of the fire, everything was quiet. The wind had faded away outside, as it often did at dusk, the snow muffled everything. Her hands were cold. She warmed them over the fire. Soon the bread would be finished. Now it was dark. The gnawing was louder now, and she did not like the sound of it anymore.

She said to her husband: Are you truly asleep?

The gnawing stopped. She thought that she saw something crawling away very rapidly through the darkness. Then she heard a noise from behind the partition. Her heart began to beat very quickly. She saw that blood was coming out of her husband. His belly was open, and inside it looked like those masses of berries that she dried on a bark tray –

Her daughter was still alive. She was sleeping soundly by the fire.

Loudly the woman said: I must go get water to rinse the bread. I shall take our daughter with us, so that she doesn't roll into the fire in her sleep. Wait patiently, husband, and I shall soon return.

She took the child up in her arms and tied her to her back in a blanket. The Moon, Whom we call Soi-ka Gawka, meaning Our Grandmother, had hidden Herself behind trees of darkness. When she reached the spring, she threw down the water-jug and began to run. There was not a sound from the lodge.

Be brave, she said to her daughter. If fortune is with us then we shall reach the village.

She ran on and on. There was not a sound. She began to believe that they were safe. Then she heard a scream of rage behind her. The dead man cried: The world is small, and I shall soon overtake you.

She looked over her shoulder and saw him. His ribs were as close-set as those of a Wendat canoe, as ripples. Cross-beams of mummy-sinew held him together. His checkered bones were yellow-white. He grinned, and his grin upturned with rage.

She tried to run faster. Tree-hills crouched on rocky claws. Soon she heard his footsteps behind her in the snow. And she was so alone in death's dream. She heard the branches creak as he pushed them aside from his face.

Again she looked over her shoulder. He was much closer. His grin was the black seam below a grosbeak's wings.

She took off her blanket and lifted her daughter into her arms. She hung the blanket from a tree and ran on.

She heard him shout with delight at seeing the blanket, believing it to be her. She heard him rip it to pieces. Then suddenly he roared, finding himself to be deceived, and came on at a redoubled pace.

She looked over her shoulder. There was an ache in her side. Her little girl felt very heavy. He was even closer. She could smell her husband's blood on his breath.

So she took off her headshawl and hung it up. Next she relinquished her daughter's blanket. Each time, the VAMPIRE SKELETON was fooled.

By now he was almost close enough to touch her. She turned her head and saw him reaching for her but she did not scream. If she screamed he would have had her. He opened his mouth and she saw something moving feebly inside. There was a little flesh still on his cheeks. It was wrinkled and blind-embossed as if with tree-bark. His nostrils stank with decay and sickness.

He lunged for her again and his boneclaws hissed through the air. Desperately, she took her robe off and hung it up. She ran on as he stopped to slaver and snatch at the furskinned thing that seemed alive –

At last she was close enough to the village to shout: *Goo-weh! Goo-weh!*

In the War-Chief's longhouse they were having games and dances when they heard her cry. They told the War-Chief, at which he said: Let us all arm ourselves and light our pitch-pine torches; let us see who is coming. Perhaps we'll catch some Crooked-Tongues . . .

They ran into the forest and found her just before the VAMPIRE SKELETON reached her. He stopped at the edge of their lights and said to her: You were fortunate that they came when they did.

The War-Chief said: Tomorrow we shall go to his lodge and destroy this serpent.

At dawn they set out. A quilt of snow-clouds rent with blue cracks streamed past the spruce-tops which half blocked the sweet white circlet of SUN, so the morning was very mild and white amidst the sound of rivers. Crows cawed in the trees. Every now and then they saw a scrap of torn and scattered clothing. They found the water-jug at the spring, just as the woman had said. They arrived at the lodge and saw her husband with a bite in his side. The dead man had drunk his blood, and he was gnawed about his ribs. The woman's bread was burned in the cold ashes. In the coffin behind the partition, the VAMPIRE SKELETON lay with his face stained with blood.

My uncle, we have come to prepare you more befittingly, said the War-Chief, as if to a Wendat he'd captured. – Uncle, we know that you're not satisfied with your present place, but when we've finished embellishing you I think you'll be pleased.

They gathered wood and piled it all about. Then they set fire to the place. Suddenly the VAMPIRE SKELETON cried: You have deceived me. If I escape, I will kill you!

He yelled, until his voice became weaker. Suddenly his skull exploded. A jackrabbit leaped out and ran between a warrior's legs and escaped into the forest. So his evil Power remained alive.

– And that is the tale, said Adodarhoh. I have spoken.

Now, bringing Adodarhoh's relation to mind so many years later, Tehorenhaennion decided to make what is known among gamblers as a sealed play. He put on his deerskin sleeves and set out to kill a jackrabbit. – Here, this hill of red and yellow trees. That was the place where jackrabbits were. He shot one with an arrow. (He listened for the Hiroquois.) There he purified himself with tobacco. ONDAKIS came bounding joyfully out of the blackness in his skull, like the animals when IOUSKEHA first let them out of the cave at the beginning of the world: moose and deer, bears and squirrels, running in the sunlight. IOUSKEHA shot them all in the hind foot, so that it would be easier for the People to hunt them – all but WOLF. So now there was something which Tehorenhaennion strove to hunt with his eye among this swarm of richness that exploded from his brain, one thing that loped rapidly into distant shadows like WOLF. Tehorenhaennion's mother had been a Wolf, so he belonged to that clan. His reason-soul ran as fleetly as WOLF, being Wolf; and

WOLF turned laughing-tongued to make certain that he followed; WOLF led him down the trail of dreams until the trees were transparent and he could see the bones inside. Tree-crowns rose into the dusk like black clouds. The grey color of ferns waving on Wendat hilltops told him that the play was almost finished. Now WOLF took him to a swamp-pool whose black leads the light still picked out between lily-crowns like the strands of a spiderweb, and WOLF laughed happily *He he he he he!* and Tehorenhaennion heard WOLF's laugh coming out of his own mouth. WOLF leaped across the pool and faced him from a fractured rock at water's edge, spruce-crowned and -shaded, and then it was dark.

Tehorenhaennion laid down a handful of deer-fat, a good present for WOLF. Beside it he stretched out the carcass of the jackrabbit that he had killed. – I consented to follow wherever you led, my UNCLE, said he. You see that there is no evil in my heart. My UNCLE, open your ears! There is a witch among us named Echon. He is one of those whom we call *Charcoal.* My UNCLE, raise my heart high! Echon is my enemy. He and I kill each other. Disturb his mind. We are in the place where trees have bones. Afflict his dreams with the VAMPIRE SKELETON. Wherever his reason-soul goes, send the VAMPIRE SKELETON to chase him. When the VAMPIRE SKELETON comes, then he must be devoured. Hear me, my UNCLE! I have spoken.

I hear you, my nephew, said WOLF. I will raise your heart high.

In the rising moonlight, Tehorenhaennion stood exultant as WOLF loped south, toward the Country of the Haudenosaunee, with the jackrabbit in his mouth. Long before dawn, WOLF returned, and a SKELETON was riding on his back . . .

Tehorenhaennion smiled.

Now it was that time of year when women got the corn in, and men set out to trade with the Neutrals and the People of the Tobacco Nation. And Père Brébeuf had a dream that he was ascending a steep snow-ridge effortlessly in his snowshoes, yearning upward for the black fringe of winter-stripped trees whose branches reached pityingly down toward him. There was a gulley ahead so that he could see through to SKY. Behind him, the indigo smudges of chilly evening clouds widened, pouring themselves out above some grand lac or sea – frozen now, glaring feebly with the last beams of daylight. Land extended endlessly behind, GOD alone knew how far. And he was leaving it all, going to SKY.

Someone was coming behind him. It comforted him to know that he was not alone. At first he was convinced that it was Père Le Jeune, and smiled to remember what Père Le Jeune so often said: *Patience abides on middle ground.*

Soon they would be together again. Père Le Jeune was proud of him; he would praise him . . . But then doubt chilled him. He turned back to see who it was, and his heart began to scream. An evil skeleton was pursuing him on snowshoes! It was running up the hill with hateful vindictive alacrity . . .

He awoke pale and sweating, knowing that as soon as he fell asleep the dream would resume. Surely the DEVIL had sent it. If only he could make the sign of the Cross in his sleep –

At the Feast of the Dead, a Sorcerer had spoken with him of the after-life, describing a Demon called HEAD-PIERCER; at once, Brébeuf's trained imagination slammed a door to keep him from visualizing this horrid figure. But a voice said to him: *Open the box, and death will be there.* – He would not! Let the box open of itself.

He fell asleep, and the VAMPIRE SKELETON was closer. It was running even more rapidly than a Neutral chasing deer in his snow-racquets. It was screaming at him through its mouth and deep black nostril-sockets. Its malice was as impassable as black spruce-ribs. It leaped upon him –

It was the morning of the seventeenth of Septembre. And, strange to say, although he had thought that he was feverish, he now felt perfectly well, but Père Jogues was feverish. On the twenty-third, one of their manservants, by name Dominique, also fell ill with a purple fever. Presently the infirmary was filled with sick Frenchmen. Père Brébeuf himself gave the invalids their medicine, which consisted of wild purslane stewed, with a dash of native verjuice. On the twenty-fourth, Père Jogues was so poorly that it was necessary to bleed him. Père Chastellain was sick also, and Père Garnier asked to be excused from the Exercises, in order to be a sick-nurse, yet he too was compelled to take to his bed (or rather, as I should say, his mat of rushes upon bark, for in Ouendaké accommodations are not as they are in France). Now of all the Black-Gowns only Père Brébeuf, Père Pijart and Père Le Mercier were well. Seeing this, the Savages came to visit, among them Tehorenhaennion (whose face was expressionless, but who gloated in his heart upon these victories which the VAMPIRE SKELETON had already won – yet he was uneasy that Echon had not yet been struck down).

To Père Le Mercier he said: I seem to see Echon also being devoured by this pestilence. Tell me truly, my brother, whether he too is feverish.

He is perfectly well, returned the priest coldly. But I must ask you as a favor, my friend, to speak a little lower, for your voice disturbs these sick men who require their rest.

You have no sense! said Tehorenhaennion contemptuously. Listen! There is a bird that speaks louder than I do, and you say nothing to him.

And he strode out.

Shortly thereafter, Tonneraouanont the Hunchback, of whom Tehorenhaennion was very jealous, came to see those who were called *Charcoal* and offered to cure them if they should give him presents, but they scorned him, which pleased Tehorenhaennion greatly when he heard. The Hunchback, it is said, then revealed to them the names of certain roots which were simples against disease, for he pitied them even when they refused to give him gifts, but the Black-Gowns only summoned their hired men to boot him out. Yet when Tehorenhaennion recounted this to Born Underwater, she said that he ought not to be so gleeful, as this was an insult to them all. Then he fell silent, and admitted that she was right.

Père Chastellain, who had the highest fever, lay raving. – Nothing but snow and birches on Cap Rouge! he shouted, and then a little later: Put your bones back in the grave, Monsieur de Champlain! Stop pinching me!

The Superior, Père Brébeuf, turned pale when he heard these words, but said nothing.

In Octobre, which is the Moon When They Cart the Net from Shore, the Black-Gowns recovered. Tehorenhaennion was dismayed. Evidently Echon had captured the VAMPIRE SKELETON, so that he now owned the disease. As a result (which could only have been expected), the People began to get sick. Echon was turning the disease upon them.

The Second Epidemic 1636–1637

That winter again there fell a great quantity of snow, so that the hunters killed many deer floundering in drifts. The men could smell them, could see their spotted coats heaving sweatily through the gaps in the trees. Antlers crowded antlers like creaking branches, and the forest flickered with tawny animals milling in their panic, trying to run, struggling against each other for the prize of arrows. But great labor it was to bring the carcasses home, and some of the meat was abandoned. Tehorenhaennion spoke against this, saying that the spirits of the deer would be angry that they had been killed for nothing, but Père Brébeuf, incensed at the man's pernicious idolatry, spoke out against him in Council, crying: Do not listen to the words of this idle fellow who cannot even make rain come! Deer have no souls. Worry rather about your own.

Presently the disease worsened, and children began to die. It leaped from village to village faster than fear, hiding in the deer-fat cakes, rustling in the corn-strings, creeping from fire to fire until it flourished loathsomely in all the twenty Huron towns (so the Black-Gowns were told, although they did not go throughout the land). The Savages, hysterical with morbid anxiety, could scarcely bear reassurance of Echon, as he learned to his great sorrow. When he told them of the marvels of eternal life, which they'd see for themselves if they died baptized in the Faith, they interrupted clamorously, crying: Speak not to us of dead things! Can you save us now, or can you not?

I am very sorry, my brothers –

(Soon he would be able to employ a more commanding language among them.)

This epidemic was much worse than the first. In Ossossané alone the Black-Gowns bled more than two hundred people, in hopes of easing them. They treated them with prunes, sugar, lemon-peel, and other French substances, knowing that these could do no harm, at least, and striving always to compete with the potions of the Sorcerers –

Tehorenhaennion and Tonneraouanont, who both recovered from the sickness early, were in great demand. In every patient that they sucked and blew upon, they discovered hairball charms which Echon or some other witch had sent into the swollen flesh.

News came from Teanaostoiaiaé that Amantacha's mother and last sister had perished, dying blind and writhing. So that family was extinguished. (As for Born Underwater, she remained in perfect health as before.)

. . . He saw a sick baby who was going to die, and he longed to send her to Heaven, but her parents were not willing. Thus he had Père Jogues distract them, while stealthily he dipped his hand in sugar water and did the deed, so that he baptized that child very opportunely.

And he wrote *The joy that one feels when he has baptized a Savage who dies soon afterwards, and flies directly to Heaven to become an Angel, certainly is a joy that surpasses anything that can be imagined.*

Painted Silhouettes
1637

You do good to your friends and you burn your enemies. GOD does the same.

PÈRE LE JEUNE, to an Algonkin chief (1637)

Another thing which can scarcely be imagined is the black-toothed shoals and rapids which wait just around the next bend of the Stream of Time; for while it is true, as the Bible says, that souls are saved by water (a fact which none save Protestants and infidels would dispute), it is also true that many are deceived and undone by it, being not simply drowned, like our martyr Père Nicolas, but also ambushed by Hiroquois who wait until those many are sufficiently close to shore to see the darkness between the trees; as happened the following summer to the Wendat when they came down to Trois-Rivières to exchange beaver-peltries for hatchets and kettles. Paddling true, they baited their hooks with frogskin and towed the lines behind them as they went. From time to time they caught a fish, and then they were very happy. The French were happy also as they awaited them, making profane Exercises to envision their Store-houses swollen with furs (although of course never never *never* could Store-houses be compensated for what the Kirke brothers had stolen away). – Be happy, Iron People! (Thus the Montagnais convert, Pigarouich.) The Huron will also bring skins to wipe away your tears for the death of your good Captain, Chawain! So I have heard. Ah, Iron People, you will be rich, rich . . . – Père Le Jeune and Père Daniel were no more or no less happy; the gift which they in their turn expected was another set of docile Huron boys for their Seminary, which Père Daniel continued to lead with great success, although two of the Seminarians, it is true, had lamentably died.

Those who survived clamored much for baptism – all three of them. Then they could live forever at *Kekwek* with baptized girls of their Nation, and the Iron People would give them gifts, and desist from trying to convert them. They would get many more gifts from the Iron People than the others . . . – One of them was named Tewatirhon. He was one of those boys who are always testing limits (he could not help himself), who must be brought up short almost every day with a blow to the wrist. And yet he was not a bad boy. His uncle was a great Captain among the Huron, by name Taratouan, so that it was to the Black-Gowns' advantage to have close dealings with him. Looking into Tewatirhon's rather gawky face, surveying the eyes high upon the forehead, the long nose and little mouth, the dark mop of hair, the skin like oak, Père Daniel said to himself: GOD grant that I make a decent Christian out of him! – even as Taratouan for his part said to the boy's mother: Do not sorrow for his loss, since he will come back to us even as Amantacha did. Nor will we permit the Iron People to carry him away to their Country; he will not be away from us as long as Amantacha. It is sufficient that they make him into one of them at *Kekwek* where the great river narrows.

I do not like the Iron People, she replied stubbornly.

You need not like them. Now that he is their nephew, they are ours as we are theirs. *Kekwek* belongs to us. The great river belongs to us. Do you want kettles? I pray you, sister, do not move me with your tears, for if my heart becomes changed, and we keep him back, then some youth other than Tewatirhon will gain the advantage for his kin.

Then you must visit him without fail in the spring. My heart is sad.

I promise you that I shall visit him.

So he did, for the forest now exploded with red and black raspberries whose subcarbuncles were reminiscent of the compound eyes of flies. But ahead of him on the Stream of Time was another uncle of Tewatirhon's, who was a War-Chief and misliked the Iron People. And he got to Three Rivers first. In this year, being somewhat in fear of the Hiroquois, he and his good grandsons and nephews took in payment for their peltries all the weapons that they could. The Iron People would not let them have firearms, but they did make available to them swords, shields, knives and poles, at which they were mollified.* A fine diversion it was to the Black-Gowns there to see

* Remember Marsolet? He was the one who'd debauched Champlain's Montagnais girls. Once Champlain croaked, he crept back into favor, married a Marie and settled down. There was no sense in bucking the Black-Gowns anymore. Marsolet was at Trois-Rivières this year. He made a killing, selling the Savages rusty iron poles . . .

them playing on the meadows by their canoes, shouting and waving their swords about. The War-Chief glanced at a Frenchman's arquebus, and his black eyes glittered angrily. But the others paid no attention to him. Some of them had lashed swords to poles and made ugly-looking pikes, so that the Black-Gowns felt that it would go ill with the Hiroquois in any battle, unless of course the latter had gotten firearms from the Hollanders in any numbers. As yet none had, although Governor de Montmagny was told by some Algonkins whom he trusted that the Mohawk now demanded them from their puppetmasters most urgently. This was no surprise to Montmagny. Of course it was in the interest of those heretics to encourage the Hiroquois to attack the Huron and the French: the ruin of the fur-trade would mean the ruin of New France – something which would be very pleasant to New Holland.

Peering most narrowly into this Huron War-Chief's visage, Montmagny's Deputy questioned him in the same terms, and the War-Chief confirmed the Hiroquois were dangerous, very dangerous, like serpents –

Montmagny had thought as much.

The Iron People conveyed the Seminarians to Three Rivers in that season, so that they might more conveniently have speech with their kindred (the Wendat had insisted upon this the previous summer). There Tewatirhon met his uncle the War-Chief, who perceived that the boy's heart was sad.

My uncle, is it true what the Montagnais say, that the Black-Gowns in Wendaké have been killed for their Sorceries? (Thus Tewatirhon.)

What! Who says this?

They all say it.

I have heard nothing of this, replied his uncle the War-Chief. But if it is true, then the Iron People will be preparing to revenge themselves upon us all. Let us steal away this night.

But the Iron People learned about it through their spies (for ever since the days of Chawain, Iron People have become very cunning in that way), and they arrested the War-Chief to prevent his escape, suspecting that it portended some plot against them. They were very sensitive about plots that summer. Then Tewatirhon dissimulated, saying that he longed only to see his relations, until at last the Iron People were tricked, and their hearts moved to pity, so they let him and his uncle go.

On the Fleuve Saint-Laurent they met Taratouan. He laughed at them. – Now I see that you have lost your intelligence among the Iron People! he cried. Indeed, I would almost look to see beards on your cheeks, so childish and without merit do your words appear to me.

So he shamed them both (it being vital to his designs that his nephew become the nephew of the Iron People), and at last Tewatirhon agreed to return to *Kekwek* for another winter. His uncle the War-Chief went on to Ouendaké, and he himself leaped into his uncle Taratouan's canoe so lightly, already making the Exercises, imagining how joyfully the Iron People would welcome him –

It was then that the Hiroquois attacked.

Tewatirhon escaped, and crawled into the post at Three Rivers naked and half-dead. The others did not.

The Iroquois paddled past Three Rivers, laughing, shouting, insulting the Iron People because they would not come out to fight.

The Fleuve Saint-Laurent was shining with whitecaps, skim-lines and ripple-lines running weirdly this way and that in the gusts.

On the eleventh of that month, two war shallops arrived from Kebec, upon one of which was Montmagny himself. The Commandant at Three Rivers, Monsieur de l'Isle, who had many arms in his Store-house, distributed his best pikes and harquebuses to those who had none, and then sent for other men to crew four additional shallops which he had on hand. – We cannot wait, said the Gouverneur. Direct them to follow us. – Yes, Seigneur. (Thus the Sieur de l'Isle.) God be with you.

They rowed all night, in a good wind. Their good Savages strained their eyes in the darkness as they crossed Lac Saint-Pierre (where the waters of the Fleuve Saint-Laurent become unequivocally free from salt), for here they might well have met with some ambush, but no yell and rattling discharge of arrows smashed the silence of that long night. Père Le Jeune could scarcely hear any sound save the quiet steady splashing at the oarlocks, and the men's fierce low breathing. He pulled at his oar with sunburned arms almost as strong and hard as those of a Savage, and suddenly a laughing exultancy rose up inside him like vomit and almost escaped between his teeth, as he thought how terrified he had been a mere four years ago when he set out to winter among the Montaignez; and now, pursuing this merciless enemy, he felt no fear! – Ah, he thought very tenderly, surely I am unworthy of this grace! . . . Now I see why God has spared my life so long, and redeemed me temporarily from His judgment – that I may strive to become hardened to my duty, and better serve Him . . . – Montmagny, too, smiled in the night. Since the Iroquois had no firearms, it would be simple to make an example of them, thereby raising the minds of his Montagnais and Algoumequins to trust in the French, and likewise the minds of his own countrymen to trust in *him* . . . The barbarians had evidently withdrawn to

Rivière des Hiroquois, down which poor dead Champlain had fought his first battle with them. Eh, that location must be pacified again, it seemed . . . – A strong southwest wind now momentarily halted their progress among the islands, as Père Le Jeune strained fruitlessly at his oar and listened to the pounding of the other men's hearts and slapped at a mosquito inside his cassock; but the Gouverneur fell upon his knees and prayed for a calm, to which entreaty Le Jeune added his own voice, and shortly thereafter GOD showed that their petition had been heard, at which they approached the mouth of Rivière des Iroquois with redoubled effort; and now they could see smoke staining the dawn and Montmagny laughed once, harshly, like the explosion of an harquebus, and said to Père Le Jeune: It is very good of these Hiroquois, to honor us by waiting upon our coming in this way! . . . – but Le Jeune, who had been in Canada longer, already felt chagrin welling up in his heart like the bitterly inky waters of some interdicted spring; and Montmagny turned to the Savage called Pigarouich and said: What is your mind, my friend? Shall we hang the enemy from good French gibbets, or shall we give them to you to be burned? – which words Père Le Jeune translated into the Montagnais tongue (he had become very ready at that in recent months) – and Pigarouich replied: I fear to spoil Onontio's pleasure by telling him that the Irocois are surely gone!

What did he say, Paul? (Thus Gouverneur Montmagny.)

He fears, Seigneur, as do I, that your exertions have been useless.

They rowed as well as they could, and so drew ever closer to that smoke. Now the Sieur des Dares exclaimed in anger, and pointed with his hand, at which Le Jeune saw that these Hiroquois robbers had stolen a crossbar of the great Cross which Monsieur the Commandant du Plessis had caused to be erected the previous year; seeing which, the men began to row still faster with wrath, despite their weariness; but Père Le Jeune only smiled thinly and said to the Gouverneur: It is only their usual impudency, Seigneur.

It was full daylight when they reached the fire which the Hiroquois had left to taunt them. In the shallows, a dead Huron knelt and nodded among the rocks, with all the complex, delicate and introverted bowings which make one hesitate to disturb a corpse in water. Pigarouich leaped out and lifted the Huron in his arms. – See how they have burned him and cut him! he shouted in his booming voice; at which Montmagny frowned and said: Tell the fellow to be quiet, for there may still be Hiroquois lurking about.

Little danger of that, Seigneur. (Thus the Sieur des Dares.)

Tell him. – No, wait – look you, there is our crossbar nailed to yonder tree! And what have they written on it?

Those are heads that they have drawn. (Thus Père Le Jeune.)

Ah. Now I see. Silhouettes in red and black. But what do these mean? Pigarouich!

Thirty heads, Onontio. (Thus Pigarouich.) The enemy have captured thirty Wendat. Two of the prisoners are Captains – those big heads. So they still have Taratouan. He has been tortured a little, as I believe. Two children's heads; and these two were destined for your Seminary. Do you comprehend me, Onontio? I tell you everything. I know everything about these Hiroquois – everything! How I would like to kill them all! . . . These heads, with the plumes of stripes, they are the brave ones. They fought the Hiroquois well.

Montmagny listened carefully. – Do you ask him, Paul, what signifies the red silhouettes and the black ones . . . – but no, why is there but one drawn in black?

That is easy, Onontio! You see how well I explain to you? The black face, he is dead. He is this man whom we found. The red ones, those are all the rest. Those are destined for the fire. Now they will all burn, for we shall never catch up with them.

Enough! Tell the Savage to shut his mouth!

Making the Exercises out of habit that he could no longer break, Père Le Jeune descended the Stream of Time an hour, a day, and saw them all wearily pulling at their oars with blistered hands, returning to Trois-Rivières where no doubt they would meet a few more Huron refugees naked and shivering and sucking up Monsieur le Gouverneur's charity; as meanwhile, trapped in the iron prison of present time, Monsieur le Gouverneur pounded his fist against the trunk of that tree, biting his lip for grief that the Christians had been denied their revenge . . .

Frenzy
1636–1637

All these people are of a very cheerful disposition, although many among them are of a sad and saturnine humour.

CHAMPLAIN, on the Huron (1615)

For Père Brébeuf the days and months were but a Savage babble of wailing and shouting and whispered menace. The Jesuits now had scarcely any friends in Ouendaké. He believed now that they never had, for the Huron were all hypocrites, as had been proved that previous Novembre when they begged him of his mercy to end the plague, and he said that they must give up divorce and Dream-Feasts and all their other filthy customs, at which they said that he was asking them to give up being Wendat, and so the meeting ended, but the next day they came to him and agreed to do these things rather than be exterminated by his disease; so he was glad, and led them in vowing themselves unalterably to CHRIST, and he was unutterably content until the following day when he found them all brutish and unclean with the masks that the Sorcerers had bade them clap over their faces, to terrify the spirits of the disease . . . So when the masks of idolatry went on, the mask of hypocrisy fell off, and he saw them now as the treacherous, dirty, lethal vilenesses that they were; and his relations with them were nothing other than war. His own life, of course, was nothing, to be expended for this cause without a thought. He strode into the longhouses and baptized the dying. Whomever he could save at this moment, he *would* save, no matter what they said or did. A woman hid her son behind a partition, so that Echon could not find him. He prowled baffled round between the hearth-fires, until a man came running at him with a hatchet and shouted: I shall split your head! – He left that longhouse and went out into the night, a winter night of vicious airs, and the snow was blowing fiercely, and he stood between the longhouses for a moment and prayed; looking up, he saw the other Black-Gowns flitting out of lodges; he went into the next lodge now where the dogs whimpered and a Savage Captain stood shouting the names of all who had died that evening and sick people lay sweating and shivering on the circle of deerskins by the hearth-embers and their eyes cringed away from him; he saw a child fur-wrapped on a cradle board; the mother sought to push him away from the babe but she herself was so weak that she could not; he baptized them both. He walked to the next fire, and the next. The smoke was so thick that it would scarcely have been possible to read a Breviary. But he peered through it; he would miss nothing. At this hearth there were children still in life, but the parents were very vigilant. He assured them that he would not baptize their little boys, since they were so much opposed to it; he would only give them water to drink. Bowing quickly over the children, he made the water holy with a silent prayer and baptized them in secret. His shadow hunched and flickered like a black bird. Moments later, the children died. These secret procedures thrilled his heart. He felt that he was carrying off spoils from SATAN in stealth. Slyly he baptized children with sugar-water. He placed his cold hand on the burning foreheads of speechless grandmothers and breathed his breath upon them. He baptized an uncle and a nephew together, and they died never knowing it. A man whose wife and sisters were dead put on his snowshoes and dragged wood on a sledge, to warm his dying son. When he came in, Echon was bending over him.

Fathers and Crows

Are these Black-Gowns friends or enemies? a Peace-Chief said. If they are friends, we may rely on them to help us in our need. Are they doing this? – He looked around him. The assembly was silent. – I remember how you jeered at Tehorenhaennion last year, when he could not make the rain come, and you were right to do so. Their magic was stronger than his. As soon as they spoke to their Cross, rain came and saved us. Is that not true? But now so many of us are dying, so many, and the Hatitsihenstaatsi do nothing to save them. Indeed, you have heard them; they are *happy* when we die! They hovered around my strong son, like crows pecking at the eyes of a fallen deer . . . Their *baptism* sends us to the Country of the Dead! Is that not true? If they can bring rain, they can cure sickness. Open your ears! Listen to the sickness flying through the air! Do you not hear it now? I hear it. It crouches on the roof; it waits by the smokehole; it scratches with its claws. The cloud-shadow is the shadow of its black wings. I ask again: are they who are called *Charcoal* friends or enemies? – I have spoken.

Diagnoses

Born Underwater said that she'd heard from her mother as a child that the Black-Gowns kept a dead corpse locked in their Tabernacle, and that the name of this corpse was JESUS. One of their secret mysteries was that they ate His flesh, even as the Wendat eat the flesh of their enemies. Now the other women said that they believed this tale; for surely the carcass of JESUS must be rotting and infecting the Country with its plague. The women remembered how in summertime, when the lodges were filled with vermin, the Black-Gowns swept their lodge, as if they wished to hide those creatures from sight. Maybe they issued from the dead body of JESUS, and spread the disease in that fashion. The women who had been baptized in sickness remembered how the Black-Gowns had urged them in low voices to *partake of the Body of Our LORD*. And as they said this, they looked right and left, as if for fear that others might hear. – Then a woman said that she believed that it was not the Black-Gowns, but Étienne Brûlé's sister who sought to kill them, in revenge because they had put him to death. She said that her uncle had heard from the Algonkin at Three Rivers that their Shamans had seen a French woman infecting the Country with her breath. Who else could this be but Brûlé's sister? – Ah, replied Born Underwater, you do wrong to believe that they who are called *Charcoal* are not allied with her, if indeed she is behind this; for it was they who summoned Brûlé to France to keep my Amantacha company. This proves that he obeyed their orders. Therefore they will be revenged for him. But I shall revenge myself on *them* in after-times, sisters, since my heart cries out for blood! – Thus she incited them. – And a woman said that her son had heard from the Montagnais at Kebec that old Chawain, who had died the previous winter, swore with his last breath that he would carry off the Wendat to the Country of the Dead. – Born Underwater had heard nothing of this, although she had once been considered Montagnais, but she fell in with it and pretended that it was familiar to her, for it seemed now to her that anyone who spoke ill of the Black-Gowns or the Iron People was surely speaking truth. – And a woman whose child had just died said that she'd seen Echon in the forest, stabbing an image of a child with a gleaming iron needle –

The Haloes

– Why, you may ask, did he move away from that upraised hatchet, if he longed so much for death? My own Sainte Catherine Tekakwitha had a similar experience in her uncle's lodge, and with a similar result. – Cowardice? – Oh, no. – When he had the fever and all the Savages seemed to wear shimmering golden haloes, an easy and detached serenity possessed him. He went about his rounds, much more slowly than usual (so he supposed, although he could not be sure), and fever tingled sensually in his fingertips, in the nape of his neck; and he felt that he could continue without ever feeling discomfort. If he had chosen to, he might have plodded round and round the outer palisade until he fell dead. Instead he chose to take to his bed for a day or two, until the fever passed, for he judged himself unready to be harvested. Soon he was well again. But as he moved among the dead in those cold days, it seemed to him that his feelings had been completely upended, like one of those light birchbark canoes which Huron travelers turned upside-down at night for a dwelling-house. The melancholy came upon him again and again, like the refrain of a melody. He ascribed it to a temptation of the DEVIL. But later he made a pretty prayer that became a rainbow trout swimming up the Stream of Time toward the Forty-Third Rapids (*viz.*, the Conversion of Magdalene), and all at once he thought: I wish Born Underwater could see. It might cure her of her delusions –

What can this mean? he said to his heart. Why am I drawn to this unbeliever?

Scourging himself would be a false humility; by such crooked ways one came into the DEVIL's house. – No, it was her *opposition* to which he was attracted – not to her; not to her! He remembered how proud Saint Ignatius had always been when his Jesuits encountered obstacles, insults, opprobrium – indeed, if a new Residence were established to the tune of approval, Ignatius would scowl and hold those priests in low esteem! He remembered a theory of Père Le Jeune's, to which he'd been subjected repeatedly (eh, he should have more charity: everyone repeats himself from time to time): – I tell you, Jean: the ENEMY who does not counterattack is dangerous, for thereby he conserves his strength. Until we're reviled, until we encounter tears and tribulations, we have *not* flushed Him out of Hell! – So it was Born Underwater's resistance that now gave him joy. Certainly he could never hate her. In his dreams she fed him to the black organs of sacrifice . . .

The Superior is incubating some notion, thought Père Le Mercier to himself. That was obvious. Ever since Joseph the Hiroquois had been burned, the Superior had begun to behave differently. He was not beside himself, as most of the other priests had been; no, this was something different.

Do you ever think upon skeletons? he asked Père Le Mercier abruptly.

In what sense, Père Superior?

In the sense of fever, I suppose. I remember how Monsieur de Champlain told me of that winter on the Isle de Sainte-Croix, thirty-odd years ago. He said that skeletons walked –

I cannot conceive of him saying such a thing, interrupted Père Le Mercier primly. Monsieur de Champellain was hardly –

Ah, you mistake me. This was nothing diabolical or supernatural, although I am sure it seemed so. It was that fever called scurvy, and so many skeletons walked –

Then Monsieur de Champlain was incorrect, Père Superior. For I have it on good authority that men afflicted with that ill suffer not from wasting, but from bloat.

No doubt of that, said Père Brébeuf absently.

The Vampire Skeleton

They threw tobacco into the fire, as an offering to the SKY. They shouted: *Taenguiaens!* – which means, *Heal us!*

But the SKY would not hear.

Kebec Years

1637

> Often they deceived an inexperienced gold-digger with documents showing that the land had belonged to them for years, or they simply shot him; often they poisoned him with brandy. Then they threw the corpse into a hole which the prospector had once dug out and abandoned, threw a bit of earth on top, and that was all. The crime was concealed for ever. It was just the same in Canada.
>
> FRANZ WELZL, *The Quest for Polar Treasures* (1933)

In this Year of Our LORD 1637, the Black-Gowns gave iron arrow-points, iron rings, iron awls and iron knives to the Montagnais children at Kebec to reward them for saying their catechism well; for the craving of these Savages for iron was a terrible thing to see in those days. Père Davost helped in this distribution of benefices when he was able to rise from his sickbed (he'd never recovered from his stay in the Huron Country). Mostly he was too weak. Out of pity, Père Le Jeune assigned him the easiest service, which was to tutor the French children. – I pity this frail soul, he said to himself, sighing; and his prayers for Père Davost's health were as the anxious pipings of nestlings in the maple trees* . . . – He saw a Savage glaring at a Cross. – Abase yourself! he shouted. – And now it was time for an interview with that Algoumequin boy whose parents had died of the plague. (Even Nations far inland were

* In Septembre of 1643, Père Davost died at sea. Having suffered for so many years from a heavy fever, he was ordered at last by the Superior to return to France for treatment. He perished on the twenty-seventh, far from land, and was cast beneath the waves. GOUGOU ate him.

dying that year, which proved that this mortality had nothing to do with the French.) – This way, Monsieur, he said. Sit down. – He closed the door. – Later, smiling with satisfaction, he sat at his writing-table and picked up the quill which he used especially for the *Jesuit Relations*, describing the conversation: *I tried, therefore, to frighten him with the fear of Hell – so that indeed I made him weep; as soon as I became aware of this, I redoubled my efforts . . .* – More effort, in the good LORD's name! That was the way! So Père Le Jeune now commenced a Habitation for the Algonkin and Montagnais at Sillery, where the Savages could learn to till the fields as they had humbly requested. Of late game had become scarcer yet, so that they frequently starved during the winter. – Of course they had always starved. But surely GOD would not turn His face away from these poor children of affliction, so how could Le Jeune refrain from such acts of charity, costly though they were? (Besides, the Habitation would also permit the Savages to be reduced to stability and more easily converted.)

In this year Père Le Jeune once more received a letter from that Ursuline nun of Tours, Marie de l'Incarnation, whom he had nearly forgotten. Her heart, as it seemed, was still fired by the accounts of the Savages which he had written for the *Jesuit Relations*. She expressed her regret that he had evidently not received her first communication (which he now withdrew from the drawer of his desk, reading it over again). She remained ardent to the point of heartsickness in her craving to render service to the Savage girls of Canada. – Sighing, Père Le Jeune took up his quill and replied in the most mortifying terms that he could, to test her. He dwelled upon the filth and ingratitude of the Savages (for example, that dying woman who'd hated his threats of eternal burning so much that she ground her teeth and wept and crawled out of the cabin into the snow . . .), of the generally poor morals of the French, of the lack of any building to house her, of the cold, cold winters and especially of the Hiroquois; and he closed advising her to remain in the Nation of her birth where she might hope to accomplish far more of the LORD's work. – I don't imagine that she will reply to that, he said to himself.

Bulwarks

The Sieur de Montmagny was now in his second year as Governor, so that men could begin to judge him. It was said that he was very conscientious, but perhaps too strict and overbearing. There were some in Kebec who now expressed longing for the days when they were ruled by the Sieur de

Champlain, who, being dead, had been polished accordingly in their memories until he shone like goldwork in a church. Yet, as Père Le Jeune well knew when these sentiments came to his ears, they were vain and false like all worldly things. As for him, he could not praise the new Governor with sufficient extravagance. Montmagny's compassion for the poor was edifying; indeed he held himself aloof from no class of men, not even the Savages. Yet he was also wise and vigilant. At Trois-Rivières he'd had erected a platform ranged with cannons. At Kebec, the Château Saint-Louys was now a good stout fortress. – Have no fear, said he to his French. Our good walls are so well strengthened with iron that they cannot be breached. What proof are Hiroquois arrows against our cannon? But take care when you travel on the Fleuve or when you go hunting in the woods, for it would be no marvel then if those DEMONS were to roast you alive.

The Second Vow

1637

Later, while preparing the altar and vesting, I felt a strong impulse to say: . . . "HOLY TRINITY, confirm me; my only GOD, confirm me!" I said this with great earnestness, and with much devotion and tears, very often repeated and deeply felt, saying once, "ETERNAL FATHER, will You not confirm me?" understanding it as a sure thing, and the same to the SON and the HOLY SPIRIT.

SAINT IGNATIUS, *Spiritual Diary*
(1544)

By the time spring came, Ihonatiria was gutted by disease and death. It was time for those called *Charcoal* to find new victims. In the month of Mai, the People at Ossossané agreed to have that honor, for the disease slumbered in exhaustion, and they feared the revenge that the Black-Gowns might take if they were refused. On the seventh of Juin their cabin was finished. Père Pijart sowed French wheat, so that in future times they could bake their own Eucharist.

But then the disease awoke once more. Warriors in the prime of health were dead in two days. Children died faster. – When this abates, said Père Brébeuf to himself, they will certainly be restored to tranquility of mind.

As it was, many of them had already begged his pardon for the slanders they had cast against him and his – which forgiveness he most freely gave. He questioned them concerning sin, and they trembled, and said: Echon, we know not what to answer you. – In this the Black-Gowns' third year among the Savages, more than two hundred of the sick and dying had been baptized – a rich harvest for JESUS; a stinging defeat for the DEVIL! Then, too, as a result of this pestilence he'd become famous throughout the Country – an advantage which could be used to draw more souls to him, if he had the wit. No one believed any longer (as until now some had erroneously done) that he was here to marry their girls or trade in beaver-skins! – From this it could be seen what marvelous use GOD makes of all things, even calamities . . . He remembered how swarms of Savages had once surrounded him, begging for iron things. He'd given one old man a handful of nails, out of pity, at which hordes came babbling and holding out their hands; he'd had to let the quietly efficient lay brothers handle it. Such events were now entirely past. The Savages rarely came to his Residence to disturb his meditations. Dully they said to him: *Your world is different from ours; the GOD who created ours did not create yours . . .*

The women greased themselves with beaver-fat and went to their cabins in the fields as usual, where they stayed with the young children, giving them suck, weeding and scaring away crows. But then they began to shake with fever. And the children died in their arms. And they themselves died.

In the lacs and rivières, lush heart-shaped pairs and clusters of leaves grew up from the muck of old sadness. Everywhere they were playing lacrosse and also the dish game of stones, believing as they did that this might cure them. It was a pitiable sight to see invalids at death's door being forced to run and shout.

The Abandonment of Iron

She knelt upon the sleeping bench, sewing some marten-skins together, and smoke twisted up from the fire and a mouse rustled in the corn above her head.

Her face was like a song sung without error.

Tehorenhaennion was saying: I consented to try your scheme, and spoke against the Hatitsihenstaatsi, thinking that would clear the Country of these witches. But now I see that your plan was without merit.

It was not my plan, but yours, she said bitterly. Do you think now to criticize me with your lies?

His eyes began to blaze.

Come now, Tehorenhaennion, said Born Underwater with weary patience. Constrain your malevolence against me, for you will require every drop of venom against our enemies –

Your words are good, he said at last. Let me tell you what is in my mind. I believe that we should abolish the use of iron and other French goods in our Country. Then we shall have no further need to tolerate the Black-Gowns. And if some poison lurks in their iron things, then we shall be safe from that also. I shall go to the Old Men –

One village has already attempted this . . . – she said slowly.

Yes, my granddaughter, yes! To see if they might save themselves!

The pestilence has not yet abated there. And I believe that to do this will be very hard.

Of course it will be hard, said Tehorenhaennion, a little contemptuously. But when the world was dry, because the GREAT FROG had hidden all the water in His armpit, then IOUSKEHA dreamed of it and came to help us. The GREAT FROG believed that He could steal our rivers forever. But IOUSKEHA undeceived Him, even though the way was difficult. Then a waterfall came out from the spear-gash, and we were happy and gave thanks –

Perhaps it is as you say, she replied guardedly. I see nothing to contradict it.

His voice dropped. – As you know, I have asked the assistance of our friend the VAMPIRE SKELETON . . .

Yes, you have told me. But Echon defeated Him, as it begins to seem.

And defeated you also, Born Underwater. Do not forget that. You are my granddaughter; your heart is pure, but is it a strong heart?

Learn now, Tehorenhaennion, once and for all: we must help one another, and not cast rebukes like stones.

I become silent, he said sheepishly.

It is well. Then let us abandon iron, little by little. If we succeed, then the others will listen to us.

There was a plant called *Tissaouhianne*, which KLUSKAP's People used to dye porcupine quills red. This hue was much more brilliant than the ocher-red with which the People sometimes daubed their faces: it was like transparent glowing blood. One morning Born Underwater set off for the forest to search for a stand of it, as she believed that the color she would gain might well be superior to that of the red glass beads of the Iron People. The Wendat women did not seem to know it. They were not forest People. They told her to be careful of the Yroquois; they always said that. She smiled; she said: the Yroquois will not catch me today; at which they were satisfied, as her words always proved true.

She killed a porcupine and brought home the meat, at which everyone in the longhouse cried: *ho, ho!* laughing so happily, and they stewed it with corn and sunflower seeds. She plucked the quills and stained them with the boiled juice of *Tissaouhianne* leaves.

Why do you do that? – the other women said. Echon's beads are better!

She still had some glass beads which Amantacha had given her. They were more beautiful than the shellbeads and bone beads that the People had always used. On their deerskin thong they now rattled faintly like uneasy dreams. She unstrung them and threw them down between the corn-hills . . . – Why do you do that? – the other women said. As soon as she had walked away, she heard them scrabbling in the dirt where she'd been, with exclamations of greed and joy.

Flames of Rapture

On the ninth day of Juin they moved to the new Mission, where they were received (says the *Relation*) "with applause." It gave him great contrition to see that they had been held in such odium in Ihonatiria. No matter; it was time to widen their reach in any event. The People louted low before them, clutching iron hatchets.

Sad to say, it no longer excited him to envision great projects –

In this year he took the Second Vow – *viz.*, never to refuse the grace of martyrdom.

The Council of State

In the Moon When Blackberries Are Ripe, the Old Men summoned those who were called *Charcoal* to a preliminary Council, to determine whether they should be put to death. He heard the teeth of the other priests chattering like skeletons (strange, how he thought about skeletons more these days), but even then they began to murmur psalms of the sweetest resignation, and seeing their Superior happy they began to be happy, too, because death would be their beginning, and the death that now began to scent their every thought made them love one another more than ever. They stood before the House of Cut-Off Heads. The door opened, and one of the Old Men came out and gazed into his eyes with the glance that seeks to turn enemy eyes aside but Echon smiled because Echon was the strongest. The Old Man staggered. He turned and opened the door again and became reincorporated into the darkness. – The door opened; a Peace-Chief beckoned them in. Well, that was good, that there were Peace-Chiefs here. It was only a civil matter. – He led his little army of saved souls in. The hearth-fires shot up with a whoosh – like eternal fires, thought Brébeuf to himself. But he remained unafraid. In this Academy he felt himself an accomplished Chevalier.

Why, Père Superior (whispered Le Mercier), they all regard one another like corpses, or men who already fear the terrors of death!

Yes, they speak in sighs . . . – said Père Brébeuf. But how will they regard us?

Be silent! cried a War-Chief. How do we know that you do not cast spells against us even now?

Echon laughed and laughed. – Yes, my uncle, he said. How will you ever know?

He spoke to clear himself and his, looking into the eyes of each of these great men; and he wanted to cry out with triumph when he saw how none of them could meet his gaze for very long; they feared the witchcraft of his blue eyes! and he said to them loudly and firmly: JESUS has blue eyes . . . ! – but this was not the bombshell that he had hoped and expected; IESVS scarcely interested them anymore . . .

They were summoned to a grand Council of State. – Come quickly, and answer to the Council! said the messenger. You are dead men!

And you, my brother (thus Echon, whispering), do you yourself have the secret of eternal life?

He was sweating, although he felt very cold. Something turned in his stomach sickly. He wondered if he would faint. (It was not fear, but the secret venom of Tehorenhaennion.) His body begged him to lie down. Instead, he fastened on his girdle of spikes and secreted himself in his good Black Gown; he made the sash fast and tied on his boots. – Come, my brothers. Fear nothing but GOD.

Again the waiting outside the longhouse, the children stoning them gleefully from hidden places, the smell of drying fish. Outside the palisadoes, where they'd bury him secretly like Brûlé, there were brilliant yellow flowers in the grass –

Aenons the War-Chief was there – he who'd offered them Brûlé's bones, he under whose authority Joseph the Iroquois had been burned. He was almost certain now that his nephew Echon was another traitor, that all the Iron People were traitors. The Old Men agreed. Aenons was prepared to split Echon's head himself if the charges were not answered. – No doubt Echon would have an answer; Echon never stopped talking. They should have cut out Echon's tongue long ago. But Echon would be lucky even in death. Aenons would not torture him. It was too dangerous to torture witches; they might escape . . . – Now the Old Men called in the *Acwentonch* speech for the warriors to send in Echon and his henchmen, and Aenons braced himself. It seemed that something vile was about to come before the flames. – Now the door was opened, and in they came . . . Sometimes Echon wore a broad-brimmed black hat that made his head cast fantastic shadows by the fire. At other times he hooded himself with a piece of blackness that drank up the firelight very thirstily, as sand drinks water, as earth swallows blood, leaving only a little stain that soon vanishes. So Echon's cowl and Black Gown drank the light. Echon himself was terribly pale, like a man without blood. Yet for all that he moved quickly on his feet, as now when he strode into the longhouse of the Council. He was very strong. Aenons had heard this from the men who had paddled the days and distances with him from the Iron People's lodge at *Kekwek*.

Aenons had prepared his speech carefully. He longed to make his enemy tremble with fear. As soon as Echon entered, and the other men began to shout at him, Aenons rose to his feet.

Hear me, Echon! he cried. I know you well. You are cunning, and seek to hide your treacheries from us; you live alone with your witches, but I am Aenons; I see through walls! You think to feed us to your MONSTER of fever and disease which you raise in your lodge. You keep Him in a cage, like a tame bear. You feed Him upon our tears and sickness in the night. I see you, Echon! I see through walls! You have forgotten that when the Grey-Gowns lived among us fifteen winters ago, there was a man of your Nation who stole a quantity of wampum-beads from us in Toanché. He fled all the way to Quieunonascaron* to hide behind the Grey-Gowns' skirts. He thought he would not be seen. But who was it who saw through walls, Echon? Now you who are called *Charcoal* steal from us once again. But this time you steal from us what is more precious than wampun: you take our lives. Our wives and grandfathers and little children you devour day by day. In the Country of the Dead which you prate of so often, the other souls speak scornfully of you, for you have respect for neither law nor life. They can see you. And I too see you. I see through walls, Echon!

He sat down. His eyes never left Echon's.

The only sound was the crackling of the fire. The Captains and War-Chiefs and others watched Echon, and hatred burned in their faces.

* Carhagouha, where Père Le Caron lived in 1615–16, was moved in 1623–4 and became Quieunonascaron.

Echon thought for a moment. Then he rose, smiling sadly.

This is very edifying, he said at length. But let us test you. You see through walls, you say. But can you see through my cassock?

He took his gown between his fingers, and raised a fold of it over his hand.

How many fingers, Aenons? Come now, you who see through walls: how many fingers do I hide in my Black Gown?

He waited.

Aenons said: It matters not what I say, for your heart is filled with lies and venom. Whatever I say, you will cry me false.

Echon laughed. – I cannot deny your cunning. Tehorenhaennion must be your familiar! I thought that for once I had trapped you in your posturings.

There was a silence for a moment, and then the others began to shout abuse at Echon.

You have a cloth of charms, Echon, and it is killing us! You must give it up to us to be destroyed!

I have no such cloth, said he. I have spoken.

How he lies! shouted the War-Chief.

If you will not believe me, go to our residence, said Echon. Search everywhere. If you are not certain which is the charm, take all our clothing and cloth, and throw them into the Sweetwater Sea.

Sorcerers always talk in that way, said Tehorenhaennion. I know. I myself am a Sorcerer.

Then what *will* you have me say? said Echon sarcastically.

Tell us the cause of the pest! the other shouted.

And you – you do not know it? But by your own admission you are a Sorcerer. How then is this? Ah, but I forgot. You Sorcerers cannot even make rain –

Produce the wicked cloth! shouted Chief Ontitarac. You whom I once called nephew, will you answer or must I kill you?

I have no such cloth, said Echon. I have only the desire to save your souls from the fires of the DEVIL, who will tie you to stakes in Hell like his henchmen the Hiroquois, and torment you in an endless burning.

What sort of men are these? said an old chief wearily. They are always saying the same things, and repeating the same words a hundred times.

The Testament

In the month of Octobre, seeing that the Huron remained so enraged against them (indeed some unknown hand had endeavored to fire the residence), Père Brébeuf sat down in the Refectory. Octobre, yes. They would be sowing winter-wheat in France. The CAPTAIN OF THE DAY had already struck four bells of the hour, so that the Savages had gone. He picked up his pen and wrote a letter to Père Le Jeune: *Reverend Père, the Peace of CHRIST! We are perhaps at the point of shedding our blood and of sacrificing our lives for the service of our good Master JESUS CHRIST. Whatever happens, I can assure you that all our Pères await the outcome of this affair with calm and untroubled spirits. And, for myself, I can tell Your Reverence in all sincerity that I have not yet had the slightest apprehension of dying in such a cause. But we are all saddened that these poor Indians, by their evil ways, close the door to the gospel and to grace.*

He heard them outside, shrilly screaming imprecations.

For the rest, he wrote, *if some survive, I have laid down everything they must do. It is my view that our Pères and lay helpers should withdraw and take shelter with those whom they will consider their better friends. I have charged them to bring to Pierre, our first Christian, everything that pertains to the sacristy, and that they take particular care to put in a safe place the dictionary and our other material on the language.*

When he had finished this letter he signed it, as did below him Père Le Mercier, Père Chastelain, Père Ragueneau, who would write a description of his martyrdom in the *Jesuit Relations*, and Père Garnier, who would also die for the Faith.

Well, said Père Brébeuf, I bear you all much love, brothers, and believe you worthy for the Crown. That's my conviction.

They blushed, and smiled at him with a young girl's timid pride.

It was the custom of these Savages to hold *festins d'adieu* if they were dying or condemned to death. Knowing that their execution had now been resolved upon, he resolved to outface his accusers by hosting one of these affairs in all boldness. – He had to smile. This whole created world was so ridiculous! Now he was sending invitations to his own funeral; for that was the custom of this Country.

But now he reached that point of epiphany which comes to every life not cut short. When he called the farewell feast, his guiding Angel, whom I shall imagine as Champlain, turned the key at last in the lock of his Store-house, and he was opened to himself, giant and radiant with treasure-light. For him the sensation was exquisite. His purpose became a Church compounded arch upon arch, in orientations parallel and perpendicular Saints stood above the doors of his heart, some with a skull at their feet. The ceiling of his soul bulged with golden flowers. Step by step, the organ which directed him ascended in pitch, pipe by golden pipe . . .

Hear me! he cried to his guests, making his face impassive, as Joseph the Iroquois had done before they burned him. – Hear me! I wish to bid you farewell! Amuse yourselves boldly with me and mine, and know that we wish you no ill will. Once you have put us to death, we will gain Power like our GREAT CAPTAIN, JESUS CHRIST. We will go up to the SKY. There we shall look down upon you, and intercede for you against your enemies. We love you. That is what I have to say to you. I have spoken.

They attended him in dreary silence, not interrupting, gazing at him as if he were already dead. The other Black-Gowns sat still, as black as mourners.

. . . And there was Born Underwater's stern silent face like a lake icebound in the middle of summer.

She stared at him, hoping that he would lower his eyes.

The love of GOD has the Power to do what death does, he whispered gently, and a woman screamed.

Power

But in the end they decided not to kill him. They were too greatly addicted to iron. – PAX CHRISTI.

The Snake

Let them make peace with me,
let them make peace with me.

Isaiah 27.5

Until now Echon had held fast to his rule, and made no full conversion among the Huron of any adult in good health, but now that his fatality had triumphed over theirs once again he was prepared to relax his strictness a little, to see what might creep into his net. – There was a man called Tsiouendaentaha, who made a public feast to announce his baptism, whereupon the Black-Gowns did the same; and when Tsiouendaentaha went to trade at Three-Rivers, the Governor's Deputy, Monsieur Delisle, gave him fine presents and entrusted him with a portrait of IESVS to bring back to the Chapel at Ossossané. Not long after he had been baptized, his wife, niece, brother-in-law and daughter all died. And then Tsiouendaentaha prudently vanishes from the *Jesuit Relations*. – But there was another man named Chihwatenah* who was not frightened. He wanted to become a Sorcerer, like the Black-Gowns. He didn't care if everyone hated him, but he *would* have Power (as the Saints very well expounded). He was like a maple leaf infected with the first scarlet blotches of autumn.

There was a Mass, and the Black-Gowns raised high the Cross upon the upturned flower-cup whose silver petals bowed only of their own will, showing that they found the Cross to be no weight or hardship; they conjured with the silver monstrance rayed like a SUN, with rubies and Angel-heads ranged in alternation around the center of the SUN so that Chihwatenah

* "He Is Brought from Afar."

MONSTRANCE (ÉGLISE DES HURONS, LORETTEVILLE/VILLAGE HURON)

thought in terror: no matter where I go, one of those SPIRIT faces can see me! and Echon prayed to *Sainct Ioseph* in loud and crashing words as the other Black-Gowns shook the brass and silver censers, with their arches and hearts and other caves for the SPIRITS to fly from, through the prickings of the golden patens! – Seeing them, Chihwatenah cried: If we look at these, we will be blinded! but Echon told him no, my nephew; these things will not weaken your vision, but *enhance* it, if they lead you to believe! – at which Chihwatenah stared at him with wide eyes. Again he studied the SUN of the monstrance, which grew like a flower from a silver-leaved stalk; ever so many tiny silver men clung to roots and shaft that Chihwatenah could not believe it. He blinked and blinked, but still the silver men were there. These must be the Saints. Above the SUN was the Cross.

He looked deep into the monstrance, whose ray-face contained a mirror as silver as a beaver-pond.

Echon whispered to him: When you are *baptized*, your name will be *Ioseph's* name!

Chihwatenah longed to shout in terror.

Echon held aloft the silver crucifix in whose gleams the reflected Wendat faces crinkled strangely, as if they were seeing themselves underwater; the chalice whose golden cup gleamed with frightening strength, this too rested in cups of silver leaves. Chihwatenah begged to take the crucifix in his hands also, but Père Brébeuf said to him: First you must be baptized! . . . – Then Chihwatenah smiled quickly and wanted Echon to pull the cup out of the leaves. Hearing this foolishness, Echon permitted him to look inside, so that they could see for themselves that the cup and the leaves were attached. – How can they be attached, scoffed Chihwatenah, when they are two different metals?

They are attached so that you will believe, said Echon.

What converted him, in the end, was the silver ciborium, in which Chihwatenah could see his face, distorted and bulging like a frog's. – That thing has great Power, he said to himself.

He watched Echon, kneeling when he knelt, clasping his hands like him, but unlike Echon he could not close his eyes, for if he did then he would not be able to see what to do next. So Echon, opening his eyes suddenly, always caught him out.

On the sixteenth day of Août, 1637, he was baptized *Joseph* most solemnly, which was a great coup for Heaven. Not long after, the Black-Gowns baptized his wife Aonetta as *Marie*, and then his entire family. For ten months, his was the only Christian family in Ossossané. Everyone ridiculed him. His sister-in-law fell sick and died within forty-eight hours of her baptism, but even then he remained steadfast in the Faith.

After his baptism, he went about preaching. He said: Brothers, just as we are superior to Born Underwater's People who wander endlessly among the trees and rocks, so the Iron People are superior to us. How can any deny it? Look at the things that they bring!

Now Chihwatenah strode about like a Captain, a rich man. He had attained everything. The Country of Heaven and Iron was his. Best of all, the Wendat would never forget him. *He was a friend of witches!* Fear him they might; hate him they certainly did; but forget him? Never!

The Soul of the Disease

So the previous stroke against Echon had not sufficed. At the time, Tehorenhaennion had scarcely recognized such a chance, for the VAMPIRE SKELETON was very Powerful, as was proved by this continuing epidemic. Yet there were other ways to continue the contest. He withdrew into the forest where red-leafed saplings girded themselves to outcrops, and he fasted until he could see the horned Serpent of witches, called ANGONT. Among the Wendat, serpents are known to be very evil. Iroquois are serpents. ANGONT is the most evil of all. If the War-Chief were to learn that Tehorenhaennion had brought Him up, then the hatchet would fall. – Ah, poor Tehorenhaennion! the Old Men would say when they'd made their investigation. The Serpent People have devoured him! – But all would know what had really happened. And no one would say anything – for to set oneself against the Old Men, why, that too is a form of witchcraft. This Chihwatenah – he would find himself skull-split soon – so Tehorenhaennion supposed. But once again the thought came that he himself could die that way, and he was afraid. – Yet I do this not to harm anybody, but solely to fight the real witches, *Those Who Are Called Charcoal!* (Thus Tehorenhaennion, crying into his heart with a very great voice, so that the hissing voices of his fears could not be heard.) After this he put such matters away from him, calming his mind with tobacco, until he could see.

Just past a ledge heaped with small grey moss-cushions, there was a swampy place between hills where the Iroquois raiders had camped the summer before last. Tehorenhaennion went there; he went sniffing and smelling for snake. Hemlocks and alders grew up through a meadow (here Amantacha's nephew had been found fresh-broiled, with his head cut off), and then the soil grew darker and soggier, until it became a wide low pond whose color was the same warm grey as the insides of mussel shells. He looked there with his eye of Power, there where the mosquitoes sang their songs. Here ANGONT slithered under the ground, where everything was so crowded together like happiness and unhappiness. – I honor You, my UNCLE, whispered Tehorenhaennion. Now let me gladden You with a song. – Slowly, singing *hé hé hé hé* and then his own special song which an OKI had given him so many years before, he placed his hand upon that liquescent earth. It pulsed under him in the way that a drowsing cat raises its ears very slowly at the sound of a mouse, and then the upcurving crevices of his sleepy eyes widen into pale green stares split by the vertical gashes of black pupils; the ears flare wider to catch the sound . . . – You know Them Who Are Called *Charcoal*, he whispered. You know how they strive to steal Your honors, greedily, falsely. Ah, my good UNCLE, how I love You! Help me to strike them with sickness . . . – Singing, he dug into the dirt of dreams and found Him. ANGONT was black and glossy. ANGONT twitched. Tehorenhaennion rubbed his fingernails against His black and glistening sides and let Him go. He covered up the hole. He trimmed his nails and stored the parings in a pouch of deerskin where he kept his magic objects. Now the cut nails had Power. Now he could send them into Echon's flesh to cause him sickness.

The Fourteenth Rapid

That night, Père Brébeuf made his prayers and lay down and for some reason he dreamed of being back in Kebec, on a summer night beside the Fleuve Saint-Laurent, and his Superior had summoned him to Champlain's Storehouse with its corner-towers shaped like fat pencils. He entered, and Père Le Jeune rose and pulled the door shut with relief. He seemed far more sprightly than was his usual manner; indeed, Père Davost and Père Daniel, who were also gathered there, wore expressions of sly triumph on their faces, as if they were boys in France playing in some spot known only to them: – a recess under stairs, or a cellar, or a thicket or the like. It was cool inside the Storehouse, and the dank smell of mortar soothed his nostrils. Something smelled like snakes. – Now you must all be very quiet, whispered Père Le Jeune gleefully. I have discovered a plan to bring us all safely to our families in France. Jean will construct effigies of ourselves. Then we shall clothe them in our Black Gowns and slip away. How easy it will be for us in France! – Then in the dream Père Brébeuf's heart was joyful, and all the Jesuits were smiling, and they sat discussing the details of the scheme. Yet it was one of those dreams whose prologue (as he later realized) was interminable; all night, it seemed, he went on dreaming, and yet he never got to France –

Again he swam to the Fourteenth Rapid (*viz.*, the Nailing to the Cross), and ascended the isle of granite. He stood upon the rock, and surveyed the bank below him, seeing a hill of red and yellow trees; a matted grove of broken-branched spruces lonely beneath the storm horizon . . . Here the river was walled by scarlet leaves. (He smelled snakes.) In the midst of the rapid was an islet of granite from which rose a single evergreen sapling. It was evident that this was something eternal, and yet he could not immediately tell what it might mean. It was as fresh as a young girl's cheek.

He fell asleep again, and when he awoke he had a slight fever, but it passed.

The Third Epidemic 1637–1638

That winter was particularly cold, and many Old Ones froze to death in the longhouses. Hardly a week went by, it seemed, that the Black-Gowns did not hear the shrill cries of mourners. Here, of course, were opportunities for saving souls through the Sacrament of holy baptism, and so they were very busy, especially since the sicknesses now seemed to worsen.

The Death of Tehorenhaennion

It was a dark night. The souls of the dead would be coming into the longhouses now to eat from the kettles, slyly, when no one could see. Tehorenhaennion smoked his pipe, whose stem was a skeleton. Smoke gives intelligence. He was as Powerful as that dead Grey-Gown, Kwer Nikoas, who'd worn the wooden skull-bead in his necklace. All the People said that it had once been the skull of a child. But they feared Tehorenhaennion more, much more – *haii haii haii!* – He'd once spent an entire day turning the leaves of a book which the Grey-Gowns had and counting them. There were images of faces in flames and faces shining in the SKY; surely all these must be alive. But that was nothing. He knew more OKIS than that!

He was enraged now. This pest that had murdered so many: he would catch it and turn it against Echon!

From beeswax he made a doll of Echon. He held the doll over the fire and roasted it slowly so that it began to sweat as if in fever. With a good stone knife he chipped away at Echon, to make him bleed inside.

I own the disease! he sang exultantly.

But he awoke, and his head hurt. There was an ache behind his eyes. Something was devouring the insides of his teeth and ears. Snakes pierced the brain behind his forehead. Despite the rigor of the cold, he felt all too warm. Then he knew that he had made a fatal play, for Echon was a greater Sorcerer than he. Echon had caught this sickness also, and turned it upon him. Now he must die.

He worsened rapidly. Born Underwater came running to his house. He saw in her face that there was no hope. Nor indeed had he expected anything different. She cried: *My heart cries out for blood!* and he smiled a little –

This was perhaps the worst sadness, that for all the passion and persistence of his gaming, no one can say whether Echon even noticed it. So Tehorenhaennion died, as quickly and insignificantly as a louse crushed between a Wendat woman's teeth.

Praising the Roy

. . . this GOD is sensuously and directly beheld as a Self, as an actual individual man . . .

HEGEL, *Philosophy of Spirit* (1807)

As always, the disease left Born Underwater unscathed.

But now her purpose was cleft like the hoof of a moose. Echon had killed Tehorenhaennion. She could do no harm to Echon. No one could. He had Power; he had *Kinap*.

She went to the longhouse of the Black-Gowns. She went to the room where the CAPTAIN OF THE DAY spoke at intervals, and the Black-Gowns sat together, bent over a single flame atop a stick of deer-fat, and they marked white leaves with little tracks as with snowshoes. She had seen all that before. But before there were many more visitors. Not so many came to the Black-Gowns' lodge now.

Père Le Mercier tried to prevent her entrance, but she called: *Echon, Echon!* and he came.

Père Chastellain ladled out a bowl of sagamite for her with ill grace; Echon brought it to her himself –

It is good, she said.

She ate.

I see that you are tongue-tied, Born Underwater. (Thus Père Le Mercier, who now sought to break the ice with her under the Superior's eyes.)

She regarded him scornfully.

Have no fear, continued Le Mercier condescendingly. I'm sure you engage in gossip and suchlike papotage with the other Savages; it takes time, I know, for such as you to become comfortable in the LORD's House.

Which Captain is that? Ah, you mean your dead IESVS, Whose flesh you gorge yourselves upon in secret . . .

Père Superior, I cannot talk with her. She really ought to be expelled.

Echon smiled a little. He had a featureless forehead of blinding white.

Please, Père Superior! I cannot compel her to do anything. But you can. I beg you . . .

Born Underwater, you must not say such things to us, he said mildly. (His hair was becoming grey-white, like caribou-hair.) It gives us sorrow, when you speak of Our LORD in such a way . . .

The other priests looked at one another significantly.

Born Underwater shifted in her seat. She was ashamed of herself for having said these things. Yet the truth was that she cared for none of the Black-Gowns save Echon. They had no Power; they knew nothing –

Strike me and kill me, she said softly. You are right to be offended. I am wrong to have angered you.

What do you mean?

I should not have spoken against you. Now or before, with Tehorenhaennion –

And do you have faith? he said.

Have pity on me, Echon! Teach me to kill those little creatures that eat the corn, for I am not from this Country. Kill the locusts for us; I know that you are a master at this.

That gives me much to consider, he said gravely, for indeed until now I had not known myself to possess such powers. I suppose your confidence is natural, if I can bring rain. – But again I ask you: Do you have faith?

What is faith? she returned coolly. You are the one who should know that.

Yes, he said, smiling terrifyingly, I am the one who should know that.

She turned and left.

No, he said to himself, I must be mistaken. That woman's heart remains frozen in ignorance and evil.

The Two Standards

1638

> The first point is to imagine how the evil leader of all the ENEMY is as if seated in that vast plain of Babylon, as on a great throne of fire and smoke in a horrible and frightening figure. The second point is to consider how He calls together countless demons, and how He scatters them, some to one city, some to another . . . missing no province, no place, no state of life, nor even any single person.
>
> SAINT IGNATIUS, *Spiritual Exercises* (*ca.* 1534)

In this year Père Le Jeune was surprised but pleased to receive a reply from that young Ursuline of Tours, Marie de l'Incarnation, whose plans he had scouted the previous year in the most discouraging terms. She now replied that her vocation to help the Savage girls remained firm in her heart. – Well, he thought. Perhaps it will be so. – Again he took up his goose-quill and wrote her a letter of chastisement and mortification, describing to her in no uncertain terms the difficulties of life among the Savages. *You have heard this from me before,* he wrote, *and yet for those who persist there is a new Cross to bear – namely, the ferocity of the Hiroquois, which increases year by year. Search your heart and consider well before you take the decision to trust yourself to the mercies of these fiends, as you would do in coming here, for they now make great boasts and threats, describing how they will raze Kebec and put us to the torture, afterwards taking our heads and scalps. Should you venture rashly here and then retreat, consider how you will weaken our cause.* – He sealed the letter and delivered it to the Captain of the ship, thinking: I hope she has the strength of heart to resist my words. A nunnery or convent would be a fine thing. (As for the Huron

Seminary, he'd closed that down, for the Black-Gowns had just learned that Savages pay little attention to young preachers. Eh, *that* had all been a waste! Even that boy they'd persuaded to mortify himself with cold water, what's-his-name, turned out to be a nobody in Ouendaké, a risible entity; nobody cared what he did . . . Time to send Père Daniel back to Ouendaké to see what he could catch!) . . . He opened the iron gates and went down into the snow. An old Montaignez woman was at death's door; her people had abandoned her in the ice, and now she was requesting baptism . . . – Come quickly, Nicanis! shouted his good Pigarouich, who had found her. – Shivering, he knelt beside her all night until she died. Her soul flew off to Heaven. Pigarouich smiled at him: You have a good heart, Nicanis! – Speak of this to no one, he replied, for I do not want to be thought of as less unworthy than I am. – Slowly they trudged back to Notre-Dame-des-Anges, carrying the corpse on their shoulders. The orange snow-dawn glared in his eyes; he felt hot and cold and dizzy . . . A Savage child peered at him from behind the tree. Seeing the anguished dead face flopping from Nicanis's shoulder, the long stringy black hair glittering with ice-crystals, he wailed. Pigarouich shouted and would have chased the boy, but Nicanis said: That is nothing. That is the merest shadow of a Cross. – And they walked on. They buried her in consecrated ground, with all the obsequies of the Church, hearing which many other Montagnets gathered round crying: *ho, ho, ho!* – which in their language means *it is well*. Stealthily one of them slipped a little bundle into the grave, but Père Le Jeune saw and began to reprove the fellow for his idolatry. – No, no, the man said. This belonged to her; I wish to bury it because the sight of it causes me sorrow – it is only for that reason, Nicanis, and none other! – Eh, go ahead and bury it, said Père Le Jeune. The next day someone wanted to exhume her, to take a lock of hair to give to a relation. – I forbid this, said Père Le Jeune. Let her rest. – The Savage began to whine, at which Le Jeune clapped him on the shoulder and said: Take some of your own hair, or the hair of a moose. It will serve the purpose just as well. – At this, the man went away laughing at the wit of Nicanis.

Night came again. There was snow on the floor of the Chapel. There was frost in the Rectory. Another stormy night between these icy walls, he sighed, and this wind . . . – Still, it's better than being in the forest . . .

Kebec Years

A Savage accused him of killing his sister by sorcery.

GOD has forbidden to kill, he said kindly. Do you think I would make you die?

A Savage came running, saying that the French were bewitching all the rivers by sorcery. Already the water tasted bitter. Would Nicanis protect him?

If a Frenchman uses sorcery, he will be put to death, said Le Jeune coldly. You ought to do the same.

He proceeded to Tadoussac, and terrified them into abolishing their naked dances; so that the late Monsieur de Champlain had his way at last, thirty-five years since Besouat's carnival of naked privities . . .

The Two Standards

On the twenty-fifth of Juin, fearing nothing save GOD, Père Brébeuf went to Teanaostoaiaié and opened the Mission there, which again was called *Saint Joseph*. This town had always been very stubbornly opposed to the Faith; yet the first convert in good health was a man of great importance – *viz.*, one Aochiati, who was Master of the Dance of Naked Ones. (Aochiati immediately resigned this office, of course.) So that was a victory. Soon there were several good Christians there, although undoubtedly they would have subscribed to the maxim written down by the lawyer Lescarbot, in regard to the legend of GOUGOU: *One must needs believe, but not everything*. Yet Brébeuf's purpose remained as cracked within him as Saint Ignatius's old death-mask with its staring white eyes. At night he lay awake, listening to the other priests' coughing and breathing; he scratched at his flea-bites, and his heart was racing.

Summer, and the hot brown river-water struggled to dislodge the greenish stones in its bed, hopeful of sliding them a foot or two closer to the ocean. When at last the rivers had carried all the land to the sea, their task would be done. – Hazelnut trees shaded islands. Ducks were still on the water. Yellow-green algæ-meadows spread upon the ponds. Few could go fishing in that season, for so many of their friends had died of disease, and fishes hate the dead. But when time purified the survivors, they'd go, in the Moon When They Cart the Net from Shore. Now came the time when the net must be married to the two virgins. They used iron awls and knives and hatchets. The boys playing ball games shouted *iron, iron!* Later there came another drought, and so once again the Black-Gowns held a Mass for rain, donning their chasubles of white with gold ripples like sun on water, upon which burned crosses of gold lace, medallions of Saint Augustine and Saint Ioseph . . . As always, the pagans said that the THUNDER-BIRD had a lack of adders and serpents; that drought comes from caterpillars gnawing in wood – but the Black-Gowns deflected that heresy with the side-edge of the golden processional Cross, like a knife-blade; the fleur-de-lys on top . . . On the first day after the Mass was completed, rain came –

Born Underwater

It happened that Père Brébeuf was paying one of his periodic visits to the longhouse of the Turtles where Born Underwater now lived, and while catechizing the little children, staring deeply into their faces so that they would not forget his teachings when he was dead, he noted that their responses were much better remembered than formerly, so, smiling, he said: Who has been teaching you? Père Jogues?

Born Underwater has! a little boy shrieked.

Born Underwater?

She helps us every day.

At once he left the children and strode down to the hearth where she lived. He did not see her. And then he heard the soft slappings of her moccasins against the longhouse floor. She had been behind him. It was very odd how he had not seen her.

You were catechizing them? he said to her sharply.

What is that?

Helping them pray, teaching them . . . (A sudden vagueness had come upon him.)

Yes, Echon. I heard your words and listened. So I was teaching them for you.

He catechized her rapidly, brutally, and she made not a single error. He was astounded. Something glowed in his heart, but he could not tell if it were gladness or anger or something else.

You must not do that anymore, he said. You do not have the Faith, and so you cannot give it.

As you wish, Echon. You want to eat?

On the fire was a stew of corn and fish and field-mice which Born Underwater had caught in the longhouse. It would be very rude to refuse.

No, he said. I am angry. O LORD, open the eyes of this woman to Your glory; help her to deliver herself from her DEMONS before it is too late!

He was groaning.

He searched the hollows of her soul for sin and found it – not only sin the garment, but sin the stain of metaphysical flesh, sin the blood, sin the lungs, sin her soft brown breast. He was enraged against her; he craved to slap her face – and then the feeling died away.

You aren't praying anymore? she said to him curiously.

No, he said, more curtly than he had intended, for this time she certainly did not mean to presume, but only to learn.

She looked away. No expression crossed her face. – Where I come from, the ones who pray, they pray always. Day and night.

Ah, but Whom do they pray to? – So saying, he turned and walked out of that longhouse.

Père Lalemant

At that time Père Brébeuf was replaced as Superior – at his own request, they said, for he had little interest in administrative work. This was true as far as it went, but since he was vowed to obedience he would certainly not have sought to lift any yoke from his shoulders. (Eh bien. As his worldly honors were lessened, so his mortifications could be increased, for which he thanked Our LORD. He went and scourged himself with the discipline until the walls were spattered with blood.) He had reason to think that Père Le Mercier or one of the others, in dismay at his softness toward Born Underwater and her kind, had sent a secret letter by some Savage to Kebec; which added to the pleasure of his mortifications, for with her he'd certainly broken no rule.

The name of the new Superior was Père Jérôme Lalemant. And he longed to begin the consolidation of Wendaké into Missions and parishes. He divided the day and the week into periods. – He went into a longhouse for the first time in his life, and emerged retching. He felt as if he had been covered with filth.

Act submissively, hissed Père Lalemant to his crew. – A blow from the hatchet is soon given by these barbarians –

Well, Jean (thus Père Lalemant), now we can finally have a chat. I congratulate you on what you've accomplished here. The Savages may love you or they may hate you, but everyone – *everyone!* has heard of Echon.

Eh, another mortification, a very appetizing one to swallow! Père Brébeuf bowed his head so meekly, slipping his neck into the silky noose of that reproof; and Père Lalemant, who watched him carefully to see how he might be taking it, became confused by his eyes so big and blue and meek.

We're going to establish a third residence at the Mission at Teanaostaiaé, Jean, do you see? And it will be my directive that you return to that place, to become the Superior there. I'm telling you this now, in case you have any business to dispose of –

Oh, no, Père Superior. I am free.

I had not finished, Jean. In case, as I was saying, you have any business to dispose of, any – inordinate attachments to break. I've known about your unwarranted leniency toward Louys Amantacha's concubine for some time now, you see. I'm not accusing you of breaking your vows, Jean. Nobody has ever found any fault in you. We all comprehend that you bear with her out of fondness for Louys Amantacha's memory; I'm well aware of your disappointment at his death. But it's a question of how we appear to others. Père Jogues was saying – no, never mind what Père Jogues was saying. But that's one of the reasons I want to send you to Teanaostaiaé. I think you'll make a better impression there.

Brébeuf was delighted with this new Cross. – And is it your will, Père Superior, that I never see her again?

Père Lalemant sat staring into the flame of his candle; his hand stroked the deerskin-covered Bible before him; he told the beads of his rosary. – That would be best, he answered at last, but I know that it would be impractical. And I comprehend that you are sincerely devoted to her and wish to guide her spirit into the safe harbor of conversion. But you must forbid her to follow you to Teanaostaiaé.

Yes, Père Superior.

You will do that?

Yes, Père Superior. I am vowed to obedience –

But you are not happy.

My happiness is of no account –

Then what do you mean to tell me?

After all, Père Superior, she is free to go where she likes. She is not yet subject to our rules. I would not like to see her flout your authority, as I sincerely believe she'd do –

She left Teanaostaiaé on your orders.

Yes, Père Superior. She obeyed me to please Amantacha.

Ah. I forgot. Well, everything comes together in the long run, doesn't it, Jean? Eh, since her paramour is dead, there is no reason to fear bad influences.

It was the other priests I worried about, their unformed speculations, and if she follows you . . . But my own authority is more important. She must not embarrass my authority.

Père Lalemant stood up. So, Jean, he said, you are right.

He strode a step away.

You are always right, as I hear, he said.

The Death of Onònkwaia the Oneida

Some few men had exchanged gifts that spring with the Neutrals, but most preferred to postpone their visiting until autumn, when they would have more blankets, kettles and peas from the Iron People. There was also a great craving among them to attack the Hiroquois in that season, and thereby obtain revenge for their previous losses – particularly for that of their great Captain, Taratouan. After some discussion in Council they decided to attack the *Onoiochihonons*, or, as they called themselves, the Oneida or Stone People. They went apart to dream, and they dreamed that IOUSKEHA caressed their faces, which meant victory.

In the Country of the Irocois it was a breathlessly hot bird-morning, the sky entirely blue save for a few albumen-streaks rising from the ridge. The sun increased in brightness until the browns and golds of the spaces between trees resembled a fawn's coat.

A great army of Crooked-Tongues was approaching, and a warrior said that it would be most prudent to run away. – Ononkwaia the Captain folded his arms across his breast. – My brothers, this resolution would be passable if ENDEKA-GAWKA the SUN were obscured by clouds, so that He could not be a spectator of our cowardice. But as it is, we must fight –

And so the Hiroquois must mourn once again. So once again DEATH THE FACELESS had kicked the logs of the longhouse apart. Skulls rolled everywhere. Their women must again march slowly down the longhouse in their best robes, while the men beat the drum. Ononkwaia's warriors had not had guns. The women's robes were dark-hemmed. Their dark pigtails hung down over their breasts. They were very stiff and glared ahead to light the road of their grief.

Now the Wendat women waited for their men to come back from war as they weeded the cornfields and examined the lovely growing corn whose green ears had begun to ripen now, and the women were shaded a little by the corn but it was very hot in the fields and they continually wiped their sweaty faces and then dried their hands on their salt-stiffened skirts of skin, and their breasts were dark and sunburned. They talked about the enemy only rarely, for fear that bad Power might hear them, but often they woke screaming from bad dreams, and they tried never to be out of sight of others among the rustling corn. And when they saw their brothers, husbands and sisters' sons home at last with many captives, they shouted with gladness. – But when Père Lalemant caught sight of those doomed men, and he comprehended that his Black-Gowns had no power to spare them or slay them, he shuddered. A hundred Oneida, and every one of them was going to be burned! (The Oneida women had to beg men from the Mohawk to marry them, to keep their Nation alive. And they swore revenge. That was how it always was.) Père Lalemant's instructions were to create a beachhead of good Christians – not a nucleus of infection as Père Brébeuf had been instructed to manufacture; not a mere retreat as the Grey-Gowns had yearned for; but a stout outpost, well palisaded, which could stand apart if need be, which would require no periodic relocations (as would have been the case if it had been set in any of the Huron villages). Times were more dangerous now. There must be a place of refuge should the hostility of these Savages increase. (And he shuddered again at the sight of the hundred Iroquois, the men and women already swarming about them tormenting them; men and women clustering upon men like maggots in a corpse . . .) – He decided upon a site upon the shores of the Isaraqui Rivière. (A Hiroquois screamed.) The season was now too advanced for ground to be broken that year, but the following spring much could be done with the force of lay brothers which the Provincial of Canada had already agreed to send. Père Lalemant turned coldly away from the sight before him, so that he wouldn't feel any more wretched . . . It was the month of Août; the sumacs bore their phalli of red berry-clusters like church candles . . .

As for Ononkwaia, Echon baptized him *Pierre*. (There were no pockets in his cassock, no hidden places. Yet beneath it he wore his iron girdle of spikes.) They fastened Pierre Ononkwaia to a stake upon a platform, and began to torture him with glowing irons and other supplices which their cruel ingeniousness easily pictured to them. Echon exhorted him to have courage. He was a Black-Gown; his determination was as thick and brawny as the upper arm of a Savage. Ononkwaia paid no attention to his bleating. The pain they gave him was as sharp as a certain kind of winter twilight when the sky, cold, glowing, separates from the snow-ridges crosshatched with trees. Drops of water (shaped like Indian snowshoes) burst out on his forehead. But he never uttered any groan. They scalped him living, and he fell beside another dead man. But he himself was not dead. When they began to attend to their other victims on that scaffold, he leaped to his feet. He snatched up a firebrand and hurled it. He wrenched himself free of the half-burned stake and began to shout against their Nation. In a great rush, they pulled him down and heaped him with burning coals until the smoke rose from his body. His countryside was opened by creeks and curvy little lakes of blood. Still he was not dead. He tottered to his feet, took up another firebrand, and began to advance toward the village, as if to set it on fire. Falling upon him with clubs, they cut off his hands and feet. Water became fire, as Captain Merveille had foretold, and fire gushed in through his nose-bays and scorched his river-veins even as his blood-springs flowed down, almost extinguishing the nine fires in which his enemies rolled him. Yet once more he rose up on the stumps of his knees, which had evidently been cauterized by the flames, and began to advance toward them. They fled screaming. At last one warrior, a little braver than the rest, cut off his head with a hatchet. Then at last, something opened out before him, something pale blue and endless: the Sweetwater Sea.

Fears and Robes

Now it was winter in the Country of the Huron as it was in Kebec, where Montmagny's cannons were covered with snow, where cannons ached beneath the weight of snow-ridges; and once more the Wendat threw on their leggings and heavy skin-cloaks. Some of the People at Teanaostoiaiaé wore the marten-robes which they had acquired in trade with the Nipissings; these were eagerly commented on and admired. Born Underwater studied these and was sure that she could make better clothes, but said nothing, having already learned how dangerous these People were when their anger or envy was excited.

. . . Born Underwater was tending the fire when he came to her.

You say that you are prepared to be baptized?

Yes, Echon.

You must give up your superstitions.

Ah, they are only sins, as you say.

And your lewdness. That was your mother's sin also, as I have heard from Père Massé –

Whatever you say must be true, Echon.

Some people love to forget the past, he said. They believe that it will then go away. But the past is always there, staining us like the dye of the *Tissaouhianne* leaves.

How do you know of that plant? cried Born Underwater in surprise.

I know what I know, he said. How is no matter. You too know your past. Your Savage half seeks to deny the French half. Yet it cannot. Although your father was a reprobate, he gave you his blood, and you can never escape him. Do you comprehend me?

No!

Perhaps you do not, but I see that you begin to reflect upon it, my dear girl. Now tell me quickly: are you satisfied to give up your sorceries and be baptized?

Yes, Echon. But wait a little longer, I pray you –

The Embroiderers

1639

> A religious, who fulfills her duty everywhere, is well everywhere, since the object of her affections is in every place.
>
> MARIE DE L'INCARNATION, to her brother (1639)

They came in the summer month of Juillet. It was the *Jesuit Relations* of Père Le Jeune that had moved them to pity and tears at the darkness of the Savage girls, who must almost always die unbaptized and therefore in great probability of burning. Marie of the Incarnation, that pious Sister of Tours, had in no wise been discouraged by the severe letters with which he had sought to test her; rather, they increased her ardency until her soul's back arched like a cat's, and she wept with longing for the privations of Canada. Indeed, seven years earlier, before Père Le Jeune had even departed for Kebec, she had dreamed of being directed by Saint Joseph to a hospice of marble, on the roof of which, in an embrasure, sat Our LADY, holding the CHILD. This hospice looked down from the brow of a great cliff, which was manifestly the precipice beneath which the Sieur de Champlain had built his Habitation. She looked at Our LADY (and here I am construing how she regarded her from my own feelings last night when I had a vision of the Blessed Sainte Catherine Tekakwitha), and there was nothing special about the way she looked or held herself or was, for she had seen her in images many times before, but this time the VIRGIN *summoned* her worshipper and lay beside her and looked deeply into her face and kissed her so that she tasted her lower lip and sucked on it and it was so beautiful and sacred that Marie felt as if she had seen her entirely in her naked glory and perfection which she knew not by seeing her but by the awe and ecstatic love she felt inside her heart, kissing it as it beat (this was where Born Underwater too had felt her revelation of Power, but for Born Underwater the Power had less to do with love than capability). The divinity of her dream was doubly proved by the fact that until then she had believed that Canada was but an imaginary country to which one threatened to send naughty children, being filled with demons and wretchedness. – They came in Juillet. (More than five hundred Montagnais and Huron Savages had been baptized in the course of that year.) Kebec was not much like Rochelle Harbor with its square sails and barrels and coaches, but they had known that: in Paris the streets were foul with dirt and garbage and excrement, over which the ladies were effortlessly borne in coaches and sedan chairs. In Kebec it was the same, except that there were no coaches to be had. – There came a cannonade of welcome. Some of them flinched. Gouverneur de Montmagny was waiting there to greet them, pathetically splendid in plumed hat and scarlet embroidered coat as he stood in that ferocious waste of wilderness. – Don't be afraid, Sisters! said the Captain. – So the nuns came ashore, white-clothed from forehead to breast, black-clothed below, with black hoods over all, and as they walked they jingled with medals and rosaries; and their eyes were dove-mild. The Savages watched. – These are the daughters of our great Sagamores, Père Le Jeune explained to them, and they have come to live out their lives here solely in order to instruct your daughters. – *Ho!* cried the Savages. That is good! – Montmagny stood smiling welcome as they trod the grassy swales.

There were two Orders. First came the Ursulines with their iron keys whose length was greater than a man's hand. They were the instructresses. Behind came the Hospitalières, whose vocation it was to care for the sick. They stood at the bottom of that cliff of dreams and looked upon the stone houses, sheds, and tenements of Kebec, the Savage wigwams scattered about among the firs . . .

Kebec grew around them (the duty of the colonists, said Père Le Jeune, is to do what Adam was commanded to do). There were more than two hundred good French Christians in residence there now. Kebec grew, and the nuns were its heart.

Sometimes the cloistered nuns heard the rattle of cartwheels in Lower Town; often they heard the cries of seagulls greedy over refuse in the harbor. In those early days there was also no end to the sour scritchings of crows, there remaining as yet many trees for those birds to perch in, and dead dogs to be devoured on the edge of town. In the summer, the torment of the *mosquitoes* (which were like small flies, but had bloodsucking habits) was very taxing, especially at night, when they hummed inside the stifling close-beds to which the Sisters retired – and if they left the door open for air, more of the vermin were certain to swarm in. In the wintertime, no matter how much they bundled up in the close-beds, no matter how many heated stones they brought between the flannels for comfort, the chill pierced through as the mosquitoes had previously done, so that the nuns more often shivered than slept, until it was four in the morning, and Marie de l'Incarnation was ringing the first bell. So they were not cloistered like corpses entombed; certainly the world's fingers found a way in to them in despite of the log palisade that they had built about their house. Yet it could truthfully be said that they took joy in these mortifications, which were not exactly the world itself: *that* they had certainly excluded – first, by sailing here to Canada, a country removed from every civilized comfort; and second, by ensconcing themselves according to their vows. The years passed, and Mère Marie recited her office, turning the pages of the Bible on the wooden lectern very very slowly. The letters, red or black like ants, crawled in swarms to frighten the Savage girls in their dreams. The skinny arms of the candelabra twisted snakily like branches or saplings caught in a frozen wind.

When they had leisure, they embroidered, making many wonderfully cunning tapisseries with silver and golden thread about whose tableaux they stuffed horsehair to form raised lozenges. Within these little oval worlds they wove such worlds as were medallions of our own. They wove, for instance, the Nativity of Our LORD and Savior, with GOD the Father bending down to see, bearded and radiant like a French King, while a chorus of Angels filled the sky. This work was more cumbrous than might be believed, since for colors other than silver and gold the Sisters must use cotton threads dyed with tinctures of flowers and vegetables – beet-juice for red; blueflower-juice for blue; these hues being susceptible to fading upon exposure to the sun, the embroiderers were obliged to keep away from the windows while they worked, sometimes even going so far as to sew by candle-light, the pale wavers and flickers of which greatly strained their poor eyes.

The embroideries with which they beautified Savage souls, however, they wove with even more facility. They took the Montagnais girls, the Huron girls, the Algonquin girls, and frenchified them into young ladies of great devotion and pudency.

And where lay the source of this fount of motherhood, which gushed so richly down upon the thirsty Savages? – The ways of GOD are sometimes horrifying. Marie was a widow with a son of eleven when she decided to become a nun. That was her epiphany. Seeing the little boy's mournful incomprehension, she tortured herself with the truth: that the action which she was about to commit was indeed very cruel in every worldly sense. For his part, he listened to what was not being said and resolved at last to run away.

Marie went to her friend Mère Françoise to beg for her advice and help. No sooner had she arrived when Dom François de Saint Bernard arrived. Marie was in tears, and so was Mère Françoise. Seeing this, and knowing full well that they expected him to console her, Dom François thought to smell the TEMPTER about. – Shame on you, he said to her in his sharpest tones. Woman of little faith, do you not see that this accident was the design of GOD Himself?

Marie fell to her knees, the better to humiliate herself while receiving his reproaches, which she knew full well that she deserved. Tears rushed down her cheeks in great streams, and she was unable to speak.

Natural feeling is still alive in you, said Dom François. This place is not for such wretches as you. Withdraw from GOD's house.

Rising to her feet, her head still bowed, Marie left the convent in silence. Her tears splashed upon the floor.

Three days later, Claude was found at Blois. They sent him back to her, and she asked his indulgence in the step that she was about to take, which he gave. Weeping, he peered at her image in her dressing-mirror. Weeping, he accompanied her to the Ursuline convent. Her sister-in-law's little girl carried the Cross. It was the twenty-fifth day of Janvier, 1633. At the door to the convent, she smiled at him. It seemed to her, she later said, as if her heart was half torn from her breast. Yes, he was crying, but undoubtedly he did not yet comprehend the endlessly bleeding wound that she was about to inflict. A small crowd of spectators did, and they were torn between horror and awe. (*Those who are surprised at Madame Martin's conduct,* says her biography, *have but to remember that the infallible Church has pronounced her virtues heroic.*) She opened the door; she went in; then she closed it upon him forever. Six years later, at the age of forty, she set out for Canada.

He'd never forgotten her. He had often come to the convent in his despair, trying to get a glimpse of her through the grille, begging the nuns to send his mother back to him or to take him in as a monk . . . Now he learned that she was about to put an ocean between them. He rushed to Orléans. He searched for her carriage desperately. Men were rolling hogsheads down the street; men bowed down beneath great burdensome bundles which they pushed away from their shoulders, bracing themselves with poles. He saw the blind man with his cup, the young man rushing by in a swish of skirts, a pair of ladies in cafalques (not her, not her); a barelegged soldier, an officer whose curls fell to his shoulders, his hat elaborate, holding his pike . . . There she was! He forced his way through the crowd and pulled the draperies aside. She looked at him gently. Her eyes were blue and white, like French glass pearls.

Where are you going, Mère? he said. Is it not strange for you to be traveling so far from your convent?

To Paris, the nun replied.

And then?

To Normandie.

I know where you're bound, he said.

My dearest son, she said to him, I love you so much. I leave you in GOD's hands.

Later, much later, he became reconciled. He became a monk. And when she was in Canada her son sent her an engraving of Sainte Scholastique with her mournful eyes and veil, holding CHRIST outstretched on a little crucifix which rested so lightly on the tips of her fingers, as if he could rest on them instead of on the bed of nails called sin; and yet He looked away from her breast. And she was uneasy that her son had sent her this.

Mère Marie passed her fingers across the band of white that covered her forehead, and to a lady of rank in Paris she wrote: *It is a singular consolation to us to deprive ourselves of all that is most necessary in order to win souls to JESUS CHRIST, and we would prefer to lack everything rather than leave our girls in the unbearable filth that they bring from their cabins. When they are given to us, they are as naked as worms and must be washed from head to foot because of the grease which their parents rub all over their bodies; and whatever diligence we use and however often their linen and clothing is changed, we cannot rid them for a long time of the vermin caused by this abundance of grease. A Sister employs part of each day at this. It is an office that everyone eagerly covets. Whoever obtains it considers herself rich in such a happy lot and those that are deprived of it consider themselves undeserving of it and dwell in humility. Madame our foundress performed this service almost all year; today it is Mère Marie de Saint-Ioseph that enjoys this good fortune.*

and to a religious of the Visitation she wrote: *O my dear Sister, what a pleasure it is to be with a great troupe of Savage women and girls, whose poor clothing, which is only a bit of fur or old blanket, has not as pleasant an odour as that of the ladies of France! But the candour and simplicity of their spirits are so delightful that they cannot be described. Those of the men are not less so. I see noble and valiant chiefs go down on their knees at my feet, begging me to make them pray to GOD before they eat. They clasp their hands like children, and I have them say everything that I wish.*

The Bite of the Hatchet

It was these good Sœurs who now received the Huron convert Joseph Chihwatenah. He'd made a pilgrimage to Kebec under the authority of the Superior, Père Lalemant. Chihwatenah never felt desperate or entangled; he'd become precisely what he wanted to be. And it was very convenient for Père Lalemant, too, that this Savage wanted to go to Trois-Rivières; for he'd just now completed the year's *Relation* (writing on birchbark for lack of paper), and as Chihwatenah stood watching, he signed it and sealed it with his seal. – Do you promise faithfully to deliver this to the Iron People? the Superior said, pursing his lips. – Yes, Père. (Thus Chihwatenah.) You'd better not be speaking falsely! If these documents get lost through your foolishness, I'll set you some pretty hard penances, d'you see? – So the *Relation* traveled downstream, passing sandy swamps, leaving behind to right and left trees uncountable all the way to the blue hills; portaging over rocky places, muddy places; paddling past blue mountains with white lakes in between, past green hills as wide as a bear's shoulders. And so the *Relation* came into Monsieur le Gouverneur's hands, and he carried it downstream in his pinnace to where the Black-Gowns were waiting at Notre-Dame-des-Anges. And they opened it to read Père Lalemant's news, and the words of the *Relation* looked about to see what they could see, and found Kebec to be more populous than last year. More souls had been saved also. In Mère Marie's convent four of the Savage girls were preparing to receive Holy Communion the next Easter, crying out in an agony of longing: Ah, when will JESUS come to kiss our hearts?

Père Le Jeune read Père Lalemant's *Relation* and said ah, so Jean has finished his Huron dictionary at last! I suppose he will feel somewhat bereft for a time, but there is much to occupy him there. Poor Jean . . .

Chihwatenah stood waiting to be rewarded and dismissed.

Eh, my good Joseph! Your *Echon* praises you highly. Come; I shall take you to meet Mère Marie. I do believe that she will have something to give you . . .

And indeed she gave him holy relics – she could almost see her son in him! – corpse-treasures, I say; the Catholic equivalent of scalps, which at no little trouble to himself he brought back with him to Wendaké. GOUGOU scented these prizes from Underwater. GOUGOU followed underneath, bloodily smiling like that Hiroquois mask with the black beak and the red veins on the black forehead and the long black hair – we know whose hair it was – but GOUGOU did not dare to eat Chihwatenah because of that dark bone-Power which Chihwatenah's heart thrilled with: – Yes! Yes! The Iron People had given him the bones of a dead Sorcerer! Now the others would fear him more than ever, particularly his brother the Shaman . . .

Open your ears! he shouted to the Old Men. I have more Power than you, for I have drunk the blood of JESUS!

This man now stood alone on the far side of a great grave-pit that separated him from his People with all their pleasures, feasts, dreams and ceremonies. They knew how he longed to yell at them: *The kettle is overturned!* – which means: *The Feast of the Dead is no more forever!* Those who had once been his kin-friends regarded him uneasily. By degrees, each of them had begun to comprehend that it was Echon's will to wrest him also from his fellows and hurl him across that loneliness the color of charcoal (with which mourners painted their faces) to where Chihwatenah stood, obscuring with his shadow that poisoned corpse called IESVS. Echon had eaten of IESVS. He had persuaded Chihwatenah to do the same. One by one, Echon would give the others that feast of flesh to eat also, until they all lived together in the Country of the Dead, excepting only a few defiant Shaman-souls who would remain among the Dream-Feasts which the rest had abandoned like worn-out cornfields. These souls would be very lonely, just as Chihwatenah was lonely now. No one could say which side of the pit would be more fearsome to stand upon when that happened.

The Fourth Epidemic *1639–1640*

That winter the snow sped down on cloudy days and sunny days and days when the sky was marbled white and Hudson blue; days when the mild cold made fingers prickle with pleasurable numbness and small birds sang while the tree-horizon greyly blurred itself with snow which cascaded like an unnumbered chute or rapid in the Stream of Time: – no matter how good the map, after all, no course can be charted down to the last foam-fleck or snowfleck. As many as were the snowflakes, still greater was the number of those who perished of disease. It began at Three Rivers, with much loss of life, for which the Montagnais condemned the custom of baptism, saying: Since we pray, we see by experience that death carries us off everywhere. – In vain the Black-Gowns sought to convince them of their folly. In vain they did their deeds of love. The Reverend Père Le Jeune, for instance, spent a night outdoors, buried in snow, because they searched for an old Savagess whom they heard was dying nearby. The next morning they found her still alive and dragged her on a piece of bark four leagues to Kebec, where she died a good death the following day. Père Le Jeune was highly praised for this charity by Mère Marie, but he was somewhat severe with her on this matter and told her not to speak of it to anyone, as it was nothing.

The disease rushed up the Fleuve Saint-Laurent, and across the lakes until it reached the Country of the Huron. This time it was smallpox. It was the last epidemic, and it completed Echon's work.

The Shamans (those who still lived) pulled the fist-sized OKIS of sickness out of so many of their patients' bellies; yet they could not cure them, for other OKIS came as fast as a torrent of snowflakes –

There was a man named Fisher, who greased the net with ashes from a burned *Onguione*-bird, as that brought him luck. He presently succumbed to the sickness, at which the Black-Gowns were glad, believing this to be a defeat for the DEVIL.

Old Captains and Seers died, who might have been able to counteract the Black-Gowns' sorceries. Children died, who might have grown into warriors to defend the People against the Iroquois.

The Arendouane prescribed dog-feasts for the sickness. They feasted naked, or with sacks over their heads, or daubed red, black or white. They wore charms of wolves' teeth and eagles' claws. And the sick ones died.

Ah, said Echon when he heard. That gives them much to reflect upon.

A man dreamed of a gull's egg, and so all the women baked corn-cakes as substitutes, hoping thereby to heal his sickness. But the man died.

The Captains paced through the longhouses, intoning in thunderous voices the names of all who had died that day. Mourners sat eating cold food. They cut the hair from the back of their heads. Weeping, a woman sat making the belt which her dying husband would wear in his grave.

Some said that the Black-Gowns surely nourished in their lodge the Serpent called ANGONT, which Tehorenhaennion had once called upon. Others said that the disease was an OKI which they who are called *Charcoal* kept hidden in the barrel of a gun. (For the Iron People still kept guns to themselves.) They could shoot it anywhere they wished; it would whoosh out and fly across Wendaké. A man dreamed of seeing the Black-Gowns standing outside the palisadoes, opening books from which disease flew like sparks. A man had a dream of IOUSKEHA saying that he was IESVS. He said that the People must drive out the Black-Gowns and drink from a kettle of sacred water. – They held the Dance of the Naked Ones, when the young girls choose the men who will sleep with them, and they copulate all together in the longhouses for the benefit of the sick, while two Captains rattle tortoise-shells. This had always brought cures before, but now it seemed of no value. The Black-Gowns had ruined that, too.

It is those who are called *Charcoal* who make us die by their spells, an Arendouane said (her words as crisp and dry as winter air). Hearken to me, my sister's sons; my mother's brothers. I will prove it by arguments which you will know to be true. They lodged in a village where everyone was well. As soon as they had ensconced themselves there, everyone was dead except for three or four persons. Is this not true? They went to the next village, and the same thing happened. They visited the longhouses in other villages, and only those which they did not enter were free of mortality. Is this not true? Do you not see that when they move their lips in the mummeries they call prayers, spells come out of their mouths? It is the same way when they read in their books. Besides, as you know, in their cabins they have helpers called arquebuses, with which they make a thunderous noise at their pleasure to spread their bad magic everywhere. You have seen people die from these arquebuses. Is this not true? If they are not promptly put to death, they will complete their overthrow of the Country! At this very moment they are ruining us, gnawing like worms in meat! They are killing you! Hurry to kill them, or of us neither great nor small shall remain.

Then she died.

On Christmas Day, Chihwatenah spoke out in the new Chapel at Ossossané, explaining to all that the candles had been sent by GOD to dissipate the Huron shadows, that the flames of rapture would soon spread – all of which the Black-Gowns thought to be prettily said, but the Old Men said: OKI! OKI!

The Black-Gowns had lived among the People for six years. When this disease finished, half the People were dead.

Power

As always, Born Underwater was unharmed by the disease.

The Hunger of Gahachendietoh
1639

And thirdly, desirous of a book of Indian stories that can be read in families and in schools, I have excluded tales with brutal and erotic themes.

ELLA ELIZABETH CLARK, *Indian Legends of Canada* (1960)

But (fearing that such hopeless scenes displease), let me now take your hand and pull you up or down the Stream of Time (as the case may be, for that aspect of things has gotten murky by now) to a happier time – *viz.*, the summer just before this final plague, when the People had a victory over the Sonontrerrhonons! – It was one of their last. – Like voyeuristic crows let us rise to see the battlefield, beginning where the sand dunes began, in the territory of the Attignawantan or Bear Nation, on the western shore, just across from Gahoendoe, where a sad remnant of the People would be starving a mere decade hence. These dunes extended southward intermittently, on the western side of the Attignawantan towns: Tondakhra, Arenté, and Ossossané, which was on the border of the lands belonging to the Tahontaenrat. South of this town the dunes continued, hiding from sight of the Sweetwater Sea a trail that led out of the Huron Country, past cranberry bogs and swamps, until at last that cousin Nation the Tionnontaté was reached. Now the dunes disappeared as the trail went inland, gaining the longhouses of the Raccoon* Nation at last. From there, stalking silently along the southern shore of the Lake called Beautiful, it was not a long walk east to the Wenroronon Nation,

* Erie.

beyond which lay the Five Nations of the Haudenosaunee, called Hiroquois, spread southward from the Lake like five fingers. The Grand League was a pillow under their heads, as they said, for they were the United People. – Shall we now invade their sleep?

There had now been peace with the Seneca or Sonontrerrhonons for four winters, at which the young men grew restive. So they caught a man of that Nation and killed him secretly. Then the Old Men were angry, but also proud, and so they decided to give no gifts to the Sonontrerrhonons to recompense them. Therefore war existed, and so the warriors were free to go raiding against them. They put on their circlets of red moosehair; they put on their wampum necklaces. And they set out to bring back captives for the House of Cut-Off Heads.

In old times there had been two boys of the Sonontrerrhonons who used to dive together in a deep lake, and one dove deeply enough to meet a sky-colored warrior named GAHACHENDIETOH, the messenger of DEATH (Who is surely GOUGOU's sister's son). GAHACHENDIETOH brought the boy into the moss-covered lodges below the water and taught him how to read portents of evil, so that later, when he swam back up to the surface of Time, he could instruct the other Hiroquois in the ways of turning doom aside. – Do you see that comet, that blue panther in the sky? he'd say. Now we must burn tobacco. Then DEATH THE FACELESS will be satisfied, and leave us undevoured on this occasion.

The Sonontrerrhonons, watching for omens, surely saw a comet (that was how they'd caught Amantacha), but GAHACHENDIETOH was hungry that night. No matter how much tobacco they burned, it was not sufficient. Though they searched nervously, like dogs before a rain, they could not discover the Wendat coming until they had been seized.

Sit down, the Wendat said very gently.

And they began to torture the Sonontrerrhonons.

The Mission to the Neutrals

1640

> It should be noted also that just as in time of consolation it is simple and light to remain in contemplation for an entire hour, so it is quite difficult in time of desolation to complete the hour. Therefore, to avoid desolation and to conquer temptation, the exercitant should continue a little beyond the full hour.
>
> SAINT IGNATIUS, *Spiritual Exercises* (?1535)

Upon the table where Père Le Jeune wrote out his *Jesuit Relations* stood a locked box. Now that he had been sent down, the box was Père Vimont's. In this box were various documents of an important and confidential nature, which only the Superior of the Canadian Mission had the authority to see. These included reports forwarded by the Society from France, concerning every one of the missionaries. After all, only by knowing the best-kept secrets of their characters could any Superior hope to fit them into the proper roles. At that time it was the custom for those who took vows to prepare a general confession of all sins committed in their earlier, worldly lives, so that these might be dealt with one by one, leaving them free to take Orders without those soiling attachments. Ignatius had done this at Manresa, as we know; Père Massé had done it, and poor Père Davost, and likewise all the rest. In his bold and steady hand (which was not entirely at variance with Champlain's), Jean de Brébeuf had prepared his own confession. Compared even to that of other missionaries, his life had been stainless. What troubled him most from his worldly years (as he had written) was a trifle, a mere episode, which had occurred when he was a little child. His mother had owned a fine glass box, which stood upon her dressing-table, not unlike our box of confessions, and she had forbidden Jean to touch it. Out of curiosity, as it seemed, he had done just that, with the foreseeable result. Jean had been thoroughly whipped, and there was the end of it as far as his parents were concerned. His father was a Seigneur; he could buy any number of boxes. But for Jean the matter was more elaborate. Writing the confession, he had discovered, as he said, that it had been not only curiosity which had drawn him to the box (although there was that, too, for the box glowed from within, like some white summer lake on a humid horizon), but also the very fear of breakage that his mother had expressed when she warned him away (leaving, as she had believed at the time, an excellent impression). Suddenly, as he looked upon it in that silent chamber, it seemed to him that the box was sliding closer and closer to the edge of the table. If he did not reach out now to save it, it would be doomed. It was the *urgency* of his desire which in fact had impelled the box from the table, to the Au-Delà past death . . . – Since he had been commanded not to touch it, of course, he should have let it fall. Obedience was simple. So he comprehended. But he unlearned the lesson every day. That was why he tormented himself. That was why on the dark and icy days he sometimes felt desperation riding his shoulders, but he welcomed it because it goaded him to work to the limit of exhaustion as the only way of shutting it out; those days, therefore, were a credit to him in the Book of Heaven. But there were also the days of the midwinter thaw, when something else stirred him, a rushing restlessness of unexplored rivers. Then the DEVIL whispered in his ear, saying: *Consider all the unknown Tribes and the Savage Nations there must be to the west! Perhaps China is not so far away; then you could convert the Grand Khan himself!* – Then he bowed his head and groaned, so beautifully did the rivers call out to him. In the spring it was much worse, when the creeks rushed more urgently than his own blood, and seeing them he felt a terrible panic, as if his life were shooting away down these waterfalls, and only by leaving the Huron and paddling up the infinities of rivers could he hope to find something new to replace the spent time (squandered or wisely invested, it mattered not at all), something somewhere in a hazy vastness of wet grass and moose and birch trees; then he remembered the tales of Père Le Jeune's wanderings with the Montagnais, and although he knew well how much the man had suffered, nothing but the *voyaging* and *journeying* could make any impression on Père Brébeuf's mind. The disease he had was the Canada-itch, which had driven Brûlé and Champlain . . . At these times, he mortified himself with penances of cold water and sleeplessness. He tightened his discipline-belt, so that its secret spikes ate deeper into his flesh. So he sought to destroy his body in order to save his soul. With bitter self-disgust he remembered the conclusion of his novitiate in France when his Superior said to him Jean, have you succeeded in becoming dead to yourself? and he said yes and the Superior said are you dead to the world? and he said yes and the Superior smiled faintly and said I believe that you *believe* you are, but remember, Jean, that the self and the world both have a way of coming back to life! and he said yes, but he had never comprehended until now.

His congregation, which before the epidemic had numbered three hundred souls, was now only three or four heads of families and a few old women. Chihwatenah, it is true, remained faithful – much more so than Amantacha had ever been. In Janvier he came to Mission Sainte-Marie to make the Exercises for eight days under Père Brébeuf's direction. Brébeuf was quite delighted with his intelligence. It seemed that he had easily reached the Thirty-Sixth Rapids (*viz.*, the Vocation of the Apostles) . . . and yet, what was the use of it? Armed with the mightiest weapons that Père Brébeuf could give him, Chihwatenah had emerged from the Mission's high palisadoes and set out to convert his fellow Savages, but he failed to move even his own brother, a reprehensible Sorcerer . . . – Brébeuf sighed most heavily. His name, *Echon*, was now a word of odium used to make children scream as if he were a WATER-MONSTER. With fearful curiosity they peeped around their mothers, while the other People turned away their faces or shouted insults. Echon did not seem to hear.

The Uprising

In Mars, which is the Moon When Flowing Water Appears, the Old Men held another Council, to discover to one another their desires concerning the Hatitsihenstaatsi. Everyone was in agreement that they ought to be killed, but no one wanted the blame for stopping the way to the Iron People. Besides, the People had now such a pressing need for iron that if the trade were halted they'd be destitute within two winters. Echon's plagues had devoured them; too few remained alive for things to be done in the old way. Nor could they leave the French and go to the Dutch, for the Hiroquois blocked the way.

The women of the Turtles asked Born Underwater what they ought to do, since she'd seen what the Black-Gowns did in other Countries. But she replied that she had neither knowledge nor desires; it did not matter anymore what Echon did. (Although Echon was no longer their Captain, she spoke only of him.) She lied, and said that she did not see-ahead. But others did. In the month of Avril the persecutions had so far increased that Crosses were torn down, and Père Brébeuf was badly beaten by the ruffianly Savages. In Mai a Sorcerer predicted that he'd soon die, and that very day he developed a high fever. The Sorcerers had poisoned him once again. But he lived –

Chihwatenah was very anxious. The Jesuits took him to Mission Sainte-Marie and tranquilized him with the Spiritual Exercises . . .

But Born Underwater continued to be Brébeuf's friend. – I see-ahead, she said. I see that they will not kill you.

He smiled. – After all, they love me . . .

They hate you, Echon.

It is the DEVIL who resists me, he said. But my MASTER is greater than he.

He went away.

He was getting old, this Black-Gown. The hairs on his head were the salt-and-pepper hairs of deerskins. She remembered how she had once touched his crow-black robe. Its texture attracted her, like the coarse hairs of moose-skins. And he had looked at her so strangely . . .

He probably did not remember that.

But Père Lalemant said to himself I must send Jean away as soon as I can. It breaks my heart to see how the Savages humiliate him.

Mission Sainte-Marie

As he thought upon this matter, he felt confirmed in the prudence of his plan to create a central Mission in Ouendaké invulnerable to Huron or Hiroquois attack. There were now twenty-eight Frenchmen at that place. The lay brothers were efficient, and much was already accomplished. Frère Guillaume, the carpenter, had proved very skillful, and Frère Charles was a master builder indeed. There were wooden chests under every staircase. Rawhide-latched cabinets filled themselves with wooden plates, and Frère Guillaume worked on with chisel and saw and pincers, making victorious Exercises of Sawdust . . . Just as a yellow sea of leaves is given form by the ivory birch-tusks that pierce it from behind like the weapons of powerful animals, so the palisade (whose construction Père Jogues had overseen) rose with high confidence above the Rivière Isaraqui. Every pole was the height of three men; every pole was sharpened. Over the points, under a sky blue and white, the woody-scaled Mission buildings could now be seen, stretching long with halls, rising tall with pointed towers. Their walls were striped and mortared. Sentries patrolled behind the gun-slits. Upon the bark-shingled roofs rose great Crosses. At Père Lalemant's command the artisans raised a splendid Chapel, in order to further cow and astonish the Savages –

He made a rule that the Savages who were infidels could neither come into the inner compound, nor sleep within the Mission's boundaries –

At the heart of everything, in splendid isolation, the Black-Gowns lived.

The Death of Chihwatenah

On the second day of the Moon When the Little Corn is Made, Chihwatenah was in the forest near Ossossané cutting wood. He knew what was going to happen. Born Underwater had told him. He'd told Echon. He liked Echon with his owlish eyes and canoe-shaped moustache, his thick beard. The creases at the corners of his eyes made them seem even wider than they were. Echon was a Bird. Echon had replied that it must be in God's hands (he did not believe that Born Underwater knew anything – for unlike the Recollect, Frère Sagard, who believed that flies were created from urine, Père Brébeuf was an educated man. How could a Savagess see the future? All his illusions, you see, had long since dispulverated into dust . . .) – *Hé é é é é!* thought Chihwatenah to himself. No matter if they kill me now. I am nephew to the Black-Gowns! My People will never forget me! After we are all dead, I will be set above this People in Heaven!

He'd already sent his nieces, including his beloved Thérèse Oionhaton, back to the longhouse. – Pick some squashes and take them home, he said. He had seen how the door of the House of Cut-Off Heads was closed. He knew that today someone would be coming . . .

The Old Men investigated his death and found that it was the work of Mohawk raiders, as could well be believed, for who but they would have slain such an exemplary Christian?

And Brébeuf said to the Superior: It is best to say nothing.

But the dead man's brother Teondechoren became a Christian, out of protest against the Old Men. Chihwatenah had told him: I shall continue to regard you as a brother only if you become a Christian. – Now his brother was dead. Now he must obey his brother.

His Monument *Midland, Ontario, 1989*

A jagged desolation of cedars at the marsh's edge; a hot autumn day, the treetops still, the sky pale blue like a dragonfly in a marsh . . . The low peninsula of trees, grey, green and black, rose above the cattail sea. (This forest had grown over an old Indian village, they said, and the trees were still sparse enough to let much light in; it was almost as hot here as in a field; it was a green humidity of leaves.) Overtopping this was a hill of darker trees. Tallest of all, the two towers of the Martyrs' Shrine.

Saint Peter, white-bearded and wise, stood holding his giant key, coloring window-radiance as usual.

Père Brébeuf lay holding a red Book upon his breast. His gold-buckled shoes peeped from the hem of his cassock. His eyes were closed so wearily, so blissfully. Above him, the red candles, then JESUS.

Kateri Tekakwitha stood at the lefthand wall, gripping her Cross just upwards of her eyes, raising her hand to it. Her dress was wood-colored, and so was her skin.

Behind the altar, the Canadian Martyrs stood or knelt on their pedestal of cloud. Brébeuf was there again. Angels above. At the center of the sun, **I.H.S.**

Outside, the Stations of the Cross, the Fountain of CHRIST. Chihwatenah's statue rose like a lighthouse above that view of the riverfall spilling into the creamy blueness of the Sweetwater Sea. Tekakwitha doubled herself to be beside him.

The Soul-Trade 1640

In the autumn, being discouraged with the reverses that they had suffered, Père Lalemant's direction decided to launch two new Missions in the event that they should be expelled from the Huron Nation. It was his duty to select the men for these Missions. One group went to the Algonkin. The other, comprised of Pères Brébeuf and Chaumonot, was sent to plant the seed of faith in the Neutral Nation. This was hardly a prudent plan, for the Huron opposed it. – No matter; Brébeuf had no fear. GOD would open His Storehouse of favors if He chose.

On the second of Novembre, they set out from Mission Sainte-Marie, between whose grey-bleached palisades the winds already blew cold.

The Neutral Captains declined to take their friendship-presents and advised them to depart, but they would not, being kin to the trees whose yellow crowns balded day by day, but still stood waiting beneath that glary white haze; their arms reached forlornly toward the SUN. Many were the longhouses they were forbidden to enter. The Savages refused even to eat from the same bowl as they, fearing them for Sorcerers. When they gave presents of their own accord, the Neutrals feared that they were poisoned. When they did not, they demanded payment. – The pride of Père Chaumonot was soon affronted, but Père Brébeuf, to whom complaint was entirely alien, embraced him, saying: My brother, we are unclean worms whose purification can come only from the fire. – Yes, and what of *them?* cried Père Chaumonot fiercely, so that the Savage children screamed. – Ah, yes, what *of* them? returned Jean de Brébeuf.

Another village expelled them screaming. He strode through the snow, and his legs ached. He comprehended that year by year he drew closer to the holocaust he sought. The backs of his thighs were numb with cold. Ahead, milky-white and brown, ice shone. Grass rose stiff and golden, glowing softer than fire beside the brown river-ice.

He was becoming thinner. He felt the cold more, and his buttocks scarcely cushioned him when he sat in their lodges.

In the middle of winter he beheld a vision of a giant Cross approaching slowly through the air, from the direction of the Hiroquois Nations.

What was it like? cried Père Chaumonot. – How large was it?

Large enough, replied Père Brébeuf, to crucify us all.

Dutch Guns

When the warriors of the Five Nations are on an expedition against an enemy, the War Chief shall sing the War Song as he approaches the Nation of the enemy and not cease until his scouts have reported that the army is near the enemy's lines. Then the War Chief shall approach with great caution and prepare for the attack.

From the Constitution of the Hiroquois

The Hiroquois children sometimes play a certain game in which they throw a bone with a hole in it high into the air, and then launch a bone peg at this whirling ivory-colored disk, seeking to interleave the two before they touch the ground. This pastime requires great skill, as might well be imagined. When the Iron People came into the land, and all Five Nations of the Hiroquois, or Haudenosaunee, began to crave iron goods as once lovers had craved lovers, one of their Rodiyaner stood up in Council and addressed them. He was a Mohawk, who had succeeded to the name of Tekarihoken, his predecessor having been killed in a raid by the Crooked-Tongues called *Wendat*. And he was in the first party of the Council. He now spoke at length, comparing the getting of iron to the children's peg game.

For this goal that we seek, he said, is a difficult one, requiring quickness and agility. We want iron and iron. But we do not have skins and skins to give these Iron People in exchange. You know that. I know that. There are not enough beaver in the Five Nations. Then, too, these Iron People wish to settle throughout the forest and dispossess us of our rights. You know them. They are liars. Worse yet, they are strangers and enemies. Their chief, Chawain, injured and insulted our fathers. So that is another difficulty. And it seems to me that this iron is a kind of poison, for by its very convenience it will make us lazy and dependent upon these Iron People. So that is a third difficulty. It is as if we were required to throw three pegs in the hole before the bone fell down! – I have spoken.

Replying to him was the man who had been clothed in the name of Oghrenghrehgowah, who was in the second party of the Council of the Mohawk. And these were the words of Oghrenghrehgowah:

Brother, in your words I perceive the Eagle atop our Tree of the Great Peace. This Eagle sees far, and his cry warns us of danger. Indeed I imagine little danger to us from these bearded Cloth-Makers, but suppose that you are right, and the Eagle sees with you. Perhaps I might then ask the Eagle to seize the bone disk in his beak and hold it, so that we can launch the three pegs that you mention. Now he has done this for me; now I can see the hole in which our iron lies. Let me launch the three pegs of bone. First, you say that we do not have enough beaver within the Five Nations. Then we must get them from elsewhere. Second, you say that the Iron People seek our ruin. Then we must be on guard against them, and put them to the torture whenever they trespass on our territories. Third, you say that iron leaves us weak. Then we must go to war to harden ourselves. Let us strike against those who possess an abundance of beaver-skins; let us attack our enemies the Crooked-Tongues! Now I believe that all three pegs have passed safely through the hole. – I have spoken.

Then one of Tekarihoken's comrades in the first party, Shadekariwade, also spoke, saying:

My brothers, both of you have enlightened my ears, and I am in full agreement. But a further point must be made. As you know, there are two Nations of Iron People. One is called *Français*, and one is called *Hollanders*. And they are enemies. If we war against the Crooked-Tongues, we will not be able to trade our skins to their allies the French. And if we cannot trade with the French we will be forced to take whatever the Hollanders choose to give us – and you all know that they are a surly and miserly people. And this may be a fourth peg to be cast into the hole. – I have spoken.

To this replied Sharenhowaneh of the second party, saying:

I see no need to cast this peg right away, for fortunes can change. Nor is there reason to fight the Wendat in a way which might irreparably break the peace. Let us slaughter them openly and in secret, but not yet strike home. – I have spoken.

Hearing this, Ayonhwhathah of the first party (who had long since succeeded to Hiawatha's name) stood up and pronounced himself in agreement, saying only: Let us get guns from the Iron People!

At this there was a great cry of excitement among the young men, who thought only of killing enemies and making great names for themselves. Although the Rodiyaner sought to keep them moderate in their emotions (for it was much easier to treat with strange Nations in that spirit), they could scarcely contain them in their lust for scalps and captives to be burned. So it was that a Mohawk who went to the Dutch post called Fort Orange knew what to ask for; he came back shouting with joy, for they had given him a gun in trade. (Why not? they said to one another. Our Indians will help keep the English down.) – Now we can kill our enemies! the warrior shouted. At once the other young men gathered around him, marveling at his Power when he stood there with the stock of his arquebus curving down against his shoulder like the upper part of a stout man's arm. They caressed the notch in the stock, wondering what it was for. They took it from him gingerly (for it might kill them); gaining confidence, they hefted it. They were amazed at how much it weighed. They stroked the long silvery tube set in wood and marveled at how finely it gleamed. It was a good Swedish gun. The French did not give the Algonkin such good guns. They took in hand his bandolier of pre-measured charges and let them clink together like sticks. Little OKIS rode the men's hearts, like the strange metal figure that squatted above the bore of that gun: it reversed the position of its head and legs when it was fed gunpowder. How lucky their kin-friend was! He could kill his enemies even as they fled from him screaming! (To terrify their enemies – ah, that Power was very dear to the Haudenosaunee.) The other braves were jealous of him. They too must go now to the Hollanders with their loads of beaver-skins. They set out easily, knowing the four directions, knowing the way that trees gathered between shore-rocks to lean a little over the water to watch it shimmering away so that their reflections continually grew beyond the low land-tongues, the pale blue mountains called by the Hollanders the *Kaatskills* . . . and in the hearts of the young men was a gloating glee: We are going to the Iron People! They ran beside snow-choked creeks, with bows cocked, arrows facing ahead. Soon they would have guns. They ran through grass as milk-bleached a yellow as the mountains were milk-bleached blue. And they came to the Hollanders.

Temptation
1641

I have two luxuries to brood over in my walks, your Loveliness and the hour of my death.

KEATS, to Fanny Brawne (1819)

Père Brébeuf and Père Chaumonot persevered among the Neutrals until the following Mars. On their return from this fruitless Mission Père Brébeuf fell while crossing a lake of ice and broke his left clavicle.

Now the hatred in which the Wendat held him was increased beyond measure by what they perceived to be his cunning and treachery in treating with another Nation. After so many attempts to murder him had failed, they did not dare to lay hands on him at once, but struck Père Chaumonot on the head with a rock. Then they became heated against Echon and got their courage and a man sought to split his head, but the other Savages intervened, for they feared the consequences to the iron trade. He withdrew into the safety of Mission Sainte-Marie. This was not his inclination, but the Superior had commanded it.

Echon has become a nephew to the Mohawk! the People whispered. He will call them here with spells. Then they will exterminate us!

But there were many in Ossossané who, fearing an Iroquois attack, asked nonetheless to be baptized, so that when they had been slain they would go to the Country of the Dead together.

Ah, that will not be possible just yet, said Echon gently. But soon. Soon, my brothers –

At Mission Sainte-Marie there were now fourteen Pères, although it was rare for them to be all together, as it was their purpose to spread the Gospel among these far-flung Savages, not to withdraw monkishly. Père Jogues and Père du Peron shared the permanent care of the residence. In this toy world where donnés and lay brothers wheeled barrels of firewood through the courtyard, or shingled the roofs or strengthened the palisadoes, the Black-Gowns were not only masters as Champlain had been at Kebec, but something more: – *viz.*, the raison d'être, to which the artisans touched their caps, louting low for love as well as for fear (the ones who felt no love did not come to Ouendaké anymore, and Brûlé was dead). They slaughtered the pigs; they tended the wheat-field across the river; they erected a longhouse for the shelter of Christian Savages; they dug a well – and all so that the Black-Gowns could grip the rough-hewn sills of windows and stare out at Heaven, regaining (if only for an hour) the blissful cloistered pallor they'd had in France, while they calculated where next to launch the heavy lead bullets of their love. Solid beams gripped darkness in rectangular criss-crosses above the dirt floors. The Store-house was filled with satiated silence, choked with the soft uneven hairs of bearskins. The sour smell of herbs echoed like an organ-chord. Withered hard brown sunflowers hung from racks in the Store-house; beaver-skin mountains rose up in the Store-house (that was how the Jesuits paid their expenses). Everywhere went the donnés in their tight red caps.

To the Superior, Père Lalemant, this place was a Paradise of his own design. But Père Brébeuf merely endured it, with a kind of stifled anguish. He was cut off from death in here –

Little wonder that Père Lalemant believed that it was his duty to send Brébeuf back to Kebec where his broken bone could be treated by a doctor –

See how they revile you, Jean! You are impeding the progress of the Mission. Have no fear; in a year or two, when they have forgotten their anger, I shall recall you here.

Yes, Père Superior, said Brébeuf. His face glowed with the fanatical joy of obedience.

Born Underwater

She stood looking across the river at the walls of Mission Sainte-Marie black and inalterable against the lavender dusk. Crosses loomed chillingly from black roof-points as sharp as arrowheads. Roof-knives cut the bleeding sky with a straightness that sickened her. The double, the reflection, trembled uncertainly silver in the river. She threw a stone at it and watched the dark double swallow the stone and heal itself, trembling darkly.

She crossed the river. She stood waiting for him to come out, as he always did.

She said: So you have gotten tired of trying to frenchify me. That is why you are leaving me.

He looked at her. – I will never give over trying to free you from your DEVIL, he said affectionately.

He explained that his Superior's command must take first place to his concern for her, but that she need have no anxiety that he would forget the needs of her soul; that he would always care for her, and many more matters of this kind – all of which she seemed to accept. Later that day, however, a Savage who happened to be passing by that longhouse, reported to him that she was crying, which those Savages very rarely do, considering it a disgrace to appear in any wise perturbed. Now he regretted his departure more keenly still, and, slipping his rosary from around his neck, he asked one of the men to take it to her – for he thought that it would be too painful if he himself were to visit her once more. – Evidently she did not think so, for she was present on the morning of his departure, her face so streaked with tears that it looked almost scandalous. – He did not look at her more than he had to.

Kebec 1641

About his journey little need be said. Kebec was as far away as his novitiate. Even the grand Fleuve Saint-Laurent was different to him now, both easier and more remorseless. He thought of a legend that they told among the Huron, how IOUSKEHA meant to establish currents in both directions on rivers, so that paddling them would be no labor, but TAWISCARON foiled him. Somehow these tales seemed more charming when one was away, and not obliged to combat them –

And what would Kebec look like? The priests and Savages said that it had grown. Three hundred French Christians, men and women, now made it their home, so that it was no longer a post, but a town. – Well, soon he would see, if GOD left him in life that long.

– Yes, he'd been withdrawn from the Huron Mission. This was a bitter mortification to him, and as such he embraced it as eagerly as he could, for he knew well that each pain flayed away another thread or rag of that splendid shirt of hopes and lusts that he had been born with, his Name-Day present from the DEVIL. – When would he be laid bare at last? How he longed to be naked and in the embrace of the Spirit!

It was a chilly Juin evening when he arrived, the sky slightly too white to be grey, and the maple trees grew high above the city walls. Churchbells tolled the hour and young birds chirped from amidst those waving leaves; treetops tossed uneasily in the breeze like restless girls leaning their heads upon each other's shoulders and then recoiling, all in the same graceful movement; and maple leaves hung over the walls like dark green thunderheads.

He knelt and made one of the Contemplations from the Exercises. When he closed his eyes, he could see how the VIRGIN held the SON, nurturing Him yet allowing Him to be seen; she already knew that she was to lose Him; for this reason His light *must* burn the brighter now . . .

And yet he knew as always that someday the Hiroquois would find him, just as the wind that gusted down the stone-walled streets of Kebec never failed to chill his bones.

Reunion

Jean, Jean, my good friend! (Thus Père Le Jeune.) The LORD be praised! And was your journey difficult? How is your shoulder?

They embraced.

Père Le Jeune stood straight and tall in his cassock. The tall black collar rose unspeakably stiff up to his chin, where it met white wisps of beard. It circled his neck in its black grip, did that collar, walling him off almost to his ears. Above its parapets, Le Jeune gazed at him almost mildly, his pupils round, French, mysterious. He had gone almost bald. An air of distinction had begun to frost him as he aged, although he would never look venerable: there would always remain something diminutive about his face, even with the stern groove now downturned at the corner of his mouth, his bird-sharp blinking eyelids . . . Perhaps it was just the Black-Gown he wore that made his head such an insignificant planet hovering above its black shoulder-reaches. But certainly distinction was there, in the grizzled ravines of his cheeks, in the strange gaze, hurt and proud to be so, that so many Black-Gowns have . . . and Brébeuf became aware of an aspect of triumph also, perhaps not fully in bloom, but budding indeed. It had not been there seven years ago, when the man returned half-dead from his winter bout with the Sorcerer. But the Sorcerer was dead, and the crusade went well, it seemed –

Ah, Jean, I have been hoping and praying daily for your arrival . . . The new Superior, Père Vimont, wishes to shake your hand (you know I'm but an ordinary missionary now?). Monsieur the Governor also longs to see you, I know . . .

Yes, I desire to meet him also, for I've heard the most edifying reports of him. And you, dear friend, tell me how things have gone with you.

Eh, the Montagnais and Algoumequins grow yearly more obedient, in part I think for fear of the Hiroquois, which is increasing in these parts. I shall be sailing soon for France, to get soldiers . . . And the pestilences among our Savages . . . – But I know it must be the same in Wendaké. You see, Jean, from time to time I read the *Relations* . . .

They both laughed at that joke.

But you must tell me, Jean, what it has been like for you. I can see pain in your face.

Can you? replied Brébeuf, astonished. For me personally it does not seem as if there's been much of that. The years have gone by; that's all. But I've wept so often for the poor Savages. In Wendaké a good half of them have died of plagues since I last set out from here.

Yes, it is the judgment of GOD. And you were persecuted among the Neutrals?

Them I pity most of all, said Père Brébeuf. In their Country the seed has fallen on barren soil.

You suffered great mortifications for our SAVIOR, Jean. Everyone here is so proud of you . . .

I suffered less than most, replied the other priest, smiling. Less than you. Remember that Sorcerer, and how they compelled you to watch his wife be murdered?

Eh, I didn't see that, exactly. I heard it secondhand from Pastedouachouan the Renegade –

That's not what they say, Paul. I will never forget the tale you told of her miserable death. Does it weigh on you still?

Somewhat . . .

And we all know how the Père Le Jeune has eaten cast-off moose-skins in his time! – continued Brébeuf, in high spirits; and then they both began to laugh again. They praised each other's sufferings and magnified them, as good friends are wont to do, and for a moment Le Jeune could almost believe that he had been gallant instead of merely steadfast, that he had met with perpetual glee the challenge of those winter night-years in Canada, when the ink froze in the ink-stand, and he could hear the frozen trees exploding in the cold night like popping harquebuses.

Kebec Years

In Avril, half a thousand Hiroquois set out on the war-path. A hundred and fifty went to attack any Huron and Algoumequin who might voyage along the Fleuve Saint-Laurent, but the plupart paddled to Trois-Rivières, where they meant to treat with the French. One of their Captains asked for three dozen muskets, in exchange for which he offered to give the Iron People peace and beaver-skins. Montmagny refused him, at which the warriors began jeering at the Iron People and shooting at them from the woods. But that was of little moment (as the French said to one another). These Savage wars were like the battles of children with slingshots in the cities of France. The children killed one another, and that was that. A stranger could hope to do nothing, unless it were to gain the Crown oneself, to be killed without pity.

That winter, as Montmagny learned from his spies, the Hiroquois pillaged five Huron canoes, torturing and devouring everyone they found. Apparently none made a successful escape.

Gougou

Père Le Jeune heard a strange noise. (Père Brébeuf never heard it.)

His heart was pounding.

But then he laughed at himself and said: After all, even at home in France there are superstitious souls, who believe in evil spirits when they hear the gnawing of a mouse!

At Kebec they had many books concerning New France, among which was the *Histoire* of that busybody Lescarbot, who'd wintered in Acadia with Poutrincourt and Champlain, a score and a half of years since. He flipped through its pages and saw something which he thought might apply equally well to the Souriquois and to certain Christians of his acquaintance: *Such is the nature and humour of many Savages, for their whole life is sullied with mutual bloodshed . . . and thus they have great fears, and invent for themselves a* GOUGOU, *Who is the Torturer of their consciences.*

The City of God

1642

> The speedy and firm establishment of Christianity was principally promoted by a belief, which originated from its founder Himself: this was the opinion *of His early return, and the revelation of His kingdom upon Earth.*
>
> JOHANN GOTTFRIED VON HERDER,
> *Reflections on the Philosophy of the History of Mankind* (1784–91)

In the midst of the Hiroquois threat, a heavy religious ecstasy had fallen upon New France. Kebec itself, of course, was becoming a city of the religious, with shady streets of churches and convents blooming year by year with more rose windows; and treetops waved above their sloping roofs. The girls at the Ursuline convent were so modest, it is said, that if one of them went about with her throat even a little uncovered, the others would cough meaningfully and say: Careful, you drive away your good Angel! – (Their virtuc, now faded to a rose color in these defrenchified times, like Montcalm's skull, then shone translucently refulgent like flowers whose soft rounded petals were sequin-tipped.) The heathen Savages were frequently to be heard lamenting and wailing: Now our dreams and prophecies are no longer true – *prayer* has spoiled everything for us! – upon being told of which, Mère Marie de l'Incarnation said to her Ursulines: Now we must rejoice, sisters, for the medicine is beginning to work! – at which they raised their white-swathed foreheads to Him in ecstasy. What was occurring in the souls of those Savages they could not know for certain, souls being windows dark to all save Him, but Mère Marie said to Sœur Marie-Josèphe that she could almost see the thousands of withered DEMONS tumbling out of the Savages' hearts like golden leaves in autumn by the Stream of Time. Sœur Marie-Josèphe was so moved by this vision that she prayed even for the poor lost DEMONS. – What further increased the Ursulines' edification, of course, was the discipline in penance shown by those Savages who had already come to a rudimentary comprehension of virtue. – On a sweet summer day when tiny clouds dotted the sky like leaves, some Christian Savages brought a kinswoman of theirs to Mère Marie. They had taken her from her husband by force, for he was a pagan (as was she), and in addition had already one wife, that being the custom with many of these filthy and despicable barbarians, be they Souriquois, Montagnais, or what have you. – Instruct this girl in the True Faith, Mère, said the Savages (so well had they been taught), then we will be able to give her in marriage to a Christian! – Mère Marie was much edified at the piety that they showed, and embraced the poor girl to give her consolation, but she would not look Mère Marie in the eyes until her chin was uplifted, and then Mère Marie saw the streams of tears that ran so silently down her chin. – Don't be afraid, child, she said, but the Savage girl said nothing. – At this, the Reverend Père de Quen took Mère Marie aside and said to her: This fillette, young though she is, is already lost, I fear, for she *loves* her husband – oh, the shame of it! I believe she will cause you no end of trouble. I will be very surprised if she does not mean to break out of the enclosure and return to her sin. – Thank you for your caution, Père, Marie replied. I will take special care with her.

For two or three days she was sad, of course, but presently Marie, watching her face, could see the moment when the DEMONS flew out of it and the HOLY SPIRIT flowed in like a Fleuve grey and remorseless thundering down great falaises and precipices to shatter the most stubborn boulders of hearts into sand which it then smoothed so sweetly on the bottom of its bed and mingled with fragments of gold and diamonds; at this she dried her tears and said: Please, Mère, give me baptism.

And your husband, child? – She was weaving a great tapisserie, in which roses, carnations, and pansies grew around the tableaux (JESUS in His crib, GOD the PÈRE, the HOLY SPIRIT). This one would take seven years.

I won't see him anymore.

You're certain of this? This is your own wish?

Yes, Mère.

Unless he receives the Faith?

Yes, Mère.

For several days longer she detained the girl, staying close by her to insure that she was hardened in her new self, until the husband, coming unrecognized to the convent, ate his sagamite with the other Savage visitors and then stood up and peered through the grille, which glowed with sunlit dust like a stained glass window in which Marie, white at breast, forehead and throat, grey elsewhere, held out her right hand toward the kneeling *filles amérindiennes* who were praying in red blankets and fringed buckskins, their headbands like apprentice haloes embroidered in the usual Savage wavy patterns like choppy rivers that ran in circles around their hair; and he saw his wife among them, staring into her close-pressed hands as Marie stared into space with her crucifix glowing black and gold in her left hand; and a leaning tree cooled all with its leaves of summer. The border of this window was blue, deep blue like the Fleuve Saint-Laurent in summer . . . – His wife looked up and saw him. She paled. He thought that she was going to scream with anguish. Silently, he swallowed his tears. Mère Marie had turned her attention instantly upon the crisis, rushing not to the swooning girl, but to the grille in order to memorize his face, but he was already gone.

Who was he? said Mère Marie. Your husband?

Yes, Mère.

And did you encourage him with your eyes?

No, Mère.

At this her kinsmen took her back to their longhouse, in order to test her resolution, for Savages are fickle, as Mère Marie well knew, and do not trust each other willingly except after a long proof of fidelity. It so happened that when this poor woman was going into the forest to butcher a deer which her brother had killed, she met her husband, who begged her to return to him. Weeping, she fled into the darkness, whose trees were as close-crowded as the ribs of a Huron canoe, for she did not know what the HOLY SPIRIT might do to her if she broke her promise. But he followed after. – Are you still my wife? he shouted after her; and she did not know what to reply, although her heart ached as Mère Marie's had when she left her son . . . He chased her into the cabin of a Frenchman, threatening and imploring in the worldly fashion of those Canadians, but she continued to say in her heart the words of the charm which Mère Marie had taught her: *I wish to believe. I long to be baptized. I love obedience.* Presently, when he could scarcely see for grief and rage, she escaped from him and returned to the longhouse of her kinsmen.

You were with your husband! shouted the Christian Savages. You were forbidden to speak to him, and you broke this commandment. We shall hold a Council and decide how to punish you.

This they did. Some were for putting her to death, being zealous for the

Faith, but others of more lenient convictions prevailed, so that she was whipped with five lashes at the railing just outside the church door, Père de Quen having given his permission. The other Christian Savagesses who witnessed the scene (as by the terms of the sentence they were bound to do) saw with what compliance she bowed her head and uncovered herself for the whip, for she believed in her heart that this must be a preparation for baptism. The morning was very clear, although the sky was soon to be overgrown with cirrus clouds. – Count the strokes! the executioner commanded her, and laid down the first line of scarlet, around which instantly appeared a collar of valencienne lace of the same hue. – *Un!* she said in a clear voice. – Now he raised the whip again and struck with all his strength, so that inside the church Père de Quen looked up and frowned, hearing the tautly liquid sound of parting flesh, and on the woman's sun-browned back appeared a second column of embroideries like scarlet butterflies, which took wing, spattering the executioner's face; and scarlet diamonds subdivided into diamonds stood breathlessly out on her skin where the teeth of the lash had been, and the woman said meekly: *Deux!* – Père de Quen came out after the third stroke and called upon the executioner to cease, believing the occasion to have been sufficiently severe. Then she asked him for baptism, but he sent her away with scornful words.

When she heard that the woman was innocent, Mère Marie was vexed at the carelessness of Père de Quen in having permitted matters to go forward, but later, when she comprehended that all had played their parts in innocence, she had to laugh with him at the simple earnestness of the Savages while remaining edified by the patience of the woman, who shortly thereafter was baptized, and the Fleuve Saint-Laurent was the pearly grey of stained glass windows at twilight –

It was another windy evening, the sky unsunny but still glowing. The gate of Governor de Montmagny's Palace creaked open, like branches creaking in a wind-gust.

Montmagny was entertaining the Captain of a ship from France which had brought settlers. The Captain was telling all the news of France, while Montmagny refilled his brandy-glass with the utmost courtesy, giving attentive ear as the man told of the doings at Court (of which he seemed to know a considerable amount), and then he launched into a long tale which Montmagny could not quite swallow, about a twelve-year-old genius named Pascal, who had invented some sort of addition machine! Now what would be the use of that? – What else? – The Roy was in bad health, it seemed, and his wars went badly . . . And that heretic Descartes had been condemned by the Senate, which was only his desert. The Captain was of the opinion that the fellow would be burned, although this too Montmagny discounted. That was his hobby – discounting things. After a day of weighing everything that his spies and minions told him, magnifying and diminishing in proportion to his own best judgement, how luxurious simply to discount! – Monsieur, he said to the Captain, I believe not a word about this addition machine. How could it operate? No, no, I do not want to hear it. You must have been mistaken. You've seen it with your own eyes, you say? Oh, faridondaine! Next you'll be telling me you shook hands with the Pope!

Actually he was not enjoying himself. The Hiroquois had invaded his brain. – Yes, he thought, I must fulfill my devoir to erect a fort at the mouth of the Rivière des Yroquois; that will keep them from infesting our Fleuve too badly . . . – as meanwhile he said aloud to the Captain: Do have some more brandy. No, this addition machine, I say it must be entirely without foundation!

The fort was well underway, but just recently some Mohawk had attacked the workmen. One good Frenchman was killed, and four wounded. The enemy had had the temerity to fire directly into the loopholes.

He was concerned to learn whether they now possessed more muskets and arquebuses than the year before – not that thirty-nine was a number to be feared, but it scarcely presaged any good for the future. A law of the world: *With increasing armaments the insolence of Savages must also increase* (which was why he had kept in force Champlain's refusal to sell arms even to allies of the French, be they Algoumequins, Montagnais or Huron). He must send out his spies again . . .

Père Le Jeune Beats the Drum

For precisely the same reason, Père Le Jeune was now in Paris. – The ship creaked all the way home. He almost thought that he could hear the grincement of GOUGOU's teeth like rocks grinding slowly together . . . He'd been instructed to deliver his cartload of alarms to the Roy himself and to Cardinal Richelieu, whose piety and goodness to the Jesuits was proverbial. So he in his turn approached the royal carpet spilling down shallow marble steps; he bent the knee at the edge of the forest of Seigneurs- and Madames-in-waiting who stood rustling with silk as if a breeze blew through leaves; he scarcely saw them. A huge Cross hung over the Roy Louys, who regarded him wearily. He'd just been compelled to execute his latest catamite, the

Marquis de Cinq-Mars, who used his favors only to gain whores and new clothes, who laughed in the Roy's face, sneering: I cannot change, or do better than before . . . – who even dared to plot Richelieu's assassination! He thought that the Roy would always forgive his trespasses according to the Bible. But the Roy had grown as old as a nerveless skull. When he'd condemned the Sieur de Chalais to death in 1625, his brother Gaston had kidnapped the executioner, and so they'd made a butcher do it. Unnerved by the crowds and the presence of De Chalais' mother, the butcher required more than thirty blows of the axe to kill his victim. Hearing this, the Roy had wept, for he'd known De Chalais since childhood. But executions have to go on, don't they? *Hé é é!* By 1630, when wives and sisters and mothers wept at the Roy's feet, imploring him to spare their good men, Louis only sucked his teeth and said: I am sorry, Madame, but he must die. – If they presumed to ask again, he'd say: I would not be Roy if I allowed myself the indulgence of private feelings. – So it came the turn of the Marquis de Cinq-Mars. The Roy was playing chess at the time. He looked at his watch and said smiling: Ah, I wonder how he looks now! – So what was Canada to him? He had indigestion, gout, insomnia, and a consumptive cough which would kill him the following year (he died in bed, with his finger on his lips, as if he meant to impart some ghoulish secret); Richelieu would croak this very Décembre . . . On the other hand, these Savage attacks seemed rather an affront. He'd eat these Savages for breakfast if they didn't behave. And Père Le Jeune would eat them, too: he knew Père Le Jeune!

Le Jeune made his submission. The Court waited. In the space of an instant, he performed the Exercises, but this time he dipped not into the Stream of Time and Sacredness which Ignatius had discovered so long ago, but simply into his stream of memories and fears. He *must* make them see the danger posed by these Yroquois! His words must be as silver and gold. (Of course they always were. Indeed, Daversière the accountant had been firmed in his holy dream of Montréal by reading the *Jesuit Relations*, for which Père Le Jeune took no credit, knowing in his simplicity that praise was due only to GOD.) – So let the bilious rapids roll! – He told the tale of the Recollect, Père Nicolas Viel, who had been basely murdered by the Huron (seventeen years ago now it had been!): they had drowned him in his canoe. Surely this man had become a Saint. Surely he'd intercede for Canada, if men only continued to have faith and perform good works there. He told the tale of his own winter among the Montagnais (a mere nine years past); how he had been tormented and reviled by the Sorcerer; how that varlet of the DEVIL had perished miserably in a fire; how his son had come to Père Le Jeune at last to drink the blood of CHRIST. Proudly he related the trials and sufferings of Père Brébeuf among the Huron Savages (at which the Mesdames of the Court wept); he detailed the multitudinous accomplishments of Mère Marie de l'Incarnation; he told of the piety of the Grey Sisters; he praised the penitences of the laity at Kebec – even the soldiers and sailors there were sometimes known to scourge themselves! – How can we abandon this land to the Hiroquois? he cried. Our great Nation of France is now literally at war with the DEVIL! If we retreat before him, we will lose more ground than we think. We will tumble backwards into the mighty Fleuve of GOD's wrath, there to be swept over terrifying cataracts into the Pit of Sin from which we came! I can see it even now before me as I speak! I see the painted imps of the Hiroquois gibbering about me in triumph; I hear the screams of mothers and children roasted slowly at adjoining stakes . . .

My Paul, you paint a fine tongue-canvas, sneezed the Cardinal. But we already knew that. Year after year we have read your *Relations* . . .

And what of the good Savages, Père? a damsel of the Court asked him. Do they truly love IESUS *in their hearts?*

For a moment, to his amazement, he was thrown into confusion. How could he say? What could he know? – But then, smiling at her his most wintry smile, he said: Madame, our Savages are always savage. They resemble the birds of passage of their Country. Do you take my imputation? And now please excuse me. – Yes, Seigneur? No, we do not have a sufficiency of *anything* for a long siege, I tell you!

He was radiant with gratitude at the benefices heaped upon him by his many friends.

Père Jogues Among the Hiroquois

If only poor Champlain weren't seven years dead and rotten! *He* would have raised that Fort in less time than it takes to say a dozen *Hail MARIES*! But Montmagny, bound by circumspection, must wait until the chests of gold were delivered into his very hands before he could set the Swiss mercenaries to capping the spot with a civilized edifice, in token of the Roy's right! – for what if the gold didn't come after all? So it was that the good Père Jogues must now prove Le Jeune's point – although I abridge his story (is it written in the ink of chalices or poison-bottles?), citing the press of so many other calamities that spew upon us pell-mell in these last and highest rapid-narrows. Suffice it to say that he'd labored most effectively among the Huron, first under Père Brébeuf, then under Père Lalemant, so that our PÈRE Who disposes all now permitted him a glimpse of the Crown which would be his reward.

Seeing-Ahead

In the *Jesuit Relations* we never read that the reason that Tekakwitha was born in the village of Ossernenon was that Père Jogues' head-blood sprayed into the longhouse darkness when he was tomahawked, scattering like a host of bitter crimson Angels to sanctify the hearth, the two nearest sleeping-benches; and later, when Tekakwitha's mother, the Algonkin slave, prepared a meal with the flesh of the THREE SISTERS she trod the bloody dirt and with her own hands broke up bloody branches for the fire. If it is as the Christians say, and blood is magic, then must not her own flesh have been transformed into a living Eucharist? Tekakwitha walked upon that same spot for ten years, rubbing the last particles of bloodclot powder with the soles of her feet until, under the leadership of that noblest of leaders, the Marquis de Tracy, six hundred men set out through the forest. They were the Carignan-Salières regiment, and it was 1666. The men trampled sunny clearings of ferns; they broke the spiderwebs between maple trees. They came to the Mohawk villages and burned them. They burned the cornfields. They dug up the caches of dried corn and burned them all, so that the Mohawk would starve that winter, like ants turned out of their hive at the end of autumn. Tekakwitha, of course, did not starve. She was needed by GOD. Neither did her uncle. GOD required him also: Moses could never have played his part without the indispensable Pharaoh. Can we agree, then, that Kateri's father was no more the man who took her mother than IESUS's father was that poor old cuckold of a Joseph who became patron Saint over Canada? The *Jesuit Relations* do not say so. They leave the inferences to us.

Père Jogues Among the Hiroquois *continued*

That year for the first time the Iroquois had begun not merely to besiege the Wendat villages as was customary, but also to sack them, to strip them of their iron things. They burned a town near Contarea, which occasioned great panic and loss of life; the Huron Christians asked Père Lalemant what should be done, and he replied: You must give yourselves to GOD. – Then the

Savages were silent. The best of them made a rendezvous at Mission Sainte-Marie, where Père Lalemant had arranged a festival for them. There they agreed to lodge only with each other when they traveled, for their clan-friends were not permitted to count for anything anymore: – Foxes, Bears, Turtles and Wolves, it made no difference. There were only Christians and infidels now. – Like children they came to Père Lalemant and asked him if that vow would be sufficient to protect them against the Iroquois. Again and again he must explain that this wretched worldly life, which can end but among worms, has no consequence except as a sort of battlefield where we make the Exercises to decide under which of the Two Standards we shall enlist; but they, still not comprehending him, vowed never to fight in the party of the Iroquois, so again he must wear out his voice. At last, realizing that deeds were better than words, he took them into the Christian Compound to see the latest improvements there. It was almost a French town now, walled and spired. Spearmint-bundles hung drying everywhere, to purify from pestilence; Swiss mercenaries marched around. His artisans had added a hospital this year, where Père Jogues did good service. This was built away from the residence proper, with a discreet tunnel-door, so that women as well as men might be cared for there. (Looking in, the Savages were terrified to see this house of living skeletons, who lay already half-devoured by the Black-Gowns' sorceries.) A Church had also been constructed, where the Savages could participate in public worship, as Père Lalemant now invited them to do. Dully, wonderingly, they made their genuflections . . . Beside the Church lay a fresh new cemetery, consecrated and hungry for corpses. The first to be buried there was a Savagess from Ossossané, who had herself carried to Sainte-Marie to die. Inspired by that woman's example, the other new Christians agreed that henceforth they would be buried only in cemeteries consecrated by those who were called *Charcoal*, thereby repudiating now and forever the Feast of the Dead in which the People's bones had once mingled . . .

At the close of the Black-Gowns' festival, a Shaman said that the Iroquois were to be found in the south, so the warriors who were Christians set off to the west, to show their scorn for the DEVIL whom that man served. As it happened, the Iroquois were indeed to the south, and the warriors who still believed in Dream-Feasts had gone that way. They were not sufficient in number to avoid defeat, thanks to the defection of the Christians. So the Iroquois devoured them. When the Christians heard, they were very joyous, for by that stroke paganism had been weakened amongst them.

Late afternoon, and the wide lakes rippled blue and white. Modest thunderheads hung in company in the sky. The People considered going to the Land of the Haudenosaunee to make their peace with them, but did not, although they had sacks filled with shell-wampum; for there was too much dissension among them. Whatever the Captains who still followed custom proposed, the Christians must contradict. And the Hiroquois laughed. The Black-Gowns throve, and saw fit to commence a new Mission to Scanonaenrat . . .

In Juin, following the command of his Père Superior, Père Jogues departed Mission Sainte-Marie for Kebec, leaving behind him the Huron hill-villages with their sandy cornfields, waiting and waiting by the streams, waiting to be abandoned, waiting for the Hiroquois to come. – There was nothing in the forest but Savages and Crosses. – He arrived without incident. The Huron Mission was in need of paper, cassocks, altar-wine, and other such necessities. These things he obtained punctiliously from Père Brébeuf, who was now the Mission Procurator. – And what is your impression now of our Huron Savages? asked Brébeuf, smiling indulgently, as exiles smile. – The watchword is that they are but louts and rustics, replied Père Jogues, for he was so piously humble that he only stated the opinions of others . . . – I, William the Blind, am sorry to say that Brébeuf was not happy. It was part of his duties to arrange the convoys to Wendaké. In this year the Hiroquois seized three of them, leaving nothing. Guilt twisted in his entrails like an arrowhead. Sweat started from his forehead, and he almost cried out. Now seeing Père Jogues (who according to Père Lalemant had described the matter of Born Underwater as excessive, who – worse still! – continued on in Wendaké, when *he* rotted in the useless ease of Kebec – his clavicle was quite healed! – when – worst of all! – Père Lalemant had evidently seen fit to ask Père Jogues to guard the convoy of paper and chalices, as a sort of steward, thus indirectly acknowledging that Brébeuf had been incompetent to permit the Hiroquois to raid those supplies), Brébeuf experienced a great rush of mortification, which showed on his face, although he was not aware of it, so that Père Jogues was moved to pity for him and stood conversing longer than he might have otherwise – in truth he *did* think that Brébeuf had gone too far with Born Underwater – and his pity increased to see how Brébeuf hung on every scrap of news about the Huron Mission – and now his pity began to show in *his* face, so that Brébeuf's mortification increased tenfold – ah, it was extremely bitter; hence extremely sweet! His face stiffened a little with anguish . . . – Once they were both Saints in Heaven together, would they continue to play those games? – I don't know. – Together, under direction of the new Superior, Père Vimont, they now made the Spiritual Exercises (which have less to do with understanding than with silence).

This time it was the Exercise of the Two Standards, which is one of the most crucial in any Black-Gown's arsenal, since it requires the Stream of Time to be peopled, in defiance of that solitude and loneliness without which one can scarcely pull himself unswervingly toward GOD. So Père Brébeuf and Père Jogues envisioned in considered detail the plain of Jerusalem where King JESUS gathers true knights beneath His standard, in the multitudinous shadow of coppery cones and domes overhanging that church-topped cliff (where three hundred years later, on the edge of Upper Town, Champlain's statue seemed to be sailing backward through the clouds), and the page-boys begin to strike the breeze-whipped tents on that last morning as their Seigneurs kneel in the grass where the horses are snorting and raking furrows with iron-shod hooves (which JESUS has washed this morning as He washed the Disciples' feet). His standard flutters overhead. The device: a white cross on a field of blue. On the bank of the Fleuve Saint-Laurent, a few portages east of where Tekakwitha made her Vow of Virginity in 1679, a knight is praying to Heaven. He prays: *GOD, Who by the predication and blood of His Martyr-Saints, Jean de Brébeuf, Isaac Jogues and their companions, consecrated the first fruits of the Faith in the vast regions of North America; accord us that by their intercession, the Christian people shall everywhere and unceasingly increase. By JESUS CHRIST. Pax CHRISTI.* His forehead is high and smooth. He is a Spaniard, whose eyelids are sly hoods, whose full mouth often smiles. His face is glowing like stained glass. His beard trembles in the wind. He clasps his hands together and prays; then he rises and takes his place at the head of the line. He is Ignatius. Seeing CHRIST, he begins to weep, whispering: I am so poor in goodness . . .

CHRIST strides down the row of Saints, breathing face against face, whispering: *Receive the HOLY SPIRIT!* at which they burn with the joy of becoming wholly His. Blood drips from His palms. He knows the agony of Père Jogues. His forehead is as beautiful as the Maison Bethanie with its white-outlined arch-windows sprouting stone blossoms. (Tekakwitha's face was never beautiful until she died.) The knights are so deeply drowned in Him that they do not look up toward those churches on the rock to see Born Underwater walking down the street in silent moccasins, stopping to peer down a narrow high-walled street in Upper Town at the Fleuve Saint-Laurent which is dark to her; she can see the longboats in a V below in the moonlight, the single column of men going up the ravine, the ships creaking at sea – the English are taking Kebec! In the Jesuit church there will soon be big holes, and the floor will be ripped up by craters. There will be holes in the ceiling, like rents in a shirt of fleurs-de-lys. But no one sees what is about to happen.

And does Born Underwater see CHRIST? Are His Knights Militant anything to her but the shafts of trees rising above tree-darkness? She hears the songs of mosquitoes. So do the Saints. Now they mount their coursers. They pull their visors down. The sunlight glitters on rounded iron kneecaps, on iron noses like crows' bills. Their eye-slits, through which the world appears so bright and airy and distant, award them a remoteness which in no way approaches serenity; the motions of their bodies are choppy, tense. Chain-mail jingles on their chests. – JESUS whispers into the ear of His courser and leaps lightly onto his back. He wears no armor; He needs no saddle. But for the first and only time He carries a sword. The standard crackles in the air. The pages strain with all their strength to hold the eager horses back; the knights pull hard at the bit so that every stallion rears and tosses his head; now at last the trumpet sounds, and CHRIST raises His arm and the knights gallop Him across that wide brightness, past Three Rivers, past Montréal with its rectangles of tan and green like arpents, its peculiar random tree-islands like forgotten trivialities, then south along the Mohawk Rivière, toward the plain of Babylon where King LUCIFER is gathering *His* army beneath a black standard whose device is a single red flame . . .

And so, in their dank stone cells, sighing and weeping, the two Black-Gowns now peeped into Hell and measured the length and breadth and depth of it and smelled its darkness. (When it is chilly and you cannot see, then it is easier for your imagination to come to grips with death.) – Under Whose standard do *you* want to die? The *Spiritual Exercises*, created by Ignatius *to conquer oneself, and to organize one's life without influencing decision by any inordinate attachment*, will force you to answer that question, if you are honest. The question is a simple one. Answering, too, is simple – as simple as pulling a trigger of an arquebus. When you answer, you cross the point of no return.

Yes, yes, murmured Père Brébeuf.

He felt himself reduced to a speck, riding upon an infinite wing of righteousness –

Pax CHRISTI, whispered Père Jogues.

Very good, said the Superior, Père Vimont.

Then Père Jogues set out on his return journey.

It was the second day of Août.

In his flotilla, a dozen canoes. There were many illustrious Huron with him, including Eustache Ahatsistari, Joseph Teondechoren, and the latter's daughter – *viz.*, Thérèse Oionhaton, the niece of the martyred Chihoaetenhwa. To her profit, she'd passed two years among the Ursulines, learning from them how to sing, read, write and accomplish many deft embroideries. Just as the Amerindian boys pouted under the Black-Gowns' care, wearing smelly skins and bead collars; walking shy and silent in pale fringed moccasins, so Mère Marie's girls wove vanneries with their own Savage motifs: Xs, square black frogs, jagged river-lines . . . Thérèse made little round ports-bijoux decorated with stars and jagged rivers. She made lung-shaped containers whose lids were nested with decorations. Marie's aim was to marry them all off into Christian families. The Duchesse d'Aiguilon sent them representations of the Saintes, painted with oils upon half a dozen copper tablets. – Very fine work, Thérèse! said Mère Marie. Your uncle would have been proud of you . . . – They came to love one another well (Mère Marie could almost imagine what it would have been like to have a real daughter), and the girl was weeping when she set out up river. But it had to be; it was her bounden duty to bring the word of God to her sisters, nieces and grandmothers in Wendaké. So the Black-Gowns had commanded, and there was no disobeying them. – Besides Thérèse was the lay brother, René Goupil, a skilled surgeon. Goupil had been forced to withdraw from his novitiate, being deaf. So it was now he who rode the Stream of Time most happily, being insulated by his deafness from the chirrings of danger. Peering into the beech-shade at the edge of the river, he saw the white line of stones that marked water.

Suddenly the sun shone on arquebus-barrels. Gun-Powder sent the Huron fleeing in terror – those who could. The others were captured. The Hiroquois, red-brown muscle-corded, strained all the tendons of their necks in yells of triumph.

Their faces were hungry and meager, their noses sharp. They were headbanded with zigzags and diamonds. Long greasy locks cloaked their necks and shoulders.

They beat Père Jogues senseless. When he recovered himself, they worried at his index finger with their teeth until it was gnawed entirely away. They laughed and pressed torches into his flesh.

Surely the Stream of Time flowed through the place where he was going. (After all, the Country of the Mohawk was streaked with rivers, just as its sky was streaked with clouds.) Where did it go? Perhaps it flowed in the east, among willows and mustard-weeds and the purple blooms of Indian tobacco glowing like cast-off treasures among the trees. Perhaps it flowed westward in the river-worried lowlands where willows formed green waterfalls. But he surely rode it now; Père Brébeuf would be envious when he heard.

The day now embruned with mist, they passed by a beaver-pond with its skinny black trees and shallow water, a stand of elms. (The beavers were all dead there, having become iron.) And they came to the Hiroquois cantons.

They sliced Père Jogues' thumb off with a knife of iron. They burned his remaining fingertips into charred and bloody bones.

The Mohawk Rivière was brown and wide between autumn leaves. The hills were red and yellow and green.

On the twenty-ninth of Septembre, a Hiroquois saw Frère Goupil making the sign of the Cross over a child. Being provoked to a fury by the sight of this pestilential sorcery, he split his head. Frère Goupil was the first of the Jesuit Martyrs.

He hadn't been the first to die, of course. How could the Irocois have waited? Indeed, the weeping French found almost at once, in the shadow of Fort Richelieu, the painted silhouettes by means of which the enemy proclaimed such doings. Just behind the ashes there rose an oak as broad as an alms-dish, its bark scorched patchily by angry fires; and this, like Père Brébeuf's tabernacle, Robert Pontgravé's altar-tree of scalps, Hélène de Champlain's hollow heart, had become a tableau of tormented souls. Here on the coarse-pored bark glowed the scarlet heads of the condemned – thirteen of those (their relics crackly underfoot like beetle-shells, their heart-drippings congealed on the bushes) – here too the black likenesses of those who'd been hoarded for other malignancies: – What grief, what grief! (thus Marie de l'Incarnation) but you say that my poor Thérèse was not painted red like the others? So there's hope, there's hope . . . and she took up one of her protégée's embroidered baskets and held it, but the echoes of the young girl were already muffled among anonymous quillwork and Marie knew that bit by bit she'd forget Thérèse's face as Thérèse must slowly forget her faith. – But no! JESUS would surely help her . . .

As for Père Jogues, he baptized sixty souls and escaped to the Dutch. He could not have the Crown yet, because his Superiors had sent him on a Mission to the Huron. He could die there, but not here. On a Dutch vessel he sailed down the Fleuve called by the Yroquois *Skä-neh'ta-de Ga-hun'-da*, which signifies the River Beyond the Openings, and so he came to the sea. And he arrived in France. He wept with longing for the Crown. At his first opportunity, he secured his passage on a ship bound for Canada.

Montréal
1642–1989

I would recommend that they be given a *small reservation* including their pueblos, the agency & sufficient lands for cultivation & grazing purposes.

JESSE FLEMING, Hopi Agent, to
Secretary of the Interior (1882)

In that same year, on the eighteenth of Mai, a companion city to Kebec was founded. – Eh, they had Trois-Rivières already, and Tadoussac, but now the French erected edifices consecrated entirely to the VIRGIN (and palisadoed around, of course; Champlain and the Iroquois still set that tone). They called it Ville-Marie. It rose upon an island where the Fleuve Saint-Laurent narrows most stringently. – Yes, Ville-Marie. Montréal was unknown then – not that it is much better known now when at night its conjectural texture is plotted by goose-pimples of light marking the perimeters of avenues and buildings, so that looking down from the air, you think that you have a very odd map rolled out before you. The city is abruptly contoured by the incurve of black water. No, at that time the map was blank, and yet someday there would be crêpes and Cinzano blanc. Squares and squares and squares would stand along that wide grey river. Inside the squares, everything was to be so smooth and colorful, like a whore in a very tight green skirt that cut into her perfect legs, her hips straining, almost bursting. In Juillet the Fleuve would be a green and silver mystery as always, over which the moon hung glowing in the evenings, filling people's lives with coolness. Everything seemed to be alight, and yet the details of things were obscured. Montréal was set among green fields and black fields and little white towns submerged in a haze of summer light.

Montréal 1989

On rue Saint-Denis it said QUÉBEC LIBRE.

The snow was still white from the previous night, and snow turned the dials of the parking meters into breasts. Snow made an upturned rowboat of the marquee roof of the Saint-Denis, where Kodo du Japon, Hi Ha Tremblay, and suchlike performers were playing. Icicles of miraculous transparency hung down the front of L'Aventurier Trailhead. Snow-covered cars labored carefully in the snowy streets. From time to time, people strode by – the women in their white or black boots, the men in dark jackets, scarves and jeans, striding briskly along through the snow. A man and a woman walked side by side, hand in hand. Suddenly she whirled against him and embraced him.

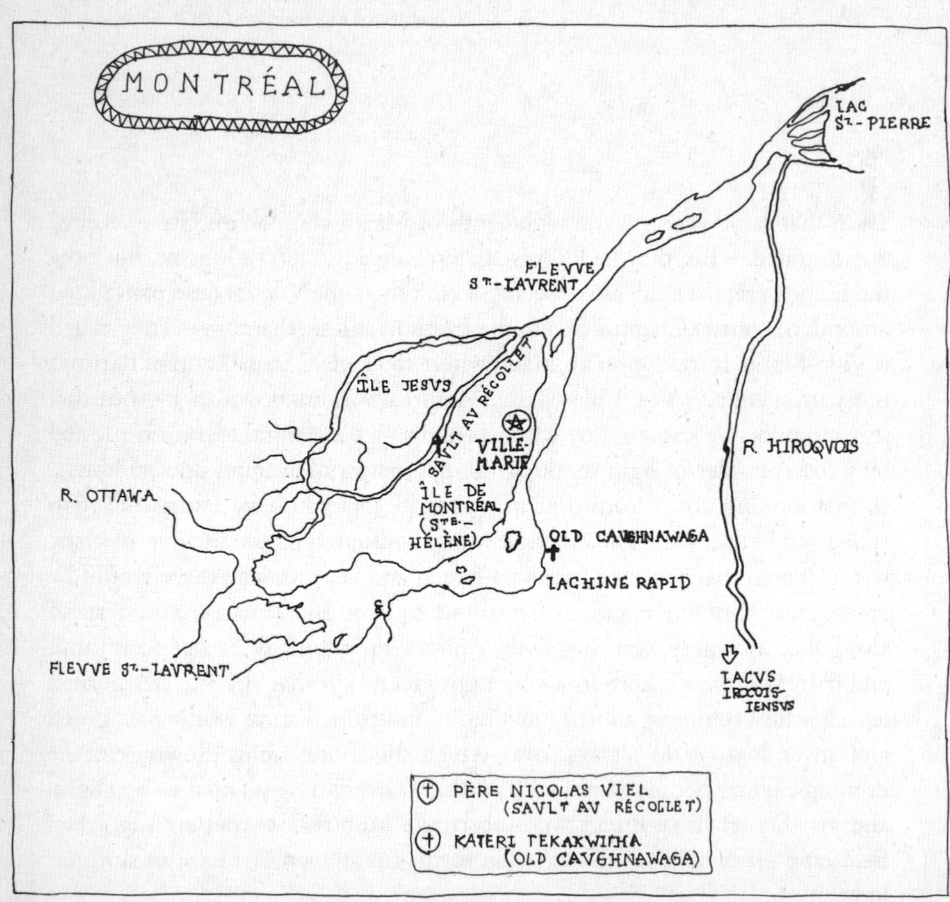

Catherine's Love

It was at Montréal that you saw Born Underwater's supplanter like a gilded Angel on a church roof, cowled and sun-warmed, extending downward to men the hand of help. *I want to have published a small favor, but to me at the time a big one,* writes Mrs. J. L. of Kingston, Ont. (1983). *I mislaid my car keys and searched everywhere through the house and to no avail. I told Kateri I would have it published if she would help me. Just then my sister from out of town chanced to phone and didn't she suggest the very place outside where I might have left them. And there they were! Kateri came through again. May she soon be canonized.* – Just across the Pont Mercier from her bones, it was a summer Sunday on Sainte Catherine street. The churches were swollen, spired pods whose seeds were old people praying in dark pews. Cyclists glided and strained, following the painted lanes reserved for them, swimming through shoulder-heat, neck-heat; gasping trees opened their leaves to the fullest, drinking light. People boiled past like sidewalk-bubbles; white cottonwood seeds streamed down like manna through the luminous air. A greenish steeple rose about the trees, ripe with stone crosses. Every chapel and basilica bore its load of Cross-fruit; light filled the interstices of every church-railing, the spaces between all church-arches. More cyclists went by, as ladies sat on a bench watching, shuffling their feet, smoothing the knee-borders of their skirts. Girls in pastel glory offered naked shoulders, naked knees to the sun. As for you, glutted with that rich summer darkness of tree-green, wiggling your toes in the hot grass of Montréal, you fell asleep in a melting puddle of church-shade and dreamed a sad dream of losing Tekakwitha, your Sainte Catherine, who now touched you and miserably confessed to you that she could not come to you anymore because you'd loved her too well . . . and you felt the hot blots of tears in your sleep, bearing you deeper and deeper underground (that is how the Stream of Time goes). – Suddenly you are awakened by the agreeable sensation that someone is astride you, hugging you, and you open your eyes to see a great round brown face, and a fat beautiful Indienne is sitting on top of you saying *Comment t'appelles-tu?* and her companion, another Indian girl, says hey, how about two dollars for a bottle? We'll bum it back for you! and you ask what's your name? and she says Marie and you turn to the one sitting on you and ask and you? and she says Catherine . . . and a chill runs down your spine and you say to her where are you from? and she points to Marie and says *she's* my home! at which you give them all the change you have, saying you don't have to give it back! at which Marie says okay, champion, we won't. – Then your Sainte kisses you and gets off you and they both go away happy and you lie in the grass feeling sweetened. A band of young people in T-shirts all the colors of glory dances by, clapping . . . And the old people are still in church.

Fishing by Night
1643

> The second way of sinning mortally is to put the thought of the sin into action.
>
> SAINT IGNATIUS, *Spiritual Exercises*

Again Governor de Montmagny sent out his spies to learn the strength and disposition of the Irocois. Upon their return from the forest they brought him news almost too dismal and distressing to be believed, for they claimed to have counted more than three hundred muskets and harquebuses among the enemy. Certainly their insolence had mounted higher than ever before. Again Père Brébeuf's succor to the Huron Mission had been seized. They stationed themselves along the Fleuve Saint-Laurent in little bands, pillaging and murdering whenever they could. When one detachment returned to the longhouses, another took its place, so that no French, Huron, Montagnais or Algonkin convoy could hope to get through that summer, unless it were formidable either in numbers or in arms. The latter was, of course, impossible, for reasons of policy, which had been determined in consultation with none other than that most pious Reverend Père, Jean de Brébeuf, SJ.

The conference had gone like this:

I beg of you, Monseigneur, to continue your strict oversight of the secondhand arquebuses. (Thus the Jesuit, Brébeuf.)

Of course, Père Jean. How could I possibly dispute a word of what you say? By your deeds as well as by your black gown you command my allegiance. However . . .

However?

Do you not perceive an ominous situation among our allies? The Hiroquois seem so strongly disposed to take their furs and iron things from them by force . . .

Ah, said Brébeuf, smiling very gently. Yes, it does seem that we have pricked the fear and rage of the DEVIL.

So you would not have us distribute arquebuses to all your Huron? We could spare plenty from the Store-house, and you know that the trade and therefore our prosperity depends on them.

Let us permit them to become a little more hard-pressed, Monseigneur, said Père Brébeuf. Then they will all long to become Christians the more ardently, in order to possess good weapons; therefore, as it seems to me, they will save their heavenly souls even as they preserve their lives on earth . . .

So be it.

Eh bien. Our Superior General will thank you by his own hand, I am sure –

And it is thanks to your views that this year I divided the Huron into Christian and non-Christian bands.

Yes, Monseigneur, I was very pleased –

. . . And the infidels did not get a very good rate this year, I am afraid! – Montmagny laughed. – Perhaps they will form a faction against us. But you know what Richelieu said.

What is that?

Nothing dispels Faction like Terror.

So those two made their usual pious plots, even as the Iroquois made a trail two leagues to the south of Fort Richelieu, so that the sentries could not see them, and came laughing silently to the Fleuve Saint-Laurent. They killed three French from Ville-Marie, and captured two others. The number of Algoumequins they slew was considerable but indeterminate, as those wandering tribes never stood still to be counted by Montmagny's spies. On the ninth of Juin (a hot white afternoon, the sky sly between green leaves), the enemy captured twenty Huron who'd come to trade at Three Rivers. Such was the terror of their muskets that they were scarcely resisted. Thirteen of their prisoners they beat to death; the remainder were led away to be adopted or burned. In Août, a convoy of a hundred Huron traders (which made up the bulk or plupart of them that year) was ambushed on their way back to Ouendaké. They lost a good part of their number to the enemy, and were compelled in fleeing to abandon almost all of the iron things which they had gotten from the French.

Mortification

In this year that good self-chastiser Père Massé, who was now quite old, removed to Sillery to minister to the needs of the Savages. Here he taught the Montaignez language to those Pères who were zealous to learn it. It is written that before he departed, Père Brébeuf bid him adieu, saying to him affectionately: It will not be long before you enter into the Kingdom.

Père Massé smiled. – I shall pray for you as long as I am able, he said. Yet I fancy my help is not needed, for your spirit continues to be as fresh and exalted as when I first knew you in your novitiate. Whatever befalls you, Jean, take confidence.

Then he smiled strangely and drew something from a chain around his neck. It was an ancient silver whistle. – This belonged to my former Superior, Père Biard. The waterfalls deafened his ears, he said. Before him I believe Robert Pontgravé owned it. You never met Robert, did you? Robert and Père Biard were great friends, which always surprised me, since they were such an unlikely pair. But many such associations have surprised me in my time, Jean . . . For instance, you and that – well. I myself never had occasion to use this whistle. I never needed anything. But if you do, then blow a hearty blast on it and see what happens. If not, then wear it, my dear brother, in memory of me . . . – And he cleared his throat and blinked vaguely.

Then he went on his way. The ground was flat, and the last-leaved trees made murky brown reflections in the grey streams.

How many novices Père Massé had confessed and inspired! Brébeuf envisioned them all for a moment, lining up to discharge their anxieties, sins and failures into Père Massé's ear, and then rising to set forth upon their duties again with renewed purity. Truly the man's patience had been a miracle . . .

But what did he mean with this whistle of his?

And Robert – and Père Biard – and the Country of the Souriquois, what had all that been like? They counted nights there, not days; so Born Underwater had said –

Brébeuf had attained the age where one begins to dwell on such things. It was only with effort that he could direct his concentration upon the Frenchmen around him – who needed him (he well knew) quite as much as the Huron Savages did. His attention remained in Wendaké. This displeased him, since, being a Black-Gown, he ought to have nothing but facility (at this stage in life) in directing his inner eye upon whatever he willed. Yet he dreamed of the great feasts at Ihonatiria, when the happy women took down smoked fishes from the racks of tree-bark, and fed the multitudes (but the Dream-Feasts he dreamed away from); he dreamed of poor Amantacha, of the more reliable but now equally dead Chihwatenah; he smelled the freshness of the Sweetwater Sea. And these memories and visions of his sparkled with hazy gold, like pollen in a ray of sunlight. They seemed far more beautiful to him than the stone houses of Kebec rising up around him year by year (more than two hundred and fifty souls dwelt there now), the gardens, the polished cannons of Champlain's Habitation, the Church, the new streets, the French fillettes throwing wide their blue shutters, singing hymns; the gold-leaf sky of sunset. It would not be long now before all the arpents between Fleuve and cliff would be built upon. Yet he persisted in his neutrality and apathy. Wendaké rang in his ears like bells.

This is not to say, of course, that he did not discharge his duties. To all save his Confessor, Père Vimont, he seemed as zealous as ever. – Eh, after all, he said to himself, I have few interior graces, being fit only to obey.

In fact he was rather too hard on himself, for his extremely perceptive nature (which he was professionally impelled to deny) was the cause of the ache he felt in Kebec. It was not so much that he pined selfishly for Wendaké (although that was how matters appeared to him). No, that was not it at all. I am sure that all of us have at one time or another stood upon the earth in darkness, watching the approach of that ever revolving line called "the terminator," which divides day and night; so presently dawn comes and we can already see the rosy gold of sacredness upon the mountains to the east; yet when dawn reaches the spot where we stand, the glow lasts only a moment, and then we find our lonely night-yearning replaced by a familiarity pedestrian in every detail. So it was on this spot called Kebec, which a mere three and a half decades since had been a rocky wilderness of screeching Savages. Now it was reclaimed, and Père Brébeuf had little reason to fault the improvement. And yet . . .

The Canadians

What he'd come to comprehend was something better not understood: – that in the same proportion that the Savages were becoming more devout and frenchified, the French were becoming less so. In those days satanic tales were gossiped about, spreading up and down the Fleuve Saint-Laurent like an infection. At first he had thought merely that Canada was becoming peopled by French superstitions, such as the White Lady at Montmorency Falls, a specter who walked upon the water calling out the name of a dead soldier whom she loved. But this was not the worst folly. One of Governor Montmagny's guards had recently related to him (swearing upon the Cross that he had seen this with his own eyes) that the drowned corpse of that ancient Grey-Gown, Père Nicolas, had been seen at Sault-au-Récollet, a falls which had been named after him almost twenty years past. He lay curled with his elbow on his knees, and waterfalls spewed from his pale and soggy flesh, but these essences of dank lifelessness made no puddles or streams, but vanished into thin air. – Monsieur, I find this incredible, said Brébeuf. – Ah, Père, there is more. – And the man said that the fire beside this revenant, beside which he seemed to be essaying to dry himself, gave off no warmth. Some fur-traders who had discovered the scene had taken firebrands in their hands and were not burned. The man who told the tale had done so himself. Suddenly a black cat appeared, mewling and glaring at them. One of the voyageurs threw a brand down its throat, and it had vanished. It was the DEVIL, of course. The DEVIL was seen everywhere along the Fleuve Saint-Laurent. At Three Rivers they saw him in the dead of winter, setting up a mirror in the crotch of a tree. At Isle d'Orléans, introducing himself as one Captain Merveille, he seduced a young mademoiselle's confidence at a dance, and abducted her following the last quadrille.

Brébeuf had almost given up attempting to convince his parishioners of the folly of their superstitions. Eh – imagine a fire that didn't burn! He'd a thousand times rather have the autos-da-fé of the Hiroquois.

But even this was not the worst of it. After all, where Frenchmen settled one must expect French DEVILS. On the very Rivière Saint-Charles where the Black-Gowns had their convent, there was, a Frenchman said, a certain Tree of Dreams, beneath which an old Savage had lain down to rest after a strenuous chase, whereupon he had a vision of Our LADY herself opening the doors of Paradise. He died soon after, and surely entered the Kingdom, for he had been very pious. To the Tree there now came a Frenchman who trafficked in rum with the Savages. He slept there in mockery, and had a vision of the Serpent MANITOU, Whom the Savages had worshipped before knowing Our LADY . . . The smuggler agreed to adore MANITOU, as the soldiers said, and received gold, a bottomless flask of brandy, and the daughter of one of the Savage Captains, so that all his lusts might be gratified. Upon his deathbed (for he was stricken soon after with sickness), MANITOU chased away the priest who sought to confess him.

What a horror! How eerie it was, to comprehend that year by year his own countrymen were becoming Canadians . . .

Sweet Water

He made the Exercises, and ascended the Stream of Time as far as the Fourteenth Rapids (*viz.*, the Nailing to the Cross) where he found the cataract much higher than usual, so that despite many bloodied efforts he was unable to surmount it, and swam to the lefthand bank to search out what the obstacle was. – On a tree was Born Underwater's heart. It was a shelf-fungus, molded and stained and frozen so that it was banded in a dozen nested arcs, like a rainbow. – He stood there looking at it. In that place the forest floor was a thin covering of pine needles and dirt over boulders, which came to an abrupt end where he had swum ashore, dropping a distance equal to half his height, deep into raspberry shade and maple sapling shade in the coolness by the water's edge.

The Murders in the Fields

In that same year, the Wendat People lost a hundred warriors, who were defeated in the Country of the Iroquois. The Haudenosaunee grilled them slowly, politely, as always, and the torturers laughed with the tortured. And that spring another calamity had happened.

Barefoot, barebreasted, with wampum strings clicking against their skirts, the Huron women went into the fields, and they took their babies with them. They must grow more corn than ever, in order to make gifts of it, for iron things . . .

It was perfectly bright at dawn, but sky and lake were a single silvery mist, the sun nowhere, the trees brownish-green silhouettes like plants seen underwater. It was very chilly. A Mohawk stood smiling in tree-darkness. Warpaint rushed across his face. He waited with charged arquebus.

Not far from him crouched another Mohawk. And another. And a hundred more.

Fathers and Crows

In the winter of this year came three hundred fugitive Savages to Kebec, in the most pitiful terror of the Hiroquois. Monsieur the Governor de Montmagny showed his usual charity by giving them all the peas and flour that they required to sustain life until spring. They built themselves wigwams near the Convent of the Ursulines. Those who were advanced enough to profit by being instructed were invited by Mère Marie into the Chapel, so that it came about that many souls were saved. By this we can see once again how all calamities are contrived by GOD to redound to our benefit, if we but throw open our arms to Him.

Reasonable Men

1644

At no period did the flow of European goods into the Huron country keep pace with the demand for these items.

TRIGGER, *The Children of Aataentsic* (1976)

Just as every chalice has its paten to cover it, so Père Brébeuf kept a lid upon his own heart, seeing no reason why he ought to leave it gaping and open for all to peer into. Was it not enough that he was here, growing white in the service of these Savages who made war on birds and beasts? Yet they'd continually reproached him for what they considered to be private and reclusive habits – in the early years, at least, when he was still welcome enough to be reproached. Now he was entrenched in their hatreds – all the more, perhaps, since absent – like a black, black crow drinking the blood from the breasts of their dying children, over whom he hovered, making the loathsome motions of *baptism*. So they believed; and he knew full well that he encouraged their terror of his supposed sorceries by keeping himself aloof from them. So he was at Kebec. This year he would go back, but it seemed likely that for his own safety the Superior maintained him at Mission Sainte-Marie . . . But it had to be that way. He had to pray for them and make the Exercises . . . Then, too, their hearts were no more transparent than his. Consider Born Underwater, for instance. She was like one of her own Indian caskets inlaid with porcupine quills, beguiling him with the richest of colored lines, like stained glass stairs and sheaves, suns and eyes – but what was inside her? What was she thinking? There had been so many times when he had thought to lift the lid and present the treasure within to GOD; but that had never come to pass. From his Exercises he knew well Saint Ignatius's Vision of the Box with the Locks, opening which Ignatius had seen with transports how the heart of his earthly adored was now proven to be that of Our LADY, the VIERGE-MARIE. But that had happened only as a result of Ignatius's desperate need, his need and also assuredly his pain. But between Born Underwater and Echon there was nothing.

Of course he had not seen her for almost two years.

Power

In a dusk of patchy brown leaves, flowers, mossy logs, groping birch-arms, Born Underwater walked, calling up her Power to see-ahead. Power was above her like the golden halo of fuzz over a cornfield. Once again she'd put on the wampum collars that Amantacha had given her; she had painted her face red. In her hand, a birchbark bowl. Power grew inside her like a rising Fleuve. It flowed out her eyes like light, so that she could see all the Persons around her in the pale light of open birch-groves. Birchbark was shining in darkness like snow. Across the wide, shallow beaver-pond, so muddy and lily-crowned, stood the beaver house with its two gables. There were no beavers there anymore; the Wendat had killed them. A crescent moon shone weakly between the branches of a dead spruce. Mosquitoes rose from the tussock-islands of the pond and began to sing. They were Persons. Born Underwater listened to them for a long time. Then she set out across a meadow of yellow sedges, looking for the place of greatest Power. It was very mucky there. She came to a narrow outflow from the beaver pond. On the water were painted the silhouettes of upside-down spruces; they were from another world. She felt very sad.

She dipped the bowl into the water. She filled it, to see-ahead in it. Then she decided against that place. She poured the water out . . .

Here, a stream of darkness. Fill the bowl. Wait for MOON; wait for KLUSKAP; wait for AATAENTSIK.

In the bowl she saw an enemy warrior, hideously painted, with the ridge of hair bristling down his otherwise naked skull, and he scowled at her, puckering his ocher-striped cheeks.

Something rose tall above her like a grey tooth.

She was afraid. She could not comprehend it. (It was the spire of Tekakwitha's church.)

The Stream of Time

On the eighteenth day of Février, the Pope signed a bull or proclamation elevating Mission Sainte-Marie to a place of pilgrimage for all Christians, hearing which the Black-Gowns were much consoled and edified. Then it was spring, and the meadow around the palisades of Notre-Dame-des-Anges was in bloom. Père Le Jeune likened it to a vestiary woven by one of the Ursulines for the Nativity of the SAINTE-VIERGE, silver with gold thread; flowers like lobsters; a dazzling explosion of gold leaves and creepers like a field of virtue coming up glowering through the snow . . .

The experiment of settling Montagnais at Sillery continued to prosper splendidly. Many more were living there now that the moose and caribou continued to decrease, and some even had stone houses! They worked the ground with sickles and hoes not unlike twisted warclubs, and the birds alighted upon tree branches twittering in hopes of eating the young corn plants that rose like green scalps from the cracked and weedy brainpan of earth, and the Savage children shinnied up trees to get honey-dripping beehives even as their fathers, soberly and modestly clad, scraped away weed-tufts from the dirt, walking moccasin-silent, out of habit, but the children would not grow up with those same habits. The girls were locked in at night to protect their virtue; this had occasioned some complaints at first, but they were fast becoming resigned to it. Unfortunately, the war with the Hiroquois obliged the Hospitalière Sisters to quit their infirmary there, at which the Savages were much distressed and cried: But what shall we do now when we are ill? – To this the poor nuns had no good reply, for they had been ordered to depart much against their own will. They returned to Kebec, and were lodged in a small hut in what would soon be Lower Town. At night worms and toads moved across their bodies.

Père Bressani Among the Hiroquois

At the end of Avril, the Huron whom Père Brébeuf had baptized left Trois-Rivières for home, where they intended to preach. With them was a new Jesuit, Père Joseph Bressani. His Faith was like a blue flag flying between tree and Church. The Savages longed to turn back, but he compelled them to obey him, believing as he did that their delay was caused by some superstition.

Almost at once, the Mohawk found them. They screamed with joy; they thanked the SUN for having given them a Black-Gown to be tortured.

After all, he thought, gazing upon these Chinamen's pigtails, these stone-black eyes, surely such people must belong to one of the outlying provinces of Cathay, as our late Sieur de Champlain has written.

They made him march barefoot and starving, day after day, among snow and rocks. The other prisoners, the Huron, showed great fortitude, although they knew that they went but to torture and death; he must endeavor to be steadfast like them. Surely this was a mercy of GOD's, to diminish his Purgatory in corresponding degree for what he'd suffer . . . (Like DEKANWIDEH, he was a great dreamer.) River-ice had lapped up onto the bank and filmed dead leaves over. His soft bare feet broke through it at every step, and it cut him like broken glass. His feet bled, but soon they were so numbed that he could scarcely feel them. The dull numbness ascended to his ankles. He endeavored most sincerely not to stumble; that would provoke them. (They longed for him to provoke them.) The low sun brushed the brown grass. Each day was white above the mountains. The heads of the frozen grasses were bent and bowed like ducks' necks. As his captors led him south, the snow and sleet became a dismal rain. He glimpsed a slender old tree, dead and bark-stripped, with only a few knots to remind him of little round eyes; otherwise the impression was one of deadness . . . He stumbled, and they shouted and hit him in the face with their fists. He knew enough not to groan. (They themselves rarely stepped falsely, for which they gave thanks to the EARTH Our Mother Who supports our feet.) They dragged him across sullen rivers. They took him to the edge of *Lacus Irocoisiensis*, where Champlain had first attacked them, thirty-five years ago now; there they forced him to labor at building canoes with them from elm-bark, although he scarcely comprehended the subtleties of that art. Whenever he made a mistake, they shouted and knocked him to the ground. They beat him whenever they pleased. At last the canoes were finished, and they paddled for half a dozen days. When they achieved the Country of the Hiroquois with its four colors – brown, green, blue and white; all pale, sunbleached, diluted hues – the first village awaited him, and a thrill passed through him, for he knew what to expect. The People awaited him in their cornhusk summer slippers. They formed the double line. They stripped him naked and made him walk the gauntlet. A man with an iron knife slit open his hand between the little and the ring fingers. – Ah, forgive me, my nephew! the man said mockingly, buffeting him forward. With an iron needle, a young girl slashed proudly at his ear. The others beat him until the blood covered his body. They were very happy; it was the Raspberry Thanksgiving, when the EARTH brings forth her first fruits . . .

He was their guest a dozen days. The children burned him with brands. That was the proper way. At night the Captains called: Young men, come and caress your prisoner!

He had to sing while they burned him. He sang: *My death will be as a Savage's quiver with its quillworked stripes and diamonds.*

On the first evening they burned one of his fingernails off. On the next, the first joint of the finger. On the next, the second joint. In the end he had only one finger left.

At night they pegged him out to sleep in the rain. So in the morning, before they came for him (they were occupied in thanking the DAWN for leaving them alive), he learned the way that meadow-grass is so green after a rain as to be almost yellow.

They haled him into the next Nation, where he had to run the gauntlet again. They beat his testicles and made him eat excrement. They hanged him by his feet, in good Dutch chains. And they told him that they would burn him soon.

His hands were crawling with worms now. Four fell out of his finger in one day. His burns striped him like a squirrel.

An old woman adopted him, in place of her grandfather who had been slain by the Huron. She did not want him burned. She gave gifts of wampum, until the others granted him his life. Then they forgot him, for that same day one of their Sachems gave a splendid feast in honor of the SKY . . .

Later the Dutch ransomed him for fifteen gold doppias. After all, they were all white men together, even though it was true that they were on rival sides of the Indian trade.

When Dirck Cornelissz, who was the Onder-Commies of New Netherland, rose puffing from his letter-table to greet him, Père Bressani's first emotion was an urgent desire to burst into tears, such as children often do who have endured their punishment stoically, waiting only for the bruises to be anointed with forgiveness before they begin to whimper. Needless to say, he did not give way to this temptation. Nonetheless, Cornelissz might have smelled the salt water held in check, for he gave a great snort, as if of embarrassment, and his piglike eyes twinkled shrewdly. For the past eighteen years it had been one of his duties to scour the nearby river-islands every autumn, laying in ripe acorns for the hog-fleet of the absentee Patroon, Killiaen van Rensaellaer. It was Cornelissz's favorite task. He loved to stroke the udders of the fecund sows as they munched, to nip the ears of the little piglets smartly between his teeth, and the Savagesses whom he secretly frequented knew no better way to make him jolly than to squeal like swine at just the right moment. There was a fine of twenty-five guilders for unchastity, of course, which doubled if a heatheness became pregnant, and quadrupled if she gave birth, so that it behoved the Onder-Commies to be aware of various abortifacients – as indeed he was. He had never had any allegation proved against him. So he was a happy man – the more so because he belonged to a Nation intelligent enough to build a brewery and a cheese-factory in this wilderness, first thing. This was the maxim of the Patroon: *If we had cattle then we should have money, and if we had horses then we should have wheat* – never forgetting to send his Onder-Commies to investigate certain rock crystals over and over, for we all believe in Canadian diamonds. But Mynheer Cornelissz preferred the more reliable wealth of pigs, squaws, beer and cheese.

I must thank you for delivering me from the fire, said Bressani abruptly, offering his hand.

Ah, thank the ALMIGHTY, Father. – What gruesome stumps! – By the way, did you happen to notice whether the Maquaqs* have much venison this year? They trade with us, you know, for butter.

I am sorry, Mynheer – I cannot say –

That's all right. The Surgeon has looked at your hands, I take it?

Yes, I thank you.

It was nothing. I commend your recovery to GOD. But I guess you won't be celebrating your Masses anymore. Don't you Papists have some kind of rule about that? No mutilations? I think Father Jogues told me –

Père Jogues received a special dispensation from the Pope, returned Bressani shortly. We must thank you for your kindness to him.

Yes, it does begin to seem that every year or two we must be getting one of you priests out of hot water. (Or should I say hot pitch? Ha, ha, ha – oh, my!) And I understand that Jogues is back in New France again!

That is correct.

I trust he's learned enough not to come proselytizing among our Savages again. We make our own efforts, as you know.

Yes, Heer Cornelissz, I have seen the effects of your doctrines for myself.

So now you're accusing us of cannibalism! (The fat face had flushed a dullish red.) Did you know that there is a law against slander in this Country? Why, I could well demand that you indemnify the Patroon!

Do as you see fit, said Bressani listlessly.

Oh, come now, Father. We're both reasonable men. I only want to reach some kind of understanding.

* Mohawk.

Yes, yes, I appreciate that . . . said Bressani.

If we treat one another as friends, the benefit will come of itself. Yes?

I am not ungrateful –

We even prohibited the trade in firearms, at the insistence of your periwigs in New France! Not that it's stopped *entirely*, of course. But at least we have the statute on the books now. It's something to strive for, Father – some kind of celestial excellence. Know what I mean?

Your Mohawk now possess guns and ammunition sufficient for four hundred men, said Bressani curtly.

What will you have? They must be armed against the incursions of your Huron! We've lost thousands of guilders!

But we do not arm our Huron, Mynheer, I assure you.

Oh?

It is a policy of the Society of JESUS that only good Christian converts should receive arms. Monsieur the Gouverneur is in accord with our opinion.

Of course we do the same, laughed the Dutchman. If our Maquaqs have more guns, it must be because we have made more converts.

Ah, perhaps they have converted you, Mynheer, for it seems that you have learned well to mock like them . . .

And why not? *You* have armed the Algoumequins, which proves your hypocrisy!

It was the English who armed them, not we. Believe me, we have no reason to encourage rebels.

Yes, you French worry a great deal about your honor and authority. (Ah, you yourself are Italian? Forgive me.) Here it is simpler. Unlike you, as I said, we are reasonable men. *Let* the Mohawk insult us, even do violence occasionally! We can suffer it; we know how to turn the other cheek, like CHRIST –

Blasphemer!*

And I should warn you, said the Dutchman coolly, that we have advised our Iroquois to plunder and ruin the Huron. We want their beaver-skins. Can we be blamed for looking out for ourselves? We mean to ruin you, and we shall do it.

They sent him home to France, and he too returned to Canada at first opportunity.

* Lest you still consider me guilty of religious digressions, I must remind you that throughout this book I have refrained from considering that much-relished stew-delicacy of Canada, the nob at a hen's anus, which Catholics call the parson's nose and Protestants call the Pope's nose.

Echon

As for Père Brébeuf, it was time for him too to re-enter the field. He stood pale-fleshed within his Black Gown like the Fleuve Saint-Laurent on a brilliant spring morning when the Fleuve itself is a warm bluish-black, with only a single streak of ice-chunks in the middle. That ice, hidden from view, would never melt except in the fire, as he knew. – Once again he took off his broadbrimmed hat; he stripped off his shoes and clambered into a Huron canoe.

With him were twenty-two of Montmagny's soldiers. Pères Chabanel and Garneau accompanied him, too – new meat for the maw of Sacrifice.

He ascended the Fleuve Saint-Laurent beyond a flowering wall of green darkness. He saw again the pines a hundred pieds in height, the tremendous corpses of trees which had surely fallen before the Deluge . . . And he passed into the forest-heart once more. (There is a special place in the Stream of Time where salt water becomes fresh. We have passed that place. There is another place where water becomes fire. We have passed that place. What next? Only the Crown.) – Now here was the Sweetwater Sea, brownish-blue and hazy, with islands of yellow-green, and streaming lines of shade continually altering it.

Born Underwater

Her face had grown broader, as it seemed to him. Her beauty was quite gone. After all, she must be nearing forty years of age, which was old among these Savages. The corners of her mouth curled down, and there were lines around her eyes from squinting through smoke. She had greased her hair, and parted it in Huron fashion, in the long plaited braids down the back. She wore no wampum anymore, but rather a single string of glass beads. Her pupils were now black wells going deep inside her; he could scarcely see their end (or was it that twin liquid glint?), and that only for a moment, when she regarded him.

There was some half-hidden sacredness in her, like a deer brown and white-dappled behind a patchy wall of yellow trees.

. . . And for a moment he almost thought that he understood her, but his comprehension was buttercups whose gold was on the point of fading in the evening shadow of that blue spruce-forest of CANADA where he now lived.

Seeing her brought on a sort of blankness, as happened sometimes when he said his *Aves*.

He stared forward a little stiffly, his neck held interminably straight by the iron-stiff collar that enveloped him even to his beard; and his pupils were huge and sad. Tufts of white hair rose above his ears like wings. He was blinking very rapidly.

He said: And surely you are a good Christian woman now?

Echon, you are already old. Therefore it is not permitted to lie to you.

Ah, he said. So that is how it is. This year, perhaps –

Yes, Echon.

Sacraments
1645

> The greatest opposition that we meet consists in the fact that their remedies for diseases; their greatest amusements when in good health; their fishing, their hunting, and their trading; the success of their crops, of their wars, and of their Councils, almost all abound in diabolical ceremonies. To be a Christian one must deprive himself not only of pastimes, and of the dearest pleasures of life, but even of the most necessary things.
>
> JÉRÔME LALEMANT, *Jesuit Relation* (1645)

In this year Père Brébeuf felt himself ready to swear his Third and final Vow, the Vow of Perfection. He made the Exercises, ascending flawlessly from the mouth of the Stream of Time as far as the Thirty-Sixth Rapids – *viz.*, the Vocation of the Apostles; but there he found the algæ-slimed boulders insurmountable, and was tumbled into an eddy by a frothy wave, so that he grieved round and round in his whirls through one of the stream's deepest pools. There he was caught in the net of trembling golden light whose form was a honeycomb. His sins were as heavy as flat-irons in his breast. They dragged him down, down under the water. But what were they? He made the Examination of Conscience to determine where the failure lay, praying while he did so for enlightenment. Someday he would find what he craved –

There were fifteen Pères in the Country of the Huron now, including two at Mission Sainte-Marie. Iron bells tolled in chapels throughout the land. One hundred and sixty-four souls were saved . . . The Huron Captains strode from longhouse to longhouse, crying out: Take pity on our half-ruined Nations, you People! Our customs are being abandoned! – and they called them to play *Yaheskara*, the Dish Game of fruit-stones, on which men sometimes wagered even their hair and fingers; but the Huron Christians jeered at them and threatened them with the flames of Hell, as Echon and his crew so often did. When the warriors of Saint-Ignace brought a captive in to be burned, one of the Christians baptized him first, even though the pagans struck and beat him for his charity. – Hearing of this, the Black-Gowns said: My son, your action was commendable! – but he only bowed his head and smote himself in the fashion of the Black-Gowns, crying: GOD performed this baptism, not I; I am only an earthworm . . .

In this year Père Lalemant was succeeded as Superior of the Huron Mission by Père Paul Ragueneau, another student of Père Massé's. This year also Brother Dominicus, the tailor, departed Sainte-Marie to return to France. Brother Ambroise the cook arrived to take his place.

As for the Savages, well, it was as always with them. That spring the Hiroquois crossed the frontier near Contarea and carried off many Huronnes, both women and fillettes. The plupart they tortured and burned, but some they adopted, to take the place of girls from their Nation who had died. – The skirmishes and treachery went on through all the dark forests of summer. At Saint-Joseph an Irocois scaled one of the watchtowers and scalped a sentry in his sleep. There was another sentry left alive on that tower; before he could shout, the warrior hurled him to his death. The other Iroquois had cut the skin from his skull by the time their companion had shinnied back down to the ground. In revenge, three Huron went by stealth to Sonnontuoan, which is the principal town of the Seneca Nation, and crept into one of their longhouses as the enemy slept. And they remembered all the injuries that the Sonontrerrhonons had ever done them as they lurked there; the Sonontrerrhonons had sawed off Amantacha's finger . . . Then they each split a head – whether man's, woman's or child's they had no care. They sliced off the scalps of their victims and set fire to the longhouse, running so happily away from the screams –

Two Streams of Blood

But Governor de Montmagny, called by the Savages Onontio, had now become happy and stout. In his belief the French in Canada were more secure than in previous years, he having concluded an agreement with the Hiroquois

– although of its two secret codicils, it is true, there is one to which he would not have agreed if refusal had been prudent; for Montmagny was by no means a treacherous or dishonorable man. Soon enough, of course, he'd reconciled himself to everything: isn't resignation the essence of piety?

It had come about in this wise: In the month of Avril of the previous year, half a dozen Algonkin set out to hunt the Hiroquois. They were all Christians; they loved the Blood of the LAMB. Falling boldly on the enemy, they killed nine before any could recover from the surprise. Two escaped into the forest. Three yet remained for the Algonkin to glut themselves on. The first they wounded almost unto death; he leaped into the river and drowned. Now the two Hiroquois who were left despaired of their lives, and fought with bitter fury. But an Algonkin said to them: Brothers, can you not see how easily we could take your lives? Surrender, and we'll treat you with consideration. – For he'd now gotten the notion of preserving him and his companion, like two live trout in a vessel filled with water; the French sometimes did this to keep them fresh. – With them he might hope even to establish peace with the Hiroquois, for which he'd be highly regarded both by his own peers and also by the Iron People. So the warriors bound them stoutly and bore them down the Fleuve Saint-Laurent in their canoes. So loving and considerate were they, as Marie de l'Incarnation remarks with astonishment, that they did not even torture them on the way! And so they brought their captives to Three Rivers.

The Commandant there, Châteaufort, was the very same who had been acting Governor of New France upon Champlain's death almost ten years before. He'd now become even more pious. – Oh, you Savages, what a worthy dream! he cried. Certainly these prisoners must go back to their kindred. And I'll also release two captives from my dungeons to underline our sincerity. – Come; dine with me; I'll give you iron!

In the following year, the Mohawk replied with an embassy of their own. On the fifth day of Juillet, 1645, the orator Kioutseaton (that is, *The Hook*) arrived at Three Rivers. He was a great Captain; he came glittering with wampum strings. With him were two of his countrymen, and they had also a French captive of theirs, by name Guillaume Couture, whom they'd made prisoner when they seized the party of Père Jogues. Jogues himself was present, and embraced his companion very gladly. Now Monsieur the Commandant welcomed the embassy with many flowery words; JESUS had told him that the wars of Canada were over at last! Governor Montmagny came himself and made his address to the Savages, so important did he conceive this meeting to be. And all were pleased to behold him, crying: *ho, ho!*

Onontio, lend me ear, said the Hook. I am the mouth for the whole of my Country. You listen to all the Hiroquois, in hearing my words. There is no evil in my heart. I have only good songs in my mouth.

Hearing this, Montmagny was moved (once or twice that had happened to him), and he almost believed that the Hiroquois had become simple children at last. Swiss mercenaries stood behind him, sporting arquebuses of the latest make. They traveled with him so much that he was barely conscious of them anymore; they but maintained his self-satisfaction at the basal level, like old concubines, old dogs to be kicked at pleasure, old idols to be adored. The Hook's warriors glared greedily at their guns. This pleased Montmagny. His pleasure increased when the Hook presented him with seventeen presents, each of which marked a word-root of that great Tree of Peace which these Hiroquois now sought to erect upon the territory of the Iron People, and Montmagny replied with fourteen gifts of a similar property, so that custom was satisfied. It is written that Huron, Algonkin and Montagnais deputies were present, but (strange to say) the men of greatest prestige and ability from those Nations were absent. Nonetheless, the aim of this meeting was achieved, as peace was made between the Hiroquois and the French, with the understanding that neither party was to molest the Nations allied to the other.

It is done, said the Hook. We are brothers! The conclusion has been reached; now we are all relatives – Hiroquois, Huron, Algoumequins and French; we are now but one and the same People. And you Huron, do not be ashamed like women, but come to our Country to visit us! (And he laughed.)

And one of the Algoumequins said: I can no longer speak. My heart is too full of joy. I have large ears, and so many good words crowd in there that they drown me in pleasure.

What a glorious resolution! the Governor exclaimed.

Now the Hook drew close to the Governor and spoke in his ear, saying that he desired speech with him in private. This favor Montmagny readily granted, being willing to oblige all such requests of Savages which cost the French nothing. So he ushered him into his private chapel, thinking to himself: Who knows? Perhaps he even wishes to make Confession.

Onontio my brother, we earnestly desire the friendship of the Iron People. – Such were the words of the Hook. Montmagny sat in silence, watching the wide red-brown face widening still more in a smile of this very friendship, as the Hook placed his hand upon his breast, and Montmagny sat musing upon that shiny Savage forehead, behind which so many secrets must be crawling like worms – how pleasant it was not to speak these Hiroquois dialects, for otherwise he would not have been able to reflect and consider his danger as he awaited delivery of the next packet of the interpreter's words! Of course the Hook had gained the same advantage. When Montmagny replied to the interpreter (that same Guillaume Couture who'd been their captive), then the Hook searched *his* face for counterpart secrets. Even now, as the Hook spoke, his eye was fixed full upon him, drilling into him with slow insolence until Montmagny could brook no more, so he drew himself up and frowned over the Hook's shoulder, in order to confuse and disarrange his thoughts. At once the Hook ceased his harangue. His head whirled backwards, and he whirled himself around, casting his vision right and left for danger so that the wampum rattled at his ear and his scalp-lock twitched, glistening sickly; then slowly he composed himself and turned back to face the Governor again, biting his lip with rage, and the Couture said: Seigneur, I pray you, you must not play with him like that! – At least he is afraid of me, thought Montmagny. Aloud he said: Tell him I was but stretching my neck. Tell him – tell him that we thank him for his friendship, and give thanks to our GOD that it has now been concluded.

At this, the Hook was mollified, and continued in his embassy. – Yes, Onontio, he continued, we are bound inseparably with the white wampum of peace. Nothing could sever us now. If your DEVIL were to throw us into the fire, we would pull you with us, such is the strength of this bond. We are content; we sing songs of rejoicing. Indeed, we love you Iron People so greatly that we desire only to lash the cord of friendship more tightly about our arms. How can we do this, Onontio? Until now, when your words in Council dispersed the clouds, our warriors and yours killed one another in ambushes every summer, and so the Fleuve Saint-Laurent was a road of menace for all who traveled it. Our hearts and yours yet weep tears of blood together for those who have died. Onontio, I pray that these twin red streams may be united in one pool. Then we will be brothers indeed. But as yet this may not be, for two great ridges separate these river-courses.

Montmagny waited.

First of all, said the Hook, we Mohawk and the other four Nations of the Haudenosaunee desire to exchange furs for iron goods with you. You grant this mark of friendship to the Huron Nation, but not to us. Therefore we are displeased. This ridge of boulders rises high, but a word from you can smooth it away. Secondly, we have suffered many injustices from the Algonkin, who always scheme against our Nation and seek our ruin. Therefore, my brother, we request you not to interfere in our wars with this enemy. You may trade with them and treat with them as you like. All we ask is that you permit us to do with them as we please. Grant this to us, Onontio, and our blood will flow together at last. – I have spoken.

At this proposal the Governor was extremely aghast, as if a harlot had sought to coax from him his snow-white virginity. – Now I see, Kioutseaton, that you are a Savage indeed! he cried. How can you ask us to abandon our allies to be roasted by your fiends of cruelty, particularly when we have just made a compact all of us together? Oh, you treacherous Hiroquois!

The Hook arose. – Onontio, I had expected better things, he said. I shall wait upon better words.

Then he strode away.

Truth to tell, Kioutseaton was chagrined with this repulse, which indeed he'd scarcely expected, for it seemed to him that the Iron People esteemed the Algonkin Nation as being of little worth. Didn't they ridicule their Sorcerers and legends, seeking always to make them believe in JESUS? So he began to grow angered with Onontio and thought himself poorly used. – Surely Onontio seeks to devour us, he said to himself. Perhaps I shall recommend to my Nation that we hang up the kettle and take up the hatchet again. Perhaps we shall pick up our War-Songs from the ground where we lately cast them. For Onontio is friends with our enemies. Therefore he must be our enemy also. We shall clear the Fleuve of these treacherous Iron People! – With these thoughts, he returned to the Council saying but little, but brown shadows flowed across the reddish face, and twin black eyeballs rolled like rocks in a cataract. The Governor, studying him, quickly saw that matters stood at a dangerous pass. He himself had prayed much, and reflected upon the importance of the Algonkin to the French. Therefore he directed Guillaume Couture, who knew him well, to summon him to another secret meeting.

You have asked me here, my brother, said the Hook curtly. He did not sit down. – Had you not asked me, I would not have come.

I have thought well upon your proposals, Kioutseaton, and wish to make some effort to roll away those ridges of boulders which you mentioned to me. Of course this is too great a labor to be undertaken by the French alone. I am sure that a Captain as honored as you will have no difficulty in putting your Hiroquois to work on this as well. As far as the beaver trade is concerned, that is easy. Bring us beaver-skins of good quality, and we will give you iron things. That leaves only the matter of the Algonkin People. Many of these people have adopted our ways and become Christians. We cannot abandon them to be killed, for that would be a sin. However, I give you my secret leave to fall upon the others and attack them. Perhaps that will encourage them to become Christians, in order to save their lives. – Kioutseaton, I have spoken. Are you content?

Yes, my brother, grinned the Hook. Now I am content indeed. Now our streams of blood can flow together.

Repercussions 1646

The Black-Gowns did not learn what had happened, it is said, until the eighth day of the following year, when on a snowy morning in Janvier a Huron named Tandihetsi arrived at Three Rivers. Some Mohawk warriors had whispered to him the secret of their country: namely, that they were preparing to exterminate the Algonkin, into whose Country three hundred Hiroquois were to come by the middle of Février. Père Lalemant and Père de Quen were very surprised by this news, and hastened to tell the Governor, who replied: Yes, I already knew it. I agreed to it. But I have consulted on this matter with Père Vimont and Père Le Jeune, and they believe that any difficulties can be smoothed over.

Now the Mohawk, hearing that their secret had come to light, proclaimed Tandihetsi's words to be false, at least in the main. In any event the Algonkin had been alarmed, and watched their borders vigilantly, so that the attack never came. Instead, the Hiroquois bided their chance to fall once again upon the French.

Sacraments

As always, he made the *Exercitia Spiritualia* of Saint Ignatius, this time lingering especially at the Sixtieth Rapid, which was the First Apparition of Our LORD JESUS CHRIST. It was winter. At length he achieved that cataract, along whose cliffy bank hung icicles white, blue and chalky-brown (these last the same hue as the Fleuve Saint-Laurent in spring) like frozen moustaches, barrels, organ-pipes, pears, immense church tapers; and the waters dark brown and chalky-brown pounded down icy rocks – a drop of some forty to fifty pieds – and sped past thick ice-crusts, creaking trees, trees wind-bent into the water and caught fast there by the weight of the lily-pads of ice which had grown in their crowns. The spruces in the hills were as snowy as clouds. The icy birches were smeared with white like pigeon dung.

Until it was night, Père Brébeuf clung to an ice-covered rock, shivering. The water numbed him. Splinters of ice whirled down and cut his shoulders.

Then suddenly he had the realization that this snowy darkness was somehow his, that his life and death here in Canada might be in the nature of things, that he could become a part of these white and black ridges . . .

The Baptism of the Hiroquois Prisoner

A Sonontrerrhonon was about to be burned. Already resounded in his ears the grésillement or crackling of the fire. For him, only for him the Black-Gowns displayed the pale SUN-face (IOUSKEHA's face) of agony and grief and love, ivory-carven, its rays the elongated arms nailed to the Cross-bar in perpetual exaltation. The man stared, speechless with incomprehension.

Don't you understand? Père Brébeuf shouted. Don't you understand even yet? When you become a Christian, you have to give up everything else! Everything!

For a long time no one said anything.

We understand, Echon, a young squaw said at last. (She was a fine Christian . . .)

But the condemned man only stared ahead as before.

A Box of Pestilence

1646

Warfare strengthened community solidarity by focusing aggression on an outside party, mainly through the ritualistic torture of male prisoners.

BRIAN YOUNG and JOHN A. DICKINSON, *A Short History of Quebec: A Socio-Economic Perspective* (1988)

In this year the Black-Gowns opened their fourth Mission in Acadia (*viz.*, the Country of the Souriquois). The Capuchin friars were also present there; they maintained a school at Port-Royal where French and Souriquois children were instructed together, in a union of faith and love. (But Père Massé, who had labored in vain among those Savages at Port-Royal, who had prayed over Born Underwater and her mother, now laid down his whip of self-mortification and died in Mai of this year, in the seventy-second year of his age. He died even while praying to GOD, as Mère Marie of the Incarnation was told. In truth his last words were these: *The silver rivers are warm to the touch.* And his colleagues praised him, writing in his epitaph the *Jesuit Relations* that *he esteemed himself less than a dog.*) In France died Champlain's old patron, the Prince of Condé. At Kebec and Three Rivers and Tadoussac the Black-Gowns continued to reduce the Montagnais to rules. In Wendaké, the Black-Gowns built Mission Sainte-Marie ever larger so that the Wendat marveled to see so many roofs and Crosses and chimneys visible over the sharpened points of the palisade; and the Hiroquois watched from the yellow trees behind, falling on women or warriors when they could and splitting their heads, at which the Black-Gowns would cry their alarms in the dark barracks of the soldiers, whose tightly set wooden posts and square windows of light wearied vigilance so that the Hiroquois always got away; and the soldiers traveled into the forest in tight bands to fell trees for winter fires.

In that year Père Brébeuf pressed Born Underwater to make the leap, as they lived in perilous times now, and he did not wish her span to run out before she received baptism. – I will come to Church then, she said unsmiling, and indeed she began to do this regularly, but he felt that something yet lay unmelted within her.

In that year also, Brother Pierre arrived at Sainte-Marie, along with the first consignment of calves. He was a replacement for Brother Dominicus the tailor; in addition he was a gardener. He stroked the bear-skins, moose-skins and beaver-skins hanging on the walls. He watched the other brothers plucking fresh-killed trumpeter swans and black ducks. – Is this a good place? he asked the others.

Oh, brother, we are all very pious here, one said to him, and thanks to the Hiroquois we daily expect the Crown.

At this, Brother Pierre went into the dim bastion, whose mortar-mottled stone benches ran all the way around the room except the doorway; and on these the soldiers were sitting quietly.

And you, he said, do you also desire the Crown?

The soldiers smiled. – No, Monsieur, said one. We will defend ourselves against the Hiroquois.

And yet the incursions of the Yroquois had suddenly ended. At Three Rivers, as I've told, Kioutseaton, *viz.*, the Hook, had brought the peace with him from within the intricacies of his wampum-strings. (Peace was indeed a delicacy as tasty to the French as the gristly fat of a beaver-tail, which they agreed was very good either boiled or fried.) Monsieur the Governor, therefore, received presents at the hands of the Hiroquois Ambassadors and bestowed as many of his own, in token that he'd henceforth love the Hiroquois and protect them as his own children (at which they bowed their heads, but smiled insolently). The fires and kettles of the Iron People would always be ready to feed them. – As proof of these things, as a mark of my special affection for you, said he, I am sending one of my great men, whom you call Black-Gowns, to your Nation to confirm the peace. Listen well to him, and benefit from his instruction. You know him well; he bears the mark of your hospitality on his hands. – (At this there was a silence.) – His name is Père Jogues. I love him as much as my own père, you Hiroquois; so give him good welcome.

We are very content, Onontio, replied the Hiroquois. We thank you for sending the Black-Gown to us. Believe us when we say that we will requite him well.

The Mission to the Hiroquois 1646

We see Jogues' face as palely luminous, with his eyes half closed; blood trickles down his forehead, down the back of his praying hands. He seems to be smiling. His beard and hair are curly, like sheep's wool. His gown is very black.

It was a hot summer evening, and that still brown river, double-algæ-walled, curved in among the trees.

Now the river was walled on either side with ferns and vines and dense shrubs all in blossom, leafing prickly and waxy-smooth, cool and wet and impenetrable.

Jogues Among the Irocois

The Savages often swam in greenish-brown lakes of water so still and impressionable that the presence of a single Savage girl so far out in the middle of it that Père Jogues could barely see the jet black crown of her head would make it shimmer with fine ripples, and when she swam to him the ripples widened in a cone behind her and cut the water with great fingernails of white light. She was Thérèse Oionhaton – Chihwatenah's niece, Marie de l'Incarnation's pet – Jogues' pet, too; it had made his heart bleed that day four years since when she'd been captured at his side; she'd only been eleven or twelve then . . . Still alive, still alive! – We've ransomed you, my child, have no fear (thus the priest). And she: Dear Père, I've never wavered in the Faith; I pray to God every day . . . Ah! We must be silent now, for the others are coming.* – Savages sat on a shelf of rock and looked down the black-and-green-marbled lip of it under the water, and when trout swam by they grabbed them with their hands. Sometimes the darkness of the water was painted on by darker clouds, and the reflections of trees like top-heavy forests weighed down the far shore. The Savages leaped into the water and let it take them and nourish them with its coolness, and they floated in it looking down into its depths very seriously as if they were holding converse with demons (while Père Jogues looked up at the sky that was like a great silver lake of haze among the trees), and presently the Savages returned with crayfish or mussels or eels, and other Savages went fishing in their canoes, and wide black branches hung out over the water. At last sunset came, and the sky was pale orange, and the hills were a purple mass bristling with trees. The clouds were like lavender puzzle-pieces floating on milk.

Père Jogues preached and preached to the Savages, in the hope that a few at least might become good Christians.

Why should we obey you? they said to him insolently, crowding him and breathing in his face. He looked into their eyes, and it was like looking into so many liquid black fires.

You should never obey *me*, he said, but the CHRIST that speaks through me.

But is this CHRIST in you all the time? they questioned him cunningly. Maybe bad SPIRITS speak through you sometimes also!

No, said Père Jogues, He is not in me all the time. I could never be as

* She was never allowed to come back. The *Jesuit Relations* say that some ten years after her capture she was married among the Onondaga.

good as He. Neither could any of you. But I stand in for Him, in His place. When one of your Great Ones dies, you call the Younger Brothers and the Older Brothers together, and the women confirm the choice of the new Great One, and he gives up his name and takes the name of the dead Great One, which was not his name, either, but the name of one of the first Great Ones who accepted the Great Peace. Now I am telling you of a Greater Peace. I have given up my name to do this. I have given up my native land, and my right to marriage and goods. I am a Black-Gown; I am nothing but the herald of CHRIST.

The Savages laughed.

Children, I mean nothing but your good, he said to them, but at this they only laughed harder. As Père Biard had written so long ago: *For they have learned from us . . . that nothing is readily given away.*

The Martyrdom

They struck him.

He looked into their faces. That is all I desire, he said, to be corrected for my faults in the hope that the correction extends to you as well. But do you correct me with love in your hearts?

They struck him again and again. Blood burst out of his nose. A warrior cut thin pieces of flesh from his arms and his back, sneering: Let us see if this white flesh is the flesh of an OKI.

I am a man like yourselves, but I do not fear death or torture, he said. I do not know why you would kill me. I come here to confirm the peace and show you the way to Heaven, and you treat me like a dog!

We would kill you for your box of pestilences! they shouted. We have sick people in our town, and the caterpillars are eating our corn! You have done it, you Black-Gown!

I am no Sorcerer, he began, but they shouted him down, saying: You shall die tomorrow!

That is of little account to me, said Père Jogues quietly, and for a moment they were amazed. Then they regained their courage – any brave captive said much the same thing, they told each other – and described to him how they'd kill him and his companion, Frère Jean, how afterwards they'd decapitate them both and affix their heads on the palisade to strike terror in any other Black-Gowns who might dare to come, but Père Jogues only smiled.

At dusk they summoned him to a feast of the Bear Clan. He knew that only the Wolf Clan and the Tortoise Clan stood in favor of his life. He looked deeply into the Savage's eye and got to his feet. The Savage led him to the Bear Chief's lodge, and then stood aside. He knew then what would happen, but shrugged wearily. As he bent his head to enter the doorway, a Savage who stood waiting in the darkness sank a hatchet into his skull.

The Father's Head

It was the month of Octobre. Upstream, the river sparkled blue and very white among the birches. There were islets carpeted with bright yellow leaves. Sharp-cornered rocks, a little softened by moss, protruded from the flesh of the hillsides. The river was white with little rapids. From the highest stake of the palisade, Père Jogues' head gazed down at this scene. On the stake adjoining, Frère Jean's head also looked outward (they had killed him on the following day). The blood was dry on their faces, and a chilly breeze blew the flies away. They could see the river braiding and meeting itself again and running white and rapid over the stones, and it glittered and twinkled through the snowdrifts and trees. The birch-trees were white like the snow.

Père Jogues' head remained with the Irocois all winter. Ten years later Tekakwitha was born in that town, and when she was small her uncle (little knowing how his susceptibilities here kissed Captain Merveille's) often told her how pleasing the head had looked with its headdress of snow, gazing mildly upon the whitish shining of the frozen river; how faithfully the head had guarded the Mohawks from other Black-Gowns and Sorcerers (for the day they struck him down the sick began to recover, and the caterpillars left the corn); but in the spring thaw Père Jogues' head began to smile on its pole, as if it were blessing them, and that was something that none of the Mohawks could abide. Then they threw it into the river, and Frère Jean's head also. The river carried them down to GOUGOU . . .

At the Gates of the Kingdom
1647

First Point. CHRIST Our LORD took with Him his beloved disciples Peter, James and John. And He was transfigured before them, and His face shone as the sun, and His garments became white as snow.

SAINT IGNATIUS, *Spiritual Exercises*
(Matthew 7.1–9)

In Kebec also it was spring, and the ice-floes were moving really rather rapidly down the Fleuve Saint-Laurent in a great herd accompanied by undisciplined strays, down below past the snowy wilderness of roofs whose tall narrow square chimneys sought to challenge the walnut trees; there were so many steep green roofs. Down the river like a scalp came the shocking news of the murder of Père Jogues. At this the French cried out and prayed, and the Christian Savages knelt with them and did likewise. As for Père Brébeuf, when the news came to Wendaké he wept with happiness for the other man, that he had won the Crown. And yet his dreams that night were not good. – How will *I* die? he wondered. – It was what he longed for, of course, but could the quivering flesh be quelled against that last and supreme mortification? It was in the hands of GOD. He had heard it said of Ignatius that whenever another Père would express his intention of doing something *tomorrow*, or *in three months' time*, the Saint would exclaim in astonishment: What! You are certain of living so long? – Père Jogues had lived and died in that spirit; he'd been a true Black-Gown . . . Then for a moment he recalled Père Jogues' allegations, and he wondered once again whether his feeling for Born Underwater partook of anything unholy which might render him less worthy for the Crown than Père Jogues? But no and no! – Mère Marie de l'Incarnation was similarly affected by the news, and wrote to her son Claude a farewell letter (like all her letters), begging him to pardon her for having left him as a child (for even now his reproaches were incessant). She admitted that she'd considered herself an eternity of times as the cruelest of mothers, but begged him to remember that life was short, so that soon she would be reunited with him forever to rejoice in the glory of GOD. (As a matter of fact, she had another quarter-century left to live.) – So tongues wagged, until there came fresher news – for that very spring the Hiroquois denuded two houses at Trois-Rivières of their furnishings while the owners were at Mass.

In that year wise Montmagny completed the construction of the Château Saint-Louis, a long narrow building, steep-roofed, with windows deep as skull-sockets. In Wendaké the priests began to fortify Mission Sainte-Marie with a stone redoubt –

It was the new Superior there, Père Ragueneau, who had conceived this prudent idea. Turning over the Spiritual Exercises in his mind, he recalled the Fourteenth Rule for the Discernment of Spirits: *The ENEMY's behavior is also like that of a Captain who wishes to conquer and plunder whatever he desires. Just as the Commander of any army pitches his camp, studies the strength and defenses of a fortress, and then attacks it on its weakest side, in like manner the ENEMY of our human nature studies from all sides our theological, cardinal and moral virtues. Wherever he finds us weakest and most in need for our eternal salvation, there He attacks and tries to take us.* He said to himself: When Ignatius wrote this rule, he had no knowledge of the enemy called Hiroquois. And yet they are servants of the EVIL ONE; and ever do they seek to study out our weaknesses. Let this redoubt then serve to protect us like virtue! And let me now walk round and round it, gazing upon it with the ENEMY's eye to find the spot most easily breached; that place my artisans will reinforce according to my commands.

He and all his Black-Gowns were in an exalted state of mind that year. The consummation of their purpose was now in sight. There were now a thousand Christians in Wendaké. Nor were these the fair-weather faithful of the early years; they genuinely comprehended that they must abandon their Savageries. The Jesuit wedge had been driven deep into the People's flesh, so that the bloody gash between those who still believed in the Dream-Feasts and those who believed in IESVS was as evident as the archways at Kebec that now divide Upper and Lower Town. Day by day, the good Pères drove it deeper and deeper, weeping at the sanguine spatters that marked their kindhearted cruelties. Their mood might best be compared to Ignatius's in his early days, when he saw the way easy and sure to pluck another Doña of the Court, and his heart was pounding and he knew that something irrevocable would happen –

In Teanaostoiaiaé Town the Christians held great processions to adore their Cross, and they did so at the times best calculated to disturb and annoy the pagans, for there could be no peace between factions anymore. Throughout the Country, marriages broke up over this magic spell called *baptism*. During the Dance of the Naked Ones, the Christians shouted wildly enough to be heard all the way to the grassy sandy shores of the Sweetwater Sea. At Echon's urging they tortured the new-dead, the turtle-dove souls, by showing their fishing nets before them; the Old Men had always said that this was evil. Echon laughed . . . For their part, the Captains who still believed in dreams called upon young girls to seduce the Christians back; but it did no good; the Christians were madmen and Sorcerers, rolling in the snow to curb their sexual desires, fleeing from women, rebuking their own uncles for lewdness! The Christian girls pretended always to be melancholy in public, so that no men would approach them. Those who had once worn as much as a dozen livres' weight of wampum now went unadorned and dirty, seeking only to lick the ashes from CHRIST's burned heart. And each side called upon the other to remove from Wendaké. The Christians were particularly blamed for assisting the Hiroquois with their sorceries, but some of the dream-believers had themselves begun to long for an Iroquois victory, for only in this way, as they thought, could they be free to keep their rituals; otherwise the Iron People would crush everything . . . – The Iroquois did not condemn all their prisoners anymore (said the Old Men). That eased their hearts as village after village fell to the Iroquois. True, there was no knowing (except by dreams, which are sometimes false) which of them the enemy would keep alive. Often they roasted a mother's children, so that she could work in their cornfields more effectively. Or they killed her – who knew why? – But to those who loved dreams, the Yroquois now seemed their only hope. And when the Irocois heard of this through their spies, they laughed.*

The People of Dreams said: Open your eyes! The Black-Gowns are warriors for IESVS. When you die and go to Heaven, if the Black-Gowns have captured you with baptism, the IESVS will be waiting to burn you. Heaven is very near the SUN, they say. We too burn prisoners for the SUN –

* This phenomenon was known also to the Nazis, who joked that once the exterminations were completed a single carload of Jews would be brought into Berlin, as a sort of curiosity. – And every Jew [cried a concentration camp commandant] secretly believes that he will be in that car!

The Christians shouted: You lie! Say nothing more, you wretches, for we stop up our ears.

And the Seneca destroyed a great town of the Neutrals, to punish that neutrality for which they stood –

Now it was the time for the women to set out to gather wood from the forest. Yet this time they were very reluctant, for fear of the Hiroquois. They had the bad dream of the Hiroquois, the nightmares of burning and screaming. When they'd started back with their bundles, the Hiroquois fell upon them. The lucky ones ran home shrieking.

At every alarm, the People rushed to Mission Sainte-Marie in terror. Built with iron, it alone could withstand the weapons of the Iron People.

But at the beginning of that summer they concluded peace with the Onondaga. The Susquehannock also agreed to be their kin-friends, for they feared the Five Nations of the Haudenosaunee. The Cayuga and the Oneida were willing to consider a peace. It was only the Mohawk and the Seneca who longed for war. – That was sufficient, of course. At Trois-Rivières the beaver-clerks waited, and the sky was variously grey like the inscription on the lead plate which we found in Kebec, in the foundations of the Moulin des Pauvres in Saint-Augustin. But the Wendat did not come. They feared the Iroquois too much, men said.

It was a fact well known to the French that all the Hiroquois on the lower Fleuve Saint-Laurent carried arquebuses now.

This year the Mohawk captured in one swoop more than a hundred Algoumequins, whom they put to the death by torture, and later on forty more, who met the same fate.

It was another overcast August in the Nations of the Haudenosaunee, the leaf-walls glowing yellow-green, as thick as feathers in a flock of birds. The great men of the Seneca and the Mohawk met together and exchanged presents. And they agreed together to exterminate their enemies the Wendat, the Crooked-Tongues. No longer would they stand outside their villages and shout at them to come out and fight. Now they would burn those villages, one by one Nation, until all that Country was empty. They would strip the Crooked-Tongues living and dead of furs; they would snatch away all their iron things. The Onondaga spoke against it, it was true, and the Oneida and Cayuga also. But they'd be bound to join them soon, when they comprehended how rich the booty was.

Père Brébeuf and Père Daniel

Now the dead Pères who had been in Canada with him seemed sometimes to cast shadows as heavily or even more so than the Pères who still lived. He felt that these brothers of his came to him to give him encouragement. And Père Daniel, who'd been first with him to Wendaké – thirteen years ago now – seemed to feel much the same, for he often sought out Brébeuf that summer, when it was the time for all the priests to make their Exercises, and said some word on Père Jogues or poor Père Davost, who'd suffered more than almost any, due to his irritable disposition, but who'd died of nothing but sickness in the end. On a night as dark as the head of a tomahawk, Père Massé came into his mind, and he smiled and said:

Do you remember how Ennemond used to cut his cord of wood faster than the hired men? And how he used to bathe in the Fleuve Saint-Laurent for his health in the summer days, no matter how fierce the mosquitoes were? And do you remember how he carried that dying Savage more than a league on his shoulders, just because the fellow asked to breathe his last in sight of a church?

I remember it all, said Père Brébeuf. Memories fill my Store-house. You have no need to tell it.

There was nothing weak about him, was there?

He gave everything. I agree.

Yet as soon as Père Daniel had commenced these reminiscences, the dead ones flew lightly from Père Brébeuf's mind, and he found himself remembering France. Why was this? He did not know. – He remembered the Mesdamoiselles whose fans had more folds than their dresses; the servant-maids in their short blouses and long underskirts; the peasants in their cloaks . . . Was all that still the fashion? There must be new costumes in Paris now, as he supposed. After all, he'd not seen his own Nation in more than a decade. He sat remembering the coaches, the Palaces, the comfortable seminaries (although they had scarcely seemed comfortable at the time), and he sighed. Due to his facility with the Exercises he could have visualized an entire city with its Rues and Avenues, down to the very cobblestones, had he chosen, but that would have been an abuse of his gift. He would not. Slowly he put France away from him, like an old Name-Day present.

And he disciplined himself *most severely*, Père Daniel was saying, with an undertone of excitement.

Again Père Brébeuf's mind skittered away.

When had this begun? He thought perhaps when the other man had been disagreeable over Born Underwater. He had always thought until then that Père Daniel was well disposed towards him. The thing had occurred at the beginning of the summer, when he'd happened to think of her (not that she was anything special to him). He was in the Superior's garden, which was flush against the inner palisado, and the sentry's boots creaked upon the platform overhead as Père Brébeuf pulled weeds (the spiked belt of discipline biting deep and secretly into his belly as he bent to murder each dandelion), when suddenly it came to him: he would administer the Exercises to her! – It was only an idle thought, of course, not even a dream (and he put no faith in dreams). He might have even had it before; such thoughts came again and again . . . But he took pleasure in imagining how he might bring it about. Assuming that she could be persuaded, where could it be done? – This train of thought was entirely natural. Incidentally, it was also inevitable. – At Mission Sainte-Marie there were a number of small cells in which the Black-Gowns could lead an Indian neophyte in the Exercises. Joseph Chihwatenah had entered one of them, to make the full Ignatian regimen in the summer before his murder. Louys Amantacha certainly would have come here also, had the Mission existed in his time, he being a great one for regaling himself upon any spiritual food. In those small chambers, whose planking blushed uncertainly beneath the wandering touch of candle-light and stray sunbeams, the Black-Gowns themselves gathered in separate proximities every summer, when the Savagesses and their children were gone to the fields, and the men were off at trading and war (at least until recently, when the war came home); so the priests could hang their black gowns upon pegs without guilt that they might be depriving the Savages of their love, and those headless shapes of darkness shivered a little upon their pegs, like Sorcerers being strangled for burning in France, and then the Père Superior came to them one by one and led them in the *Anima CHRISTI* before directing their contemplations upstream; then he slipped out to launch the next man. – There was the difficulty – that the cells were only for the use of men. Those sanctuaries for the Book, the candle and the rosary abutted the priests' Residence. Women could not be permitted there. – Besides, she was not even a Christian! (It was not with her as with others, that the Exercises could be given to refine and temper the Faith already received; rather, it was Brébeuf's aim to have the Exercises bring her *to* the Faith. Her mind was logical and intelligent, though Savage; if he could guide her past the river's mouth into that last great canyon of rapids where everything narrowed, how would she be able to escape him then?) – Eh bien. He'd install her in the west Store-house –

She refused him, of course. (So now she had become déniaisé; she had lost her innocence.) She put him off, saying that she did not yet believe herself ready to be instructed in that way.

She went away, and Père Daniel stood watching.

Jean is full of secrets and contradictions, isn't he? said Père Daniel a few days later, as if to Père Ragueneau.

What do you mean? said Père Brébeuf.

He says much more to a Savagess – an old concubine! – than he does to any of us. I sometimes wonder if . . .

Yes? said Père Brébeuf sharply. What is it that you wonder?

But Père Daniel said nothing. And the Superior was likewise silent.

The same wearisome question! Could it be that he flew a double standard? Père Daniel, Père Jogues, Père Castellain, Père Massé, Père Lalemant – they'd all implied it! But he was *obedient!* Had any Superior ever told him to desist? His purpose here was consistent even though it might sometimes seem otherwise, in just the same way that morning trees are light on the edges and dark green in the center.

He must ask Père Daniel to forgive him.

Power

Now it was autumn, and the maple-trees donned their chasubles of red and scarlet. Soon there would be no place to hide from the Irocois. That was why the Rock Nation of the Wendat abandoned their villages and moved to well-walled Taenhatentaron. In the summer it was an easy matter for the People to fly from their enemies: the dense green forest offered many hiding-places, and game could be had without trouble. But when winter came, the leafless forests hid nothing, and the refugees must leave their tracks upon the snow for the Irocois to find. If they sought to withdraw to some island in the Sweetwater Sea they were in no better wise, as their enemies came upon the ice-bridges that formed in that season, scouring island upon island until they discovered them. – So the Wendat were in terror. JESUS had given them iron arrowheads, but help they might have only at the hands of GOD.

The Song of Heaven
1648

> The Third Form of Humility is the most perfect. This exists when . . . in order to be more like CHRIST Our LORD, I desire and choose poverty with CHRIST rather than riches, insults with CHRIST . . . rather than honor, and desire to be considered worthless and a fool for CHRIST . . .
>
> SAINT IGNATIUS, *Spiritual Exercises*

In this year, Governor de Montmagny, now sixty-five years of age, was replaced by Louis d'Ailleboust. Of late Montmagny had been severely criticized for vacillation in the face of the danger constituted by those painted imps of Hell called *Yroquois*, for which reason the two and a half hundreds who now dwelled at Kebec considered him approaching unfitness; then, too, as the Jesuits reminded those who consulted them, he was a Knight of Malta like his predecessor Châteaufort, and it was necessary to guard against that Order's designs. – Montmagny, it is written, received the new Governor with courtesies as elaborate as a Spanish altar; at which worldly malice, disappointed in its hope of spying resentment on the face of him who'd been so discarded, now changed its key if not entirely its tune, to insinuate that he was weary of his position, believing the perilous state of New France to be beyond remedy. Despite the urgent prayers of the Jesuits, people said, he'd refused to arm the Huron with arquebuses, and now the trade would be ruined . . . It was on the twentieth day of Août that he received D'Ailleboust so graciously. On the twenty-third of Septembre he set sail for France, never to return, and many there were who wept for their own vain and worthless lives, now certain that they had been abandoned to the Hiroquois. – Governor d'Ailleboust was quick to read this panic between their hymn-lines, but he said to himself:

we need only another decade or two to be entirely safe from any Savage impudence, for look! in 1608 we were but twenty-eight here under Champlain; seven years ago we numbered three hundred; and now we approach a thousand! (He was reading off Montmagny's figures.) Indeed there seemed to be little peril here at Québec. The fortress clove the sky with reassuring massiveness; the Algoumequins still brought in their peltries for trade; in the convent of Marie de l'Incarnation the Savage girls still wove their vanneries cunningly from native grass, called le tressage, and the nuns wove costumes for the Image of the VIERGE MARIE. (So also did Champlain's widow, Hélène de Saint-Augustin. This year she completed her novitiate and removed to another convent at Meaux, where she requested the privileges of a maid, unfettered correspondence with her brother, and exemption from rising at four in the morning, all of which were granted her, in consideration of the twenty thousand livres which she brought. She had six years left to live.) – Mère Marie loved the little Savagesses yet more ardently each year. She took in as many as she could, and so they watched her praying. (I wish that I had the space to describe for you how each was defeated, how each gave in and was converted. It was like suicide, but beautiful, a sexual act.) She had a very pale yellow face; she was faded, having reached the age of almost fifty years. Her face was almost like a burn. Everything in her heart's tapisserie was earth-yellow or earth-red. As she prayed, Mère Marie kept looking sideways so that the Savagesses could see her face. She was showing herself so that the Savagesses might learn.

As for Gouverneur d'Ailleboust, he and his wife Marie-Barbe ate off pewter plates incised with his coat of arms. And New France exported twenty-two thousand four hundred skins –

The Yroquois seemed to have disappeared from the earth – a conclusion which would have rejoiced him exceedingly, had he believed it. Surely they plotted some cunning ruse. He'd heard tell of a certain tribe of Savages who disguised their footprints by wearing moose-hooves on their feet, so that they could lure hunters afield and then slaughter them. Even this device was surely inferior in evil calculation to whatever the Iroquois might be planning.

The Death of Jacques Douart

Wild strawberries grew in the charred clearings, where last year there had been Wendat villages. But there were now almost two thousand Christians in the Country. Ossossané, Teanaostaiaé and Scanonaenrat were so crowded with the devout that the Chapels filled to overflowing, and People stood outside. The thought of death was always among them. So many had died. It seemed that the Black-Gowns knew of death, and could comfort them. No matter anymore whether or not they brought it. – At the beginning of the year, in the Moon called Day Will Become Longer, the People had sent a wampum-embassy to the Onondaga to confirm the peace, but the Mohawk fell upon them and killed them. So the Onondaga Captain whom the Wendat had as a hostage cut his own throat in dishonor, and to revenge him the Onondaga agreed to war alongside the Mohawk and the Seneca. Now the Oneida remembered how the Wendat had put a hundred of their men to the torture a decade past, and the Cayuga had no desire to stand by themselves in this matter; so the Five Nations of the Iroquois resolved together to complete the extermination of the Crooked-Tongues, the Wendat. The Death Wampum Belt flew from town to town. The young girls sang songs to incite their men to war. The men danced faster and faster, screaming. – This news only enhanced the Christians' resignation, but those who still followed dreams were desperate, and decided to try one last time to eliminate the Black-Gowns. Perhaps then the Iroquois would not kill all of them –

The Christians thought differently. They fled screaming from the Iroquois; they begged to be admitted to Mission Sainte-Marie . . .

Père Brébeuf sometimes reflected on the contrast between his lot and that of the refugees who shivered and sickened in the Indian Compound. There, ground corn was as precious as CHRIST. But to the Black-Gowns it only meant another meal to strengthen them: thankfully partaken of, it is true, but consumed in a spirit of tranquil appreciation, not desperate hunger.

He wondered if he ought to suggest to the Superior Père Ragueneau that they share it all out with the Christians and be done with it. Then the priests would eat, or not eat, as they did. But if Père Ragueneau were to do this he would lose one of his most effective means of control over them. They were simply not strong enough in their faith for him to forego such control.

. . . In the Moon When the Pickerel Run, six of the staunchest Captains resolved to go to Mission Sainte-Marie and kill the first Frenchman they met. Then they'd demand that the Black-Gowns be expelled from their Country.

Père Brébeuf had been thinking of taking his accustomed walk at that time. He passed through the Indian Compound, where the Savages confessed themselves to him and ridiculed all their dreams, at which he rejoiced; he ascended the ladder to the observation platform, in order to bring the sentry fresh milk (which was a charity he often performed). – Eh, Père, we keep up a decent front against the Iroquois! cried the soldier, proud and sweating.

He drained the cup. – Thank you, Père. You're the best, you know that? I can always count on you, to come up and think of me . . . Is it hard to be so good? – Ah, smiled Brébeuf, it is not so hard as that. – And he looked smiling out upon the rivière whose trees already glowed with red berries; the brown rivière rippled on down, algæ-marbled, and there were lilies on the far side where he sometimes met Born Underwater to instruct her, but she was not there. Turning away, he descended back into his nest of angular roofs and towers and Crosses where the skinny Savages sang hymns and wept. The black hen had gotten loose again. He must catch her; otherwise the Savages would eat her.

No, she was not there. So it befell that a lay brother, by name Jacques Douart, was the first to go out. Frère Douart was the one.

A sentry in a bastion peered out through green leaf-light and shouted. He seized his arquebus from between the radiating beams and took aim. But by then the murderers had run away into the twilight. Yet other soldiers blew dust from the barrels of their wheel-lock pistols and began to fire through the slit-windows so that the dirt leaped up along the edge of the rivière where the killers had run. Forest darkness, so different from that of a longhouse, now fell over everything, and the soldiers desisted, trapped between the curvy lines of their own wood-beams . . . Now the Iron People made a great tintamarre, and closed Sainte-Marie against the entire Country. In the *Jesuit Relations* Père Ragueneau wrote: *there are, altogether, many and considerable influences which not only hinder our work, but even seem to threaten the ruin of the entire Mission. Some of these, indeed, are common to us with all the Huron, – especially the enemy, which we call by the name of Iroquois; they, on the one hand, close the roads and obstruct trade, and, on the other, devastate this region by frequent massacre. In short, they fill every place with fear.* He sighed, and dipped the quill in ink to continue: *Other hindrances, however, are altogether peculiar to us – notably, the hatred toward us of certain infidel Huron . . .* And Mission Sainte-Marie held its watchful breath. The gates stayed closed, until all who dwelled there began to feel like De La Roche's convicts on that earlier toy world, Sable Island, who had to lie underground like foxes for seven years . . .

And the Old Men met to discuss the question. But while many hated the Black-Gowns, they said: We fear the Iroquois too much to rid ourselves of them. Only the Black-Gowns can save us now, for are they not Sorcerers?

So those who loved dreams lost once and for all. Now they must pay the forfeit. Throughout the vastness of Canada, they must pay, and they would, patiently, as the Souriquois did when they had lost the gambling-game of Waltes, as the Hiroquois did, as the Huron did, even when they gambled away their wives and wigwams, their hair and fingers . . . This time they'd gambled away everything. And the Wendat stripped themselves to render presents and presents – more than ever in their history – until those called *Charcoal* were satisfied.

The Village of Christians

Now Ossossané was purified and perfected, and thus (we can only assume) ripe for GOD to pluck, for it would be among the next to fall (although Père Brébeuf would die first). The Christians ruled it. They'd called a Council to denounce the Captains who still believed in dreams, and proclaimed that henceforth the priest would be the principal Captain of that place. Any deed contrary to the Faith was forbidden. Husbands and wives prayed to GOD when they quarreled, and one mother even beat her child for offenses committed – a new and eminently French innovation, which pleased the Black-Gowns. The dream-Captains sought to protest, but the Christians would not listen to them, and so they withdrew from Ossossané with sadness in their eyes, saying that nothing but selfishness and witchcraft held sway there any longer. After that, it was called *The Village of Christians*. Their fears were as dense as trees.

Each of the conquered Huron villages had become a note in a lament of deep descending organ-tones – as bright as the windows glazed with images of Saints, as desolate as the snow-choked arched turrets of Kebec by night. Hundreds of the Savages, Christians and pagans alike, had fled to the stout walls of Mission Sainte-Marie. Ossossané's burning would be a beautiful chord –

The Death of Père Daniel

On the second of Juillet, Père Daniel completed a retreat of eight days during which he made the Exercises most fervently at Sainte-Marie, so that he was prepared for eternity. When Père Ragueneau had led him to the Fourteenth Rapids, which is the Nailing to the Cross, he saw a very strange sight: in place of the JESUS he'd always found before, he saw Père Jogues. He wanted to weep. He kissed Père Jogues on the lips, as the early Christians would have done . . . Bidding farewell to the other Black-Gowns, he set out that very day for Saint-Joseph, where he arrived the following day. The following morning he reached his destination and confessed a great number of Christians. – Ready yourselves for death! he told them. There is no certainty in this world.

On the fourth of Juillet, the Hiroquois attacked Saint-Joseph and Ekhiondastsaan, taking seven hundred prisoners. Père Ragueneau wrote in the *Jesuit Relations* that this victory was easy for them, for most of the defenders of those two towns were absent, being engaged in trade at Three Rivers, or else in desperate, futile raids against the Country of the Hiroquois. – The Hiroquois had approached by stealth during the previous night, and now fell upon Saint-Joseph shortly after dawn, while the Christian Huron were making their devotions in Père Daniel's church. When he heard the first screams, perhaps he hoped a little that GOD would let him out of his body so that he could watch himself being tortured without feeling it – ah, then he'd confound them! – His heart beat indiscriminately now with a rabbity terror; he believed for a moment that no device of the Savages could be worse than that; but then he laughed, thinking that he'd soon learn the contrary. (Actually his death would be very easy.) Looking upon his flock, he perceived how they feared to go and feared to stay, and the screams were louder outside and he smelled smoke and roasting flesh, and the congregation was on its feet and outside he heard the high-pitched scream that only a little child could make, and then that stopped and he heard the Hiroquois singing.

Escape, brothers, and leave me alone, said Père Daniel. I will face them. As for you, bear your faith with you even to the last sigh.

He stepped outside the church and stared those DEVILS down, with his arms folded across his breast. – Shame on you for this treachery! he shouted. Have you no understanding of GOD? The sin that you are about to commit will redound to your harm. Have a care!

For a moment they stood silent. He had time to close his eyes once more. This time he did not see Jogues, but Brébeuf. The blue gaze of that other was not loving as Jogues' had been, but emptily, utterly merciless; it riddled him with terror. Why did he have that vision at the end, why? He opened his eyes, shuddering. Then they rushed forward whooping and shot him with arrows until he bristled. Even then he did not fall. So they aimed their arquebuses at him and fired. And so his soul left the world red with the blood of JESUS . . . He was the next of the Jesuit Martyrs.

They dragged his bleeding body into the church without troubling to remove their arrows, and threw him down at the foot of the altar. They mutilated him, stripping him of everything except an integrity more bitter than tears. (The old scars on his back were as white water-lines on a grey rock. Like the other Black-Gowns, he had mortified himself.) Then they set the premises on fire, throwing into the flames the corpses of men, women and children. Furiously, feverishly, they convoyed their prisoners away toward their Country, making them bear the iron and other riches of Teanaostaiaé on their backs. Any who displayed weakness were killed – by torture if leisure permitted; otherwise by a quick blow of the tomahawk. Out of the two thousand people who'd dwelled there, seven hundred fell into the hands of the enemy.

The Exercise of Consolation

The news of the destruction of Teanaostaiaé Town shattered Père Brébeuf at first, for while he'd always expected the Crown it had been an article of faith with him that his empire of Huron souls would endure to the end of time, like France. No, there was no mistaking the current. But he calmed himself. Blessed Ignatius's face swam fishily before him in a black darkness, and the dark eyes glowed beneath the thick brows; the moustache was like a shadow . . . A white finger's width of collar ran around his throat like a wound. – He knew that Born Underwater would be crying. (She wept whenever any one of the good Pères suffered the slightest misfortune, so tender and pious had she become.) The Savages came screaming and wailing and bleeding. The wounded were perishing now in the hospital at Mission Sainte-Marie, choking in a few last breaths of dirt and sawdust, while Père Ragueneau's crew strode from bed to bed like black shadows, encouraging each to die well. Yet he knew, too, that his FATHER was the GOD of Revelation who revealed Himself daily, in every action, in violence as in rivers, wherever Truth might be sought or denied (it could never be destroyed).

Again Sainte-Marie was shut off – this time for fear of the refugees who kept coming and coming. Brébeuf spoke to the Superior about this, saying that one must succor these poor people, to which Père Ragueneau replied: Of course you are right, Jean. But they've disappointed me so many times before. What if they seek to murder one of us again, to revenge this misfortune which we did not cause? – They will not do that this time, replied Brébeuf. They are broken now to our will. – Do you really think so? You are such an optimist! But you are right, of course; we must be optimists for GOD! – And he commanded that the gate be opened. Savages rushed in, terrified, desperate and starving. The donnés, throwing slops to the grunting pigs whose dirty faces quivered with greed, whose huge pink ears flapped without scaring the flies, regarded them uneasily. The donnés milked the mooing and shining-eyed cows of sleek blackness, whose swollen brown udders proclaimed their wealth: milk glistened in pail after pail. The Savages watched. Cows lowed loudly in the hay. A brown calf frisked. Quietly, Père Ragueneau posted a guard over those animals. The European Compound was sealed off. Corn-ears hung yellow-bright from the beams. The Black-Gowns prayed and lay down on their wooden cots softened with blankets and deer-skins.

The next day they gathered in the refectory, sitting on the long benches, surrounded by pewter orbs gleaming and scratched. – Let us pray to GOD that their obedience continues, said Père Ragueneau.

Père Brébeuf said nothing. The others waited respectfully.

Well, brothers, I shall speak to the donnés, said Ragueneau at last. The Savages shall be given their portion –

So the Black-Gowns gave up their hard-gathered corn. And the Savages were fed. But great wheels of cheese lurked in the Store-house, and quarters of smoked pork loomed there, too. It was necessary to save these for more difficult times.

Père Ragueneau knelt before the Cross at the foot of his bed and requested guidance from Heaven. A breeze blew in the window, rippling the hairs of the great bearskin which some Christian Savages had given him for a coverlet (when no one could see, he slept on the floor, as Père Massé had done, as the Savages now did in his courtyard). Slowly he slid out the map from its birchbark case and spread it out on that elliptical table of rippled wood that Frère Guillaume had made. – When the enemy came, where then? It was all very well for Jean to be so cavalier; Jean was not the Superior anymore; he had no responsibility for the lives of others –

They will devour us from the south and the east, he said to himself. Contarea and Teanaostaiaé are gone. Old Taenhatentaron is ashes. Next will go Scanonaenrat, and Saint-Joachim, I suppose. Then Saint-Jean, Saint-Anne, Saint-François-Xavier. And they will move into those territories. They will cut us off, here on our peninsula.

He took his dividers, and began to measure the way to various islands in the Sweetwater Sea which could be fortified . . .

As for Père Brébeuf, he went to the compartment at the top of the stairs where extra hay was kept. This would be a good place to make the Exercises and mortify himself . . . – After all, he must now make preparation to follow Père Daniel. Thinking this, he slowly began to feel refreshed and renated in his innermost spirit.

He swung open the window and looked out at neighboring roof-bark, dull and brown. The other building was almost close enough to touch. He peered down at the rusty buckets in the grass.

And Born Underwater, would the Hiroquois burn her, too? (Her soul was softly mottled, like cod-skin.) When the moment came, he wanted to say goodbye to her. The fact that he could never do this pierced his heart.

She dwelled at Saint-Ignace now. She continued to come to church, and knew all the important doctrines well. But then she always had.

That summer Père Brébeuf preached in all the towns where his Superior commanded him to go, joyously, with no fear of the enemy. He ducked his head when he passed through the longhouses, for they seemed much lower to him now. He presided when a Savage rang the bell. So many towns had Chapels now, altared and tapestried **I.H.S.**, with silver candlesticks upon which burned flames sustained by brown cylinders of bear-fat. He swished in his long black robe which hung like scalps from his bony limbs, and the People cried desperately: *Echon, Echon!* He prepared them for Heaven. Then he went through the winding tunnel between the palisadoes and emerged from the village to look upon the green shimmer of the cornfields so sweet in the sun. That Recollect, Père Le Caron, always used to say that one could find one's way in their towns without difficulty, but their cornfields were a maze of the DEVIL. Poor Le Caron! Surely he must still be in Purgatory. Père Brébeuf's lips began to move of their own accord, saying a prayer for him. How long ago had it been since he himself first came here? Eh, twenty-one years ago! Amantacha had been a stripling then, Père Nicolas freshly drowned, Brûlé soon to be murdered . . . And in those days the Hiroquois had seemed of no more account than the downy pollens of trees, floating through the humid days of Août and Septembre . . .

Born Underwater

Born Underwater was filling a kettle from the stream when Echon came to her.

I don't want to, she said. Why must I see your JESUS tortured? Isn't there torture enough?

Such ignorance and pride no longer shocked him very deeply, for he'd heard them so many times, but he cried: Be careful, woman, lest you mock Him Who died for you! Do you still not understand how close to mortal sin you come in uttering such words?

It will be done, she said suddenly.

What do you mean?

I said that I shall do it. Isn't that what you have desired of me?

She gazed upon him like Sainte Agnès looking up with glazed eyes as the headman held her head back by the hair and pushed the sword deeper and deeper into her throat and blood came out like a fountain, missing her clothes, vanishing into the dry straw-colored earth while a little lamb watched and two Angel-boys came with the Martyr's crown.

He thought for a moment that he had heard her say to him: *Iatenonhwé* – which means *I love you* – but of course her lips had not moved.

Prelude to Epiphany

So it had come to this. Yes. She had not painted her face with red ocher, because Echon had said that doing that would displease him. But around her neck she wore wampum-strings, and also the Cross that Amantacha had given her. It was very important that Echon see that. There was no birchbark bowl of water from a beaver-stream; Echon's gaze upon her would be that. There would be no singing of her song of Power; Echon would sing the Song of IESVS. But the smooth stone that she had been given with her Power (thirty winters ago now and more), that she had. She could not hold it in her hand, of course; Echon would never permit that. But she had lashed it round and round against her thigh, with deer-sinew, where Echon would never see.

The purpose of these Exercises, began Echon, is to assist your soul in relinquishing worldly, devilish or other inordinate attachments. Do you comprehend me?

Yes, Echon.

Echon's face was half-bright in the darkness, his beard silky and almost handsome. His nose had become sharper with the years; it was like a crow's beak.

I am going to lead your heart in certain secret directions, just as I once did for Louys Amantacha de Saincte-Foy.

Will I see him now?

Certainly not. You must loose him from you, my dearest daughter . . .

He was silent for a moment.

These Exercises are to bring your vision nowhere but to GOD in His three PERSONS, he said, in a dryer voice.

It was very dark.

Eh bien, said Echon. Close your eyes. You are now to imagine a river before you. This river's mouth waits to devour you. And it is good that it desires to do so. For it is the way to GOD. But you must comprehend another thing. To be devoured is a great labor and mortification. You must go upstream, surmounting new rapids, to reach the narrow place where it shall be finished at last. It is only when this occurs that you are in Heaven. Do you comprehend?

Yes, Echon.

Why is it, he cried fiercely, that none of you ever tell me when you do not comprehend?

She said nothing.

Now let us make the *Anima CHRISTI* together, he said after a time. Repeat after me: *Soul of CHRIST, sanctify me . . .*

Soul of CHRIST, sanctify me . . .

And she heard the Power crying out. As ever, she offered it her entire will.

The Stream of Time

Just as an Lnu'k woman must first cut off the large quills from a porcupine's back before she roasts it, so Born Underwater must prepare herself before she began her journey to Ghost World. She sang Echon's song: *In the hour of my death call me and bid me come to Thee . . .* – The stone of Power burned against her thigh.

She passed by the great rock called by the Wendat *Ecaregniondi*, which is smeared with red-ocher from the painted faces of the dead. The Black-Gowns know this rock also. But they call it the Rock of Our Heavenly KING.

She could already see a dead birch lying in the Stream of Time like a shaggy skeleton hand. The water was eating channels into orange and grey flat rocks . . .

She came to the lodge where PIERCE-HEAD lived. He opened the door, and was much dismayed at seeing her, for He could not take her brains out and put them in one of His pumpkins, as He did with the dead souls of the Wendat. He had done that to Amantacha –

She crossed the Stream of Time on the narrow tree-trunk bridge guarded by the wicked dog that sought to tumble her into the rapids, but she kicked him in the snout. GOUGOU waited at the bottom as GOUGOU had always been waiting, snapping His bloody beak, insinuating His stinging tentacles through the water like a net, peering unwinking through the greenish pillars of a bell cupola rising from the back of a greenish seashell . . . but she made the crossing safely. The Stream of Time was the Milky Way, as the Wendat said, but still it was mild. As soon as she had crossed it, it seemed to her that she could have lain on her back on the flat rocks of it and not been submerged . . . She bested its waterfalls spilling around steep hill-curves, its dark brown steps of rock connected by white water-bridges to light brown steps below, in sluggish pools possessed in all confidence by water-striders, whose legs trapped bubbles to help them skate along, postponing the moment when some fish would eat them; and the Stream ducked down around the side of flat-topped mossy boulders, and came into wide shallow canyons of its own making.

Upstream? Downstream? The current went in both directions, as the Old Men said.

Now she was in Ghost World where the souls complained day and night; it was all that their Captains could do to keep them from lamenting too miserably. She could hear them dancing now. Their cries rang. Perhaps AATAENTSIC was ill, and the dead were dancing to cure Her. Or was she home with the Lnu'k now? PAPKUTPARUT was the Captain there.

Membertou was not there. He had been *baptized*.

Amantacha, too, of course –

She went further.

An island appeared before her eyes, perhaps because she'd been staring at the SUN.

So she ascended even to the Seventy-Third Rapid, above which towered a grey tooth of rock like a Church. And beyond that was the SKY.

The ice was silver and crackly at the edge of the grass where the SKY began. Time struck the SKY in the same way that sunlight struck the Stream, making its ripples and white flashes into rapids pretending the existence of rocks. Everything was mild.

In the SKY where the waters boomed, there stood a woman with Power. She seemed to be a woman also of great weakness and sickness. Her thin oval face, so meek, so delicate, rested against the cheek of darkness inside her veil, and her right hand was drawn against her heart as she gazed through closed eyelids at the Cross she held outstretched. She stood in a shallow depression like a grave; perhaps it was her own grave, for she was to be buried near her Cross in the spot she loved to pray in. There was an open field behind her. Little cabins stood on the slope of Mount Royal very far away. And the woman said: *I am your sister Kateri.*

KLUSKAP appeared. KLUSKAP wore Born Underwater's face. The woman scalped Him with her Cross and threw the scalp into the rapids. The scalp became GOUGOU. KLUSKAP screamed as Born Underwater screamed –

Born Underwater

I promised you that I would make the Exercises and I made them, she said. I made them, didn't I?

She was shouting.

Did you? said Père Brébeuf skeptically. And what did you see?

I saw – Him . . .

And?

I saw HEAD-PIERCER and AATAENTSIC, and They were in chains. KLUSKAP was screaming in the fire. MN'TU' was lost in a house of mist . . . He was never your MN'TU'; He was our MN'TU'. He was not GOD. That is why He must be lost now.

And?

I won't be able to see-ahead anymore, she said. That's gone, too.

Père Brébeuf said nothing for a moment. Then he put his hand on her shoulder and said as gently as he could: Child, this seeing-ahead of yours was a black and devilish art, and it is a sign of grace that GOD has caused you to relinquish it.

She looked down at the ground. He saw that she was utterly tamed and broken.

So you made the First Contemplation, he continued. What happened?

I came to the Stream of Time . . .

How did you succeed in swimming it?

I threw myself in, as you commanded, and – I don't know. I couldn't see anything. I got weaker and weaker, but then the river got slower . . .

And you ascended the First Rapids?

I saw HEAD-PIERCER, but He only laughed at me and said I was your wife. He was in iron chains, I said . . .

He found her trembling mouth very oppressive.

He said to himself: Now, like Amantacha and Chihwatenah and all the others, she has achieved her epiphany.

But he was wrong; that had not happened quite yet . . .

Suddenly it occurred to him that he should ask what (if anything) she still remembered from her seeing-ahead concerning the Hiroquois, and whether it was possible to act a certain way so that all the Huron who remained might yet save themselves. But at once he recognized this as a temptation of the DEVIL.

The Crown
1649

> Whenever a war against a foreign Nation is pursued until that Nation is about to be exterminated because of its refusal to accept the Great Peace, and if that Nation shall by its obstinacy become exterminated, all its rights, property and territory shall become the property of the Five Nations.
>
> From the Constitution of the Hiroquois

In that last autumn, the forest was glorious like altar-fringe with silver threads and red velvet, like silver lace for a ciborium veil. Hidden behind these colors came upwards of a thousand Hiroquois. Hardly a twig crackled under their step. They were heavily armed with Dutch arquebuses. Such was their craft that the Huron had no suspicion of them, although (as the *Jesuit Relations* later marveled) their bloody designs compelled them to hunt in the forest all winter, meanwhile making a journey of two hundreds of leagues. Descending the snowy grooves in the earth, whose slippery sides could be passed through only by clinging to trees, the Hiroquois crept northwest. In their dreams they already saw the lake called *Beautiful* shining ahead with clouds sealed like Huron faces in its ice. When the rivers froze, snow covered them like fog, and the Hiroquois traveled along their margins, ready always to duck into the darkness so that they would not be seen. The cold shriveled their skins, but fierceness warmed them. Their War-Chief gave an oration calling upon them to do deeds of bravery; he sang to them the War-Song: *My warriors shall be mighty in the strength of the* CREATOR. *Between Him and my Song they are, for it was He who gave the Song, this War-Song that I sing!* And he sang it to them without ceasing. They clambered over little walls of ice-shards set in ice. They looked across windows of ice to the hills ahead, where thin birches stood like the skeletons of wrists. The War-Chief sang the War-Song. This year they would not be home to celebrate the Maple Thanksgiving. Their sons would play snow-snake; their laughing daughters would toss the ball of deer-hair from hand to hand; the Elders would tell the tale of the VAMPIRE SKELETON, but they would not be there. The War-Chief sang the War-Song. At twilight the trees were the same color as the rocks, and the War-Chief sang the War-Song. Later, when the color went out of everything, the grass became the hue of rust, the bare trees, rocks and dirt all the same grey, the cold grey sky no different. Then it was night, and white trees reached out like the ghosts of dead souls. At this, the War-Chief raised his hand, and all fell silent. The muffled rattle of their snowshoes was barely perceptible; and even if the Wendat had heard it they would have thought it to be nothing but icy branches scraping in some feeble breeze. It was very dark. – On the night of the fifteenth of Mars they crossed into the Country of the Huron and approached the first of the places which they meant to conquer. This was Saint-Ignace. Reconnoitering, they were apprised of this town's defenses: – *viz.*, a stout palisado of pine stakes fifteen to sixteen feet high and well-sharpened, and a dry-moat (filled in this season, however, by deep snow-drifts) formed by deep ravines on three sides, and a trench on the fourth. Perceiving this trench to be narrow, the Hiroquois decided to make their approach from that side. At dawn, while the Huron still slept, they clambered silently over the palisade and landed like cats. Crouching in a circle around the longhouses as their companions dropped down lightly as snow, the Hiroquois gaped their mouths in noiseless glee. Then they made their rush. Hardly a gunshot was fired, so quickly did they seize the place. Now the frozen lake of silence found its outlet in a cataract of screams as the Hiroquois slaughtered the Huron. Only ten Hiroquois were killed. As for the Wendat, three men escaped, running across the snow almost naked to give the alarm to another village at a league's distance. The rest – men, women and children – were either slain on the spot or else reserved for tortures.

The day was still very early. The black legs of trees were muffled in snow. In the Country of the Huron was nothing but snow and trees and darkness. A portion of the Hiroquois remained in Saint-Ignace to guard the position and begin upon the captives. The rest went running lightly through the snow. Soon the screams were drowned among the trees behind them. A mist of grief hung grey and white between winter birches. Before dawn the Hiroquois reached Saint-Louis, which was quite well-fortified. Most of the women and children had fled, thanks to the warning they received from that trio of lonely desperate fugitives, but perhaps eighty men remained to offer some defense. These succeeded in killing thirty of the thousand before they met their doom. With great strokes of their iron hatchets, the Hiroquois breached the palisade and ran inside, yelling. From their guns they shot fear and terror. The old people and children who had been unable to escape were hurled screaming into the flames of the burning village; the sick and the wounded met the same end.

Among those captured were Père Jean de Brébeuf and Père Gabriel Lalemant.

The Seventy-Third Rapid

Of Père Brébeuf it must be told that, like his predecessor in martyrdom, Père Daniel, he had already been prepared for death. Indeed, during the month of Février he had made the Exercises privately in his residence, not being able to spare the time to attend a retreat at Mission Sainte-Marie. On this occasion he was able to ascend the entire Stream of Time, including the Seventy-Third and final Rapid (*viz.*, The Ascension of Our LORD), without once finding fault with himself. At the base of this final and most formidable fall he swam, looking up the pounding white walls of water to the summit where water blue-green and white rolled past tree-islands and rocks to the edge and then fell so loud and far, raising mist through which black gulls flew; below this, all was lathered white, mist rising in a triangular cloud of greater height than the falls itself; birds swooped below like the water that became dark green-blue at last, but marbled with lather; foam-clouds drifted down from that immensely wide white wall . . . Knowing that he could never ascend this cataract under his own power (for it fell full two hundred feet), he made his prayers to GOD and Saint Joseph, the patron of this Country, and found himself lifted up easily to one of those summit-islands surrounded by green water beneath which rocks showed green and black; this water curled over the lip of the rock in a steady mass; just at the edge it turned a paler green; there was nothing but foam below . . . – Now for a moment he felt anguish on his island, for there were no more rapids to ascend (he had not yet the presumption to look upon the Source of the Fleuve). What was he to do now with his urgent love? He stood very still. He knelt and prayed for a new burden. Then he stood up and climbed a scrubby little alder on his island to gain a better view, and looked down. Struggling in the foam of these very rapids he saw Born Underwater.

Born Underwater

I'm no good, Born Underwater said. You think I'm good but I'm not. Every time I meet you I want to pray some new prayer, but now I can't anymore. I don't have anything left to give you except things that were never mine.

But why must it be a new prayer? said Père Brébeuf.

A tear crawled down to her chin and hung there. – I don't know, she said. You Black-Gowns always bring new things . . .

The Destruction of Saint-Louis

On the sixteenth of Mars, the last day of Père Brébeuf's life (it was nine days to his fifty-fourth birthday), the Hiroquois attacked the palisado of Saint-Louis, as we have seen. Twice the Huron braves repelled them, although they were outnumbered a dozen to one. On the third sally, the enemy breached the palisade.

When he saw the Mohawk warriors running at them, waves and waves of them, Père Brébeuf felt a sense of shocking exultancy. He had long expected the Hiroquois to keep their rendezvous. Now he was on the Strait Road, and there was nothing to do but walk it. How easy everything was!

But then for a moment it seemed that the enemy did not see him, and he almost believed that she hadn't lost her Power after all and had cloaked him in protective sorceries in spite of himself; and he took out Père Massé's whistle and blew a merry blast –

After that, just as a seagull, having alighted, may raise his wings above his back and flutter them as if in triumph, so the Irocois pagans upraised their arms about him, stabbing the air and shrieking and howling, so that he had no uncertainty regarding his fate.

The Epiphany of Born Underwater

Well, it seems we are to follow the road of Père Jogues, said Brébeuf to young Gabriel Lalemant. – Do not despair, boy – do not despair! for like Our MASTER we are but going down to Jerusalem.

The lad was very pale, but he choked back his tears and nodded.

What do you see? said Brébeuf.

They are forming in a double line.

Ah, then they will beat us. Louys Amantacha told me of that.

Being ready, he now folded his cassock tight around his body and waited. They shouted in his ears; they struck him.

What is it, Père Brébeuf asked himself, that compels me to go on like this when I know what will happen? – A cowardly thought, that, for – yes! – I *do* know what will happen; I desire it to happen, as the Pilgrim going to Heaven desired to be drowned swimming toward that City. I must be burned under this sun that the Souriquois used to call JESUS. And yet it is so easy. And I am not afraid. I am here for love. – But that poor boy! He's not ready. Eh, soon he'll be safe in Heaven. I hope he dies quickly; he cannot hold fast in much pain. He's like Père Davost . . . Fortunately his constitution is weak. If only he could die now! I'm sure Our gracious LORD would count him just as much a martyr!

He stood among them like a great maple offering all its leaves to GOD with upraised arms. Tearing his Black Gown from him, they slowly poured boiling water upon his head in a parody of baptism. He said: Oh, you are bold and valiant, you Iroquois! You know not the DEVILS you serve. – He stood with his crossed wrists lashed to a pole. A Hiroquois with meager features rushed forward and sliced a ribbon of flesh from his arm, devouring it greedily like a dog. Another had already honored him with the collar of red-hot axeheads. These sizzled upon his naked chest, which the Savages laughed to see, saying: So we replace the collar of your Black Robe which we stripped from thee! – Others crowded near, seeking to string more axeheads about his neck. He said nothing. He looked sideways, past the fire which they had prepared for him, waiting to see CHRIST appear to him for his consolation. His eyes were resigned, and yet the Savages discovered something in them that was seeking, seeking . . . – What a Sorcerer he is! they said to one another. Even now he seeks to poison us with his JESUS. – And some among them grew apprehensive lest they be stricken with some new disease. – The firelight was ruddy on his bald forehead. He smiled suddenly, and Lalemant, seeing this, was reminded of the engravings of the Blessed Ignatius which he had so often seen in France, the sly dart of a smile between moustache and beard – and Ignatius had been bald also, which he well knew, so that now at the threshold of his torments as he looked upon his companion it seemed to him that the man and the Saint had become one, which exalted and terrified him. He called: you have no need of my prayers, Jean! – but then two Irocois forced him to his knees and swung their tomahawks high above his head and their sweating distorted faces were puffed with pride and lust like the countenances of demons, and their greasy bodies smelled abominable; and he clasped his hands together like the white wings of a butterfly and closed his eyes and composed his long pale face as he began to pray O LORD and FATHER, I who now am about to return into Your hands entreat You to grant me grace to remain steadfast in my trials, however undeserving I may be . . . – and his mouth was very dry; he could not swallow; and still the tomahawks had not descended; and he heard the cries of a Huron woman and then he heard an axe split her skull open and still the tomahawks had not descended to end this unbearable eternity; he heard the flame-crackle consuming the village behind him; the church that the Black-Gowns had built glowed with orange glory; and a Hiroquois discharged his musket into a Huron's breast; and a laughing rosy-breasted Huronne stabbed her spear into Père Brébeuf's side, shouting *now you are opened like JESUS!* and the Huron Christians were praying in low voices and the tomahawks had not yet descended and the Irocois shot arrows into the heaps of arrow-bristling corpses and fought shrilly over scalps and the tomahawks came swishing down at last but did not touch him, at which joke the Irocois shrieked with glee, and he could not pray anymore because his heartbeats overwhelmed his thoughts, so he crouched like an animal until the tomahawks came down.

With that first blow, although his skull was laid open to such an extent that his brains were exposed, his agony was of course not ended. Yet now in a flood of relief he found himself able, if not yet to pray, at least to make the Exercises, and he made the Contemplation of Jean the Baptist waiting at the River Jordan for JESUS and the river was very calm and blue like the Fleuve Saint-Laurent, with green fingers of light in its depths, and Saint Jean stood in the knee-deep water of the Thirty-Fourth Rapid, attending he knew not what, as JESUS left His blessed Mother and journeyed toward him through the Savage forest (that was the First Point); but when JESUS came Jean sought to be excused, saying my dear LORD I am unworthy to baptize You; – but JESUS said (this was the Second Point): Let it be so now, for it becomes us to fulfill all justice; and then in the Third Point the Holy Spirit descended upon JESUS and the Voice of the FATHER testified from Heaven, saying: Here is my beloved SON, in whom I am well pleased. – So he comforted himself, knowing that JESUS would forgive him his unworthiness for the Crown if he strove manfully to be patient among these torments; and yet he still could not pray, although his lips moved and the Hiroquois believed him to be praying.

His end, as it proved, was fifteen hours away. Père Brébeuf suffered but three; such being their hatred for him as to distract them from their usual ingenuities. When he began to preach to them of Our PÈRE, they hacked his mouth off in pieces. At the vanguard of his torturers, it is said, were a shrill flock of Huron converts, pecking about him like crows, screaming menace and abuse. Foremost among them was the Souriquois woman, Born Underwater.

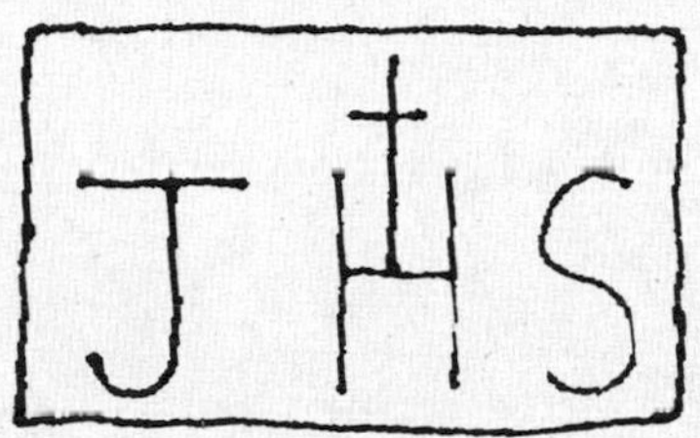

VII
Our Father
or,
The Ascension of the Hiroquois Virgin

Catherine Tegahkouita

1656–1680

Copper, which is "soft" and therefore extremely malleable, could be hammered into other shapes easily . . .

GINA LACZKO, *Iroquois Silverwork* (1978?)

We recognized that this folk could easily be converted to our faith.

JACQUES QUARTIER, *Voyages* (1535)

My children, Kateri has just died.

PÈRE CHOLONEC, to the Christian Hiroquois at Kahnawaké (1680)

Elle était charmante à la manière indienne, says one of her condescending biographers, and Père Lecompte comments very favorably on her leggings, "enriched with brilliantly colored porcupine quills," in which she walked timidly toward the altar on that Easter Sunday in 1676, four years before the Sun King's bust was installed in Kebec's Lower Town – but I, who was there, remember more vividly the worn buckskins that she wore earlier that morning, the garb of the outcast; – the clothes that she wore to receive her new name were borrowed. She was to be called *Kateri* – which means Catherine. Her old name, *Tekakwitha* – "she who goes searching in front of her," the name they called her since childhood because the smallpox that had orphaned her also damaged her vision, so that she must peer before her as she went – this name was to be stripped from her; so that as she approached the altar, arrayed in those many-hued quill-clothes, she felt as if it were autumn and her clothes were all the colors of turning leaves; the torch-lamps that burned so numerously before her blinking eyes were great yellow maple-leaves; the beaver-furs that hung on the walls in offering were oak leaves past their season. She could smell the low sun dripping like honey through the trees, and a warm wind blew and leaves pelted her; the trees were stripping themselves. Hour by hour she could see more of their trunks, dark and thin, like long lines of rain. As she climbed the hill of dead leaves she saw striated and mossy boulders resting in hollows like islands, and she continued to ascend, striving to rise above the yellow leaf-horizon to her Cross. She had forgotten where she was. *They contemplated her with admiration and respect,* says the biographer previously quoted. *Something divine emanated from her frail person. She glowed with joy, and her happiness communicated itself mysteriously to the congregation. It was an unforgettable hour . . . From that moment on, the life of the new Christian was nothing but a marvel of sanctity.* She stood like a bare and naked tree, in short, offering up her suppliantly skinny branches.

Perhaps it was because she had not married the Fox. She did not dislike him, but when she was affianced to him she tried not to think about him and went outside the palisade to the summer woods and fetched water from the spring that now bears her name; there she had a revelation from the SKY that comforted her and made her feel so sweet and sad and solitary that she could not bear to be any other way; squinting, scratching a mosquito bite on her pockmarked cheeks, Tekakwitha tried not to think about the evening when the Fox must come and sit beside her in her uncle's longhouse and all the aunts would be sending her eye-flickers to make her offer him meat, at which time she'd be married – and she would *not* be married; so when the dreaded evening came, displacing the Little Festival of Green Corn beyond which she'd also striven not to think, and she narrowed her feeble gaze to exclude the Fox who squatted at her side, his hair shining so bright with grease that she could have almost seen herself in it if she turned towards him which she would not do but would *have* to do very soon because he could not eat until she had offered him food and her uncle was sitting with his eyes upon her, only puzzled as yet because she'd never failed to do what he wished, and her fat aunts were watching her and no one was eating and she heard her heart and her heart and her heart until one of her aunts said

But, Tekakwitha, why haven't you offered this young man some meat? then the girl sprang up and rushed from the wigwam.

The blood rushed to the Fox's face. – Does she go to cast spells? he shouted.

Of course we must speak with her, the uncle said. Now comfort your heart and have some meat.

And the aunts put the nicest pieces of fat before him.

As for Tekakwitha, she ran into the forest, in terror of its darkness and panthers and MONSTERS, but fearing her uncle even more, because he would come looking for her, along with the Fox, and perhaps they'd remember now that she was the daughter of Prairie Flower the Algonquin woman, the enemy woman.

Here I should say, if I have not already, that Tekakwitha had inherited the Advance-Knowing from her mother, Fleur-de-la-Prairie, who'd inherited it from her mother, who had traded certain other magics to get it from a wise woman of the *L'nuk* People named Born Underwater. No doubt this was an iron thing given her by CHRIST in compensation for her nearsightedness. So she could see – not only up to the Seventy-Third Rapids, like the Black-Gowns; but also downstream to the mouth of the Fleuve and beyond.

This made her unhappy.

The Eagle protected her and hid her behind a cache of corn until it was agreed that she would not have to marry the Fox. Then he brought her home. But after this her uncle and aunts were always angry, as the *Relation* says. They treated her as a slave. Whenever she went to chapel they caused her to be followed by swarms of men pretending to be drunk, who rained stones upon her or seized her as if to drag her into the woods. The children called her *Chrétienne* as if she were a dog, until none remembered that she had ever had any other name. Still her uncle sought to turn the evil aside with the smoke of tobacco-prayers. (He did not hate her, no matter what she thought. He only wished to prevent her from going to church. If she were *baptized*, she'd leave the Country like all the others.) She defied him. Growing impatient, he gave a man presents to come rushing into the lodge one day as she sat sewing; the man raised his tomahawk over her head and screeched: I will kill Chrétienne! – Kateri bowed her head and waited for the blow. For a long time the silver edge hung over her, as it had over Père Brébeuf; then silently the man departed. One of her aunts, hearing her address an uncle by his given name rather than by the name Uncle as was customary, spread a calumny that she had gone into the woods with him for her pleasure. Hearing this, she became as pale as a cloudberry. When she took the Sacrament of baptism and so became a *chrétienne* in truth (how sensual it sounded!) they despised her more than ever.* On Sundays they refused to give her food, since she would not work in the cornfields on those days. *I want to be chrétienne, even though I die for it,* said Kateri. She would not attend the Festivals and Thanksgivings of the Haudenosaunee anymore. She chose not to attend the Great Feather Dance, in which HÄ-WEN-NÉ-YU the GREAT SPIRIT was praised. She turned away when the False Faces came to purify her longhouse, crawling slowly about, spreading ashes; and the False Faces said that she'd ruined their ceremony, at which her aunts berated and mocked her. They even accused her of Sorcery, which among the Haudenosaunee is an offense meriting death. At last some other converts, one called Ogenheratarihiens, and the other an adopted Huron prisoner whose name is not recorded, decided to help her flee. And the Eagle said goodbye to them in the darkness –

After Kateri was gone, riding down the river to become Catherine, the Eagle returned to the village, but the Fox was suspicious; and the Eagle hated the Fox more each day because he'd made Kateri cry and when the Raspberry Thanksgiving was over, and clouds flew through the crowns of high maples, he went into the forest determined to follow her to the Mission to declare his heart, and as he went he heard the Fox sneaking behind him and he could not bear it; he'd do a deed of love and hate that would increase his credit; he'd slice the Fox from ear to ear; he'd cleave his skull; his uncle had done that to Père Jogues. He bounded ahead. Then he hid in a hollow between two granite slabs, just downstream of a little waterfall. The rock-slabs met in darkness beneath a ceiling of roots roofed with ferns and mosses; here he lurked, waiting for the Fox. He could not kill him openly, for that would begin a blood-feud which he was bound to lose. – So he waited until the Fox came, and the Eagle gazed at him from his cave making sure that there was no one with him, and then he came out noiselessly and the Fox was staring about nervously and the Eagle said enlighten your ears, my enemy and his face was like the Mohawk faces three hundred years later in the Mission Sainte-Marie to which Catherine had fled but by then it had become the Caughnawagwa Mohawk Reserve where they played soccer dirty, where if the home team lost they came after the outsiders with bricks and stones,

*"As for de-construction of texts," says Trigger, "I think it is reasonable to assume either that French writers stressed the Mohawk abuse of Kateri because that was *their* paradigm of how native saints were to be treated by their pagan kin or because Kateri said she was treated that way because she knew that that was the way that the French expected her to have been treated. Comparative ethnography suggests that [the] least likely alternative was that she was really treated that way."

where Pierre's friend once dropped a Coke can on the ground and some Mohawk men came up to him and said pick up that can and Pierre's friend said but be reasonable; just look around! It's so littered here, one more can won't matter! and they said pick up the can and he picked up the can. And the Eagle said in the same voice I'm going to kill you.

The Fleuve Saint-Laurent, *or,* Catherine's Epiphany

At last they came to the Fleuve Saint-Laurent, which was broad, deep, gracious, and Catherine prayed as Ogenheratarihiens and the Huron drew their paddles through the water, which was very blue and orange like the evening sky that shone so cold; and there was a river of clouds of blue. She still wore wampum, with which the Haudenosaunee adorn themselves and wipe away the bloody places of mourning when the great ones have disappeared into the earth. She had not yet put off that vanity, the correction of which would soon regale her with mortifications. In the gently rocking canoe with the breathing of her two friends in her ears, she traveled farther from her life, and at sunset the river was a dull blue, and blue clouds swam between the bare trunks of trees. (Beneath swam the Fox's scalp – *viz.*, GOUGOU, Whom the cheerfully skeptical Lescarbot knew to be no greater danger than the Phantom Monk of Paris. GOUGOU swam sadly. He loved Catherine. He sought to make Himself beautiful for her in all His heartleaves and brainleaves, but the season was too far advanced for Him to bloom in His favorite clusterhead of violet flowers arranged almost like sumac berries, which He'd copied from cordate pickerelweed. He loved her like a fly drowning in the waxy maw of a pitcher-plant. He outstretched His arms – which were covered with little sacs like the ramifications of a bladderwort's stem – and Ogenheratarihiens clove them with the blade of the paddle and GOUGOU even let him do it.)

Presently they came into the *écumen*, or settled district, and arpents of French land, with their narrow frontages of river, flashed past them. Catherine marveled to see the tall black roofs rising so high above the trees.

They have big families, the Huron told her. More of their children live than ours.

As the twilight murdered itself, the blue clouds glowed more coldly, and the sky became white. The river had its own light, although that too was fading like the mournful green-brown fields; and house-ends swam up to the canoe – they were massive stone pentagons – then they too were gone. It was very cold.

Catherine glimpsed the silhouette of a church that had not been built yet. She could see sky between the pillars of the belfry as if it were some skeleton. Then trees and twilight grew up through it, and the Fleuve Saint-Laurent carried her past it, and she was gone. She felt so alone . . . But Ogenheratarihiens and the Huron were beside her. They were her dear friends, and their care clothed her like a shining blanket, like the Fleuve that flowed white and liquid through the forest. It was actually an indescribable color, neither white nor orange nor blue, that dazzled Catherine as she looked at it. For awhile it seemed to be getting richer and richer in milkiness, but then she saw that that too was an illusion, that the river and sky were not getting lighter; they were simply getting paler and darker at the same time. The trees were black now, and the river light was bleeding out of them before her eyes.

It was almost dark now. The water flowed bluish-grey and the trees were reddish-grey. Silently, they passed square houses of pale mortar and stone at the riverside, ever so many of them, and the grass was brownish.

There are no deer here anymore, said Ogenheratarihiens, and the Huron said nothing.

The houses had gable-windows. Their mortar was black-speckled with stones; their two chimneys and four chimneys rose up against the sunset.

They cut down so many trees for their fireplaces, said Ogenheratarihiens, and still the Huron said nothing, and Catherine was praying, and suddenly Ogenheratarihiens said Kateri, my sister, can't you make us go down a different river than this? and she saw that he was shaking with fear and anger.

My friend, said Catherine weeping . . .

. . . Old people from Ville-Québec will say to you yes yes I grew up by the sea, meaning the Fleuve Saint-Laurent, for it is so wide (as much as sixty-nine miles) that anything can happen between its shores, and it is possible that if Catherine had prayed hard enough she could have found a place where there were no Christians ever and no tall grey-painted houses standing in a row as in the village of Saint-Sulpice, their A-frame roofs steeply sloping, no town of Saint-Ignace-de-Loyola with its fields of cattails and orange-roofed gas stations, its green sheds framing Petrol Canada sheds, upon which darkness must fall as surely as JESUS CHRIST descending each day to the altar; but Catherine would never have prayed such a prayer for the same reason that she never would have married the Fox even though she loved her uncle and liked the boy and knew that her refusal humiliated them so much

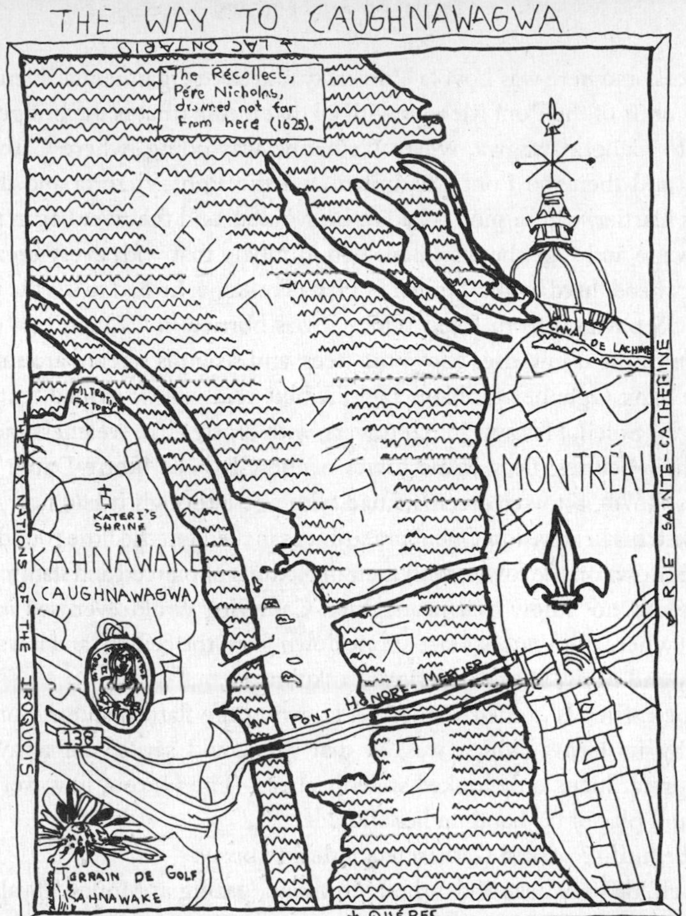

more than she herself was worth. – It was dark now, and the settlements could not be seen.

We camp here, the Huron said, and Ogenheratarihiens said nothing.

The next day they came in sight of Ville-Marie, now known as Montréal, and they heard the wind blow through the cobblestone streets. The Huron looked about him with awe, but Ogenheratarihiens refused to see anything but the river-course that lay straight ahead when the island city began to crowd them with its low old buildings with stone walls (they were not as old, of course, as Catherine's holy bone-dust), its buildings with red bricks and green roofs, its old buildings with crosses, and the wide mossy front of the Montréal Seminary, and then they were downtown among glittering gilded windows, smart businesswomen getting into their cars, their pretty scarves fluttering in their faces, and here was Loyola University, but here Ogenheratarihiens had to take account of the Pont Mercier with all that traffic (that is the bridge to take to get to Caughnawagwa, where Catherine was going, where Catherine is buried) and then the Pont Champlain and the Pont Victoria and the Pont Jacques Cartier, whose pilings had to be avoided; and the river began to smell like sewage and Ogenheratarihiens had to inhale that with every breath; and straight ahead, hard by the Tunnel L. H. La Fontaine, he had to see the remains of the US pavilion from Expo 1967 – it was burned in '77, and now just the skeleton of the dome rises above the trees, and seagulls scream around it. On the left bank Ogenheratarihiens saw the blue and yellow striped tents of the Cirque du Soleil. He saw church towers, with crosses like weathervanes rising from their belfries; he saw the tower of the Chapelle Notre-Dame de Bon Secours (1678), a tower green-stained with age although it had not yet been built; with his keen vision Ogenheratarihiens picked out the little round stained glass windows on the tower, with their depictions of pierced and flaming hearts (but he did not know that nearsighted Catherine could even see *inside* the church, where the VIRGIN's face shone down from the ceiling, and it was bright and airy and stony, like the interior of a skull).

– Look, friends! cried Catherine, knowing the flattish summit of Mount Royal by its Cross (which was all that she could see so far away) – but Ogenheratarihiens only looked sullenly ahead. The Huron, however, smiled at her and placed his hand on her shoulder.

Is it beautiful? asked Catherine a little anxiously.

Yes, child. Very beautiful, the Huron said, gazing at Mount Royal with its thin autumnal trees, in whose crotches were so many birds' nests, and the ground was gilded with leaves. (From its shoulder, Montréal with its rectangular buildings spreads below you. On the summit, there is a parking lot with parking meters, added after too many loving couples came there to park all night, and a traffic light with the usual sign: ATTENDEZ LE FEU VERT,* which Catherine, for whom French was not a native language, would interpret to mean ATTEND THE GREEN FIRE as if she were a vestal.) At the foot of this grand hill were the pillared mansions. An old woman in black walked slowly up the steps of a church. Down the avenue was the building called the Virgin Tower, because when the female students first inhabited it the rules were very strict, and then the Oratory of Saint-Joseph with its greenish dome, where miracles have occurred – cripples have thrown away their crutches –

They wait, the Huron said, and at this Ogenheratarihiens did look up, out

* "Wait for the green light."

of habit, to make certain that no enemies were waiting. Catherine with her weak eyes could not quite see the people who waited, so she looked through them and saw the girls coming home from school on the wide snowy street, their plump cheeks red with cold, and they walked sedately in the snow while the boys behind them leaned against bare trees and walls and threw snowballs at each other and the girls did not look but walked on in their beaver hats and red scarves, holding their books against their breasts as if they were very precious, and snow was on the cornerposts and the house-gables, and the girls walked on in their shiny black galoshes, talking two by two. Then for just a moment Catherine became anxious, and she asked of CHRIST: What's happened to all *my* brothers and sisters? – and she could feel CHRIST's hand on her shoulder (it was actually still her friend the Huron's) as He said to her just wait until we get closer, child, and you'll see them! – and He was right because Ogenheratarihiens and the Huron paddled them skillfully to the shore and there they were! – *On all these more or less uncouth faces,* writes the biographer, with her usual tact and empathy, *she could read genuinely sincere sympathy. She felt almost as if she were in Paradise.*

Mission Saint-François-Xavier de la Prairie

The name of the Black-Gown at the Mission was Père Cholenec. When the Huron brought her to him (for *he* could not be expected to wait at the river's edge for *her*), she made obeisance and gave him a letter composed by Père de Lamberville.

And what is this piece of birchbark, child? said Père Cholenec very playfully.

The letter said:

> Catherine – or Kateri – Tekakwitha will be living at Sault. I pray you to take responsibility for guiding her. Before very long you will recognize the treasure that we give you. Preserve it well. In your hands may there be profit to the glory of GOD and salvation for a soul that is assuredly dear to Him.

Père Cholenec stared at the young woman. He read the letter again. When he looked up at her, she smiled very timidly. He raised his hand to pat her cheek, and she flinched a little. Then he comprehended that she must have often been struck.

Let me show you our pretty little Chapel, child, he said.

He led her past the bookstores and erotica shops of rue Sainte-Catherine, which he could not see, and they turned onto rue Saint-Denis and he pointed to the yellow light shining from the nested pair of belfries of the church tower, but before he drew her up to the church, whose stones, stained white and black, rose in a gilded arch above the massive door (the sides of the tower were already drawing together in the darkness, as Catherine saw when she lifted up her eyes in wonder – this was the great tooth in Born Underwater's dream) and through the balcony's ribs shone the light from the belfries, which glowed yellow like bone against the cold dark night; – before they got there three prostitutes came strolling up from rue Sainte-Catherine and they were chewing gum and their lips were made up and their faces were fat and brutal and they jostled Catherine and Père Cholenec aside (Père Cholenec thought he felt a gust of wind through the fields) and they stood blocking the sidewalk, laughing stupidly, and one of them put a hand on Père Cholenec's cheek just as Père Cholenec had done to Catherine and the whore said *hey* Father you wanna go out? and Père Cholenec said to Catherine the autumn winds are strong today I'm glad we have the harvest almost in and the whores said to Catherine what's *your* problem you bitch you got nothing to say to us is that it? and Père Cholenec, suddenly understanding that Catherine was beset by DEMONS, cried out in a commanding voice *you shall not see!* but Catherine did see and she knew in spite of all her reverence for the Black-Gowns that Père Cholenec was wrong in saying this, and she smiled at the whores and said good evening to you, sisters.

Here ends the

Second Dream

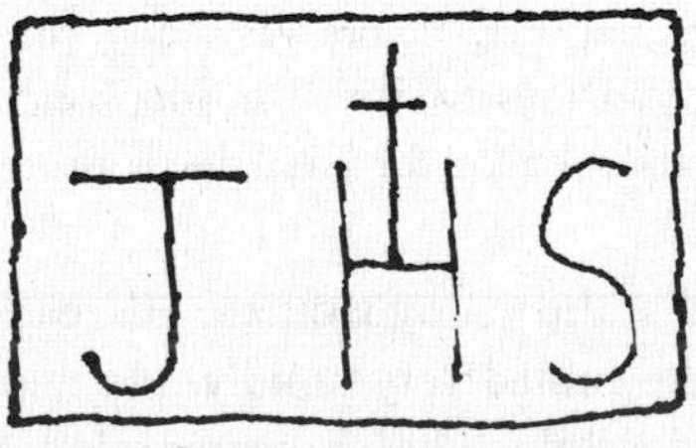

Black Wings

1611–1990

Further History of the Savages

1649–1990

The United States is not a Nation of people which in the long run allows itself to be pushed around.

DOROTHY PARKER, *On the Record*

After a summer's rain, the Fleuve Saint-Laurent was immaculately blue and grey. Gulls spiraled about the harbor and the roofs of Lower Town. Kebec smelled like new cedar-wood in the hot sun. Mère Marie de l'Incarnation stood gazing through the windows of her convent and saw more thunderheads coming up river edge-on. Many of the trees in the cliff-shade below her were in bloom; their blossoms twinkled in the breeze like stars. The wet spires of churches shone in the sun. The roofs of Lower Town were green and grey like forest, shadowing and angling among the lush green bushes. It was the Year of Our LORD 1668. She picked up her pen and finished the letter to her very dear son, in which she praised the virtues of the Hospitalière religious, Mère de Saint-Augustin, who had but lately died. It was this good Mother who'd watched over the bedside of a girl harassed by the DEMONS of a French Sorcerer whom she would not marry. Praying by day and by night, she protected the girl's purity. Although the DEMONS flew into a rage, Mère de Saint-Augustin bore them patiently, even when they pinched her arms as black as ink. *GOD strengthened her in this great travail,* wrote Mère Marie, *with the help of the Reverend Père de Brébeuf, who often appeared to her and consoled her in her travails.* By this token we know that Brébeuf has attained the source of the Stream of Time, that crystal spring in Heaven.* He stands at the bank of this, the Seventy-Third Rapid, and peers

* He was canonized in 1930.

over the edge of the falaise down which the water plunges. Beside him are Saint Peter and Saint Ignatius. – Brébeuf turns to them smiling. – Here in this place it must be permissible to see downstream, is it not, brothers? he says. (Saint Ignatius bows his head and turns away.) – Is it not? he says again. – Saint Peter regards him for a moment: When I was on Earth I refused to hear, and denied Him, he says. – Never will I compound that sin by refusing to see, or to show another. Look, then.

Further History of the Huron Nations 1649–1989

There can be no rest on the flight into Egypt, said the Black-Gowns gently. – The Huron were starving. Those members of their flock who were not running desperately through the woods, seeking to be adopted into the Neutral Nation, the Tobacco Nation, any Nation, the Black-Gowns led in orderly retreat to Saint Joseph's Isle in the middle of the Sweetwater Sea. The buildings of Mission Sainte-Marie, which alone had not been captured, Père Ragueneau put to the torch.

That winter was bitterly cold, and the Hiroquois snapped about them like wolves, slaughtering all within reach. The Black-Gowns doled out what they could from their Store-house of Huron corn, but that was hardly enough, even for the most pious of the Savages, whom they fed almost as well as themselves. As for the others, they ate moss, bark and fungus. Later they ate their own excrement and the bodies of those who had died. – At least, said the Black-Gowns, the meager shares of food we possess will give them time enough to prepare for Heaven. – (That year, as the *Jesuit Relations* boasted, three thousand Wendat were converted!) – By springtime, the People were so weak that they could no longer bury the corpses. In the month of Mars, small bands of survivors set out to search for acorns. Their children fell through the rotten ice of the Sweetwater Sea and were drowned. The others went on, weeping. On the mainland the Hiroquois were waiting. None of the foragers ever came back. Yet remaining on the island meant dying, so again a contingent of Huron set out, making the Black-Gowns their heirs, for they had no great hopes. The Hiroquois captured them all – what a fine Floating Island had come in! They burned them all alive, down to the last infant, and the shrieks drifted slowly up to Heaven. How easily smoke rises, compared with the labor of swimming upstream! . . .

Now came news that two great armies of Hiroquois were coming north to complete the butchery. On the tenth day of Juin, 1650, the Black-Gowns set out for Kebec at the head of their flock, which by now had dwindled to three hundred. They reached their destination after fifty days of great distress, and through the charity of the French were given land not far from the Hôtel-DIEU. With her usual generosity, Marie de l'Incarnation took one of their fillettes to be reared as a French girl . . . The following year, another three hundred arrived, creeping and crawling feebly from diverse places. The Black-Gowns resettled them all on the Isle d'Orléans.

In 1656, the year of Tekakwitha's birth, a band of Mohawk landed there and surprised them as they were planting their Indian corn. Six they killed at once, and all the others whom they had captured, to the number of eighty five, they carried off, *including many young women,* say the *Jesuit Relations, who were the flower of that Colony.* They paddled away in full sight of the fort, even making their prisoners sing to mock them, and the French did not dare to fire. They spared the lives of all save the six principal Christians, one of whom, by name Jacques Oachonk, they burned with such cleverness that he lasted three days. Seeing now that even in the bosom of the French they had no haven, the Huron sent a desperate peace embassy, but the Mohawk replied that there would never be any peace until they gave themselves up to be adopted; the Huron Nations must be dissolved. – We can do nothing for you, said the French Governor. – Some of the Huron went to the Mohawk, and some to the Onondaga. On the journey, a Seneca chief split open the skull of a Huron woman who refused to submit to his lewdness. The Onondaga then killed all the Huron men and robbed the women and children of their possessions, treating them as prisoners of war. Père Ragueneau attempted to help them, but the Hiroquois laughed and said: You Frenchmen have abandoned these people! They are our enemies. We will treat them as we like.

A few souls remained in Kebec. They lived in a fortified village under the loving supervision of the Black-Gowns. From time to time, the Hiroquois carried a couple of them off. (By 1668, Huron and Algonkin captives composed two-thirds of the Oneida Nation.) In 1697 the Huron moved to Jeune Lorette, where they still live. Others, scattered like a few white kernels of corn, became the Wyandots. *From this time onward,* writes Trigger, *the Huron country and much of the region to the north remained desolate and uninhabited, while the Huron were scattered in every direction.* But in the nineteenth century, when Wendaké was being cleared by English farmers, so many iron implements were turned up by the ploughs that scrap dealers traveled from town to town buying up these rusted relics of the Huron, or rather of the Iron People . . .

In time, of course, the gate to the very Iroquois was opened, and many souls were saved, including that of the Venerable Kateri Tekakwitha, so that in after times, though the Black-Gowns shed many tears for the failure of the Huron

Mission, they agreed that it had been a wise action, this sacrifice of a part to save the rest.

Further History of the Nipissing Nation 1649

Destroyed by the Iroquois.

Further History of the Neutral Nation 1650–1651

Destroyed by the Iroquois.

Further History of the Erie Nation 1651–1680

Destroyed by the Iroquois.

Further History of the Montagnais 1650–1683

Now at long last the tribes at Tadoussac, who had always refused passage to the French, came to the Black-Gowns in all humility and asked to be converted . . . In 1646 they abandoned their custom of holding eat-all feasts, of which the Iron People had disapproved. In their banquets they now became civilized and decorous, the sexes eating separately. For the first time, it is said, the women no longer got enough to eat at these affairs. But the tongue that uttered that lie was surely an organ of the DEVIL.

In 1653, in the month of Juillet, the Montagnais, Souriquois and Etechemins attacked the Hiroquois.

In 1661 the Hiroquois destroyed the Porcupine Nation of the Montagnais.

The Betsiamite Nation, it is reported, had moose and caribou in plenty much longer than any other Montagnais, because they got arquebuses later.

The Montagnais continued to settle in houses at Sillery, where the Black-Gowns ruled them. Year by year this village grew. In 1678 it was considered a model for the land. In 1683 it was wracked by drunkenness, and presently abandoned.

Further History of the Souriquois 1693

In this year the French traded with them five hundred pounds of gunpowder, two muskets, six hundred pounds of shot, a hundred pounds of bar lead . . . Oddly enough, game in their Country had become quite scarce. The Sieur Denys, who'd spent many years cod-fishing in Acadia, reported that the Jesuits were compelled to abandon the missions at Miscou and Nepisiguit because the morals of the Savages had been ruined by brandy. They'd quite lost the generosity which Père Biard once praised, and were quick to profit from the wars of the French Lords one upon the other. The beaver-skins and pelts which they brought in trade were no longer worth nearly as much, which embittered them. Being but ungrateful Savages, they threatened to take goods by force, and in particular the liquor to which they were addicted. – They gave the very robes they wore in exchange for this poison. Once they began drinking they never failed to fight, for each claimed to be a greater Saqmaw than the others. Bones were broken, and heads split with warclubs, and hearts bullet-pierced (although this harm was not so severe as it might have been, the Savages being very cunning to heal themselves with balsams). When the women saw them about to begin one of these amusements, they took everything sharp from them, even the knives that they wore about their necks; then they fled to the woods with their children, to avoid being hurt themselves. They always fled to the same place. The fishermen knew where to find them, and they prostituted themselves for brandy.

Further History of the Christians 1650–1989

The Fox's scalp had long since taken root in the bed of the Fleuve Saint-Laurent, as we know, and the Christians continued to leave their families and shatter the families of others for its sake, *even as Cain,* says Lescarbot, *after the murder of his brother Abel, had the wrath of* GOD *ever at his heels, and could nowhere find peace of soul, thinking ever he had this* GOUGOU *before his eyes; so that he was the first who tamed the horse wherewith to flee, and who shut himself in with walls in the town which he built . . .* – which certainly describes Lescarbot, Champlain, Saint Ignatius, Saint Peter, Soranhes, Père Biard, Père Le Jeune, Marie de l'Incarnation, Père Jogues, Père Brébeuf, and by contagion poor Tekakwitha – but yet it does not describe them, either, because what they did they did for love of something, bravely doing what worldly minds must call insane actions. Without them the disasters would probably have happened anyway.

Further History of Katherine Tegakouïtha 1680–1700

The *Jesuit Relations* tell us that on the eve of Kateri Tekakwitha's passing, a certain woman retired to a private place in the forest, in order to mortify herself as an offering for the happy death. The violets were not yet in flower, neither yellow nor white; the raspberries had not yet opened their leaves. We may well surmise that this woman was her friend Marie-Thérèse. It is also safe to imagine as we make this Exercise that Marie-Thérèse applied herself even more diligently than usual to the task of making her flesh burst smartly open, out of charity for her dear one's sake. She approached the deathbed. She knelt down. Catherine clasped her arms and whispered: *Courage, dear sister. Oh, how delighted I am with the life you lead! Know that I not only know your life, but that I know also the place from which you came, and what you did there just now. Go, my dear sister; take courage; continue in the same way.* – The Black-Gowns said that this was one of her first miracles; for she knew without leaving the place where she lay what her companion had done. But if it was Marie-Thérèse, then she would not have needed the Power of Seeing-Ahead to imagine what she might have been doing. Indeed, it could have been anybody. The Great Mohawk constricted his body with iron bands every Friday; then there was Anne, who plunged herself beneath the ice in winter, dragging her three-year-old Marie with her, so that the half-dead child would store up penance in advance for any sins committed when she was older –

Kateri's last words to Marie-Thérèse were these: *I am leaving you. I am about to die. Always remember what we have done together since we knew each other; if you change I will accuse you before the tribunal of GOD . . . Never give up mortification. I will love you in Heaven; I'll pray for you; I'll assist you.*

Fifteen minutes after her death, came the second miracle. The pockmarks vanished from her face, and she became beautiful.

She began appearing to everyone in dreams.

A Frenchman named Claude Caron was the first to be cured. A priest made him promise her three Masses, and the congestion in his chest went away. Then a Christian Iroquois regained his health by eating some of the earth from her grave. Soon there were many others. *She does not act in the same way toward the sick children for whom prayers are said,* a Black-Gown cautions terrifyingly. *Experience shows that the earth from her tomb, which cures persons of an advanced age, seems rather to draw these little ones to Heaven.*

In his life of her, our good Père Chauchetière writes what must be considered her epitaph:

SHE WAS VERY FAR REMOVED FROM THE CORRUPTION OF THE SAVAGES. SHE WAS GENTLE, PATIENT, CHASTE, INNOCENT, AND BEHAVED LIKE A WELL-BRED FRENCH CHILD.

Further History of the Iroquois 1700

If the English sell goods cheaper than the French, we shall have ministers; if the French sell them cheaper we shall have priests, said a sensible Iroquois.

Further History of the Iroquois 1837–1875

So the New York ladies sat at table, smiling behind their bonnets, and their waists were drawn marginally inward by secret compressions, and their eyes were sad and delicate and dreamy. At night the clouds were white above, the moon-ball yellow on the water below. Boats sailed noiselessly in the harbor. In the morning, the golden river lowlands were so wide between low mountains, with the sun streaming through the sky's blue window. Cattle waded in the river to drink. Cows lay or browsed in the shady dead-leaf spaces between the trees, and the light was white on the river, where it was so bright. Along the bank, two American girls stood in sunbonnets, picking berries at the edge of that soothing spacious shade. In the spring, the flowers by the river were white, and the clouds were the color of cream. Cows stood breast-deep in the cool, fast water. Sheep nipped at the grass. Deeper into what had once been Indian Country, dead trees clutched treacherously just above the surface of a wide lake. A twin-sailed boat passed. In the distance, high above the banks, curved the great hook of Mount Chocorua. Of the Iroquois villages, there was not one to be seen.

Debts and Debtors

1989

> A reference, at least, to the missionary efforts of the French, while in the occupation of Canada, ought not to be omitted.
>
> LEWIS HENRY MORGAN, *League of the Iroquois* (1851)

Eleven days before the English conquered Québec forever, they burned a little French town. The Captain of the HMS *Scarborough* (Admiralty 1022) sat looking at the flames for a moment and opened the log. Now he made the easy march back through the foliage of the previous hours' memories which rustled about him like the maples around that settlement: *. . . all the inhabitance was run in the woods,* he wrote, *where we searched strictly and found an Indian cannue and several other things, but most of their affects they carried with them, so we left 30 men in the ridout all night and had shooting parties out all day . . .*

The Anglophones, they don't know exactly nothing! shouted Pierre.

He wedded his pretty Marie-Claude in the month of Août, when the mosquitoes and blackflies were not too bad, so that they could have the reception at their country house. In the photograph, he grins holding his champagne glass, bearing the confetti in his hair, and she is laughing so hard she is almost crying. The forest rises behind them. Confetti spangles his dark suit.

I visited them in Novembre. They lived in Montréal. The Fleuve Saint-Laurent was the hue of a tarnished mirror which split the whole world of Canada in two (all the way to China, as far as the Sieur de Champlain could tell). Over the Fleuve hung clouds fire-red at the edges like hellish essences, votive candles. Below these stretched an evening of white-roofed blocks of houses, brassy yellow eyes of automobiles in the narrow crevices between the house-encrusted plates of ivory. The roofs bore their snow more thickly at their eaves than in the middle. Trees were frosted grey with snow. Puzzle pieces of snow-white and tree-grey alternated outside of the town. A bluish-grey chill was manifest over all. I walked through slushy icy streets whose nested curves were like the ridges of some colossal fingerprint, and reached rue Sainte-Catherine. The whores were smiling and shivering; the department stores glittered with Christmas. Snow thickened on everyone's shoulders.

The light was on. When I rang the bell, Pierre buzzed me in. I could see him waiting for me at the top of the stairs, smiling. He shook my hand; Marie-Claude kissed me *salut!* – smack, smack! Pierre was saying: Do you want some juice? Do you want some coffee? Treat this house as yours; open everything! – and I gave Marie-Claude a vase and she kissed me again, saying delightedly: yes, we don't have!

Pierre and Marie-Claude were Québecois. They were the Old Canadians now, like Champlain, like Amantacha, like Born Underwater.

The Cross

The most difficult part of our identity right now is to understand exactly what we are and what we were before, when the Canadian spirit came to reality. (Thus Pierre.) For me, the problem is this: we never governed ourselves – never! Champlain was the Governor. It was always Paris or London. We were always the colony. It's hard in that situation. You create a national identity, but you don't have the political power to assure this identity. And so it's always a failure. We were New France. After, we were French-Canadian, when the British won the war, and now we're Canadian because the British decide that. That's the only way we're Canadian.*

So, do you think Canada would have been better if Wolfe had been defeated?

No, I don't say that. The English people, they're like United States: they don't like Inuit or Indians. And the French had a lot of *mépris*, a lot of suspicion and bad feeling about the Indians. Some people don't bother about that. They just say: oh well, it's another Country, a great space, a beautiful Country, bizarre

* "I'm sure this is what M[arie-Claude] and P[ierre] would say." (Thus Trigger.) "But they have had great political power to regulate the life of everyone in Quebec since a provincial parliament was established in 1867, & great economic power since the Quiet Revolution of the 1960s. This sense of powerlessness is a manifestation of false consciousness that powerfully reinforces cultural identity at the expense of individual fulfillment (& justifies individual failures such as we all have)."

people . . . I have no bad feeling; I'm happy to know who I was. But many Québecois don't want to admit they were a part of an Indian kind of life before. How can you analyze our people today with such progress, with white people, television, comfort economically, and so and so, and say: well, not long time ago we were in the bush; we were like those Indians? You look at Indians now and it is hard to say: oh, we were similar. Do you understand? It's hard to figure that we were like them. Now the ideology try to tell us: you are white, and you are pure white. And the Indians have the same ideology for them: we are Indian, we are red, and we are pure red.

Do you think that started with the Catholics?

Oh yes. The Jesuits did it. And then Marguerite Bourgeoys, she opened the first school here in Montréal, and she tried to educate the young Canadian girls and the young Indian girls. She had a very big problem with the young Canadian girls, because they want to become *Indian!* (The Indians, they were okay; they listened quite well.) Marguerite Bourgeoys, she said: those young Canadian girls are so wild! And many, many Jesuits said the same. What was the purpose of the Jesuits? To penetrate the Country, firstly, to penetrate the hearts of those first Indian people. Secondly, to help French grab the Country. The best way to do that is by the religion. We know that the Indians are a very spiritual People. I don't know exactly why they played that game with the Jesuits and the Recollects and every kind of priest that came here. But they did. They played the game, and they lost the game.*

You know, Pierre, when I first started reading about Tekakwitha, I said: What a sad victim she was! She ended up being someone who thought she was so bad that she literally had to torture herself to death. Because she killed herself, she became a Sainte. That doesn't seem right.

But the Catholics at that time always had that kind of ideology, of education. We learned, ever since we came into the life, that we are guilty for something –

For Adam?

Maybe, he laughed. And we have to live with that. The educational system here, family system, work system, political system, all work with the same idea.

When you were a boy, and went to church, what did they say to you about the Indians then? Did they say anything?

No. Only in school. And there we had the old books, the old ideas. The Indians were the hypocrite, they were Savage, wild . . .

When was the first time you saw an Indian?

* "A profound observation," returns Trigger. "My suspicion is that they played the religious game even more seriously as a consequence of knowing they had lost."

I was young. My parents lived near from Oka. I saw there poverty. I saw criminals. I said: oh, all that the books have told me is true. It took a long time before I analyzed and said to myself: it's not so simple like that. And I'm afraid that the majority of people here don't make the same distance. It's the same for black and white, for everything. You know, the government here never recognize that Métis can exist here. No half-breeds in Québec.

So a person is either Indian or white?

Yes.

Do the Indians in Québec consider themselves Québecois?

No.

Do they consider themselves Canadian?

Oh, it's hard for them. It's a failure. I remember ten years ago they said: we are Canadian; we are proud of it. And we are Indian. – Five years ago they began to say: we are the first Canadians. We were here before you. – And now they say: We are Indian. We are not Canadian.

When you used to go to Caughnawagwa, did you feel that the Indians there felt any kinship toward you as a human being?

Not really. The last time that I go there, I play before at a sport called lacrosse. And we played against Caughnawagwa. The RCMP* had to come after the game, to escort us out of the reserve.

For your safety?

Exactly. It was tough. Very tough. They looked for fight.

What would they have thought if you'd worn relics of Tekakwitha around your neck? Would they have thought about you any differently?

I hope not, because I'm not agreeing with Kateri Tekakwitha. I don't understand why many Indians respect that kind of symbol. For me it means colonialism, alienation. I feel a little painful. For myself, if I were an Indian, I would put fire to those things on my reserve.

The Doll

In Montréal at the dawn of a hot August day surrounded by the sounds of cats and birds, your prayer sits aching, unsleeping, rubbing eyes with wingtips. The grey cat is also awake, and she comes to your prayer's bed with raised ears, turning her head to follow the car-sounds with such regularity that it makes your

* Royal Canadian Mounted Police.

prayer weary to hear it. Sweat breaks out on your prayer's shoulders. Today at last your prayer will kiss Catherine's relics.*

The shrine dedicated to her is indeed, as Pierre has implied, at Kahnawaké, which place – although it has moved several times since 1668, it is true – may now be reached by taking the number ten autobus to the Pont Mercier, disembarking, and *walking* that bridge's shuddering length (having no other option due to the Voyageur bus strike, now in its second year – well, your prayer could fly, it is true, but the distance is now so negligible!) Upon making this portion of the Exercises it is customary for the pilgrim to gaze down into the Fleuve Saint-Laurent with its dull whitecaps of toilet paper from the sewage outflow. Now in the humid haze of the day your prayer sees the greenness of the far side, from which a gilded steeple rises, and your prayer keeps walking, inhaling perforce the exhaust of the big trucks or camions that shake the bridge and make your prayer wobble in their air-wash; and then there is a gap in the walkway through which workmen's curses ascend, and then your prayer arrives at the Caughnawagwa side. Your prayer descends the embankment and passes through the ditch of sumacs and thistles (that is the First Prelude) into the aforementioned Kahnawaké, where brown moths follow your prayer, clinging to sweaty trousers and sweaty wings. The Mohawk, who are not unfriendly, direct your prayer past the cemetery and up the hill to the shrine, just before which your prayer buys itself a Canada Dry. The lady at the cash register says that the temperature will reach 30° Celsius. *C'est bien dommage.*

Now here is the Church with its many ribboned bouquets, its marriage bouquets posted on the door. This is a living Church. Above the altar, high above, is JESUS, arms in Jansenist position. Ignatius is on His left, holding aloft a monstrance. François Xavier with the crucifix is on His right. Just over the flickering candles, an arrow-sign says **RELICS OF KATERI TEKAKWITHA.**

Your prayer's heart beats painfully.

There is her tomb, a block of white marble delectably candied with a golden turtle to represent her clan, and the words

KAIATANORON

KATERI TEKAKWITHA

1656–1680

* "For the true sense we must have in the Church Militant we should observe the following rules," begins Ignatius. "The sixth: to praise the relics of the Saints by venerating them and praying to these Saints."

CHURCH AT KAHNAWAKE (1989)

behind which stands her wooden statue with its tall elongated shadow. She stands staring ahead of her, clasping her arm over her breast, her robe pulled tight as a shroud. A Crucifix sprouts from her left hand; rosary-roots descend from her right. A pink blossom rests between her crossed palms. Her eyes stare so far away . . . Before her, like another offering, is the text of a prayer to GOD, Who is called in the Mohawk language SEWENNIIO.

A Mohawk woman approaches the tomb. With her is a girl of six or seven years. They kneel. – Ask her to bless everybody, the mother says.

Is she in there? asks the child.

No, but her bones are.

There are two portraits, one on each side of the altar. On the right she is in profile praying. On the left she stands spreading her arms to release a corona of stars. Her hair is jet-black. Her lips are as pink as the flowers of the raspberry called *ronce odorante*. She stands upon a crescent. Above her are two Faces. She is beautiful.

A Hiroquoise genuflects at the altar-rail, hiding herself in jet-black hair.

(Saint Kateri is part of the altar also. Angels hold an immense Crown over her. She is a little unadorned doll in her buckskins, her head on her shoulder, her arms crossed.)

On the wall of the old fortress abutting the Church it says **SMOKE WEED, DRINK BEER, GET LAID.**

The Martyr

At the country house, it was snowing again, and one of the cats was curled up on the sofa by the bearskin which clings to the wall with outstretched claws as if it were flying. Marie-Claude's father had shot it. Pierre mixed me up a Clamato juice just right, with lemon and Worcestershire, and I sat thinking about how Tekakwitha's fingers were reddish-brown but she wanted them to become as white as snowy alder-twigs transfixed by darkness.

Marie-Claude was always singing and kissing Pierre. (He said to me confidentially: She is an Angel!)

Pierre sat beside me, and I toasted him, saying: Here's to the Roy de Clamato! Here's to the Roy de Sentier! – and Pierre laughed, and Marie-Claude shouted at a woman on television, calling her tart and pig, and the other cat scratched at the window from outside, waiting and licking its snowy paw, and Pierre let him in while Marie-Claude sang a song as beautiful as anything out of the Mohawk hymnal or gradual which the Black-Gowns had composed at Kahnawaké, with its square notes of praise-music rising and falling, and Pierre said:

Here in Québec, you know, many people call Québec *Réserve du Québec*. Because our history is like Indian in a way. And we even have accommodators like Tekakwitha! When French Canadians become Prime Minister of the Canada, they come to speak English and only English. They become proud of the Crown, the British Queen. For me it's exactly the same. And also wc have our Saints and Martyrs, killed by the Indians. They tortured them. They too were

Tekakwithas. And this is what they tell us: Our good Saint-Fathers were killed by the bad ugly Savage Indians!

Statement at the Beatification Mass 1980

The last months of her life, said Pope John Paul II, *are an even clearer manifestation of her solid faith, straightforward humility, calm resignation and radiant joy, even in the midst of terrible sufferings.*

Canadians

Since three hundred years, with Jesuit, with intellectual people, they try to tell us we are not Indian, said Pierre. Since three hundred years! And this still continue today, more than ever. Because we don't want to be an Indian. I know for myself I'm not an Indian: little, blond, blue eyes . . . But somatically I think I was. I am, and historically I was. I believe that we half-breed with Indian, we take part in their point of view of the world. We approach the whole continent that way.

I think the best thing for our strength now, said Marie-Claude, is for the Indian, to not search for purity, and the same for us. We should say with the Indian: come on, let's get together and *act* for our land! It's not the English one way, the French one way, and the Indian another way. It's the same fight. So we should work together. And the Indian must lose this damn search for the red – *red, red, red!* "You're a Métis; you're not an Indian." Like us, we say: "If you don't have grandparents that come from Normandie, you're not a real one." That's one of the things that makes me angry, that bothers me! And one mistake is, we always look what was before. The Indians say: We were here before! Stop fighting like that. In each Canadien Français there is a little bit of Savage. There's no solution as long as the Canadien Français say: We don't want the Indian inside us! And the Indian the same. – What is a Canadian? It's a European that came here, that went Métis, and stayed here. If you admit that, there's no problem.

I said nothing.

We are angry about our dominator, said Marie-Claude. Either France, then England. Of course we are near French, because we speak French. But a French that stay here and doesn't métis, who doesn't breed with the Indian, for me he is as bad as the English that did the same thing. Our identity is here.

So would you say that Tekakwitha was one of the first Canadians in a way? Because she represented that movement, that mixing between Indians and French.

No! cried Pierre. For me, she tried to become a beautiful white, and because of that failure, she kill herself.

She didn't try to become a Canadian! said Marie-Claude. She try to be a French. She did not want to admit that she was Indian.

(But at this I could not but think of Sainte Catherine her namesake being stretched between two spiked wheels, throwing out her hands and screaming with anguish while a light like radioactivity had already begun to glow around her face and JESUS leaned down from the clouds with His arms outstretched for her and a little cherub came flying down with a garland and a river of light and blood flowed upward from her soul-spring.)

What if there were Indians who didn't want to be Canadians? I said. The French and the English who came here had a choice. If they didn't want to become Canadians, as you say, they could go back to France. But the Indians had nowhere else to go.

But, Bill, said Marie-Claude, in 1989 you don't have the choice. You must be Canadian here or you die. You don't have the choice to be Métis, to be free; you don't have a chance.

What about the reserves like Kahnawaké? Are they useless?

It's like a zoo! When you have extinctious animal, you put them there, so you can make experiments, and maybe breed them there . . . But when the last tiger come in the zoo, it will be the last. Maybe if you keep the tiger out, and he try to breed, maybe he have more chance like that! If their soul want to live, they must extend their people!

But, Marie, said her husband, if the Indians go outside the reserve, if you abolish the reserve, in ten years there will be no Indians.

We had already advanced three good leagues, and had dropped anchor in the middle of the river waiting for the tide, when we discovered six Armouchiquois canoes coming towards us. There were twenty-four persons there, all warriors. They went through a thousand maneuvers and ceremonies before accosting us, and might have been compared to a flock of birds which wants to go into a hemp-field but fears the scarecrows.

PÈRE BIARD, letter of 31 Janvier 1612

Glossaries

Glossaries

* See the Orthographic Notes

Note

I have tried to define every term which may not be readily comprehensible. (1) Because this is a novel, not a treatise in linguistics, the words are entered as they appear in the text. For example, I refer to the organization founded by Ignatius de Loyola as the Society of JESUS, which was in fact born in Paris and so obviously was not christened in English. – Too bad; my pedanticism can only go so far. (2) Source citations for terms are not in any way exhaustive; they merely indicate where I have seen them in my reading. Thus, for instance, GOUGOU was so called not only by the Etechemin, but also by the Micmac and others, as I have in fact assumed. (3) The same word is often spelled a variety of ways in this book (e.g., "Catherine Tegahkouita" and "Kateri Tekakwitha"; "Louis" and "Louys"; "Saint Peter" and "Saint Pierre"; "Hiawatha" and "Ayonhwhatha"; "DEKANWIDA" and "DEKANWIDEH"; "Iroquois", "Yroquois", "Irocois" and "Hiroquois" – which of course are all three the same as "Haudenosaunee" or "Hodinhsioni" or "League of the Five Nations"; "Québec" and "Kebec"; "Moor" and "Morisco"; "Acadia" and "Acadie"). I am sadistic but not unjust: every spelling is taken from a primary source. Rather than be a totalitarian, I have preferred to let the variants stand in all their charm.

Orthographic Notes

Note on Micmac Orthography

Many of the Micmac words listed are from the dictionary of the Rev. Silas T. Rand (1888), from the *History* of Marc Lescarbot (researched 1606–7), or from the Relation of Father Sebastien Le Clercq (*ca.* 1680). The written Micmac language has since been standardized, and many of these spellings are obsolete. Following the convention established in the first volume of *Seven Dreams*, *The Ice-Shirt* (and explained there), I generally have Europeans use European spellings, and Micmac use the standard orthography, which has been given to me by Ruth Holmes Whitehead of the Nova Scotia Museum and Bernard Francis of the Micmac Language Institute. I've deviated from this when a word or name appears so briefly that variant spellings would be confusing. Thus, the Jesuits use the spelling "Cacagous" for a certain man's name. Whitehead's orthography is "Ka'qaqus." Although a Jesuit addresses this man, I have used only Whitehead's orthography, as the reference is so brief.

Note on French Orthography

I have tried to integrate French words into the text whenever possible, to enhance the fiction that this is a sort of Jesuit Relation. Thus, I use "Fleuve Saint-Laurent" rather than "Saint Lawrence River," "rivière" rather than "stream" (except to vary syntax), "Père" rather than "Father," etc. This strategy has required a few odd compromises. For instance, in French the names of months are not capitalized. But because in English they are, and because I sometimes use Micmac or Iroquoian month-names, which are capitalized, I've done the same for French names: "Avril" rather than "avril," etc. May the Sorbonne forgive me. I also make use of Old French on occasion: "Roy" not "roi," etc. My Québecois friends Pierre and Marie-Claude Paiement have corrected some of my misspellings.

Note on Huron Orthography

I have used words as spelled by Sagard, Champlain, Trigger and the *Jesuit Relations* except when I have different information from Prof. John Steckley, who is the best living authority. Steckley writes: "The only Huron dictionary that is any good (Sagard's phrasebook is incredibly misleading; even fooled Voltaire) is the Fifteenth Report of the Bureau of Archives for the Province of Ontario, published in 1920 . . . The orthography I typically use is the one developed by the Jesuits" (letter to author, 2 February 1990). Steckley has kindly suggested for me the Huron pronunciations of various French words: "Kwer Nikoas" for "Père Nicolas," "Chawain" for "Champlain," "Kekwek" for "Kebec," etc. But I have disregarded Steckley's spellings in cases paralleling those for the Micmac, listed above. Two examples: (1) Brébeuf believes that he knows his *Arendouane* from his *Aescara*. These are his own spellings, and have nice alliteration, so for the latter I avoid Steckley's "yaheskara." (2) "Soranhes," not "Shorenhes" (except in a footnote).

NOTE ON IROQUOIS ORTHOGRAPHY

Most of the proper names of Iroquois leaders are taken from Hale and Hewitt's versions of the Ritual of Condolence in Bierhorst's *Four Masterworks of American Indian Literature* (see Sources). I also make some use of the spellings in Morgan's *League of the Iroquois*.

NOTE ON MONTAGNAIS ORTHOGRAPHY

All spellings of these words are taken from the *Jesuit Relations*.

NOTE ON PLURALS

Many books call the Micmac "Micmacs," the Huron "Hurons," etc. Whitehead argues that saying "Micmacs" is like saying "mens." Trigger sometimes says "Hurons"; in *The Children of Aataentsic*, however, he uses "Huron." In this book I decided to drop the "s" in pluralizing the names of tribes except in a few old forms such as Champlain's "Algoumequins" for "Algonkin."

NOTE ON NATIONAL AND TRIBAL NAMES

Generally, a people's name for itself is different than others' name for them. The people we call French call themselves Français. The people called Huron by the French call themselves Wendat. The people called Souriquois or Micmac call themselves Ln'uk, the people called Iroquois call themselves Haudenosaunee. I have endeavored to adhere to this rule in the text. When a Huron person is thinking of his people, I have him use the word "Wendat." When a Frenchman thinks of them, I have him use "Huron." The case is complicated by the fact that Iroquois names for the Huron are not the same as French names for them, and so on and so forth. By and large, however, I believe that I have already used names enough to tax your patience. So French, Iroquois, Montagnais and Souriquois alike generally say "Huron" in this book – likewise for similar cases.

1
Glossary of Personal Names

Aataentsik [*Huron*; lit., "She Is Old" – Steckley] A pregnant Sky Woman Who fell to earth, which was at that time covered with water. Animals dived down to get mud to make land for Her. She was the Mother of humankind. (Also, in Trigger: Aataentsic; in *Jesuit Relations*: Eataentsic. The Iroquois called her simply Sky Woman.)

Abadon the Destroyer [*Hebrew*] According to Francis Barrett in *The Magus or Celestial Intelligencer* (1801), the chief of demons of the Seventh Hierarchy. Name given by St. John in the Apocalypse to the King of Grasshoppers.

Adodardoh [*Iroquois*] A malignant Onondaga sorcerer whose Power (see Glossary 2) maintained strife among the Iroquois Nations. **Dekanwideh** brought goodness into his mind, and he became one of the great chiefs of the Iroquois confederacy. Each successive chief who inherits his position also takes on his name. (This has been a general rule with positions among the Iroquois and elsewhere; see, e.g., **Onontio**.) (Variant: *Adadardoh*, *Adadarhoh*, etc.)

Aktowtinji'j [*Micmac*] A son of **Membertou**. (Lescarbot's orthography: *Actcoudinech*.)

Louys **Amantacha de Saincte-Foy** [*Huron*; Steckley is uncertain of the meaning of "Amantacha": an odd name since the Huron language has no "m"] Son of **Soranhes**. Taken to France by the Black-Gowns in 1626; baptized Louys de Saincte-Foy. His return was delayed by the war between France and England, and he was kidnapped by the **Kirke** brothers. But he reached Québec in 1629. In 1634, while raiding against the Seneca, he was captured and lost a finger to torture. In 1636 he was captured again on another raid and (probably) tortured to death.

Amiskoueian [*Montagnais*] A girl's name. Champlain leaves no record of the real names of the three Montagnais girls he adopted in 1628 and baptized Foy (Faith), fifteen; Espérance (Hope), twelve; and Charité (Charity), eleven. I have supposed that Foy, the eldest, who ran away, was called Amiskoueian. It is unclear how much duress was involved in the girls' adoption.

Amortortak [*Greenlandic*] A Demon with black hands, Whose touch is death. (See volume 1, *The Ice-Shirt*.)

Anadabijou [*Montagnais*] Sagamore who gave **Champlain** and the **Pontgravés** hospitality at Tadoussac in 1603, where Champlain saw his first dance of naked privities. In 1607 he joined **Membertou** in the latter's raid on Saco. Anadabijou died in 1611.

ANIMAL PERSONS [*Micmac*] See **PERSONS**.

Claudius Aquaviva [*Italian*] A Superior General of the Jesuits. He ruled on the case of Père de **Nobili**; and would have been in charge of the Order when Père de **Brébeuf** took his novitiate.

Captain Samuel Argall [*English*] A pirate in the service of the Virginia colony. He kidnapped Pocahontas in 1613. The same year he destroyed the Jesuit settlement at Mount Desert Island, disrupting the plans of Pères **Biard** and **Massé**. He will be featured in the following volume, which bears his name.

Ayonhwhatha [*Iroquois*: "He Makes Rivers"] An Onondaga whose daughters were all killed by sorcery. Ayonhwhatha is credited with the invention of wampum. His "elder brother," the wise **DEKANWIDEH**, used the wampum to soothe his grief according to the Iroquois Rite of Condolence. Once Ayonhwhatha's mind was cleared, he was able to take part in forming the League of the Iroquois, or Haudenosaunee (see Glossary 2). (Also: *Haio^{n}hwa'tha*, *Hiawatha*, *Hayenhwatha*, etc.)

Bashaba [*Armouchiquois*] Sagamore of a band at what is now Saco, Maine. According to some accounts, he'd built up a superconfederacy. The Armouchiquois and the Micmac had a long-standing blood feud, which Bashaba's warriors advanced a little by killing **Panoniac**. The French gave the Micmac arquebuses for a counterattack – the first recorded instance of the use of firearms by one Amerindian group against another. After the French were expelled from Acadia in 1613, the Micmac killed Bashaba.

BEELZEBUB [*Hebrew*] A particular infernal spirit in Hell; the Jesuits, however, often used this word as an appellation for SATAN.

Père Pierre Biard, SJ [*French*] Attempted to convert the Micmac at Port-Royal, Acadia, from 1611 to 1613. He and his colleague Père **Massé** were the first Jesuits to come to the New World. In 1613 they removed to Mount Desert Island and built a new retreat, which was destroyed by Captain **Argall**. Died in France in 1622.

Biencourt [*French*] See **Poutrincourt**.

BLUE-SHIRT [*Norse*] Name for a large glacier in east Greenland; used in *The Ice-Shirt* as an appellation for **AMORTORTAK**.

Born Swimming [*Micmac*] A woman who first foresaw the arrival of the Black-Gowns in a dream. Raped by **Pontgravé the Younger**. Their daughter was **Born Underwater**.

Born Underwater [*Micmac*] Daughter of **Born Swimming** and Robert **Pontgravé**. A Métis woman with Power. An outcast and barren wife, she left her mother's people to marry **One-Eye** of the Montagnais, leaving him also to become the *asqua* (unmarried companion) of **Amantacha**.

Saint Jean de Brébeuf, SJ [*French*] Born 1593. Led the Huron Mission 1626–9; returned to it 1634–41, 1644–9. Tortured to death by the Iroquois in 1649. Canonized in 1930. (Called *Echon* by the Huron.)

Saint Brendan the Navigator [*Irish*] According to legend he sailed from Ireland to the New World and back again in an open boat (*ca.* 550).

Père Joseph Bressani, SJ [*Italian*] Captured by the Iroquois while en route to the Huron Mission (1644), he was adopted after prolonged tortures, and then escaped to the Dutch.

Étienne Brûlé [*French*] A subaltern of **Champlain**'s. Sent by him to Wendaké to learn the Huron language. At this time he might have been ten or eleven years old (but some say seventeen or eighteen). He was an interpreter for the French and later for the English, living most of the time with the Huron, although he may have come to Paris with **Amantacha**. In 1633 or thereabouts he was killed by the Huron for treachery after he had sought to open French trade with the Neutral Nation, or possibly the Seneca. Some Huron blamed the French for subsequent epidemics, accusing them of taking witch-vengeance for Brûlé's death.

Emery de Caën [*French*] **Champlain**'s deputy at Kebec in 1626. He conveyed **Amantacha** to France to be educated. He was Roman Catholic, his cousin Guillaume "was a heretic. Hence Emery was able to go on having dealings with Richelieu and others as Protestants fell out of favor — a nice arrangement for the family," — Trigger. Against Emery's will they succeeded in sending **Brûlé** and the other "insubordinate" interpreters to France. In 1628 the expectation of receiving supplies from him encouraged Champlain to hold out against the **Kirke** brothers (who later in fact captured those ships). In 1632, when the French regained control of Kebec, De Caën was made Champlain's deputy once more. Guillaume was excluded; he might have been in league with the Kirkes.
the Kirkes.)

Capitanal [*Montagnais*] A Captain or headman (son of a man with whom **Champlain** had fought against the Iroquois). Not as docile as Champlain would have liked.

Carigouan [*Montagnais*] See **Manitousiou**.

Jacques Cartier [*French*] Born 1494. First sailed to Canada in 1534. Said to have visited **Membertou**. A kidnapper of Indians. (Also: *Quartier.*)

Saint Catherine Tegakouitha See **Tekakwitha**.

Samuel de Champlain [*French*] Born in 1567 (?) (see Chronology). Sea-Captain, King's Quartermaster to 1598, geographer of New France beginning 1603; founder of Kebec 1608, proxy military commander of New France until his death in 1635. He launched a century of French–Iroquois war in 1609 by assisting the Montagnais–Algonkin–Huron alliance. (The Huron would probably have pronounced his name *Chawain*, and so have I done in the Huron parts.)

Charité [*Montagnais*] One of the Amerindian girls adopted by **Champlain**. See **Amiskoueian**.

Père Claude Chauchetière, SJ [*French*] Born 1645; died 1701. Principal biographer of **Tekakwitha**.

Chawain [*Huron*] See **Champlain**.

Joseph Chihwatenah [*Huron*] Born 1600 (?) The Jesuits' most famous Huron convert, he was also among the first adults in full health to be baptized (1637). Chihwatenah is also known as the uncle of **Oionhaton**. Noting his sponsors' propaganda that he'd married only once and had never used charms or relied on curing rites, Trigger says:

"These claims are hagiographic and almost certainly exaggerated. If only partly true, however, they suggest that his personality was an abnormal one by Huron standards . . . he seems also to have been attracted by . . . the notoriety that accrued from being the Jesuits' favored disciple . . ." (*The Children of Aataentsic*, p. 550). In 1640 he was murdered, ostensibly by the Seneca but probably by other Huron who believed him guilty of sorcery. There is a statue of him at the Martyrs' Shrine in Midland, Ontario. (Also: *Chihoatenhwa*, *Chihaetenhwa*.)

CHRIST [*Greek*: "The Anointed One"] When asked how he thought the Amerindians would have understood Him, Trigger replied: "I would think mainly as 'GOD's son,' kinship being the clearest concept to the Huron."

Père **Cotton**, SJ [*French*] Father Confessor to **Henri IV** of France. (Also: *Coton.*)

Saint Antoine **Daniel**, SJ [*French*] Accompanied Père **Brébeuf** on the Huron Mission of 1634. Schoolmaster at the Huron Seminary at Kebec, 1636–8. Martyred by the Iroquois in 1648. (Called by the Huron *Anouemen.*)

Darontal [*Huron*] **Champlain**'s host and fellow fighter on the 1615 campaign against the Iroquois. He was the At(t)ironta, or principal headman, of the Arenharhonon Nation of the Huron. As such he was the first Huron of any prestige to visit Kebec in 1616, to strengthen the alliance with the French (and possibly, by Huron custom, to claim any lucrative new trade routes for himself).

Père Ambroise **Davost**, SJ [*French*] Accompanied Père **Brébeuf** on the Huron Mission of 1634. Died at sea, 1643.

DEKANWIDA [*Various Iroquois*: "Two River Currents Flowing Together," or perhaps "Double Rows of Teeth"] Born of a Huron virgin, he united the Iroquois (see Glossary 2) in the Great Peace. He was aided in this by his "younger brother," **Ayonhwhatha**. (Also: DEKANWIDEH, DEKANWITHA, DEKANAHOUIDED, etc.)

Donnaconna [*Stadaconnan*] Chief kidnapped by **Cartier**, 1536.

DREAM PERSON [*Micmac*] See **PERSONS**.

DURGA [*East Indian*] A Hindu goddess. The Destroyer.

Jean **Duval** [*French*] A crony of young **Pontgravé**'s, this secretive locksmith hoarded various schemes in the Acadian years (1603–7); in 1608 he went as far as outright conspiracy at Kebec. **Champlain** sentenced him to death.

The **Eagle** [*Mohawk*] Warrior; a friend and protector of **Tekakwitha**'s. (NOTE: The names of many of the people in Tekakwitha's life have been lost. Her biographers often invent plausible names. "The Eagle" comes from the Lavergne book, a "popular" tract with little claim to accuracy.)

Echon [*Huron*] See **Brébeuf**.

Espérance [*Montagnais*] One of the Amerindian girls adopted by Champlain. See **Amiskoueian**.

EVIL-MINDED [*Various Iroquois*] See **HĂ-NE-GO-ATÉ-GEH**.

Fernando and **Isabella** [*Spanish*] "Their Catholic Majesties." It was under this royal pair that Columbus discovered America. They unified Spain, reconquered the province of Granada from the Moors, and expelled apostates. Bully for them.

Florinda [*Spanish*] Apocryphal. Raped by Roderick King of Spain, she supposedly opened the gates to the Moors, *ca.* 714.

The Fox [*Mohawk*] Warrior; a suitor for **Tekakwitha**; rejected by her and killed by the **Eagle**. (This name is probably apocryphal: see Note for the **Eagle**.)

Foy [*Montagnais*] One of the Amerindian girls adopted by Champlain. See **Amiskoueian**.

GAHACHENDIETOH [*Seneca*] The messenger of death. Lives at the bottom of a lake.

GOUGOU [*Etechemin*] "Demon feared by the Indians" – *Jesuit Relations.* Possibly some PERSON or Power consulted by Shamans. Mentioned by Champlain, who believed the tale. ("GOU-GOU IS a WHIRLPOOL PERSON, I think, rather than a sea monster. *Kuku* or *Ku'ku* is probably the correct orthography. It is a common Micmac last name nowadays. *Kukukwes* is the word for owl" – Whitehead.)

GREAT SPIRIT See **HÄ-WEN-NÉ-YU**.

Marquise Antoinette [de Pons] de Guercheville [*French*] A rich widow with time on her hands, she was at first the unrequited love of **Henri IV**, then, continuing in her piety, funded the mission of Pères **Biard** and **Massé** to Port-Royal. (Apparently **Champlain** also had besought her aid at Kebec, but she refused him since he seemed to prefer Recollects to Jesuits.) Later most of the known territory in North America (excepting only Port Royal) was granted to her; she speedily passed it on to the Jesuits. With such an empire, it was little effort for her to re-establish Biard and Massé in their own colony at Mount Desert Island, where they remained until the unpleasant visit of Captain **Argall**.

HÄ-NE-GO-ATÉ-GEH [*Various Iroquois*: "The Evil-Minded"] Brother of the GREAT SPIRIT, **HÄ-WEN-NÉ-YU**. Creator of monsters, poisons, etc.; discord-sower among human beings. Same as the Huron **TAWISCARON** ("Flint").

HÄ-WEN-NÉ-YU [*Various Iroquois*: "The Great Spirit," or "The Great Creator." Says Morgan: "This is an original uncompounded word, and in the Seneca dialect. It means simply 'A Ruler'"] The One Who cares for the People; the One to Whom they give thanks. Equivalent to the Huron **IOUSKEHA**.

HEAD-PIERCER [*Huron*] A sort of Charon on the road of the dead souls. Rather than convey them anywhere, however, He seizes the dead souls and sucks their brains out. (Also: PIERCE-HEAD.)

The Roy Henri IV [*French*] King of France at the beginning of our Canadian adventure. A womanizer. He had little trust in the Jesuits, but seems to have been compelled by policy to agree to the Mission of **Biard** and **Massé**. Assassinated by a religious fanatic, Ravaillac, in 1610.

Hiawatha See **Ayonhwhatha**.

Saint Ignatius de Loyola [*Spanish*] Born 1491; died 1556. Wrote the *Spiritual Exercises*. Founder of the Society of JESUS (1534). (Also: *Saint Ignace, Iñigo, the Pilgrim.*)

IOUSKEHA [*Huron*] The GREAT SPIRIT, according to Morgan's analogue. "Son or more often grandson of **AATAENTSIC**" – Trigger. "I believe He was not originally the 'Great Spirit,' as that concept developed after contact" – Steckley. Same as the Iroquois

HÄ-WEN-NÉ-YU. Invoked by Huron warriors. Also identified with the SUN. Prisoners of war were tortured to death in His name. (Also: *Jouskeha*.)

Iroquet [*Algonkin*] "An Onontchataronon or Petit Nation Algonkin" – Trigger. **Champlain** confided Étienne **Brûlé** to him to take to Wendaké, as he usually wintered there. Iroquet was probably present at all three of Champlain's battles with the Iroquois, and it was possible that he shot the rapids of Lachine with him in 1611.

Queen **Isabel La Católica** [*Spanish*] See **Fernando and Isabella**.

JASCONIUS [*Latin*] Great fish that befriended Saint **Brendan**.

Père Isaac **Jogues**, SJ [*French*] One of the Jesuit Martyrs. Jogues was assigned to the Huron Mission and assisted in the construction of Mission Sainte-Marie in 1639. In 1642 he was captured by the Mohawk, along with Thérèse **Oionhaton**. Tortured and so mutilated that he'd afterwards require a dispensation from the Pope to perform Mass, he was eventually adopted by an old woman from whom he escaped. In 1646 he was sent back to the Mohawk to "confirm the peace." The Mohawk had suffered severely from epidemics and blamed a box of his effects which he'd left among them before. They split his head. This occurred in the same village where **Tekakwitha** was born in 1656.

Kaiatanoron [*Mohawk*] Native name for Catherine **Tekakwitha**.

Ki'kwa'ju [*Micmac*] Wolverine, a personage in Micmac myths.

Ki'kwa'jusi's [*Micmac*] Wolverine's little brother. (See preceding entry.)

Kinebji'j-koji'j [*Micmac*] A friend of Born Swimming's. All we know of her historically is that she helped to execute an Armouchiquois slave-girl, *ca*. 1607. (Lescarbot's orthography: *Kinibech'coech'*.)

Kioutseaton [*Mohawk*; lit., "The Hook"] Chieftain and orator sent to conclude peace with the French in 1645–6.

The **Kirke brothers** [*English*] David, Thomas and Lewis. Sons of Gervase Kirke by a (naturalized?) Frenchwoman. Requested **Champlain**'s surrender in 1628; got it in 1629, and so conquered New France, which they held until 1632. David was knighted in 1633, Lewis in 1643. David became the Governor of Newfoundland (Terre-Neuve) in 1639, but died in prison in 1654. Apparently there were two other Kirke brothers, John and James, but nothing is known of them. (Also: *Querque*.)

KISU'LKW [*Micmac*: "He Makes Us"] A **PERSON** or Power among the Micmac.

KJIKINAP [*Micmac*: lit., "Great Power"] The "GREAT SPIRIT." According to one creation myth, He made the world (and hence **KLUSKAP**, with whom he dueled). As Whitehead points out, the fact that the world was thus literally created *by* Power (see Glossary 2) underscores the importance of Power for the Micmac.

KLUSKAP [*Micmac*] A powerful **PERSON** Who appears in some Micmac legends. "The character KLUSKAP was first recorded about 1850 . . ." says Whitehead. "By 1930, He had taken on some of the attributes of **CHRIST**." In spite of this problem with dates, Whitehead agreed that it was reasonable to have Him be one of the Persons invoked by the Micmac in the Norse era, since nothing is known of their legends from that time. So I kept Him in for this volume, too. (Rand's obsolete spelling is GLOOSKAP.)

KUKWESK [*Micmac*] Hairy cannibal giants who lived in the forest. ("The plural is *Kukwesk*, 'k' being one of the animate plurals" – Whitehead.)

Père Gabriel Lalemant, SJ [*French*] The brother of Jérôme **Lalemant**. He was born in 1610 and became a Jesuit in 1630. His Huron name was *A(t)tironta*, meaning "Big Stone" or successful trader (**Soranhes** was also a Big Stone). In 1649, only six months after having joined the Huron Mission, he was captured with Père **Brébeuf** and tortured with him. Apparently his agony lasted longer than Brébeuf's because the Iroquois (and their Huron-born "apostates") hated Brébeuf so much that they could not restrain themselves; Lalemant they treated more carefully. "Those wild men gouged out the eyes of Father Gabriel Lalemant and put red-hot coals in the sockets . . . He survived from six-o'-clock in the evening until nine-o'-clock the next morning, March 17th . . . From head to foot every part of his body was broiled and burned raw . . ." – Père Paul Ragueneau, SJ. (Also: *Lallemant.*)

Père Jérôme Lalemant, SJ [*French*] Père **Brébeuf**'s replacement as Superior of the Huron Mission, 1638–44. After this time he became Superior of the entire Canadian Mission. An orderly fellow, who dreamed up Mission Sainte-Marie. By all accounts he was a good administrator, but rigid in his dealings with the Huron. (Also: *Lallemant.*)

Père Joseph Le Caron [*French*] A Recollect; missionary at Kebec and in Wendaké from 1615 until 1628, when the English conquered New France. After this the Jesuits got a monopoly on missionary work. Died of plague, 1632.

Père Paul Le Jeune, SJ [*French*] Superior of the Kebec Mission, 1632–9. Wintered among the Montagnais in 1633–4, attempting to convert them. Called by them *Nicanis* ("my well-beloved"). Wrote many of the *Jesuit Relations* (see Glossary 4) for our period. Died in 1664.

Marc Lescarbot [*French*] A lawyer friend of **Poutrincourt**'s who was at Port-Royal in 1606–7. Enemy of **Champlain**'s.

The Roy Louis XIII [*French*] Son of **Henri IV**. Born 1601; died 1643. Very pious.

MANITOU [*Algonkian*; *Micmac*, **M'NTU'** – Whitehead] A Power or spirit. There were several MANITOUS, with different motivations, a fact which the Black-Gowns did not always understand. (See also Glossary 2, s.vv. OKI, Power, and the entry for "The Sorcerer's Wife" in the Source-Notes.)

Manitousiou [*Montagnais*: "The Married Man," or "Most Famous," according to Father **Le Jeune**; but suggesting to me "He Who Knows **MANITOU**," or something of the kind] A Montagnais shaman with whom Le Jeune was at odds in the winter of 1632–3. (Probably an appellation given to any Shaman.) His given name was Carigouan. A brother to Pierre-Antoine **Pastedouachouan**. Falling sick, he was burned alive by his relatives in the winter of 1633–4.

Mère Marie [Guyart] de l'Incarnation, OSU [*French*] A pious lady who forsook her own child to minister to the Indian children. In her long life (1599–1672) she accomplished quite a lot in the way of frenchifying Canada. She entered the Ursuline Order in 1631 and arrived at Kebec in 1639 to found a convent there. Much of what we know about New France at that time comes from her surviving letters. She was beatified on 22 June 1980. One of her characteristic maxims: "We must begin anew everyday to love GOD, and believe today that we did not truly love Him yesterday."

VIERGE-MARIE [*French*] The BLESSED VIRGIN MARY; the woman who gave birth to **CHRIST** after a heavenly or "immaculate" conception. Her purity was a grave point of faith to Saint **Ignatius**, who once contemplated killing a Moor for arguing that her hymen must have been torn after the birth of CHRIST. In the other Black-Gowns in this book her name inspired much the same feelings. The mystery of the virgin birth lay far beyond earthly logic, and was defended all the more fiercely for that.

Marie-Claude See **Pierre et Marie-Claude**.

Marsolet [*French*] Champlain's Montagnais interpreter. He lost his heart to Champlain's Indian girls. Born 1587 (?); died 1677.

PÈRE ENNEMOND (or **Ennemonu**) **Massé**, SJ [*French*] Entered the Order aged twenty. Companion of Père **Biard** in Acadia, 1611–13. Later returned to the New World under Père **Le Jeune**, 1625–9, and 1632–46, when he died, aged 72. A devotee of mortification.

Membertou [*Micmac*] Sagamore among the Micmac at Port-Royal. Said to be over a hundred years old in 1604. A friend of the **Poutrincourts**. Given guns by them in 1607, he led the first raid involving the use of firearms by one native group against another. **Born Swimming** was in his band. Converted by the French. Baptized 1610. Died 1611.

Membertouji'j [*Micmac*] Son of **Membertou**. (Also *Membertouchis* in the *Jesuit Relations*.)

Captain Merveille [*French*] The familiar or evil genius of Robert **Pontgravé**. Related to **GOUGOU**.

M'NTU' [*Micmac*] See **MANITOU**.

Marquis de Montcalm [*French*] The last French Governor at Québec. Defeated by the English General Wolfe in 1759, in a battle in which both were killed.

Charles Huault de Montmagny [*French*] The new Governor of New France after **Champlain**'s death, from 1636 to 1648. (Champlain never actually got the title of Governor.) Montmagny's name, which means "Grand Mountain," was literally translated *Onontio* by his Amerindian allies. He and all succeeding Governors of New France were known to them by that name. He died in 1653, five years after his removal. Replaced by Governor d'Ailleboust.

Nicanis [*Montagnais*: "My well-beloved"] Nickname for Père **Le Jeune**. (Not exclusively Le Jeune's appellation in reality, as the Indians sometimes used it among themselves; but applied only to him in this text.)

Père Nicolas See Père Nicolas **Viel**.

NIKSKAM [*Micmac*: "Our Grandfather"] Micmac word for GOD.

Père Roberto de Nobili, SJ [*Italian*] Converted the Indians of Goa. Born in 1577; died 1656. His example showed that it would have been possible to Christianize without frenchifying.

ODIN [*Norse*] King of the Gods. See *The Ice-Shirt* for more information.

Thérèse **Oionhaton** [*Huron*] The niece of **Chihwatenah**. In 1640, aged eleven or twelve, she was brought to **Marie de l'Incarnation** in Québec and instructed in the Faith. Marie called her "our good Huron girl." She preached zealously and lived like a nun. While returning home in 1642 she was captured by the Mohawk.

One-Eye [*Montagnais*] A widower. Married **Born Underwater**.

Onontio [*French*] Amerindian name for any Governor of New France excepting **Champlain**. See Charles Huault de **Montmagny**.

Panoniac [*Micmac*] Son-in-law of **Membertou**. A Sagamore. He sought to impress the Armouchiquois with French trade goods, for which presumption he was put to death by them in 1606. The French later gave Membertou some guns to help avenge his murder. (Also: *Panounias*.)

PAPKOOTPAROUT [*Micmac*] The Sagamore or Chief of Ghost World. (LeClerq's orthography; Whitehead spells it PAPKUTPARUT.)

Pierre-Antoine **Pastedouachouan** [*Montagnais*] A youth taken by the Recollects to France in 1620 to be baptized and instructed. He returned to Canada in 1625, an acculturated misfit who barely remembered his own language. Later he renounced Christianity and became an alcoholic. He was the one whom Père **Le Jeune** called "the Renegade" when he wintered among the Montagnais in 1633–4. Pastedouachouan had several wives, but they all ridiculed him and left him because he did not know how to hunt. He starved to death in the winter of 1634–5. (Also: *Pastedouchouan, Pastedechouan.*)

PERSONS [*Micmac, Huron, Iroquois, etc.*] Conscious entities (plants, animals, stars, legendary personages) who could affect life for better or worse, had Power, and could be addressed. Same as **MANITOUS**, OKIS, POWERS (see Glossary 2, and also the entry for Power in the Source-Notes to "The Dream of the Floating Island").

Saint Peter The Vicar of **CHRIST**. (Also: *Saint Pierre.*)

Pierre et Marie-Claude [*Canadian*] My Francophone friends in Montréal.

Étienne de **Pigarouich** [*Montagnais*] One of the Sorcerers converted by Père **Le Jeune**. In 1640, **Marie de l'Incarnation** praised him in a letter, calling him, in words uniquely suited to the times, "a man on fire." Citing Pigarouich's trick of putting red-hot cinders on the heads of the disobedient (which I fancy he'd learned from Le Jeune), Marie remarked: "One cannot see this good Christian without a sense of devotion."

PLANT PERSONS [*Micmac*] See **PERSONS**.

Pontgravé the Elder (François) [*French*] A merchant of St.-Malo. Born *ca.* 1554. A gambler. At Tadoussac 1603, Port-Royal 1605–6, Kebec 1608–29 (intermittently). Returned to France after the conquest by the **Kirkes** in 1629. He may have died on the voyage, as we know nothing further of him.

Pontgravé the Younger (Robert) [*French*] Born *ca.* 1585. Son of **P. the Elder**. Sailed to Port-Royal, Acadia. In 1607 he survived an attack of Armouchiquois. In 1610 (or earlier – the sources are vague) he raped an Etechemin or Micmac woman (whom I have imagined to be **Born Swimming**), and hid in the woods until Père **Biard** obtained his pardon from **Poutrincourt**. Later he and his associate Captain **Merveille** plotted against Poutrincourt. He was captured in 1611 and promised to reform. In 1618 he returned to France; in November 1621 he was killed in a sea-battle with the Dutch.

The Sieur de Poutrincourt [*French*] A credulous loyalist. He held Port-Royal in fief to the French crown from 1604 until 1611, when the Jesuits got it from him. Died in the French civil war, 1615.

Charles Biencourt de Poutrincourt [*French*] Son of the Sieur de **Poutrincourt**. Ruled Port-Royal in his absence and after him. Born *ca.* 1590; died *ca.* 1630.

Claudette de Poutrincourt [*French*] Poutrincourt's wife; Biencourt's mother.

Jacques Quartier See **Cartier**.

Rev. Père Jean de Quen [*French*] Missionary and priest at Kebec; friend of **Marie de l'Incarnation**.

Père Paul Ragueneau, SJ [*French*] Third and last Superior of the Huron Mission (after **Brébeuf** and **Lalemant**); from 1644 to 1650.

The Renegade [*Montagnais*] See **Pastedouachouan**.

Frère Gabriel Sagard [*French*] A Recollect lay brother who accompanied Père Nicolas **Viel** and Père Joseph **Le Caron** to Wendaké in 1623. The book he wrote about his trip is a valuable ethnographic record.

Satouta [*Huron*] One of the first Huron seminarians at Kebec. Died in the winter of 1636–7, following a quarrel with a Frenchman.

Savignon [*Huron*] A young man whom **Champlain** took to France in exchange for sending Étienne **Brûlé** to Wendaké. Savignon seems not to have liked France much. He was the brother to **Tregouaroti**.

SEWENNIIO [*Mohawk*] GOD.

SKY WOMAN [*Iroquois*] See the Huron **AATAENTSIK**.

Soranhes [*Huron*: "Tall Tree"] Father of **Amantacha**. A successful trader with the French. Lived in Teanaostaiaé. Probably committed suicide upon his son's capture in 1636. (Trigger's spelling, and therefore generally mine, is *Soranhes*. John Steckley, the Huron linguist, spells it *Shoranhes*).

The Sorcerer [*Montagnais*] See **Manitousiou**.

Taratouan [*Huron*] A headman near Teanaostaiaé. Uncle of **Tewatirhon**. Captured and killed by the Iroquois in 1637.

TAWISCARON [*Huron*: "Flint"] "Evil" Spirit (according to Morgan); brother of the "GREAT SPIRIT," **IOUSKEHA**. "Son or more often grandson of **AATAENTSIC**," says Trigger. Steckley adds: "I would not refer to him as 'evil'; that is a Western concept, not a Native one. Both twins had elements that could be thought of as 'good' and 'bad.'" Same as Iroquois **HÄ-NE-GO-ATÉ-GEH**.

Tehorenhaennion [*Huron*] Famous shaman in Ihonatiria who, along with Père **Brébeuf**, tried to invoke the rain during the drought of 1634–5. He vanishes from the *Jesuit Relations* after 1637–8. When I asked Trigger what he thought happened to him, he replied: "He had a 50 percent chance of dying of smallpox in 1639–40." (Steckley's orthography; also *Tehorenhaegnon* – Trigger and *Dictionary of Canadian Biography*.)

Tekakwitha or **Tegahouitha** [*Mohawk*: "She who goes searching in front of her"] Born of an Algonquin mother in Ossernenon, 1656. Converted by the Black-Gowns, she fled to Caughnawagwa (see Glossary 3), where she died in 1680. Called "Lily of the Mohawk," "Star of the Natives," etc. Beatified 1980, she has not yet been formally canonized and so is not officially a saint, although some call her so anyway. (Also: *Tegahkouita*, *Tekagouitha*, *Sainte Catherine*, *Kateri*, *Kaiatanoron*, etc.)

Teondisewan [*Huron*] Elder sister of **Amantacha**. (NOTE: For almost all Huron female characters I've had to supply names myself, since the *Relations* rarely give them, probably to avoid any charges which might reflect badly on the Jesuits' celibacy. What I did was to get Steckley to give me a list of Huron women's names with their meanings, and picked the one I thought appropriate. Steckley says: "Huron names can refer to events in their clan's origin story or to characteristics of their clan totem animal.")

Tewatirhon [*Huron*] One of the first students at the Jesuit seminary at Kebec, 1636.

Gilbert du Thet, SJ [*French*] A lay brother who came to Canada in 1613. Killed in **Argall**'s raid that year, he became the first Jesuit to die in Canada.

The Three Sisters [*Hiroquois*] Corn, squash and beans, personified as PLANT **PERSONS**.

Tonneraouanont [*Huron*] A hunchbacked Sorcerer. Chief rival of **Tehorenhaennion**. Died in the epidemic of 1637–8.

Tregouaroti [*Huron*] Conducted Étienne **Brûlé** to Wendaké in 1613. His brother **Savignon** went to France to be educated by **Champlain**.

Père Nicolas Viel [*French*] A Recollect missionary in the Huron country in 1625–6. Returning to Kebec to make a spiritual retreat, he drowned accidentally. His death was later attributed to Huron malignancy, in order to give the Recollects a martyr (or possibly because the Algonkin started that rumor, seeking to estrange the Huron from the French).

Whore of Babylon A Biblical symbol or DEMON of lust and license, whose appearance foretells the end of the world.

Major General James Wolfe [*English*] Led the assault upon Québec in 1759 and took the city. Both he and his French counterpart, **Montcalm**, were killed in the battle.

Yatera [*Huron*] Wife of **Soranhes**; mother of **Amantacha** and **Teondisewan**.

Yroquet [*Algonkin*] See **Iroquet**.

2
Glossary of Orders, Isms, Nations, Races, Hierarchies, Shamans, Tribes and Monsters

Agnierrhonons [*Huron*] **Mohawk** (Jesuit orthography). See also **Haudenosaunee**.

Agonha [*Various Indian*: "Iron People"] Name for the French. Which Indian tribes used it is controversial. Trigger, for instance, speaks of "the Huron's 'men of iron.'" But Steckley says: "Yannionyenhak (rather than Agonha) did not mean 'Iron People' in Huron. I believe they borrowed the term from another Iroquian speaking group." I have used the term herein fairly indiscriminately, both because of the importance of iron goods to the Amerindians and because it seemed desirable to have a general label for Europeans to form a counterpart to the Europeans' "Savages."

Algonkians North American Indian tribes; **Algonquian**-speaking inhabitants of the Ottowa River Valley. (Also: *Algoumequins, Algonkin.*)

Algonquian Group of languages spoken by the **Algonkians**. (This according to Whitehead. But Trigger says that "both should be either *k* or *qu* – difference is *ian/in* ending." – So I figure I can follow my own whims in this matter.)

Angont [*Huron*] "Witches were believed to harm people by supernaturally causing charms to enter their bodies . . . In order to make the object enter a body, it had to be rubbed with the flesh of an *angont*, or mythical serpent that lived under the ground or in the water . . ." – Trigger.

Arendouane [*Huron*] Shaman. According to Father Brébeuf there were three kinds of these: prognosticators, curers and seers.

Armouchiquois [*French*] Name for various agricultural tribes living in southern New England, including the **Etechemins** according to the *Jesuit Relations*. However, Champlain and Lescarbot seem to intimate that the Armouchiquois were a more southerly group than the Etechemins. (According to Alvin Morrison, a western subgroup of the Etechemins was allied with them.) In any event, both the **French** and the **Souriquois** were on bad terms with the Armouchiquois. Membertou went to war against them; Robert Pontgravé was almost killed by them. Morrison calls this name "a blanket term as imprecise as our own current label of 'Latin Americans' for all our neighbors to the south." Peter Bakker suggests that the *-quois* suffix may be "a remnant of Basque pidgin."* Whitehead adds: "You must know [that] Armouchiquois is probably a Micmac insult-name, based on their word for dog. Plus the *-kws* or *-ikwa* ending." (Also: *Almouchiquois*.)

Assirioni [*Mohawk*: "Cloth-makers"] Iroquois name for the Dutch.

Atiwaronta [*Huron*: "Big Stone"] A Huron headman who profited from the fur trade without trading himself.

Attignawantan One of the four Nations in the **Huron** confederacy.

Attiwandarons [*Huron*] Members of the Neutral Nation, on whose territory were extensive beds of chert, said to be required by the **Huron** and the **Irocois** for spear-points. ("No!" says Trigger. "This is an old white myth. Huron got their chert from pebbles in till [gravel] or used quartz.")

Autmoinos [*Etechemin*] Medicine man.

Basques [?] "Among the European peoples visiting Canada's east coast, the Basques had the most intensive contacts with some of the Amerindian nations . . . notably with the Micmac, Montagnais and Maliseet from the late 1540s to the first decades of the seventeenth century."*

Black-Gowns [*Various Indian*; *French* = *Robes-Noires*] Jesuit Fathers. According to Steckley, the Huron word was **Hatitsihenstaatsi**, or *they are called Charcoal*. "As far as I know," he says, "they were never called black robes or black gowns by the Huron." – But see, for instance, *Jesuit Relations*, vol. 39 (1638–9), p. 13, in which Brébeuf seems to suggest the opposite. In any event, I have not stinted to use the term evenhandedly throughout the book.

Cat Nation [?] Another name for the Erie (also Raccoon Nation). This **Iroquoian** group, which possibly had poisoned arrows, "lived near the southwestern end of Lake Erie. Like their neighbors, the Eries were horticulturalists inhabiting a number of sedentary communities" – Trigger. In 1654–6 they too would be scattered by the **Iroquois**.

Cayuga [*Iroquois*] A tribe of the **Haudenosaunee**. One source claims that the name means "the place where locusts were taken out." Other possibilities: "Mountain rising from water," "when they drew their boat ashore," "at the mucky land."

Charistooni [*Mohawk*: "Iron-makers"] Iroquois name for the Dutch.

Chrétien (m.), **chrétienne** (f.) [*French*] **Christian**.

Christians Originally followers of CHRIST, they later grafted various other tenets to His, dividing into factions in the process. In seventeenth-century Canada, they thought to coerce, and so combined with their beauty of purpose an ugliness of execution.

Crooked-Tongues See **Huron**.

Decuriae [*Latin*] Groups of ten. The **Jesuits** subdivided their student classes into *decuriae* to better manage them. Each *decuria* was comprised of nine students and a tenth who

* Peter Bakker, Institute for General Linguistics (University of Amsterdam): "A Basque etymology for the word 'Iroquois'." This is a forthcoming article which Whitehead was kind enough to send me.

was their monitor. The *decuriae* were sometimes pitted against each other in scholastic competitions.

Delaware [?*Delaware*] An **Algonkian** people who lived north of Delaware Bay. They were bounded by the **Dutch** on the east and the **Susquehannock** on the west. Like the **Iroquoians**, they were matrilineal. In the 1700s they sold their lands to the whites and moved west.

Donné [*French*] Lay worker in a religious Order (esp. the **Jesuits**). Donnés worked without pay, in exchange for which the Jesuits promised to support them all their lives and tend them in sickness. Because the donnés did not have to take religious vows, they were free to bear arms, which made them and the Pères they served more attractive to the Indians among whom they lived.

Dutch They discovered the Hudson River in 1609, Mr. Hudson having (in the words of the incorrigible Washington Irving) "laid in abundance of gin and sour crout, and every man was allowed to sleep quietly at his post." They settled at Manhattan and played their own hand in the fur trading game, being enemies of the **French** and therefore uneasy allies of the **Iroquois**. They were about as cruel as the **English**.

English A Caucasian people of mixed stock. After the defeat of the Spanish Armada in 1588, the English became a much greater presence in the world. They battled with the French for possession of North America from *ca.* 1600 to 1763, at which time they won the prize. Later supplanted in lower North America by their own colonists, the so-called "Americans." (Called by the Huron *Hatiwendoyeronnon*, or "They Are People of the Island.")

Eskimo [?*Indian*] Foreigners' name for the **Inuit**. The literal meaning is "eater of raw meat." Many Inuit now consider it derogatory. (See also **Excomminqui**.)

Esquimaux [?*Indian, frenchified*] See **Eskimo**.

Etechemins [*Etechemin*] Abenakis; Algonquin-speaking western neighbors of the **Micmac**. "Mainly hunter-gatherers," says Trigger. According to Thwaites, these consisted of three tribes: (1) the Tarratines (Penobscotts – but some say Micmac), (2) the Openagos (Quoddys), (3) the Marachites. The *Dictionary of Canadian Biography* simply calls them Malecites. Alvin Morrison divides them into Eastern Etchemin (allied with Micmac) and Western Etchemin (allied with **Armouchiquois**). Like all the Indians in this area before the French came, they were nomads. They lived in the Acadia area, probably between the St. John and the Kennebec Rivers. "By 1620 some had moved north and joined the Montagnais" – Trigger. My layman's opinion is that nobody knows who they were. (Also: *Etchemin, Estechemins, Etheminquins.*)

Excomminqui [*French*] Hudson Bay **Inuit** (17c). Probably derived from "excommunicated" and "Exquimau."

False Faces [*Various Iroquois*] Members of a curing society who wear gruesome masks (often globular) which gape serenely, representing a spirit whose face was crushed by a mountain in a contest with the GREAT CREATOR, after which the spirit promised to be good and heal diseases.

French A European people who proudly traced their descent from the ancient Gauls.

They were less cruel to the Amerindians than their rivals the **English** and the **Spaniards**, however odious their program might seem to us now. In short, they encouraged conversion, intermarriage and assimilation rather than conversion, expropriation and extermination.

Gallicanism A militant form of Catholicism which claimed the right and power of the Pope to depose a King if he were an enemy of the Church. Expounded by the Spanish Jesuit Mariani; approved by the General of the Jesuits in 1625. The Gallicans were sometimes, however, allied with the **Jansenists**.

Grey-Gowns [*My own neologism, to parallel "Black-Gowns"*] Name for the **Recollects**.

Hatitsihenstaatsi [*Huron*: "They are called *Charcoal*"] According to Steckley, the appellation for the **Jesuits** (see **Black-Gowns** for a further note on this).

Hatiwendarons [*Huron*] "Term referring to Iroquoian-speaking peoples who were not part of the Iroquois confederacy. They lived in what is now Ontario and western New York" – Steckley.

Hatiwendoyeronnon [*Huron*] Name for the **English**, meaning "They Are the People of the Island."

Haudenosaunee [*Various Iroquois*: lit., "the People of the Long House"] What the **Iroquois** call themselves. The League of Five Nations: **Mohawk** (also *Agnierrhonons*, or Flint People), **Oneida** (also *Onoiochihonons*), **Onondaga** (also *Onontaerrhonons*), **Cayuga** (also *Ouioenihonons*), and **Seneca** (also *Sonontrerrhonons*). In *ca*. 1712 the Tuscarora joined the Haudenosaunee, so it is now called the League of Six Nations. Founded by Hiawatha and DEKANWIDEH (see Glossary 1). "To this Indian League," says Morgan (1851), "France must chiefly ascribe the final overthrow of her magnificent schemes of colonization in the northern part of America." For a discussion of Huron *vs*. Iroquois myths, see the Source-Notes to the DEKANWIDEH tale. (Also: *Hodinhsioni*, *Ongwanonsionni*, etc.)

Hiroquois [*French*] A variant name for **Iroquois**. See also **Haudenosaunee**.

Hodinhsioni See **Haudenosaunee**; see also **Iroquois**.

Hollanders See **Dutch**.

Huron [?*French*; sometimes called *Chariquois* or *Good Iroquois* by Champlain; also: *Ochateguins*. Their real name – i.e., what they called themselves, was **Wendat**. Their enemies the **Iroquois** called them "Crooked-Tongues"] A confederacy of four Iroquoian-speaking tribes (the Attignawantan, Attigneenongnahac, Arendarhonon and Tahontaenrat) who lived in the Simcoe County area of Canada, north of the St. Lawrence. There were eight clans among them, each named after an animal. The Jesuits estimated a population of 30,000 in their twenty towns. They called them "the granary of the **Algonquin**" as they grew corn to trade with the Algonkin and related peoples. Half the population was lost to epidemics in 1634–40. The confederacy was destroyed by the Iroquois in 1649–50, "but the Huron lived on in two groups. Some became the group known as the Huron of Lorette, having a community near Quebec. Others joined their Petun and Neutral neighbors to form the Wyandot of Michigan, Ohio and Oklahoma" – John Steckley.

Indian [*Various European*] Appellation for native Americans, originally so given in the belief that North America was really India.

Innuat (sing. **Innu**) [*Montagnais*] What the Montagnais called themselves: "the People."

Inuit (sing. **Inuk**) [*Inuktitut*; lit., "the People"] The principal native people of the Arctic (= **Eskimo**).

Irocois [*French*] See **Iroquois**.

Iron People [*Various Indian*] See **Agonha**.

Iroquoian [*Various anthropologists*] Not Iroquois, but the culture including them, the Huron, Neutrals, Eries, Susquehannock, etc. in a common family of languages, horticultural pursuits, etc.

Iroquois [*French*] The League of Five (later Six) Nations, or **Hau-de-no-sau-nee**. "Iroquois," says one source, is a corruption of the Algonquin "Ee-reen-ah-krah" or "Irinakhoiw," meaning "real adders." But Trigger says: "Not clear what it is derived from. Recent suggestions that it is of **Basque** origin." Whitehead agrees. Their enemies the **Huron** called them "Serpents." (Also: *Hiroquois*, *Irocois*, etc.)

Jansenism Founded by Cornelius Jansen (1585–1638), Bishop of Ypres. One of the many religious movements based on the idea that only the elect, who have divine grace, will be saved. As such it was of course opposed to the orthodox Catholicism of the **Jesuits**. In the early eighteenth century miracles took place at the grave of a Jansenist. The cemetery was finally closed, but the sect endured until 1788. Jansenists played a role in the temporary suppression of the Jesuits in 1773.

Jesuit [*French; various European*] Originally derisive; now a standard term for a member of the Society of JESUS. With one exception, all Jesuits have been male. Members are either priests, candidates for the priesthood or lay brothers. The procedure is the same for all (except that the lay brothers must first pass through a six-month postulancy). A Jesuit spends two years in a novitiate and then takes simple perpetual vows of poverty, chastity and obedience. Approved scholastics (who take a fourth vow of obedience to the Pope) then may enter into Sacred Orders, studying liberal arts for two years, philosophy for three, a varying number of years as a teacher or prefect (this period is known as "regency"), theology for four years (they are ordained at the third), and "spiritual formation" or "tertianship" for one, according to the *New Catholic Encyclopedia* (1967), which also says: "Jesuit obedience is not military but religious." According to the *Encyclopedia Americana* (1984), "No other religious Order has been as widely admired or as bitterly hated as the Jesuits."

Jenuaq (sing. **Jenu**) [*Micmac*] Northmen, or northern demons, according to the Rev. S. T. Rand (who spells it *Chenoo*). In one of the Micmac legends in his compilation, they have hearts of solid ice. But Ruth Holmes Whitehead, who knows more, says: "It does NOT mean 'Northern Devil' . . . A Jenu is a human who has become transformed (probably by fat deprivation in winter). These people become psychotic and eat and kill other humans. They can be cured by drinking fat and being thawed out."

Jipijka'maq [*Micmac*] Race of horned Serpent-PERSONS. They had two horns – one red, one yellow.

Kinap [*Micmac*] Ruth Whitehead translates this word as "**Power**."

Knights of Malta [*French; various European*] Originally the Hospitaliers de St.-Jean. Formed in Jerusalem hospitals in 1048 to care for the sick. They later took up knighthood against the Muslim "infidels." The isle of Rhodes was their base until they were driven from it in 1522. Charles V gave them Malta, which became one of the best-fortified places in the world. Bonaparte overran them in 1798, after which they had little more than a paper existence. Governor Montmagny (see Glossary 1) was one of them.

Lnu'k [*Micmac*] What the **Micmac** called themselves: "the People."

Mahican [?*Mahican*] An **Algonkian** people who lived south of Albany between the Hudson and Connecticut Rivers. In 1628 the **Iroquois** subjected them to the Great Peace.

MANITOU See Glossary 1.

Martyr "The definition of a Christian martyr is one who is put to death out of hatred for the faith" – Angus J. Macdougall, SJ.

Métis [*French*] White-Indian halfbreeds.

Micmac [*French*; from a misunderstanding of the word *nikmaq* used in greeting, meaning "my kin-friends"] An **Algonkian** people once widespread in Nova Scotia, Prince Edward Island, New Brunswick, Gaspé Québec and environs. Still in existence. Also called **Souriquois** by the French. (The Recollect missionary LeClerq [1657–1736] calls them "Migmagi," and divides them into three subgroups, one of which, the Gespogoitg, he subdivides into three again: one of these latter bands he calls "Souriquois.") Like many Indian tribes, they called themselves "the People" – in their language, **Lnu'k**. Quite possibly it was the Micmac whom Norse Greenlanders encountered at the beginning of the eleventh century. ("Personally," says Trigger, "I doubt this.") See the Note on Micmac Orthography immediately preceding these Glossaries.

Mi'kmwesu'k [*Micmac*] "Beautiful and strong – flute players whose music enchants . . . they appear to humans lost in the woods. They themselves are thought to have once been People, having become through Power the ultimate realization of human potential" – Whitehead, *Stories from the Six Worlds*.

MN'TU' [*Micmac*] That People's spelling for **MANITOU**.

Mohawk [?*French*] One of the five (later six) Nations of the **Iroquois** or **Haudenosaunee**. Sixteenth-century French sometimes called this tribe the "Lower Iroquois," the other four comprising the "Upper Iroquois." Kateri Tekakwitha (see Glossary 1) was a Mohawk. Before 1666 they had three main villages: Ossernenon, Tionnontoguen, and Gandagaron. The Mohawk were the first of the Five Nations to get guns in significant numbers. They and the **Seneca** led the drive to destroy the **Huron** confederacy in the 1640s. (Also: *Agnierrhonons*, or Flint People; called *Maquaqs* by the Dutch.)

Montagnais [*French*] A nomadic people calling themselves the *Innuat*, who commanded a territory from Côte-Nord south to the Saguenay River and west as far as St.-Augustin: so says the Secrétariat des activités gouvernementales en milieu amérindien et inuit's *Native People of Québec*. But Trigger ends the above " . . . south to the St.

Maurice River." Père Le Jeune (see Glossary 1) wintered among them in 1633–4 and sought to convert them. Because they chafed at his fur trade monopoly, Champlain (see Glossary 1) once called them his "worst enemies." Enemies of the **Iroquois**. (Also: *Montagnes, Montagnets, Montagnaits, Montaignez*, etc.)

Morisco [*Spanish*] Moor.

Népissingue See **Nipissing**.

Neutral Nations This **Iroquoian** confederacy lived near the western end of Lake Ontario. They were "neutral" because they feuded with the **Algonkin** instead of with the **Huron** or the **Iroquois**. Their territory may have supported more hunting than the Hurons'. Like the **Tionnontaté**, they tattooed themselves lavishly. They and the Huron called each other **Attiwandarons**, meaning "people who speak a slightly different language." In 1647 the **Seneca** fell on one of their Nations (the Neutral had access to beaver-pelts but not to guns, a double enticement for the Iroquois). In 1650–1, the Seneca, joined by other Iroquois Nations, dispersed them in a series of merciless raids.

Nikani-kjijitekewinu [*Micmac*: lit., "one who knows in advance"] Someone gifted with precognition. Born Underwater (see Glossary 1) was one of these.

Nipissing [?*Nipissing*] An **Algonkian** group "that had its headquarters near Lake Nipissing and traveled as far north as James Bay each summer" – Trigger. Many wintered among the corn-rich **Huron**. Champlain visited them in 1615, en route to the Huron villages to attack the **Iroquois**. As the Huron confederacy collapsed in 1649–50, the Nipissing, too, were dispersed by the Iroquois.

OKI [*Huron; various Iroquois*] ". . . the Indian believes in supernatural existences, known among the Algonquins as **MANITOUS**, and among the Iroquois and Hurons as *Okies* or *Otkons*. These words comprehend all forms of supernatural being . . . with the exception, possibly, of certain diminutive fairies or hobgoblins . . ." – Parkman (I, 385–6). But Steckley says, "This is a Huron, not an Iroquois term." According to Trigger, "Persons who had unusual powers or characteristics, such as shamans and . . . valiant warriors . . . were believed [by the Huron] to possess companion spirits . . . Because of this power, they, too, were considered to be *oki*." See Glossary 1, s.v. PERSONS.

ONDAKI A variant of **OKI**.

Oneida [?*French*] One of the tribes of the **Haudenosaunee**. Their name means "Stone People." They had good reason to hate the **Huron** after 1638, when the latter wiped out most of their warriors in a single raid. (Also: *Onoiochihonons.*)

Onondaga [?*French*] One of the tribes of the **Haudenosaunee**. Their capital was Onnontagué, which was situated between two deep ravines. There was a Grand Council of the Haudenosaunee there, which was abandoned in 1680. It was either the **Oneida** or the Onondaga whose town Champlain and his Huron–Algonkin allies besieged in 1615. (Also: *Onontaerrhonons.*)

Orenda [*Various Iroquois*] The magic force which controls all natural phenomena. Equivalent to the **Power** or **Kinap** of the **Micmac**.

People [*Various Indian*] What the **Inuit**, Maliseet and **Micmac** called themselves (possibly also the Beothuk, but Trigger says, "I don't think we know enough about these to say").

Petuns [*Various Indian*] The **Tobacco Nation**. (Also: *Khionontateronons.*)

Power A numinous Being or capability in stars, plants, animals, etc., which were thought of as PERSONS (see Glossary 1). People could acquire Power for hunting, etc.; Shamans could use it more grandly. (See also the entry for Power in the Source-Notes to "The Dream of the Floating Island.")

Provincial An officer of the Society of JESUS who represents a specific province.

Puoin (plur. **Puoninaq**) [*Micmac*] Witch or warlock; Shaman. (A synonym is *Puolni'skq*, which the more phonetic if less fashionable Rand spells *Boooineskwa.*)

Récollets [*French*] Strictest of the Franciscan Orders. Began work in France in 1597. Co-operated with the Jesuits in New France 1624–8. After the English interregnum, 1629–33, they were not permitted to return during the period of this story. (Also: *Recollects.*)

Robes-Noires [*French*] Black-Gowns.

Rodiyaner [*Various Iroquois*] "Members of Iroquois lineage from which chiefs were selected," says Trigger. Same meaning as **Saqmaw**.

Sagamore [*English*] Corruption of **Saqmaw** (?).

Saqmaw [*Micmac*] Tribal elder, sachem. (Also: *sagmaw.*)

Savage [*English*] Common appellation (later derogatory) from the 1500s onward, referring to native peoples. (French: *Sauvage*; English (sometimes): *Salvage.*)

Seneca [*Seneca*] One of the Five Nations of the **Haudenosaunee**, sometimes called *Chouontouaronon* or *Tsonnontuan* by the **French**; called *Sonontrerrhonons* by the **Huron**. It was they who tortured Étienne Brûlé (see Glossary 1) and later, perhaps, made a secret deal with him, for which he was executed by the Huron. They also captured Amantacha on both of his two known raids against them. They played a leading role in the destruction of the Huron confederacy in the late 1640s.

Serpents See **Iroquois.**

Skrælings [*Old Norse*] Generic and derogatory term used in the Saga Era to describe the **Inuit** of Greenland and Helluland and also the Red Indians (**Micmac** and/or Beothuk) of **Vinland** – in short, the aboriginal inhabitants of the New World. See *The Ice-Shirt.*

Society of JESUS See **Jesuits.**

Sonontrerrhonons [*?Huron*] **Seneca** (a tribe of the **Haudenosaunee**). Their chief town was Sonontoen.

Souriquois [*French*] **Micmac** (Indians). Referencing Peter Bakker, Whitehead says that the *-quois* suffix may be "a remnant of Basque pidgin."

Spanish A Nation caught between Europe and Africa, and so originally torn between Christianity and Islam. Perhaps as a result, Christian organizations formed there tended to be militant. The Spaniards perpetrated great cruelties in the New World, for both religious and economic reasons. Washington Irving quotes a Spanish Father as saying:

"Can anyone have the presumption to say, that these savage Pagans, have yielded any thing more than an inconsiderable recompense to their benefactors; in surrendering to them a little pitiful tract of this dirty sublunary planet, in exchange for a glorious inheritance in the kingdom of Heaven!"

Superior General The head of the Society of JESUS, subject only to the Pope. Ignatius was the first Superior General. Elected for life. The only officer of the Society to be elected.

Susquehannock [?] An **Iroquoian** Nation to the south of the **Iroquois**. Allies of the **Huron**. Brûlé wintered among them in 1615–16. "They were the last northern Iroquoian people who remained unconquered by the Iroquois" – Trigger.

Tahontaenrat One of the four Nations in the **Huron** confederacy. (Also: *Tohontahenrat.*)

Tionnontaté [?*Tionnontaté*: "Mountain People"] A Nation living just south of the **Huron**. They grew tobacco, much of which they traded; hence they were known to the French as the Petun or Tobacco Nation. They spoke the same dialect as the **Attignawantan**. "The Huron and the Tionnontaté were differentiated politically rather than culturally" – Trigger. The Iroquois fell upon the Tionnontaté in 1649–50. "The number of Tionnontaté–Huron refugees who survived the decade was no more than 500" – Trigger.

Tobacco Nation See **Tionnontaté**.

Wendat [*Huron*] What the **Huron** called themselves, meaning "Island People" or "Dwellers on a Peninsula." According to Trigger, the implication is "the People at the Center of the World."

Wenroronon [?*Wenroronon*: "People of the Floating Scum" (?)] An Iroquoian group, possibly allied with the **Neutral** confederacy, who lived in what is now New York State; exactly where is unclear. In 1639, being under irresistible attack by the **Iroquois**, a number of them became refugees among the **Huron**. (Also: *Wenro*; the *-onon* suffix is a standard plural.)

3
Glossary of Places

Acadia [*French*] "A peninsula of triangular form, which bounds America on the southeast" – Lescarbot. More or less equal to the maritime Provinces of Canada. "The word is said to derive from the Indian *Aquoddiauke*, or *Aquoddie*, supposed to mean the fish called the pollock . . . This derivation is doubtful. The Micmac word, *Quoddy*, *Katy*, or *Cadie*, means simply, a place or region, and is properly used in conjunction with some other noun; as, for example, *Katakady*, the Place of Eels . . ." – Parkman. "Acadie: *-akati* is a Micmac suffix which means 'place where —— (preceding morphemes) is/are found'" – Whitehead. "More likely," says Trigger, "Lescarbot's Arcadia corrupted & moved north." (Also: *Acadie, La Cadie.*)

Açores [*French*] The Azores.

Antarctic France French name for the Americas, or maybe South America (*ca.* 1550).

Baccalos [*French*] Early name for **Terre-Neuve, Labrador** and other parts of **Canada**. *Baccalaos* is Basque for codfish.

Ca Pocoucachtechokhi Cachagou Achiganikhi, Ca Pakhitaouananiouikhi [*Montagnais*] Name for a certain rocky island in the St. Lawrence; meaning unknown. Père Le Jeune was taken there when he wintered with the Montagnais.

Canada [*Stadaconnan*] Name for the St. Lawrence River, or, more likely, for a native settlement on it. (Trigger says more crisply: "Word applied to Iroquoian settlements around Québec City.") Originally adopted by the French to describe the vast region around the river. Not until much later (say, mid 17c), was Canada synonymous with the even vaster **New France**, which also contained the Louisiana territory and (according to some) the expanse called Florida.

Cap Finneterre [*French*] Cape Finnister, on the Iberian peninsula. Champlain passed by it on his first voyage, to the West Indies.

Carhagouha [*Huron*] A town in **Wendaké**. The Recollect Père Le Caron set up a short-lived Mission here; Champlain passed through it in 1615.

Carontouan [*Susquehannock*] A principal town of this Iroquoian Nation. Brûlé wintered here in 1615–16.

Caughnawagwa [*Various Iroquois, corrupt*] Mohawk reservation near Montréal. The location has changed slightly several times. The name comes from *Kahnawaké* (lit., "At the place of rapids"), as the place was called when it was a little village of Indian converts at the Mission St.-François-Xavier de la Prairie. Tekakwitha fled there to become a Christian. Her relics are preserved in the church.

Deyoswege Kaniodai [*Mohawk*: "Beautiful Lake"] Lake Ontario.

Écumen [*French*] Inhabited part. Québec Province has a small écumen even today; the rest is wilderness.

Emenemic [?*Etechemin*] Now Caton's Island, on the St. John River, in Nova Scotia. Where Robert Pontgravé established his trading post *ca.* 1610.

Fleuve [*French*] Large river.

Fonda, New York Site where Kateri Tekakwitha was baptized.

Gethsemane [*Hebrew*] Garden where CHRIST went after the Last Supper with His Apostles; where He was taken into custody.

Golgotha [*Hebrew*: "The Place of Skulls"] The hill outside Jerusalem where CHRIST was crucified.

Grand Cibou [*French*] Early French name for Cape Breton, Nova Scotia.

Grand Banc [*French*] A fishing-ground for cod, a little east of **Terre-Neuve**. Frequented by Basques as early as 1500. One of the most important resources of French Acadia. (Also: *Great Bank.*)

Hochelaga [*Iroquoian*] According to Parkman (I.155), Hochelaga was the country to the north of the Fleuve **Saint-Laurent** (which one of Cartier's maps called the "River of Hochelaga"). Hochelaga was originally an Iroquoian town on the future site of Montréal. The Hochelagans were discovered and abused by Cartier in 1535. When Samuel de Champlain (see Glossary 1) came to the area in 1603, they had mysteriously vanished.

Huronia [*Spurious*] See **Wendaké**. "'Huronia' sounds like a tourist gimik," says Trigger.

Ihonatiria [*Huron*] Large village in **Wendaké** where Père Brébeuf and other Black-Gowns first had their mission. Brébeuf first came there with the Recollect Le Caron (see Glossary 1) in 1626. After the expulsion of the French by the English, Brébeuf returned to Ihonatiria in 1634. Ihonatiria was a town in the Bear Nation. Abandoned after epidemics, spring 1638.

Isles of Demons "The islands are perhaps those of Belle Isle and Quirpon [north of Newfoundland]," says Parkman. "More probably, however, that most held in dread . . . is a small island near the northeast extremity of Newfoundland, variously called, by Thevet, Isle de Fiche, Isle de Roberval, and Isle des Démons. It is the same with . . . the Fishot Island of many modern maps." I have chosen to imagine it as the Isle of Dew where Leif Eiriksson landed in *The Ice-Shirt*.

Kah-ha-nah-yenh [*Various Iroquois*] The Huron town where DEKANWIDEH was born. According to the Six Nations' Council (Ontario, 1900), this place was "somewhere in the neighborhood of the Bay of Quinte." In the Seth Newhouse version of the legend, the town was close to "the great hill, Ti-ro-nat-ha-ra-da-donh." These are our only clues as to the whereabouts of Kah-ha-nah-yenh.

Kahnawaké [*Various Iroquois*] See **Caughnawagwa**.

Kebec [*Indian*] Original (now archaic) spelling for **Québec**.

Labrador [?*Latin*] "Labrador – *Laboratoris Terra* – is so called from the circumstance that Cortoreal in the year 1500 stole thence a cargo of Indians for slaves" – Parkman. Trigger adds: "Named after him because he was a farmer (*labrada*)."

Lachine [*French*] Rapid upstream of Montréal. The name meant "China" and mocked those who thought that the Fleuve **Saint-Laurent** would easily take them to that Nation. Later called St.-Louis, like so many other places.

Lacus Irocoisiensis [*Latin*: "Lake of the Iroquois"] Early Jesuit name for Lake Champlain.

Mechique [*French*] Mexico.

Mer des Iroquois [*French*: "Sea of the Iroquois"] Lake Champlain.

Mer douce [*French*: lit., "Sweetwater Sea"] Lake Huron.

MVNDVS NOVVS [*Latin*] New World.

New France Shifting fortunes of war sometimes made the French claim the entire continent of North America as New France, and other times made them moderate their claims. For all practical purposes, New France was the same as **Canada**. "The common consent of all Europe is to represent New France as extending at least to the thirty-fifth and thirty-sixth degrees of latitude . . ." – Champlain (1632).

New Spain What the Spanish called the New World. In Ignatius's time all that was known of it was the Caribbean islands, Central America and bits of South America.

Oceanus Occidentalis [*Latin*] The Caribbean Sea (?).

Mount Olivet [?] The hill just outside Jerusalem where CHRIST ascended into Heaven. (Also: *Mount Olive, Mount of Olives.*)

Ossernenon [*Mohawk*: "The Land of Many Crosses"] One of the principal Mohawk villages, on a hilltop not far from the Mohawk River in what is now Auriesville, New York. Tekakwitha was born there (1656) not long after Père Isaac Jogues was murdered at the same place (1646). After the town was razed in 1666 by the Marquis de Tracy, it was rebuilt at a slight distance as Gandaouagué. There is now a Catholic shrine on this site.

Ossossané [*Huron*] A large town in **Wendaké**. Tehorenhaennion the Shaman was invited here in 1637 to try to cure the third major epidemic.

Otoüacha [*Huron*] The first Huron town visited by Champlain.

Ouendaké [*Huron*] See **Wendaké**.

Pampeluna [*Spanish*] Old name for Pamplona, the border town where Ignatius was wounded.

Port-Royal [*French*] Original name for Annapolis Royal, Nova Scotia.

Prima terra vista [*Latin*] First landing (on a new land).

Québec [*French*] Corruption of *Kebec* or possibly *Kaybekog*, an Indian word meaning "the closed-up place." Trigger says simply: "Narrows of River." Lescarbot expounds: "This is a narrow strait of the great Fleuve of Canada, which Jacques Quartier calls *Achelaci*; where M. de Monts has built a fort and dwelling-place for Frenchmen. Near at hand is a stream which falls from a high crag." Here the St. Lawrence River is only

1320 feet wide. Champlain began a settlement there in 1608. The Huron place-name was **Teyiatontariye**.

Quieunonscaran [*Huron*] Huron village. Successor of **Carhagouha**, where Père Le Caron made his first Mission.

River Beyond the Openings [*Various Iroquois*] The Hudson River.

The **Road that Walks** [*Various Indian*] The Fleuve **Saint-Laurent**, or St. Lawrence River.

Sable Island A little experimental world of colonization. Each experiment was a failure. The Baron de Léry tried it in the sixteenth century and left cattle; De la Roche's convicts were cast off there and ate the cattle; Champlain looked it over speculatively but did nothing, and Killiaen van Rensellaer declared himself its Patroon in 1632.

Saguenay [?*Iroquoian*] According to Parkman (I.155), Hochelaga was the country to the north of the Fleuve **Saint-Laurent** (which one of Cartier's maps called the "River of Hochelaga"), and Saguenay was the country to the south. "Saguenay" now refers to a river. Trigger adds: "Cartier refers to Saguenay River & land to north & west of St. Lawrence, perhaps including . . . Lake Superior."

le **Fleuve Saint-Laurent** [*French*] The Saint Lawrence River. Called by the Amerindians "The Road That Walks."

Rue **Sainte-Catherine** [*French*] A long street in Montréal with shops and cafés. Sainte-Catherine extends from the west side of the city, which is English-speaking, to the French-speaking east side. Prostitutes frequent Sainte-Catherine a few blocks east of the dividing line.

Sault [*French*] Rapids.

Sheol [*Hebrew*] Hell, but probably a Hell of dry nothingness that predates the Christian tradition.

Sillery [*French*] An experimental settlement not far west of **Kebec**, modeled after the Jesuit "reductions" in South America. Here cabins were built for the Montagnais in hopes of "rendering them sedentary and subject to rules."

Skä-neh'-ta-de [*Seneca*: "Beyond the Openings"] Later Fort Orange, or Albany, New York. The present-day city of Schenectady took its name from this.

Stadaconna [?*Iroquoian*] A series of Iroquoian towns along the Fleuve **Saint-Laurent**, beginning about 32 miles upriver of the future site of Québec City. Jacques Cartier explored this region in the 1530s and kidnapped the Stadaconnans' chief, Donnaconna (see Glossary 1). When Champlain came to the area in 1603, the Stadaconnans had mysteriously vanished. Morgan (1851) supposes the Stadaconnans to have been Adirondacks dispossessed by the Iroquois. Others suppose differently.

Sweetwater Sea [*French*; lit., *la mer douce*] Lake Huron.

Teanaostaiaé [*Huron*] A town in **Wendaké** where Amantacha (see Glossary 1) lived.

Terre-Neuve [*French*] Newfoundland.

Teyiatontariye [*Huron*: "Where two large bodies of water join"] Québec.

Ti-ro-nat-ha-ra-da-donh [*Various Iroquois*] See **Kah-ha-nah-yenh**.

Ville-Marie [*French*] Original name for Montréal.

Vinland [*Norse*: "Vine-Land" or "Wine-Land"] North America. The Norse thought of it as a promontory, and I have imagined it as being the Great Northern Peninsula of Newfoundland.

Wendaké [*Huron*: "The Land Apart," or possibly "the Island" or "the Peninsula"] The place where the Huron lived, now in Simcoe County, Ontario, abutting Lake Huron's Georgian Bay. (Also: *Ouendaké*.)

4
Glossary of Texts

Cramoisys So called after their first printer, Sebastien Cramoisy of Paris. Duodecimal volume versions of the ***Jesuit Relations***, published once a year from 1632 until 1673, when no approval was forthcoming from the Roman Congregation of Propaganda. Thus there were forty such (the 1637 edition had a different printer).

Jesuit Relations Yearly compilations and extracts made by the Provincial Superior in Montréal or Québec from the daily journals of the missionaries. These were further refined and edited by the Jesuit Superiors in Paris before being published. The introduction to the Martyrs' Shrine version of Père Brébeuf's "Huron Relation" of 1635 claims that the first Relation was Père Le Jeune's, in 1632. The *Relations* of poor Père Biard were "never considered popular publications such as our *Relations*." – How sad! – R. G. Thwaites, however, who edited the seventy-three-volume series of "Jesuit relations and allied documents" did begin the tale, as I have done, with Père Biard. In general I have labeled anything which appears in the Thwaites version a Jesuit Relation. (Brébeuf, by the way, wrote only the "Huron Relations" of 1635 and 1636. Père Le Mercier wrote those of 1637–8, Père Lalemant wrote those of 1639–45, and Père Ragueneau wrote those of 1646–50.)

Vulgate The ancient Latin text of the Holy Scriptures.

5
Glossary of Calendars, Currencies and Measures

As the majority of entries here are dates and times, the others have been prefaced with a bullet (•). For Micmac months, the initial words "Moon of" have not been taken into consideration when alphabetizing. The same applies to the initial "When" in Huron months.

Moon of **All Saints** [*Micmac*] November. (It seems likely that the missionary who recorded this made his own substitution.)

Août [*French*] August.

• **Arpent** [*French*] 100 square perches (191.85 English feet). In short, an acre.

Avril [*French*] April.

When **Bear Cubs Are Born** [*Huron*] December. (Also: *When Deer Again Form Bands.*)

When **Blackberries are Ripe** [*Huron*] July.

• **Brass** [*French*] A measurement of distance. Used so inconsistently in the *Jesuit Relations* that its equivalent is conjectural.

Chief Moon [*Micmac*] December.

Cod-Rising Moon [*Micmac*] December.

Day Will Become Longer [*Huron*] January.

Day Will Be Long Again [*Huron*] February.

Décembre [*French*] December.

When **Deer Again Form Bands** [*Huron*] December. (Also: *When Bear Cubs Are Born.*)

• **Doppia** [?*Italian*/?*Dutch*] Père Bressani's ransom, paid by the Dutch, was fifteen doppias (? doubloons), which was "$80 in gold," or, according to another source, two thousand French **livres** (which does not conform to the value of a livre given below. C'est bien dommage).

Egg-Laying Moon [*Micmac*] April.

Moon of **Fat Animals** [*Micmac*] August (although one source says October).

Février [*French*] February.

When **Flowing Water Appears** [*Huron*] March.

Frost-Fish Moon [*Micmac*] January.

Green Corn Festival [*Iroquois*] Midsummer festival of thanksgiving for the ripening of beans, squash, corn (the THREE SISTERS).

Harvest Thanksgiving [*Iroquois*] Autumn festival of thanks for the harvest.

Janvier [*French*] January.

Jeudi [*French*] Thursday.

Juillet [*French*] July.

Juin [*French*] June.

Leaf-Opening Moon [*Micmac*] June.

• **League** A measurement of distance equivalent to French *lieue* used by Champlain. One league was about 2.5 to 3 miles.

When the **Little Corn is Made** [*Huron*] August.

When the **Little Corn is Ripe** [Huron] September.

• **Livre** [*French*] A unit of currency; also a measure of weight. In weight the livre was a pound; in money it was about twenty cents, if we accept S. E. Morison's claim that 14 to 15 livres was "$3.00 in gold."

Mai [*French*] May.

Maple Thanksgiving [*Iroquois*] First festival of the spring (March or April).

Mars [*French*] March.

Moose-Calling Moon [*Micmac*] September.

New Year's Thanksgiving [*Iroquois*] Major festival, usually at the beginning of February. Morgan claims that a white dog was sacrificed.

Novembre [*French*] November.

Octobre [*French*] October.

When **One Sows** [*Huron*] May. (Also: *Strawberry Flowers Open.*)

When the **Pickerel Run** [*Huron*] April.

• **Pied** [*French*] Unit of measurement; a foot.

Planting Festival [*Iroquois*] Second festival of the year, when corn was ready to be planted.

Raspberry Thanksgiving [*Iroquois*] Same as **Strawberry Thanksgiving**.

River-Freezing Moon [*Micmac*] November.

Moon When **Seafowl Shed Feathers** [*Micmac*] July.

Septembre [*French*] September.

Snow-Blind Moon [*Micmac*] February.

• **Sol** [*French*] Unit of currency. According to the Sieur de Dièreville, a laborer's wages were about 25 to 30 sols a day (1708).

Spring Moon [*Micmac*] March.

When **Strawberries Are Ripe** [*Huron*] June.

When **Strawberry Flowers Open** [*Huron*] May. (Also: *When One Sows.*)

Strawberry Thanksgiving [*Iroquois*] Festival to celebrate the first fruits of the earth (? June). (Also: *Raspberry Thanksgiving.*)

When **They Cart the Net from Shore** [*Huron*] October.

• **Toise** [*French*] 6.4 English feet.
When **Whitefish Come** [*Huron*] November.
Moon When **Young Birds Are Full-Fledged** [*Micmac*] August.
Moon of **Young Seals** [*Micmac*] May.

6
General Glossary

Aboteaux [*French*] Clappered dykes.

Acwentonch [*Huron*] A formal mode of speech used in councils, involving quavers of the voice. (Brébeuf's orthography.)

A.D.M.G. [*Latin*] "Ad majorem Dei gloriam." The Jesuit motto, meaning "for the greater glory of GOD."

Aescara [*Huron*] A gambling game of straws. (Sagard's orthography, 1632; Steckley prefers *yaheskara.*)

Anedda [?*Montagnais*] A tree (possibly spruce or some other evergreen with vitamin C) used to cure scurvy.

Armadille [*French*] Armadillo; wood-louse.

Asataion [*Huron*] Farewell feast, given by those about to die.

Asqua [*Huron*] Unmarried female companion (Sagard). Trigger says that this is probably a mistake of Sagard's – actually a corruption of Micmac "squaw." But Steckley says: "I suspect that this is a use, now obscure (but I'm working on it) of the Huron term *yaskwak*, meaning 'daughter-in-law.' The Huron use of kin terms had cultural usages not readily understood by the French." Used in this book mainly to refer to Born Underwater's relationship to Amantacha (see Glossary 1).

Attimonai oukhimau [*Montagnais*] "He is a Captain of the Dogs."

Mon **calice** [*Québecois French*; lit., "my chalice"] A way to call someone a sonofabitch.

C'est bien dommage. [*French*] That's really too bad.

Mon **CHRIST** [*Québecois French*; lit., "my CHRIST"] A way to call someone a sonofabitch.

Mon **ciboire** [*Québecois French*; lit., "my ciborium [= sacred vessel]"] A way to call someone a sonofabitch.

Cou ouaboucho ouichitoui [*Montagnais*] "He is bearded like a hare."

Danseuses nues [*French*] Nude dancers.

Farandole [*French*] A Provençal dance.

Faridondaine [*French*] Nonsense word, similar to "fiddlesticks!"

Fleur-de-lys [*French*] A stylized lily, with one long flared petal flanked on the left and the right by a shorter. An ancient symbol, supposedly first used by Solomon to symbolize purity. Later appeared on the coats-of-arms of many European rulers, including the King of France and the Queen of England. Also used extensively by religious Orders as a sign of Heaven and holiness.

Fleuve [*French*] Large river. (French usage: one flowing into the sea.)

Foudrille [*French, archaic*] Blizzard. (Used by the Sieur de Dièreville, 1708.)

Frère [*French*] Brother.

Les **grands** [*French*] Important personages.

Gringalet [*French*] Weakling.

Haouaoutont [*Huron*] Quarrelsome.

Institutum [*Latin*] The official directives that bound the Society of JESUS (see Glossary 2): papal documents, the Constitutions, the *Spiritual Exercises*, the rules and statutes of the General Congregations, the instructions of the Superiors General, the *Epitome instituti*, and the ***Ratio Studiorum***.

Ji'nm [*Micmac*] Man. (S. T. Rand: *Cheenum*.)

Ka'kaquj [*Micmac*] Crow.

Kayenesha' Kowa [*Mohawk*] The Great Law of Peace.

Kijimij [*Micmac*] Your cunt. Also "a curse which men yell at men, and here it means more 'your hole' rather than implying 'you're a cunt'" – Francis and Whitehead.

Kwe! [*Micmac*] "Greetings!" (S. T. Rand: *Kwa!*)

Lac [*French*] Lake.

Leindohy [*Huron*] "Stinking corn" – Sagard. "Small ears of corn . . . permitted to ferment in a stagnant pond for several months before being eaten" – Trigger. Steckley adds: "The term means 'corn in a liquid.' The stinking corn bit comes from the cultural prejudice of the French writers." (Steckley's orthography: *yandohi*.)

Nicanis [*Montagnais*] My well-beloved. (Nickname for Père Le Jeune.)

Nsi'siknm [*Micmac*] My prick. (Francis/Whitehead orthography.)

Ondachienroas [*Huron*] A poisonous root (possibly May apple) which the Wendat sometimes used for medicine, or, in larger doses, to commit suicide.

Oniondechouten [*Huron*] "Such is the custom of our country."

Mon **ostie** [*Québecois French*; lit., "my Host"] A way to call someone a sonofabitch.

Palisade "Two to five rows of stakes reinforced with trees, bark and sticks to form a single barrier" – Trigger.

Pax CHRISTI [*Latin*] The peace of CHRIST be with you.

Père [*French*] Father.

Plupart [*French*] The most part, the majority.

Prima terra vista [*Latin*] First landing (on a new land).

Puktew [*Micmac*] Fire. (Francis/Whitehead orthography.)

Raquettes [*French*] Snowshoes.

Ratio Studiorum [*Latin*] The plan of studies followed by the Jesuits.

Rihouiosta [*Huron*] "I believe."

Rivière [*French*] Small river. (French usage: river which does not flow into the sea.)

Rougeole [*French*] Measles.

Mon **sacrement** [*Québecois French*; lit., "my sacrament"] A way to call someone a sonofabitch.

Sagamite [?*Various Indian*] "A sort of porridge of water and powdered maize" – Père Le Caron, 1615.

Samuquan [*Micmac*] Water. (Francis/Whitehead orthography.)

Mon **tabernacle** [*Québecois French*; lit., "my Tabernacle"] A way to call someone a sonofabitch.

Tissaouhianne [*Micmac*] A plant used to dye porcupine quills red. (Le Clerq's orthography.)

Toupillon [*French*] Hair-tuft.

Trental A set of thirty requiem masses, for which payment must be made.

Ultramontane Bearing allegiance to the Pope.

Waltes [*Micmac*] Gambling game played with moose-bone dice. (Le Clerq's/Lescarbot's orthography: *Leldestaganne*.) Whitehead says: "Lescarbot heard the *l* prefix in another context. His *aganne* is *aqn*, which means 'a thing for doing whatever the previous morpheme indicates,' so Lescarbot is really giving the word for some of the implements involved, rather than the game itself. See? Waltes is still its name . . . It is . . . scored first in base ten, using stick counters of different shapes, then (I think) in base seven, base three, base five."

Wampum [*Various Indian*; from Algonquian *wampumpeak*] A white string of shell-beads, used either for currency, for ceremony, or for official remembrance of treaties, obligations, etc.

Wigwam or **wikuom** [*Micmac*: "Shelter"] A house of pole-frame construction, covered with bark.

Yandawa [*Huron*] River.

Yandohy [*Huron*] See **leindohy**.

A Chronology of the Second Age of Wineland

Note

The dates in this Chronology are considerably less provisional than those in *The Ice-Shirt*. But difficulties remain. The foundation of the League of the Haudenosaunee, for instance, which I follow Iroquois reckoning in dating to the very distant past, has been dated *ca.* 1390 by some historians, and *ca.* 1570 by others. Be warned. – The Chronology is lengthier than its predecessor because more nations and interests are involved in this story.

The Age of Fathers and Crows

??	A SKY WOMAN named AATAENTSIC falls to the watery earth. Birds dive down and bring up mud in their beaks to make land for Her. The world is created.	
??	DEKANWIDEH and Hiawatha found League of the Haudenosaunee (Iroquois).	
4 BC	Jesus the CHRIST is born.	
AD ?30	CHRIST is crucified	
?500		Iroquoian peoples begin to adopt agriculture around the eastern Great Lakes.
?500	Saint Brendan the Navigator travels by curragh to the Promised Land of the Saints.	
710–14		Roderic, son of Theodofridus, reigns, the last Gothic King of Spain. He rapes Florinda, La Cara, daughter of Count Julian; in revenge Florinda opens the gates of the Peninsula to the Moors.
714–1087		The Moors occupy Toledo.
?1070		Iroquoian peoples begin to cultivate maize, beans and squash.
1231		Pope Gregory IX institutes the Papal Inquisition.
1252	Pope Innocent IV authorizes the use of torture by the Inquisition.	
?1330		Iroquoian peoples begin building large villages inside palisades.
?1440		The Attignawantan and Attigneenongnahac tribes of the Huron band together, founding the Huron confederacy.

1451		Queen Isabel the Catholic (Isabella I) born.
1474		Isabel wins a civil war and ascends to the throne of Castile and Aragon.
1478		Pope Sixtus IV authorizes the establishment of the Spanish Inquisition to combat heretics and apostate Jewish and Moorish converts. The first proceedings of the Inquisition in Seville are so cruel that Sixtus intervenes.
1480		The Spanish Inquisition is established in Andalusia.
1482		Ferdinand and Isabel begin the reconquest of Granada from the Moors.
1483		Sixtus authorizes the establishment of a Grand Inquisitor for Castile. The first is Torquemada, who burns approximately 2,000 persons.
1488		Cousins, a French Navigator, is blown west to a new land.
?1491	Ignatius of Loyola born.	
1492	Columbus discovers the Bahamas, Cuba, Haiti. His sailors bring syphilis back to Europe.	Granada is conquered. Torquemada persuades Fernando and Isabel to expel all Jews who refuse baptism.
1493		On a subsequent voyage, Columbus discovers Puerto Rico, Jamaica.
1497		John Cabot reaches the North American coast.
1498		Cabot sails along the northeast coast and vanishes. Columbus discovers Trinidad.
1500		Gaspar Corte Real, a Portuguese, sails along the east coast.
?1500		Norman, Basque, Breton fishermen establish temporary settlements in Newfoundland. The Micmac population is estimated at 12,000 + (says Trigger; others say 4,500). (See entry for 1616.)

1502		In his last voyage, Columbus discovers Honduras and Panama.
1504		Death of Queen Isabel the Catholic.
1506	Francis Xavier born	Denis de Honfleur explores the Gulf of St. Lawrence.
		Death of Columbus.
1506/7	Ignatius becomes a page at the court of Don Juan Velasquez.	The German cartographer Martin Waldseemüller is the first to use the name "America."
1513		Ponce de Léon, searching for the Fountain of Youth, claims Florida for Spain.
1515	Ignatius is charged in court of law with some serious offense now unknown.	
1516		Death of King Fernando of Spain. He is succeeded by King Charles I (who will become Charles V of the Holy Roman Empire).
		Jerusalem falls under Ottoman rule.
1517	Ignatius joins the Spanish army under Antonio Manrique de Lara, Duke of Nájera and Viceroy of Navarre.	
1518		Juan de Grijalva lands in Mexico and hears of Montezuma's empire.
		The Baron de Léry attempts to settle Sable Island.
1519		Cortés conquers Montezuma's capitol, Tenochtitlán.
1520	Ignatius serves among the Duke's occupying forces in Nájera.	
1521	Ignatius receives a leg wound in the battle of Pampeluna (Pamplona). In his sickbed he receives his conversion vision.	
1522–3	Ignatius begins work on the *Spiritual Exercises* at Manresa. He meditates here for a year, and then makes a pilgrimage to Jerusalem.	
1524		Under the auspices of Francis I, Verazzano the Florentine explores the coast of the New World from present-day North Carolina to Newfoundland.

1524–5	Ignatius returns to Barcelona from Jerusalem. He spends a year there studying grammar.	
1525–1600		European trade goods first reach the Iroquois.
1526	Ignatius goes to Alcalá for general studies. The Inquisition investigates him. He and his three companions are commanded not to wear the same clothing, since they are not members of any religious order.	
1527	The Inquisition investigates Ignatius on suspicion of fornication. He is cleared.	
1528–33	Ignatius studies philosophy and theology in Paris. In 1532 he becomes a bachelor of arts.	
1530		King Charles I of Spain is crowned King Charles V of the Holy Roman Empire. The Bible is first printed in French in its entirety.
1532		Pizarro conquers the Inca capital of Cuzco, seizes the Inca king, Atahualpa, and murders him after extorting the proverbial king's ransom.
1534	St. Ignatius Loyola becomes a master of arts and builds an apostleship in Paris with six companions. They hope to go on a mission to the Holy Land; failing that, they will put themselves at the service of the Pope. Jacques Cartier makes first voyage to the New World, claims Gaspé Peninsula for France; encounters the Micmac, kidnaps two Indians.	
1535	Cartier ascends the St. Lawrence, discovers the sites of Québec and Montréal, and kidnaps an Indian King, Donnaconna, along with his chiefs. The Indians die a year or two later in France. Ignatius completes the *Spiritual Exercises*.	Ursuline order of nuns founded in Italy.

1537	Ignatius is ordained as a priest.	First complete edition of the Bible published.
1537–41		Suleiman the Magnificent fortifies Jerusalem.
1538	War between Venice and Turkey blocking the way to the Holy Land, Ignatius and his six companions found the Society of JESUS, which puts itself at the service of the Pope.	
1539		DeSoto lands in Florida.
1549	The Society of JESUS is approved by the Pope.	Coronado leads an expedition into the American southwest, discovers the Grand Canyon and the Pueblos of New Mexico.
1540/1	Francis Xavier, SJ, begins missionary work in India.	
1541	Ignatius is elected General of the Society of JESUS.	
	Jean François de la Rocque, Sieur de Roberval, founds a short-lived settlement at Québec, with Cartier for a guide and convicts for colonists. Cartier deserts and returns to France.	
1542	Roberval casts off his niece, Marguerite, on one of the Isles of Demons.	
1543		Protestants burned at the stake by the Spanish Inquisition.
		First printing of the New Testament in Spanish.
1549		Jesuits convert 300,000 Japanese to Christianity.
1552	Francis Xavier dies.	
1553		Henry of Navarre (Henri IV of France) born.
		First printing of the Old Testament in Spanish.
1556	St. Ignatius dies.	Pope Paul IV issues the Catholic Church's first list of banned books.
		The Society of JESUS counts 938 members.

1557	In France, Père Pierre Biard is born at Grenoble.	
1558		In France, a beaver-skin sells for 2½ livres.
?1560		The French begin buying bison-skins from the Indians.
1562		Jean Ribaut claims Florida for France.
1564		The French Huguenots establish the settlement of Fort Caroline in Florida. The next year, the Spanish massacre them.
1565		The Society of JESUS counts 1,565 members.
1566		The Jesuits establish a mission in Florida.
		St. Francis de Borja, General of the Society of JESUS, forbids Jesuits from reading the *Autobiography* of St. Ignatius.
1567	Samuel Champlain born, according to older historiography ("now thought *ca.* 1580 according to paper in *Revue d'histoire de l'Amérique française*" – Trigger; *Dictionary of Canadian Biography* says "*ca.* 1570").	
?1570		The Hochelagans are destroyed, possibly by Iroquois (Mohawks).
1572		In France, Catherine de Medici organizes the St. Bartholomew's Day Massacre of the Huguenots.
1577	Roberto de Nobili born in Rome.	
1578		150 French fishing vessels in Newfoundland, and 200 of other nationalities.
1579		Beginning in this year, all Dukes of Bavaria have a Jesuit confessor.
1580		Spain invades Portugal.
		One source estimates the number of European men in eastern Canada as 17,000: 15,000 in the fisheries, and 2,000 in whaling.
?1580		European trade goods begin to reach the Huron on a regular basis.

1580		Demand for beaver-wool hats in Paris inaugurates the French fur trade in North America. Claudius Aquaviva becomes Superior General of the Society of Jesus.
1588		St. Peter of Canisius condenses Saint Ignatius's *Spiritual Exercises* from thirty days into a shorter retreat. The British defeat the Spanish Armada.
1589		In France, King Henri III is assassinated.
1590		The Jesuits establish a mission in India.
?1590		In Canada, the Arendarhonon Nation joins the Huron confederacy.
1591	Paul Le Jeune born at Vitry-le-François.	
1593	Jean de Brébeuf born in Normandy.	
1594		In France, a man named Chastel attempts to assassinate Henri IV. Popular prejudice blames the Jesuits.
1595		As a result of the Chastel affair, the Jesuits are temporarily expelled from France as 'corrupters of youth and disturbers of the Nation's repose.'
1597		The Recollects begin work in France.
1598	Samuel de Champlain, a quartermaster in the King's army, finds himself out of work after the victorious Brittany campaign and undertakes a voyage to the West Indies (?1599–1601).	The Sieur de la Roche attempts to build a colony with convicts on Sable Island. A storm blows him back to France, and the convicts are abandoned.
1599		Claudius Aquaviva, General of the Society of Jesus, issues the official version of the *Ratio Studiorum*, which further codifies (some say regiments) study in Jesuit institutions.
1600		Pierre de Chauvin de Tonnetuit establishes a fur trading post at Tadoussac.

1600–1700 Various native American populations are decimated by epidemics of smallpox, measles, etc. As one source explains it: "Throughout the sixteenth century, then, and continuing after it, first hundreds and then thousands of European men . . . yearly left the crowded, dirty streets of that continent and a month or two later were breathing into the faces of Algonkian Indians." Trigger notes: "Decimated SE U.S. by 1530; E New England 1616–19; upper NY S[tate] & S Ont. 1634–40s."

1603 Roberto de Nobili is ordained.

De la Roche's convicts are rescued.

King Henri IV permits the Jesuits to return to France and makes Père Coton his Royal Confessor.

Samuel de Champlain, in company with the merchant Pontgravé, sails up the Fleuve Saint-Laurent in his first Canada expedition, meeting Montagnais and Algonkin.

1604 Pierre du Gast, the Sieur de Monts, establishes the first permanent French settlement in North America at Port-Royal (now Annapolis Royal), Nova Scotia. He is accompanied by Champlain, Pontgravé, and the Sieur de Poutrincourt. Poutrincourt obtains a grant of the place from De Monts and returns to France. De Monts meanwhile builds a fort on the isle of Ste.-Croix, but abandons it after a year and removes to Port-Royal. They find a faithful friend in a Micmac Sagamore named Membertou.

Roberto de Nobili sails for India. He will make fifty converts in his first eighteen months.

1606 Poutrincourt and the lawyer Marc Lescarbot leave Rochelle for Port-Royal.

The Jesuits are authorized once again to reside in Paris.

1607	Champlain's first general map.	The Acadian colonists learn that De Monts' patent of monopoly on the fur trade has been rescinded. The colony is abandoned, and reverts to Poutrincourt.
	Père Isaac Jogues born.	Henry Hudson discovers Spitzbergen.
		First permanent white settlement in Virginia, at Jamestown.
1608	Champlain establishes a post at Québec and crushes a conspiracy to assassinate him.	A Bavarian, Simon Marius, names the moons of Jupiter.
	King Henry IV asks the Jesuits to save the souls of the Souriquois (Micmac) Indians.	English settle at mouth of Kinibéqui River.
	Membertou and his allies attack Armouchiquois using French guns. (First use of firearms by one native group against another.)	Henry Hudson searches the Russian Arctic for a northeast passage.
1609–12		Free trade in Canada.
1609	In India, Father Roberto de Nobili baptizes Sivadarma the Brahmin. A few months later he is censured for not compelling his converts to conform to European habits.	English settlers on the Kinibéqui mistreat the Indians, who stab 11 of them; the colony is abandoned.
		Kepler affirms that Mars's trajectory is elliptical.
	Champlain aids the Huron and Algonkin against the Iroquois, thereby commencing a century of war. Champlain shoots one Iroquois prisoner to end his torture by the victors.	Henry Hudson makes contact with the Iroquois in the name of the Dutch, who soon enter the beaver trade.
	Père Pierre Biard, SJ, and his companion Père Ennemond Massé wait vainly for a year at Bordeaux to be taken to Acadia.	
1610	Hoping to forestall the Jesuits, Poutrincourt arrives at Port-Royal with a lay priest, Messire Jessé Fléché, who baptizes 21 Abenakis, including Membertou.	The Tahontaenrat tribe joins the Huron confederacy, which is now complete with four tribes. (Date approximate.)
	Champlain marries Hélène Boullé.	

	Champlain joins battle with the Montagnais against the Iroquois. His side is victorious; the Montagnais torture their captives to death.	
?1610	Amantacha the Huron born.	In France, King Henri IV is assassinated. His nine-year-old son, Louis XIII, succeeds him; the Queen-Mother is Regent.
1611	Père Biard and Père Ennemond Massé finally arrive at Port-Royal and begin the work of the Society of JESUS in the New World.	The King James Bible is printed in England. Louis XIII grants all the territory of North America (except Port-Royal) to Madame de Guercheville, a puppet of the Jesuits. In France, a beaver-skin sells for 8½ livres. (See entry for 1558.)
1612		The last heretics (Unitarians) are burned at the stake in England. Champlain creates a new organization called the Company of Associates, its members to share profit and loss in the beaver trade. Merchants from Rouen, Havre and St. Malo agree to join; those from La Rochelle decline, and trade illicitly with the Indians. 12,000–15,000 beaver pelts a year exported from Canada. The Dutch enter the fur trade.
1612–?1615		Iroquois raids on Huron and Algonquin traders on the Ottowa River (the object being to steal European trade goods) provoke reprisals. "As a result of these raids," says Trigger, "the Huron were drawn into a conflict with the Onondaga and Oneida that probably had not existed . . . prior to the development of the fur trade" (293).
1613	The Jesuits remove to Mt. Desert Island. Samuel Argall destroys their settlement. Gilbert du Thet, a lay brother, dies in the attack. Argall casts Père Massé and others into an open boat; they are rescued by French traders. He takes Père Biard and 13 others prisoner and brings them to Virginia.	In Virginia, Captain Samuel Argall abducts Pocahontas.

	Paul Le Jeune enters the novitiate.	
	Champlain becomes deputy to the Prince de Condé.	
1614		The French open a fur trading post in Albany, New York.
	Père Biard is repatriated.	Captain Argall returns to Acadia with Père Biard and destroys Fort Ste.-Croix and Port-Royal.
		New Netherlands Company of Amsterdam given a 3-year monopoly of the fur trade in North America by the Dutch.
1615	The Society of Jesus now counts 13,112 members.	Poutrincourt dies in battle in the French civil war.
	Champlain assists the Huron in an attack upon an Onondaga village	Franciscan friars (Récollets) begin missionary work in Québec. One of their number, Joseph Le Caron, commences operations among the Huron.
		The Récollets build a residence at Three Rivers. Father Le Caron winters among the Huron.
		Death of Claudius Aquaviva, Superior General of the Jesuits.
1615–16		Lost in the woods, Brûlé surrenders to the Iroquois, who give him food, torture him, and then treat him kindly upon his promise to make peace between them and the French.
1616		The Micmac population is estimated at slightly more than 3,000. (See entry for *ca.* 1500, and for *ca.* 1700.)
1616–29		"The Huron country remained the granary for the Ottowa River Algonkin . . ." (Trigger, 359).
1618		In France, a beaver-skin sells for 10 livres. (See entry for 1611.)
1620	Champlain voyages to Canada with Hélène.	The Récollets bring the Montagnais child Pastedouachouan to Paris, where he learns French and Latin. In later life, having no hunting skills, he becomes an alcoholic among his own people and starves to death in the forest.

		Two illegal ships from La Rochelle trade firearms to the Montagnais. Most of these guns soon wear out.
?1620–??		Having received iron axes from the French in trade, the Micmac become more successful in warfare, and drive the Etechemins north. Both Iroquois and Huron now have iron arrowheads capable of piercing Iroquois slat armor. Open encounters give way to ambushes.
?1620–5		About 500 Huron a year raid the Iroquois.
1621		The Récollets build their first chapel and convent in New France, on the St. Charles River.
1622	Ignatius is canonized.	Père Biard dies at Avignon. Iroquois attack Québec. In France, Richelieu becomes Cardinal.
1623	In India, Roberto de Nobili, SJ, is permitted to resume his baptisms.	Québec Montagnais now spend so much time fur-trapping as to rely on French for sea biscuits, etc. Father Le Caron and others undertake another Récollet mission to the Huron. A young Huron from Quieunonscaran leads a raiding party to victory over 60 Iroquois.
1624	Champlain and Hélène return from Canada, Hélène for good.	The Dutch buy New Amsterdam (Manhattan) from the Delawares. Concerned about a possible Dutch rapprochement with their enemies, the Mohawk make peace with the French and their allies. Le Caron and Sagard return to Québec. In France, peasants revolt at Quercy.
1625	The Récollets invite the Jesuits to join them. By this time the Récollets have 5 missions in New France. Pères Lalemant, Brébeuf and Massé arrive in Canada.	Father Nicholas Viel, who is carrying on the Huron mission alone, drowns in a portage. Nine years after the fact, the accident is attributed to Huron malignancy.

?1625		The Mohawk go to war against the Mahican.
1625–6	Unable to proceed immediately to the Huron, Père Brébeuf winters among the Montagnais.	
1625–40		The Iroquois trade 5,000–6,000 beaver-skins a year with the Dutch.
1626	Brébeuf, Daillon, and de Nouë begin their mission among the Huron.	The Society of JESUS numbers 15,544 worldwide. The Mahican destroy an eastern village of the Mohawk. Later, the war goes against the Mahicans, and Dutch traders, who want to trade with others than the Iroquois, commission Dutch troops to aid the Mahican. The Iroquois catch them and roast them alive. Then the Dutch traders apologize to the Iroquois and resume their neutrality.
1626–8	Amantacha, son of a Huron headman, is taken to France and baptized publicly in Rouen cathedral in 1627. He is kept in Paris until 1628.	Père Daillon, the last Récollet to visit the Huron, tries to go over the Huron's heads and open up independent trade with the Neutral Nation. He fails, and creates suspicion among the Huron.
1627	In Québec, Champlain advocates the extermination of the Iroquois because they menace trade and travel.	
1628	His companions having left, Brébeuf is now the sole missionary among the Huron.	The Mohawk defeat and disperse the Mahican.
1628–9	On his voyage back from Paris. Amantacha's ship is captured by the English. Hearing that he is the son of a King, they take him to London and detain him for a year, giving him fancy clothing to console him. When they bring him back to Ontario and meet his father, who is but a "hungry, naked Indian," they want to take his clothes away, but in the end they find it more politic to relent.	New France conquered by the Kirke brothers of England. Champlain, Jesuits expelled.
1629	Brébeuf recalled to Québec, and there captured by the English.	Iroquois raids force the abandonment of an Algonquian-Montagnais village at Three Rivers.

?1630		Beavers have been overhunted to extinction in Wendaké.
1630		Year of "mortality" in France (famine and epidemic).
1631		Thirty Dutch settlers come to New Amsterdam. The colony is wiped out by Indians a year later.
1632	Père Paul Le Jeune leads a new mission in Québec.	England restores New France to France. The Jesuits return, but (per Richelieu's orders) not the Récollets. Thus the Jesuits have a missionary monopoly on the Canadian mainland.
		Year of "mortality" in France. Père Le Caron dies there of plague.
		Iroquois defeat a party of Algonquians in battle.
1633	Brébeuf and Massé return to Québec. Champlain tells the Huron that if they love the French they will allow the Jesuits to live in their villages.	Brûlé is murdered by the Huron, probably because he has been dealing with the Iroquois (Seneca), or the Neutral. (See entry for 1615–16.)
	Amantacha the Huron meets Born Underwater at Kebec.	Two French traders are ambushed on the St. Lawrence River by Iroquois and scalped.
	Champlain makes his twelfth and last voyage to Canada.	A Dutch trader murders a Mohawk chief by castration. The Mohawk retaliate. Then they make peace with the Algonkin, hoping thereby to trade with the French. The following year, six French traders visit the Oneida.
1633–4	Le Jeune winters among the Montagnais.	
1634		[4 July] Settlement begins at Three Rivers, on the site of the old Récollet residence. Three Rivers will become an important spot in the fur trade.
1634	Père Jean de Brébeuf and Père Antoine Daniel re-establish the Huron mission.	The Algonquin accuse the Huron of Père Viel's murder in order to create dissension between the Huron and the French.
	500 Huron attack a Seneca village. The Seneca kill 200 Huron and cut off one of Amantacha's fingers.	

	Epidemics begin to decimate native populations in the upper Great Lakes. Between 1634 and 1640 the Huron lose half their population	
1634–5		The Mohawk are decimated by smallpox. Some Mohawk possess Dutch-made doors with iron hinges.
1634–70	The Jesuits convert the Micmac.	
1635	Brébeuf's baptisms of the sick give him a reputation as a good shaman. Nevertheless, he offends the Huron by calling for separate burial of Christians during the Feast of the Dead.	Père Le Jeune opens a school for Huron boys at Québec. The Seneca make peace with the Huron. Some Kichespirini, attempting clandestine trade with the Dutch, are slain by Mohawk while passing through their territory. This puts an end to good relations between the Mohawk and the French, and ties the Mohawk more securely to the Dutch. Perhaps, says Trigger, the Dutch persuaded the Kichespirini to come in the first place.
	Champlain dies at Kebec. Pastedouachouan starves to death.	
1636	Amantacha and other Huron raiders are captured by Mohawk. Amantacha is most likely tortured to death. His father kills himself out of grief. Père Jogues comes to live among the Huron.	Charles Huault de Montmagny becomes Governor of New France. An August eclipse appears to the Huron an omen of Iroquois victory. Tehorenhaegnon the Shaman holds a ceremonial feast to counteract the omen. The Jesuits baptize their first Iroquois prisoner.
1636–7		A more serious epidemic strikes Wendaké. The Jesuits are sick, but recover.
1637	The Jesuits are placed in spiritual charge of the Indians and settlers in Canada. Another epidemic. This time the Jesuits are unaffected. The Huron now consider them witches, and refrain from killing them only because they are dependent on French trade goods.	The Iroquois re-invade the St. Lawrence, raiding and killing Huron, among them a council chief named Taratouan. Montagnais and Algonquin successfully repel an Iroquois assault but their own raid on the Iroquois fails. One of the Huron boys at the Jesuit school in Québec is persuaded to mortify himself with cold water.

		Chihouatenhoua the Huron baptized as Joseph Chihwatenah.
1638		A Huron vengeance raid against the Iroquois for the killing of Taratouan and the others (1637) is successful. Almost 100 Oneida are killed in battle or tortured to death in Wendaké. Oneida women are forced to ask for Mohawk men to marry to keep their tribe from extinction.
		The Jesuits hold a Mass for rain when Wendaké is drought-ridden. Three days of rain come, restoring the Jesuits to favor.
		Brébeuf holds a feast to speak on the subject of hell. After this he is considered a headman.
		The first chapel in Wendaké is erected, near the town of Ossossané.
		Père Jérôme Lalemant replaces Père Brébeuf as Superior of the Huron Mission.
		The Dutch governor William Kieft arrives in New Amsterdam. His policies kill a thousand Indians between 1640 and 1645.
1639	Père Le Jeune is replaced as Superior of Kebec.	The Huron launch their first raid against the Seneca, breaking the peace of 1635.
	The Ursulines arrive at Kebec.	Almost 100 Huron are professing Christians. More than 200 more have been baptized.
		A saint's name is given to each Huron village.
		Thousands of Huron die in a smallpox epidemic. The Algonkin death rate is so high that the living cannot bury the dead. The Huron assault Brébeuf and the other Jesuits and set their house on fire.
?1640	The Haudenosaunee begin trading for firearms, first with the English, but then mainly with the Dutch. In reaction, the French trade a few guns to Christian Algonquin and Montagnais.	

1640	Brébeuf and his brethren establish the central mission house of Wendaké, Sainte-Marie. Against Huron wishes, without Huron knowledge, he undertakes a mission to the Neutral Nation. He is charged with sorcery and conspiracy with the Iroquois.	There are now 100 converts out of 16,000 Huron.
		"By 1640 not only the Huron but most of the Indians in eastern Canada and adjacent parts of the United States had become dependent on the fur trade" (Trigger, 603).
		Joseph Chihwatenah is murdered, probably by Huron.
		The Neutral Nation captures 100 Assistaronon (Algonkian-speaking group) in Michigan.
		The good harvest of this year renders the Jesuits less suspicious to the Huron.
1640–1		Smallpox strikes the Seneca.
		Mohawk raid in Kichespirini.
1640–2		Chihwatenah's young niece Oionhaton is brought to Québec to be instructed by the Ursulines.
1641		Following his baptism, Charles Tsondatsaa becomes the first Huron to possess a gun.
		The Iroquois offer to make peace with the French, but not with the Algonquin or Huron. Governor Montmagny realizes that this would be unacceptable to his Indian allies, and refuses.
		Ahatsistari, a renowned Huron warrior, scatters 300 Iroquois with a force of 50 men.
		The Tionnontaté mission ends, due to Huron opposition.
1641–4	His life endangered because of the Huron's anger at his mission to the Neutral of 1640, Brébeuf remains at Québec for this time.	En route to Wendaké with Jogues, Chihwatenah's niece Oionhaton is captured by Mohawk, who later refuse to let her be ransomed.
		Iroquois expel the Potawatomi from their territory.
1642	Père Jogues and his donnée, Goupil, tortured by the Iroquois, Goupil to death. Jogues rescued by the Dutch.	Mohawk set out to attack Huron fur traders but are repulsed by the French.

Permanent settlement, Ville-Marie, established on the site of present-day Montréal.

Iroquois burn a Huron village.

Ahatsistari is baptized. Later that year, following a raid on the Iroquois, he is captured and tortured to death.

A band of Huron Christians announce that they do not wish to be reburied after death in their community's Feast of the Dead.

1643 Iroquois expel the Wenro from western New York State.

The Neutral Nation captures 800 Assistaronon, torturing 70 to death immediately and blinding and muzzling the old men so that they will starve in the forest.

The Mohawk establish continual "shifts" of raiders in ambush along the St. Lawrence so that the Huron cannot safely get through to trade. The Mohawk seize so many Huron furs that they cannot carry them all.

Huron coming to trade at Three Rivers are publicly separated into Christian and non-Christian groups, the former to receive preferential exchange rates.

The Iroquois continue to attack Huron villages. Many women are killed in the fields. Hundreds of prisoners are taken. Meanwhile the Huron suffer from famine, making them more vulnerable still.

Under their governor, William Kieft, the Dutch massacre 100 Wiechquaeskeck Indians, precipitating the Esopus Wars, which continue until the British takeover in 1664.

In France, Louis XIV begins his 72-year reign.

1643–4 The Mohawk hold peace talks with the Huron.

1644	Francis Joseph Bressani captured and tortured by Mohawks. Adopted after torture and sold to the Dutch.	The Mohawk have guns, ammunition sufficient for 400 warriors.
1645	Lalemant leaves Wendaké to become Superior for New France. His place is taken by Père Paul Ragueneau.	30,000 pounds of beaver-skins exported from Canada. Iroquois carry off a group of Huron women from the fields. At the torture of an Iroquois prisoner, a Huron convert performs baptism. The Mohawk make peace with the French, requesting as a secret condition that they refrain from protecting the Algonquin. Pères Le Jeune and Vimont persuade Governor Montmagny to accede to this provided that the Iroquois leave Christian Algonquin unharmed. (This is in defiance of a treaty between the French and the Algonquin.) Mohawk attack the Abenaki. Governor Kieft is recalled from New Amsterdam and replaced by Peter Stuyvesant.
1646	Père Jogues and his donné are hatcheted to death by the Bear Clan of the Mohawk. (The Turtle and Wolf Clans oppose this action.) Hélène de Champlain takes the veil.	There are about 500 devout Huron Christians. The Jesuits renew their mission to the Tionnontaté.
1647		Iroquois raid the Algonquin, capturing 40. The Huron make peace with the Onondaga. The Cayuga also express a willingness for peace. The Mohawk and Seneca remain bellicose. Out of fear of these tribes, the Huron decide not to go downriver to trade with the French. The Seneca wipe out the Neutral village of Aondironnon. The Arendarhonon retreat to other Huron villages.

		Seneca and Mohawk attack two Huron groups near the village of Taenhatentaron. This village is nearly abandoned by the following year.
1648		Twenty percent of the Huron are now nominally Christian.
		The Onondaga begin to raid the Huron again. Huron traditionalists murder a Frenchman and call for the expulsion of Jesuits and Christians from Wendaké. However, most Huron do not feel able to leave their trading relationship with the French. The Jesuits call for the largest reparations payment ever made by the Huron.
	The Iroquois destroy the well-fortified town of Teanaostaiaé, where Père Daniel becomes the first Jesuit martyr for the Huron. Ten percent of the Huron are wiped out in this raid.	On route to trade at Three Rivers, the Huron have a victory over Iroquois raiders.
		The Iroquois and the French again have peace negotiations.
		Montmagny is succeeded by Louis d'Aillebout, who permits the colonists to trade in Wendake independent of the Jesuits.
		The Huron town of Ossossané becomes "the village of Christians."
		Year of "mortality" in France.
1649	The Iroquois destroy the Huron villages of Taenhatentaron, St.-Louis (where Père Brébeuf and young Gabriel Lalemant are captured and tortured to death), and possibly two other villages. The Huron confederacy disperses in terror. The Jesuits accompany a remnant to Gahoendoe Island. Starvation and cannibalism ensue that winter.	The Iroquois destroy the Tionnontaté village of Etharita.
		The Iroquois destroy the Nipissing Nation.
		Charles I beheaded in England.
1650	Huron missions abandoned. Some Huron refugees arrive at Québec.	The Tionnontaté abandon their country.
	"By 1650 almost all the original native inhabitants of the St. Lawrence Valley had been killed by disease or warfare, with the few survivors distancing themselves from white settlements" – *A Short History of Quebec.*	

1650–1		The Iroquois destroy the Neutral Nation.
		The only remaining Huron Nation, the Tahontaenrat, goes to live among the Seneca.
1651		Huron refugees leave Québec for the Île d'Orléans. Harassed and hunted by the Iroquois, they return to Québec a year later.
1651–80		The Iroquois destroy the Erie Nation.
1652		The Iroquois menace reaches such proportions that Montréal is unable to buy a single beaver-skin.
1653		Père Joseph Anthony Poncet captured by Iroquois, but not killed.
		The Iroquois make peace with the French.
1653		The Iroquois nearly exterminate the Eries.
1654	Roberto de Nobili retires. Fifty years earlier, when he first arrived in south India, there were no Christian converts. Now there are 4,183.	
	Hélène de Champlain dies.	
1655	Jesuit mission to the Iroquois.	Huron refugees at Québec are attacked by the Mohawk; the French do not intervene.
1656	Roberto de Nobili dies in Mylapore.	The Jesuits first visit the Cayuga.
	St. Kateri Tekakwitha born at Ossernenon (now Auriesville, New York).	
1658		The Huron refugees leave Québec for Beauport.
1659		Bishop Laval founds the Seminary at Québec.
		Ascendancy of France over Spain confirmed in the Treaty of the Pyrenees.
1660		The Cayuga population is estimated to be 1,500.

1661		Louis XIV ("the Sun King") comes to power in France.
1664	The Jesuits number 35,968 worldwide.	New Amsterdam passes from Dutch to English control, and is renamed New York.
1665	New France goes to war against the Iroquois and burns many of their villages.	
1666	Under the Marquis de Tracy, the 600 men of the Carignan-Salières regiment burn Mohawk cornfields and villages, bringing that Nation to its knees for seven years. Peace is concluded in 1667.	
1667–8	There is now a Jesuit mission in each of the five Iroquois nations.	
1667	Tekakwitha meets her first Black-Gown.	
1670		Hudson's Bay Company established. At least 10 million beaver in Canada. The Iroquois complete the subjugation of the Adirondacks and Huron.
1673		The Huron refugees leave Beauport for Ancienne Lorette.
1676	Catherine Tekakwitha is baptized on Easter Sunday at what is now Fonda, New York.	
1677	Tegahkouita joins the mission at Sault-St.-Louis. At Christmas, she receives her first communion.	
1678		Chapelle Notre-Dame de Bon Secours erected in Montréal.
1679	Tekakwitha vows herself to CHRIST.	
1680	Tekakwitha dies at Sault-St.-Louis, aged twenty-four.	The Iroquois invade the Country of the Illinois.
1687		The French abandon their Iroquois missions, due to increasing danger from the English.

1690		Québec City weathers an attack from Sir William Phipps of Massachusetts.
1696		Frontenac burns Iroquois villages and crops and disperses the Five Nations.
1697–present		The Huron survivors settle at Jeune Lorette.
?1700		The population of the Five Nations is estimated at 16,000. The Micmac population is estimated at 2,200. (See entry for 1616.)
1700–1800	Many bullets are fired. "In the eighteenth century it was calculated that it took a man's weight in lead to kill him" (Lower and Chafe).	
1701	French and Iroquois sign a peace treaty.	
1711		Québec City remains unconquered after an attack by Admiral Howedon Walker.
?1712	The Tuscarora join the League of the Haudenosauneee.	
1713		Treaty of Utrecht transfers Terre-Neuve, Acadia and Hudson Bay to the British.
1715		The Sun King dies.
1749	The Society of JESUS numbers 22,589 worldwide. Jesuit missioners make up a quarter of the entire Catholic apostolate.	
1754		Benjamin Franklin suggests that the Thirteen Colonies form a confederation similar to that of the Haudenosaunee.
1759	Québec City is conquered by Major General James Wolfe.	
1759–68		The Jesuits are expelled from South America.
1762–5		The League of the Iroquois adopts the Delaware, Tutelo and Nanticoke tribes.
1763	Final downfall of New France.	

??	KLUSKAP leaves the Micmac.	
1764		The Society of JESUS is declared illegal in France and her colonies. The Jesuits are expelled "irrevocably and without return."
1767		Spain confiscates the property of the Order and expels more than 5,100 Jesuits.
1773	Pope Clement XIV dissolves the Society of JESUS "to restore peace to the Church." Lorenzo Ricci, the Superior General, is imprisoned until his death in 1775. Jesuit lands in Canada revert to the British Governor.	
1774		The population of the Six Nations is estimated at 10,000–12,500.
1775		Benedict Arnold fails to conquer Québec from the British.
1777	In the American War of Independence, the Oneida and half of the Tuscarora ally themselves with the Colonies; the remainder of the Haudenosaunee side with the British.	
1778		The Cayuga population is estimated to be 1,100.
1780		Out of thirty Iroquois towns, two remain habitable. The Iroquois name for George Washington is "Town-Destroyer."
1789		Ganioda'yo (Handsome Lake) has a vision and tells the Iroquois to live at peace with the whites but keep some of the ancient ceremonies.
1808		Joseph Bonaparte finally suppresses the Spanish Inquisition.
1814	The Society of JESUS is restored by Pope Pius VII.	The Spanish Inquisition is also restored.
1820		It is suppressed again . . .
1823		. . . and restored . . .
1834		. . . and suppressed for good.

1842		The Jesuits are permitted to return to Canada.
1853–77		Hudson's Bay Company sells 3 million beaver-skins.
1867	The nation of Canada is formed by the British North America Act. Macdonald is the first Prime Minister.	
1870		Red River Uprising in Canada.
1884	The Council of Baltimore proposes canonization for Jogues, Goupil and Tekakwitha.	
1885		Northwest Rebellion – religious hatreds in Québec.
1888		The Jesuit Estates Act pays compensation to the Jesuits for their lands seized in the suppression of 1773.
1899		Out of 100,000 Canadian Indians, 15,000 are listed as "pagan" by a government census, 14,000 are recorded "religion unknown," and the rest are Christian.
1890	Separate Catholic schools are abolished in Manitoba.	
1912	The last Huron speaker dies.	
1922	St. Ignatius is proclaimed Patron of all Spiritual Exercises.	
1925	Père Jogues, Père Brébeuf, and their six lay brothers are all beatified as the "North American Martyrs."	
1930	The North American Martyrs are canonized.	
1943	Kateri Tekakwitha declared Venerable by Pope Pius XII.	
1954	Discovery of Père Brébeuf's grave in the ruins of Mission Sainte-Marie.	
1960		In Québec Province, the Quiet Revolution brings about "the liquidation of the Catholic church as the embodiment of the French nation" (Herbert Guindon).

1980	Kateri Tekakwitha declared Blessed by Pope John Paul II.	
1986		Hudson's Bay Company's profit for the year is $6 billion.
1987		Hudson's Bay Company sells most of its fur auction business and all of its 178 retail stores.
1989		William the Blind visits Kateri Tekakwitha's relics at Kahnawaké.

Sources

And a few notes

The poet will see only the inherent beauty of the story, and perhaps failing to find any beauty, will invent it and produce a tale that no Indian would ever recognize. Plot and detail will be changed, fine flowery language will be used, and perhaps the whole given the swing and meter of blank verse. This is all very well for the poet, but he has buried the personality of the folk tale, albeit in petals of roses – instead of allowing it nakedly to appear the living thing it is.

ARTHUR C. PARKER
(GAWASOWANEH), *Seneca Myths and Folk Tales* (1923)

Note

It may be of interest to the reader to know what use I have made of my sources. My aim in *Seven Dreams* has been to create a "Symbolic History" – that is to say, an account of origins and metamorphoses which is often untrue based on the literal facts as we know them, but whose untruths further a deeper sense of truth. Here one walks the proverbial tightrope, on one side of which lies slavish literalism; on the other, self-indulgence. Given these dangers, it seemed wise to have this source list, so as to provide those who desire with easy means of corroborating or refuting my imagined versions of things, to monitor my originality,* and to give leads to primary sources and other useful texts for interested non-specialists such as myself. I have tried to do this as fully as seemed practical. As in the first volume, Ruth Holmes Whitehead of the Nova Scotia Museum was kind enough to read the parts bearing on Micmac characters; Bruce G. Trigger of McGill University did the same for the Huron parts. Of course they are not responsible for my errors or my perverse rejection of their advice on some occasions.

As in *The Ice-Shirt*, I have not hesitated to portray very far-off and uncertain places in a way that makes them more North American. For example, my descriptions of Golgotha and the mount called Olivet in the time of CHRIST are in fact based on my notes on Joshua Tree National Monument (California) in February 1988. And I have continued to ascribe motivations to characters which can in no wise be literally justified. Offering us a model of the responsible approach, Prof. Trigger says the following in his history of the Huron:

> First, while not completely suppressing the individuality of historical figures, I have concentrated on those aspects of people's behaviour that reflect their roles as members of one or more interest groups. Secondly, while the motivations of the members of each interest group have been presented as clearly as possible, I have tried to do this impartially and in such a manner that the interest of the reader focuses on the total situation rather than on the passions or problems of any one group.
>
> This approach is necessary, because, for the most part, we lack the documentation to

* For two explanatory cases, see my examples in the Source-List for volume 1, *The Ice-Shirt.*

> adequately reconstruct the psychological framework that is associated with Indian behaviour.*

Because, as I said, I have followed the opposite course, this book is perforce a tissue of speculations, prejudices and falsehoods. I cannot describe the people who used to live in Canada as they were; I do not even know enough to direct my imagination very far in specific directions. But I have done my best.

For similar reasons, I have sometimes appropriated churches, spires, crypts, etc. from Québec City which date from *after* 1649. These anachronisms are generally founded in religious monuments growing out of the events related here. Not making use of them in my tropes would have required using more French cathedralscapes, which would have correspondingly diminished the Canadian flavor of this enterprise.

All quotations, excerpts and epigraphs in the text, by the way, are genuine unless stated below.

W.T.V.

* Bruce G. Trigger, *The Children of Aataentsic: A History of the Huron People to 1660* (Montreal: McGill-Queen's University Press, 1987), pp. 25–6. This massive study will be cited more than once in the work at hand.

Fathers and Crows

page viii Bressani epigraph – *Breve Relatione d'alcune Missioni nella Nuova Francia* (1653), trans. in Horace Kephart, ed., *Captives Among the Indians: Firsthand Narratives of Indian Wars, Customs, Tortures, and Habits of Life in Colonial Times* (New York: Outing Adventure Library, 1815), pp. 118–19.

Crow-Text

NOTE Throughout this book I have described religious artifacts at the Museum of the Laval Seminary, the Museum of the Ursuline Sisters, and the Museum of the Augustine Sisters; all in Québec City. While I have sometimes cited these places specifically, I have often not, particularly in cases of numerous brief similes or descriptions.

page 3 Parkman on priests and forests – ibid., p. 15 ("Pioneers of France in the New World" [1885 rev. ed.], intro.).

page 3 "my love, my Saint, Catherine Tekakwitha" – "Not officially," reminds Trigger (note to author, 15 May 1989). "The Vatican is very slow." In fact Tekakwitha is only "Venerable" as of this writing (1989).

page 4 "I will deprive myself of all light . . ." – Ignatius of Loyola, *Exercitia Spiritualia S. Ignatii eorumque Directoria* (?1535), additional direction to the Fifth Exercise of the First Week. See, e.g., Antonio T. de Nicolas, ed., *Powers of Imagining: A Philosophical Hermeneutic of Imagining through the Collected Works of Ignatius de Loyola, with a Translation of These Works* (Albany: State University of New York Press, 1986, p. 121, para. 79). I have generally referred to this edition while writing *Fathers and Crows*. Another fine version of the Exercises, which is free from De Nicolas's structuralist disease but does not contain the other works, is Luis J. Ruhl, SJ, *The Spiritual Exercises of St. Ignatius, Based on Studies in the Language of the Autograph* (Chicago: Loyola University Press, 1951).

page 5 Description of the Stream of Time – from a visit to the woods near Livingston Manor, New York, in October 1988.

page 5 Footnote on Canada – Trigger notes: "Canada never referred to the Mississippean part of New France" (note to author, 28 May 1989).

page 6 Père Biard on the supposed addiction of the Inuit to cannibalism – *The Jesuit*

Relations, ed. Reuben Gold Thwaites (Cleveland: The Burrows Brothers Company, 1896), vol. 1 (Acadia 1610–13): "Missio Canadensis: Epistola ex Porto-regali in Acadia," 1611. (NOTE (1) *The Jesuit Relations* is a series of parallel texts. In every case, for the convenience of the English-language reader, I have cited the right-hand English pages. (2) The various volumes have different publishing dates. (3) Henceforth in this Source List *The Jesuit Relations* will be referred to as *JR*.)

page 8 Description of the unheard rapids – from a visit to the countryside near Lac Sainte-Rose, Québec Province, in October 1988.

page 11 "Love ought to be manifested in deeds . . ." – Ignatius, *Exercitia Spiritualia*, "Contemplation to Attain Love."

page 15 Episodes of "austerities" – *JR*, vol. 62: Lower Canada, Iroquois, Ottawas 1681–3 (MDCCXCVII): "Lettre du P. Claude Chauchetière touchant de la mission des Iroquois du Sault S[t]. Francois Xavier proche Montreal" (*sic*), 15e octobre 1682, pp. 175–9.

page 17 ". . . one must always be prepared for death . . ." – ibid., p. 169.

page 17 ". . . they deplore the misfortune of their birth . . ." – ibid., p. 189.

page 17 In his concise and useful study *Moon of Wintertime: Missionaries and the Indians of Canada in Encounter Since 1534* (University of Toronto Press, 1984), John Webster Grant says: "The effective transfer of a message requires that it be both offered and received. Paying most attention to the offer, we have commonly pictured the Indians as reluctant and recalcitrant. Much evidence suggests, rather, that most of them were eager for Christianity but that they were allowed to receive it only on terms destructive to their culture and humiliating to their pride" (263).

page 17 Description of Auriesville, New York – from a visit in September 1989.

page 18 Iroquois description of the FACELESS ONE – a common appellation in their Ritual of Condolence. Cf., e.g., John Bierhorst, ed., *Four Masterworks of American Indian Literature* (Tucson: The University of Arizona Press, 1974), p. 144 ("The Fourth Article").

page 19 "a few arpents of snow" – sometimes ascribed to Voltaire.

page 19n *Dictionary of Canadian Biography* – vol. 1: 1000–1700 (University of Toronto Press, 1966), p. 4 (Jacques Rousseau and George W. Brown, "The Indians of Northeastern North America").

page 20 Père Biard on gains and losses – lettre du Père Biard au R. P. Provinciale à Paris, Port-Royal, 31 janvier 1612; in *JR*, vol. 2 (Acadia 1612–14) (pub. 1896), p. 5.

page 21 Errors and libraries – Ludwig Marase, *Soldier of the Church*, trans. Christopher Lazare (New York: Simon and Schuster, 1939), pp. 341–2.

page 22 Thwaites's confession – *JR*, vol. 1, pp. viii–ix.

page 22 "Nothing to report about St. Ignatius," writes Jonathan Franzen from Italy (postcard to author, 11 June 1989). "In Siena two days ago, though, we did see the HEAD and NECK of another saint of interest to you; namely, Catherine. They were brought back to Siena four years after her death, by none other than her biographer, and put in a glass box . . . The monks we saw in the abbey pictured here were smoking cigarettes of black tobacco." – None of which has anything to do with Catherine Tekakouitha, but one must believe in the correspondences between namesakes: indeed, the latter was named after the former.

page 22 I have omitted to mention the town of Sainte-Catherine's with its hotels, white sky and ragweed pollen. The maple-leaf flag waves high over the Electronic Supermarket.

Fathers and Crows

page 24 Train oil and candles epigraph – Harriet Beecher Stowe, *Oldtown Folks* (1869), bound with *Uncle Tom's Cabin* and *The Minister's Wooing* (New York: Library of America, 1982), p. 1406.

page 24 Jesuit epigraph – *Jesuit Relations*, 1660, as quoted in Francis Parkman, *France and England in North America*, vol. 1 (New York: Library of America, 1983), p. 1153 ("The Old Régime in Canada" (1894), ch. VI).

Wearing the Black Shirt

page 27 Epistle on waterfalls and forests – *De Regione et Moribus Canadensium seu Barbarorum Novae Franciæ* (Auctore Josepho Juvencio, Societatis Jesu, Sacerdote), Rome, 1710: in *JR*, vol. 1, pp. 245–7.

page 28 Incident of the Fox's scalp – cf., e.g., Juliette Lavergne, *La Vie Gracieuse de Catherine Tekakwitha* (Montréal: Éditions Fides, 1955 – "7e édition, 14e mille," says the title page proudly, and "Prix Albert Lévesque, 1933"), pp. 100–3, "Le sacrifice de l'Aigle."

page 29 The chant of the Clear-Minded orator – adapted from the Iroquois ritual of condolence in Bierhorst, p. 161 ("The Thirteenth Article").

page 30 The Fifth Seal – from a painting by El Greco, "The Vision of Saint John" (Metropolitan Museum, New York).

page 30 The Whore of Babylon and the scarlet Beast – Revelation 17–19.

The Games of Waterfalls

page 31 Description of the gorges – from a visit to Ithaca, New York in August 1979–August 1981. The pool where the Iroquois children swam corresponds most particularly to places at Robert Treman State Park, about ten miles south of Ithaca.

The Dream of the Floating Island

page 32 In this book as in the previous volume, I have referred to Ruth Holmes Whitehead's *Elitekey: Micmac Material Culture from 1600 to the Present* as a basis for my descriptions of Micmac clothing, canoes, wigwams, baskets, etc.

page 32 Description of the country of the Souriquois – from a visit to Bar Harbor, Maine, and environs in 1966.

page 32 Power – "Modern science maintains that all matter is energy, shaping itself to particular patterns. The Old Ones of the People took this a step further: they maintained that patterns of Power could be conscious, manifesting within the worlds as acts of *will*. They thought of such entities as Persons . . ." – Whitehead, *Stories from the Six Worlds: Micmac Legends* (Halifax: Nimbus, 1988), p. 3.

page 33 The dream of the floating island – Ella Elizabeth Clark, *Indian Legends of Canada* (Ontario: McClelland & Stewart, 1960), pp. 151–2.

NOTE The original Dream of the Floating Island, which Born Swimming dreams that she dreamed, might have happened as early as 1521 (Ruth Holmes Whitehead, letter to author, 31 January 1989). See note to "The Magic Words," below. Although Whitehead was not happy with what I have done here in setting the dream in the seventeenth century, I felt it necessary to proceed this way in order to avoid starting a hundred years earlier. And the dream is appropriate symbolically as a contrast to the days of iron which have already come. The careful reader will see from the beginning of the section "Robert Pontgravé's Sweetheart" that the dream is in fact a dream within a dream, and therefore, being free from historical imputation (as a myth should be) does not violate either letter or spirit. Nonetheless, Whitehead's continuing reservations about what I have done are worth quoting, since this is my most gaping anachronism:

> A point could be made that since [Membertou]'s supposed to be over 100 in 1607, he could have encountered [Europeans] in 1520 in the manner that you describe. But he would not have been a chief then, an elder, a puoin. And he sure as hell isn't meeting Poutrincourt in this manner. He spoke Montagnais-Basque pidgin to the French, anyway, not Micmac. Lescarbot is most explicit on this point. Mesimuet, chief at La Havre, had been to France as the guest of the Mayor of Bayonne, stayed in his house, all before 1580, when M. de Grandmont died, and Mesimuet is piloting these guys around the Bay of Fundy, and all of this European weirdness is now a long-accepted phenomenon to the Micmac. Whatever will you do? This is quite a lot of artistic license to take – history 100 years out of sync. Transfer that to Europe, and you'd really be laughed out of court. Champlain even found a decaying European cross, set up at the head of the Bay of Fundy. [Letter to author, 24 April 1990]

Again, I feel that I had to do what I did, just as with the ice-heart business in the previous volume, because in each case the dream is a myth which informs and structures the text, and I feel that it would be disrespectful to the myth to tell it in any way which weakens it. – But this note should give the reader sufficient information to judge whether my disregard for facts in this case makes sense or is imbecilic.

page 36 Women and bears – According to the Recollect priest Le Clercq (cited below), when a bear was killed, the girls and childless women had to leave the wigwam. They could not return until all was eaten. Later, a new door was made in the wigwam, since women were "not sufficiently deserving" to pass through the place where a bear had passed. More likely, the women stayed away because bear-Power would not mix with woman-Power.

page 37 The priest – I suppose here that he was either Messire Jessé Fléché, who baptized Membertou and others in 1610, as described below, or else his predecessor Messire Aubry. "George Hamell (NYS Museum, Albany) suggests he was originally seen as a White Rabbit ancestor figure" (Trigger to author, 15 May 1989).

Saint Pierre and His Shadow

page 38 William Byrd epigraph – *William Byrd's Histories of the Dividing Line Betwixt Virginia and North Carolina* (Raleigh: William K. Boyd, ed., 1929), from pp. 52–86, as excerpted in the Encyclopædia Britannica's *Annals of America, vol. 1, 1493–1754: Discovering a New World* (Chicago, 1968), pp. 378.

page 39 The Visitation at Emmaus – Luke 24.13–31.

page 40 Spread of the Christian faith after Christ's death – Acts 1–4.4.

A Concise History of the Middle Ages

page 41 Herder – Johann Gottfried von Herder, *Reflections on the Philosophy of the History of Mankind*, trans. T. O. Churchill (1880), abr. Frank E. Manuel (Chicago: The University of Chicago Press, 1968), p. 317.

Further History of the Christians

page 42 Epigraph – Thomas à Kempis, *The Imitation of Christ* (*ca.* 1413), trans. Leo Sherley-Price (New York: Penguin, 1952), p. 110.

page 42 Various little vignettes of saintliness and asceticism in this section were inspired by the engravings in *Sadler's Hermits and Saints* (1594).

page 43 Saint Ignatius on eating – adapted from the Mottola version of the *Spiritual Exercises* (see subsection "Love" in the section "Saint Ignatius" immediately following), p. 97.

page 43 Saint Augustine on remembered colors – *Confessions*, trans. E. B. Pusey, DD (New York: Dutton, Everyman's, 1962), p. 211.

page 43 The schematic of medieval Christianity given to me by the late Mary C. Mansfield is analogous to my parable of Saint Peter's life. Mary begins by citing the sixth-century letter of Pope Gregory on tolerance in the conversion of foreigners. The basic rule then was compromise. The Church was happy to turn a "pagan" site into a "holy" one, and pagan holidays were not dangerous. Some peasants from this time who venerated a dog as a Saint were considered "silly but not disloyal." But after the Reformation both Catholic and Protestant élites became more rigid, as they had to be to fight against each other. At this point, says Mary, "you had to be educated; you had to understand what you said, not just say it." Most interesting of all is her comment that there was "less acceptance of a symbolist mentality. Each rite must now call up only one picture."

MAPS OF CANADA

page 44 Welzl epigraph – op. cit., p. 22.

THE KHANS OF CANADA

page 45 "Thirty-three days . . ." – R. H. Major, ed., *Select Letters of Columbus* (London: 1847), p. 1.

page 46 "The inhabitants . . ." – ibid., p. 2.

page 46 An interesting and amusing account of Canadian history in newspaper form is Mgr. Albert Tessier et al., *Le Boréal Express: Journal d'histoire du Canada 1524–1760* (Sillery, Québec: Les éditions du Boréal Express, 1978).

THE MAGIC WORDS

page 48 Commenting on Membertou's unusual tallness (he had a thin beard as well), Whitehead suggests that he may have been Métis, or half-French (letter to author, January 1989). In such a case, of course, intimate relations between the French and the Micmac would have been in effect for some time, as I have suggested in various places in this book. Whitehead also cites the case of another chief called the Flemish Bastard, and a chief mentioned by Champlain called "Juan Chou" or "Iuan Chou." She believes this name is the Micmac "Wenju" = (W + Anjou), or "the Frenchman."

BLACK-GOWNS

page 52 Epigraph – Ignatius, *Spiritual Diary*, 2 February 1544 to 12 March 1544, in De Nicolas ed., p. 212.

page 52 Parkman excerpt – op. cit. ("The Jesuits in North America" [1867]), pp. 409–10.

page 53 Painting of the Saints Martyrs Canadiens – by Mother Mary Nealis. This painting now (1989) hangs at the Martyrs' Shrine in Midland, Ontario.

page 53 Prof. Trigger, whose remarks on the Order could also rarely be considered benedictions, said (op. cit., pp. 469–70):

> The intellectual approach of these seventeenth-century Jesuits to the task of conversion and their careful reporting of strange customs strikes a sympathetic chord in modern scholars who, for this reason, are tempted to regard the Jesuits as entertaining more modern views than they in fact held . . . While [they] may have been able to treat cultural variations in what they regarded as relatively trivial or morally neutral matters with equanimity or even intellectual curiosity, they were wholly unprepared to extend the same toleration to the sphere of religious beliefs or morality . . . It was therefore their

ambition, wherever possible and by whatever means, to win converts to Roman Catholicism and to stamp out other religions.

page 53 For information on Jesuit costume, see Patrick Folkes and Nancy Penny, *Cassocks, Doublets, and Deerskins* (Midland, Ontario: The Friends of Sainte-Marie, 1988).

Toy Islands

page 54 Rockwell Kent epigraph – *Rockwell Kent's Greenland Journal* (New York: Ivan Obolensky, 1962), entry for 13 February 1932.

page 54 One of my under-themes is the transformation of French *habitants* into French-Canadians. A fine book on this subject is Philippe Jacquin's *Les indiens blancs: Français et Indiens en Amérique du Nord (XVIe–XVIIIe siècle)* (Paris: Payot, 1987). I have gained understanding from it, particularly when recreating the characters of Brûlé, Robert Pontgravé, and other French who "went Indian" to some extent.

Acadia

page 55 "seeing our France seeming to languish . . ." – Lescarbot, op. cit. (*JR*, vol. 1, p. 61.)

page 55 Poutrincourt's thought on the arms of the Savages – Lescarbot, *The History of New France, Containing the Voyages, Discoveries, and Settlement made by the French in the West Indies and New France, by Commission from our Most Christian Kings; and their Diverse Fortunes in the Execution of these matters; from one hundred years ago until now . . .* (3rd ed., 1618), trans. W. L. Grant, MA (Oxon.) (Toronto: Champlain Society, vol. 7, 1907), vol. 3, p. 265.

The Voyage

page 63 The sailors' dirty hands, the sand as white as salt, and two or three like details – the Sieur de Dièreville, *Relation of the Voyage to Port Royal in Acadia or New France, etc.* (1708), trans. Mrs. Clarence Webster, ed. John Clarence Webster (Toronto: Champlain Society, 1933).

The Prize

page 67 Description of Acadia – from a visit to Annapolis Royal, Nova Scotia in May 1987, and a visit to the river-coast of New Jersey near Manhattan in August 1988.

Naked Privities

page 72 Unnerving companion epigraph – William A. Bary, SJ, *Jesuit Formation Today:*

An Invitation to Dialogue and Involvement (St. Louis, Missouri: The Seminar on Jesuit Spirituality, 20/5 November 1988), p. 9.

page 72 Little information about Champlain exists outside of his own writings. A reasonably fair summary taken from them, with some personal additions of landscapes, but little analytical sifting of Champlain's claims, is Samuel Eliot Morison's *Samuel de Champlain: Father of New France* (Boston: Little, Brown, 1972). Trigger paints a fairly detailed and far more jaundiced picture of Champlain's Canadian career in *The Children of Aataentsic.* In creating my version of Champlain, I have cribbed shamelessly from his treatise on seamanship (1632), which, being a set of rules and instructions, gives a good opportunity to see what sort of general principles Champlain believed in.

AVOCADOS AND DRAGONS

page 76 Champlain's first voyage – *Brief discovrs des choses plvs remarqvables qve Samvel Champlain des Brovage* (1599, 1601), in H. P. Biggar, gen. ed., *The Works of Samuel de Champlain in Six Volumes,* "repr., trans. & annot. by five Canadian scholars" (Champlain Society, 1922–36), vol. 1.

page 76 The *Dictionary of Canadian Biography* casts doubt on many of the particulars of Champlain's Spanish voyage, and indeed on the very authorship of the *Brief Discovrs.* But, as the *DCB* itself admits, "there is no good reason why one should reject this declaration [of a trip to New Spain] by a man at the end of his career" (vol. 1, p. 187). Given that, and given that the *Brief Discovrs* is the only record of the voyage that we have, be it true or false, I've felt free to use it. Conscientious objectors may stop reading here.

THE RIVER'S MOUTH

page 79 Champlain's second voyage – *Des Savvages, ov Voyage de Samuel Champlain, de Brovage, fait en france novvelle, l'an mil Six cens trois* in Biggar, op. cit., vol. 1.

page 81 Trigger footnote – letter to author, 19 March 1990.

THE PROMISE

page 82 Meeting at Tadoussac; the feast; naked dancing; religious stories – Biggar, op. cit., vol. 1, pp. 98–114.

page 86 "When the Hiroquois burn their prisoners . . ." – Trigger asks: "Would Champlain have known about Iroquois tortures at this point?" (letter to author, 19 March 1990). It seems likely to me that the Montagnais and Algonkin would have told Pontgravé.

More Pleasant Reflections

page 87 Trigger footnote – first part (before ellipses) from letter to author, 19 March 1990. Second part from *The Children of Aataentsic*, p. 263.

Iron

page 98 Marie de l'Incarnation epigraph – Marie de l'Incarnation to her son, Québec, 1670, in Joyce Marshall, trans. and ed., *Word from New France: The Selected Letters of Marie de l'Incarnation* (Toronto: Oxford University Press, 1967), p. 362.

page 98n Kettles – "'Kettles' is a confusing term", says Whitehead. "These are really pots. In the 1500s and 1600s they were copper, then brass. There were no iron pots until long after Membertou's death. We have a whole bunch from burials, and they are huge. Iron would have been impossibly heavy" (letter to author, 14 April 1990).

page 99 Membertouji'j – "Membertouchis" in the *Jesuit Relations*. "Ji'j or sis's (a dialectical difference) is the diminutive" (Whitehead again, same letter).

Pontgravé's Reward

page 100 Enemy epigraph – *Spiritual Exercises* (slightly altered from Mottola ed.).

A Dream of Meadows

page 107 Subterranean epigraph – Herder, op. cit., p. 309 fn.

Fishing

page 108 Champlain's calculations, etc. – H. P. Biggar, gen. ed., *Des Savvages . . .* in Champlain's *Works*, vol. 1, pp. 256–300.

Robert and the Souriquois

page 113 "pidgin wasn't good enough . . ." – "All the people spoke pidgin Basque, and so did most of the 'Normans,'" says Whitehead (letter to author, 24 April 1990).

The Wolverine-Brothers

page 114 The tale of Ki'kwa'ju and Ki'kwa'jusi's – Ruth Holmes Whitehead, *Six Micmac Stories* (The Nova Scotia Museum, 1989), pp. 27–32. S. T. Rand is sourced for this tale (see *The Ice-Shirt*, Glossaries and Source Notes, for information on Rand). (Whitehead notes, by the way, that most retellings of this tale wrongly translate Ki'kwa'ju as "Badger" when he should be "Wolverine.")

EFFECTS

page 124n Although Captain Merveille is indeed mentioned briefly in the *DCB*, it is needless to add that he was not mentioned in quite this way. My citation of Lescarbot is an outright lie.

page 125n Extract from Tekakwitha's biography – Lavergne again, op. cit., p. 96.

THE LAWYER'S HOLIDAY

page 126 ". . . this vacation season in the year 1608" – Lescarbot, *The History of New France* (Toronto: Champlain Society, vol. 1, 1907), vol. 1, p. 30.

ROBERT PONTGRAVÉ'S SWEETHEART

page 127 Lescarbot epigraph – op. cit., vol. 3, p. 208.

THE STORYTELLER

page 132 "They are great trees; you cannot fell them all at once" – inspired by a remark in *JR*, vol. 16 (1639), p. 159.

THE EXERCISE OF HELL

page 133 Dialogue on christening and Hell – almost verbatim from Père Le Clercq, *Premier establissment de Foy* (Toronto: Champlain Society, 1910).

WEARING THE WOMAN-SHIRT

page 134 The tale of KLUSKAP – Rev. Silas T. Rand, *Legends of the Micmacs* (New York: Longmans, Green & Co., 1894).

IRONLESS NIGHTS

page 137 "He had hung Moose's bones in a tree" – "Moose bones are not thrown in the river. They are put up in trees. Fish and beaver bones are put in the river. Because moose don't give birth in water, hokay?" (Whitehead, letter to author, 24 April 1990.)

page 137 Etiquette of bringing home animals – see Adrian Tanner, *Bringing Home Animals: Religious Ideology and Mode of Production of the Mistassini Cree Hunters* (Memorial University of Newfoundland, Social and Economic Studies No. 23), a portion of which Whitehead kindly sent me.

MEMBERTOU'S GUNS

page 139 Our main account of Membertou's raid and its background is given in a pompous verse by Lescarbot, entitled "La Deffait des Savvages Armovchiqvois" in *Les Muses de la Novvelle-France*. Whitehead kindly drew my attention to an English translation by Thomas H. Goetz (State University College, Fredonia, New York). This translation accompanies an essay by Alvin H. Morrison (same institution) entitled "Membertou's Raid on the Chouacoet 'Almouchiquois' – The Micmac Sack of Saco in 1607" (National Museum of Man Ethnology Service – Mercury Series Paper No. 23, 6th Algonquian Conference, 1974). Concerning Lescarbot's account, Morrison says: ". . . 'poetic license' seldom was more overworked before or since." So I have not hesitated to put my oar in, either.

page 140 The Micmac vengeance song – based on the version of S. T. Rand (on whose career see Source Notes to the previous volume), as given in Penny Petrone, ed., *First People, First Voices* (Buffalo: University of Toronto Press, 1983), p. 32. Following Whitehead's recommendation, I have transliterated "Hey-yeh!" as "Kwe! Ya!" both here and in *The Ice-Shirt*. I have made some other minor changes.

MORE GOOD TIMES FOR ROBERT

page 144 The pounding of Robert's heart – "If you'll pardon my saying so, Pontgravé seeing Born Swimming naked and his heart pounding has been used in too many historical romances about white/red sex. Forgive the snottiness of that remark, but it has, my son, it has." (Whitehead to author, 14 April 1990.)

GLEAM AND GLITTER

page 145 Orientation of landmarks at Saco Bay – after Champlain's chart from *Les Voyages* . . . (1613).

HOW THEY ALL TOOK IT

page 149 The poem – somewhat perversely translated by me, and yet the meaning of Lescarbot's original (Lescarbot, op. cit., p. 491) is not so far off:

Car d'un fleuve infini tu cherches l'origine
À fin qu'à l'avenir y faisant ton séjour,
Tu nous fais par là parvenir à la Chine.

HOSPITALITY

page 150 Description of making port in France – after an engraving by Theodore de Bry, "Départ pour le Nouveau Monde à partir d'un port européen" (1594).

NO NEED OF ANY LEARNED DOCTORS

page 157 Lescarbot on amiability as pliability – *The Conversion of the Savages*, op. cit., p. 69.

page 157 "Now, for the present . . ." – ibid., pp. 81–3.

ANNUNCIATIONS

page 165 Ignatius epigraph – Spiritual Exercises, Second Week, First Day, First Contemplation; in De Nicolas, op. cit., p. 125, para. 106.

A REPRESENTATION OF THE IDEAL

page 167 "I don't know about rape-propitiation," Whitehead wrote me (24 April 1990), "except probably Membertou would bring it up with the French, indirectly, over a smoke, and many diplomatic orations would be made, and many presents given to soothe the hearts and ease the pains, all in very literal language, not in terms of concepts of honour, property, etc."

THE FIRST CONVERSION

page 175 "Your name is Jacob . . ." – Genesis 35.10.

THE DISAPPOINTMENT

page 176 Parkman on Mme. de Guercheville – op. cit. ("Pioneers of France," ch. V), p. 214.

page 177 Conversation of Mme. de Guercheville and the Queen – from a painting by Georges de la Tour, "Edification of the Virgin" (Frick Museum, New York).

page 180 Description of Bordeaux – from a painting by Claude Joseph Vernet (attrib.), ?1714–?1789, "Port de Bordeaux" (Musée de Québec, no. 983.65).

PÈRE BIARD

page 182 Brébeuf epigraph – *JR*, vol. 8, p. 121.

page 182 Parkman epigraph – op. cit. ("The Jesuits in North America"), p. 409.

page 182 A good concise reference on Jesuit organization in France at this time is given in R. Poncet, *Les institutions de la France au XVI*[e] *siècle* (Paris: Éditions Picard, 1948), vol. 2, pp. 772–8 ("La Compagnie de Jésus"). I have also made occasional use of Roland Mousner's *The Assassination of Henry IV: The Tyrannicide Problem and the Consolidation of the French Absolute Monarchy in the Early Seventeenth Century*, trans. Joan Spencer (London: Faber and Faber, 1973). Still another useful book is the *Dictionnaire historique de la France* of Lalanne (New York: Burt Franklin, 1968 repr. of 1877 ed.), 2 vols.

THE CONVERSION OF THE SOURIQUOIS

page 185 "the envy of the French . . ." – Nicolas Denys, *The Description and Natural History of the Coasts of North America (Acadia)* (MDCLXXII), trans. ed. (Champlain Society, vol. 2, 1908), p. 106.

page 186 "you do not desire to go straight to GOD" – this sentence based on one in the "Introduction into Making an Election of a Way of Life" in the *Spiritual Exercises* (De Nicolas, op. cit., p. 134, para. 169).

page 186 Geography of the mouth of the Stream of Time – based on a description of the entrance to the River Saint-Jean, in Denys, op. cit., p. 113.

page 187 "to think of living as the Savages do" – Lescarbot, *The Conversion of the Savages*, op. cit., p. 83.

page 188 Poutrincourt to Père Biard on their respective paths – Parkman, op. cit., p. 217 ("Pioneers of France in the New World," ch. VI).

THE WORK AHEAD

page 193 "Here then are our occupations . . ." – *JR*, vol. 2, p. 5.

page 193 CHRIST in the color of a flame of fire – Ignatius, *Spiritual Diary*, Monday, 11 February 1544 (De Nicolas, op. cit., p. 1919).

THE EDUCATION

page 197 "The first things the poor Savages . . ." – *JR*, vol. 2, p. 9.

MEMBERTOU

page 197 The Souriquois prayer – *JR*, vol. 1, p. 165. Whitehead, unimpressed, writes: "At best it is misheard Micmac, or misprinted Micmac, but it may be pidgin Basque" (letter to author, 24 April 1990).

page 198 Membertou on bread – *JR*, vol. 1, p. 165.

KA'QAQUS

page 198 The interrogation of Cacagous – *JR*, vol. 1, p. 165.

page 198 In *JR*, Ka'qaqus is written *Cacagous*. Whitehead gave me the Micmac form – which could also be *Ka'qaquj* ("*j* and *s* are often interchanged in Micmac," she says).

page 198 Ignatius on revealing the sins of others – *Spiritual Exercises*, op. cit., p. 52.

page 199 "But let it be enough to keep before our eyes the vision of these poor natives . . ." – verbatim (with minor punctuation changes) from *JR*, vol. 4 (Acadia and Quebec 1616–29) (pub. MDCCXCVII), p. 117.

PROVIDENCE

page 201 Antoynette de Pons' namesake; the words of Joseph – *JR*, vol. 2, pp. 9–15.

BIRDS IN SPRING

page 216 Pamphlet epigraph – ISBN 0-921709-24-2. Text by Dan Strickland, third page for Post 5.

page 219 Poutrincourt's inner prisons – from "The Prisons" (*Le Carceri*) of Giovanni Battista Piranesi (*ca.* 1745, 1761).

PÈRE MASSÉ'S EPIPHANY

page 222 Saint Ignatius holding the *Constitutions* – unattributed engraving, *Encyclopedia Americana*, vol. 17, p. 35 (1984 ed.), caption: "Bibliothèque Nationale, Paris/Giradon."

page 222 Saint Ignatius in the waterfall – unattributed engraving, repeated several times in De Nicolas, op. cit.

page 223 "My dear Canada . . ." – *JR*, vol. 29 (Iroquois, Lower Canada, Huron 1646) (1898).

SMOKING THE PIPE

page 225 Micmac tradition of the SUN and the deluge – Le Clercq, op. cit., p. 64.

MAKING THE EXERCISES

page 226 "Eels run in the fall, and were [the Micmac's] favorite food," says Whitehead. "Eels are easily trapped in weirs, very fat, pure protein, and one can put up tons of them by smoking, without all the cutting of meat necessary when smoking jerky" (letter to author, 24 April 1990).

THE WARMAKER

page 233 I have generally relied on the De Nicolas edition of Ignatius's *Autobiography*. Another version I have sometimes referred to is *The Autobiography of Ignatius Loyola and Related Documents*, trans. Joseph F. O'Callaghan, ed. with intro. and notes (New York: Harper Torchbooks, 1974). This edition is graced with several beautiful illustrations which have been of great help to me.

page 233 A fine reference on Ignatius's conversion is *Saint Ignatius Loyola, The Pilgrim Years 1491–1538*, by James Brodrick, SJ (New York: Farrar, Straus & Giroux, 1956). I have gleaned a number of details from this book.

page 233 Champlain epigraph – *Works*, vol. 6, p. 103.

page 233 Ignatius considering Saint Peter – it was to him that Iñigo made the one poem of his life, which has since been lost.

Love

page 235 ". . . not a Countess nor a Duchess . . ." – *Autobiography* (De Nicolas ed.), ch. 1, para. 6, p. 250.

page 236 The anagram – "He seems to have fallen in love [at court] with a lady of noble blood, perhaps Doña Catarina, daughter of Philip the Fair," says Robert W. Gleason, SJ (*The Spiritual Exercises of St. Ignatius*, trans. Anthony Mottola, PhD (Garden City, New York: Doubleday [Image Books], 1964), p. 12.

Machinations of His Destiny

page 238 Description of Ferdinand and Isabella praying – from a painting by an anonymous Flemish master, "The Virgin of the Catholic Kings."

page 238 Ignatius's recollection of Ferdinand – from a reproduction of a likeness by Cristofano dell' Altissimo, Collezione Gioviano, Uffizi Gallery, Florence.

Pampeluna

page 238 Description of Pamplona – from city plan AMS-1, M981, 1st edition 1943 1:100,000 US Army (copied from Spain 1:50,000 map 141, 1931).

In France

page 240 Description of Francis and his mistress on the sofa – from Charles Heath's engraving of a likeness by R. P. Bonington, "Francis the first and his Sister," n.d.

page 241 Francis's face – from an engraving by I. Jacob Lacroix, "François Ier," *ca.* 1550.

The Books

page 244 An excellent schematic of pre-Reformation thinking about the Saints and the Holy Family is given in the beginning of John Bossy's *Christianity and the West 1400–1700* (New York: Oxford, 1987). I have kept this schematic in mind from time to time in *Fathers and Crows*.

page 246 The extracts supposedly from a *Vita Christi* are in fact taken from *The*

Imitation of CHRIST, a book which Ignatius is known to have read and profited from. As it is very clear and specific, I have preferred to use it here.

page 246 On vanity – Thomas à Kempis, *Imitation*, op. cit., p. 28.

page 247 . . . on affection for beauty of body – ibid., p. 34.

page 247 . . . on affection for the invisible – ibid., p. 28.

page 247 . . . on the fierceness of the struggle for self-conquest – ibid., p. 31.

THE SECOND LOCK

page 248 The fields and forests in the box – from a visit to the northeast of Montréal in October 1988.

THE ELECTION

page 250 Ignatius's declaration – "For just as soon as you determined to bend every effort to procure the praise, honor, and service of God our Lord, you declared war against the world and raised your standard in its face, and got ready to reject what is lofty by embracing what is lowly . . ." – Ignatius to Isabel Roser, 10 November 1532 (De Nicolas, op. cit., p. 315).

THE PILGRIM

page 251 Epigraph – Rev. Père F. X. de Charlevoix, SJ, *The History and General Description of New France* (1743), trans. Dr. John Gilmary Shea (New York: Francis P. Harper, 1900), vol. 1, p. 123.

THE UNBELIEVER

page 252 *Autobiography* – De Nicolas ed., p. 255, para. 17.

MONTSERRAT

page 253 Description of Montserrat and the Abbey – from a view entitled "Maison et Chambre Angélique de la Vierge-Marie de MONT-SERRAT située en Catalogne a sept lieues et demi au Nord de *Barcelone* . . ." in *L'Atlas Curieux ou le Monde dressé et Dedié A Nos Seigneurs les Enfans de France par leur tres humble et tres Obeissant Serviteur, N. de Fer* (1701).

page 254 Further description of the Abbey – from illustrations in Alexandre de Laboude, *Voyage pittoresque et historique en Espagne* (1806).

The Vigil

page 255 The vigil of Ignatius with his armor – El Greco, "Vincentio Anastagi" (Frick Museum, New York).

Manresa

page 256 Ignatius praying – El Greco, "Saint Francis in Prayer" (1580–5). Joslyn Museum, Omaha, Nebraska.

Rome

page 260 The various Contemplations here and elsewhere in the text are generally from the "Mysteries of the Life of Our Lord" at the end of the Fourth Week of the *Spiritual Exercises*. Otherwise, as with some of the purported Exercises in the "Crow-Text," or Père Biard's Contemplation of Ignatius, I have invented them for use as devices or metaphors. The reader who disparages this liberty of mine is invited to write his own book.

page 262 Description of St. Peter's – in *L'Atlas Curieux* . . . "L'Église de St. Pierre a Rome," p. 48.

Jerusalem

page 263 The round, large gold thing – *Autobiography*, De Nicolas ed., p. 267, para. 45.

page 264 "the ENEMY behaves like a woman . . ." – "Rules for the Discernment of Spirits," 12th, in the *Spiritual Exercises*, De Nicolas ed., p. 165, para. 325.

page 264 "the ENEMY also behaves like a false lover . . ." – ibid., 13th, p. 166, para. 326.

page 265 The Provincial – after Piero della Francesca, "Augustinian Monk" (Frick Museum, New York).

page 267 Description of the mount called Olivet – from a trip to Sunset Crater, Arizona and Wupatki Pueblo, Arizona, in June 1988.

The Black-Gown

page 270 Epigraph on Asiatic bishops – Herder, op. cit., p. 282.

page 270 Epigraph on the Pope's chair – John Donne, op. cit., p. 97.

page 270 Aquinas on man and sperm – *Selected Writings of Thomas Aquinas*, trans. Robert P. Goodwin (Indianapolis: Bobbs-Merrill, 1965), p. 7.

Barcelona (1525)

page 271 On contrition – *Imitation*, op. cit., p. 27.

THE FIRST INVESTIGATION

page 272 View of Toledo – from a painting by El Greco of the same title (*ca.* 1597).
page 272 The Grand Inquisitor – from a painting by El Greco of Cardinal Don Fernando Niño de Gredain (1541–1609), painted *ca.* 1599–1601.
page 273 Ignatius's conversation with Figueroa – *Autobiography*, De Nicolas ed., p. 274, para. 59.

THE OATH

page 274 The tale of Maurus – told in Saint Ignatius's letter on obedience to the Fathers and Brothers at Coimbra (Rome, 26 March 1553): De Nicolas ed., p. 310.

THE SOCIETY OF JESUS

page 276 Ignatius to Father Nicolás Bobadilla – letter MI I 277–282, Rome, 1543: De Nicolas ed., p. 327.
page 277 Ignatius's instructions – letter to Fathers Salermón and Bröet, September 1541: De Nicolas ed., pp. 323–4.

THE SCRUPLES OF PÈRE BIARD

page 281 Anti-idleness epigraph – Edward Payson Morton, PhD, *Lake Huron and the Country of the Algonquins* (Chicago: Ainsworth & Co., 1913, Great Lakes Series, 1913), p. 5.

THE CONVERSION OF THE FRENCHMEN

page 282 William Byrd epigraph – loc. cit.

THE THREE MIRACLES

page 285 The kind devotion of the Marshal of Virginia – ibid., p. 53.
page 285 "For this reason, he began to look for a Savage . . ." – *JR*, vol. 4, p. 39.
page 286 "a gentle people who extend to us their hands . . . defeated" – ibid., p. 113.

THE AGREEMENT

page 288 "O wonderfull *Hypercritiques* . . ." – John Donne, *Ignatius His Conclave* (1611), ed. T. S. Healy, SJ (Oxford: Clarendon Press, 1969), p. 27.
page 289 First part of Argall's song – from John Oldham, *Satires upon the Jesuits*

(1768–81), III, lns 445–8, in Elias F. Mengel, Jr., *Poems on Affairs of State*, vol. ii, *Augustan Satirical Verse 1660–1714* (New Haven: Yale, 1965).

page 289 Second part of Argall's song – ibid., II.210–13.

The Meaning of the Falls

page 289 Anecdote of the log in the Acadian falls – Denys, op. cit., p. 117.

Further History of the French Acadians

page 292 Epigraph – Herbert Guindon, *Québec Society: Tradition, Modernity, and Nationhood* (University of Toronto Press, 1988), p. 104.

page 293 The death of Poutrincourt – see, e.g., the pamphlet given as an appendix to Lescarbot, *History of New France*, vol. 3, p. 534. Parkman merely says euphemistically: ". . . command was given him of the royal forces destined for the attack on Méry; and here, happier in his death than in his life, he fell, sword in hand" (*Pioneers of France*, p. 239).

page 293 Description of Père Le Clercq – from an illustration in his *New Relation* (see the full citation in the section "Born Underwater," below).

page 295 Description of the harbor of Annapolis Royal – engaving in the Dominion Archives, pub. J. F. W. des Barres, 1781, in Captain John Knox, *An Historical Journal of Campaigns in North America for the Years 1757, 1758, 1759 and 1760*, ed. Arthur G. Doughty, vol. 1 (Toronto: Champlain Society, 1914), p. 497.

page 295 Extract on the Micmac girl – ibid., p. 89.

page 295 Footnote on "these Tribes" – Dièreville, op. cit., p. 116.

Further History of the Armouchiquois

page 297 Père Lalemant epigraph – *Lettre dv Père Charles L'Allemant Superievr de la Mission des Canadas de la Compagnie de IESVS. Au Père Hierosme l'Allemant son frère* (1627) (*JR*, vol. 4, p. 197).

page 297 The Englishman – Sir Ferdinando de Gorges, *A Briefe Narration of the Originall Undertakings of the Advancement of Plantations Into . . . New England* (1658), quoted by Morrison, op. cit., pp. 154–5.

Out of the Kingdom

page 298 "Jacob left Beer-sheba . . ." – Genesis 28.10.

BORN UNDERWATER

page 299 Epigraph – Carl Jung, *Dreams* (from *Collected Works* of C. G. Jung, vols. 4, 8, 12, 16), trans. R. F. C. Hull (Princeton: Princeton University Press, Bollingen Series, 1974), p. 96.

page 299 Whitehead footnote – note to author, 24 April 1990.

page 299 A good background reference for Micmac life in the 1600s is Father Christien Le Clercq, *New Relation of Gaspesia, with the Customs and Religion of the Gaspesians*, trans. with repr. of orig. by William F. Ganong, PhD (Toronto: Champlain Society, 1910). A more general work on the ceremonies of North American Indians, to which I have occasionally referred throughout this book, is Ruth M. Underhill, *Red Man's Religion: Beliefs and Practices of the Indians North of Mexico* (Chicago: University of Chicago Press, 1965).

SAULT OF ELECTION

page 301 According to Le Clercq, moose-bones could yield six or seven pounds of fat.

page 302 The awakening of the waterfalls – from a visit to Livingston Manor, New York, in March 1989.

page 303 The pain in her belly – according to Whitehead, the solar plexus was often the seat of an individual's Power.

TWO WINNERS

page 305 Some details of the scoring of Waltes are taken from a 2-page document entitled "Waltes, for Mary Spaulding, from Marion Walter", which Whitehead kindly sent me.

THE DREAM OF THE IROCOIS

page 311 "As we began to approach the said rapids . . ." – *Les Voyages dv Sievr de Champlain Xaintongeoius, Capitaine ordinarie pour le Roy, en la Marine (M.DC.XII)*, in Biggar, op. cit., vol. 1, p. 180.

page 311 Description of the rivers half-frozen in ignorance – from a visit to the Saint Lawrence River (Fleuve Saint-Laurent) in March 1989.

page 312 "Navigation seemed to him the highest art . . ." – from Biggar, op. cit., vol. 1, p. 209.

page 314 "The Savages assured him that this brackishness increased . . ." – "This does not follow the original," says Trigger (note to author, 17 March 1990), "but perhaps that is artistic license." In fact Champlain's description goes on at somewhat tedious length, and I have simplified it, and therefore Canadian geography, at this point. As this section has more to do with his hopes and illusions than with his knowledge, I feel justified in doing so. (Authors always do, don't they?)

THE HODINHSIONI

page 316 Epigraph – Petrone, op. cit., p. 39. She cites J. Hewitt's translation of 1928.

page 316 In my recreation of Wendaké I have made use not only of Trigger's *The Children of Aataentsic* but also of his *The Huron: Farmers of the North*, 2nd ed. (Montréal: Stanford University Press, Case Studies in Cultural Anthropology Ser., ed. George and Louise Spindler, 1990).

page 316 Founding date of the confederacy – "It has been proposed that Dekanwideh's blotting out of the sun, an event that is part of the traditional account of the founding of the Iroquois league, refers to a solar eclipse visible in upper New York State in AD 1451 . . ." (Trigger, *The Children of Aataentsic*, pp. 162–3, citing the *Handbook of North American Indians*, vol. 15, p. 420). See the Chronology for other dates.

page 316 "What similarities and differences would you say there were between Huron and Iroquois myths of this period?" I asked Trigger. He replied (19 March 1990): "We really don't know – creation myths similar; no evidence of a Huron Great Peace myth; clan myth etc. probably structurally similar."

page 316 Huron coats – from one displayed at the Museum of the American Indian (Heye Foundation), New York.

page 316 ". . . but always the torturers laughed" – reading this (27 March 1990), Trigger added: "And so did the victims" – an important point about Iroquoian mores which I should have stressed, and now have. I am especially grateful for this correction.

page 318 "Men were ragged with sacrifice" – Parker, op. cit., p. 17.

THE PEACEMAKER

page 318 Foundation of the League – best described in A. C. Parker, *The Constitution of the Five Nations or the Iroquois Book of the Great Law* (Ontario: Iroqrafts Ltd, 1984 [repr. of 1916 ed.]). This book contains two versions of the legend: the Seth Newhouse version (Mohawk), and the version of Six Nations Chiefs. As with the conflicting saga-version sources in the previous volume, I have felt free to use whatever details from each suited me.

page 318 For my descriptions of Iroquoian (i.e., Huron and Iroquois) features, beginning here and continuing throughout this book, I have made some use of John G. Garratt's *The Four Indian Kings / Les Quatre Rois Indiens* (Public Archives Canada, 1985), which contains a number of portrait reproductions.

page 318 The Huron village – see, for instance, Trigger, *The Children of Aataentsic*, ch. 2.

page 318 Trigger footnote – note to author, 2 June 1989.

page 323 Attempted drownings of DEKANWIDEH – again, based on the Mohawk story collected by Newhouse. "Is there a basis for this?" writes Trigger. "It seems very unHuron – only case I can think of was story of shaman reincarnated in woman – she aborted fetus and hid it in forest but it lived. – Huron normally loved children and would not do this. To make reactions 'realistic' you have to stress fear of mother and lodgemates that baby is an evil spirit" (note to author, 15 May 1989). I hope I have now done this.

page 324 "When DEKANWIDA had grown to manhood . . ." – Parker, op. cit., p. 14.

page 324 ibid. – "The Huron did not approve of anything that was extraordinary unless it justified its existence by serving the people," notes Trigger (communication to author, Easter Sunday 1990).

page 327 Père Cholonec's encomium on Kateri Tekakwitha – actually written two years after her death. I use the translation given in the Catholic *Positio* on her canonization (sourced in full in the notes to Part V), p. 81.

page 330 Ayonhwhatha, Hiawatha and Hayonhwhatha are all, of course, the same. If you want it simple, read Longfellow.

page 330 The domain of Adadarhoh – from a visit to Lake George, New York in July 1989.

FROM THE CONSTITUTION OF THE FIVE NATIONS

page 336 Extract – Parker, op. cit., p. 54.

THE FUTURE

page 337 Père Biard on torture – *JR*, vol. 1, pp. 221–3.

THE ISLES OF DEMONS

page 338 In this part of the book, I have made occasional use of the *Handbook of North American Indians* (Washington: Smithsonian, 1978), vol. 15, *Northeast*, ed. Bruce G. Trigger.

page 338 Epigraph – Alfred Goldsmith Bailey, *The Conflict of European and Eastern Algonkin Cultures 1504–1700: A Study in Canadian Civilization*, 2nd ed. (Toronto: University of Toronto Press, 1969), p. 10.

page 338 Champlain on GOUGOU – Biggar, vol. 3, pp. 186–8. A note in Biggar claims identity between GOUGOU and the Micmac (Souriquois) Power of earthquakes, KEWKW or KUKHW (see *The Ice-Shirt*, Glossary I).

CURRENTS

page 340 The coronation of Charles V – from an engraving of N. Hogenberg, Antwerp, 1632.

The Enmity of Mapmakers

page 340 By "America" in this section I mean South America, as the Spaniards probably did. I have probably been too succinct. And I am using "Canada" wrongly here, in place of "New France," which would not read as well immediately following "Antarctic France." – "Antarctic France really S. America, esp. Brazil," notes Trigger (27 March 1990). "Canada always referred to the St. Lawrence – New France to a larger area = ½ N. America? Champlain divided N. Amer. into N. France & Florida."

The Ants

page 342 Verazzano being "permitted by the sea-demons to reach Canada" – here again I am using Canada only in the poetic sense. Would actually have been New France; see Trigger note immediately above.

page 342 "They are of color russet . . ." – "Hakluyt's translation from Ramusio, in *Divers Voyages* (1582)," cites Parkman, who tells this episode after brief mention of Honfleur, Aubert and Léry (*Pioneers of France*, pp. 149–51).

page 342 temples of silver and gold – extrapolated from some Mayan ruins I saw in Belize.

page 343 In the annals of generosity we must never forget Jacques Quartier, who gave tiny bells to the Souriquois women near Chaleur Bay, at which they caressed him gratefully and sang songs. He was afraid of the Souriquois who held beaver-skins on sticks and shouted eagerly at him, so he sailed away, but they pursued him, being greedy for iron, so he launched two fire-darts over their heads, and still they came on, so he shot two fire-darts among them, and they scattered screaming. The next day, seeing more (or perhaps the same people), he gave them iron, with a red hat for their Captain.

The Dream of the Hiroquois

page 344 Lescarbot excerpt – *History of New France*, op. cit., vol. 2, p. 125.

A Toy Island Broken

page 345 Epigraph – F. X. Weiser, SJ, *Kateri Tekakwitha* (Caughnawagwa, P.Q., Canada: The Kateri Center, 1972), p. 115.

page 345 Champlain's measurement of Sable Island – in part from Biggar, op. cit., vol. 1, p. 240.

The City of God

page 346 First para. – in part from Biggar, op. cit., vol. 1, pp. 130–40.

page 347 Champlain footnote – ibid., vol. 4, p. 31.

KEBEC

page 357 Herder epigraph – op. cit., p. 305.

page 358 Description of church-rays – from an oil painting by Arthur Villeneuve, "L'Angélus" (1962) (in *Cahiers des arts visuels au Québec*, vol. 10, no: 39 [hiver 1988], p. 18).

page 360 The altar and the figures of Jogues and Brébeuf – from a visit to the Chapelle des Jésuites de Québec, March 1989.

page 360 Description of Governor Montcalm – from an anonymous painting, "Le Marquis de Montcalm" (Musée du Séminaire du Québec, 983.1).

THE SHOALS OF HELL

page 361 "Canadians share that most enlightened of systems . . ." – A. R. M. Lower and J. W. Chafe, *Canada – A Nation and How It Came to Be* (Longmans, Green & Co., 1958), p. 6.

MY RESEARCHES

page 362 Montcalm's tomb-inscription – the original reads: ***HONNEUR À MONTCALM! LE DESTIN EN LUI DÉROLANT LA VICTOIRE L'A RÉCOMPENSÉ PAR UNE MORT GLORIEUSE!***

READYING HIS SPORTSMEN

page 364 Description of Montagnais war-clothes – from Biggar, op. cit., vol. 1, p. 180.

COMMENCEMENT OF THE IROCOIS WAR

page 364 The island of birds "in perfect order by species" – actually, a recollection of Frère Sagard's.

page 364 Description of Iroquois country – from a visit to Ithaca, New York in August 1988.

page 367 For a good résumé of the battles of 1609 and 1610, with interesting discussions of motivations, misunderstandings, etc., see Trigger, *The Children of Aataentsic*, pp. 249–61.

IRON

page 371 Description of the Ritual of Condolence – see Bierhorst, op. cit., pp. 109–86. Wherever possible, the tropes in my first paragraph are Iroquois figures of speech used in the actual Ritual.

page 371 Trigger points out that the Ritual of Condolence was held only for Council chiefs (sachems), who would have been unlikely to accompany a war party. Obviously I want to have the Ritual here, to tie in with the DEKANWIDEH myth earlier. So I asked Trigger to help me rationalize. He replied: "You could just ignore my point – few if any will ever notice. Alternatively, you might argue that one of the things this 'war party' was hoping to do was meet & trade with Basques or other Europeans & that council chiefs had come along with them for this reason . . ." (note to author, Easter Sunday 1990).

HENRY HUDSON

page 372 On the plan of the Iroquois to trade with the Dutch, see Trigger, *The Children of Aataentsic*, pp. 260–1.

IN THE SHALLOWS

page 374 Epigraph – U.S.D.I. pamphlet, p. 5.

page 376 Little information is available on the life of Hélène Boullé de Champlain. An excellent summary and analytical portrait is given in René Bauchi's "Madame de Champlain" in *Les Cahiers de Dix*, numéro 32 (Montréal, 1968, pp. 27–52). There are numerous differences between that account and that in the *Dictionary of Canadian Biography*. In its long article on her husband, for instance, it says: "Of the promised dowry (6,000 livres), Champlain received 4,500 livres the day before the ceremony . . ." (vol. 1, p. 191), but the *Cahiers de Dix* article presents evidence which suggests that Champlain signed a quittance for this amount. A number of other inconsistencies and vagaries exist, which I have capitalized upon to create the account most pleasing to me.

THE TWENTIETH RAPIDS

page 387 "This account does not follow historical setting," says Trigger, "perhaps for good reason. Huron & Ottawa Valley Algonquins wanted secret meeting with Champlain – agreed to return him to trading station via Lachine – 8 canoes involved Huron/Algonquins – not Montagnais as far as we know" (note to author, Easter Sunday 1990).

page 393 Description of Rochelle in the peach-colored dusk – after an oil painting by Claude-Joseph Vernet, "Vue du port de La Rochelle" (1762), Musée de la Marine, Paris; in André Vachon, m.s.r.c., *Les documents de notre histoire*, vol. 2 (Ottawa: Public Archives Canada, 1985, p. 57).

THE EXCHANGE STUDENTS

page 400 The character of Étienne Brûlé – "Like many others in his situation," writes Trigger, "Brûlé seems to have felt little genuine attachment to his identity either as a

Frenchman or as a Huron, but was capable of sacrificing either in order to accomplish whatever duties he was hired to perform" (*The Children of Aataentsic*, p. 372).

THE WATERFALL OF HUMILITY

page 405 Lower and Chafe epigraph – op. cit., p. 36.

THE THIRD CAMPAIGN

page 413 Champlain's astrolabe – "It was sold to a U.S. collector & Canadians have grumbled about this ever since," says Trigger (27 March 1990). "I believe I heard the Canadian government has ransomed it for the New Museum of Civilization (?). Heidenreich proved that the astrolabe found was too crude to make the observation Champlain recorded – was it his # 2 instrument?"

page 416 "their breasts hang down . . ." – ibid., p. 136.

page 416 Flogging of the cabin boy to bring on good weather – an actual episode in Denys.

page 417 Champlain's solemn declaration – from his *Works*, vol. 3, *Voyages et descovvertvres faites en la Novvelle France, depuis l'année 1615 iusques à la fin de l'année 1618* . . ., p. 9.

page 423 Description of the Onondaga village – unattributed French engraving, 1615. Many of the illustrations in Champlain, once thought to be faithful engravings of his drawings, seem now to be of less certain provenance. Trigger has little use for most of them. He remarks on the palm trees depicted in the Lac Champlain battle scene, on the nakedness of the Amerindians in that sketch and in the one for the battle of the following year; as for the engraving of this battle with the Onondaga, he has little faith in the hexagonal shape in which the village has been drawn. But as it seems likely that Champlain looked at the drawing and approved it, I have allowed the image to stand, not because it was true, but because after all this time the illustration deserves its own status as an icon of an important battle the very location of which is now unknown. Indeed, almost everything about the battle is obscure. Whether or not these Iroquois were Onondaga, for instance, is conjectural. Many historians have believed so. Trigger, however, advances arguments to suggest that they were Oneida. Champlain's whereabouts during this battle cannot be deduced with any certainty.

page 423 "Those who know the least shout the loudest" – Champlain, *Voyages*, 1632, p. 367. (I am sorry that some of the Champlain citations are inconsistent in form.)

A LOST BET

page 431 Champlain's and Darontal's conflicting motivations are well analyzed by Trigger in *The Children of Aataentsic*. Trigger sees this period as epochal in the snowballing of Champlain's paranoia, remarking (p. 330): "The winter that Champlain was compelled to spend among the Huron seems to have enlarged a basic fear and mistrust of the Indians, which had hitherto been concealed by a sense of superiority and of his ability to control them."

THE FRENCH DRESS

page 433 Epigraph – Marie de l'Incarnation to her son, Québec, 1670; in Marshall, op. cit., p. 369.

page 434 "Barren women could be used as light sexual relief by male Micmac hunters, and had no recourse. Husbands dumped barren women" – Whitehead to author (31 January 1989).

A PERFECT MATCH

page 435 Description of One-Eye's outfit – after an engraving of a Montagnais man on Champlain's map of 1612. However, the man in the engraving wears a sort of skirt decorated with leaf designs. Whitehead corrects: "One-Eye would wear a robe . . . Montagnais designs were linear and geometric, with caribou and other realistic art, not leaves" (letter to author, 24 April 1990).

THE FRENCH DRESS

page 437 A few of the descriptions of Montagnais artifacts, etc. in this section are based on photographs in *Oti il no Kaepe / Les Indiens Montagnais du Québec* by Alfred Connolly (Ottawa: Collection Plumes d'Outarde 1, 1972).

KEBEC YEARS

page 439 My descriptions of the Habitation at Kebec from this point on are informed by the beautiful illustrations in a children's book entitled *Québec 1616: Un comptoir au bord du Saint-Laurent* by Jean Hamelin and Carlo Wieland (Rennes: Éditions Ouest-France, 1989).

FURTHER PLEASURES OF THE TOY WORLD

page 448 The Montagnais murder of the two Frenchmen, and its punishment – told in Champlain's *Voyages* of 1619, vol. 4.

HÉLÈNE IN CANADA

page 455 The Roy's letter – Champlain, vol. 5, p. 13.

KEBEC YEARS

page 461 Description of Kebec seen from the river by the Hiroquois in 1622 – Légaré, "Québec au soleil couchant," 1885–98 (Musée de Québec, 58.326). "The later claim of this attack probably not true. But why not?" (Trigger to author, May 1990).

PÈRE DE NOBILI

page 472 Goa footnote – from Edward Thornton, Esq., *A Gazateer of the Territories under the Government of the East India Company, and of the Native States on the continent of India, compiled by the authority of the Honourable Court of Directors, and chiefly from documents in their possession* (Delhi: Neeraj Publishing House, 1858 ed., repr. 1984).

page 472 Description of Goa – from a visit there in January 1990.

page 475 Description of Père Roberto de Nobili – unattributed engraving, *Catholic Encyclopedia*, vol. x, p. 478.

GLORY, OR, THE CONVERSION OF THE HURON SAVAGES

page 479 Again, various vignettes of saintliness and asceticism in this section were inspired by the engravings in *Sadler's Hermits and Saints* (1594). In the dialogues between Born Underwater and Père Brébeuf, I have occasionally put into the latter's mouth words from the letters to me of Michael Remshard, SJ, in 1988 and 1989. Mostly these have been sourced in the text. The descriptions of Huron villages and longhouses are based not only on written sources but also on a visit in September 1989 to replicas erected at the Mission Sainte-Marie restoration and the Huronia Museum, both at Midland, Ontario.

THE HURON YEARS

page 481 Epigraph on dying for JESUS – Marie de l'Incarnation to her son, Québec, 1647, in Marshall, op. cit., p. 167.

THE CURRENTS OF PATIENCE

page 483 Herder epigraph – op. cit., p. 304.

page 485 The fifth rule – *Spiritual Exercises*, para. 318: "Rules for the Discernment of Spirits," First Week (De Nicolas ed., p. 164).

page 485 "It was the Recollects who sent for the Black-Gowns . . ." – Trigger and others have suggested that the Recollects were intimidated by them even then, and would have kept them out of Canada if they'd had the power; failing this they felt forced to welcome them. We may be sure that there was tension between the two Orders almost immediately.

page 487 Père Le Caron on the Huron – Trigger sums up the position of the Père's Order as follows: "The fundamental problem that the Récollets saw impeding their work was that the Indians were too 'primitive' to be converted. From this they drew the devastatingly simple conclusion that if they were to convert the Indians they had first to find ways of 'civilizing' them" (p. 378).

The Martyrdom of Père Nicolas

page 490 "the artless simplicity of my usual manner" – Gabriel Sagard, *The Long Journey to the Country of the Hurons* (1632), ed. George Wrong, trans. H. H. Langton (Toronto: Champlain Society, 1939), p. 8.

page 490 The Stinkards, Coppermines, etc. – "Not on route to Huron," says Trigger, "or am I being too literal?"

page 491 "this Nation was very docile, and when influenced by temporal considerations . . ." – Père Le Jeune's *Relation* of 1633 (Paris: Sebastien Cramoisy, 1643), *JR*, vol. 6 (Québec: 1633–4), p. 42.

page 494 Père Nicholas's underwater view – from a study by snorkel of the bottom of Grand Lake, Algonquin Park, Ontario.

page 494 "almost in sight of the Cross where Kateri Tekakwitha was going to be buried" – "She was buried south of the St. Lawrence," says Trigger, "not by the Rivière des Prairies" (note to author, January 1990). But I am protected by my "almost."

page 495 I have already noted above Trigger's statement that Père Nicolas met his end accidentally. Even now, however, the religious do not seem to accept this view. For instance, in the Jesuit biography of Père Brébeuf (Angus J. Macdougall, SJ, *Brébeuf: A Giant in Huronia* (Martyrs' Shrine: Midland, Ontario, 1970) we read that Père Nicolas "was apparently drowned by his unfriendly Huron companions in Rivière-des-Prairies to the north of Montréal Island at a spot called today, in his memory, Sault-au-Récollet" (p. 7).

Amantacha's Sponsors

page 498 Note on nephews – Tregouaroti was Arendarhonon. And "Iroquet's ties would have been to Rock Tribe, not Cord, to which Soranhes belonged. Still, Soranhes could have been nephewing here in a general way" (Trigger to author, 8 May 1990).

The Education

page 501 Description of Paris – from a city plan dated 1610.

page 501 Trigger footnote – note to author, 28 May 1990.

FAITH, HOPE AND CHARITY

page 509 Pontgravé's figures on the skin trade – according to Trigger (*Children of Aataentsic*, pp. 336–7), the French were exporting twelve to fifteen thousand skins a year at this time, of which perhaps ten thousand were purchased from the Huron. In contrast, the total Dutch volume was something like five thousand skins per year. This helps to explain why the Dutch and the Iroquois were becoming so desperate to disrupt the French–Huron trade.

page 512 "with French speech . . . they may also acquire a French heart and spirit" – Champlain, *Works*, vol. 2 (1615–18), trans. H. H. Langton and W. F. Ganong, gen. ed. Biggar (Toronto: Champlain Society, 1929), p. 6.

THE HONEYMOON

page 515 Trigger expresses doubt that Brûlé would have returned to Canada before 1628–9 when he was in the pay of the English. I have preferred to retain the contrary supposition held by some earlier commentators, in order to advance the plot.

ECHON ALONE

page 517 The Huron language "among the first of those which sprang up so suddenly at the Tower of Babel" – Père François du Creux, SJ, *The History of New France* (1664), trans. Percy J. Robinson, ed. James B. Conacler, vol. 1 (Toronto: Champlain Society, 1951), p. 24.

page 517 Pronunciation of the Huron language from the pit of the stomach – "It is not necessary to pronounce this language from the pit of the stomach, as with Huron, Swiss or German" (Pére Le Clercq, op. cit., p. 141).

THE THREE DASTARDS

page 519 The Three Dastards – "[The] Kirkes had grown up in France," says Trigger. "Their father probably in league with Guillaume de Caen – Brûlé and some other employees of de Caen had gone over to the Kirkes & sailed with them from England" (note to author, January 1990).

page 524 Dialogue between Brébeuf, Kirke and Michel – taken almost verbatim from Parkman, *Pioneers of France in the New World*, pp. 321–2.

HOPE AND CHARITY ABANDONED

page 532 Marsolet's letter – abridged from Champlain, vol. 6 (1629–32) (Champlain Society, 1936; trans. W. D. Le Sueur and H. H. Langton), p. 104.

page 532 "in a c-c-canoe . . ." – cribbed from S. E. Morison.

Two Dispositions

page 537 "If thou suffer to issue from thy lips . . ." – *JR*, vol. 29, p. 35.

The River's Mouth

page 546 Epigraph – Thomas à Kempis, op. cit., p. 39.

The Treachery of the Huron Savages

page 549 Again, the events related here are based on Père Jeune's *Relation* of 1633, *JR*, vol. 6.

Winter at Kebec

page 557 Description of the cliffs and the Fleuve Saint-Laurent – from a painting by Joseph LeGaré, "Le manoir Caldwell et les moulins de l'Etechimin vers 1845" (Musée de Québec, 56.404).

The Sorcerer's Wife

page 558 The winter of 1633–4 – Lettre du P. Paul le Jeune, au R. P. Provincial de France à Paris (Québec, 1634), *JR*, vol. 6. Many incidents have been rearranged for artistic effect.

page 558 "There is not an insect . . ." – *JR*, vol. 6, p. 261.

page 558 "I am rather tired . . ." – loc. cit.

page 560 ". . . foul odor of the sewers . . ." – ibid., p. 253.

page 568 MANITOU – says Whitehead in her *Tales from the Six Worlds* (p. 5): "*Mn'tu'* is another word for Power . . . which seems to refer more to its conscious aspects than does the word *kinap*."

page 568 Description of the shooting stars and the shapes of spruces (in Le Jeune's search for MANITOU) – from a tapisserie haute lisse by Suzanne Paquette, "Tenue de soirée" (1987) (in *Cahiers des arts visuels au Québec*, vol. 10, no. 39 [hiver 1988], p. 41).

Consolation

page 570 "I wanted to describe this journey . . ." – *JR*, vol. 7, p. 209.

The Dream of the Iron People

page 571 Epigraph – Donne, op. cit., p. 15.

THE PLAN

page 580 Jesuit policy – see, for instance, Trigger, *The Children of Aataentsic*, pp. 467–9.

AN EXTRACT FROM THE HURON RELATION OF 1649

page 581 The extract – although this appears in Thwaites's version of the *Jesuit Relations*, I have here drawn on the more available Fallon translation: Rev. Paul Ragueneau, SJ, *Shadows Over Huronia* (1650), trans. Rev. J. Fallon, SJ (Midland, Ontario: The Martyrs' Shrine, 1965), p. 54.

THE COMPANIONS

page 582 Epigraph – Weiser, op. cit., p. 149.
page 582 Champlain's chat with Capitanal – partly based on the record in *JR*, vol. 5, pp. 205–11.
page 586 The religious articles – as seen in the Musée du Séminaire du Québec.

THE STREAM OF TIME

page 586 The journey – *JR*, vol. 8. (NOTE A reprint of Brébeuf's Huron Relation in this volume is available from the Martyrs' Shrine, Midland, Ontario.)
page 588 Sagard on Chaudière Falls – op. cit., p. 260.

THE KINGDOM

page 594 Description of the Huron men in the village – after an engraving by Champlain (1632).

MARIE AEOSWINA

page 604 "I see only the liberty . . ." – *JR*, vol. 8, p. 151.
page 604 Part of the description of the Huron in council – from a painting by Zacharie Vincent, 1815–86, "Jeune-Lorette" (Musée du Séminaire de Québec).
page 604 Description of Saint Michael chastising the rebellious Angels – from a painting by Claude Vignon, 1593–1670, "St. Michel chassant les anges rebelles" (Musée du Séminaire de Québec, 983.5).

THE SIN OF AMANTACHA

page 608 Brébeuf's criticisms of Amantacha – *JR*, vol. 8, p. 149.

The Flames of Time

page 611 "On a sunny granite shelf adjoining the water . . ." – "No granite bedrock in Huronia," says Trigger, "or any rock outcrops – could be a granite boulder – glacial erratic" (note to author, 28 May 1990). So what Amantacha actually lay on was a granite boulder sunken into the lake shore.

page 613 The custom of pyromancy – described by Brébeuf in *JR*, vol. 8, p. 125.

Amantacha Among the Hiroquois

page 614 Description of Iroquoia – from a visit to Livingston Manor, New York, in May 1989.

page 615 Amantacha's capture – some of the details are based on James Smith's "Prisoner of the Caughnawagwas" and Moses van Campen's "An Inch of Ground to Fight On," in Frederick Drimmer, ed., *Captured by the Indians: Fifteen Firsthand Accounts 1750–1870* (New York: Dover, 1985 repr.).

The First Epidemic

page 618 Whitehead notes that for the Micmac (Souriquois) as well as for the Huron, "the collapse of the fur trade through overhunting had not yet occurred in 1630: disease was factor that destabilized."

page 618 Epigraph – *JR*, vol. 16 (1639), p. 185.

page 619 Nature of the various epidemics in Wendaké – according to Trigger, the first epidemic, of 1634, might have been measles or influenza but was definitely not smallpox; it was the least severe of any. The second, beginning in the fall of 1636, was probably influenza. The third, which occurred in the summer of 1637, while the second was still running its course (in the text I have lumped them together) "is more likely to have been a European childhood ailment against which most Frenchmen had already acquired immunity" (*The Children of Aataentsic*, p. 528). The fourth, which struck in the summer of 1639, was smallpox and by far the most serious. It continued until spring 1640, by which time the Huron population was about 50 percent of what it had been in 1634.

Kebec

page 619 Le Jeune's writing in this section is based on the *Relation de ce qvi s'est passé en la Nouvelle France en l'Annee 1635. Enuoyé au R. P. Provincial de la Compagnie de Iesvs en la Province de la France. Par le P. Paul le Ieune de la mesme Compagnie; de la residence de Kebec* (Paris: Cramoisy, 1636), in *JR*, vol. 7.

page 619 "If these people receive the faith . . ." – *JR*, vol. 6, p. 57.

THE FIRST EPIDEMIC

page 622 Episode of Khionngnona – *JR*, vol. 13 (1637), p. 135.

AMANTACHA AND JESUS

page 623 Description of grave-flowers – from a collage painting by Françoise Bujold, "Hommage à Lionel Groulx" (1968) (in *Cahiers des arts visuels au Québec*, vol. 10, no. 39 [hiver 1988], p. 20).

A FUNERAL FEAST

page 626 Epigraph – Kempis, op. cit., p. 81.

THE DROUGHT

page 628 Epigraph – Ignatius, *Spiritual Diary*, entry for 22 February 1544, in De Nicolas ed., p. 201, para. 64.

POST MORTEM

page 637 "We are responsible for the sterility or fecundity of the earth . . ." – based on Le Jeune's *Relation* of 1636, in *JR*, vol. 9 (Québec) (Cramoisy, 1637), p. 95.

THE CUSTOM OF THE COUNTRY

page 638 "It is the nature of our ENEMY to become weak . . ." – *Spiritual Exercises*, "Rules for the Discernment of Spirits," 12th, De Nicolas ed., pp. 165–6, para. 325.

THE LOSER

page 640 The five parts of the soul – "This does not precisely correspond with John Steckley's analysis in an unpublished MA thesis – but is close enough to let stand – esp. since John doesn't manage to relate living & dead souls" (Trigger to author, January 1990).

THE THIRTEEN CONTEMPLATIONS

page 650 Guy La Flèche epigraph – from an extract from his book, in *Le Québec littéraire*, hiver 1989, no. 2, "Martyrs canadiens ou 'Canadiens' donc martyrs?", p. 91.

Brûlé's Bones

page 656 The women making cord – Trigger notes that it is actually unknown whether women or men made this (note to author, June 1990).

The Death of Amantacha

page 666 "During her life she considered herself to be a great sinner . . ." – Père Chauchetière's *Life of the Good Katherine Tekagoüitha, Now Known as the Holy Savage* (1685, rev. 1695), in the *Positio* on her beatification (see Part V, below, for full citation), p. 121.

page 666 "Ah, my Père, I will not marry . . ." – Père Cholonec's *Life of Katherine Tekagouitha, First Iroquois Virgin* (1696), in the *Positio*, p. 276.

page 668 The incantation of the Iroquois medicine men – based on Bierhorst, *In the Trail of the Wind: American Indian Poems and Ritual Orations* (New York: Farrar, Straus & Giroux/Sunburst, 1971), p. 163 ("Magic Formula"); Bierhorst cites Parker as the collector of this incantation.

page 668 Soranhes' mourning speech – beginning based on a speech in *JR*, vol. 8, p. 251 (1636).

page 668 In the *Jesuit Relations* Brébeuf makes a pretty epitaph for Amantacha, saying: "He has not yet returned, but I have confidence in him" (vol. 10, p. 81).

The Huron Seminary

page 669 Indian destiny epigraph – Lewis Henry Morgan, *League of the Iroquois, or Ho-dé-no-sau-nee* (Rochester: Sage and Brothers, 1851), p. 447.

page 670 "I fear they may be satisfied with their old kettles . . ." – *JR*, vol. 13 (Hurons 1637) (1898), p. 7.

page 673 Le Jeune's plea for more Demons – *JR*, vol. 11, p. 89.

Echon's Mercy

page 679 The baptism of the Iroquois prisoner – said the late Mary C. Mansfield, a medievalist: "Look for baptism before being burned as a point of identity between Canada and the Spanish Inquisition."

page 679 "Charity causes us to overlook many considerations" – *JR*, vol. 13, p. 39.

page 680 "Good God, what a compliment!" – ibid., p. 41.

page 680 The uncle's speech – ibid., p. 53.

The Vampire Skeleton

page 685 Tale of the Vampire Skeleton – Jesse J. Cornplanter, as told to Sah-Nee-Weh, the White Sister (Mrs. Walter A. Henricks), *Legends of the Longhouse* (Ohsweken,

Ontario: Iroqrafts repr., 1986), XIII, "The Vampire Skeleton," pp. 140–50. Cornplanter was a Seneca. An Onondaga version appears in Bierhorst, op. cit., pp. 236–8. It is very similar, except that at the end the dead man becomes a fox with red eyes rather than a jackrabbit. Bierhorst says that the fox was "at one time recognized . . . as a symbol of sexual love."

page 686 Description of the Harvest Thanksgiving – based on Morgan, op. cit., pp. 198–207, 279–83 (Feather Dance).

page 691 Tehorenhaegnon, on the bird – *JR*, vol. 13, p. 101. In fact the identity of the Wendat who said this is not given.

THE SECOND EPIDEMIC

page 693 Le Jeune's theory of the DEVIL's counterattacks – from his *Relation de ce qvi s'est passé en la Nouvelle France en l'Annee 1637* (Paris: Jean le Boullenger, 1638), in *JR*, vol. 11 (Hurons and Quebec 1636–7) MDCCCXCVIII, pp. 41–3.

page 693 "The joy that one feels . . ." – *JR*, vol. 8, p. 169.

PAINTED SILHOUETTES

page 694 This incident is told in *JR*, vol. 12, pp. 211–17.

page 699 Marie de l'Incarnation suggests that the black-painted heads have a different meaning, when, writing of the capture of Jogues, she says, "At the same spot were found twelve heads painted red, which is a sign that those they represented are to be burned; six others painted black, which is a sign that these are not yet condemned, and a single one raised above the others . . ." (letter to a Superior of Tours, Kebec, 29 September 1642, in Marshall, op. cit., p. 112).

FRENZY

page 700 Champlain epigraph – Biggar, op. cit., vol. 3, *Voyages et descovvertvres faites en la Novvelle France, depuis l'année 1615 iusques à la fin d'année 1618*, p. 135.

KEBEC YEARS

page 705 Welzl epigraph – op. cit., p. 19.

page 706 "I tried, therefore, to frighten him . . ." – *JR*, vol. 11, p. 107.

page 706 My favorite epigram by Père Le Jeune is this: "All things are yellow to the yellow eyes of the jaundiced" (*JR*, vol. 12, p. 87).

The Second Vow

page 708 Ignatius epigraph – De Nicolas ed., p. 198 ("He Asks for Divine Acceptance – Second Time," para. 48).

page 708 "they will be restored to tranquility of mind" – Le Jeune, op. cit., in *JR*, vol. 11, p. 17.

page 709 "Your world is different from ours . . ." – *Epistola P. Joannis de Brébeuf ad R. P. Mutium Vitellschi, Præpositum Generalem Societatis Jesu, Romae* (*ca.* 1636), in *JR*, vol. 11, p. 9.

The Council of State

page 712 ". . . they regard one another like corpses . . ." – *JR*, vol. 15 (Hurons and Quebec 1638–9) (1638), p. 41.

page 712 "Come quickly . . ." – ibid., p. 59.

The Testament

page 715 The testament – abbreviated and slightly edited from the version given in Macdougall, op. cit., pp. 32–4.

page 716 "The love of God has the Power . . ." – *JR*, vol. 10, p. 83.

Praising the Roy

page 725 "Strike me and kill me . . ." – a common Micmac apology, according to Le Clercq, op. cit., p. 244.

page 725 "Teach me to kill these little creatures . . ." – a Huron woman said this to the Black-Gowns, according to *JR*, vol. 14.

The Two Standards

page 726 Ignatius epigraph – De Nicholas ed., pp. 129–30 ("Fourth Day," paras, 140–1).

The Two Standards

page 728 Lescarbot on Gougou – *History of New France*, p. 176.

page 729 The religious articles – as seen in the Musée du Séminaire de Québec.

Père Lalemant

page 730 "Act submissively . . ." – *JR*, vol. 29, p. 15.

THE DEATH OF ONONKWAIA THE ONEIDA

page 732 "This resolution would be passable . . ." – *JR*, vol. 17 (Huron and Three Rivers 1639–40) (1898), p. 73. An account of his baptism and death follows.

THE EMBROIDERERS

page 737 Marie de l'Incarnation's dream – letter to Dom Raymond de Saint-Bernard, 3 May 1633, in Marshall, op. cit., pp. 51–2.

page 737 The arrival of the Ursulines – from a painting in the Musée des Ursulines de Québec. Ditto for the description of the first monastery, and other scenes in this section too numerous to mention.

page 737 In strict fact the Ursulines did not take possession of their convent until 21 November 1642, it being unready for them previous to that time. During the first three years they were lodged in a small house in the Lower Town. It was needlessly cumbersome to go into this in the text.

page 739 "Those who are surprised at such conduct . . ." – An Ursuline of Québec, *Mary of the Incarnation: Foundress of the Ursuline Monastery Québec* (1939), p. 19.

page 740 Letter on degreasing the naked Savage girls – Marie de l'Incarnation to a lady of rank, Québec, 3 September 1640, in Marshall, op. cit., p. 75.

page 740 Letter on the stink of the Savage girls – Marie de l'Incarnation to Mère Marie-Gilette Roland, Kebec, 4 September 1640, in Marshall, op. cit., p. 79. Even in this century an Ursuline could write (An Ursuline of Quebec, op. cit., p. 42):

> For persons of delicate constitution brought up in seventeenth-century France, dwelling in such close quarters with Indian women and girls presupposes continual abnegation and entire mortification. A great spirit of faith renders life endurable, and no natural repugnance would ever cause them to dismiss this rather unpleasant company, no more than a feeling of disgust will make them refuse a dish seasoned with tallow, a bunch of hair or an old shoe! Far from it! Madame de Peltrie liked going to the huts of Father Le Jeune's neophytes; she even lodged under his roof.

page 740 The habit of the Ursulines was the same from 1659 to 1965.

page 740 In 1988 I asked an Ursuline if the young at Québec were beginning to return to the Church. "It's better now," she replied. "But still in their songs love and war are all mixed up. They simply do not have the resources to make moral choices. They do whatever is easiest."

THE FOURTH EPIDEMIC

page 742 "It . . . seems reasonable to conclude," says Trigger in *The Children of Aataentsic*, p. 602, "that the Huron and Iroquois had been roughly equal in numbers before the epidemics began and that both had lost approximately one half of their population by 1640. In strictly demographic terms this gave neither side an advantage over the other."

page 744 The old Arendouane on the sorceries of the Black-Gowns – this whole speech taken almost verbatim from the words of "one of the oldest and most prominent women of [the Huron] nation," as told by Marie de l'Incarnation to the Superior of the Ursulines at Tours, 13 September 1640, in Marshall, op. cit., p. 82.

page 744 Chihwatenah's sermon on candles – *JR*, vol. 17 (Huron and Three Rivers 1639–40) (1898), p. 41.

The Hunger of Gahachendietoh

page 745 Epigraph – Clark, op. cit., p. ix.

page 746 The tale of Gahachendietoh – Arthur C. Parker, *Seneca Myths and Legends* (1923) (Lincoln: University of Nebraska Press, 1989), p. 78.

The Mission to the Neutrals

page 747 Ignatius epigraph – De Nicolas ed., p. 107, para. 12.

Mission Sainte-Marie

page 750 For information on Mission Sainte-Marie I have relied upon notes I took of my visit to this site (Midland, Ontario) in September 1989, and upon the following two books (which are well illustrated): Barbara McConell and Michael Odesse, *Sainte-Marie among the Hurons* (Toronto: Oxford University Press, 1980), and Huronia Historical Parks, *Images of/de Sainte-Marie* (Midland, 1989).

The Soul-Trade

page 752 "The major dispersals of tribes in the lower Great Lakes area do not seem to have begun with the militancy of the Iroquois, but as a result of the Neutral exploiting the advantages that accrued to them from their geographical position in relation to contemporary trading networks" (Trigger, op. cit., p. 625).

Dutch Guns

page 754 Hiroquois epigraph – Parker, *Constitution of the Iroquois*, p. 53, para. 82.

page 756 The nontraditional nature of this type of warfare cannot be overemphasized. In the 1530s two Iroquoian peoples, the Stadaconnans and the Hochelagans, lived on the Saint Lawrence. By Champlain's time they had disappeared. The destruction of the Stadaconnans by the Hochelagans, and that of the Hochelagans by the Mohawk, is hypothetical. Grounds for believing that it may have happened, however, are supplied by Trigger, who says:

> If our interpretation of these events is correct, we have in these early conflicts on the Saint Lawrence the first evidence of the Iroquois becoming involved in wars that were not of a traditional type. The motive for this conflict was clearly economic and was connected with the fur trade. Instead of seeking to take individual prisoners, the Mohawk sought to annihilate or disperse whole populations whose activities were felt to be a threat to their well-being. In traditional warfare, the aim was to preserve one's enemies as a group in order to go on fighting with them indefinitely. Wars may have been fought in prehistoric times to eliminate an enemy completely, but all known wars of this sort are in some way connected with trade with Europeans.

page 756 It is said that the Iroquois had their first dozen arquebuses at the end of this year.

REUNION

page 760 Description of Père Le Jeune – after an engraving of him by R. Lochon (1665).

GOUGOU

page 762 Lescarbot citation – *The History of New France*, op. cit., p. 174.

THE CITY OF GOD

page 763 Epigraph – Herder, op. cit., p. 273.
page 764 The tale of the Savage girl taken from her pagan husband – Marie de l'Incarnation to Mère Ursule de Sainte-Catherine of Tours, Kebec, 29 September 1642, in Marshall, op. cit., pp. 104–6.
page 765 The husband's view through the grille – scene on a stained glass window in the Chapelle des Ursulines de Québec.

PÈRE LE JEUNE BEATS THE DRUM

page 769 "Our Savages are always savage . . ." – *JR*, vol. 11, p. 81.

PÈRE JOGUES AMONG THE IROQUOIS

page 773 The Exercise of the Two Standards – De Nicolas ed., pp. 129–30, paras. 136–48 (Second Week, Fourth Day).
page 773 In this description, Jerusalem is, of course, Québec.
page 773 Ignatius's prayer – Novena to the Canadian Martyrs, printed at the Martyrs' Shrine in Midland, Ontario.

page 773 Description of the English longboats – from an engraving by Captain Hervey Smith, "A View of the Taking of Quebec, Sept. 13, 1759," in Captain John Knox, *An Historical Journal of Campaigns in North America for the Years 1757, 1758, 1759 and 1760*, ed. Arthur G. Doughty, vol. 2 (Toronto: Champlain Society, 1914), p. 94.

page 773 Description of the wrecked Jesuit Church at Kebec – from a drawing by Richard Short, in Knox, op. cit., p. 244.

page 774 Ignatius on the purpose of the Spiritual Exercises – Annotations, para. 21, in De Nicolas ed., p. 110.

Montréal

page 777 Epigraph – Fleming to Secretary of the Interior, 27 March 1882, BIA Letters Received, 6230/1882 encl., US Archive.

page 777 Description of Montréal in summer – from visits in July 1987, August 1988, October 1988, May 1989 and July 1989.

Catherine's Love

page 779 Mrs. J. L.'s thanks – in the magazine *Kateri: Lily of the Mohawks*, spring 1983 (no. 135, bol. 35 no. 2), p. 5.

Fishing by Night

page 781 Epigraph – De Nicolas ed., p. 113, para. 37.

The Canadians

page 784 The tale of the White Lady, of Père Nicolas, of the Devil at Three Rivers, of the Devil at Isle d'Orléans, of the Tree of Dreams – Jean-Claude Dupont, *Légendes du Saint-Laurent: I: De Montréal à Baie-Saint-Paul*, 5ième édition (Légendes du Saint-Laurent: Sainte-Foy, Québec, 1988), pp. 39, 11, 18, 44, 31. Most of these legends are set in times after 1643. However, as I am describing the evolution of the French settlers into Canadians, which these tales reflect, I am not bothered a whit by such anachronisms. If you are, too bad.

Reasonable Men

page 788 Trigger epigraph – *The Children of Aataentsic*, op. cit., p. 361.

The Stream of Time

page 790 Description of the Montagnais working the ground at Sillery – after an "encre brune" by Père Claude Chauchetière, entitled "On travaille aux champs," accompanying his *Narration annuelle de la mission du Sault* [i.e., Old Caughnawagwa] *depuis sa fondation jusques à l'an 1686.*

PÈRE BRESSANI AMONG THE HIROQUOIS

page 790 The tale of Bressani – in Kephart, loc. cit.

page 792 Description of New Netherland – after A. J. F. Van Laer, trans, & ed., *Van Renssaelaer Bowier Manuscripts* (Albany: New York State Library, University of the State of New York, 1908). For the maxim of the Patroon (1632), see p. 199. For the text of the prohibition on firearms (1641), see p. 568. For the text of the prohibition on intercourse with Amerindiennes (1643), see p. 644.

SACRAMENTS

page 797 Epigraph – *JR*, vol. 28, p. 53.

TWO STREAMS OF BLOOD

page 799 Preserving the Iroquois – some sources say that it was Pieskaret himself who wanted to spare the Mohawks' lives. This version, however, is Marie de l'Incarnation's (letter to her son, Québec, 14 September 1645, in Marshall, op. cit., p. 135–6).

page 800 Public words of the Hook – almost verbatim, from *JR*, vol. 26 (1642–5), pp. 253–61, 291, 303.

SACRAMENTS

page 803 Description of the Sixtieth Rapid – from a visit to Pont des Menteurs, near Lac Sainte-Rose, Québec Province, in November 1989.

THE BAPTISM OF THE HIROQUOIS PRISONER

page 804 Baptism of the Iroquois prisoner – *JR*, vol. 29, p. 263.

A BOX OF PESTILENCE

page 805 Epigraph – Brian Young and John A. Dickinson, *A Short History of Quebec: A Socio-Economic Perspective* (Toronto: Copp Clark Pitman Ltd., Toronto, 1988).

JOGUES AMONG THE IROCOIS

page 808 Description of Iroquois country in summer and early autumn – from a visit to Ithaca, New York in August 1988, and a visit to Livingston Manor, New York in October 1988.

page 808 The doctrine of obedience – cf., for instance, Saint Ignatius's already cited letter on this subject to the Fathers and Brothers at Coimbra, Rome, 26 March 1553: De Nicolas ed., pp. 303–11.

page 809 "For they have learned from us . . . that nothing is readily given away" – *JR*, vol. 2, p. 79.

THE MARTYRDOM

page 809 "That is all I desire . . . to be corrected . . ." – Ignatius to Father Nicolás Bobadilla, Rome, 1543: "This will be my lifelong desire, to be corrected for my faults in the hope that the correction extend to all of them and be given with brotherly affection" (De Nicolas ed., p. 326).

page 809 Trigger expresses reservations about the violence offered to Jogues before his death. My account follows Parkman's, which sources Marie de l'Incarnation (see Marshall, op. cit., p. 166).

THE FATHER'S HEAD

page 809 Description of Iroquois country in late autumn – from a visit to eastern Massachusetts in November 1988.

AT THE GATES OF THE KINGDOM

page 811 Epigraph – De Nicolas ed., p. 155, para. 284.

page 812 Mère Marie begs pardon of her son – Québec, 1647 (in Marshall, op. cit., pp. 163–4).

page 812 The Fourteenth Rule for the Discernment of Spirits – *Spiritual Exercises*, in De Nicolas ed., p. 166, para. 327.

THE SONG OF HEAVEN

page 818 Epigraph – De Nicolas ed., p. 134 ("The Second Week"), para. 167.

THE DEATH OF JACQUES DOUART

page 821 The *Relation* of Père Ragueneau – *JR*, vol. 32, p. 61.

page 821 "lie underground like foxes for seven years . . ." – Champlain, *Voyages*, 1632.

THE DEATH OF PÈRE DANIEL

page 823 The martyrdom of Père Daniel – Ragueneau (Fallon trans.), pp. 16–20.

THE EXERCISE OF CONSOLATION

page 824 The GOD of Revelation – much of this sentence is based on a letter from Michael Remshard to the author, 1988.

BORN UNDERWATER

page 827 The martyrdom of Sainte Agnès – after a painting by Paolo Veronese (attr.), 1528–88, 'Martyre de Ste. Agnès' (Musée de Québec, 983.20).

THE STREAM OF TIME

page 828 Ecaregniondi, PIERCE-HEAD, the log-bridge and the Country of the Dead – all described in various places in Brébeuf's Huron Relation, *JR*, vol. 10.
page 828 We know that the most rapid watercourse must contain the least vegetation. In the case of the Stream of Time, this seems especially cruel, since it is precisely in such places that multitudes perish, and it seems unfair to have no water-lily to mourn them. A rolling stone gathers no moss, as the saying goes – how much truer of water!
page 829 Born Underwater's dream of the woman praying – after an engraving of the posthumous portrait of Catherine Tegahkouita by Père Claude Chauchetière.

THE CROWN

page 831 Hiroquois epigraph – Parker, *Constitution of the Iroquois*, p. 53, para. 85.
page 831 War-Song – loc. cit., para. 81.

THE SEVENTY-THIRD RAPID

page 833 Description of the Seventy-Third Rapids – from a visit to Niagara Falls, in September 1989.

THE EPIPHANY OF BORN UNDERWATER

page 835 Description of the deaths of Brébeuf and Lalemant – from the gravure of Grégoire Huret (*ca.* 1650). A reproduction of reasonable size may be found in *Le Québec littéraire*, hiver 1989, numéro 2, p. 86.

CATHERINE TEGAHKOUITA

page 841 The best source of eyewitness documents about Kateri Tekakwitha is published by the Catholic Church: *The Positio of the Historical Section of the Sacred Congregation of Rites on the Introduction of the Cause for Beatification and Canonization and of the Virtues of the Servant of God Katharine Tekakwitha: The Lily of the Mohawks* (New York: Fordham University Press, 1940). Many of the texts included here appear in the *Relations.*

page 841 Copper epigraph – Gina Laczko, *Iroquois Silverwork from the Collection of the Museum of the American Indian – Heye Foundation* (Gallery Association of New York State, n.d.), p. 3.

page 841 "Elle était charmante . . ." – Lavergne, p. 61.

page 841 Père Lecompte's assessment – ibid.

page 842 "They contemplated her with admiration . . ." – ibid., p. 62.

page 844 The abuse of Kateri – "Artifice having proved unsuccessful," says Père Cholonec, SJ, "they had recourse to violence" (letter to Père Le Blanc, SJ, 27 August 1715, in the *Positio*, p. 347). Cholonec goes on to cite the stone-throwing and the tomahawk incident. Other sources mention the children's name-calling and the compulsory fasting on Sundays. Trigger's view of these official biographies (note to author, February 1990) is given in a footnote to the text at this point.

page 845 Killing of the Fox – "Iroquois could not kill each other without starting a blood feud between clans – unless they made it look like work of enemies or accused was a recognized witch" (Trigger to author, 15 May 1989).

The Fleuve Saint-Laurent

page 845 Description of the St. Lawrence River – from a visit to Montréal in October 1988.

page 849 White girls coming home from school – from an oil painting by F. M. Bell-Smith, "Daughters of Canada" (1884), on display in the McCord Museum in Montréal.

page 849 "On all these more or less uncouth faces . . ." – Lavergne, op. cit., p. 75.

page 849 Of course Kateri would have gone straight to Kahnawaké/Caughnawagwa across the river, not to Montréal proper as described here.

Mission Saint-François-Xavier de la Prairie

page 849 Letter from Père de Lambertville – loc. cit.

page 850 Says Trigger (*The Children of Aataentsic*, p. xxix):

> [The Jesuits] hoped that if native people could be induced through constant persuasion, rewards and punishments to speak and act like Christians they might eventually think and believe like Christians. Yet they understood the ambiguities involved in such a process of conversion and in their more reflective moments realized that only God could distinguish between true belief and the mere appearance of it. In their missions at Kahnawaké and Lorette there were many more women and children than men, and the economic dependence of these Indians on the Jesuits made them anxious to please them . . . Yet the Jesuits could never be certain what these Indians did behind their backs . . . Gossip even called into question the conduct of Kateri Tekakwitha when she left Kahnawaké to accompany a winter hunting party.

FURTHER HISTORY OF THE SAVAGES

page 853 The tale of Brébeuf and Mother de Saint-Augustin – Marie de l'Incarnation to her son, Kebec, 7 September 1668, in Marshall, op. cit., p. 344.

FURTHER HISTORY OF THE HURON NATIONS

page 855 Trigger on the dispersal of the Huron – *The Children of Aataentsic*, op. cit., p. 788.

page 856 Describing events after 1650, Trigger writes (ibid., pp. 813–14):

> Out of self-interest French government officials and Jesuits had delivered many of the Huron refugees who sought their protection into the hands of the Iroquois. Thus the Huron joined the growing ranks of Indians who ceased to be treated with respect by Europeans once they ceased to be an economic asset . . . The Huron believed that bonds of religion and the economic and military alliances that had linked them with the French gave them a special claim on the latter's friendship and support. It was their misfortune that at the height of their adversity they had to learn otherwise.

page 856 And what does Wendaké look like now? It has been flattened and farmed and marked with the half-cylinders of hay-bales. Fields are dark green and shaggy with vegetables; fields glisten with corn. A sign says *HURONIA BAIT – MINNOWS.* Tawny fields, white cows, and grey barns bring you to the next sign: *WE LOVE HURONIA*, signed Realty World and McDonald's.

FURTHER HISTORY OF THE SOURIQUOIS

page 857 Denys – op. cit., last chapter.

FURTHER HISTORY OF THE CHRISTIANS

page 857 Lescarbot – *History of New France*, op. cit., vol. 2, p. 174.

FURTHER HISTORY OF KATHERINE TEGAKOUÏTHA

page 858 "Courage, dear sister . . ." – *Positio*, op. cit., p. 83.

page 858 "I am leaving you . . ." – ibid., p. 204.

page 858 "She does not act in the same way toward the sick children . . ." – ibid., p. 90.

page 859 Epitaph – actually, a description of her childhood: ibid., p. 121.

FURTHER HISTORY OF THE IROQUOIS

page 859 The landscape descriptions here are based on the following paintings, all by Jasper F. Cropsey (and on exhibit at the New York Historical Society, December

1987): "Castle Garden, New York City" (1859), "River View I" (1874), "River View II" (1871), "Greenwood Lake" (1862), "Springtime on the Hudson" (1856), "Lake at Mt. Chocorua" (1875).

Debts and Debtors

page 860 Epigraph – Morgan, op. cit., p. 23.

page 860 Log of the HMS *Scarborough* – Lieutenant Colonel William Wood, ed., *The Logs of the Conquest of Canada* (Toronto: The Champlain Society, 1909), p. 293.

page 860 Description of Montréal under snow – from a visit in November 1989.

page 861 Trigger footnote – from a note to the author, February 1990.

The Cross

page 861 "Champlain was the Governor" – "Never in title," reminds Trigger, "tho it is metaphorically true" (note to author, February 1990).

The Doll

page 864 Description of Catherine Tegakouitha's shrine – from a visit to Caughnawagwa in August 1989.

page 864n Ignatius's sixth rule – *Spiritual Exercises*, "Rules for Conforming with the Church," in De Nicholas ed., pp. 170–1, paras. 352, 358.

page 865 One thing I would have liked to devote more space to is the magical properties of Catherine's remains. Père Rémy, a good Pastor, often distributed her grave-earth or shroud-ashes to his flock for sickness. In his accounts, the invalid often vomits up a fat live worm after partaking of one of these panaceas. – Skeletons, teeth, spines and spicules all form minerals; Catherine's bones may perhaps biomineralize gold . . .

Canadians

page 867 Marie-Claude on the Métis – see Whitehead's note to "The Magic Words," above.

page 868 Description of the martyrdom of the other Sainte Catherine – from a painting by François Chaveau (attr.), "Martyre de Ste.-Catherine" (Musée du Séminaire de Québec, 983.14).

Epitaph

page 869 Père Biard on fathers and crows – *JR*, vol. 2, p. 35.

GLOSSARIES

NOTE Most quoted extracts here are so short that I have not bothered to source them. Most of Trigger's remarks come either from notes written on a draft of the Glossaries, or else extracts from *The Children of Aataentsic*. Whitehead's remarks similarly are usually from notes to me.

CHRONOLOGY

page 918 1600–1700 ("breathing into the faces of Algonkian Indians") – Alice Bleckenhoe, *North American Indians: A Comprehensive Account* (Englewood Cliffs, NJ: Prentice-Hall, 1981), pp. 234–5.

page 930 1650 (death from disease and warfare) – Young and Dickinson, op. cit., p. 72.

page 933 1700–1800 – see A. R. M. Lower and J. W. Chafe, *Canada – A Nation; and How It Came to Be*, op. cit.

page 935 Herbert Guindon on the Quiet Revolution of 1960 – op. cit., p. 104.

SOURCES

page 938 Epigraph – Parker, *Seneca Myths*, p. xxv.

NOTE A good bibliography is given in Trigger's book. A more extensive one, which covers Micmac ("les Algonquiens maritimes"), Montagnais ("les Algonquiens du Subarctique") and Iroquoians, is Richard Dominique and Jean-Guy Deschènes, *Cultures et sociétés autochtones du Québec: Bibiographie critique* (Québec: Institut Québecois de Recherche sur la Culture, 1985). Sources listed are both French and English.

SOURCES FOR ILLUSTRATIONS

The Micmac quillwork design "Kagwet" on page 202 and the Waltes equipment were both drawn from photographs in Whitehead's *Elitekey*. (By the way, Whitehead now believes that "Kagwet" represents a sun design, not a starfish.) The Indian sign for MANITOU on page 569 was scanned from Ernst Lehner, *Symbols, Signs and Signets* (New York: Dover, 1950), p. 28. In drawing the maps I made use of Trigger's books, Morgan's *League of the Iroquois*, which has a detailed map of Iroquois place-names in New York State and environs, the *Historical Atlas of Canada*, vol. 1, and Canadian topographic maps.

Acknowledgements

CANADA

The two people to whom Dream 2 owes the most are Mme. Ruth Holmes Whitehead of the Nova Scotia Museum (Halifax), who came to my rescue once again on the Micmac parts ("keep those moose bones out of the river!"), and Professor Bruce Trigger at McGill University's Department of Anthropology (Montréal), who gave unstintingly of his time and expertise when the manuscript was still in a very rough state. My ignorance astounded even me, so I am grateful that now the Rivière Saint-Charles is where it belongs, that Born Underwater isn't given a crash course in shamanism by Smoking the Pipe, that some doubt is cast on the violence supposedly offered Tekakwitha by her family, etc., etc. – that all the details, in short, are more likely to be accurate and that my characters might actually behave in keeping with their respective cultures (if they don't, of course, the fault is mine – especially since I sometimes went my own perverse and exasperating way). I cannot sufficiently express my appreciation.

Anyone who has been kind enough to read this book will also see how indebted I am to my friends Pierre and Marie-Claude. They loaned me books, gave me reading lists and addresses, let me stay with them innumerable times at short notice, and most importantly offered me friendship. (While I'm at it, let me thank Marie-Claude's mother for the delicious strawberry pie.)

Professor John Steckley at Humber College gave valuable corrections and replies on Huron linguistics and orthography. I am also grateful to Mr. Bernard Francis of the Micmac Institute for his answers to queries (via Ruth Whitehead).

In Québec I would like to thank everyone at the Musée des Ursulines, especially Sonia, and the staff of the Centre de Marie de l'Incarnation, especially the Directrice, Sr. Gabrielle Noël, OSU, who was kind enough to explain Marie's life to me in French that I could understand, and who let me purchase her last copies of various books on Marie which I could not have found elsewhere.

I would also like to express my appreciation to M. Marc Brousseau, SJ, Secrétaire provincial (Maison provinciale de Montréal, province du Canada Français de la Compagnie de Jésus), and M. Georges Sioui (Village-des-Hurons).

United Kingdom

I am fortunate to have had the help of Mr. Howard Davies in preparing many of my books for press – a task he has fulfilled again with his usual care. Any remaining typographical blemishes should be blamed on the Devil. Mr. Tom Rosenthal sighed and agreed to pay a few billion quid to put the book into production. He'll never see *that* money again. Ms. Esther Whitby stayed my friend through it all.

United States

Here my main debt is to the Mrs. Giles Whiting Foundation, which gave me $25,000 to play with in 1988. In a long project such as *Seven Dreams*, support such as this makes all the difference. My books don't tend to make much money, so without the generosity of the Whiting Foundation I would have had a lot less hope about being able to do this part of the series right.

Mr. Paul Slovak at Viking-Penguin has been a fine advocate for me and my projects. If he ever gets another job, I'd better give up eating. Mr. Scott Anderson likewise did his best for this book, which encountered such great difficulties on both sides of the Atlantic that at times I expected it to be published only in a mutilated form, if at all. Mr. Lee Smith, then at Macmillan, read it and told me it was good. Thank you one and all.

Mr. Brad Edmondson (Ithaca, New York) helped me with my Iroquois research; Mr. Richard Estell (New York City) located period landscape and costume representations for France and Spain in the Metropolitan Museum; Mr. Jacques Sapriel (Philadelphia) encouraged my project and introduced me to Mr. Michael Remshard, who kindly took the time to answer a number of religious questions bordering on the personal.

I would like to remember my friend Professor Mary Claire Mansfield of Berkeley, California, for her help on certain most cunning and subtle matters of doctrine. I had often looked forward to showing her the manuscript of this book which doubtless her comments could have further improved. Her recent death made this impossible. I will always miss Mary.

I thank Janice Ryu for accompanying me on so many book-expeditions and being (relatively) patient with capsized canoes, maps scattered on the floor, mosquitoes in the tent and half-raw, half-burned beans on the stove.